JINXWORLD PRESENTS

JINX™

JINXWORLD PRESENTS

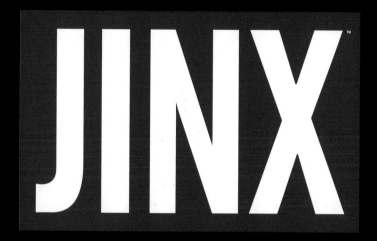

Created by
BRIAN MICHAEL BENDIS

DARK HORSE BOOKS

DARK HORSE EDITION

PUBLISHER
MIKE RICHARDSON

COLLECTION EDITOR
DANIEL CHABON

ASSISTANT EDITORS
CHUCK HOWITT AND
MISHA GEHR

DESIGNER
KATHLEEN BARNETT

DIGITAL ART TECHNICIAN
BETSY HOWITT

ORIGINAL PRINTING

JINXWORLD PUBLISHER
ALISA BENDIS

COLLECTION EDITOR
JENNIFER GRÜNWALD

COVER AND PUBLICATION DESIGN
TIM DANIEL, PATRICK MCGRATH,
AND **CURTIS KING JR.**

To find a comics shop in your area, visit comicshoplocator.com.

JINX

Published by Dark Horse Books. A division of Dark Horse Comics LLC
10956 SE Main Street, Milwaukie, OR 97222 | DarkHorse.com

Neil Hankerson Executive Vice President | **Tom Weddle** Chief Financial Officer | **Dale LaFountain** Chief Information Officer | **Tim Wiesch** Vice President of Licensing | **Matt Parkinson** Vice President of Marketing | **Vanessa Todd-Holmes** Vice President of Production and Scheduling | **Mark Bernardi** Vice President of Book Trade and Digital Sales | **Randy Lahrman** Vice President of Product Development | **Ken Lizzi** General Counsel | **Dave Marshall** Editor in Chief | **Davey Estrada** Editorial Director | **Chris Warner** Senior Books Editor | **Cary Grazzini** Director of Specialty Projects | **Lia Ribacchi** Art Director | **Matt Dryer** Director of Digital Art and Prepress | **Michael Gombos** Senior Director of Licensed Publications | **Kari Yadro** Director of Custom Programs | **Kari Torson** Director of International Licensing

First edition: July 2022 | Ebook ISBN 978-1-50673-032-5 | Trade paperback ISBN 978-1-50673-015-8

10 9 8 7 6 5 4 3 2 1

Printed in China

THANKS

One area of thanks that I don't think I have sufficiently covered in previous editions of this work is specifically thanking my fellow pros/friends that physically helped me produce this book.

Michael Gaydos for illustrating the Jinx fantasy section.

Mark Ricketts for production help on the original series.

David Mack and Galen Showman for inking assists they probably don't even remember doing.

Roxanne Starr and Jared Bendis for lettering for me when I didn't even own a computer.

My sincerest apologies to Sal Buscema for the cheesy homage.

A huge thank-you to the retail community for always keeping this book in print and to the fans who are always reporting to me that they lent out their copy. Keep lending out your comics.

I check my messages. There's one from Brian Bendis.

BRIAN: Hey, it's me. Subtle reminder—I need your *Jinx* trade intro ASAP, as I am putting the book to bed ASAP. That's all. I hope you had a good weekend. Wa wa wu hu hun wha wha [direct quote].

I go to sleep anyway.

Then, I'm sound asleep with my girlfriend, Anh, smelling good beside me, when the phone rings and a voice on the machine interrupts my needed rest.

VOICE: Dave, it's Dan Brereton [the painter]. Come on. Answer the phone. I know you're awake, Dave!!!!

I'm so asleep that I actually answer it—partly because he left five messages on my machine over the weekend and I haven't called him back. I answer with the wrong phone, so the machine never cuts off; instead, it records the whole conversation.

ME: Hello, Dan.

DAN: What are you doing?

ME: Sleeping.

DAN: No you're not.

ME: It's true.

DAN: Is Anh there?

ME: Yes.

DAN: Put her on the phone.

ME: She's sleeping.

DAN: Did she wake up with the phone?

ME: Yes.

DAN: Then put her on.

ME: She pulled the covers over her head to shut out the talk.

DAN: Then why did you answer the phone?

ME: Because you left five messages.

DAN: I only left two messages.

ME: You left two messages and three hang-ups.

DAN: Oh, so you have caller ID. Oh, well, me and Kieron Dwyer [artist] still want you to share that endcap of tables with us at the San Diego Comic-Con. Kieron is on his way for sure with. And we carefully considered who to invite to share a setup with us. Seriously, we did, and me and Kieron love your stuff.

ME: That's encouraging.

DAN: Well, that's why we asked you first. Are you in?

ME: You didn't ask me first.

DAN: Well, that's true, we asked Bendis first. But we asked you next.

ME: Thanks.

DAN: Bendis wasn't sure if he was going, and he didn't want to plan so far in advance. I told him if he doesn't show, he can still pay for a table. But he said he was way too Jewish to let that happen. But if you go, we can watch a crazy person sit with us and later you can do tricks. Hey, why don't you cut loose around Alex Ross [the really famous painter]?

ME: What are you talking about?

DAN: Alex thinks you're some respectable, literary philosopher-artist type. Why don't you cut loose around him?

ME: I do. I've jumped all over him before. And then we went to a dance club.

DAN: What happened?

ME: He didn't dance.

DAN: I can understand that . . .

ME: Me and Anh and Rick Mays were all getting our groove on and trying to get Alex to move.

DAN: I know what this is like. I was at a wedding and everyone was trying to get me to dance. Finally some girls said they would show me how and I got out on the floor and danced with them and everyone was happy. People always like to see a fat guy dance.

NEW VOICE BREAKS IN: You fuckin' cocksucker. I was waiting for you to say something bad about me.

I realize it's Alex Ross on Brereton's three-way calling. He's been listening silently the whole time like some kind of weirdo.

ME: Hi, Alex.

DAN: We were hoping I could get you to say something funny about him. But this is great. Yeah, now I should call Bendis and wake him up, too.

ME: That's a great idea. I'm supposed to write an introduction for him. I could just use this conversation with us and him as the intro. So I don't spend extra time writing shit.

ALEX: I saw your new book.

ME: Which one?

ALEX: The *Kabuki Reflections*. The one with all the photos in the back with you and all those girls. What's that about? That you have to rub it in our faces?

ME: Did you look at the rest of the book?

ALEX: Not yet, I just saw those pictures. And why are you painted blue in one? What's that about?

ME: Why'd you buy the book?

ALEX: I have the store get all the *Kabuki* books— they pull them for me. And there you are, holding hands with Susie Owens—like you have to taunt us with that.

ME: That picture was us modeling for Brian Bendis's photo reference.

DAN: Dave's a porn star.

ALEX: Stop all your John Holmes shit.

DAN: You're Dirk Diggler. Come on, Dave, what's your porn name?

ME: It's David Mack.

ALEX: You know what, Dave? I hate you.

DAN: No, you're my hero.

ALEX: I've seen a woman naked, like, once. And I think I remember liking it. And you have pictures in the back of naked women posing for sculptures. I should tell all the weird stories to Colleen Doran.

ME: What are you talking about?

ALEX: She always says nice shit about you. So I should tell her all the weird shit.

DAN: Is Colleen a different person than Amanda Conner?

ME: Yes, Dan. They are two completely different people. Are we going to call Bendis for that intro?

DAN: Don't feel bad that he was first on the list. Alex wasn't on the list at all. Actually, I can't tell if Alex listens to me anyways. I can't tell if he likes me.

ME: I can't tell if he likes you either.

DAN: Put Anh on. I need to talk to her.

ME: Every time you talk about her you start breathing heavy.

ALEX: Just one time I want to get laid from being in comics. I'm at the pinnacle of my career; I got everything I want except groupies.

DAN: I got laid once for being a comics artist.

ALEX: Yeah, fag hags.

DAN: No, she was a brunette. Chicks dig me. I'm very easy for girls to be friends with. They can let their defenses down, and sooner or later they get bored and fuck me.

ALEX: You're making a great argument for yourself.

It became clear real fast that we weren't calling Bendis. And I was going to have to write this introduction myself after all. Hopefully this telephone masturbation will work in here. After all, it's got lots of similarities to Bendis's work:

- Witty dialogue
- Real-sounding conversation—like a play
- Integrates real life with art (one of my favorite things about Bendis's work, from his photo-reference acting to his real-life stories)
- Uses the word "fuck" a lot . . . and "shit" . . . and "cocksucker" . . .

I could make a cocksucking fuckload of a shit list of things that I enjoy about Brian Bendis's work:

- The design sense
- The pacing
- The humor
- The poetry
- The artistic therapy that it obviously is for him
- The boldness of the art
- The uncompromising dialogue
- The often self-derisive charm
- The best letters column in the business

I could talk at length about the groundbreaking storytelling techniques, or how I learn things just looking at the pacing, or how it is one of the few books that make me laugh out loud. Maybe someday I will talk at length about these things. But the fact is, the real magic of the book is undefinable. It happens between the panels. It happens in your mind. Bendis puts just enough on the page in both word and image to make the reader's mind piece it together. And that's why it stays in your head after you put the book down. That's why you pick up the next issue, read the next chapter. That's why I'm up all night writing this introduction.

—DAVID MACK

With acknowledgments to the verbal acts of Dan Brereton and Alex Ross. These guys are seriously amazing artists and wonderful, charming human beings. I've had dozens of all-night conversations with each of them separately, and they've always been deep, insightful, intelligent, educational, and thought provoking. But this is the one that got recorded. Next time I'll tell some Bendis stories. Every time I'm with him, it's like an episode of Seinfeld.

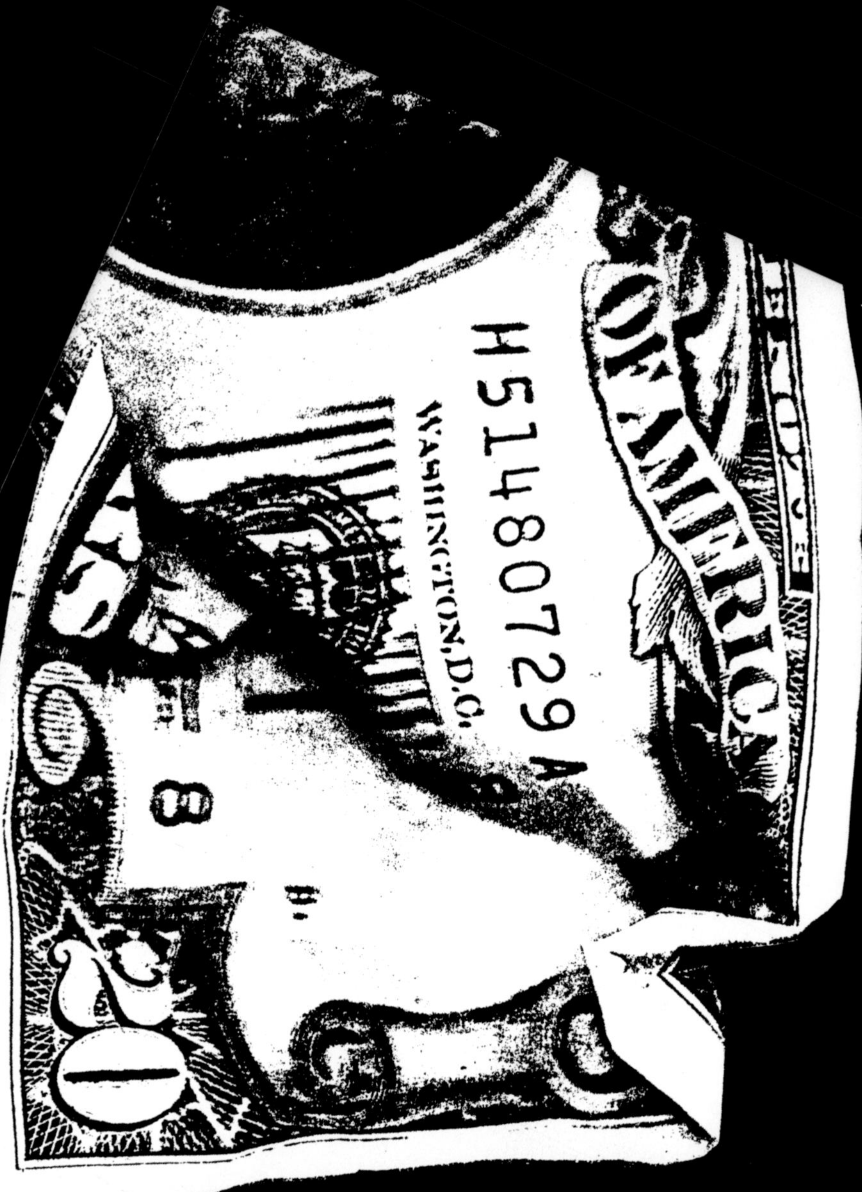
OF AMERICA
H51480729 A
WASHINGTON, D.C.

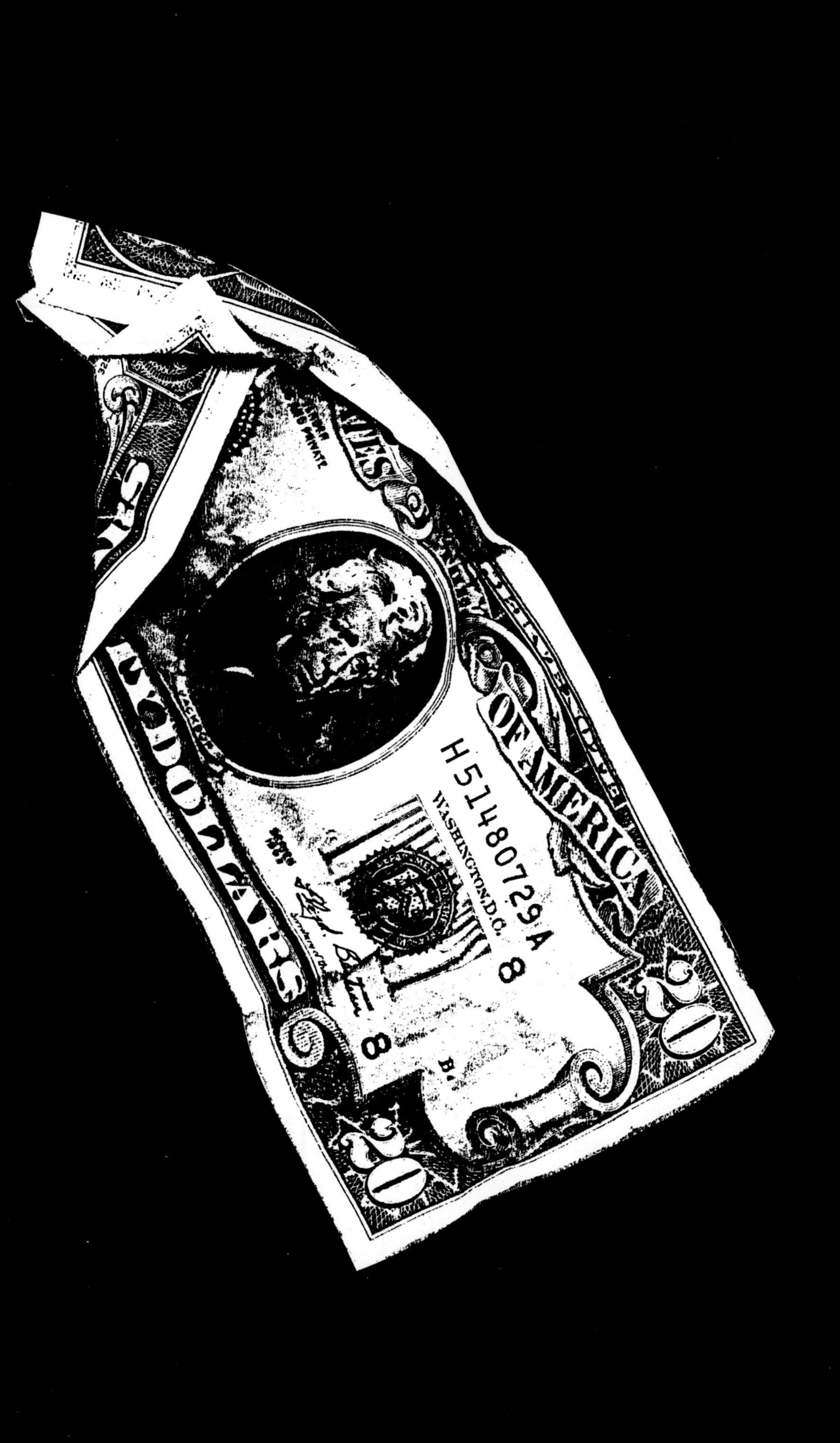
OF AMERICA
H51480729A
WASHINGTON,D.C.
20

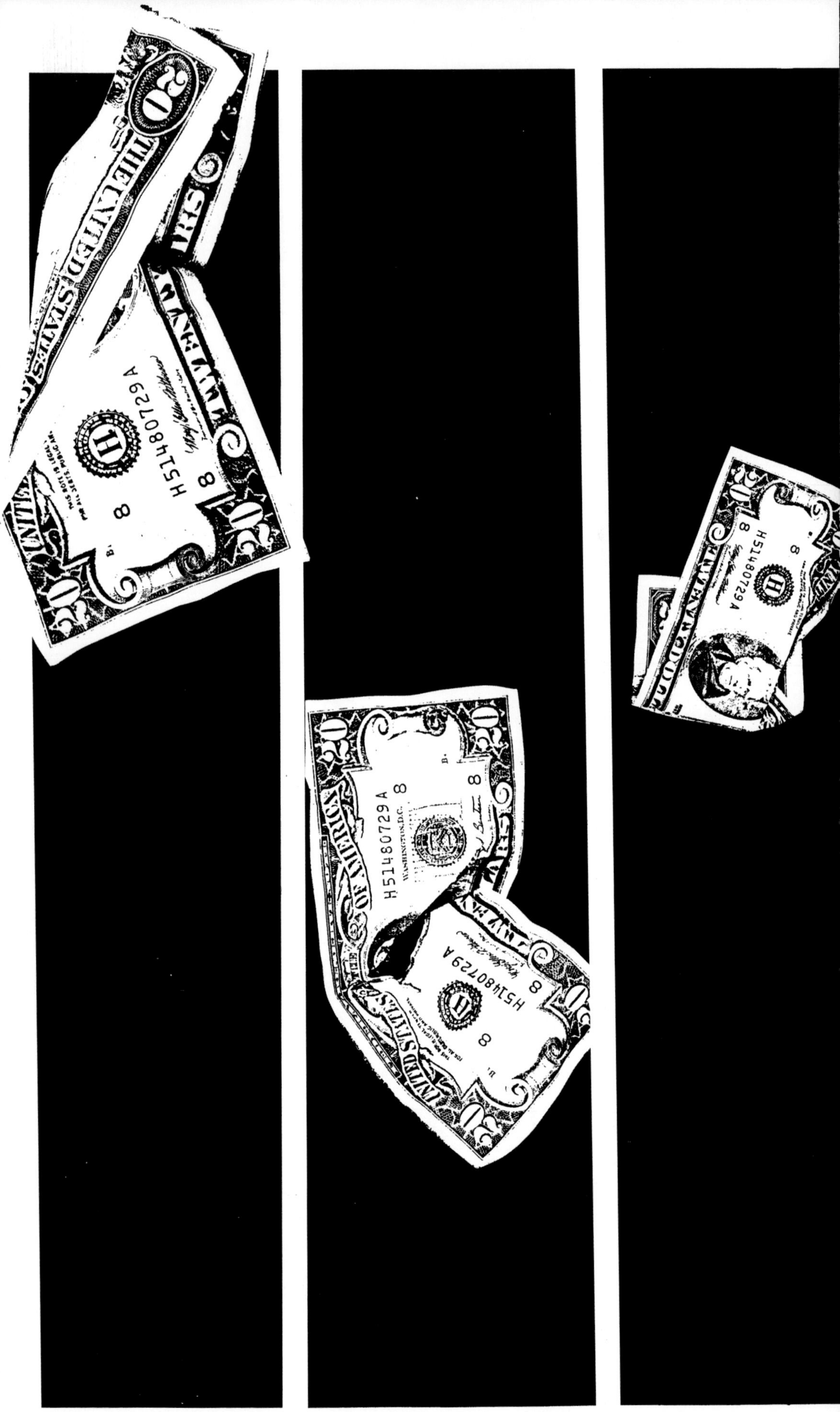

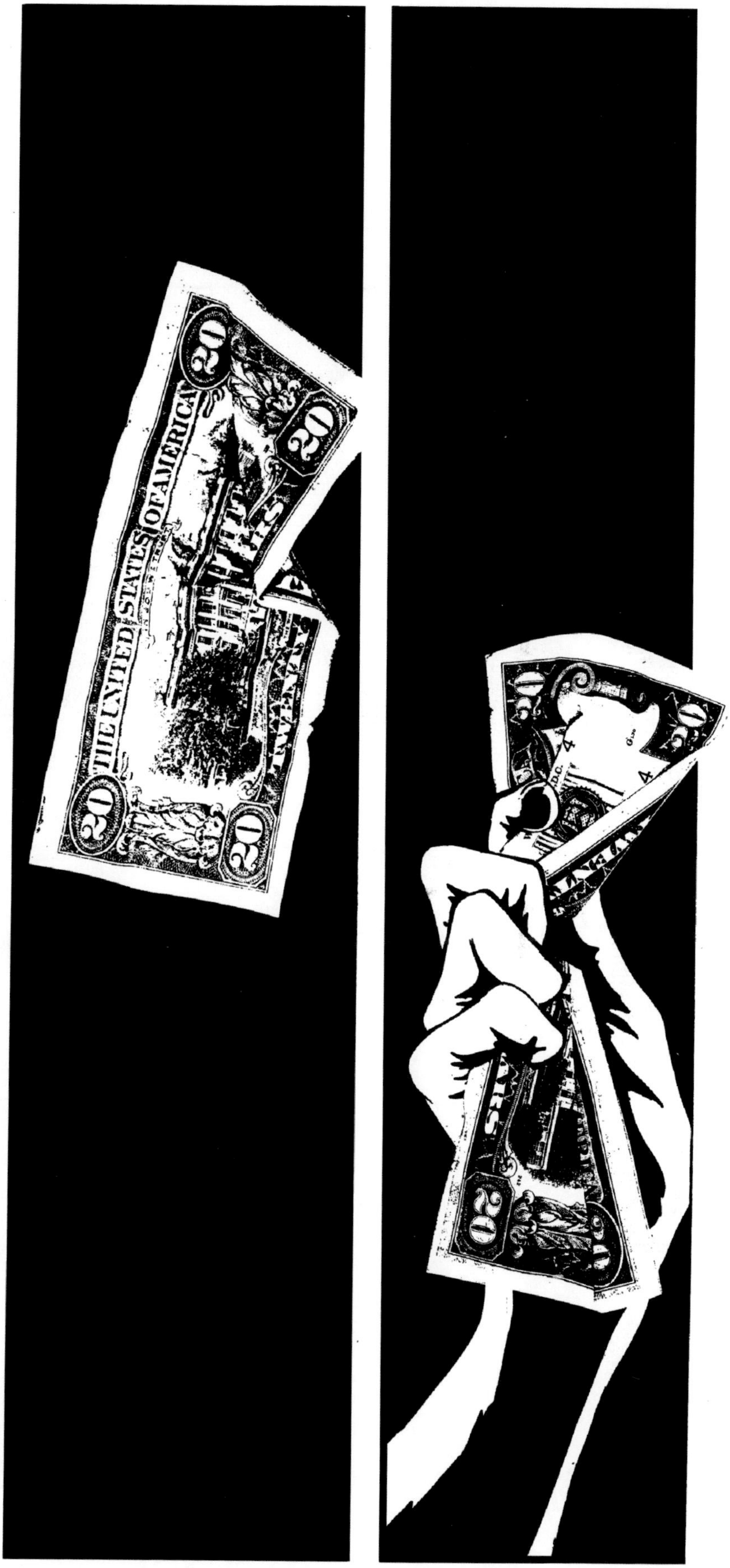
THE UNITED STATES OF AMERICA
20

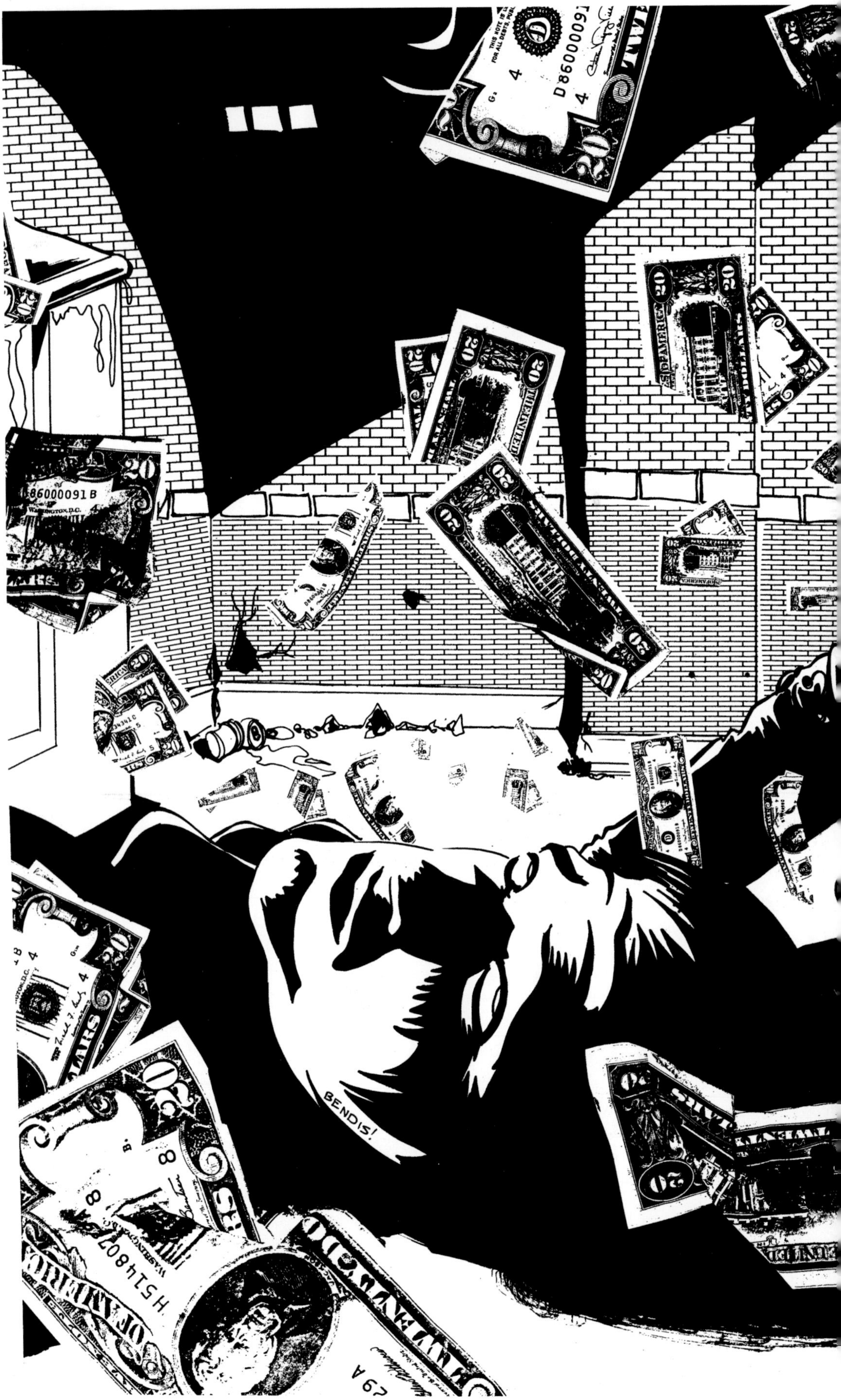
BENDIS!

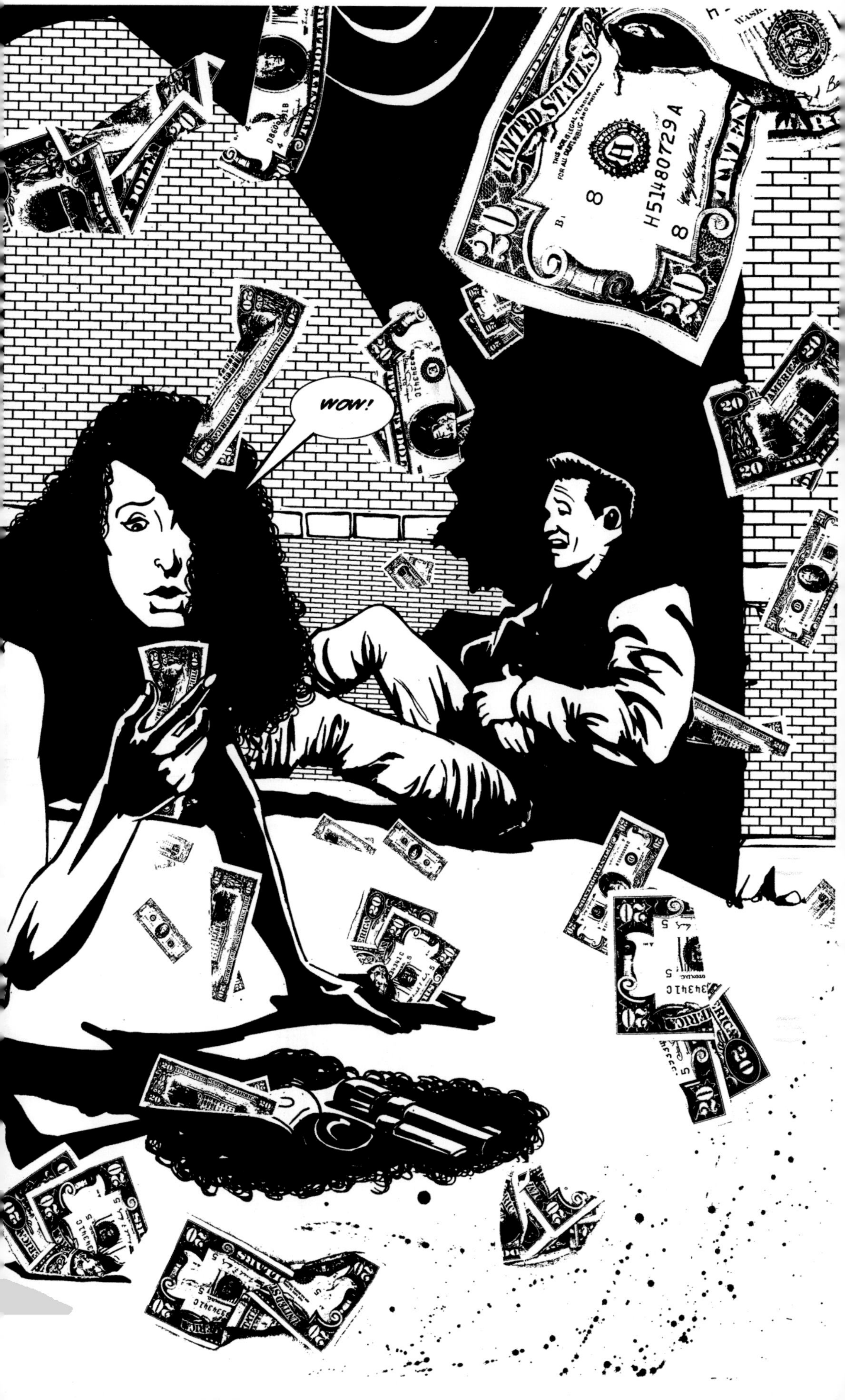
WOW!

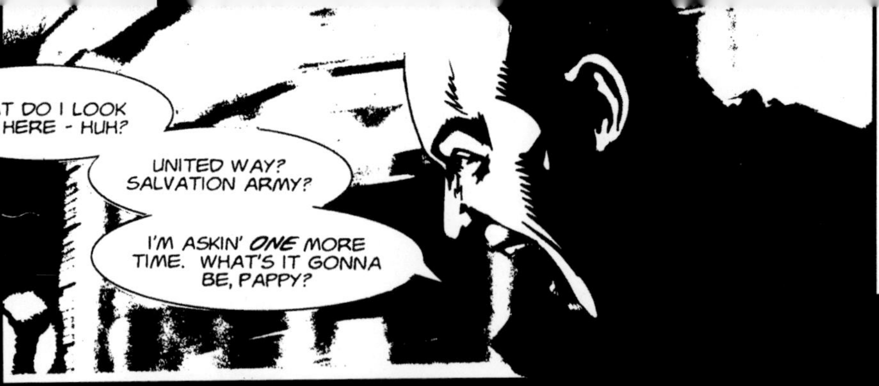
WHAT DO I LOOK LIKE HERE - HUH?
UNITED WAY? SALVATION ARMY?
I'M ASKIN' ONE MORE TIME. WHAT'S IT GONNA BE, PAPPY?

"...I am not a loser."

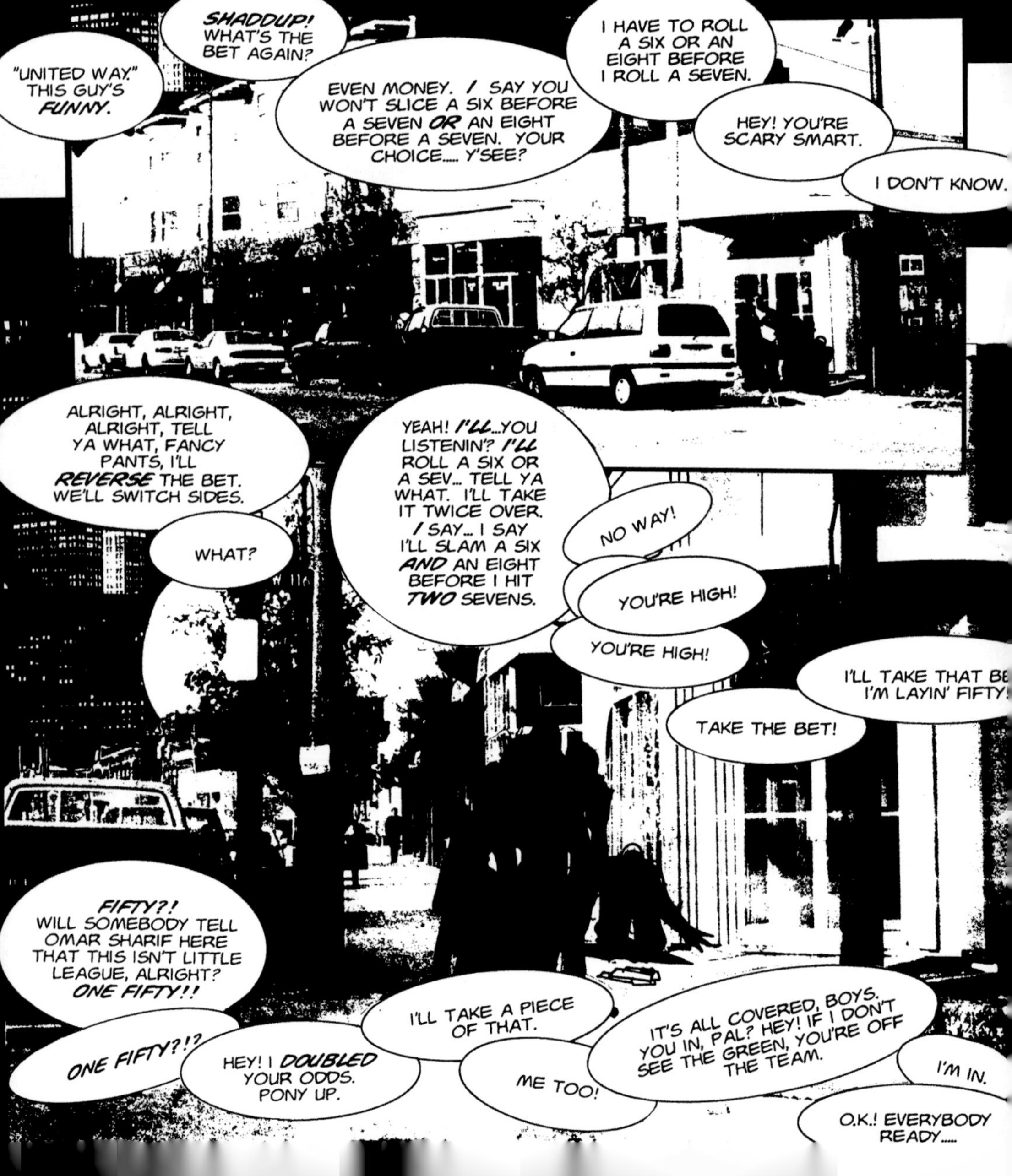
"UNITED WAY." THIS GUY'S FUNNY.
SHADDUP! WHAT'S THE BET AGAIN?
EVEN MONEY. I SAY YOU WON'T SLICE A SIX BEFORE A SEVEN OR AN EIGHT BEFORE A SEVEN. YOUR CHOICE.... Y'SEE?
I HAVE TO ROLL A SIX OR AN EIGHT BEFORE I ROLL A SEVEN.
HEY! YOU'RE SCARY SMART.
I DON'T KNOW.
ALRIGHT, ALRIGHT, ALRIGHT, TELL YA WHAT, FANCY PANTS, I'LL REVERSE THE BET. WE'LL SWITCH SIDES.
WHAT?
YEAH! I'LL...YOU LISTENIN'? I'LL ROLL A SIX OR A SEV... TELL YA WHAT. I'LL TAKE IT TWICE OVER. I SAY... I SAY I'LL SLAM A SIX AND AN EIGHT BEFORE I HIT TWO SEVENS.
NO WAY!
YOU'RE HIGH!
YOU'RE HIGH!
I'LL TAKE THAT BE
I'M LAYIN' FIFTY
TAKE THE BET!
FIFTY?! WILL SOMEBODY TELL OMAR SHARIF HERE THAT THIS ISN'T LITTLE LEAGUE, ALRIGHT? ONE FIFTY!!
ONE FIFTY?!?
HEY! I DOUBLED YOUR ODDS. PONY UP.
I'LL TAKE A PIECE OF THAT.
ME TOO!
IT'S ALL COVERED, BOYS. YOU IN, PAL? HEY! IF I DON'T SEE THE GREEN, YOU'RE OFF THE TEAM.
I'M IN.
O.K.! EVERYBODY READY.....

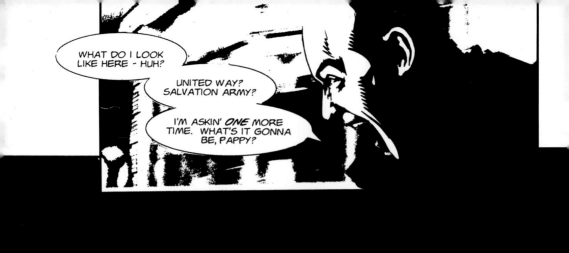

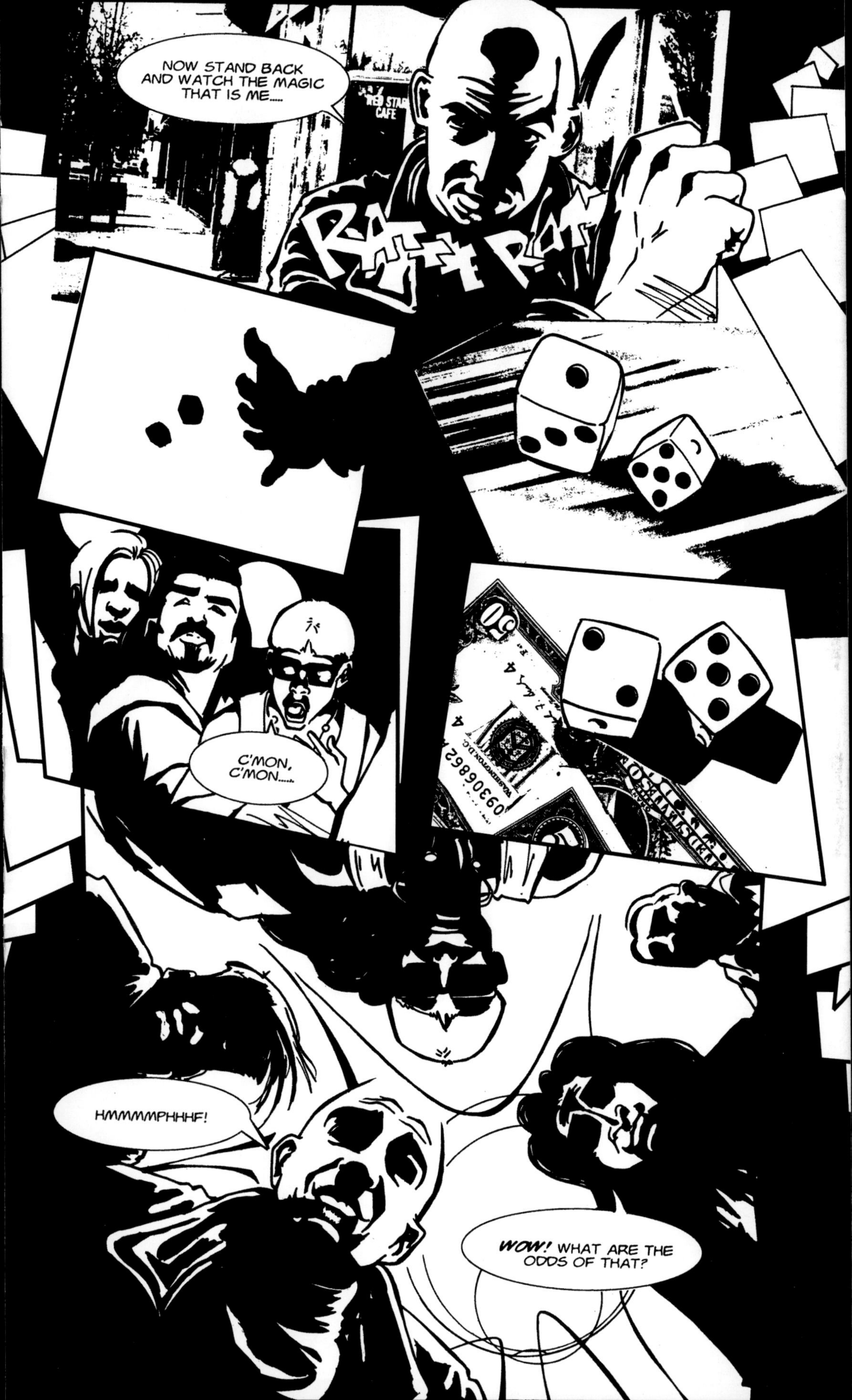
NOW STAND BACK AND WATCH THE MAGIC THAT IS ME.....
RED STAR CAFE
C'MON, C'MON.....
HMMMMPHHHF!
WOW! WHAT ARE THE ODDS OF THAT?

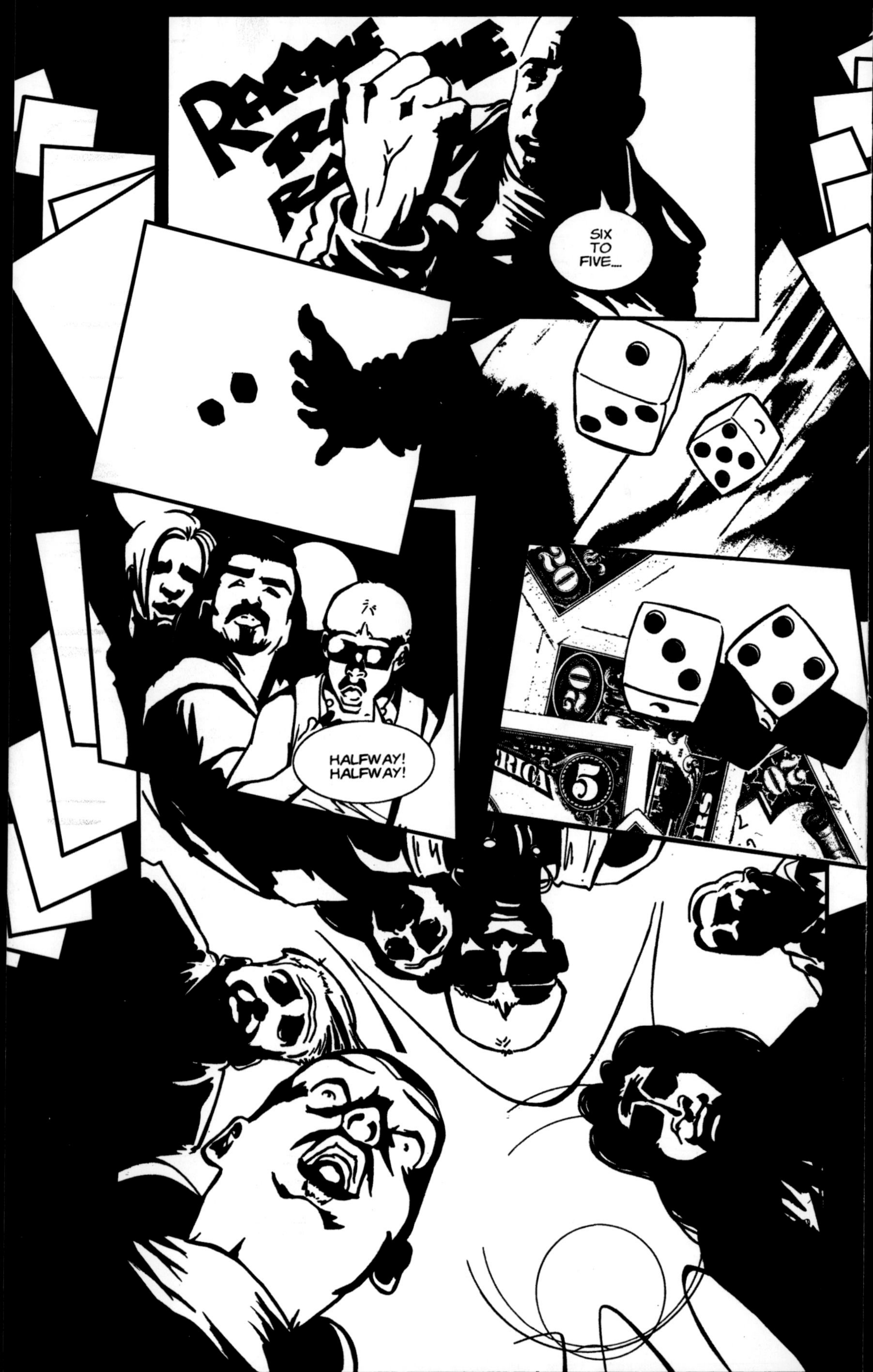
SIX TO FIVE....
HALFWAY! HALFWAY!

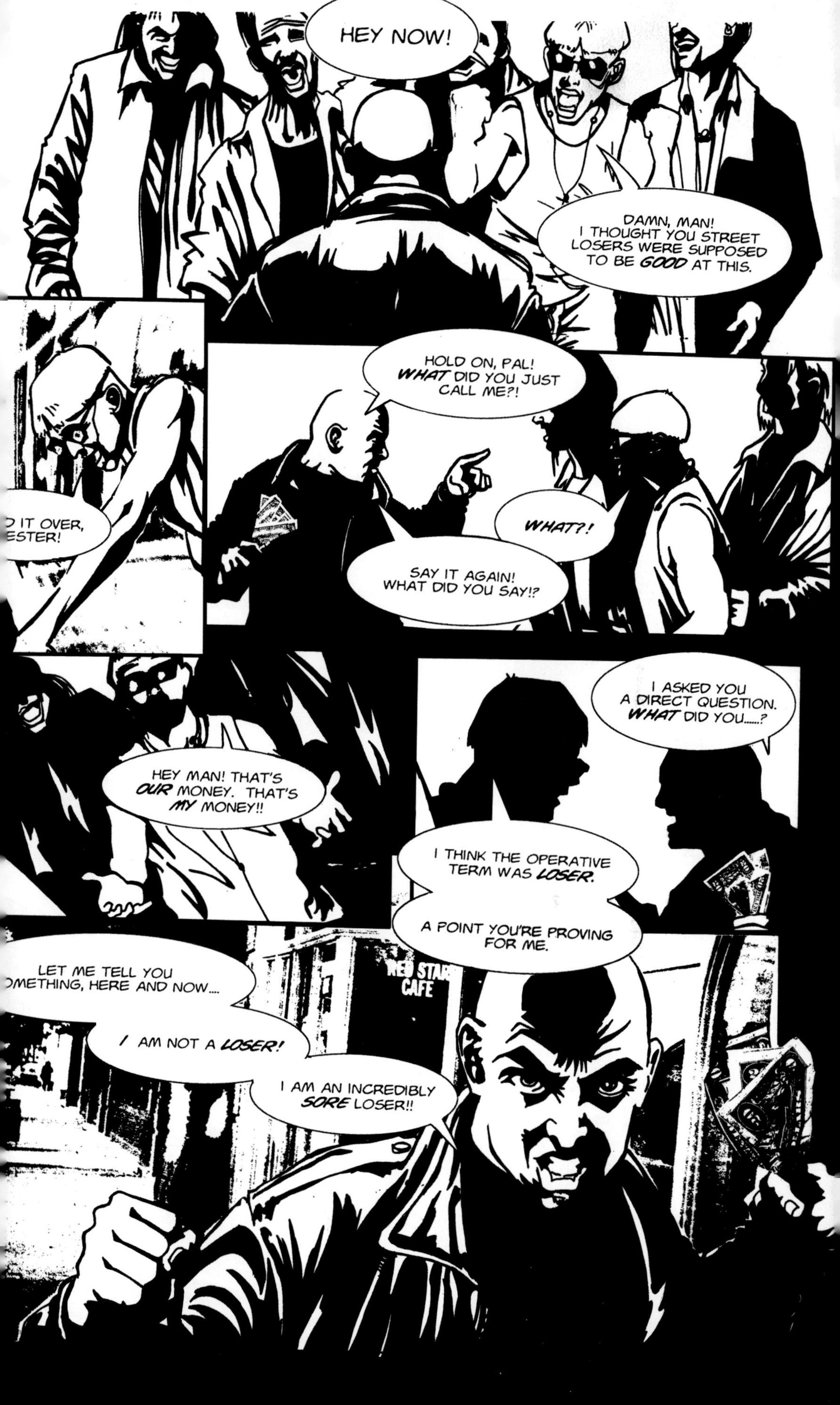
HEY NOW!
DAMN, MAN! I THOUGHT YOU STREET LOSERS WERE SUPPOSED TO BE GOOD AT THIS.
D IT OVER, ESTER!
HOLD ON, PAL! WHAT DID YOU JUST CALL ME?!
WHAT?!
SAY IT AGAIN! WHAT DID YOU SAY!?
HEY MAN! THAT'S OUR MONEY. THAT'S MY MONEY!!
I ASKED YOU A DIRECT QUESTION. WHAT DID YOU.....?
I THINK THE OPERATIVE TERM WAS LOSER.
A POINT YOU'RE PROVING FOR ME.
LET ME TELL YOU OMETHING, HERE AND NOW....
I AM NOT A LOSER!
I AM AN INCREDIBLY SORE LOSER!!
RED STAR CAFE

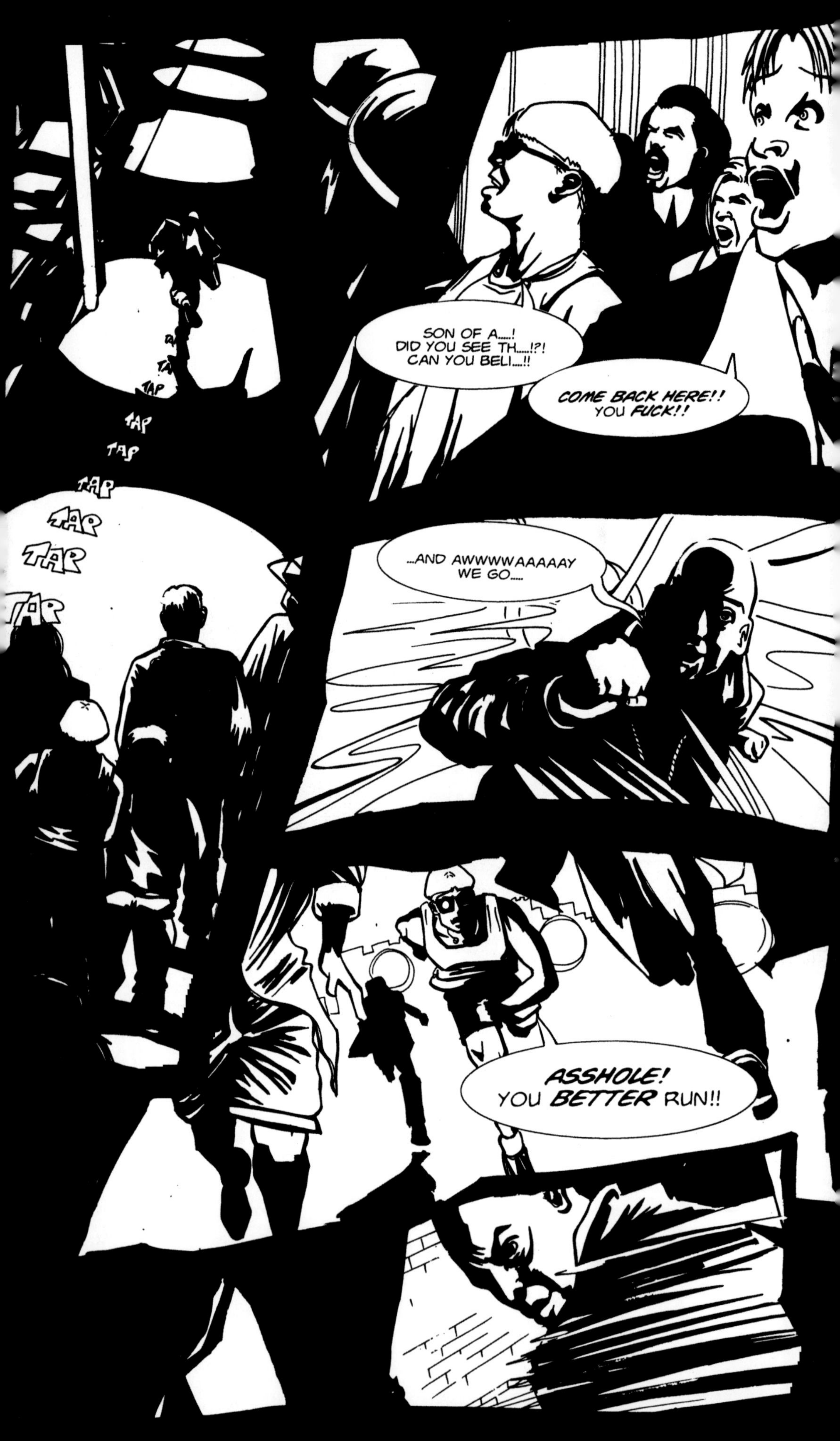
TAP
TAP
TAP
TAP
TAP
TAP
TAP
TAP
TAP
SON OF A....! DID YOU SEE TH....!?! CAN YOU BELI....!!
COME BACK HERE!! YOU FUCK!!
...AND AWWWWAAAAAY WE GO.....
ASSHOLE! YOU BETTER RUN!!

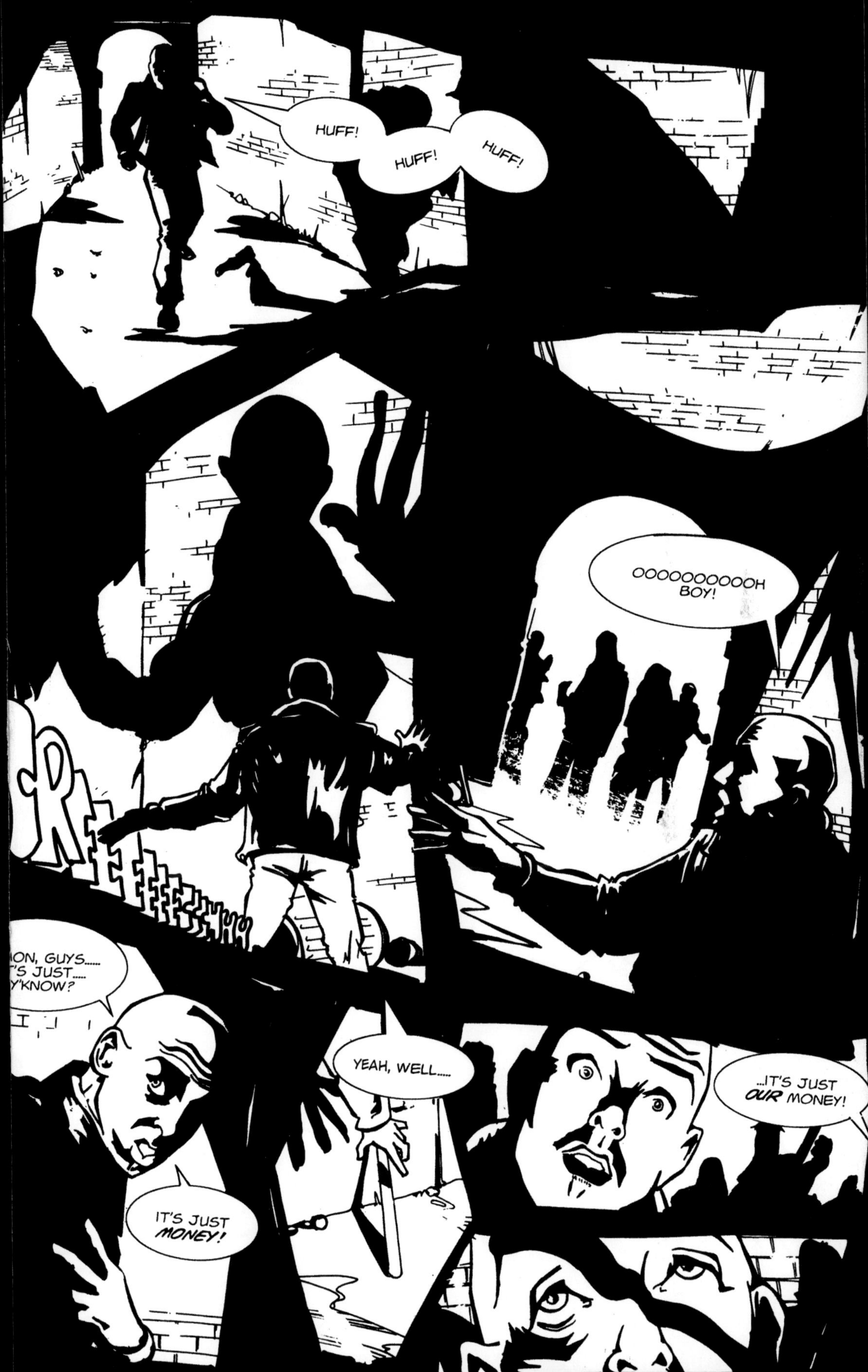
HUFF!
HUFF!
HUFF!
OOOOOOOOOOH BOY!
FFFSHHH
ON, GUYS...... T'S JUST..... Y'KNOW?
IT'S JUST MONEY!
YEAH, WELL.....
...IT'S JUST OUR MONEY!

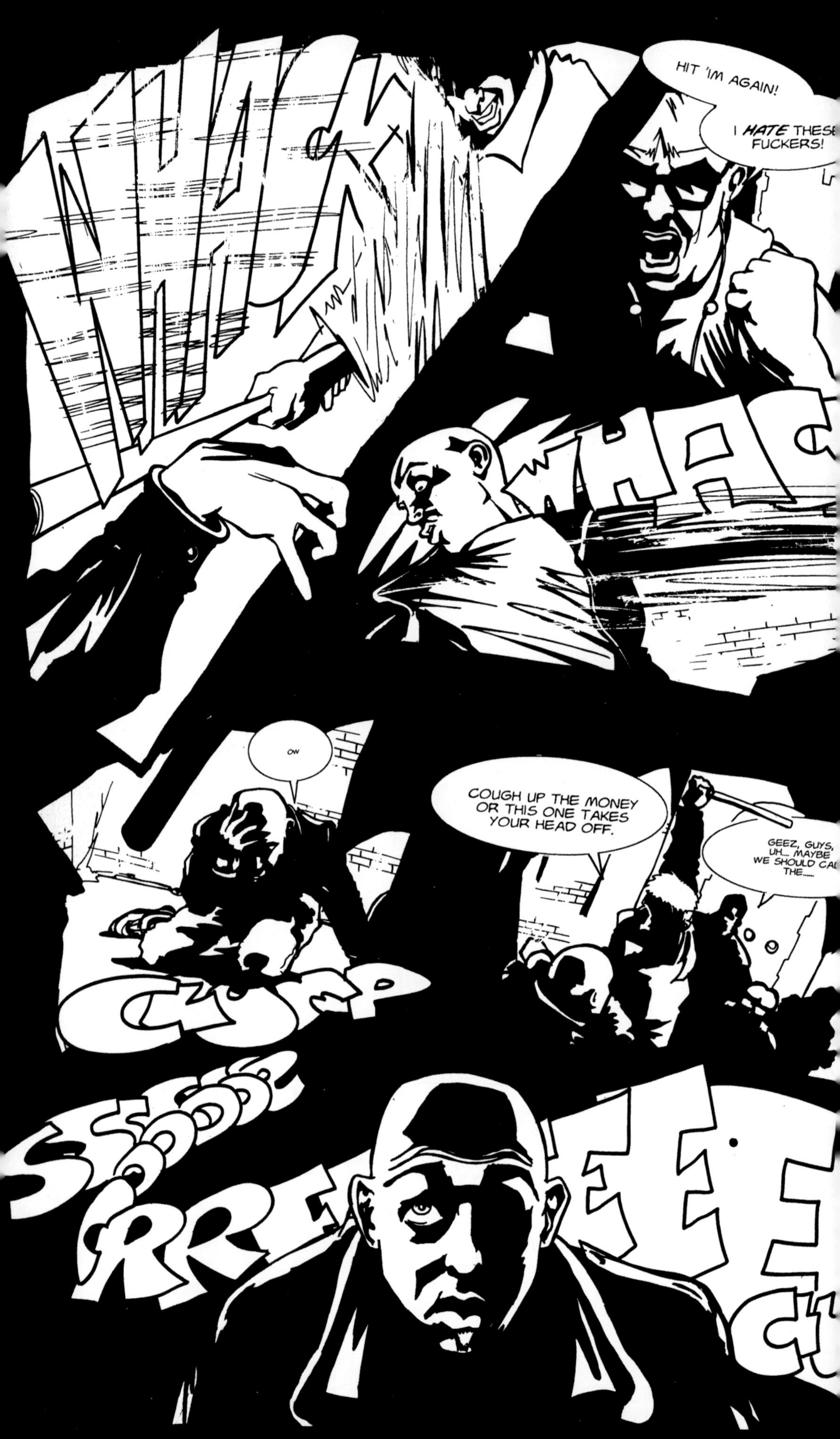
HIT 'IM AGAIN!
I HATE THESE FUCKERS!
OW
COUGH UP THE MONEY OR THIS ONE TAKES YOUR HEAD OFF.
GEEZ, GUYS, UH... MAYBE WE SHOULD CAL THE.....

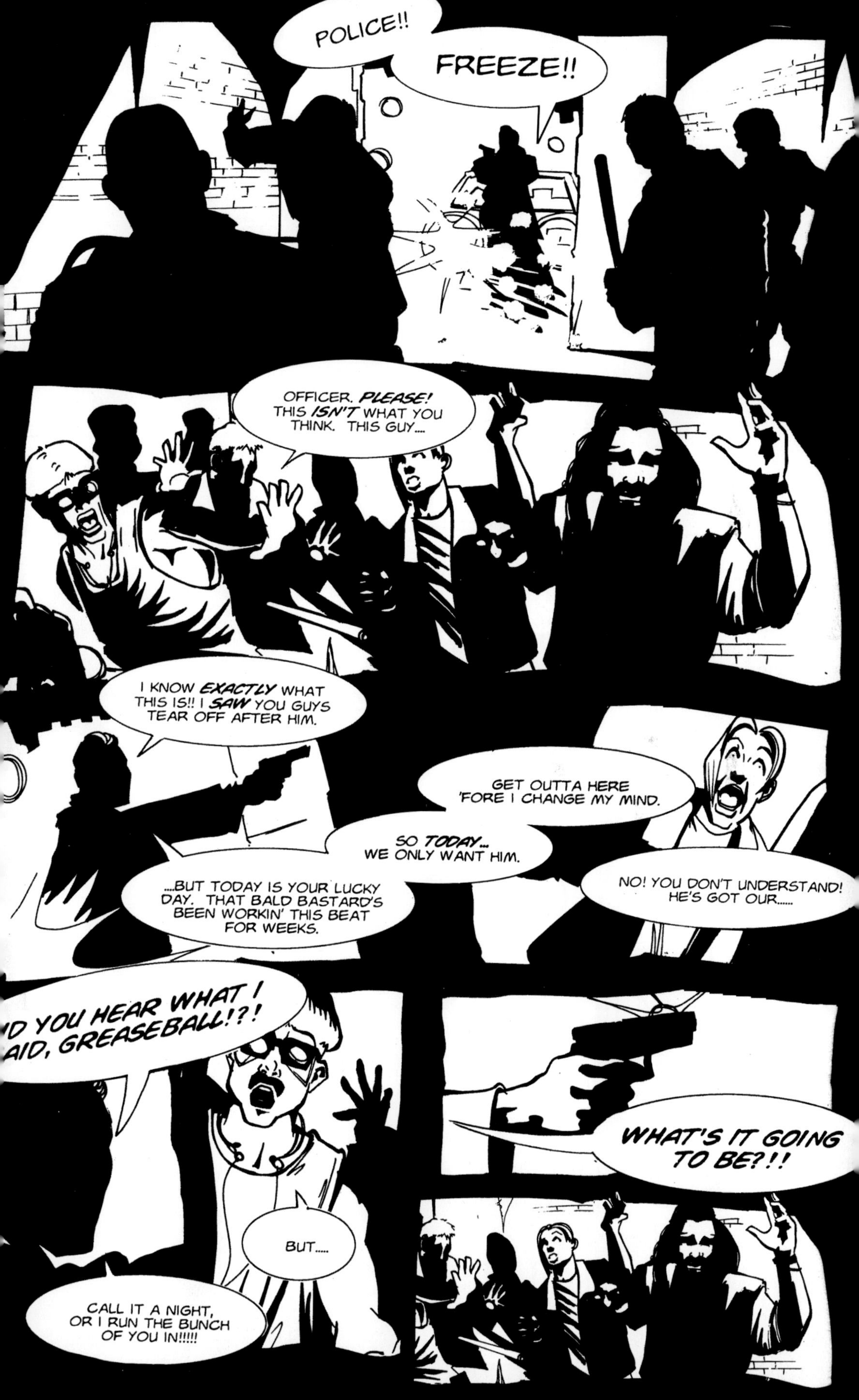
POLICE!!
FREEZE!!
OFFICER. PLEASE! THIS ISN'T WHAT YOU THINK. THIS GUY....
I KNOW EXACTLY WHAT THIS IS!! I SAW YOU GUYS TEAR OFF AFTER HIM.
...BUT TODAY IS YOUR LUCKY DAY. THAT BALD BASTARD'S BEEN WORKIN' THIS BEAT FOR WEEKS.
SO TODAY... WE ONLY WANT HIM.
GET OUTTA HERE 'FORE I CHANGE MY MIND.
NO! YOU DON'T UNDERSTAND! HE'S GOT OUR......
D YOU HEAR WHAT I AID, GREASEBALL!?!
BUT....
CALL IT A NIGHT, OR I RUN THE BUNCH OF YOU IN!!!!!
WHAT'S IT GOING TO BE?!!

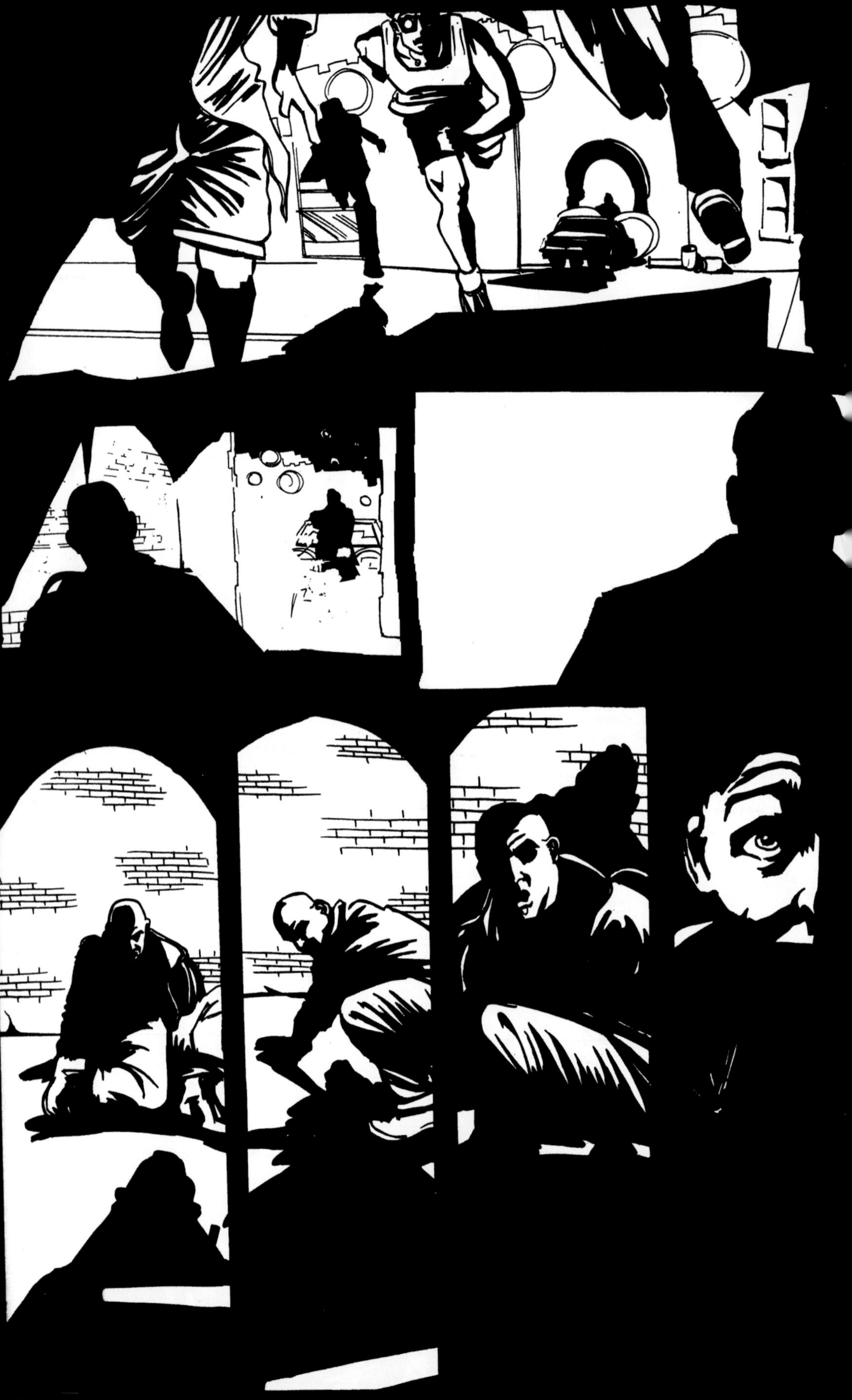

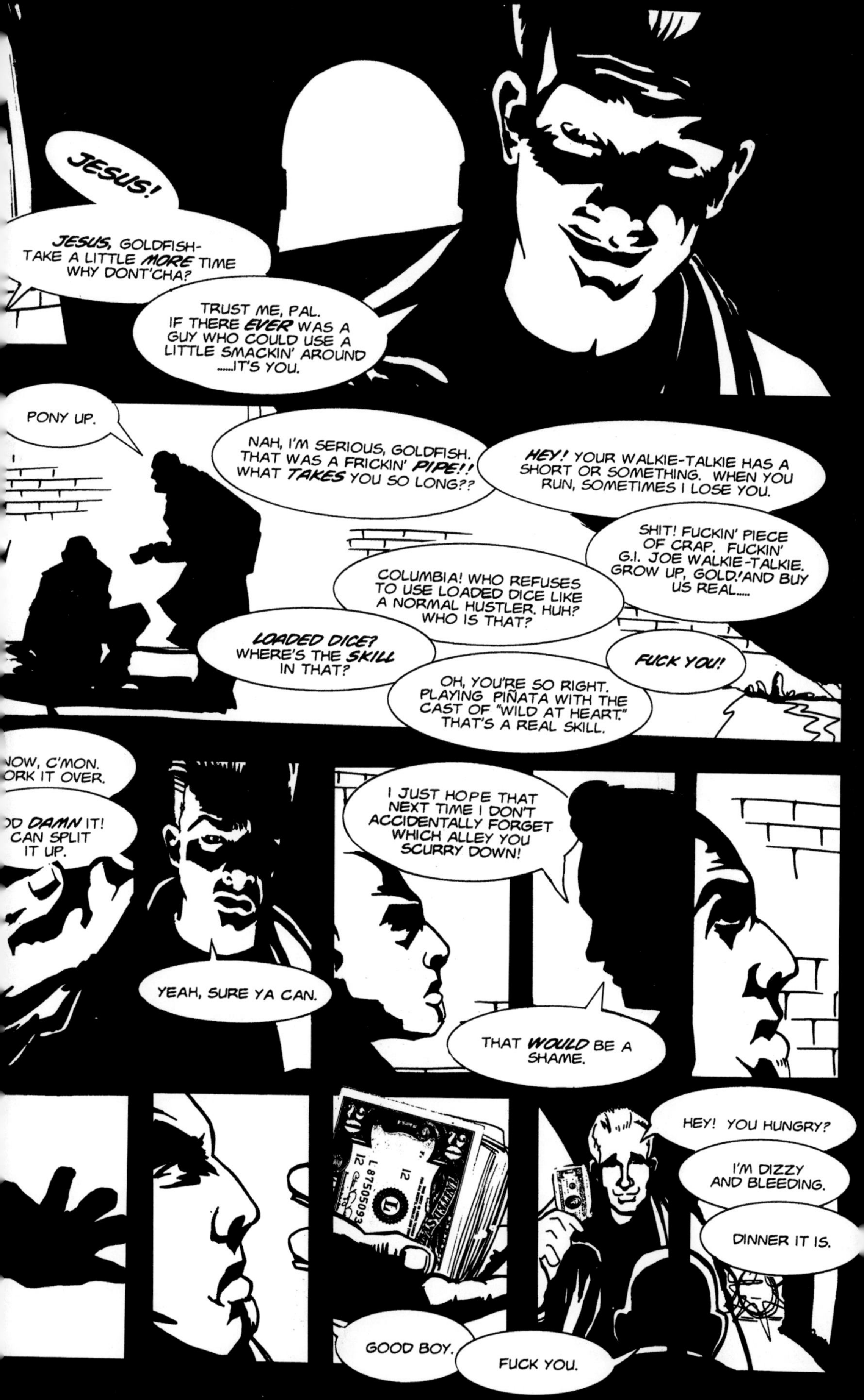
JESUS!
JESUS, GOLDFISH- TAKE A LITTLE MORE TIME WHY DONT'CHA?
TRUST ME, PAL. IF THERE EVER WAS A GUY WHO COULD USE A LITTLE SMACKIN' AROUND .....IT'S YOU.
PONY UP.
NAH, I'M SERIOUS, GOLDFISH. THAT WAS A FRICKIN' PIPE!! WHAT TAKES YOU SO LONG??
HEY! YOUR WALKIE-TALKIE HAS A SHORT OR SOMETHING. WHEN YOU RUN, SOMETIMES I LOSE YOU.
SHIT! FUCKIN' PIECE OF CRAP. FUCKIN' G.I. JOE WALKIE-TALKIE. GROW UP, GOLD, AND BUY US REAL.....
COLUMBIA! WHO REFUSES TO USE LOADED DICE LIKE A NORMAL HUSTLER. HUH? WHO IS THAT?
LOADED DICE? WHERE'S THE SKILL IN THAT?
FUCK YOU!
OH, YOU'RE SO RIGHT. PLAYING PIÑATA WITH THE CAST OF "WILD AT HEART." THAT'S A REAL SKILL.
NOW, C'MON. ORK IT OVER.
OD DAMN IT! CAN SPLIT IT UP.
YEAH, SURE YA CAN.
I JUST HOPE THAT NEXT TIME I DON'T ACCIDENTALLY FORGET WHICH ALLEY YOU SCURRY DOWN!
THAT WOULD BE A SHAME.
GOOD BOY.
FUCK YOU.
HEY! YOU HUNGRY?
I'M DIZZY AND BLEEDING.
DINNER IT IS.

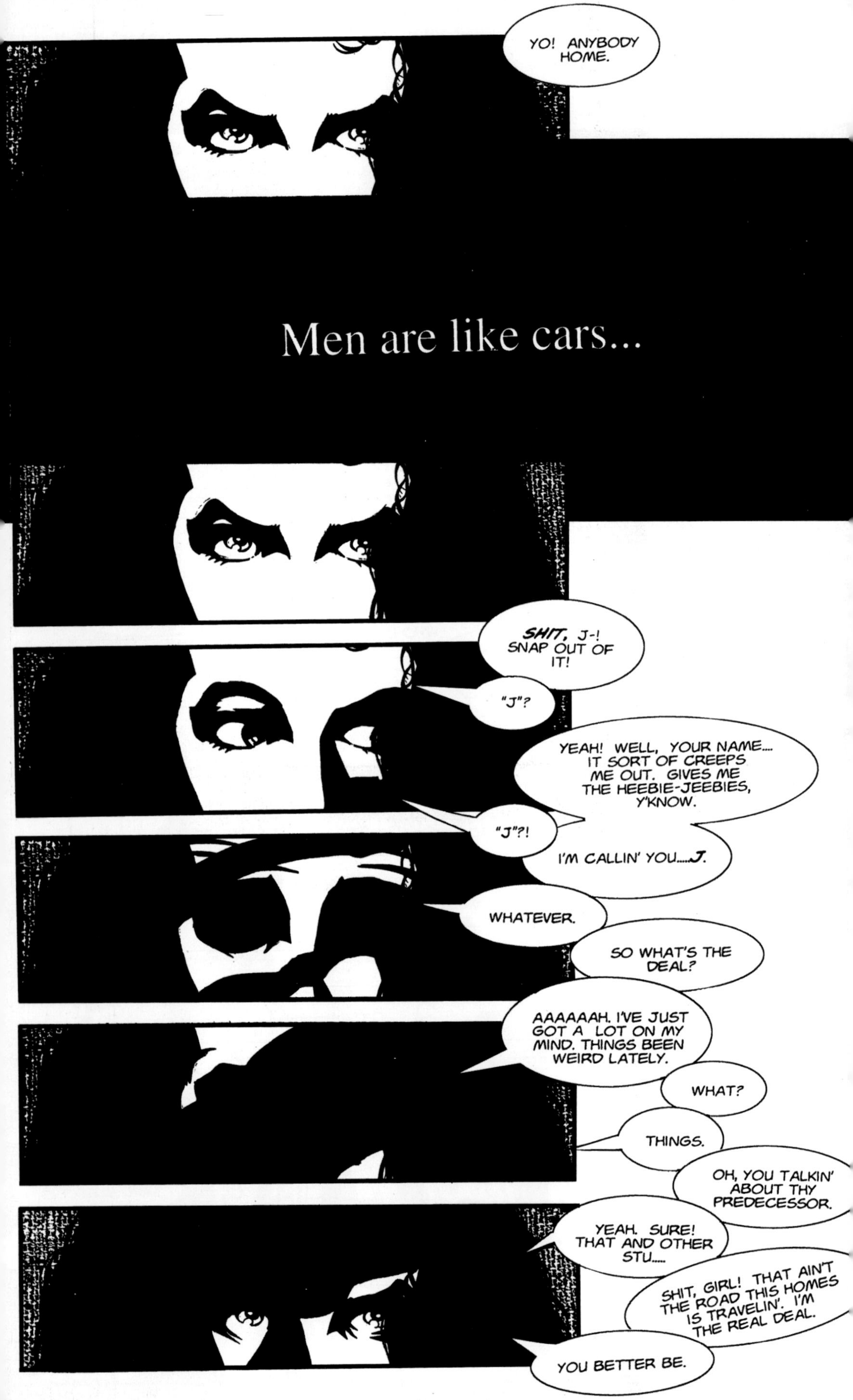
YO! ANYBODY HOME.
Men are like cars...
SHIT, J-! SNAP OUT OF IT!
"J"?
YEAH! WELL, YOUR NAME.... IT SORT OF CREEPS ME OUT. GIVES ME THE HEEBIE-JEEBIES, Y'KNOW.
"J"?!
I'M CALLIN' YOU.....J.
WHATEVER.
SO WHAT'S THE DEAL?
AAAAAAH. I'VE JUST GOT A LOT ON MY MIND. THINGS BEEN WEIRD LATELY.
WHAT?
THINGS.
OH, YOU TALKIN' ABOUT THY PREDECESSOR.
YEAH. SURE! THAT AND OTHER STU.....
SHIT, GIRL! THAT AIN'T THE ROAD THIS HOMES IS TRAVELIN'. I'M THE REAL DEAL.
YOU BETTER BE.

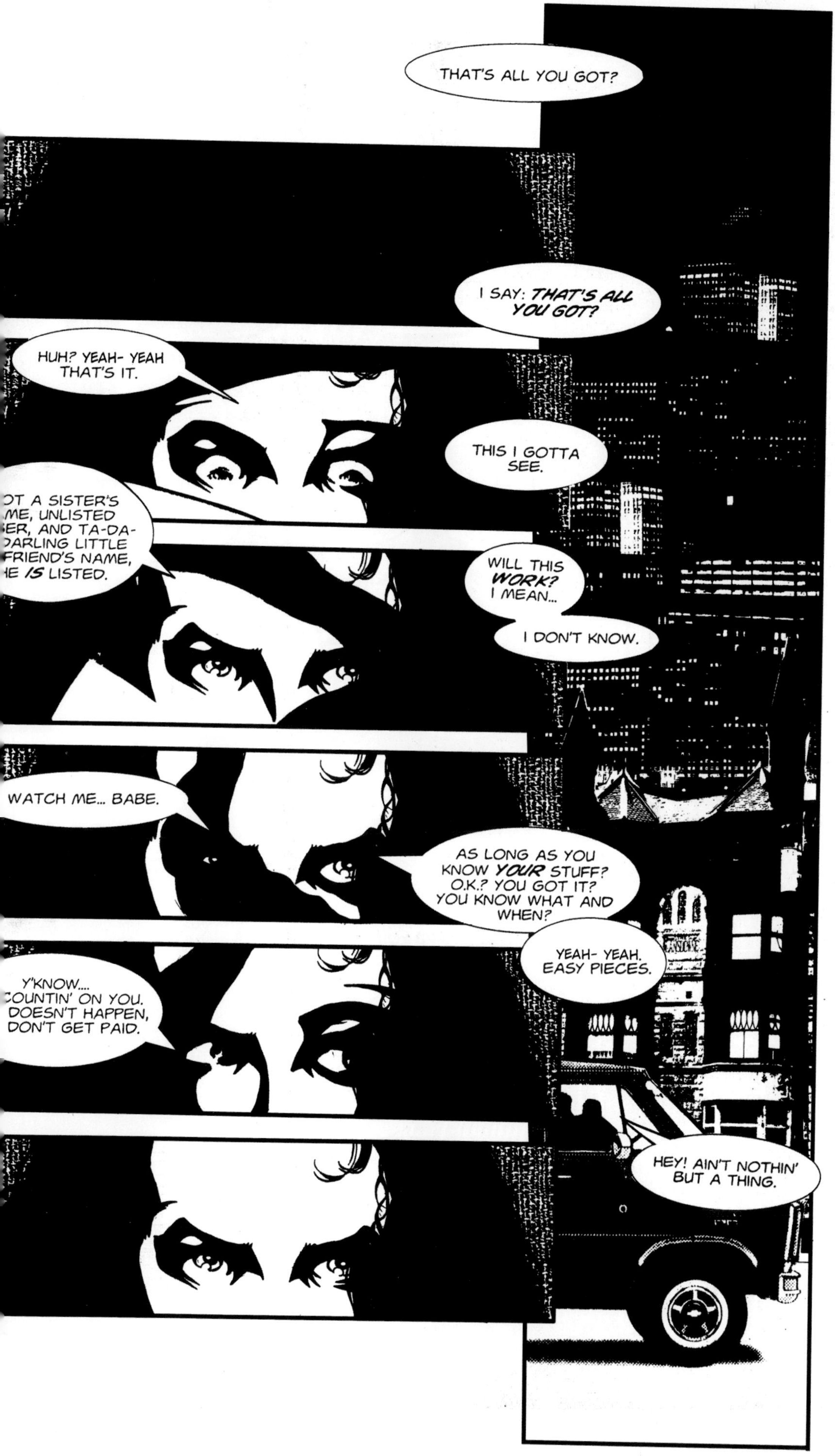
THAT'S ALL YOU GOT?
I SAY: THAT'S ALL YOU GOT?
HUH? YEAH- YEAH THAT'S IT.
THIS I GOTTA SEE.
OT A SISTER'S ME, UNLISTED ER, AND TA-DA- DARLING LITTLE FRIEND'S NAME, IE IS LISTED.
WILL THIS WORK? I MEAN...
I DON'T KNOW.
WATCH ME... BABE.
AS LONG AS YOU KNOW YOUR STUFF? O.K.? YOU GOT IT? YOU KNOW WHAT AND WHEN?
YEAH- YEAH. EASY PIECES.
Y'KNOW.... COUNTIN' ON YOU. DOESN'T HAPPEN, DON'T GET PAID.
HEY! AIN'T NOTHIN' BUT A THING.

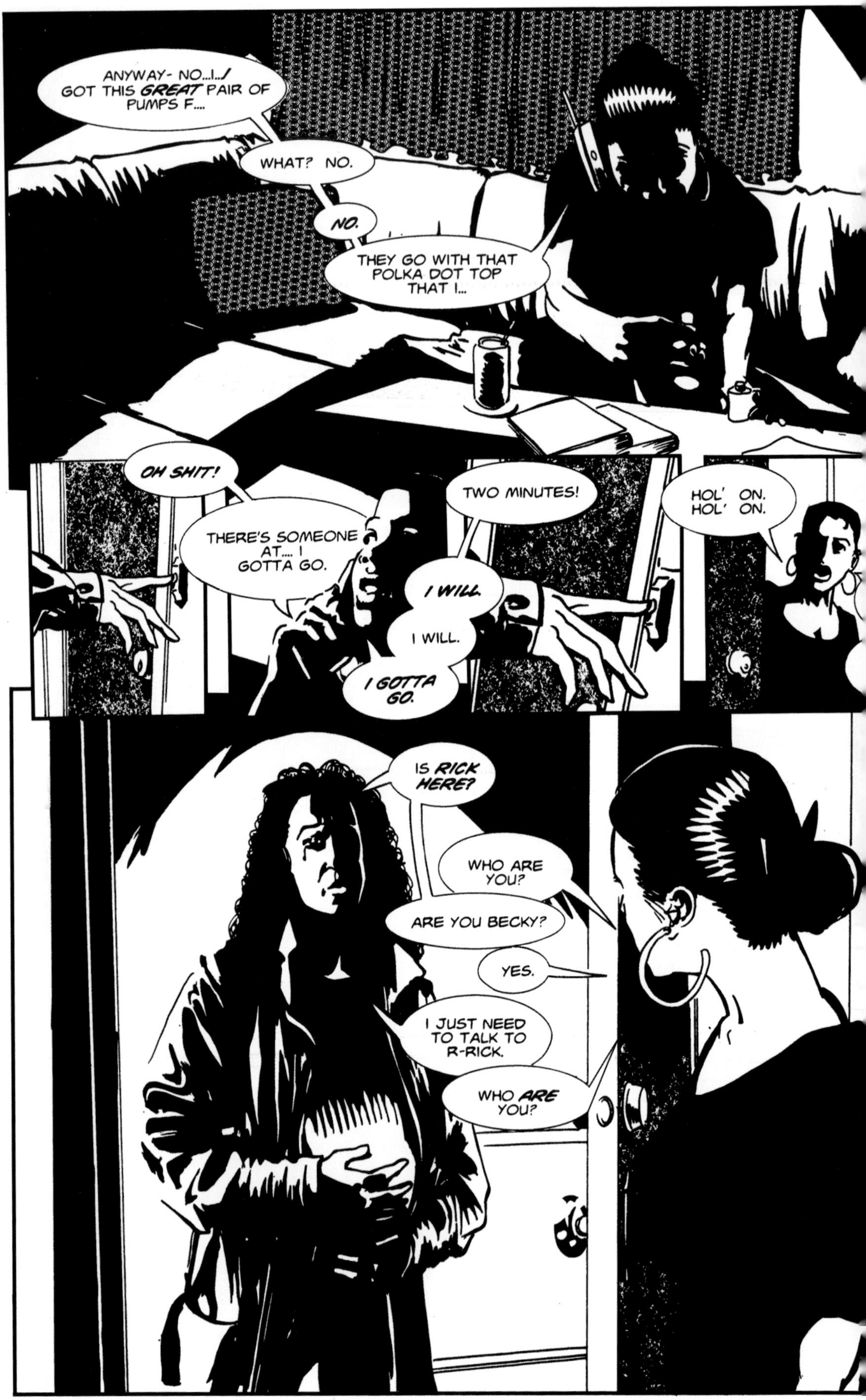
ANYWAY- NO...I...! GOT THIS *GREAT* PAIR OF PUMPS F....
WHAT? NO.
NO.
THEY GO WITH THAT POLKA DOT TOP THAT I...
OH SHIT!
THERE'S SOMEONE AT.... I GOTTA GO.
TWO MINUTES!
I WILL.
I WILL.
I GOTTA GO.
HOL' ON. HOL' ON.
IS *RICK HERE?*
WHO ARE YOU?
ARE YOU BECKY?
YES.
I JUST NEED TO TALK TO R-RICK.
WHO *ARE* YOU?

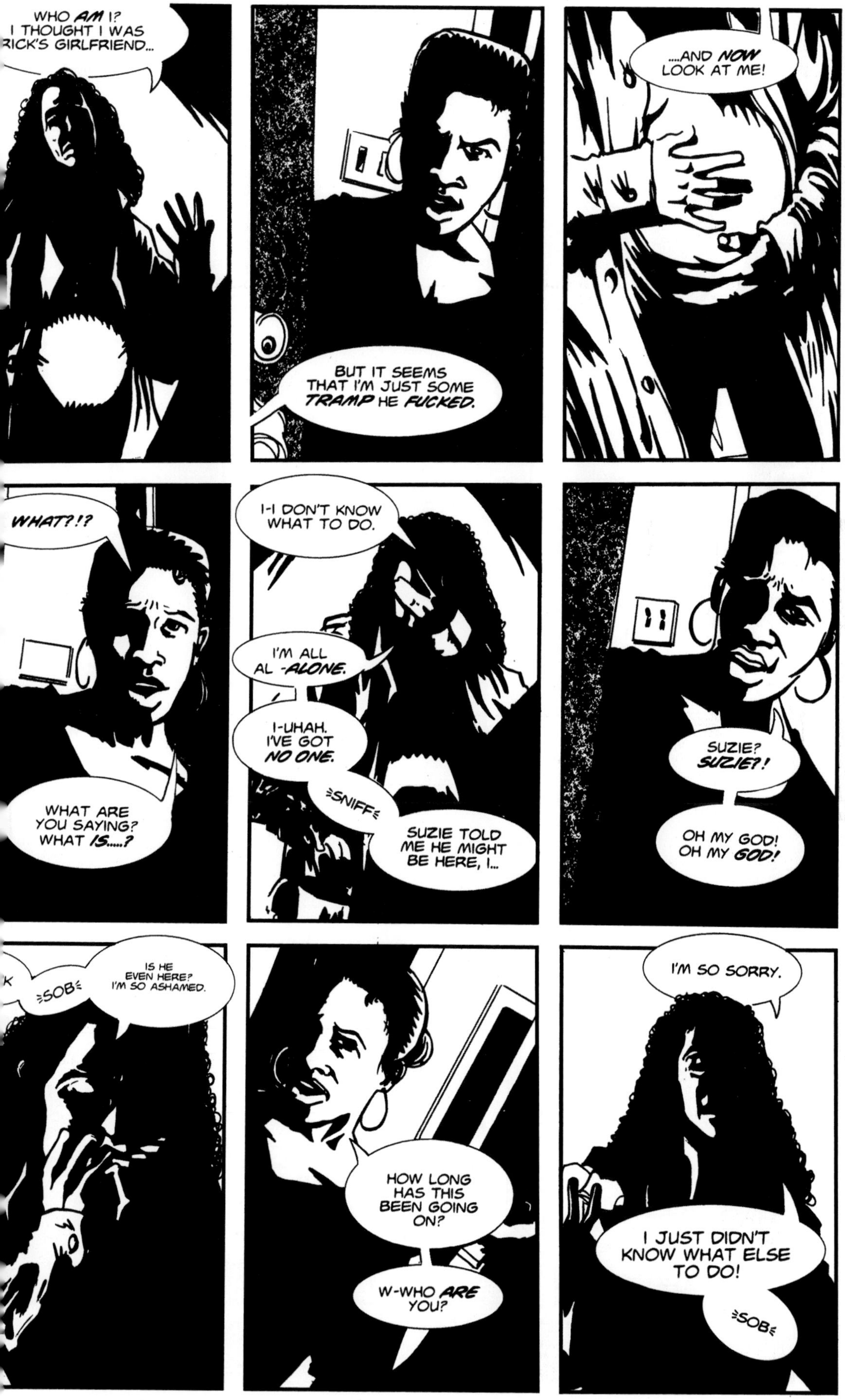

WHO AM I? I THOUGHT I WAS RICK'S GIRLFRIEND...
BUT IT SEEMS THAT I'M JUST SOME TRAMP HE FUCKED.
...AND NOW LOOK AT ME!
WHAT?!?
WHAT ARE YOU SAYING? WHAT IS.....?
I-I DON'T KNOW WHAT TO DO.
I'M ALL AL-ALONE.
I-UHAH. I'VE GOT NO ONE.
SNIFF
SUZIE TOLD ME HE MIGHT BE HERE, I...
SUZIE? SUZIE?!
OH MY GOD! OH MY GOD!
SOB
IS HE EVEN HERE? I'M SO ASHAMED.
HOW LONG HAS THIS BEEN GOING ON?
W-WHO ARE YOU?
I'M SO SORRY.
I JUST DIDN'T KNOW WHAT ELSE TO DO!
SOB

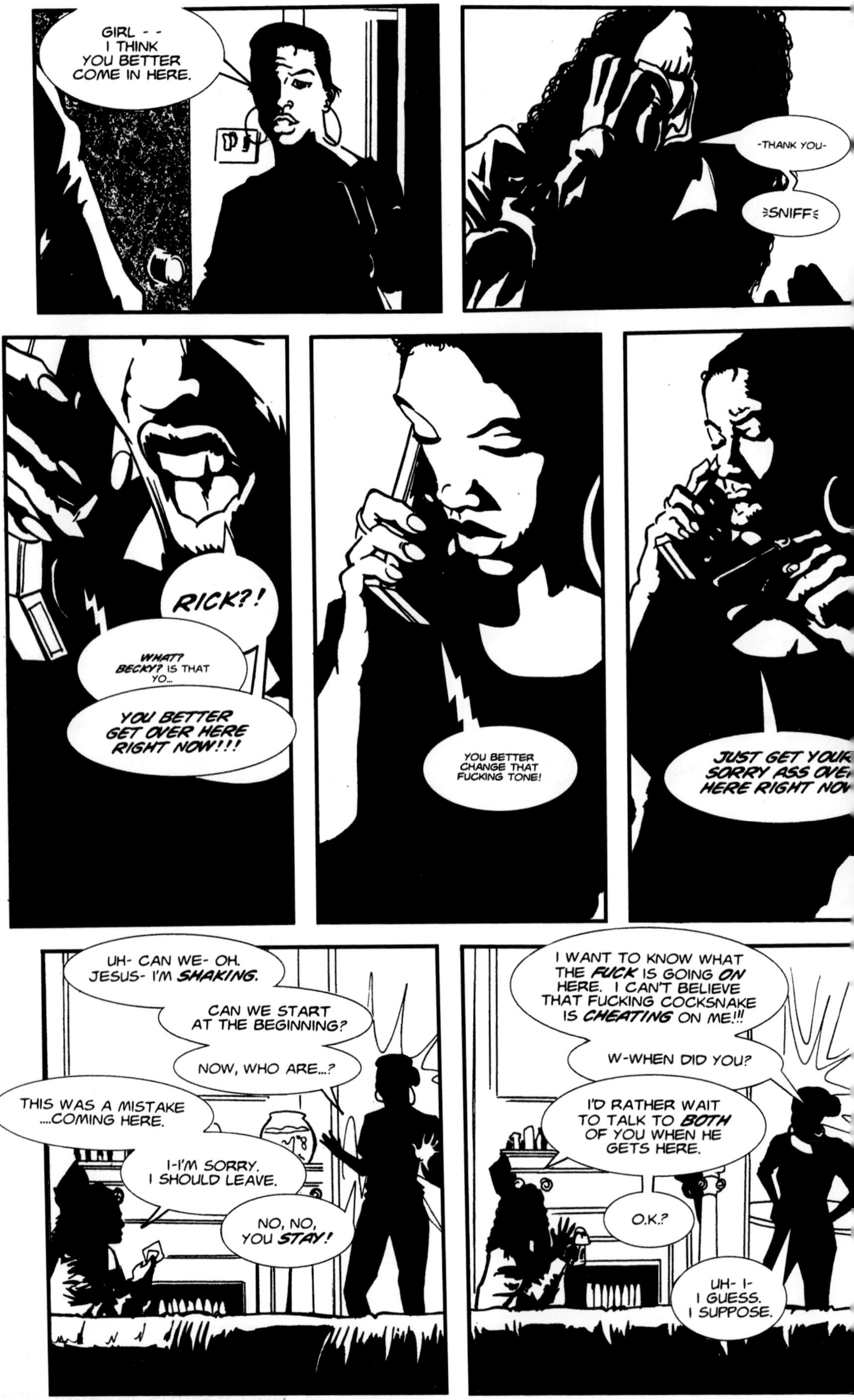
GIRL - - I THINK YOU BETTER COME IN HERE.
-THANK YOU-
SNIFF
RICK?!
WHAT? BECKY? IS THAT YO...
YOU BETTER GET OVER HERE RIGHT NOW!!!
YOU BETTER CHANGE THAT FUCKING TONE!
JUST GET YOUR SORRY ASS OVER HERE RIGHT NOW
UH- CAN WE- OH. JESUS- I'M SHAKING.
CAN WE START AT THE BEGINNING?
NOW, WHO ARE...?
THIS WAS A MISTAKE ....COMING HERE.
I-I'M SORRY. I SHOULD LEAVE.
NO, NO, YOU STAY!
I WANT TO KNOW WHAT THE FUCK IS GOING ON HERE. I CAN'T BELIEVE THAT FUCKING COCKSNAKE IS CHEATING ON ME!!!
W-WHEN DID YOU?
I'D RATHER WAIT TO TALK TO BOTH OF YOU WHEN HE GETS HERE.
O.K.?
UH- I- I GUESS. I SUPPOSE.

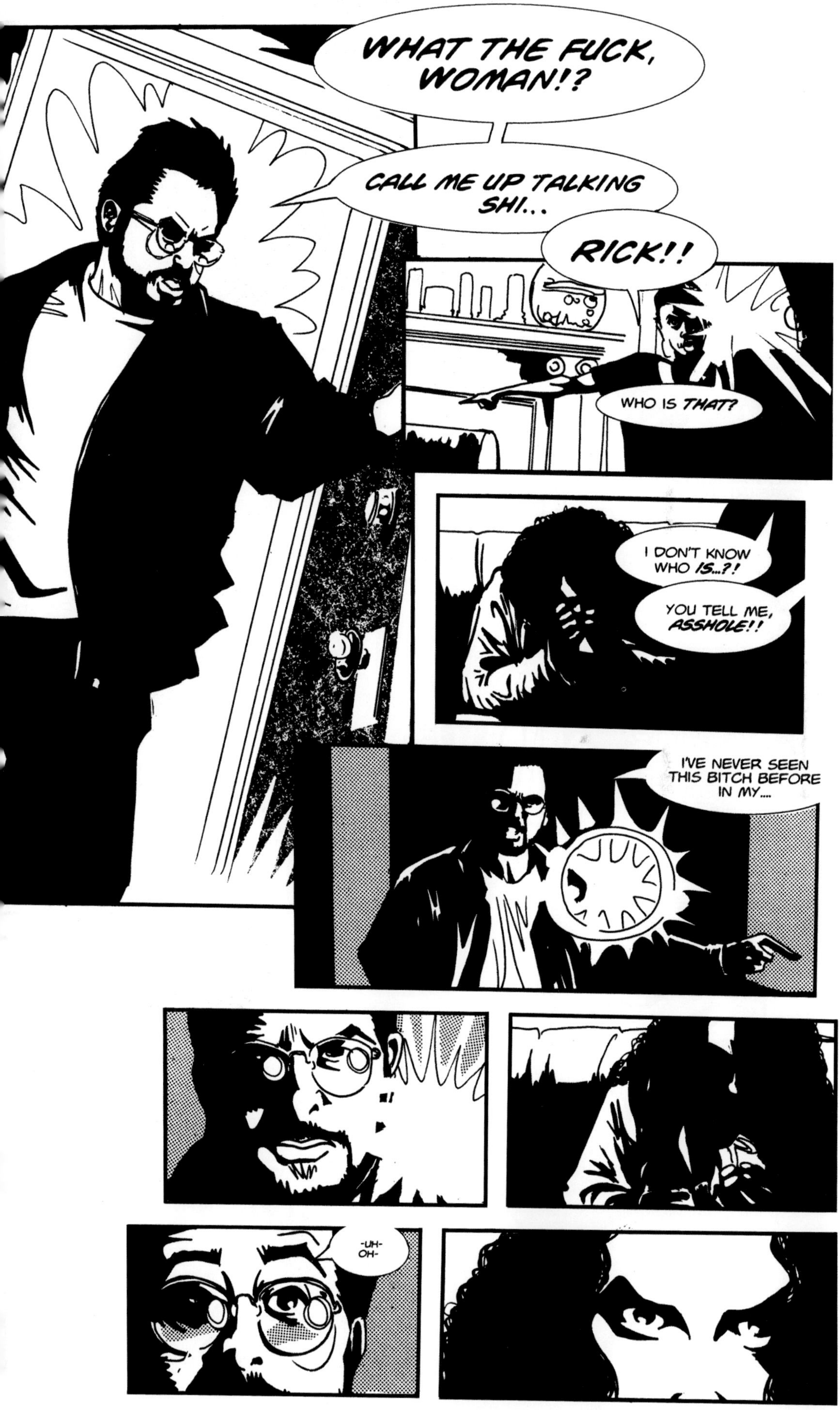
WHAT THE FUCK, WOMAN!?
CALL ME UP TALKING SHI...
RICK!!
WHO IS THAT?
I DON'T KNOW WHO IS...?!
YOU TELL ME, ASSHOLE!!
I'VE NEVER SEEN THIS BITCH BEFORE IN MY....
-UH-OH-

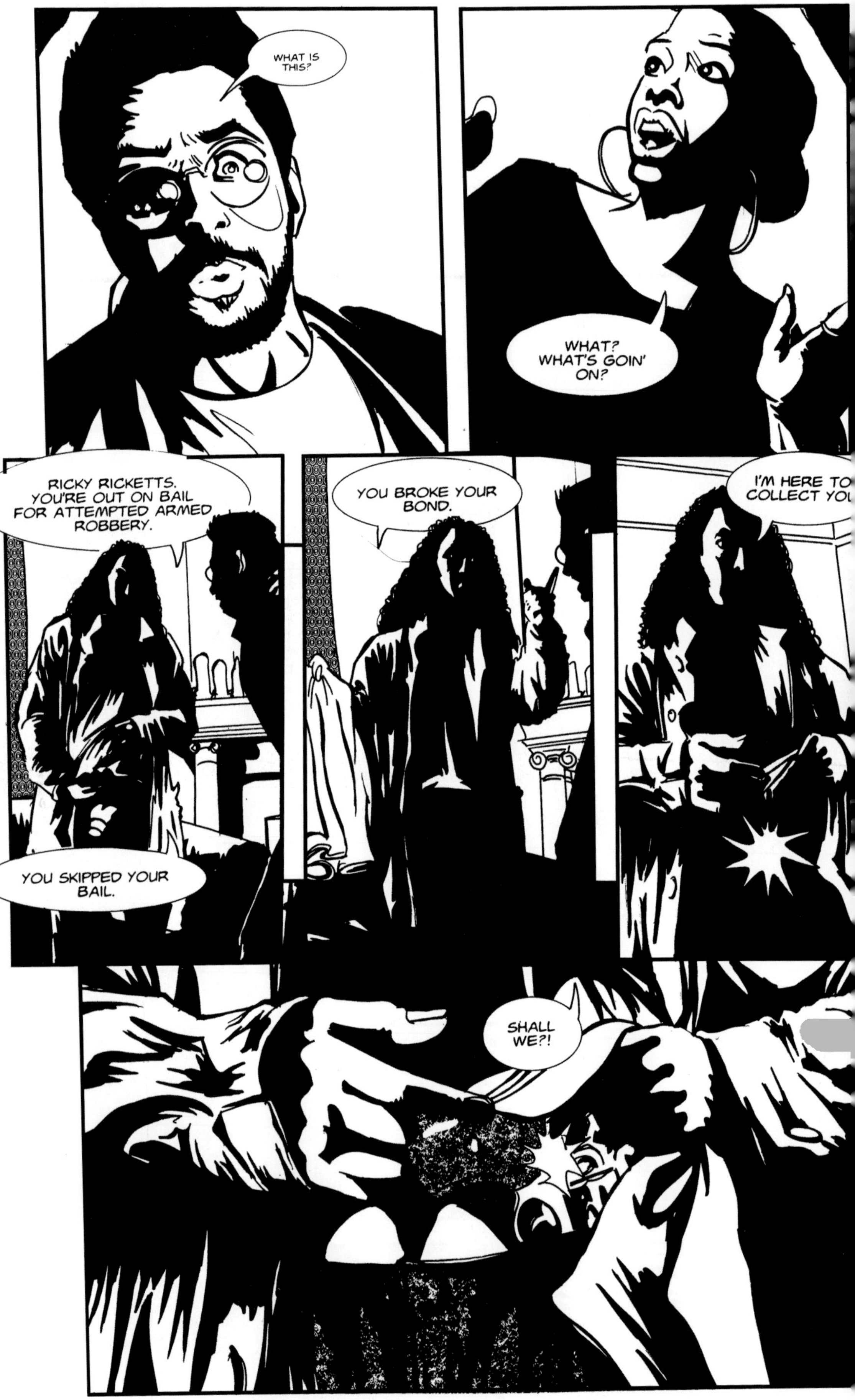
WHAT IS THIS?
WHAT? WHAT'S GOIN' ON?
RICKY RICKETTS. YOU'RE OUT ON BAIL FOR ATTEMPTED ARMED ROBBERY.
YOU SKIPPED YOUR BAIL.
YOU BROKE YOUR BOND.
I'M HERE TO COLLECT YOU
SHALL WE?!

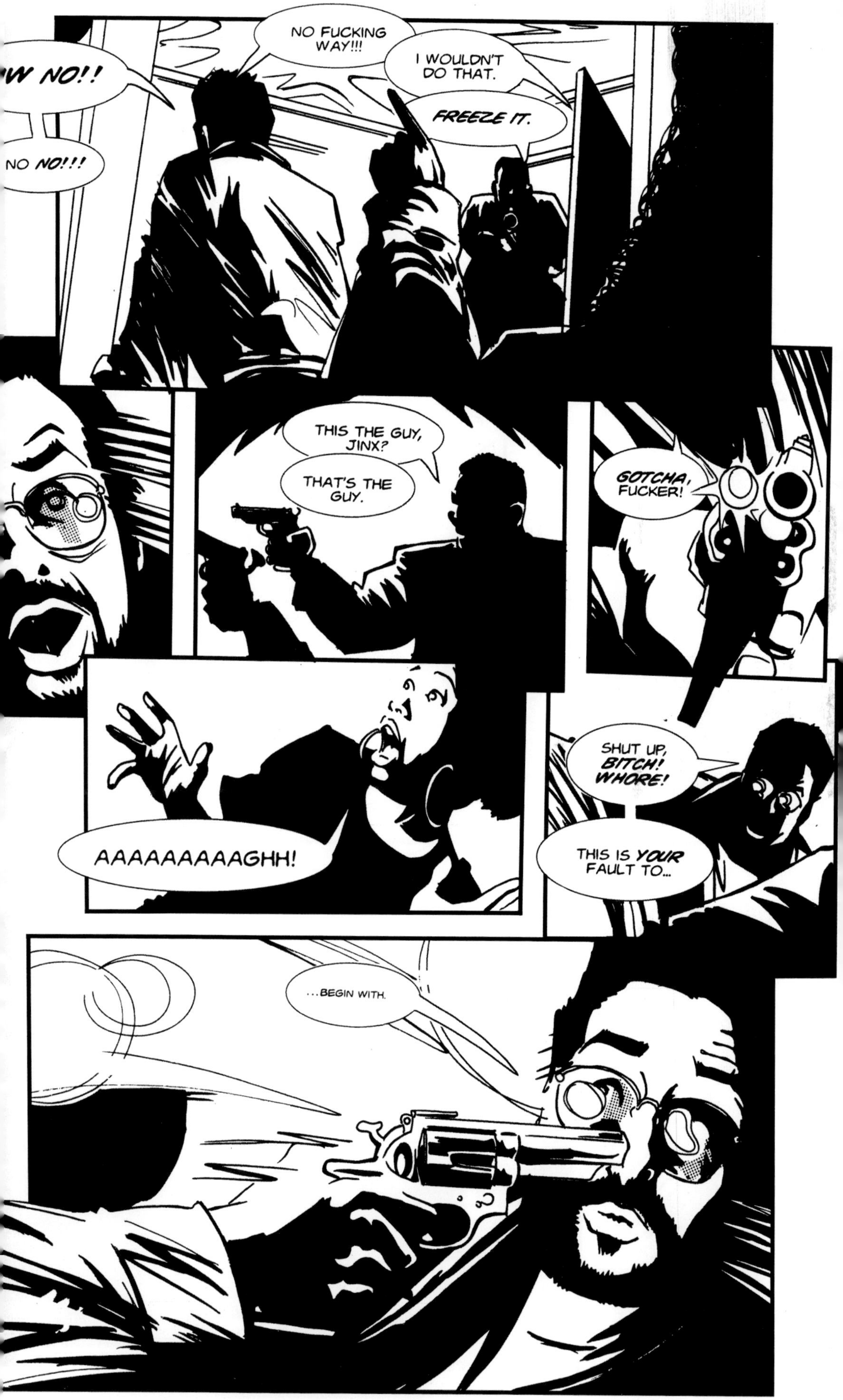

W NO!!
NO NO!!!
NO FUCKING WAY!!!
I WOULDN'T DO THAT.
FREEZE IT.
THIS THE GUY, JINX?
THAT'S THE GUY.
GOTCHA, FUCKER!
AAAAAAAAAAGHH!
SHUT UP, BITCH! WHORE!
THIS IS YOUR FAULT TO...
...BEGIN WITH.

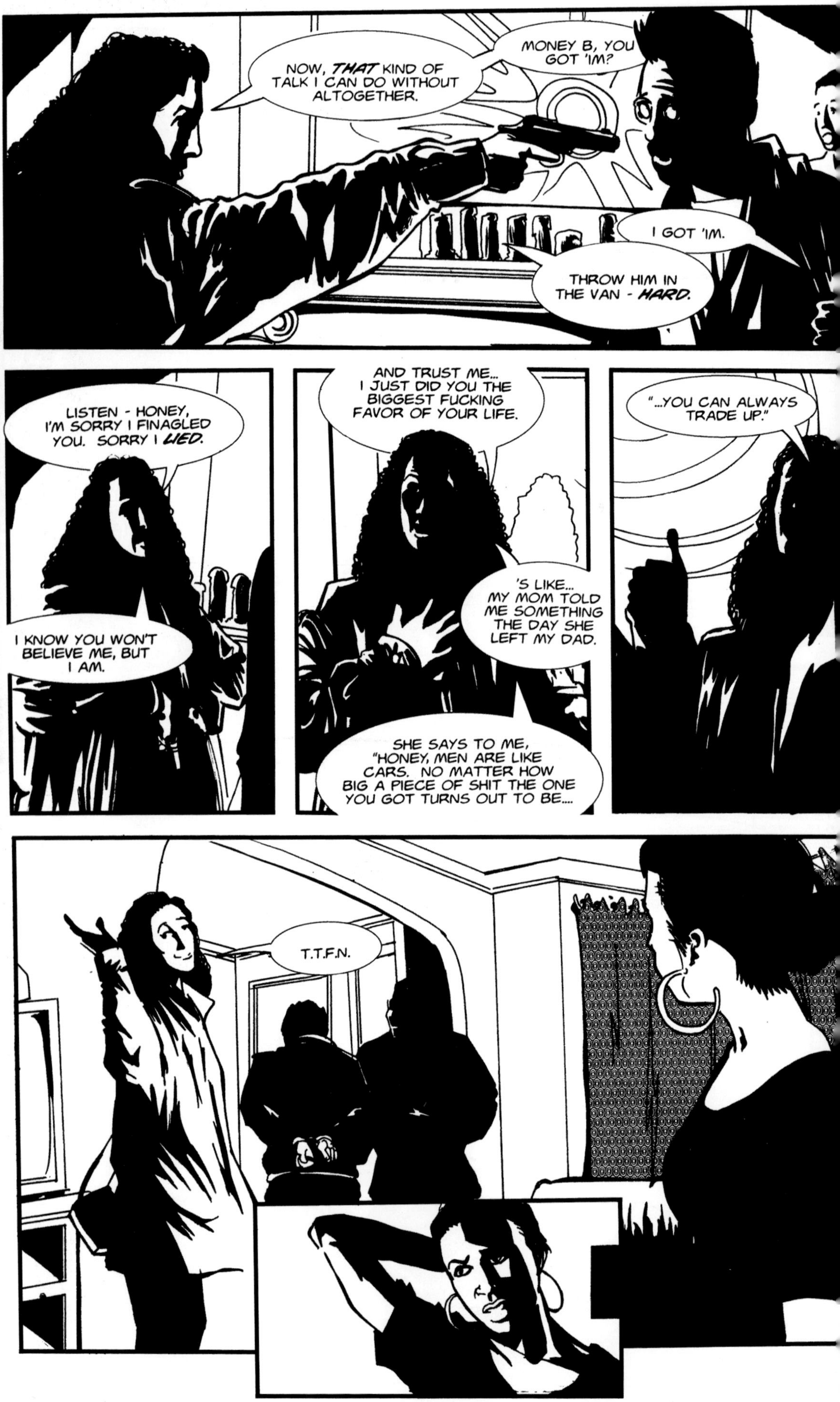

NOW, THAT KIND OF TALK I CAN DO WITHOUT ALTOGETHER.
MONEY B, YOU GOT 'IM?
I GOT 'IM.
THROW HIM IN THE VAN - HARD.
LISTEN - HONEY, I'M SORRY I FINAGLED YOU. SORRY I LIED.
I KNOW YOU WON'T BELIEVE ME, BUT I AM.
AND TRUST ME... I JUST DID YOU THE BIGGEST FUCKING FAVOR OF YOUR LIFE.
'S LIKE... MY MOM TOLD ME SOMETHING THE DAY SHE LEFT MY DAD.
SHE SAYS TO ME, "HONEY, MEN ARE LIKE CARS. NO MATTER HOW BIG A PIECE OF SHIT THE ONE YOU GOT TURNS OUT TO BE....
"...YOU CAN ALWAYS TRADE UP."
T.T.F.N.

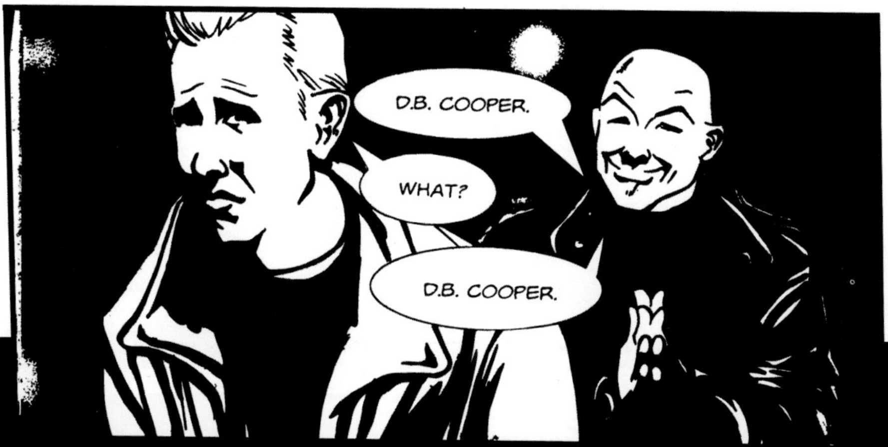
D.B. COOPER.
WHAT?
D.B. COOPER.

Real Money

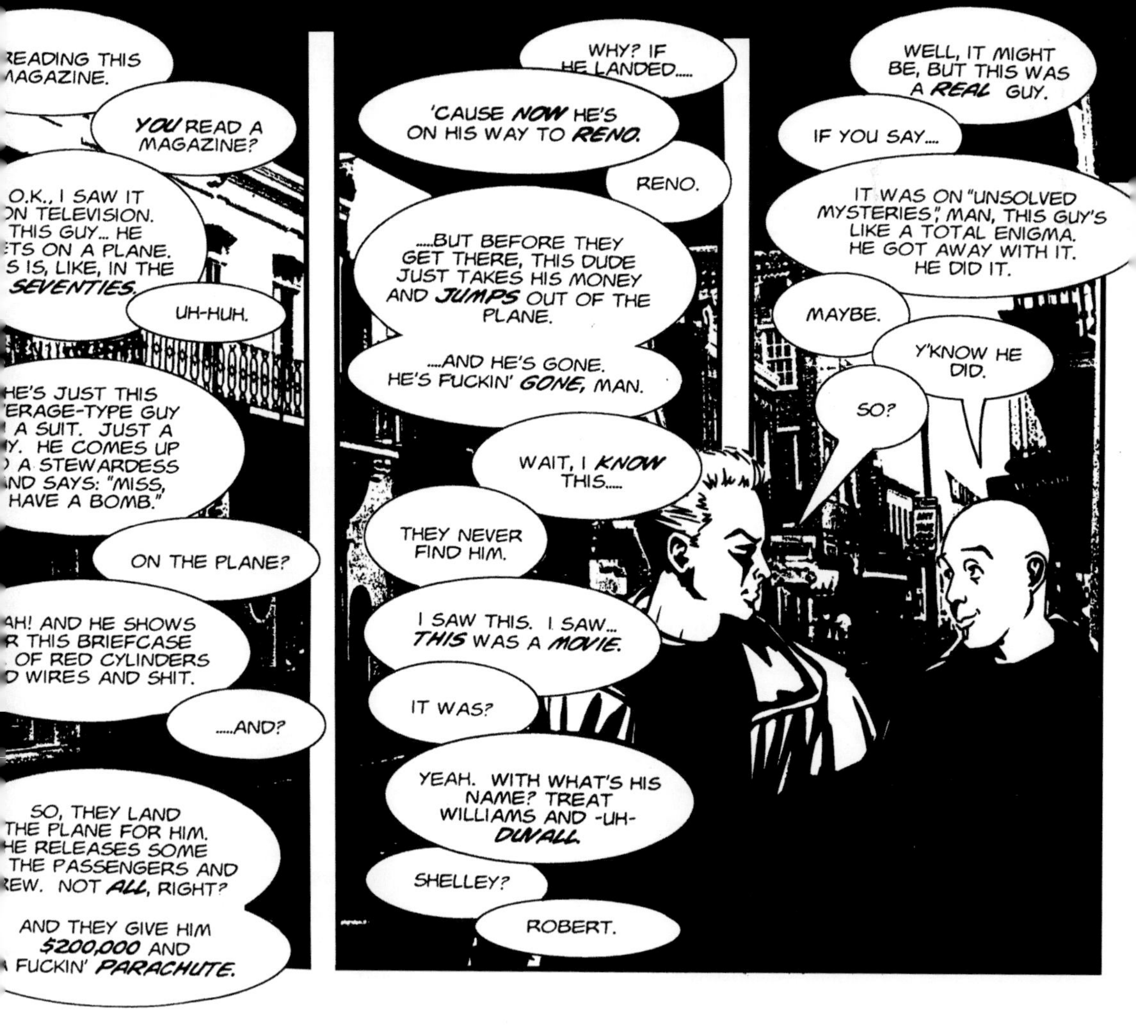
READING THIS MAGAZINE.
YOU READ A MAGAZINE?
O.K., I SAW IT ON TELEVISION. THIS GUY... HE ETS ON A PLANE. S IS, LIKE, IN THE SEVENTIES.
UH-HUH.
HE'S JUST THIS ERAGE-TYPE GUY A SUIT. JUST A Y. HE COMES UP A STEWARDESS ND SAYS: "MISS, HAVE A BOMB."
ON THE PLANE?
AH! AND HE SHOWS R THIS BRIEFCASE OF RED CYLINDERS D WIRES AND SHIT.
.....AND?
SO, THEY LAND THE PLANE FOR HIM. HE RELEASES SOME THE PASSENGERS AND REW. NOT ALL, RIGHT?
AND THEY GIVE HIM $200,000 AND FUCKIN' PARACHUTE.
WHY? IF HE LANDED.....
'CAUSE NOW HE'S ON HIS WAY TO RENO.
RENO.
.....BUT BEFORE THEY GET THERE, THIS DUDE JUST TAKES HIS MONEY AND JUMPS OUT OF THE PLANE.
....AND HE'S GONE. HE'S FUCKIN' GONE, MAN.
WAIT, I KNOW THIS.....
THEY NEVER FIND HIM.
I SAW THIS. I SAW... THIS WAS A MOVIE.
IT WAS?
YEAH. WITH WHAT'S HIS NAME? TREAT WILLIAMS AND -UH- DUVALL.
SHELLEY?
ROBERT.
WELL, IT MIGHT BE, BUT THIS WAS A REAL GUY.
IF YOU SAY....
IT WAS ON "UNSOLVED MYSTERIES," MAN, THIS GUY'S LIKE A TOTAL ENIGMA. HE GOT AWAY WITH IT. HE DID IT.
MAYBE.
Y'KNOW HE DID.
SO?

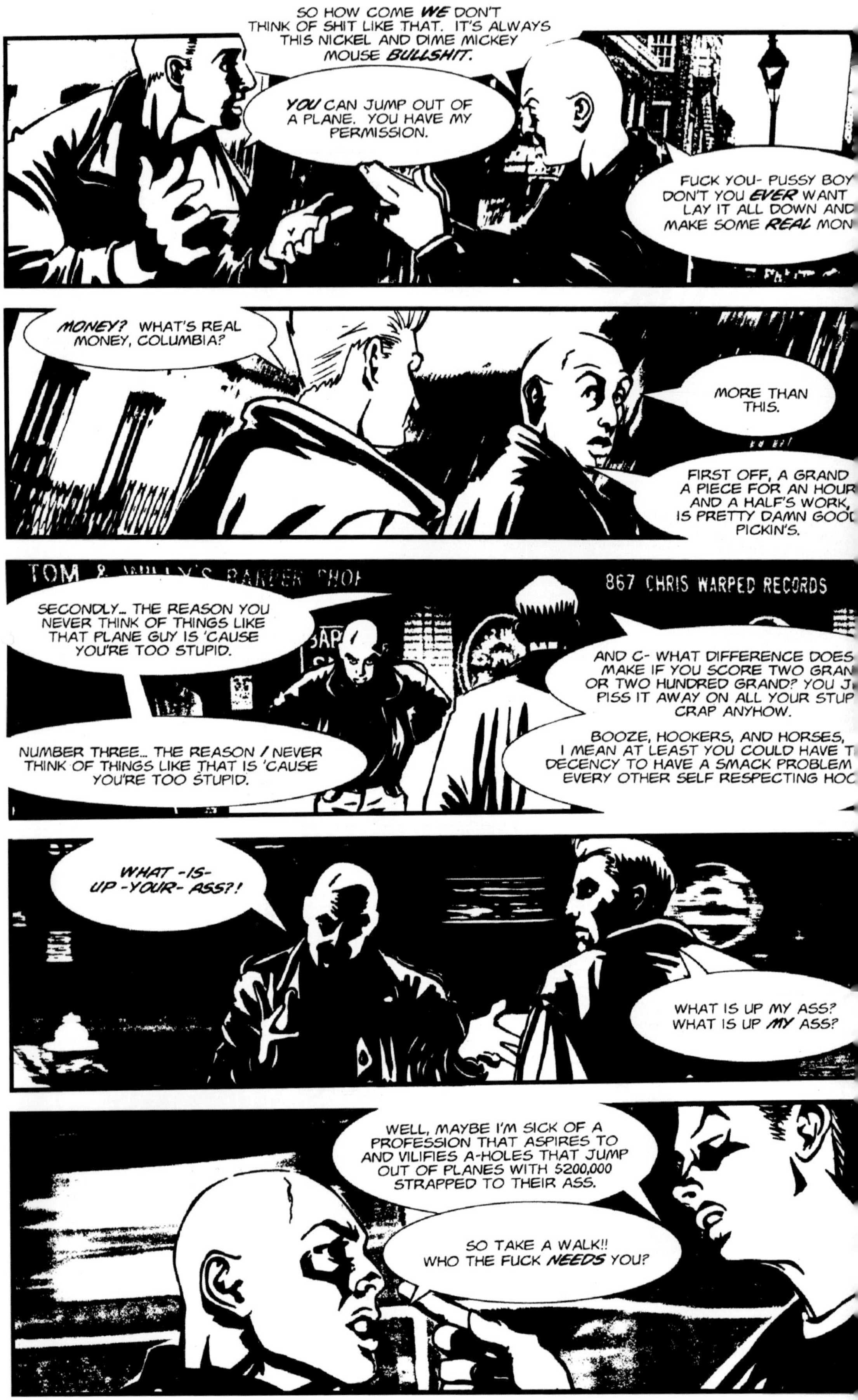
SO HOW COME WE DON'T THINK OF SHIT LIKE THAT. IT'S ALWAYS THIS NICKEL AND DIME MICKEY MOUSE BULLSHIT.
YOU CAN JUMP OUT OF A PLANE. YOU HAVE MY PERMISSION.
FUCK YOU- PUSSY BOY DON'T YOU EVER WANT LAY IT ALL DOWN AND MAKE SOME REAL MON
MONEY? WHAT'S REAL MONEY, COLUMBIA?
MORE THAN THIS.
FIRST OFF, A GRAND A PIECE FOR AN HOUR AND A HALF'S WORK, IS PRETTY DAMN GOOD PICKIN'S.
TOM &
867 CHRIS WARPED RECORDS
SECONDLY... THE REASON YOU NEVER THINK OF THINGS LIKE THAT PLANE GUY IS 'CAUSE YOU'RE TOO STUPID.
NUMBER THREE... THE REASON I NEVER THINK OF THINGS LIKE THAT IS 'CAUSE YOU'RE TOO STUPID.
AND C- WHAT DIFFERENCE DOES MAKE IF YOU SCORE TWO GRAN OR TWO HUNDRED GRAND? YOU J PISS IT AWAY ON ALL YOUR STUP CRAP ANYHOW.
BOOZE, HOOKERS, AND HORSES, I MEAN AT LEAST YOU COULD HAVE T DECENCY TO HAVE A SMACK PROBLEM EVERY OTHER SELF RESPECTING HOC
WHAT -IS- UP -YOUR- ASS?!
WHAT IS UP MY ASS? WHAT IS UP MY ASS?
WELL, MAYBE I'M SICK OF A PROFESSION THAT ASPIRES TO AND VILIFIES A-HOLES THAT JUMP OUT OF PLANES WITH $200,000 STRAPPED TO THEIR ASS.
SO TAKE A WALK!! WHO THE FUCK NEEDS YOU?

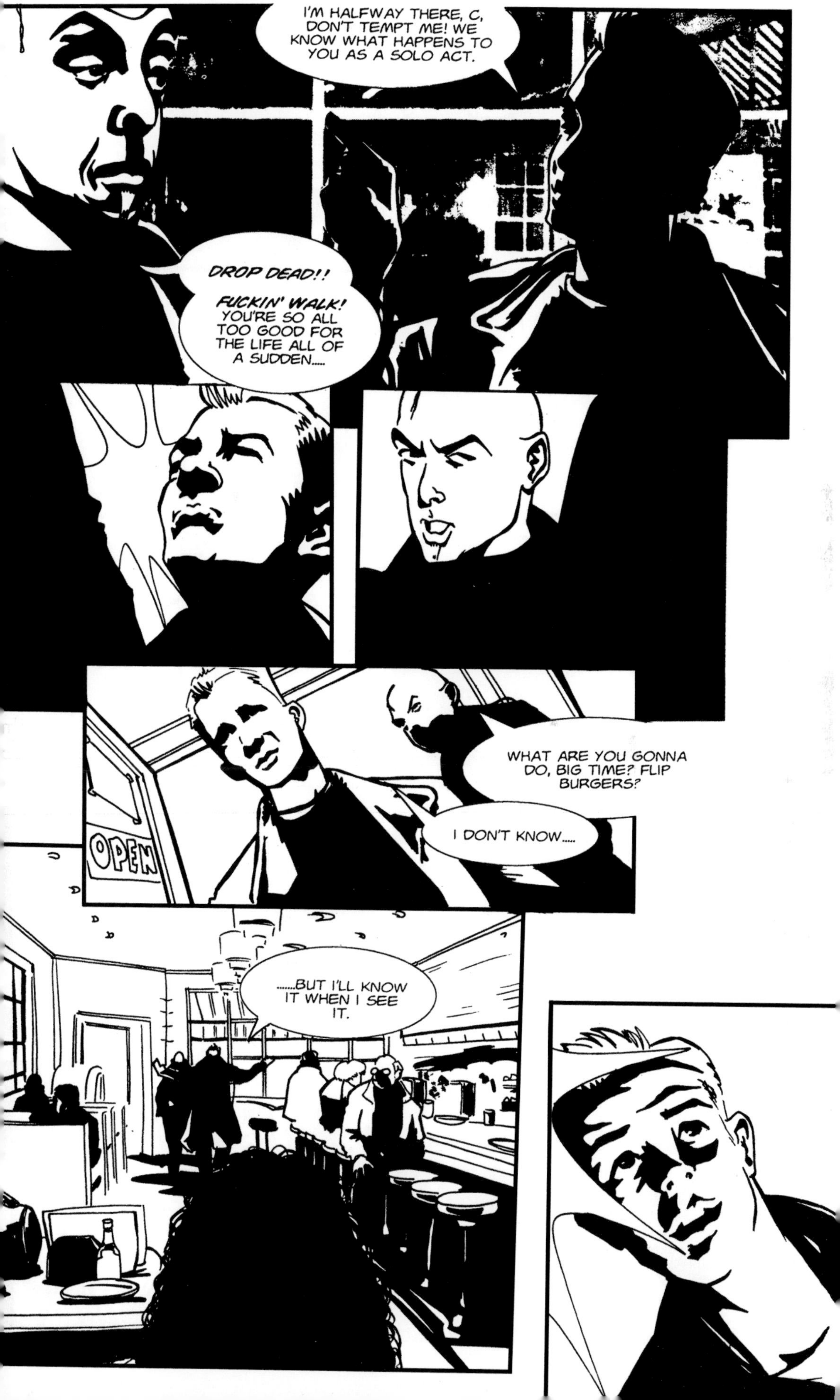
I'M HALFWAY THERE, C, DON'T TEMPT ME! WE KNOW WHAT HAPPENS TO YOU AS A SOLO ACT.
DROP DEAD!!
FUCKIN' WALK! YOU'RE SO ALL TOO GOOD FOR THE LIFE ALL OF A SUDDEN.....
OPEN
WHAT ARE YOU GONNA DO, BIG TIME? FLIP BURGERS?
I DON'T KNOW.....
......BUT I'LL KNOW IT WHEN I SEE IT.

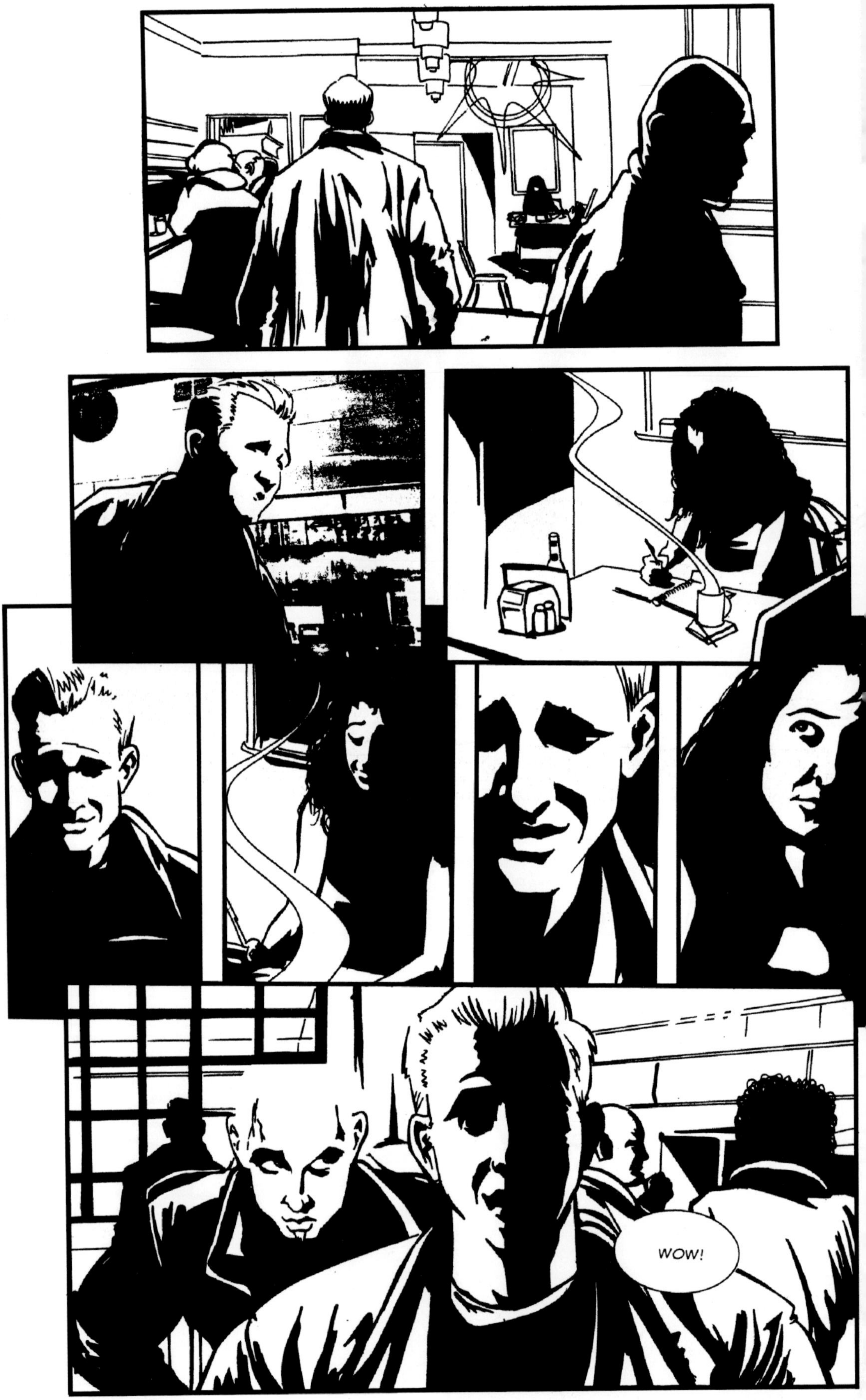
WOW!

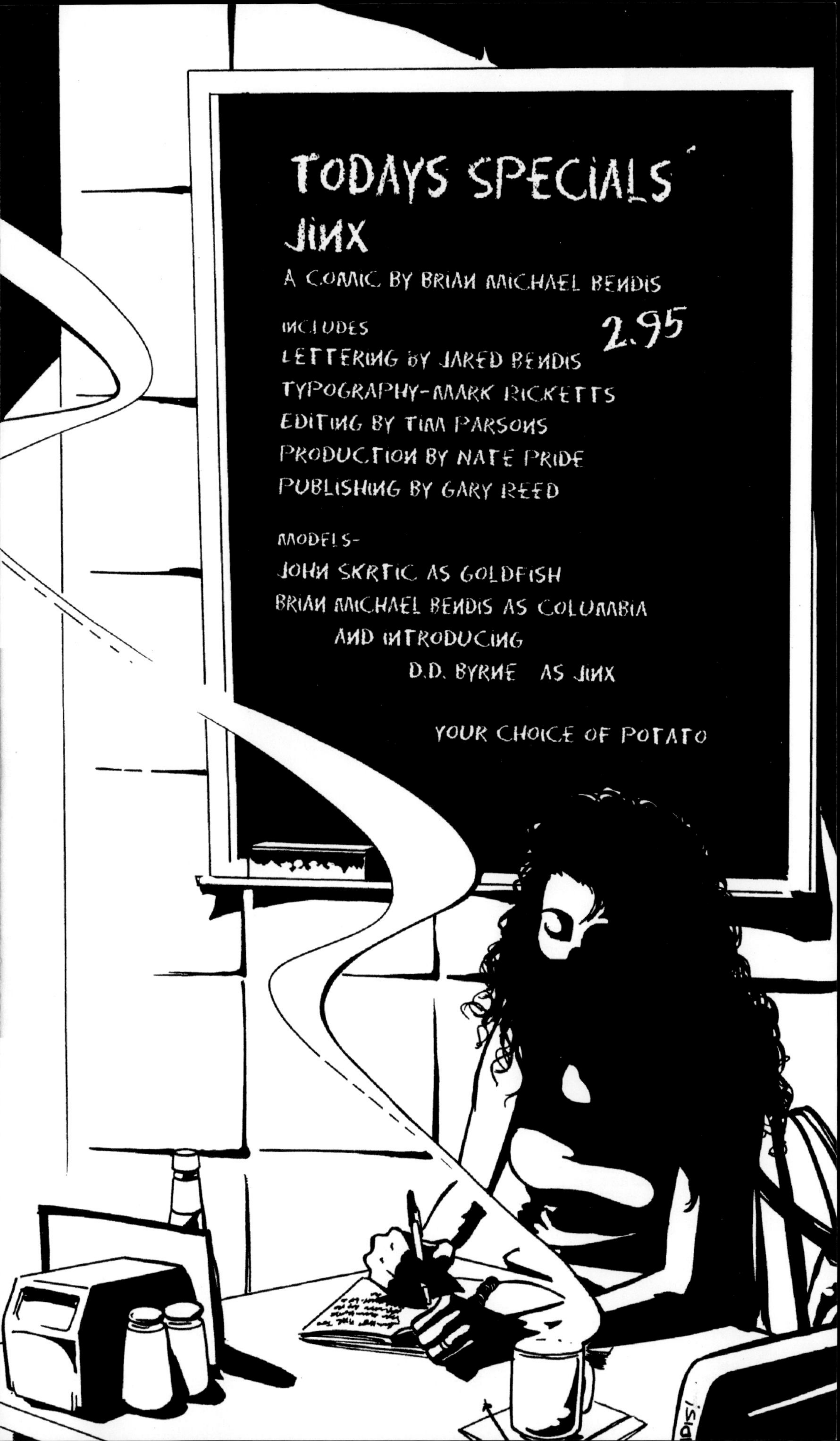
TODAYS SPECIALS
JINX
A COMIC BY BRIAN MICHAEL BENDIS
INCLUDES
2.95
LETTERING BY JARED BENDIS
TYPOGRAPHY-MARK RICKETTS
EDITING BY TIM PARSONS
PRODUCTION BY NATE PRIDE
PUBLISHING BY GARY REED
MODELS-
JOHN SKRTIC AS GOLDFISH
BRIAN MICHAEL BENDIS AS COLUMBIA
AND INTRODUCING
D.D. BYRNE AS JINX
YOUR CHOICE OF POTATO

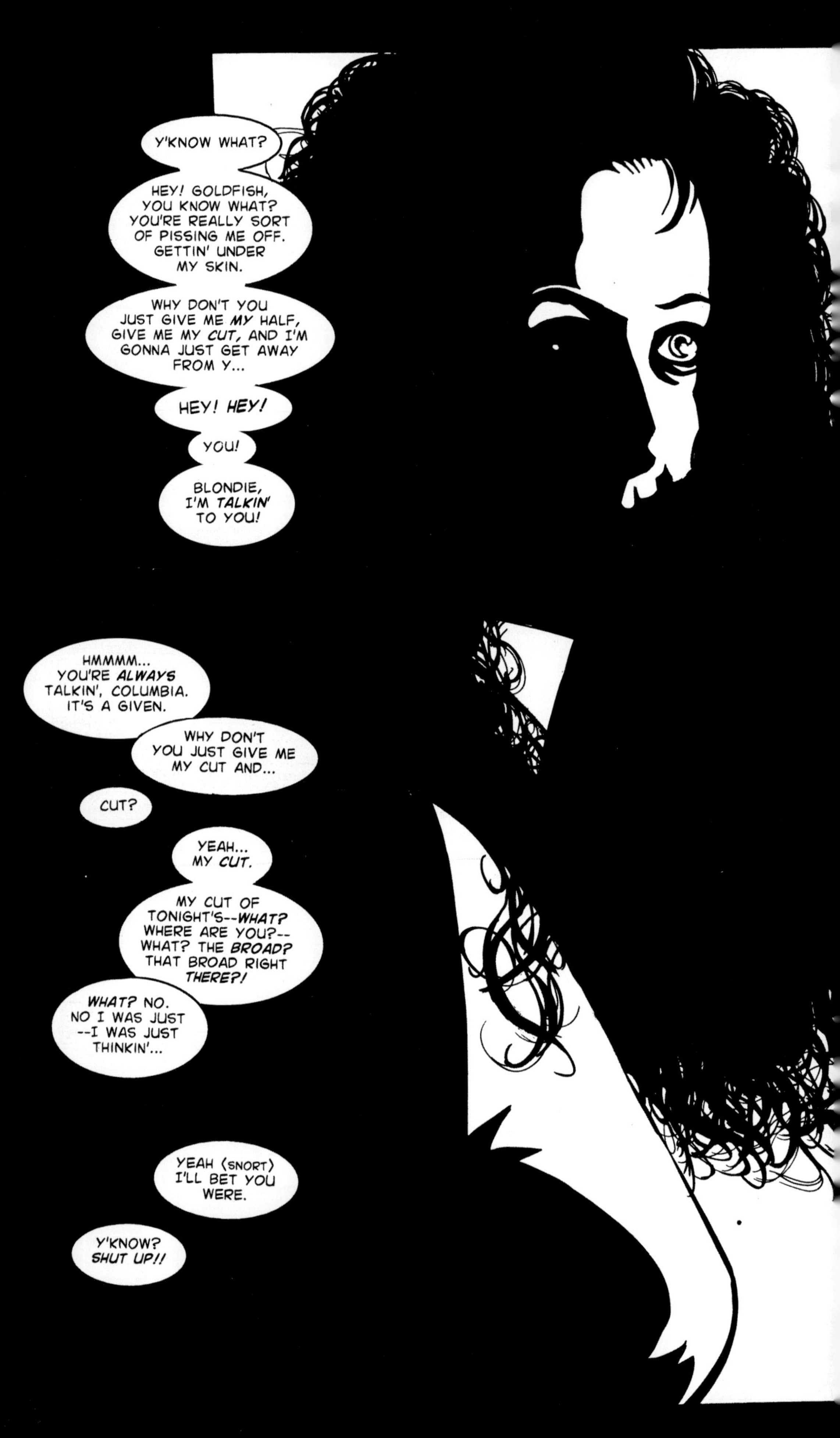
Y'KNOW WHAT?
HEY! GOLDFISH, YOU KNOW WHAT? YOU'RE REALLY SORT OF PISSING ME OFF. GETTIN' UNDER MY SKIN.
WHY DON'T YOU JUST GIVE ME MY HALF, GIVE ME MY CUT, AND I'M GONNA JUST GET AWAY FROM Y...
HEY! HEY!
YOU!
BLONDIE, I'M TALKIN' TO YOU!
HMMMM... YOU'RE ALWAYS TALKIN', COLUMBIA. IT'S A GIVEN.
WHY DON'T YOU JUST GIVE ME MY CUT AND...
CUT?
YEAH... MY CUT.
MY CUT OF TONIGHT'S--WHAT? WHERE ARE YOU?--WHAT? THE BROAD? THAT BROAD RIGHT THERE?!
WHAT? NO. NO I WAS JUST --I WAS JUST THINKIN'...
YEAH (SNORT) I'LL BET YOU WERE.
Y'KNOW? SHUT UP!!

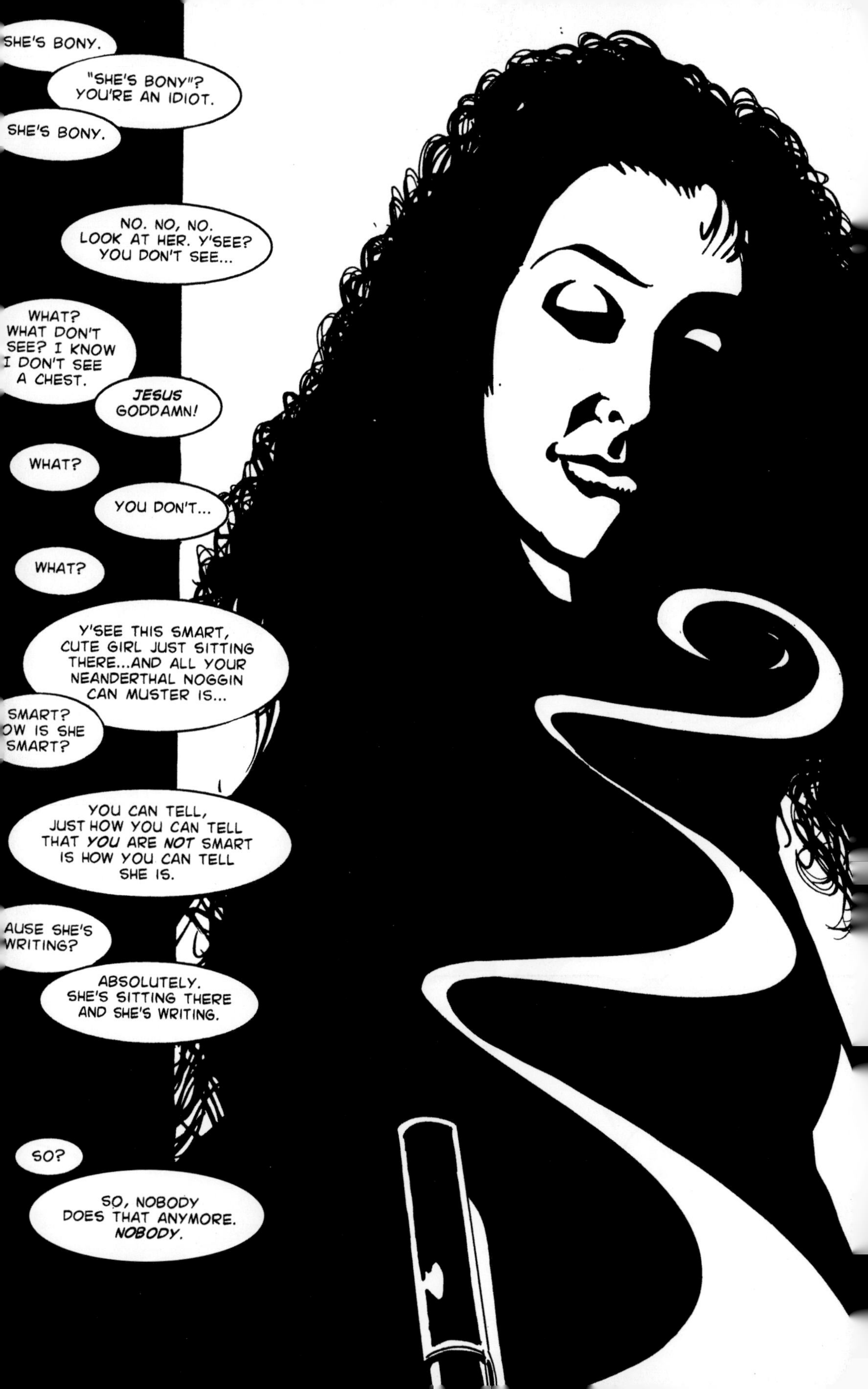
SHE'S BONY.
"SHE'S BONY"? YOU'RE AN IDIOT.
SHE'S BONY.
NO. NO, NO. LOOK AT HER. Y'SEE? YOU DON'T SEE...
WHAT? WHAT DON'T SEE? I KNOW I DON'T SEE A CHEST.
JESUS GODDAMN!
WHAT?
YOU DON'T...
WHAT?
Y'SEE THIS SMART, CUTE GIRL JUST SITTING THERE...AND ALL YOUR NEANDERTHAL NOGGIN CAN MUSTER IS...
SMART? OW IS SHE SMART?
YOU CAN TELL, JUST HOW YOU CAN TELL THAT *YOU* ARE *NOT* SMART IS HOW YOU CAN TELL SHE IS.
AUSE SHE'S WRITING?
ABSOLUTELY. SHE'S SITTING THERE AND SHE'S WRITING.
SO?
SO, NOBODY DOES THAT ANYMORE. *NOBODY.*

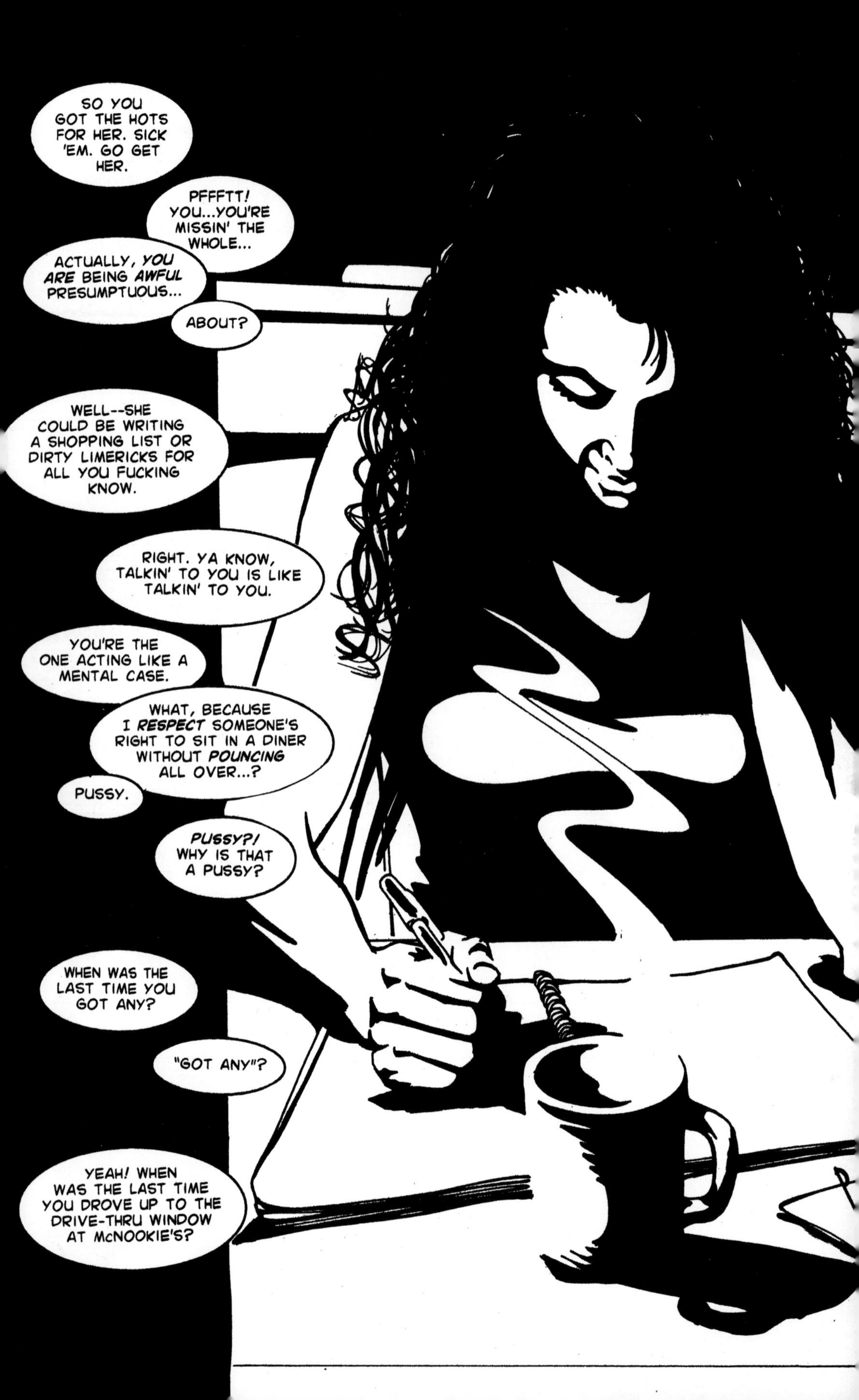
SO YOU GOT THE HOTS FOR HER. SICK 'EM. GO GET HER.
PFFFTT! YOU...YOU'RE MISSIN' THE WHOLE...
ACTUALLY, *YOU ARE* BEING *AWFUL* PRESUMPTUOUS...
ABOUT?
WELL--SHE COULD BE WRITING A SHOPPING LIST OR DIRTY LIMERICKS FOR ALL YOU FUCKING KNOW.
RIGHT. YA KNOW, TALKIN' TO YOU IS LIKE TALKIN' TO YOU.
YOU'RE THE ONE ACTING LIKE A MENTAL CASE.
WHAT, BECAUSE I *RESPECT* SOMEONE'S RIGHT TO SIT IN A DINER WITHOUT *POUNCING* ALL OVER...?
PUSSY.
PUSSY?! WHY IS THAT A PUSSY?
WHEN WAS THE LAST TIME YOU GOT ANY?
"GOT ANY"?
YEAH! WHEN WAS THE LAST TIME YOU DROVE UP TO THE DRIVE-THRU WINDOW AT McNOOKIE'S?

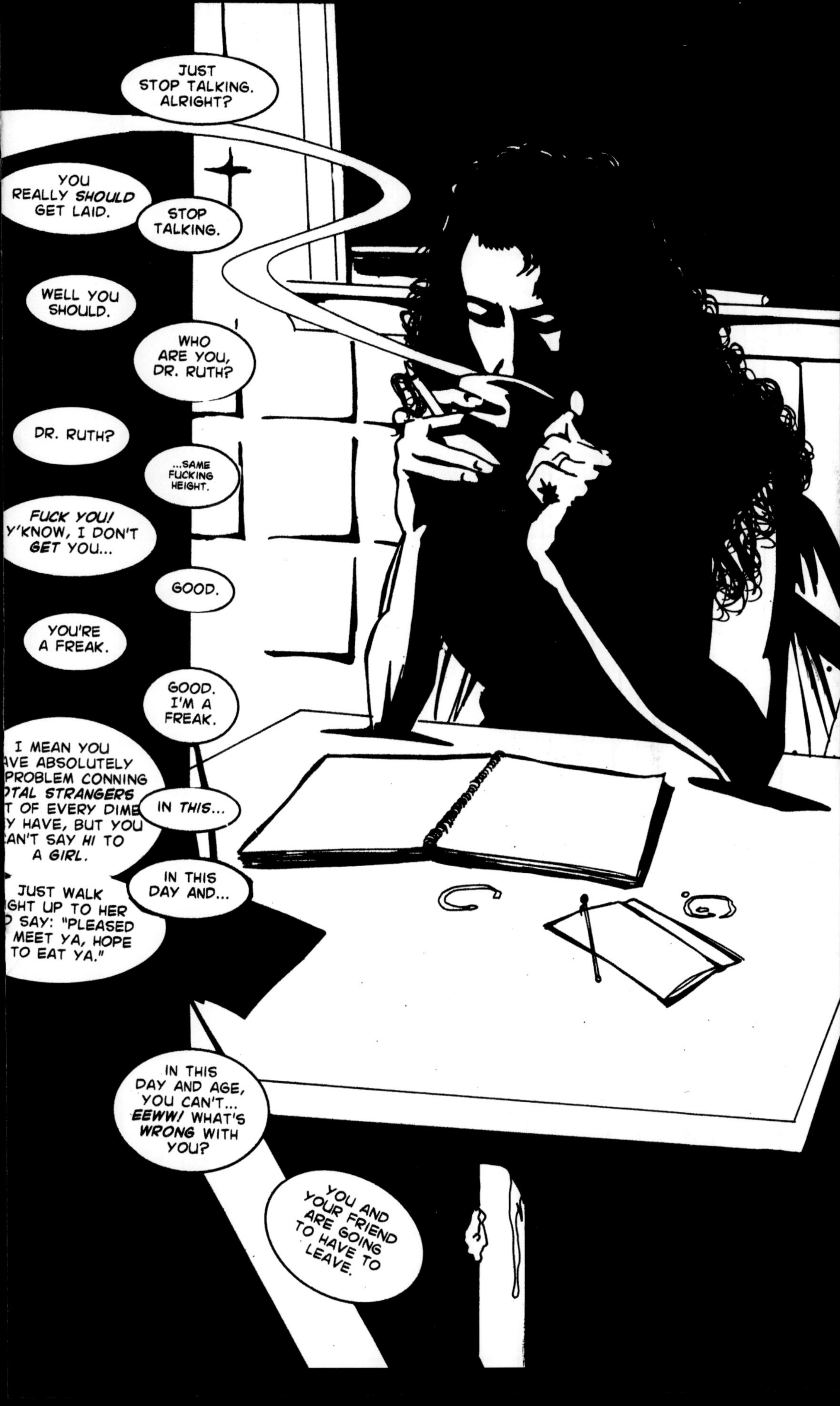
JUST STOP TALKING. ALRIGHT?
YOU REALLY *SHOULD* GET LAID.
STOP TALKING.
WELL YOU SHOULD.
WHO ARE YOU, DR. RUTH?
DR. RUTH?
...SAME FUCKING HEIGHT.
FUCK YOU! Y'KNOW, I DON'T *GET* YOU...
GOOD.
YOU'RE A FREAK.
GOOD. I'M A FREAK.
I MEAN YOU AVE ABSOLUTELY PROBLEM CONNING *OTAL STRANGERS* T OF EVERY DIME Y HAVE, BUT YOU AN'T SAY *HI* TO A *GIRL*.
IN *THIS*...
IN THIS DAY AND...
JUST WALK IGHT UP TO HER D SAY: "PLEASED MEET YA, HOPE TO EAT YA."
IN THIS DAY AND AGE, YOU CAN'T... *EEWW!* WHAT'S *WRONG* WITH YOU?
YOU AND YOUR FRIEND ARE GOING TO HAVE TO LEAVE.

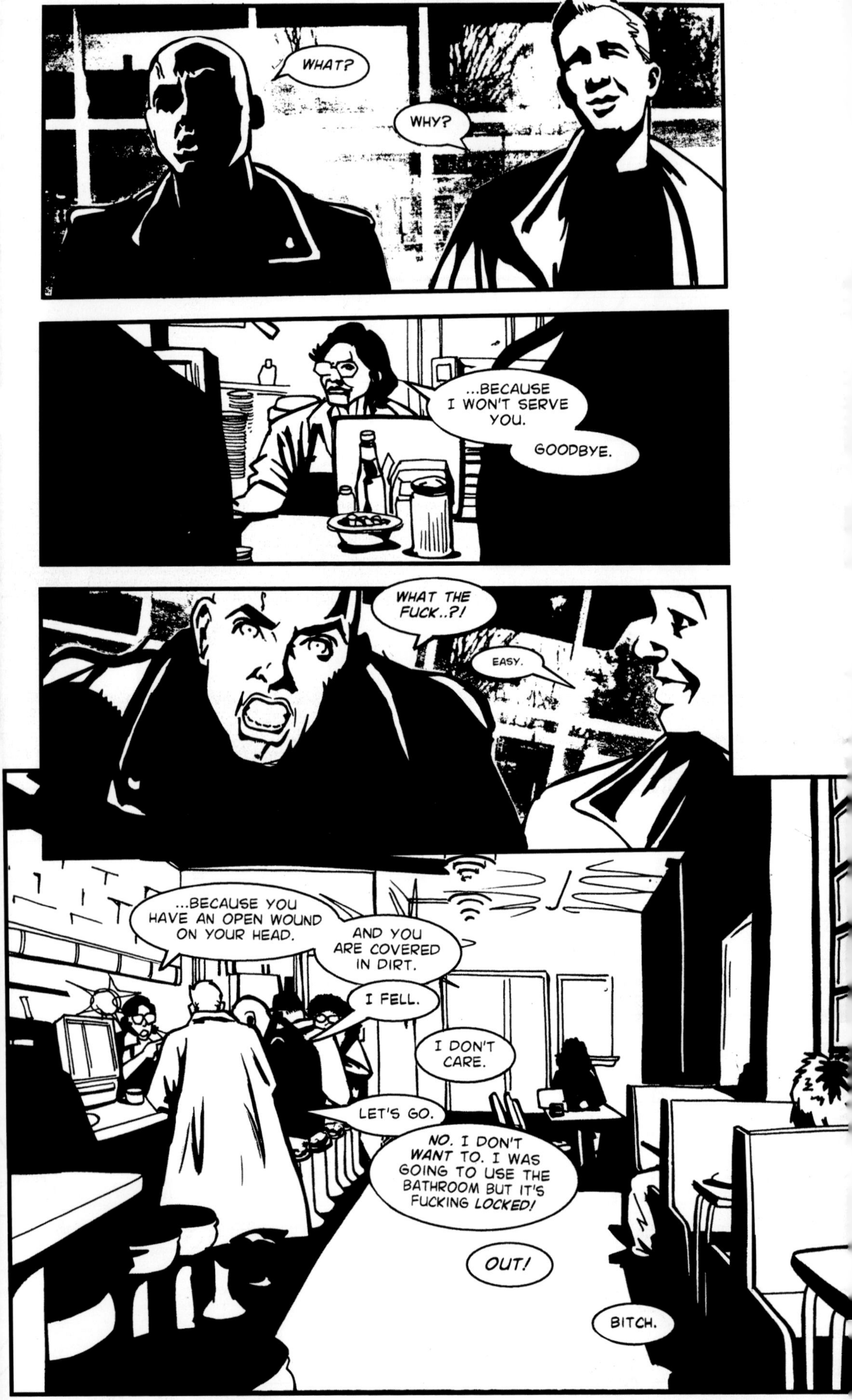
WHAT?
WHY?
...BECAUSE I WON'T SERVE YOU.
GOODBYE.
WHAT THE FUCK..?!
EASY.
...BECAUSE YOU HAVE AN OPEN WOUND ON YOUR HEAD.
AND YOU ARE COVERED IN DIRT.
I FELL.
I DON'T CARE.
LET'S GO.
NO. I DON'T WANT TO. I WAS GOING TO USE THE BATHROOM BUT IT'S FUCKING LOCKED!
OUT!
BITCH.

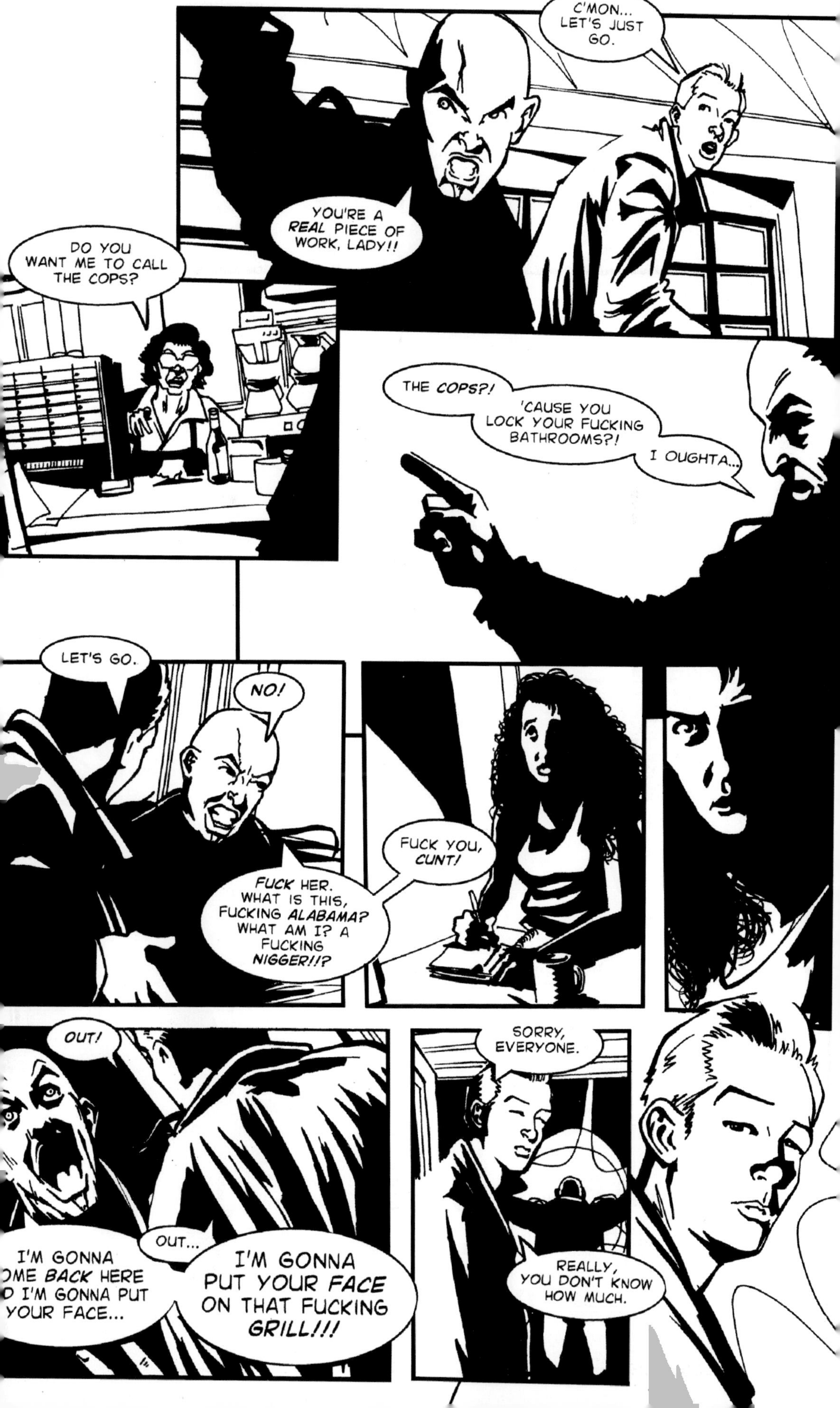
C'MON... LET'S JUST GO.
YOU'RE A REAL PIECE OF WORK, LADY!!
DO YOU WANT ME TO CALL THE COPS?
THE COPS?!
'CAUSE YOU LOCK YOUR FUCKING BATHROOMS?!
I OUGHTA...
LET'S GO.
NO!
FUCK HER. WHAT IS THIS, FUCKING ALABAMA? WHAT AM I? A FUCKING NIGGER!!?
FUCK YOU, CUNT!
OUT!
I'M GONNA
OME BACK HERE
D I'M GONNA PUT
YOUR FACE...
OUT...
I'M GONNA PUT YOUR FACE ON THAT FUCKING GRILL!!!
SORRY, EVERYONE.
REALLY, YOU DON'T KNOW HOW MUCH.

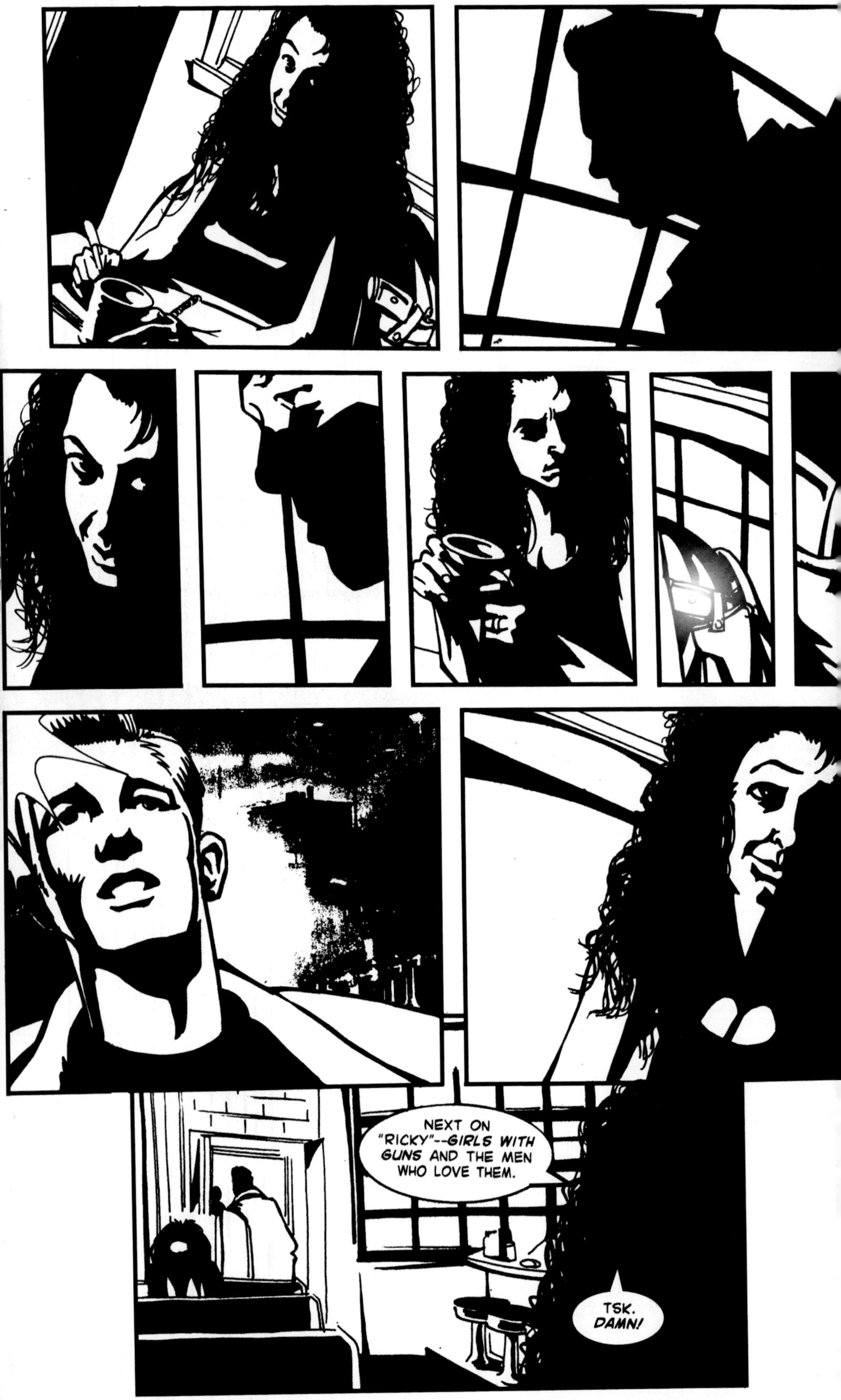
NEXT ON "RICKY"--GIRLS WITH GUNS AND THE MEN WHO LOVE THEM.
TSK. DAMN!

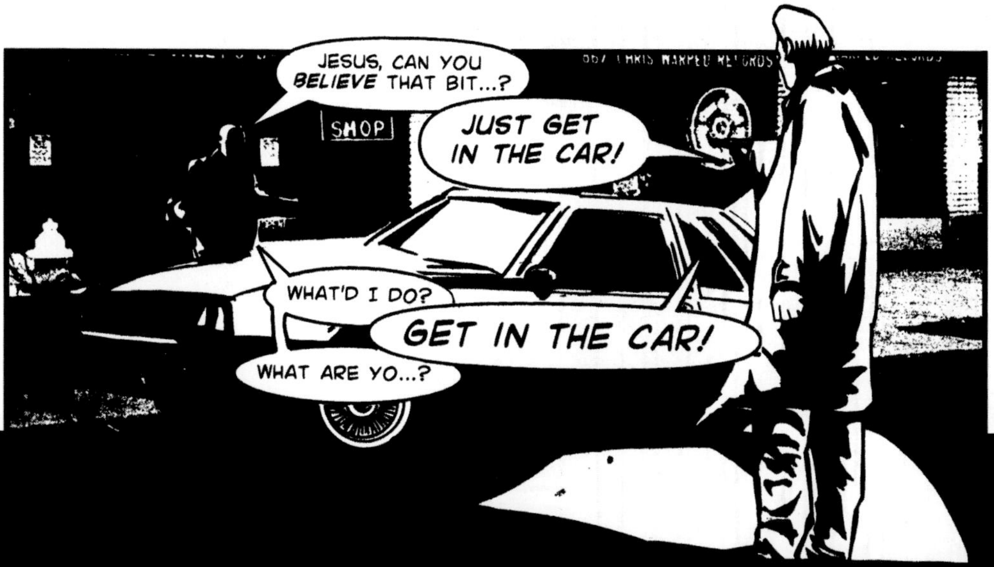
JESUS, CAN YOU *BELIEVE* THAT BIT...?
SHOP
JUST GET IN THE CAR!
WHAT'D I DO?
GET IN THE CAR!
WHAT ARE YO...?

The Keys

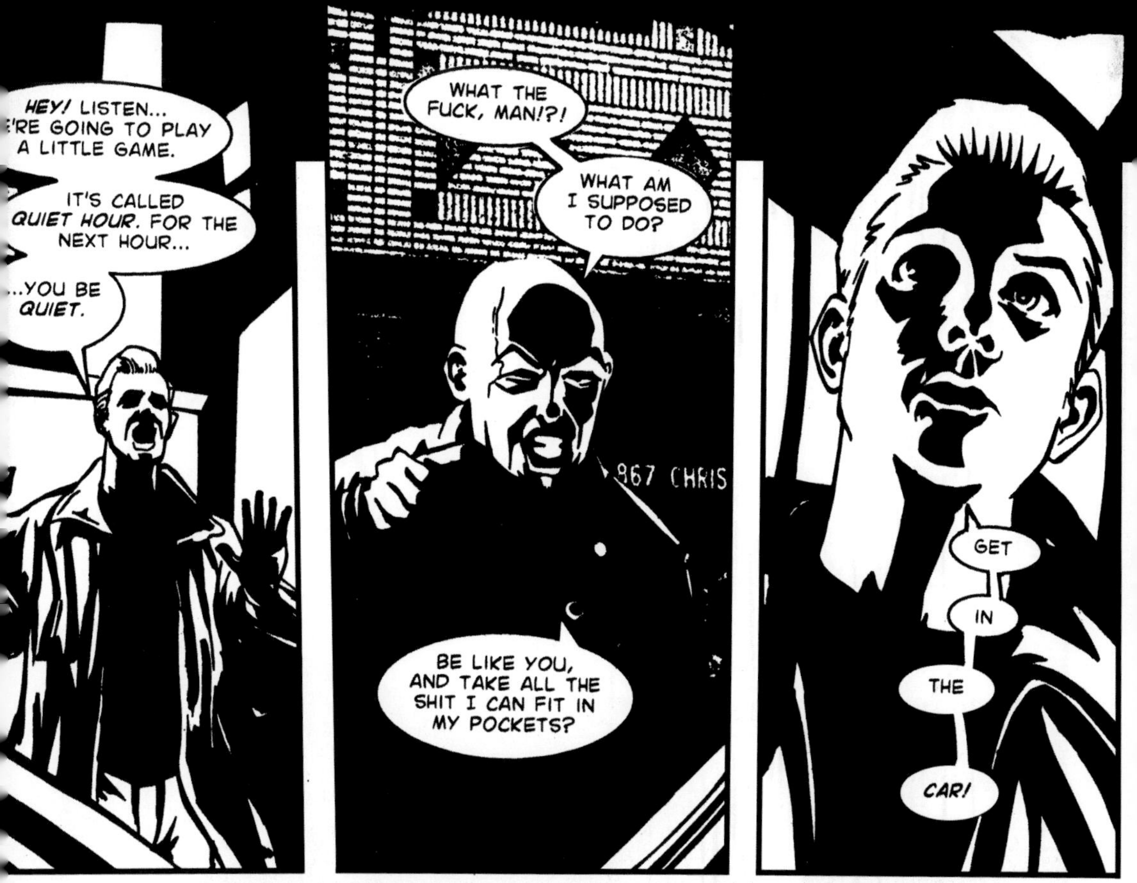
HEY! LISTEN... E'RE GOING TO PLAY A LITTLE GAME.
IT'S CALLED *QUIET HOUR*. FOR THE NEXT HOUR...
...YOU BE *QUIET*.
WHAT THE FUCK, MAN!?!
WHAT AM I SUPPOSED TO DO?
867 CHRIS
BE LIKE YOU, AND TAKE ALL THE SHIT I CAN FIT IN MY POCKETS?
GET
IN
THE
CAR!

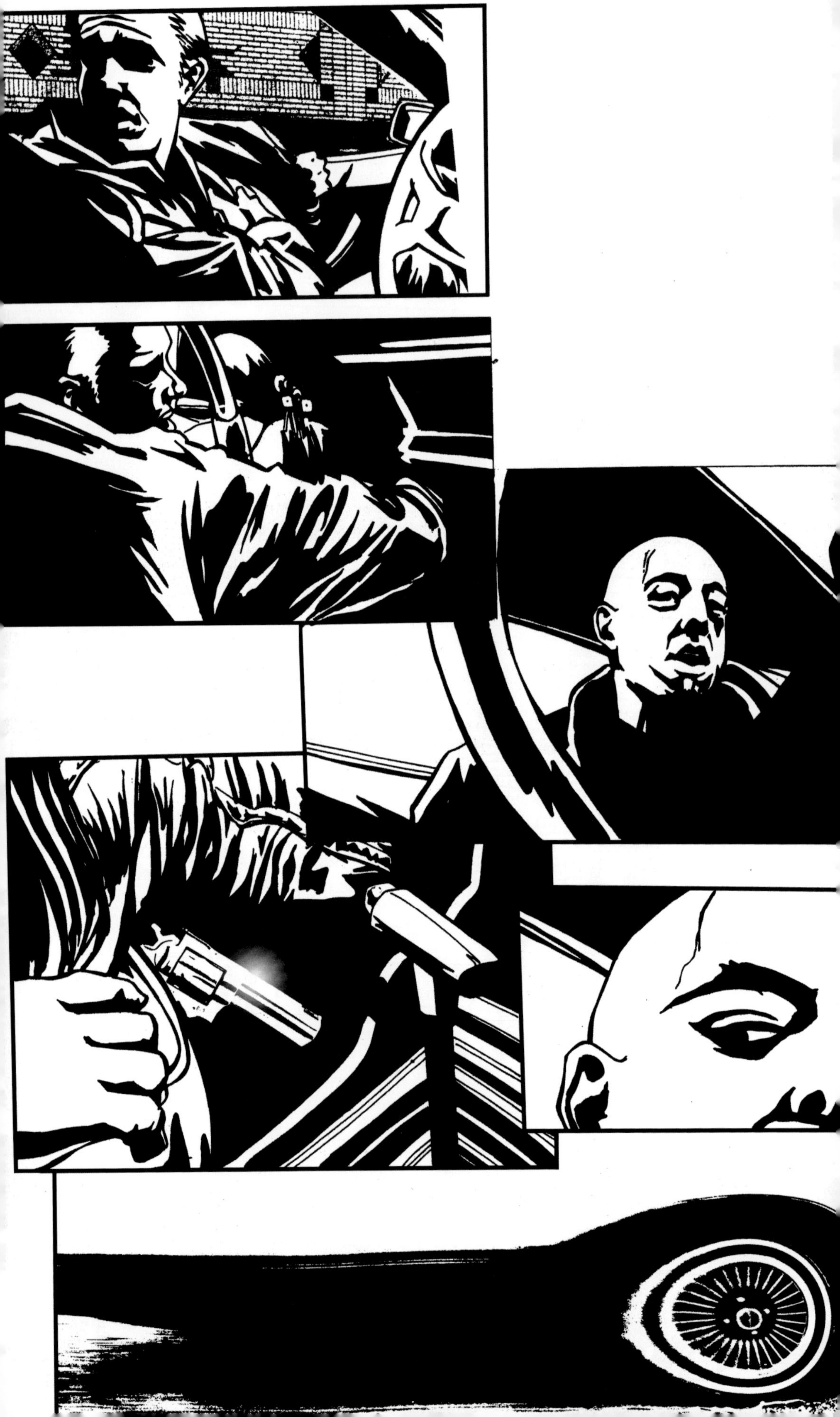

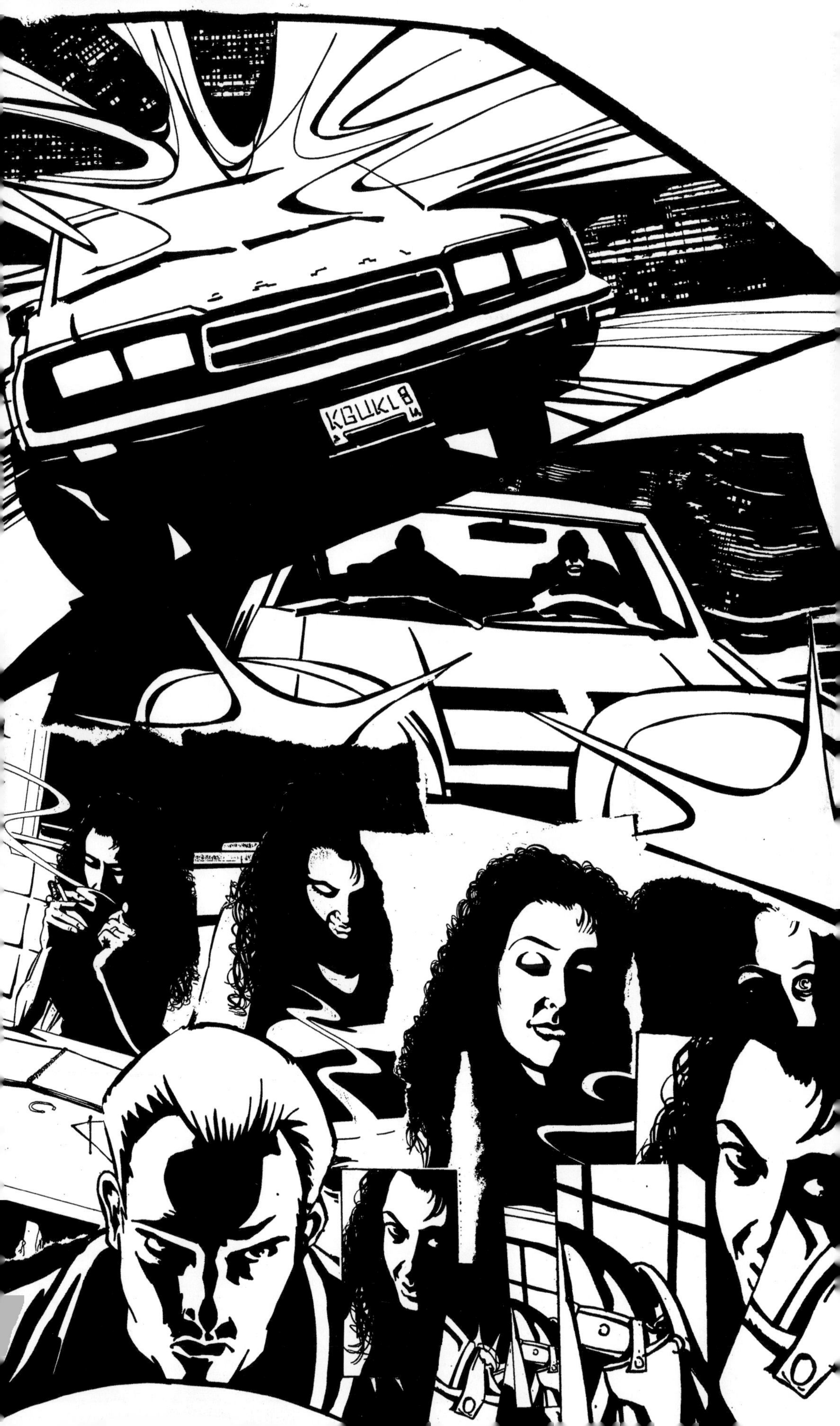

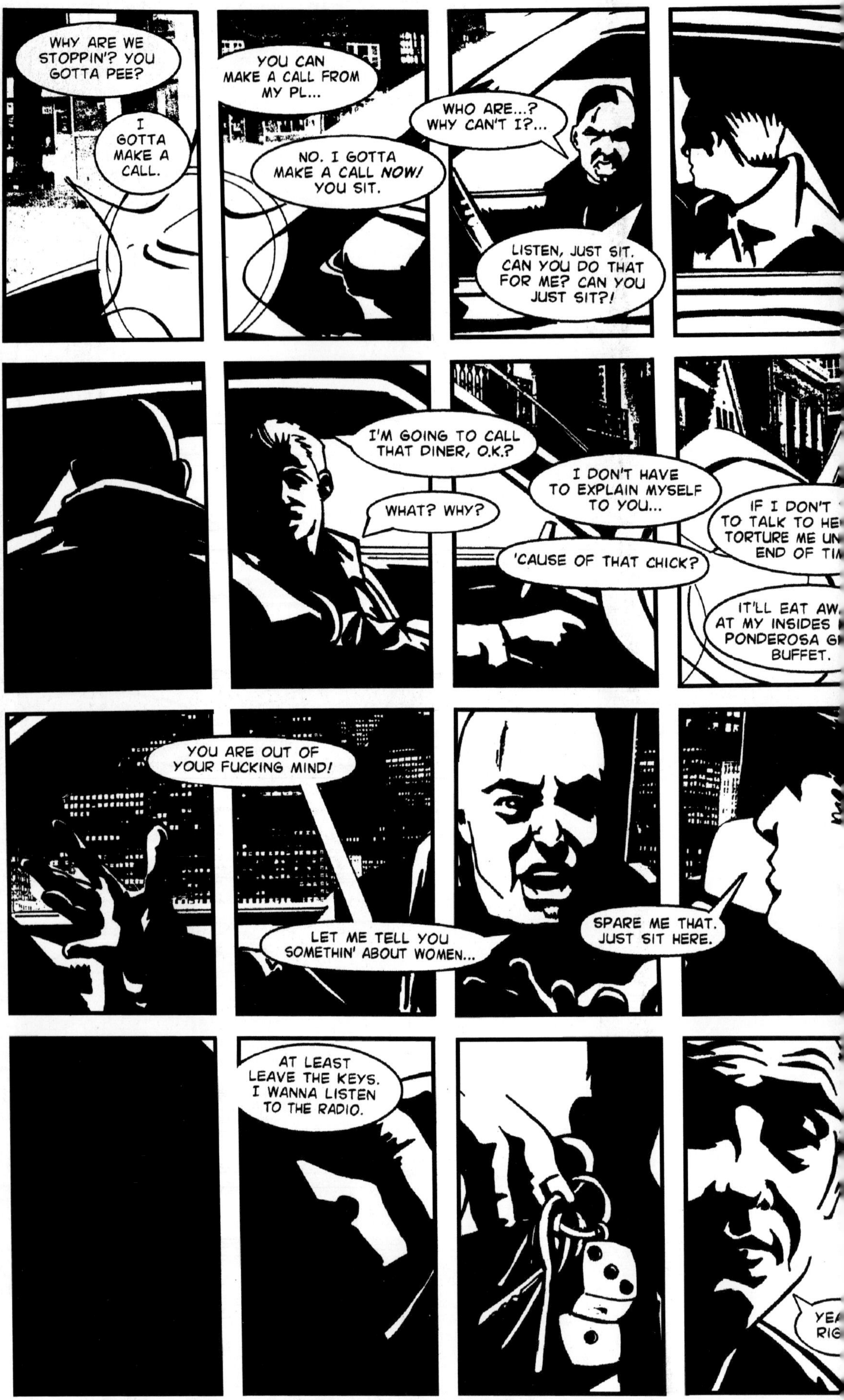

WHY ARE WE STOPPIN'? YOU GOTTA PEE?
I GOTTA MAKE A CALL.
YOU CAN MAKE A CALL FROM MY PL...
NO. I GOTTA MAKE A CALL *NOW!* YOU SIT.
WHO ARE...? WHY CAN'T I?...
LISTEN, JUST SIT. CAN YOU DO THAT FOR ME? CAN YOU JUST SIT?!
I'M GOING TO CALL THAT DINER, O.K.?
WHAT? WHY?
I DON'T HAVE TO EXPLAIN MYSELF TO YOU...
'CAUSE OF THAT CHICK?
IF I DON'T
TO TALK TO HE
TORTURE ME UN
END OF TI
IT'LL EAT AW
AT MY INSIDES
PONDEROSA G
BUFFET.
YOU ARE OUT OF YOUR FUCKING MIND!
LET ME TELL YOU SOMETHIN' ABOUT WOMEN...
SPARE ME THAT. JUST SIT HERE.
AT LEAST LEAVE THE KEYS. I WANNA LISTEN TO THE RADIO.
YE
RIG

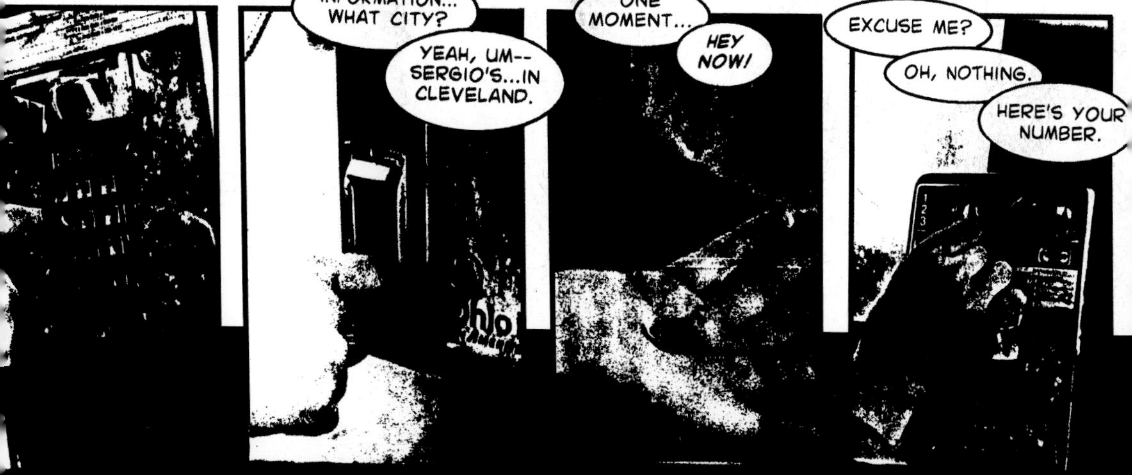
INFORMATION... WHAT CITY?
YEAH, UM-- SERGIO'S...IN CLEVELAND.
ONE MOMENT...
HEY NOW!
EXCUSE ME?
OH, NOTHING.
HERE'S YOUR NUMBER.

A Sociological Catastrophe

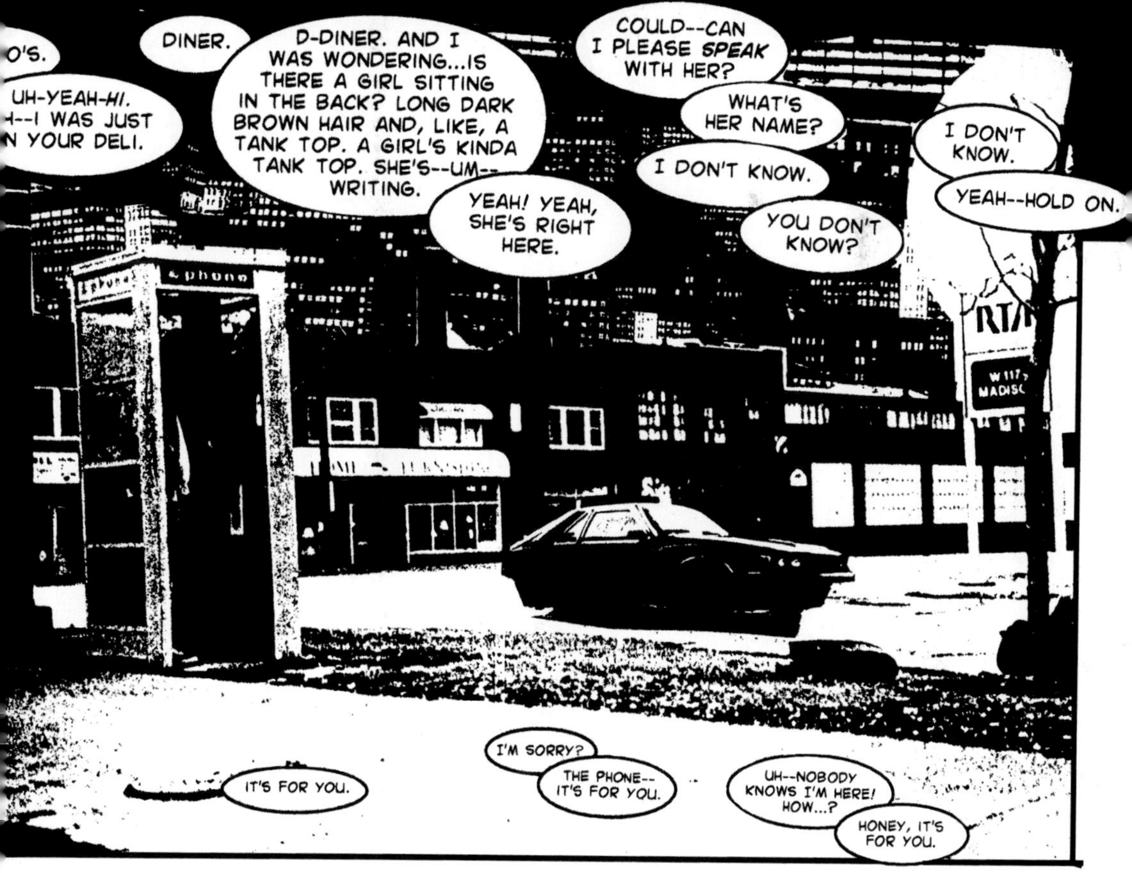
O'S.
UH-YEAH-HI. H--I WAS JUST N YOUR DELI.
DINER.
D-DINER. AND I WAS WONDERING...IS THERE A GIRL SITTING IN THE BACK? LONG DARK BROWN HAIR AND, LIKE, A TANK TOP. A GIRL'S KINDA TANK TOP. SHE'S--UM-- WRITING.
YEAH! YEAH, SHE'S RIGHT HERE.
COULD--CAN I PLEASE SPEAK WITH HER?
WHAT'S HER NAME?
I DON'T KNOW.
YOU DON'T KNOW?
I DON'T KNOW.
YEAH--HOLD ON.
IT'S FOR YOU.
I'M SORRY?
THE PHONE-- IT'S FOR YOU.
UH--NOBODY KNOWS I'M HERE! HOW...?
HONEY, IT'S FOR YOU.

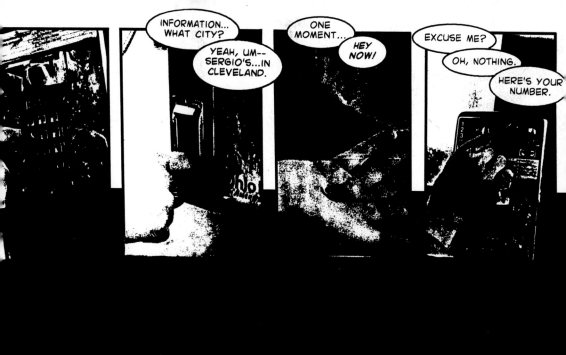

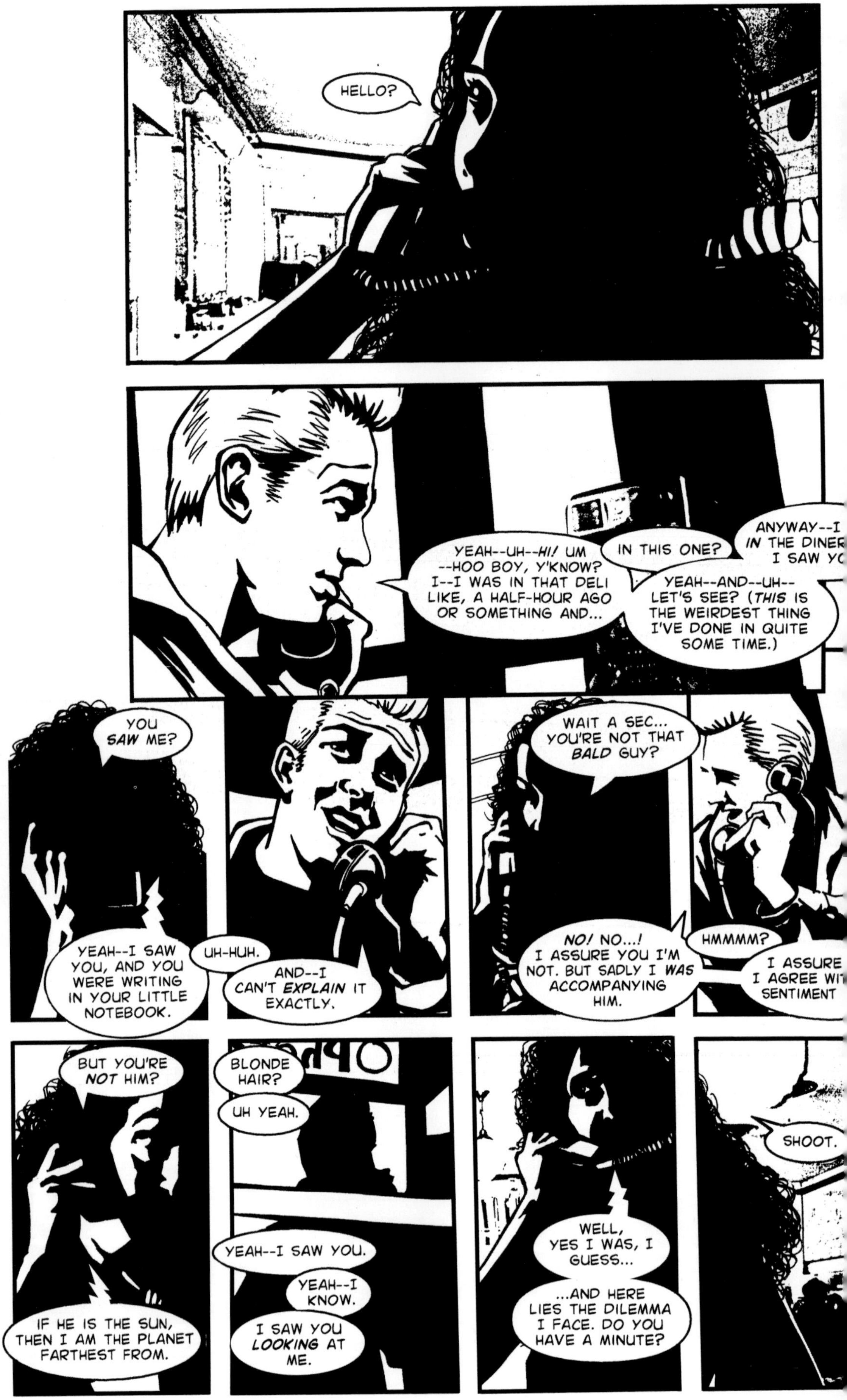
HELLO?
YEAH--UH--*HI!* UM --HOO BOY, Y'KNOW? I--I WAS IN THAT DELI LIKE, A HALF-HOUR AGO OR SOMETHING AND...
IN THIS ONE?
ANYWAY--I *IN* THE DINER I SAW YO
YEAH--AND--UH-- LET'S SEE? (*THIS* IS THE WEIRDEST THING I'VE DONE IN QUITE SOME TIME.)
YOU *SAW* ME?
YEAH--I SAW YOU, AND YOU WERE WRITING IN YOUR LITTLE NOTEBOOK.
UH-HUH.
AND--I CAN'T *EXPLAIN* IT EXACTLY.
WAIT A SEC... YOU'RE NOT THAT *BALD* GUY?
NO! NO...! I ASSURE YOU I'M NOT. BUT SADLY I *WAS* ACCOMPANYING HIM.
HMMMM?
I ASSURE I AGREE WIT SENTIMENT
BUT YOU'RE *NOT* HIM?
IF HE IS THE SUN, THEN I AM THE PLANET FARTHEST FROM.
BLONDE HAIR?
UH YEAH.
YEAH--I SAW YOU.
YEAH--I KNOW.
I SAW YOU *LOOKING* AT ME.
WELL, YES I WAS, I GUESS...
...AND HERE LIES THE DILEMMA I FACE. DO YOU HAVE A MINUTE?
SHOOT.

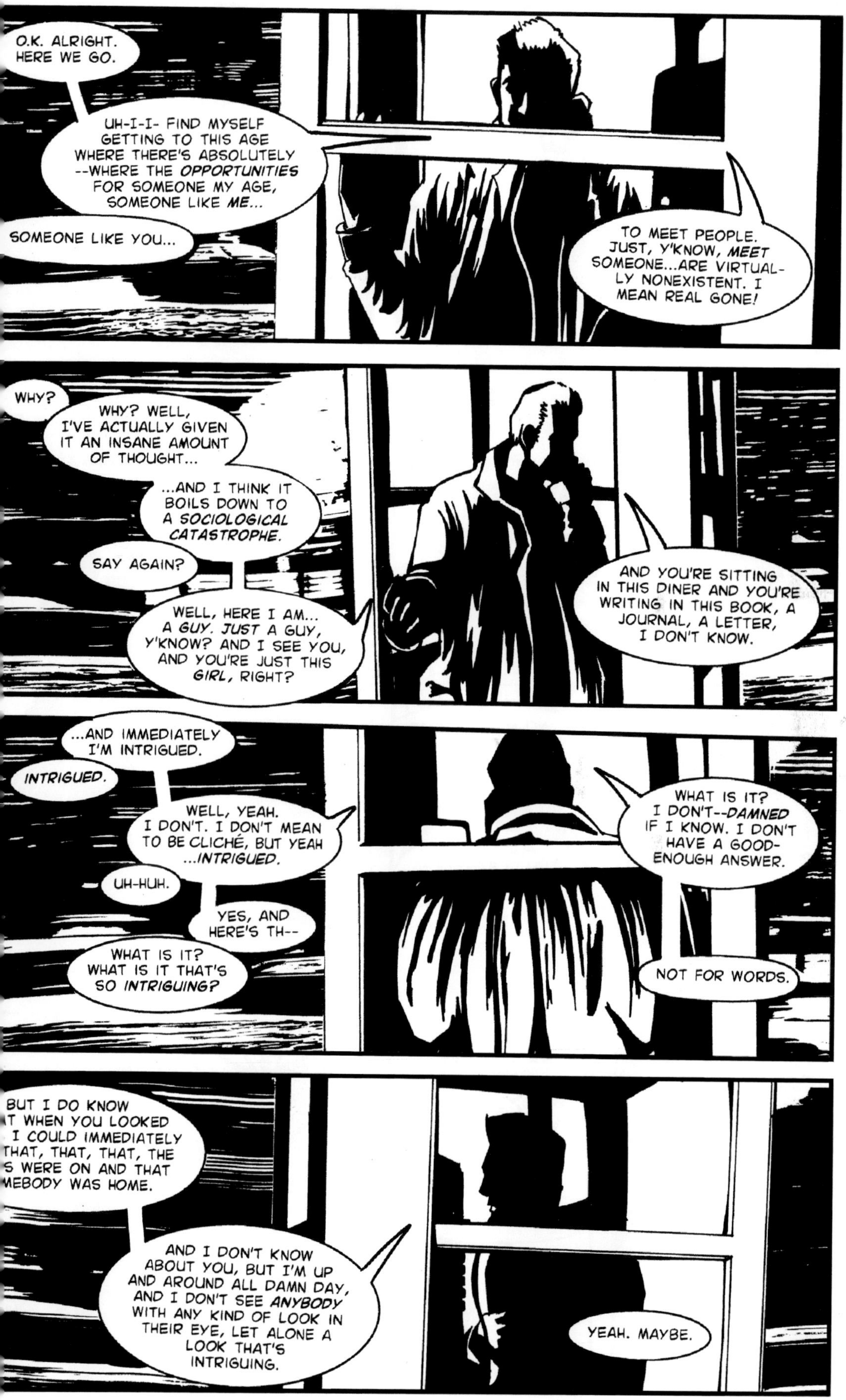
O.K. ALRIGHT. HERE WE GO.
UH-I-I- FIND MYSELF GETTING TO THIS AGE WHERE THERE'S ABSOLUTELY --WHERE THE *OPPORTUNITIES* FOR SOMEONE MY AGE, SOMEONE LIKE *ME*...
SOMEONE LIKE YOU...
TO MEET PEOPLE. JUST, Y'KNOW, *MEET* SOMEONE...ARE VIRTUAL-LY NONEXISTENT. I MEAN REAL GONE!
WHY?
WHY? WELL, I'VE ACTUALLY GIVEN IT AN INSANE AMOUNT OF THOUGHT...
...AND I THINK IT BOILS DOWN TO A *SOCIOLOGICAL CATASTROPHE*.
SAY AGAIN?
WELL, HERE I AM... A *GUY*. *JUST* A GUY, Y'KNOW? AND I SEE YOU, AND YOU'RE JUST THIS *GIRL*, RIGHT?
AND YOU'RE SITTING IN THIS DINER AND YOU'RE WRITING IN THIS BOOK, A JOURNAL, A LETTER, I DON'T KNOW.
...AND IMMEDIATELY I'M INTRIGUED.
INTRIGUED.
WELL, YEAH. I DON'T. I DON'T MEAN TO BE CLICHÉ, BUT YEAH ...*INTRIGUED.*
UH-HUH.
YES, AND HERE'S TH--
WHAT IS IT? WHAT IS IT THAT'S SO *INTRIGUING?*
WHAT IS IT? I DON'T--*DAMNED* IF I KNOW. I DON'T HAVE A GOOD-ENOUGH ANSWER.
NOT FOR WORDS.
BUT I DO KNOW T WHEN YOU LOOKED I COULD IMMEDIATELY THAT, THAT, THAT, THE S WERE ON AND THAT MEBODY WAS HOME.
AND I DON'T KNOW ABOUT YOU, BUT I'M UP AND AROUND ALL DAMN DAY, AND I DON'T SEE *ANYBODY* WITH ANY KIND OF LOOK IN THEIR EYE, LET ALONE A LOOK THAT'S INTRIGUING.
YEAH. MAYBE.

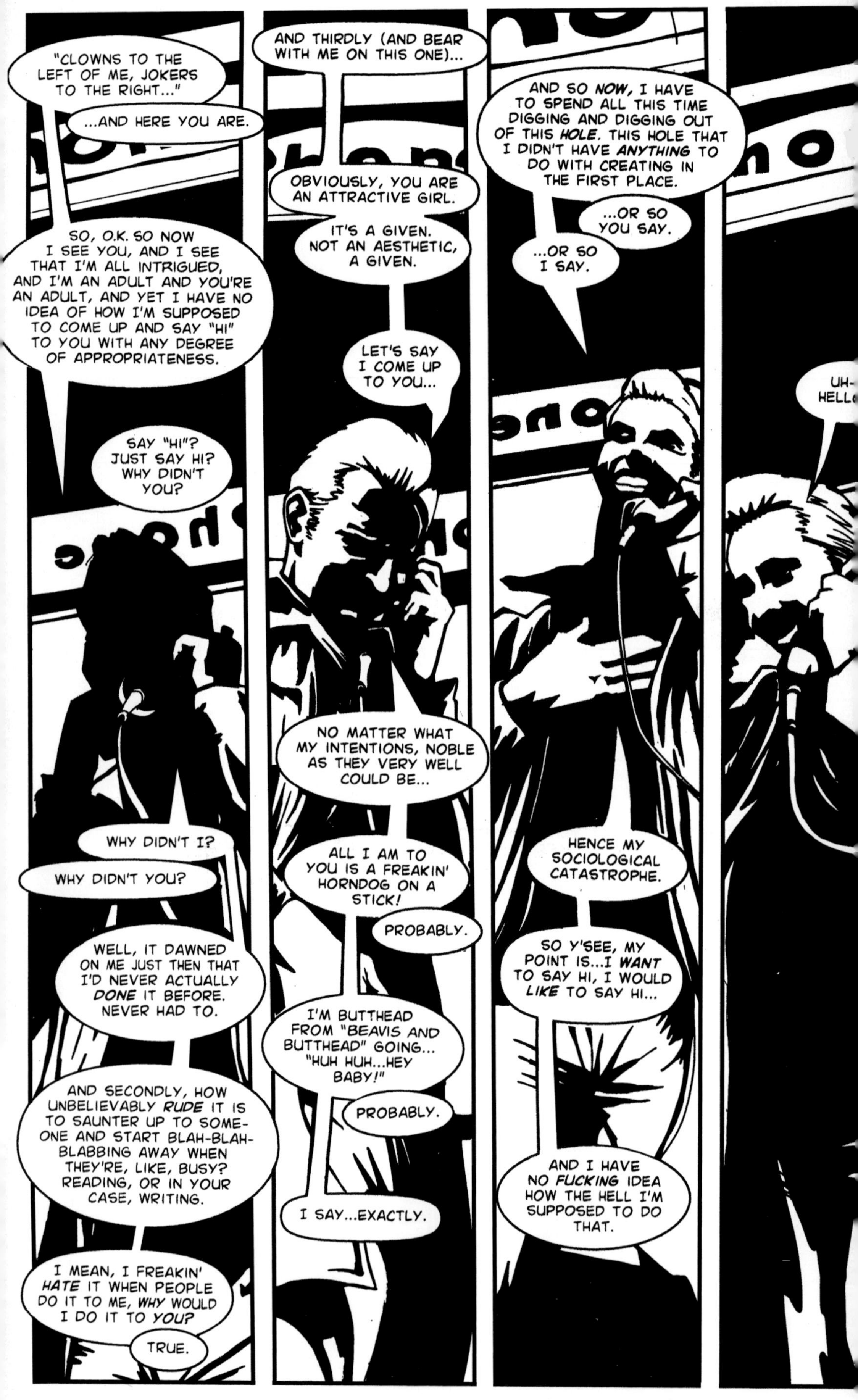
"CLOWNS TO THE LEFT OF ME, JOKERS TO THE RIGHT..."
...AND HERE YOU ARE.
SO, O.K. SO NOW I SEE YOU, AND I SEE THAT I'M ALL INTRIGUED, AND I'M AN ADULT AND YOU'RE AN ADULT, AND YET I HAVE NO IDEA OF HOW I'M SUPPOSED TO COME UP AND SAY "HI" TO YOU WITH ANY DEGREE OF APPROPRIATENESS.
SAY "HI"? JUST SAY HI? WHY DIDN'T YOU?
WHY DIDN'T I?
WHY DIDN'T YOU?
WELL, IT DAWNED ON ME JUST THEN THAT I'D NEVER ACTUALLY *DONE* IT BEFORE. NEVER HAD TO.
AND SECONDLY, HOW UNBELIEVABLY *RUDE* IT IS TO SAUNTER UP TO SOME-ONE AND START BLAH-BLAH-BLABBING AWAY WHEN THEY'RE, LIKE, BUSY? READING, OR IN YOUR CASE, WRITING.
I MEAN, I FREAKIN' *HATE* IT WHEN PEOPLE DO IT TO ME, *WHY* WOULD I DO IT TO *YOU?*
TRUE.
AND THIRDLY (AND BEAR WITH ME ON THIS ONE)...
OBVIOUSLY, YOU ARE AN ATTRACTIVE GIRL.
IT'S A GIVEN. NOT AN AESTHETIC, A GIVEN.
LET'S SAY I COME UP TO YOU...
NO MATTER WHAT MY INTENTIONS, NOBLE AS THEY VERY WELL COULD BE...
ALL I AM TO YOU IS A FREAKIN' HORNDOG ON A STICK!
PROBABLY.
I'M BUTTHEAD FROM "BEAVIS AND BUTTHEAD" GOING... "HUH HUH...HEY BABY!"
PROBABLY.
I SAY...EXACTLY.
AND SO *NOW,* I HAVE TO SPEND ALL THIS TIME DIGGING AND DIGGING OUT OF THIS *HOLE.* THIS HOLE THAT I DIDN'T HAVE *ANYTHING* TO DO WITH CREATING IN THE FIRST PLACE.
...OR SO YOU SAY.
...OR SO I SAY.
HENCE MY SOCIOLOGICAL CATASTROPHE.
SO Y'SEE, MY POINT IS...I *WANT* TO SAY HI, I WOULD *LIKE* TO SAY HI...
AND I HAVE NO *FUCKING* IDEA HOW THE HELL I'M SUPPOSED TO DO THAT.

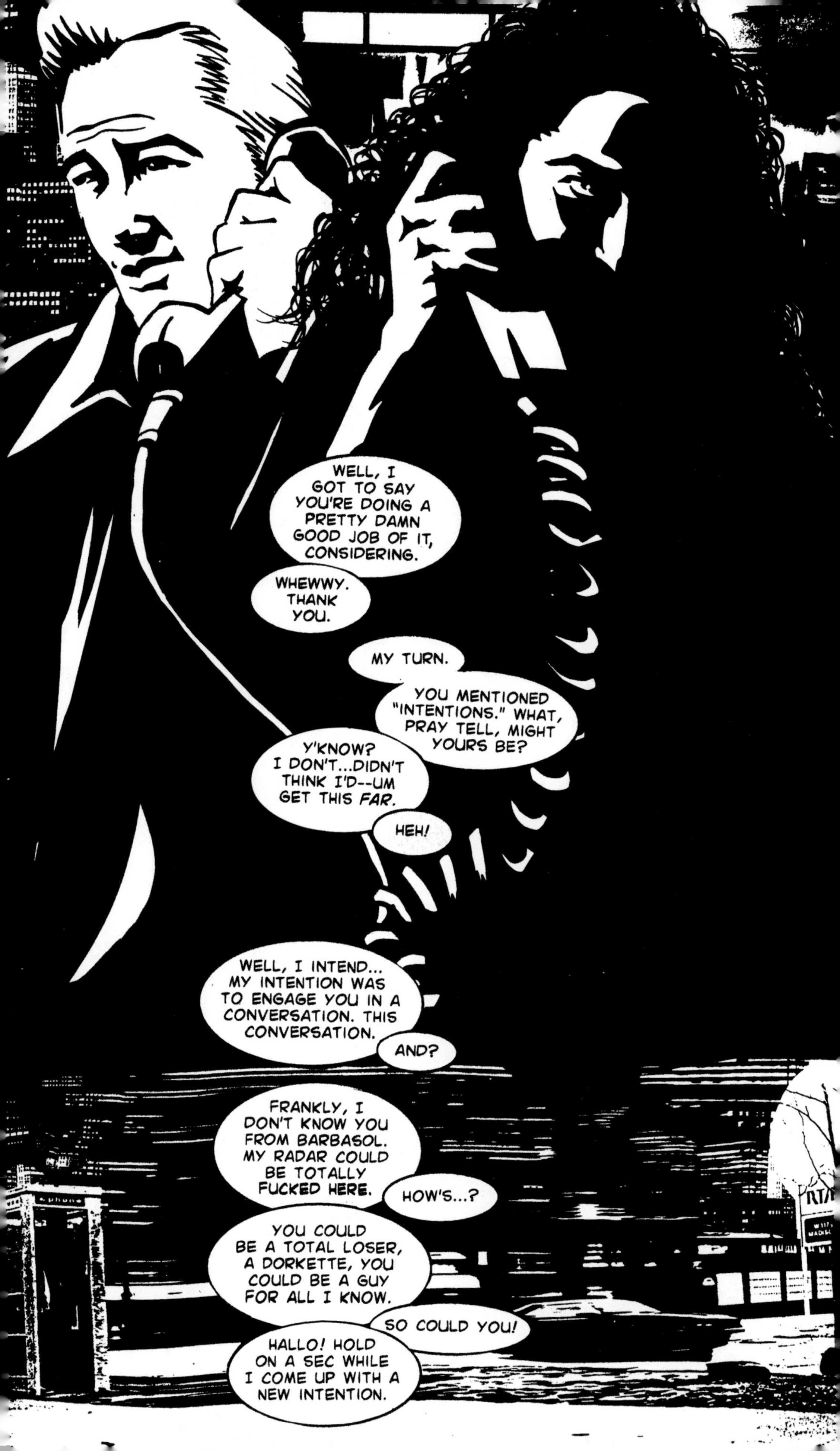
WELL, I GOT TO SAY YOU'RE DOING A PRETTY DAMN GOOD JOB OF IT, CONSIDERING.
WHEWWY. THANK YOU.
MY TURN.
YOU MENTIONED "INTENTIONS." WHAT, PRAY TELL, MIGHT YOURS BE?
Y'KNOW? I DON'T...DIDN'T THINK I'D--UM GET THIS *FAR*.
HEH!
WELL, I INTEND... MY INTENTION WAS TO ENGAGE YOU IN A CONVERSATION. THIS CONVERSATION.
AND?
FRANKLY, I DON'T KNOW YOU FROM BARBASOL. MY RADAR COULD BE TOTALLY FUCKED HERE.
HOW'S...?
YOU COULD BE A TOTAL LOSER, A DORKETTE, YOU COULD BE A GUY FOR ALL I KNOW.
SO COULD YOU!
HALLO! HOLD ON A SEC WHILE I COME UP WITH A NEW INTENTION.

WH-WHAT'S THE LOOK ON YOUR FACE RIGHT NOW?

I'M SMILING.

REALLY?

YES.

YOU'RE NOT ROLLING YOUR EYES UP IN THE BACK OF YOUR HEAD AND SPINNING YOUR FINGER AROUND YOUR EAR?

NO.

I'M-UM-I'M DAVID, DAVID GOLD.

BY THE WAY.

BIBLICAL, NICE. I'M JINX ALAMEDA.

JINX? IS THAT A NAME OR A LIFESTYLE?

I'LL LET THAT ONE SLIP BY...

WHERE ARE YOU? WHERE ARE YOU CALLING...

I'M AT-- I'M AT A PAY PHONE.

ARE YOU SERIOUS?

WELL, YEAH. I DIDN'T WANT TO MISS YOU, SO...

THAT'S CUTE. THAT'S, THAT'S ADORABLE.

WELL, BEING ADORABLE IS REA[L] PRIORITY OF M[Y]

TELL YA WHAT, I THINK Y[OU] DEFINITELY EARNE[D] RIGHT TO BUY ME[A] AND A MUFFI[N]

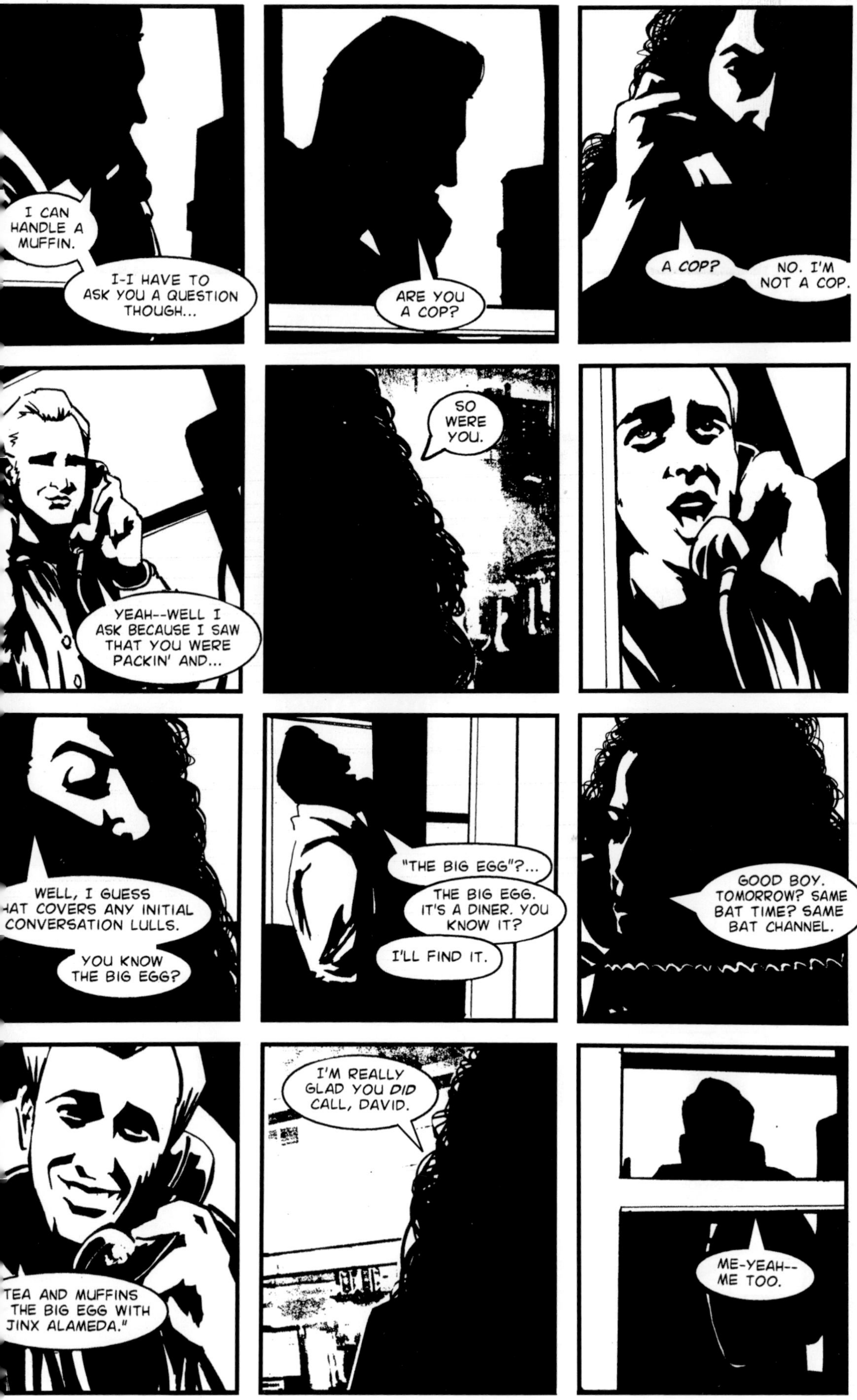
I CAN HANDLE A MUFFIN.
I-I HAVE TO ASK YOU A QUESTION THOUGH...
ARE YOU A COP?
A COP?
NO. I'M NOT A COP.
YEAH--WELL I ASK BECAUSE I SAW THAT YOU WERE PACKIN' AND...
SO WERE YOU.
WELL, I GUESS HAT COVERS ANY INITIAL CONVERSATION LULLS.
YOU KNOW THE BIG EGG?
"THE BIG EGG"?...
THE BIG EGG. IT'S A DINER. YOU KNOW IT?
I'LL FIND IT.
GOOD BOY. TOMORROW? SAME BAT TIME? SAME BAT CHANNEL.
TEA AND MUFFINS THE BIG EGG WITH JINX ALAMEDA."
I'M REALLY GLAD YOU DID CALL, DAVID.
ME-YEAH-- ME TOO.

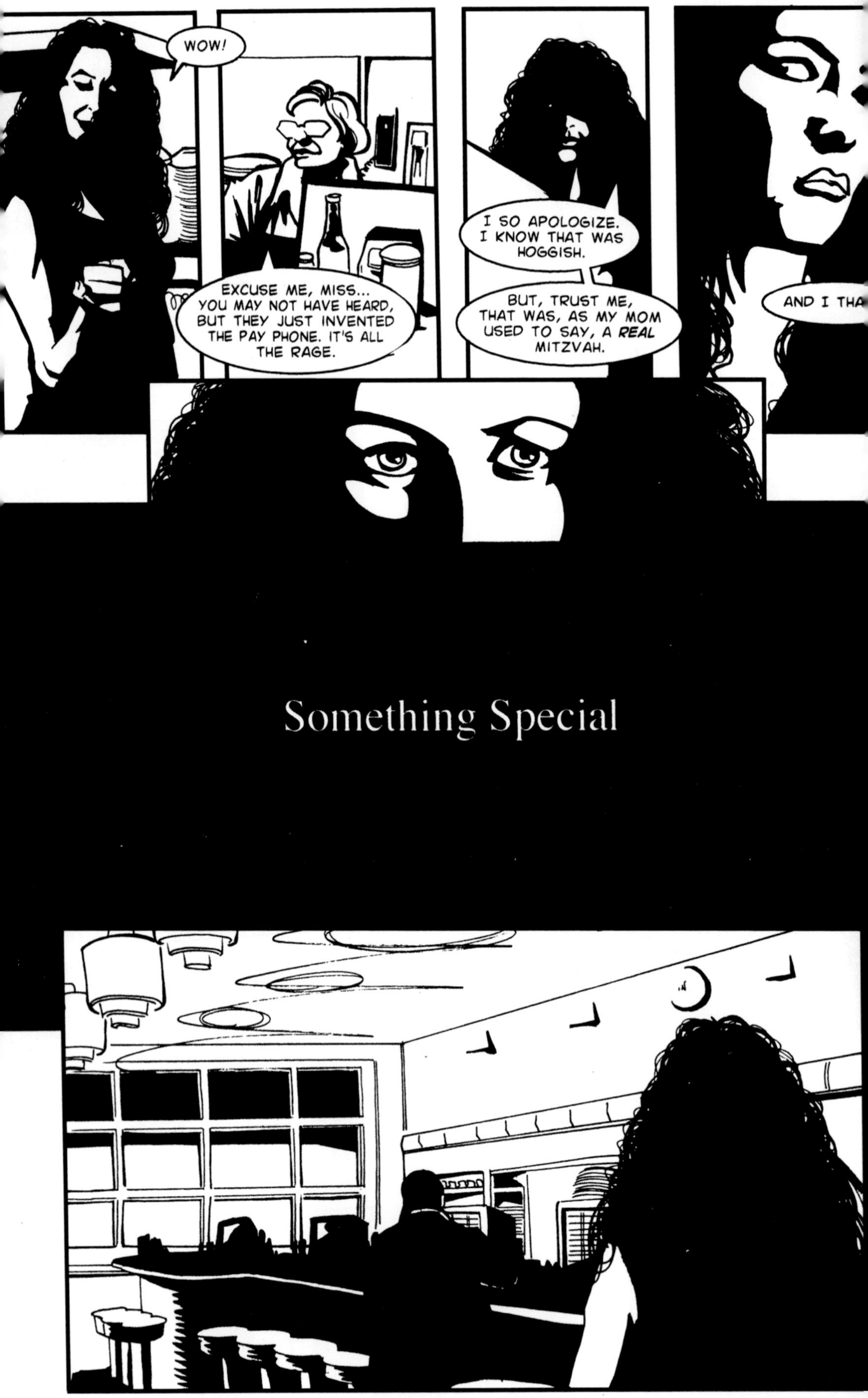
WOW!
EXCUSE ME, MISS... YOU MAY NOT HAVE HEARD, BUT THEY JUST INVENTED THE PAY PHONE. IT'S ALL THE RAGE.
I SO APOLOGIZE. I KNOW THAT WAS HOGGISH.
BUT, TRUST ME, THAT WAS, AS MY MOM USED TO SAY, A REAL MITZVAH.
AND I THA
Something Special

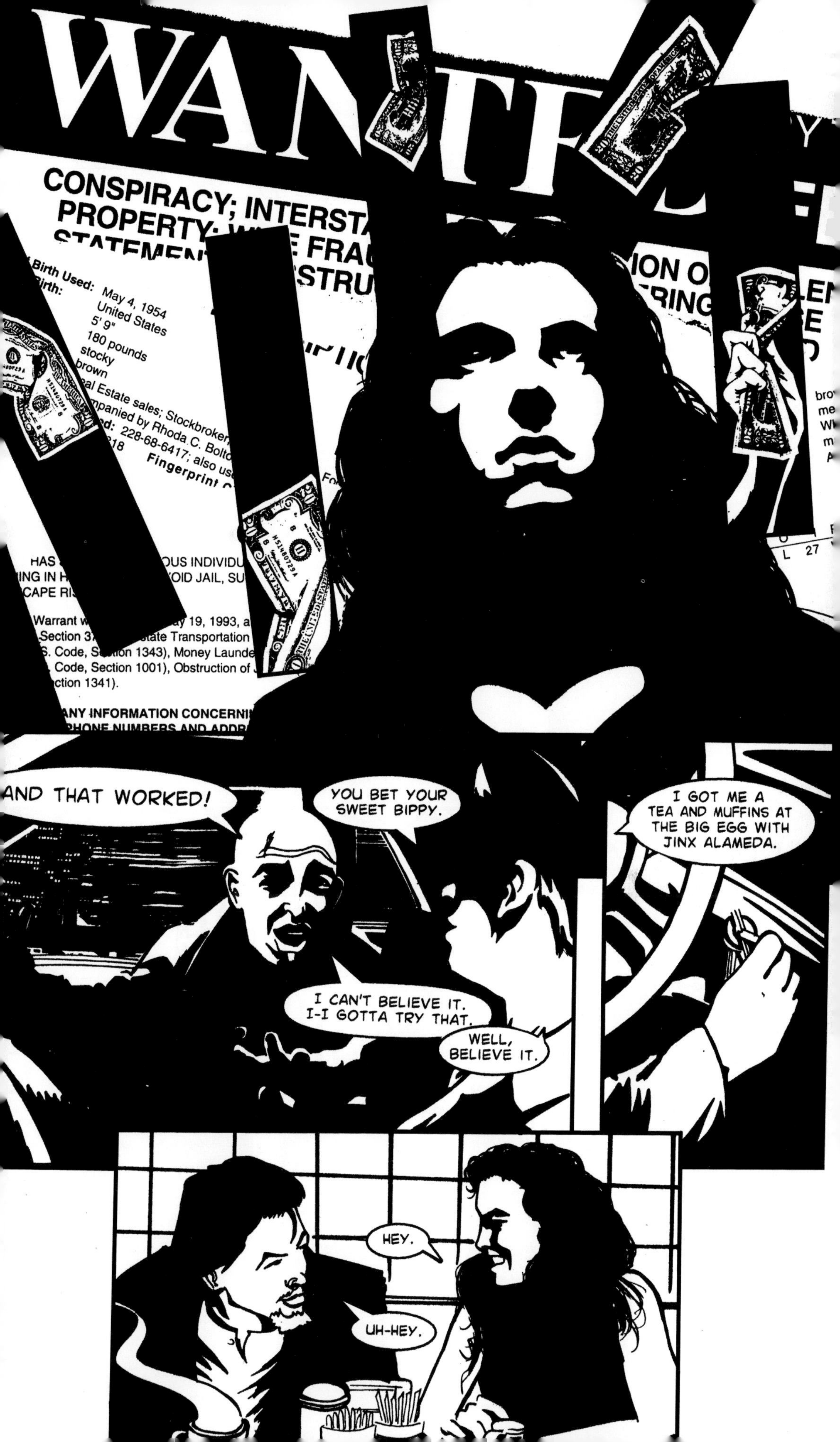
WAN
CONSPIRACY; INTERSTA
PROPERTY
FRA
STRU
Birth Used: May 4, 1954
United States
5' 9"
180 pounds
stocky
brown
al Estate sales; Stockbroker
panied by Rhoda C. Bolto
ed: 228-68-6417; also us
Fingerprint
HAS
OUS INDIVIDU
OID JAIL, SU
Warrant w
y 19, 1993, a
Section 37
tate Transportation
S. Code, S
tion 1343), Money Launde
Code, Section 1001), Obstruction of
ction 1341).
ANY INFORMATION CONCERNI
L 27
AND THAT WORKED!
YOU BET YOUR SWEET BIPPY.
I GOT ME A TEA AND MUFFINS AT THE BIG EGG WITH JINX ALAMEDA.
I CAN'T BELIEVE IT. I-I GOTTA TRY THAT.
WELL, BELIEVE IT.
HEY.
UH-HEY.

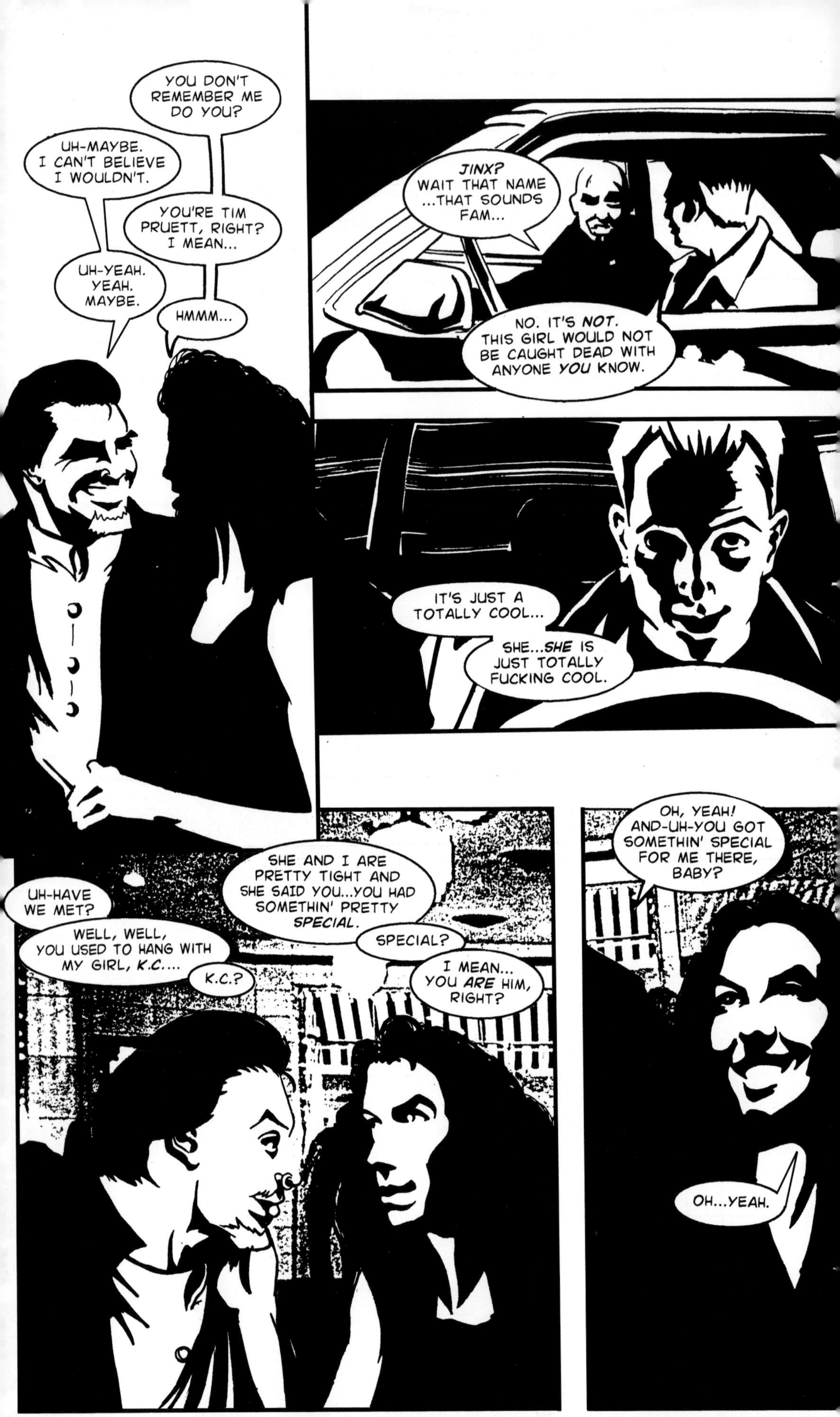
YOU DON'T REMEMBER ME DO YOU?
UH-MAYBE. I CAN'T BELIEVE I WOULDN'T.
YOU'RE TIM PRUETT, RIGHT? I MEAN...
UH-YEAH. YEAH. MAYBE.
HMMM...
JINX? WAIT THAT NAME ...THAT SOUNDS FAM...
NO. IT'S NOT. THIS GIRL WOULD NOT BE CAUGHT DEAD WITH ANYONE YOU KNOW.
IT'S JUST A TOTALLY COOL...
SHE...SHE IS JUST TOTALLY FUCKING COOL.
UH-HAVE WE MET?
WELL, WELL, YOU USED TO HANG WITH MY GIRL, K.C....
K.C.?
SHE AND I ARE PRETTY TIGHT AND SHE SAID YOU...YOU HAD SOMETHIN' PRETTY SPECIAL.
SPECIAL?
I MEAN... YOU ARE HIM, RIGHT?
OH, YEAH! AND-UH-YOU GOT SOMETHIN' SPECIAL FOR ME THERE, BABY?
OH...YEAH.

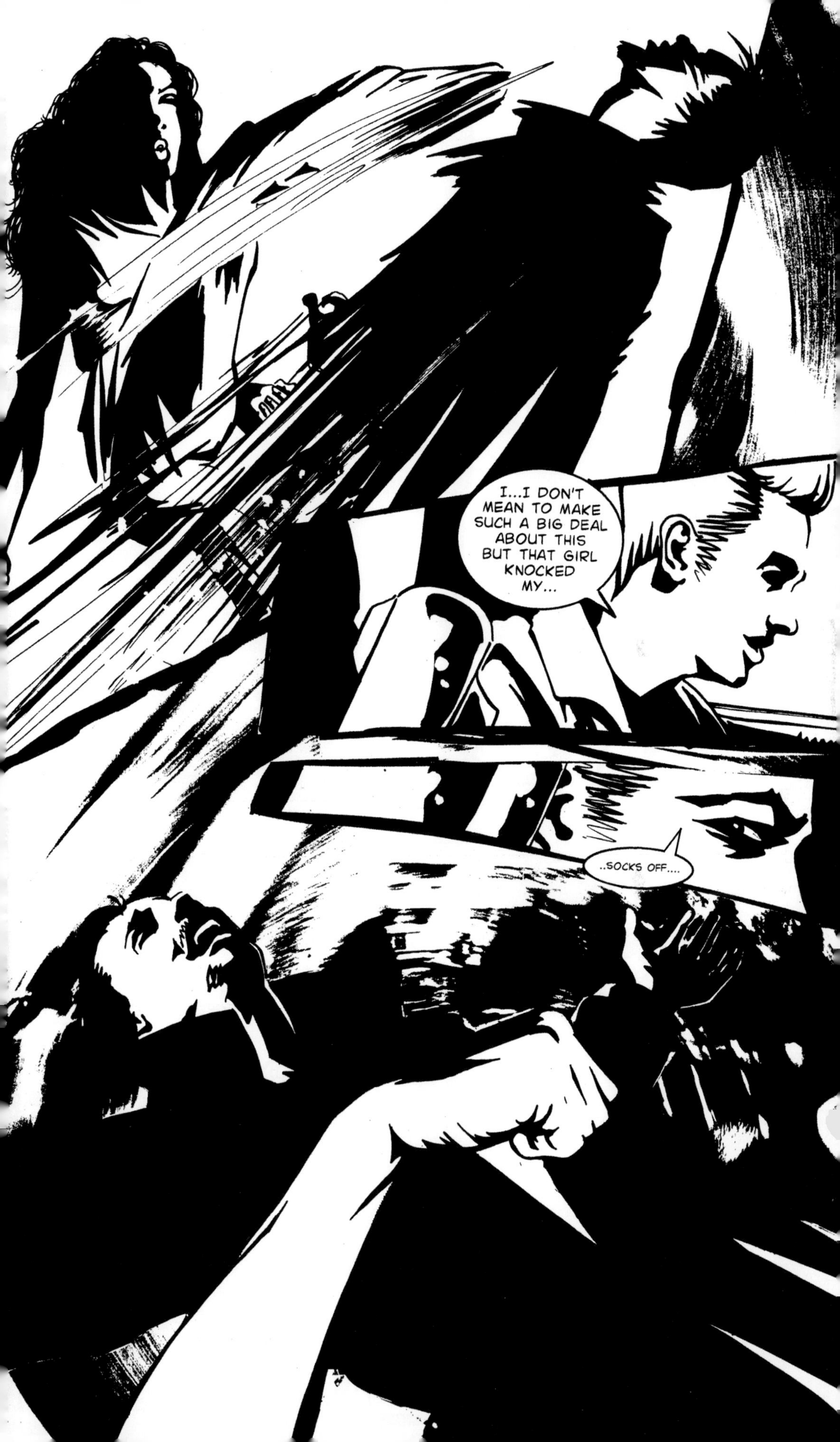
I...I DON'T MEAN TO MAKE SUCH A BIG DEAL ABOUT THIS BUT THAT GIRL KNOCKED MY...
..SOCKS OFF....

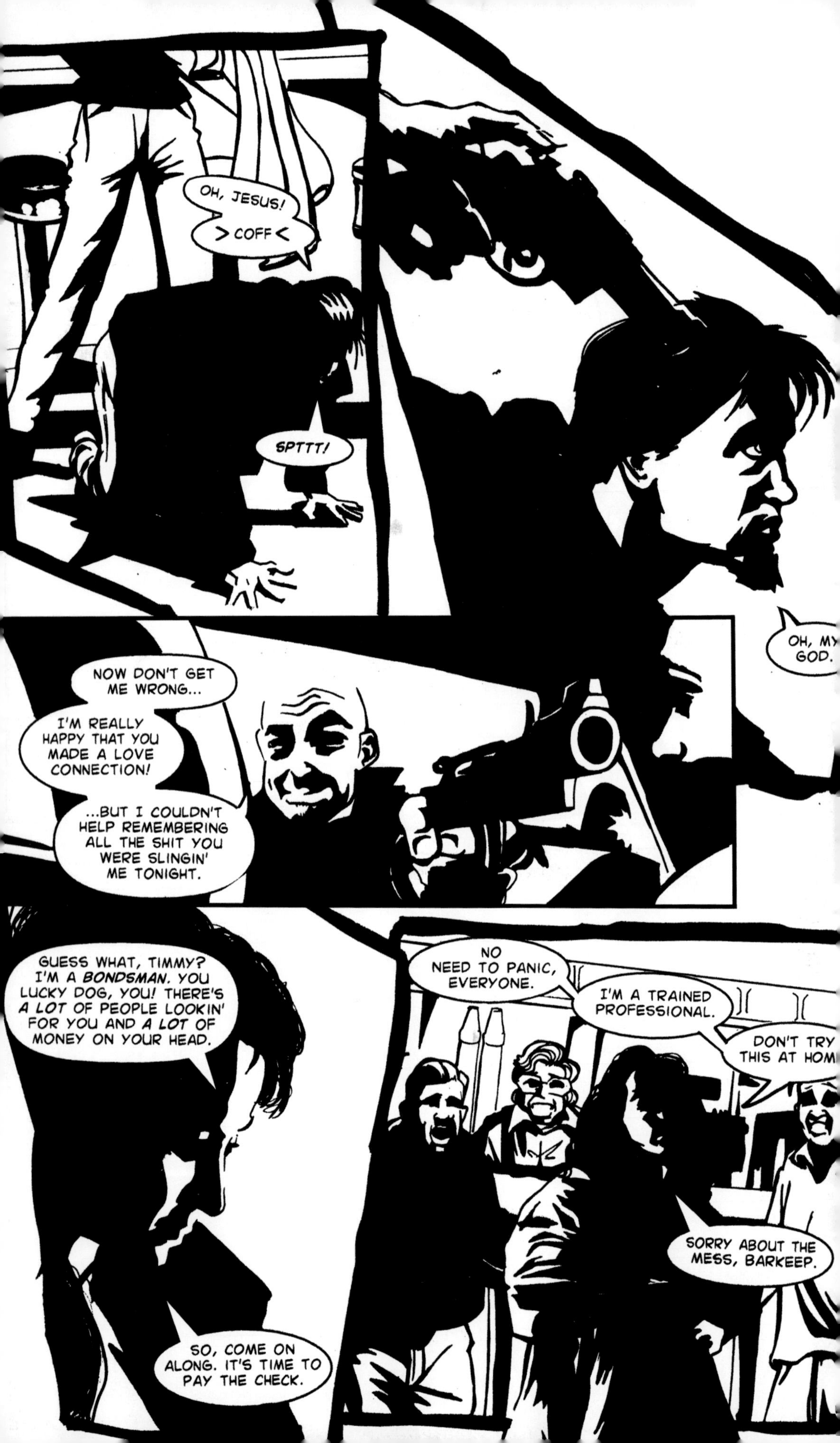
OH, JESUS!
>COFF<
SPTTT!
OH, MY GOD.
NOW DON'T GET ME WRONG...
I'M REALLY HAPPY THAT YOU MADE A LOVE CONNECTION!
...BUT I COULDN'T HELP REMEMBERING ALL THE SHIT YOU WERE SLINGIN' ME TONIGHT.
GUESS WHAT, TIMMY? I'M A BONDSMAN. YOU LUCKY DOG, YOU! THERE'S A LOT OF PEOPLE LOOKIN' FOR YOU AND A LOT OF MONEY ON YOUR HEAD.
SO, COME ON ALONG. IT'S TIME TO PAY THE CHECK.
NO NEED TO PANIC, EVERYONE.
I'M A TRAINED PROFESSIONAL.
DON'T TRY THIS AT HOM
SORRY ABOUT THE MESS, BARKEEP.

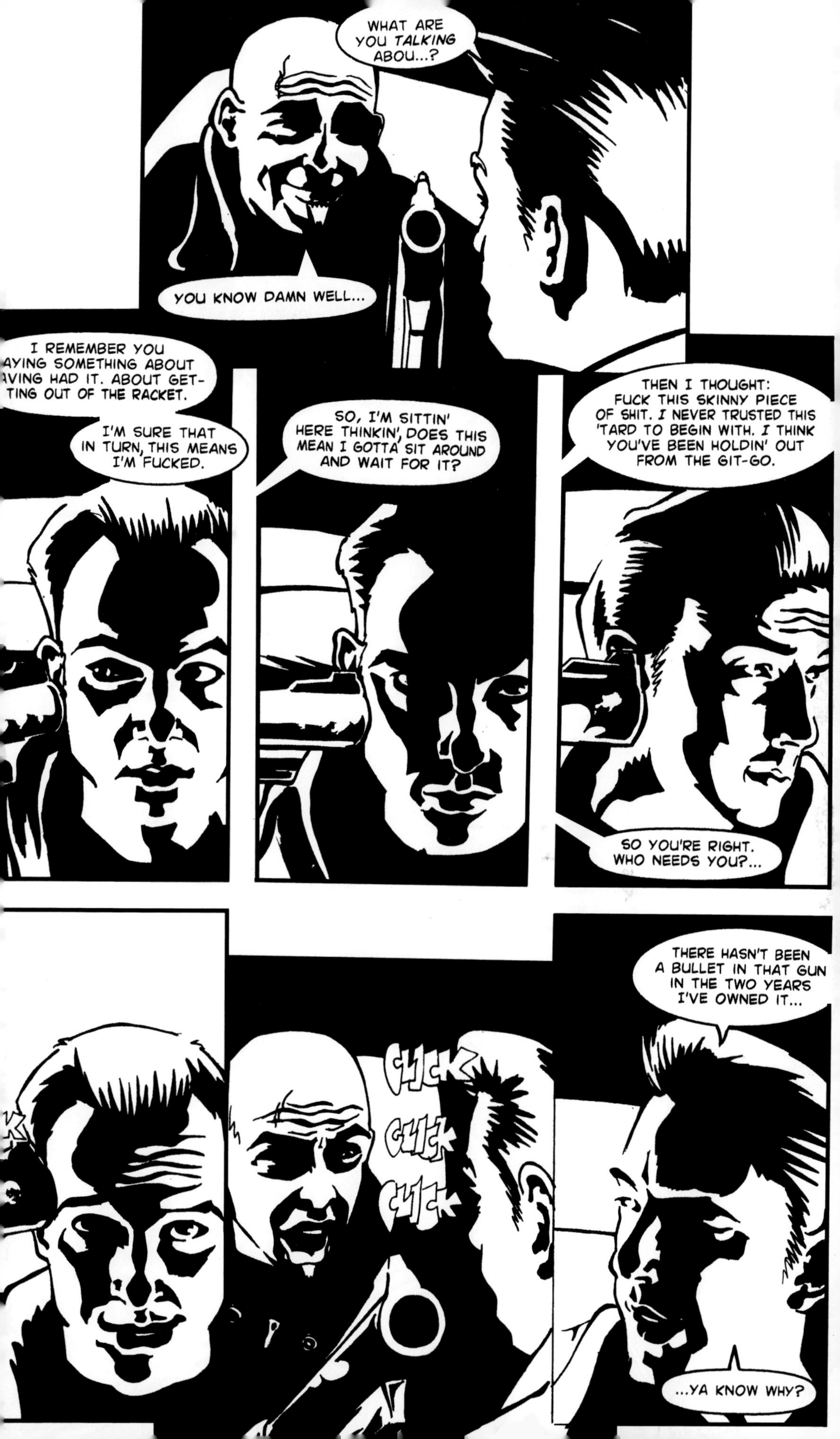
WHAT ARE YOU *TALKING* ABOU...?
YOU KNOW DAMN WELL...
I REMEMBER YOU AYING SOMETHING ABOUT AVING HAD IT. ABOUT GETTING OUT OF THE RACKET.
I'M SURE THAT IN TURN, THIS MEANS I'M FUCKED.
SO, I'M SITTIN' HERE THINKIN', DOES THIS MEAN I GOTTA SIT AROUND AND WAIT FOR IT?
THEN I THOUGHT: FUCK THIS SKINNY PIECE OF SHIT. I NEVER TRUSTED THIS 'TARD TO BEGIN WITH. I THINK YOU'VE BEEN HOLDIN' OUT FROM THE GIT-GO.
SO YOU'RE RIGHT. WHO NEEDS YOU?...
CLICK
CLICK
CLICK
THERE HASN'T BEEN A BULLET IN THAT GUN IN THE TWO YEARS I'VE OWNED IT...
...YA KNOW WHY?

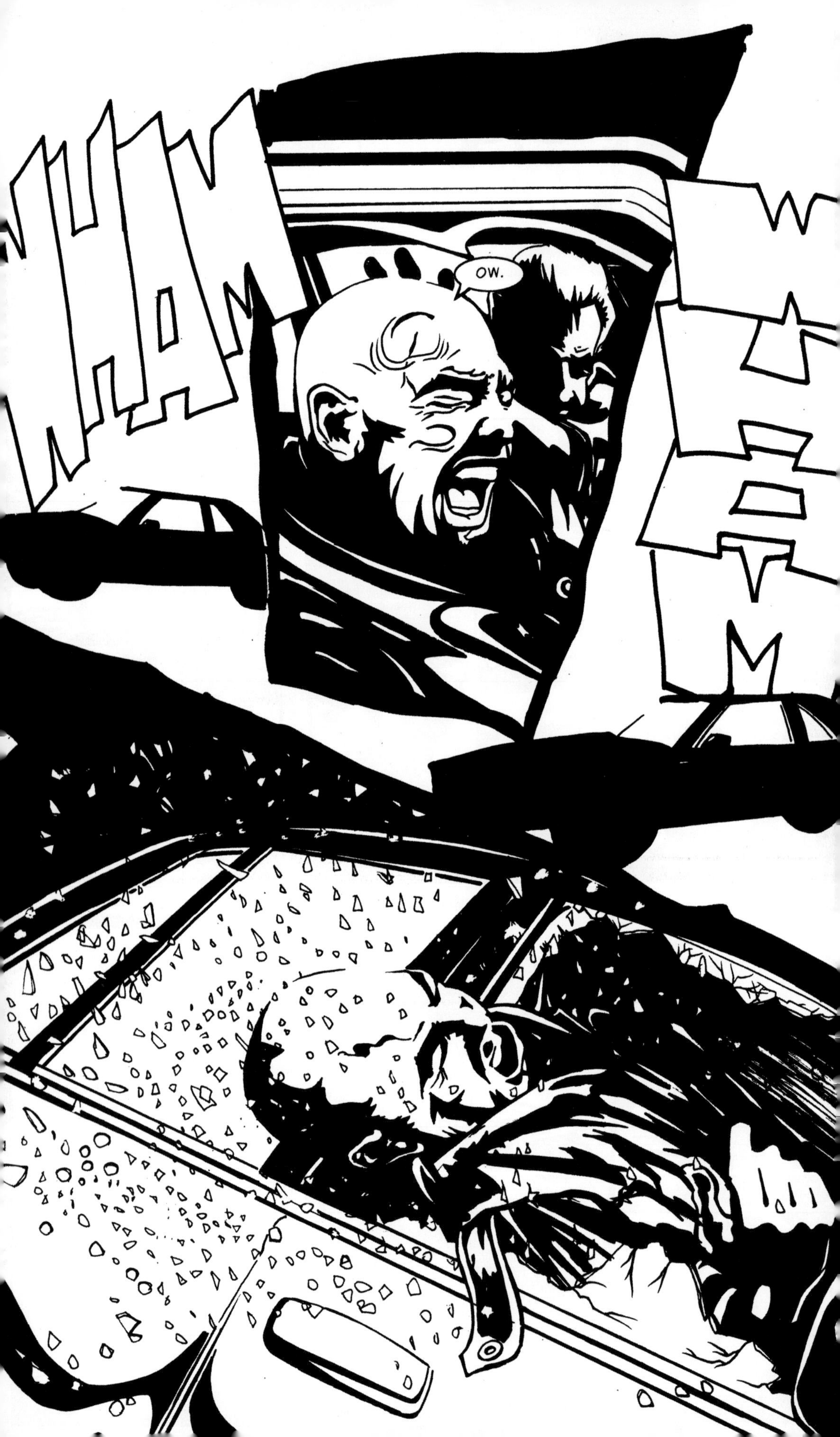
WHAM
OW.
WHAM

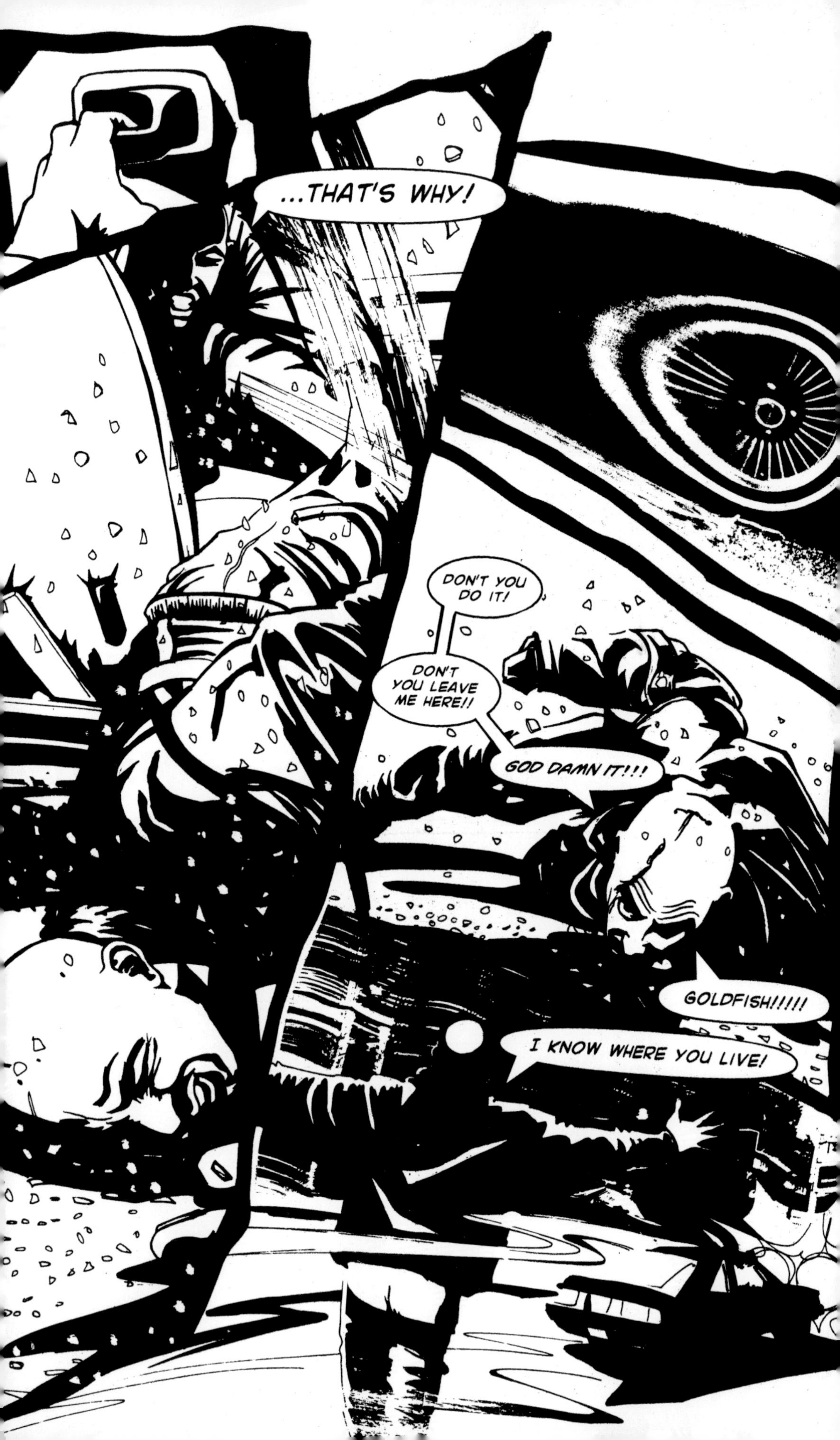
...THAT'S WHY!
DON'T YOU DO IT!
DON'T YOU LEAVE ME HERE!!
GOD DAMN IT!!!
GOLDFISH!!!!!
I KNOW WHERE YOU LIVE!

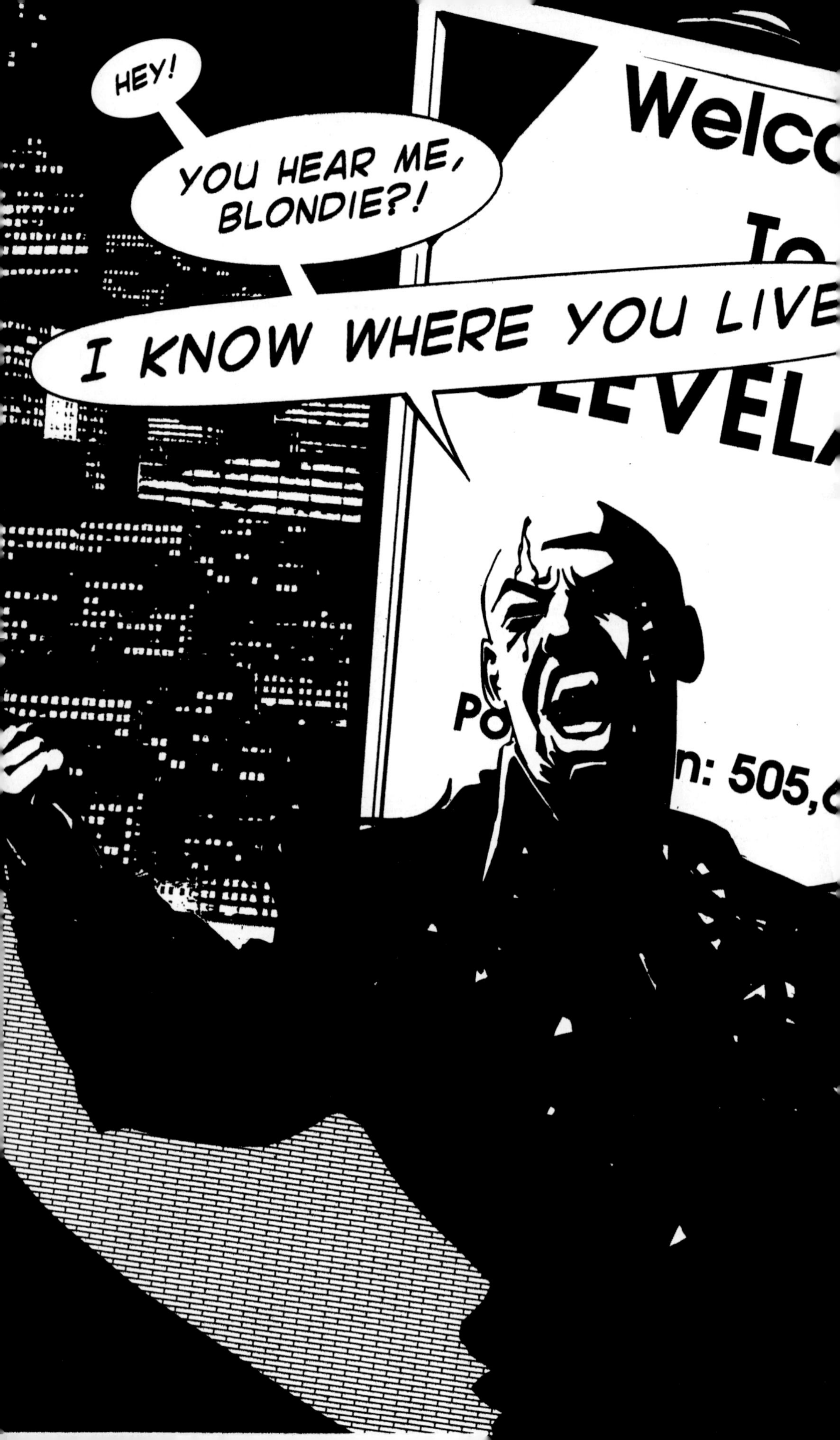
HEY!
YOU HEAR ME, BLONDIE?!
I KNOW WHERE YOU LIVE
Welc
To
EVEL
Po
n: 505,

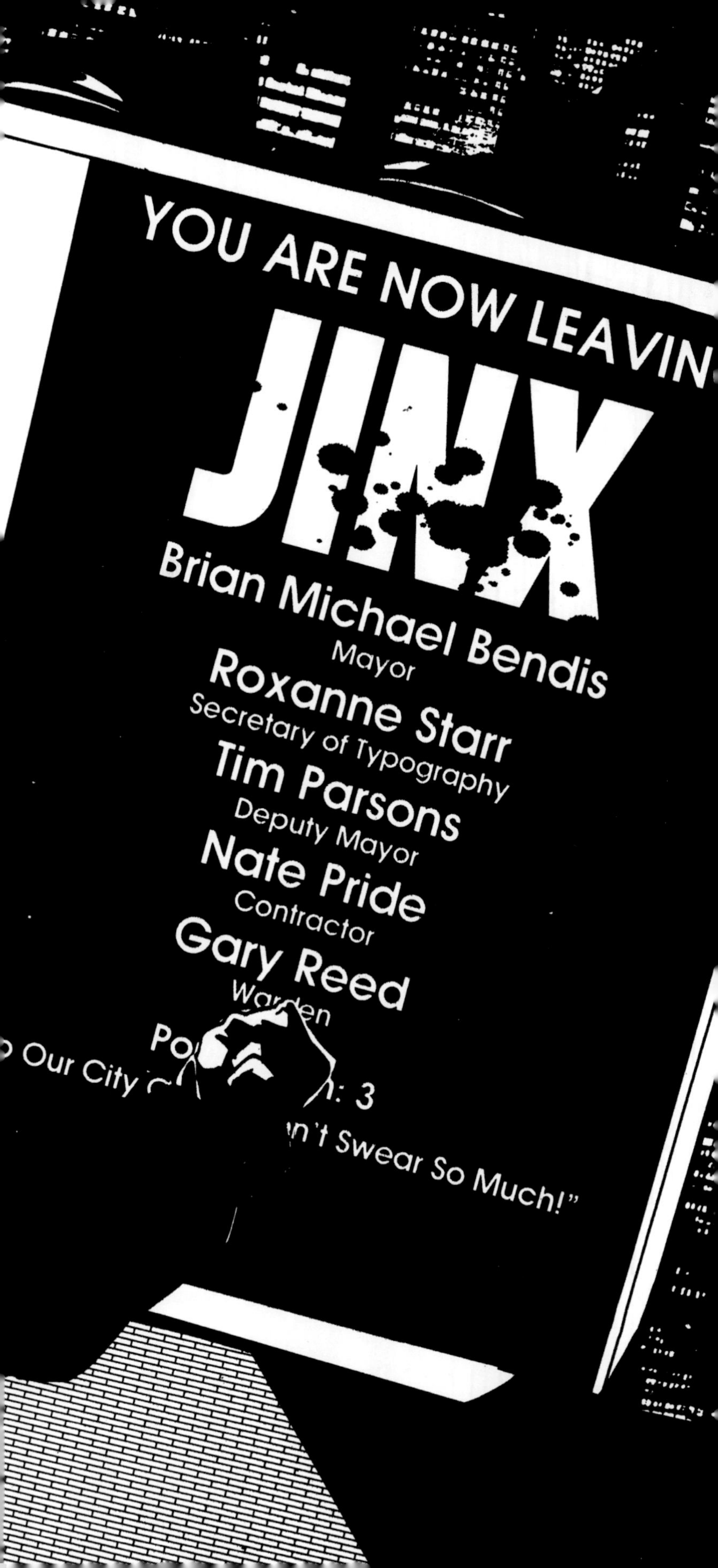
YOU ARE NOW LEAVIN
JINX
Brian Michael Bendis
Mayor
Roxanne Starr
Secretary of Typography
Tim Parsons
Deputy Mayor
Nate Pride
Contractor
Gary Reed

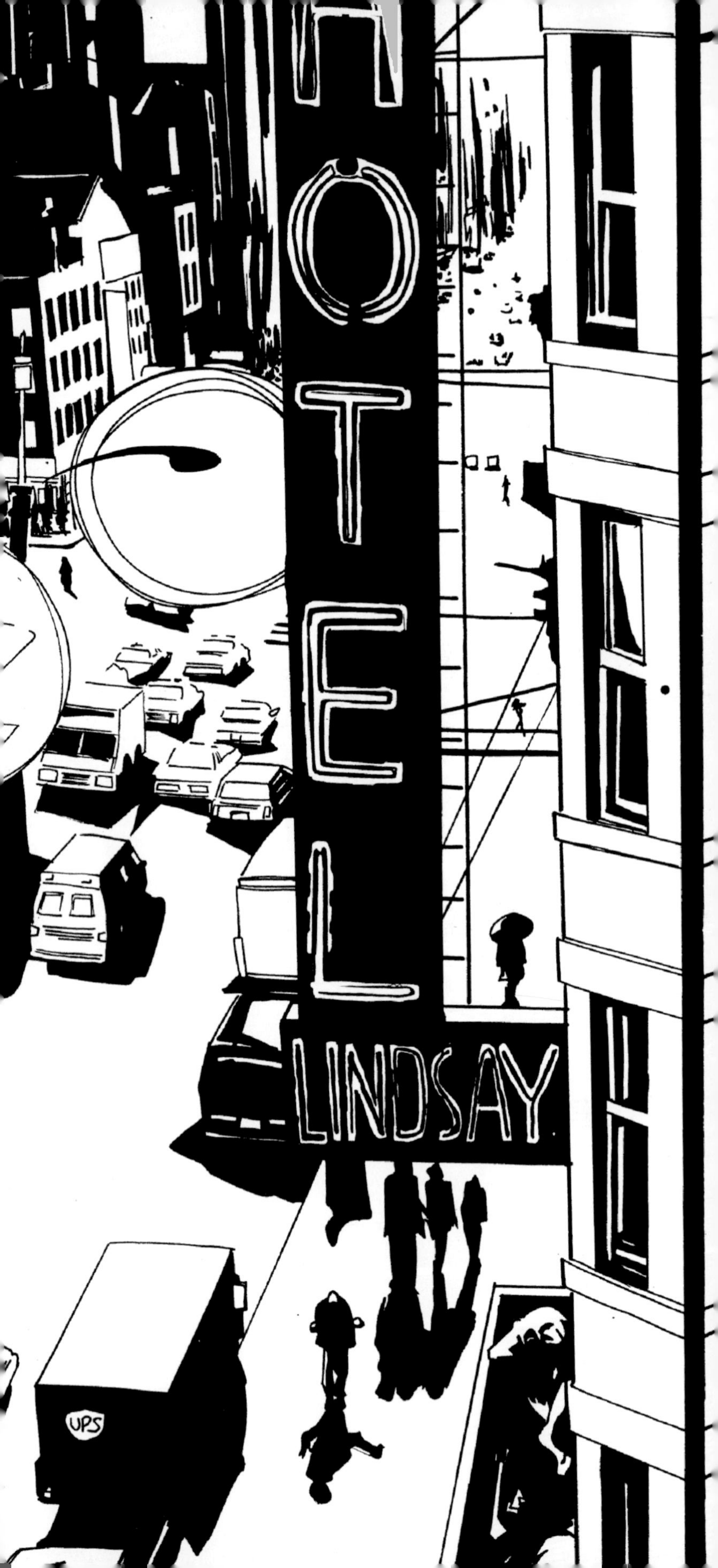
HOTEL
LINDSAY

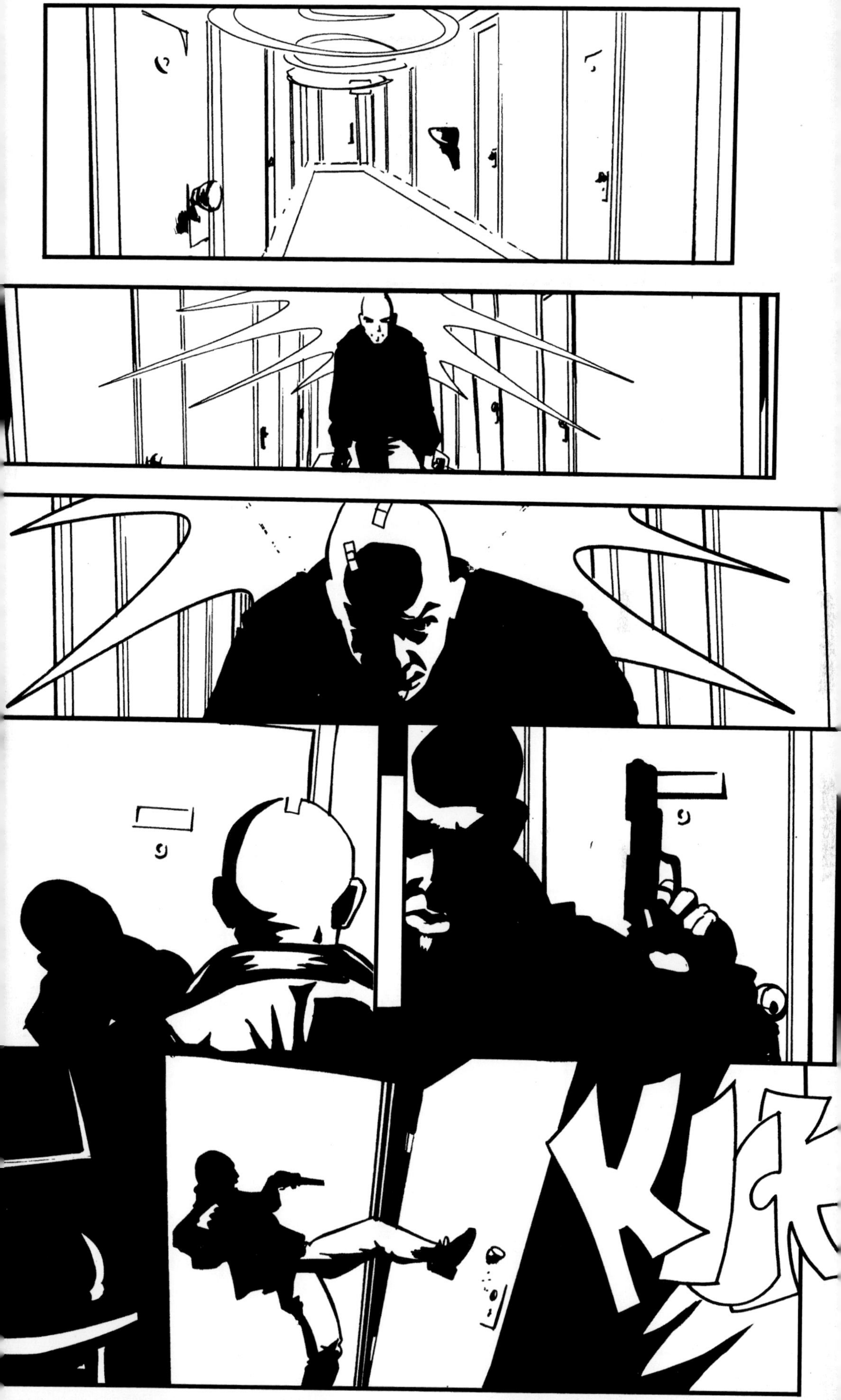

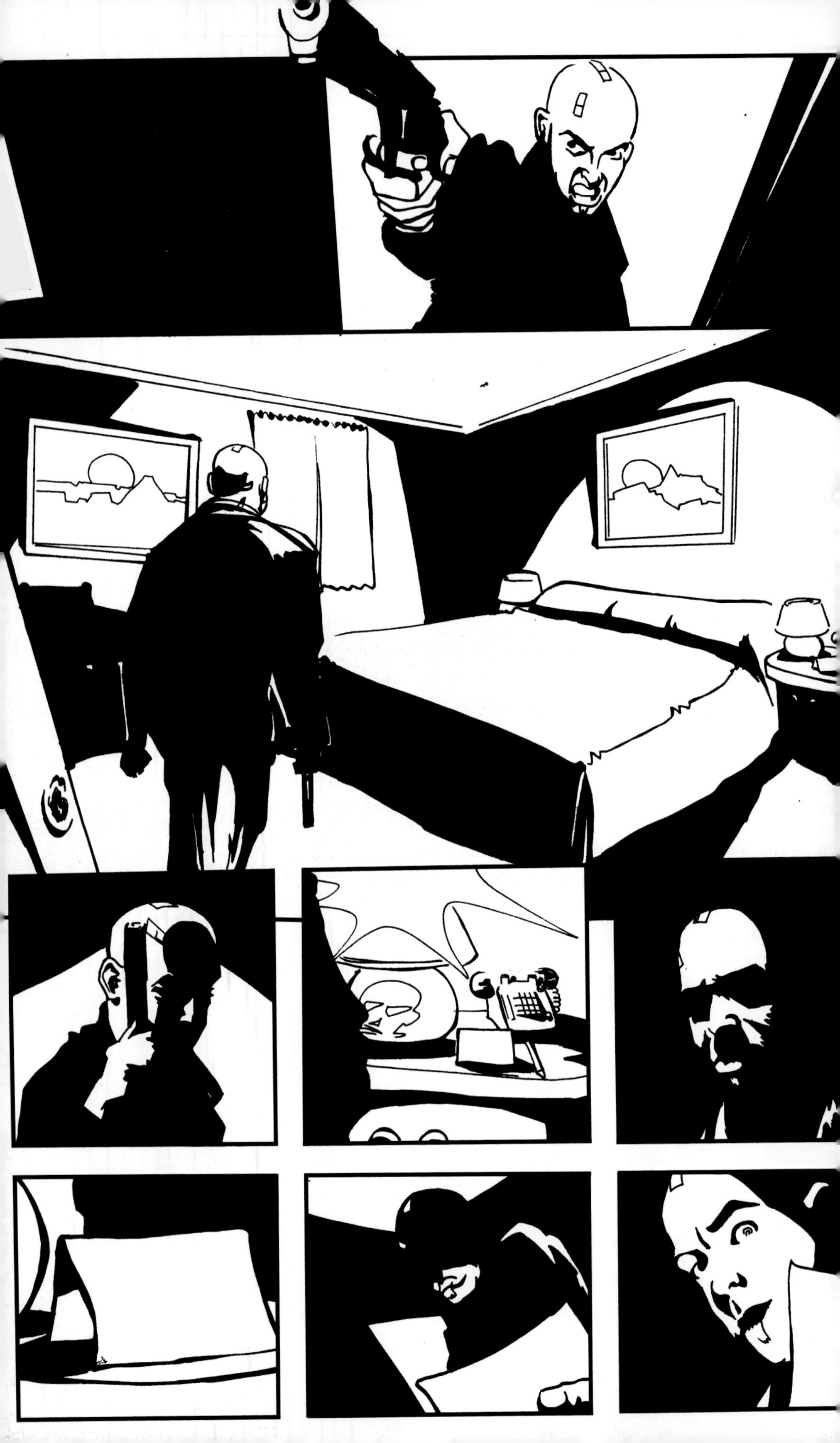

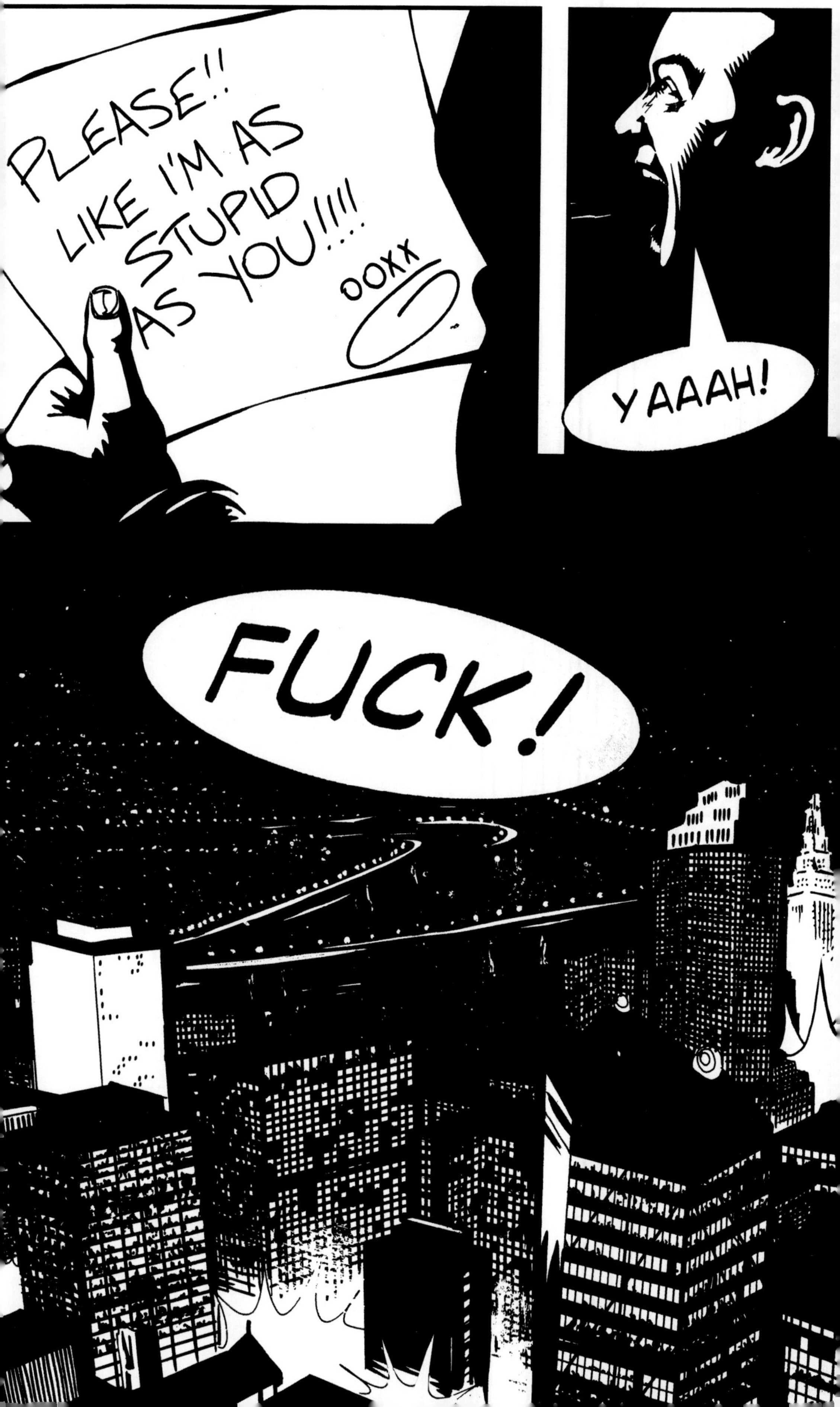
PLEASE!! LIKE I'M AS STUPID AS YOU!!!!!
OOXX
YAAAH!
FUCK!

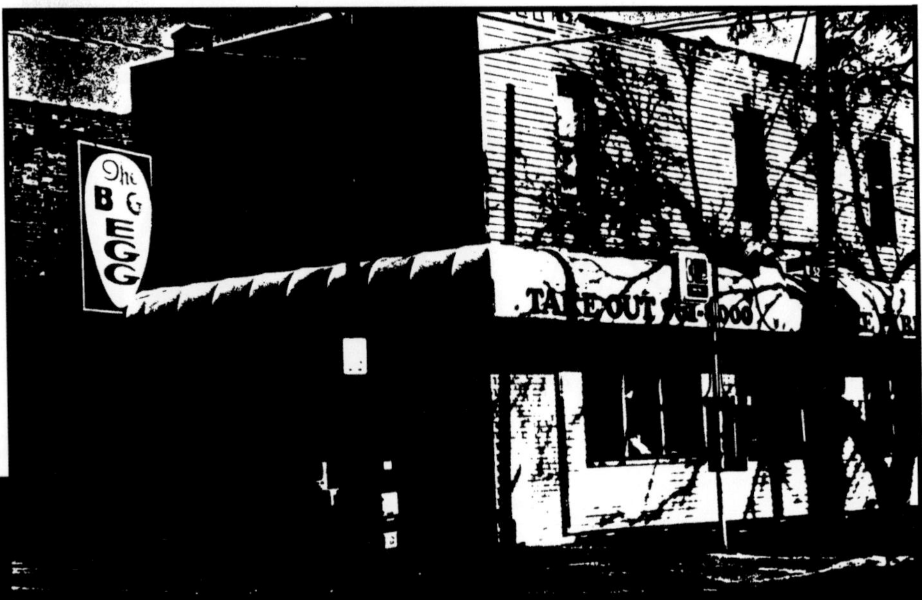
The
B G
EGG
TAKE OUT

Dick Cavett

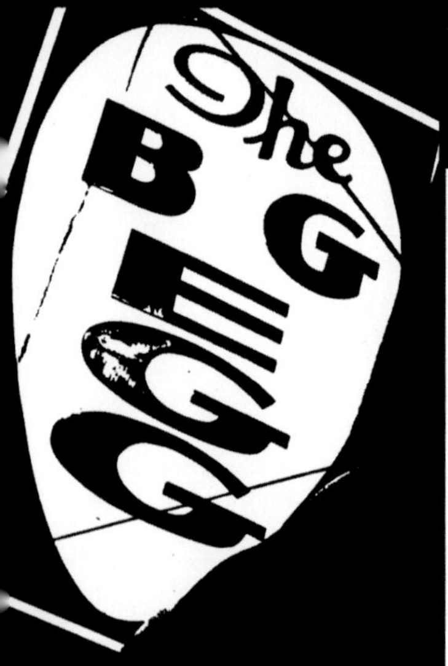
The
B G
EGG

"HERE YA GO, M'LADY, YOUR TEA AND YOUR MUFFIN."

"*YAY!* VERY GOOD... VERY NICE."

"SWEET'N LOW?"

"THANKS A MIL. SO WHAT'S ON YOUR *MIND,* MYSTERY DATE?"

"WHAT'S ON MY MIND?"

"DAVID...*DAVID.* YOUR NAME. IT'S A BEAUTIFUL NAME."

"YOU THINK?"

"OH YEAH. I *ALWAYS* HAVE. PLANNED ON NAMING MY KIDS DAVID."

"ALL OF THEM?"

"EVERY SINGLE ONE. SO WHAT'S ON YOUR MIND?"

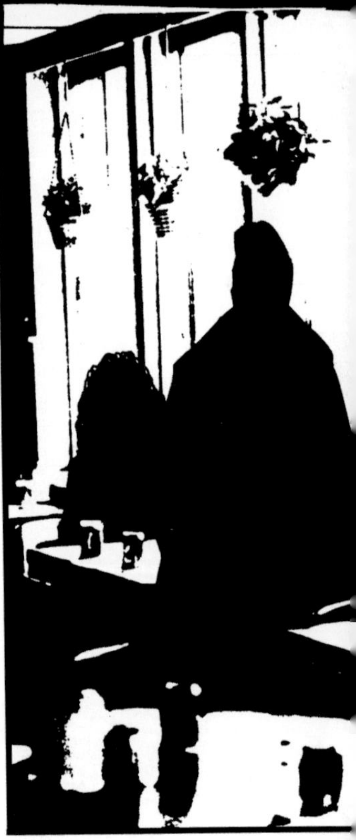

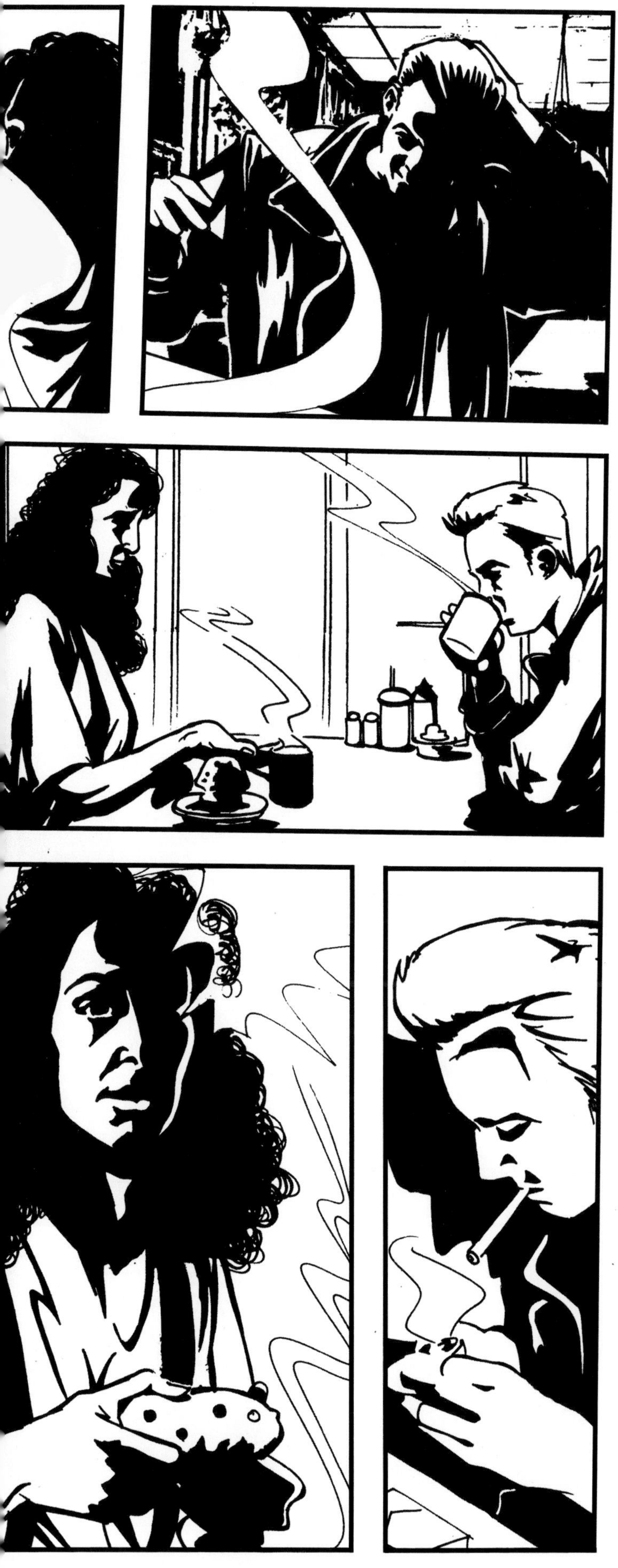

"WHAT'S?...NOTHING. NOTHING'S...WELL, QUITE FRANKLY, I FIND MYSELF WITH SO *MUCH* TO SAY AND *SO* MUCH...SO MANY QUESTIONS, THAT I CAN'T READILY THINK OF ANYTHING...WHERE DO YOU START? *YOU* ARE A TOTAL BLANK SLATE TO ME."

"I THOUGHT OF THAT TOO, AS I WAS COMING OVER HERE. BUT, Y'KNOW, IT'S SORT OF A KEEN OPPORTUNITY FOR US."

"HOW SO?"

"WELL, CHECK IT OUT. I HAVE NO PRECONCEIVED NOTIONS OF YOU. YOU CAN PRESENT YOURSELF IN ANY WAY YOU SEE FIT. YOU CAN BE THE MAN YOU'VE ALWAYS DREAMED YOU'D BE."

"THE MAN I'VE ALWAYS *DREAMED* I'D BE?"

"YEAH, Y'KNOW? YOU CAN GET PIGEONHOLED INTO BEING A CERTAIN *KIND* OF PERSON. YOUR REPUTATION CAN PRECEDE YOU, RIGHT? AND ALL OF YOUR WORDS AND ACTIONS ARE FUNNELED THROUGH THIS REPUTATION LIKE A...LIKE A *WHAT?* WHAT AM I THINKING OF?"

"WHAT...A *FUNNEL?*"

"NO."

"A...A *SIEVE?*"

"NO, NO...A *PRISM*. A *PRISM*. AND SOMETIMES THAT'S A RAW DEAL. SOMETIMES THAT'S A BAD RAP."

"GOOD POINT."

"SO NOW, HERE WE ARE, TWO BLANK SLATES."

"WE CAN BE WHOEVER WE WANT TO BE."

"TA-DAA."

"ARE *YOU* NOT HAPPY WITH WHO *YOU* ARE NOW?"

"TOTALLY? *NO*. NOBODY IS. JINX ALAMEDA IS A WORK IN PROGRESS..."

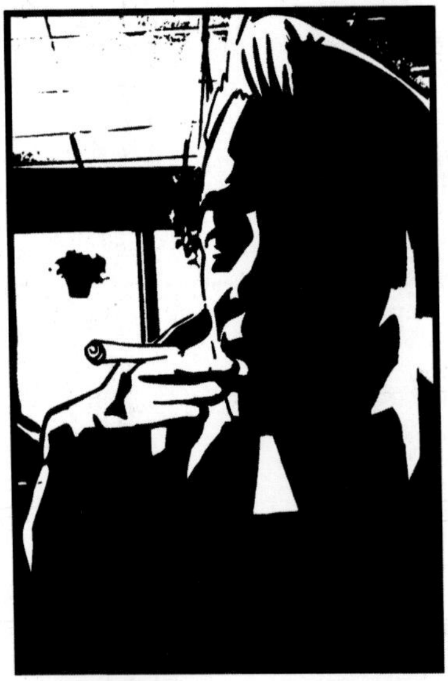

"SO AM I, Y'KNOW? I BET IT'S NOT SO EASY."

"WHAT?"

"TO FLIP A SWITCH AND JUST BE THIS PERFECT VERSION OF ME."

"MAYBE, MAYBE NOT."

"MAYBE NOT."

"WELL, I BET IT PRETTY MUCH DEPENDS ON HOW CLOSE YOU ARE TO BEGIN WITH."

"OLD HABITS DIE HARD."

"MAYBE, MAYBE NOT."

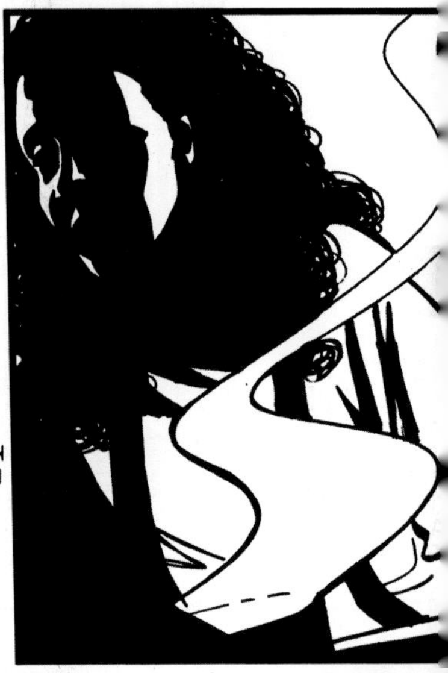

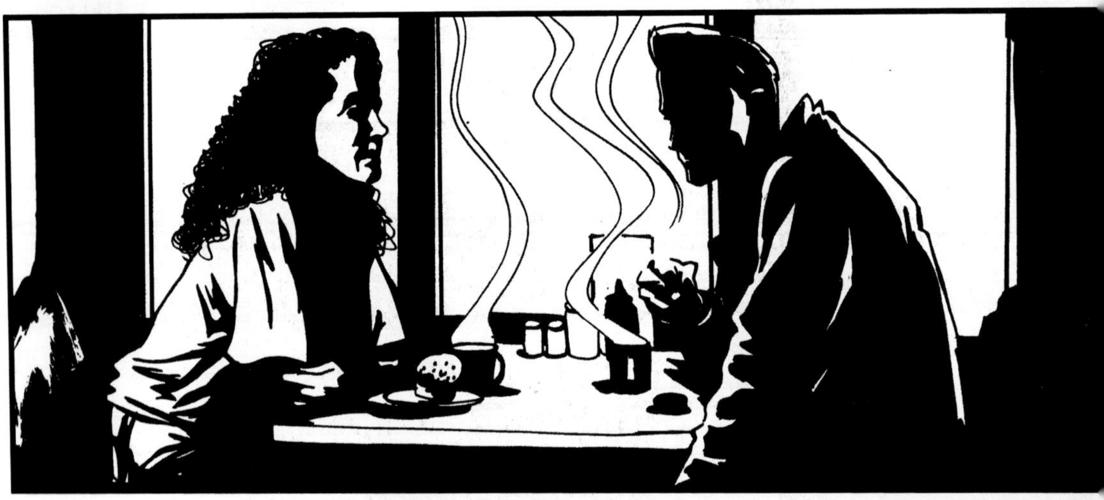

"I'LL HAVE TO THINK ABOUT IT. GOOD MUFFIN?"

"ALL MUFFINS ARE GOOD MUFFINS, SHE REPLIED WITH MUCH VERVE...WHAT?"

"WHAT?...*OH*... OH NOTHING."

"WHAT WERE YOU *SMILING* ABOUT?"

"OH SHIT! WAS I SMILING? *GREAT!* I'M COMING OFF LIKE A *MENTAL PATIENT!*"

"NOT YET."

"I'LL, I'LL, I'LL BE *HONEST* WITH YOU. I HAVE...I HAVE BEEN LOOKING FORWARD TO THIS. I MEAN. ALREADY THIS IS NICE. WHATEVER THIS IS."

"SO FAR."

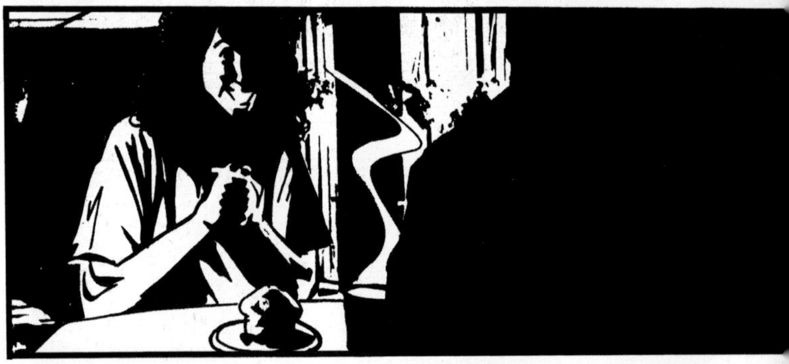

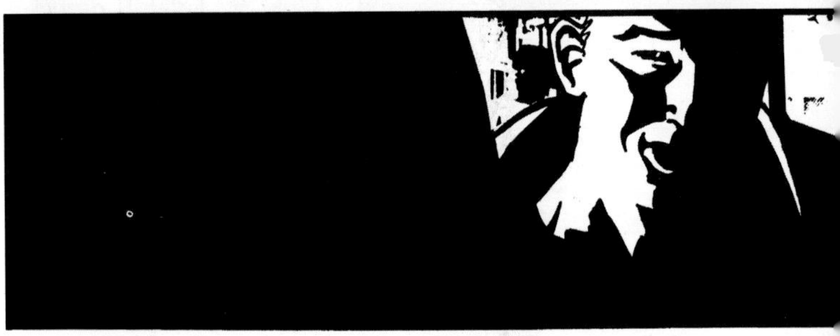

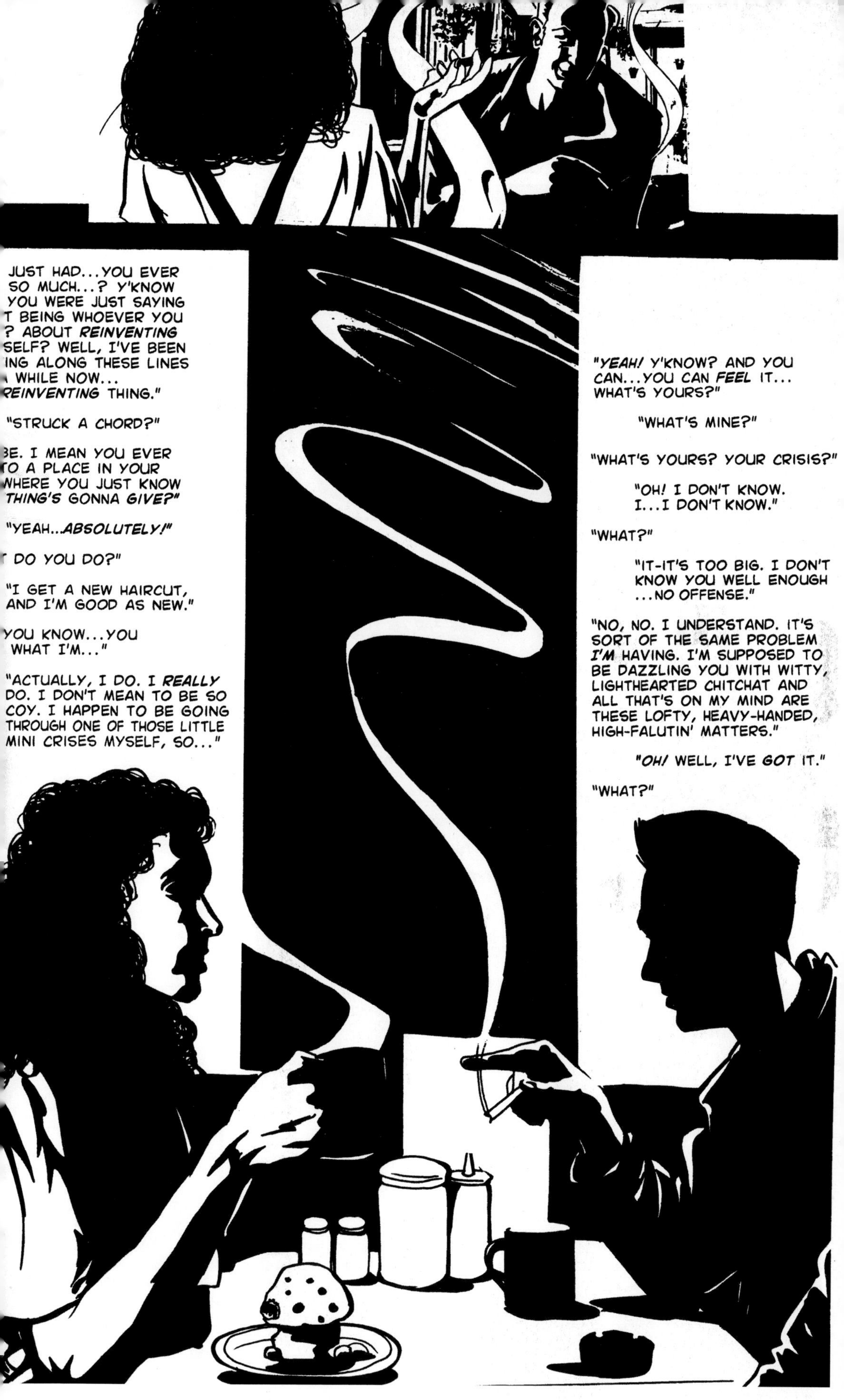

JUST HAD...YOU EVER SO MUCH...? Y'KNOW YOU WERE JUST SAYING T BEING WHOEVER YOU ? ABOUT *REINVENTING* SELF? WELL, I'VE BEEN ING ALONG THESE LINES WHILE NOW... *REINVENTING* THING."
"STRUCK A CHORD?"
BE. I MEAN YOU EVER TO A PLACE IN YOUR WHERE YOU JUST KNOW *THING'S* GONNA *GIVE?"*
"YEAH...*ABSOLUTELY!"*
DO YOU DO?"
"I GET A NEW HAIRCUT, AND I'M GOOD AS NEW."
YOU KNOW...YOU WHAT I'M..."
"ACTUALLY, I DO. I *REALLY* DO. I DON'T MEAN TO BE SO COY. I HAPPEN TO BE GOING THROUGH ONE OF THOSE LITTLE MINI CRISES MYSELF, SO..."
"*YEAH!* Y'KNOW? AND YOU CAN...YOU CAN *FEEL* IT... WHAT'S YOURS?"
"WHAT'S MINE?"
"WHAT'S YOURS? YOUR CRISIS?"
"OH! I DON'T KNOW. I...I DON'T KNOW."
"WHAT?"
"IT-IT'S TOO BIG. I DON'T KNOW YOU WELL ENOUGH ...NO OFFENSE."
"NO, NO. I UNDERSTAND. IT'S SORT OF THE SAME PROBLEM *I'M* HAVING. I'M SUPPOSED TO BE DAZZLING YOU WITH WITTY, LIGHTHEARTED CHITCHAT AND ALL THAT'S ON MY MIND ARE THESE LOFTY, HEAVY-HANDED, HIGH-FALUTIN' MATTERS."
"*OH!* WELL, I'VE *GOT* IT."
"WHAT?"

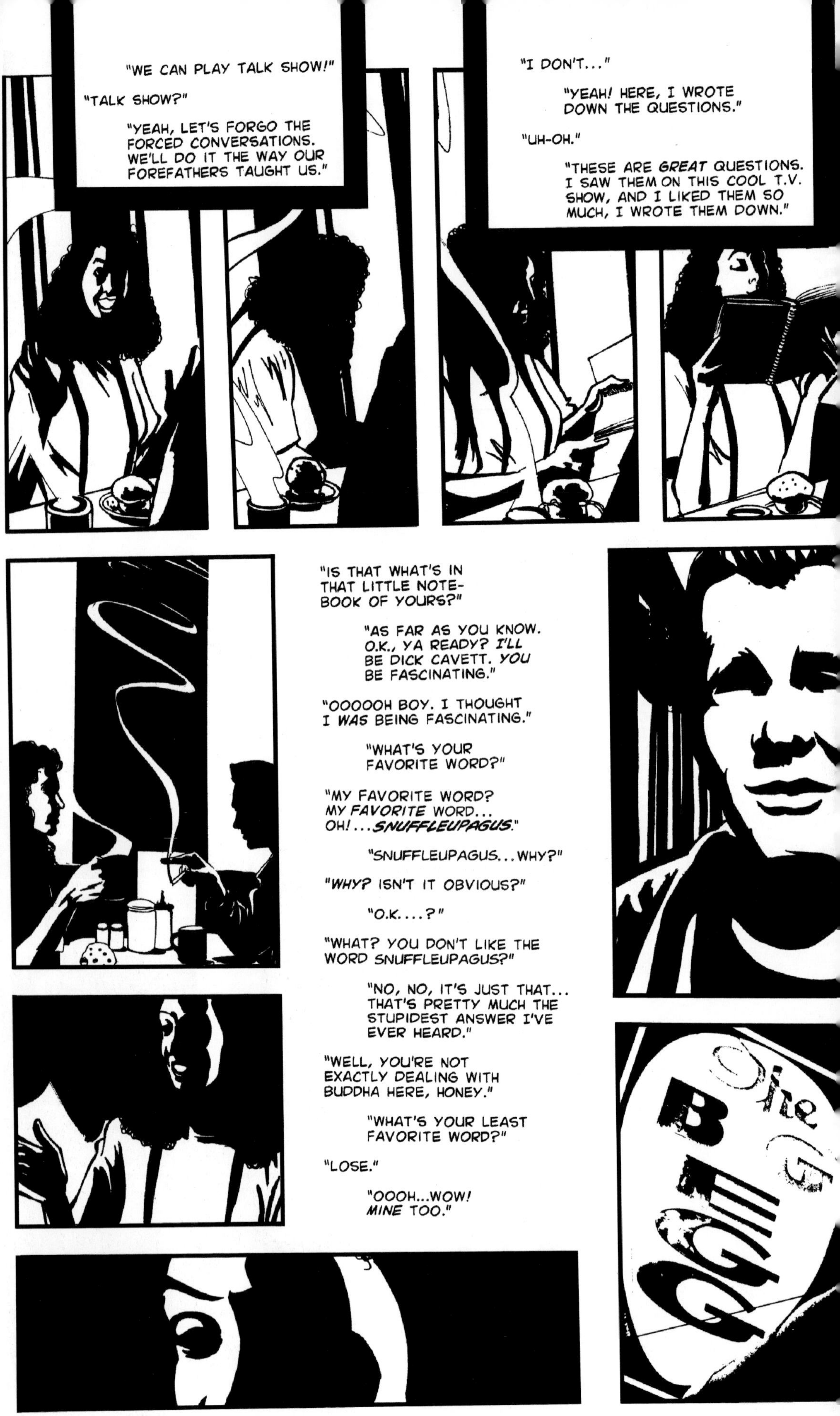
"WE CAN PLAY TALK SHOW!"
"TALK SHOW?"
"YEAH, LET'S FORGO THE FORCED CONVERSATIONS. WE'LL DO IT THE WAY OUR FOREFATHERS TAUGHT US."
"I DON'T..."
"YEAH! HERE, I WROTE DOWN THE QUESTIONS."
"UH-OH."
"THESE ARE *GREAT* QUESTIONS. I SAW THEM ON THIS COOL T.V. SHOW, AND I LIKED THEM SO MUCH, I WROTE THEM DOWN."
"IS THAT WHAT'S IN THAT LITTLE NOTE-BOOK OF YOURS?"
"AS FAR AS YOU KNOW. O.K., YA READY? *I'LL* BE DICK CAVETT. *YOU* BE FASCINATING."
"OOOOOH BOY. I THOUGHT I *WAS* BEING FASCINATING."
"WHAT'S YOUR FAVORITE WORD?"
"MY FAVORITE WORD? MY *FAVORITE* WORD... OH!... ***SNUFFLEUPAGUS***."
"SNUFFLEUPAGUS... WHY?"
"*WHY?* ISN'T IT OBVIOUS?"
"O.K....?"
"WHAT? YOU DON'T LIKE THE WORD SNUFFLEUPAGUS?"
"NO, NO, IT'S JUST THAT... THAT'S PRETTY MUCH THE STUPIDEST ANSWER I'VE EVER HEARD."
"WELL, YOU'RE NOT EXACTLY DEALING WITH BUDDHA HERE, HONEY."
"WHAT'S YOUR LEAST FAVORITE WORD?"
"LOSE."
"OOOH...WOW! *MINE* TOO."

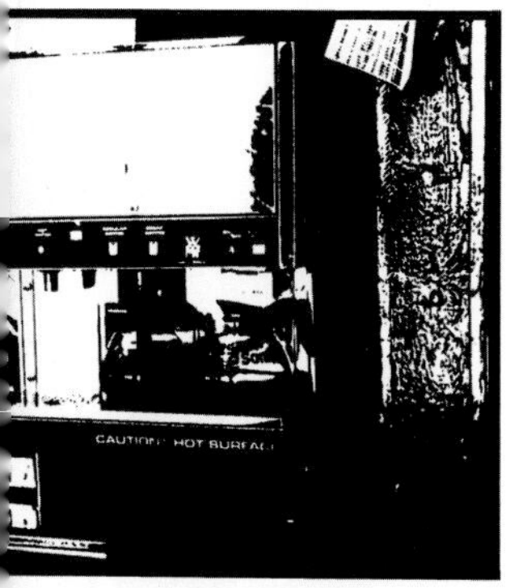
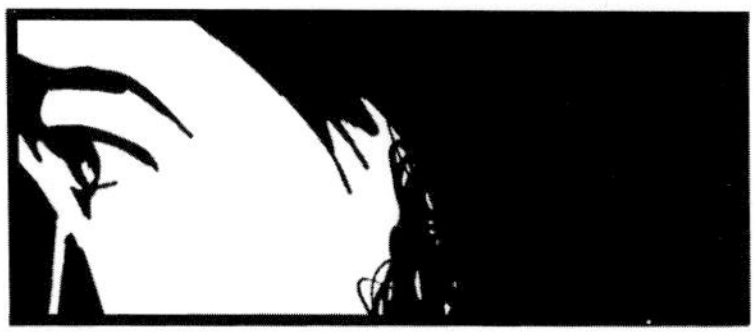
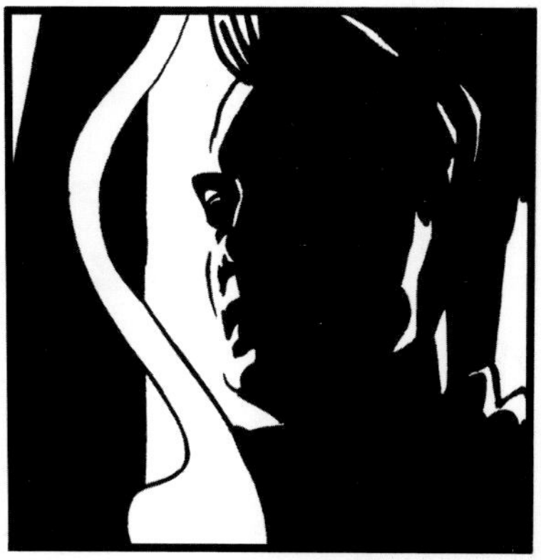

"I SHOULD SAY *LOSE* OR *CAN'T*."

"HMMMM. WHAT'S YOUR FAVORITE SOUND?"

"SOUND... THE SOUND EFFECT WHERE LETTERMAN THROWS A PENCIL THROUGH HIS FAKE WINDOW. *PSSHH!!*"

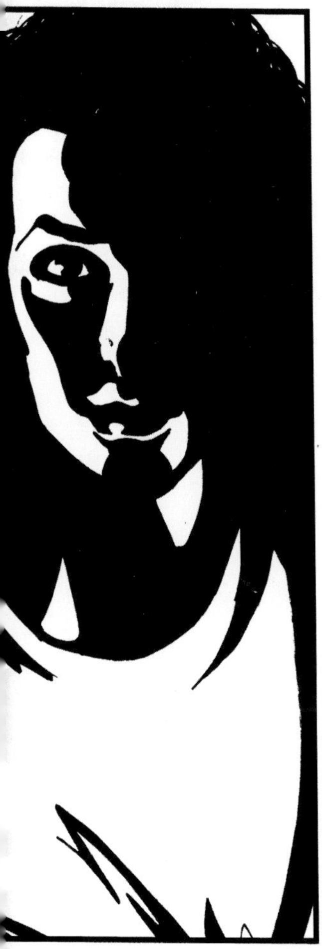
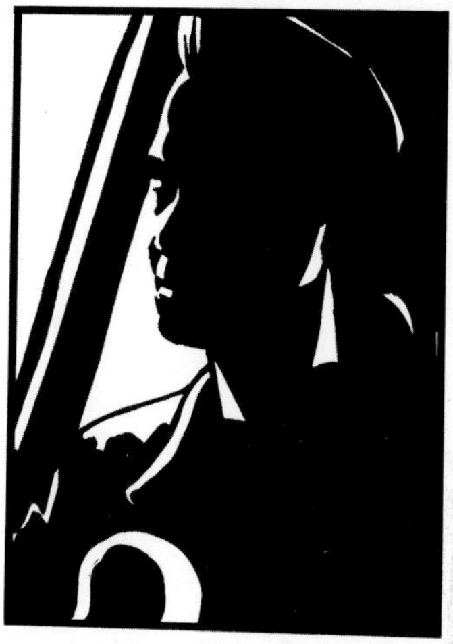

"DOES HE STILL DO THAT?"

"Y'KNOW? I DON'T KNOW."

"WHAT'S *YOUR* LEAST FAVORITE SOUND?"

"OH...IT'S THE HISS. *HISSSSSSSS!!!* THAT IS THE WORST. WHEN I SEE A COMEDIAN ON-STAGE OR ON T.V., AND I HEAR SOMEONE HISS, I JUST *CRINGE*. IT'S THE *MEANEST*, MOST *VULGAR* SOUND A HUMAN CAN MAKE."

"WELL, IT'S SUPPOSED TO BE, YOU'RE SUPPOSED TO HATE IT."

"WELL, THEN, GOOD NEWS FOR ME."

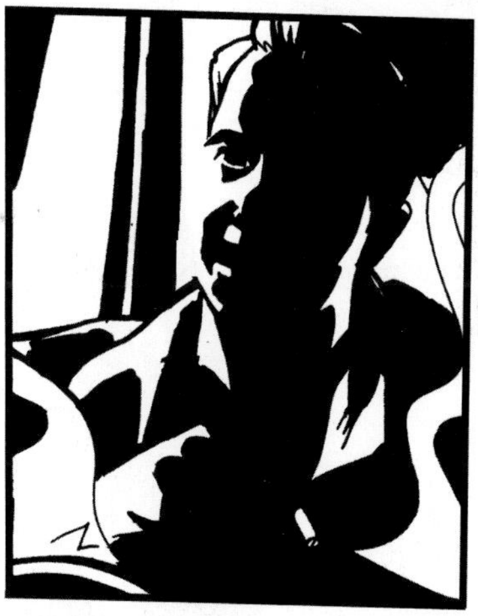

"WHAT'S YOUR FAVORITE CURSE WORD?"

"OH EASY... *FUCK!!!*"

"THAT'S EVERYBODY'S."

"NO. IT'S NOT THE WORD. IT'S THE *EXECUTION*. YOU'VE GOT TO LET IT BUILD UP STEAM AND THEN... *BOOM...* FFFFFFFFFFUCK!"

"POINT WELL MADE. O.K. THIS IS A WEIRD QUESTION, BECAUSE I DON'T KNOW WHAT IT IS THAT YOU *DO* FOR A LIVING."

"WHAT'S THE QUESTION?"

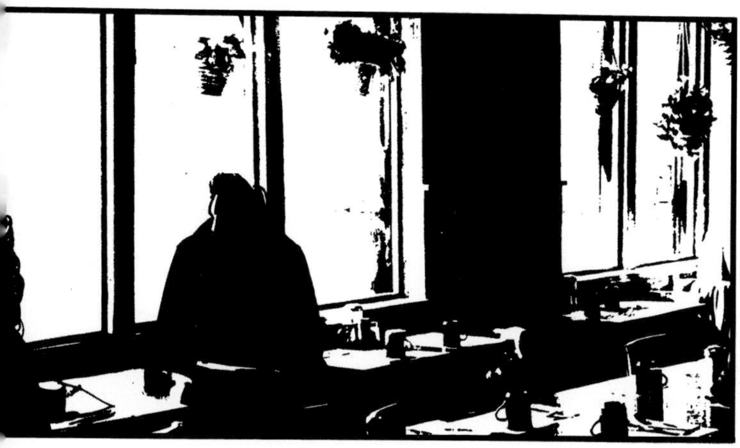
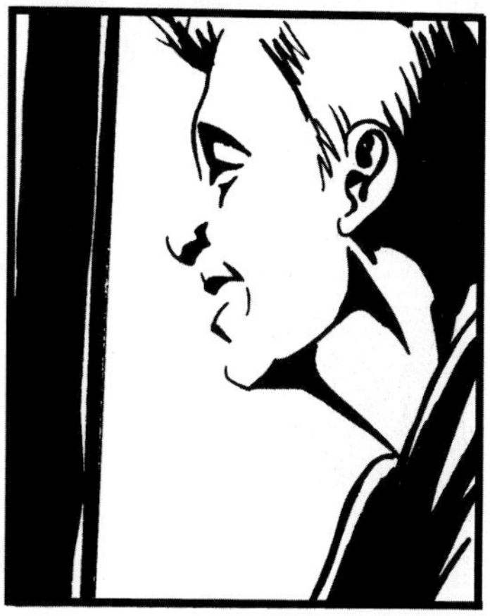

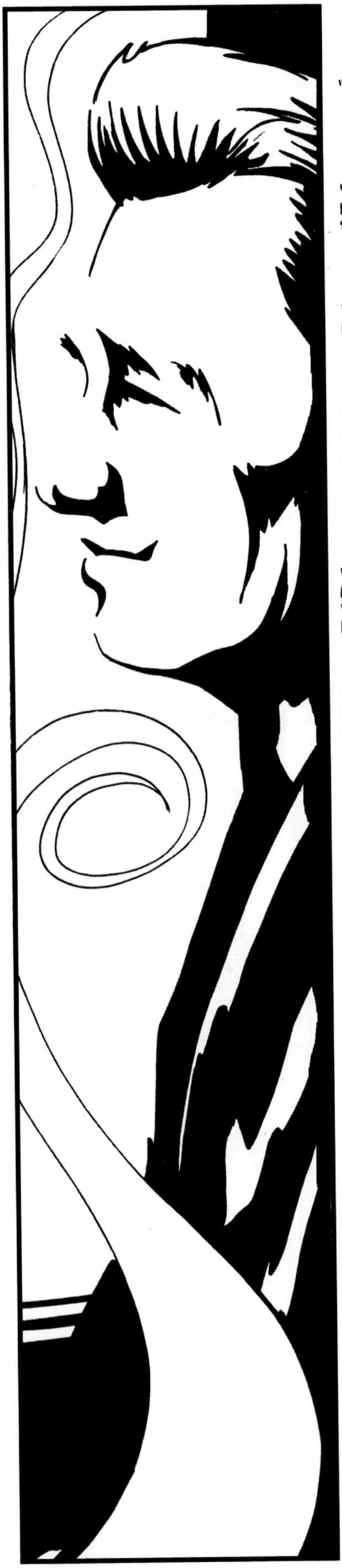

"WHAT PROFESSION *OTHER* THAN YOUR OWN WOULD YOU MOST LIKE TO HAVE?"

"CULT LEADER."

"WHAT PROFESSION OTHER THAN YOURS WOULD YOU *LEAST* LIKE TO HAVE?"

"OH...THE AGENT WHO BOOKS TALENT FOR SALLY JESSY RAPHAEL."

"AREN'T YOU THE CLEVER ONE. SO, WHAT *DO* YOU DO?"

"WHAT DO *I* DO? I HAVE INVESTMENTS."

"WHAT KIND OF BULLSHIT ANSWER IS *THAT?"*

"IT'S THE WAY IT IS. MY GRANDMA LEFT ME LIKE THIS PORT-FOLIO OF STUFF AND I'M SORT OF TAKEN CARE OF."

"REALLY...WOW!"

"YEAH. I JUST HAVEN'T DECIDED WHAT TO *DO* WITH IT YET. I HAVEN'T FOUND MY *NICHE."*

"MUST BE NICE."

"WELL, I'M NOT...OBVIOUSLY I'M NOT A GAZILLIONAIRE. I CAN SWING A *MUFFIN."*

"HMMM..."

"NEXT..."

"OH--LAST ONE. IF HEAVEN EXISTS WHAT WOULD YOU LIKE TO HEAR GOD SAY TO YOU WHEN HE MEETS YOU AT THE GATE?"

"I'D LIKE HIM TO SAY: DO YOU THINK I LOOK LIKE GEORGE BURNS? 'CAUSE I DON'T SEE IT."

"YOU'RE A NUT-BALL."

"THAT VERY WELL COULD BE. SO WHAT DO *YOU* DO?"

"OH--I DON'T--I DON'T WANT TO TALK ABOUT IT. I--"

"WHAT? WHY?..."

"IT'S BORING."

"IT'S BORING?...DO YOU WORK AT FOTOMAT?"

"NO."

"DO YOU WORK IN REAL ESTATE?"

"NO."

"ACCOUNTING?"

"NO."

"INSURANCE?"

"NO."

"THEN I CAN HANDLE IT."

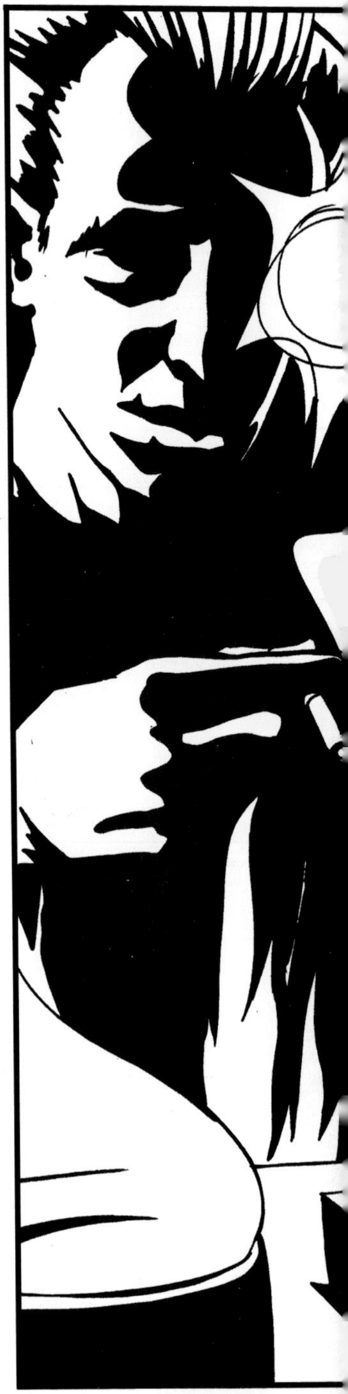

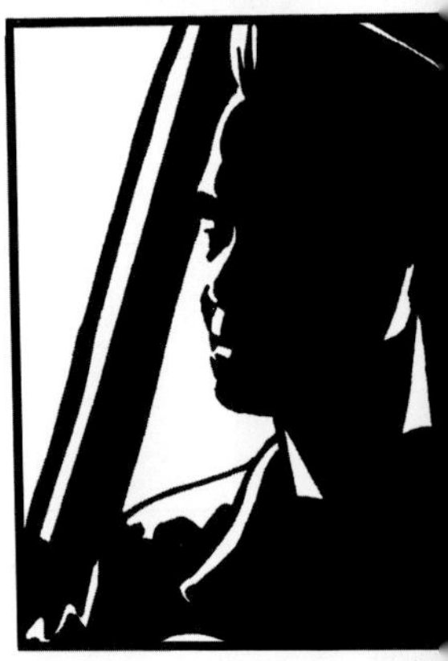

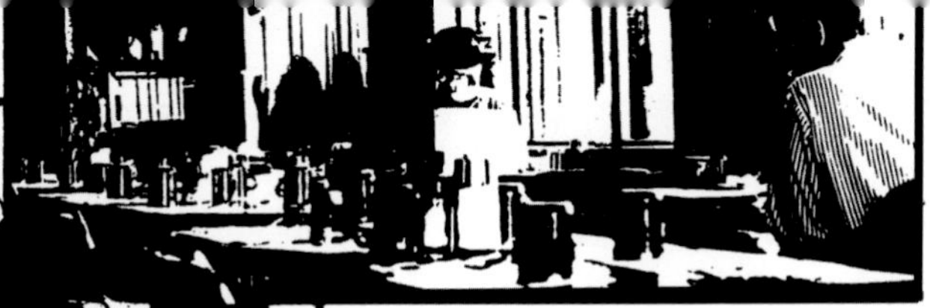

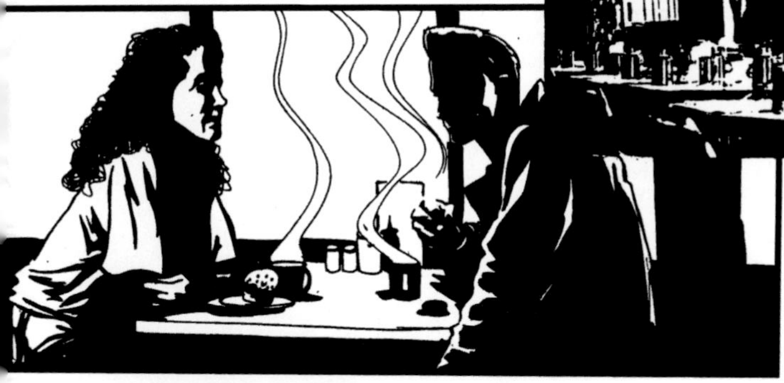

"I...Y'KNOW? I DON'T. HERE. WHY DON'T YOU ASK ME THESE...?"

"UH-UH. NO WAY. YOU'VE HAD TIME TO COME UP WITH CLEVER ANSWERS, NO FAIR... BUT LISTEN, I DON'T THINK IT'S BORING AT ALL. *I* THINK IT HAS SOMETHING TO DO WITH THE FACT THAT YOU CARRY A *GUN.*"

"*WOW!* YOU TOOK YOUR TIME WITH *THAT* ONE."

"WELL, I'M *RIGHT,* RIGHT? MEAN, I CAN TELL."

"YOU CAN *TELL?*"

"YOU KNEW TO KEEP YOUR HOLSTER EXPOSED. YOU DON'T CARRY IT *CONCEALED.*"

"YOU DO."

"YOU DID THAT TO ME ONCE ALREADY."

"I KNOW, BUT YOU *DO.*"

"C'MON, WHAT'S YOUR DEAL?"

"WHAT'S MY DEAL?"

"YEAH, O.K. SO YOU CARRY A GUN. MAYBE I DO TOO."

"MAYBE I JUST...MAYBE I'M JUST TRYING TO... I-I-IT'S *HARD* TO BE A SINGLE GIRL IN THE '90S."

"YOU DON'T COME OFF AS SOMEONE WHO IS EASILY FUCKED WITH."

"YOU NEVER KNOW WHEN..."

"AND YOU ALSO DON'T COME OFF AS A *BULLSHIT* SLINGER. I KNOW I DON'T KNOW YOU ALL THAT WELL, BUT, I DON'T KNOW, THIS *SURPRISES* ME."

"WOULD IT *BOTHER* YOU? *DOES* IT BOTHER YOU? ...A GIRL WHO CARRIES ...DOES THE POWER BALANCE...?"

"*POWER BALANCE?*"

"YEAH...I MEAN WE'RE QUITE A COUPLE HERE."

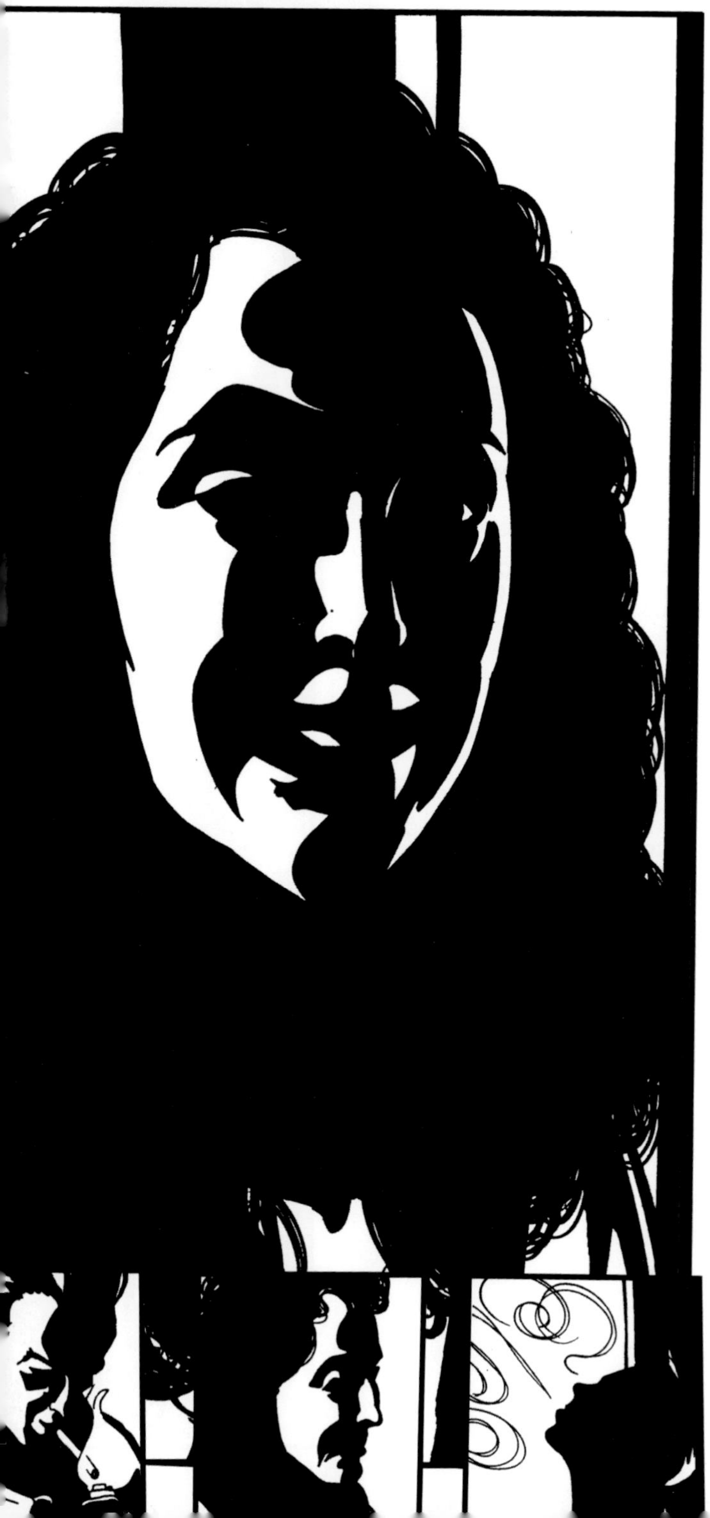

"I'VE MET *A LOT*...I'VE KNOWN SOME PEOPLE OVER THE YEARS WHO HAVE CARRIED...AND... IT USUALLY HAS ABSOLUTELY NOTHING TO DO WITH POWER. IN FACT, IT USUALLY RUNS IN DIRECT OPPOSITION TO..."

"'INVESTMENTS.' YOU'RE SO FULL OF SHIT. I MEAN ...COME ON."

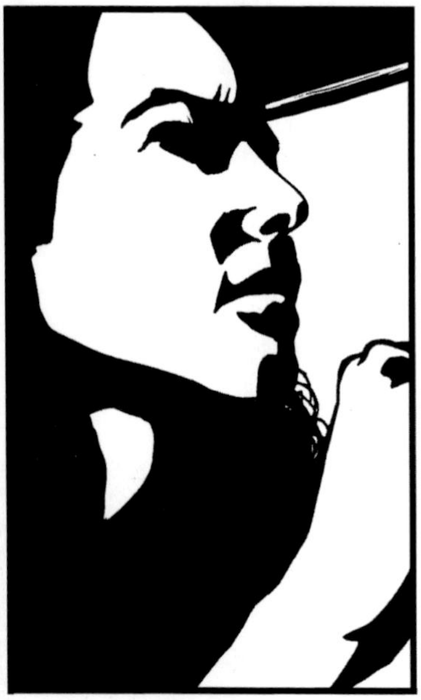

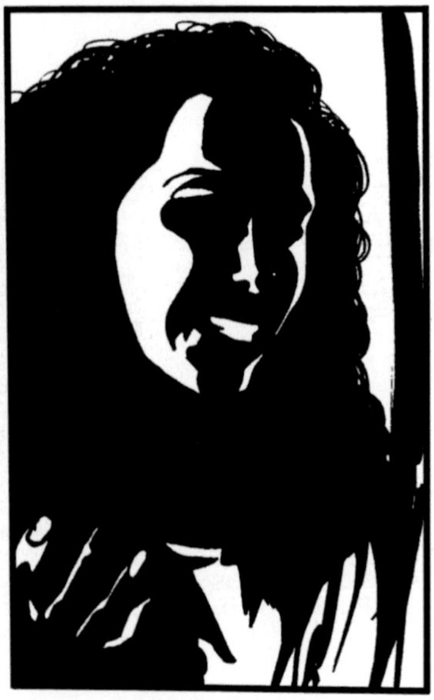

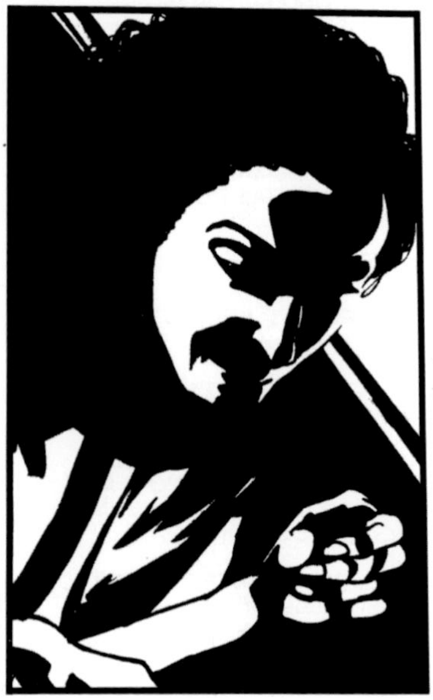

"WELL, IT'S BETTER THAN WHAT *YOU'VE* COME UP WITH. WHAT...I...*LISTEN!* I KNOW IT'S NONE OF MY FUCKIN' BUSINESS WHAT YOU DO. I'M NOT TRYING TO PRY OR TO GET YOU TO SAY STUFF YOU'RE NOT COMFORTABLE WITH..."

"YEAH, I KNOW."

"BUT IT'S JUST THAT. I MEAN, THERE'S, IT'S JUST *HANGIN'* THERE NOW AND ...AND IT...YOU SEEM TO HAVE SET THIS UP AS AN OBSTACLE OF A SORT."

"YEAH...I DIDN'T MEAN..."

"AND I CAN'T TELL IF YOU *REALLY* WANT ME TO DROP IT OR IF YOU'RE JUST SHY ABOUT IT OR *EMBARRASSED* OR WHAT?"

"I...YOU'RE RIGHT. I JUST ...I'VE LOST SO MANY... I DON'T MEAN TO BULLSHIT YOU. I HATE IT WHEN PEOPLE DO IT TO ME. I CAN SMELL IT FOR MILES. I DON'T MEAN TO DO THAT TO YOU."

"YOU WANT TO COME CLEAN. GET REAL. NO MORE TALK SHOW. I MEAN, THERE'S A REASON DICK CAVETT KEEPS GETTING CANCELED."

"YOU ARE HILARIOUS."

"TELL YOU WHAT. I'M GOING TO ADMIRE MYSELF IN THE MEN'S ROOM MIRROR FOR A MINUTE...'CAUSE I'M *LONG* OVERDUE."

"HA HA...O.K."

"AND WHEN I GET BACK, IT'S *TRUE CONFESSIONS.* YOU CAN GO FIRST. I'LL GO FIRST, WHATEVER..."

"WHATEVER."

"IT'LL GIVE US A MINUTE TO GET OUR NERVE UP. I'LL COME BACK. WE'LL SPILL THE BEANS AND THEN BASED ON THAT WE'LL EITHER GET *MARRIED* OR WE'LL BOTH RUN SCREAMING OFF INTO THE NIGHT IN OPPOSITE DIRECTIONS. *O.K.?*"

"O.K."

"Y'KNOW, YOU'VE GOT *GREAT* HAIR."

"OH...IT'S A PAIN IN THE ASS!"

"IT'S...IT'S *GREAT* THOUGH. THAT COLOR...IT'S..."

"BLACK."

"REALLY? IT'S SO..."

"NO...TRUST ME IT'S BLACK."

"OH..."

"BUT THANKS. THANKS...I MEAN."

"I'LL BE BACK."

"I'LL BE HERE."

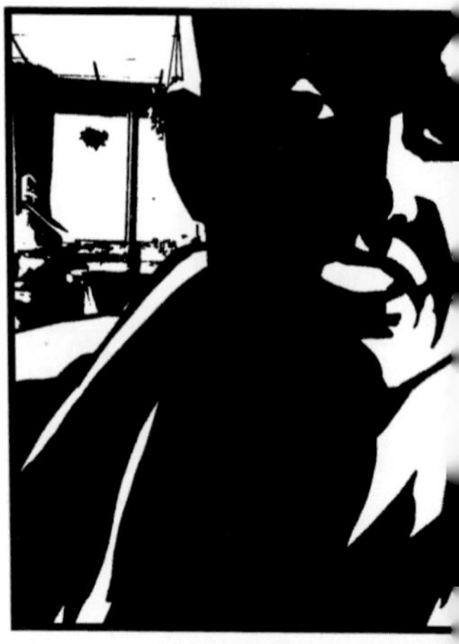

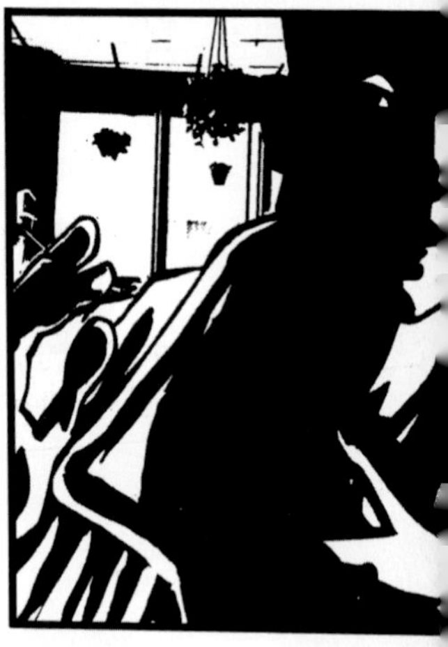

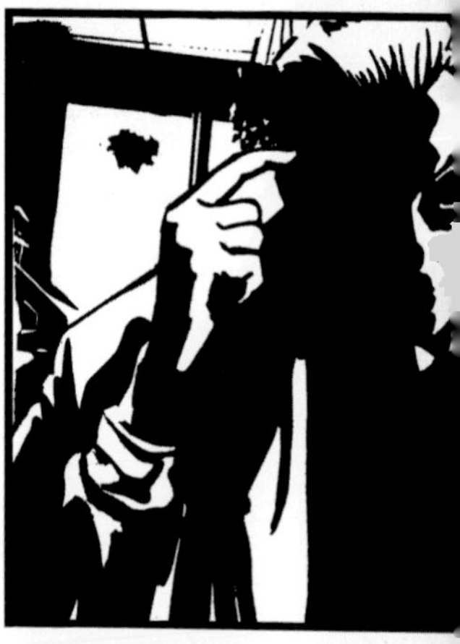

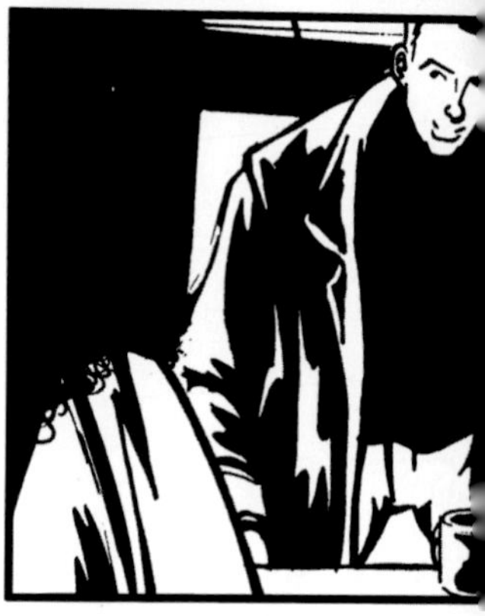

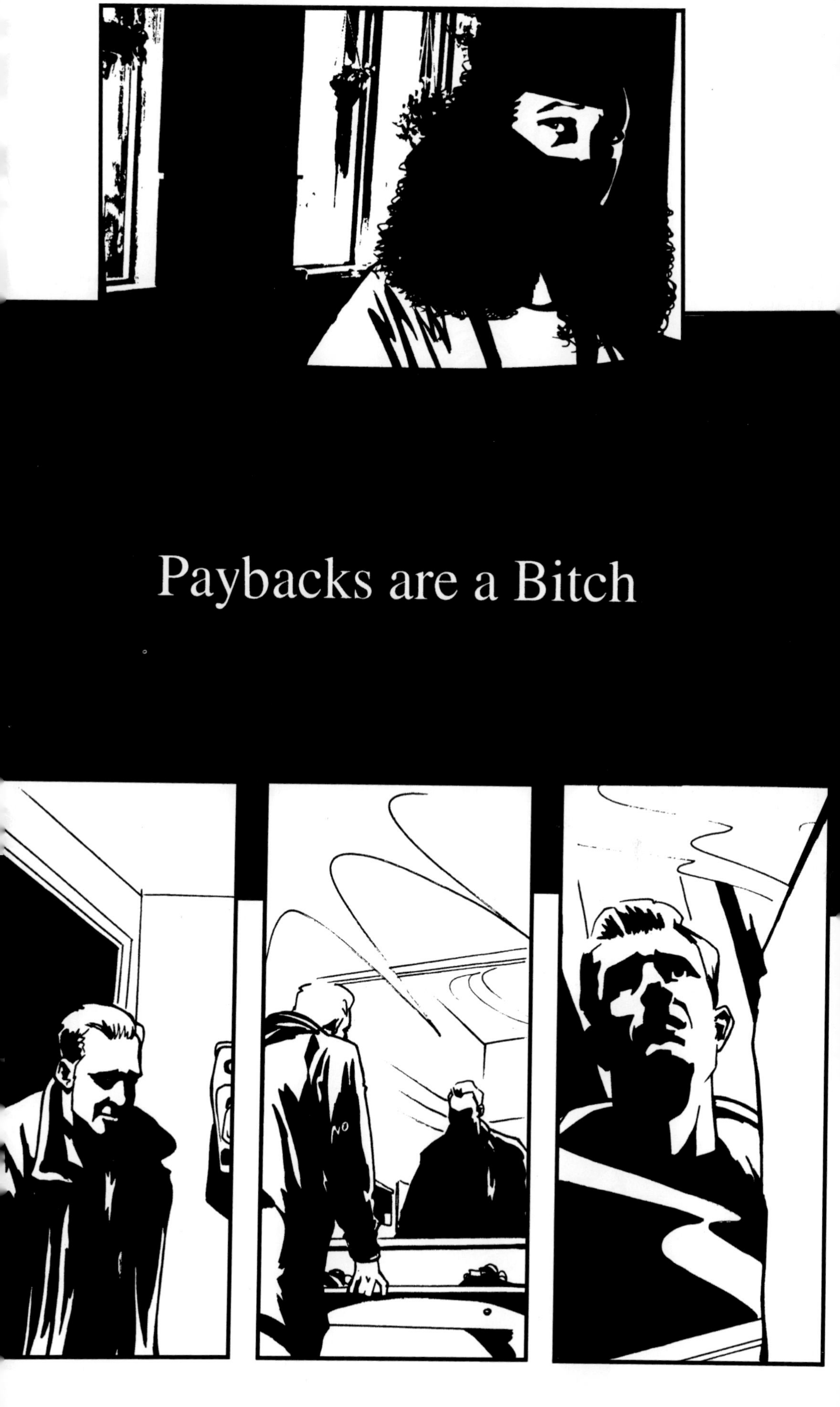
Paybacks are a Bitch

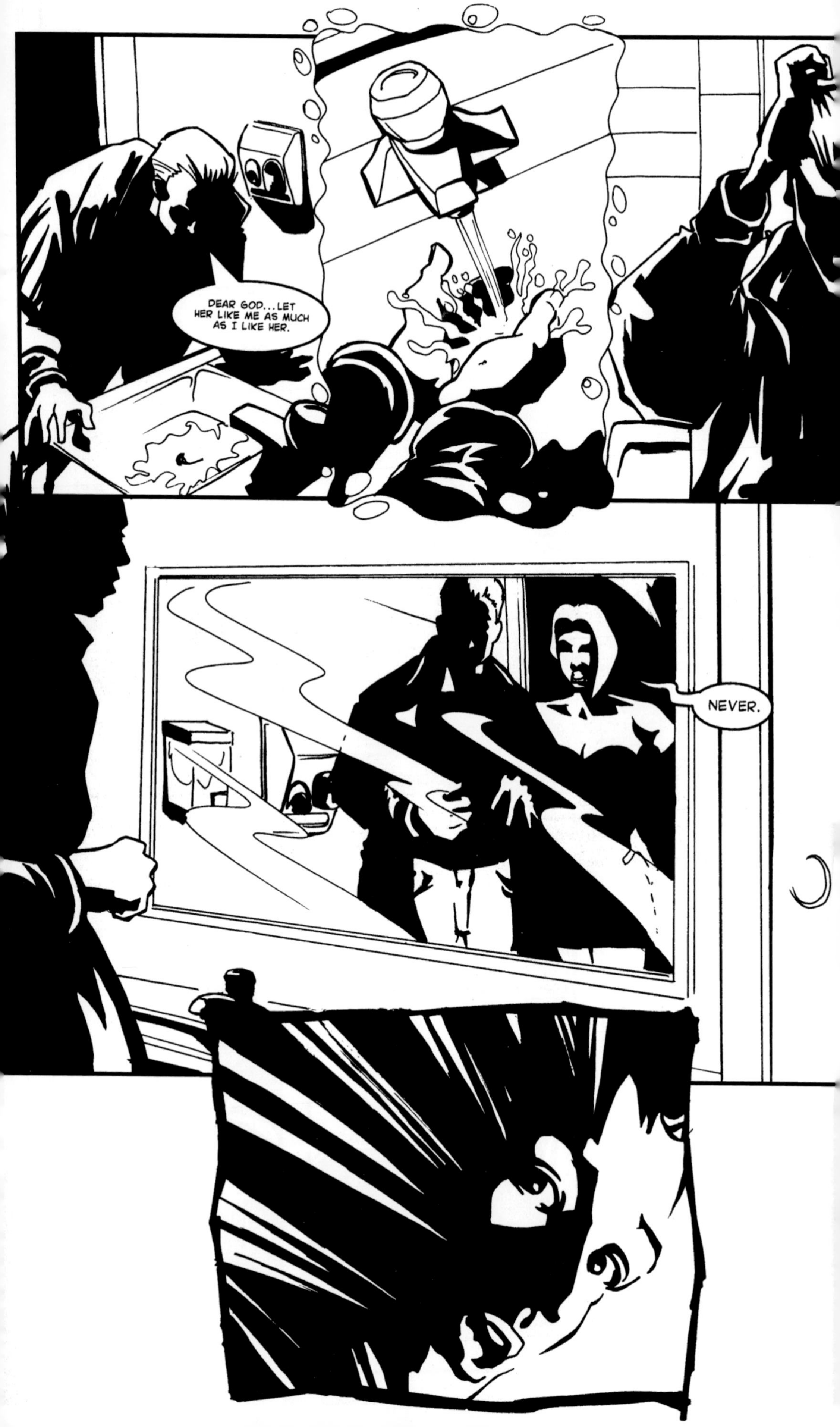
DEAR GOD...LET HER LIKE ME AS MUCH AS I LIKE HER.
NEVER.

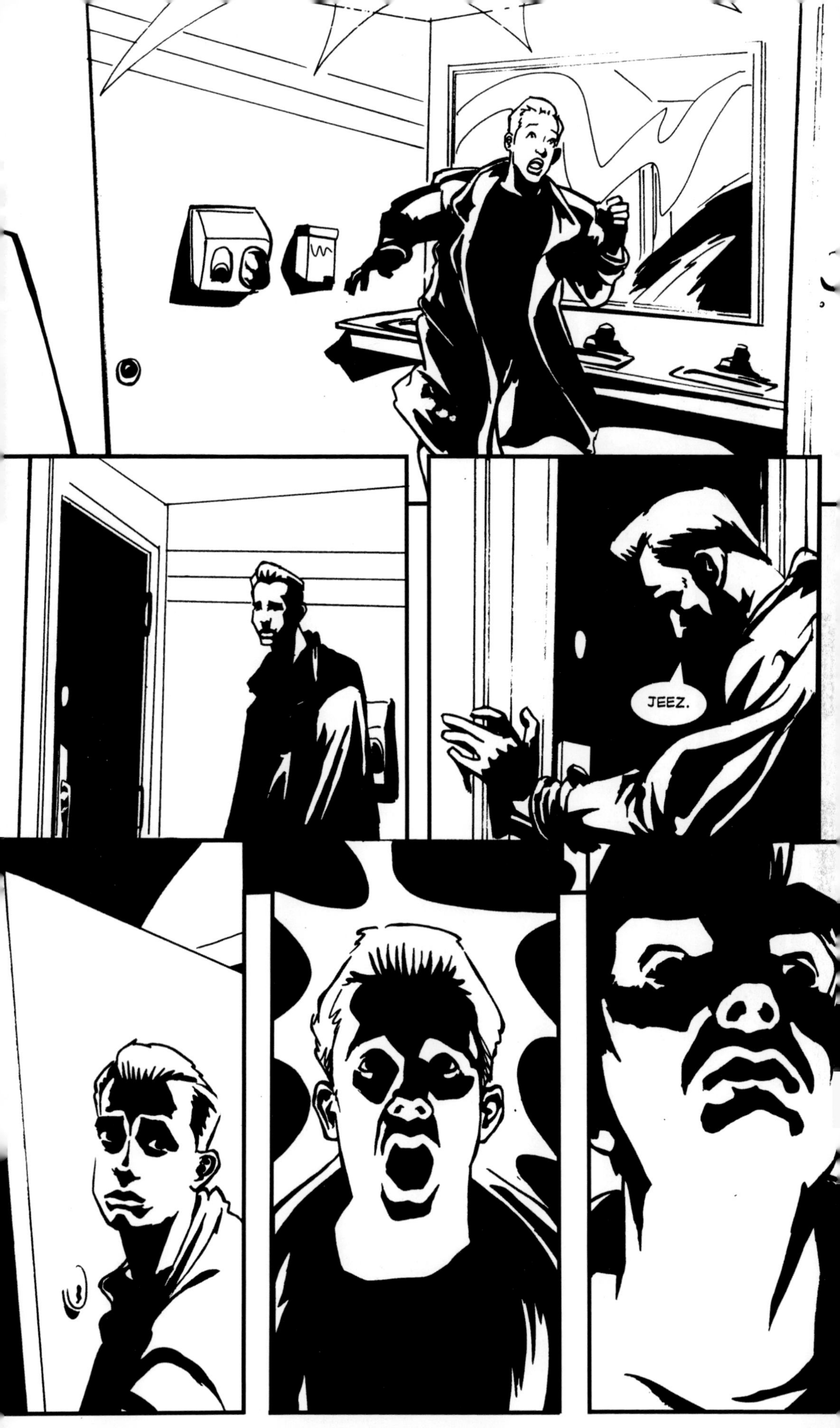
JEEZ.

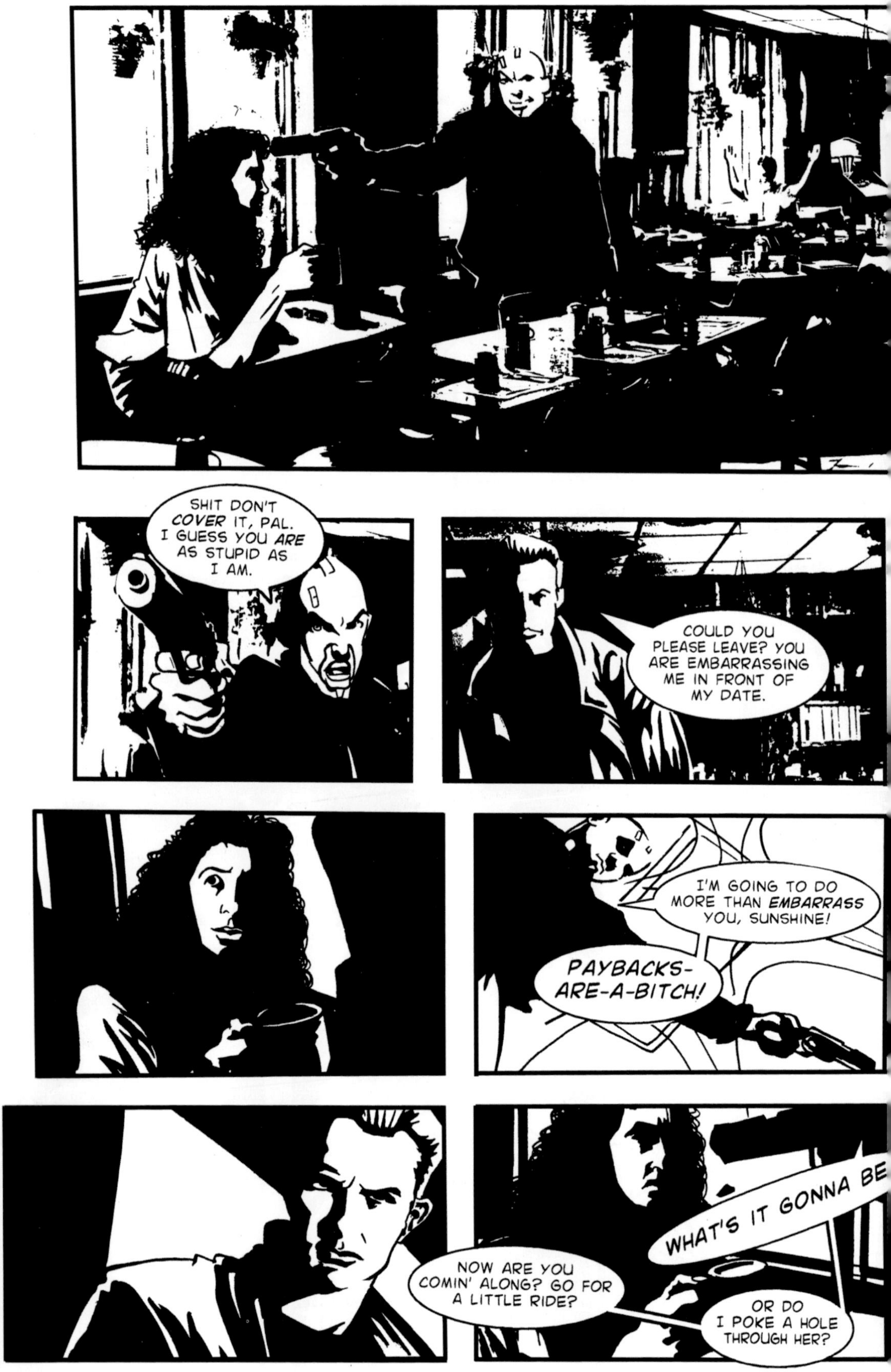
SHIT DON'T COVER IT, PAL. I GUESS YOU ARE AS STUPID AS I AM.
COULD YOU PLEASE LEAVE? YOU ARE EMBARRASSING ME IN FRONT OF MY DATE.
I'M GOING TO DO MORE THAN EMBARRASS YOU, SUNSHINE!
PAYBACKS-ARE-A-BITCH!
NOW ARE YOU COMIN' ALONG? GO FOR A LITTLE RIDE?
WHAT'S IT GONNA BE
OR DO I POKE A HOLE THROUGH HER?

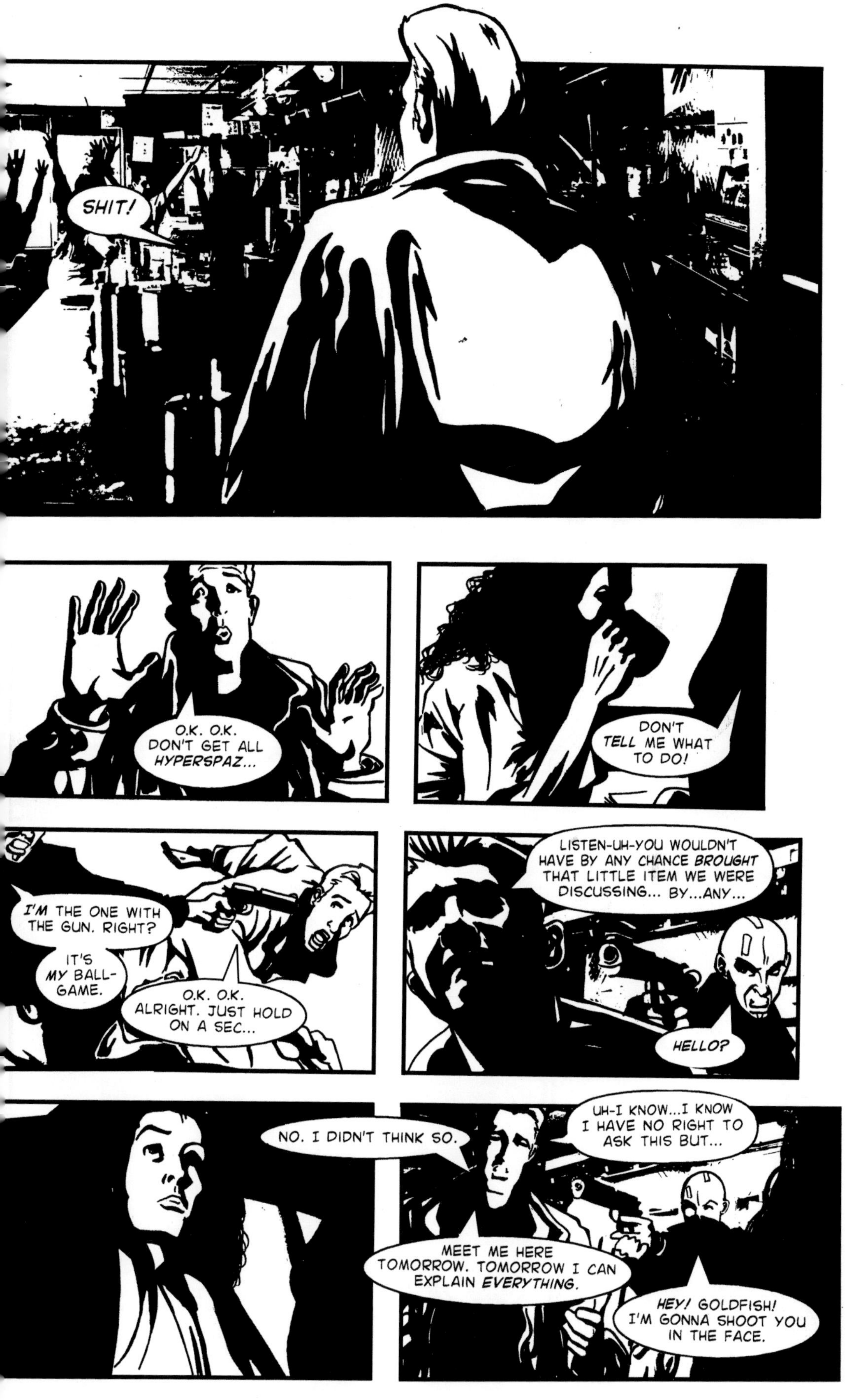
SHIT!
O.K. O.K. DON'T GET ALL HYPERSPAZ...
DON'T TELL ME WHAT TO DO!
I'M THE ONE WITH THE GUN. RIGHT?
IT'S MY BALL-GAME.
O.K. O.K. ALRIGHT. JUST HOLD ON A SEC...
LISTEN-UH-YOU WOULDN'T HAVE BY ANY CHANCE BROUGHT THAT LITTLE ITEM WE WERE DISCUSSING... BY...ANY...
HELLO?
NO. I DIDN'T THINK SO.
UH-I KNOW...I KNOW I HAVE NO RIGHT TO ASK THIS BUT...
MEET ME HERE TOMORROW. TOMORROW I CAN EXPLAIN EVERYTHING.
HEY! GOLDFISH! I'M GONNA SHOOT YOU IN THE FACE.

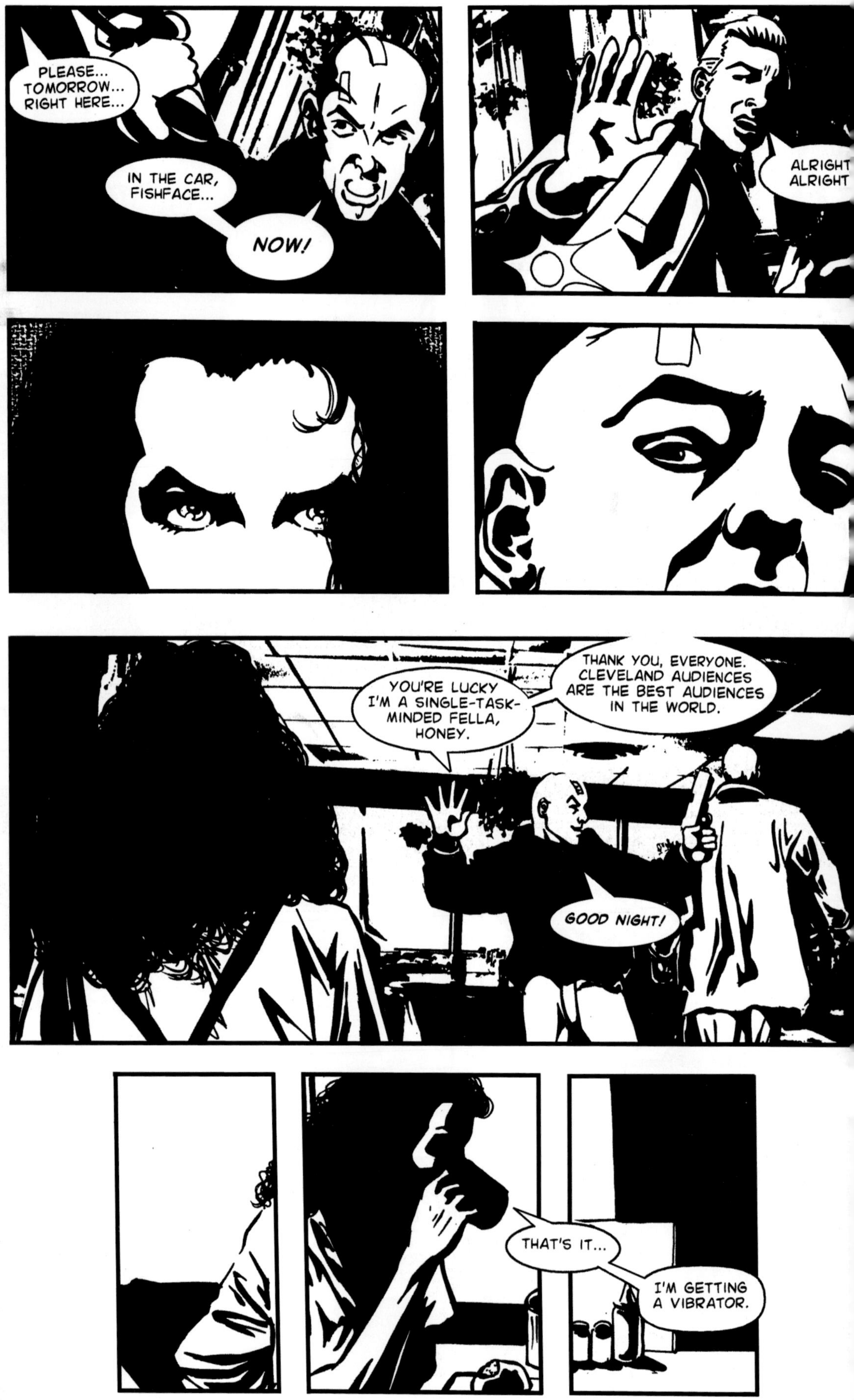
PLEASE... TOMORROW... RIGHT HERE...
IN THE CAR, FISHFACE...
NOW!
ALRIGHT ALRIGHT
YOU'RE LUCKY I'M A SINGLE-TASK-MINDED FELLA, HONEY.
THANK YOU, EVERYONE. CLEVELAND AUDIENCES ARE THE BEST AUDIENCES IN THE WORLD.
GOOD NIGHT!
THAT'S IT...
I'M GETTING A VIBRATOR.

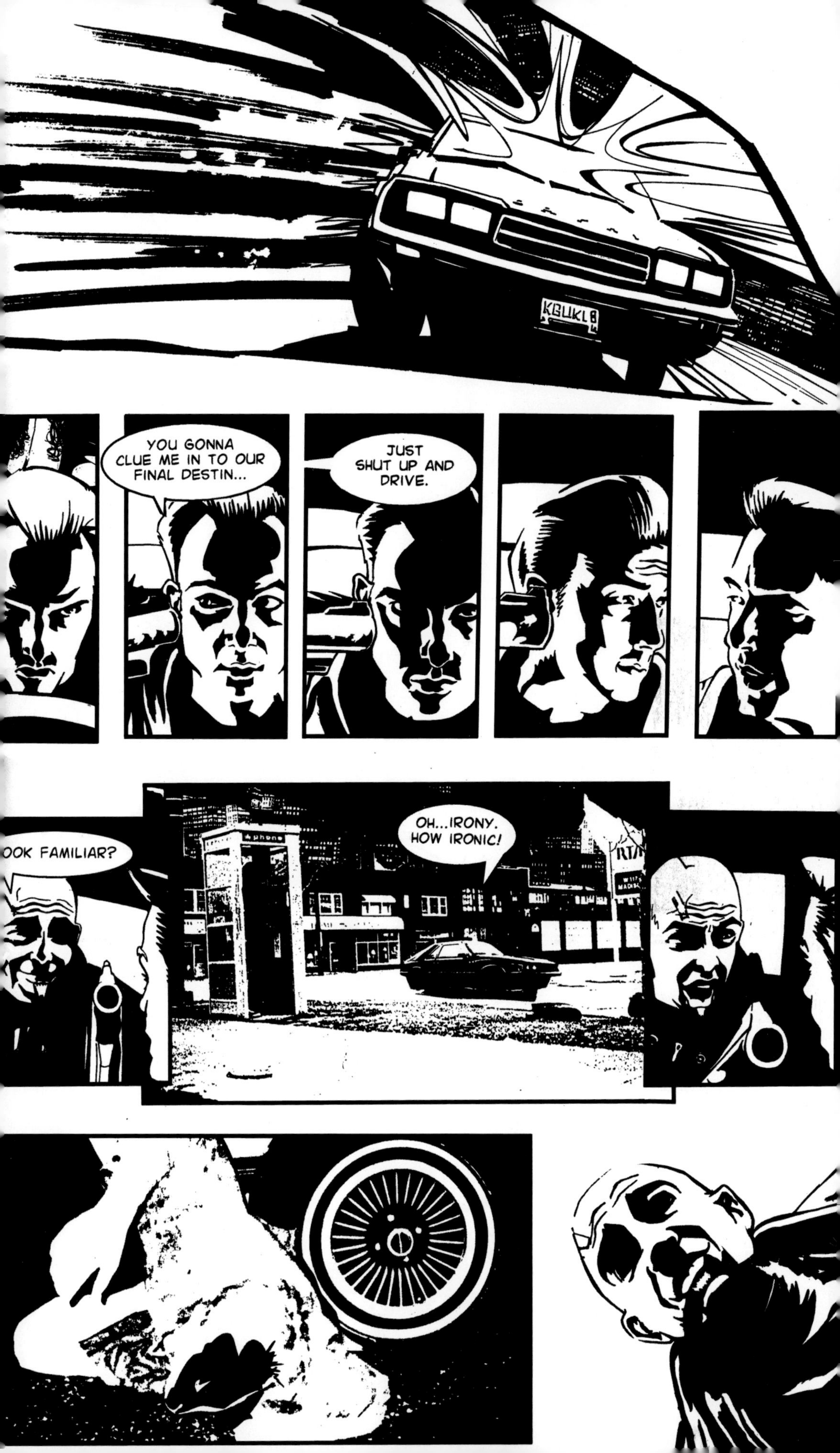
YOU GONNA CLUE ME IN TO OUR FINAL DESTIN...
JUST SHUT UP AND DRIVE.
OOK FAMILIAR?
OH...IRONY. HOW IRONIC!

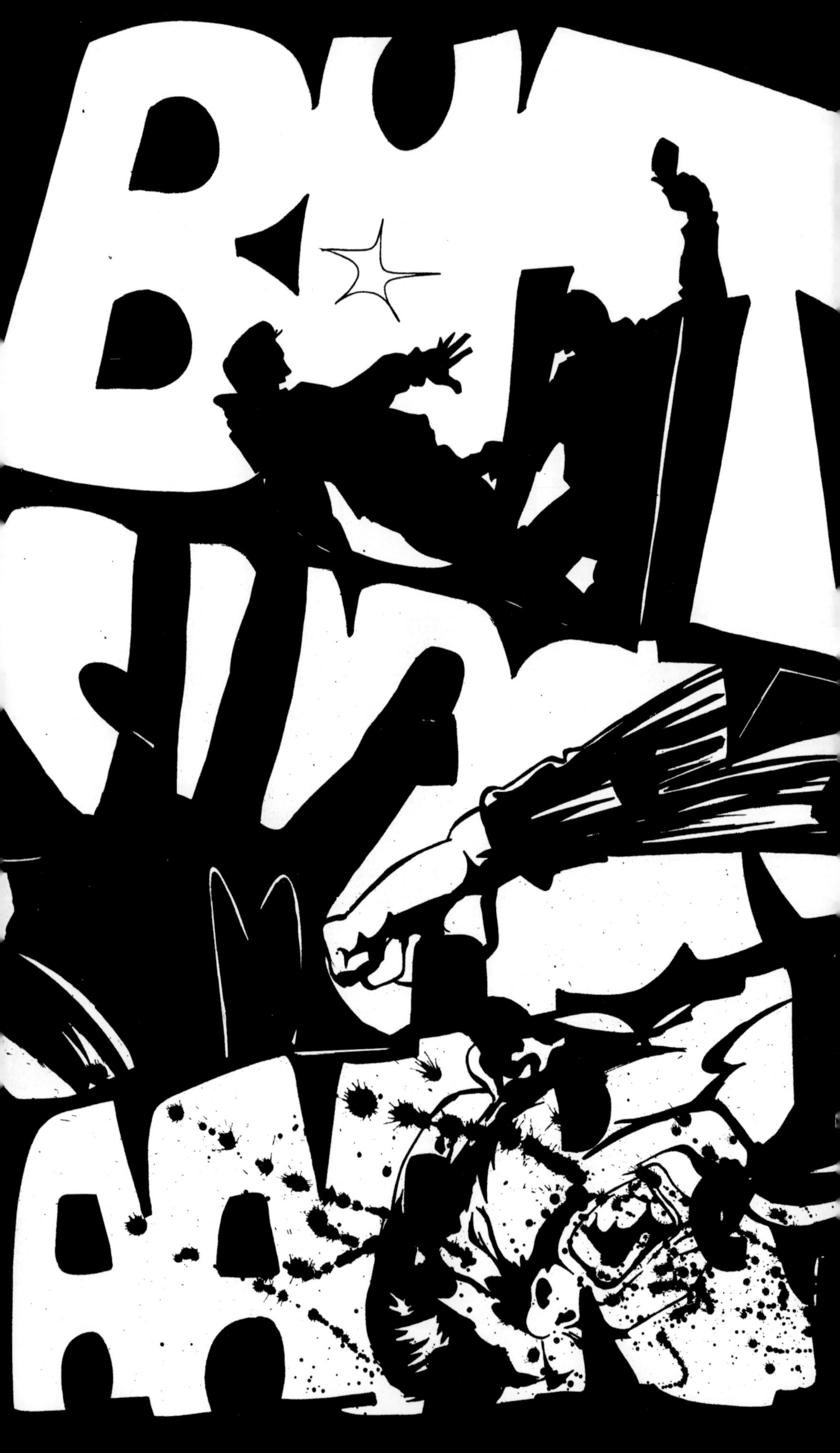

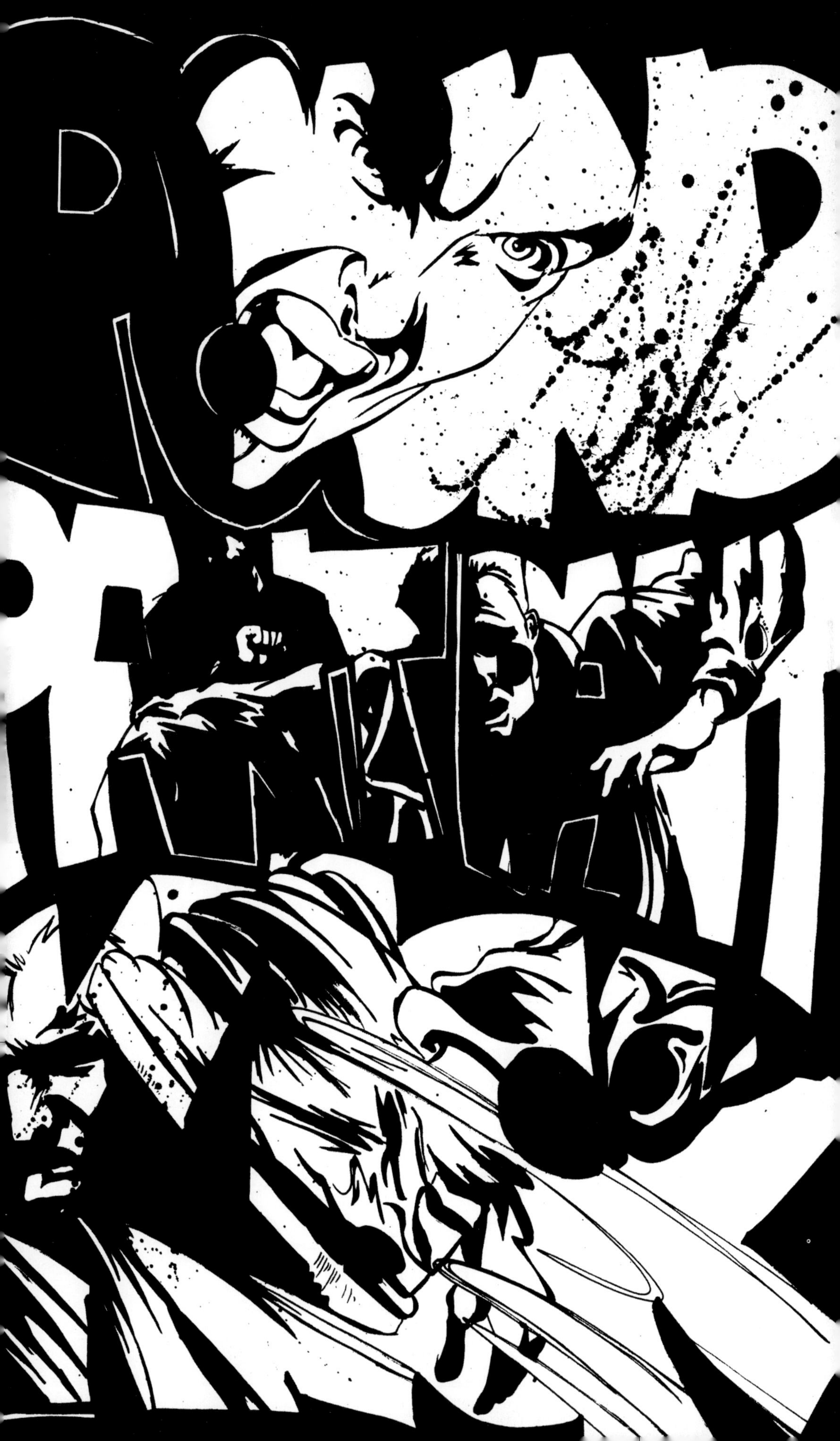

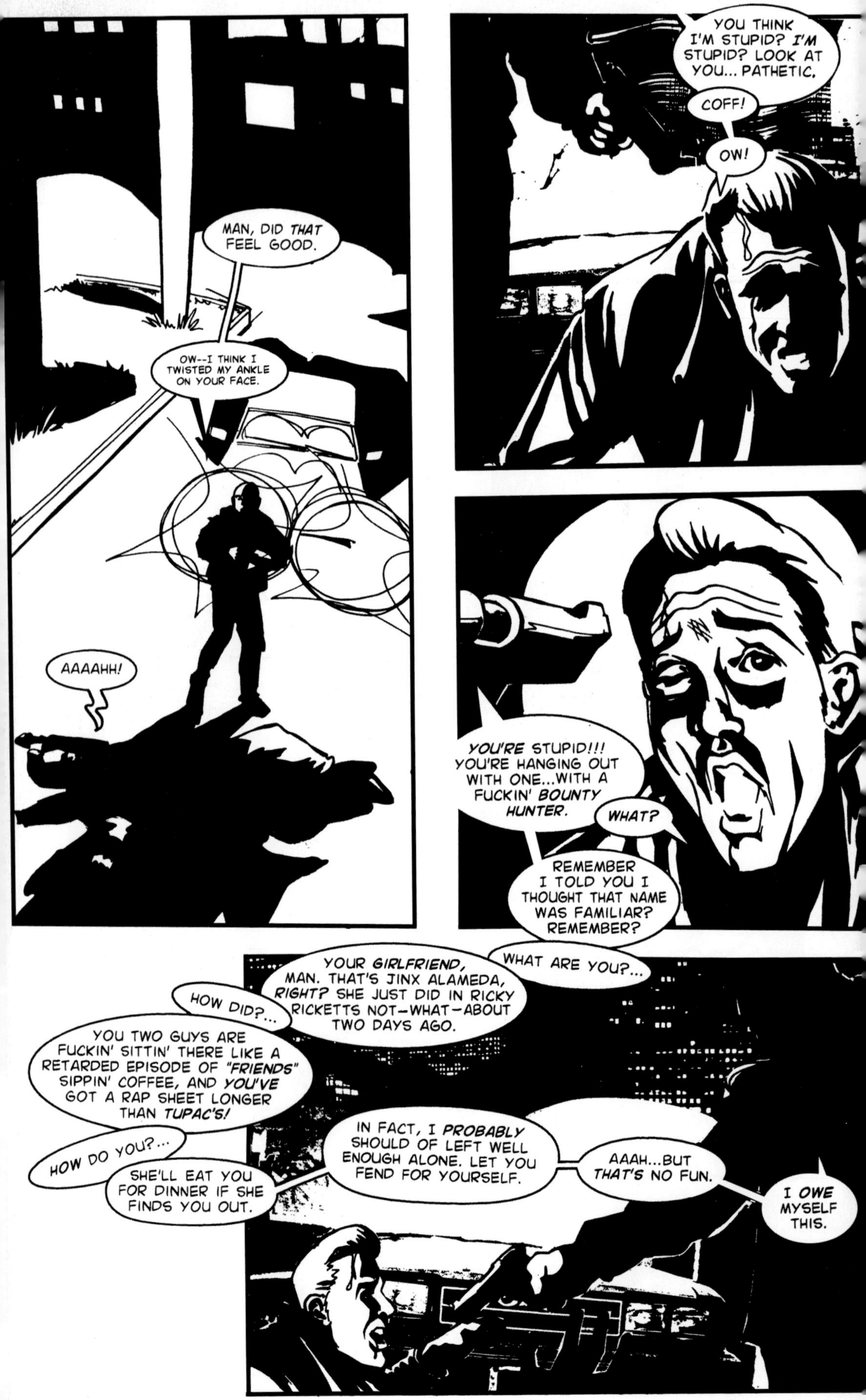
MAN, DID THAT FEEL GOOD.
OW--I THINK I TWISTED MY ANKLE ON YOUR FACE.
AAAAHH!
YOU THINK I'M STUPID? I'M STUPID? LOOK AT YOU... PATHETIC.
COFF!
OW!
YOU'RE STUPID!!! YOU'RE HANGING OUT WITH ONE...WITH A FUCKIN' BOUNTY HUNTER.
WHAT?
REMEMBER I TOLD YOU I THOUGHT THAT NAME WAS FAMILIAR? REMEMBER?
WHAT ARE YOU?...
YOUR GIRLFRIEND, MAN. THAT'S JINX ALAMEDA, RIGHT? SHE JUST DID IN RICKY RICKETTS NOT-WHAT-ABOUT TWO DAYS AGO.
HOW DID?...
YOU TWO GUYS ARE FUCKIN' SITTIN' THERE LIKE A RETARDED EPISODE OF "FRIENDS" SIPPIN' COFFEE, AND YOU'VE GOT A RAP SHEET LONGER THAN TUPAC'S!
HOW DO YOU?...
SHE'LL EAT YOU FOR DINNER IF SHE FINDS YOU OUT.
IN FACT, I PROBABLY SHOULD OF LEFT WELL ENOUGH ALONE. LET YOU FEND FOR YOURSELF.
AAAH...BUT THAT'S NO FUN.
I OWE MYSELF THIS.

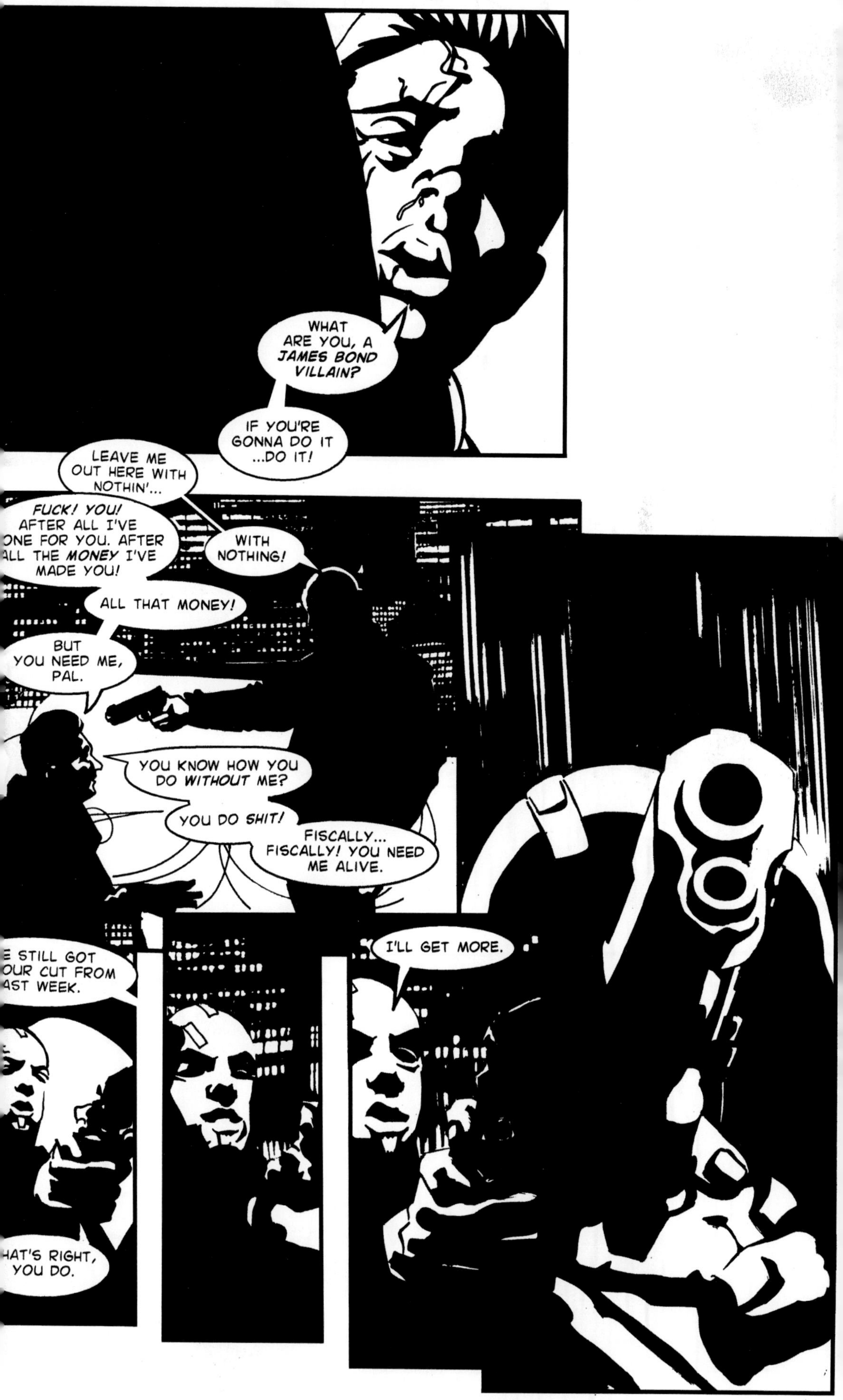
WHAT ARE YOU, A *JAMES BOND VILLAIN?*
IF YOU'RE GONNA DO IT ...DO IT!
LEAVE ME OUT HERE WITH NOTHIN'...
FUCK! YOU! AFTER ALL I'VE ONE FOR YOU. AFTER ALL THE *MONEY* I'VE MADE YOU!
WITH NOTHING!
ALL THAT MONEY!
BUT YOU NEED ME, PAL.
YOU KNOW HOW YOU DO *WITHOUT* ME?
YOU DO *SHIT!*
FISCALLY... FISCALLY! YOU NEED ME ALIVE.
E STILL GOT OUR CUT FROM AST WEEK.
HAT'S RIGHT, YOU DO.
I'LL GET MORE.

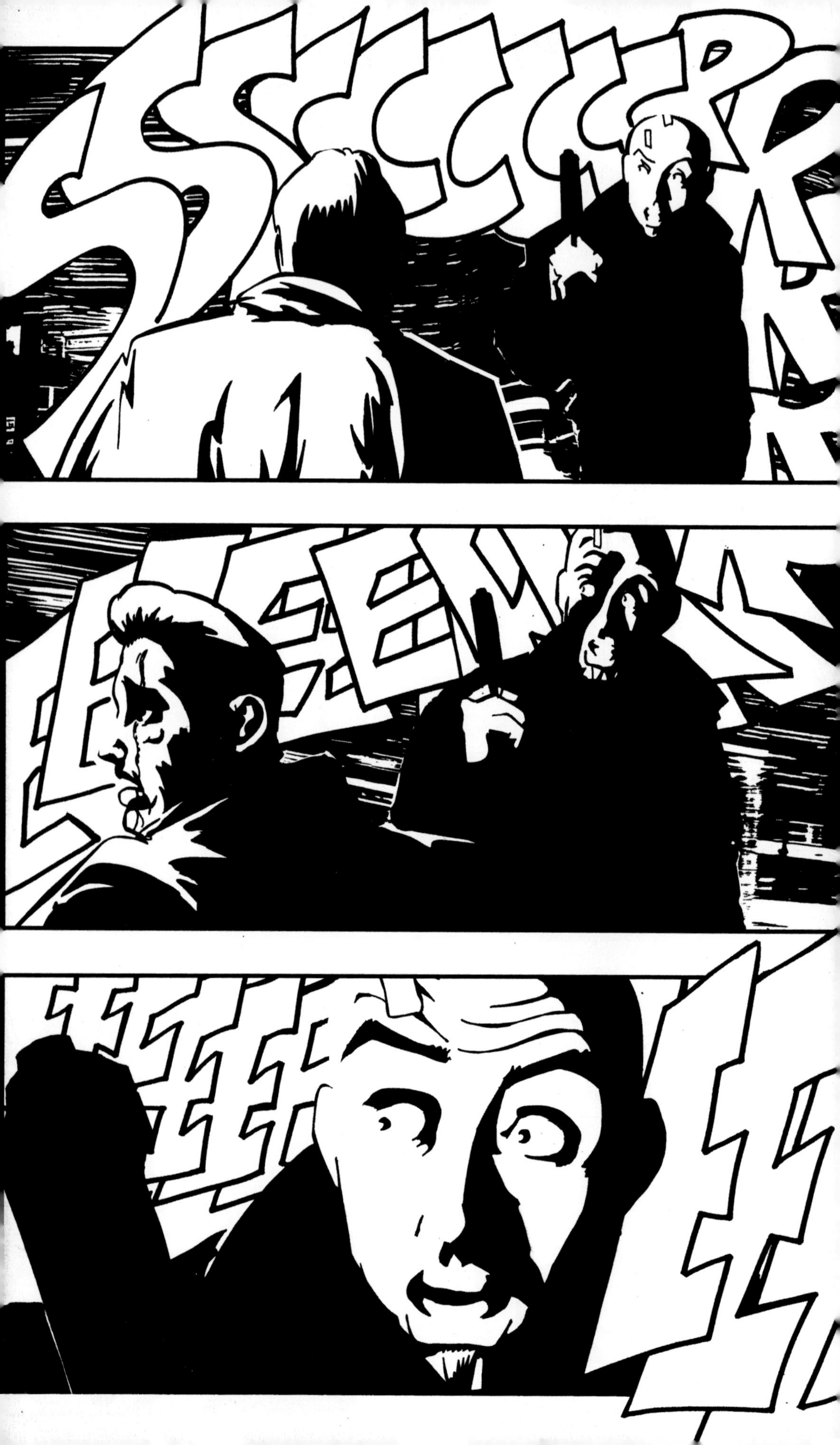

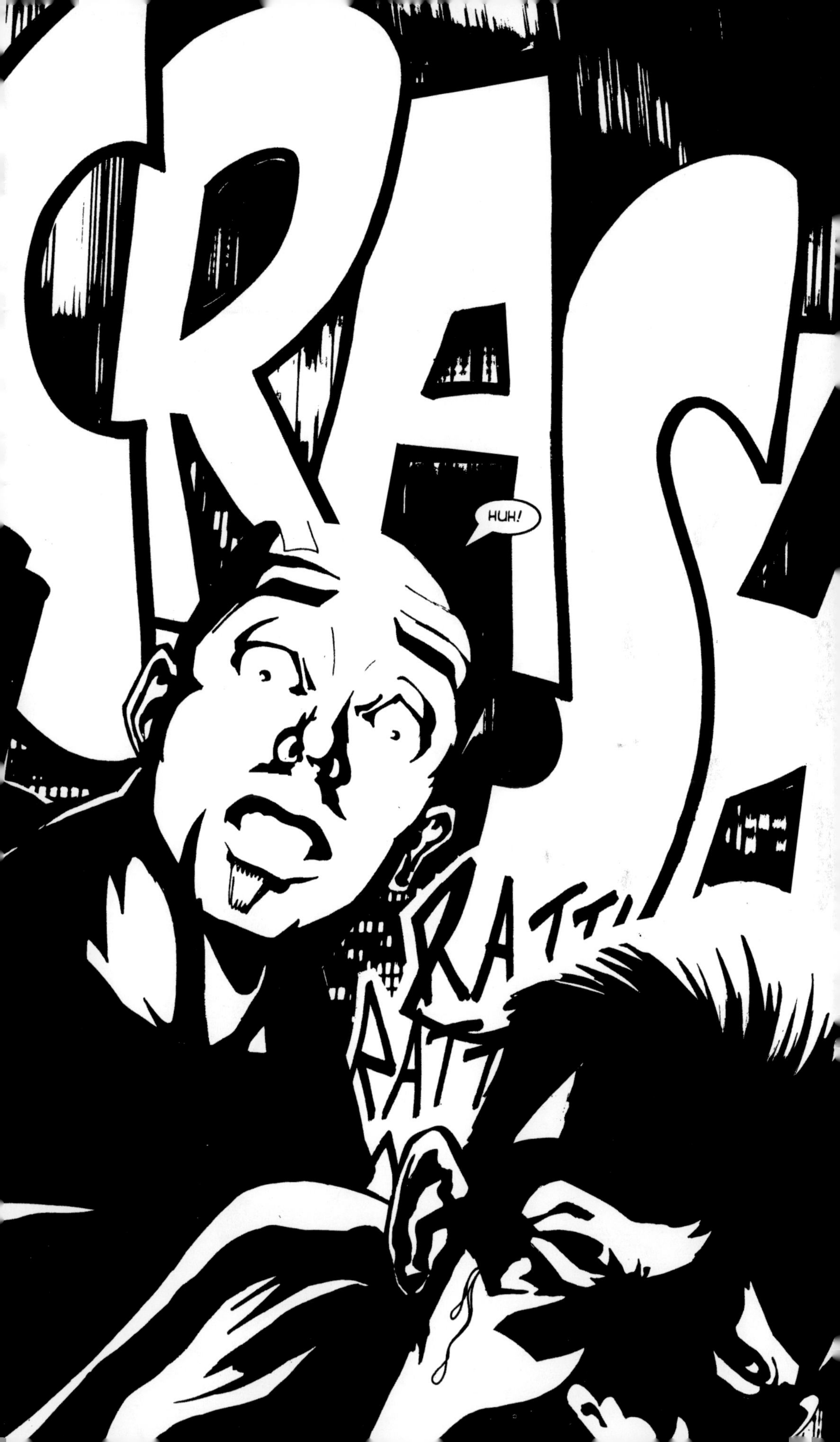
CRACK
HUH!
RATT!
RATT

I Hate Everything

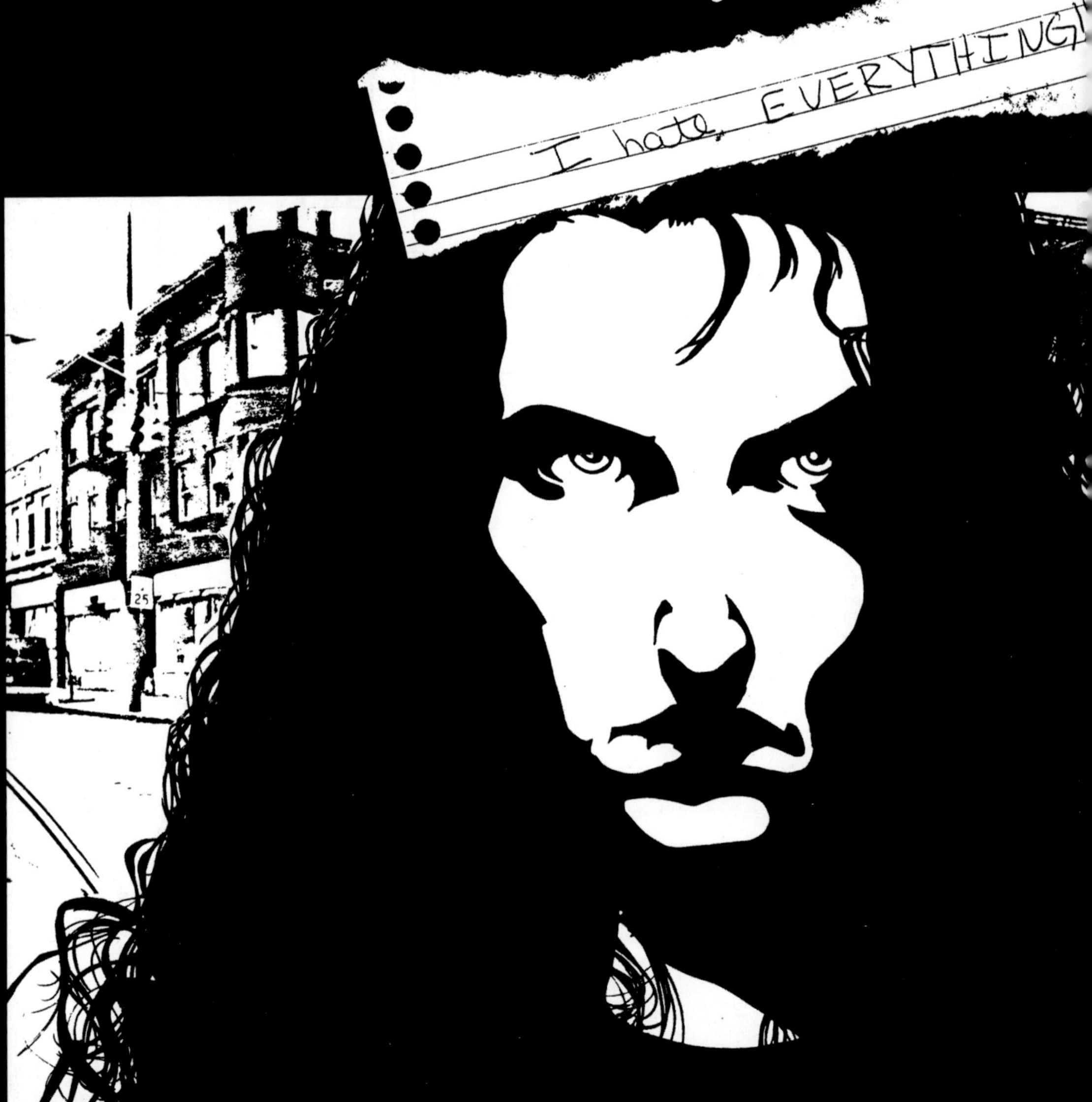
I hate EVERYTHING!

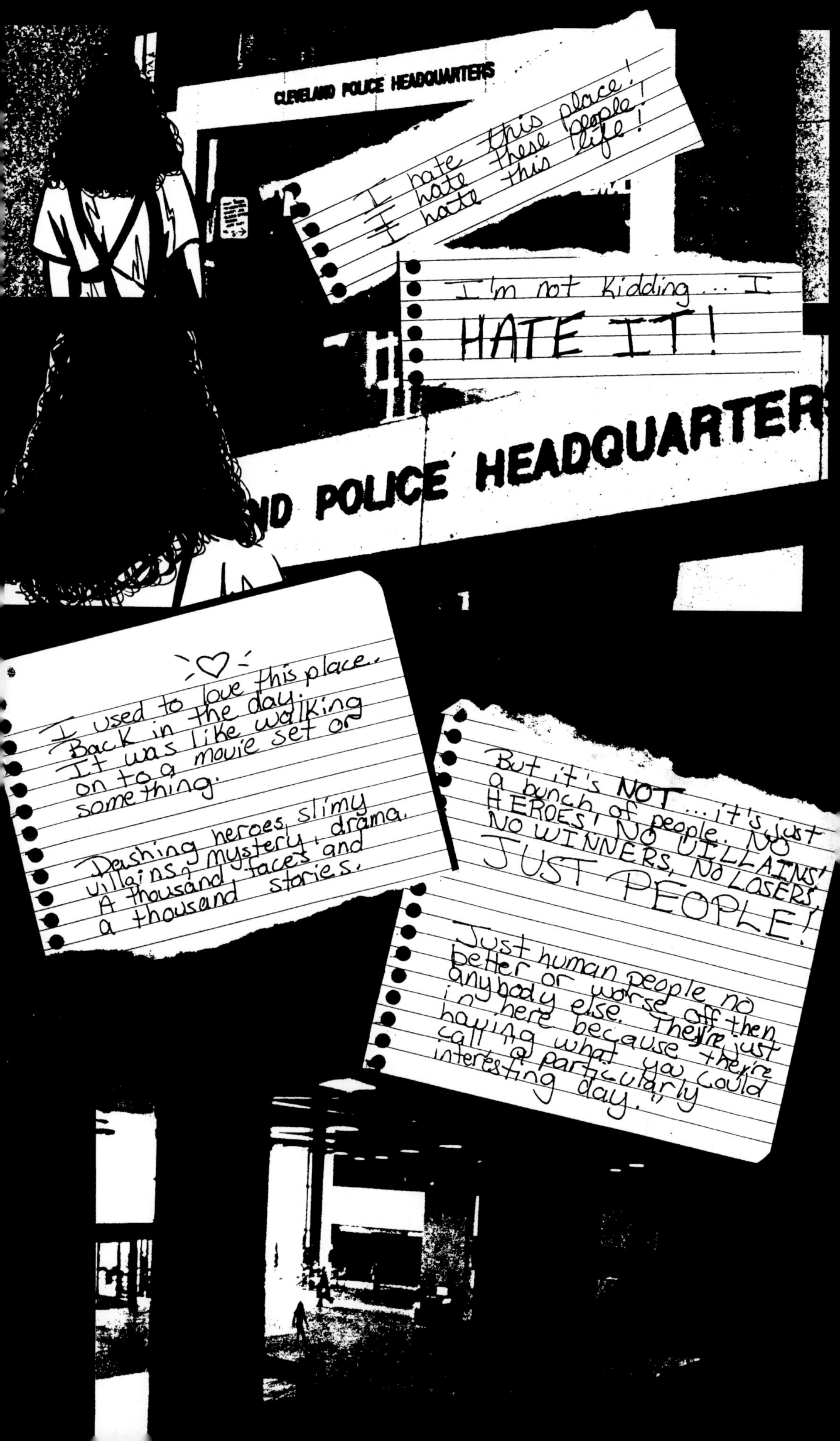
CLEVELAND POLICE HEADQUARTERS
I hate this place!
I hate these people!
I hate this life!
I'm not kidding... I HATE IT!
ND POLICE HEADQUARTERS
I used to love this place. Back in the day. It was like walking on to a movie set or something.
Dashing heroes, slimy villains, mystery, drama. A thousand faces and a thousand stories.
But it's NOT... it's just a bunch of people. NO HEROES, NO VILLAINS! NO WINNERS, NO LOSERS. JUST PEOPLE!
Just human people no better or worse off then anybody else. They're just in here because they're having what you could call "a particularly interesting day."

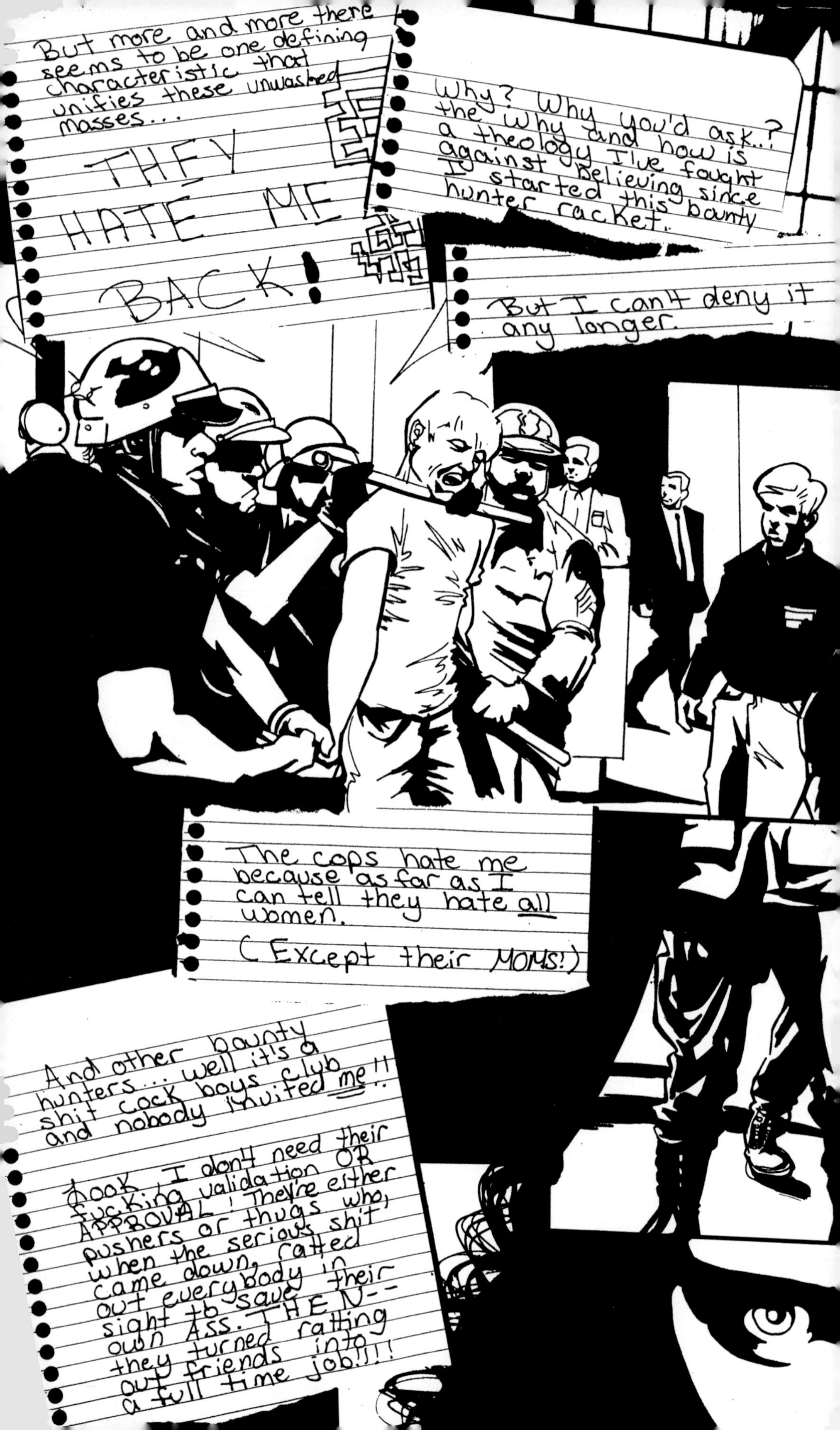
But more and more there seems to be one defining characteristic that unifies these unwashed masses...
THEY HATE ME BACK!
Why? Why you'd ask..? the why and how is a theology I've fought against believing since I started this bounty hunter racket.
But I can't deny it any longer.
The cops hate me because as far as I can tell they hate all women.
(Except their MOMS!)
And other bounty hunters... well it's a shit cock boys club and nobody invited me!!
Look, I don't need their fucking validation OR APPROVAL! They're either pushers or thugs who, when the serious shit came down, ratted out everybody in sight to save their own ASS. THEN-- they turned ratting out friends into a full time job!!!

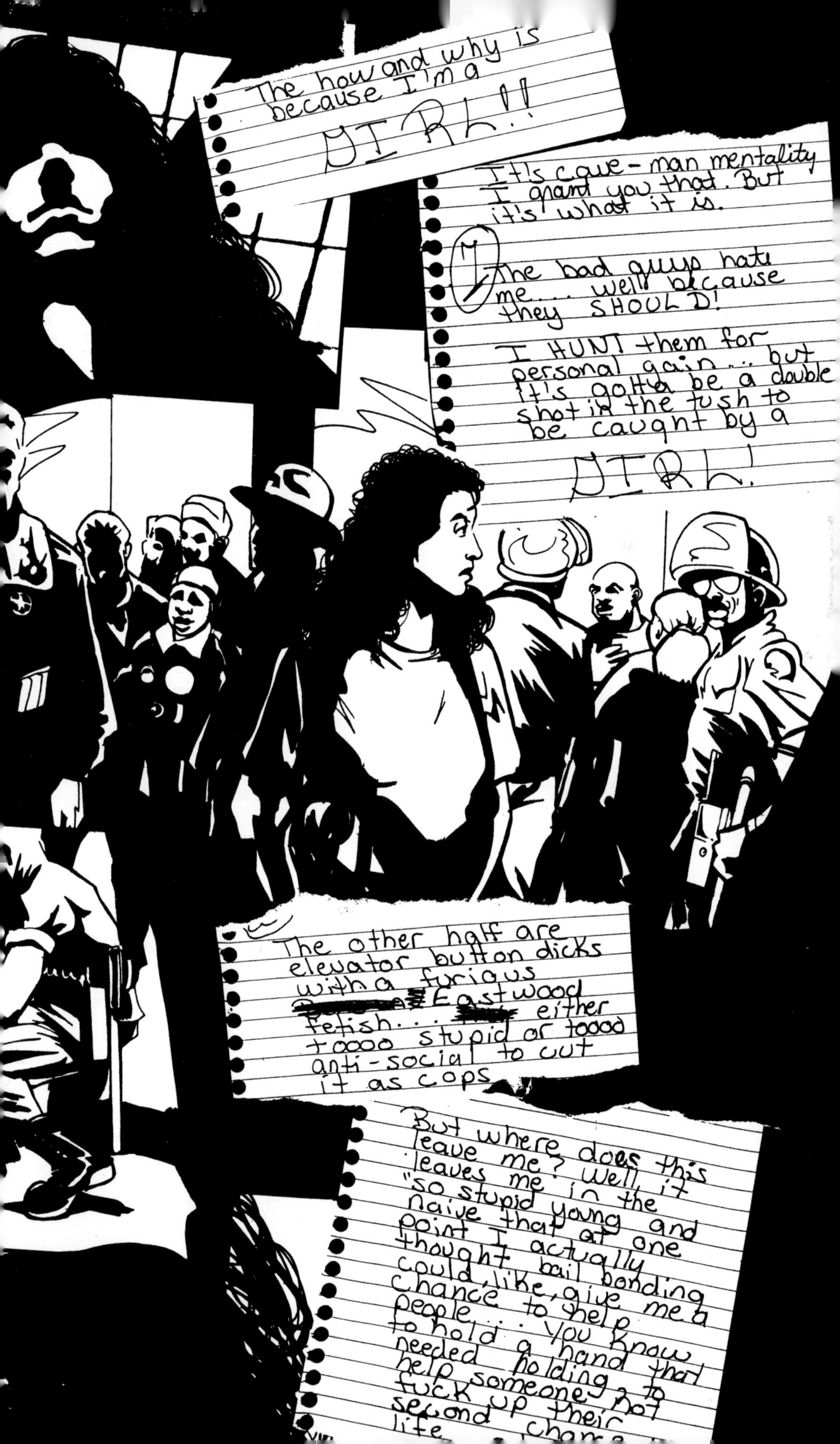
The how and why is because I'm a
GIRL!!
It's cave-man mentality I grant you that. But it's what it is.
The bad guys hate me... well because they SHOULD!
I HUNT them for personal gain... but it's gotta be a double shot in the tush to be caught by a
GIRL!
The other half are elevator button dicks with a furious [redacted] Eastwood fetish... [redacted] either toooo stupid or toood anti-social to cut it as cops
But where does this leave me? Well, it leaves me in the "so stupid young and naive that at one point I actually thought bail bonding could, like, give me a chance to help people... you know, to hold a hand that needed holding, to help someone not fuck up their second chance...
life

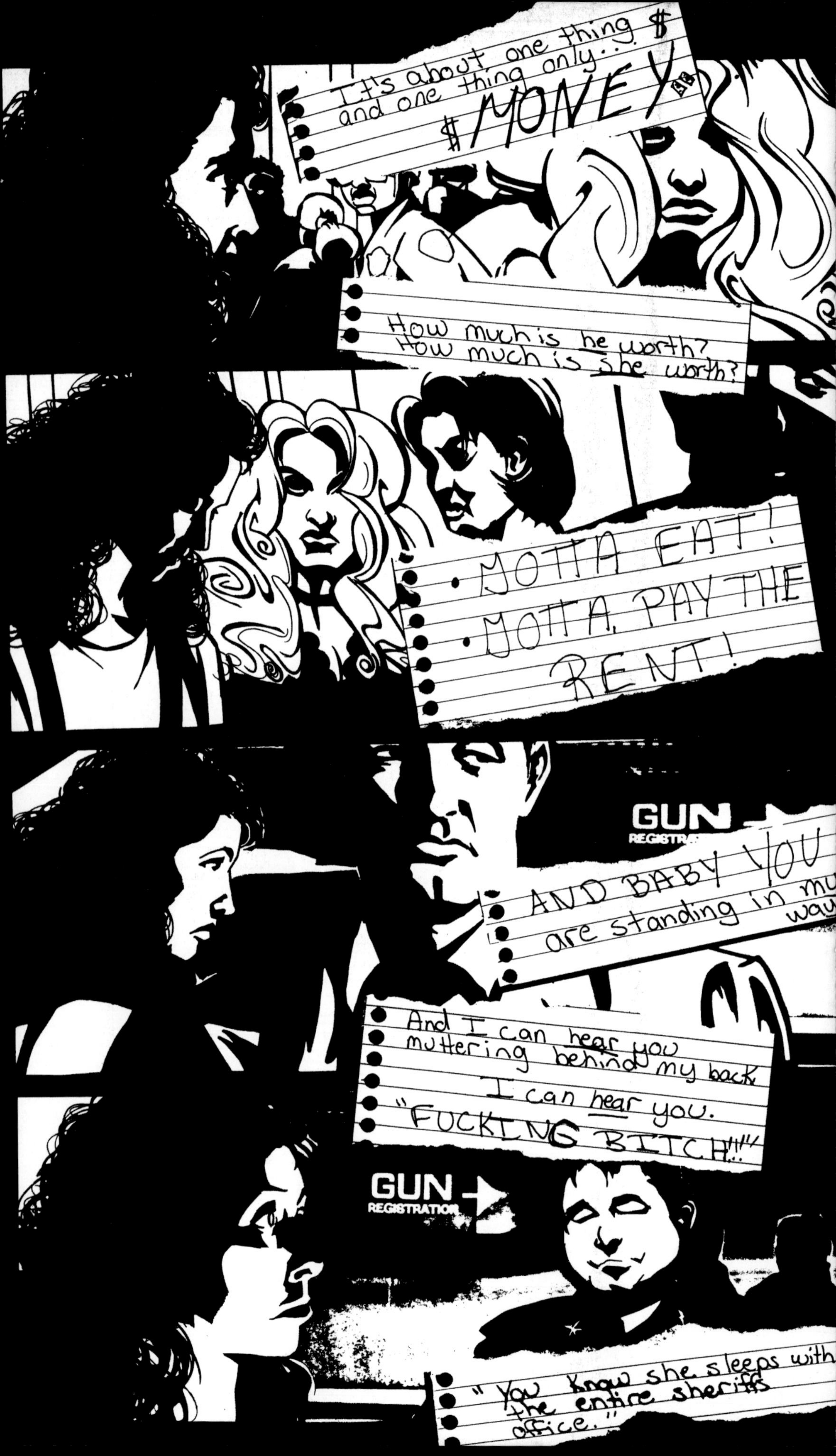

It's about one thing $ and one thing only... $MONEY$
How much is he worth? How much is she worth?
• GOTTA EAT! • GOTTA PAY THE RENT!
AND BABY YOU are standing in my way
GUN REGISTRATION
And I can hear you muttering behind my back I can hear you. "FUCKING BITCH!!!"
GUN REGISTRATION
"You know she sleeps with the entire sheriffs office."

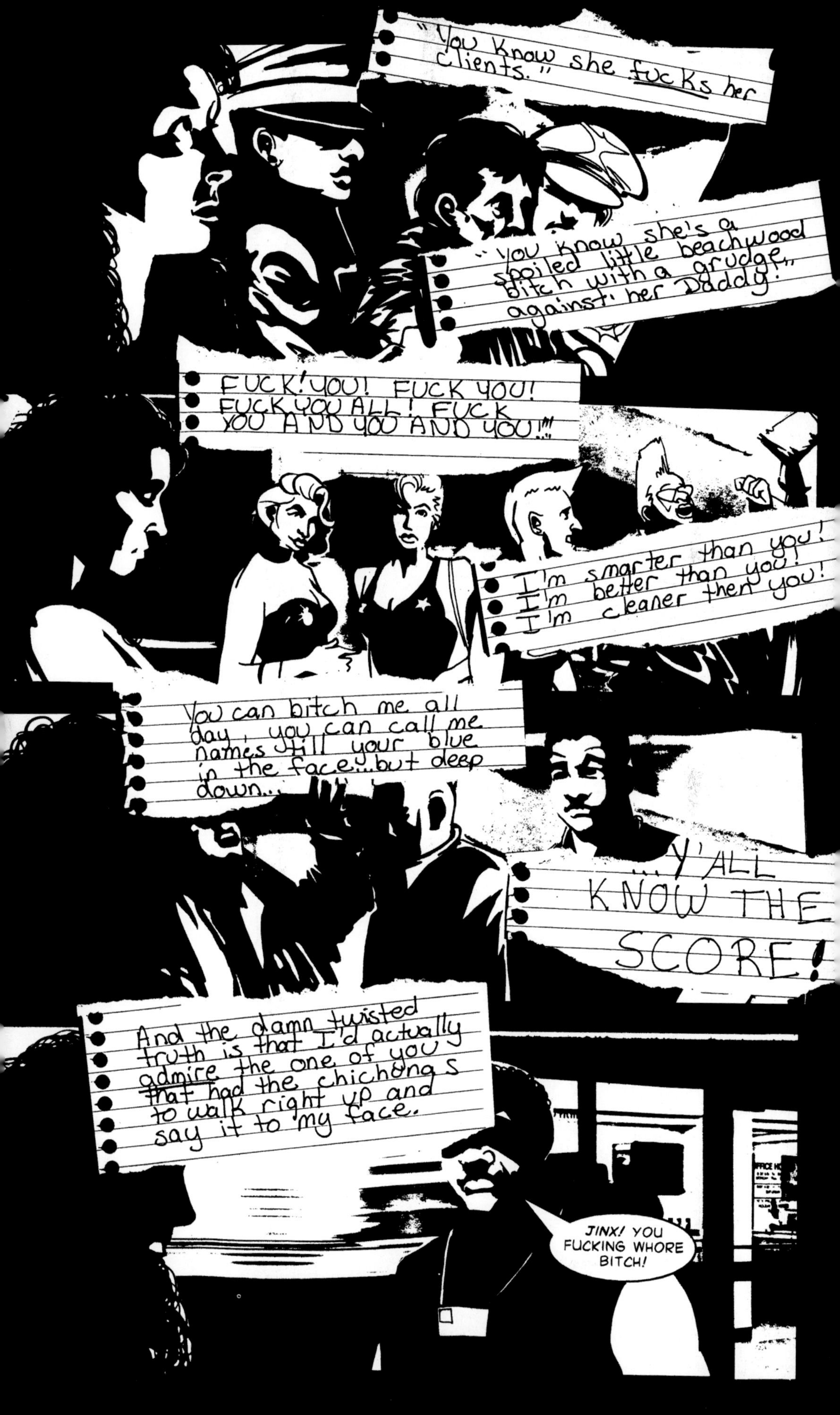
"You know she fucks her clients."
"You know she's a spoiled little beachwood bitch with a grudge against her Daddy!"
FUCK! YOU! FUCK YOU! FUCK YOU ALL! FUCK YOU AND YOU AND YOU!!!
I'm smarter than you! I'm better than you! I'm cleaner then you!
You can bitch me all day, you can call me names till your blue in the face...but deep down...
...Y'ALL KNOW THE SCORE!
And the damn twisted truth is that I'd actually admire the one of you that had the chichongs to walk right up and say it to my face.
JINX! YOU FUCKING WHORE BITCH!

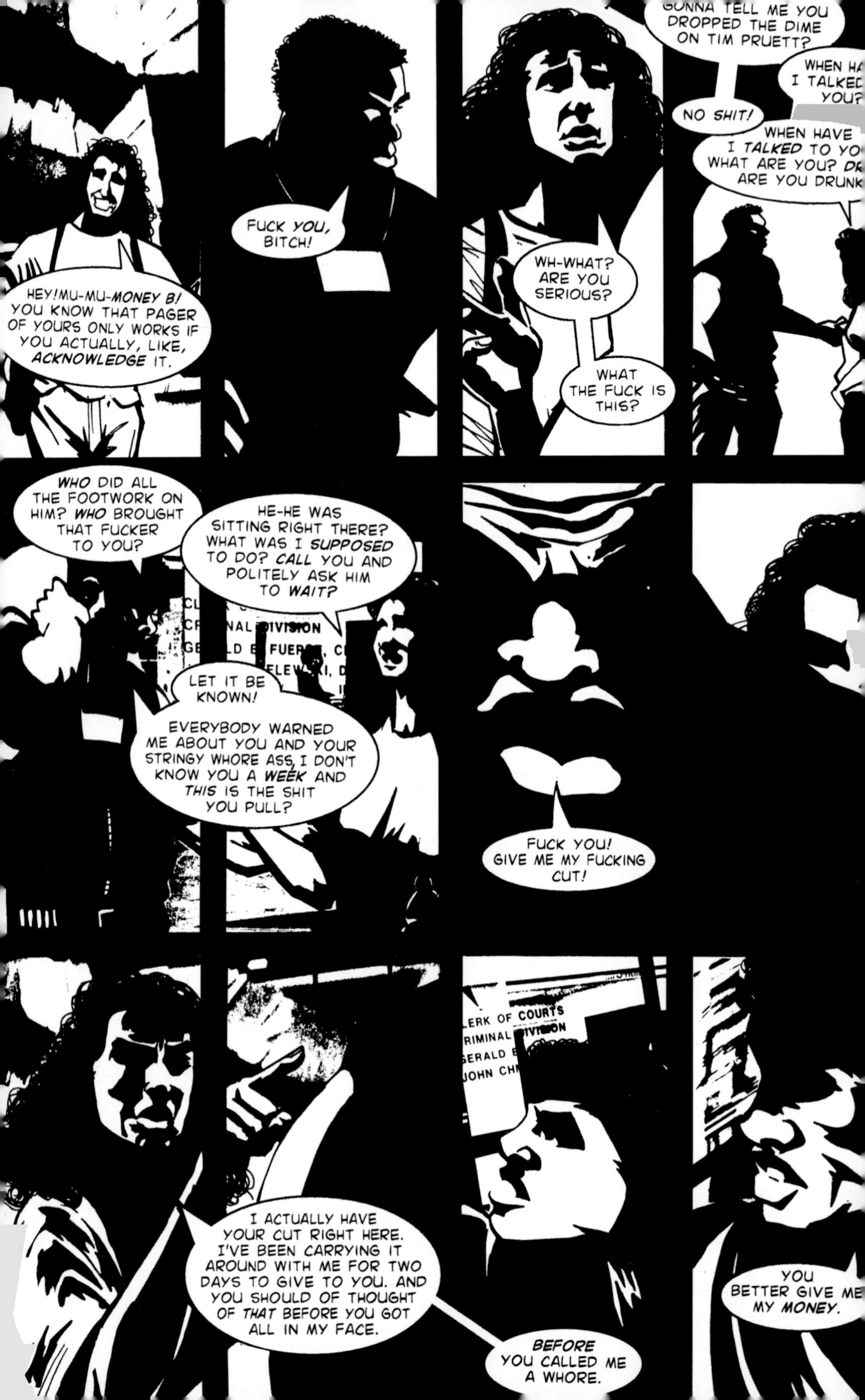
HEY! MU-MU-MONEY B! YOU KNOW THAT PAGER OF YOURS ONLY WORKS IF YOU ACTUALLY, LIKE, ACKNOWLEDGE IT.
FUCK YOU, BITCH!
WH-WHAT? ARE YOU SERIOUS?
WHAT THE FUCK IS THIS?
GONNA TELL ME YOU DROPPED THE DIME ON TIM PRUETT?
NO SHIT!
WHEN HA
I TALKED
YOU?
WHEN HAVE I TALKED TO YO
WHAT ARE YOU? DR
ARE YOU DRUNK
WHO DID ALL THE FOOTWORK ON HIM? WHO BROUGHT THAT FUCKER TO YOU?
HE-HE WAS SITTING RIGHT THERE? WHAT WAS I SUPPOSED TO DO? CALL YOU AND POLITELY ASK HIM TO WAIT?
LET IT BE KNOWN!
EVERYBODY WARNED ME ABOUT YOU AND YOUR STRINGY WHORE ASS, I DON'T KNOW YOU A WEEK AND THIS IS THE SHIT YOU PULL?
FUCK YOU! GIVE ME MY FUCKING CUT!
I ACTUALLY HAVE YOUR CUT RIGHT HERE. I'VE BEEN CARRYING IT AROUND WITH ME FOR TWO DAYS TO GIVE TO YOU. AND YOU SHOULD OF THOUGHT OF THAT BEFORE YOU GOT ALL IN MY FACE.
BEFORE YOU CALLED ME A WHORE.
YOU BETTER GIVE ME MY MONEY.

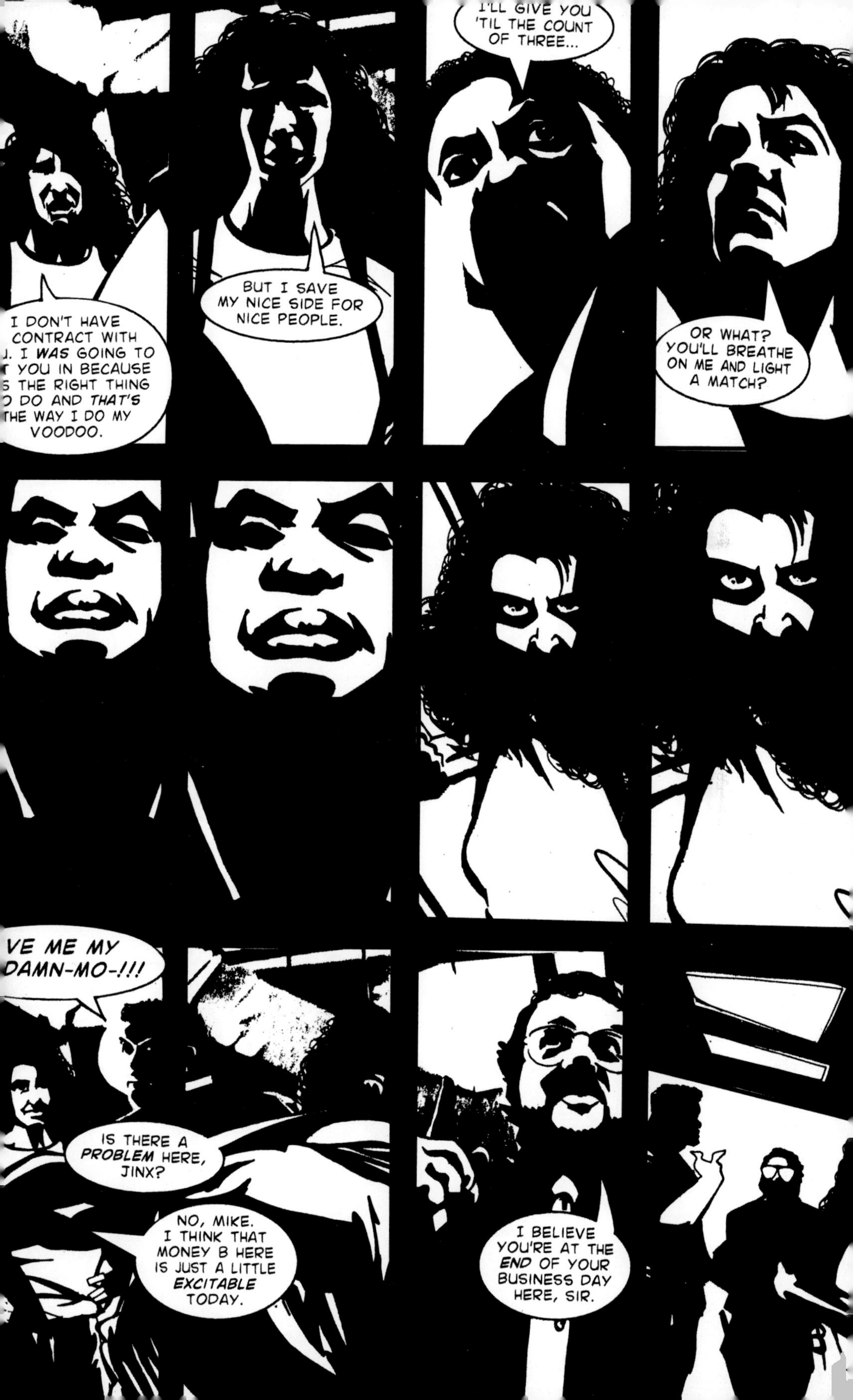
I DON'T HAVE
CONTRACT WITH
J. I WAS GOING TO
T YOU IN BECAUSE
S THE RIGHT THING
O DO AND THAT'S
THE WAY I DO MY
VOODOO.
BUT I SAVE MY NICE SIDE FOR NICE PEOPLE.
I'LL GIVE YOU 'TIL THE COUNT OF THREE...
OR WHAT? YOU'LL BREATHE ON ME AND LIGHT A MATCH?
VE ME MY DAMN-MO-!!!
IS THERE A PROBLEM HERE, JINX?
NO, MIKE. I THINK THAT MONEY B HERE IS JUST A LITTLE EXCITABLE TODAY.
I BELIEVE YOU'RE AT THE END OF YOUR BUSINESS DAY HERE, SIR.

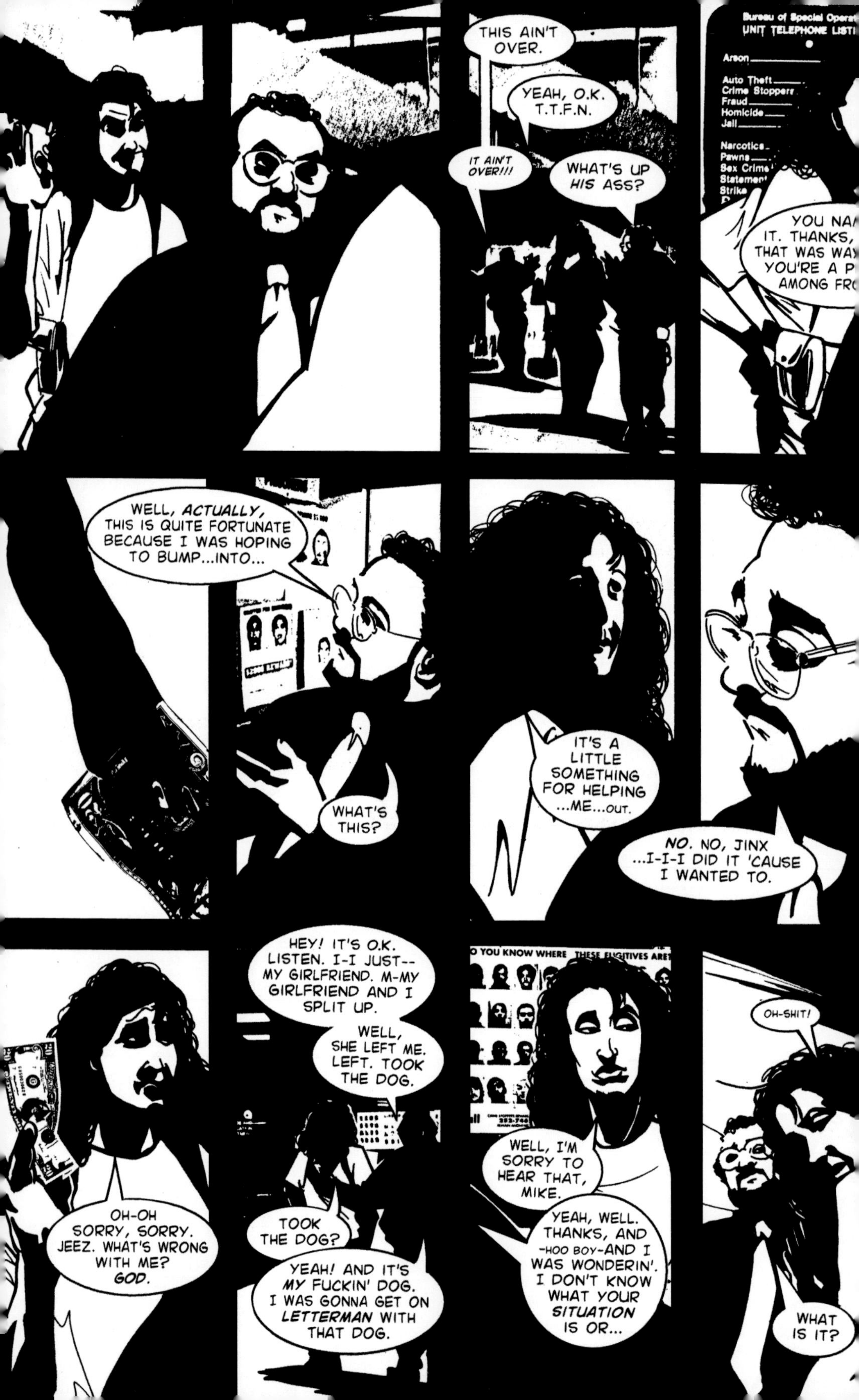
THIS AIN'T OVER.
YEAH, O.K. T.T.F.N.
IT AIN'T OVER!!!
WHAT'S UP HIS ASS?
Bureau of Special Operat
UNIT TELEPHONE LISTI
Arson
Auto Theft
Crime Stopperr
Fraud
Homicide
Jail
Narcotics
Pawns
Sex Crime
Statement
Strike
YOU NA IT. THANKS, THAT WAS WAY YOU'RE A P AMONG FR
WELL, ACTUALLY, THIS IS QUITE FORTUNATE BECAUSE I WAS HOPING TO BUMP...INTO...
WHAT'S THIS?
IT'S A LITTLE SOMETHING FOR HELPING ...ME...OUT.
NO. NO, JINX ...I-I-I DID IT 'CAUSE I WANTED TO.
OH-OH SORRY, SORRY. JEEZ. WHAT'S WRONG WITH ME? GOD.
HEY! IT'S O.K. LISTEN. I-I JUST-- MY GIRLFRIEND. M-MY GIRLFRIEND AND I SPLIT UP.
WELL, SHE LEFT ME. LEFT. TOOK THE DOG.
TOOK THE DOG?
YEAH! AND IT'S MY FUCKIN' DOG. I WAS GONNA GET ON LETTERMAN WITH THAT DOG.
O YOU KNOW WHERE THESE FUGITIVES ARE?
WELL, I'M SORRY TO HEAR THAT, MIKE.
YEAH, WELL. THANKS, AND -HOO BOY- AND I WAS WONDERIN'. I DON'T KNOW WHAT YOUR SITUATION IS OR...
OH-SHIT!
WHAT IS IT?

252-7463
DAVID GOLD
(a.k.a. Goldfish)
Ht- 5' 7"
Wt- 160 lbs.
Eyes- Blue
Hair- Blonde
Panhandling, Solicitation,
Acceptance of stolen proper
Wanted for questioning
n the fatal shooting
Det. Ralph Mathieu
OOOOH! OH FUCK!
RRRRRGGHH!
WHAT'S GOIN' ON?
It's just like Mom used to say..."MEN ARE LIKE CARS."
Fuck Mom! Men are like getting HIT by a car!

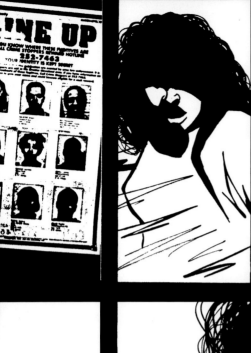

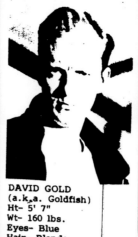

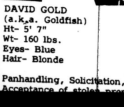

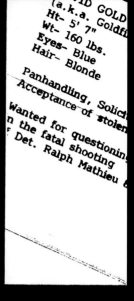

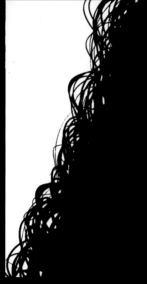

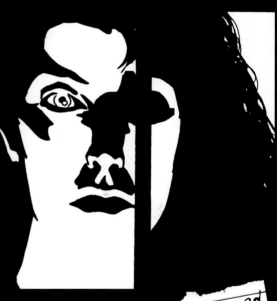

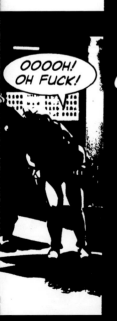

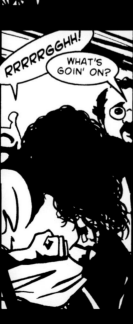

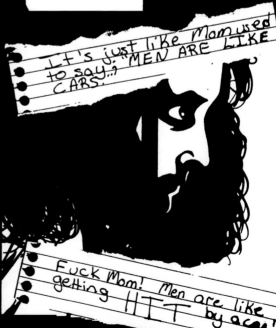

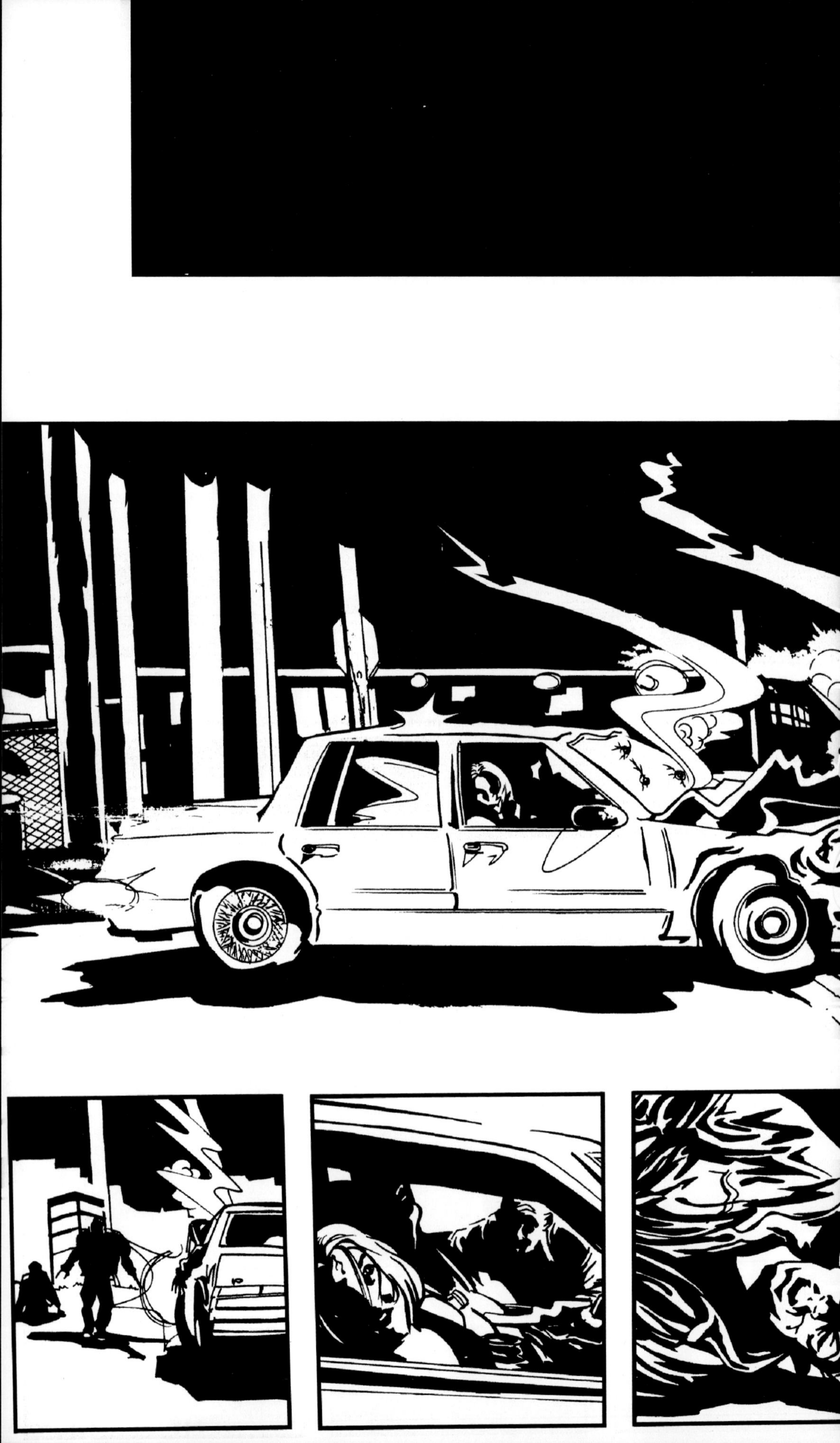

So, did You Hear the one about the Two Dead Wiseguys who...

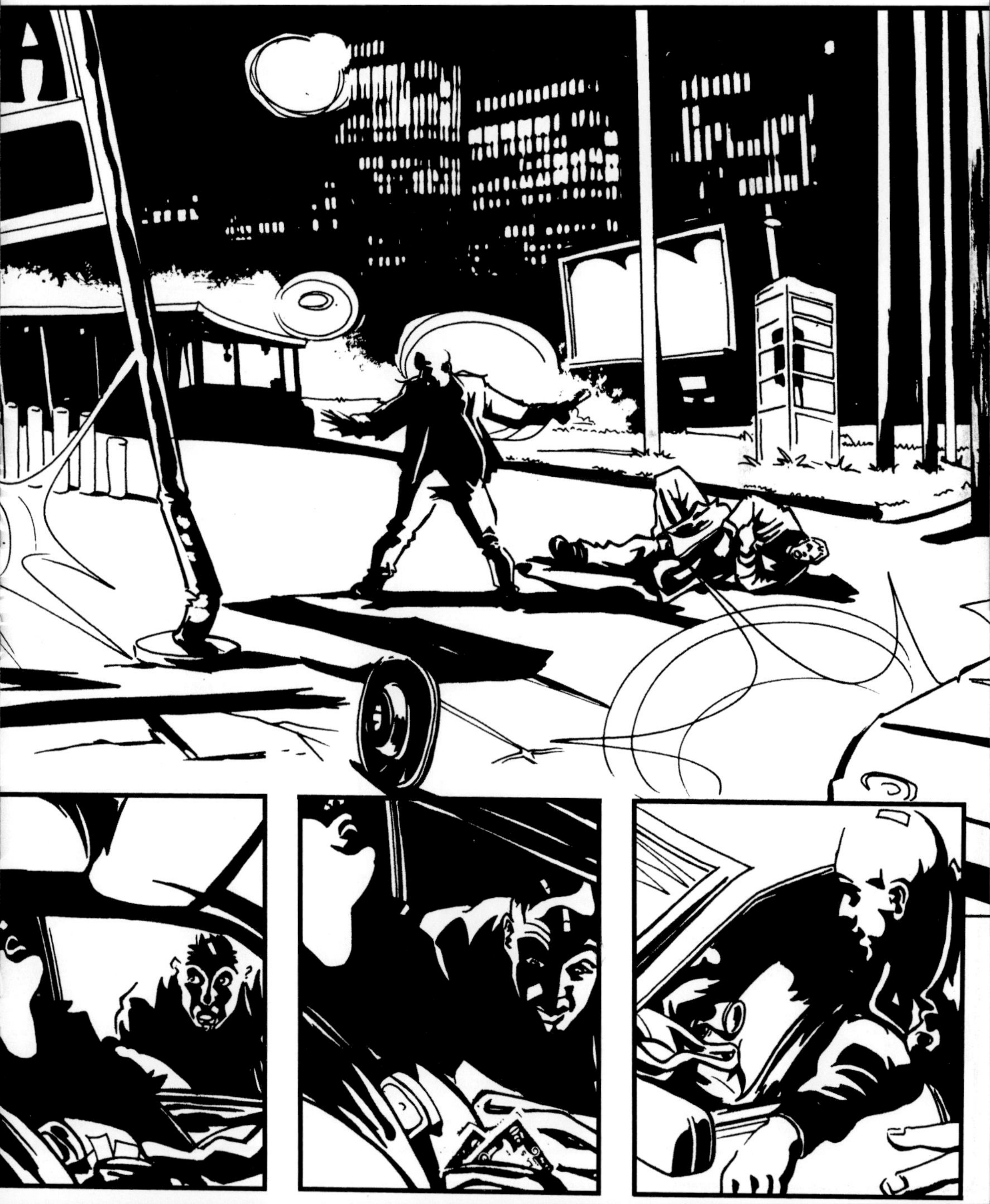

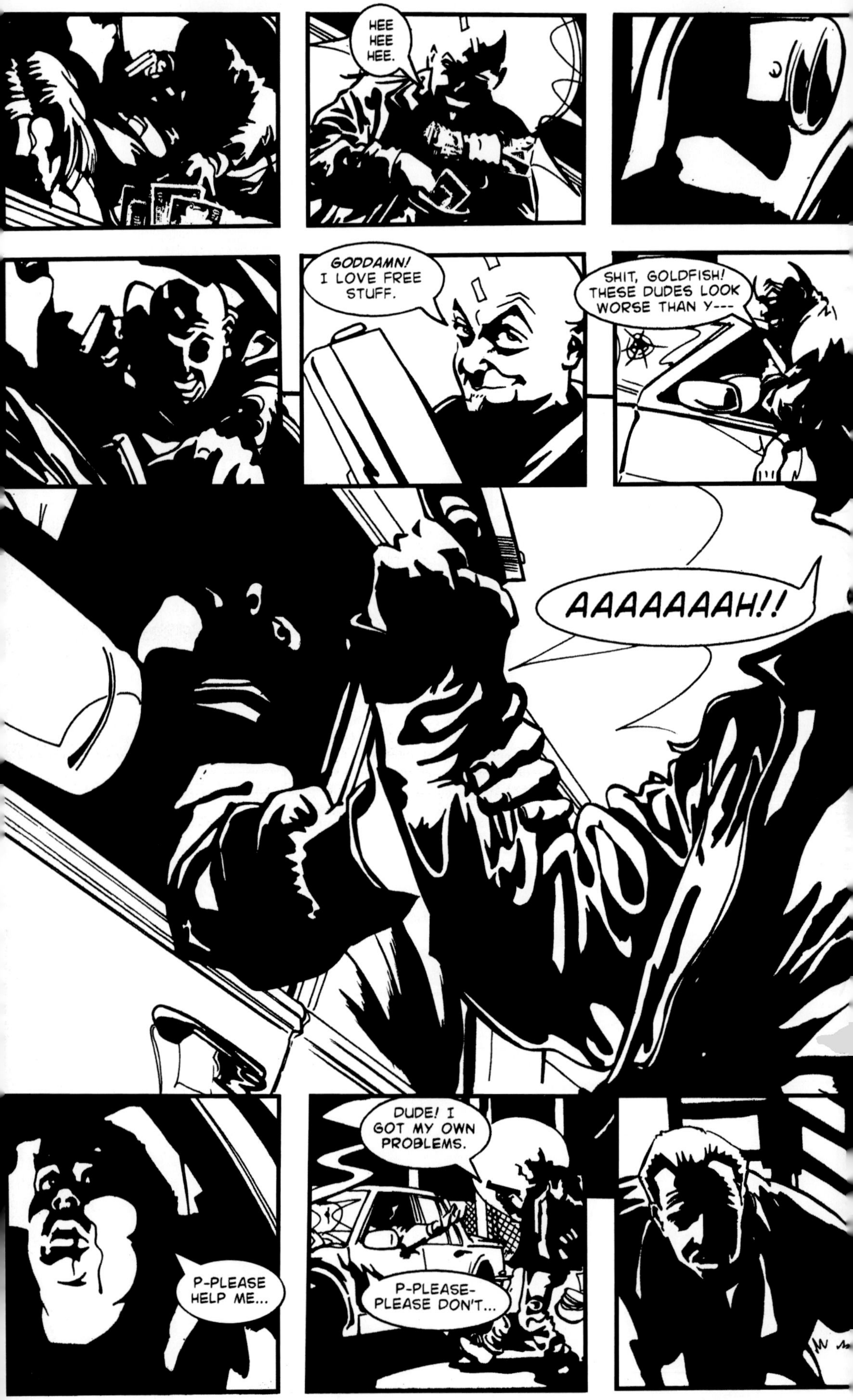
HEE HEE HEE.
GODDAMN! I LOVE FREE STUFF.
SHIT, GOLDFISH! THESE DUDES LOOK WORSE THAN Y---
AAAAAAAH!!
P-PLEASE HELP ME...
DUDE! I GOT MY OWN PROBLEMS.
P-PLEASE- PLEASE DON'T...

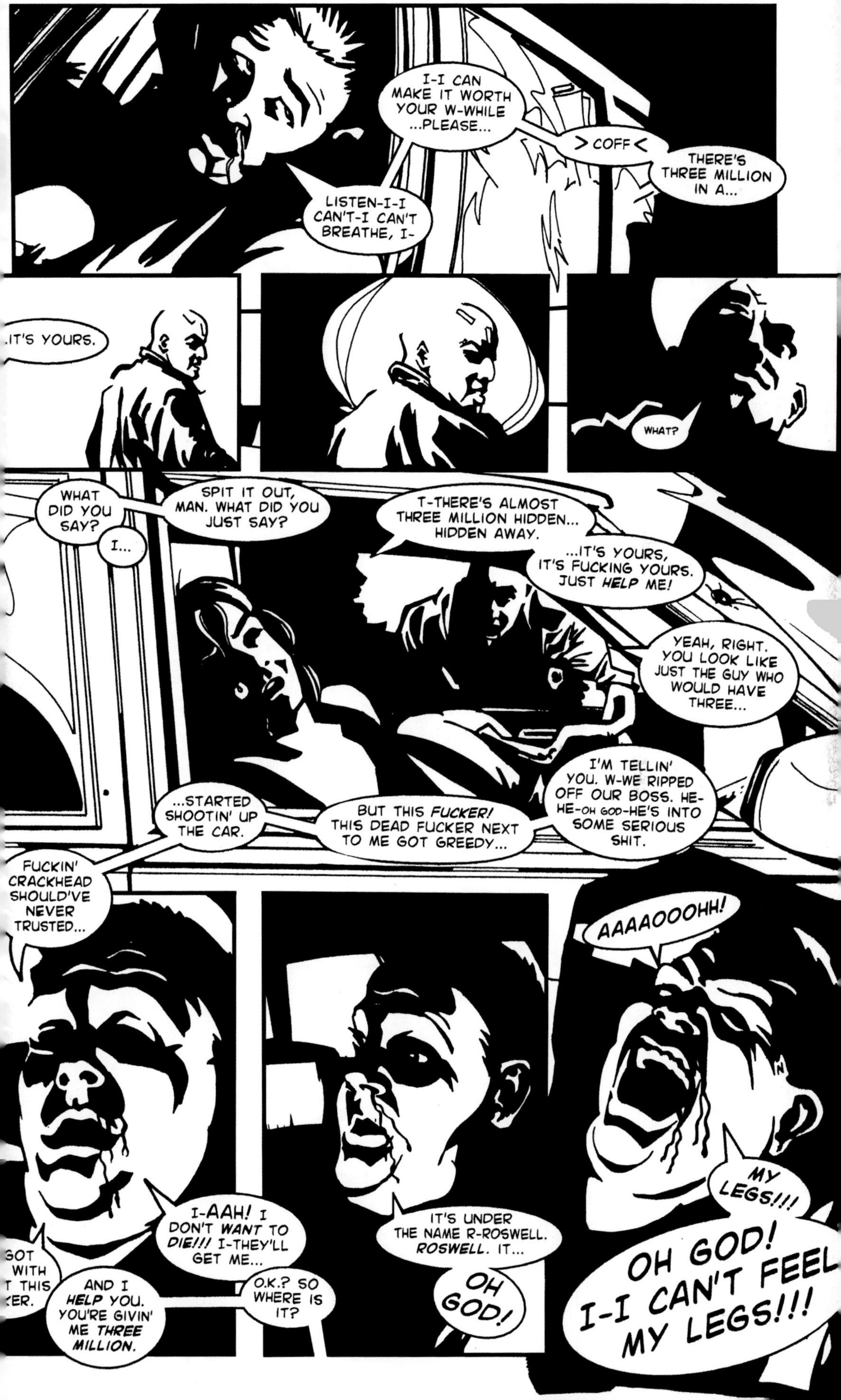
LISTEN-I-I CAN'T-I CAN'T BREATHE, I-
I-I CAN MAKE IT WORTH YOUR W-WHILE ...PLEASE...
>COFF<
THERE'S THREE MILLION IN A...
...IT'S YOURS.
WHAT?
WHAT DID YOU SAY?
I...
SPIT IT OUT, MAN. WHAT DID YOU JUST SAY?
T-THERE'S ALMOST THREE MILLION HIDDEN... HIDDEN AWAY.
...IT'S YOURS, IT'S FUCKING YOURS. JUST HELP ME!
YEAH, RIGHT. YOU LOOK LIKE JUST THE GUY WHO WOULD HAVE THREE...
I'M TELLIN' YOU. W-WE RIPPED OFF OUR BOSS. HE-HE-OH GOD-HE'S INTO SOME SERIOUS SHIT.
BUT THIS FUCKER! THIS DEAD FUCKER NEXT TO ME GOT GREEDY...
...STARTED SHOOTIN' UP THE CAR.
FUCKIN' CRACKHEAD SHOULD'VE NEVER TRUSTED...
I-AAH! I DON'T WANT TO DIE!!! I-THEY'LL GET ME...
AND I HELP YOU. YOU'RE GIVIN' ME THREE MILLION.
O.K.? SO WHERE IS IT?
IT'S UNDER THE NAME R-ROSWELL. ROSWELL. IT...
OH GOD!
AAAAOOOHH!
MY LEGS!!!
OH GOD! I-I CAN'T FEEL MY LEGS!!!

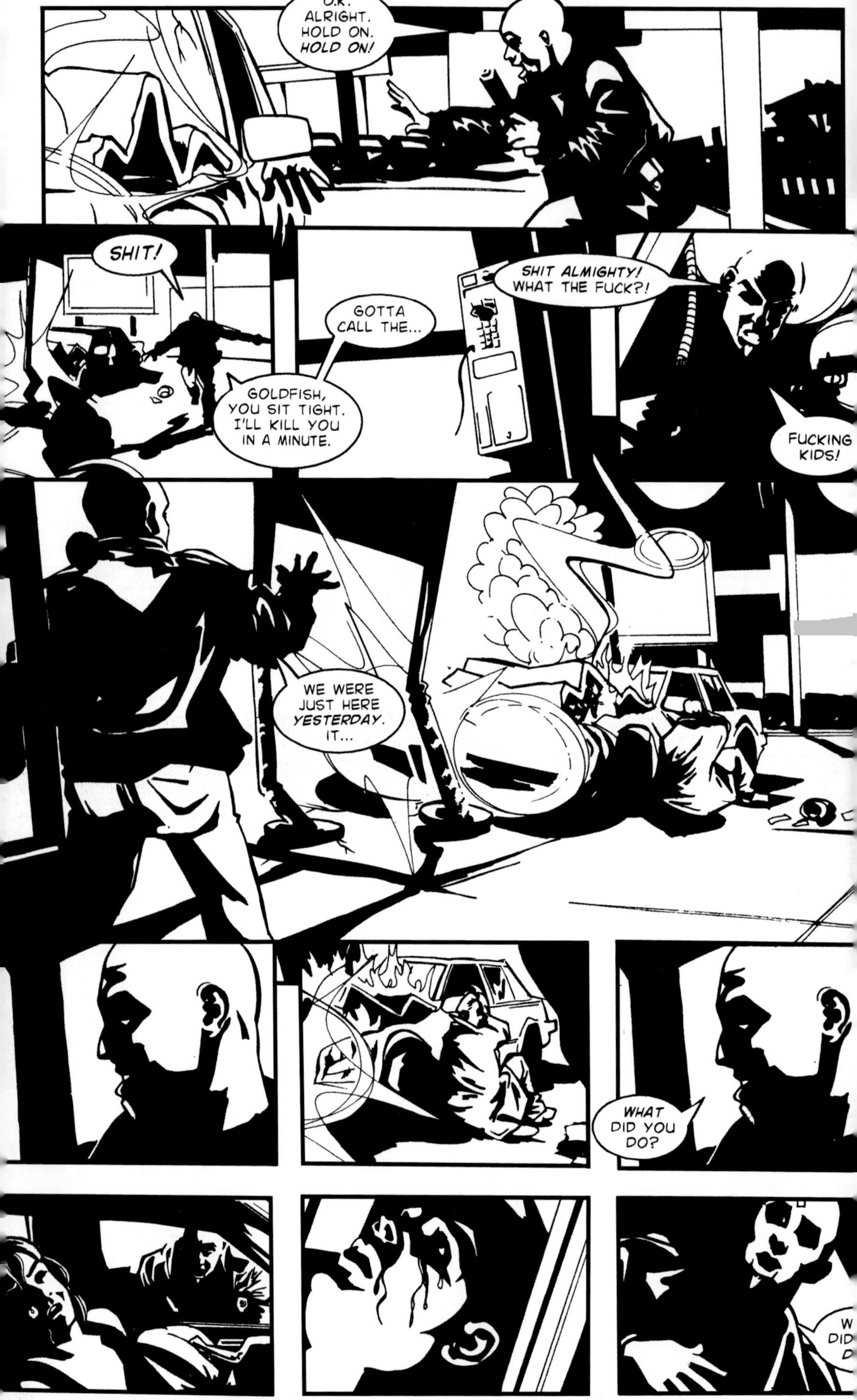
O.K. ALRIGHT. HOLD ON. *HOLD ON!*
SHIT!
GOTTA CALL THE...
GOLDFISH, YOU SIT TIGHT. I'LL KILL YOU IN A MINUTE.
SHIT ALMIGHTY! WHAT THE FUCK?!
FUCKING KIDS!
WE WERE JUST HERE *YESTERDAY*. IT...
WHAT DID YOU DO?

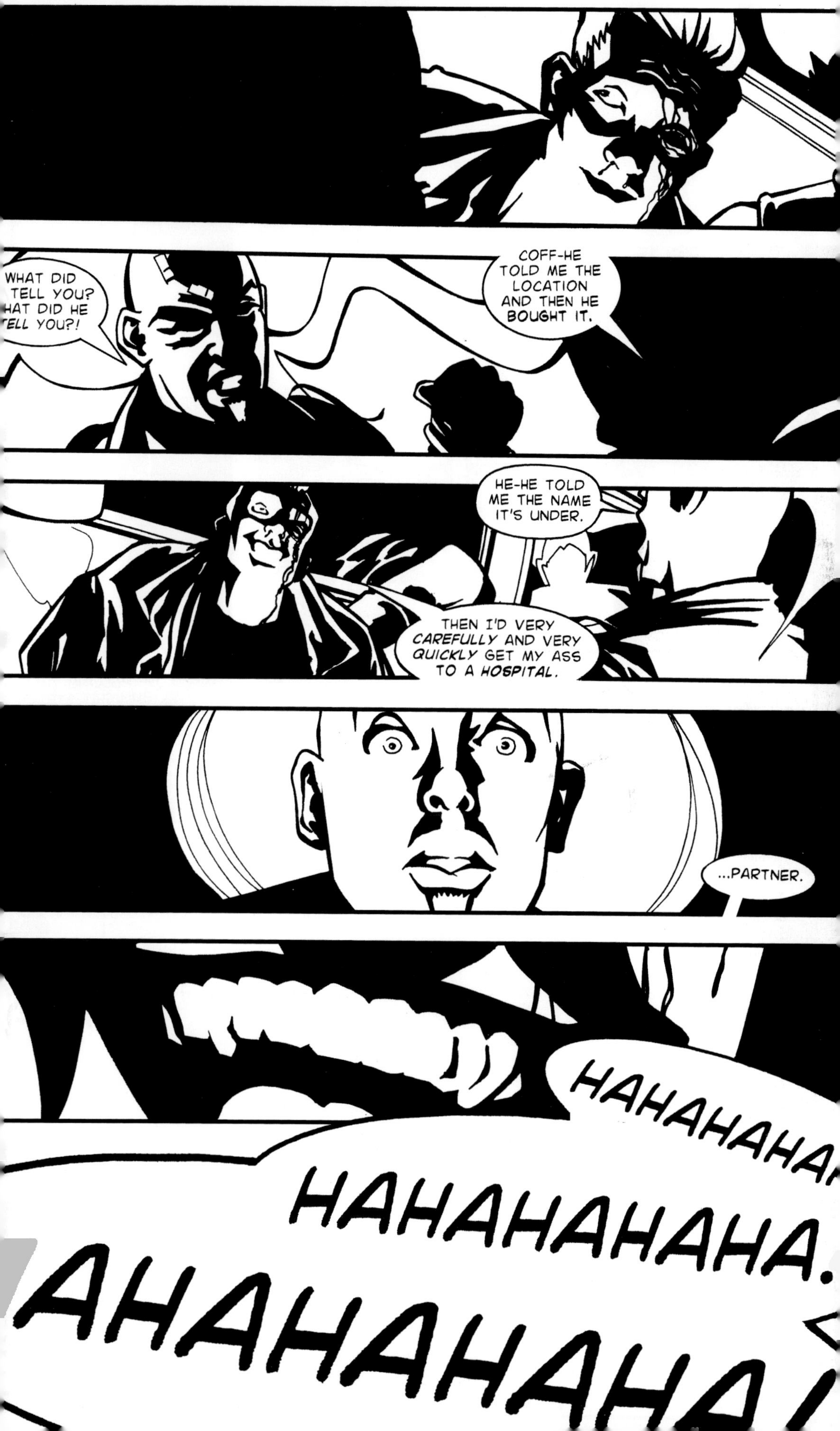
WHAT DID
TELL YOU?
HAT DID HE
TELL YOU?!
COFF-HE TOLD ME THE LOCATION AND THEN HE BOUGHT IT.
HE-HE TOLD ME THE NAME IT'S UNDER.
THEN I'D VERY CAREFULLY AND VERY QUICKLY GET MY ASS TO A HOSPITAL.
...PARTNER.
HAHAHAHA
HAHAHAHAHA.
AHAHAHAHA!

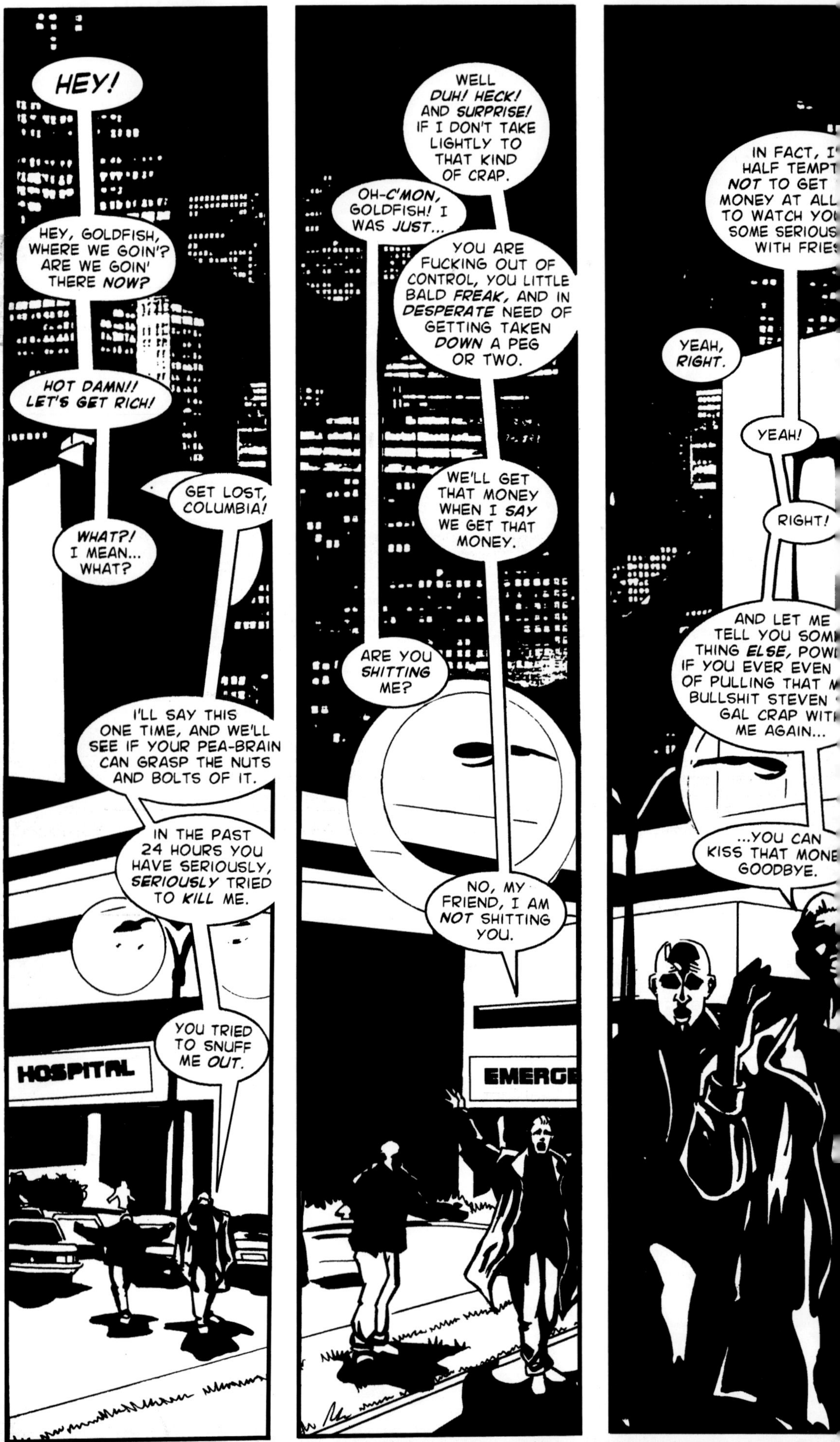
HEY!
HEY, GOLDFISH, WHERE WE GOIN'? ARE WE GOIN' THERE NOW?
HOT DAMN!! LET'S GET RICH!
GET LOST, COLUMBIA!
WHAT?! I MEAN... WHAT?
I'LL SAY THIS ONE TIME, AND WE'LL SEE IF YOUR PEA-BRAIN CAN GRASP THE NUTS AND BOLTS OF IT.
IN THE PAST 24 HOURS YOU HAVE SERIOUSLY, SERIOUSLY TRIED TO KILL ME.
YOU TRIED TO SNUFF ME OUT.
HOSPITAL
OH-C'MON, GOLDFISH! I WAS JUST...
WELL DUH! HECK! AND SURPRISE! IF I DON'T TAKE LIGHTLY TO THAT KIND OF CRAP.
YOU ARE FUCKING OUT OF CONTROL, YOU LITTLE BALD FREAK, AND IN DESPERATE NEED OF GETTING TAKEN DOWN A PEG OR TWO.
WE'LL GET THAT MONEY WHEN I SAY WE GET THAT MONEY.
ARE YOU SHITTING ME?
NO, MY FRIEND, I AM NOT SHITTING YOU.
EMERGE
YEAH, RIGHT.
IN FACT, I' HALF TEMPT NOT TO GET MONEY AT ALL TO WATCH YO SOME SERIOUS WITH FRIES
YEAH!
RIGHT!
AND LET ME TELL YOU SOM THING ELSE, POW IF YOU EVER EVEN OF PULLING THAT M BULLSHIT STEVEN GAL CRAP WIT ME AGAIN...
...YOU CAN KISS THAT MONE GOODBYE.

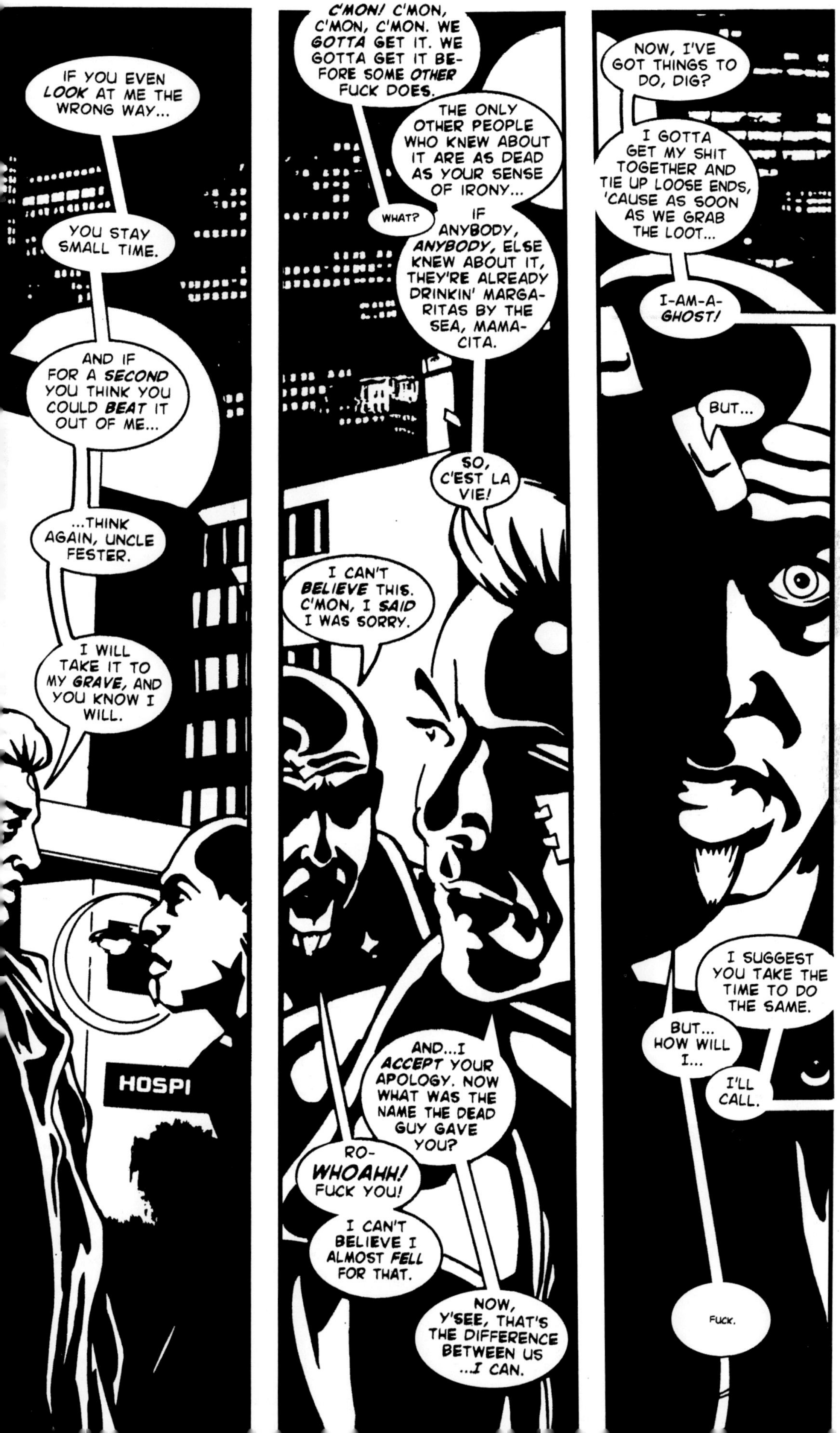

IF YOU EVEN LOOK AT ME THE WRONG WAY...
YOU STAY SMALL TIME.
AND IF FOR A SECOND YOU THINK YOU COULD BEAT IT OUT OF ME...
...THINK AGAIN, UNCLE FESTER.
I WILL TAKE IT TO MY GRAVE, AND YOU KNOW I WILL.
HOSPI
C'MON! C'MON, C'MON, C'MON. WE GOTTA GET IT. WE GOTTA GET IT BEFORE SOME OTHER FUCK DOES.
WHAT?
THE ONLY OTHER PEOPLE WHO KNEW ABOUT IT ARE AS DEAD AS YOUR SENSE OF IRONY...
IF ANYBODY, ANYBODY, ELSE KNEW ABOUT IT, THEY'RE ALREADY DRINKIN' MARGARITAS BY THE SEA, MAMACITA.
SO, C'EST LA VIE!
I CAN'T BELIEVE THIS. C'MON, I SAID I WAS SORRY.
AND...I ACCEPT YOUR APOLOGY. NOW WHAT WAS THE NAME THE DEAD GUY GAVE YOU?
RO-WHOAHH! FUCK YOU!
I CAN'T BELIEVE I ALMOST FELL FOR THAT.
NOW, Y'SEE, THAT'S THE DIFFERENCE BETWEEN US ...I CAN.
NOW, I'VE GOT THINGS TO DO, DIG?
I GOTTA GET MY SHIT TOGETHER AND TIE UP LOOSE ENDS, 'CAUSE AS SOON AS WE GRAB THE LOOT...
I-AM-A-GHOST!
BUT...
I SUGGEST YOU TAKE THE TIME TO DO THE SAME.
BUT... HOW WILL I...
I'LL CALL.
FUCK.

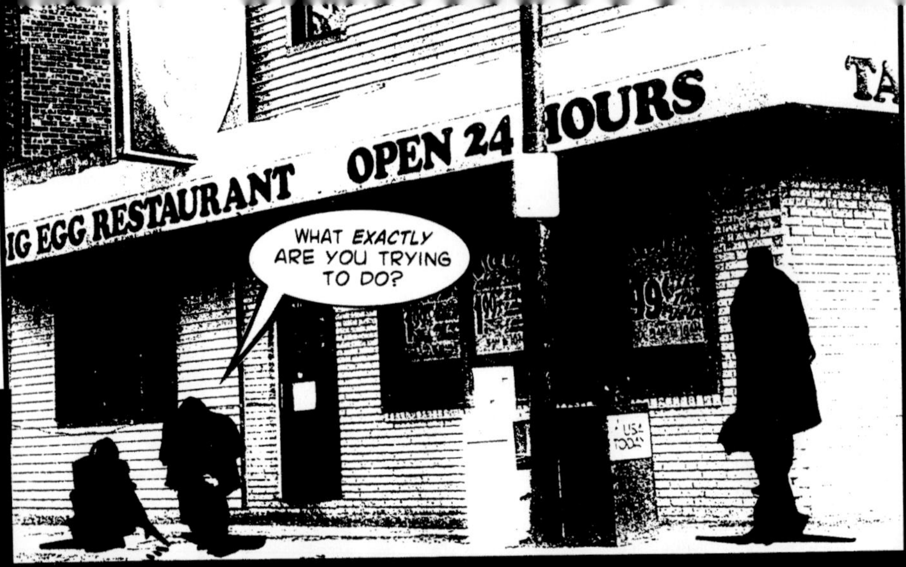
IG EGG RESTAURANT
OPEN 24 HOURS
WHAT *EXACTLY* ARE YOU TRYING TO DO?

Nowheresville

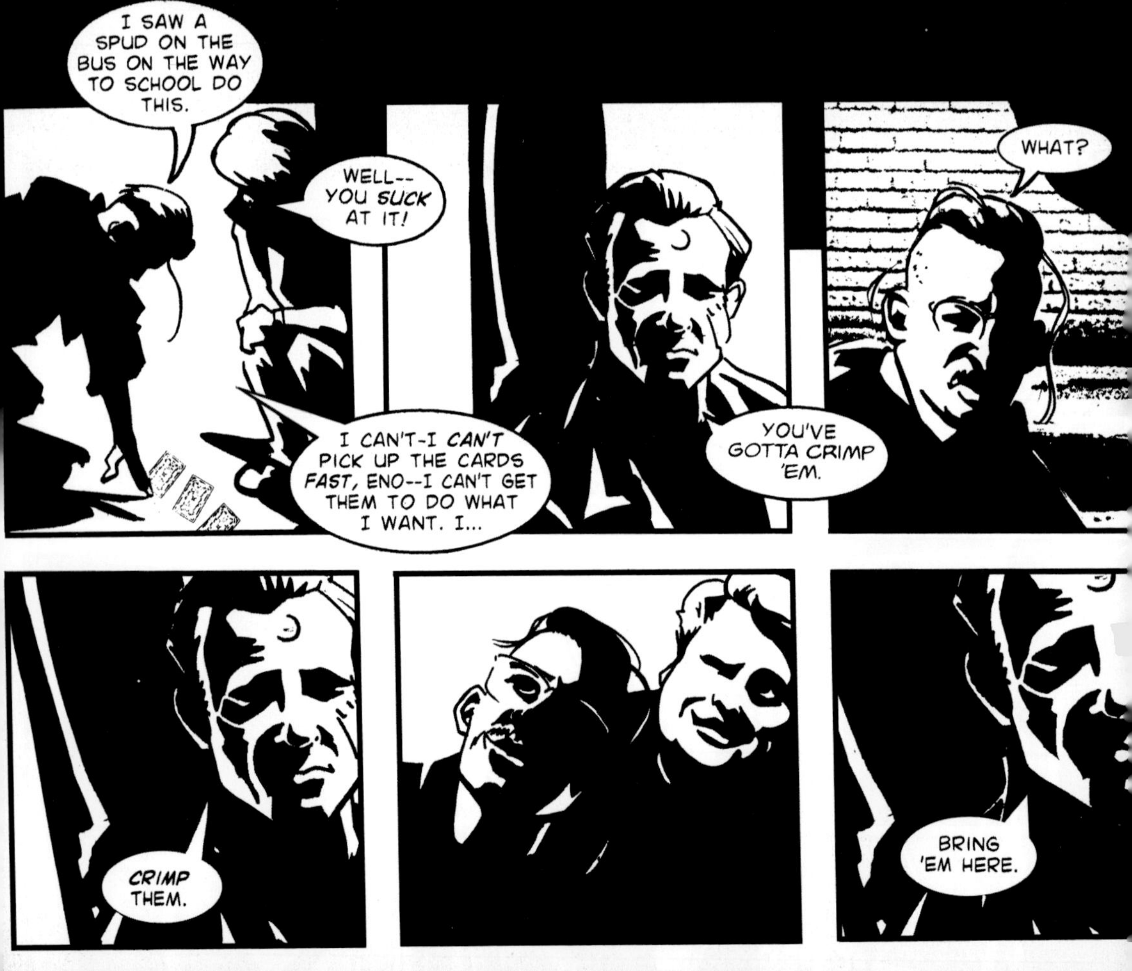
I SAW A SPUD ON THE BUS ON THE WAY TO SCHOOL DO THIS.
WELL-- YOU *SUCK* AT IT!
I CAN'T-I *CAN'T* PICK UP THE CARDS *FAST,* ENO--I CAN'T GET THEM TO DO WHAT I WANT. I...
YOU'VE GOTTA CRIMP 'EM.
WHAT?
CRIMP THEM.
BRING 'EM HERE.

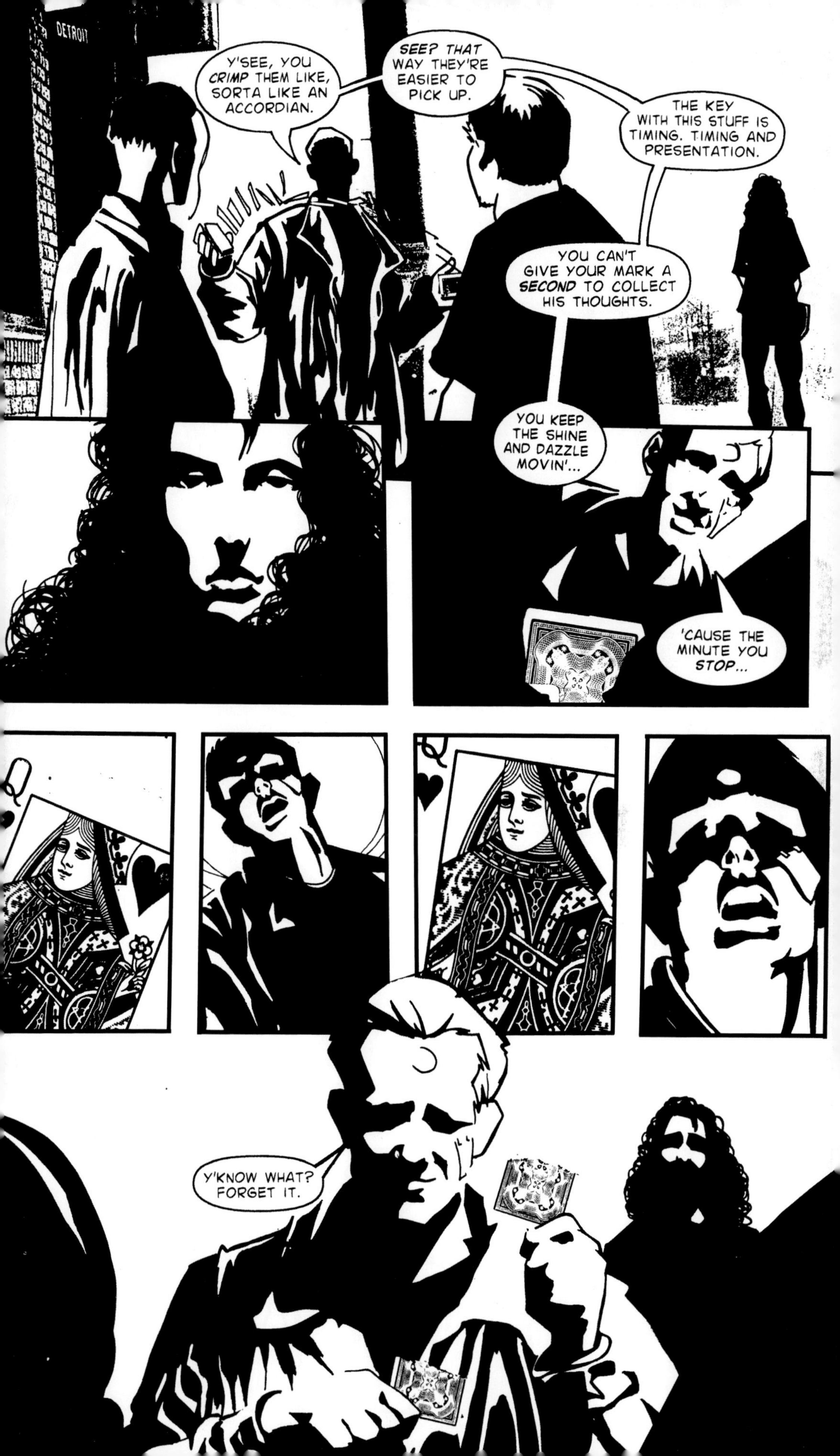
DETROIT
Y'SEE, YOU CRIMP THEM LIKE, SORTA LIKE AN ACCORDIAN.
SEE? THAT WAY THEY'RE EASIER TO PICK UP.
THE KEY WITH THIS STUFF IS TIMING. TIMING AND PRESENTATION.
YOU CAN'T GIVE YOUR MARK A SECOND TO COLLECT HIS THOUGHTS.
YOU KEEP THE SHINE AND DAZZLE MOVIN'...
'CAUSE THE MINUTE YOU STOP...
Y'KNOW WHAT? FORGET IT.

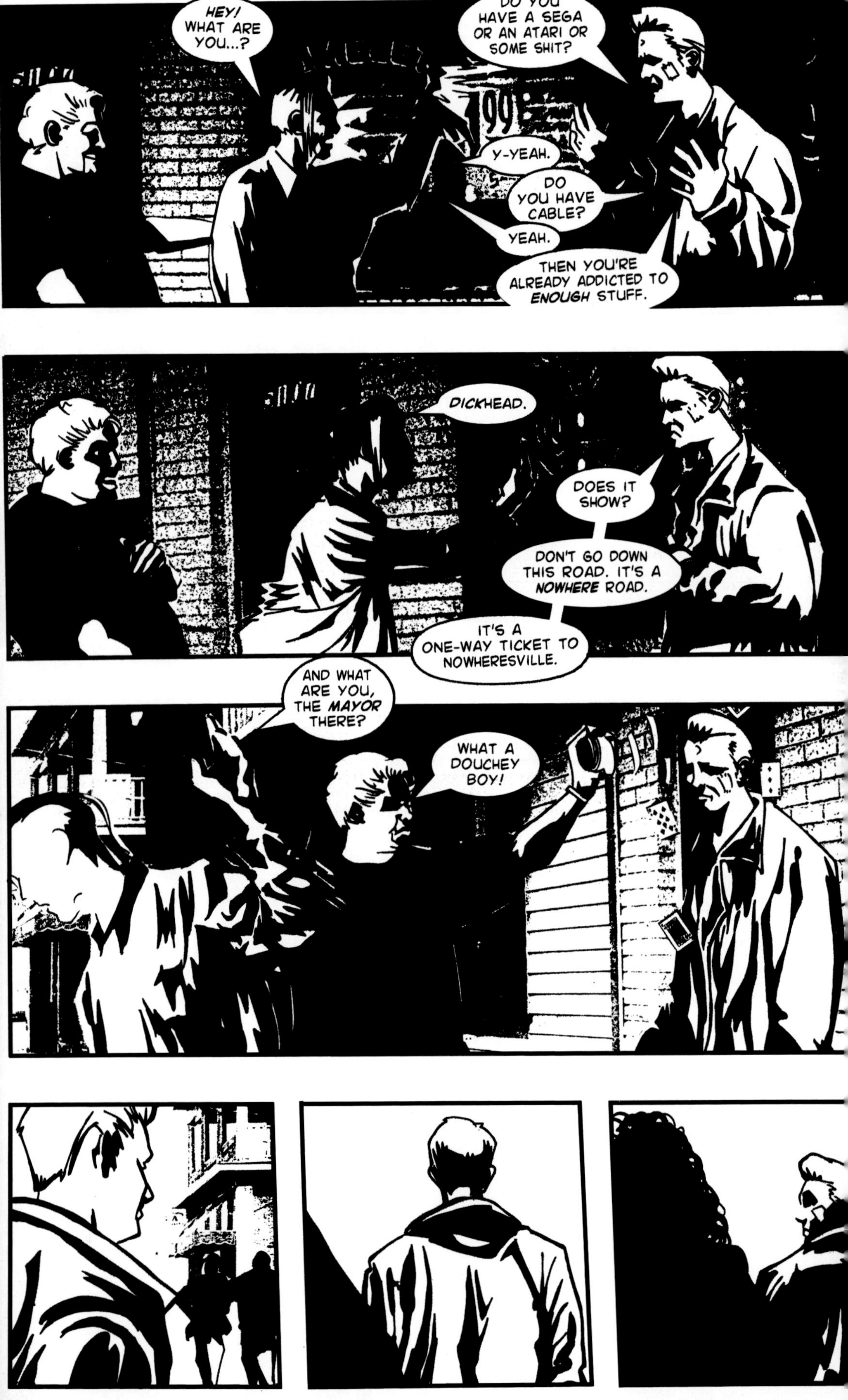

HEY! WHAT ARE YOU...?
DO YOU HAVE A SEGA OR AN ATARI OR SOME SHIT?
Y-YEAH.
DO YOU HAVE CABLE?
YEAH.
THEN YOU'RE ALREADY ADDICTED TO *ENOUGH* STUFF.
*DICK*HEAD.
DOES IT SHOW?
DON'T GO DOWN THIS ROAD. IT'S A *NOWHERE* ROAD.
IT'S A ONE-WAY TICKET TO NOWHERESVILLE.
AND WHAT ARE YOU, THE *MAYOR* THERE?
WHAT A DOUCHEY BOY!

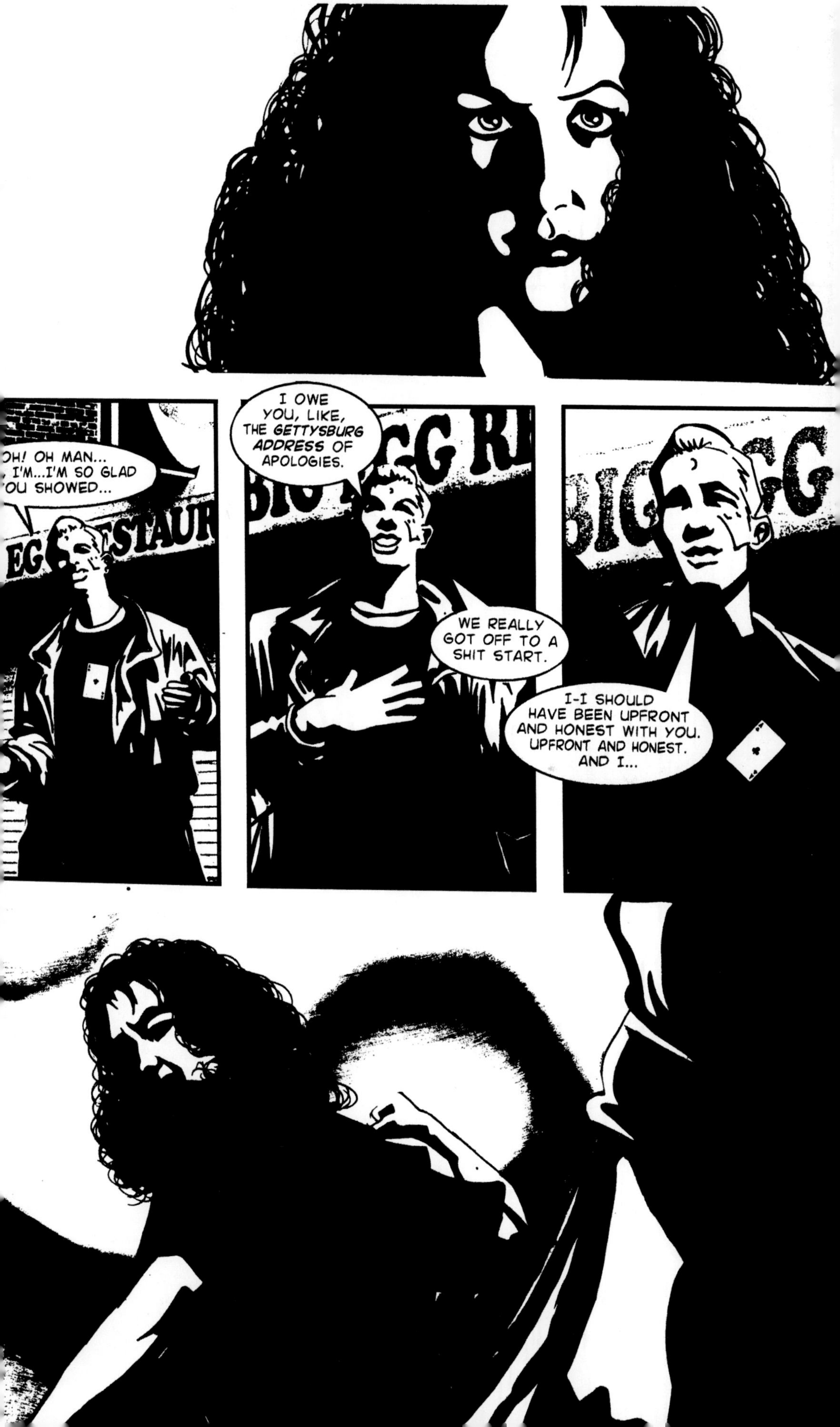
OH! OH MAN...
I'M...I'M SO GLAD
YOU SHOWED...
I OWE YOU, LIKE, THE GETTYSBURG ADDRESS OF APOLOGIES.
WE REALLY GOT OFF TO A SHIT START.
I-I SHOULD HAVE BEEN UPFRONT AND HONEST WITH YOU. UPFRONT AND HONEST. AND I...

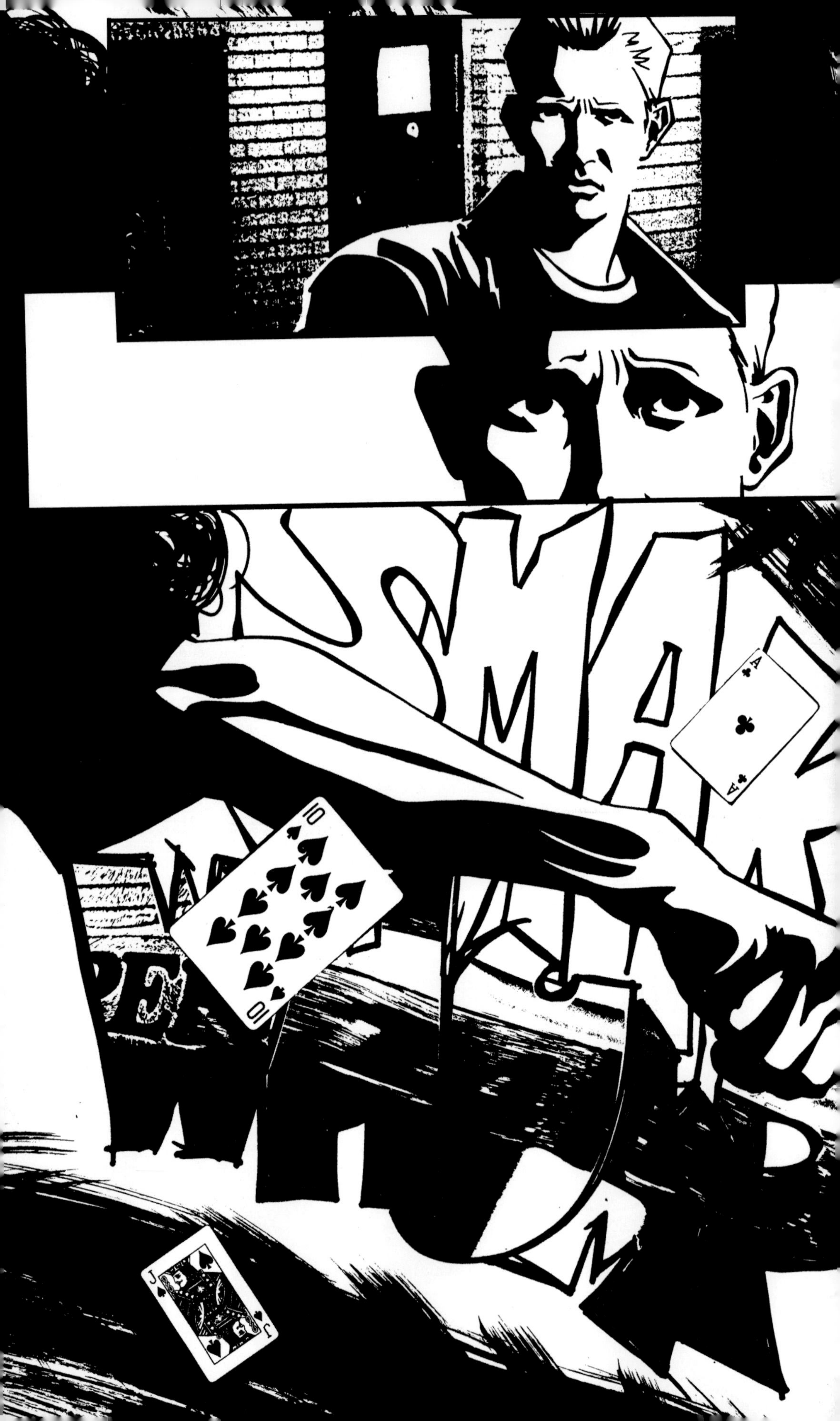

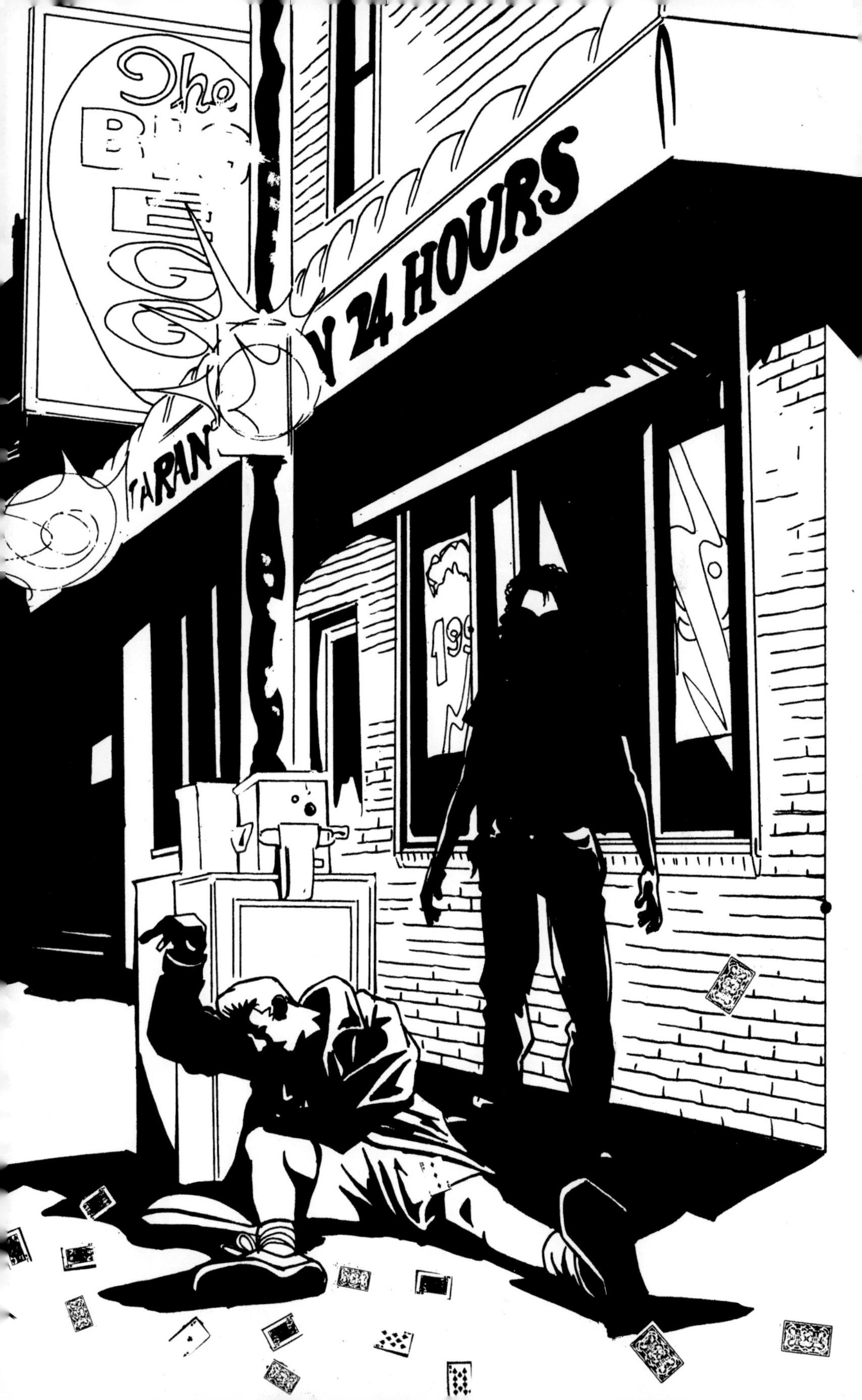

The
Y 24 HOURS
TARAN

EGG RESTAURANT   OPEN 24 HOURS   TAKE OUT

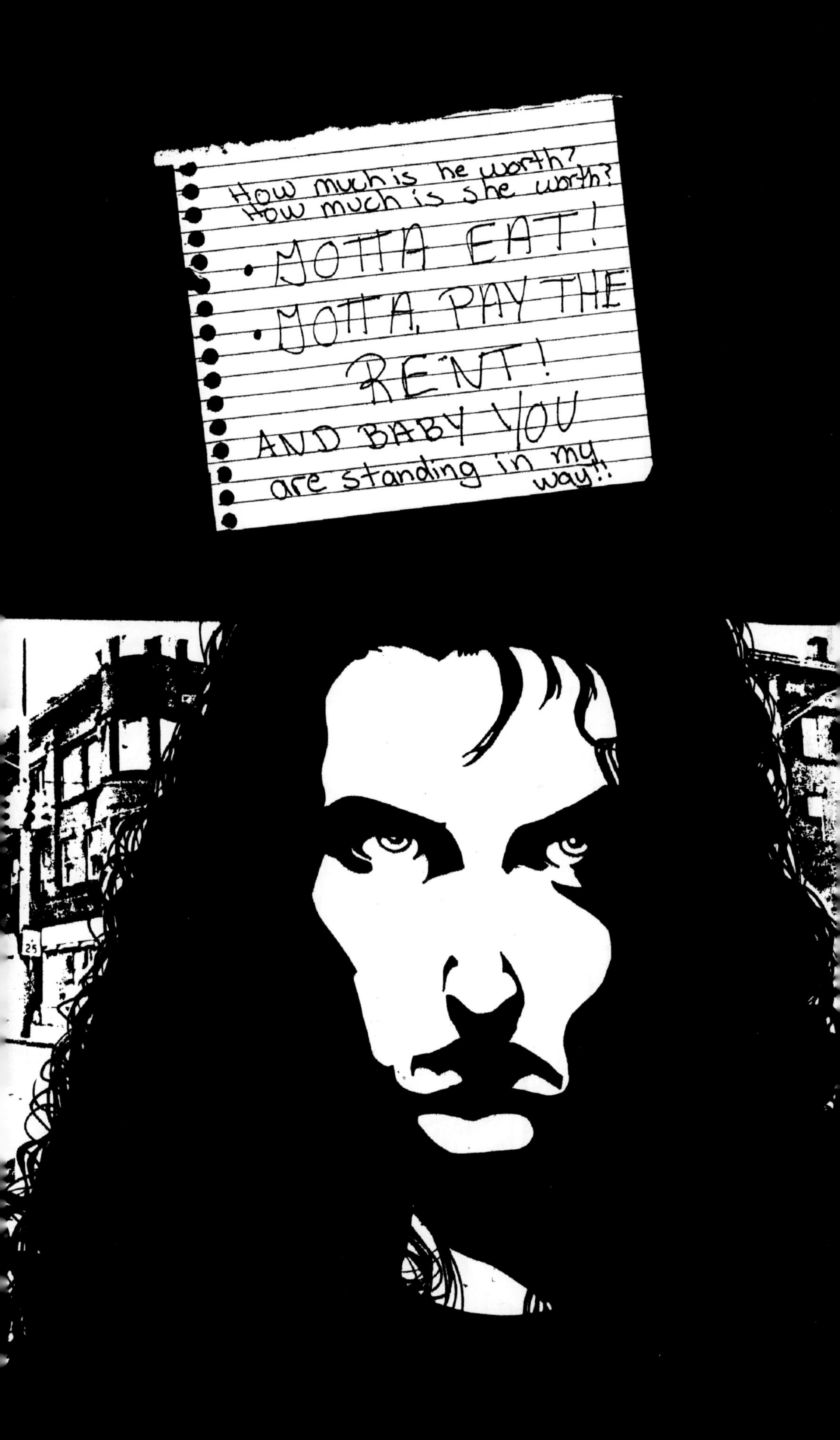
How much is he worth?
How much is she worth?
• GOTTA EAT!
• GOTTA PAY THE RENT!
AND BABY YOU
are standing in my way!!

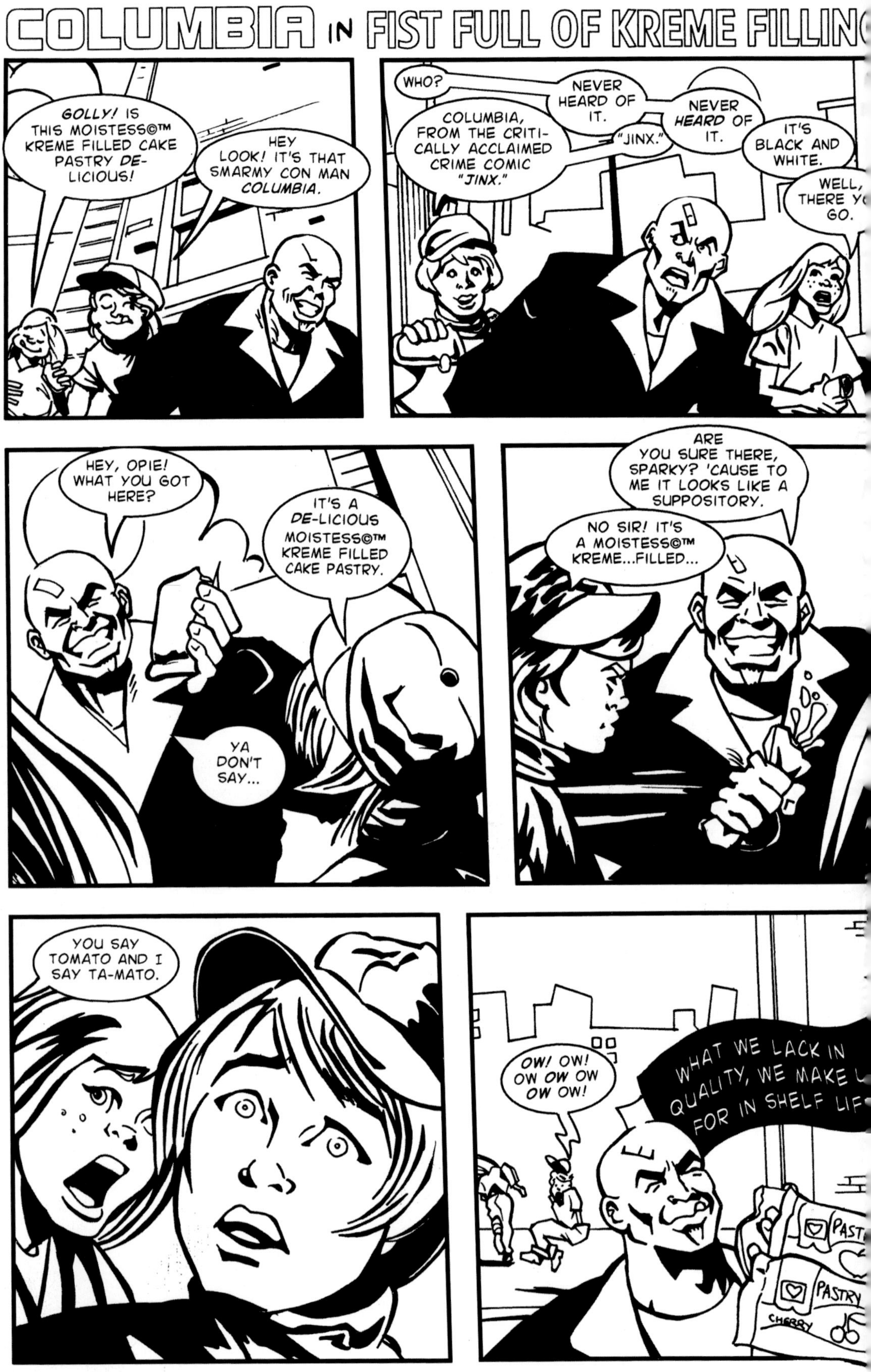
COLUMBIA IN FIST FULL OF KREME FILLING
GOLLY! IS THIS MOISTESS©™ KREME FILLED CAKE PASTRY DE-LICIOUS!
HEY LOOK! IT'S THAT SMARMY CON MAN COLUMBIA.
WHO?
COLUMBIA, FROM THE CRITI-CALLY ACCLAIMED CRIME COMIC "JINX."
NEVER HEARD OF IT.
"JINX."
NEVER HEARD OF IT.
IT'S BLACK AND WHITE.
WELL, THERE YO GO.
HEY, OPIE! WHAT YOU GOT HERE?
IT'S A DE-LICIOUS MOISTESS©™ KREME FILLED CAKE PASTRY.
YA DON'T SAY...
ARE YOU SURE THERE, SPARKY? 'CAUSE TO ME IT LOOKS LIKE A SUPPOSITORY.
NO SIR! IT'S A MOISTESS©™ KREME...FILLED...
YOU SAY TOMATO AND I SAY TA-MATO.
OW! OW! OW OW OW OW OW!
WHAT WE LACK IN QUALITY, WE MAKE U FOR IN SHELF LIF
PASTRY
PASTRY
CHERRY

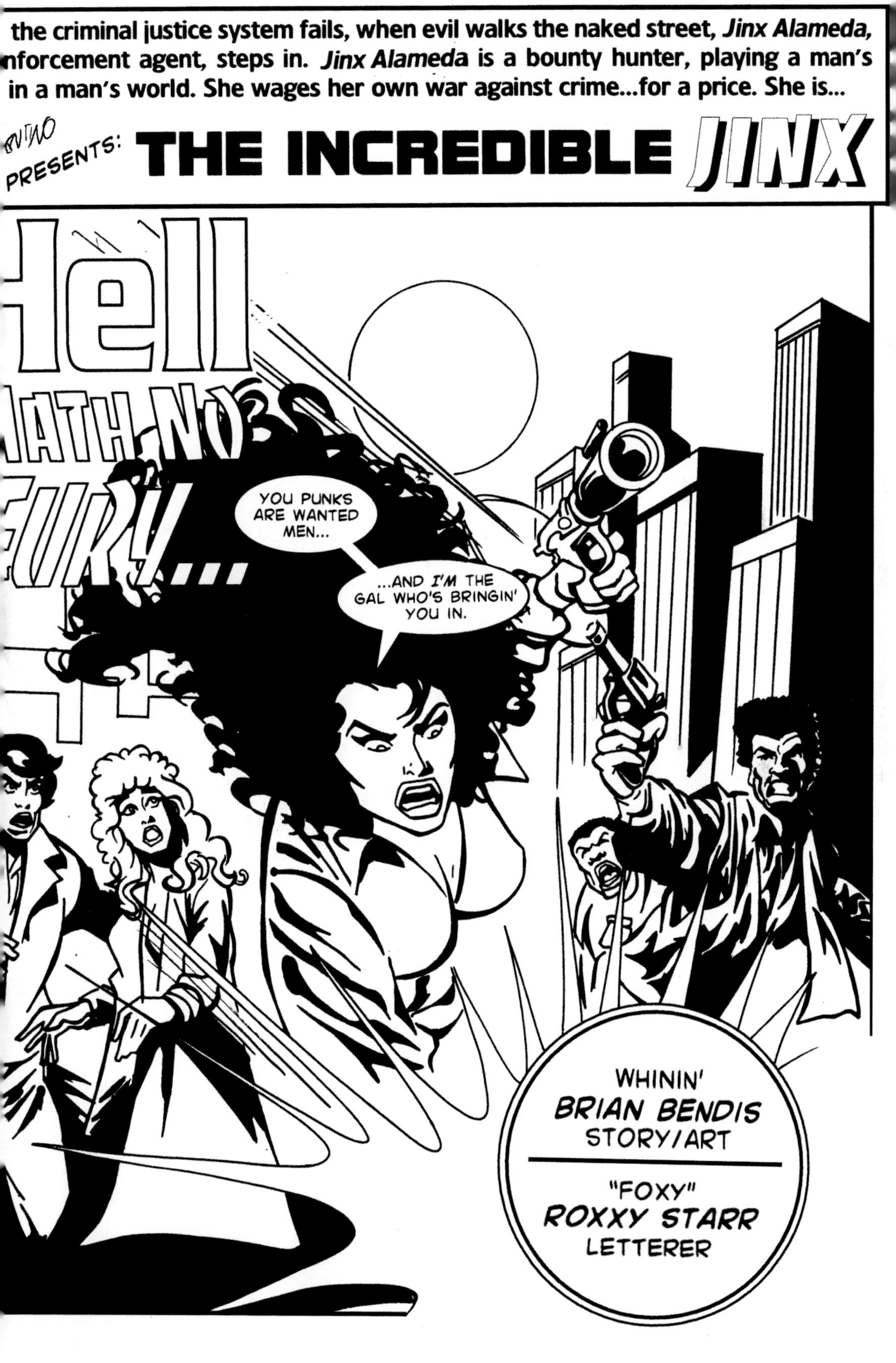
the criminal justice system fails, when evil walks the naked street, Jinx Alameda,
nforcement agent, steps in. Jinx Alameda is a bounty hunter, playing a man's
in a man's world. She wages her own war against crime...for a price. She is...
PRESENTS: THE INCREDIBLE JINX
Hell
YOU PUNKS ARE WANTED MEN...
...AND I'M THE GAL WHO'S BRINGIN' YOU IN.
WHININ' BRIAN BENDIS STORY/ART
"FOXY" ROXXY STARR LETTERER

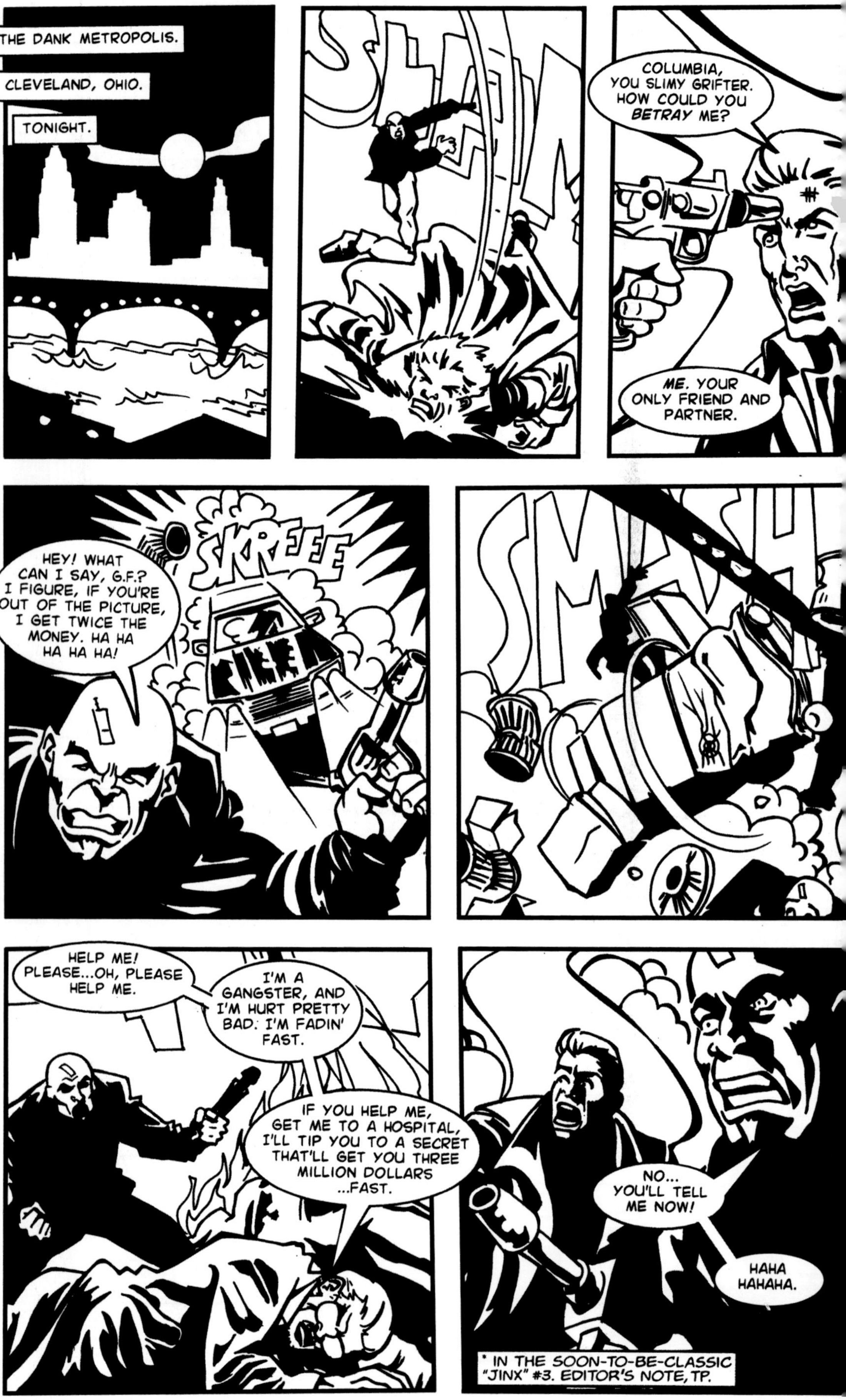
THE DANK METROPOLIS.
CLEVELAND, OHIO.
TONIGHT.
COLUMBIA, YOU SLIMY GRIFTER. HOW COULD YOU BETRAY ME?
ME. YOUR ONLY FRIEND AND PARTNER.
SKREEE
HEY! WHAT CAN I SAY, G.F.? I FIGURE, IF YOU'RE OUT OF THE PICTURE, I GET TWICE THE MONEY. HA HA HA HA HA!
HELP ME! PLEASE...OH, PLEASE HELP ME.
I'M A GANGSTER, AND I'M HURT PRETTY BAD. I'M FADIN' FAST.
IF YOU HELP ME, GET ME TO A HOSPITAL, I'LL TIP YOU TO A SECRET THAT'LL GET YOU THREE MILLION DOLLARS ...FAST.
NO... YOU'LL TELL ME NOW!
HAHA HAHAHA.
* IN THE SOON-TO-BE-CLASSIC "JINX" #3. EDITOR'S NOTE, TP.

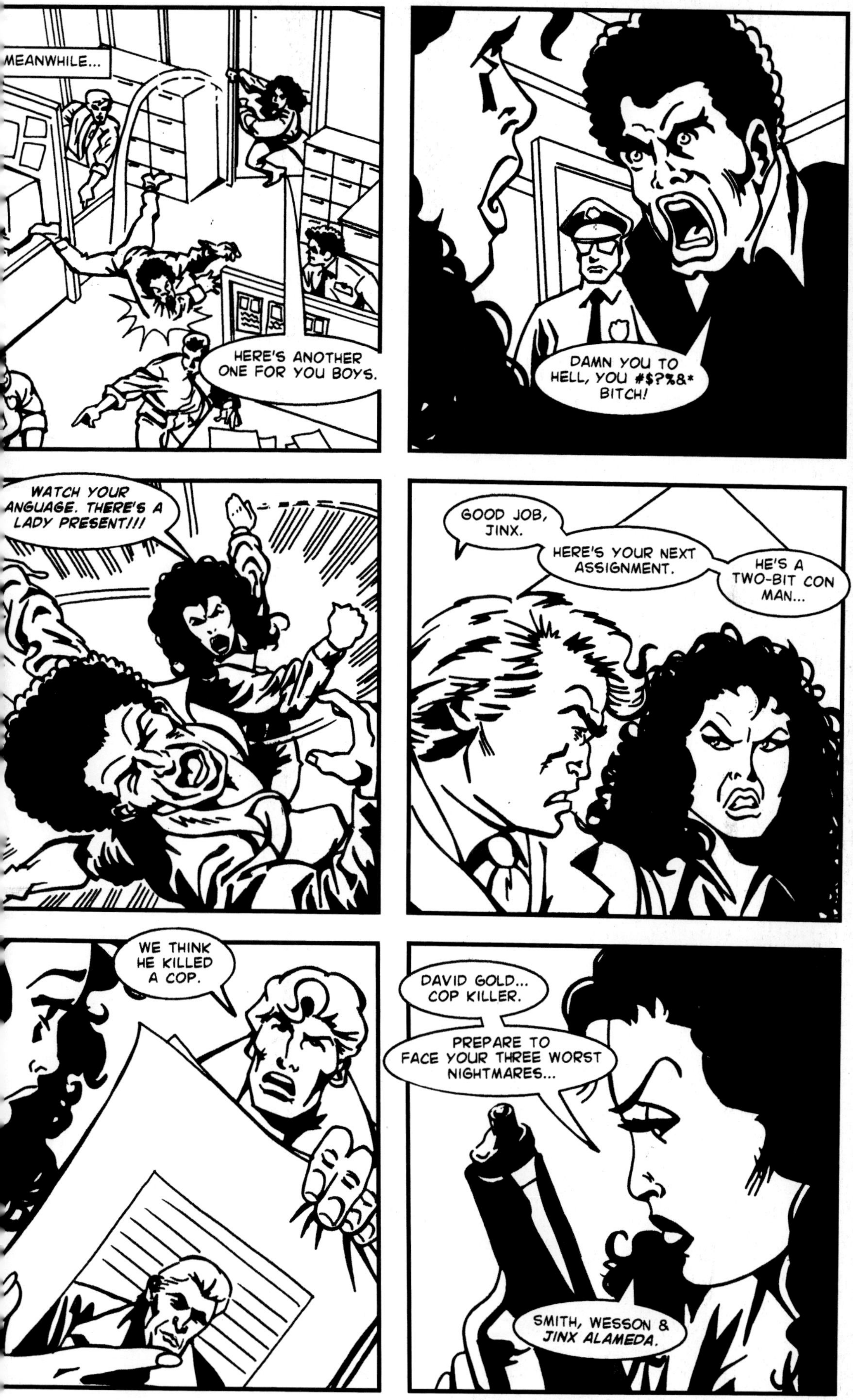
MEANWHILE...
HERE'S ANOTHER ONE FOR YOU BOYS.
DAMN YOU TO HELL, YOU #$?%&* BITCH!
WATCH YOUR LANGUAGE. THERE'S A LADY PRESENT!!!
GOOD JOB, JINX.
HERE'S YOUR NEXT ASSIGNMENT.
HE'S A TWO-BIT CON MAN...
WE THINK HE KILLED A COP.
DAVID GOLD... COP KILLER.
PREPARE TO FACE YOUR THREE WORST NIGHTMARES...
SMITH, WESSON & JINX ALAMEDA.

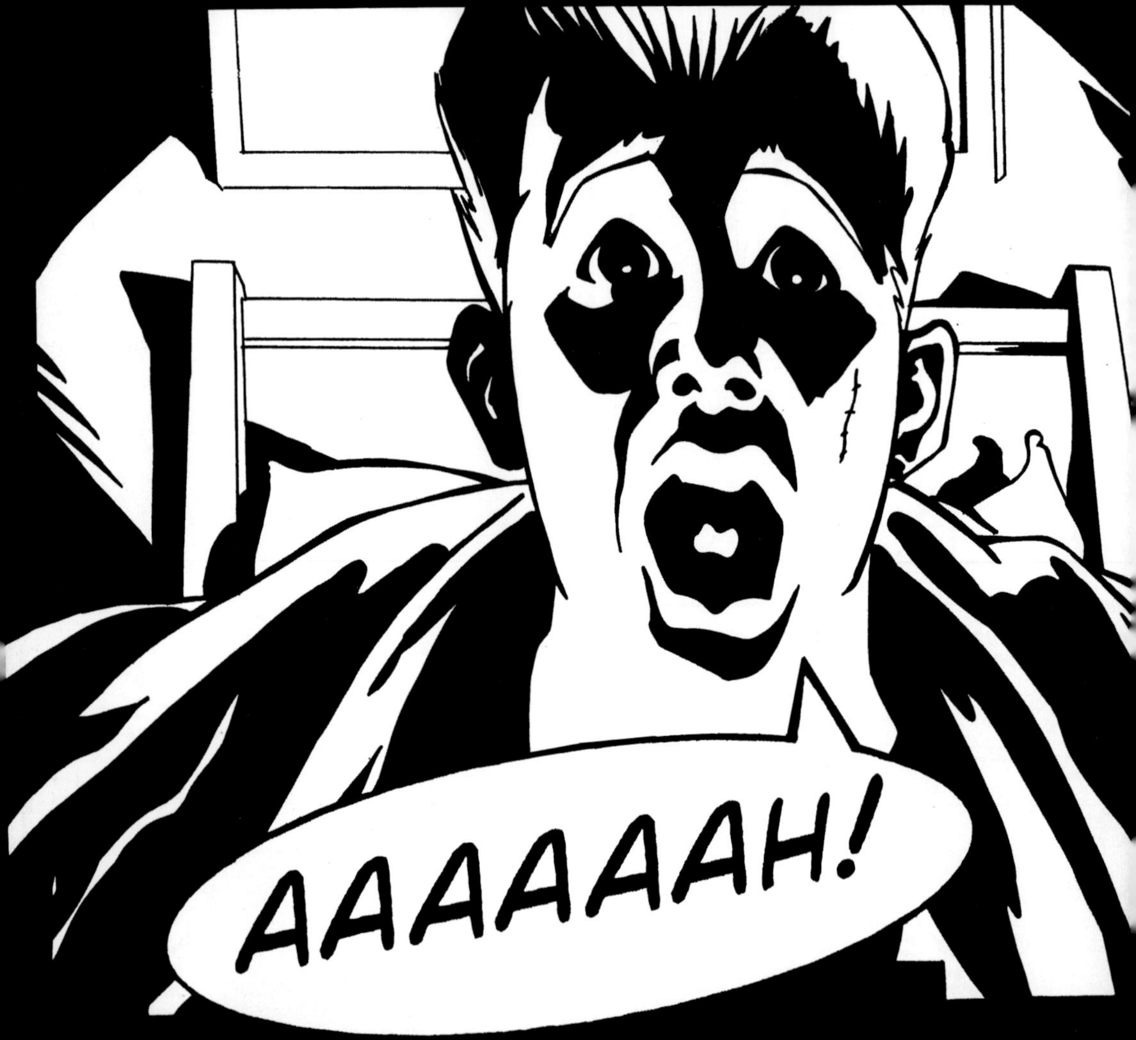
AAAAAAH!

Liar, Liar

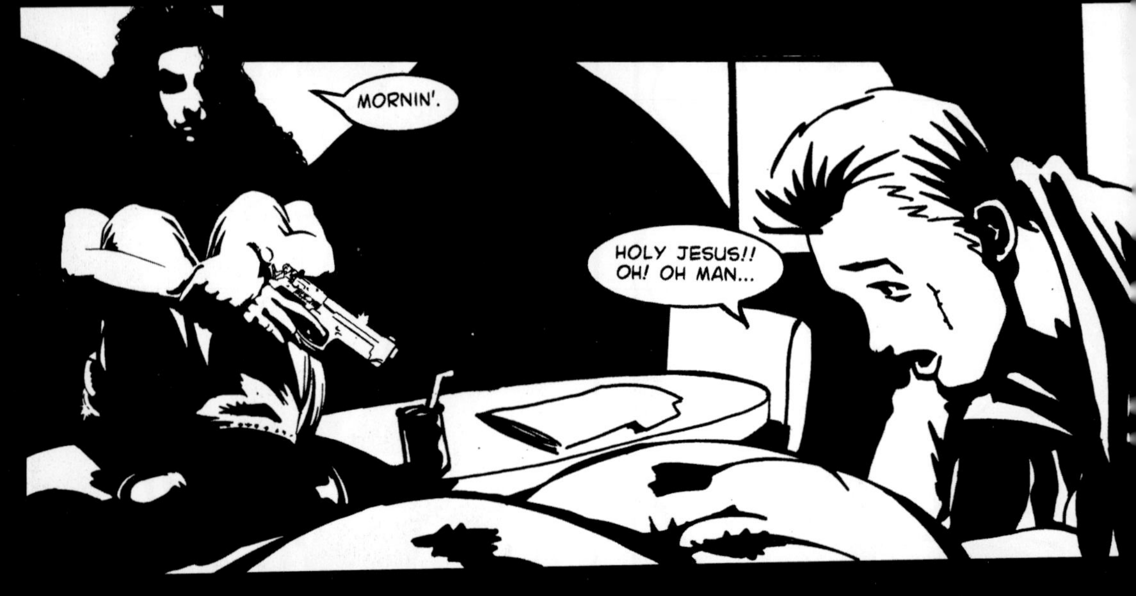
MORNIN'.
HOLY JESUS!! OH! OH MAN...

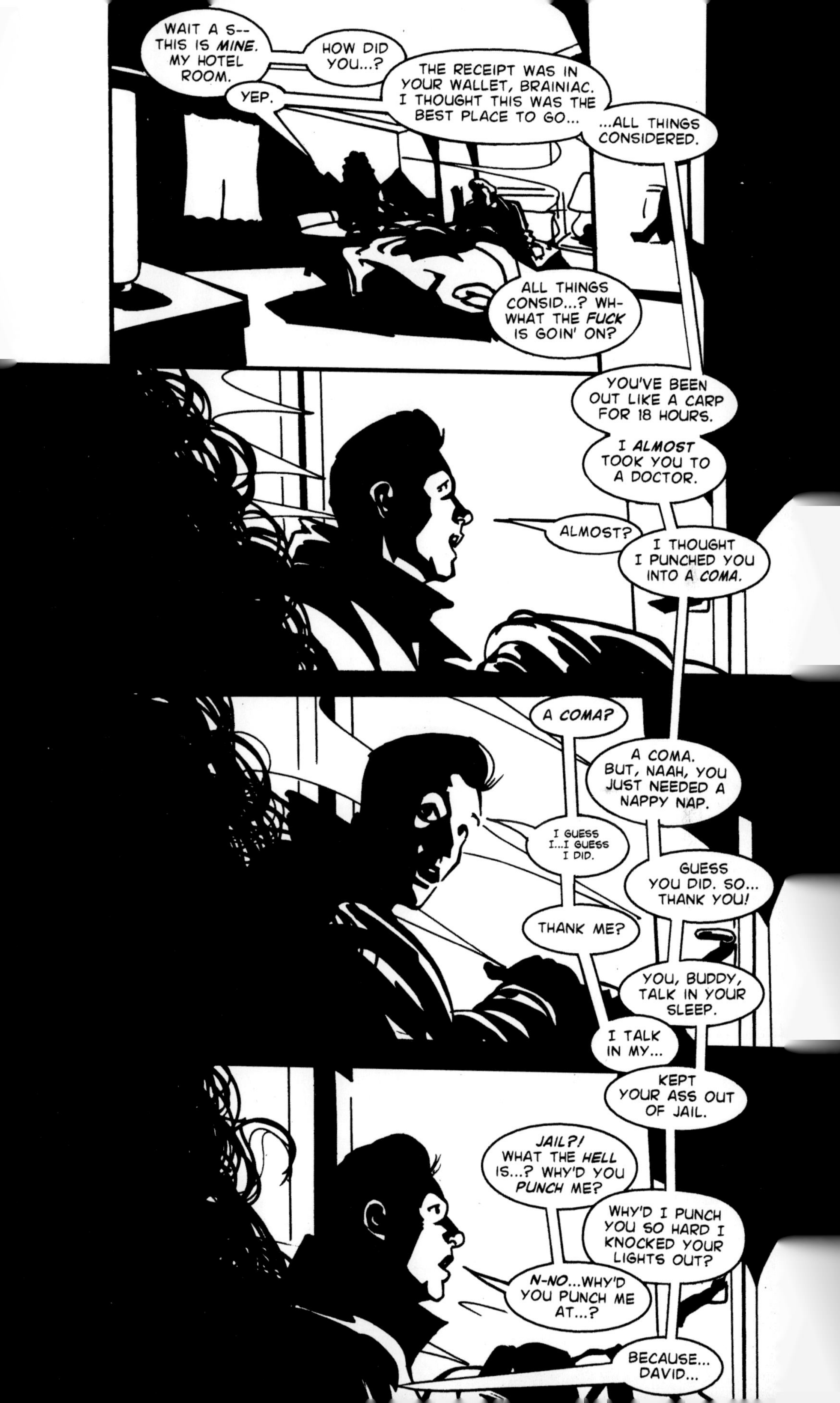
WAIT A S-- THIS IS MINE. MY HOTEL ROOM.
HOW DID YOU...?
YEP.
THE RECEIPT WAS IN YOUR WALLET, BRAINIAC. I THOUGHT THIS WAS THE BEST PLACE TO GO...
...ALL THINGS CONSIDERED.
ALL THINGS CONSID...? WH- WHAT THE FUCK IS GOIN' ON?
YOU'VE BEEN OUT LIKE A CARP FOR 18 HOURS.
I ALMOST TOOK YOU TO A DOCTOR.
ALMOST?
I THOUGHT I PUNCHED YOU INTO A COMA.
A COMA?
A COMA. BUT, NAAH, YOU JUST NEEDED A NAPPY NAP.
I GUESS I...I GUESS I DID.
GUESS YOU DID. SO... THANK YOU!
THANK ME?
YOU, BUDDY, TALK IN YOUR SLEEP.
I TALK IN MY...
KEPT YOUR ASS OUT OF JAIL.
JAIL?! WHAT THE HELL IS...? WHY'D YOU PUNCH ME?
WHY'D I PUNCH YOU SO HARD I KNOCKED YOUR LIGHTS OUT?
N-NO...WHY'D YOU PUNCH ME AT...?
BECAUSE... DAVID...

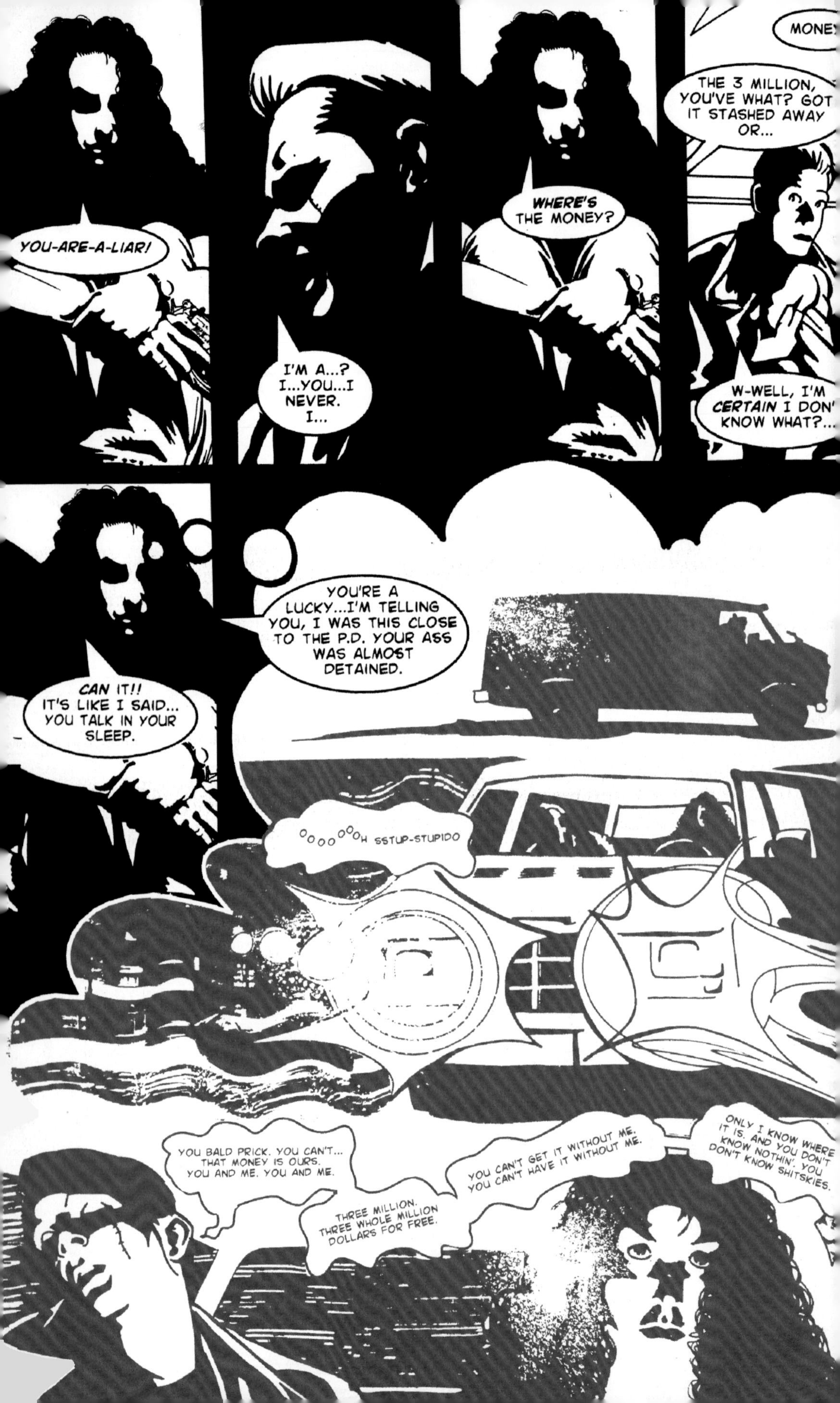

YOU-ARE-A-LIAR!
I'M A...? I...YOU...I NEVER. I...
WHERE'S THE MONEY?
MONEY
THE 3 MILLION, YOU'VE WHAT? GOT IT STASHED AWAY OR...
W-WELL, I'M CERTAIN I DON' KNOW WHAT?...
CAN IT!! IT'S LIKE I SAID... YOU TALK IN YOUR SLEEP.
YOU'RE A LUCKY...I'M TELLING YOU, I WAS THIS CLOSE TO THE P.D. YOUR ASS WAS ALMOST DETAINED.
OOOOOOH SSTUP-STUPIDO
YOU BALD PRICK. YOU CAN'T... THAT MONEY IS OURS. YOU AND ME. YOU AND ME.
THREE MILLION. THREE WHOLE MILLION DOLLARS FOR FREE.
YOU CAN'T GET IT WITHOUT ME. YOU CAN'T HAVE IT WITHOUT ME.
ONLY I KNOW WHERE IT IS. AND YOU DON'T KNOW NOTHIN'. YOU DON'T KNOW SHITSKIES.

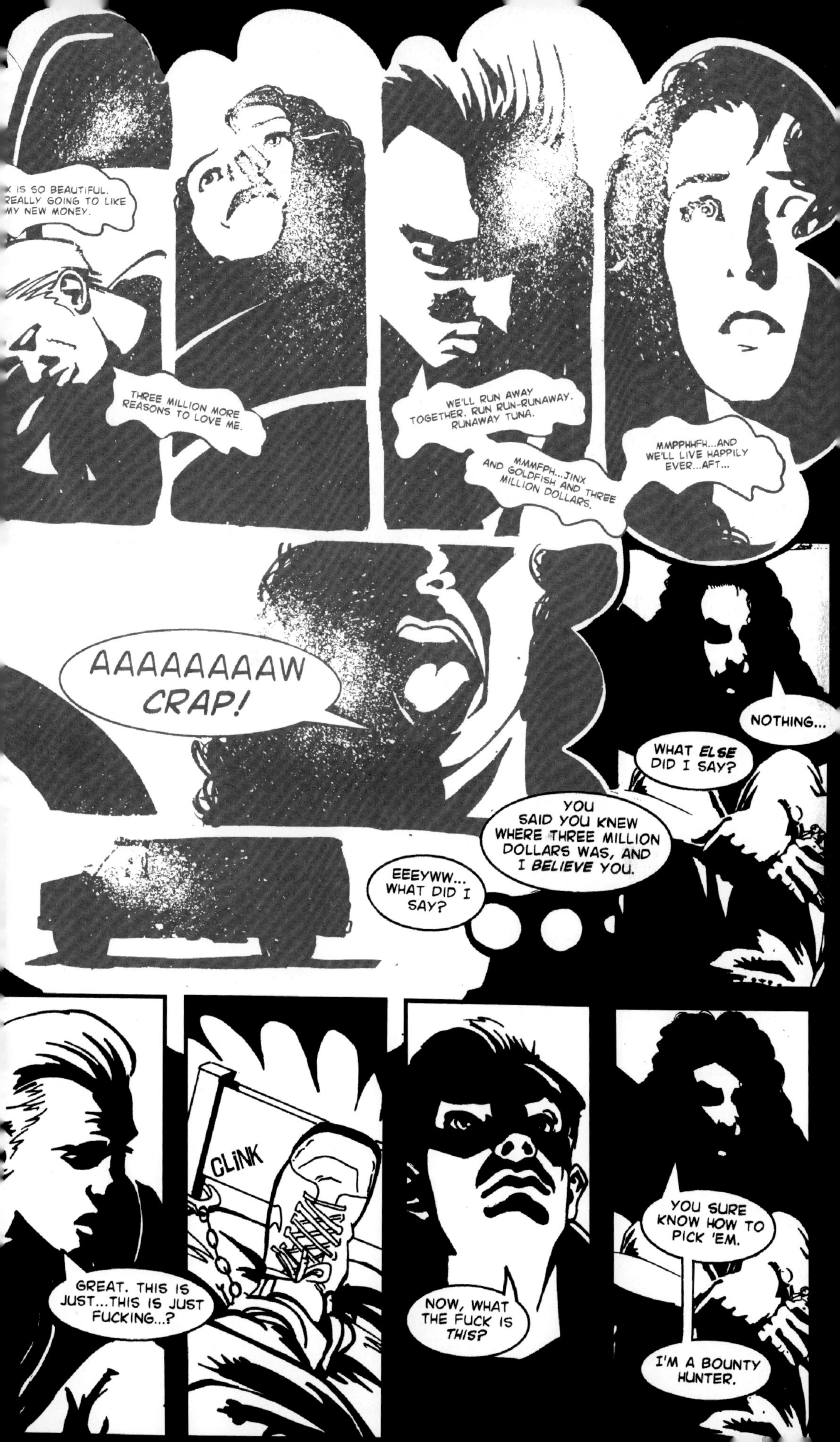

X IS SO BEAUTIFUL. REALLY GOING TO LIKE MY NEW MONEY.
THREE MILLION MORE REASONS TO LOVE ME.
WE'LL RUN AWAY TOGETHER. RUN RUN-RUNAWAY. RUNAWAY TUNA.
MMMFPH...JINX AND GOLDFISH AND THREE MILLION DOLLARS.
MMPPHHFH...AND WE'LL LIVE HAPPILY EVER...AFT...
AAAAAAAAW CRAP!
NOTHING...
WHAT ELSE DID I SAY?
YOU SAID YOU KNEW WHERE THREE MILLION DOLLARS WAS, AND I BELIEVE YOU.
EEEYWW... WHAT DID I SAY?
GREAT. THIS IS JUST...THIS IS JUST FUCKING...?
CLINK
NOW, WHAT THE FUCK IS THIS?
YOU SURE KNOW HOW TO PICK 'EM.
I'M A BOUNTY HUNTER.

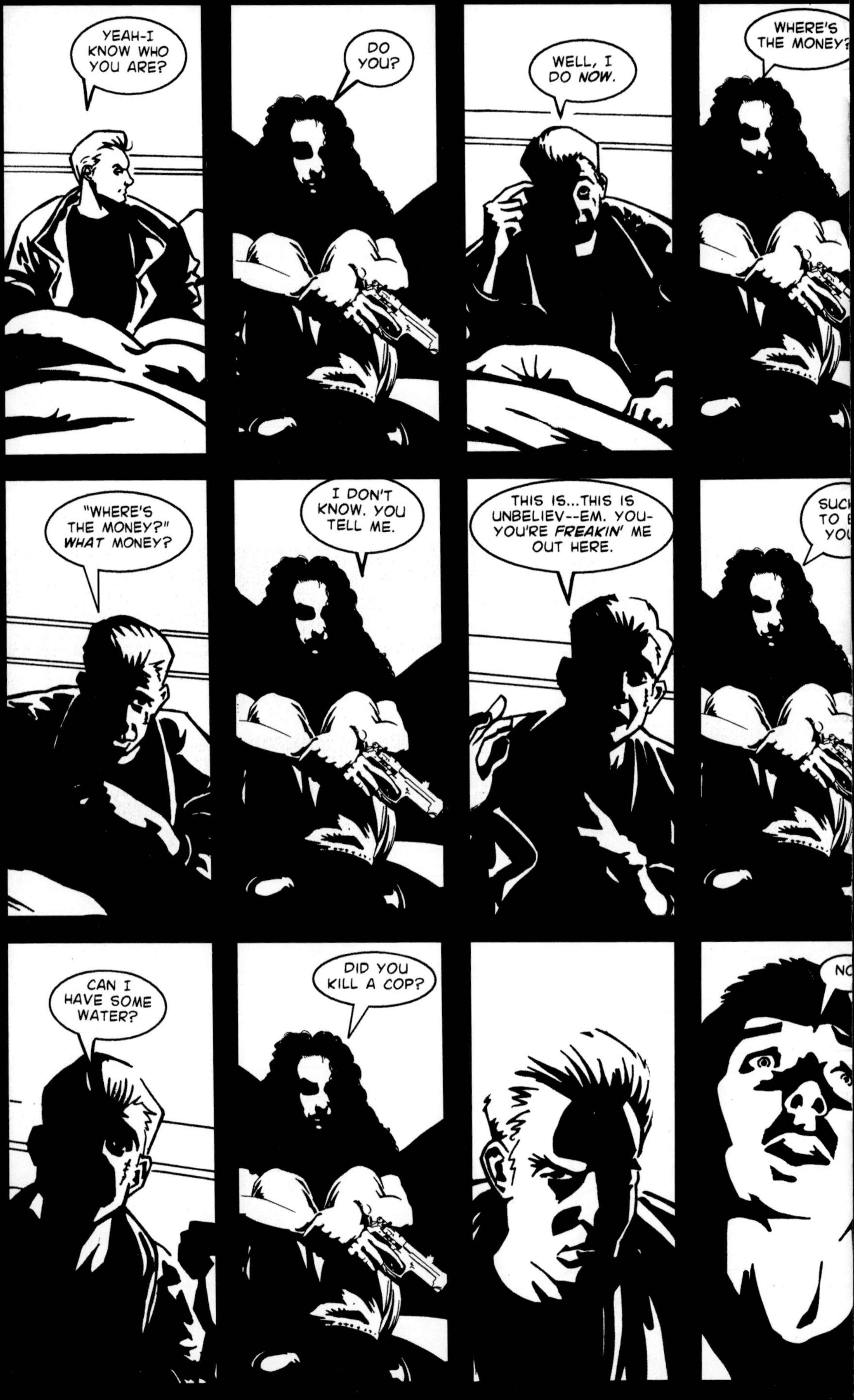
YEAH-I KNOW WHO YOU ARE?
DO YOU?
WELL, I DO *NOW*.
WHERE'S THE MONEY?
"WHERE'S THE MONEY?" *WHAT* MONEY?
I DON'T KNOW. *YOU* TELL ME.
THIS IS...THIS IS UNBELIEV--EM. YOU-YOU'RE *FREAKIN'* ME OUT HERE.
CAN I HAVE SOME WATER?
DID YOU KILL A COP?

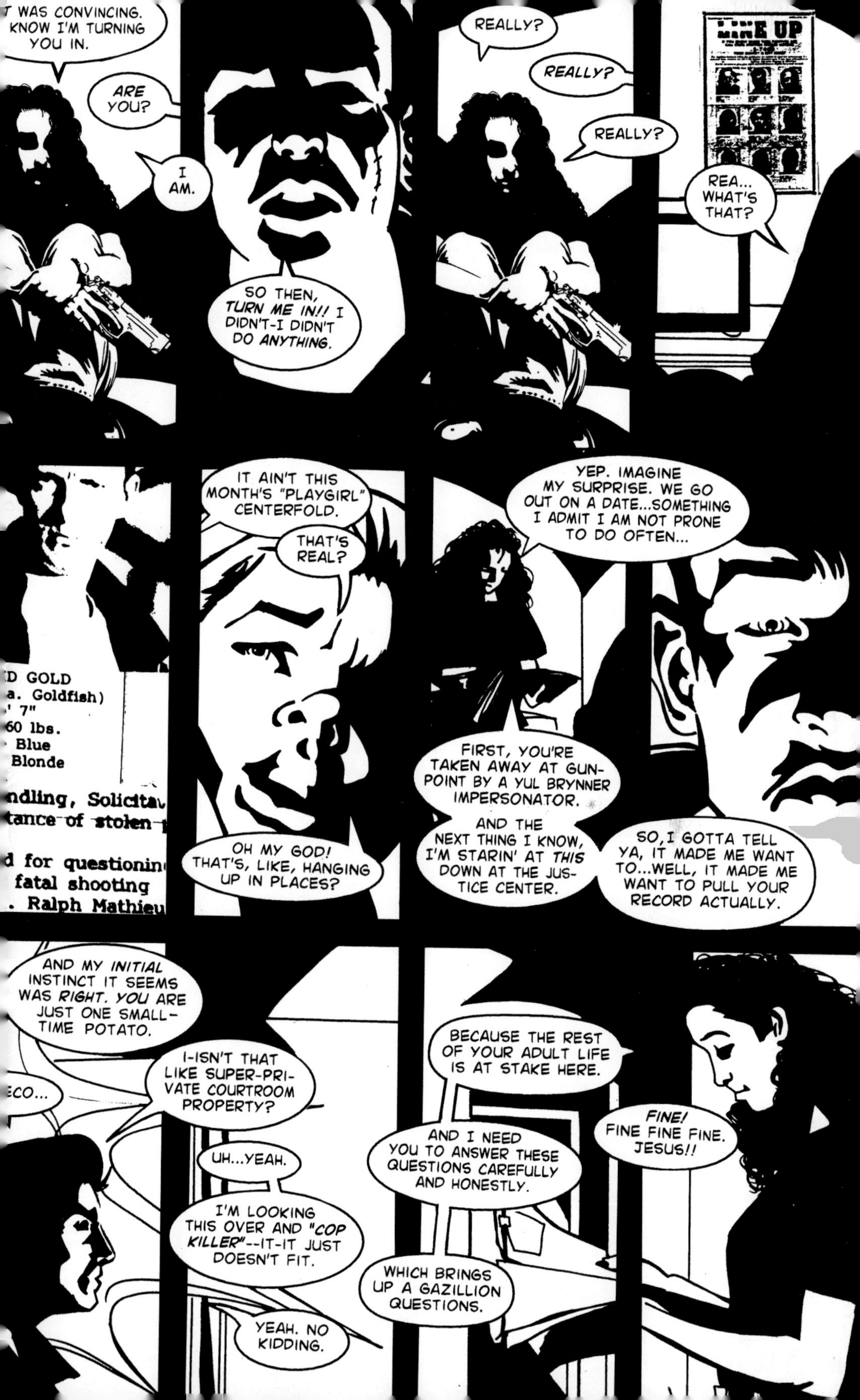
T WAS CONVINCING. KNOW I'M TURNING YOU IN.
ARE YOU?
I AM.
SO THEN, TURN ME IN!! I DIDN'T-I DIDN'T DO ANYTHING.
REALLY?
REALLY?
REALLY?
REA... WHAT'S THAT?
LINE UP
D GOLD
a. Goldfish)
' 7"
60 lbs.
Blue
Blonde
ndling, Solicita
tance of stolen
d for questionin
fatal shooting
. Ralph Mathieu
IT AIN'T THIS MONTH'S "PLAYGIRL" CENTERFOLD.
THAT'S REAL?
OH MY GOD! THAT'S, LIKE, HANGING UP IN PLACES?
YEP. IMAGINE MY SURPRISE. WE GO OUT ON A DATE...SOMETHING I ADMIT I AM NOT PRONE TO DO OFTEN...
FIRST, YOU'RE TAKEN AWAY AT GUN-POINT BY A YUL BRYNNER IMPERSONATOR.
AND THE NEXT THING I KNOW, I'M STARIN' AT THIS DOWN AT THE JUS-TICE CENTER.
SO, I GOTTA TELL YA, IT MADE ME WANT TO...WELL, IT MADE ME WANT TO PULL YOUR RECORD ACTUALLY.
AND MY INITIAL INSTINCT IT SEEMS WAS RIGHT. YOU ARE JUST ONE SMALL-TIME POTATO.
ECO...
I-ISN'T THAT LIKE SUPER-PRI-VATE COURTROOM PROPERTY?
UH...YEAH.
I'M LOOKING THIS OVER AND "COP KILLER"--IT-IT JUST DOESN'T FIT.
YEAH. NO KIDDING.
BECAUSE THE REST OF YOUR ADULT LIFE IS AT STAKE HERE.
AND I NEED YOU TO ANSWER THESE QUESTIONS CAREFULLY AND HONESTLY.
WHICH BRINGS UP A GAZILLION QUESTIONS.
FINE! FINE FINE FINE. JESUS!!

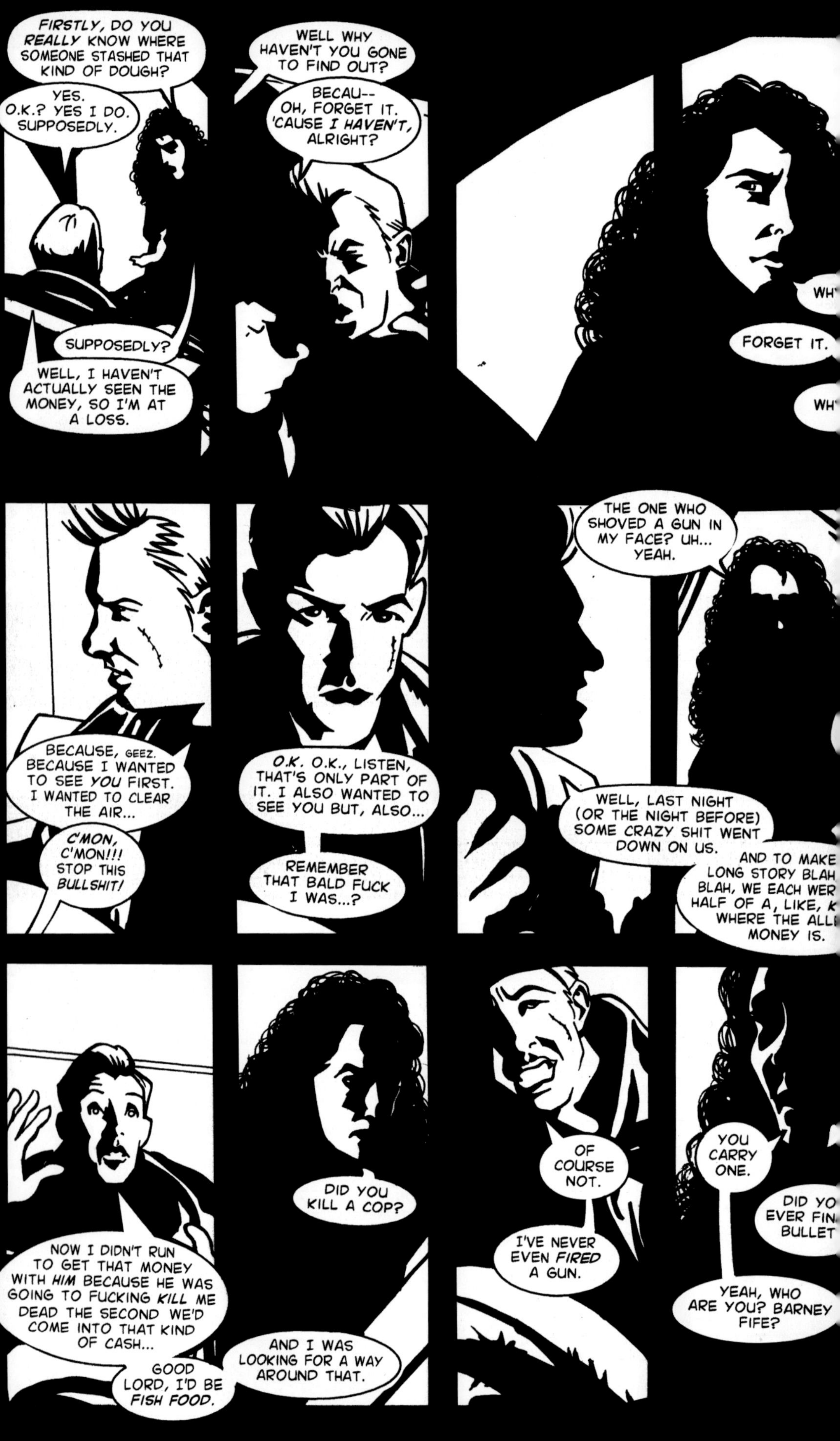
FIRSTLY, DO YOU REALLY KNOW WHERE SOMEONE STASHED THAT KIND OF DOUGH?
YES. O.K.? YES I DO. SUPPOSEDLY.
SUPPOSEDLY?
WELL, I HAVEN'T ACTUALLY SEEN THE MONEY, SO I'M AT A LOSS.
WELL WHY HAVEN'T YOU GONE TO FIND OUT?
BECAU-- OH, FORGET IT. 'CAUSE I HAVEN'T, ALRIGHT?
FORGET IT.
BECAUSE, GEEZ. BECAUSE I WANTED TO SEE YOU FIRST. I WANTED TO CLEAR THE AIR...
C'MON, C'MON!!! STOP THIS BULLSHIT!
O.K. O.K., LISTEN, THAT'S ONLY PART OF IT. I ALSO WANTED TO SEE YOU BUT, ALSO...
REMEMBER THAT BALD FUCK I WAS...?
THE ONE WHO SHOVED A GUN IN MY FACE? UH... YEAH.
WELL, LAST NIGHT (OR THE NIGHT BEFORE) SOME CRAZY SHIT WENT DOWN ON US.
NOW I DIDN'T RUN TO GET THAT MONEY WITH HIM BECAUSE HE WAS GOING TO FUCKING KILL ME DEAD THE SECOND WE'D COME INTO THAT KIND OF CASH...
GOOD LORD, I'D BE FISH FOOD.
AND I WAS LOOKING FOR A WAY AROUND THAT.
DID YOU KILL A COP?
OF COURSE NOT.
I'VE NEVER EVEN FIRED A GUN.
YOU CARRY ONE.
YEAH, WHO ARE YOU? BARNEY FIFE?

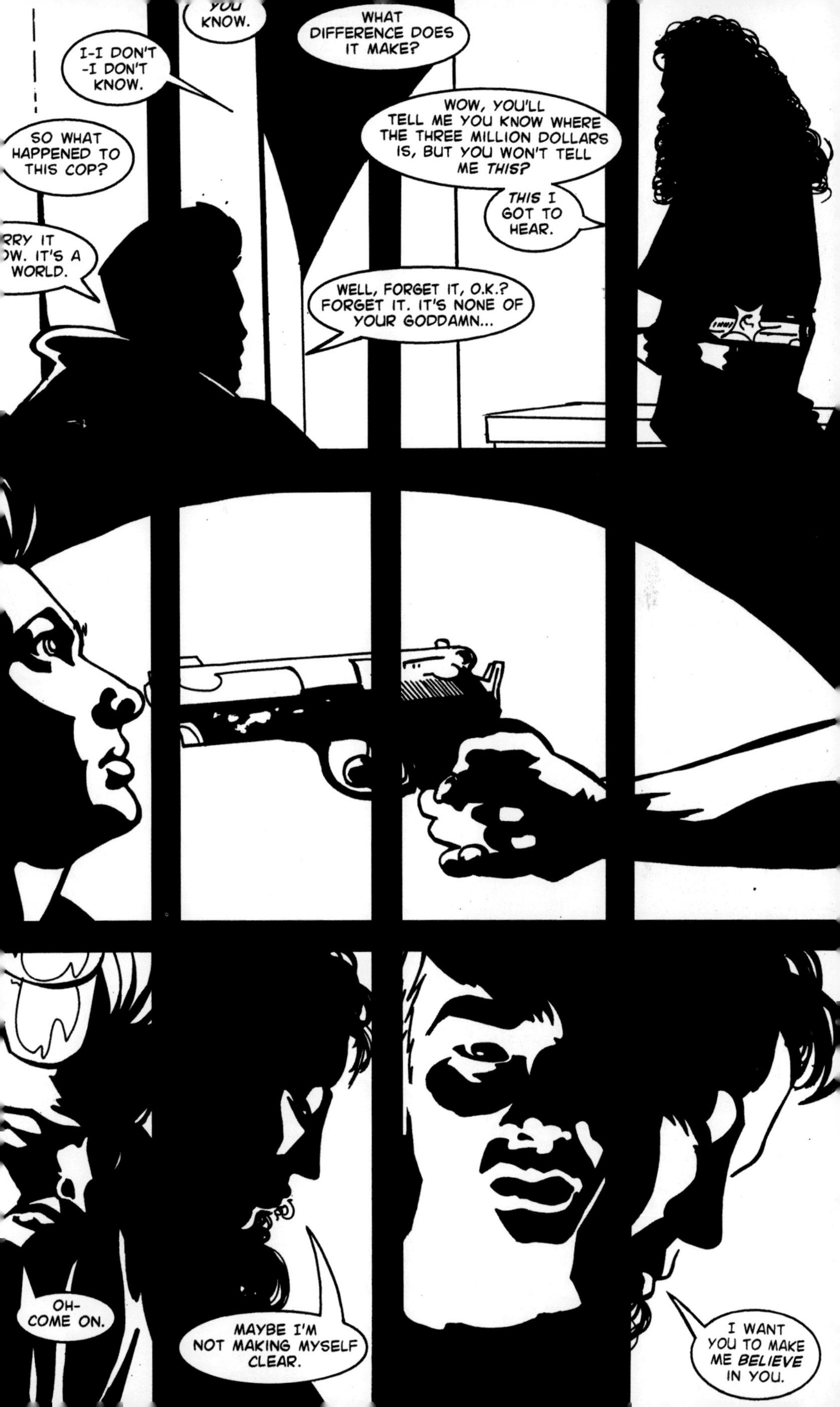

YOU KNOW.
WHAT DIFFERENCE DOES IT MAKE?
I-I DON'T -I DON'T KNOW.
SO WHAT HAPPENED TO THIS COP?
WOW, YOU'LL TELL ME YOU KNOW WHERE THE THREE MILLION DOLLARS IS, BUT YOU WON'T TELL ME THIS?
THIS I GOT TO HEAR.
RRY IT OW. IT'S A WORLD.
WELL, FORGET IT, O.K.? FORGET IT. IT'S NONE OF YOUR GODDAMN...
OH- COME ON.
MAYBE I'M NOT MAKING MYSELF CLEAR.
I WANT YOU TO MAKE ME BELIEVE IN YOU.

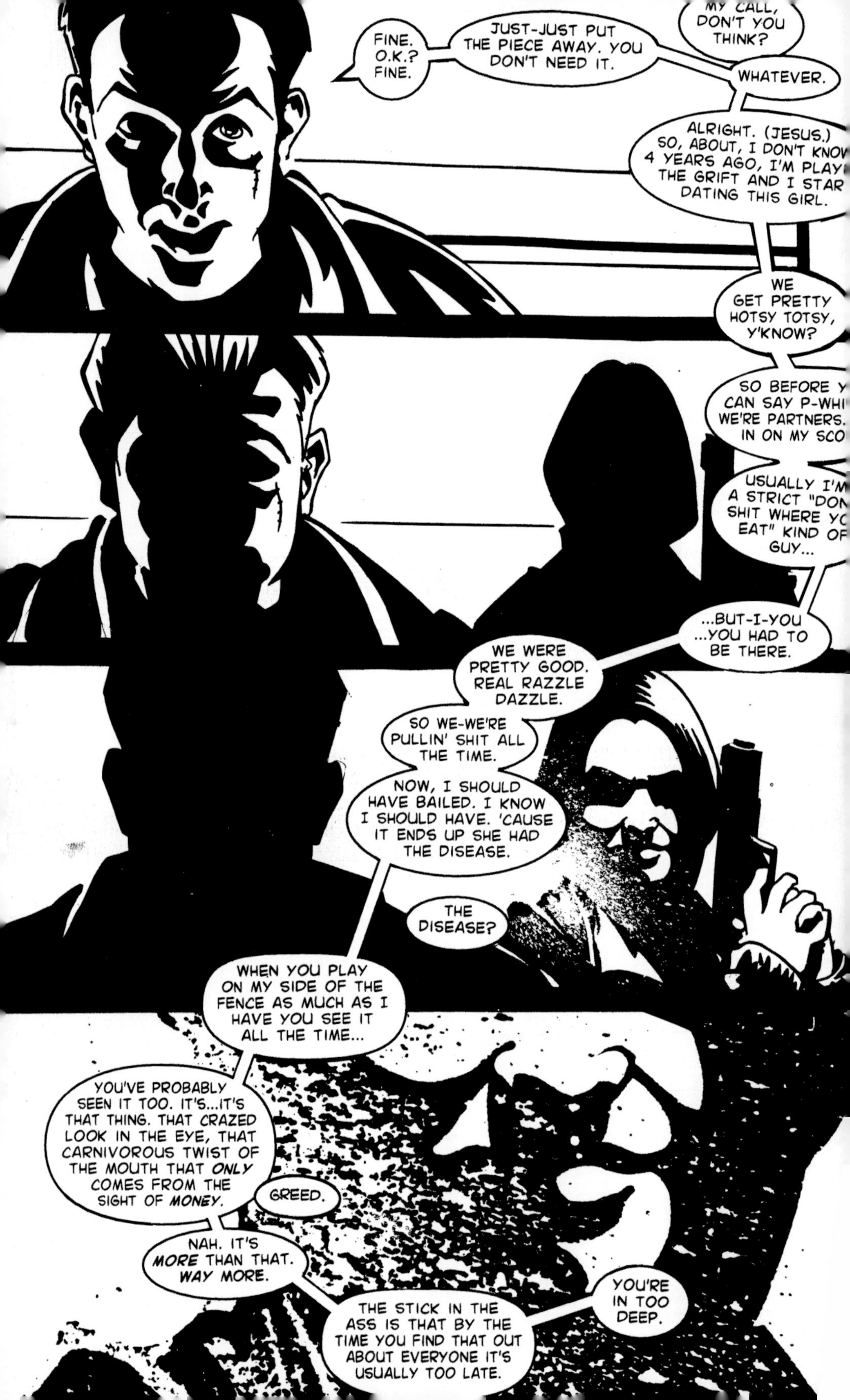

MY CALL, DON'T YOU THINK?
JUST-JUST PUT THE PIECE AWAY. YOU DON'T NEED IT.
FINE. O.K.? FINE.
WHATEVER.
ALRIGHT. (JESUS.) SO, ABOUT, I DON'T KNOW 4 YEARS AGO, I'M PLAY THE GRIFT AND I STAR DATING THIS GIRL.
WE GET PRETTY HOTSY TOTSY, Y'KNOW?
SO BEFORE Y CAN SAY P-WH WE'RE PARTNERS. IN ON MY SCO
USUALLY I'M A STRICT "DON SHIT WHERE YO EAT" KIND OF GUY...
...BUT-I-YOU ...YOU HAD TO BE THERE.
WE WERE PRETTY GOOD. REAL RAZZLE DAZZLE.
SO WE-WE'RE PULLIN' SHIT ALL THE TIME.
NOW, I SHOULD HAVE BAILED. I KNOW I SHOULD HAVE. 'CAUSE IT ENDS UP SHE HAD THE DISEASE.
THE DISEASE?
WHEN YOU PLAY ON MY SIDE OF THE FENCE AS MUCH AS I HAVE YOU SEE IT ALL THE TIME...
YOU'VE PROBABLY SEEN IT TOO. IT'S...IT'S THAT THING. THAT CRAZED LOOK IN THE EYE, THAT CARNIVOROUS TWIST OF THE MOUTH THAT *ONLY* COMES FROM THE SIGHT OF *MONEY*.
GREED.
NAH. IT'S *MORE* THAN THAT. *WAY MORE*.
THE STICK IN THE ASS IS THAT BY THE TIME YOU FIND THAT OUT ABOUT EVERYONE IT'S USUALLY TOO LATE.
YOU'RE IN TOO DEEP.

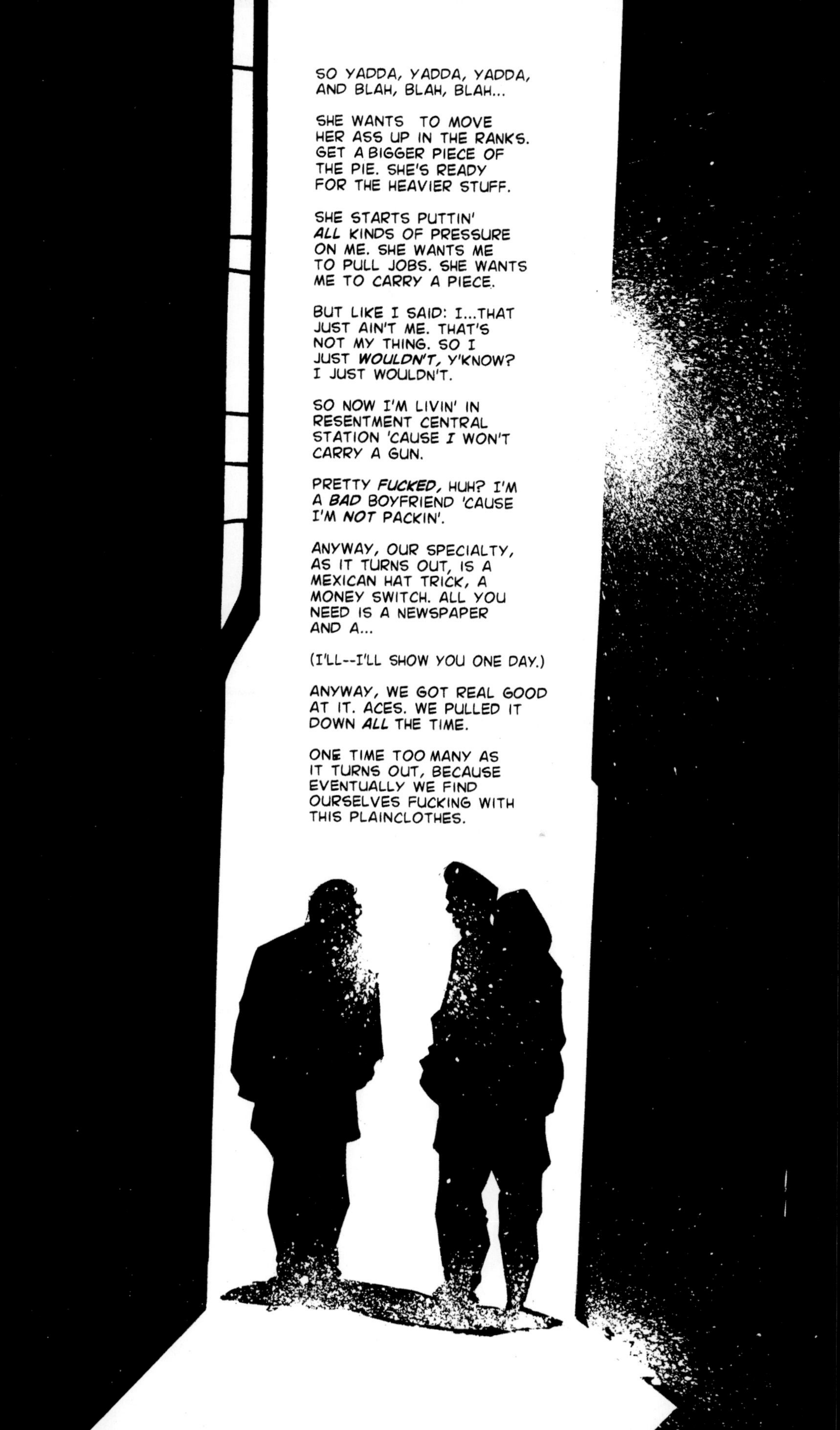
SO YADDA, YADDA, YADDA, AND BLAH, BLAH, BLAH...
SHE WANTS TO MOVE HER ASS UP IN THE RANKS. GET A BIGGER PIECE OF THE PIE. SHE'S READY FOR THE HEAVIER STUFF.
SHE STARTS PUTTIN' ALL KINDS OF PRESSURE ON ME. SHE WANTS ME TO PULL JOBS. SHE WANTS ME TO CARRY A PIECE.
BUT LIKE I SAID: I...THAT JUST AIN'T ME. THAT'S NOT MY THING. SO I JUST WOULDN'T, Y'KNOW? I JUST WOULDN'T.
SO NOW I'M LIVIN' IN RESENTMENT CENTRAL STATION 'CAUSE I WON'T CARRY A GUN.
PRETTY FUCKED, HUH? I'M A BAD BOYFRIEND 'CAUSE I'M NOT PACKIN'.
ANYWAY, OUR SPECIALTY, AS IT TURNS OUT, IS A MEXICAN HAT TRICK, A MONEY SWITCH. ALL YOU NEED IS A NEWSPAPER AND A...
(I'LL--I'LL SHOW YOU ONE DAY.)
ANYWAY, WE GOT REAL GOOD AT IT. ACES. WE PULLED IT DOWN ALL THE TIME.
ONE TIME TOO MANY AS IT TURNS OUT, BECAUSE EVENTUALLY WE FIND OURSELVES FUCKING WITH THIS PLAINCLOTHES.

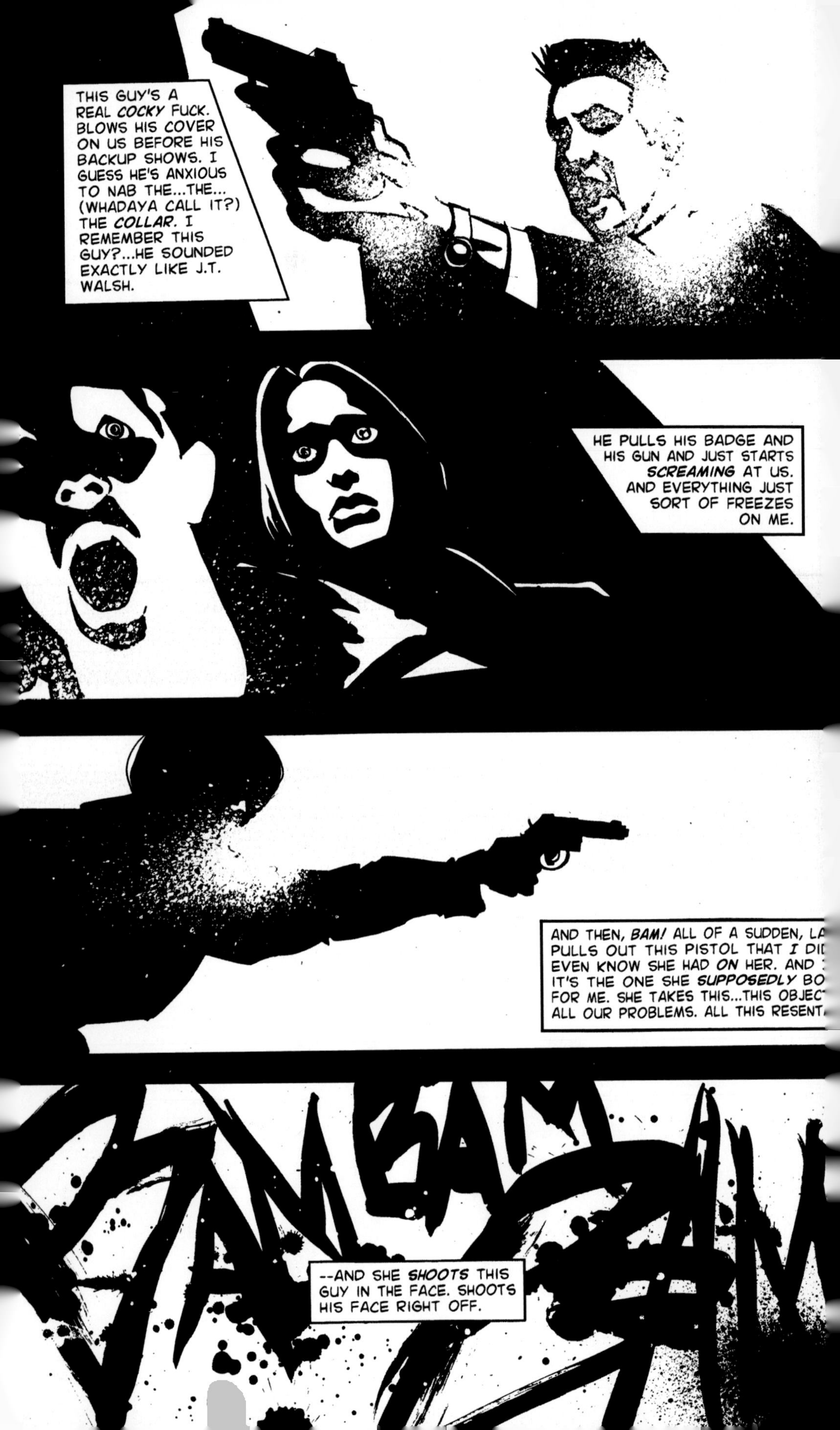
THIS GUY'S A REAL COCKY FUCK. BLOWS HIS COVER ON US BEFORE HIS BACKUP SHOWS. I GUESS HE'S ANXIOUS TO NAB THE...THE... (WHADAYA CALL IT?) THE COLLAR. I REMEMBER THIS GUY?...HE SOUNDED EXACTLY LIKE J.T. WALSH.
HE PULLS HIS BADGE AND HIS GUN AND JUST STARTS SCREAMING AT US. AND EVERYTHING JUST SORT OF FREEZES ON ME.
AND THEN, BAM! ALL OF A SUDDEN, PULLS OUT THIS PISTOL THAT I EVEN KNOW SHE HAD ON HER. AND IT'S THE ONE SHE SUPPOSEDLY FOR ME. SHE TAKES THIS...THIS ALL OUR PROBLEMS. ALL THIS
--AND SHE SHOOTS THIS GUY IN THE FACE. SHOOTS HIS FACE RIGHT OFF.

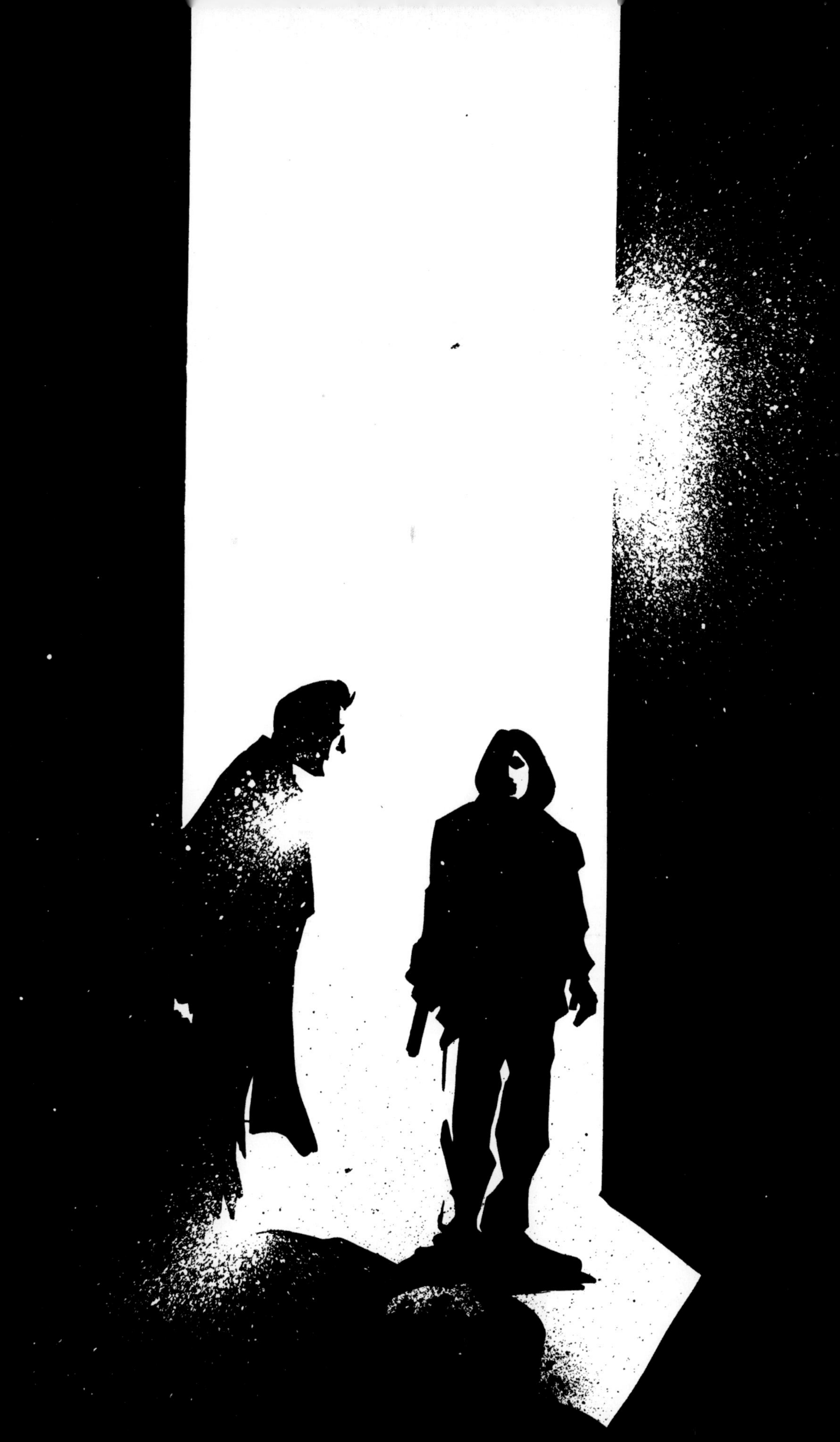

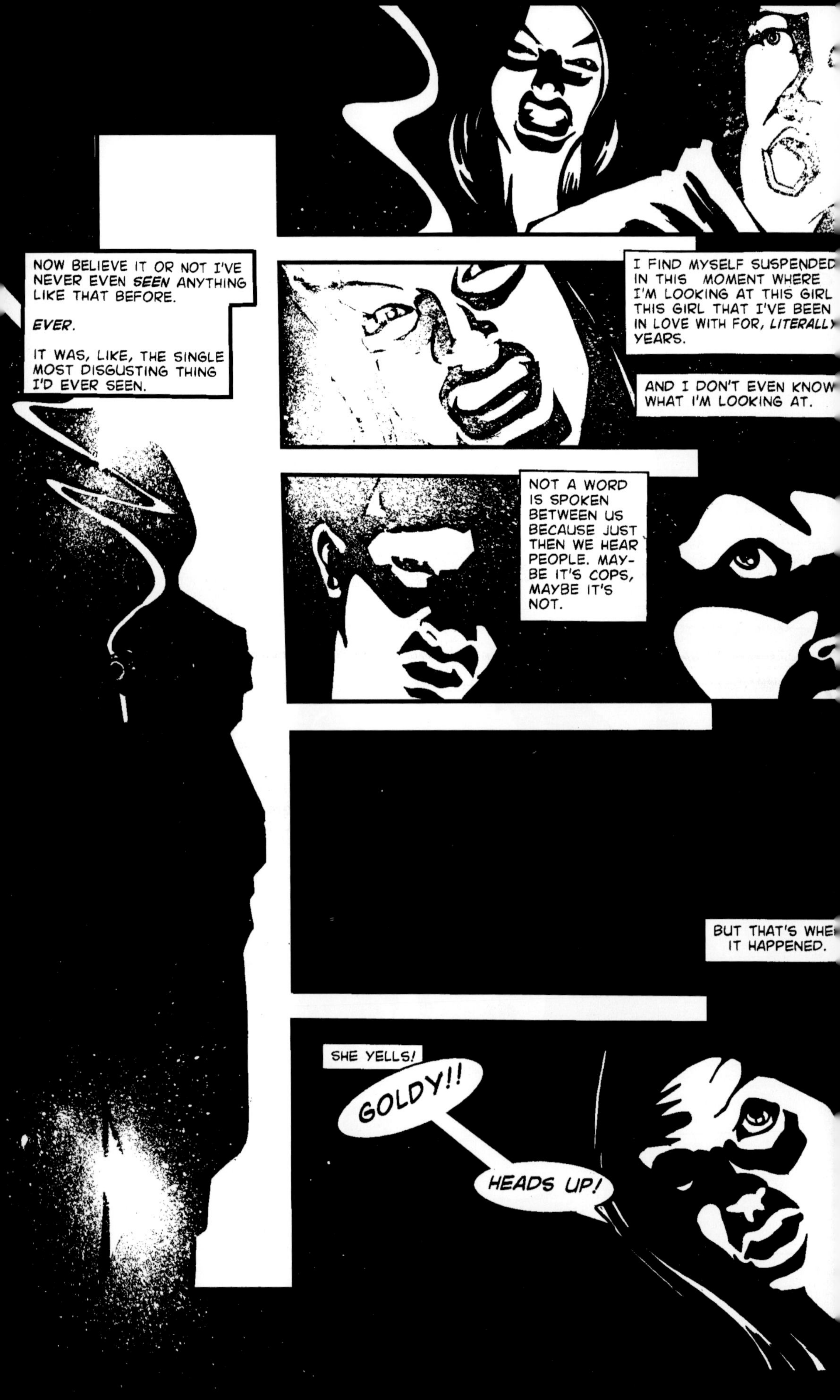
NOW BELIEVE IT OR NOT I'VE NEVER EVEN *SEEN* ANYTHING LIKE THAT BEFORE.
EVER.
IT WAS, LIKE, THE SINGLE MOST DISGUSTING THING I'D EVER SEEN.
I FIND MYSELF SUSPENDED IN THIS MOMENT WHERE I'M LOOKING AT THIS GIRL THIS GIRL THAT I'VE BEEN IN LOVE WITH FOR, *LITERALLY* YEARS.
AND I DON'T EVEN KNOW WHAT I'M LOOKING AT.
NOT A WORD IS SPOKEN BETWEEN US BECAUSE JUST THEN WE HEAR PEOPLE. MAYBE IT'S COPS, MAYBE IT'S NOT.
BUT THAT'S WHE
IT HAPPENED.
SHE YELLS!
GOLDY!!
HEADS UP!

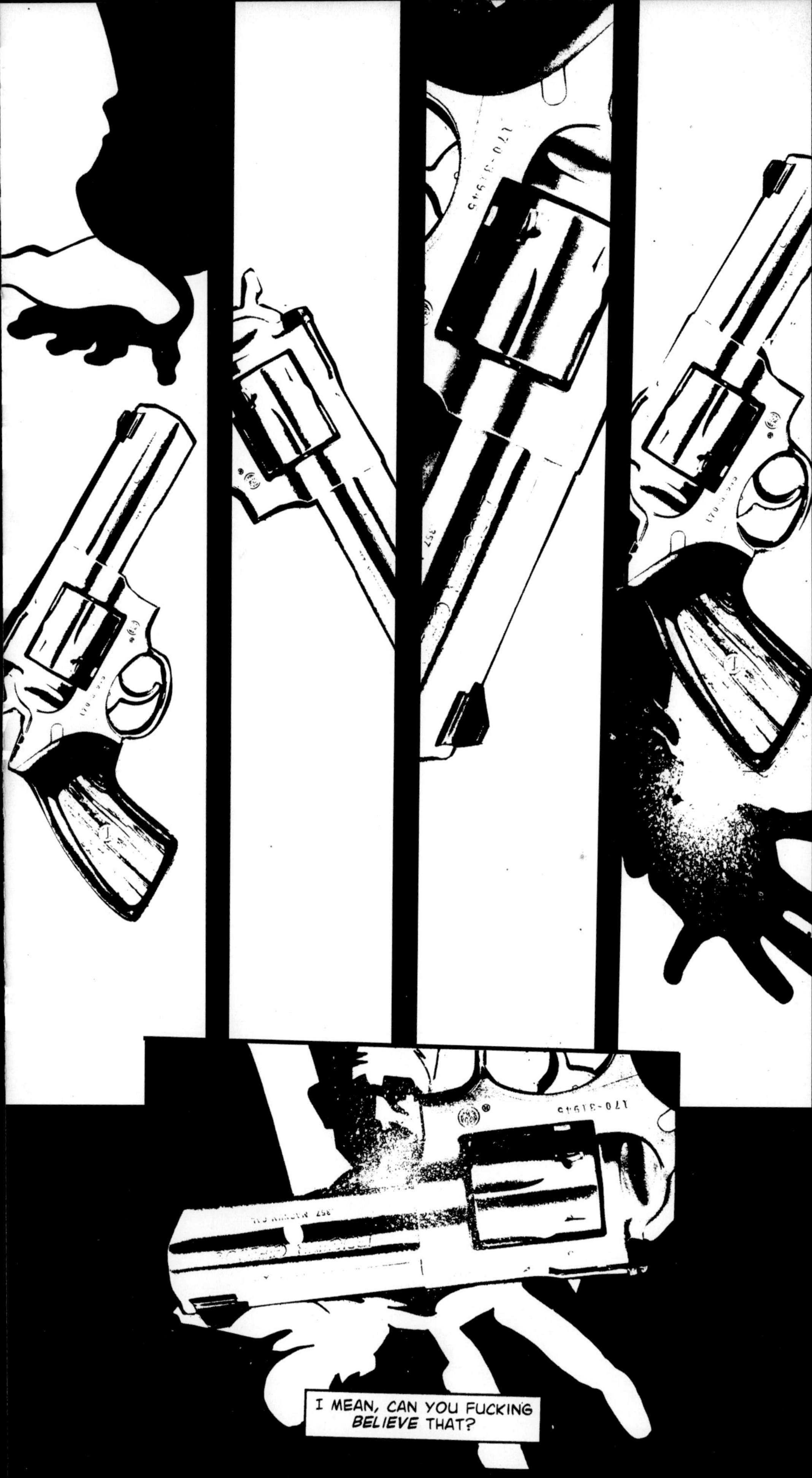
I MEAN, CAN YOU FUCKING *BELIEVE* THAT?

LAURY?
...WHY?

THE SOUNDS OF THE ONCOMING WERE GETTING CLOSER AND CLOSER SO I HIGHTAILED IT THE HELL OUT OF THERE.

FUNNY THING IS...YOU KNO
IN THOSE MOVIES WHEN
COPS CHASE THE BAD GU
AND THEY ALWAYS "GET
FROM AROUND THE CORN

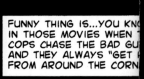

AND I NEVER SAW HIDE NOR HAIR OF HER EVER AGAIN.

THAT'S LIKE *TOTAL BULLSHIT*. I JUST RAN THROUGH THIS BUILDING OUT ONTO THE OPPOSITE STREET, HOPPED ONTO AN R.T.A, AND NEVER LOOKED BACK.

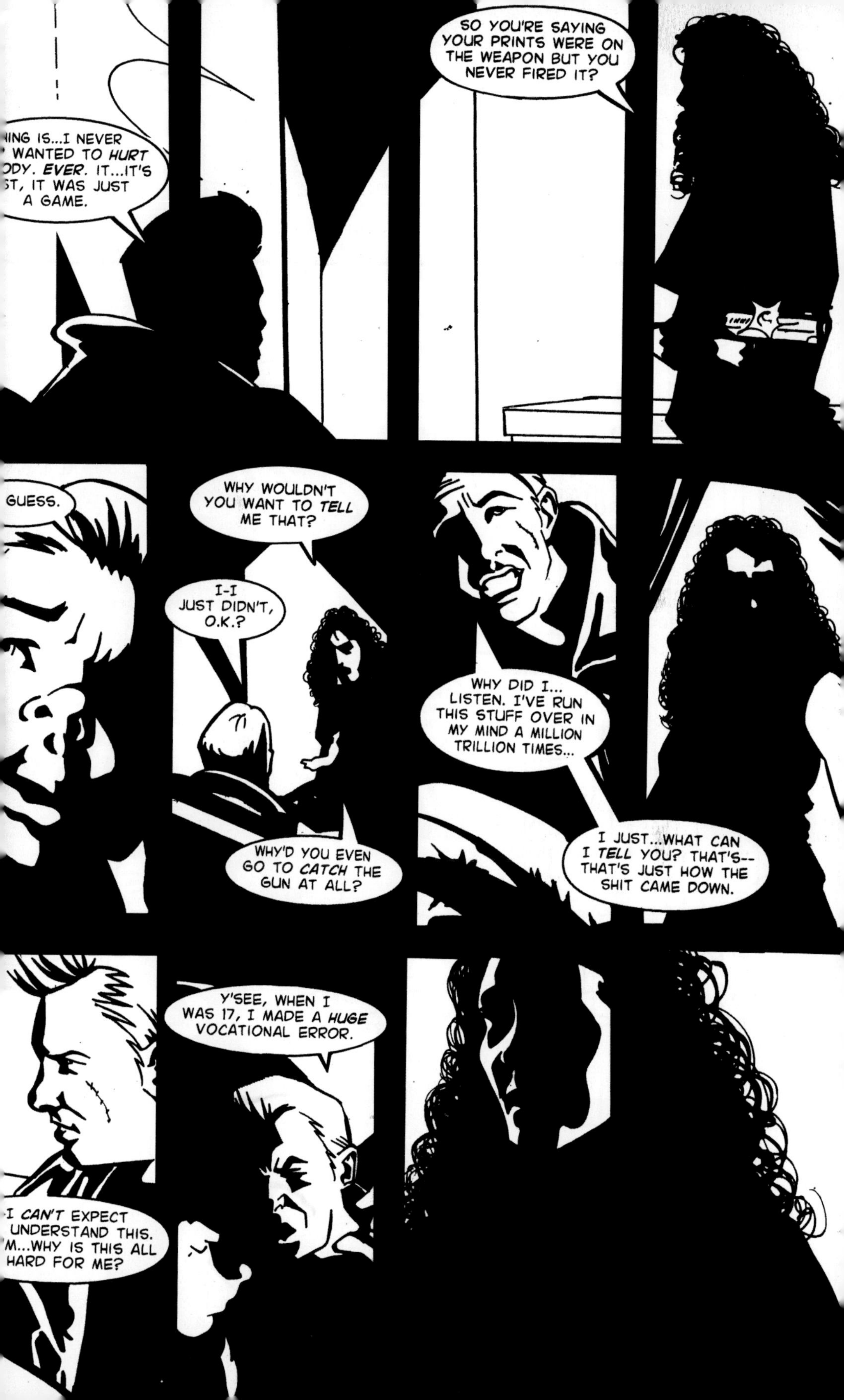
ING IS...I NEVER WANTED TO HURT ODY. EVER. IT...IT'S ST, IT WAS JUST A GAME.
SO YOU'RE SAYING YOUR PRINTS WERE ON THE WEAPON BUT YOU NEVER FIRED IT?
GUESS.
WHY WOULDN'T YOU WANT TO TELL ME THAT?
I-I JUST DIDN'T, O.K.?
WHY'D YOU EVEN GO TO CATCH THE GUN AT ALL?
WHY DID I... LISTEN. I'VE RUN THIS STUFF OVER IN MY MIND A MILLION TRILLION TIMES...
I JUST...WHAT CAN I TELL YOU? THAT'S--THAT'S JUST HOW THE SHIT CAME DOWN.
I CAN'T EXPECT UNDERSTAND THIS. M...WHY IS THIS ALL HARD FOR ME?
Y'SEE, WHEN I WAS 17, I MADE A HUGE VOCATIONAL ERROR.

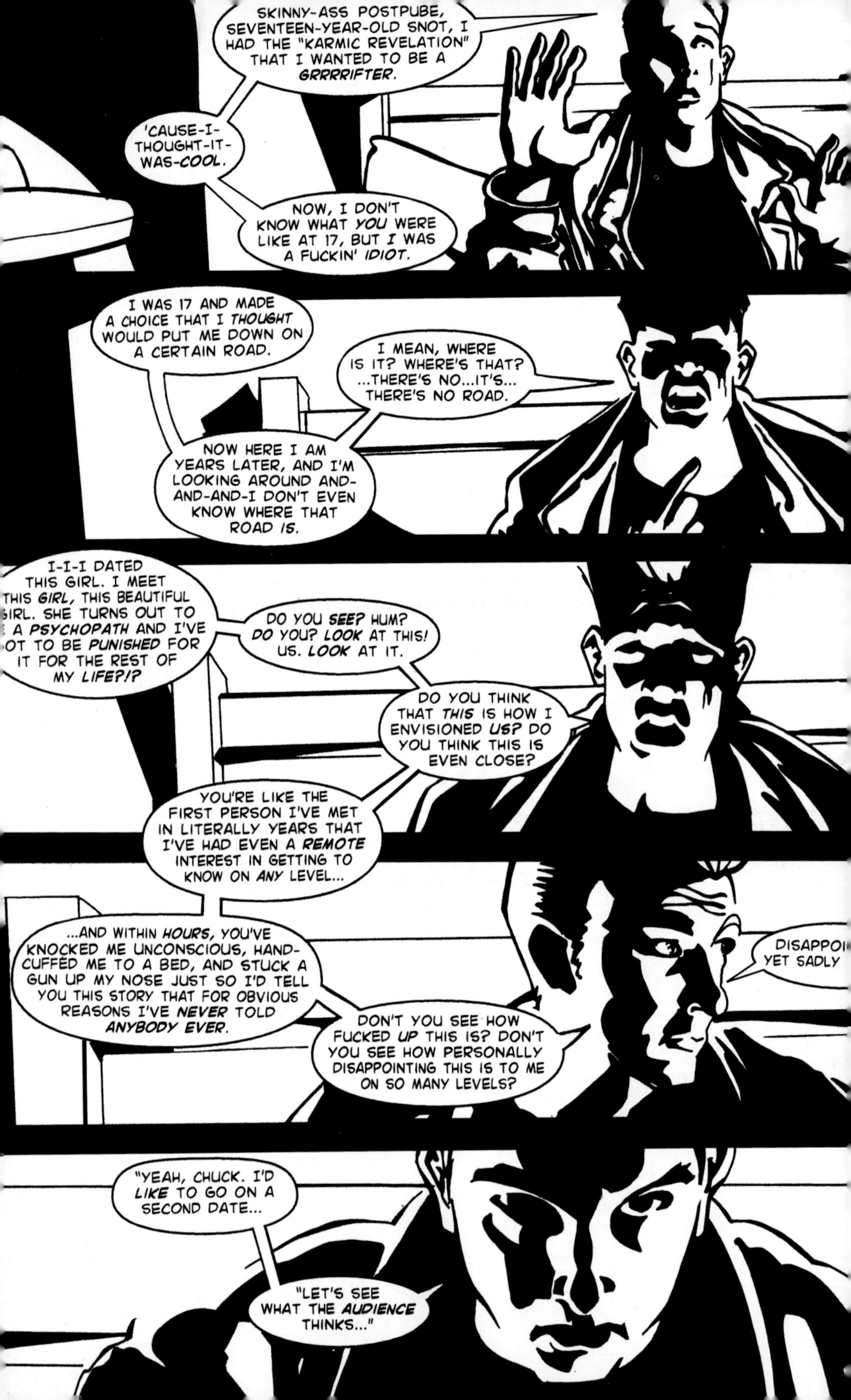
SKINNY-ASS POSTPUBE, SEVENTEEN-YEAR-OLD SNOT, I HAD THE "KARMIC REVELATION" THAT I WANTED TO BE A GRRRRIFTER.
'CAUSE-I-THOUGHT-IT-WAS-COOL.
NOW, I DON'T KNOW WHAT YOU WERE LIKE AT 17, BUT I WAS A FUCKIN' IDIOT.
I WAS 17 AND MADE A CHOICE THAT I THOUGHT WOULD PUT ME DOWN ON A CERTAIN ROAD.
I MEAN, WHERE IS IT? WHERE'S THAT? ...THERE'S NO...IT'S... THERE'S NO ROAD.
NOW HERE I AM YEARS LATER, AND I'M LOOKING AROUND AND-AND-AND-I DON'T EVEN KNOW WHERE THAT ROAD IS.
I-I-I DATED THIS GIRL. I MEET THIS GIRL, THIS BEAUTIFUL IRL. SHE TURNS OUT TO A PSYCHOPATH AND I'VE OT TO BE PUNISHED FOR IT FOR THE REST OF MY LIFE?!?
DO YOU SEE? HUM? DO YOU? LOOK AT THIS! US. LOOK AT IT.
DO YOU THINK THAT THIS IS HOW I ENVISIONED US? DO YOU THINK THIS IS EVEN CLOSE?
YOU'RE LIKE THE FIRST PERSON I'VE MET IN LITERALLY YEARS THAT I'VE HAD EVEN A REMOTE INTEREST IN GETTING TO KNOW ON ANY LEVEL...
...AND WITHIN HOURS, YOU'VE KNOCKED ME UNCONSCIOUS, HAND-CUFFED ME TO A BED, AND STUCK A GUN UP MY NOSE JUST SO I'D TELL YOU THIS STORY THAT FOR OBVIOUS REASONS I'VE NEVER TOLD ANYBODY EVER.
DON'T YOU SEE HOW FUCKED UP THIS IS? DON'T YOU SEE HOW PERSONALLY DISAPPOINTING THIS IS TO ME ON SO MANY LEVELS?
DISAPPOI YET SADLY
"YEAH, CHUCK. I'D LIKE TO GO ON A SECOND DATE...
"LET'S SEE WHAT THE AUDIENCE THINKS..."

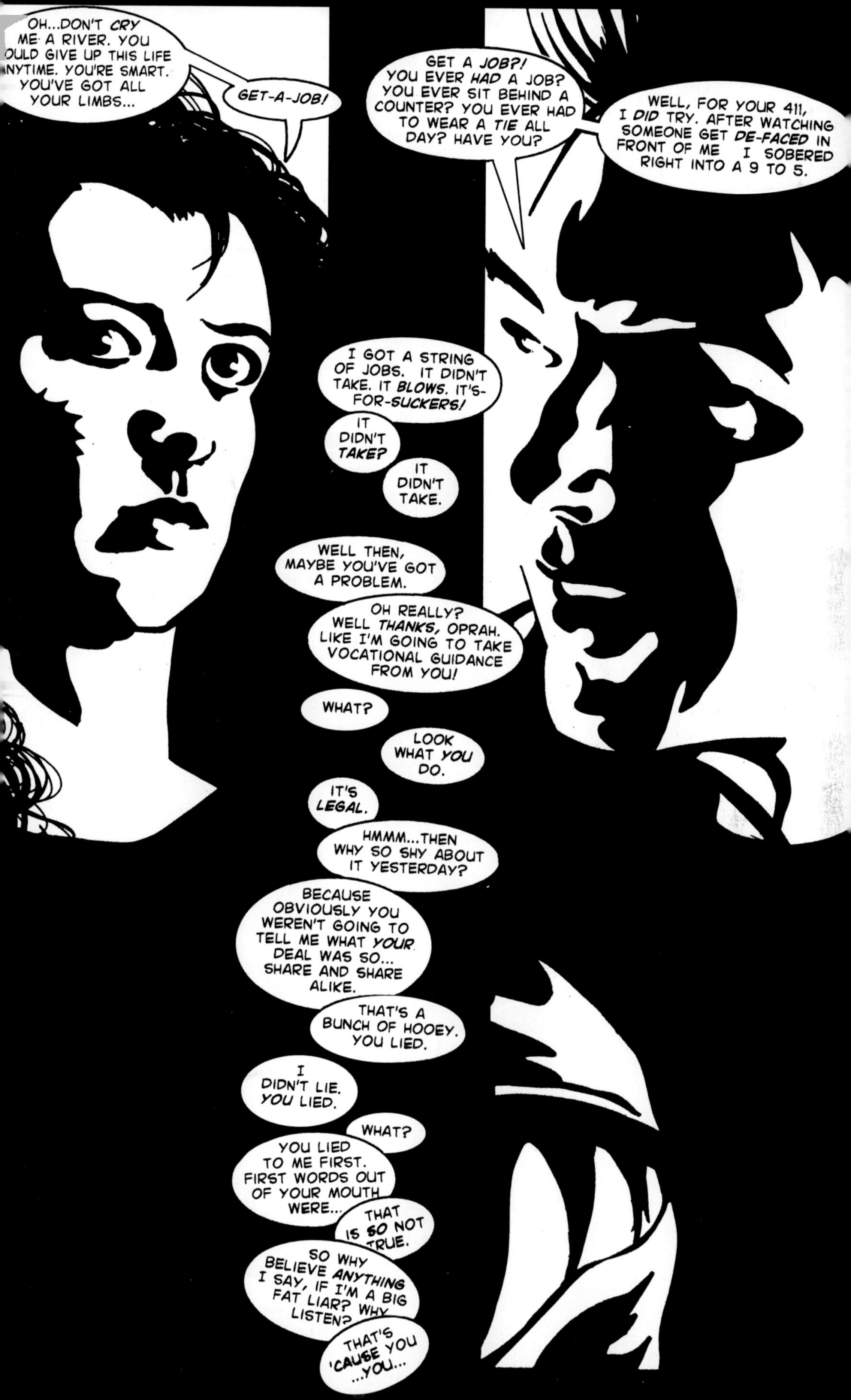
OH...DON'T CRY ME A RIVER. YOU OULD GIVE UP THIS LIFE NYTIME. YOU'RE SMART. YOU'VE GOT ALL YOUR LIMBS...
GET-A-JOB!
GET A JOB?! YOU EVER HAD A JOB? YOU EVER SIT BEHIND A COUNTER? YOU EVER HAD TO WEAR A TIE ALL DAY? HAVE YOU?
WELL, FOR YOUR 411, I DID TRY. AFTER WATCHING SOMEONE GET DE-FACED IN FRONT OF ME I SOBERED RIGHT INTO A 9 TO 5.
I GOT A STRING OF JOBS. IT DIDN'T TAKE. IT BLOWS. IT'S-FOR-SUCKERS!
IT DIDN'T TAKE?
IT DIDN'T TAKE.
WELL THEN, MAYBE YOU'VE GOT A PROBLEM.
OH REALLY? WELL THANKS, OPRAH. LIKE I'M GOING TO TAKE VOCATIONAL GUIDANCE FROM YOU!
WHAT?
LOOK WHAT YOU DO.
IT'S LEGAL.
HMMM...THEN WHY SO SHY ABOUT IT YESTERDAY?
BECAUSE OBVIOUSLY YOU WEREN'T GOING TO TELL ME WHAT YOUR DEAL WAS SO... SHARE AND SHARE ALIKE.
THAT'S A BUNCH OF HOOEY. YOU LIED.
I DIDN'T LIE. YOU LIED.
WHAT?
YOU LIED TO ME FIRST. FIRST WORDS OUT OF YOUR MOUTH WERE...
THAT IS SO NOT TRUE.
SO WHY BELIEVE ANYTHING I SAY, IF I'M A BIG FAT LIAR? WHY LISTEN?
THAT'S 'CAUSE YOU ...YOU...

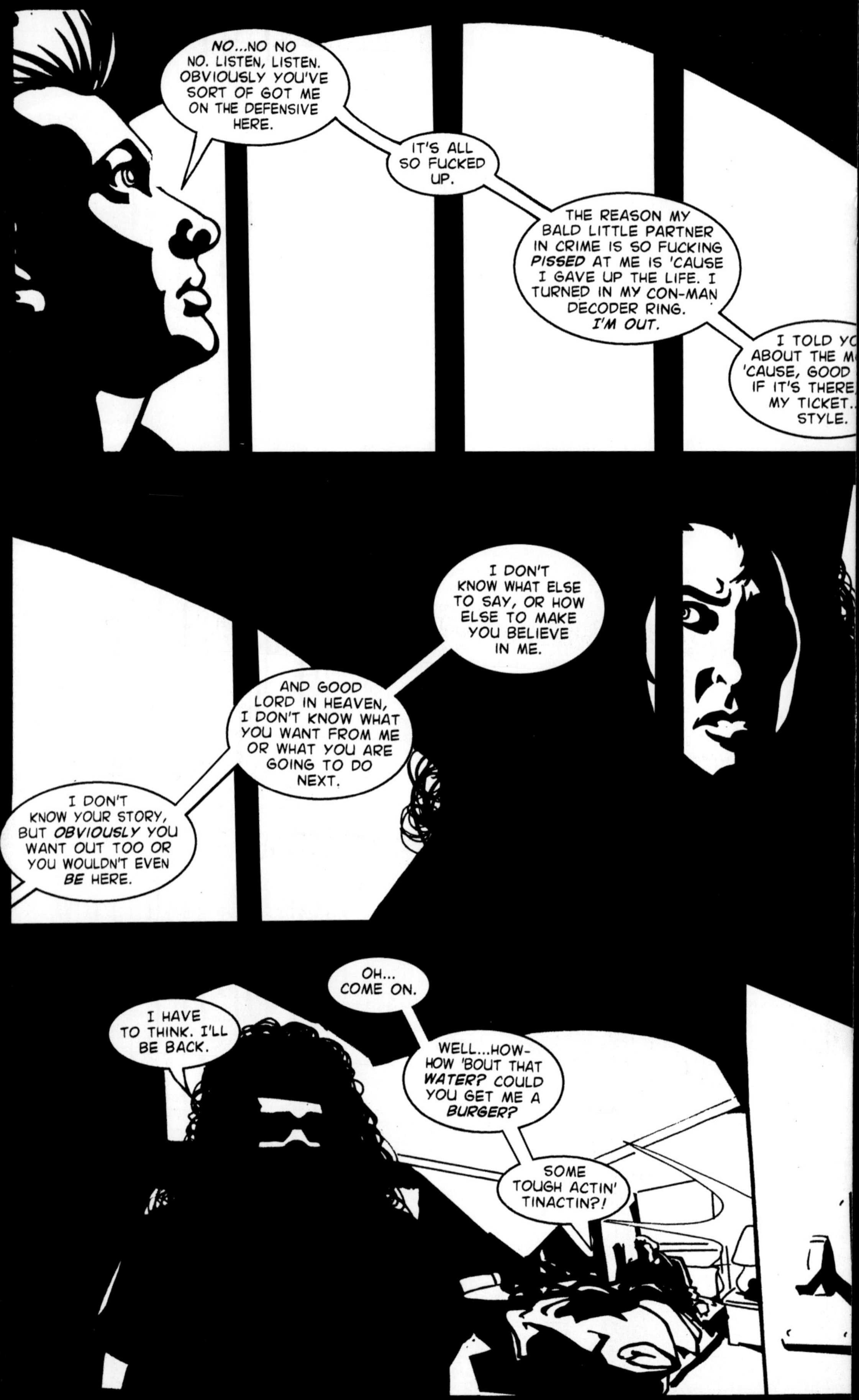
NO...NO NO NO. LISTEN, LISTEN. OBVIOUSLY YOU'VE SORT OF GOT ME ON THE DEFENSIVE HERE.
IT'S ALL SO FUCKED UP.
THE REASON MY BALD LITTLE PARTNER IN CRIME IS SO FUCKING PISSED AT ME IS 'CAUSE I GAVE UP THE LIFE. I TURNED IN MY CON-MAN DECODER RING. I'M OUT.
I DON'T KNOW YOUR STORY, BUT OBVIOUSLY YOU WANT OUT TOO OR YOU WOULDN'T EVEN BE HERE.
AND GOOD LORD IN HEAVEN, I DON'T KNOW WHAT YOU WANT FROM ME OR WHAT YOU ARE GOING TO DO NEXT.
I DON'T KNOW WHAT ELSE TO SAY, OR HOW ELSE TO MAKE YOU BELIEVE IN ME.
I HAVE TO THINK. I'LL BE BACK.
OH... COME ON.
WELL...HOW-HOW 'BOUT THAT WATER? COULD YOU GET ME A BURGER?
SOME TOUGH ACTIN' TINACTIN?!

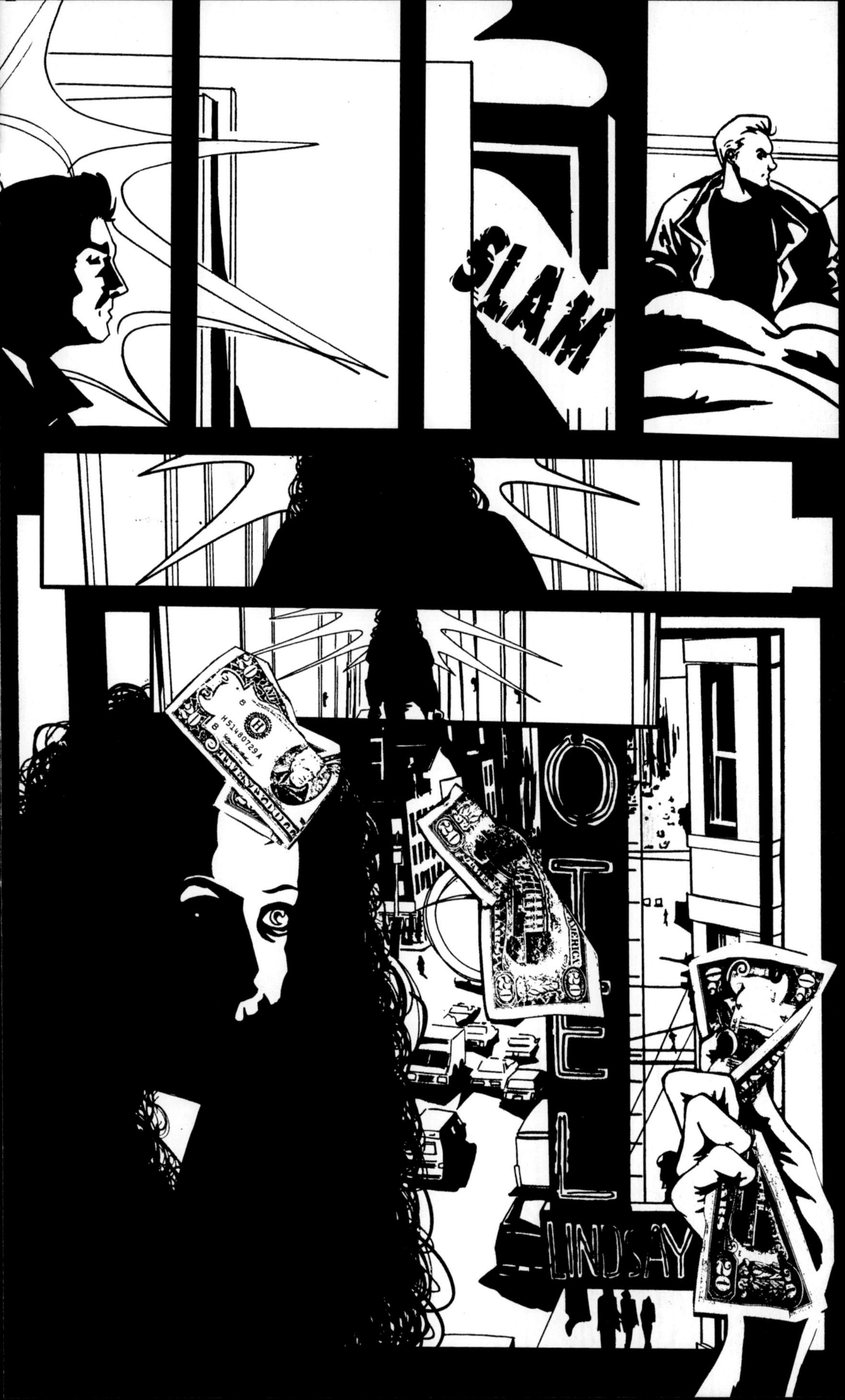

SLAM
LINDSAY

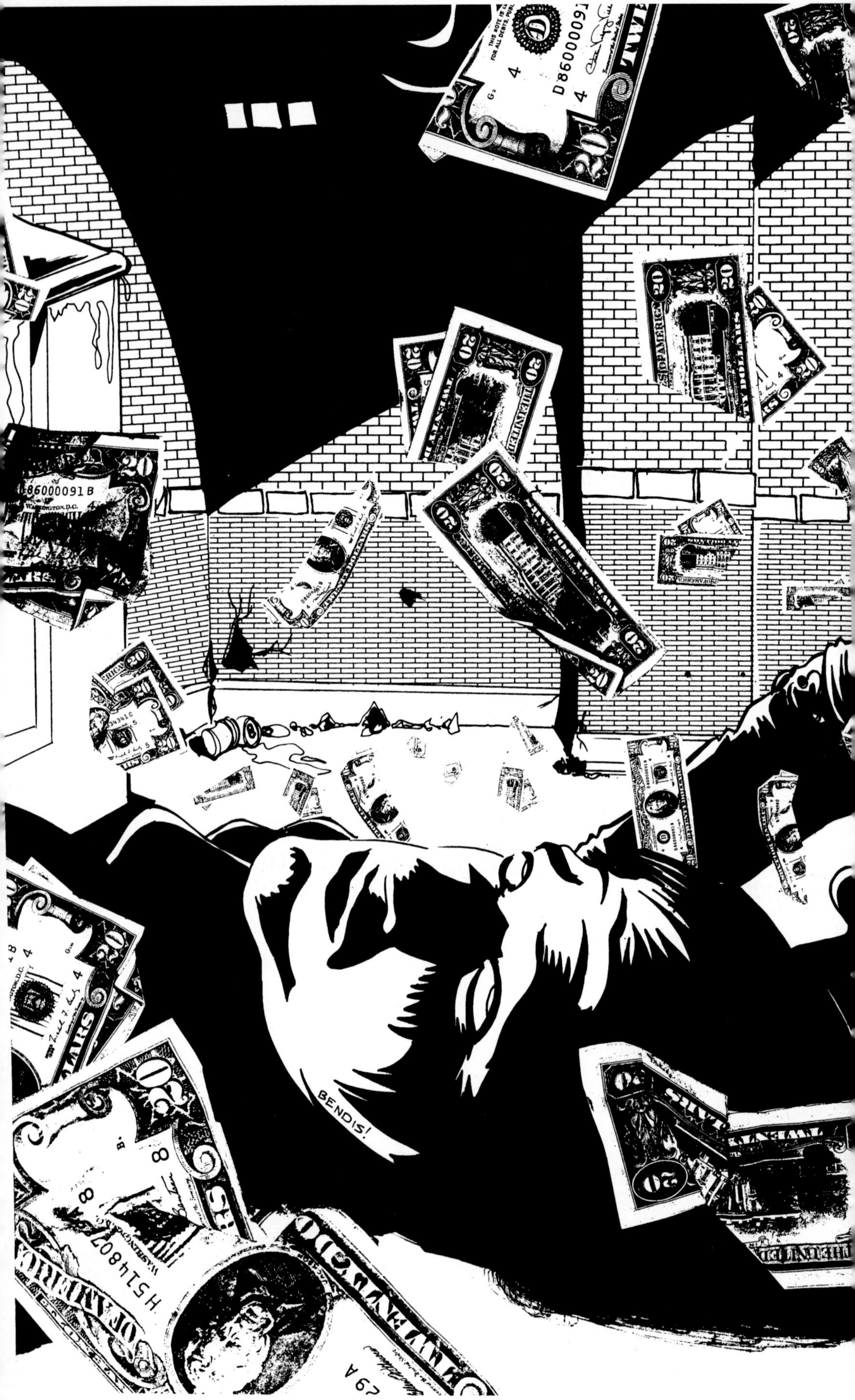
BENDIS!

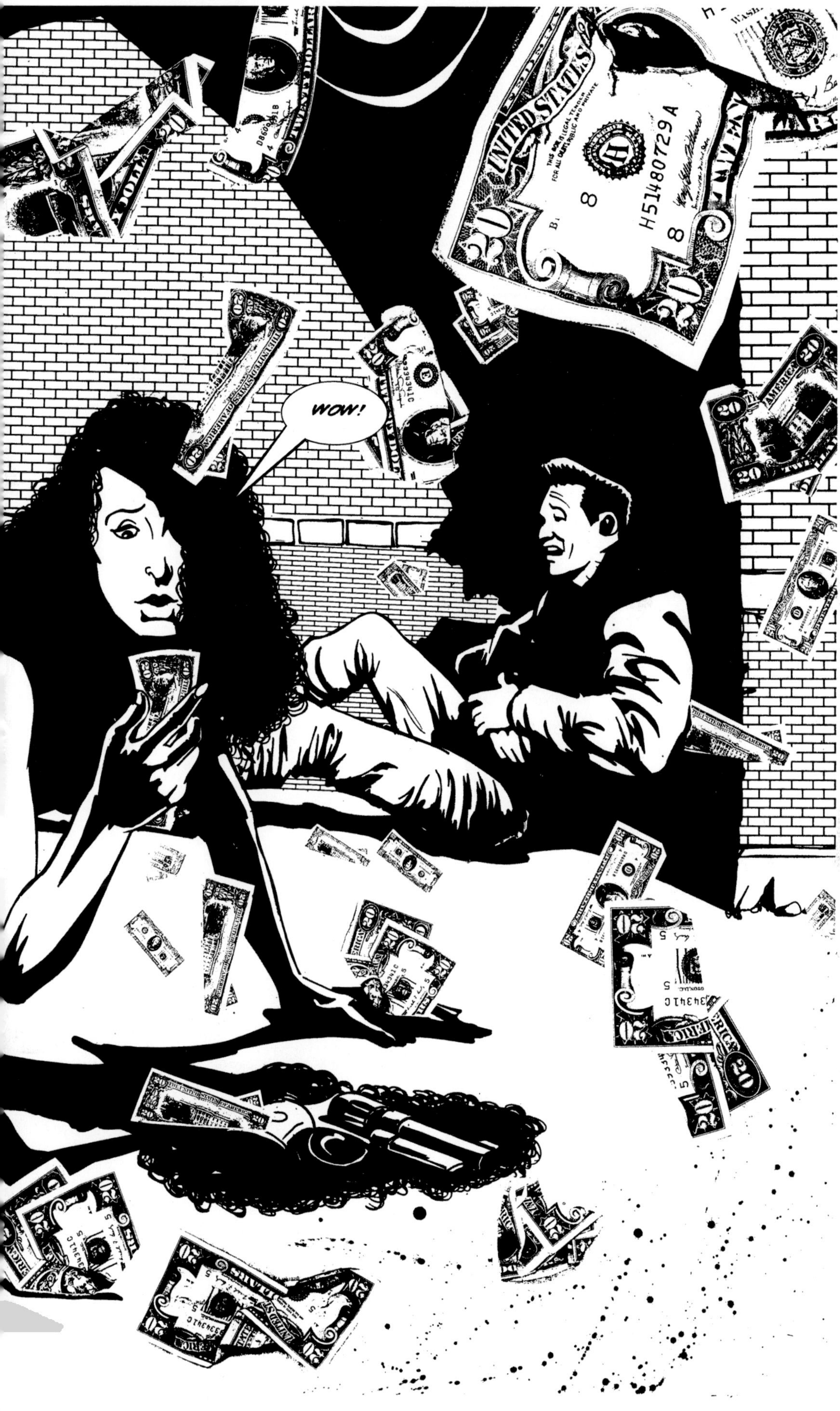
WOW!

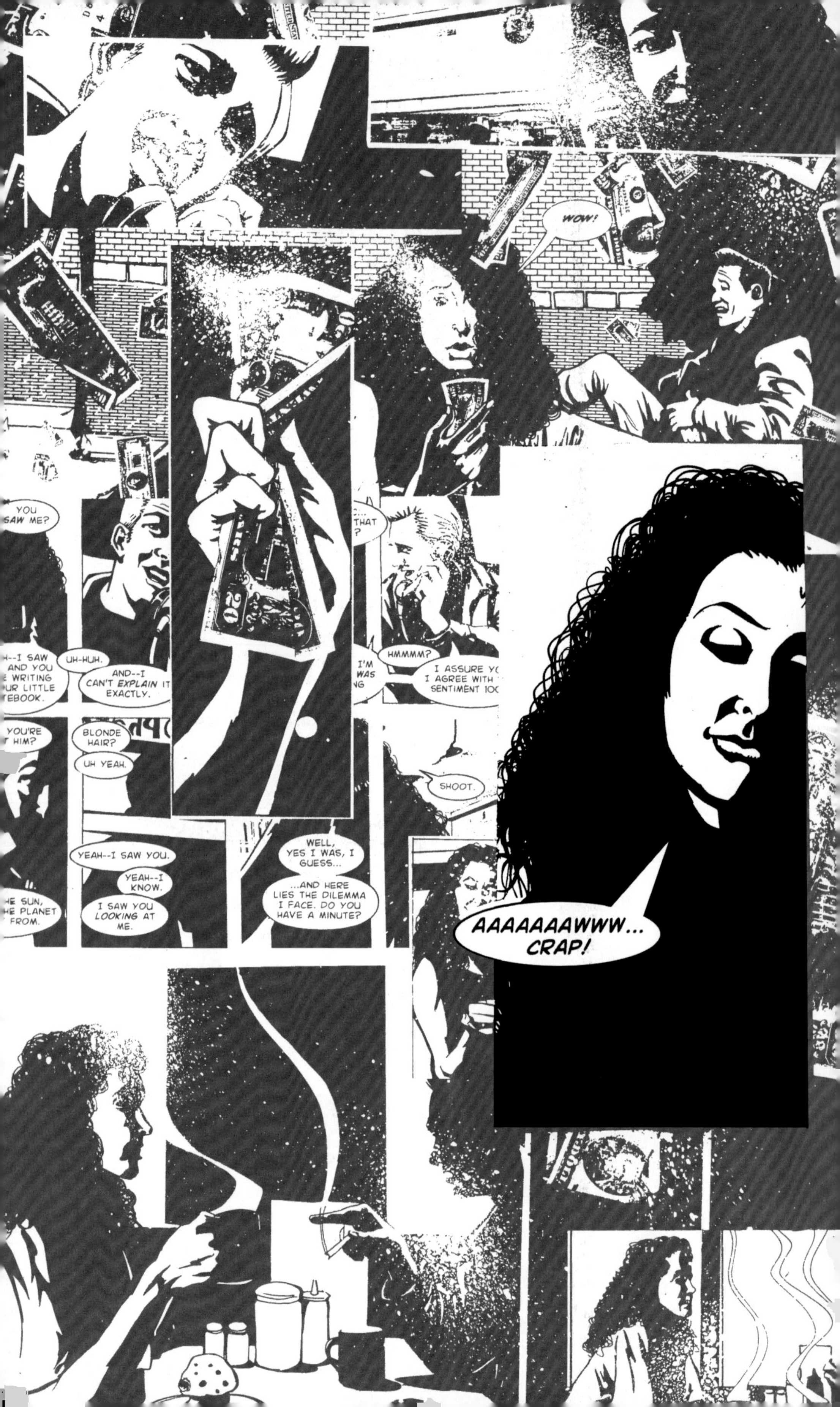
WOW!
YOU SAW ME?
UH-HUH.
AND--I CAN'T EXPLAIN IT EXACTLY.
BLONDE HAIR?
UH YEAH.
HMMMM?
SHOOT.
YEAH--I SAW YOU.
YEAH--I KNOW.
I SAW YOU LOOKING AT ME.
WELL, YES I WAS, I GUESS...
...AND HERE LIES THE DILEMMA I FACE. DO YOU HAVE A MINUTE?
AAAAAAAWWW... CRAP!

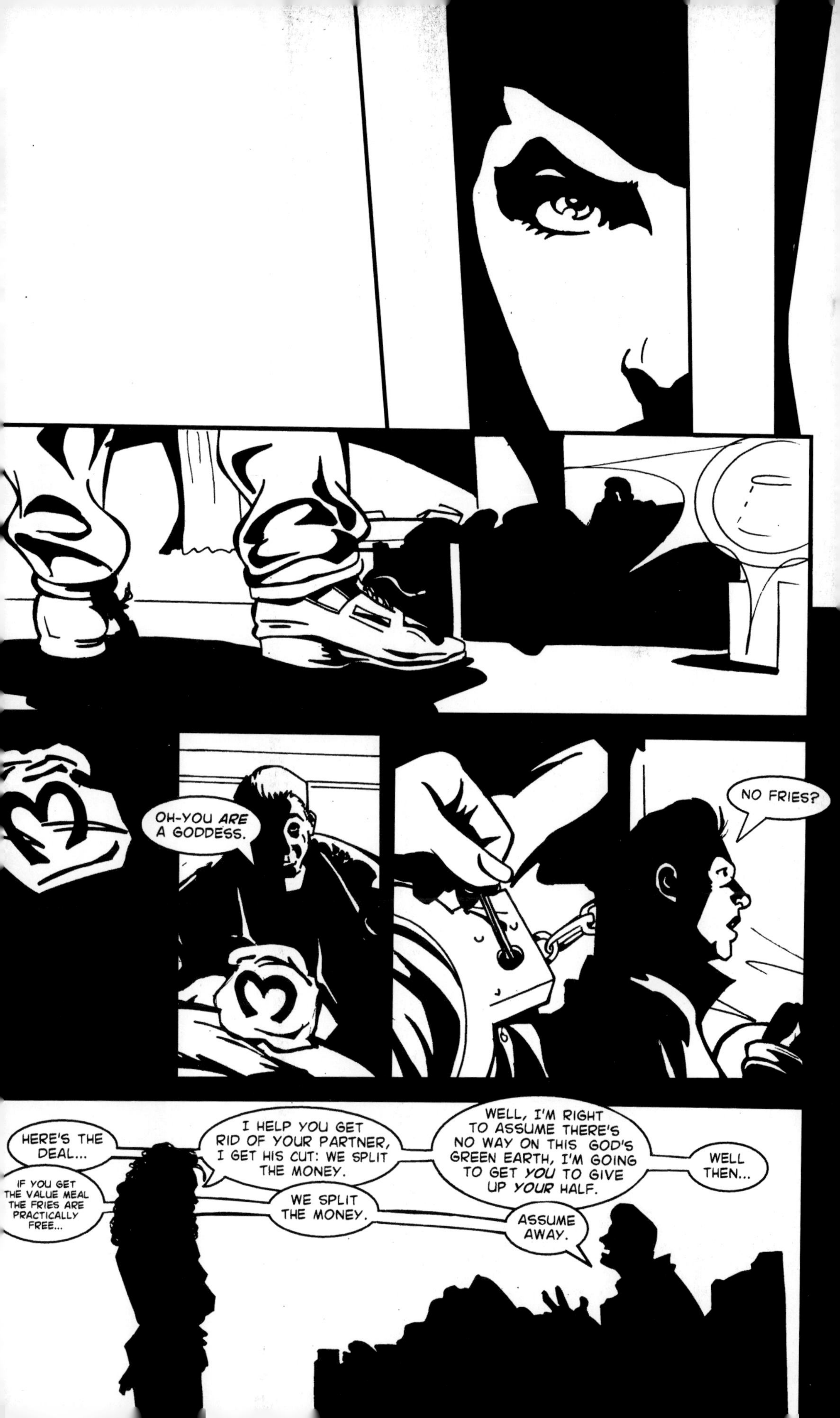
OH-YOU *ARE* A GODDESS.
NO FRIES?
HERE'S THE DEAL...
IF YOU GET THE VALUE MEAL THE FRIES ARE PRACTICALLY FREE...
I HELP YOU GET RID OF YOUR PARTNER, I GET HIS CUT: WE SPLIT THE MONEY.
WE SPLIT THE MONEY.
WELL, I'M RIGHT TO ASSUME THERE'S NO WAY ON THIS GOD'S GREEN EARTH, I'M GOING TO GET *YOU* TO GIVE UP *YOUR* HALF.
ASSUME AWAY.
WELL THEN...

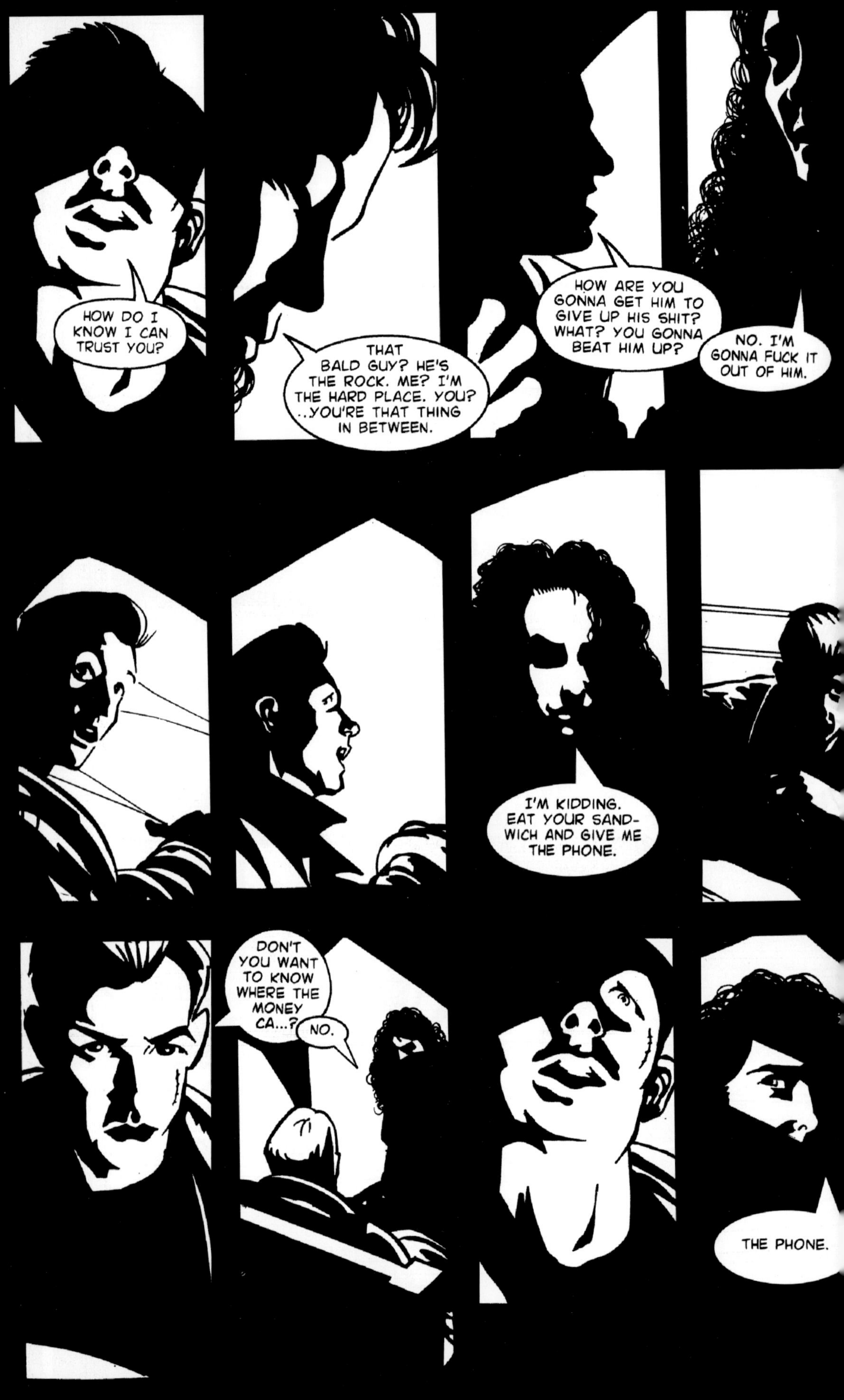
HOW DO I KNOW I CAN TRUST YOU?
THAT BALD GUY? HE'S THE ROCK. ME? I'M THE HARD PLACE. YOU? ..YOU'RE THAT THING IN BETWEEN.
HOW ARE YOU GONNA GET HIM TO GIVE UP HIS SHIT? WHAT? YOU GONNA BEAT HIM UP?
NO. I'M GONNA FUCK IT OUT OF HIM.
I'M KIDDING. EAT YOUR SAND-WICH AND GIVE ME THE PHONE.
DON'T YOU WANT TO KNOW WHERE THE MONEY CA...?
NO.
THE PHONE.

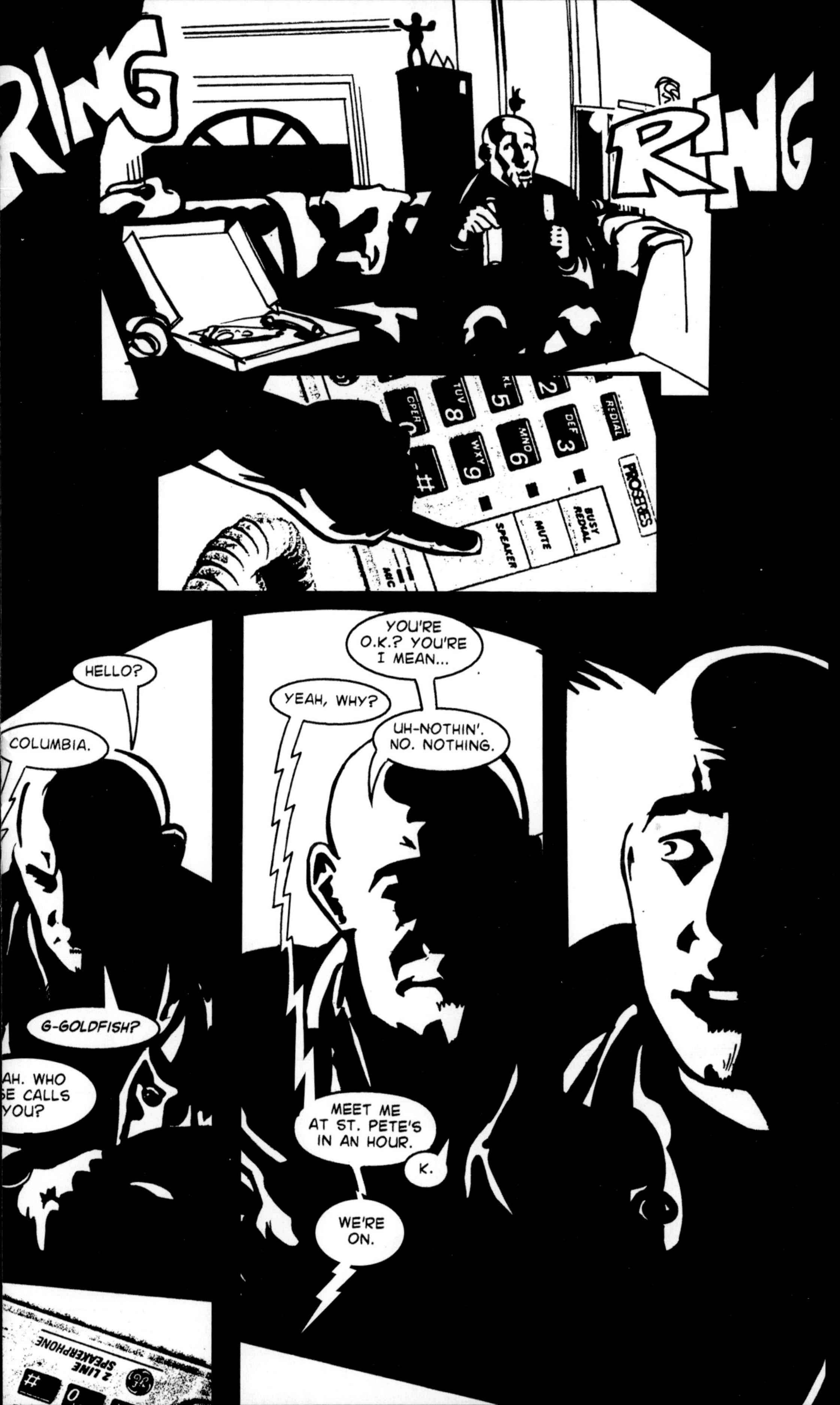
RING
RING
HELLO?
COLUMBIA.
G-GOLDFISH?
AH. WHO
E CALLS
YOU?
YEAH, WHY?
YOU'RE O.K.? YOU'RE I MEAN...
UH-NOTHIN'. NO. NOTHING.
MEET ME AT ST. PETE'S IN AN HOUR.
K.
WE'RE ON.

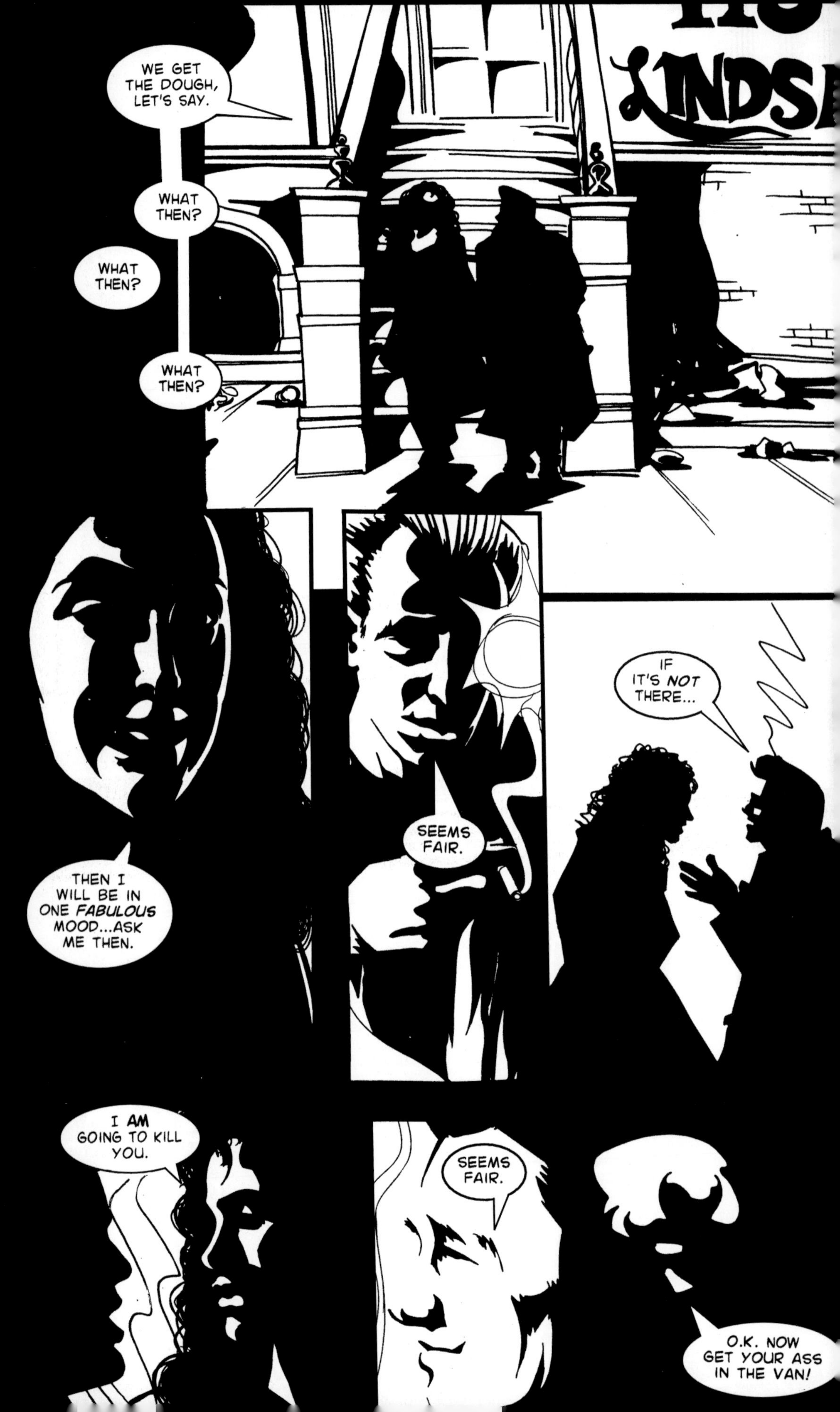
WE GET THE DOUGH, LET'S SAY.
WHAT THEN?
WHAT THEN?
WHAT THEN?
THEN I WILL BE IN ONE *FABULOUS* MOOD...ASK ME THEN.
SEEMS FAIR.
IF IT'S *NOT* THERE...
I *AM* GOING TO KILL YOU.
SEEMS FAIR.
O.K. NOW GET YOUR ASS IN THE VAN!

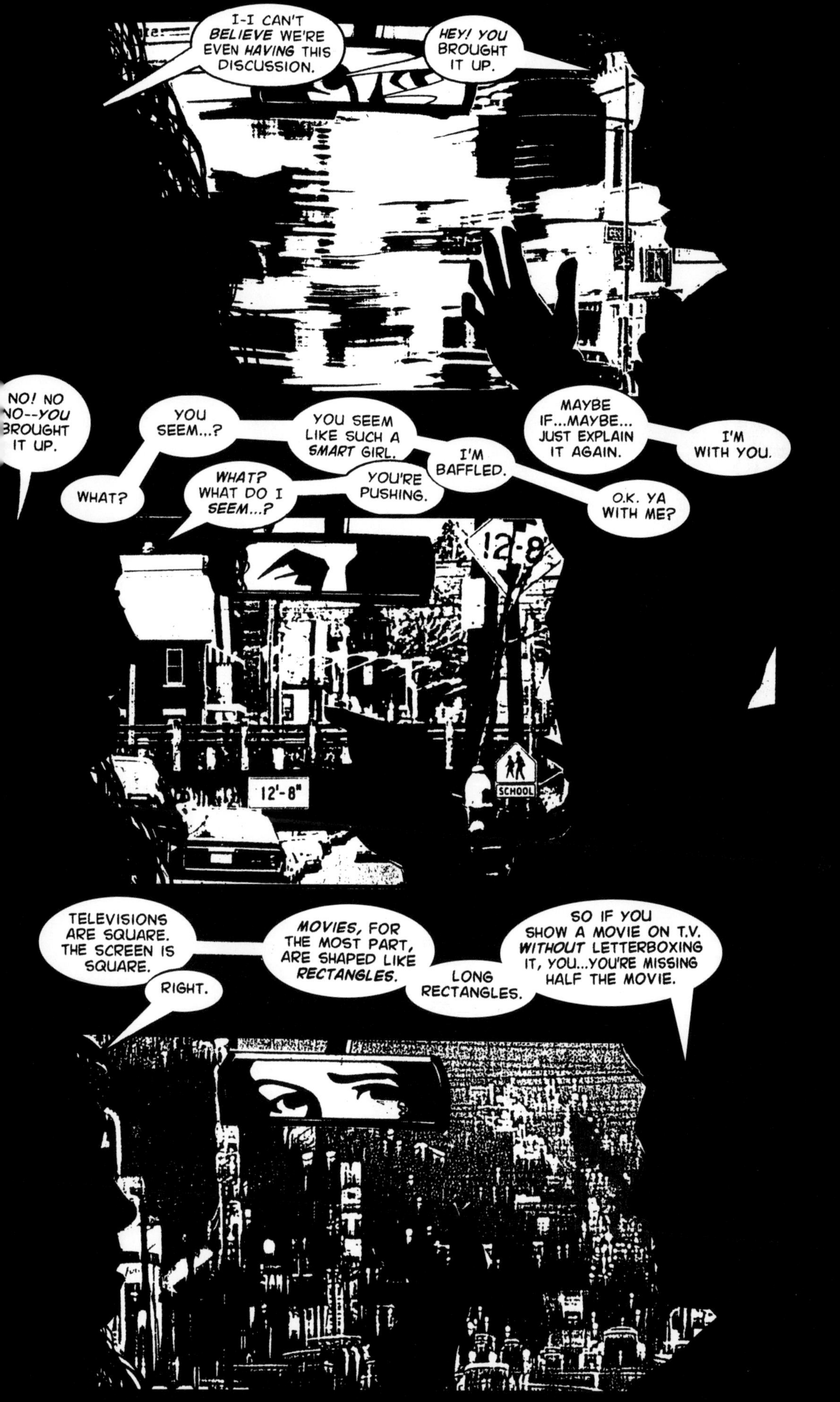

I-I CAN'T *BELIEVE* WE'RE EVEN *HAVING* THIS DISCUSSION.
HEY! YOU BROUGHT IT UP.
NO! NO NO--*YOU* BROUGHT IT UP.
WHAT?
YOU SEEM...?
WHAT? WHAT DO I *SEEM...?*
YOU SEEM LIKE SUCH A *SMART* GIRL.
YOU'RE PUSHING.
I'M BAFFLED.
O.K. YA WITH ME?
MAYBE IF...MAYBE... JUST EXPLAIN IT AGAIN.
I'M WITH YOU.
12'-8"
SCHOOL
12'-8"
TELEVISIONS ARE SQUARE. THE SCREEN IS SQUARE.
RIGHT.
MOVIES, FOR THE MOST PART, ARE SHAPED LIKE *RECTANGLES.*
LONG RECTANGLES.
SO IF YOU SHOW A MOVIE ON T.V. *WITHOUT* LETTERBOXING IT, YOU...YOU'RE MISSING HALF THE MOVIE.

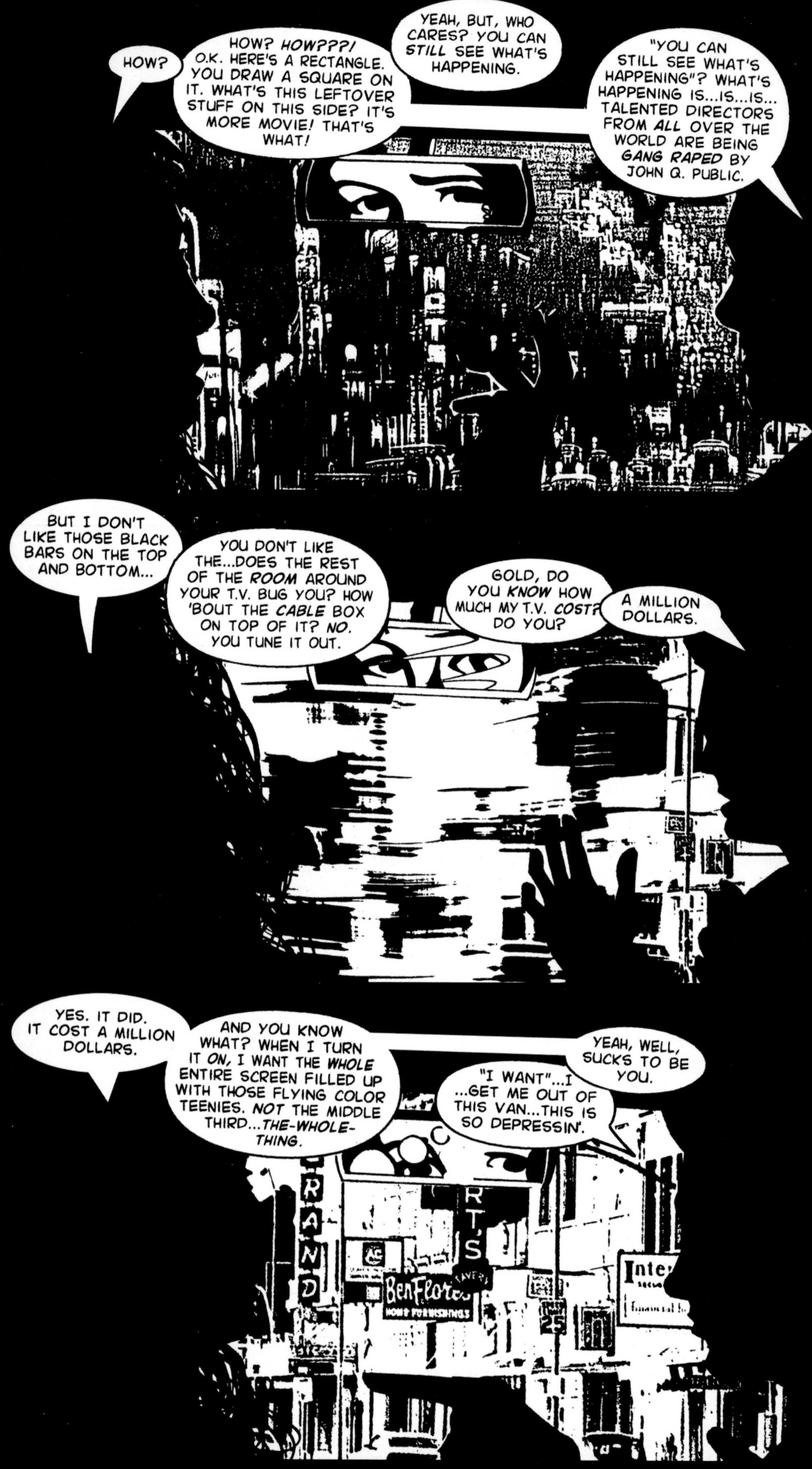
HOW?
HOW? HOW???! O.K. HERE'S A RECTANGLE. YOU DRAW A SQUARE ON IT. WHAT'S THIS LEFTOVER STUFF ON THIS SIDE? IT'S MORE MOVIE! THAT'S WHAT!
YEAH, BUT, WHO CARES? YOU CAN STILL SEE WHAT'S HAPPENING.
"YOU CAN STILL SEE WHAT'S HAPPENING"? WHAT'S HAPPENING IS...IS...IS... TALENTED DIRECTORS FROM ALL OVER THE WORLD ARE BEING GANG RAPED BY JOHN Q. PUBLIC.
BUT I DON'T LIKE THOSE BLACK BARS ON THE TOP AND BOTTOM...
YOU DON'T LIKE THE...DOES THE REST OF THE ROOM AROUND YOUR T.V. BUG YOU? HOW 'BOUT THE CABLE BOX ON TOP OF IT? NO. YOU TUNE IT OUT.
GOLD, DO YOU KNOW HOW MUCH MY T.V. COST? DO YOU?
A MILLION DOLLARS.
YES. IT DID. IT COST A MILLION DOLLARS.
AND YOU KNOW WHAT? WHEN I TURN IT ON, I WANT THE WHOLE ENTIRE SCREEN FILLED UP WITH THOSE FLYING COLOR TEENIES. NOT THE MIDDLE THIRD...THE-WHOLE-THING.
YEAH, WELL, SUCKS TO BE YOU.
"I WANT"...I ...GET ME OUT OF THIS VAN...THIS IS SO DEPRESSIN'.
GRAND
ART'S
Ben Flores
HOME FURNISHINGS
TAVERN
25

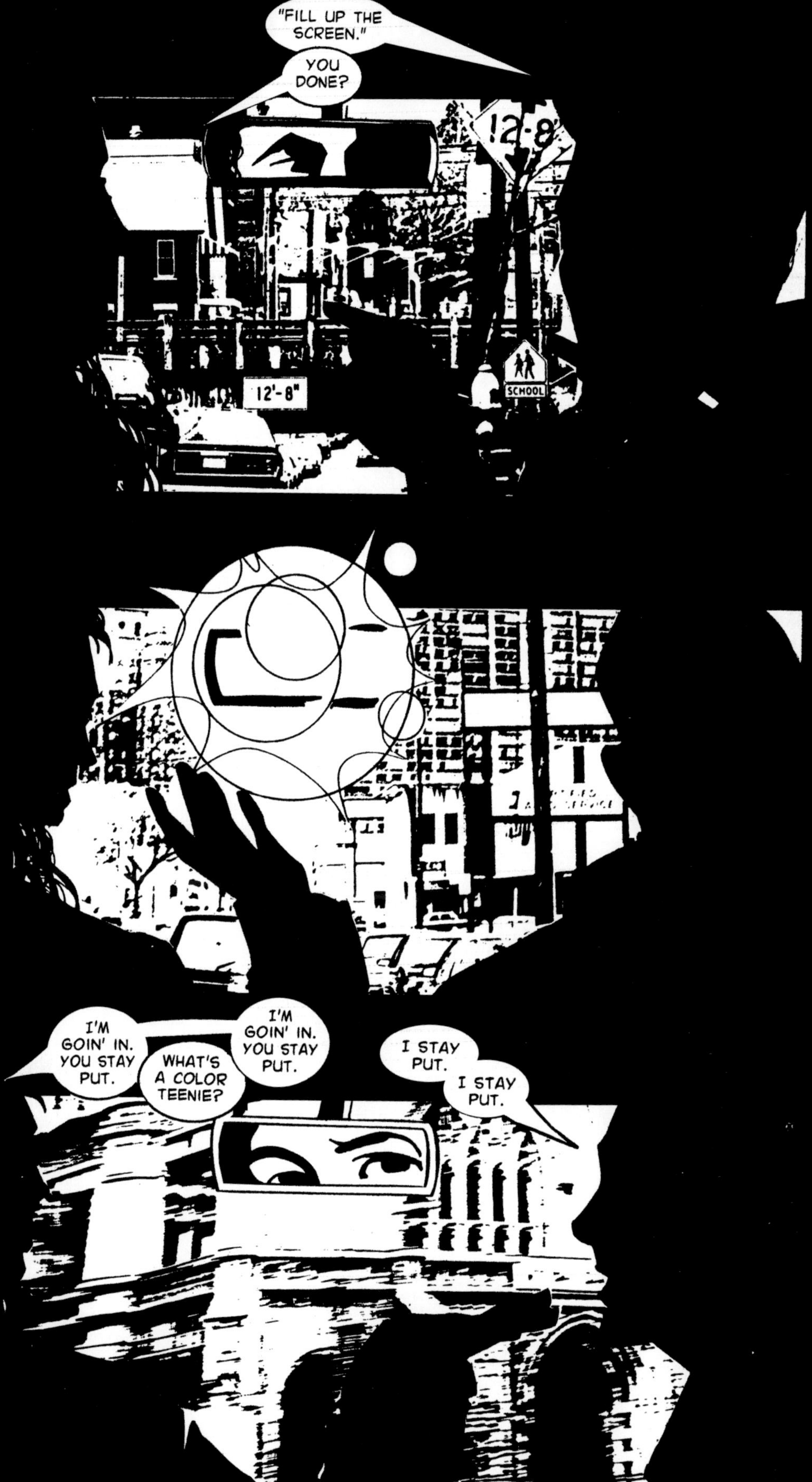
"FILL UP THE SCREEN."
YOU DONE?
12'-8"
SCHOOL
12'-8"
I'M GOIN' IN. YOU STAY PUT.
WHAT'S A COLOR TEENIE?
I'M GOIN' IN. YOU STAY PUT.
I STAY PUT.
I STAY PUT.

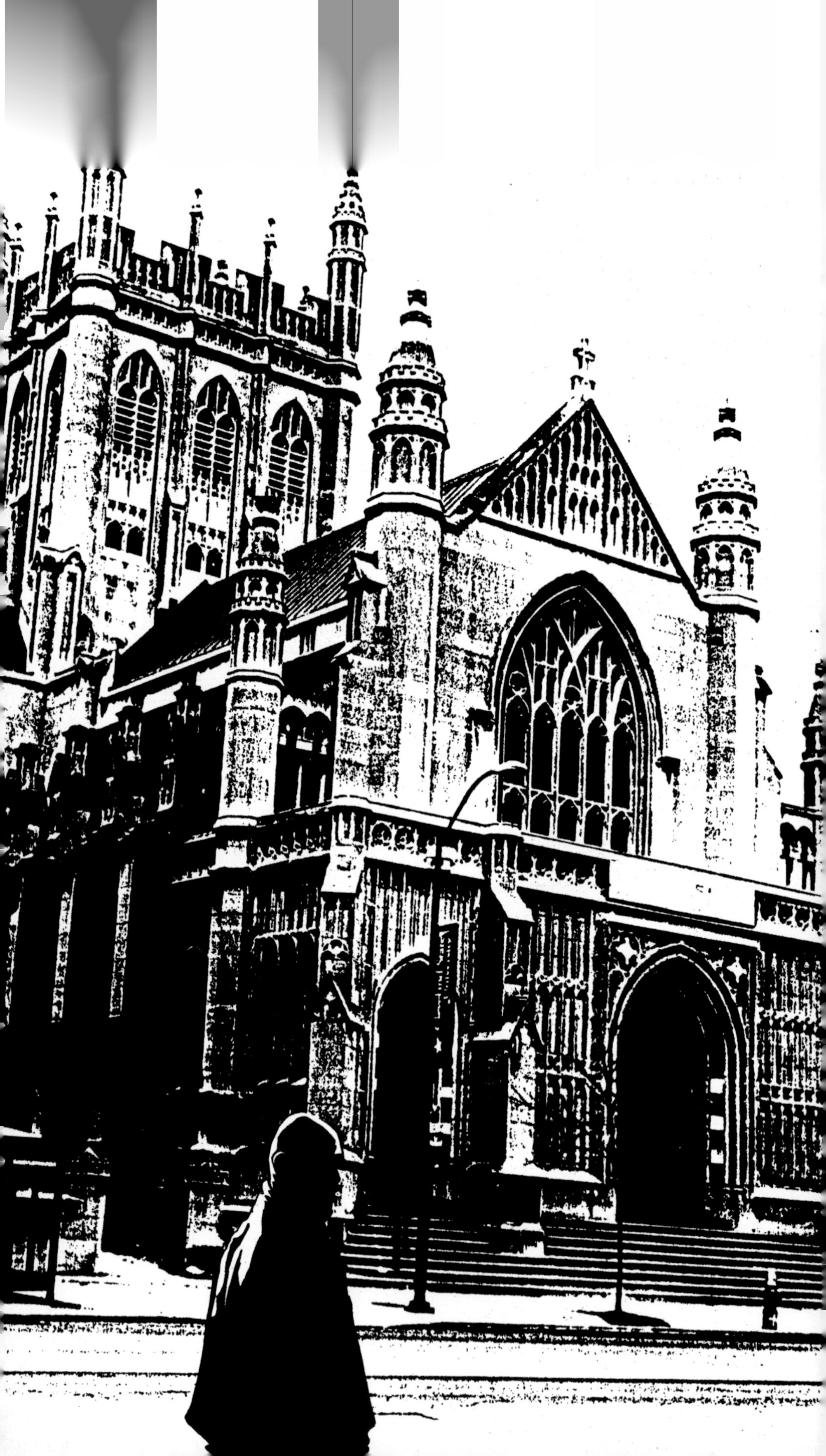

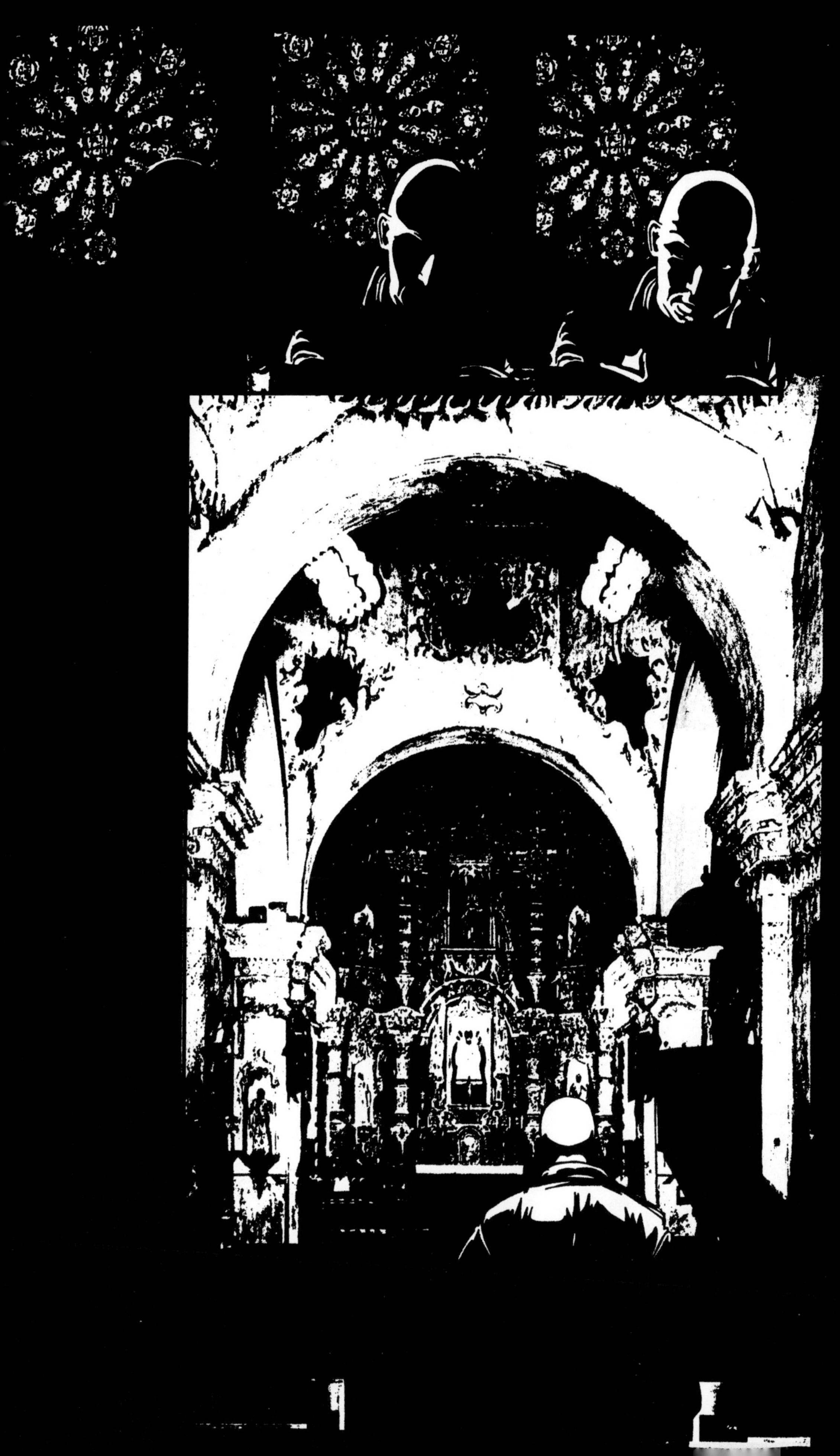

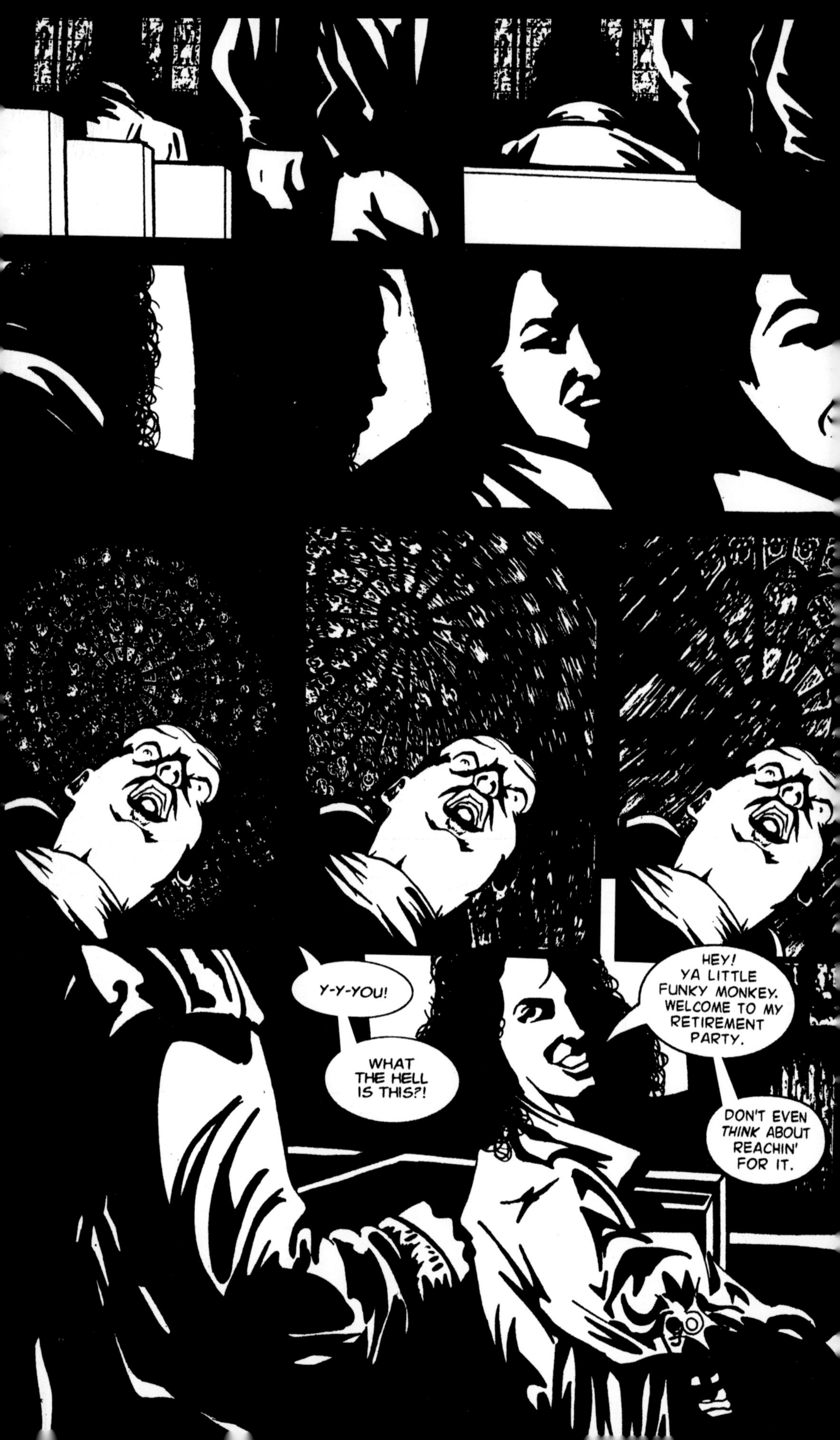
Y-Y-YOU!
WHAT THE HELL IS THIS?!
HEY! YA LITTLE FUNKY MONKEY. WELCOME TO MY RETIREMENT PARTY.
DON'T EVEN *THINK* ABOUT REACHIN' FOR IT.

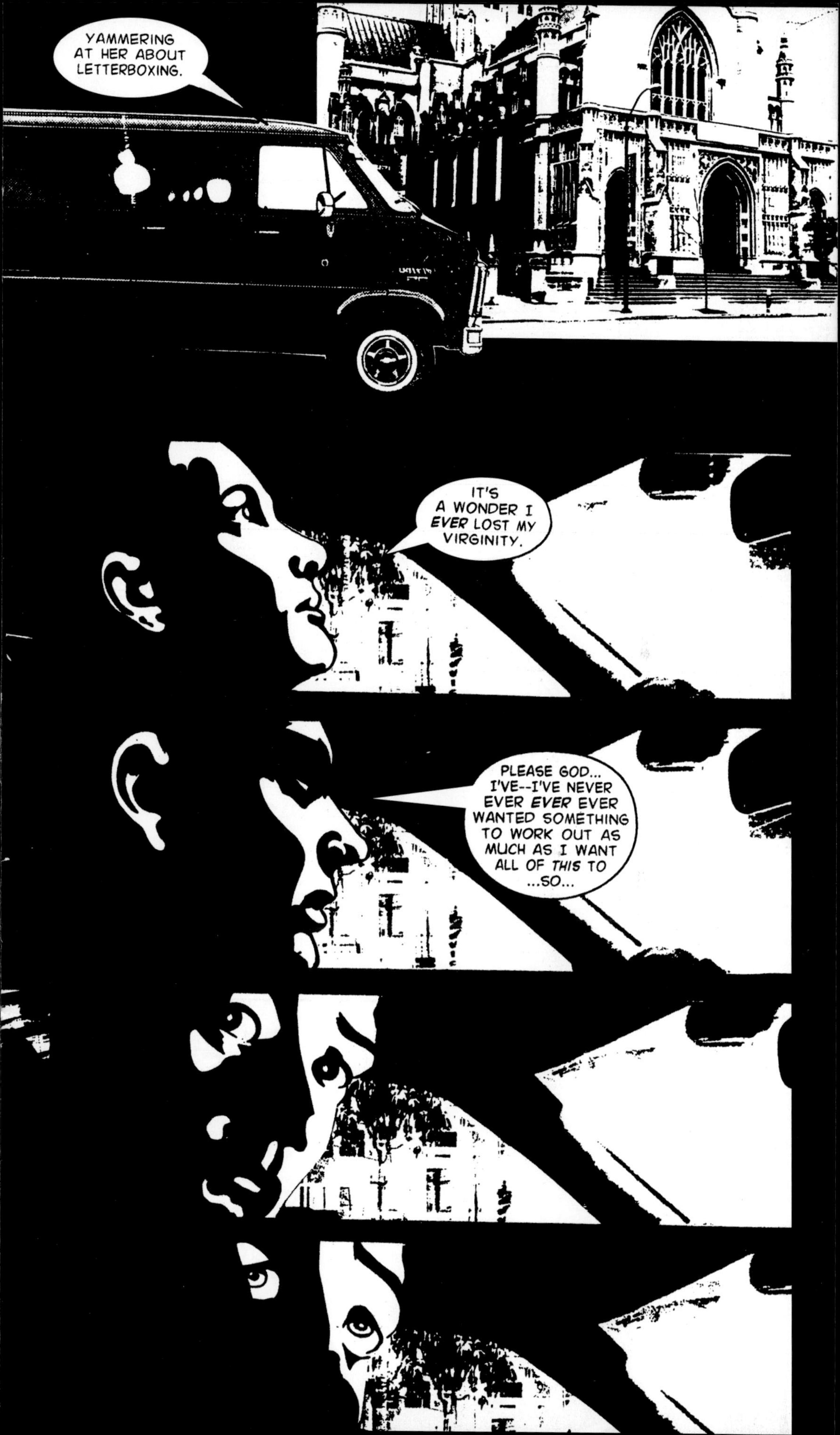
YAMMERING AT HER ABOUT LETTERBOXING.
IT'S A WONDER I *EVER* LOST MY VIRGINITY.
PLEASE GOD... I'VE--I'VE NEVER EVER *EVER* EVER WANTED SOMETHING TO WORK OUT AS MUCH AS I WANT ALL OF *THIS* TO ...SO...

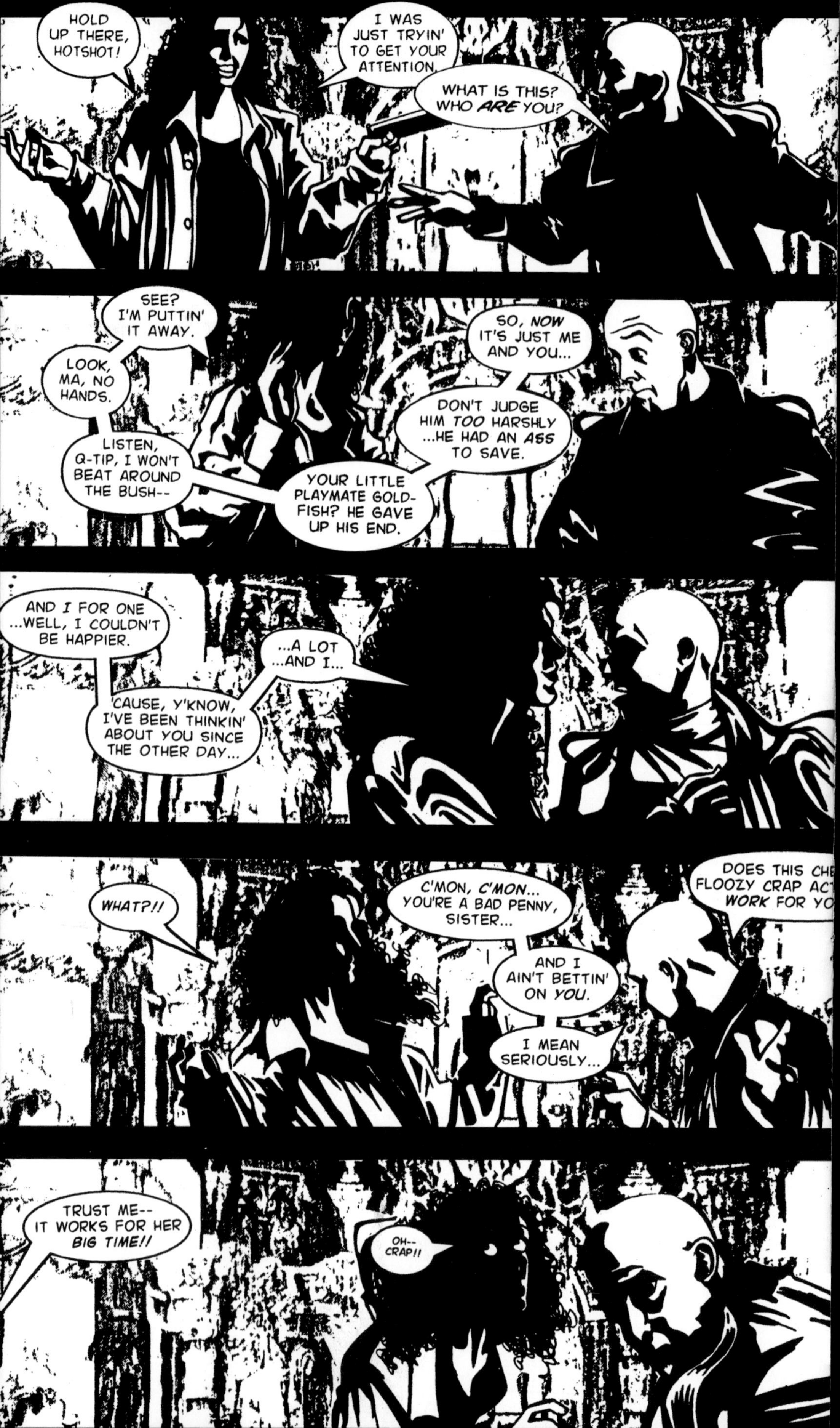
HOLD UP THERE, HOTSHOT!
I WAS JUST TRYIN' TO GET YOUR ATTENTION.
WHAT IS THIS? WHO ARE YOU?
SEE? I'M PUTTIN' IT AWAY.
LOOK, MA, NO HANDS.
LISTEN, Q-TIP, I WON'T BEAT AROUND THE BUSH--
SO, NOW IT'S JUST ME AND YOU...
DON'T JUDGE HIM TOO HARSHLY ...HE HAD AN ASS TO SAVE.
YOUR LITTLE PLAYMATE GOLD-FISH? HE GAVE UP HIS END.
AND I FOR ONE ...WELL, I COULDN'T BE HAPPIER.
'CAUSE, Y'KNOW, I'VE BEEN THINKIN' ABOUT YOU SINCE THE OTHER DAY...
...A LOT ...AND I...
WHAT?!!
C'MON, C'MON... YOU'RE A BAD PENNY, SISTER...
AND I AIN'T BETTIN' ON YOU.
I MEAN SERIOUSLY...
TRUST ME-- IT WORKS FOR HER BIG TIME!!
OH-- CRAP!!

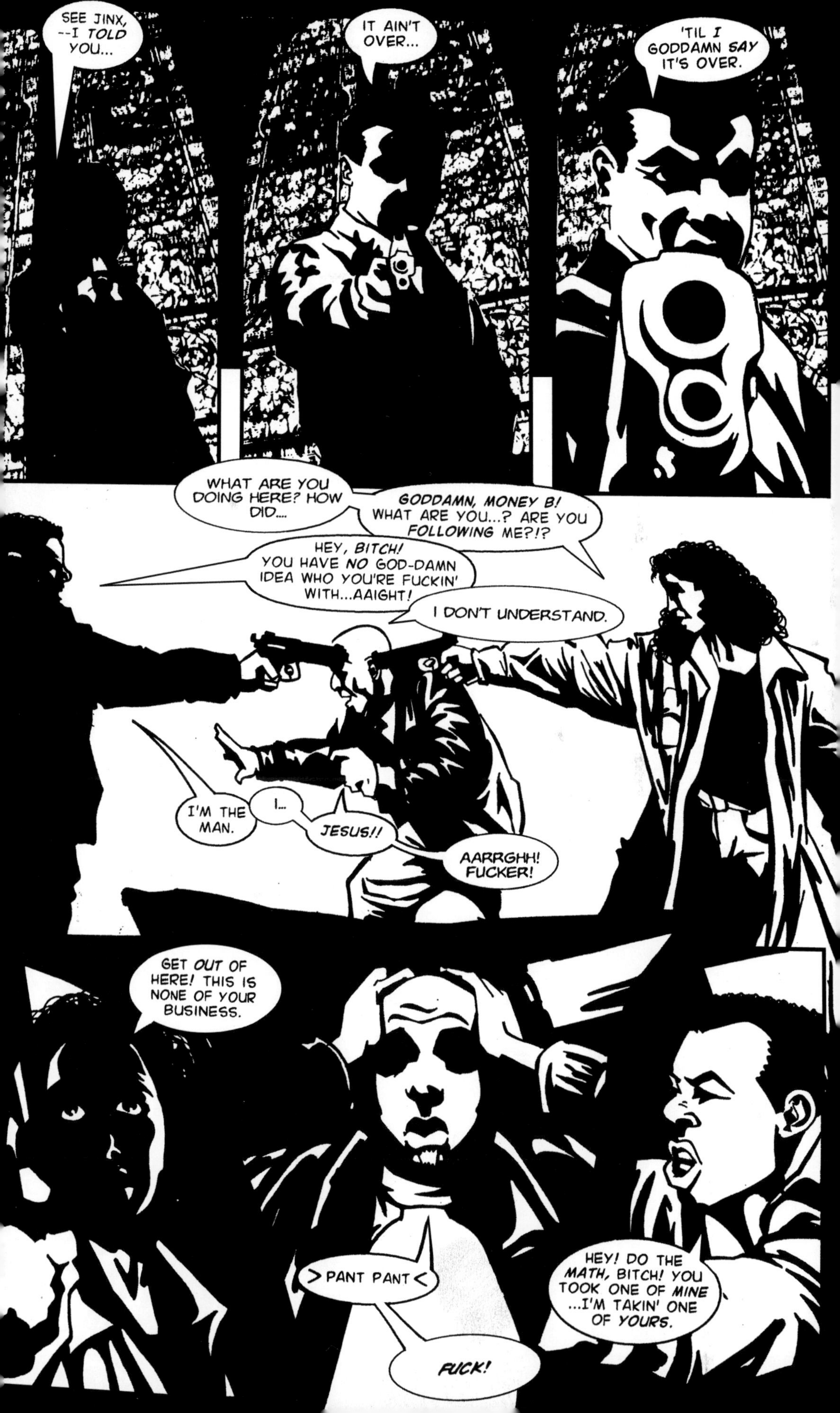
SEE JINX, --I TOLD YOU...
IT AIN'T OVER...
'TIL I GODDAMN SAY IT'S OVER.
WHAT ARE YOU DOING HERE? HOW DID...
GODDAMN, MONEY B! WHAT ARE YOU...? ARE YOU FOLLOWING ME?!?
HEY, BITCH! YOU HAVE NO GOD-DAMN IDEA WHO YOU'RE FUCKIN' WITH...AAIGHT!
I DON'T UNDERSTAND.
I'M THE MAN.
I...
JESUS!!
AARRGHH! FUCKER!
GET OUT OF HERE! THIS IS NONE OF YOUR BUSINESS.
>PANT PANT<
FUCK!
HEY! DO THE MATH, BITCH! YOU TOOK ONE OF MINE ...I'M TAKIN' ONE OF YOURS.

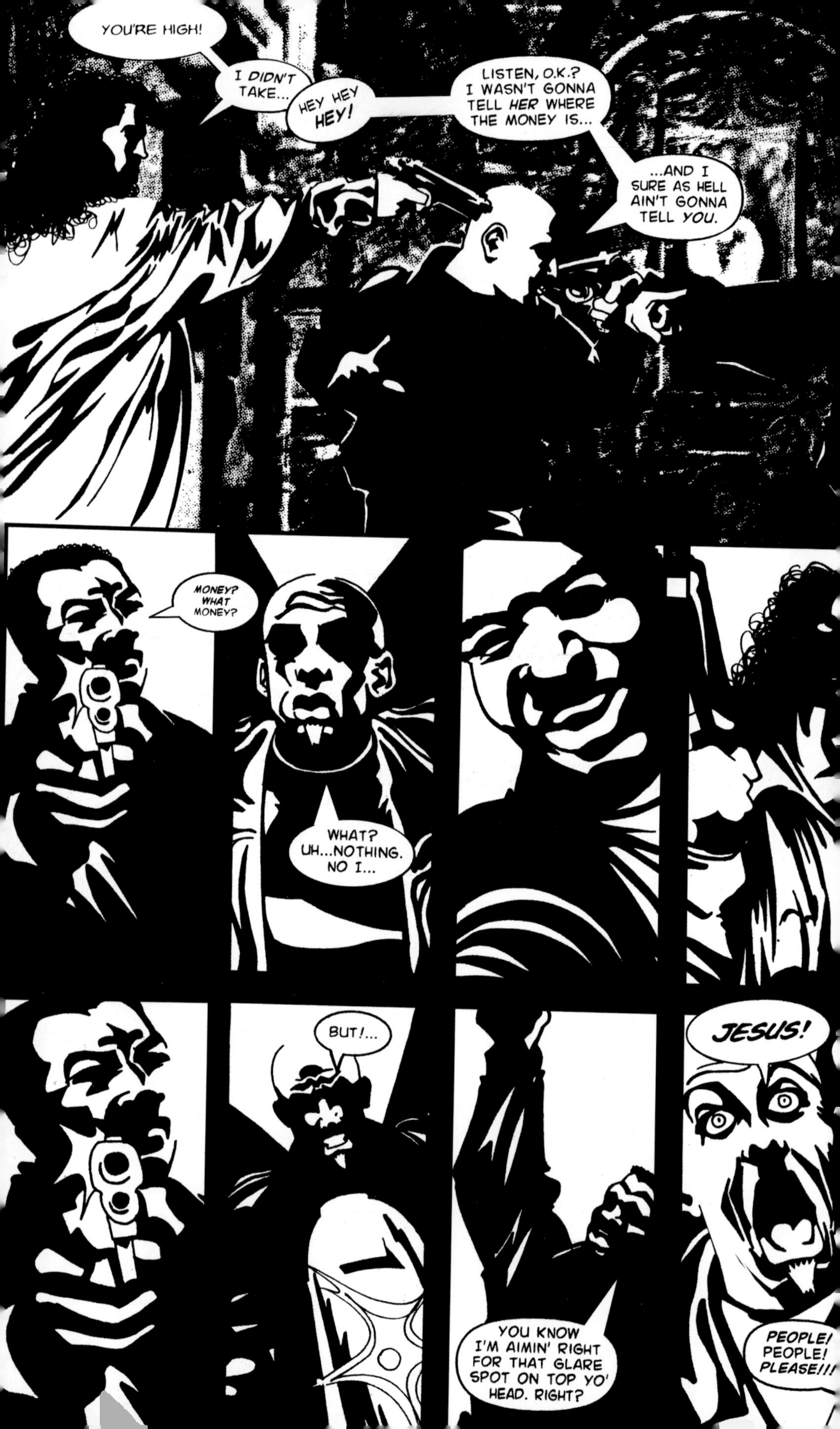

YOU'RE HIGH!
I DIDN'T TAKE...
HEY HEY HEY!
LISTEN, O.K.? I WASN'T GONNA TELL HER WHERE THE MONEY IS...
...AND I SURE AS HELL AIN'T GONNA TELL YOU.
MONEY? WHAT MONEY?
WHAT? UH...NOTHING. NO I...
BUT!...
YOU KNOW I'M AIMIN' RIGHT FOR THAT GLARE SPOT ON TOP YO' HEAD. RIGHT?
JESUS!
PEOPLE! PEOPLE! PLEASE!!!

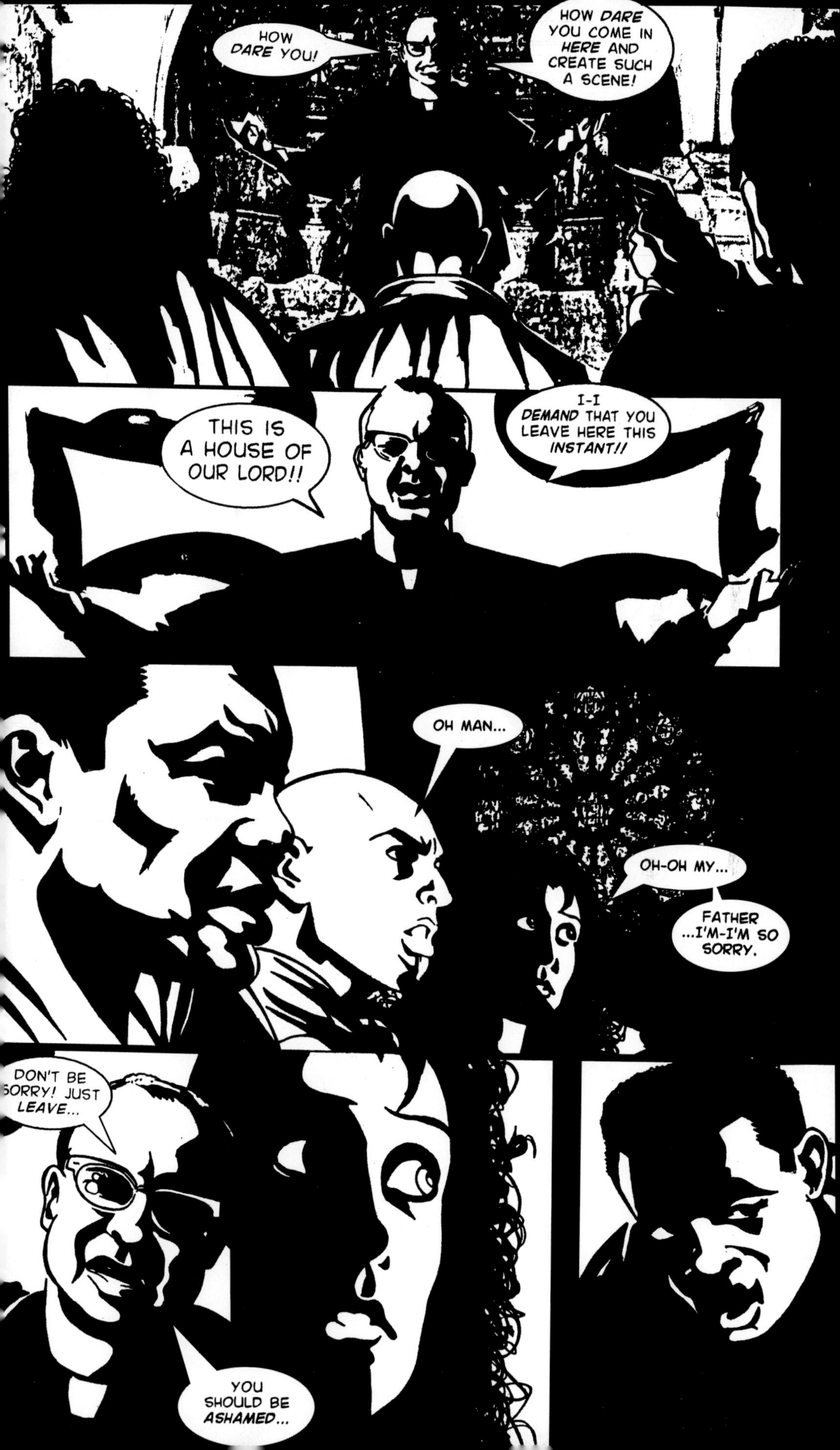
HOW DARE YOU!
HOW DARE YOU COME IN HERE AND CREATE SUCH A SCENE!
THIS IS A HOUSE OF OUR LORD!!
I-I DEMAND THAT YOU LEAVE HERE THIS INSTANT!!
OH MAN...
OH-OH MY...
FATHER ...I'M-I'M SO SORRY.
DON'T BE SORRY! JUST LEAVE...
YOU SHOULD BE ASHAMED...

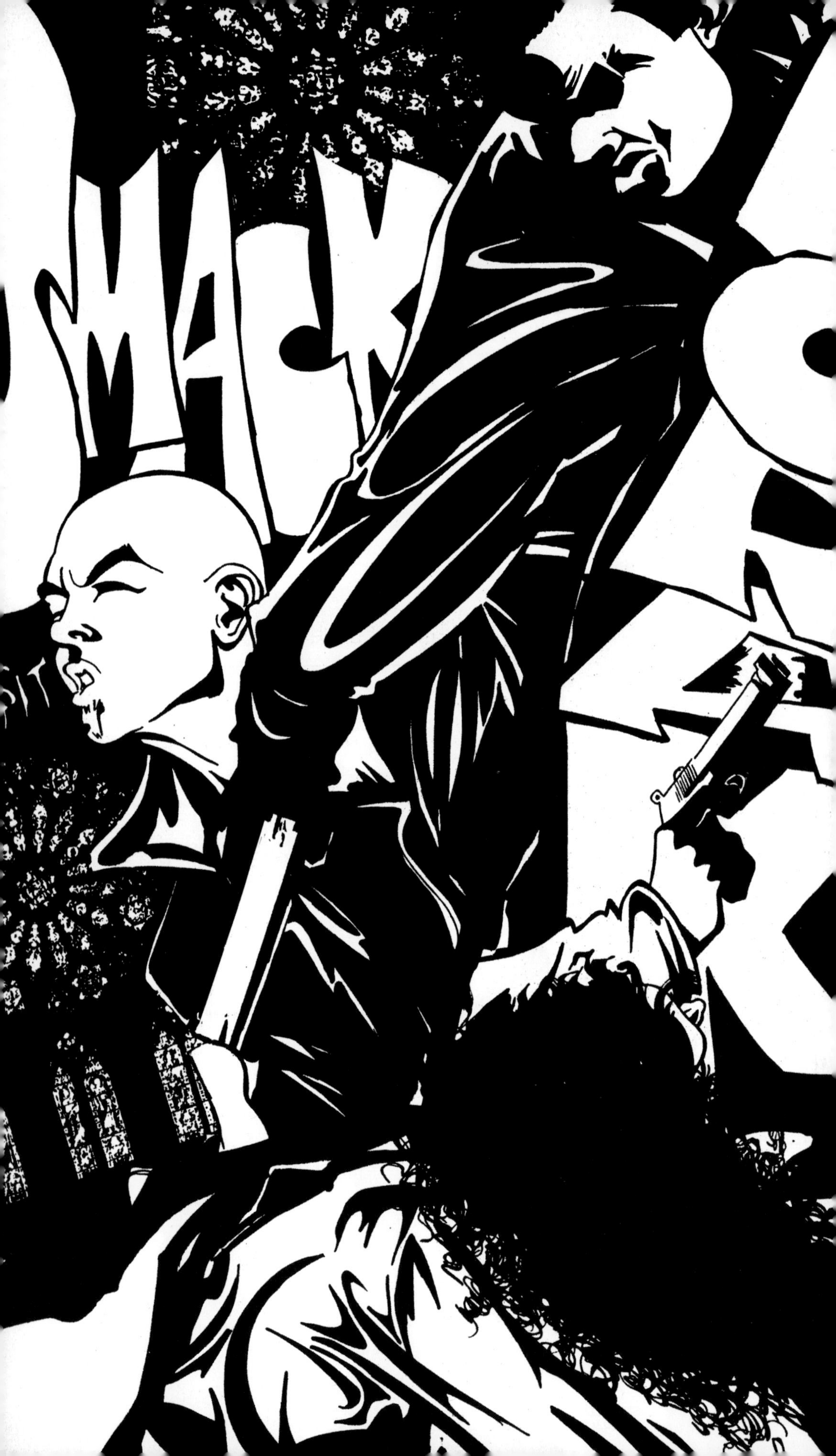
MACK

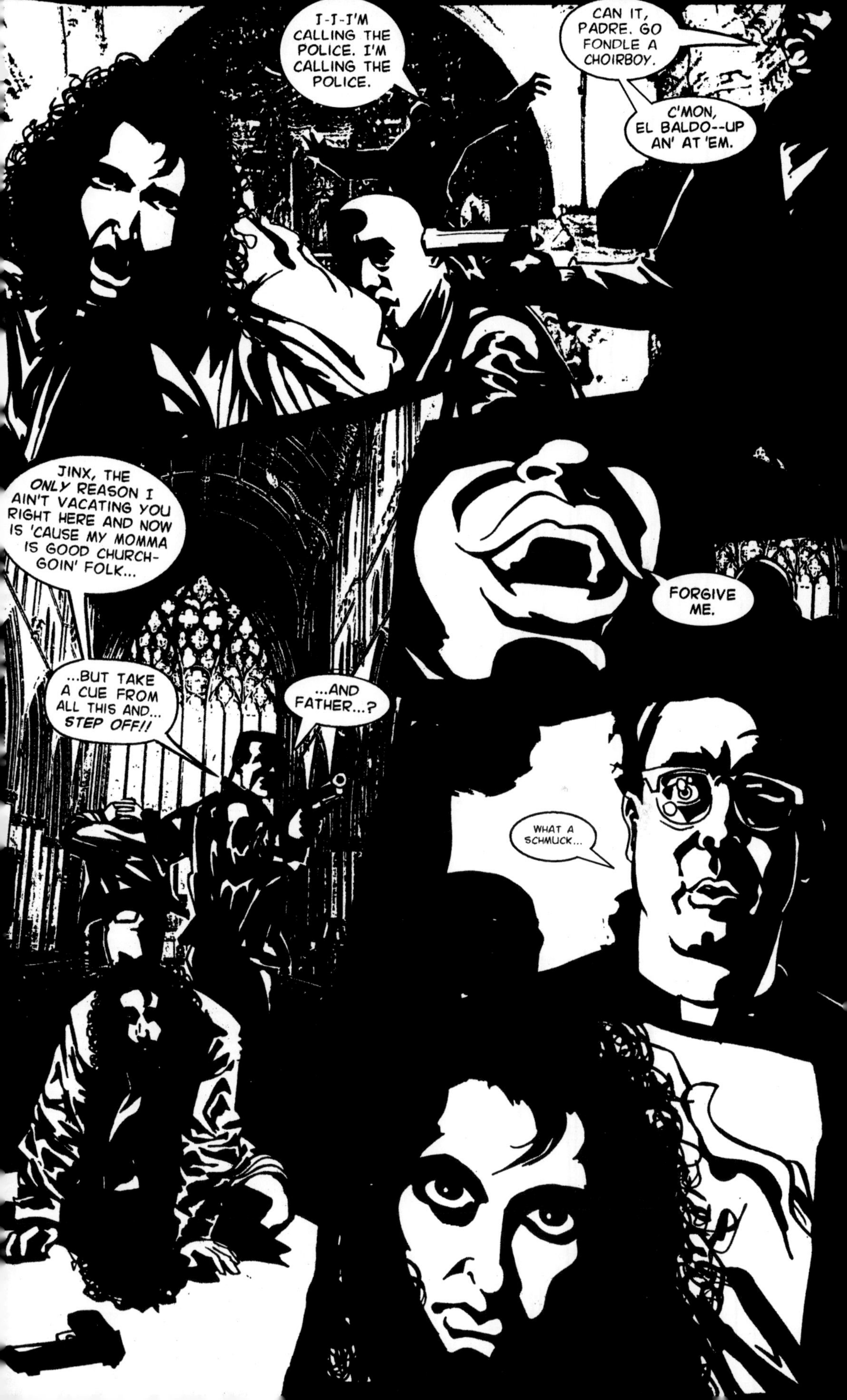
I-I-I'M CALLING THE POLICE. I'M CALLING THE POLICE.
CAN IT, PADRE. GO FONDLE A CHOIRBOY.
C'MON, EL BALDO--UP AN' AT 'EM.
JINX, THE *ONLY* REASON I AIN'T VACATING YOU RIGHT HERE AND NOW IS 'CAUSE MY MOMMA IS GOOD CHURCH-GOIN' FOLK...
...BUT TAKE A CUE FROM ALL THIS AND... *STEP OFF!!*
...AND FATHER...?
FORGIVE ME.
WHAT A SCHMUCK...

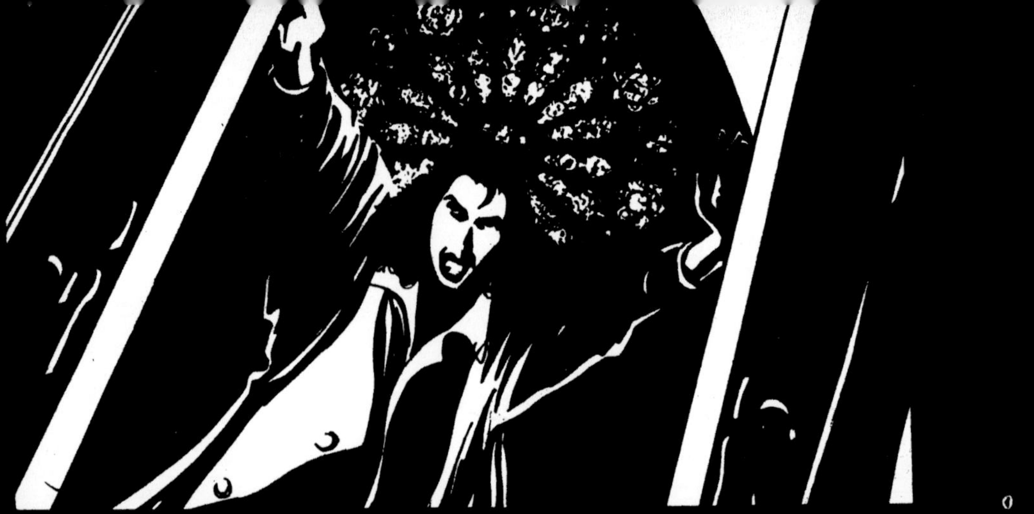

Men Are Like Cars
Part II

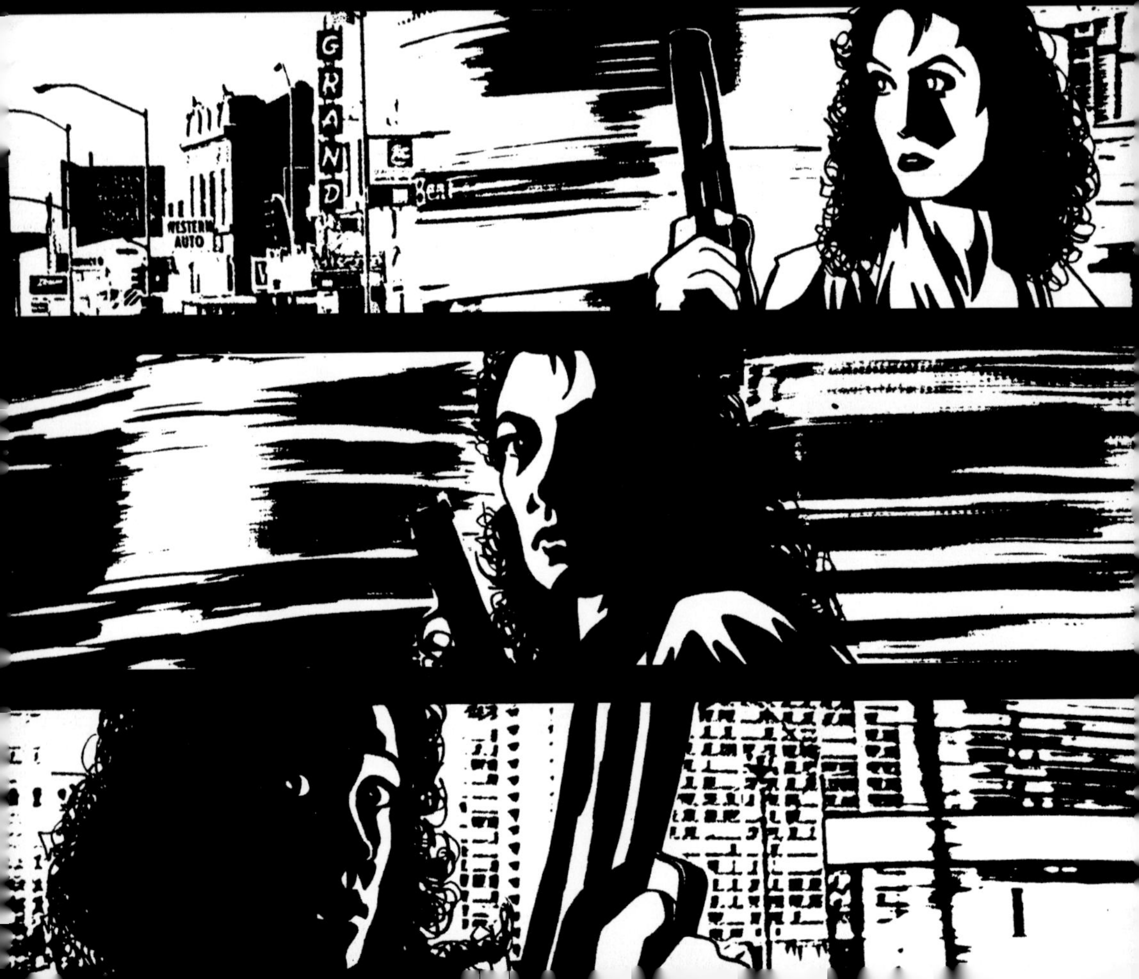
GRAND
WESTERN AUTO

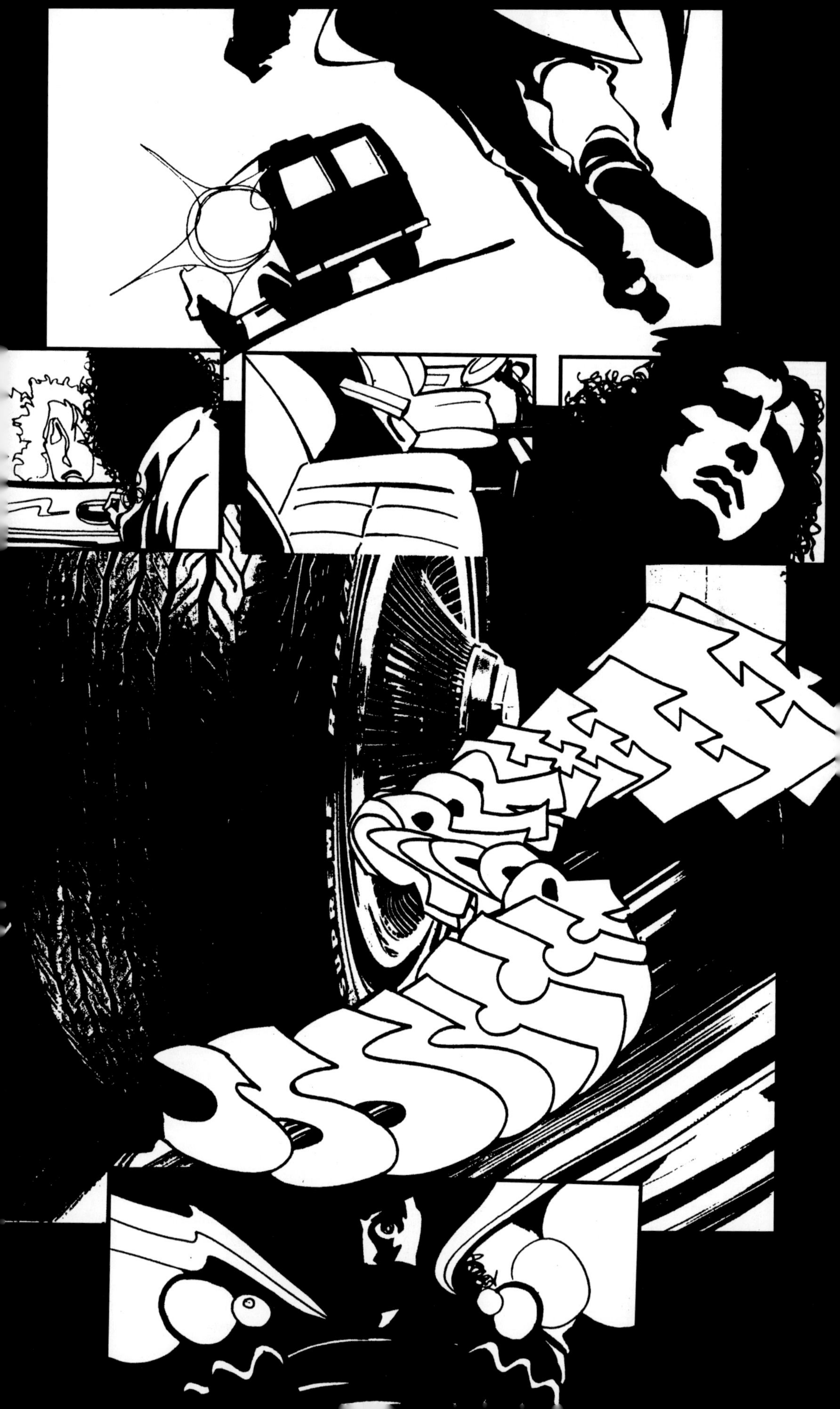

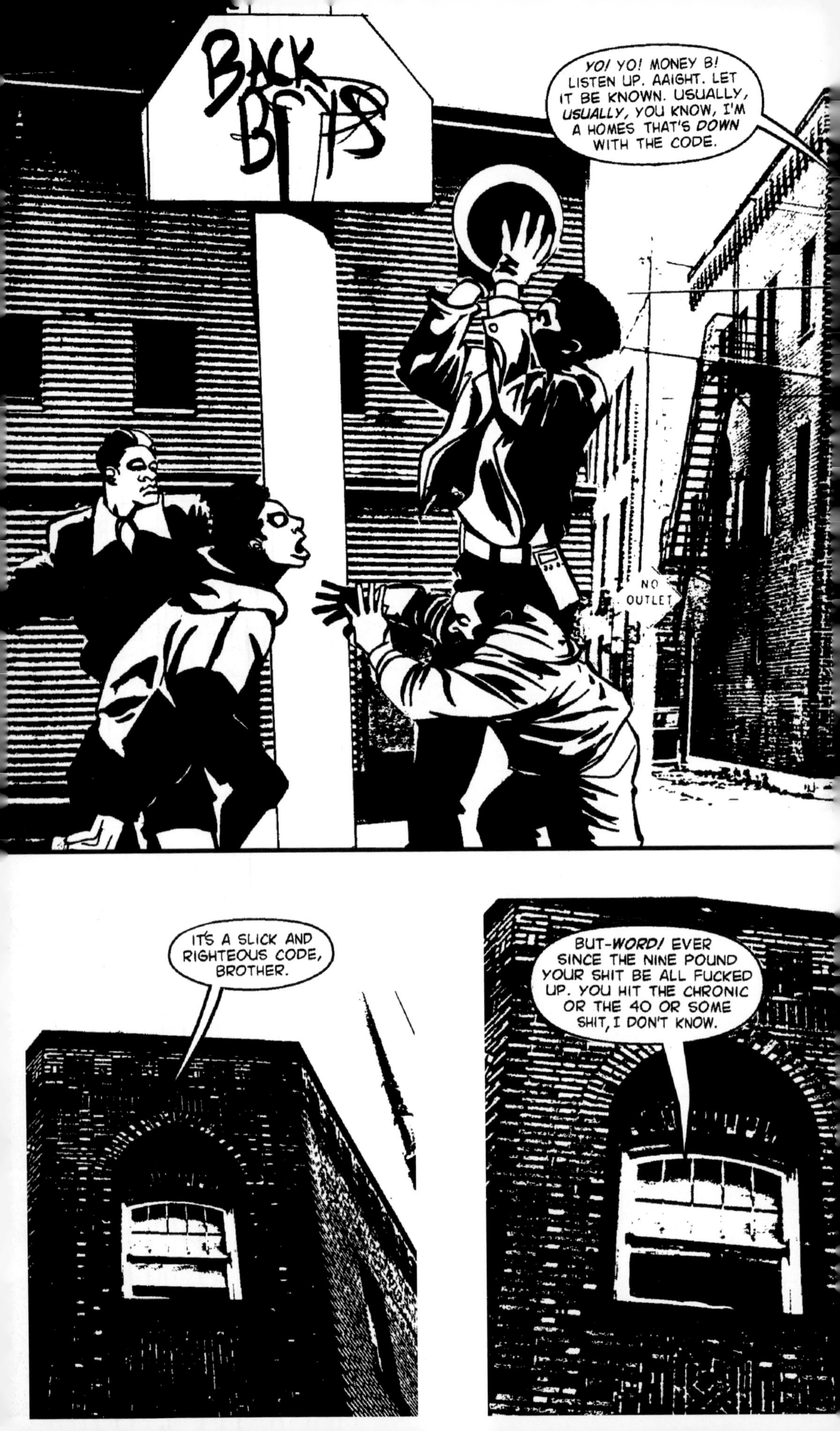
BACK BOYS
YO! YO! MONEY B! LISTEN UP. AAIGHT. LET IT BE KNOWN. USUALLY, USUALLY, YOU KNOW, I'M A HOMES THAT'S DOWN WITH THE CODE.
NO OUTLET
IT'S A SLICK AND RIGHTEOUS CODE, BROTHER.
BUT-WORD! EVER SINCE THE NINE POUND YOUR SHIT BE ALL FUCKED UP. YOU HIT THE CHRONIC OR THE 40 OR SOME SHIT, I DON'T KNOW.

Ziggy

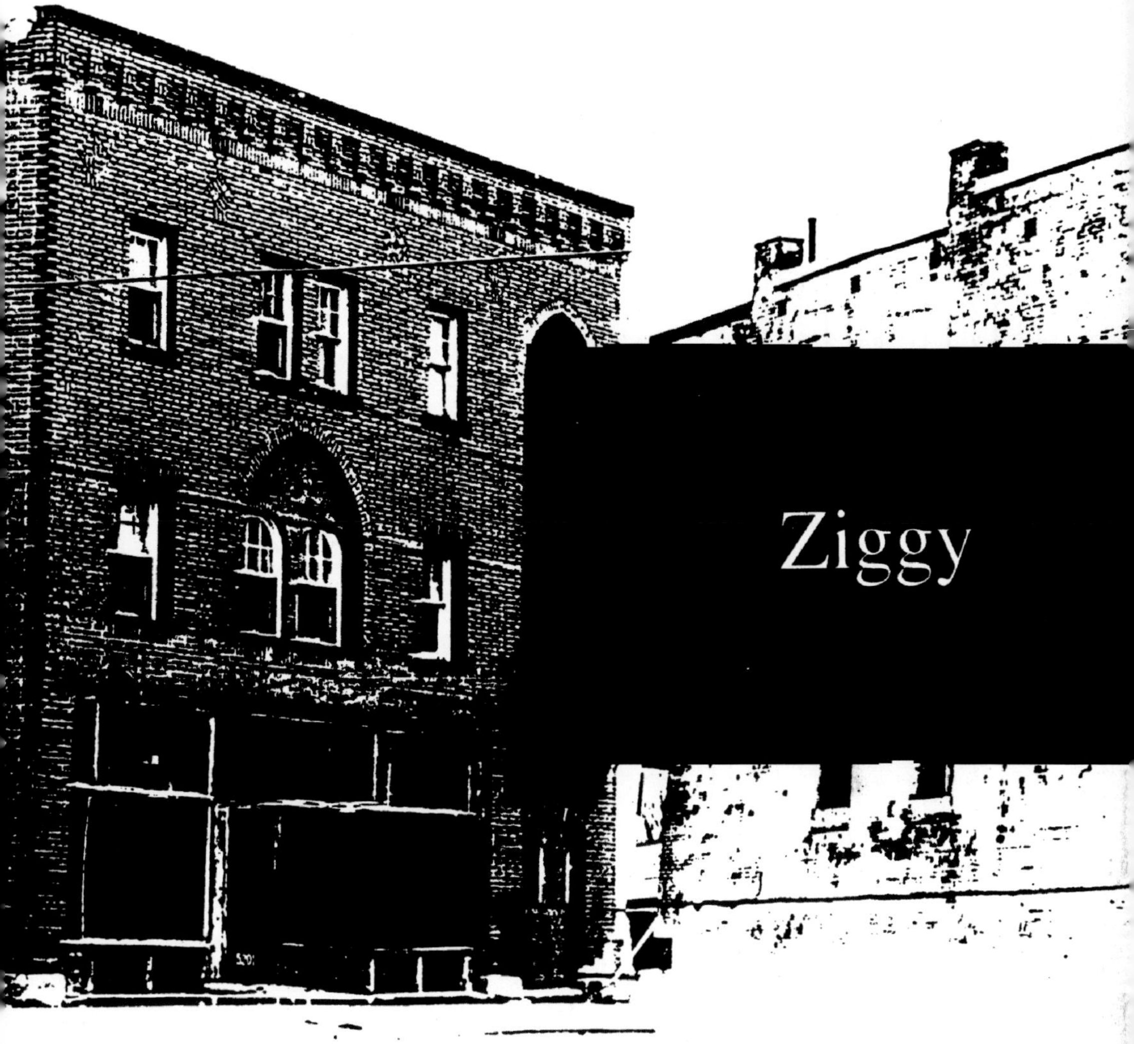

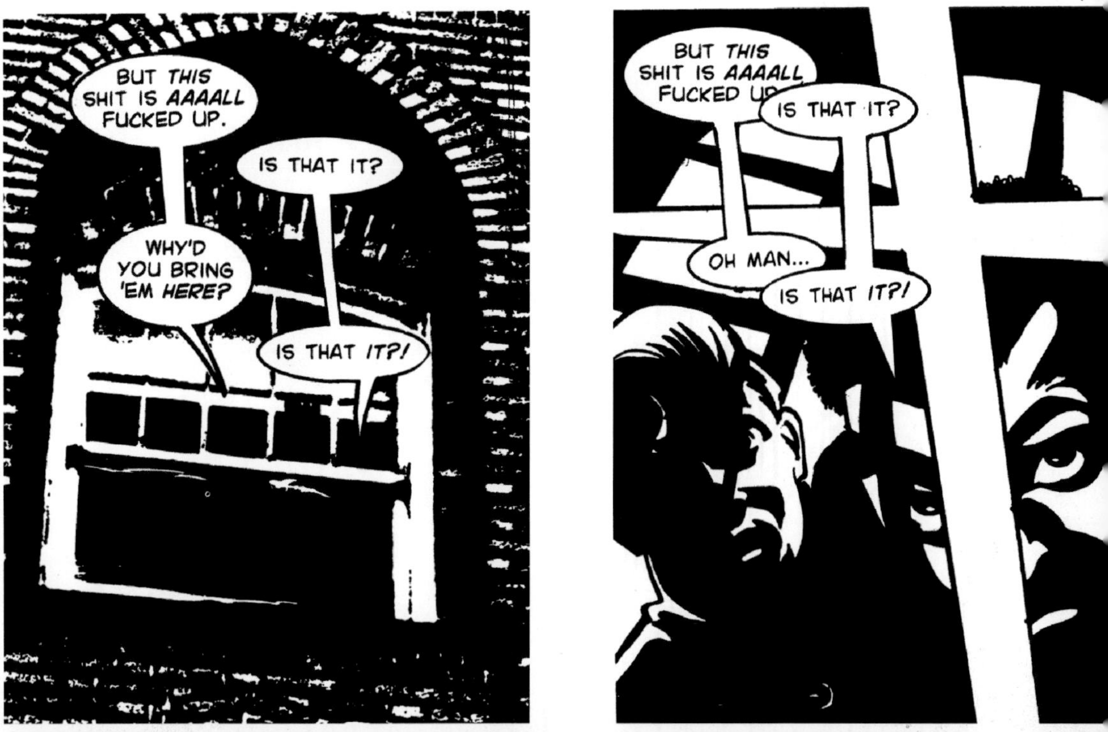
BUT *THIS* SHIT IS *AAAALL* FUCKED UP.
IS THAT IT?
WHY'D YOU BRING 'EM *HERE?*
IS THAT *IT?!*
BUT *THIS* SHIT IS *AAAALL* FUCKED UP
IS THAT IT?
OH MAN...
IS THAT *IT?!*

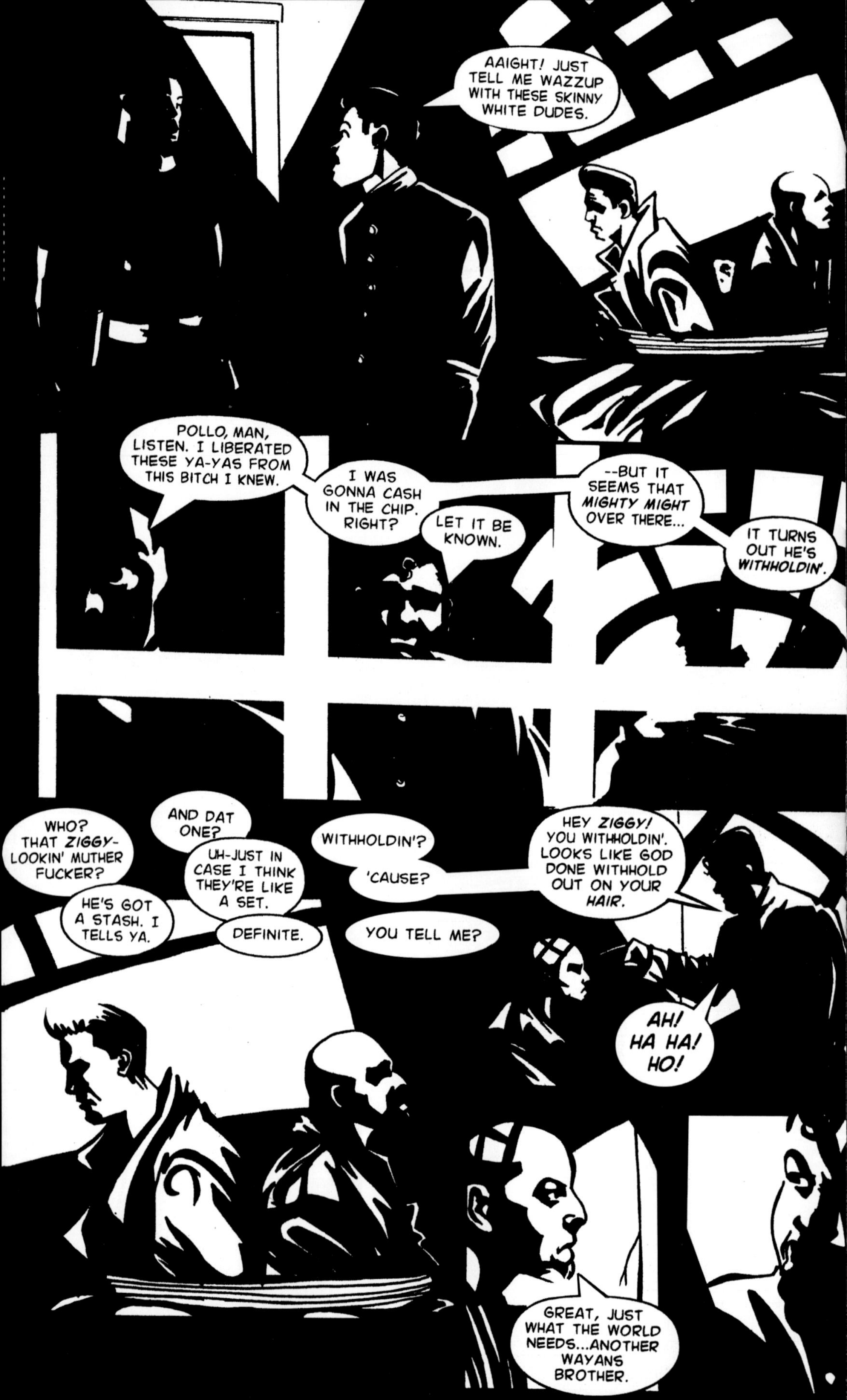
AAIGHT! JUST TELL ME WAZZUP WITH THESE SKINNY WHITE DUDES.
POLLO, MAN, LISTEN. I LIBERATED THESE YA-YAS FROM THIS BITCH I KNEW.
I WAS GONNA CASH IN THE CHIP. RIGHT?
LET IT BE KNOWN.
--BUT IT SEEMS THAT MIGHTY MIGHT OVER THERE...
IT TURNS OUT HE'S WITHHOLDIN'.
WHO? THAT ZIGGY-LOOKIN' MUTHER FUCKER?
HE'S GOT A STASH. I TELLS YA.
AND DAT ONE?
UH-JUST IN CASE I THINK THEY'RE LIKE A SET.
DEFINITE.
WITHHOLDIN'?
'CAUSE?
YOU TELL ME?
HEY ZIGGY! YOU WITHHOLDIN'. LOOKS LIKE GOD DONE WITHHOLD OUT ON YOUR HAIR.
AH! HA HA! HO!
GREAT, JUST WHAT THE WORLD NEEDS...ANOTHER WAYANS BROTHER.

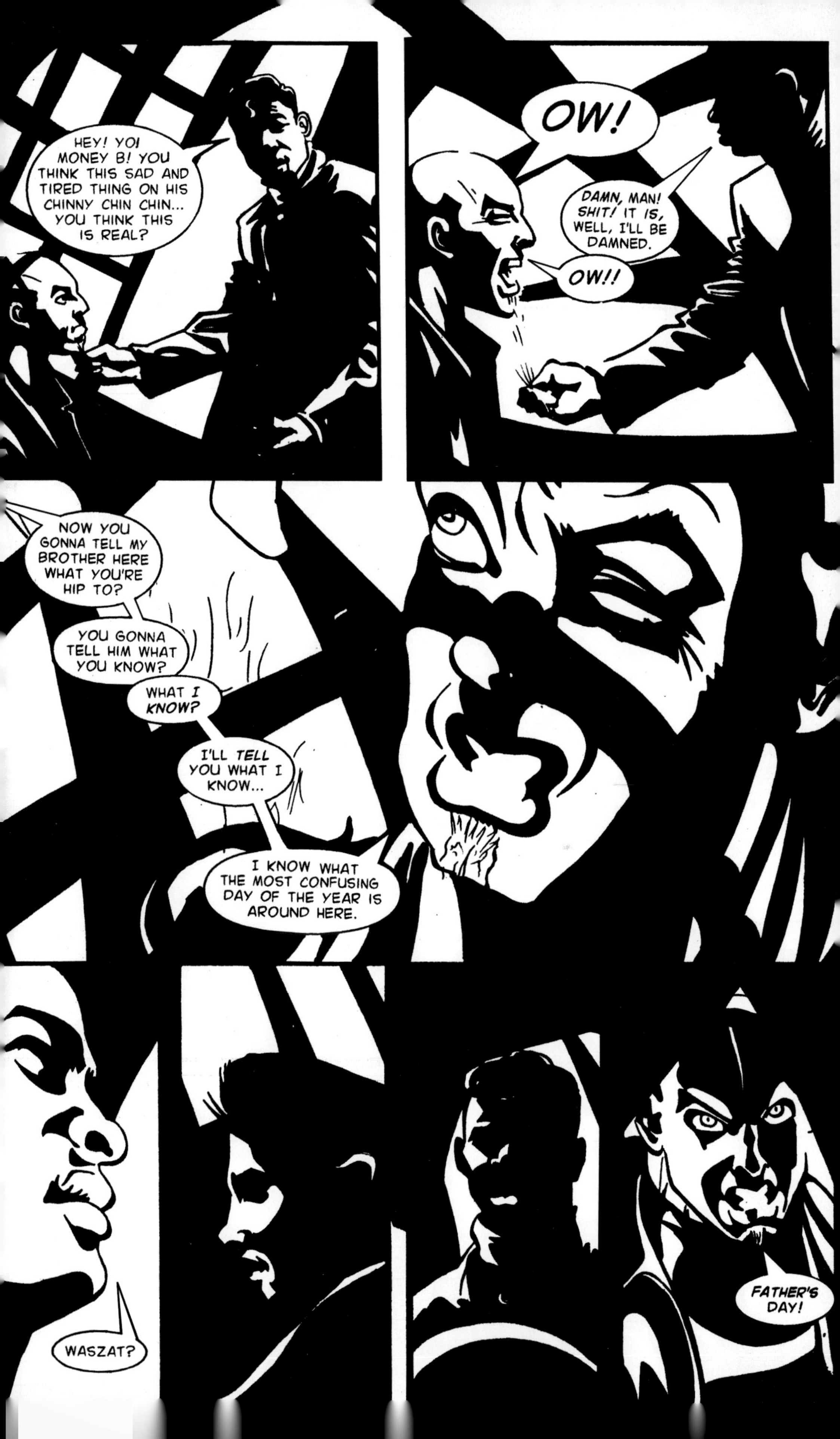
HEY! YO! MONEY B! YOU THINK THIS SAD AND TIRED THING ON HIS CHINNY CHIN CHIN... YOU THINK THIS IS REAL?
OW!
DAMN, MAN! SHIT! IT IS, WELL, I'LL BE DAMNED.
OW!!
NOW YOU GONNA TELL MY BROTHER HERE WHAT YOU'RE HIP TO?
YOU GONNA TELL HIM WHAT YOU KNOW?
WHAT I KNOW?
I'LL TELL YOU WHAT I KNOW...
I KNOW WHAT THE MOST CONFUSING DAY OF THE YEAR IS AROUND HERE.
WASZAT?
FATHER'S DAY!

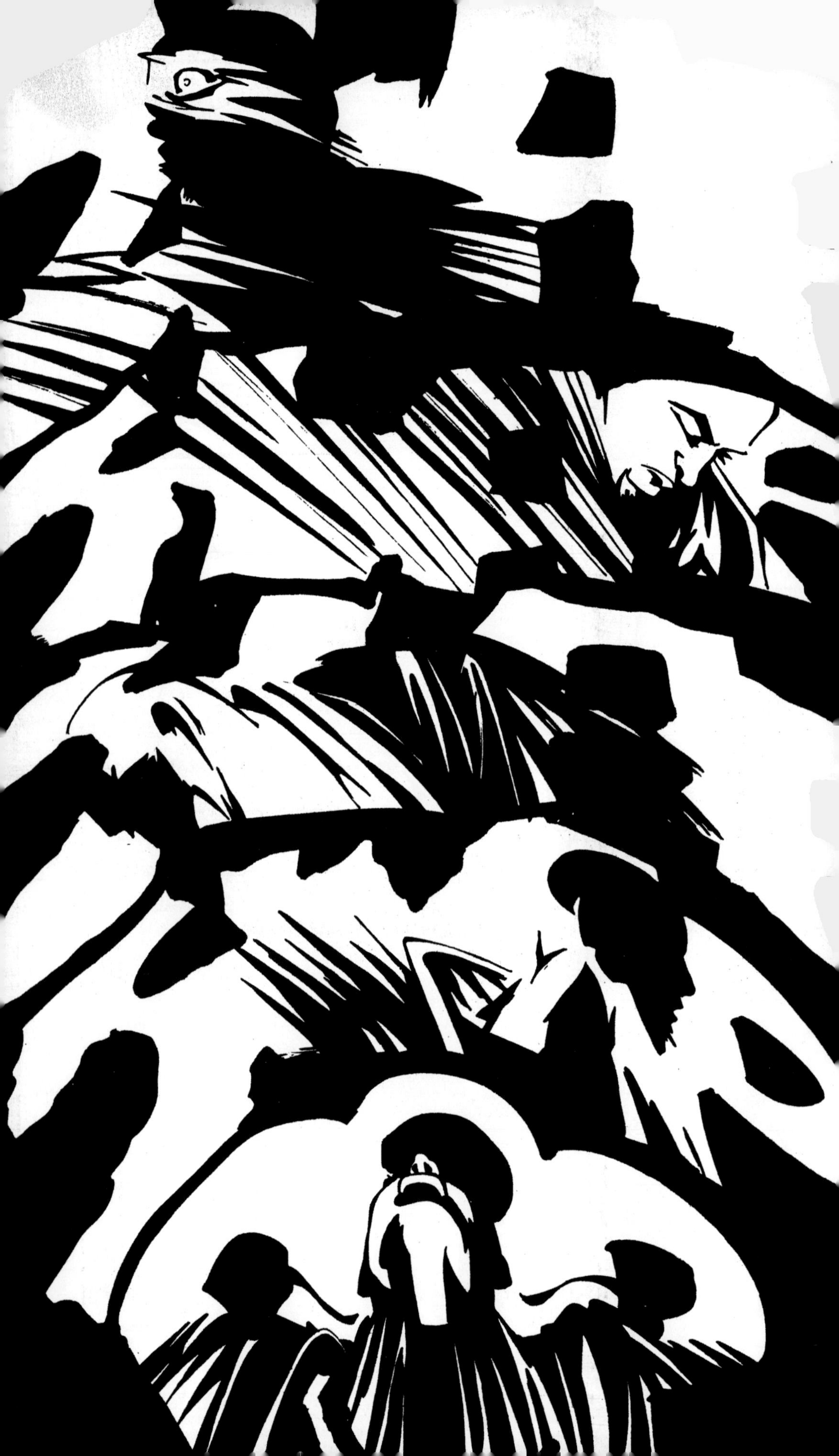

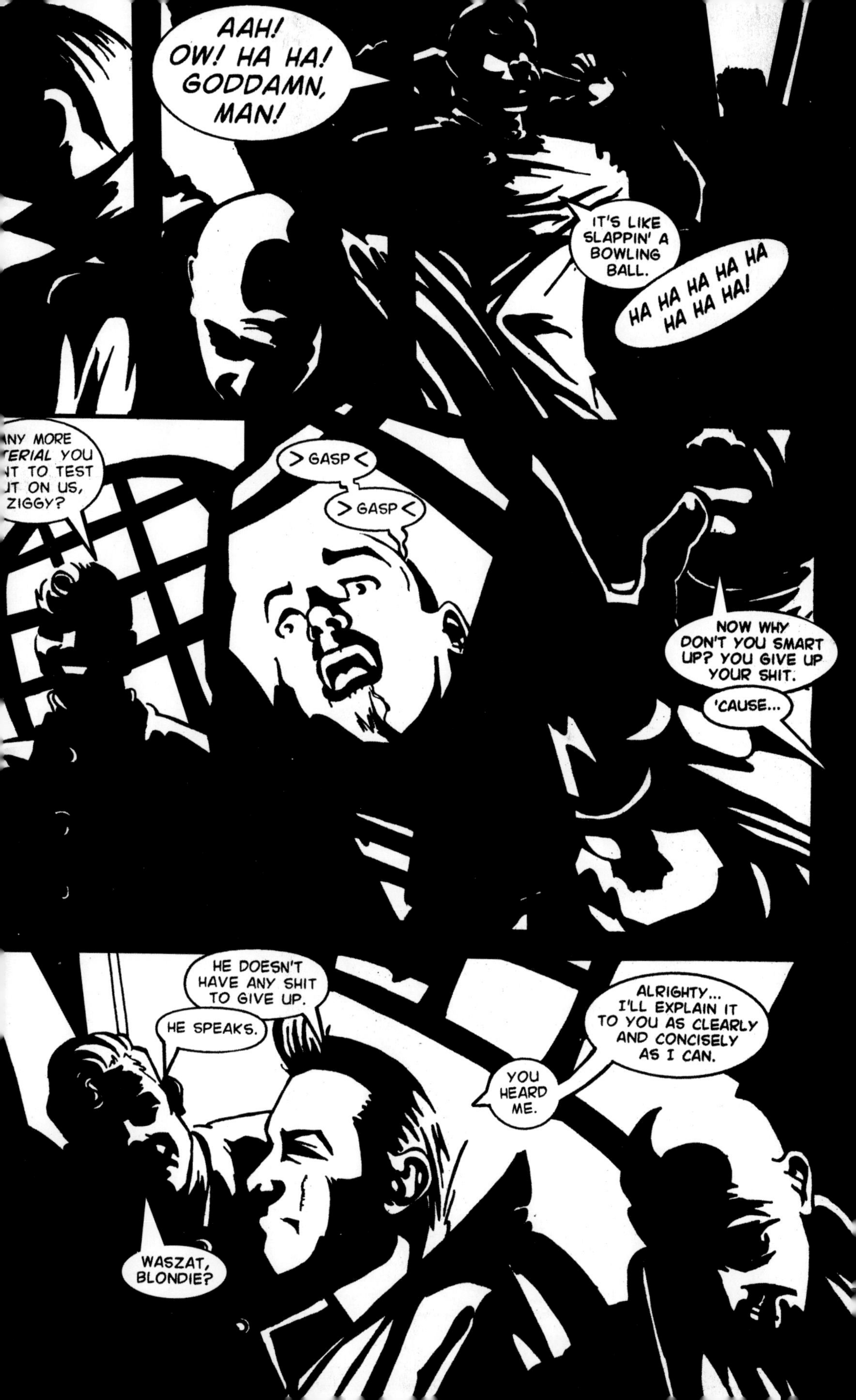
AAH! OW! HA HA! GODDAMN, MAN!
IT'S LIKE SLAPPIN' A BOWLING BALL.
HA HA HA HA HA HA HA HA!
NY MORE TERIAL YOU NT TO TEST UT ON US, ZIGGY?
>GASP<
>GASP<
NOW WHY DON'T YOU SMART UP? YOU GIVE UP YOUR SHIT.
'CAUSE...
HE DOESN'T HAVE ANY SHIT TO GIVE UP.
HE SPEAKS.
WASZAT, BLONDIE?
YOU HEARD ME.
ALRIGHTY... I'LL EXPLAIN IT TO YOU AS CLEARLY AND CONCISELY AS I CAN.

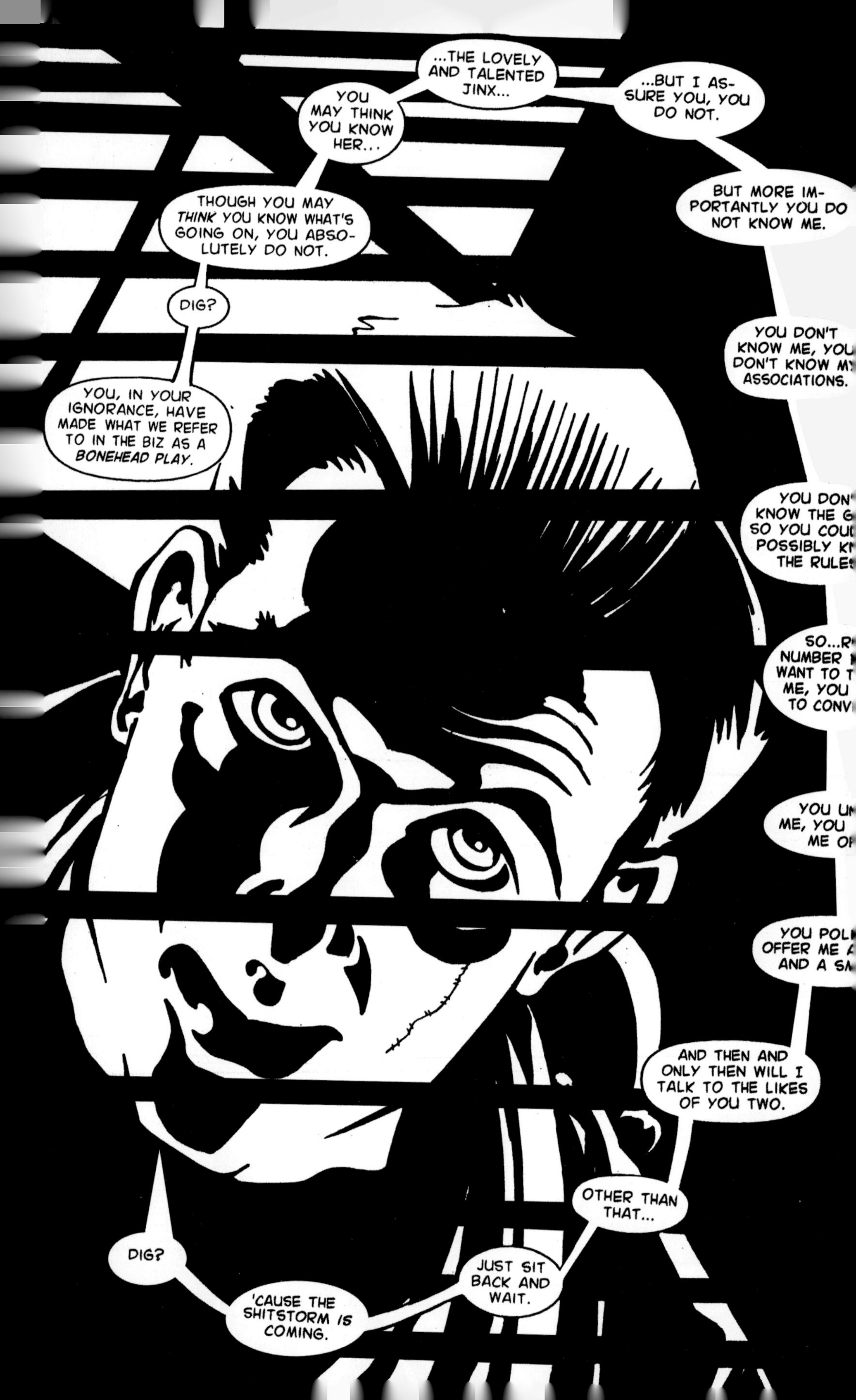

YOU, IN YOUR IGNORANCE, HAVE MADE WHAT WE REFER TO IN THE BIZ AS A *BONEHEAD PLAY.*
DIG?
THOUGH YOU MAY *THINK* YOU KNOW WHAT'S GOING ON, YOU ABSOLUTELY DO NOT.
YOU MAY THINK YOU KNOW HER...
...THE LOVELY AND TALENTED JINX...
...BUT I ASSURE YOU, YOU DO NOT.
BUT MORE IMPORTANTLY YOU DO NOT KNOW ME.
YOU DON'T KNOW ME, YOU DON'T KNOW ASSOCIATIONS.
KNOW THE SO YOU POSSIBLY
NUMBER WANT TO ME, YOU
AND THEN AND ONLY THEN WILL I TALK TO THE LIKES OF YOU TWO.
OTHER THAN THAT...
JUST SIT BACK AND WAIT.
'CAUSE THE SHITSTORM *IS* COMING.
DIG?

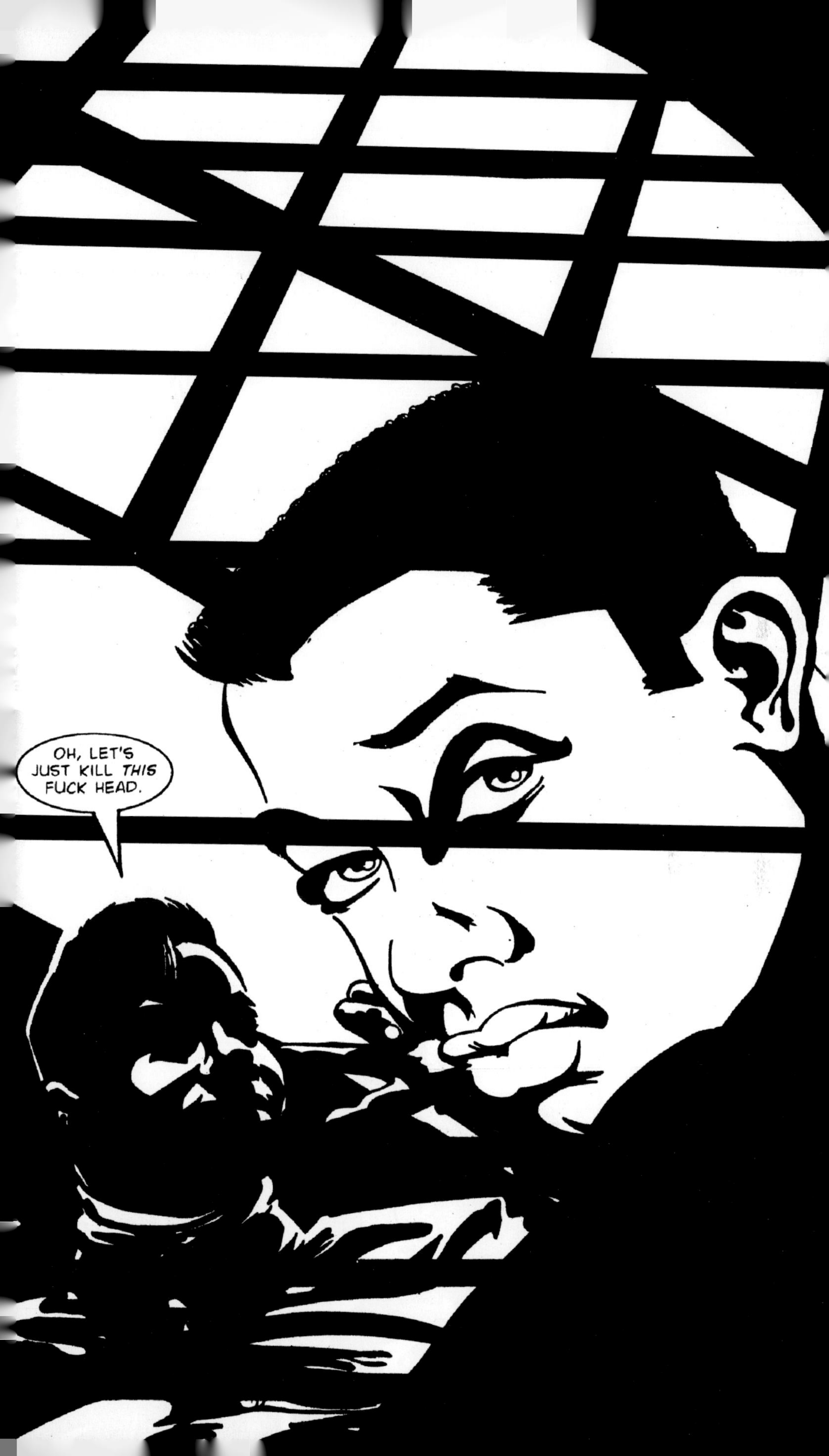
OH, LET'S JUST KILL *THIS* FUCK HEAD.

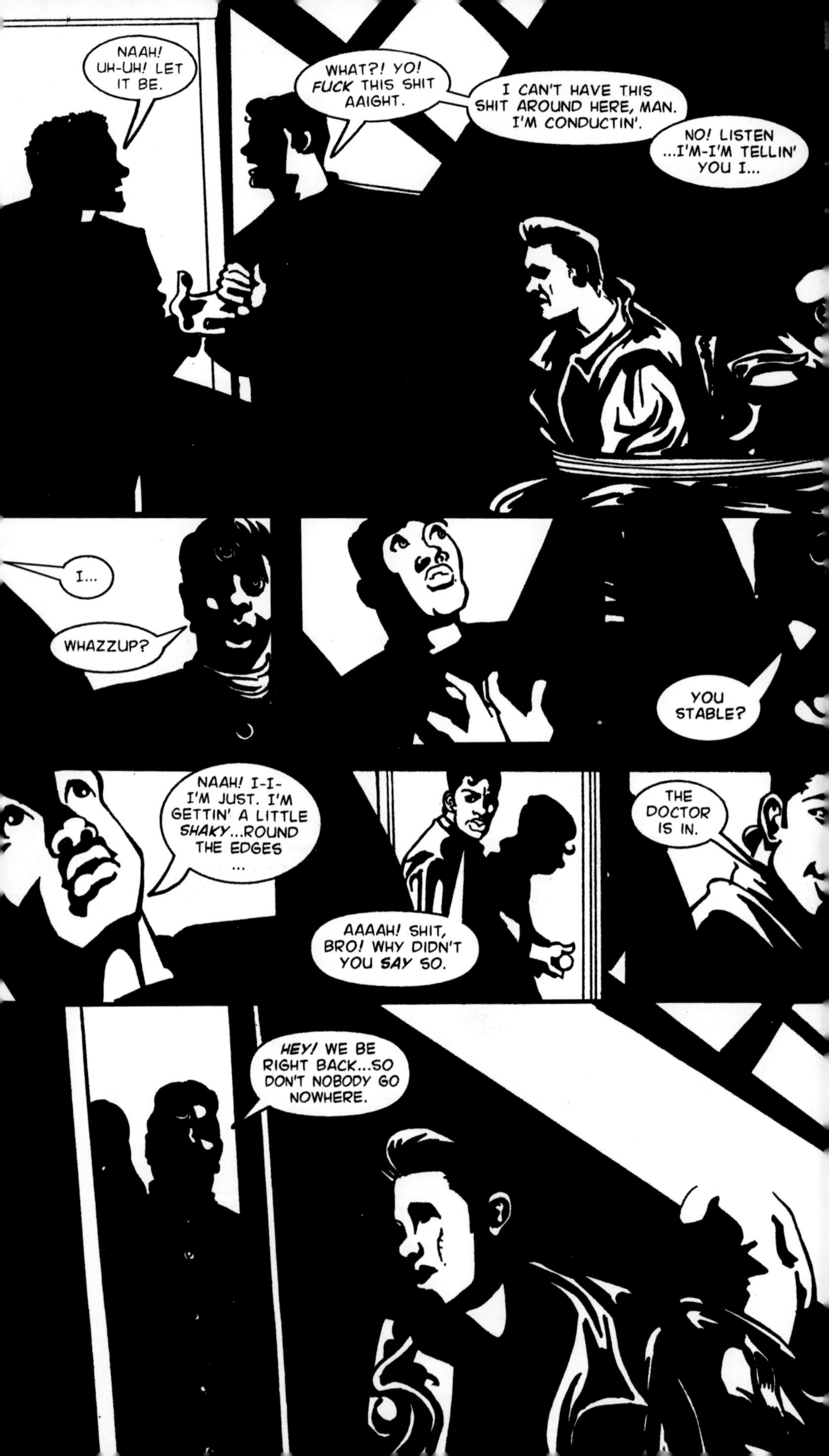
NAAH! UH-UH! LET IT BE.
WHAT?! YO! FUCK THIS SHIT AAIGHT.
I CAN'T HAVE THIS SHIT AROUND HERE, MAN. I'M CONDUCTIN'.
NO! LISTEN ...I'M-I'M TELLIN' YOU I...
I...
WHAZZUP?
YOU STABLE?
NAAH! I-I-I'M JUST. I'M GETTIN' A LITTLE SHAKY...ROUND THE EDGES ...
AAAAH! SHIT, BRO! WHY DIDN'T YOU SAY SO.
THE DOCTOR IS IN.
HEY! WE BE RIGHT BACK...SO DON'T NOBODY GO NOWHERE.

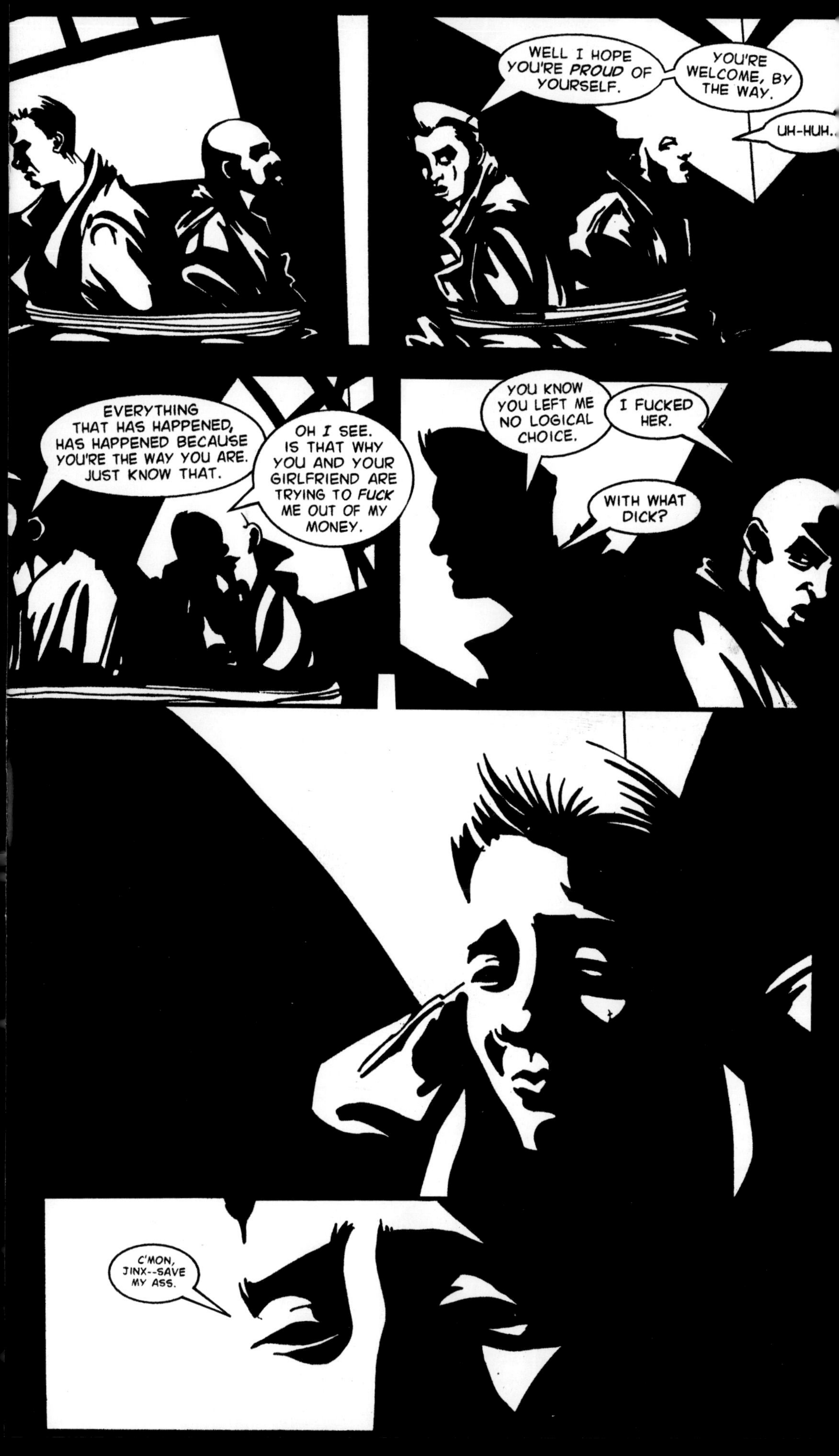
WELL I HOPE YOU'RE *PROUD* OF YOURSELF.
YOU'RE WELCOME, BY THE WAY.
UH-HUH.
EVERYTHING THAT HAS HAPPENED, HAS HAPPENED BECAUSE YOU'RE THE WAY YOU ARE. JUST KNOW THAT.
OH *I* SEE. IS THAT WHY YOU AND YOUR GIRLFRIEND ARE TRYING TO *FUCK* ME OUT OF MY MONEY.
YOU KNOW YOU LEFT ME NO LOGICAL CHOICE.
I FUCKED HER.
WITH WHAT DICK?
C'MON, JINX--SAVE MY ASS.

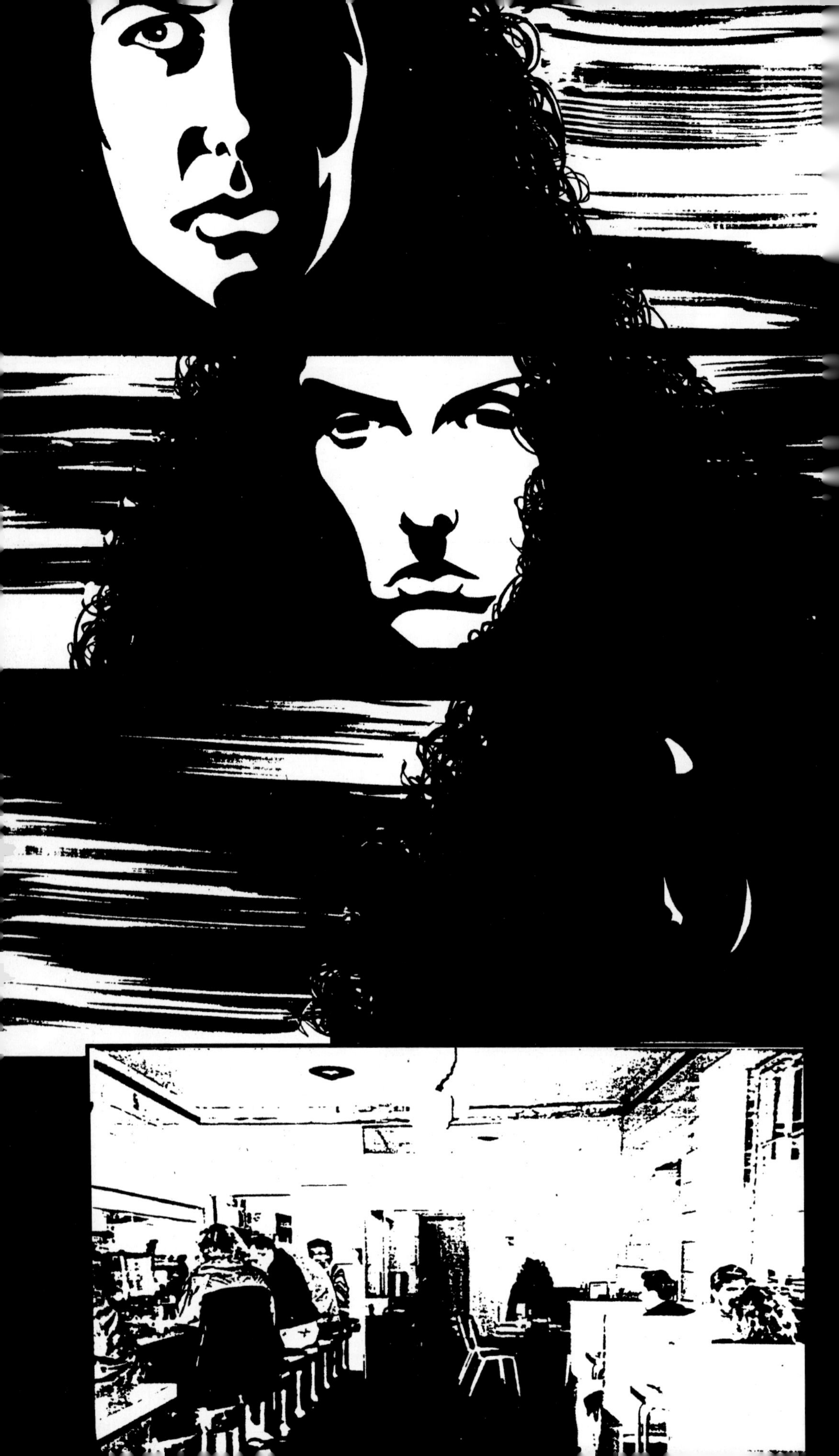

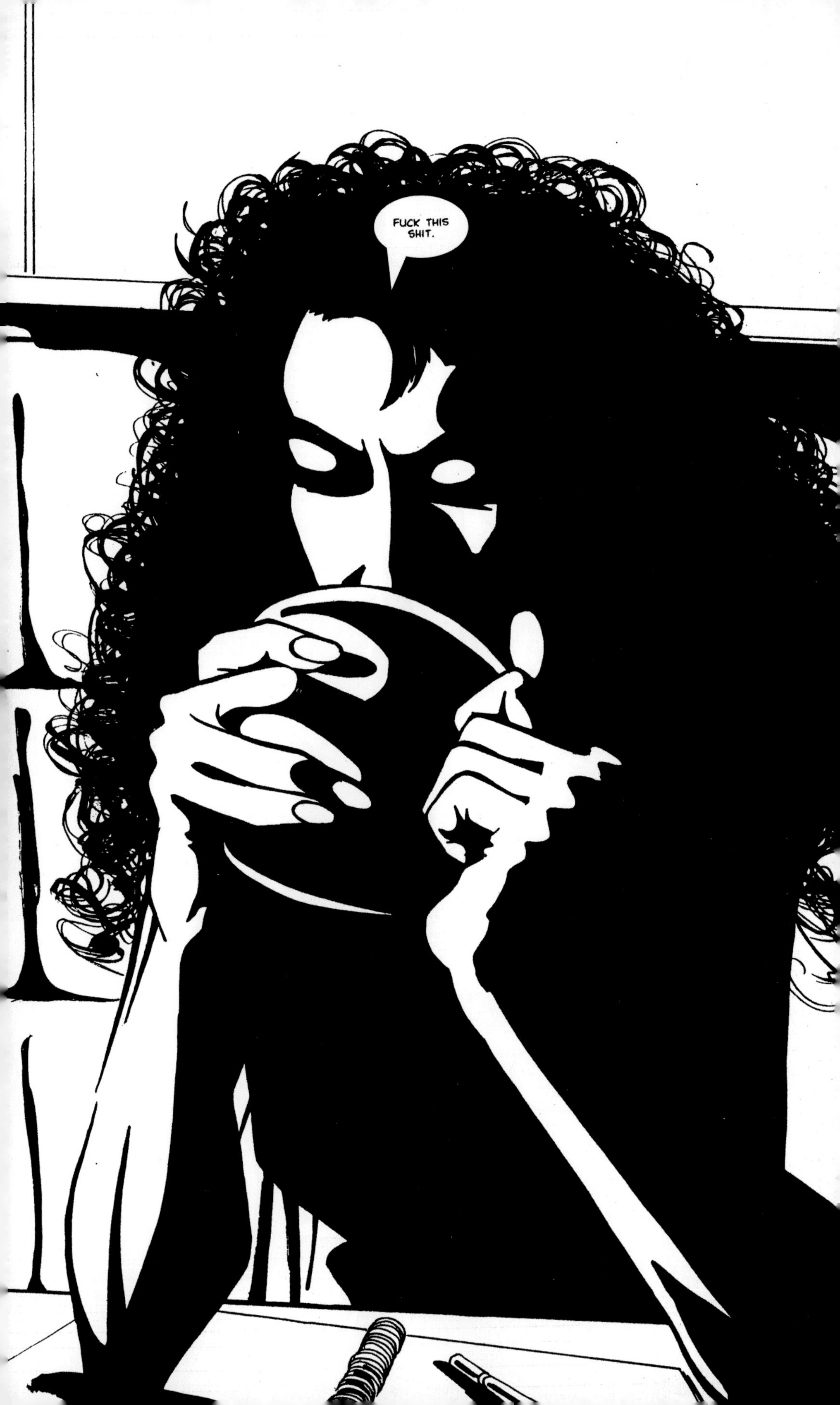
FUCK THIS SHIT.

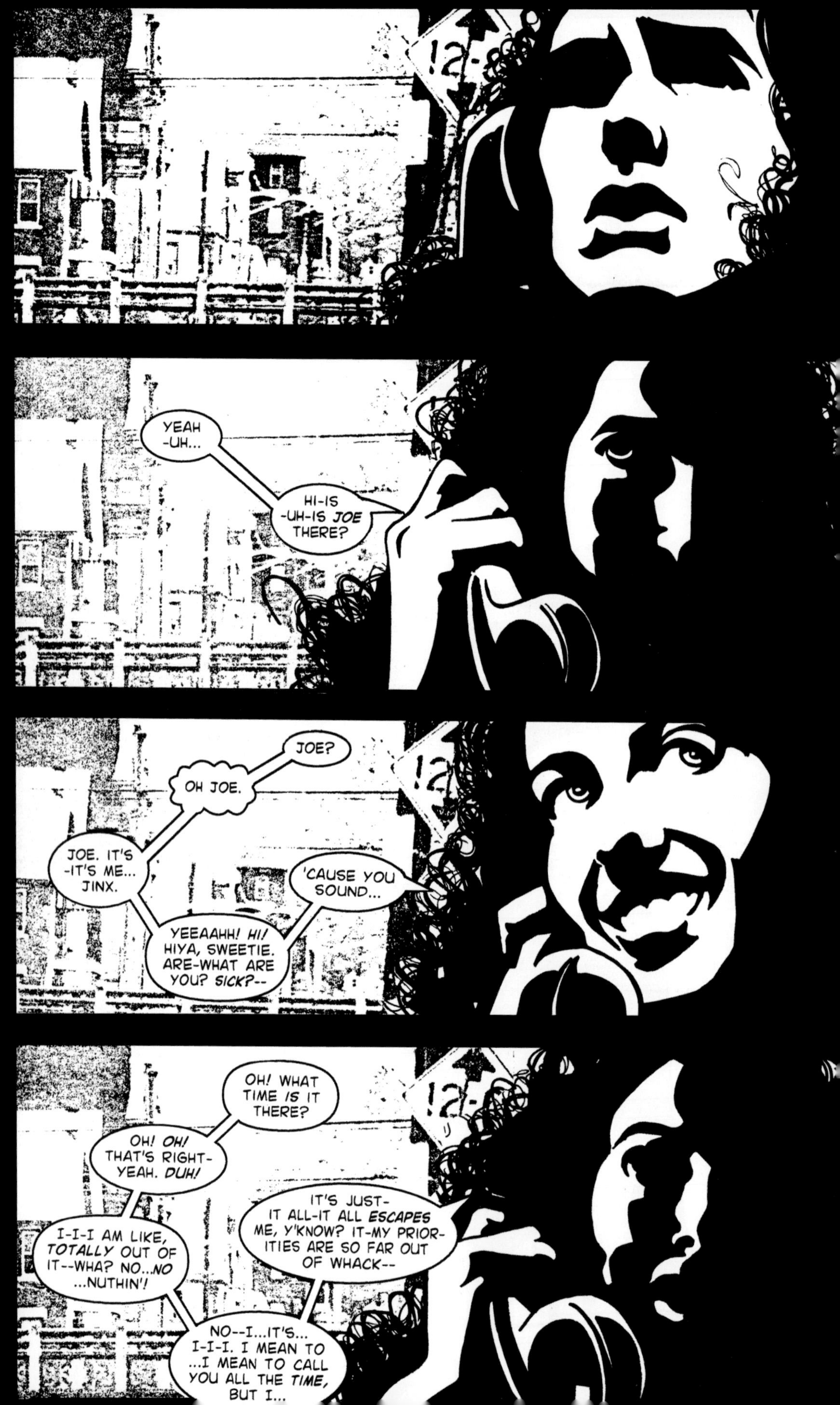
YEAH -UH...
HI-IS -UH-IS JOE THERE?
JOE?
OH JOE.
JOE. IT'S -IT'S ME... JINX.
'CAUSE YOU SOUND...
YEEAAHH! HI! HIYA, SWEETIE. ARE-WHAT ARE YOU? SICK?--
OH! WHAT TIME IS IT THERE?
OH! OH! THAT'S RIGHT- YEAH. DUH!
IT'S JUST- IT ALL-IT ALL ESCAPES ME, Y'KNOW? IT-MY PRIOR- ITIES ARE SO FAR OUT OF WHACK--
I-I-I AM LIKE, TOTALLY OUT OF IT--WHA? NO...NO ...NUTHIN'!
NO--I...IT'S... I-I-I. I MEAN TO ...I MEAN TO CALL YOU ALL THE TIME, BUT I...

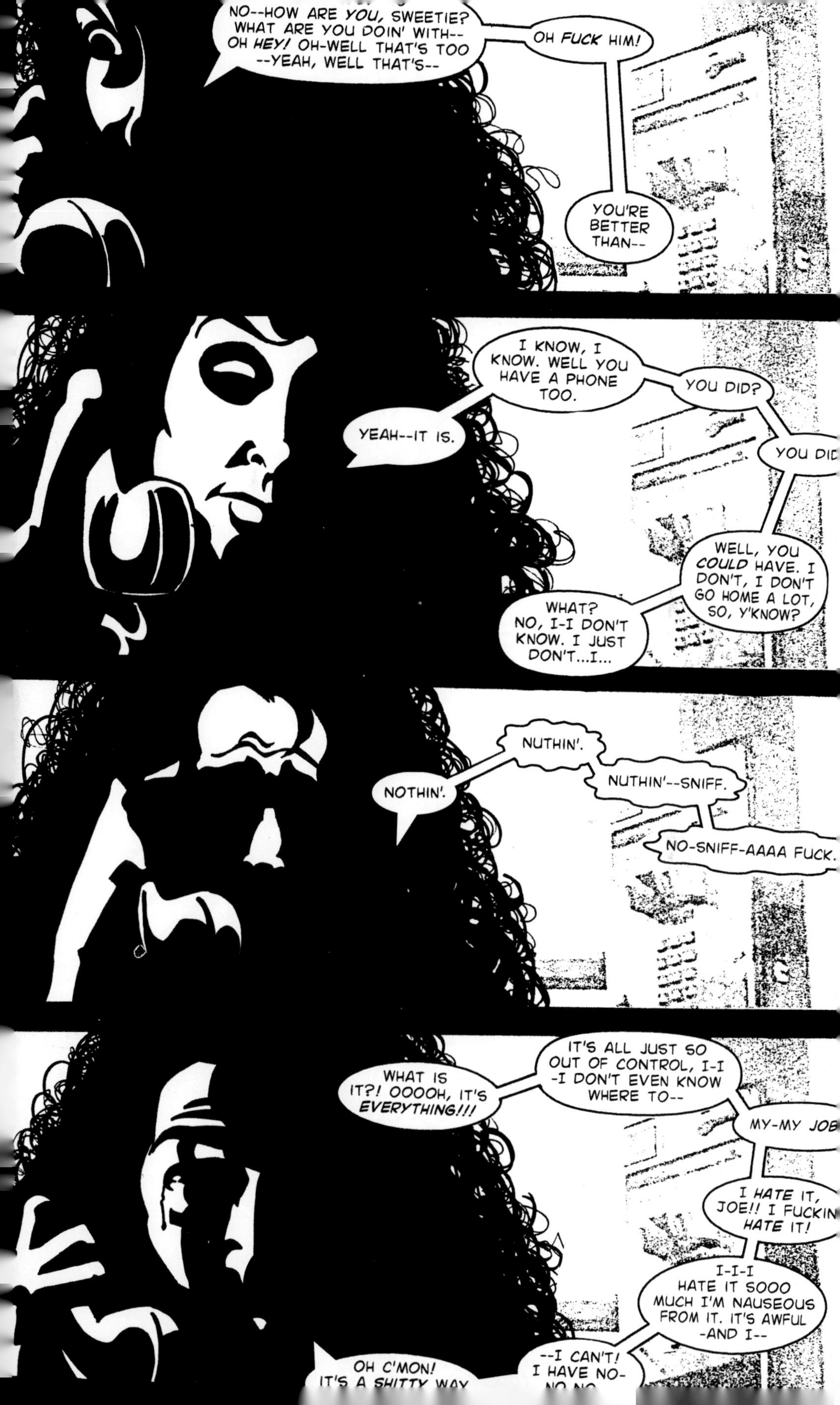
NO--HOW ARE *YOU,* SWEETIE? WHAT ARE YOU DOIN' WITH-- OH *HEY!* OH-WELL THAT'S TOO --YEAH, WELL THAT'S--
OH *FUCK* HIM!
YOU'RE BETTER THAN--
YEAH--IT IS.
I KNOW, I KNOW. WELL YOU HAVE A PHONE TOO.
YOU DID?
YOU DID
WELL, YOU *COULD* HAVE. I DON'T, I DON'T GO HOME A LOT, SO, Y'KNOW?
WHAT? NO, I-I DON'T KNOW. I JUST DON'T...I...
NOTHIN'.
NUTHIN'.
NUTHIN'--SNIFF.
NO-SNIFF-AAAA FUCK.
WHAT IS IT?! OOOOH, IT'S *EVERYTHING!!!*
IT'S ALL JUST SO OUT OF CONTROL, I-I -I DON'T EVEN KNOW WHERE TO--
MY-MY JOB
I *HATE* IT, JOE!! I FUCKIN *HATE* IT!
I-I-I HATE IT SOOO MUCH I'M NAUSEOUS FROM IT. IT'S AWFUL -AND I--
--I CAN'T! I HAVE NO-
OH C'MON!

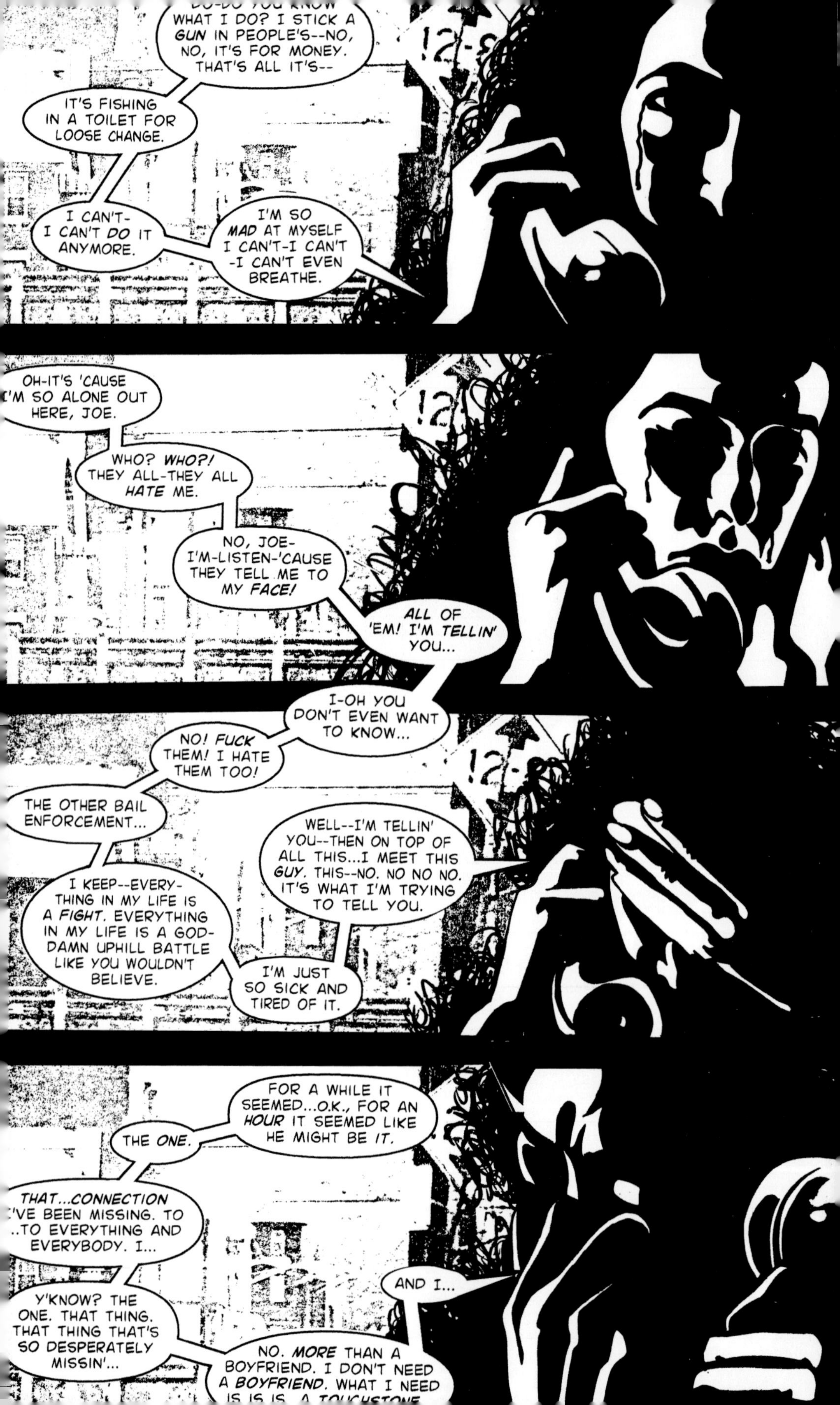

WHAT I DO? I STICK A GUN IN PEOPLE'S--NO, NO, IT'S FOR MONEY. THAT'S ALL IT'S--
IT'S FISHING IN A TOILET FOR LOOSE CHANGE.
I CAN'T- I CAN'T DO IT ANYMORE.
I'M SO MAD AT MYSELF I CAN'T-I CAN'T -I CAN'T EVEN BREATHE.
OH-IT'S 'CAUSE I'M SO ALONE OUT HERE, JOE.
WHO? WHO?! THEY ALL-THEY ALL HATE ME.
NO, JOE- I'M-LISTEN-'CAUSE THEY TELL ME TO MY FACE!
ALL OF 'EM! I'M TELLIN' YOU...
I-OH YOU DON'T EVEN WANT TO KNOW...
NO! FUCK THEM! I HATE THEM TOO!
THE OTHER BAIL ENFORCEMENT...
I KEEP--EVERY-THING IN MY LIFE IS A FIGHT. EVERYTHING IN MY LIFE IS A GOD-DAMN UPHILL BATTLE LIKE YOU WOULDN'T BELIEVE.
I'M JUST SO SICK AND TIRED OF IT.
WELL--I'M TELLIN' YOU--THEN ON TOP OF ALL THIS...I MEET THIS GUY. THIS--NO. NO NO NO. IT'S WHAT I'M TRYING TO TELL YOU.
FOR A WHILE IT SEEMED...O.K., FOR AN HOUR IT SEEMED LIKE HE MIGHT BE IT.
THE ONE.
THAT...CONNECTION I'VE BEEN MISSING. TO ..TO EVERYTHING AND EVERYBODY. I...
Y'KNOW? THE ONE. THAT THING. THAT THING THAT'S SO DESPERATELY MISSIN'...
AND I...
NO. MORE THAN A BOYFRIEND. I DON'T NEED A BOYFRIEND. WHAT I NEED

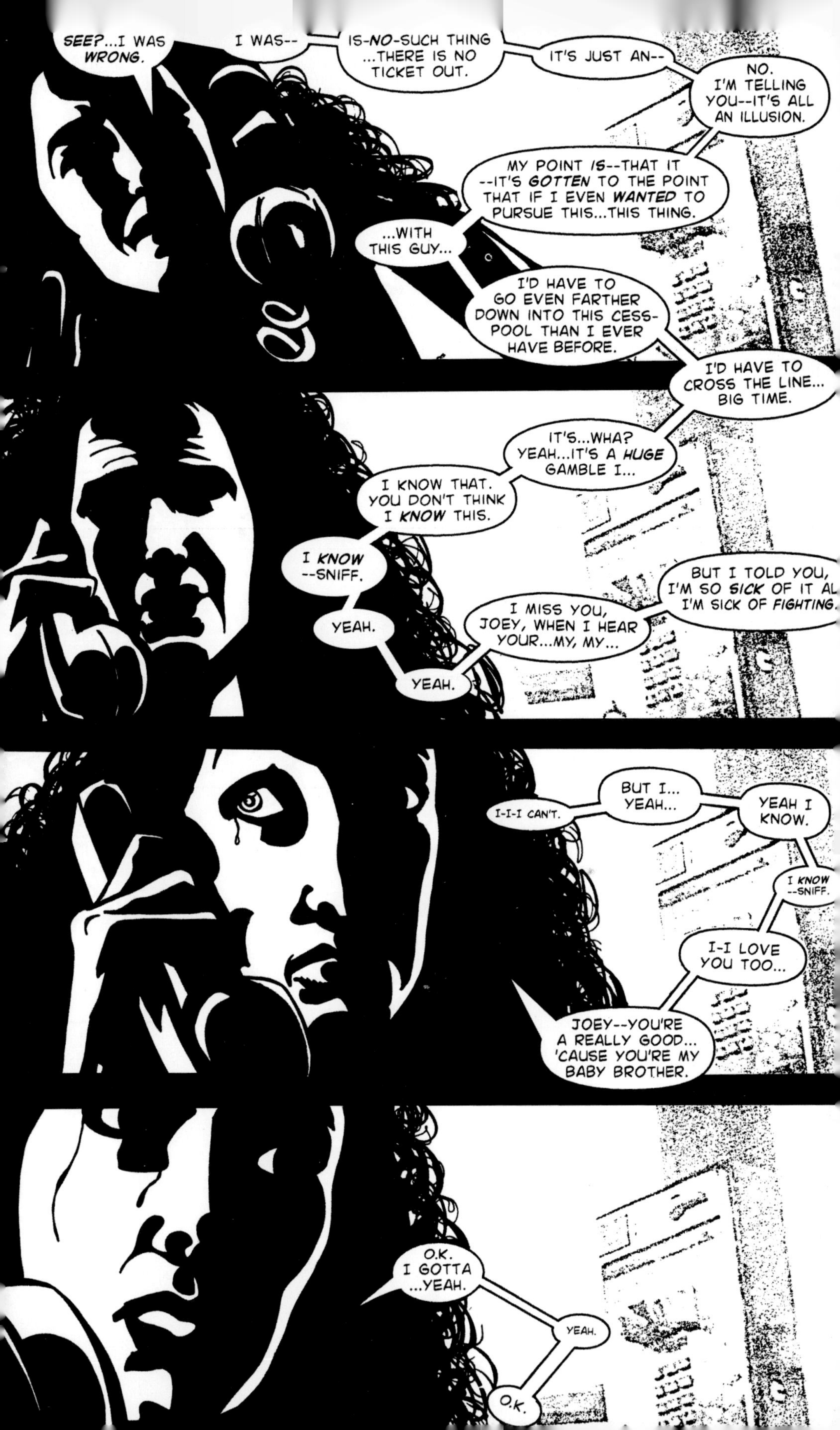
SEE?...I WAS WRONG.
I WAS--
IS-NO-SUCH THING ...THERE IS NO TICKET OUT.
IT'S JUST AN--
NO. I'M TELLING YOU--IT'S ALL AN ILLUSION.
MY POINT IS--THAT IT --IT'S GOTTEN TO THE POINT THAT IF I EVEN WANTED TO PURSUE THIS...THIS THING.
...WITH THIS GUY...
I'D HAVE TO GO EVEN FARTHER DOWN INTO THIS CESS-POOL THAN I EVER HAVE BEFORE.
I'D HAVE TO CROSS THE LINE... BIG TIME.
IT'S...WHA? YEAH...IT'S A HUGE GAMBLE I...
I KNOW THAT. YOU DON'T THINK I KNOW THIS.
I KNOW --SNIFF.
YEAH.
YEAH.
I MISS YOU, JOEY, WHEN I HEAR YOUR...MY, MY...
BUT I TOLD YOU, I'M SO SICK OF IT AL I'M SICK OF FIGHTING.
I-I-I CAN'T.
BUT I... YEAH...
YEAH I KNOW.
I KNOW --SNIFF.
I-I LOVE YOU TOO...
JOEY--YOU'RE A REALLY GOOD... 'CAUSE YOU'RE MY BABY BROTHER.
O.K. I GOTTA ...YEAH.
YEAH.
O.K.

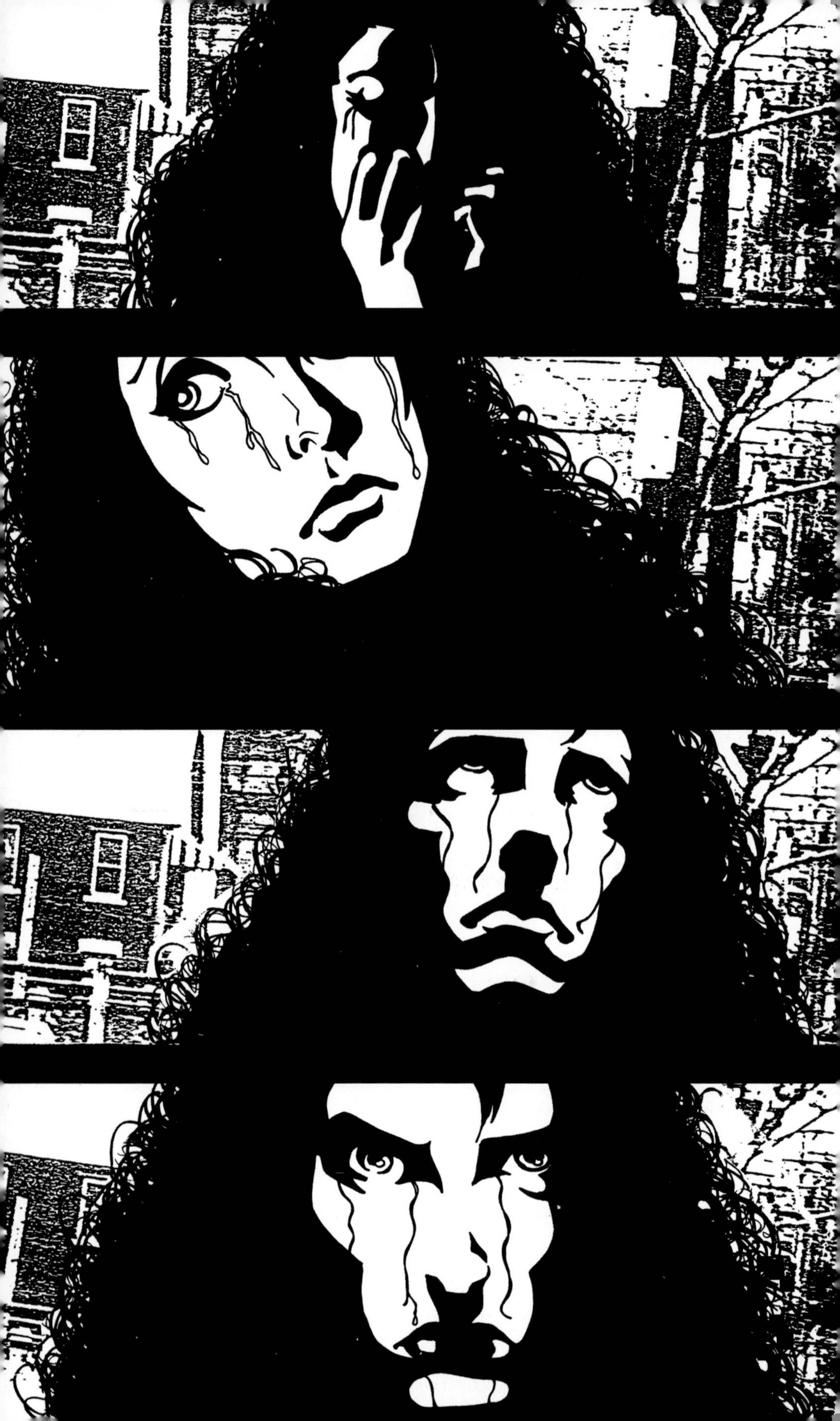

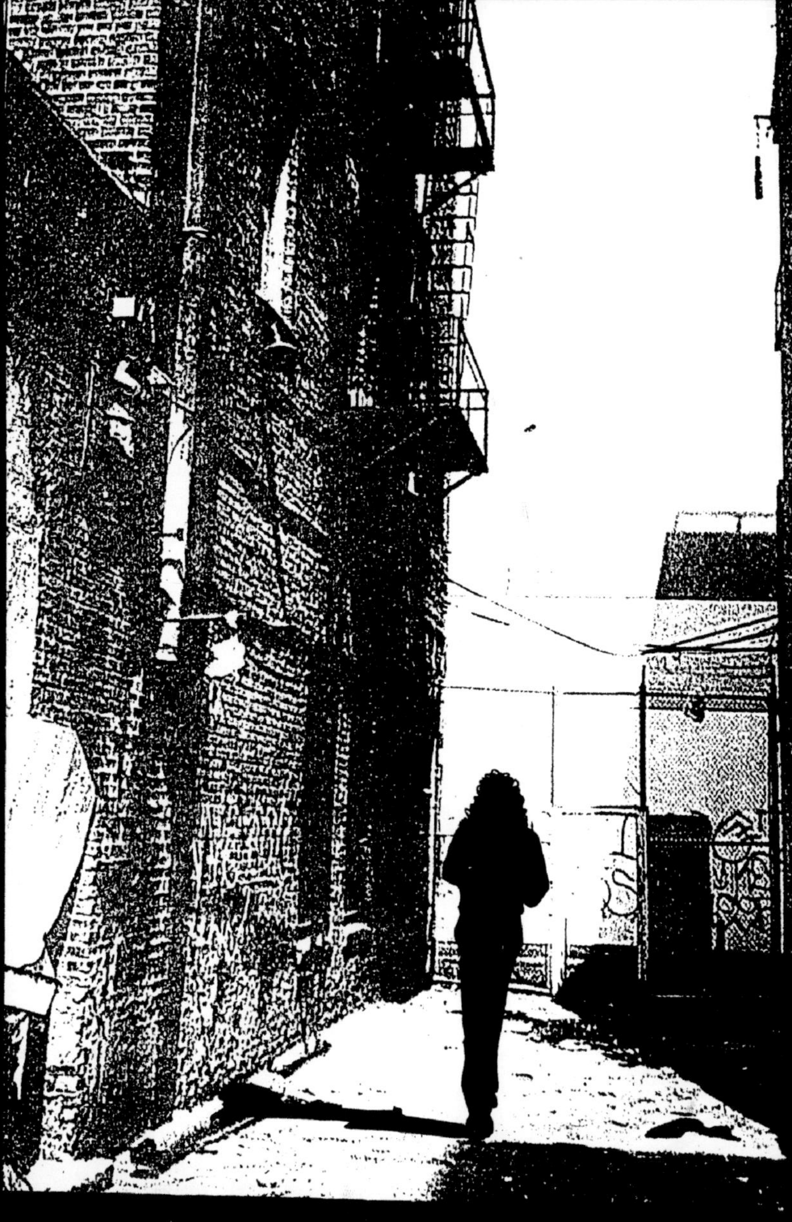

If It's Not There In An Hour...It's Free

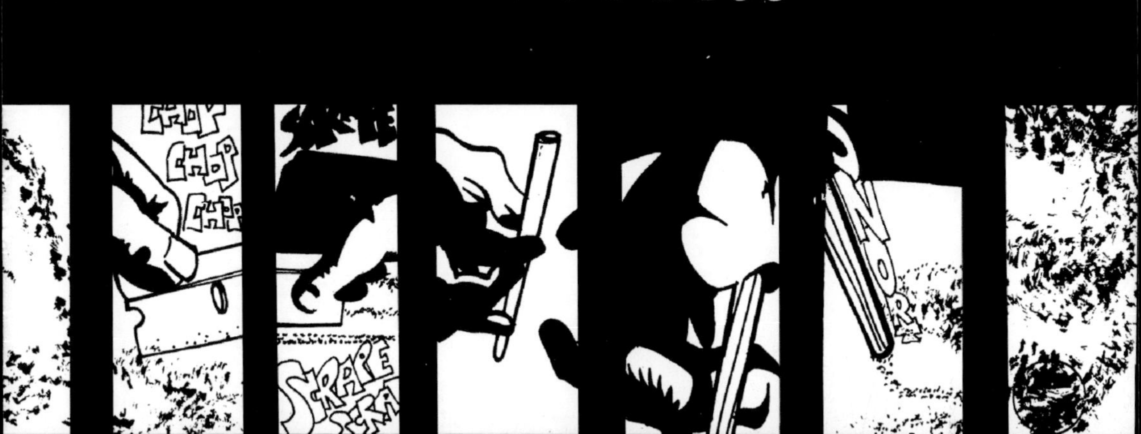
CHOP

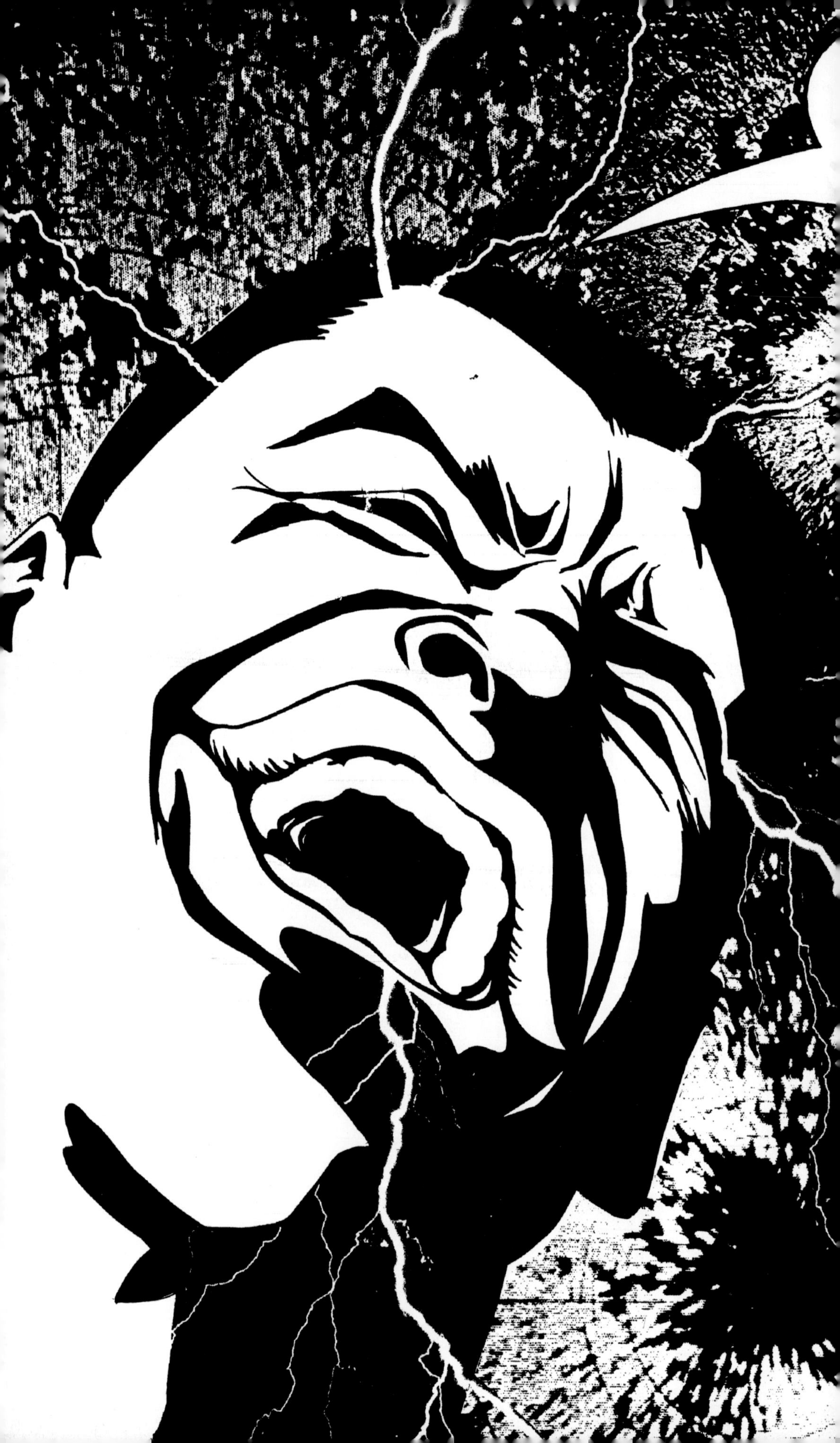

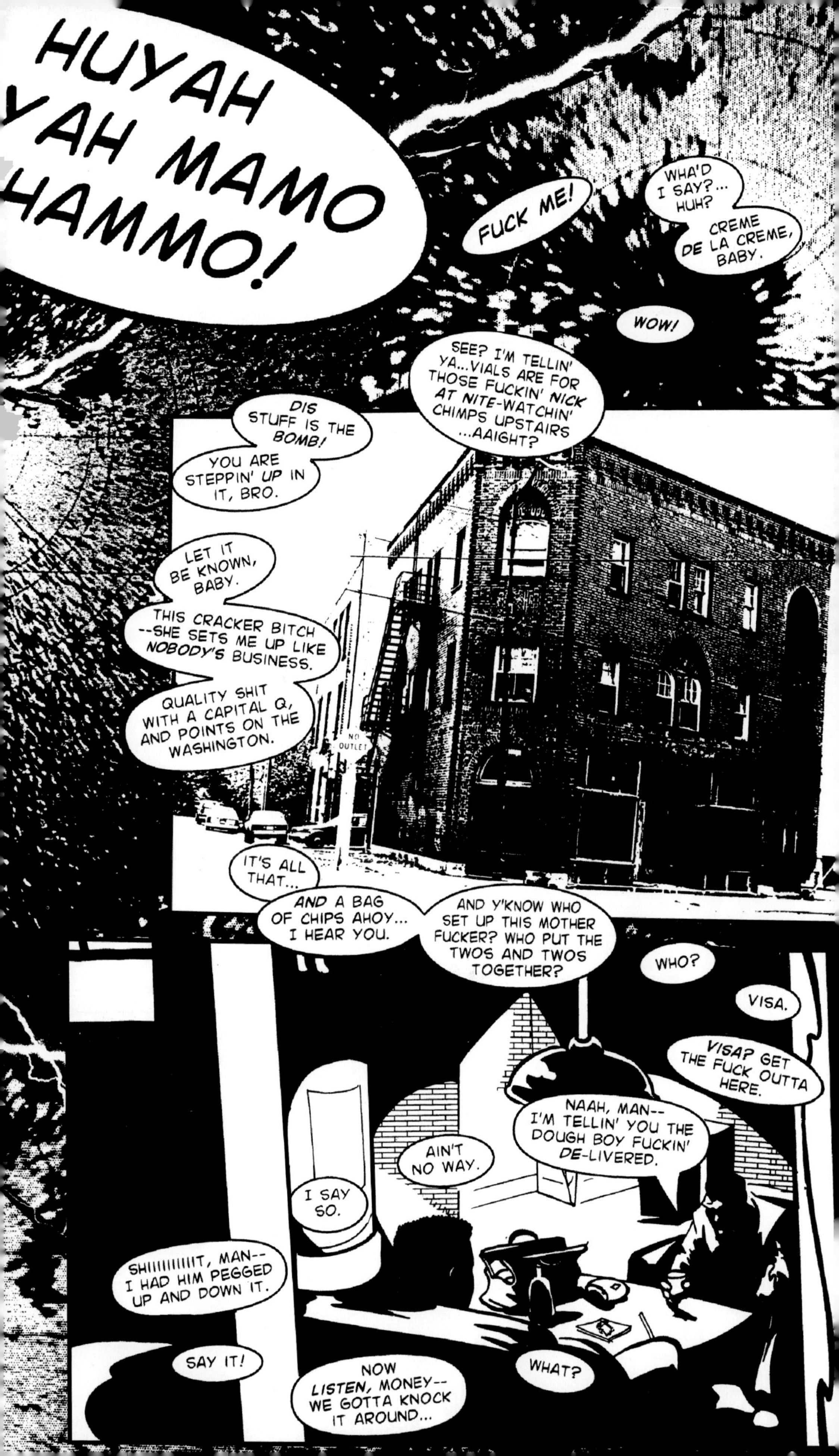
HUYAH YAH MAMO HAMMO!
FUCK ME!
WHA'D I SAY?... HUH?
CREME DE LA CREME, BABY.
WOW!
SEE? I'M TELLIN' YA...VIALS ARE FOR THOSE FUCKIN' NICK AT NITE-WATCHIN' CHIMPS UPSTAIRS ...AAIGHT?
DIS STUFF IS THE BOMB!
YOU ARE STEPPIN' UP IN IT, BRO.
LET IT BE KNOWN, BABY.
THIS CRACKER BITCH --SHE SETS ME UP LIKE NOBODY'S BUSINESS.
QUALITY SHIT WITH A CAPITAL Q, AND POINTS ON THE WASHINGTON.
NO OUTLET
IT'S ALL THAT...
AND A BAG OF CHIPS AHOY... I HEAR YOU.
AND Y'KNOW WHO SET UP THIS MOTHER FUCKER? WHO PUT THE TWOS AND TWOS TOGETHER?
WHO?
VISA.
VISA? GET THE FUCK OUTTA HERE.
NAAH, MAN-- I'M TELLIN' YOU THE DOUGH BOY FUCKIN' DE-LIVERED.
AIN'T NO WAY.
I SAY SO.
SHIIIIIIIIIT, MAN-- I HAD HIM PEGGED UP AND DOWN IT.
SAY IT!
WHAT?
NOW LISTEN, MONEY-- WE GOTTA KNOCK IT AROUND...

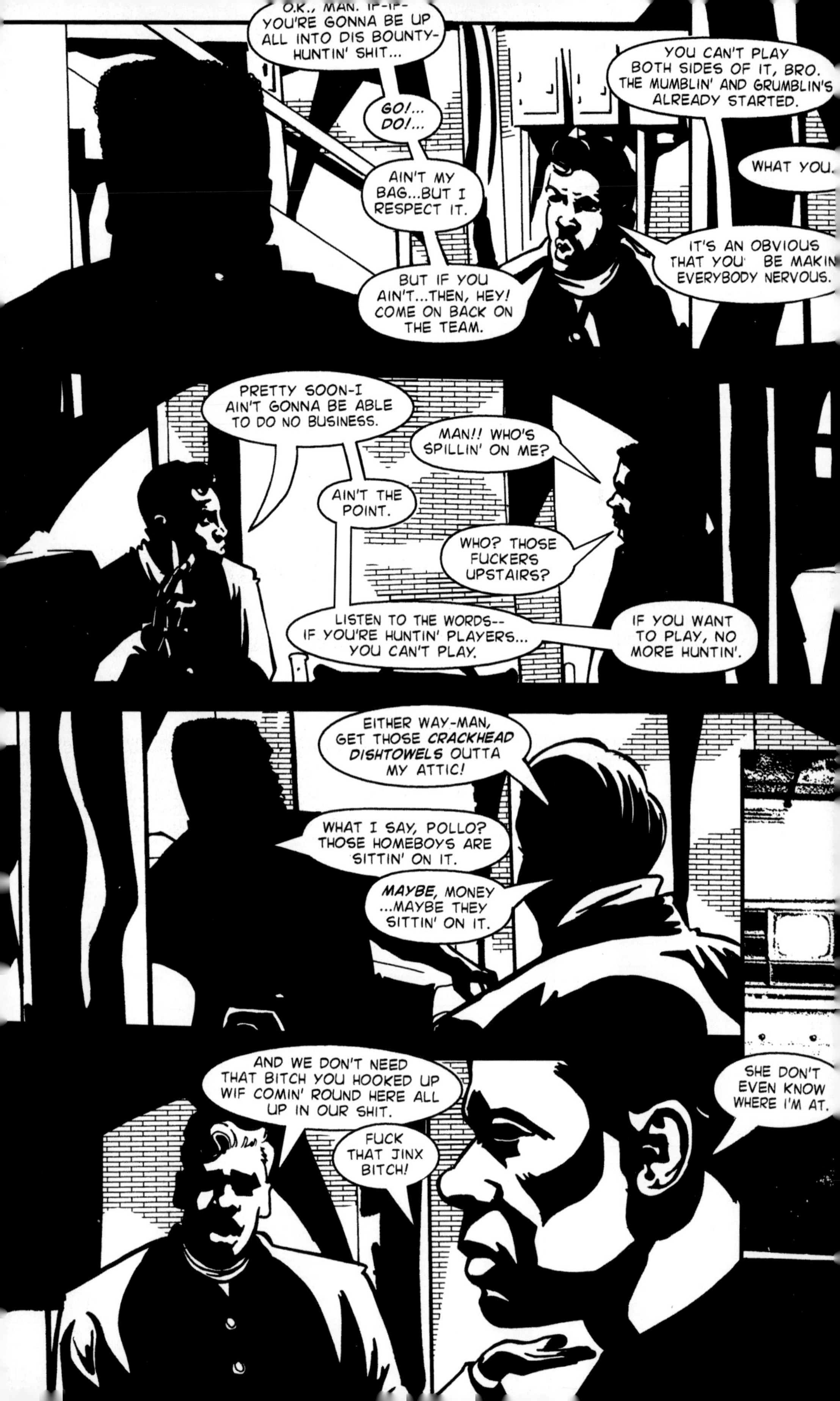

O.K., MAN. IF-IF-
YOU'RE GONNA BE UP ALL INTO DIS BOUNTY-HUNTIN' SHIT...
GO!... DO!...
AIN'T MY BAG...BUT I RESPECT IT.
BUT IF YOU AIN'T...THEN, HEY! COME ON BACK ON THE TEAM.
YOU CAN'T PLAY BOTH SIDES OF IT, BRO. THE MUMBLIN' AND GRUMBLIN'S ALREADY STARTED.
WHAT YOU
IT'S AN OBVIOUS THAT YOU BE MAKIN EVERYBODY NERVOUS.
PRETTY SOON-I AIN'T GONNA BE ABLE TO DO NO BUSINESS.
AIN'T THE POINT.
MAN!! WHO'S SPILLIN' ON ME?
WHO? THOSE FUCKERS UPSTAIRS?
LISTEN TO THE WORDS-- IF YOU'RE HUNTIN' PLAYERS... YOU CAN'T PLAY.
IF YOU WANT TO PLAY, NO MORE HUNTIN'.
EITHER WAY-MAN, GET THOSE CRACKHEAD DISHTOWELS OUTTA MY ATTIC!
WHAT I SAY, POLLO? THOSE HOMEBOYS ARE SITTIN' ON IT.
MAYBE, MONEY ...MAYBE THEY SITTIN' ON IT.
AND WE DON'T NEED THAT BITCH YOU HOOKED UP WIF COMIN' ROUND HERE ALL UP IN OUR SHIT.
FUCK THAT JINX BITCH!
SHE DON'T EVEN KNOW WHERE I'M AT.

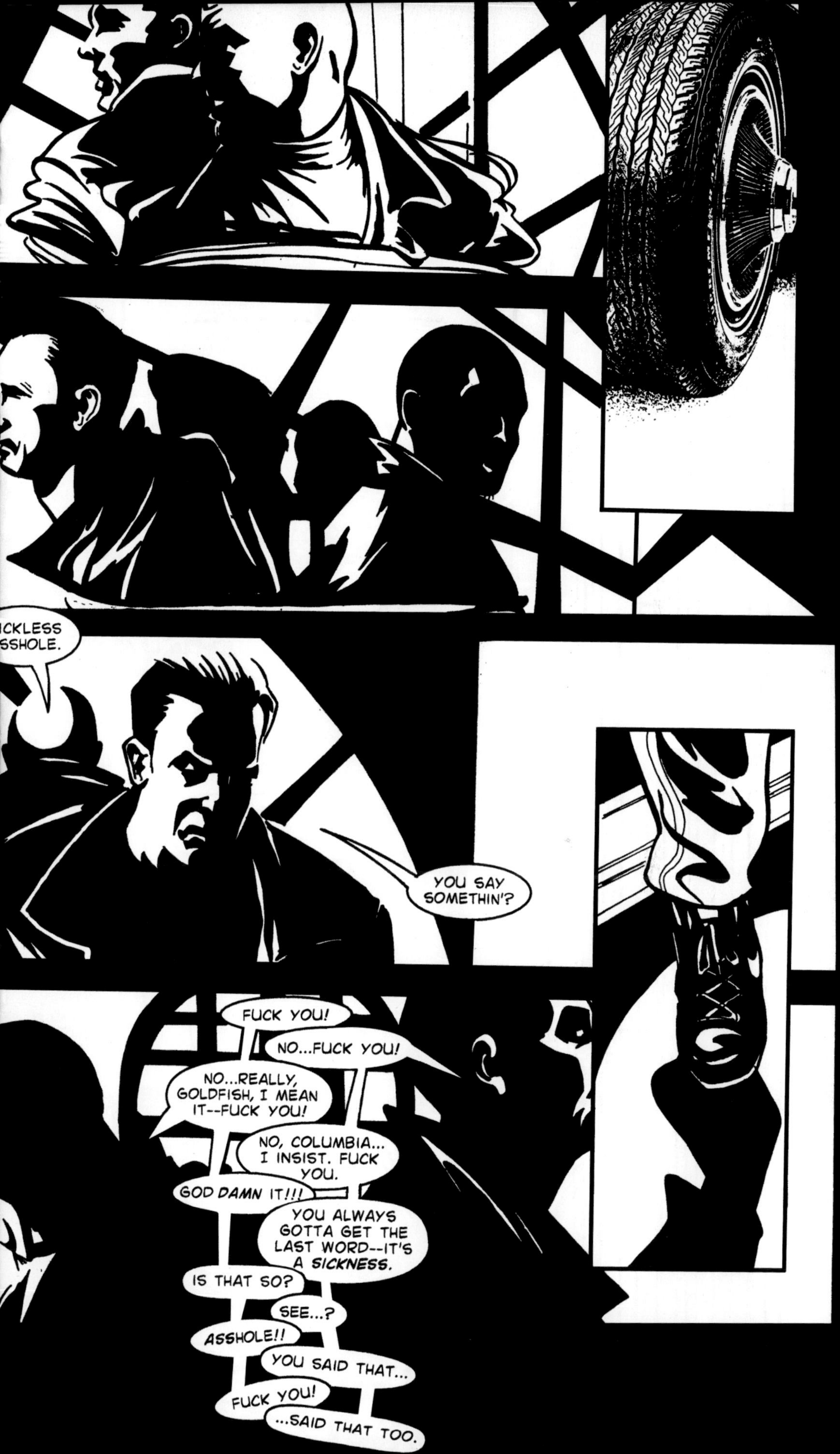

ICKLESS SSHOLE.
YOU SAY SOMETHIN'?
FUCK YOU!
NO...FUCK YOU!
NO...REALLY, GOLDFISH, I MEAN IT--FUCK YOU!
NO, COLUMBIA... I INSIST. FUCK YOU.
GOD DAMN IT!!!
YOU ALWAYS GOTTA GET THE LAST WORD--IT'S A SICKNESS.
IS THAT SO?
SEE...?
ASSHOLE!!
YOU SAID THAT...
FUCK YOU!
...SAID THAT TOO.

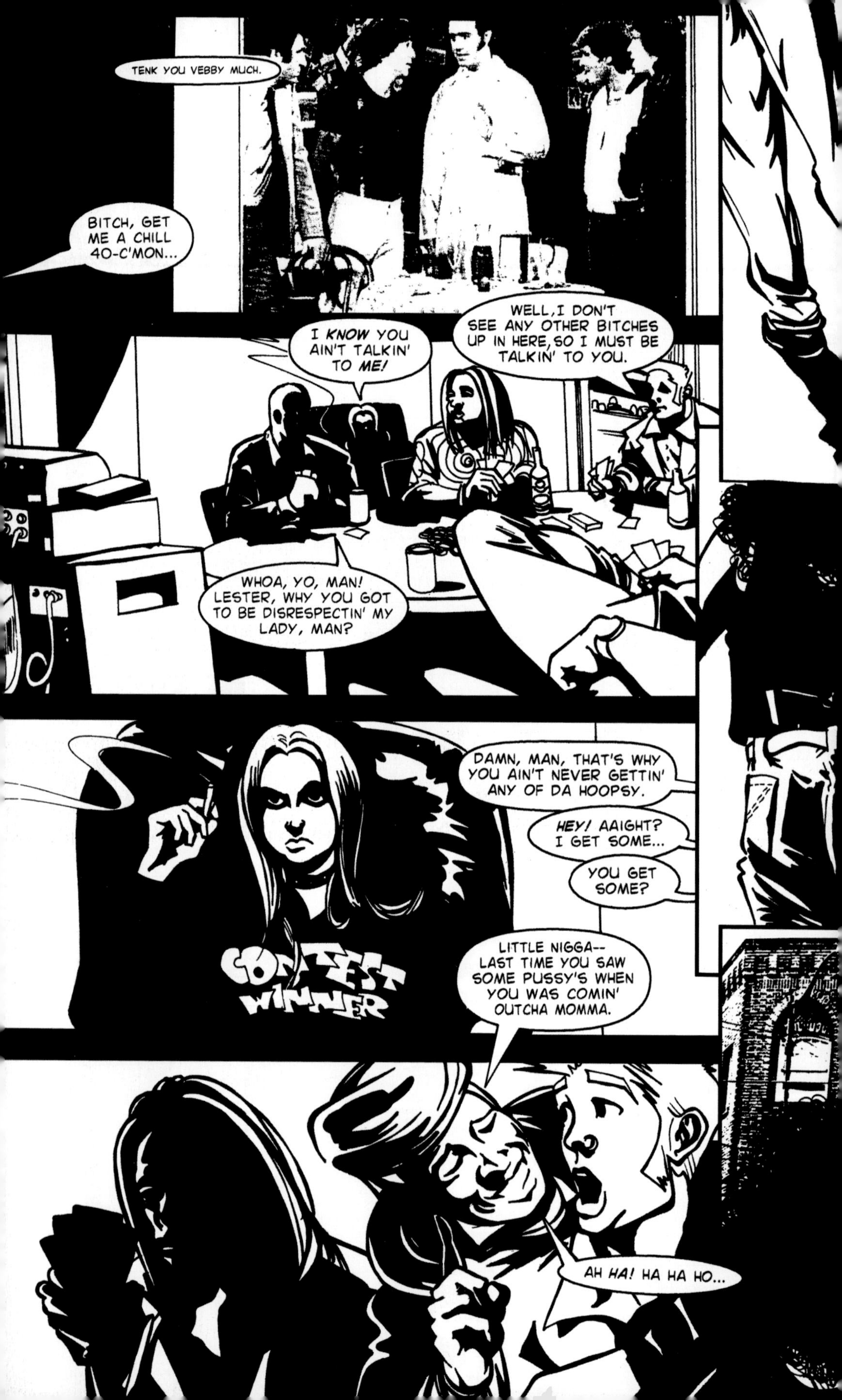
TENK YOU VEBBY MUCH.
BITCH, GET ME A CHILL 40-C'MON...
I *KNOW* YOU AIN'T TALKIN' TO *ME!*
WELL, I DON'T SEE ANY OTHER BITCHES UP IN HERE, SO I MUST BE TALKIN' TO YOU.
WHOA, YO, MAN! LESTER, WHY YOU GOT TO BE DISRESPECTIN' MY LADY, MAN?
CONTEST WINNER
DAMN, MAN, THAT'S WHY YOU AIN'T NEVER GETTIN' ANY OF DA HOOPSY.
HEY! AAIGHT? I GET SOME...
YOU GET SOME?
LITTLE NIGGA-- LAST TIME YOU SAW SOME PUSSY'S WHEN YOU WAS COMIN' OUTCHA MOMMA.
AH *HA!* HA HA HO...

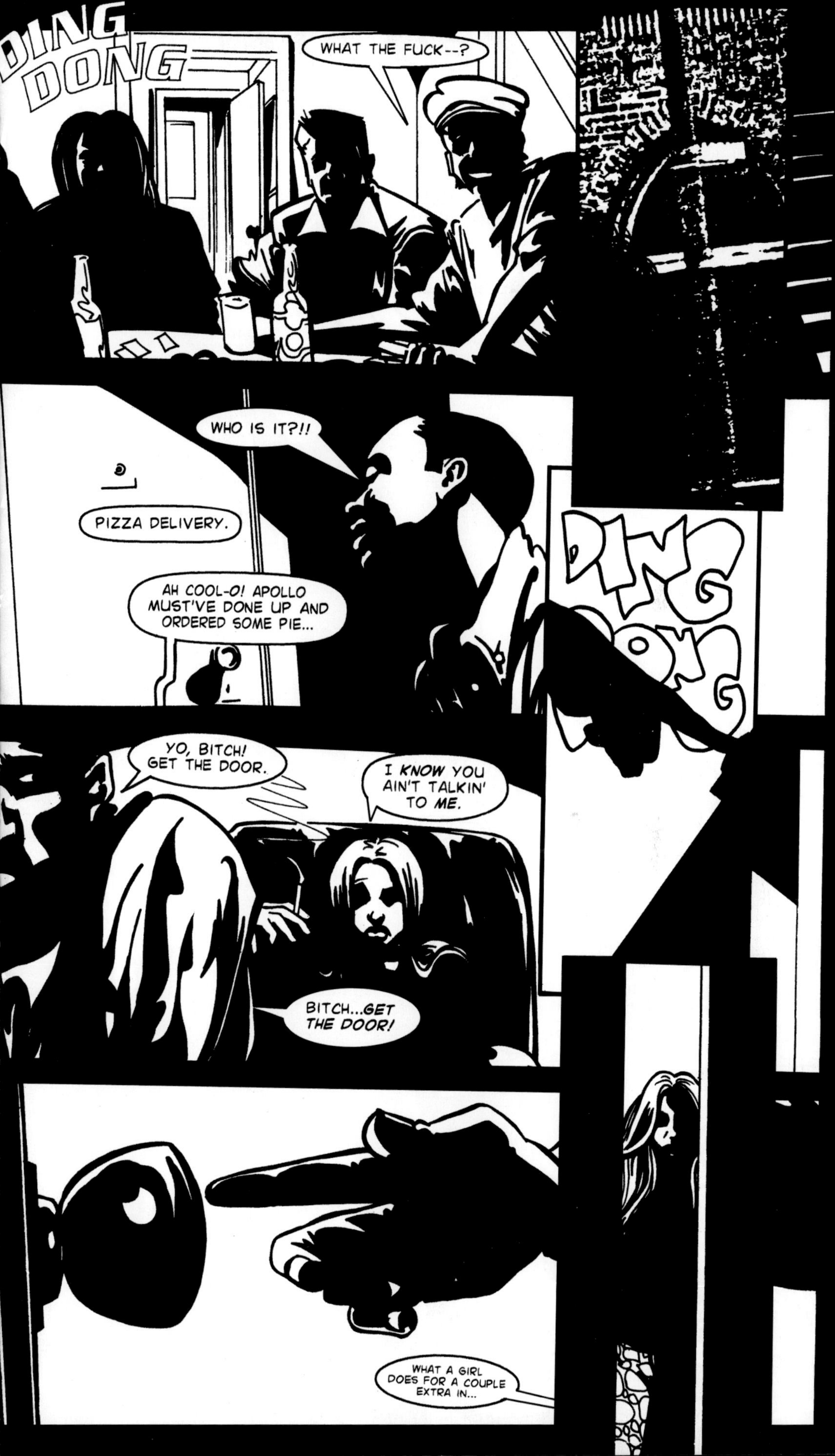
DING DONG
WHAT THE FUCK--?
WHO IS IT?!!
PIZZA DELIVERY.
AH COOL-O! APOLLO MUST'VE DONE UP AND ORDERED SOME PIE...
DING DONG
YO, BITCH! GET THE DOOR.
I KNOW YOU AIN'T TALKIN' TO ME.
BITCH...GET THE DOOR!
WHAT A GIRL DOES FOR A COUPLE EXTRA IN...

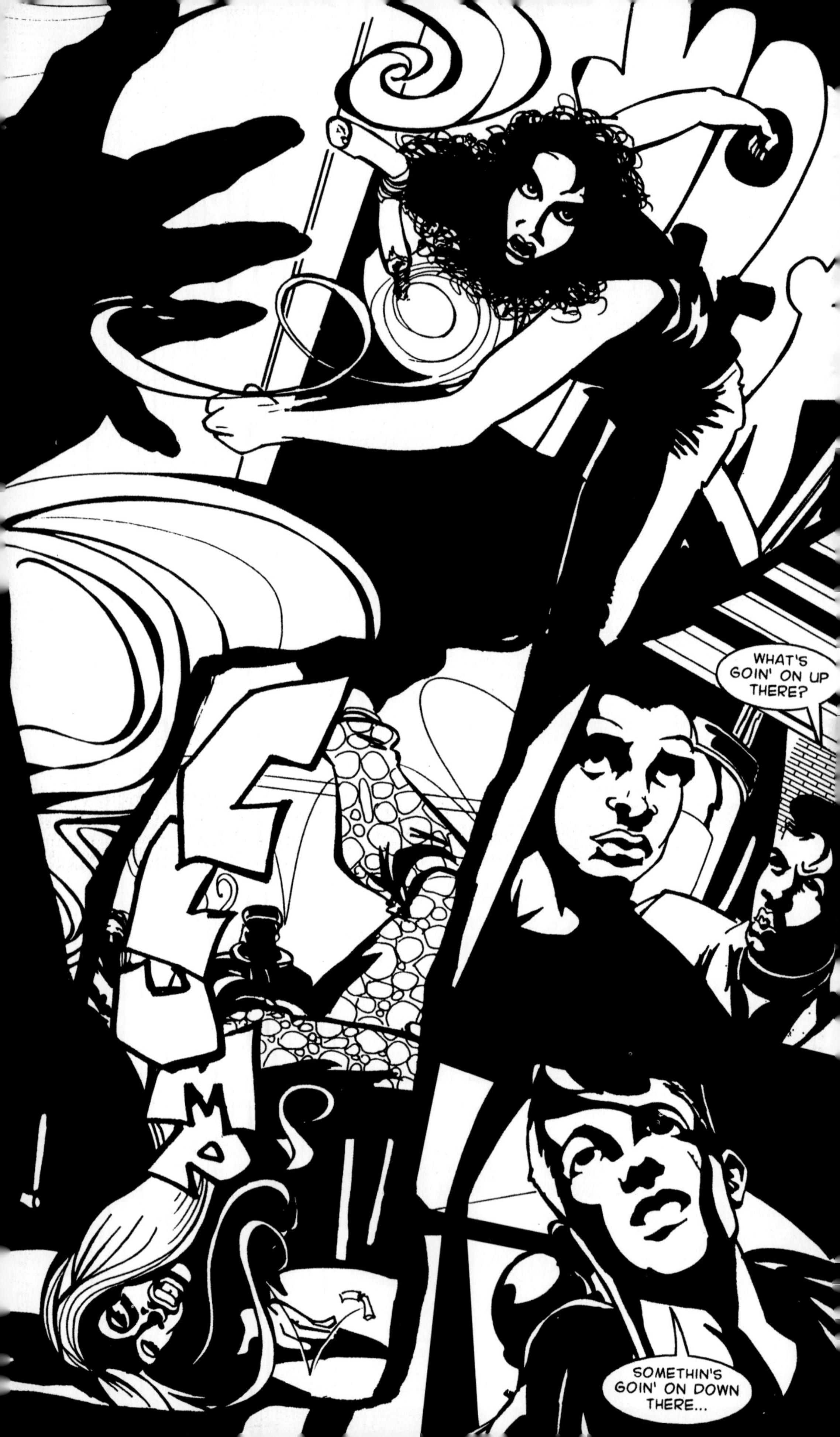
WHAT'S GOIN' ON UP THERE?
SOMETHIN'S GOIN' ON DOWN THERE...

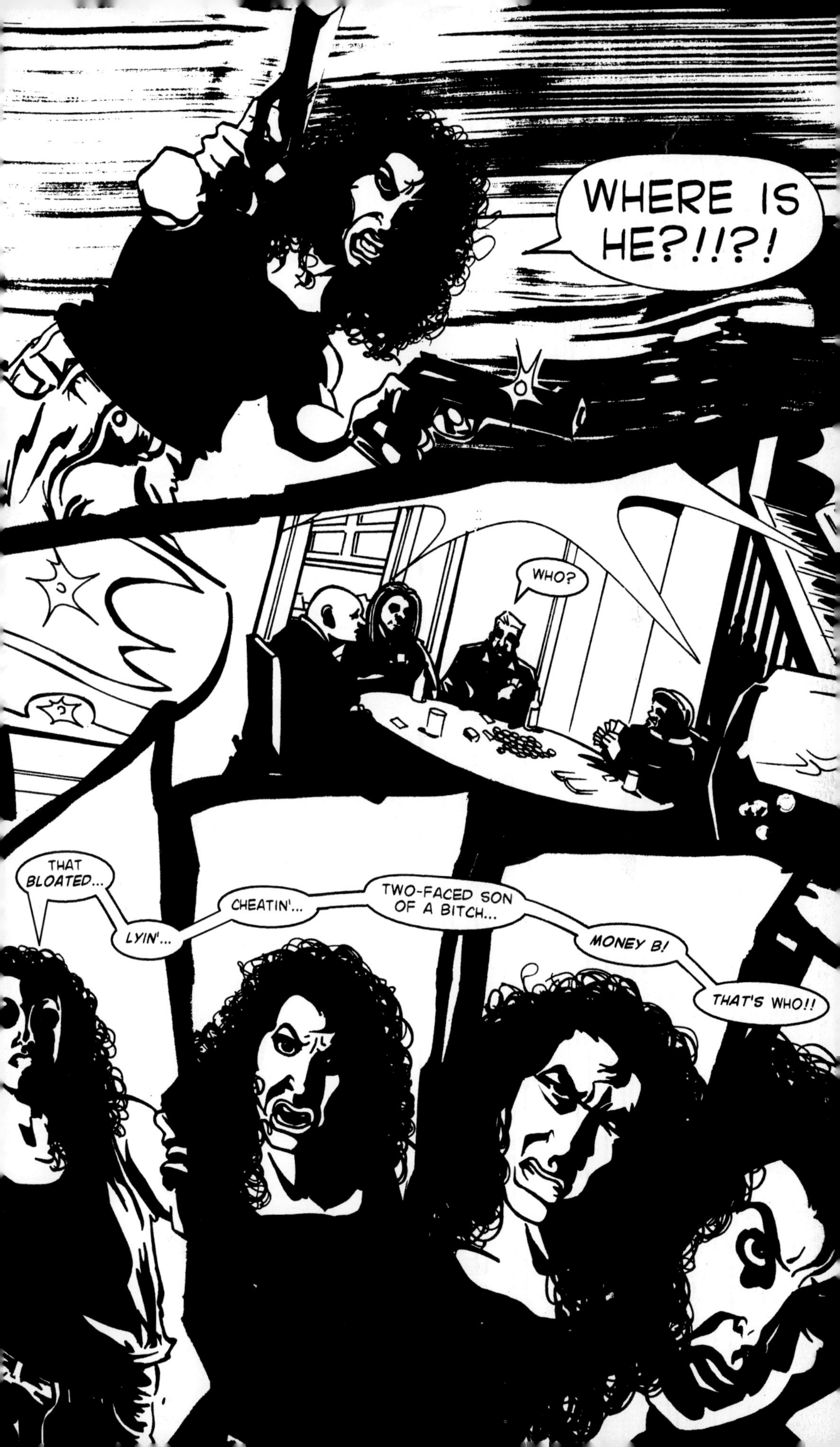
WHERE IS HE?!!?!
WHO?
THAT BLOATED...
LYIN'...
CHEATIN'...
TWO-FACED SON OF A BITCH...
MONEY B!
THAT'S WHO!!

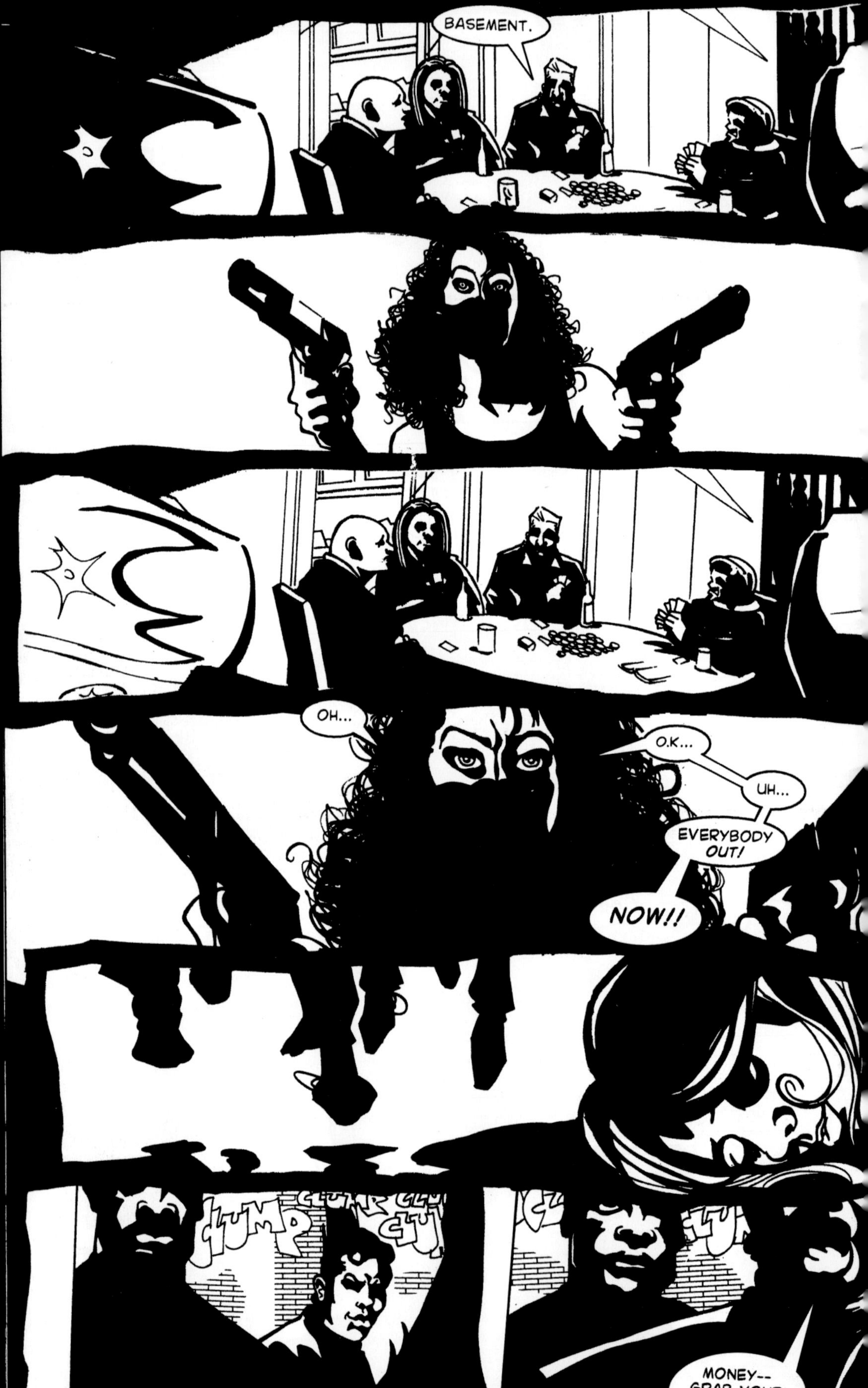
BASEMENT.
OH...
O.K...
UH...
EVERYBODY OUT!
NOW!!
MONEY-- GRAB YOUR PIECE...

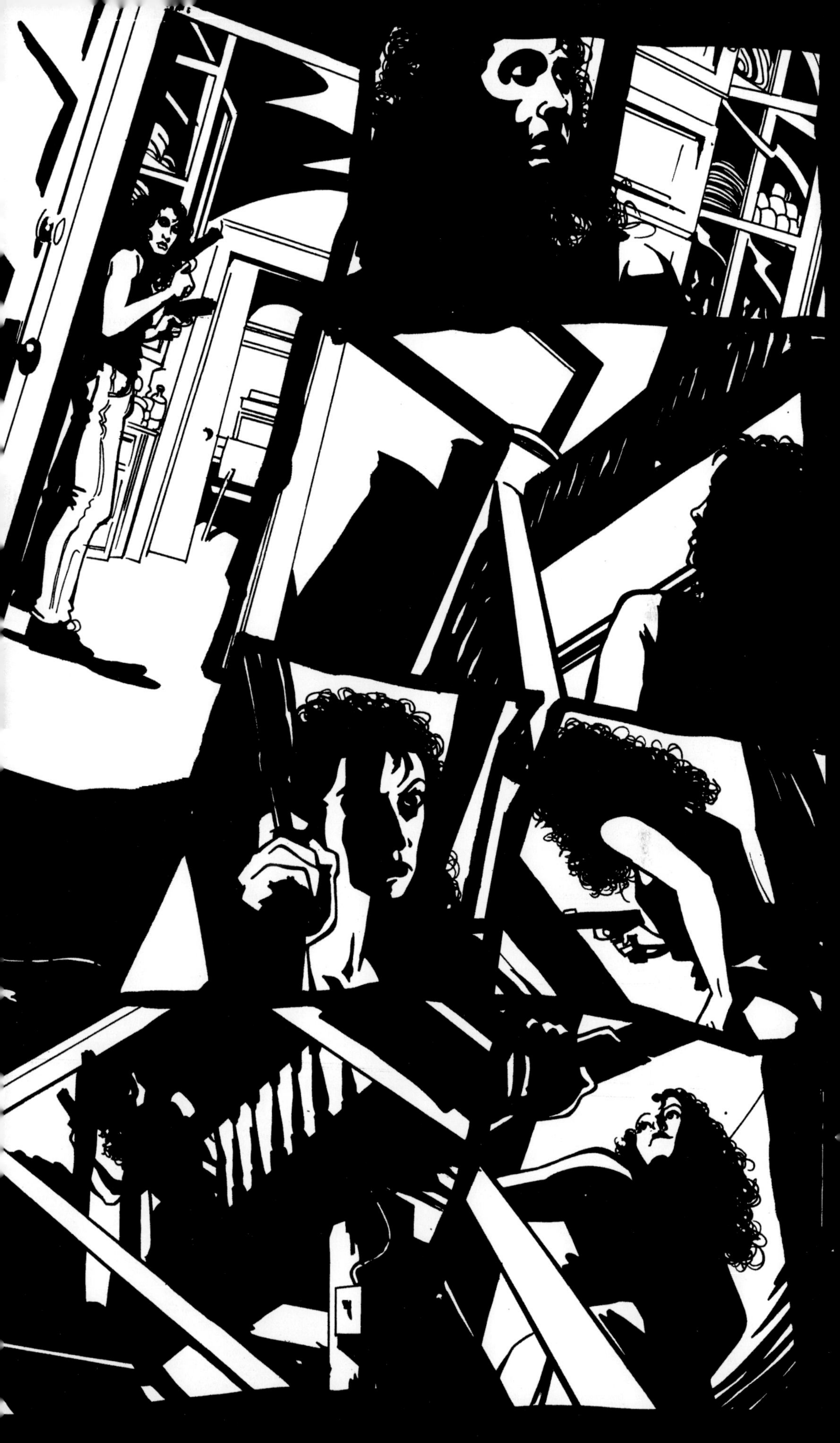

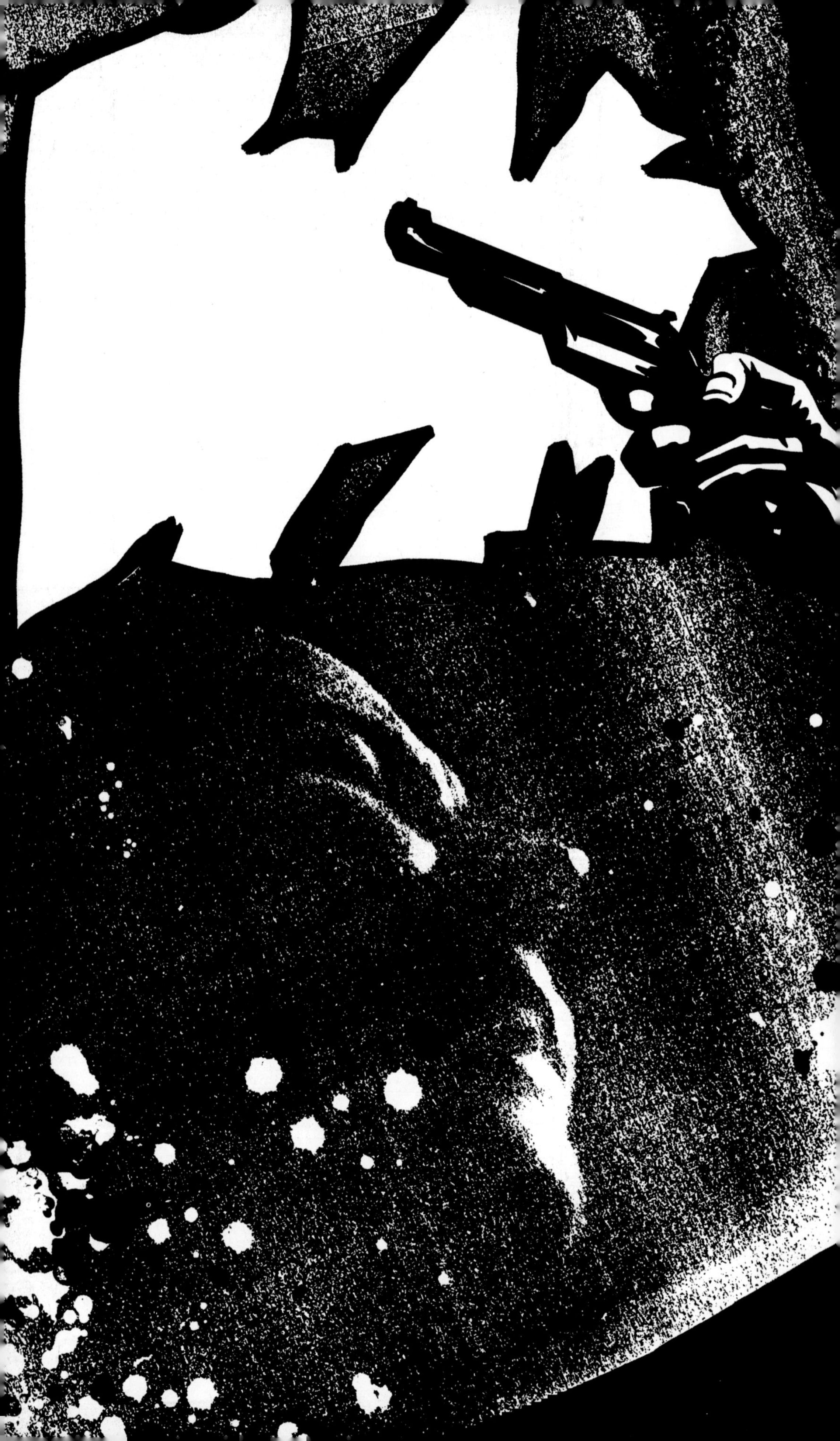

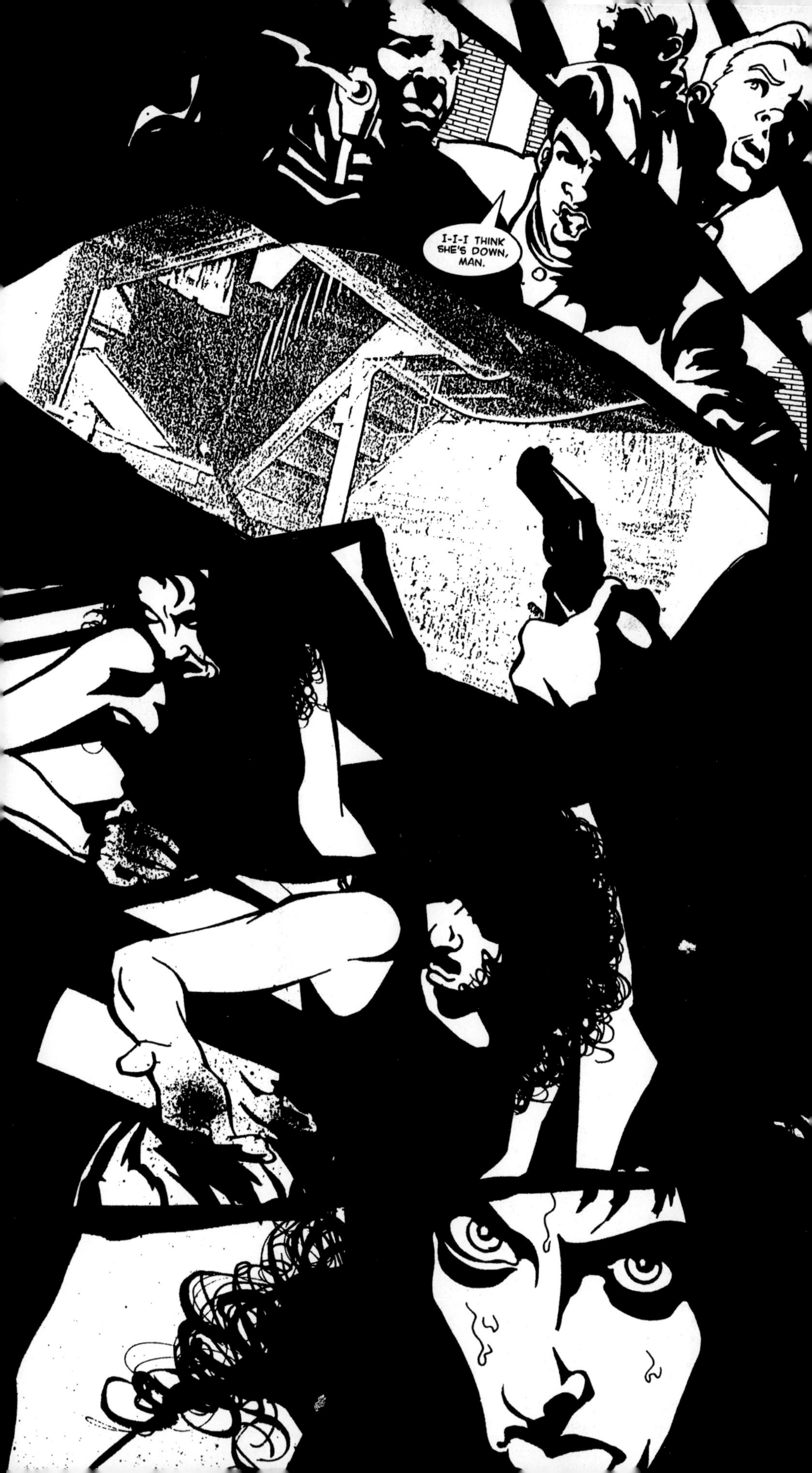
I-I-I THINK SHE'S DOWN, MAN.

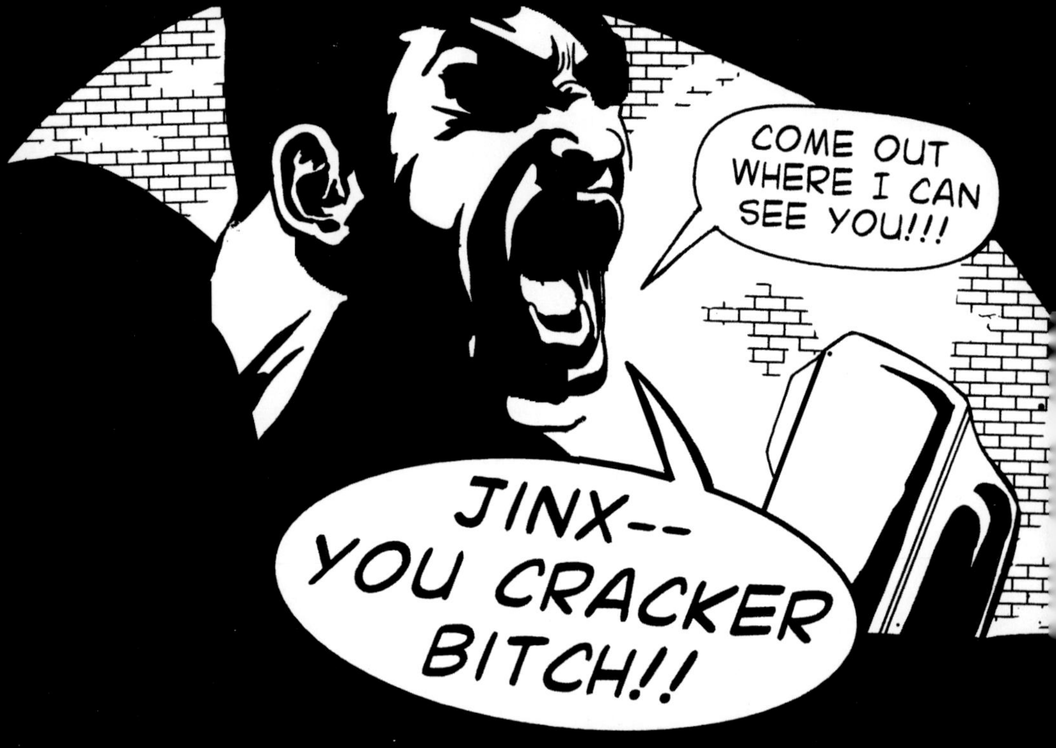
COME OUT WHERE I CAN SEE YOU!!!
JINX-- YOU CRACKER BITCH!!

Playin' Possum

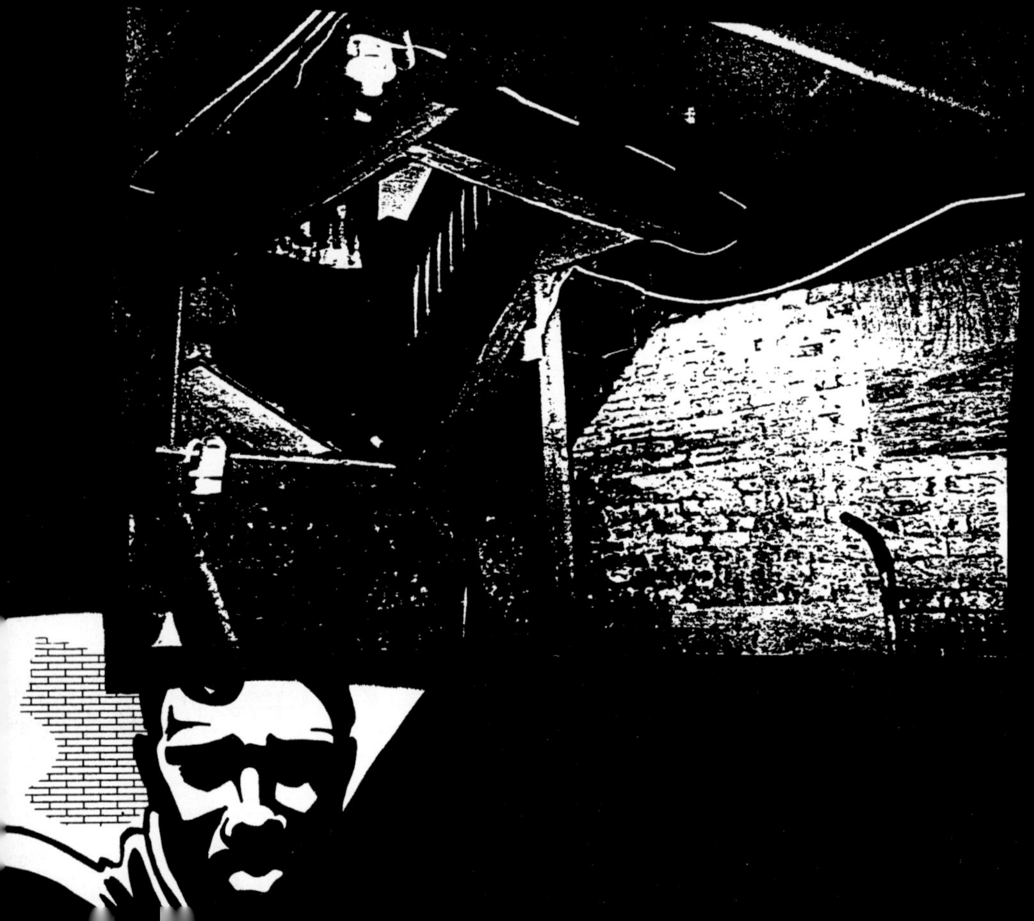

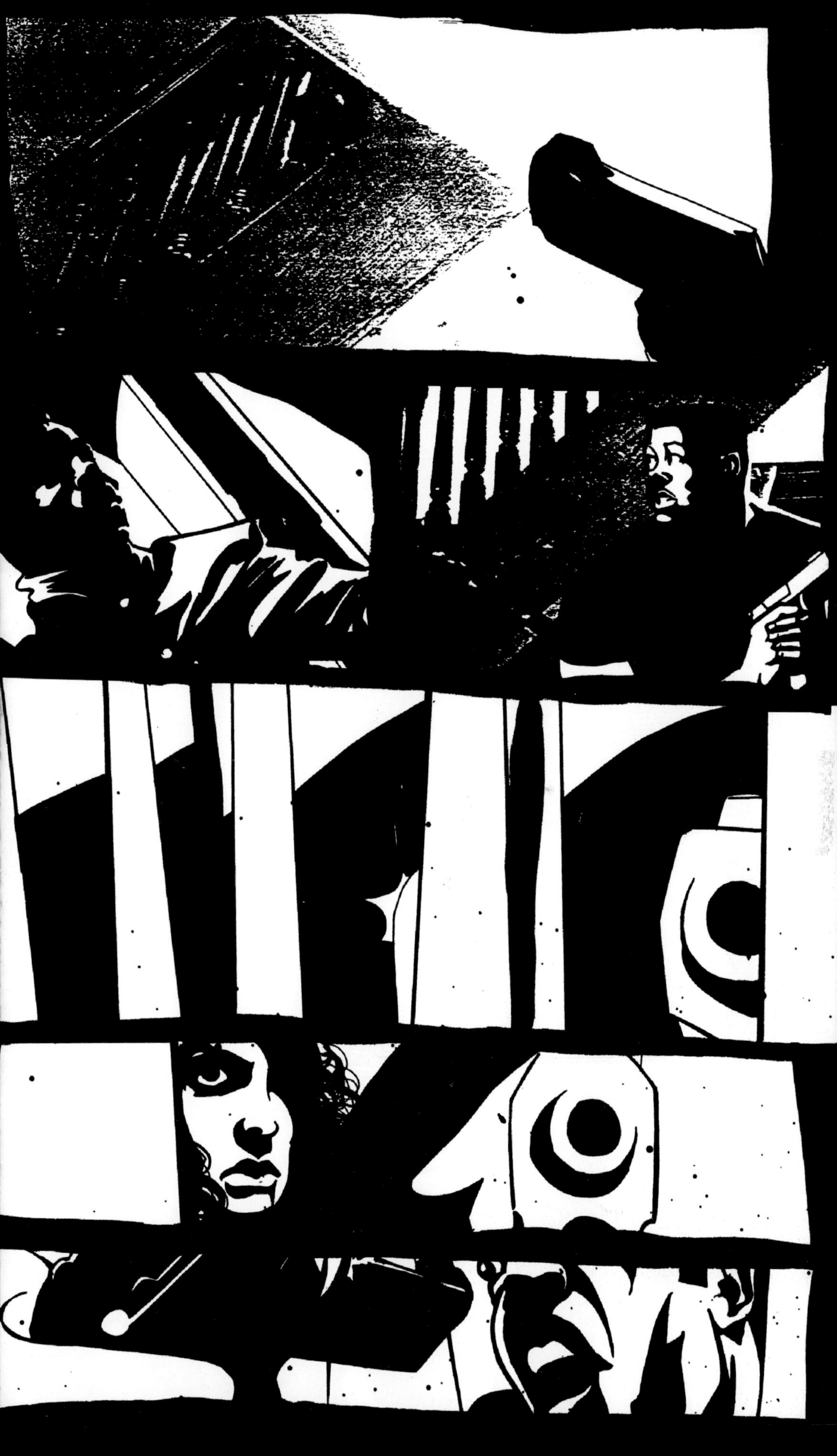

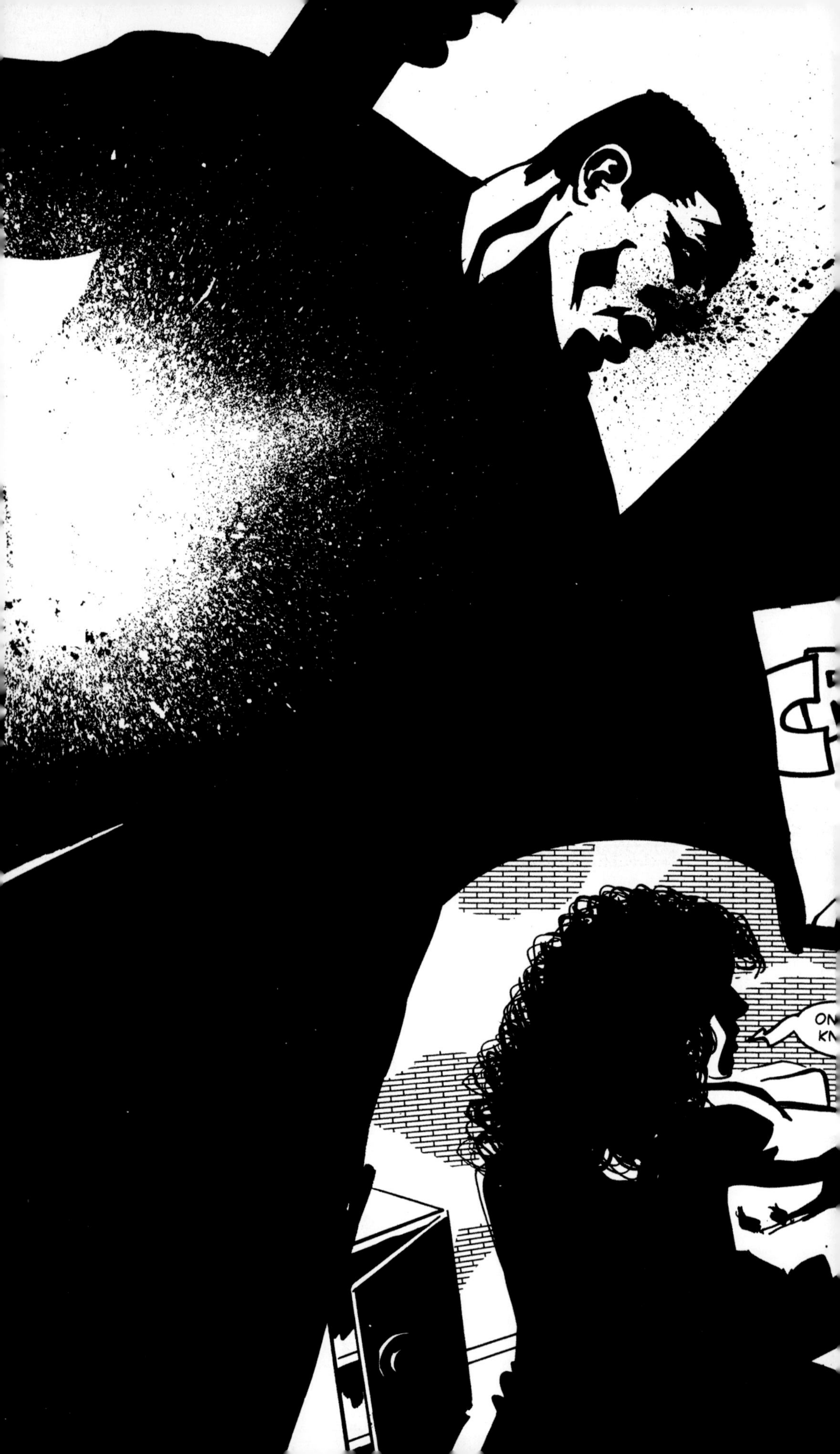

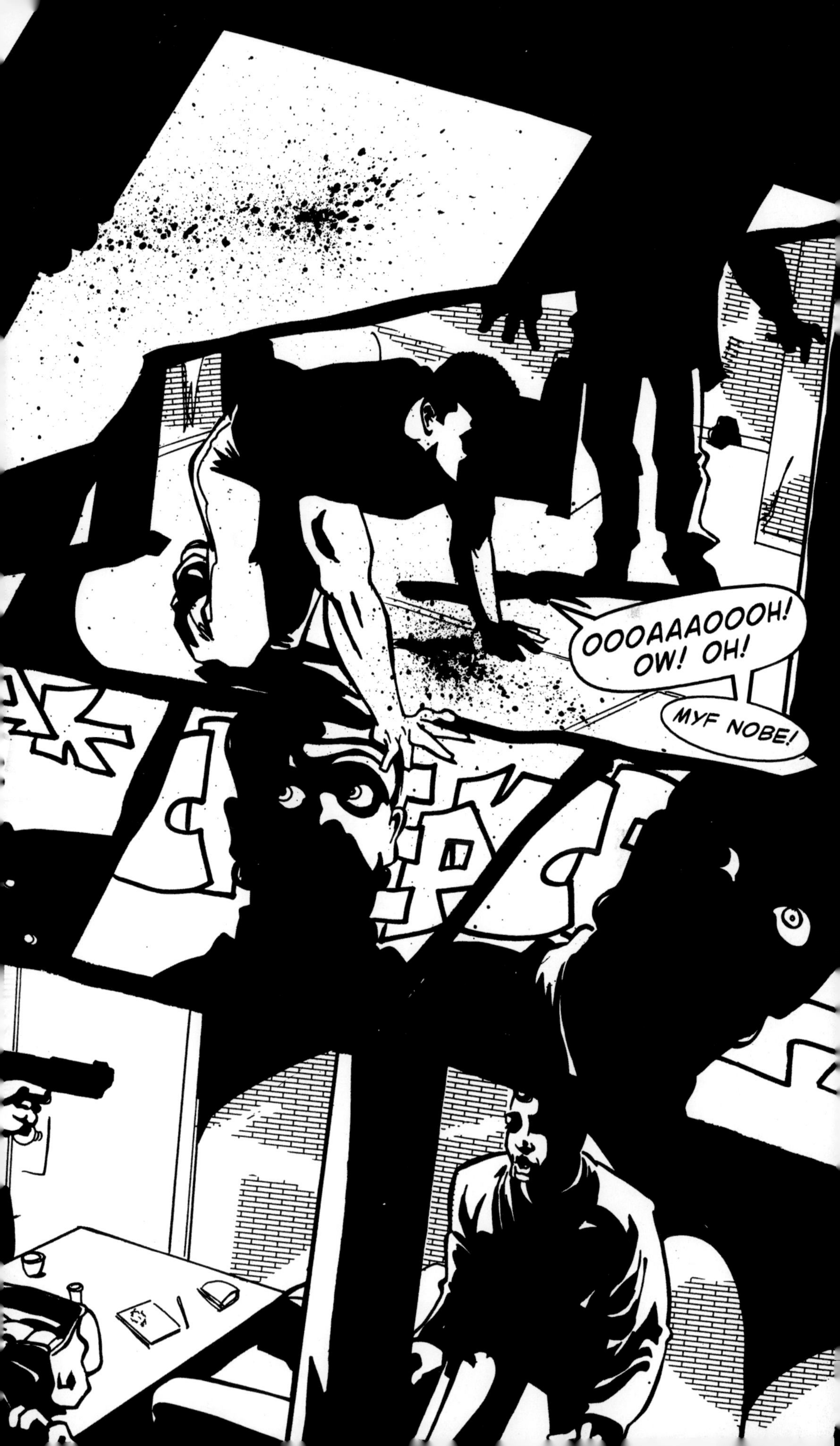
OOOAAAOOOH! OW! OH!
MYF NOBE!

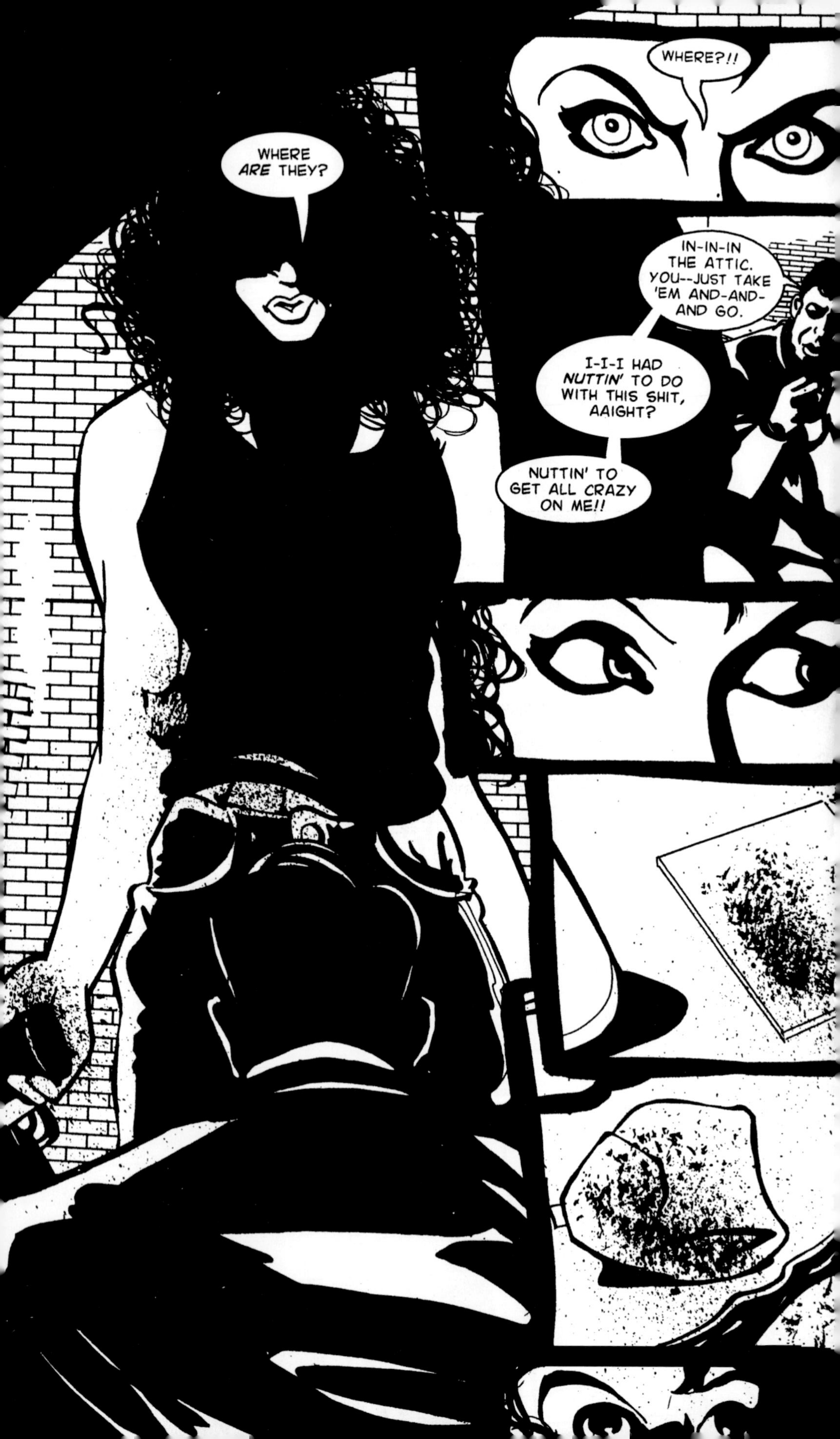
WHERE ARE THEY?
WHERE?!!
IN-IN-IN THE ATTIC. YOU--JUST TAKE 'EM AND-AND-AND GO.
I-I-I HAD NUTTIN' TO DO WITH THIS SHIT, AAIGHT?
NUTTIN' TO GET ALL CRAZY ON ME!!

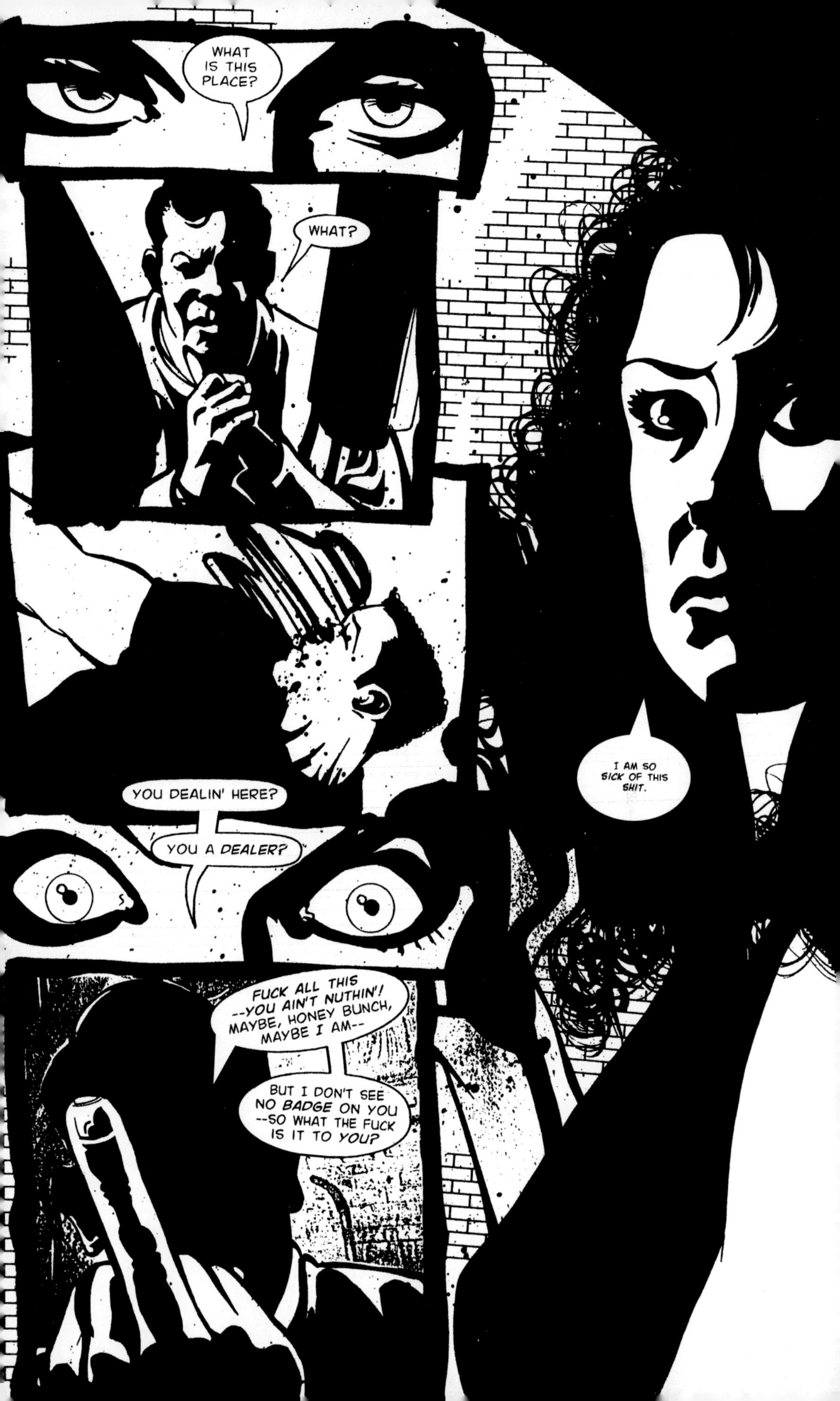
WHAT IS THIS PLACE?
WHAT?
YOU DEALIN' HERE?
YOU A DEALER?
I AM SO SICK OF THIS SHIT.
FUCK ALL THIS --YOU AIN'T NUTHIN'! MAYBE, HONEY BUNCH, MAYBE I AM--
BUT I DON'T SEE NO BADGE ON YOU --SO WHAT THE FUCK IS IT TO YOU?

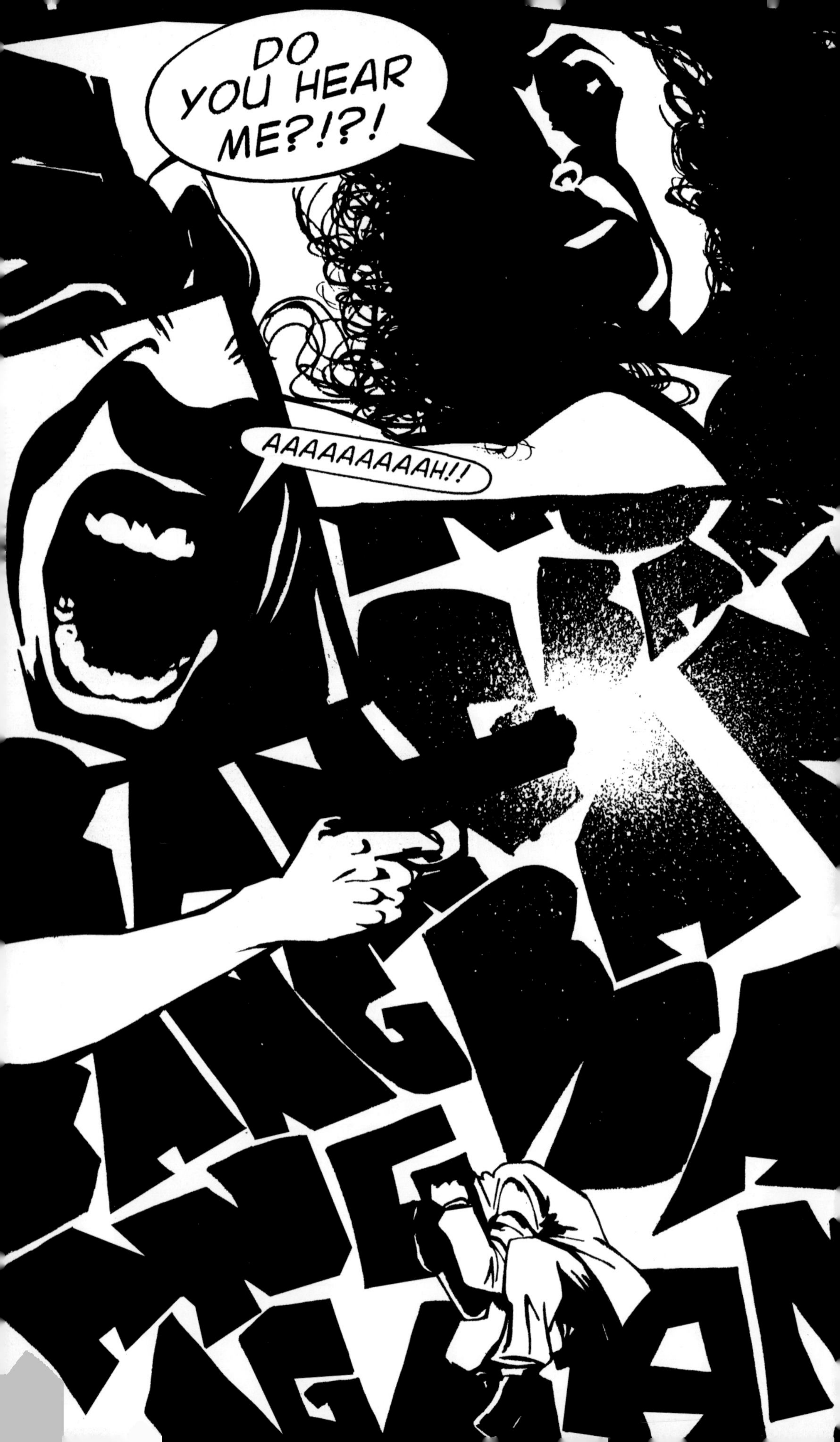
DO YOU HEAR ME?!?!
AAAAAAAAAH!!

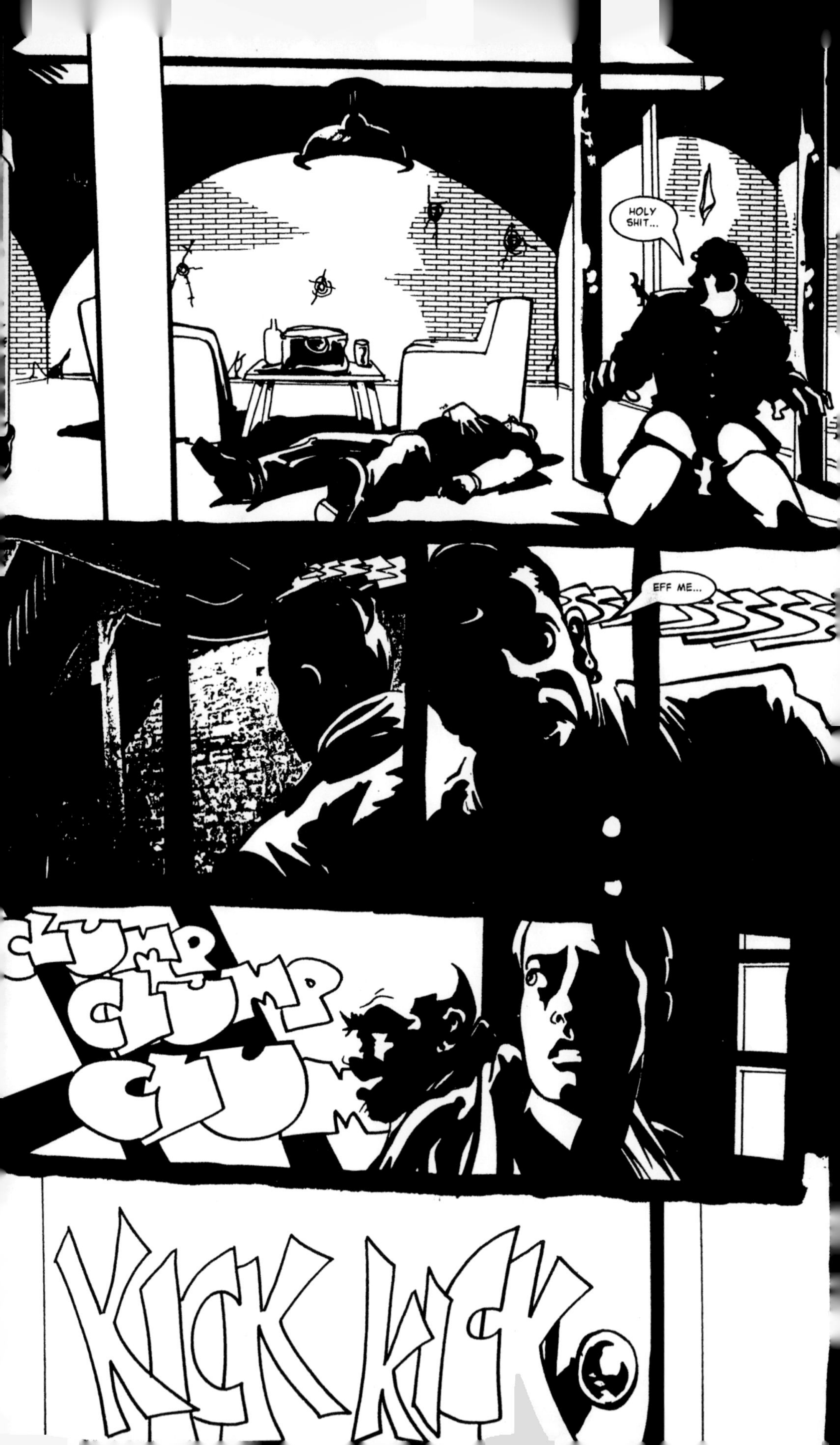
HOLY SHIT...
EFF ME...
CLUMP CLUMP CLU
KICK KICK

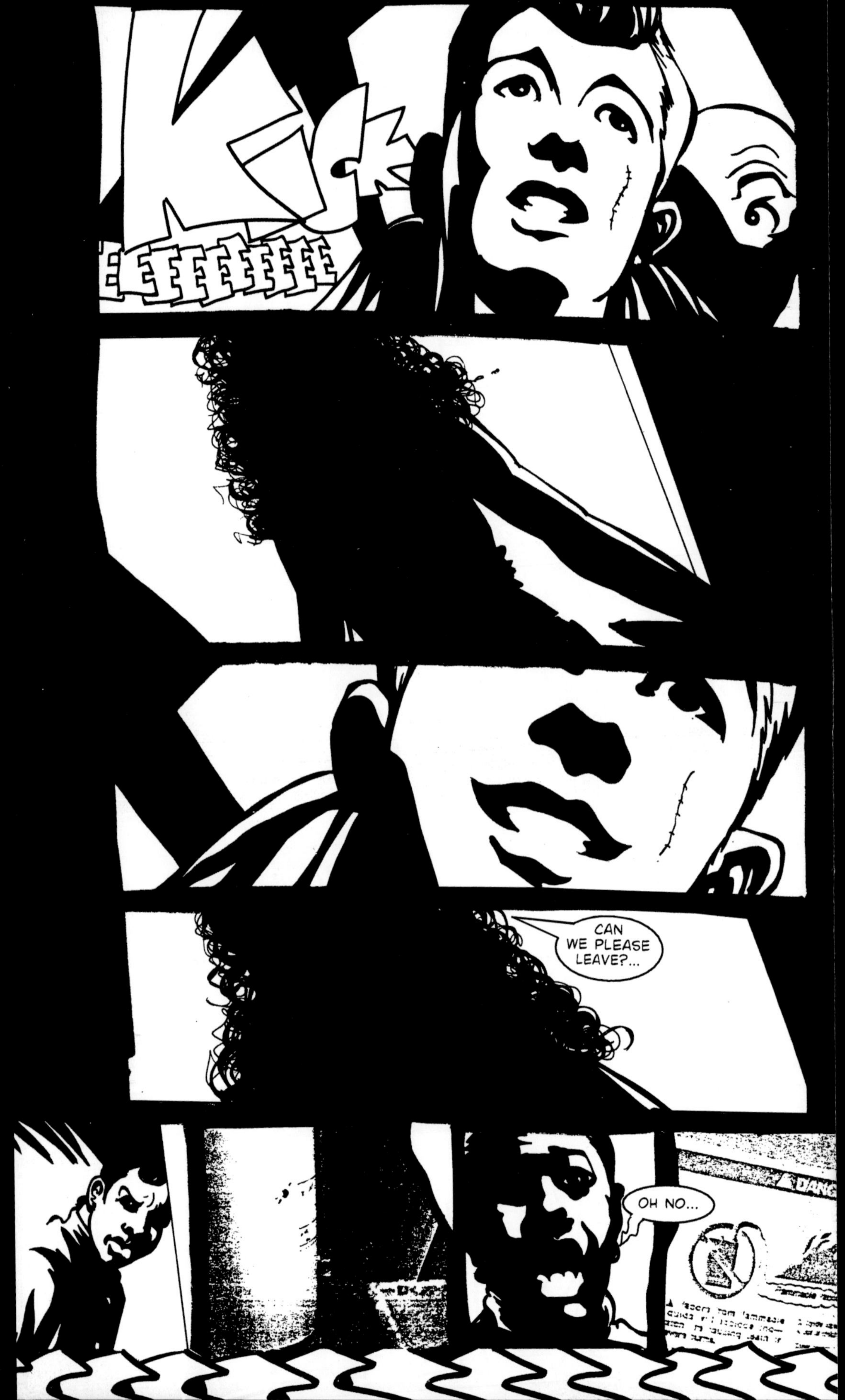
CAN WE PLEASE LEAVE?...
OH NO...

BOOM

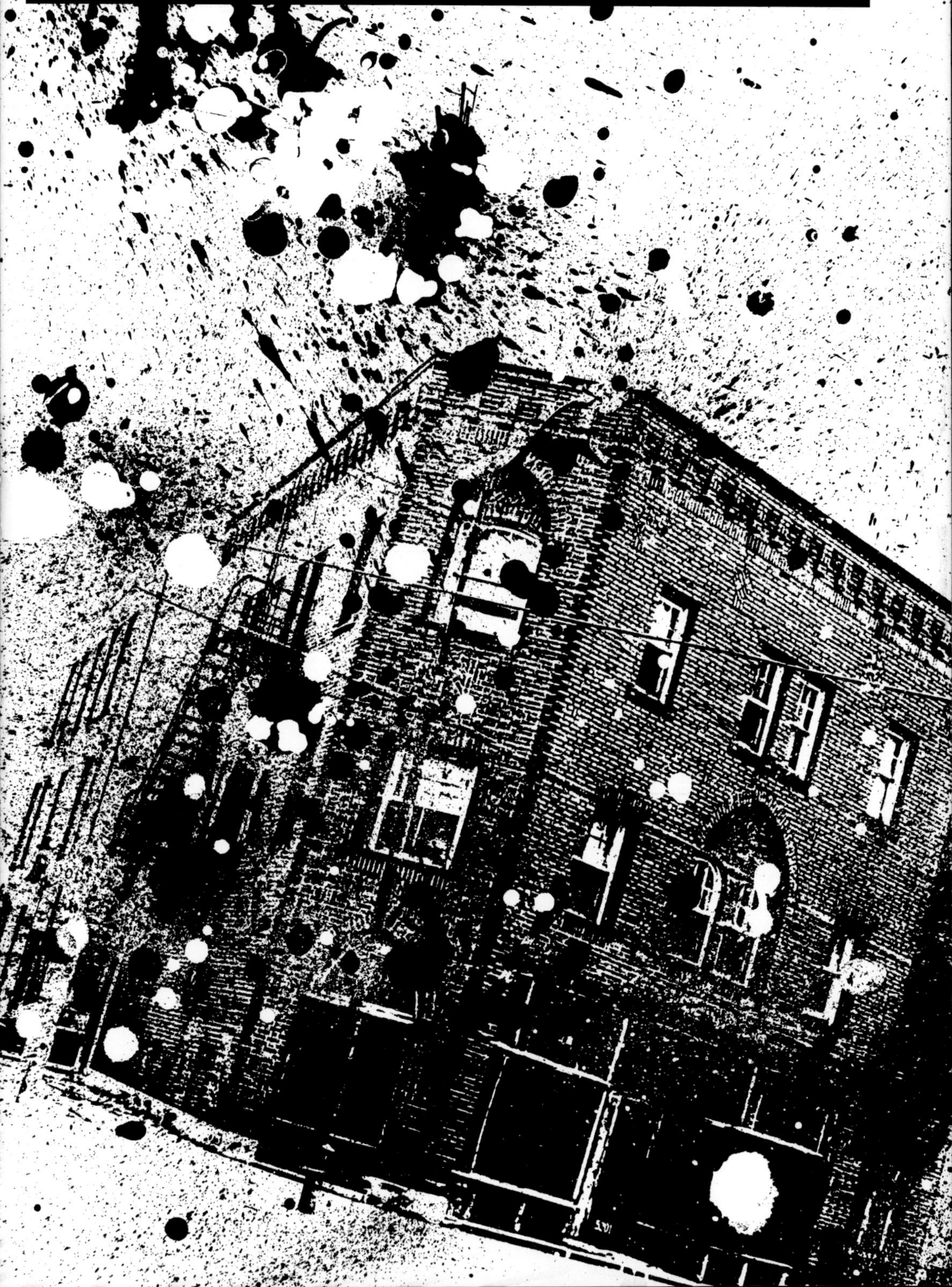

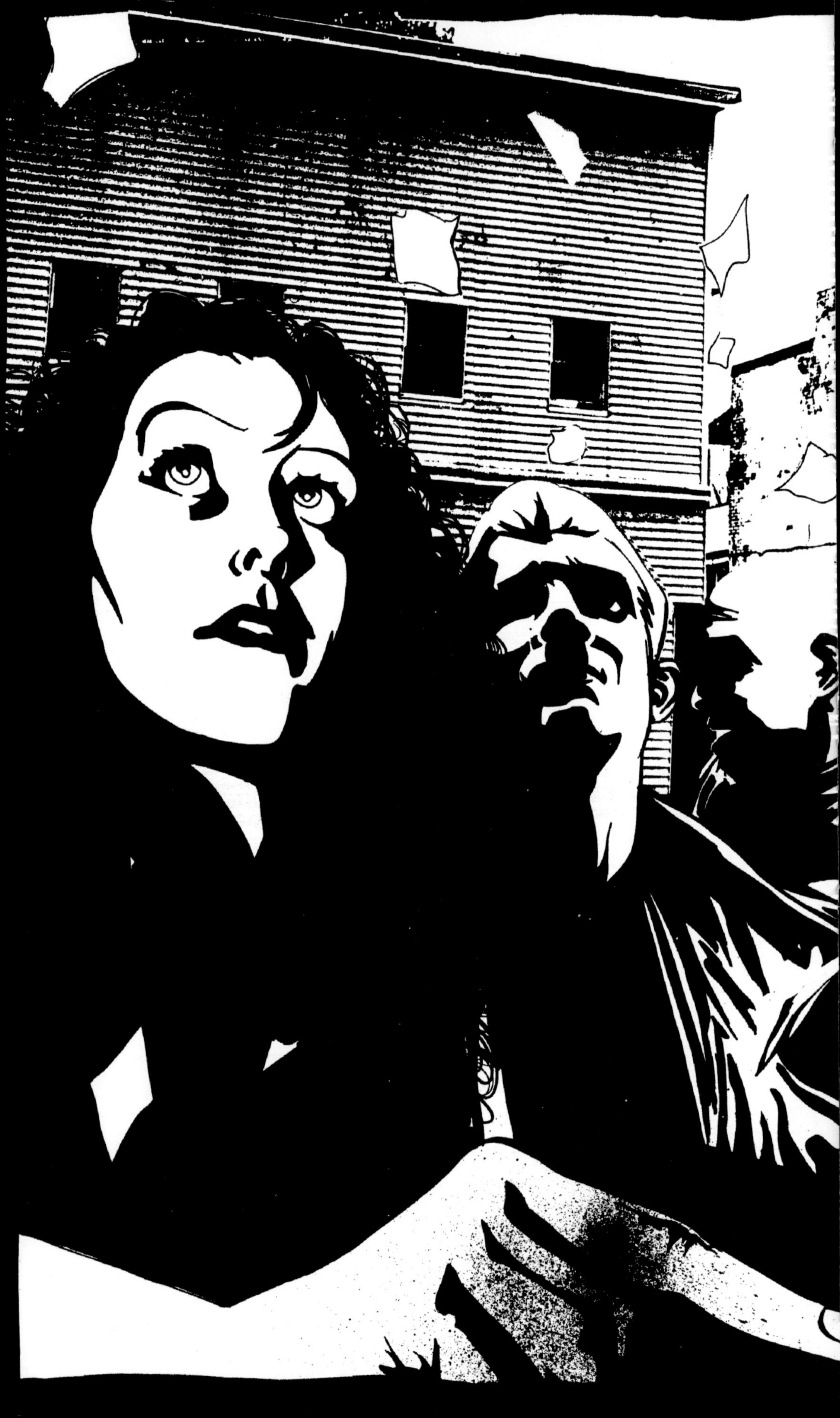

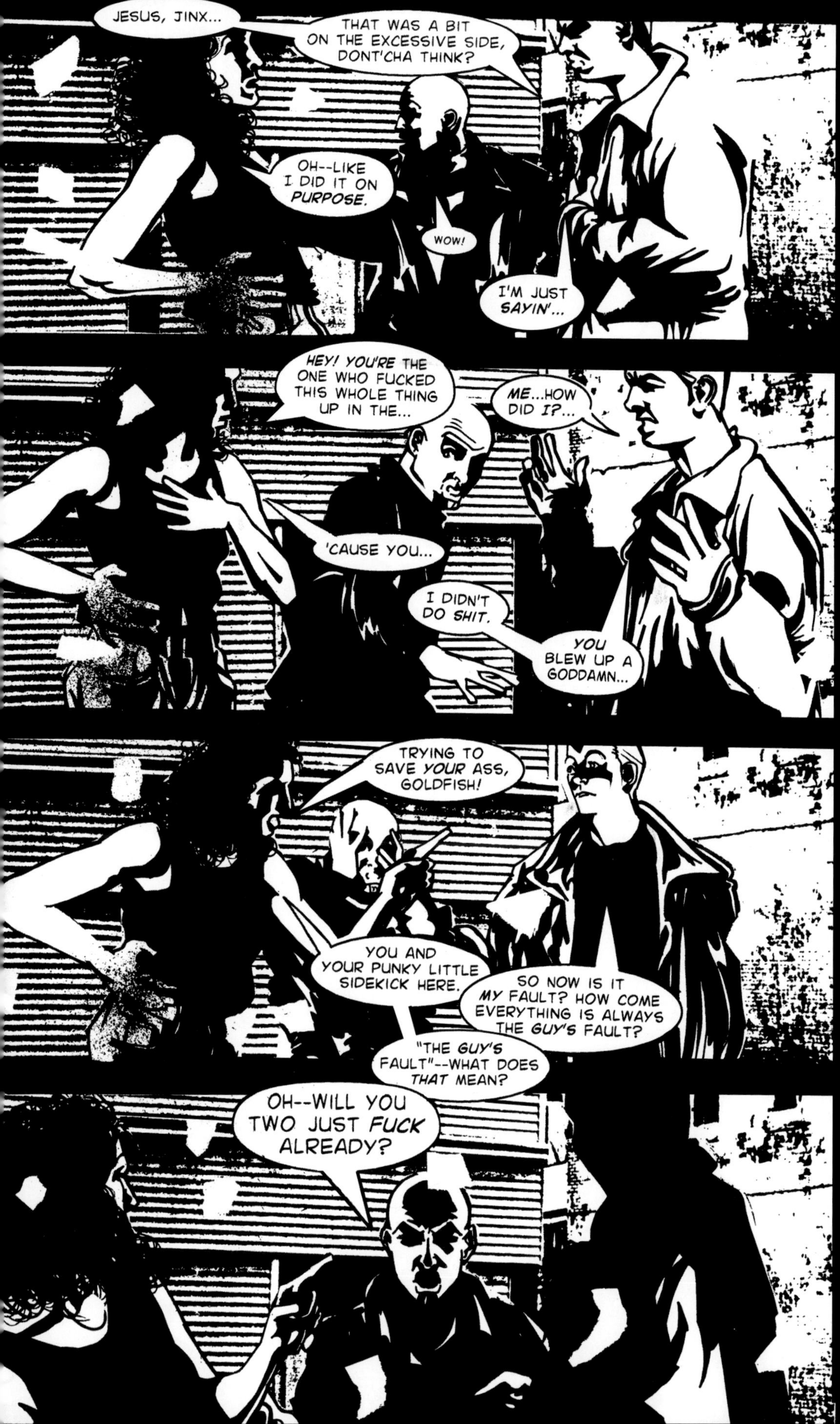
JESUS, JINX...
THAT WAS A BIT ON THE EXCESSIVE SIDE, DONT'CHA THINK?
OH--LIKE I DID IT ON PURPOSE.
WOW!
I'M JUST SAYIN'...
HEY! YOU'RE THE ONE WHO FUCKED THIS WHOLE THING UP IN THE...
ME...HOW DID I?...
'CAUSE YOU...
I DIDN'T DO SHIT.
YOU BLEW UP A GODDAMN...
TRYING TO SAVE YOUR ASS, GOLDFISH!
YOU AND YOUR PUNKY LITTLE SIDEKICK HERE.
SO NOW IS IT MY FAULT? HOW COME EVERYTHING IS ALWAYS THE GUY'S FAULT?
"THE GUY'S FAULT"--WHAT DOES THAT MEAN?
OH--WILL YOU TWO JUST FUCK ALREADY?

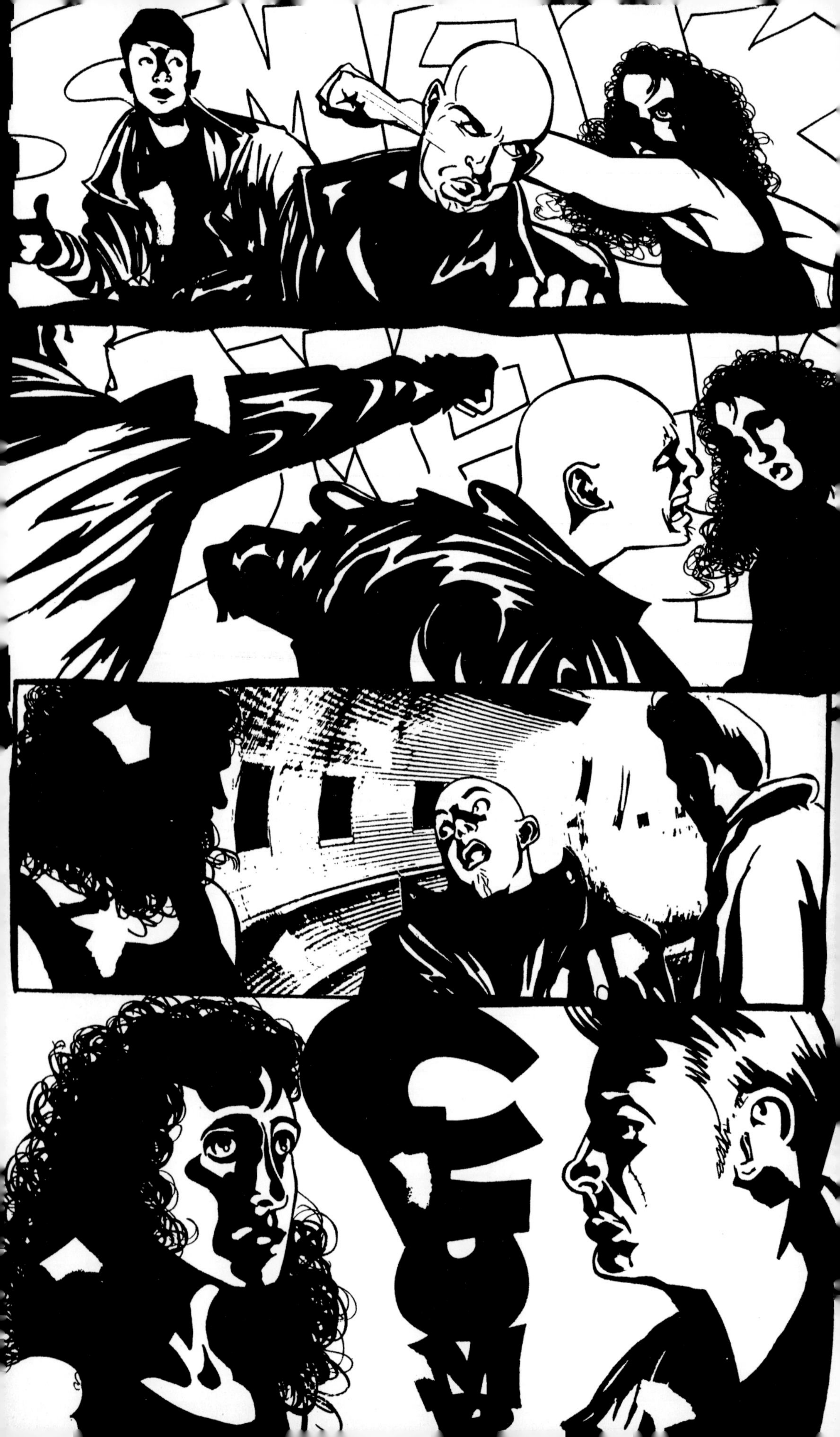

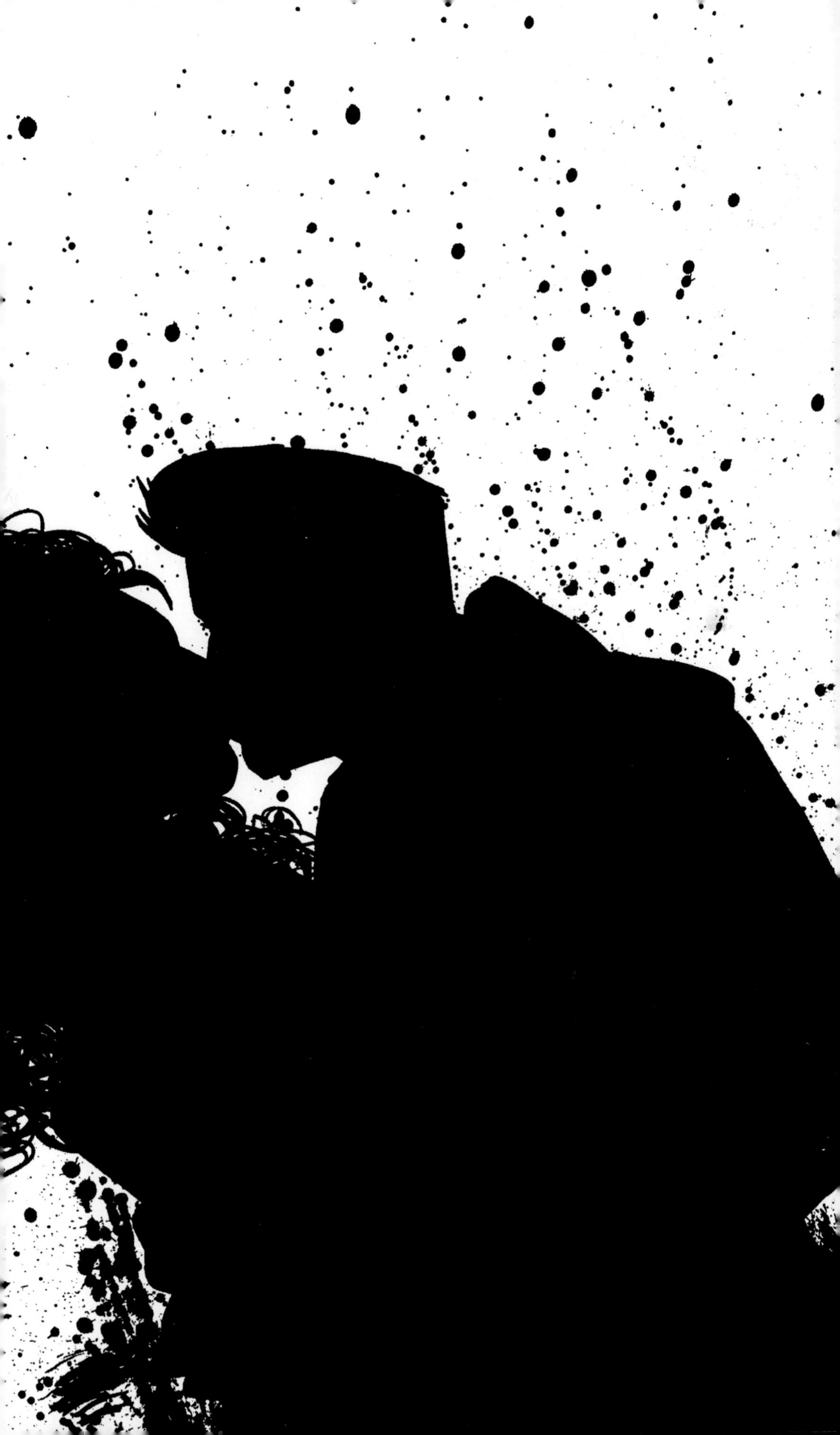

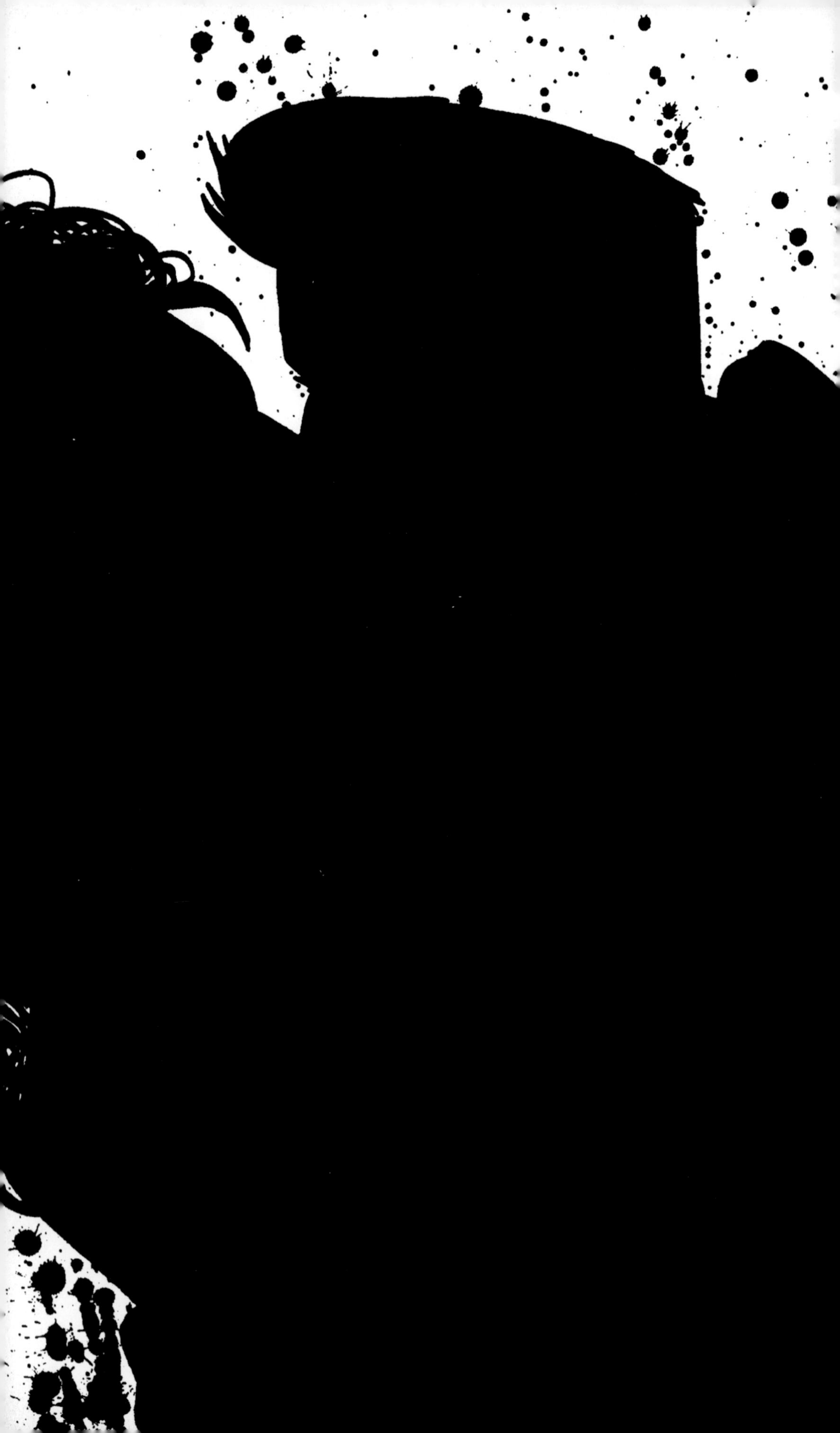

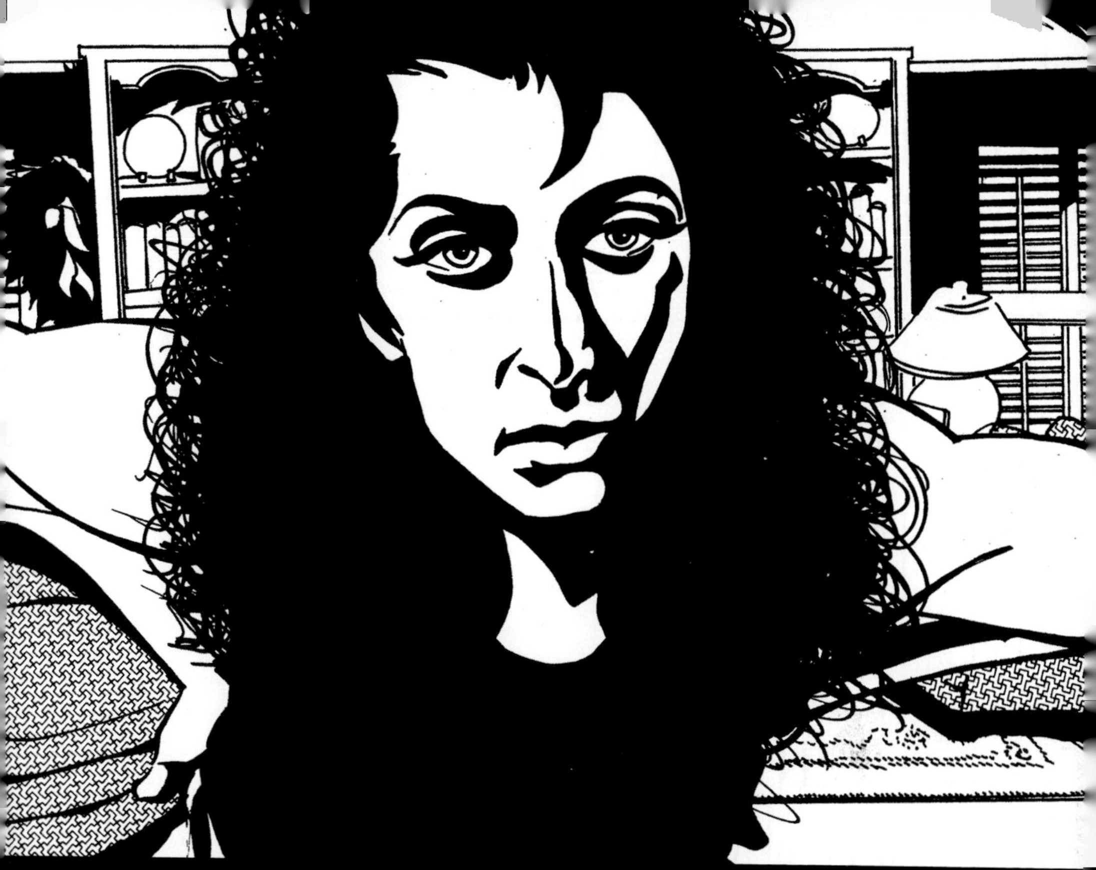

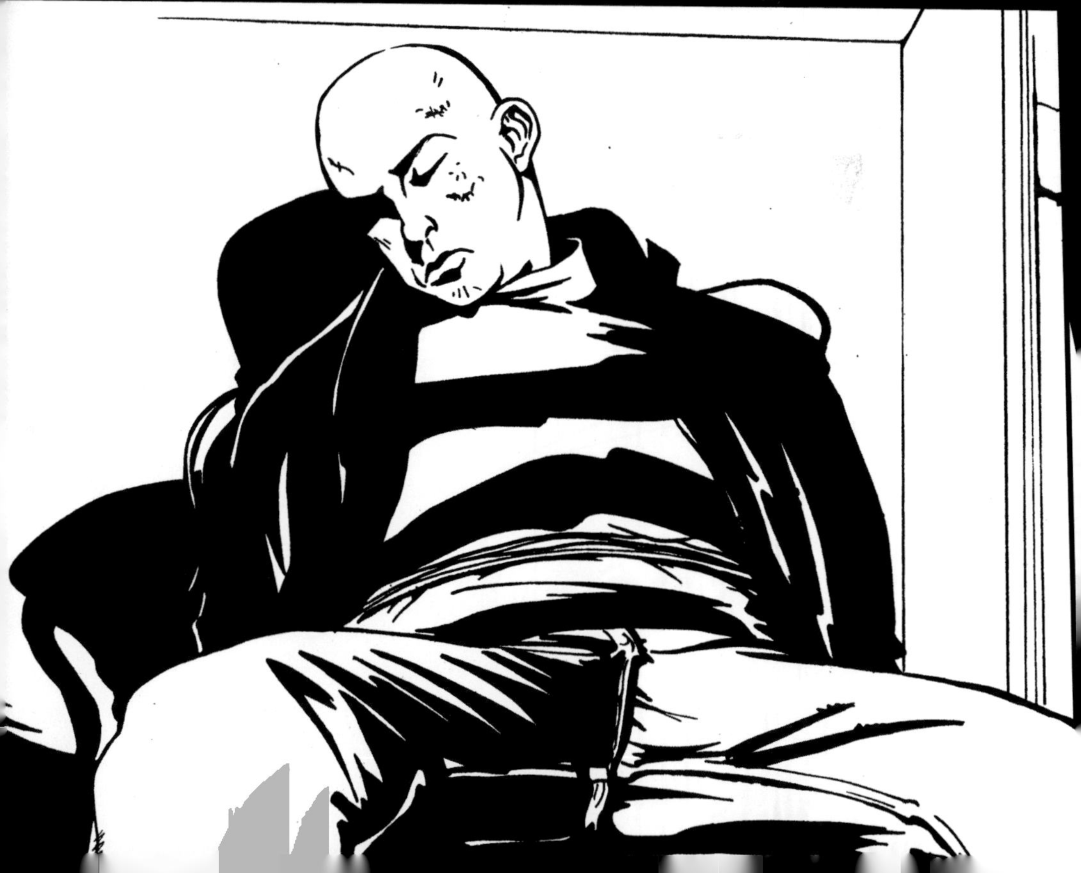

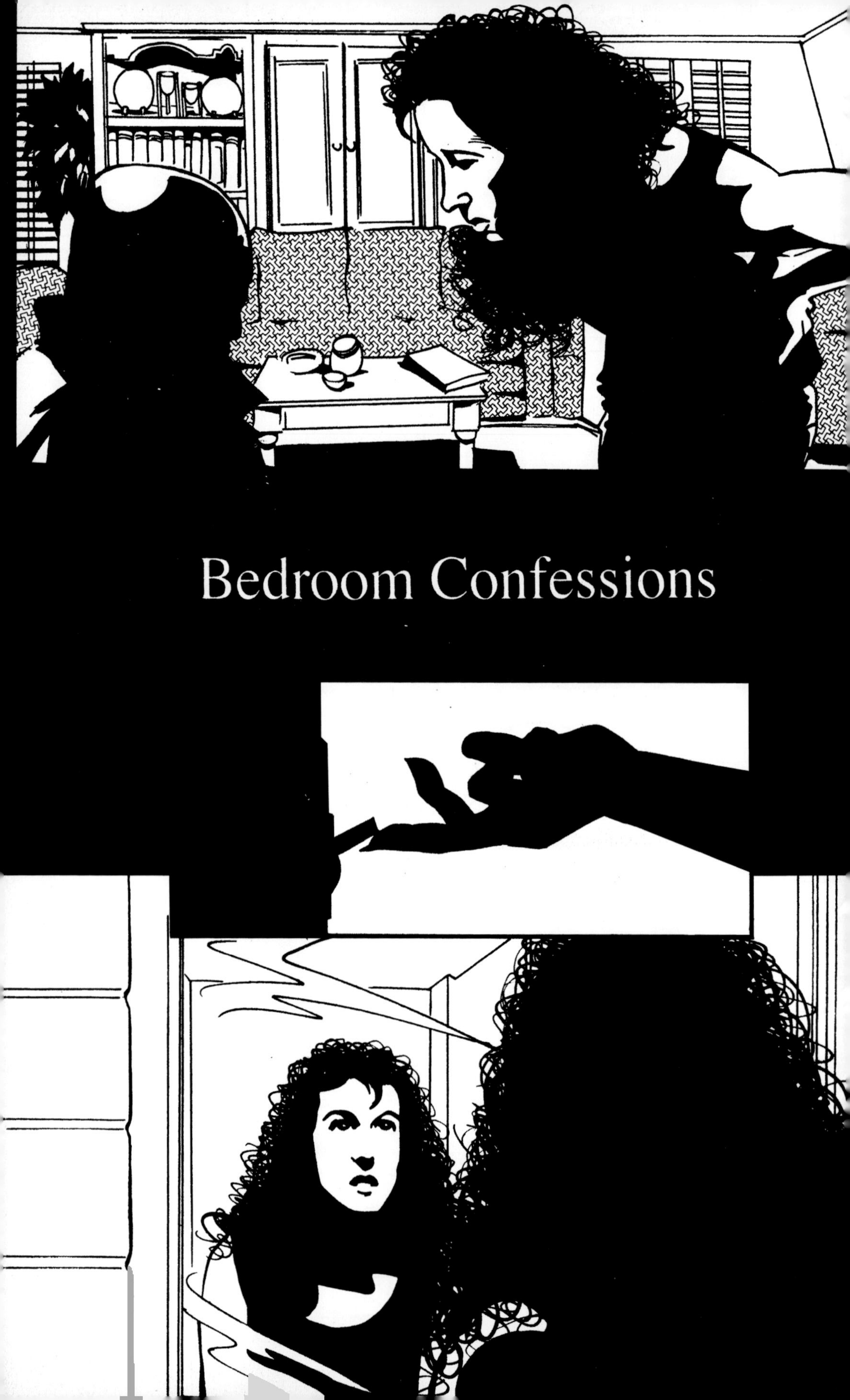
Bedroom Confessions

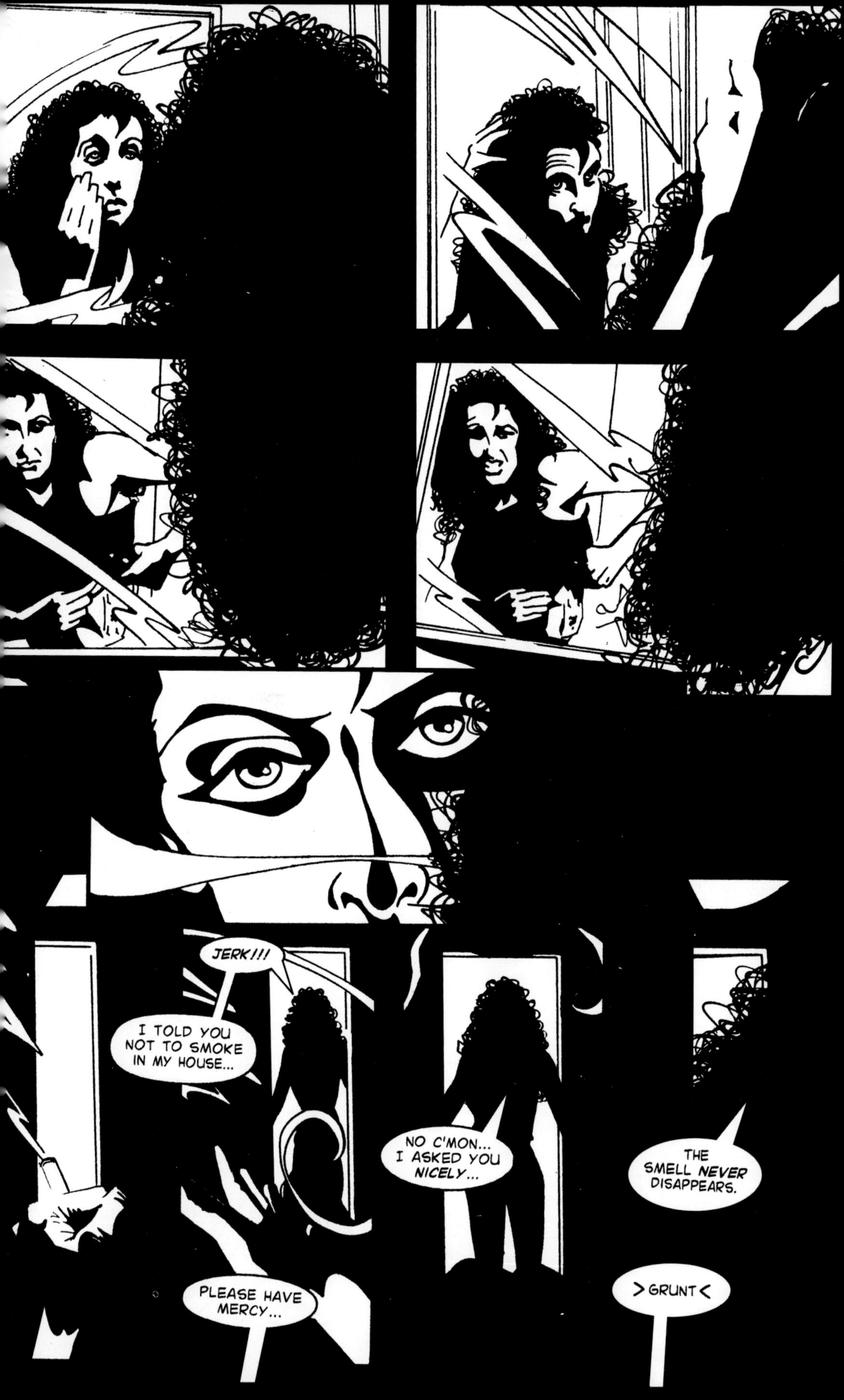
JERK!!!
I TOLD YOU NOT TO SMOKE IN MY HOUSE...
PLEASE HAVE MERCY...
NO C'MON... I ASKED YOU NICELY...
THE SMELL NEVER DISAPPEARS.
>GRUNT<

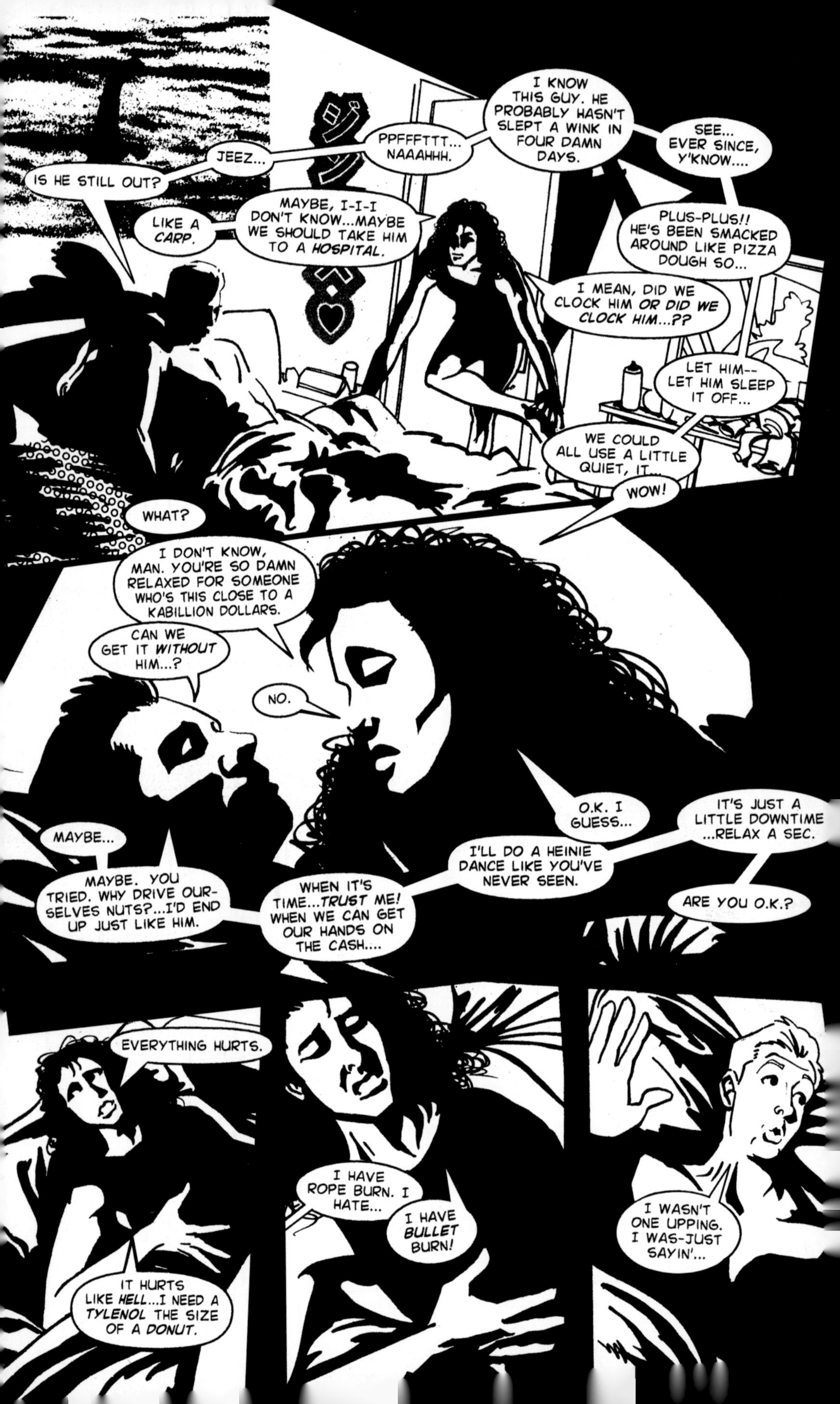
IS HE STILL OUT?
JEEZ...
PPFFFTTT... NAAAHHH.
I KNOW THIS GUY. HE PROBABLY HASN'T SLEPT A WINK IN FOUR DAMN DAYS.
SEE... EVER SINCE, Y'KNOW....
LIKE A CARP.
MAYBE, I-I-I DON'T KNOW...MAYBE WE SHOULD TAKE HIM TO A HOSPITAL.
PLUS-PLUS!! HE'S BEEN SMACKED AROUND LIKE PIZZA DOUGH SO...
I MEAN, DID WE CLOCK HIM OR DID WE CLOCK HIM...??
LET HIM-- LET HIM SLEEP IT OFF...
WE COULD ALL USE A LITTLE QUIET, IT...
WOW!
WHAT?
I DON'T KNOW, MAN. YOU'RE SO DAMN RELAXED FOR SOMEONE WHO'S THIS CLOSE TO A KABILLION DOLLARS.
CAN WE GET IT WITHOUT HIM...?
NO.
O.K. I GUESS...
IT'S JUST A LITTLE DOWNTIME ...RELAX A SEC.
MAYBE...
MAYBE. YOU TRIED. WHY DRIVE OURSELVES NUTS?...I'D END UP JUST LIKE HIM.
WHEN IT'S TIME...TRUST ME! WHEN WE CAN GET OUR HANDS ON THE CASH....
I'LL DO A HEINIE DANCE LIKE YOU'VE NEVER SEEN.
ARE YOU O.K.?
EVERYTHING HURTS.
IT HURTS LIKE HELL...I NEED A TYLENOL THE SIZE OF A DONUT.
I HAVE ROPE BURN. I HATE...
I HAVE BULLET BURN!
I WASN'T ONE UPPING. I WAS-JUST SAYIN'...

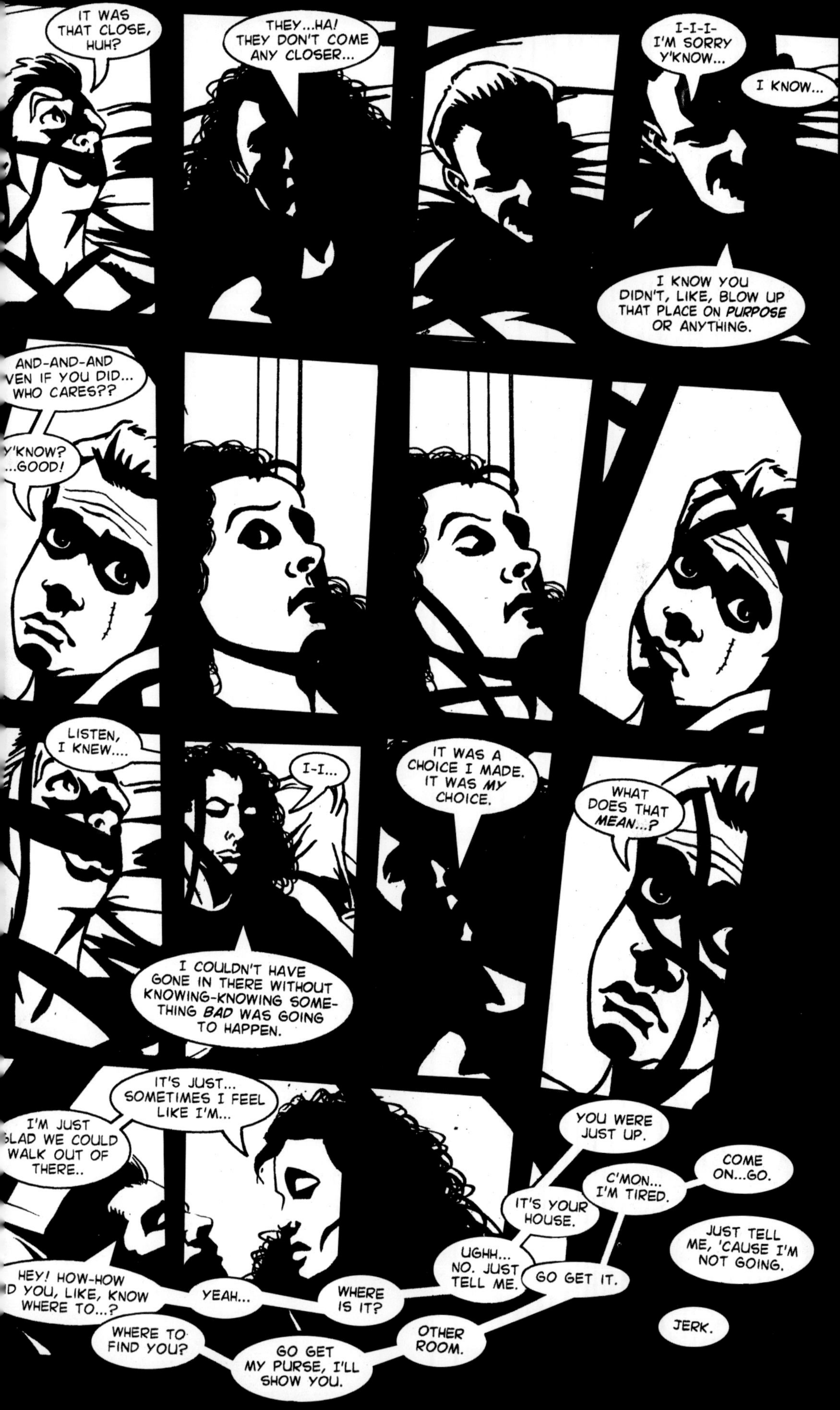
IT WAS THAT CLOSE, HUH?
THEY...HA! THEY DON'T COME ANY CLOSER...
I-I-I- I'M SORRY Y'KNOW...
I KNOW...
I KNOW YOU DIDN'T, LIKE, BLOW UP THAT PLACE ON PURPOSE OR ANYTHING.
AND-AND-AND VEN IF YOU DID... WHO CARES??
Y'KNOW? ...GOOD!
LISTEN, I KNEW....
I-I...
I COULDN'T HAVE GONE IN THERE WITHOUT KNOWING-KNOWING SOMETHING BAD WAS GOING TO HAPPEN.
IT WAS A CHOICE I MADE. IT WAS MY CHOICE.
WHAT DOES THAT MEAN...?
I'M JUST LAD WE COULD WALK OUT OF THERE..
IT'S JUST... SOMETIMES I FEEL LIKE I'M...
HEY! HOW-HOW D YOU, LIKE, KNOW WHERE TO...?
WHERE TO FIND YOU?
YEAH...
GO GET MY PURSE, I'LL SHOW YOU.
WHERE IS IT?
OTHER ROOM.
UGHH... NO. JUST TELL ME.
GO GET IT.
IT'S YOUR HOUSE.
YOU WERE JUST UP.
C'MON... I'M TIRED.
COME ON...GO.
JUST TELL ME, 'CAUSE I'M NOT GOING.
JERK.

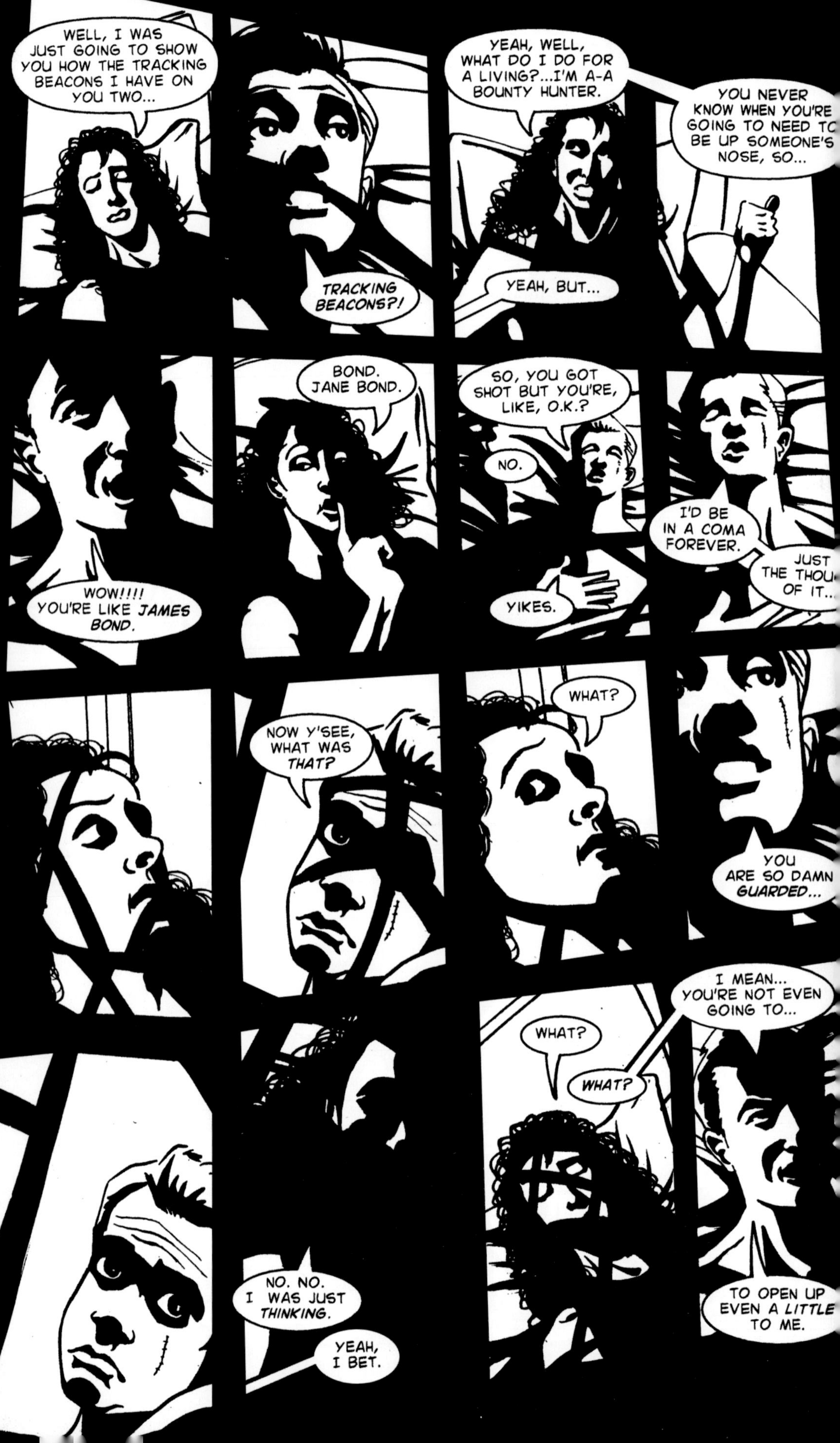
WELL, I WAS JUST GOING TO SHOW YOU HOW THE TRACKING BEACONS I HAVE ON YOU TWO...
TRACKING BEACONS?!
YEAH, WELL, WHAT DO I DO FOR A LIVING?...I'M A-A BOUNTY HUNTER.
YEAH, BUT...
YOU NEVER KNOW WHEN YOU'RE GOING TO NEED TO BE UP SOMEONE'S NOSE, SO...
WOW!!!! YOU'RE LIKE JAMES BOND.
BOND. JANE BOND.
SO, YOU GOT SHOT BUT YOU'RE, LIKE, O.K.?
NO.
YIKES.
I'D BE IN A COMA FOREVER.
JUST THE THOU OF IT...
NOW Y'SEE, WHAT WAS THAT?
WHAT?
YOU ARE SO DAMN GUARDED...
NO. NO. I WAS JUST THINKING.
YEAH, I BET.
WHAT?
WHAT?
I MEAN... YOU'RE NOT EVEN GOING TO...
TO OPEN UP EVEN A LITTLE TO ME.

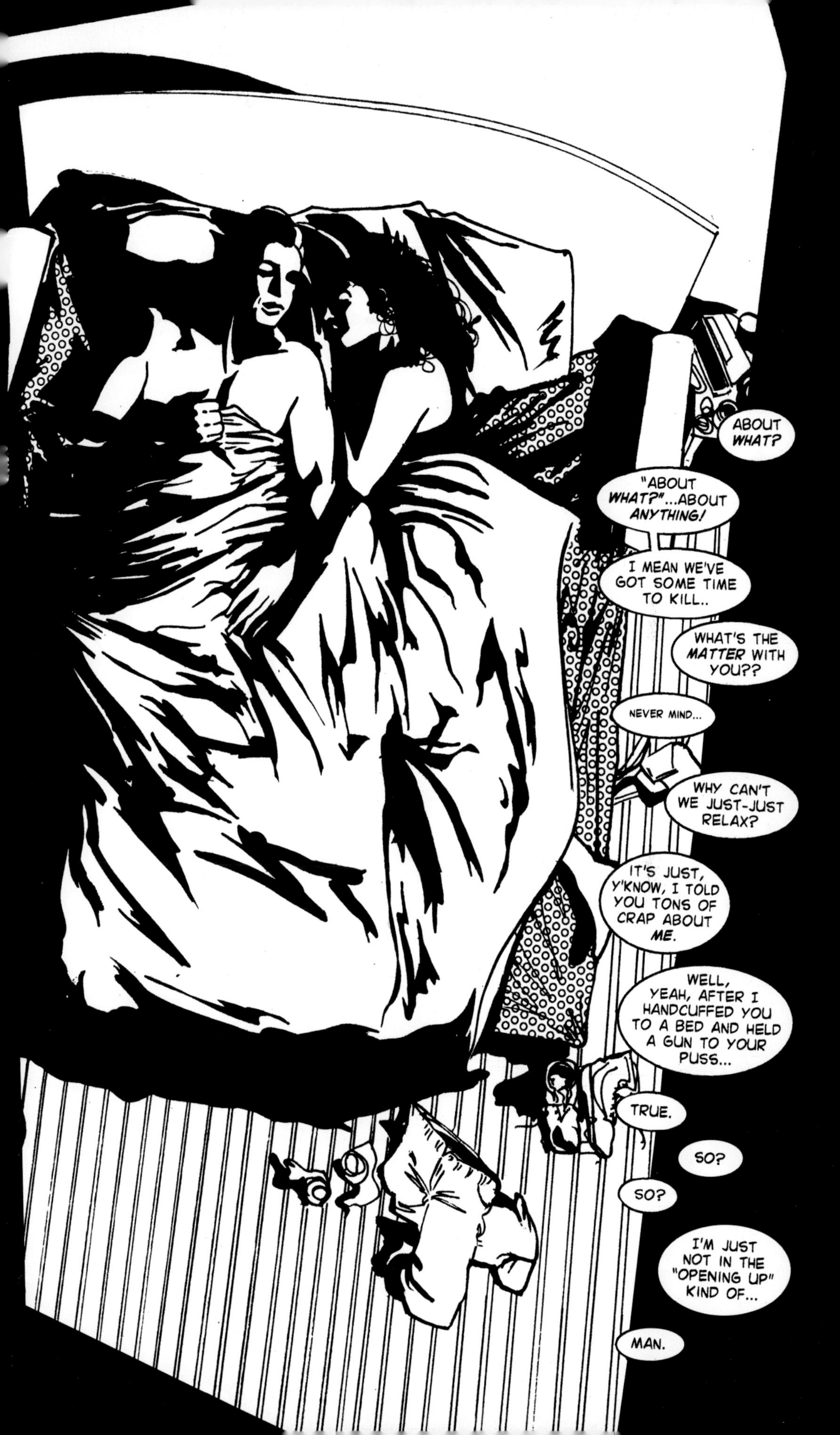

ABOUT *WHAT?*
"ABOUT *WHAT?*"...ABOUT *ANYTHING!*
I MEAN WE'VE GOT SOME TIME TO KILL..
WHAT'S THE *MATTER* WITH YOU??
NEVER MIND...
WHY CAN'T WE JUST-JUST RELAX?
IT'S JUST, Y'KNOW, I TOLD YOU TONS OF CRAP ABOUT *ME*.
WELL, YEAH, AFTER I HANDCUFFED YOU TO A BED AND HELD A GUN TO YOUR PUSS...
TRUE.
SO?
SO?
I'M JUST NOT IN THE "OPENING UP" KIND OF...
MAN.

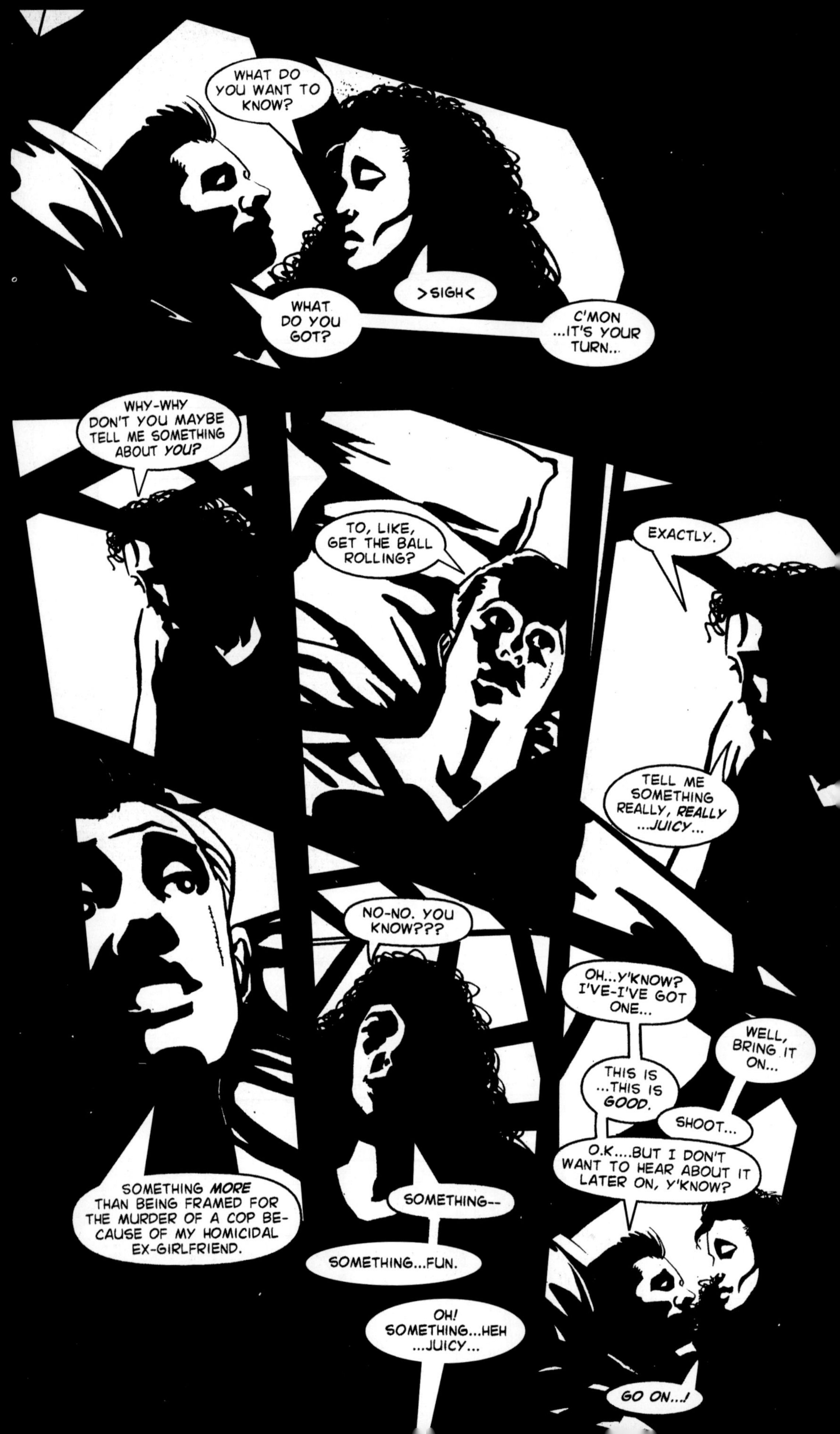
WHAT DO YOU WANT TO KNOW?
>SIGH<
WHAT DO YOU GOT?
C'MON ...IT'S YOUR TURN...
WHY-WHY DON'T YOU MAYBE TELL ME SOMETHING ABOUT YOU?
TO, LIKE, GET THE BALL ROLLING?
EXACTLY.
TELL ME SOMETHING REALLY, REALLY ...JUICY...
SOMETHING MORE THAN BEING FRAMED FOR THE MURDER OF A COP BE-CAUSE OF MY HOMICIDAL EX-GIRLFRIEND.
NO-NO. YOU KNOW???
SOMETHING--
SOMETHING...FUN.
OH! SOMETHING...HEH ...JUICY...
OH...Y'KNOW? I'VE-I'VE GOT ONE...
THIS IS ...THIS IS GOOD.
WELL, BRING IT ON...
SHOOT...
O.K....BUT I DON'T WANT TO HEAR ABOUT IT LATER ON, Y'KNOW?
GO ON...!

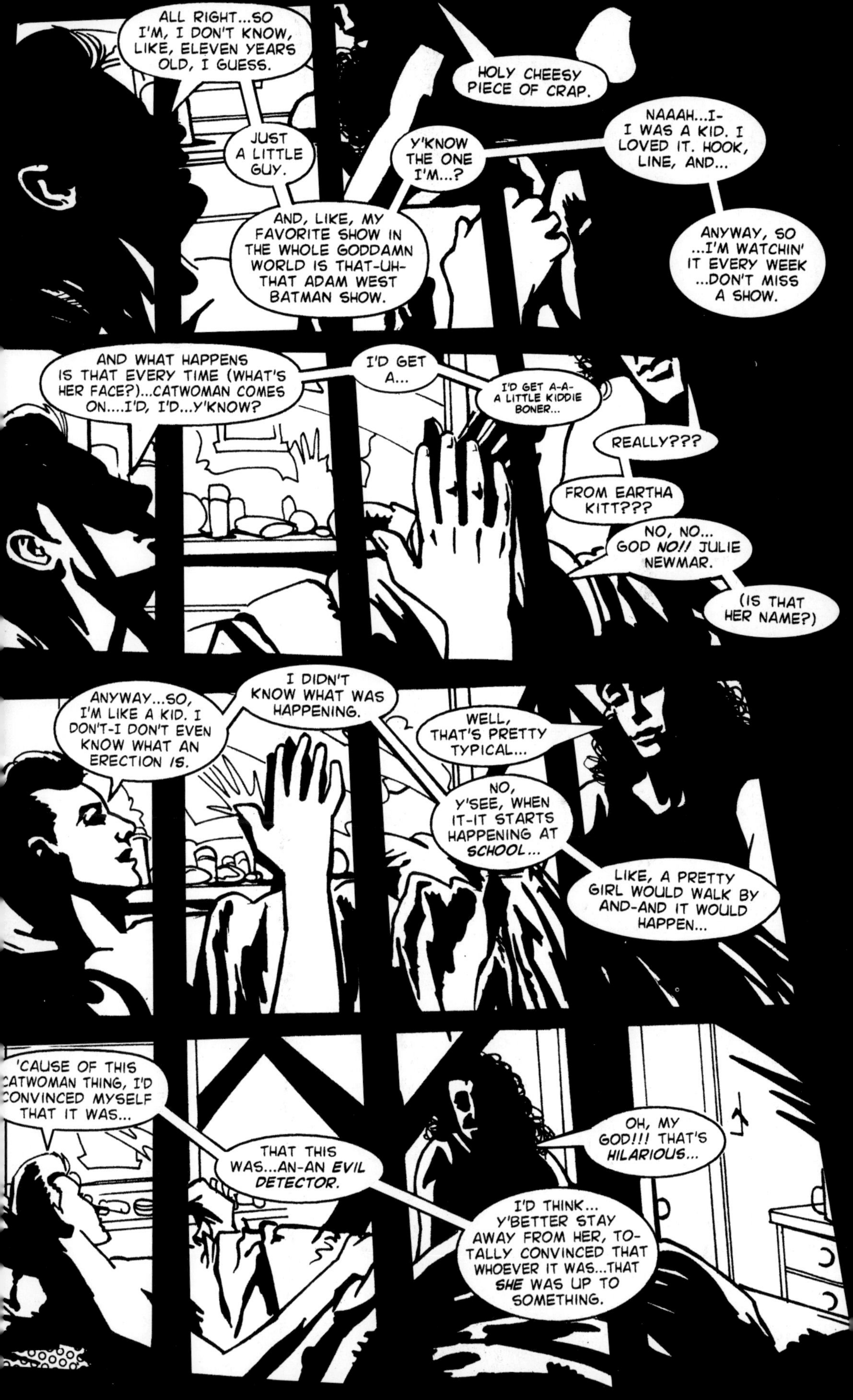
ALL RIGHT...SO I'M, I DON'T KNOW, LIKE, ELEVEN YEARS OLD, I GUESS.
JUST A LITTLE GUY.
AND, LIKE, MY FAVORITE SHOW IN THE WHOLE GODDAMN WORLD IS THAT-UH- THAT ADAM WEST BATMAN SHOW.
Y'KNOW THE ONE I'M...?
HOLY CHEESY PIECE OF CRAP.
NAAAH...I- I WAS A KID. I LOVED IT. HOOK, LINE, AND...
ANYWAY, SO ...I'M WATCHIN' IT EVERY WEEK ...DON'T MISS A SHOW.
AND WHAT HAPPENS IS THAT EVERY TIME (WHAT'S HER FACE?)...CATWOMAN COMES ON....I'D, I'D...Y'KNOW?
I'D GET A...
I'D GET A-A- A LITTLE KIDDIE BONER...
REALLY???
FROM EARTHA KITT???
NO, NO... GOD NO!! JULIE NEWMAR.
(IS THAT HER NAME?)
ANYWAY...SO, I'M LIKE A KID. I DON'T-I DON'T EVEN KNOW WHAT AN ERECTION IS.
I DIDN'T KNOW WHAT WAS HAPPENING.
WELL, THAT'S PRETTY TYPICAL...
NO, Y'SEE, WHEN IT-IT STARTS HAPPENING AT SCHOOL...
LIKE, A PRETTY GIRL WOULD WALK BY AND-AND IT WOULD HAPPEN...
'CAUSE OF THIS CATWOMAN THING, I'D CONVINCED MYSELF THAT IT WAS...
THAT THIS WAS...AN-AN EVIL DETECTOR.
OH, MY GOD!!! THAT'S HILARIOUS...
I'D THINK... Y'BETTER STAY AWAY FROM HER, TO- TALLY CONVINCED THAT WHOEVER IT WAS...THAT SHE WAS UP TO SOMETHING.

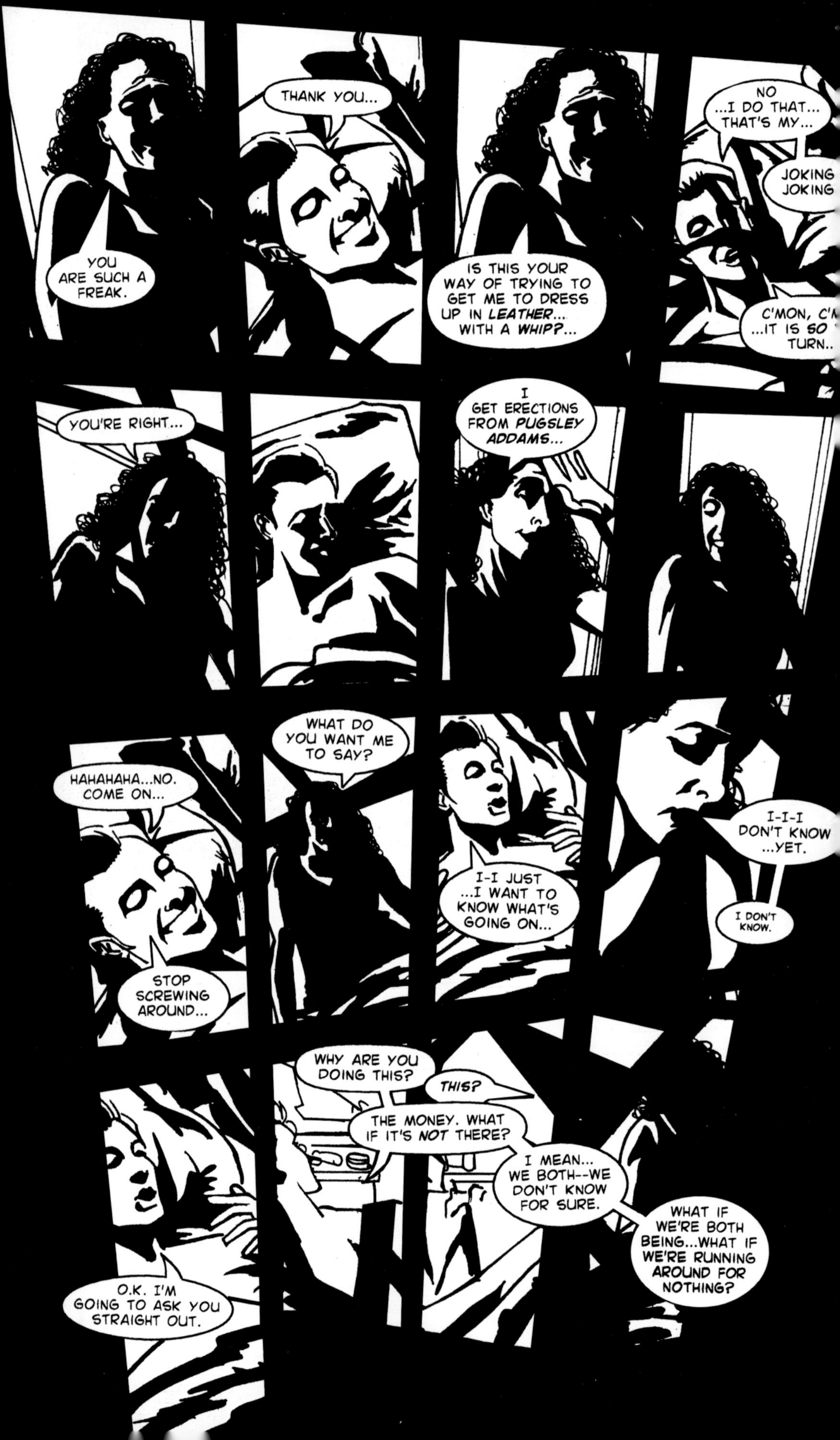
YOU ARE SUCH A FREAK.
THANK YOU...
IS THIS YOUR WAY OF TRYING TO GET ME TO DRESS UP IN *LEATHER*... WITH A *WHIP?*...
NO ...I DO THAT... THAT'S MY...
JOKING JOKING
C'MON, C' ...IT IS *SO* TURN..
YOU'RE RIGHT...
I GET ERECTIONS FROM *PUGSLEY ADDAMS*...
HAHAHAHA...NO. COME ON...
STOP SCREWING AROUND...
WHAT DO YOU WANT ME TO SAY?
I-I JUST ...I WANT TO KNOW WHAT'S GOING ON...
I-I-I DON'T KNOW ...YET.
I DON'T KNOW.
O.K. I'M GOING TO ASK YOU STRAIGHT OUT.
WHY ARE YOU DOING THIS?
THIS?
THE MONEY. WHAT IF IT'S *NOT* THERE?
I MEAN... WE BOTH--WE DON'T KNOW FOR SURE.
WHAT IF WE'RE BOTH BEING...WHAT IF WE'RE RUNNING AROUND FOR NOTHING?

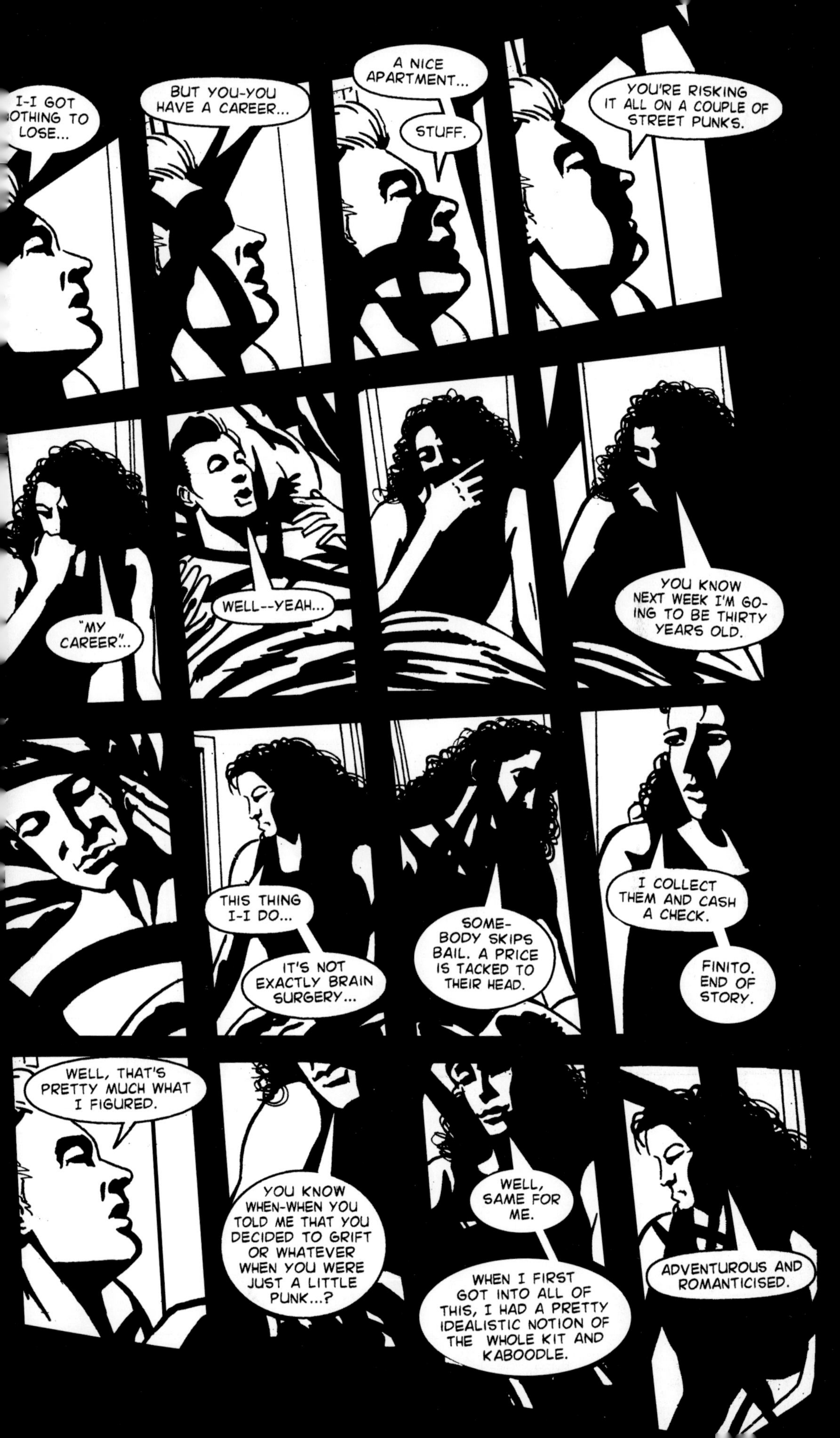
I-I GOT
OTHING TO
LOSE...
BUT YOU-YOU HAVE A CAREER...
A NICE APARTMENT...
STUFF.
YOU'RE RISKING IT ALL ON A COUPLE OF STREET PUNKS.
"MY CAREER"...
WELL--YEAH...
YOU KNOW NEXT WEEK I'M GO-ING TO BE THIRTY YEARS OLD.
THIS THING I-I DO...
IT'S NOT EXACTLY BRAIN SURGERY...
SOME-BODY SKIPS BAIL. A PRICE IS TACKED TO THEIR HEAD.
I COLLECT THEM AND CASH A CHECK.
FINITO. END OF STORY.
WELL, THAT'S PRETTY MUCH WHAT I FIGURED.
YOU KNOW WHEN-WHEN YOU TOLD ME THAT YOU DECIDED TO GRIFT OR WHATEVER WHEN YOU WERE JUST A LITTLE PUNK...?
WELL, SAME FOR ME.
WHEN I FIRST GOT INTO ALL OF THIS, I HAD A PRETTY IDEALISTIC NOTION OF THE WHOLE KIT AND KABOODLE.
ADVENTUROUS AND ROMANTICISED.

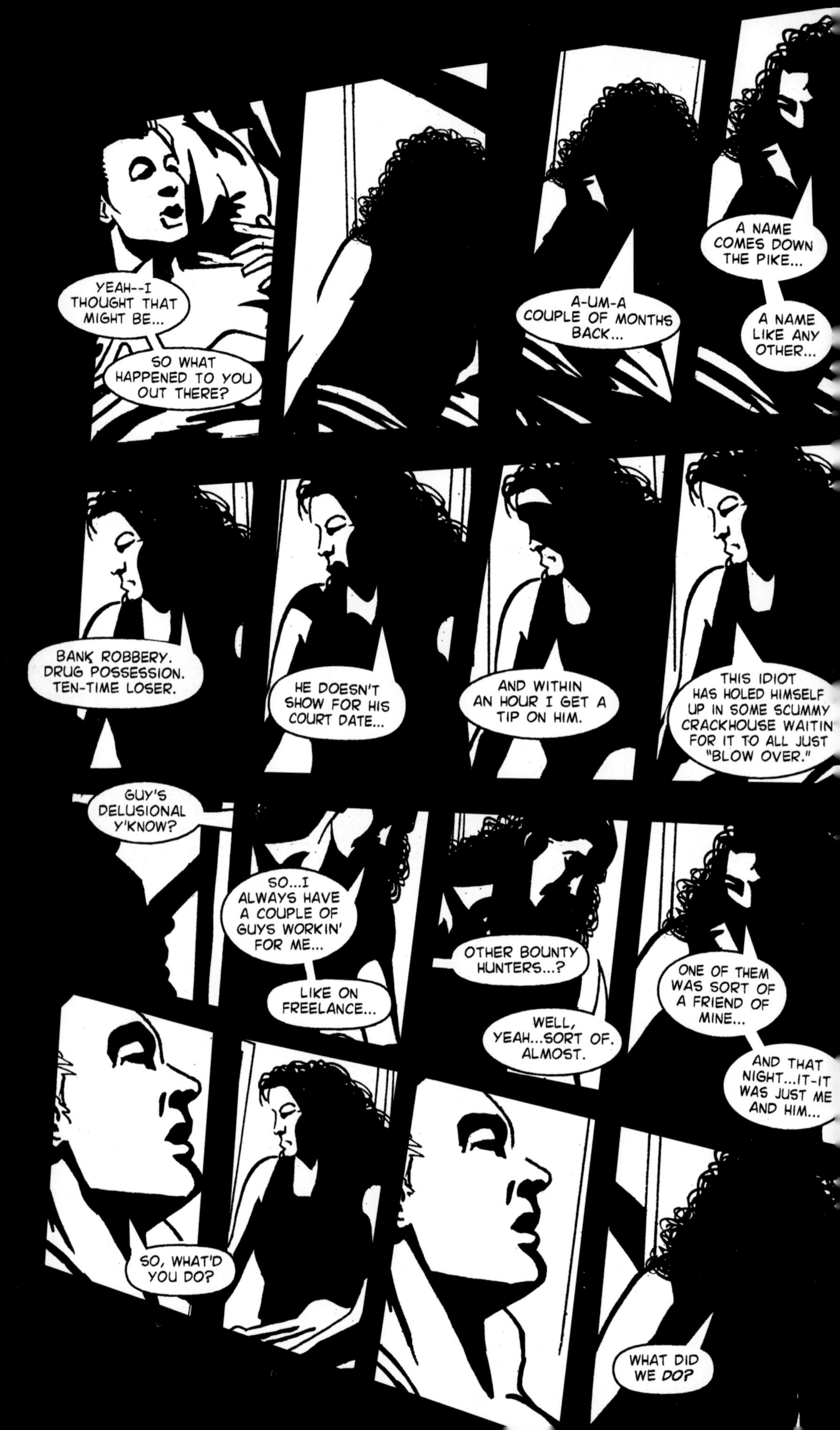
YEAH--I THOUGHT THAT MIGHT BE...
SO WHAT HAPPENED TO YOU OUT THERE?
A-UM-A COUPLE OF MONTHS BACK...
A NAME COMES DOWN THE PIKE...
A NAME LIKE ANY OTHER...
BANK ROBBERY. DRUG POSSESSION. TEN-TIME LOSER.
HE DOESN'T SHOW FOR HIS COURT DATE...
AND WITHIN AN HOUR I GET A TIP ON HIM.
THIS IDIOT HAS HOLED HIMSELF UP IN SOME SCUMMY CRACKHOUSE WAITIN FOR IT TO ALL JUST "BLOW OVER."
GUY'S DELUSIONAL Y'KNOW?
SO...I ALWAYS HAVE A COUPLE OF GUYS WORKIN' FOR ME...
LIKE ON FREELANCE...
OTHER BOUNTY HUNTERS...?
WELL, YEAH...SORT OF. ALMOST.
ONE OF THEM WAS SORT OF A FRIEND OF MINE...
AND THAT NIGHT...IT-IT WAS JUST ME AND HIM...
SO, WHAT'D YOU DO?
WHAT DID WE *DO?*

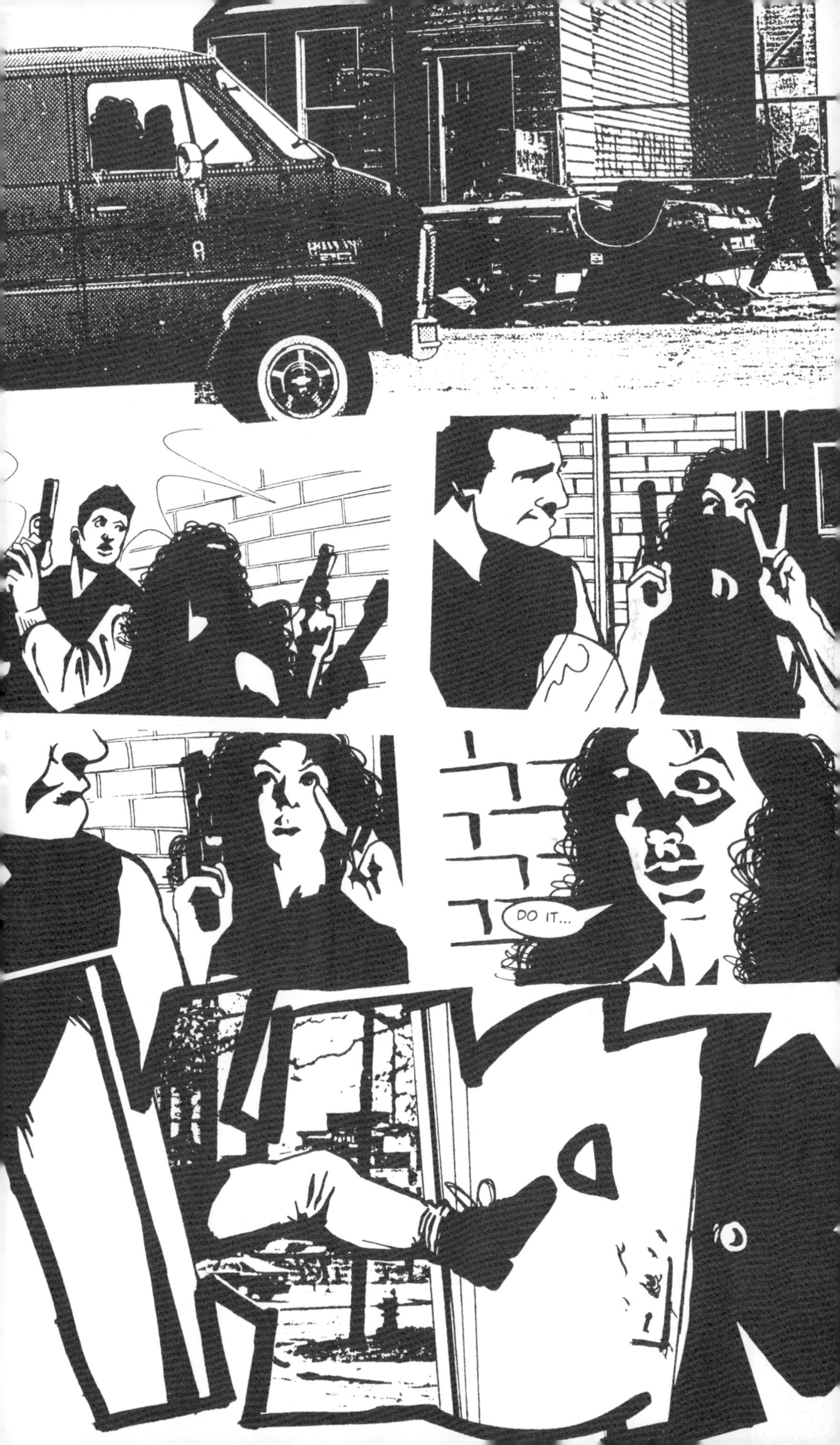
DO IT...

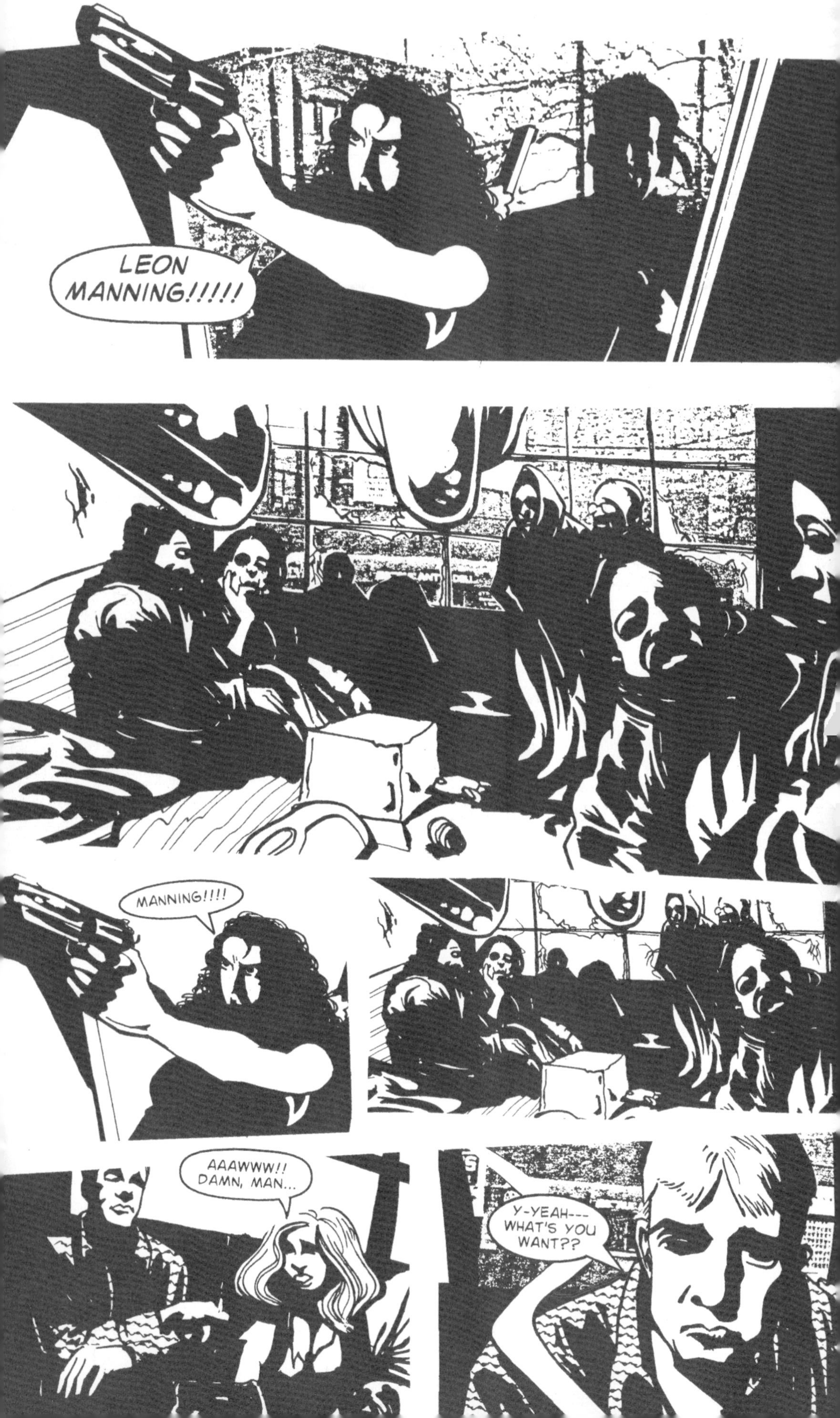
LEON MANNING!!!!!
MANNING!!!!
AAAWWW!! DAMN, MAN...
Y-YEAH--- WHAT'S YOU WANT??

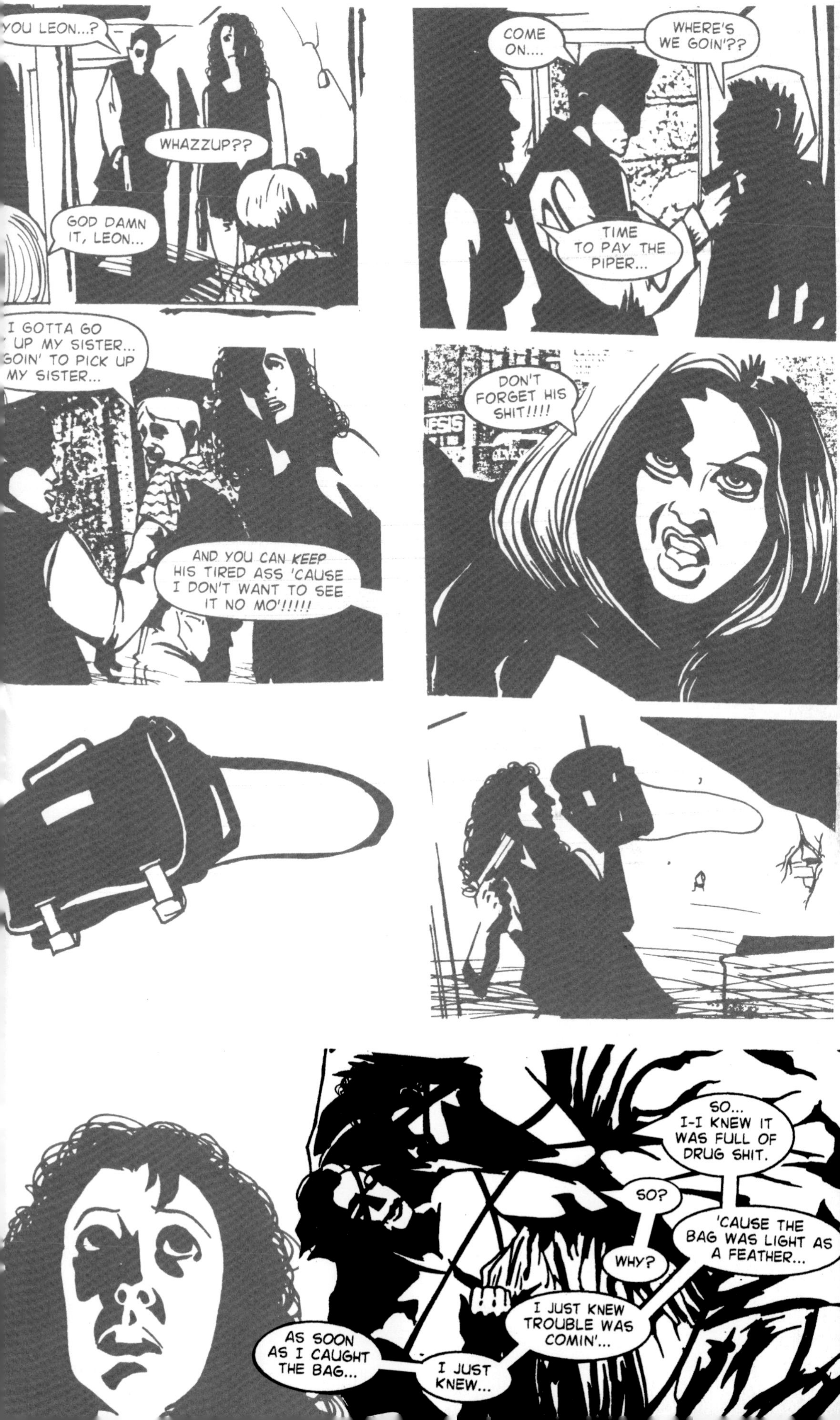
YOU LEON...?
WHAZZUP??
GOD DAMN IT, LEON...
COME ON....
WHERE'S WE GOIN'??
TIME TO PAY THE PIPER...
I GOTTA GO
UP MY SISTER...
GOIN' TO PICK UP MY SISTER...
AND YOU CAN *KEEP* HIS TIRED ASS 'CAUSE I DON'T WANT TO SEE IT NO MO'!!!!!
DON'T FORGET HIS SHIT!!!!
AS SOON AS I CAUGHT THE BAG...
I JUST KNEW...
I JUST KNEW TROUBLE WAS COMIN'...
WHY?
'CAUSE THE BAG WAS LIGHT AS A FEATHER...
SO?
SO... I-I KNEW IT WAS FULL OF DRUG SHIT.

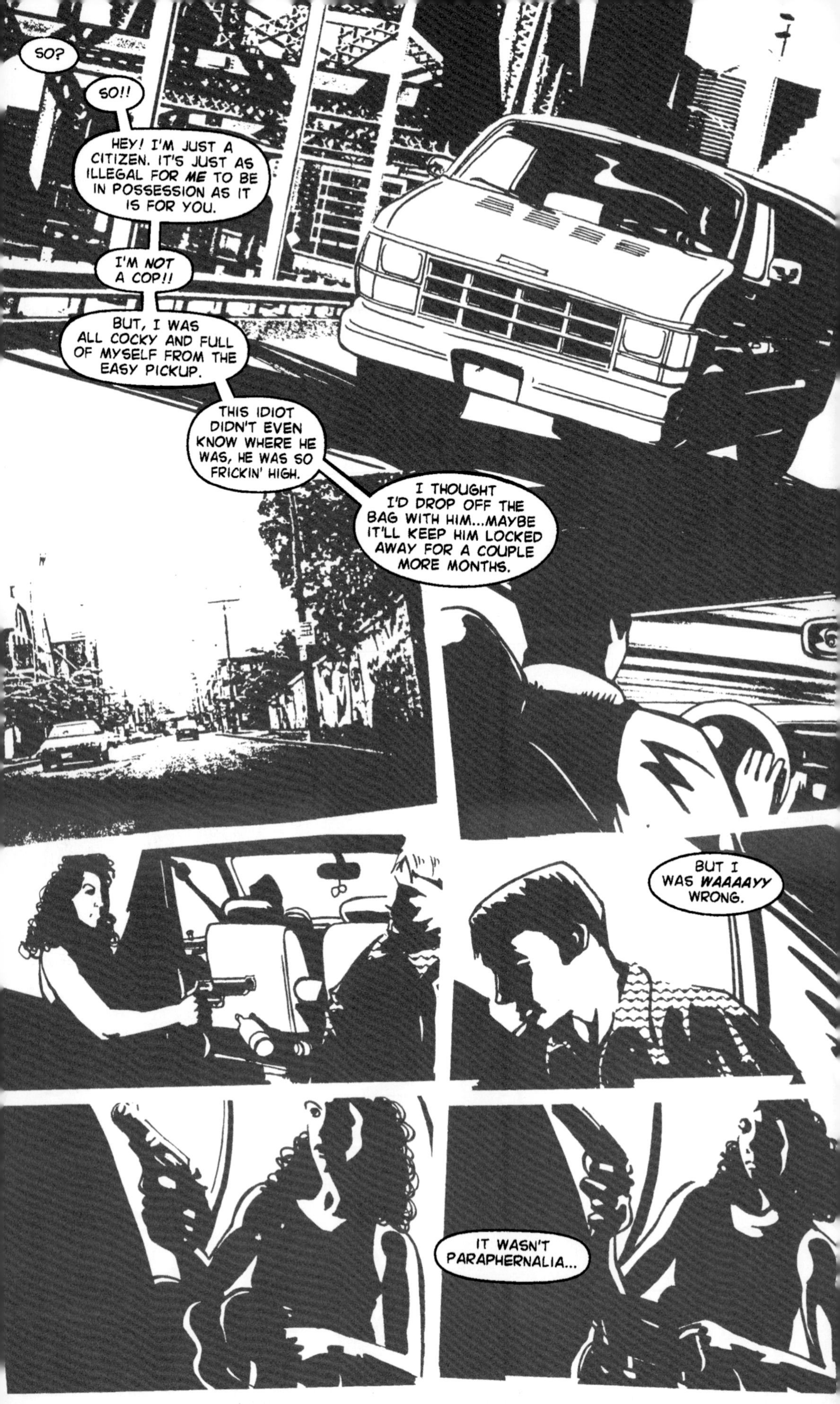
SO?
SO!!
HEY! I'M JUST A CITIZEN. IT'S JUST AS ILLEGAL FOR *ME* TO BE IN POSSESSION AS IT IS FOR YOU.
I'M *NOT* A COP!!
BUT, I WAS ALL COCKY AND FULL OF MYSELF FROM THE EASY PICKUP.
THIS IDIOT DIDN'T EVEN KNOW WHERE HE WAS, HE WAS SO FRICKIN' HIGH.
I THOUGHT I'D DROP OFF THE BAG WITH HIM...MAYBE IT'LL KEEP HIM LOCKED AWAY FOR A COUPLE MORE MONTHS.
BUT I WAS *WAAAAYY* WRONG.
IT WASN'T PARAPHERNALIA...

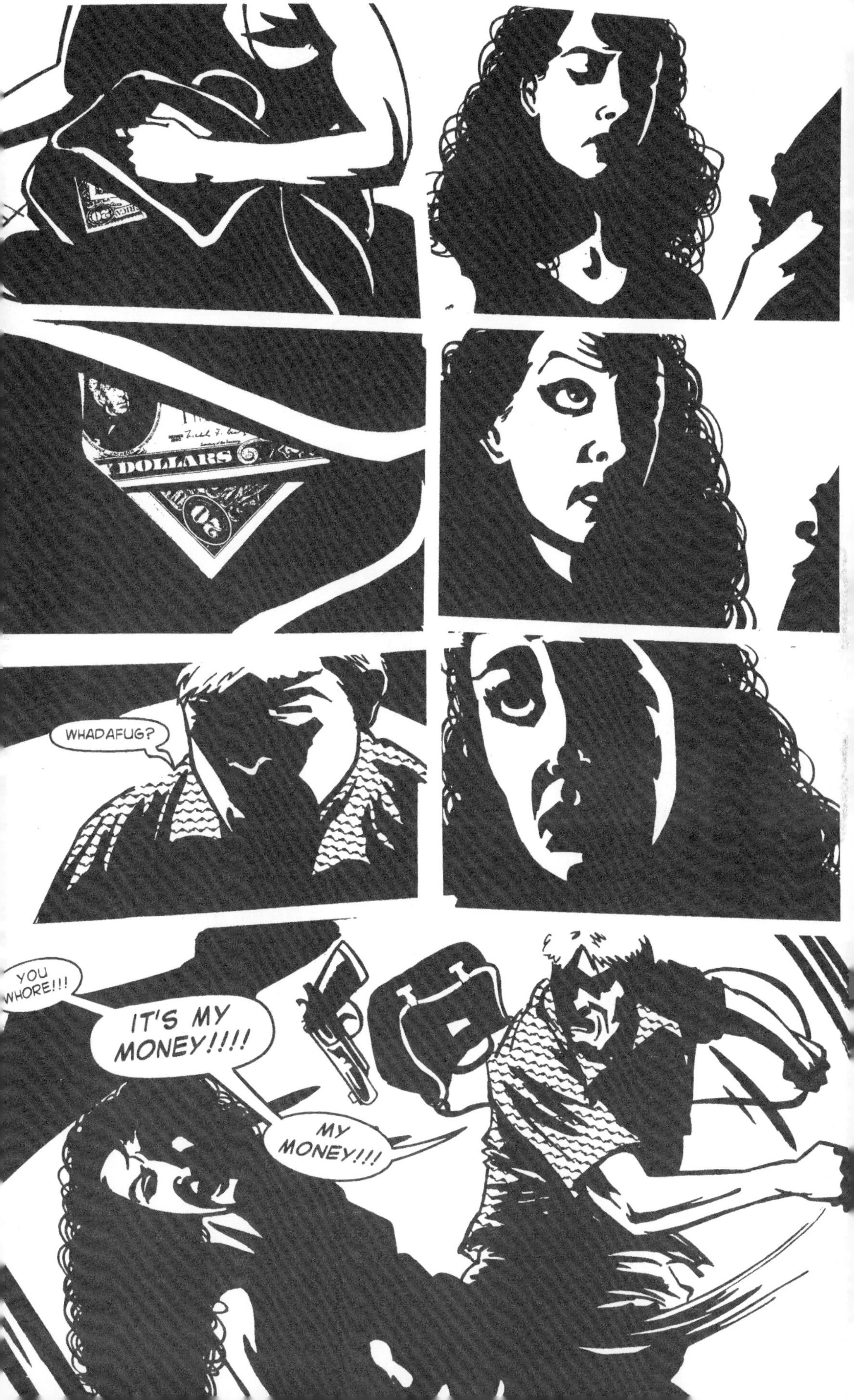
WHADAFUG?
YOU WHORE!!!
IT'S MY MONEY!!!!
MY MONEY!!!

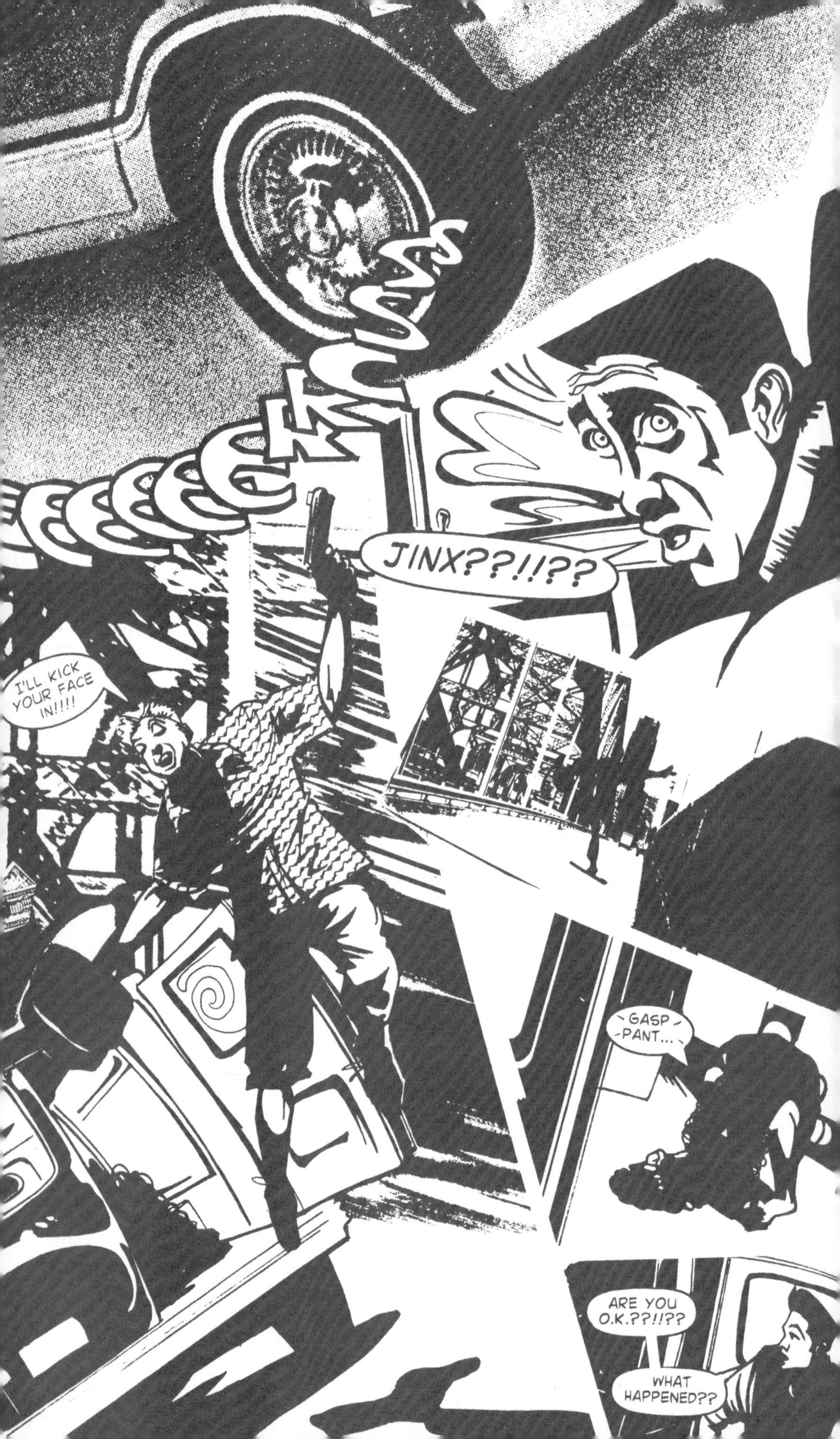
JINX??!!??
I'LL KICK YOUR FACE IN!!!!
GASP PANT...
ARE YOU O.K.??!!??
WHAT HAPPENED??

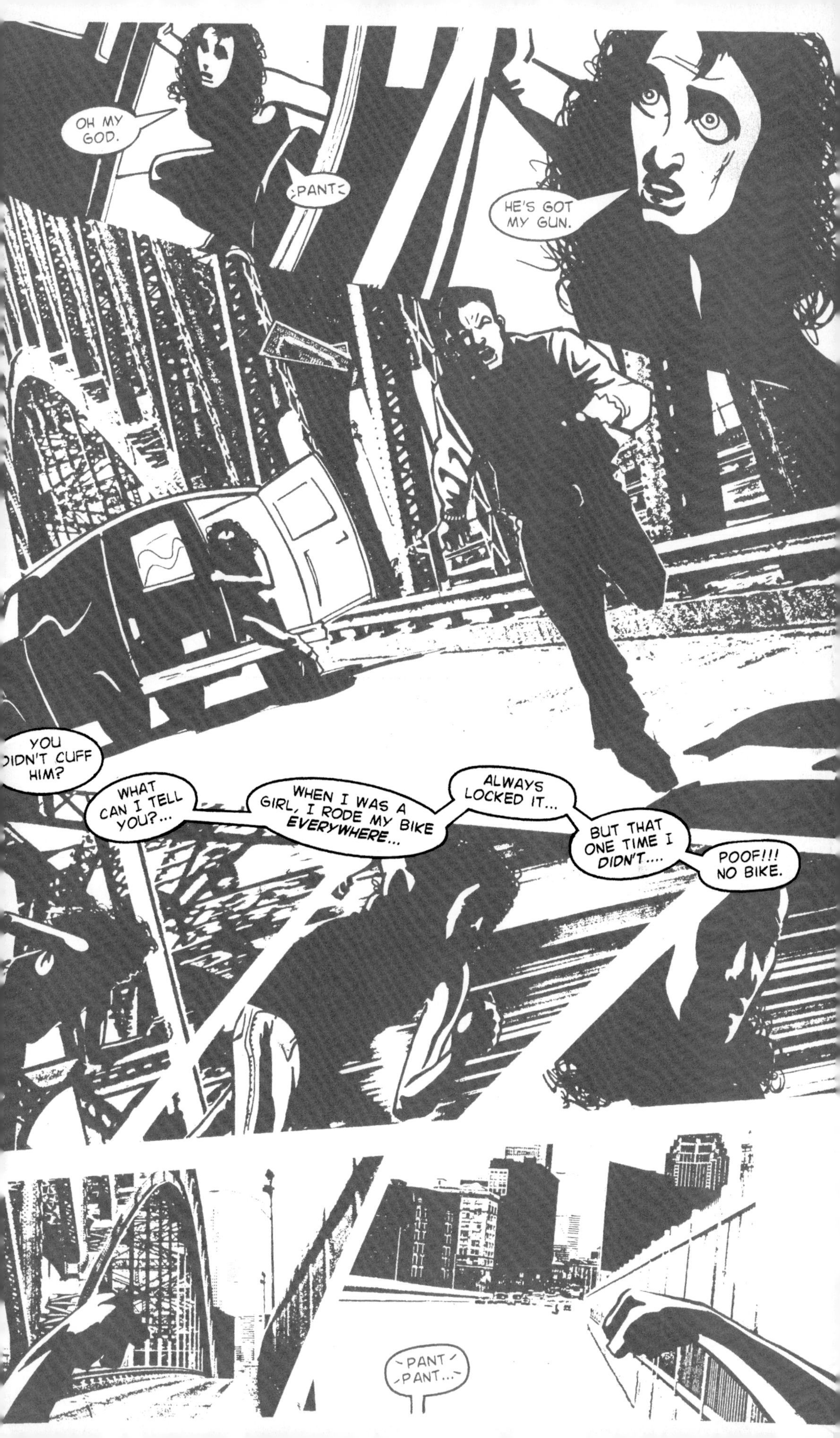
OH MY GOD.
PANT
HE'S GOT MY GUN.
YOU DIDN'T CUFF HIM?
WHAT CAN I TELL YOU?...
WHEN I WAS A GIRL, I RODE MY BIKE EVERYWHERE...
ALWAYS LOCKED IT...
BUT THAT ONE TIME I DIDN'T....
POOF!!! NO BIKE.
PANT PANT...

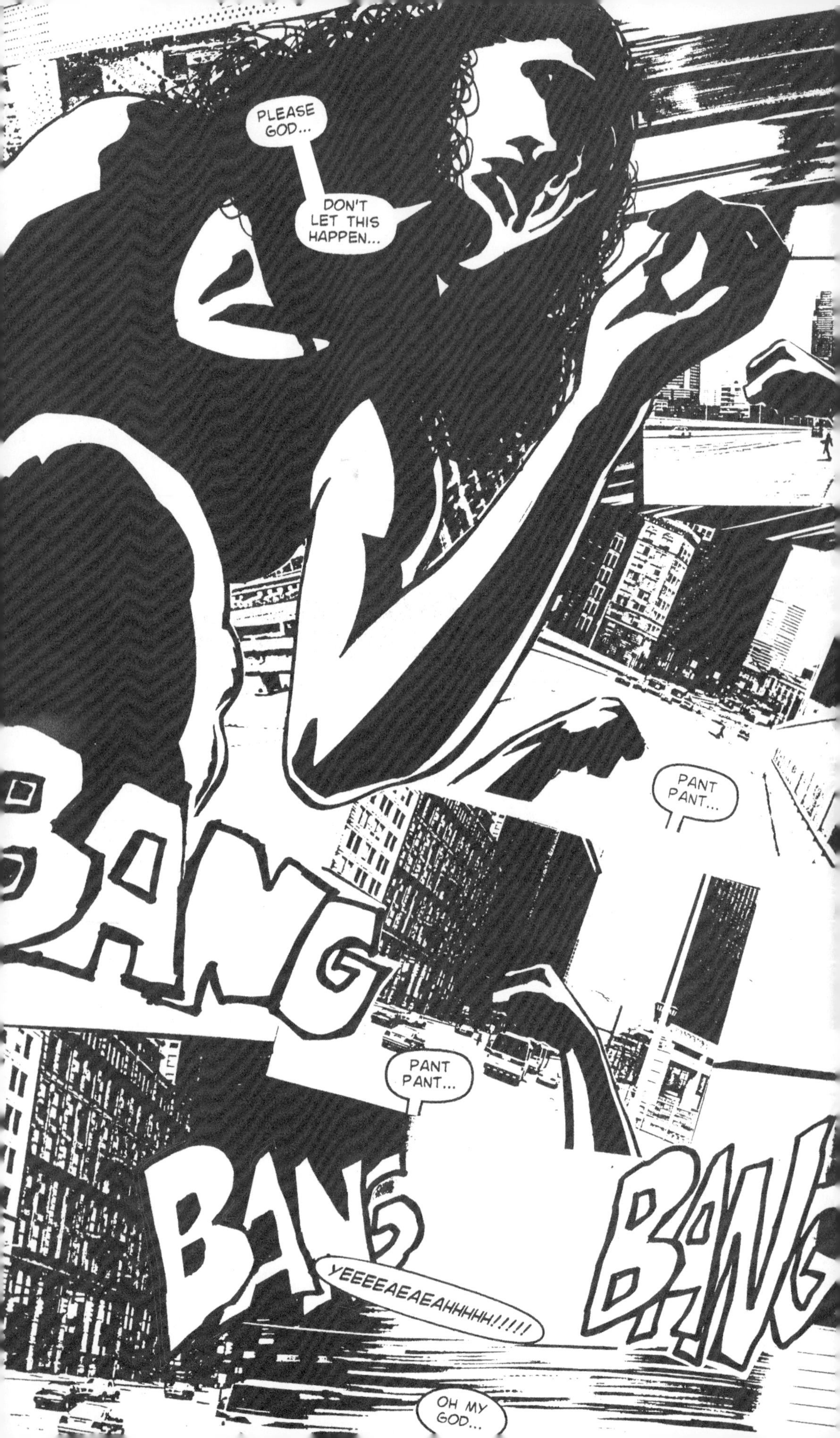
PLEASE GOD...
DON'T LET THIS HAPPEN...
BANG
PANT PANT...
PANT PANT...
BANG
BANG
YEEEEAEAEAHHHHH!!!!!
OH MY GOD...

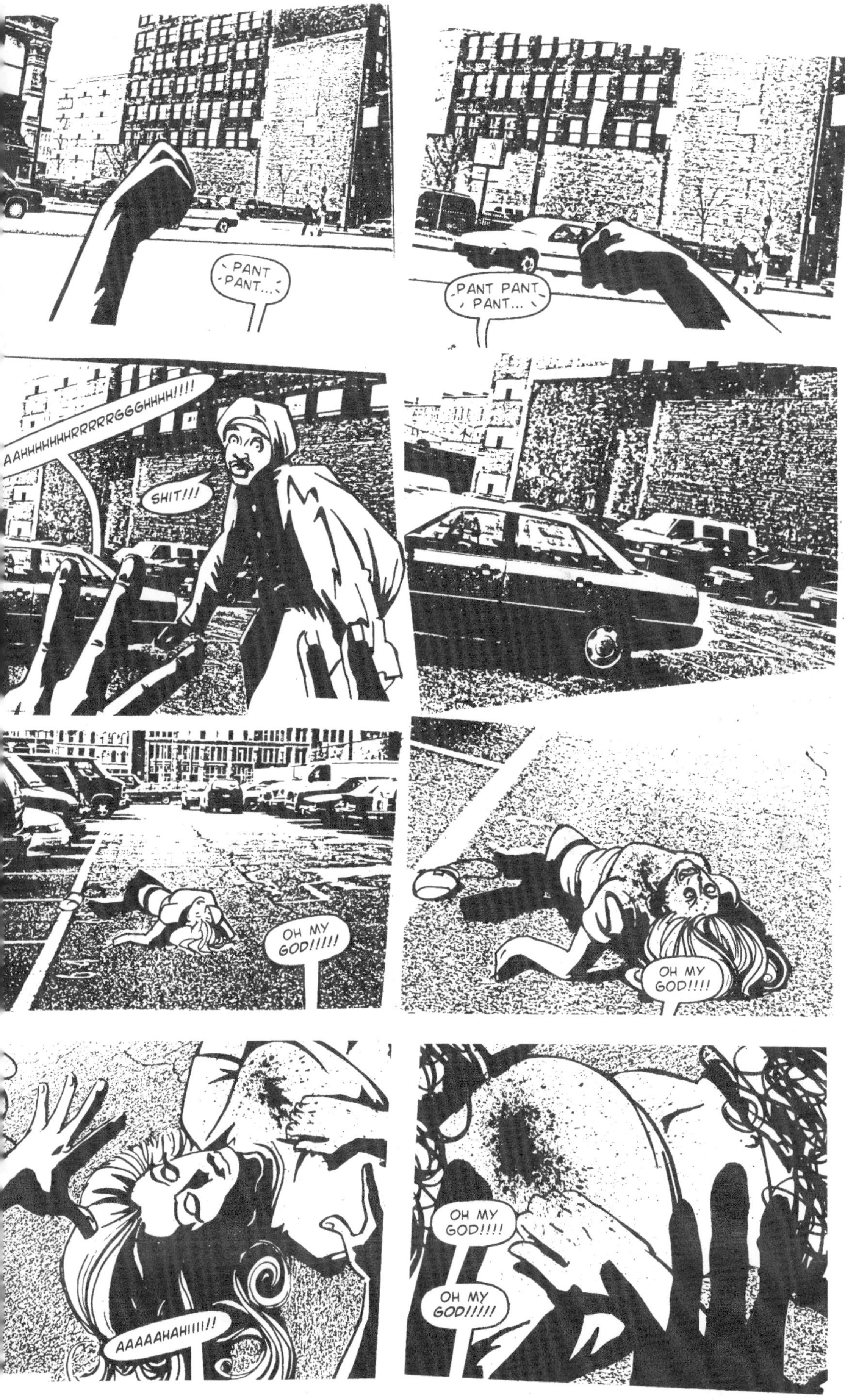
PANT PANT...
PANT PANT PANT...
AAHHHHHHHHRRRRRGGGHHHH!!!!
SHIT!!!
OH MY GOD!!!!!
OH MY GOD!!!!
AAAAAHAH!!!!!
OH MY GOD!!!!
OH MY GOD!!!!!

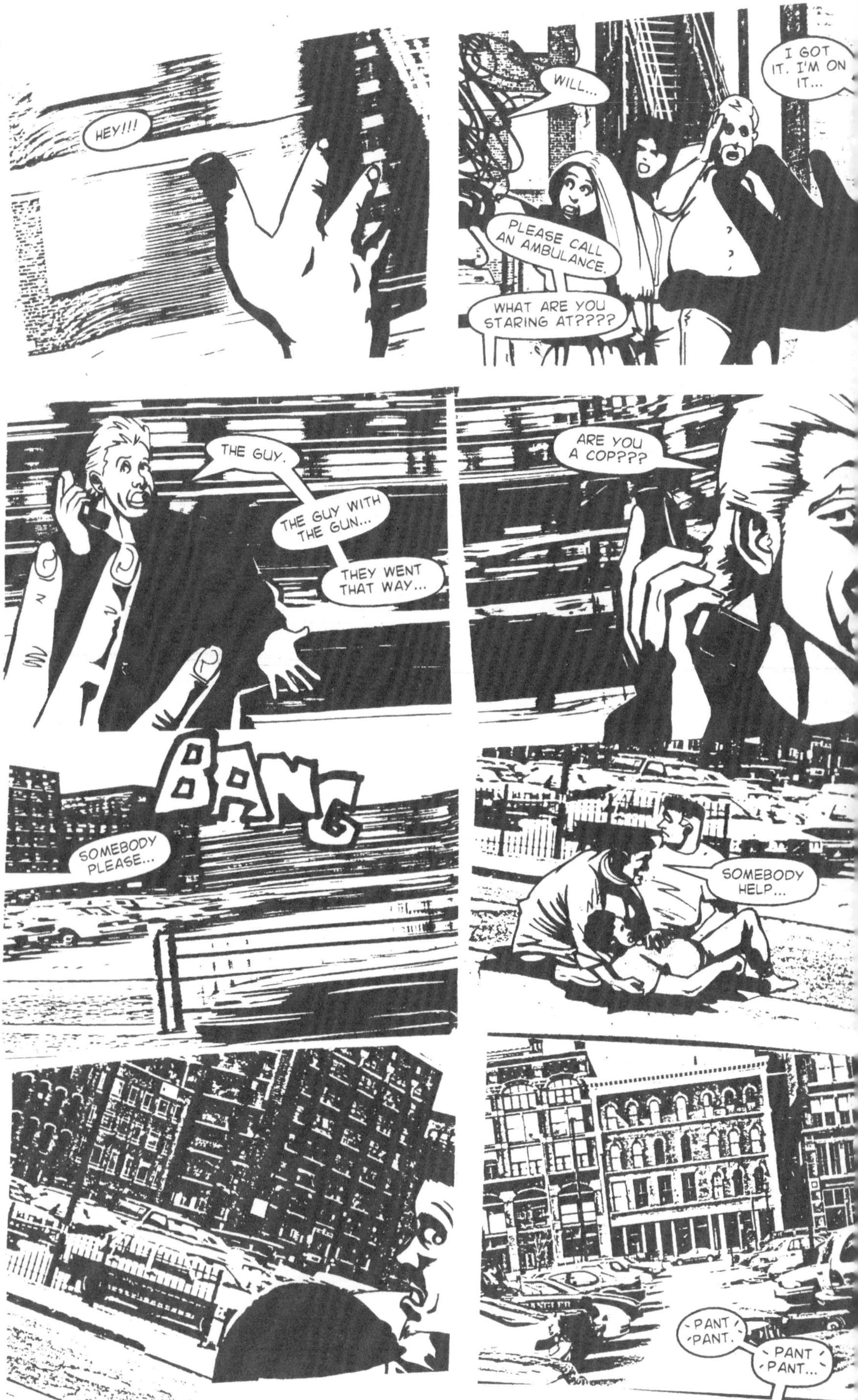
HEY!!!
WILL...
I GOT IT. I'M ON IT...
PLEASE CALL AN AMBULANCE.
WHAT ARE YOU STARING AT????
THE GUY.
THE GUY WITH THE GUN...
THEY WENT THAT WAY...
ARE YOU A COP???
BANG
SOMEBODY PLEASE...
SOMEBODY HELP...
PANT PANT.
PANT PANT...

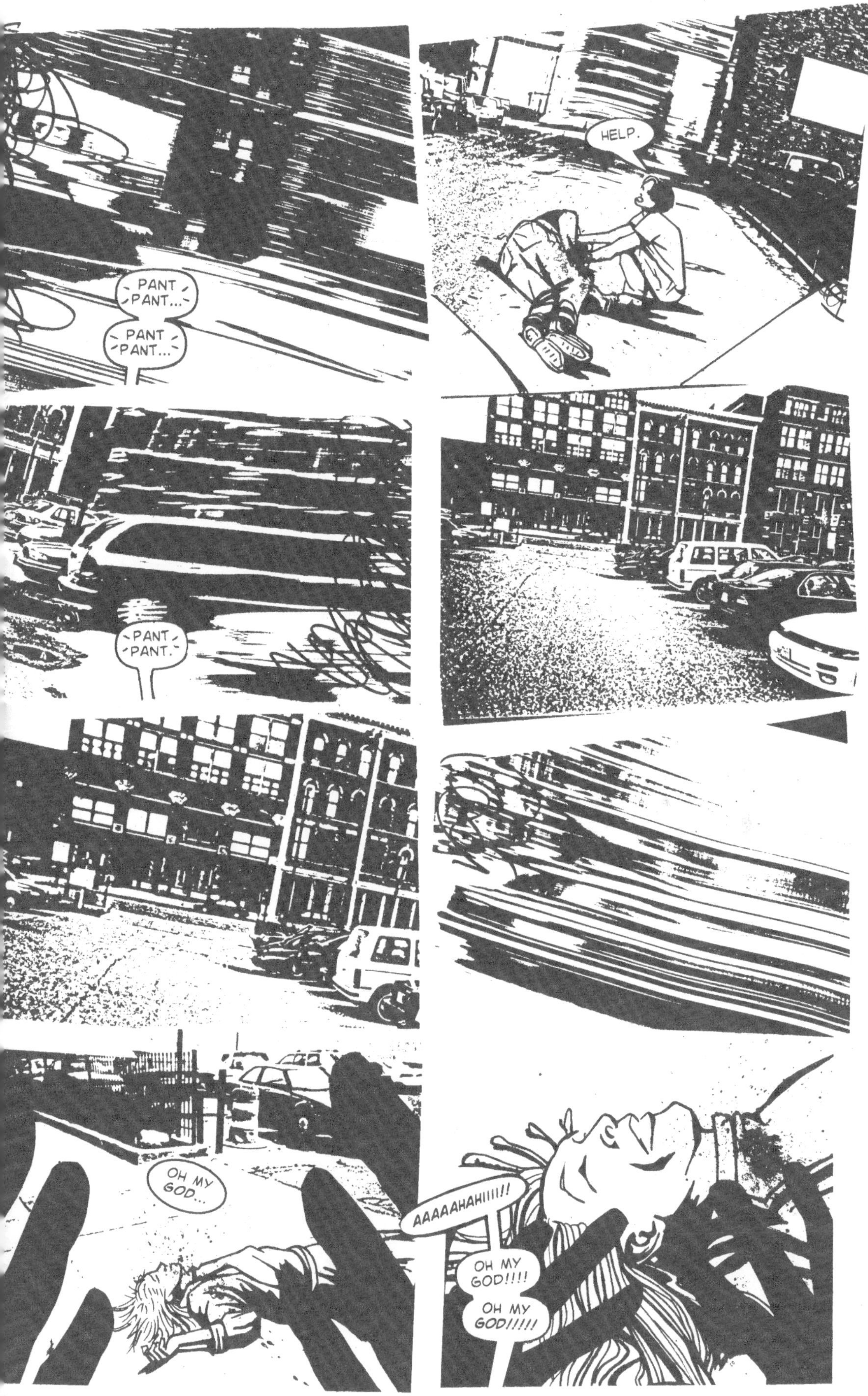
PANT PANT...
PANT PANT...
HELP.
PANT PANT.
OH MY GOD...
AAAAAHAH!!!!!!
OH MY GOD!!!!
OH MY GOD!!!!!

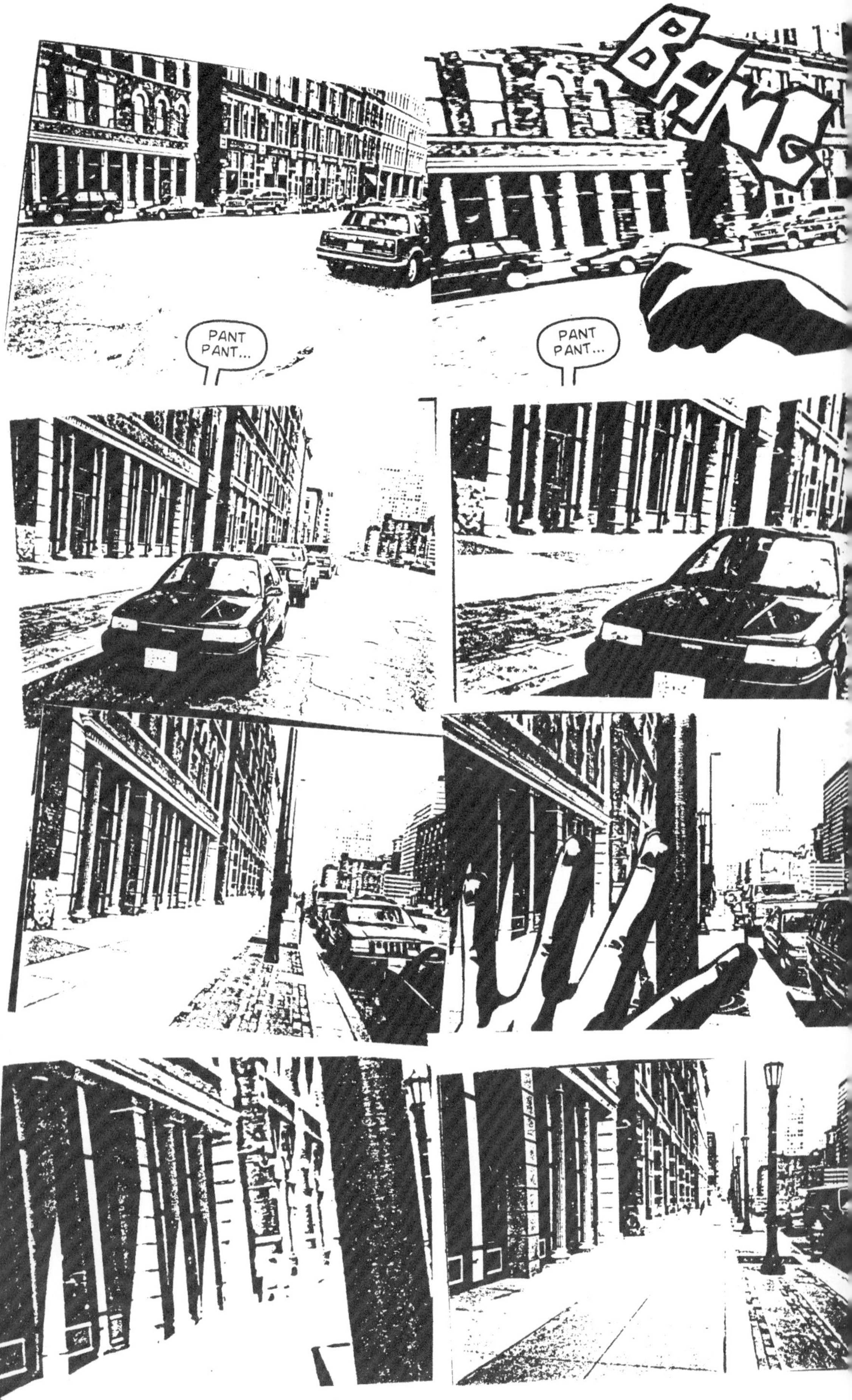
PANT PANT...
BANG
PANT PANT...

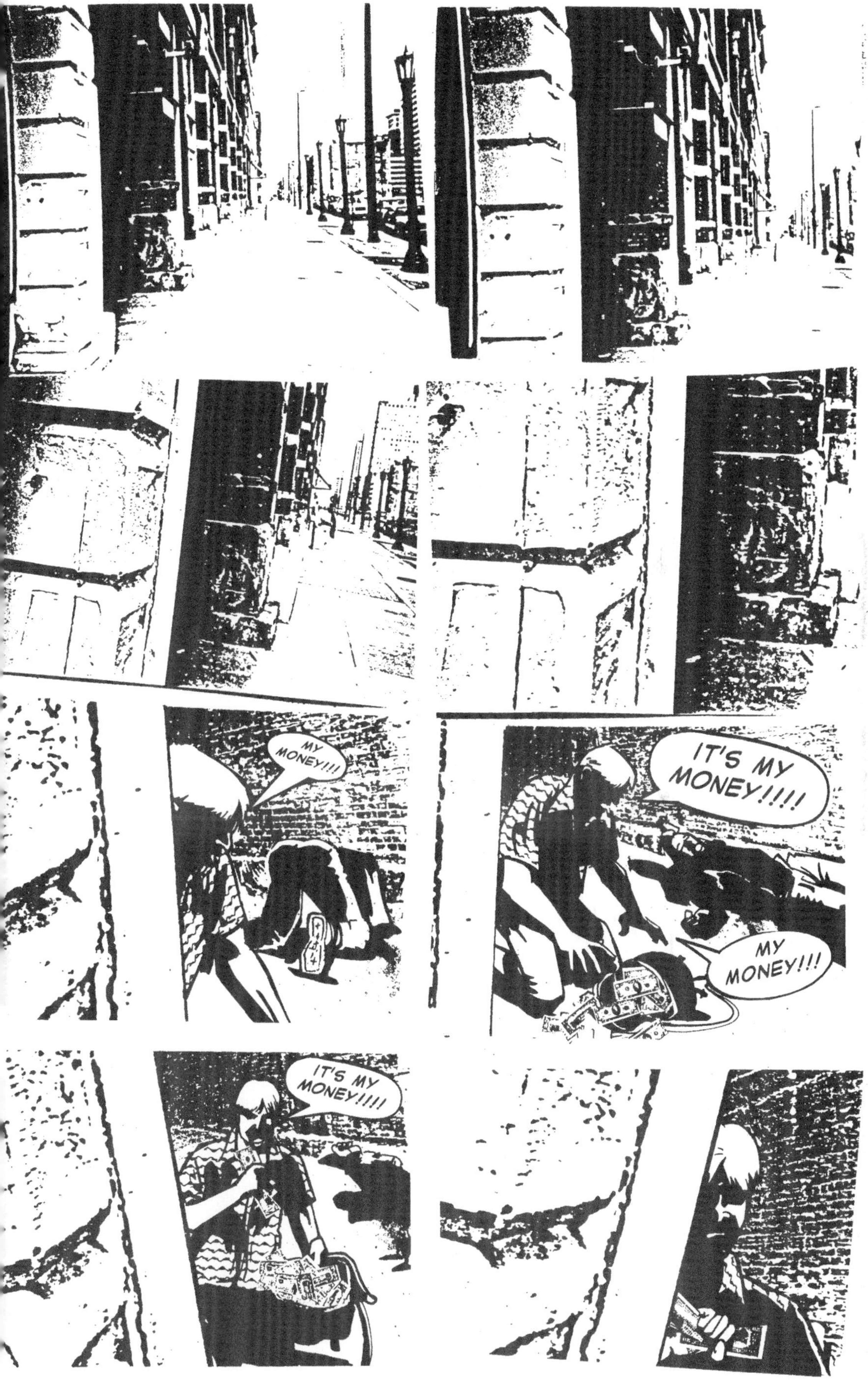
MY MONEY!!!
IT'S MY MONEY!!!!
MY MONEY!!!
IT'S MY MONEY!!!!

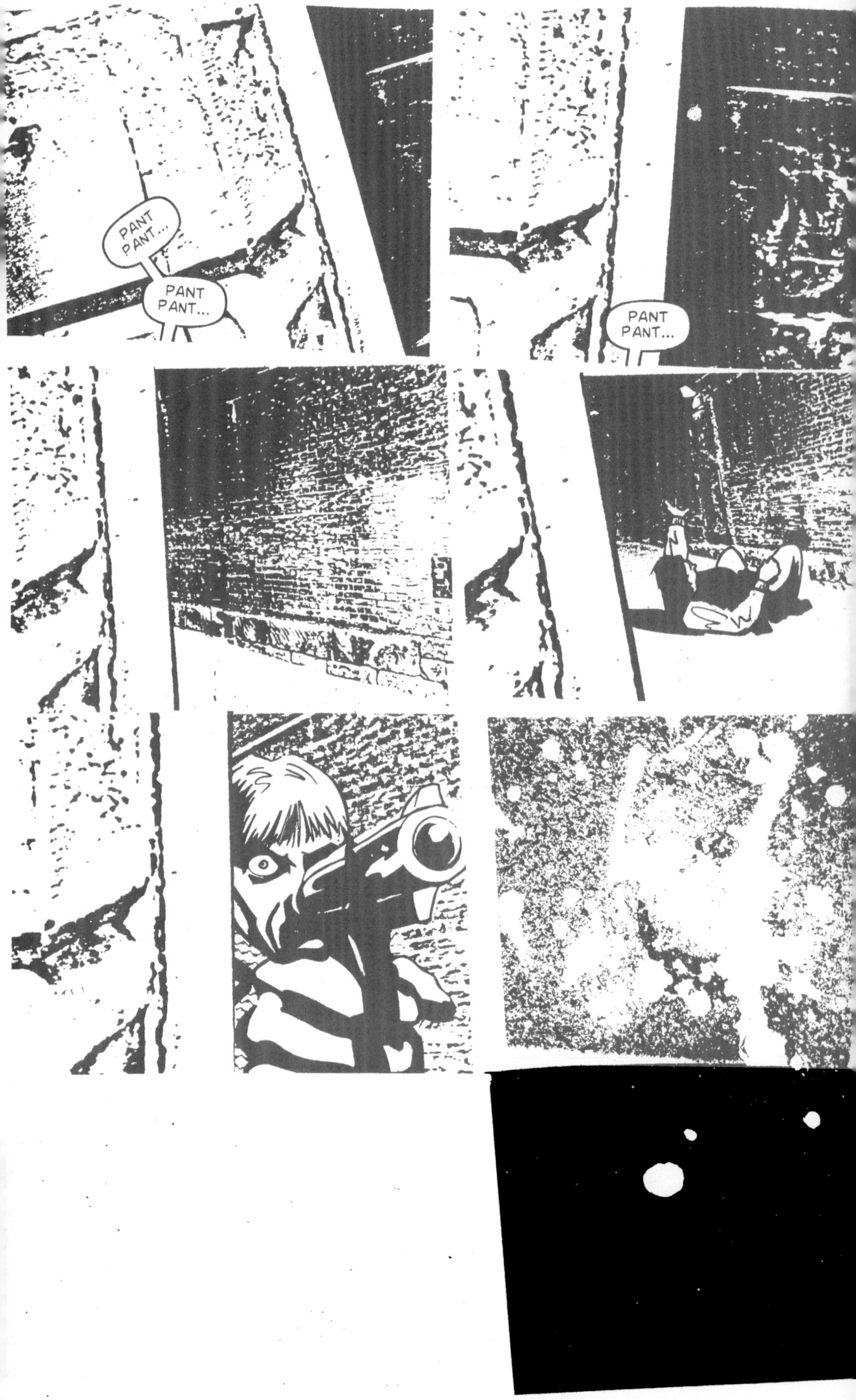
PANT PANT...
PANT PANT...
PANT PANT...

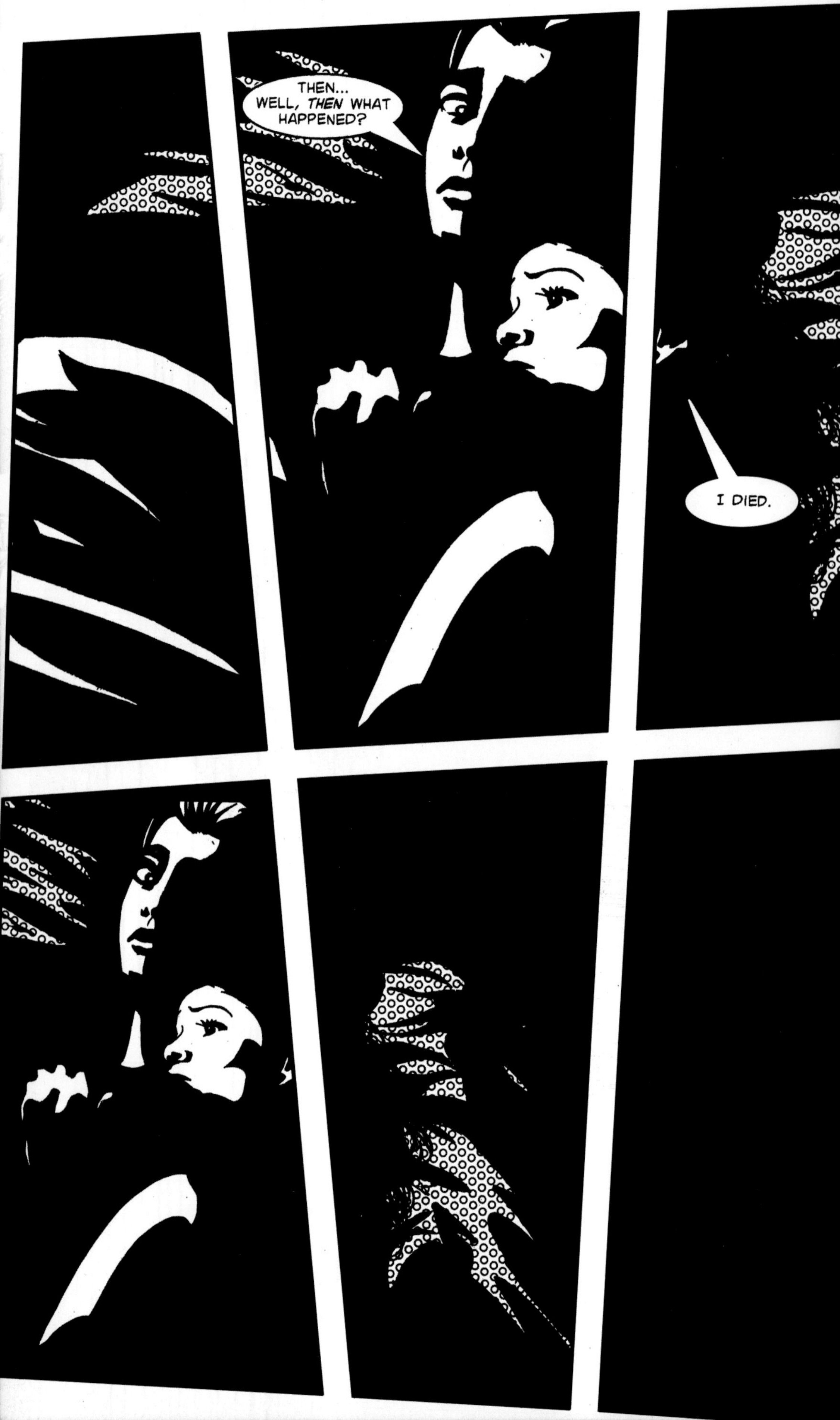
THEN... WELL, *THEN* WHAT HAPPENED?
I DIED.

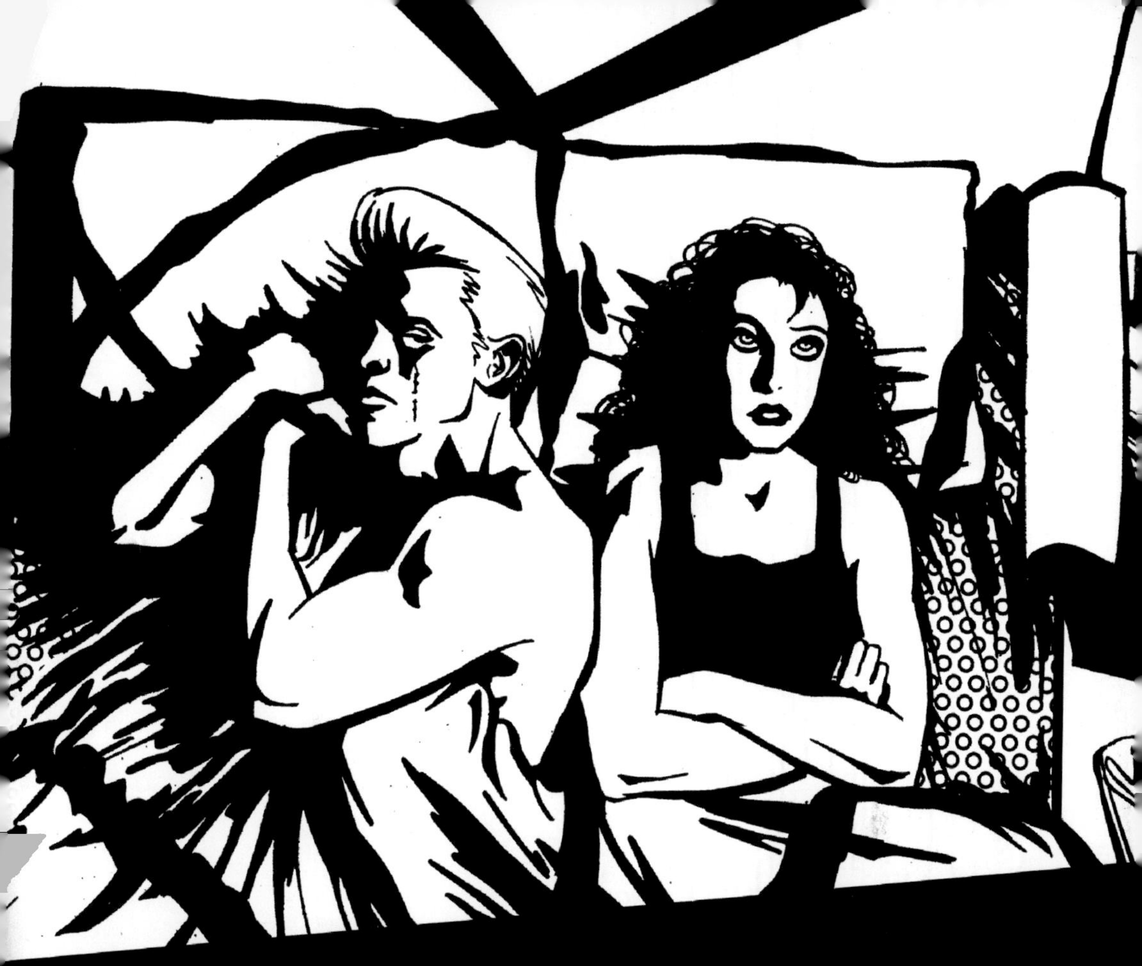

Game Show

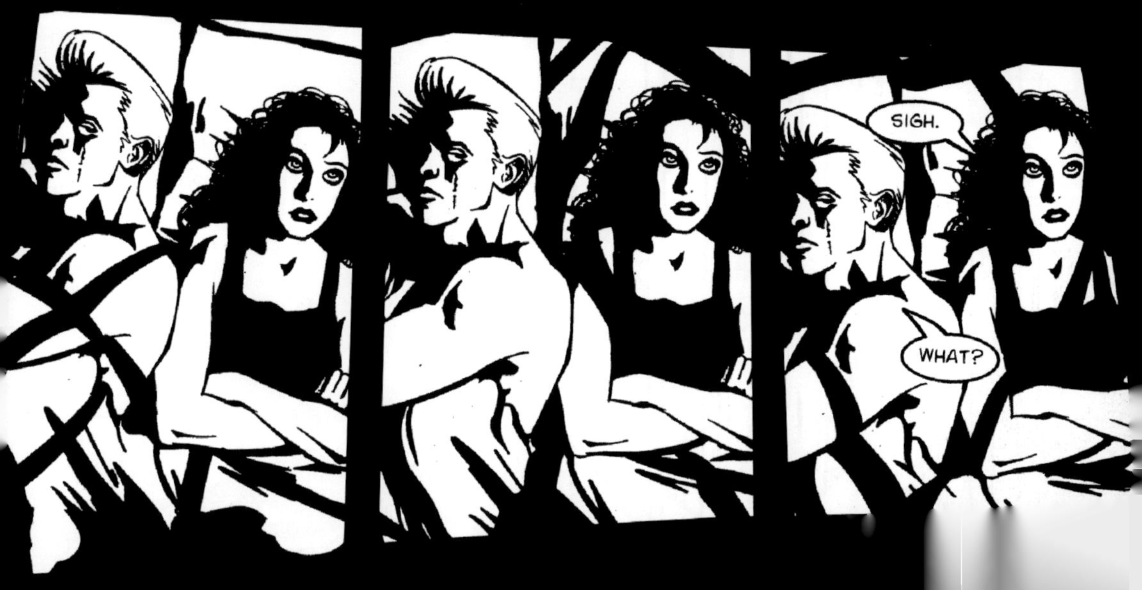
SIGH.
WHAT?

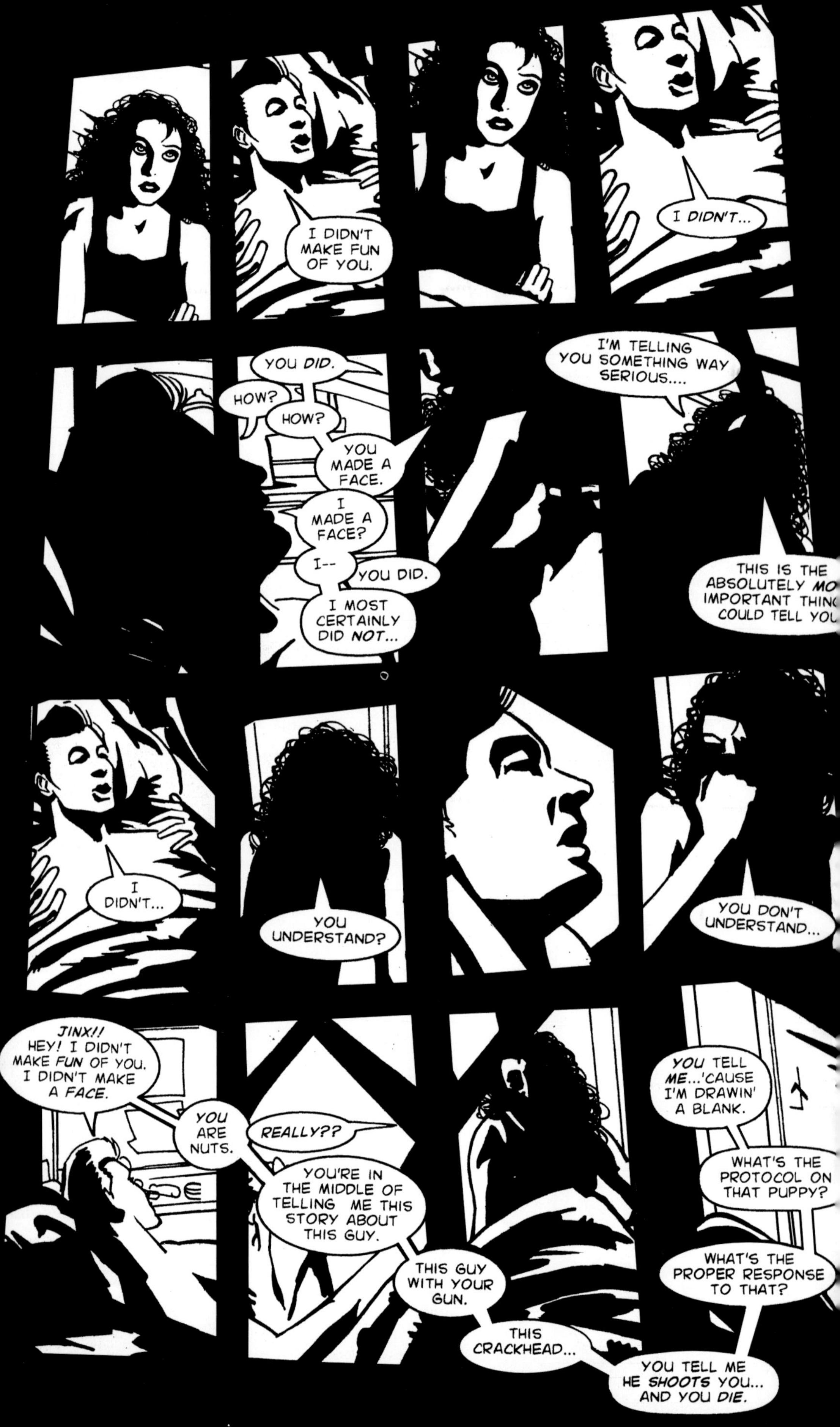
I DIDN'T MAKE FUN OF YOU.
I DIDN'T...
YOU DID.
HOW?
HOW?
YOU MADE A FACE.
I MADE A FACE?
I--
YOU DID.
I MOST CERTAINLY DID NOT...
I'M TELLING YOU SOMETHING WAY SERIOUS....
THIS IS THE ABSOLUTELY MO
IMPORTANT THING
COULD TELL YOU
I DIDN'T...
YOU UNDERSTAND?
YOU DON'T UNDERSTAND...
JINX!! HEY! I DIDN'T MAKE FUN OF YOU. I DIDN'T MAKE A FACE.
YOU ARE NUTS.
REALLY??
YOU'RE IN THE MIDDLE OF TELLING ME THIS STORY ABOUT THIS GUY.
THIS GUY WITH YOUR GUN.
THIS CRACKHEAD...
YOU TELL ME HE SHOOTS YOU... AND YOU DIE.
YOU TELL ME...'CAUSE I'M DRAWIN' A BLANK.
WHAT'S THE PROTOCOL ON THAT PUPPY?
WHAT'S THE PROPER RESPONSE TO THAT?

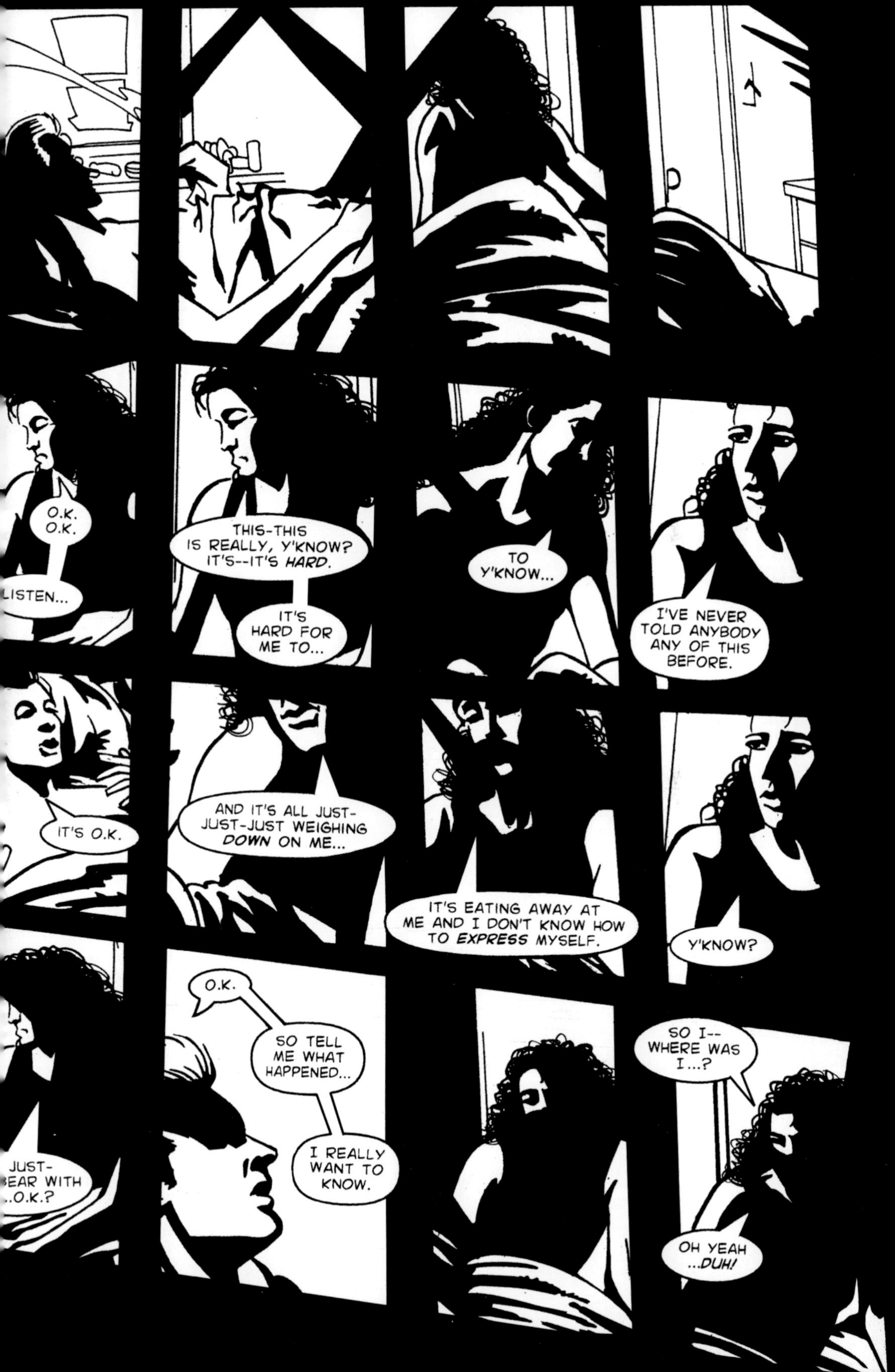
O.K. O.K.
LISTEN...
THIS-THIS IS REALLY, Y'KNOW? IT'S--IT'S HARD.
IT'S HARD FOR ME TO...
TO Y'KNOW...
I'VE NEVER TOLD ANYBODY ANY OF THIS BEFORE.
IT'S O.K.
AND IT'S ALL JUST-JUST-JUST WEIGHING DOWN ON ME...
IT'S EATING AWAY AT ME AND I DON'T KNOW HOW TO EXPRESS MYSELF.
Y'KNOW?
O.K.
SO TELL ME WHAT HAPPENED...
I REALLY WANT TO KNOW.
SO I--WHERE WAS I...?
OH YEAH ...DUH!

I *FINALLY* CATCH
UP TO THIS GUY.
HE'S CORNERED HIMSELF
IN ONE OF THOSE--
THOSE...WHAT?
YOU KNOW--
THOSE DELIVERY ALLEYS.

AND I'M, LIKE,
JUST TRYING TO
FIGURE OUT WHAT
TO DO NEXT.
AND I SEE THIS
A-HOLE IS HUNCHED
OVER IN AN ALLEY,
AND HE'S STUFFING
HIS SHIRT FULL OF
THE MONEY
FROM HIS BANK JOB.

NOW *WHY* HE'S DOING THIS IS
BEYOND *ME,* BUT AT *LEAST* HE'S
STOPPED SHOOTING PEOPLE.

THEN I SEE THIS KID--
THIS KID PARTNER OF MINE.

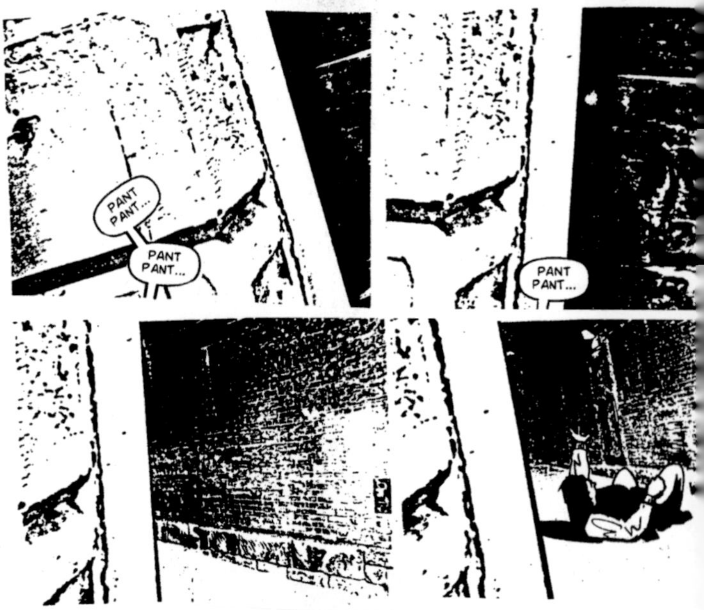
PANT PANT...
PANT PANT...
PANT PANT...

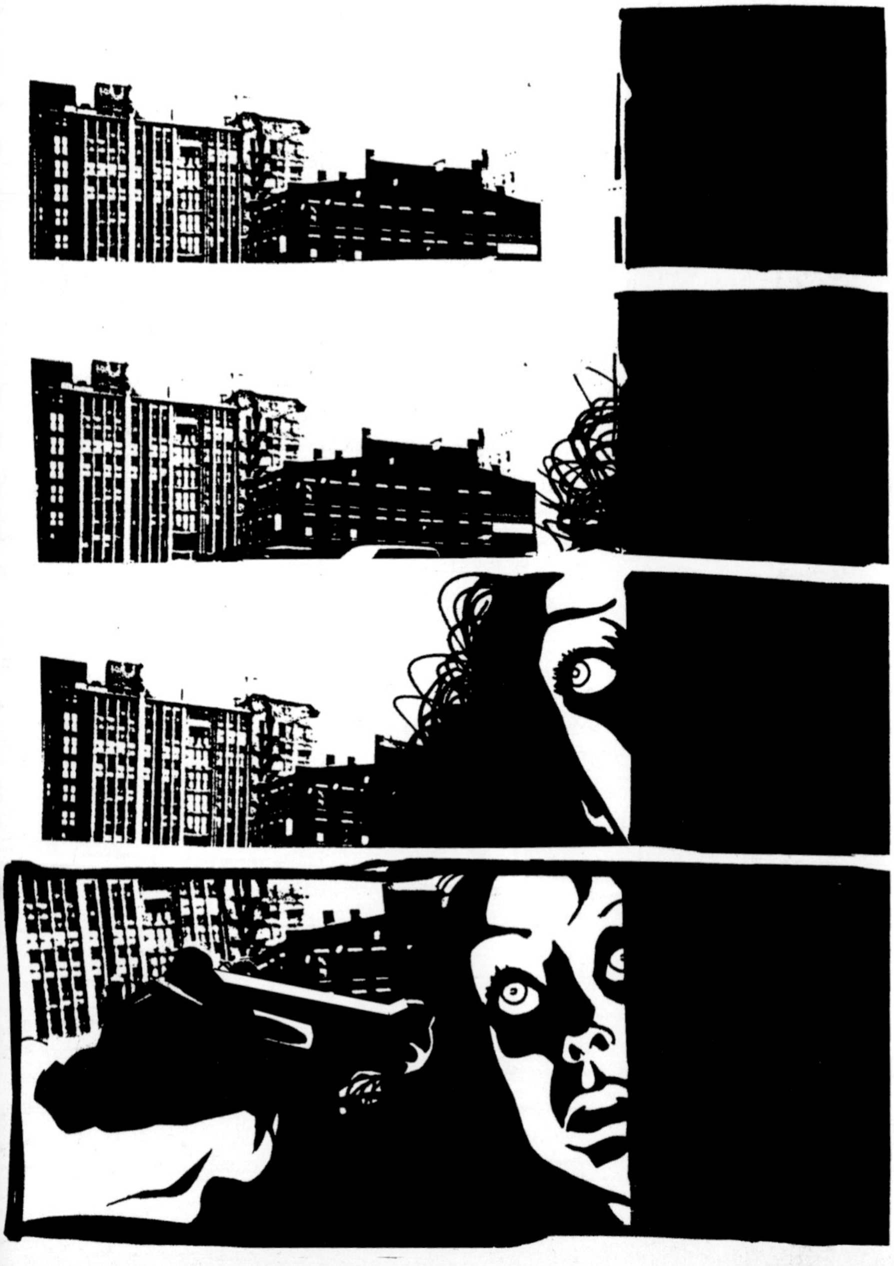

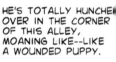

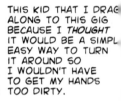

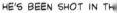

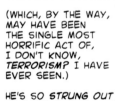

THIS KID THAT I DRAG
ALONG TO THIS GIG
BECAUSE I *THOUGHT*
IT WOULD BE A SIMPL
EASY WAY TO TURN
IT AROUND SO
I WOULDN'T HAVE
TO GET MY HANDS
TOO DIRTY.

HE'S TOTALLY HUNCHE
OVER IN THE CORNER
OF THIS ALLEY,
MOANING LIKE--LIKE
A WOUNDED PUPPY.

HE'S BEEN SHOT IN TH

NOW I GOTTA REITER
TO YOU THAT THIS GU
WERE HUNTIN' DOWN...

HE WAS REAL SMALL T
HE WAS STRICTLY FAS
A SUPER DUPER POOP
LOSER, Y'KNOW?

PICK HIM UP
AND DROP HIM OFF.

BUT--BUT THIS THING
SO OUT OF HAND *SO*

HE'S GOT MY GUN.
HE'S RUNNING THROUG
DOWNTOWN
ALL WHACKED OUT
ON CRACK FUMES
(OR GOD KNOWS WHA
SHOOTING AT TOTAL
INNOCENT STRANGERS

(WHICH, BY THE WAY,
MAY HAVE BEEN
THE SINGLE MOST
HORRIFIC ACT OF,
I DON'T KNOW,
TERRORISM? I HAVE
EVER SEEN.)

HE'S SO ***STRUNG OUT***
HE DOESN'T EVEN KNO
WHAT HE'S DOING.

WHEN I FINALLY, *FINAL*
CATCH UP TO HIM, TO

I-I-I WAS SO FRAZZL

AND THAT'S WHEN...

WHEN
THE GUN WENT OFF
IN MY FACE

POINT BLANK

AND MY WORLD
WENT WHITE

OR WHAT I *SHOULD* SAY--
IS THAT IT BECAME
ABSOLUTELY *NOTHING.*

ALL OF MY SENSES,
ALL OF MY BODY FUNCTIONS,
ALL THE THINGS THAT ARE
...THAT ARE *ME*...

CEASED

I COULDN'T SEE
I COULDN'T FEEL
I COULDN'T HEAR
I COULDN'T SMELL

NOTHING

AND-AND THIS *SENSATION,*
IT WAS SO *COMPLETE*
SO INSTANTANEOUS
SO *ALL CONSUMING*

THAT I HAD ABSOLUTELY *NO DOUBT*
IN MY MIND THAT I HAD CHECKED OUT

THAT *THIS* WAS *IT!*

THAT I HAD DIED
AS VIOLENTLY AS--AS
I HAD LIVED

AND MY FIRST THOUGHT,
I REMEMBER,
WAS THAT SOMEBODY, SOME *GUY,*
WAS GOING TO HAVE TO *SCOOP UP*
MY EMPTY--MY EMPTY LEFTOVERS...

AND SHOW THEM TO MY MOM

SO SHE COULD BURY ME...

HOW VULGAR IS *THAT?*

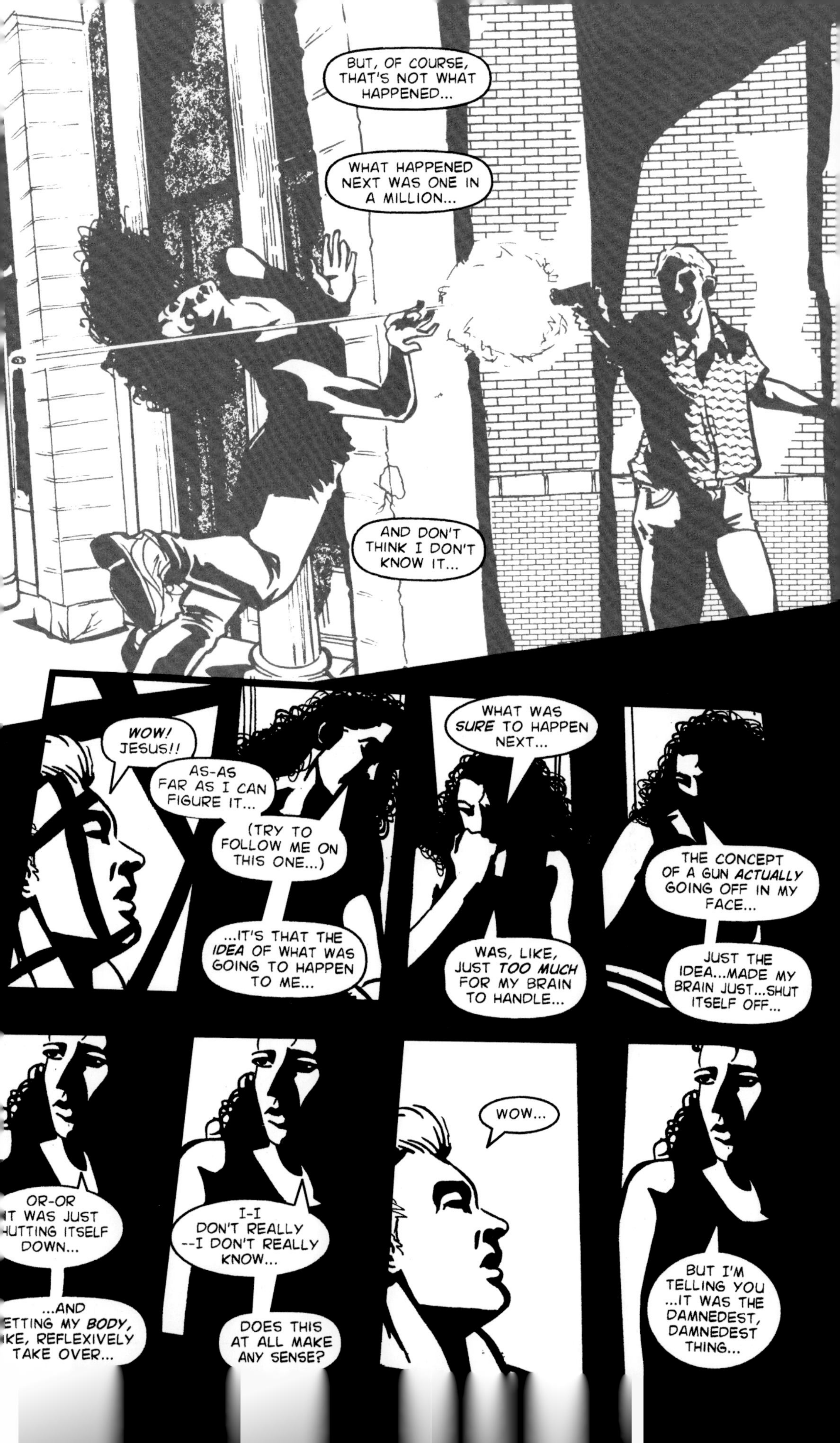
BUT, OF COURSE, THAT'S NOT WHAT HAPPENED...
WHAT HAPPENED NEXT WAS ONE IN A MILLION...
AND DON'T THINK I DON'T KNOW IT...
WOW! JESUS!!
AS-AS FAR AS I CAN FIGURE IT...
(TRY TO FOLLOW ME ON THIS ONE...)
...IT'S THAT THE *IDEA* OF WHAT WAS GOING TO HAPPEN TO ME...
WHAT WAS *SURE* TO HAPPEN NEXT...
WAS, LIKE, JUST *TOO MUCH* FOR MY BRAIN TO HANDLE...
THE CONCEPT OF A GUN *ACTUALLY* GOING OFF IN MY FACE...
JUST THE IDEA...MADE MY BRAIN JUST...SHUT ITSELF OFF...
OR-OR IT WAS JUST HUTTING ITSELF DOWN...
...AND ETTING MY *BODY*, KE, REFLEXIVELY TAKE OVER...
I-I DON'T REALLY --I DON'T REALLY KNOW...
DOES THIS AT ALL MAKE ANY SENSE?
WOW...
BUT I'M TELLING YOU ...IT WAS THE DAMNEDEST, DAMNEDEST THING...

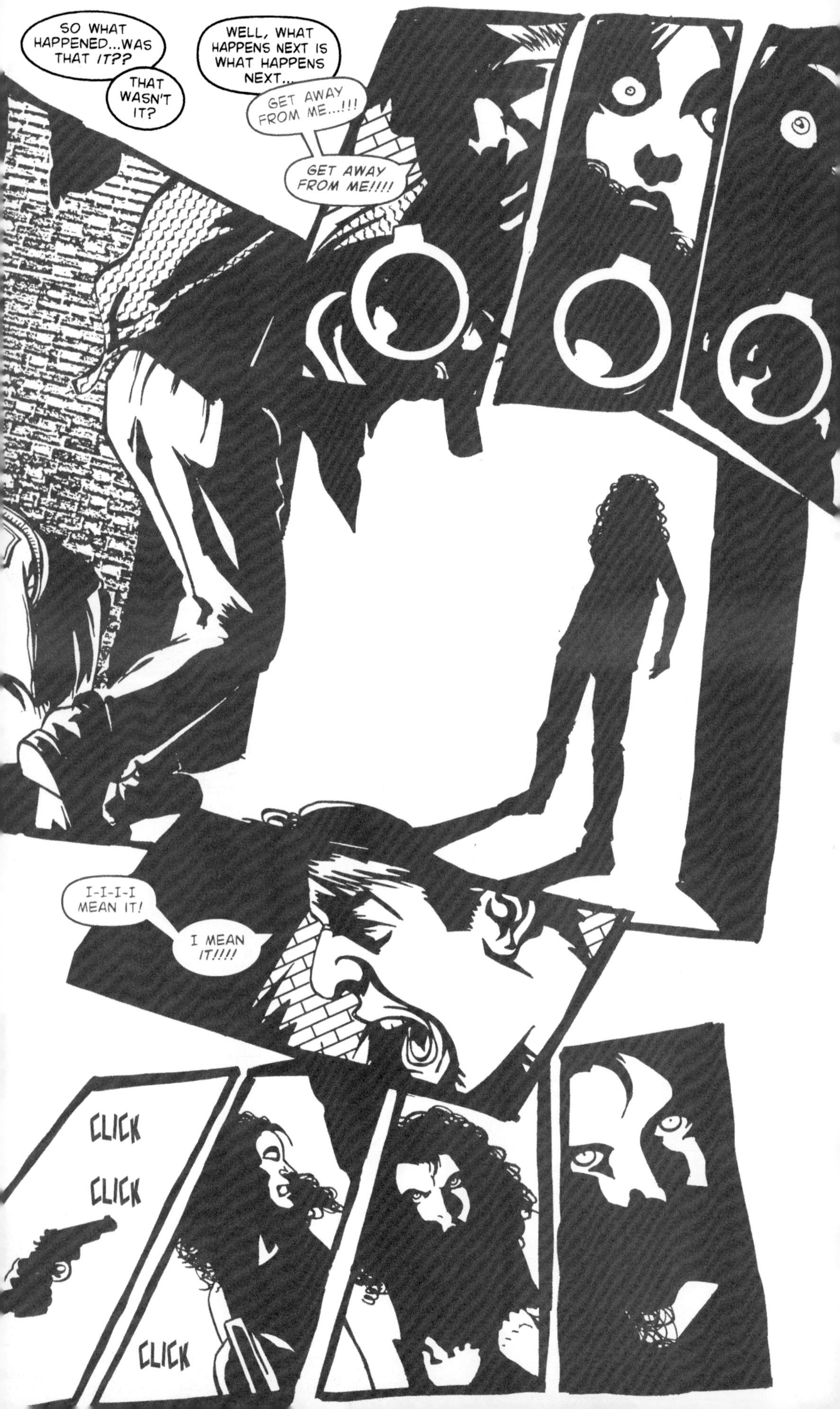
SO WHAT HAPPENED...WAS THAT IT??
THAT WASN'T IT?
WELL, WHAT HAPPENS NEXT IS WHAT HAPPENS NEXT...
GET AWAY FROM ME...!!!
GET AWAY FROM ME!!!!
I-I-I-I MEAN IT!
I MEAN IT!!!!
CLICK
CLICK
CLICK

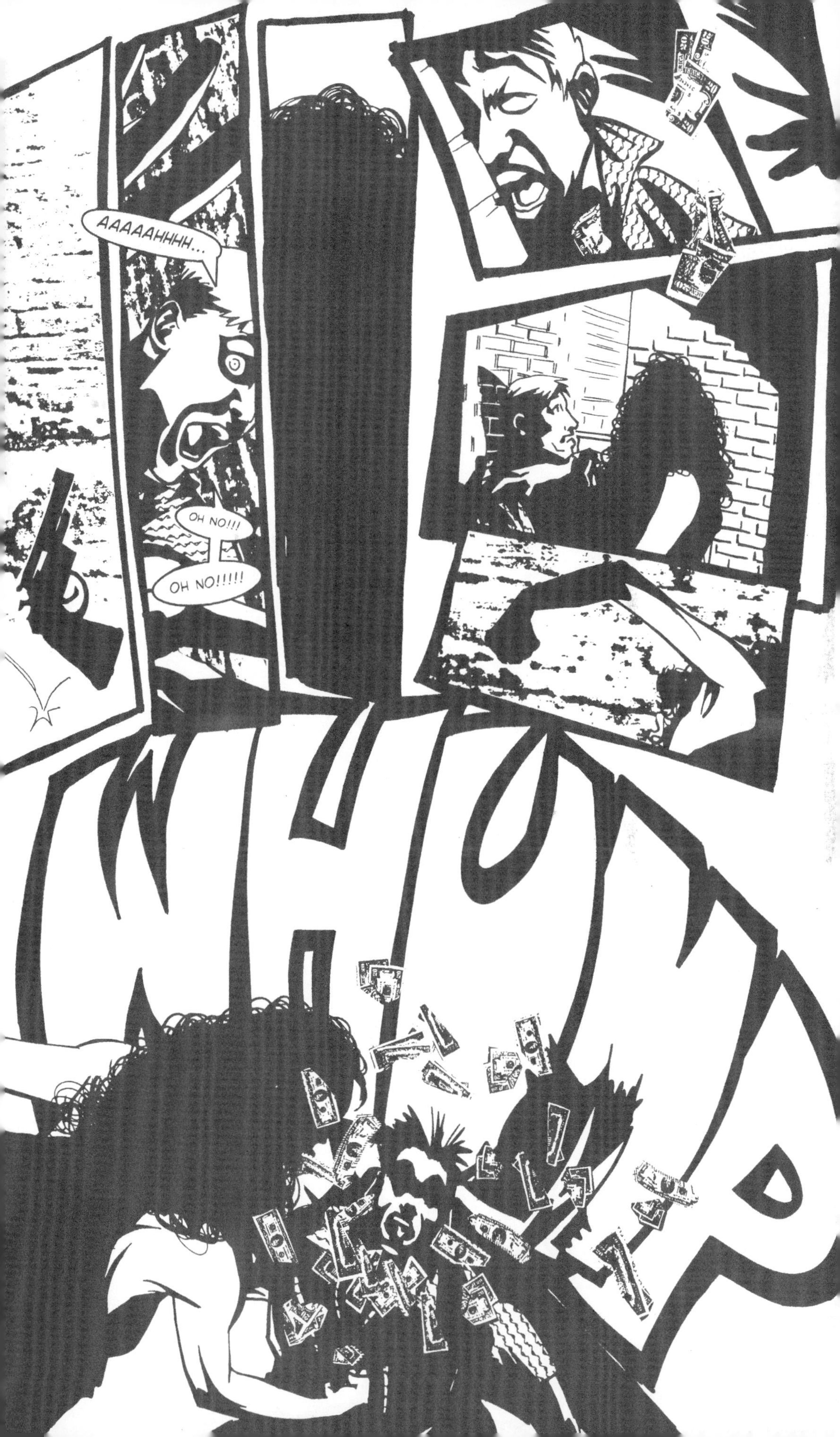
AAAAAHHHH...
OH NO!!!
OH NO!!!!!

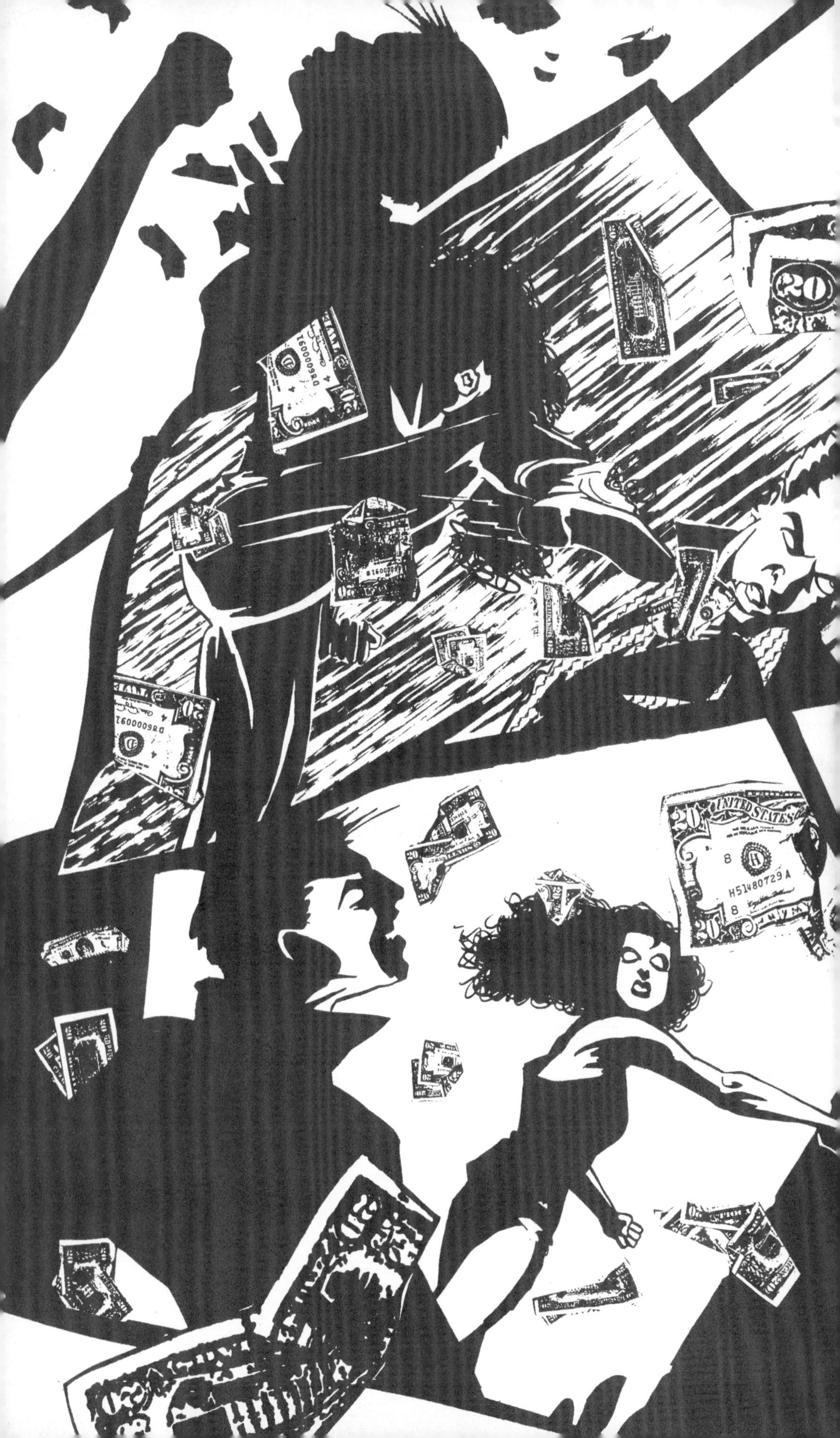
UNITED STATES
H51480729 A

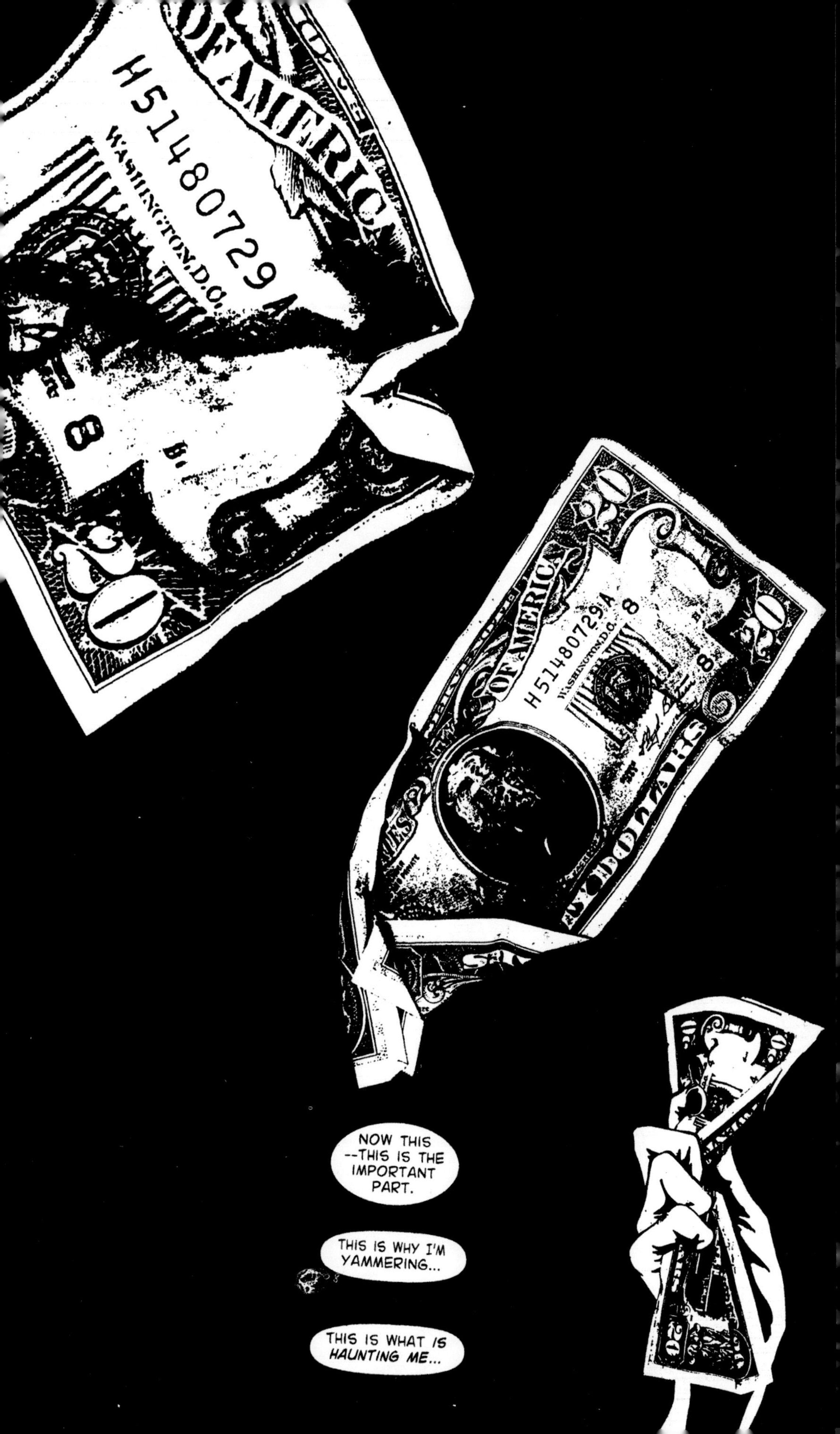
NOW THIS --THIS IS THE IMPORTANT PART.
THIS IS WHY I'M YAMMERING...
THIS IS WHAT IS HAUNTING ME...

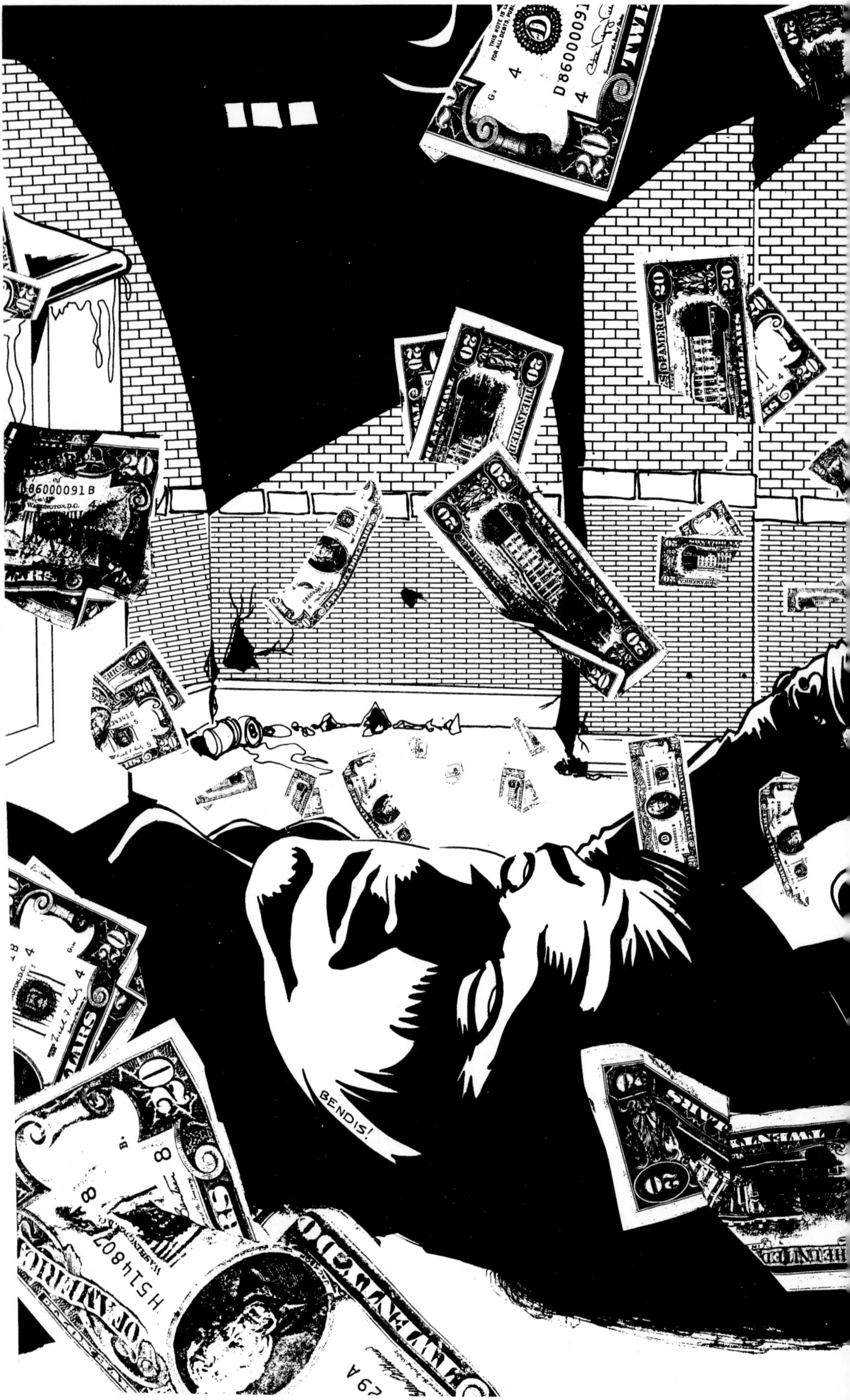
BENDIS!

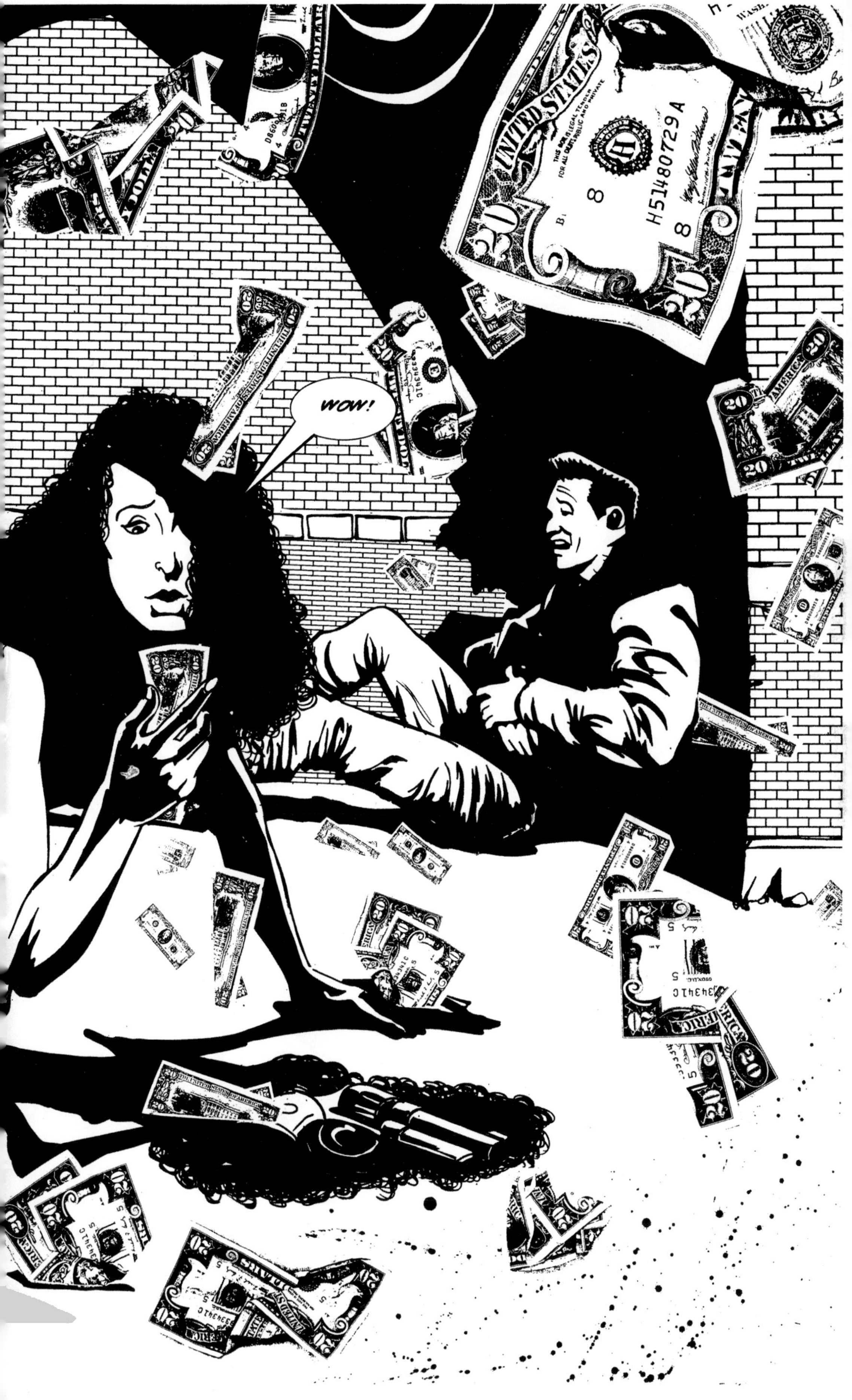
WOW!

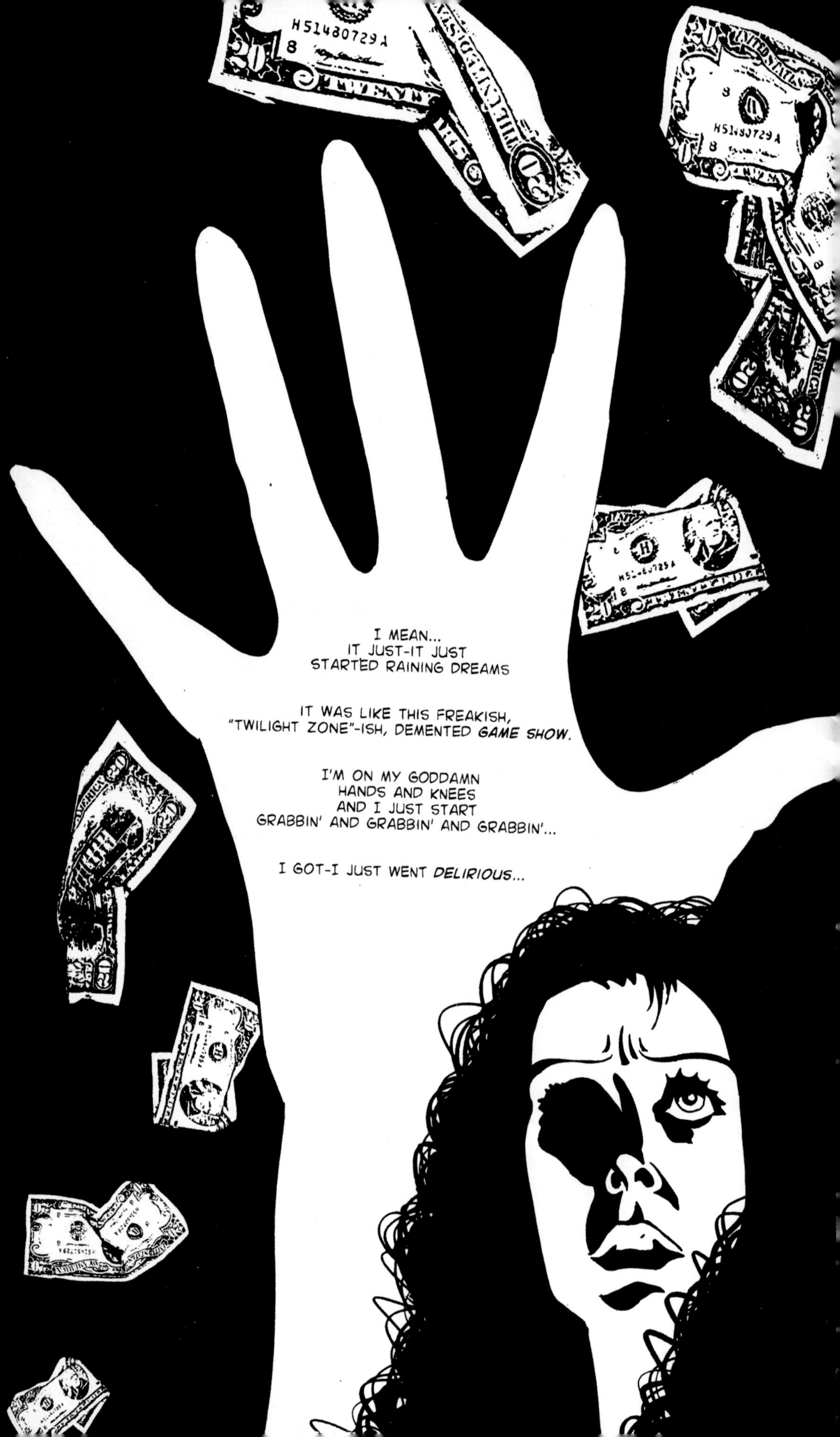
I MEAN...
IT JUST-IT JUST
STARTED RAINING DREAMS
IT WAS LIKE THIS FREAKISH,
"TWILIGHT ZONE"-ISH, DEMENTED *GAME SHOW*.
I'M ON MY GODDAMN
HANDS AND KNEES
AND I JUST START
GRABBIN' AND GRABBIN' AND GRABBIN'...
I GOT-I JUST WENT *DELIRIOUS*...

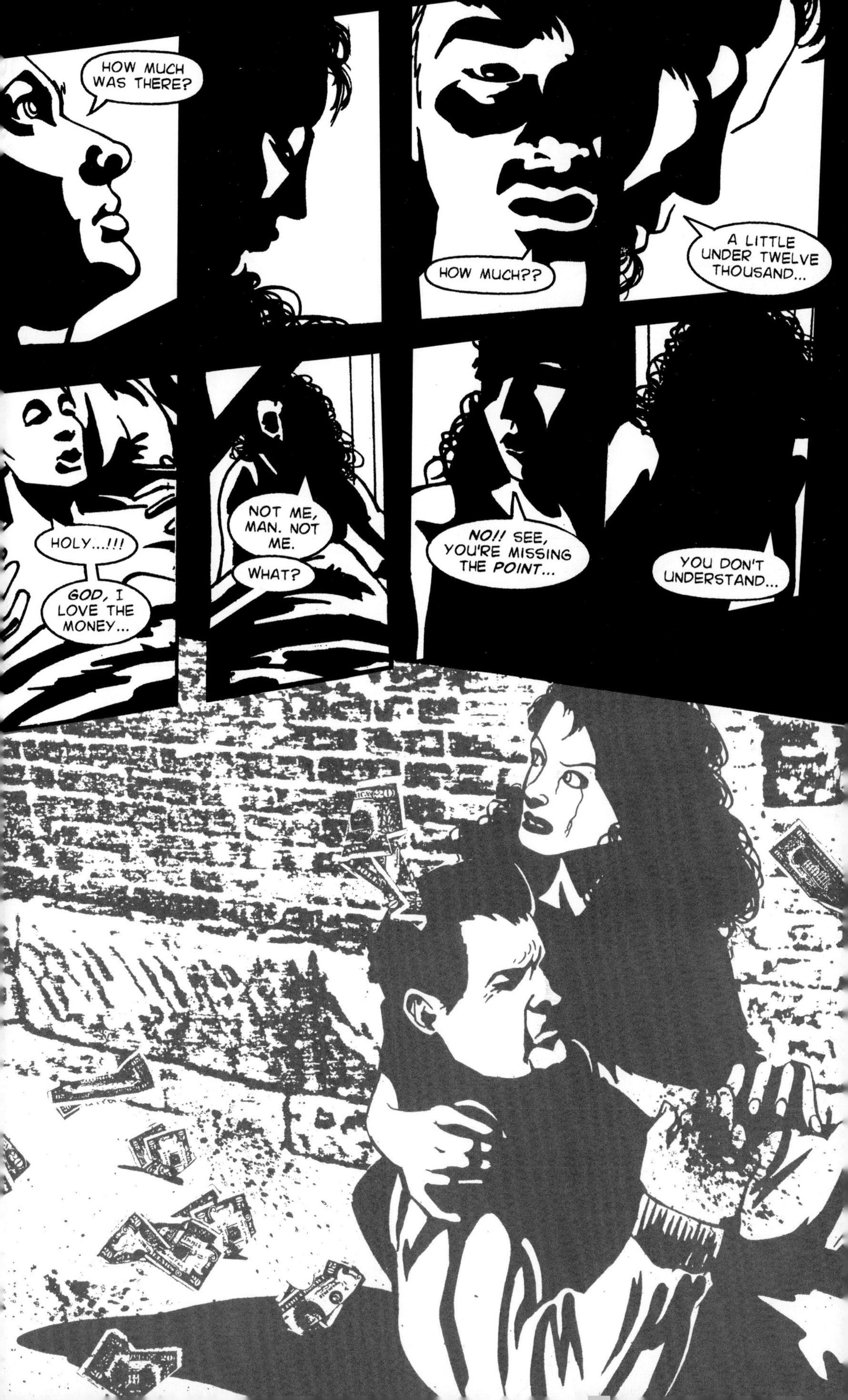
HOW MUCH WAS THERE?
HOW MUCH??
A LITTLE UNDER TWELVE THOUSAND...
HOLY...!!!
GOD, I LOVE THE MONEY...
NOT ME, MAN. NOT ME.
WHAT?
NO!! SEE, YOU'RE MISSING THE POINT...
YOU DON'T UNDERSTAND...

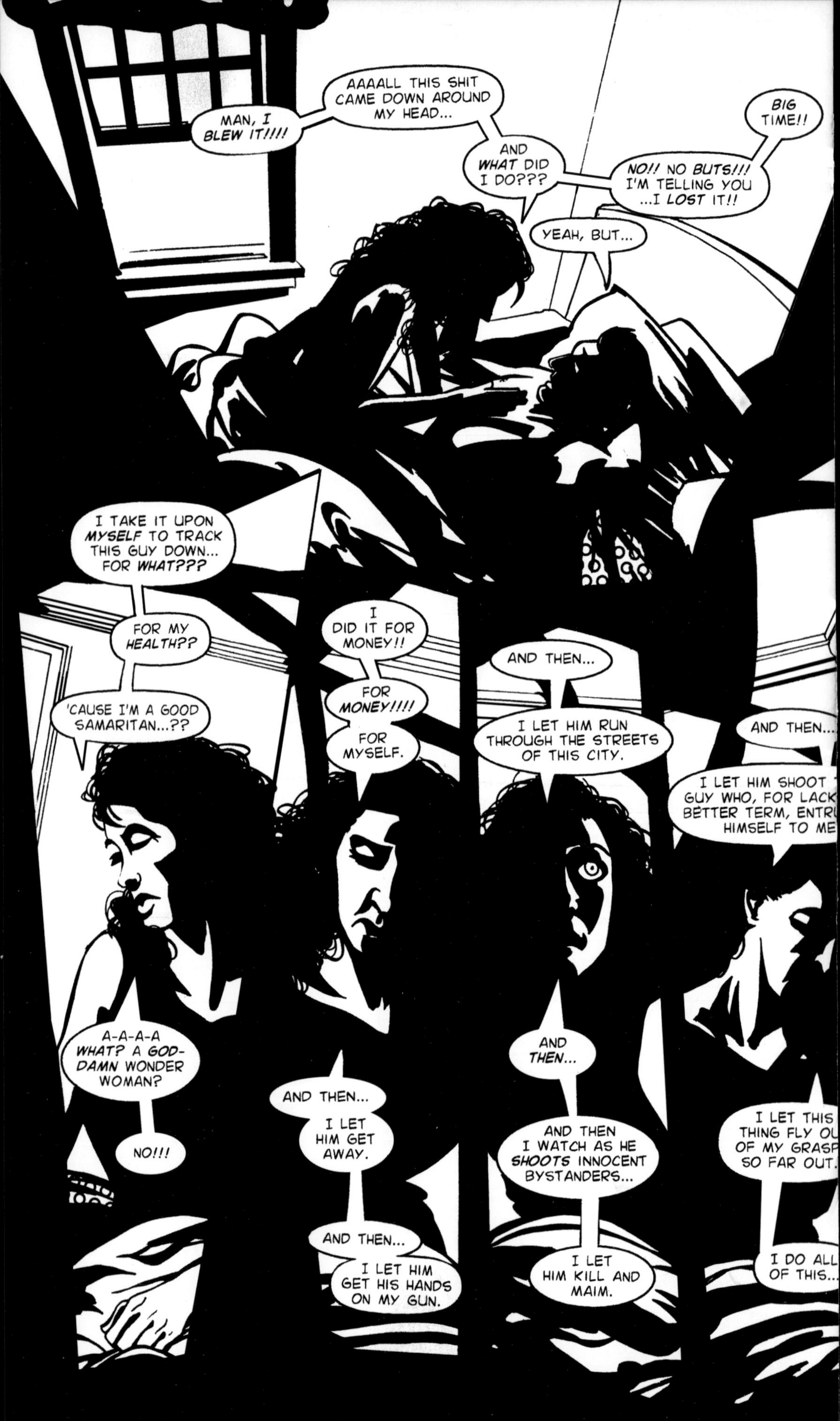
MAN, I BLEW IT!!!!
AAAALL THIS SHIT CAME DOWN AROUND MY HEAD...
AND WHAT DID I DO???
YEAH, BUT...
NO!! NO BUTS!!! I'M TELLING YOU ...I LOST IT!!
BIG TIME!!
I TAKE IT UPON MYSELF TO TRACK THIS GUY DOWN... FOR WHAT???
FOR MY HEALTH??
'CAUSE I'M A GOOD SAMARITAN...??
A-A-A-A WHAT? A GOD-DAMN WONDER WOMAN?
NO!!!
I DID IT FOR MONEY!!
FOR MONEY!!!!
FOR MYSELF.
AND THEN...
I LET HIM GET AWAY.
AND THEN...
I LET HIM GET HIS HANDS ON MY GUN.
AND THEN...
I LET HIM RUN THROUGH THE STREETS OF THIS CITY.
AND THEN...
AND THEN I WATCH AS HE SHOOTS INNOCENT BYSTANDERS...
I LET HIM KILL AND MAIM.
AND THEN...
I DO ALL OF THIS...

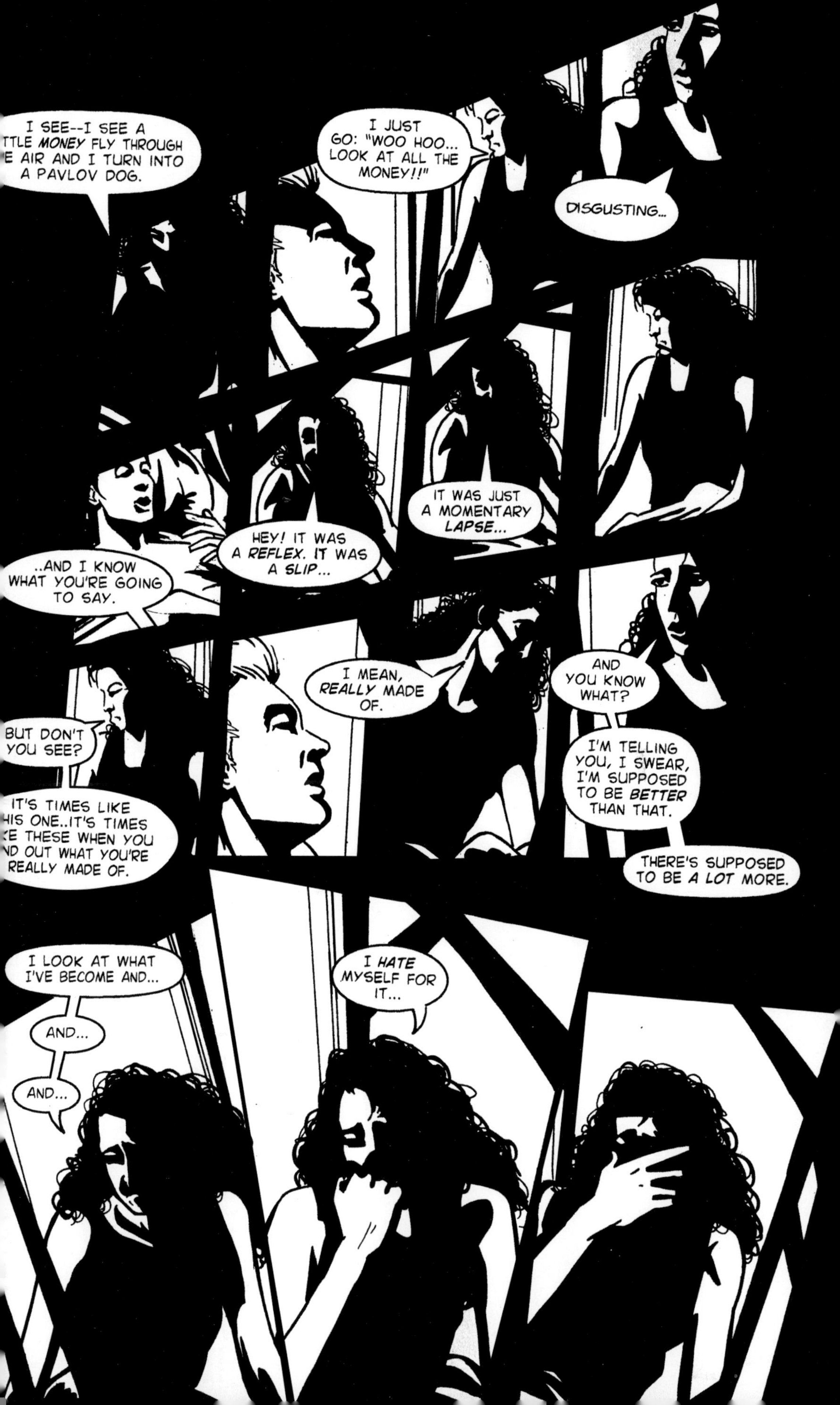

I SEE--I SEE A
TTLE MONEY FLY THROUGH
E AIR AND I TURN INTO
A PAVLOV DOG.
I JUST GO: "WOO HOO... LOOK AT ALL THE MONEY!!"
DISGUSTING...
..AND I KNOW WHAT YOU'RE GOING TO SAY.
HEY! IT WAS A REFLEX. IT WAS A SLIP...
IT WAS JUST A MOMENTARY LAPSE...
BUT DON'T YOU SEE?
IT'S TIMES LIKE
HIS ONE..IT'S TIMES
E THESE WHEN YOU
D OUT WHAT YOU'RE
REALLY MADE OF.
I MEAN, REALLY MADE OF.
AND YOU KNOW WHAT?
I'M TELLING YOU, I SWEAR, I'M SUPPOSED TO BE BETTER THAN THAT.
THERE'S SUPPOSED TO BE A LOT MORE.
I LOOK AT WHAT I'VE BECOME AND...
AND...
AND...
I HATE MYSELF FOR IT...

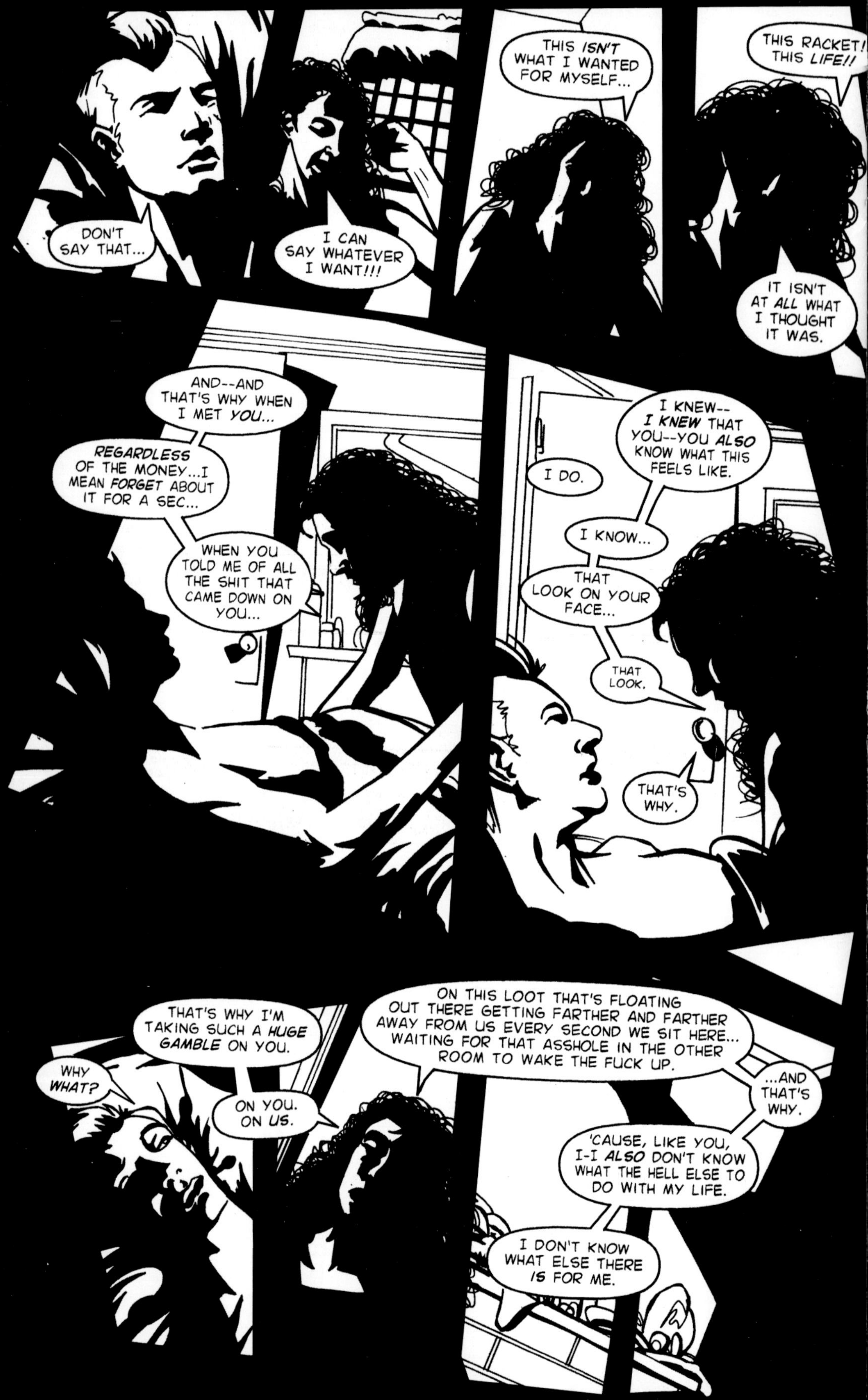
DON'T SAY THAT...
I CAN SAY WHATEVER I WANT!!!
THIS ISN'T WHAT I WANTED FOR MYSELF...
THIS RACKET! THIS LIFE!!
IT ISN'T AT ALL WHAT I THOUGHT IT WAS.
AND--AND THAT'S WHY WHEN I MET YOU...
REGARDLESS OF THE MONEY...I MEAN FORGET ABOUT IT FOR A SEC...
WHEN YOU TOLD ME OF ALL THE SHIT THAT CAME DOWN ON YOU...
I DO.
I KNEW-- I KNEW THAT YOU--YOU ALSO KNOW WHAT THIS FEELS LIKE.
I KNOW...
THAT LOOK ON YOUR FACE...
THAT LOOK.
THAT'S WHY.
WHY WHAT?
THAT'S WHY I'M TAKING SUCH A HUGE GAMBLE ON YOU.
ON YOU. ON US.
ON THIS LOOT THAT'S FLOATING OUT THERE GETTING FARTHER AND FARTHER AWAY FROM US EVERY SECOND WE SIT HERE... WAITING FOR THAT ASSHOLE IN THE OTHER ROOM TO WAKE THE FUCK UP.
...AND THAT'S WHY.
'CAUSE, LIKE YOU, I-I ALSO DON'T KNOW WHAT THE HELL ELSE TO DO WITH MY LIFE.
I DON'T KNOW WHAT ELSE THERE IS FOR ME.

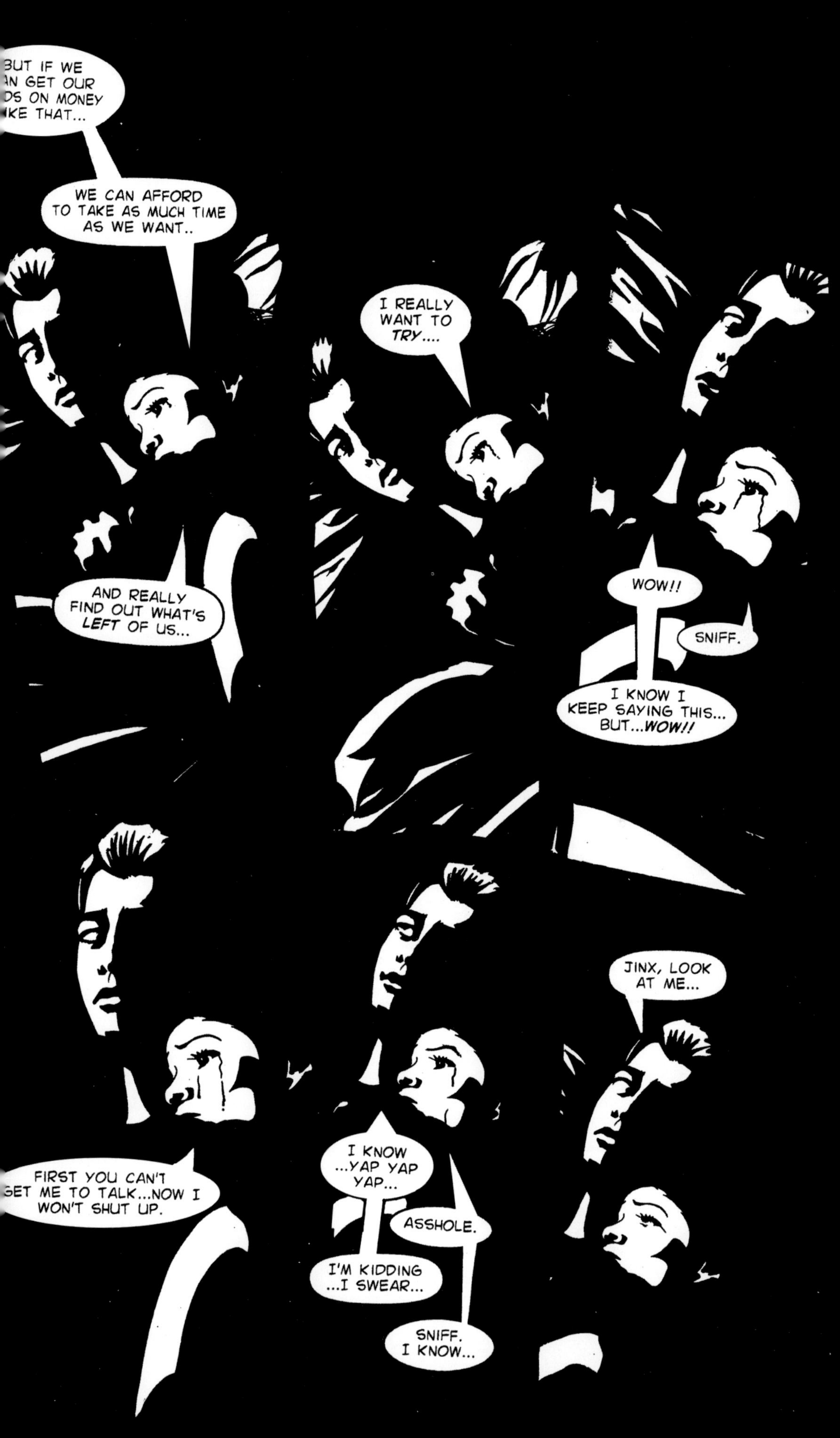
BUT IF WE
AN GET OUR
DS ON MONEY
IKE THAT...
WE CAN AFFORD TO TAKE AS MUCH TIME AS WE WANT..
AND REALLY FIND OUT WHAT'S *LEFT* OF US...
I REALLY WANT TO *TRY*....
WOW!!
SNIFF.
I KNOW I KEEP SAYING THIS... BUT...*WOW!!*
FIRST YOU CAN'T
GET ME TO TALK...NOW I WON'T SHUT UP.
I KNOW ...YAP YAP YAP...
ASSHOLE.
I'M KIDDING ...I SWEAR...
SNIFF. I KNOW...
JINX, LOOK AT ME...

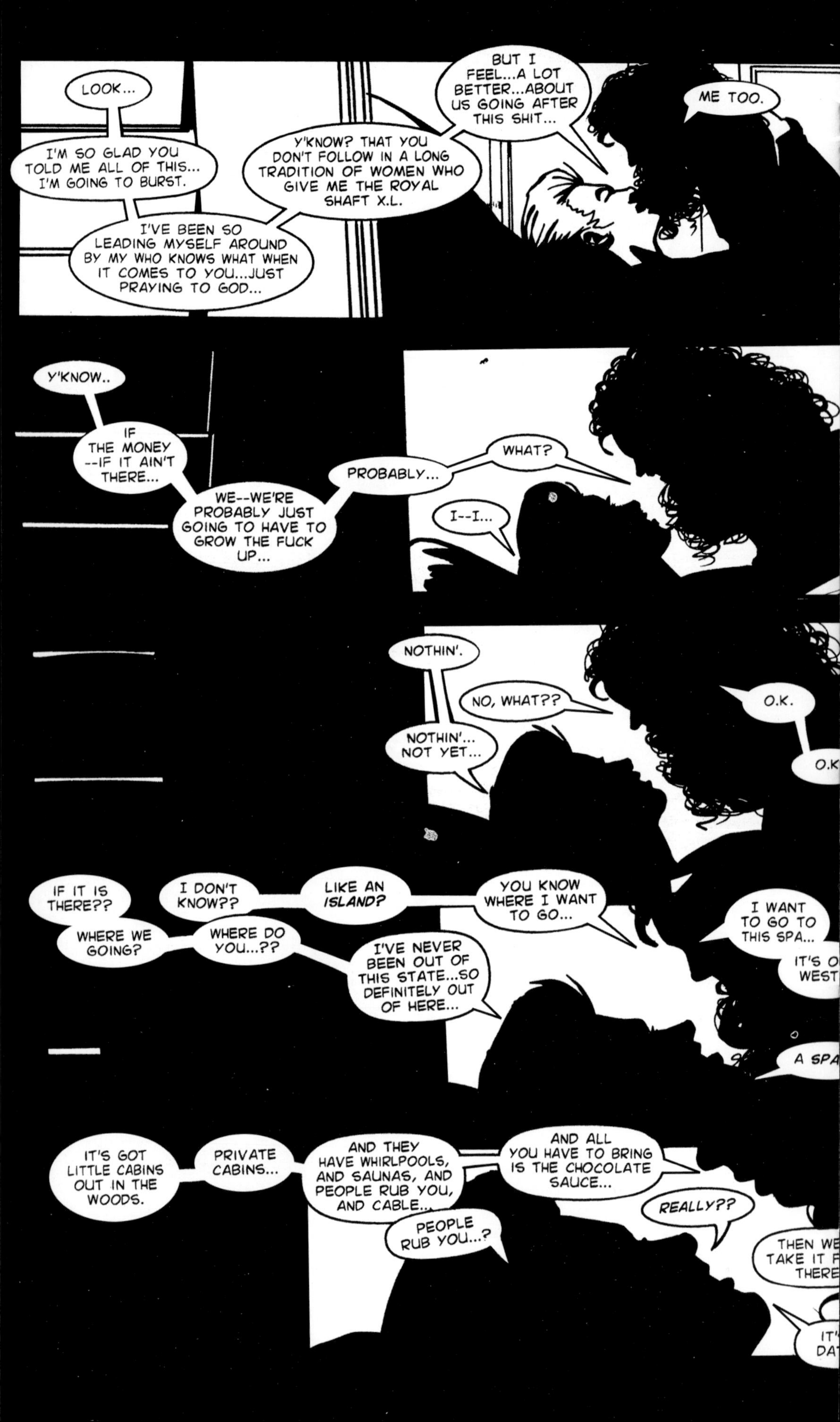
LOOK...
I'M SO GLAD YOU TOLD ME ALL OF THIS... I'M GOING TO BURST.
I'VE BEEN SO LEADING MYSELF AROUND BY MY WHO KNOWS WHAT WHEN IT COMES TO YOU...JUST PRAYING TO GOD...
Y'KNOW? THAT YOU DON'T FOLLOW IN A LONG TRADITION OF WOMEN WHO GIVE ME THE ROYAL SHAFT X.L.
BUT I FEEL...A LOT BETTER...ABOUT US GOING AFTER THIS SHIT...
ME TOO.
Y'KNOW..
IF THE MONEY --IF IT AIN'T THERE...
WE--WE'RE PROBABLY JUST GOING TO HAVE TO GROW THE FUCK UP...
PROBABLY...
WHAT?
I--I...
NOTHIN'.
NO, WHAT??
NOTHIN'... NOT YET...
O.K.
O.K
IF IT IS THERE??
WHERE WE GOING?
I DON'T KNOW??
WHERE DO YOU...??
LIKE AN *ISLAND?*
I'VE NEVER BEEN OUT OF THIS STATE...SO DEFINITELY OUT OF HERE...
YOU KNOW WHERE I WANT TO GO...
I WANT TO GO TO THIS SPA...
IT'S O
WEST
A SPA
IT'S GOT LITTLE CABINS OUT IN THE WOODS.
PRIVATE CABINS...
AND THEY HAVE WHIRLPOOLS, AND SAUNAS, AND PEOPLE RUB YOU, AND CABLE...
PEOPLE RUB YOU...?
AND ALL YOU HAVE TO BRING IS THE CHOCOLATE SAUCE...
REALLY??
THEN WE
TAKE IT F
THERE
IT'
DA

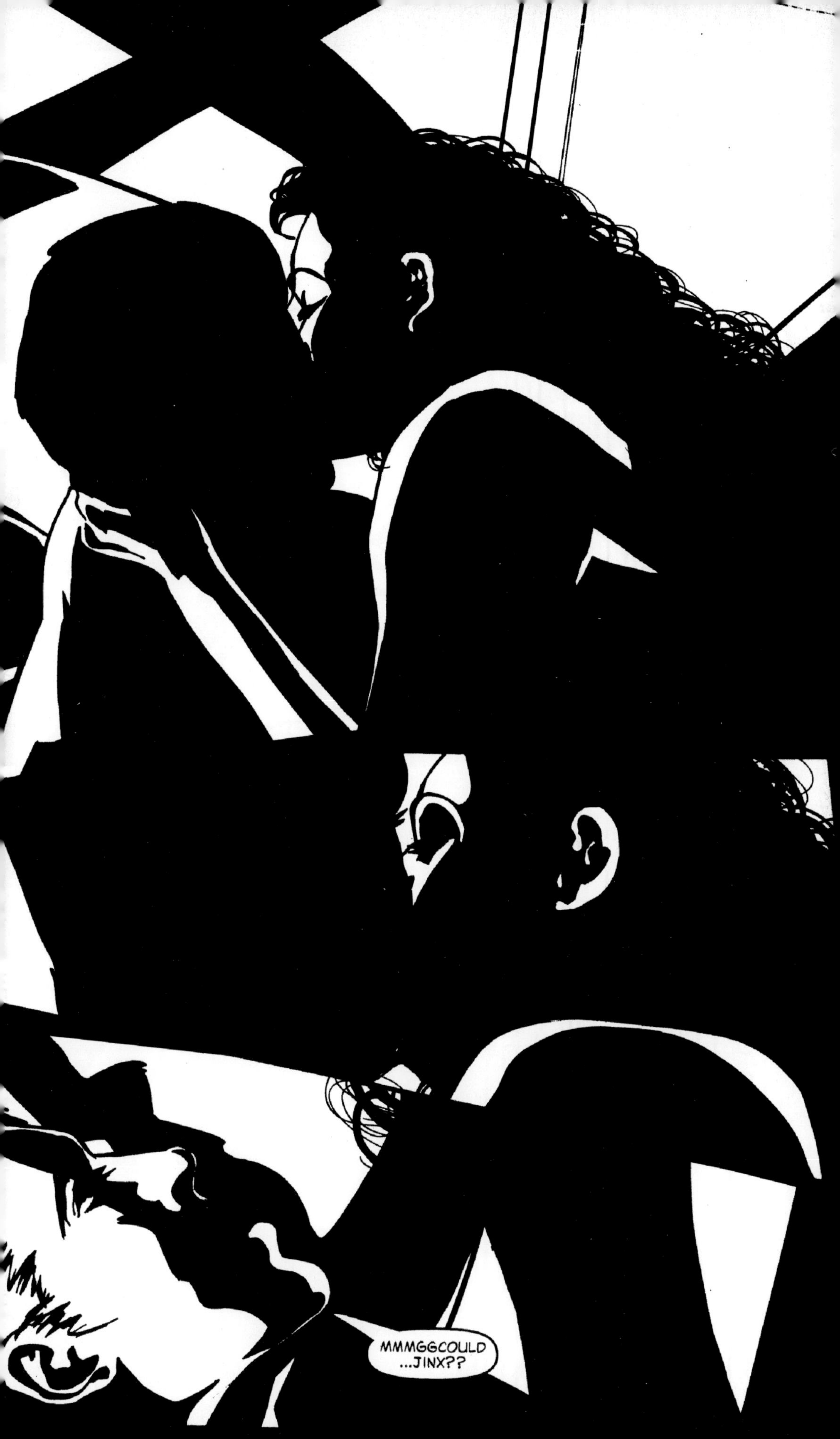
MMMGGCOULD
...JINX??

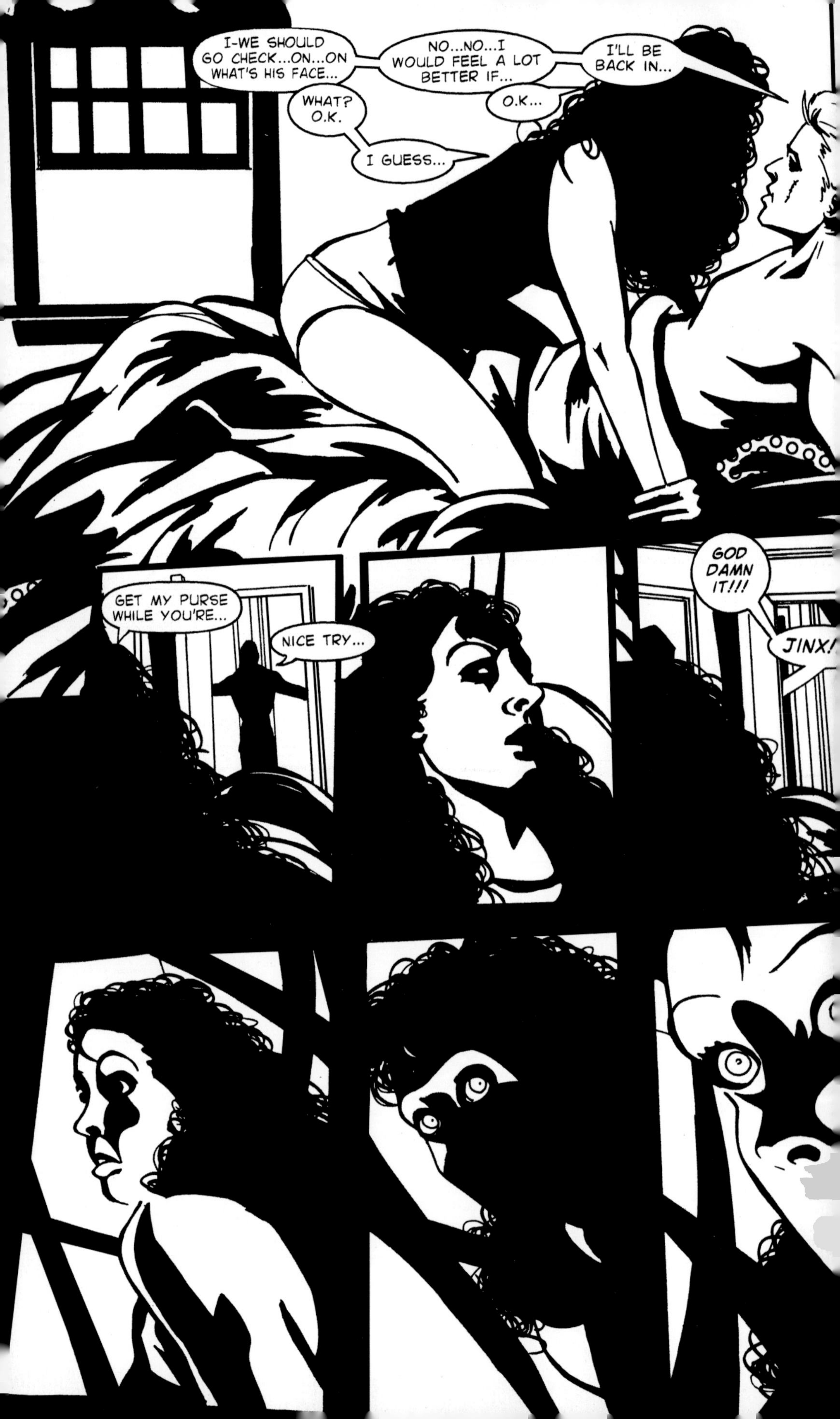
I-WE SHOULD GO CHECK...ON...ON WHAT'S HIS FACE...
WHAT? O.K.
I GUESS...
NO...NO...I WOULD FEEL A LOT BETTER IF...
O.K...
I'LL BE BACK IN...
GET MY PURSE WHILE YOU'RE...
NICE TRY...
GOD DAMN IT!!!
JINX!

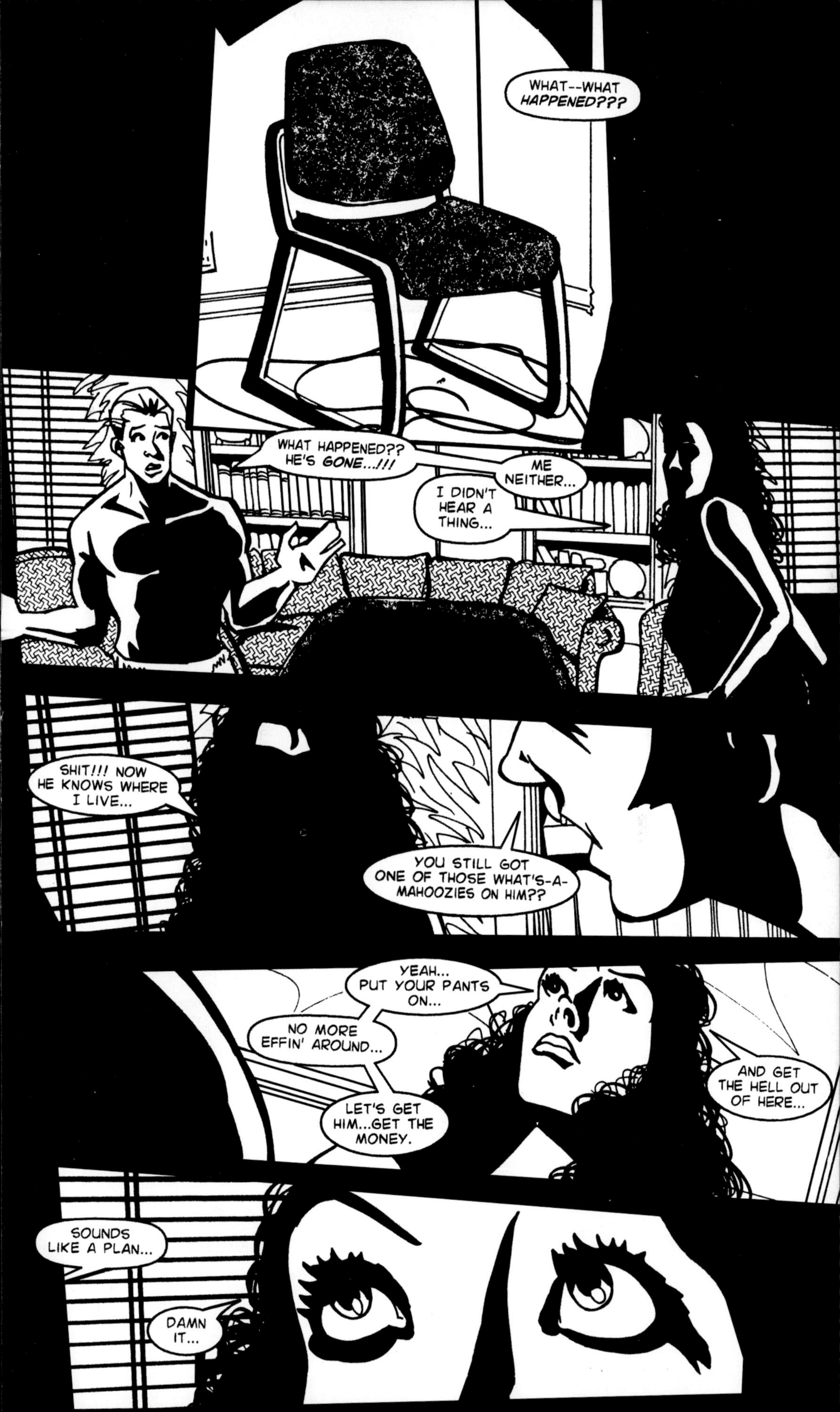
WHAT--WHAT HAPPENED???
WHAT HAPPENED?? HE'S GONE...!!!
ME NEITHER...
I DIDN'T HEAR A THING...
SHIT!!! NOW HE KNOWS WHERE I LIVE...
YOU STILL GOT ONE OF THOSE WHAT'S-A-MAHOOZIES ON HIM??
YEAH... PUT YOUR PANTS ON...
NO MORE EFFIN' AROUND...
LET'S GET HIM...GET THE MONEY.
AND GET THE HELL OUT OF HERE...
SOUNDS LIKE A PLAN...
DAMN IT...

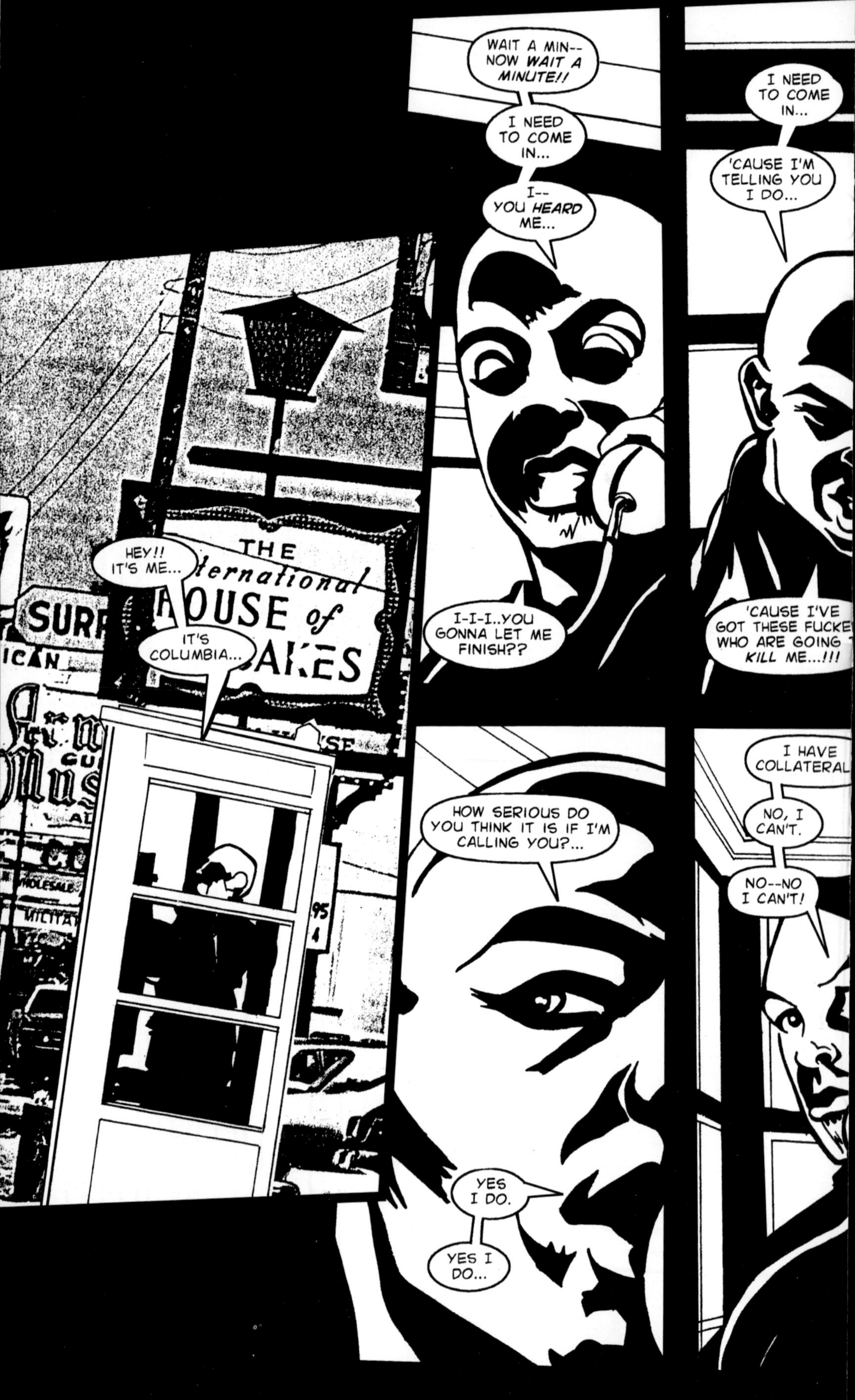
HEY!! IT'S ME...
IT'S COLUMBIA...
THE International HOUSE of PANCAKES
SURF
WAIT A MIN-- NOW WAIT A MINUTE!!
I NEED TO COME IN...
I-- YOU HEARD ME...
I-I-I..YOU GONNA LET ME FINISH??
I NEED TO COME IN...
'CAUSE I'M TELLING YOU I DO...
'CAUSE I'VE GOT THESE FUCKE WHO ARE GOING KILL ME...!!!
HOW SERIOUS DO YOU THINK IT IS IF I'M CALLING YOU?...
YES I DO.
YES I DO...
I HAVE COLLATERAL
NO, I CAN'T.
NO--NO I CAN'T!

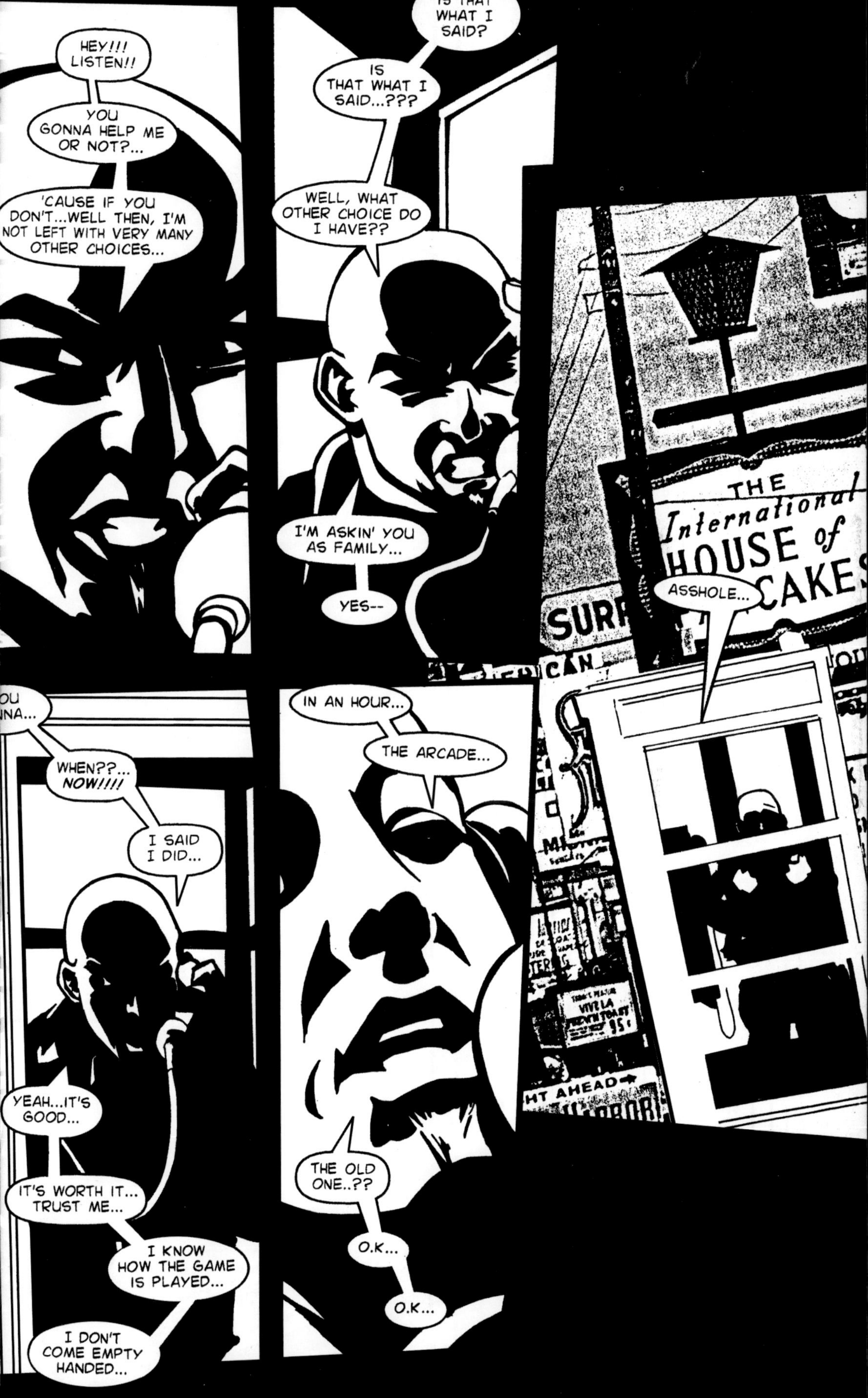
HEY!!! LISTEN!!
YOU GONNA HELP ME OR NOT?...
'CAUSE IF YOU DON'T...WELL THEN, I'M NOT LEFT WITH VERY MANY OTHER CHOICES...
IS THAT WHAT I SAID?
IS THAT WHAT I SAID...???
WELL, WHAT OTHER CHOICE DO I HAVE??
I'M ASKIN' YOU AS FAMILY...
YES--
THE International HOUSE of
CAKES
ASSHOLE...
SURF
CAN
OU
NNA...
WHEN??... NOW!!!!
I SAID I DID...
YEAH...IT'S GOOD...
IT'S WORTH IT... TRUST ME...
I KNOW HOW THE GAME IS PLAYED...
I DON'T COME EMPTY HANDED...
IN AN HOUR...
THE ARCADE...
THE OLD ONE..??
O.K...
O.K...
VIVE LA FRENCH TOAST 95¢
HT AHEAD

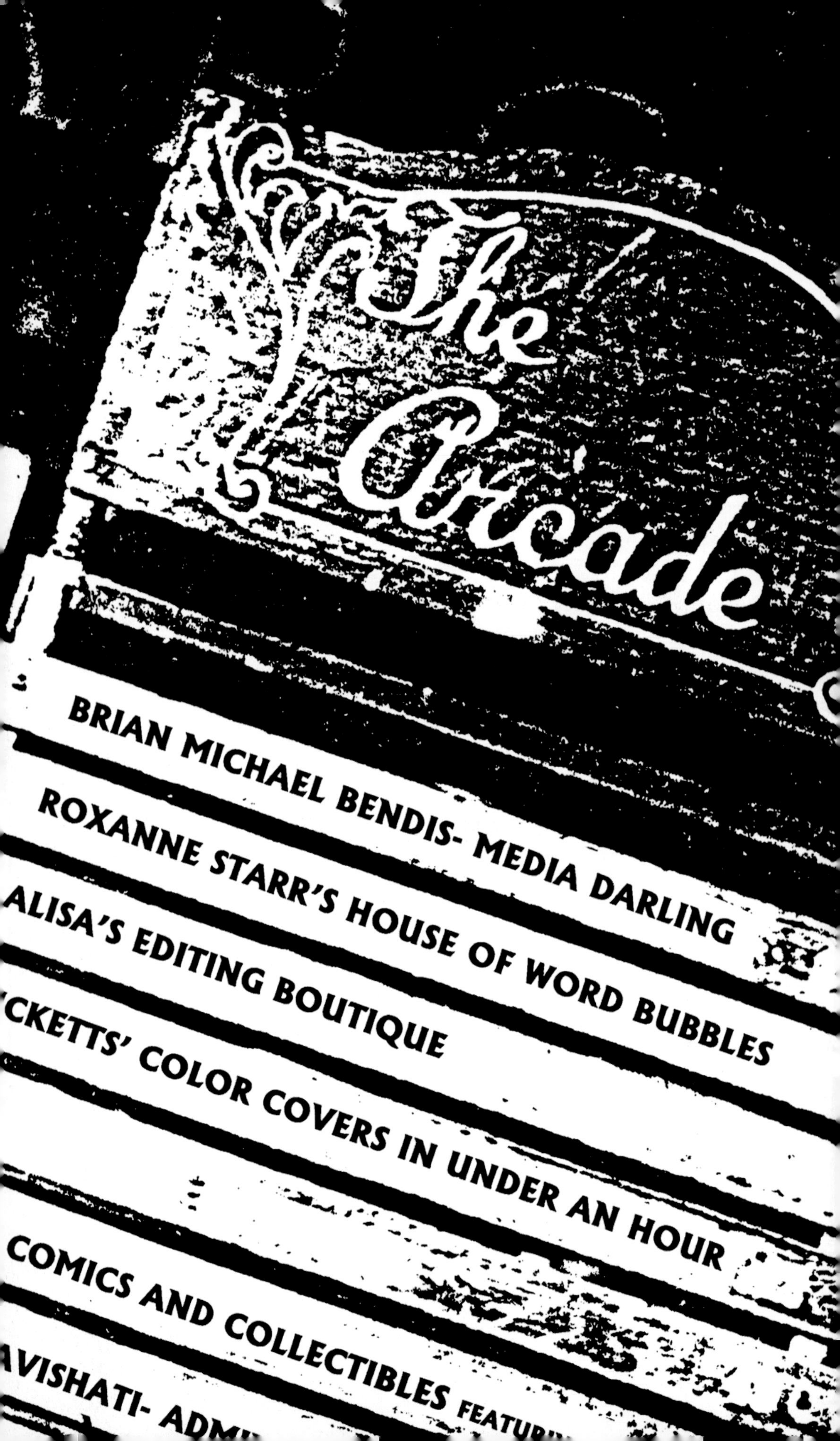
The Arcade
BRIAN MICHAEL BENDIS- MEDIA DARLING
ROXANNE STARR'S HOUSE OF WORD BUBBLES
ALISA'S EDITING BOUTIQUE
CKETTS' COLOR COVERS IN UNDER AN HOUR
COMICS AND COLLECTIBLES

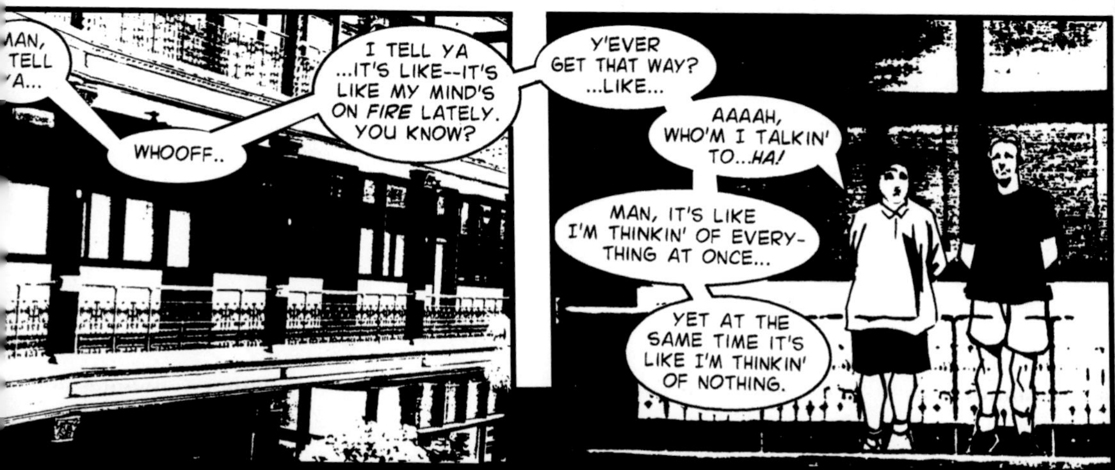
AN, TELL A...
WHOOFF..
I TELL YA ...IT'S LIKE--IT'S LIKE MY MIND'S ON FIRE LATELY. YOU KNOW?
Y'EVER GET THAT WAY? ...LIKE...
AAAAH, WHO'M I TALKIN' TO...HA!
MAN, IT'S LIKE I'M THINKIN' OF EVERY-THING AT ONCE...
YET AT THE SAME TIME IT'S LIKE I'M THINKIN' OF NOTHING.

Stoplights

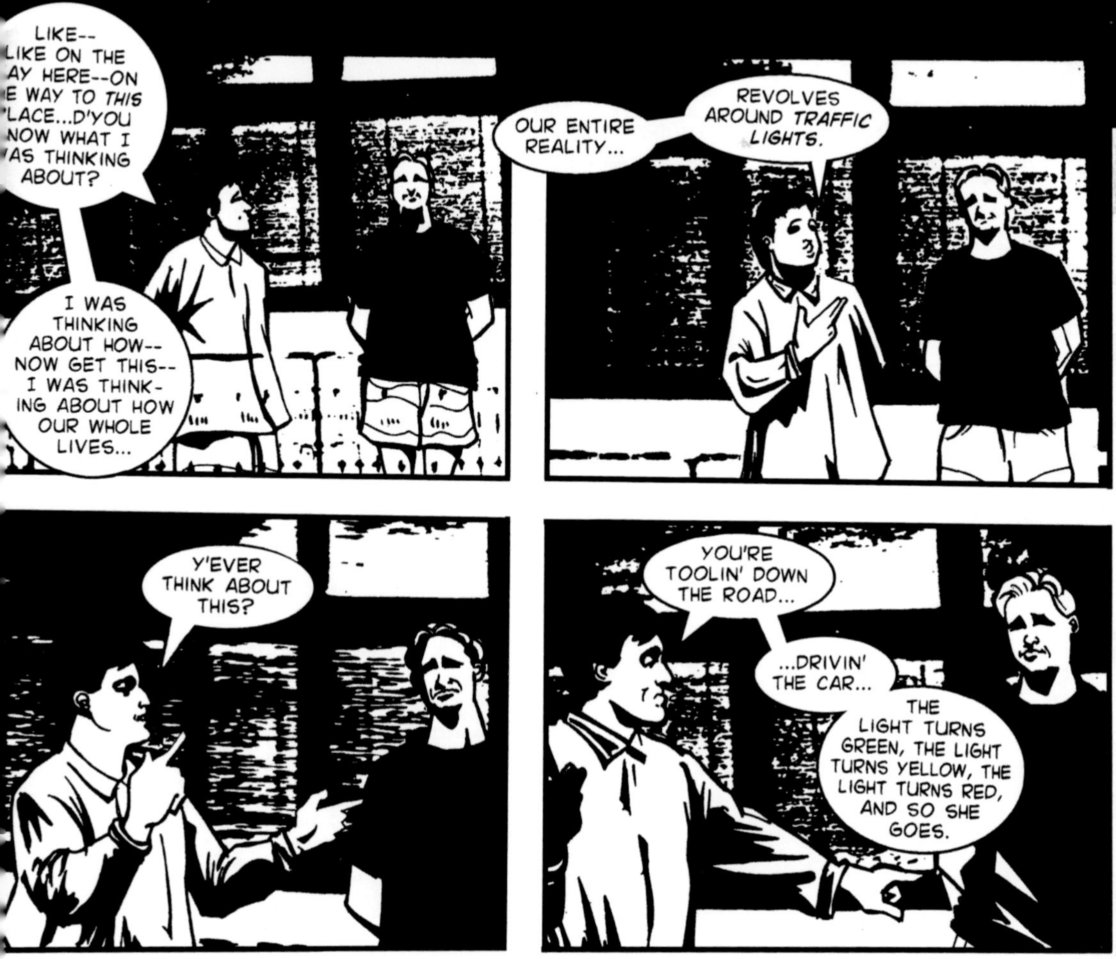
LIKE-- LIKE ON THE AY HERE--ON E WAY TO THIS LACE...D'YOU NOW WHAT I AS THINKING ABOUT?
I WAS THINKING ABOUT HOW-- NOW GET THIS-- I WAS THINK-ING ABOUT HOW OUR WHOLE LIVES...
OUR ENTIRE REALITY...
REVOLVES AROUND TRAFFIC LIGHTS.
Y'EVER THINK ABOUT THIS?
YOU'RE TOOLIN' DOWN THE ROAD...
...DRIVIN' THE CAR...
THE LIGHT TURNS GREEN, THE LIGHT TURNS YELLOW, THE LIGHT TURNS RED, AND SO SHE GOES.

LET'S SAY YOU'RE COMING UP ON A YELLOW...

SOMETIMES IT'S LIKE THE DIFFERENCE OF A SECOND...

A 200TH OF A SECOND...

WHETHER YOU HIT THE BRAKE OR FLOOR IT.

AN IMPULSE ON WHETHER YOU GO THROUGH THAT YELLOW LIGHT.

NOW WHAT BLOWS MY MIND ABOUT THIS IS THAT I DON'T THINK IT'S JUST A DECISION TO MAKE A LIGHT.

HOW MANY TIMES THIS HAPPEN TO YOU? A MILLION, RIGHT?

HOW MANY TIMES IN ONE DAY ALONE??

THIS CROSSROADS...

IT'S--IT'S LIKE YOU'RE PICKING A WHOLE NEW LIFE FOR YOURSELF.

I THINK THAT EVERY TIME YOU'RE CONFRONTED WITH THIS...

LIKE--LET'S SAY YOU BITE THE BULLET AND STOP AT THE LIGHT...

THAT DECISION COULD OF MADE YOU AVOID HITTING ONE OF THOSE A-HOLE KIDS WHO'VE CUT THE BRAKES ON THEIR BICYCLE FOR THE THRILL RIDE...

OR STOPPING AT THAT LIGHT-- THAT 30-SECOND DELAY OF YOUR LIFE AS YOU SIT THERE TRYING NOT TO PICK YOUR NOSE IN PUBLIC...

THIS COULD HAVE PREVEN[T] YOU FROM MEE[T] THE GIRL OF Y[OUR] DREAMS LATER IN THE DAY[?]

THINK OF IT!

OR LET'S SAY--LET'S SAY YOU GO THROUGH THE LIGHT, RIGHT?

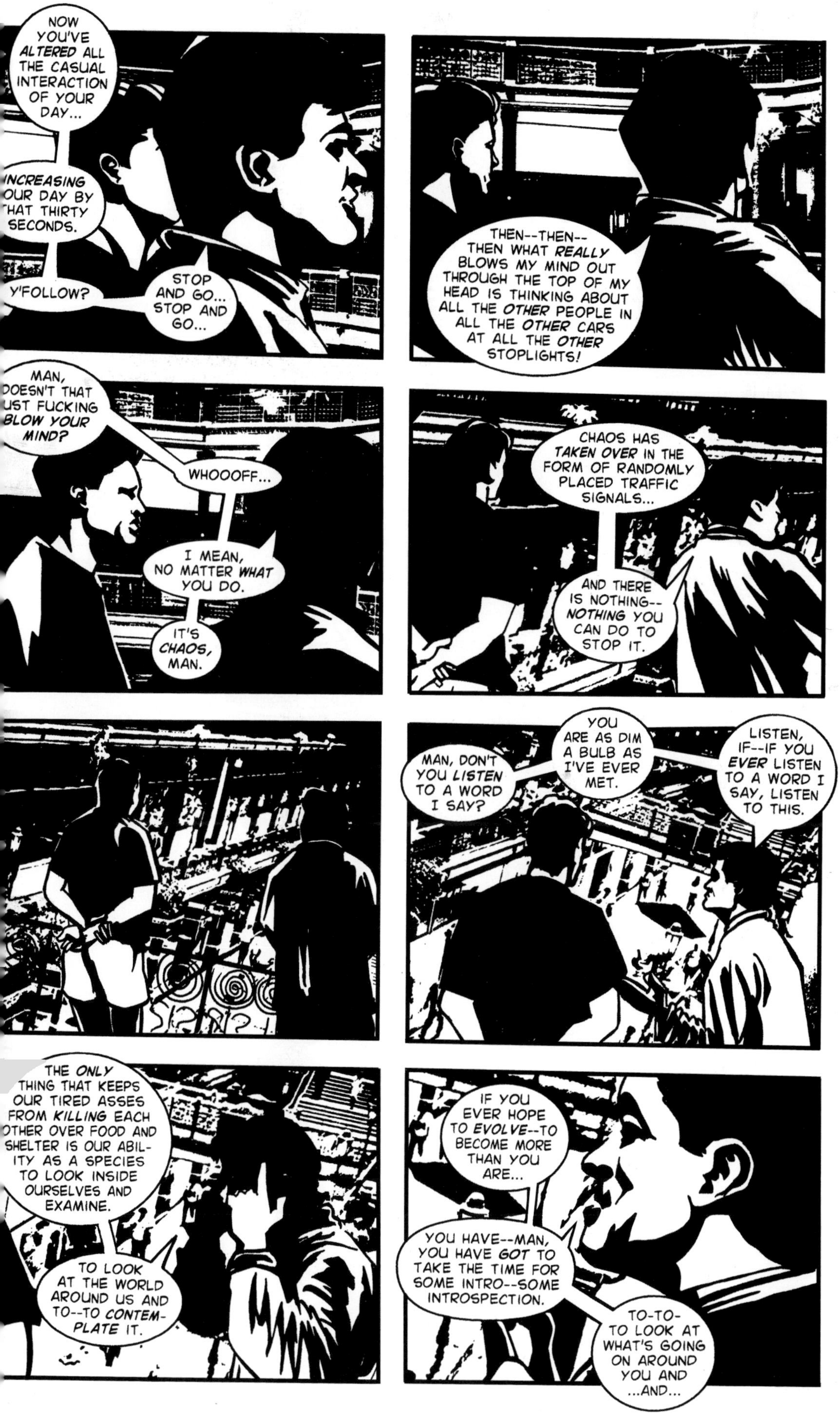
NOW YOU'VE ALTERED ALL THE CASUAL INTERACTION OF YOUR DAY...
INCREASING OUR DAY BY THAT THIRTY SECONDS.
Y'FOLLOW?
STOP AND GO... STOP AND GO...
THEN--THEN-- THEN WHAT REALLY BLOWS MY MIND OUT THROUGH THE TOP OF MY HEAD IS THINKING ABOUT ALL THE OTHER PEOPLE IN ALL THE OTHER CARS AT ALL THE OTHER STOPLIGHTS!
MAN, DOESN'T THAT JUST FUCKING BLOW YOUR MIND?
WHOOOFF...
I MEAN, NO MATTER WHAT YOU DO.
IT'S CHAOS, MAN.
CHAOS HAS TAKEN OVER IN THE FORM OF RANDOMLY PLACED TRAFFIC SIGNALS...
AND THERE IS NOTHING-- NOTHING YOU CAN DO TO STOP IT.
MAN, DON'T YOU LISTEN TO A WORD I SAY?
YOU ARE AS DIM A BULB AS I'VE EVER MET.
LISTEN, IF--IF YOU EVER LISTEN TO A WORD I SAY, LISTEN TO THIS.
THE ONLY THING THAT KEEPS OUR TIRED ASSES FROM KILLING EACH OTHER OVER FOOD AND SHELTER IS OUR ABIL-ITY AS A SPECIES TO LOOK INSIDE OURSELVES AND EXAMINE.
TO LOOK AT THE WORLD AROUND US AND TO--TO CONTEM-PLATE IT.
IF YOU EVER HOPE TO EVOLVE--TO BECOME MORE THAN YOU ARE...
YOU HAVE--MAN, YOU HAVE GOT TO TAKE THE TIME FOR SOME INTRO--SOME INTROSPECTION.
TO-TO- TO LOOK AT WHAT'S GOING ON AROUND YOU AND ...AND...

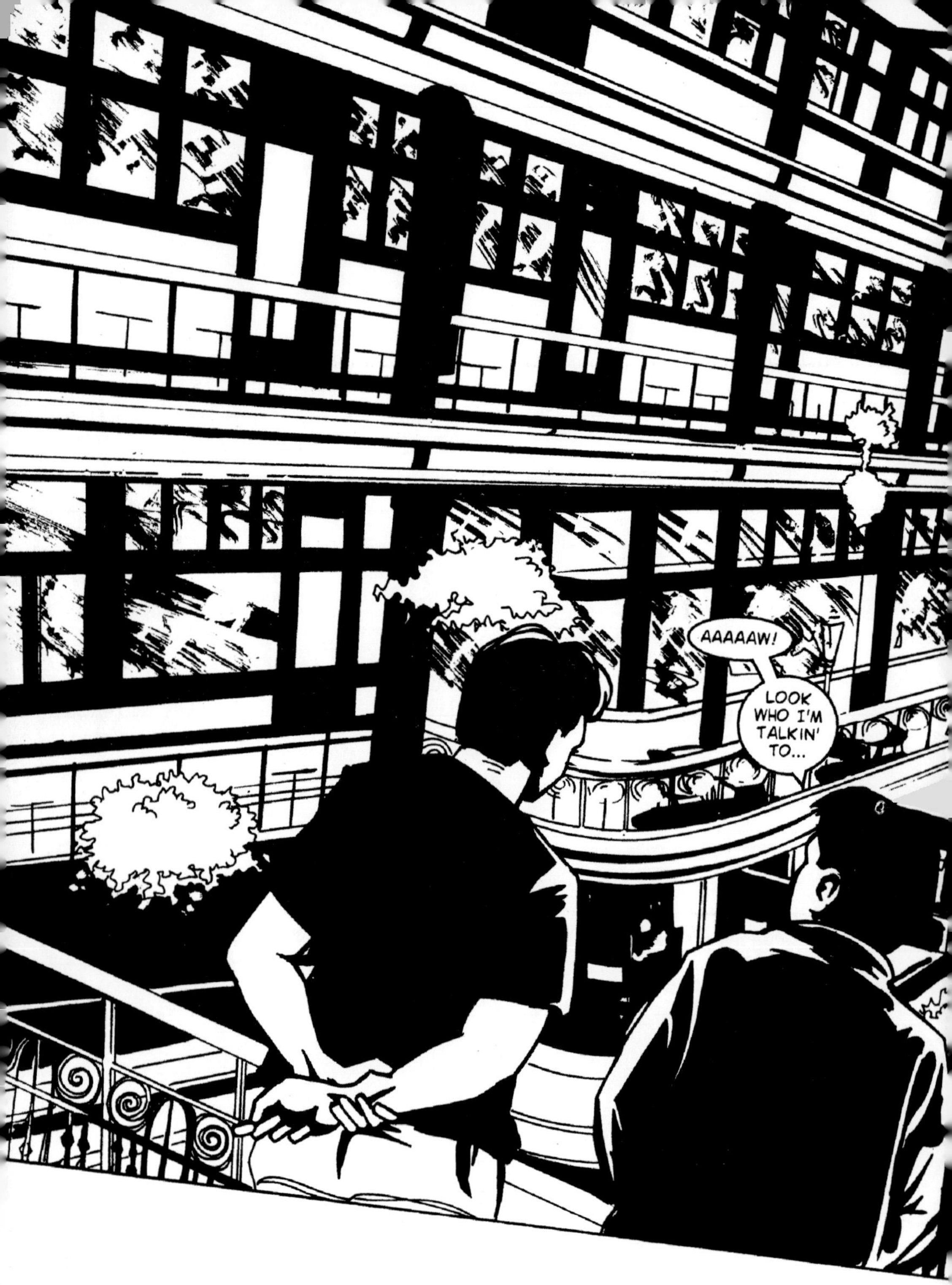
AAAAAW!
LOOK WHO I'M TALKIN' TO...

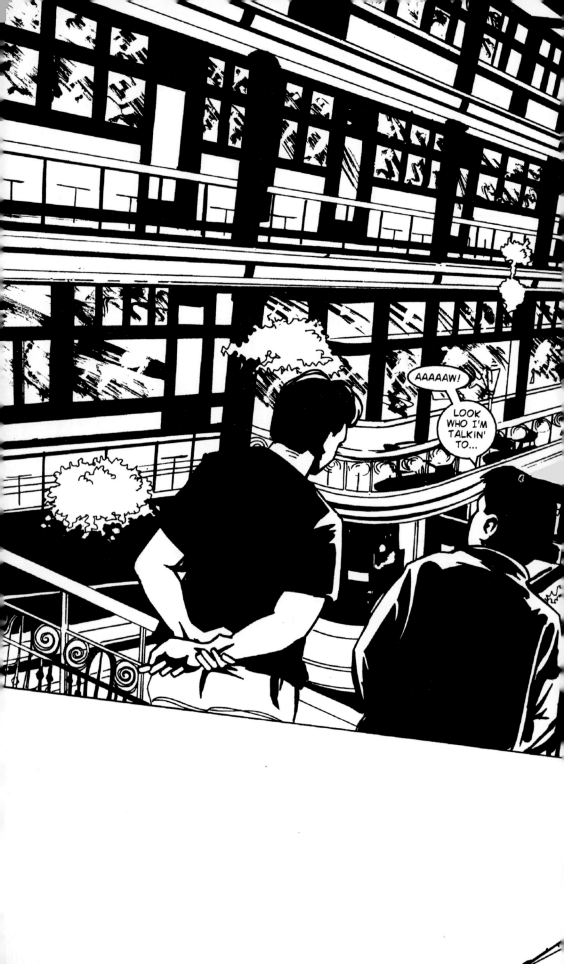

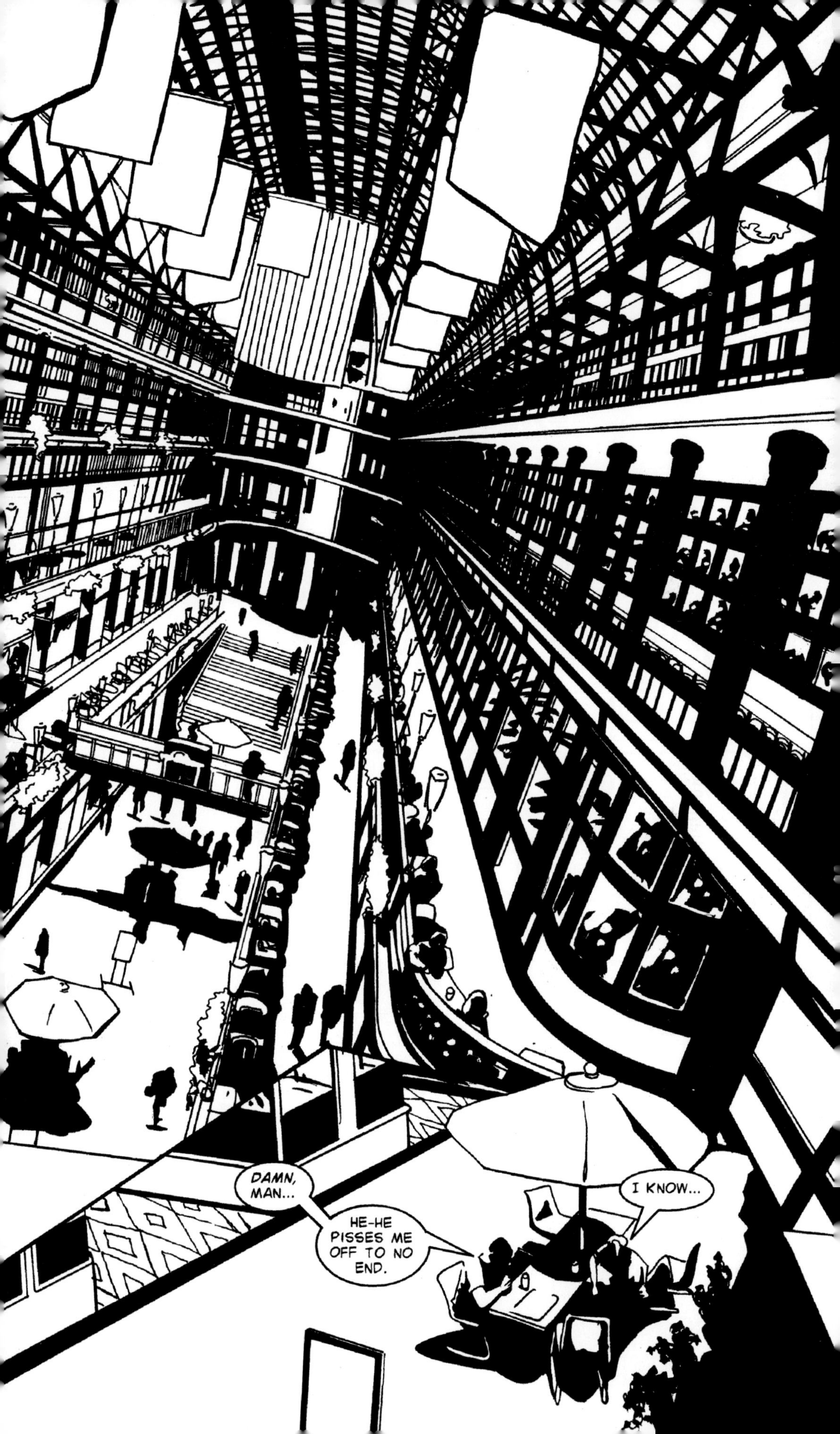
DAMN, MAN...
HE-HE PISSES ME OFF TO NO END.
I KNOW...

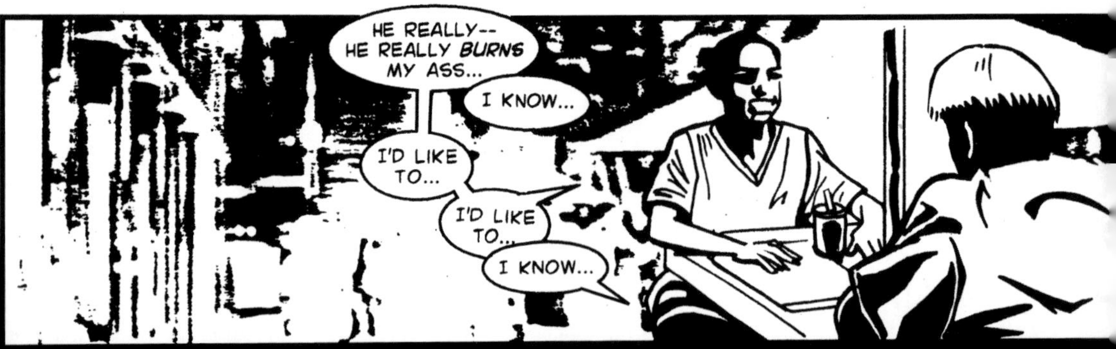
HE REALLY-- HE REALLY BURNS MY ASS...
I KNOW...
I'D LIKE TO...
I'D LIKE TO...
I KNOW...

David Hasselhoff

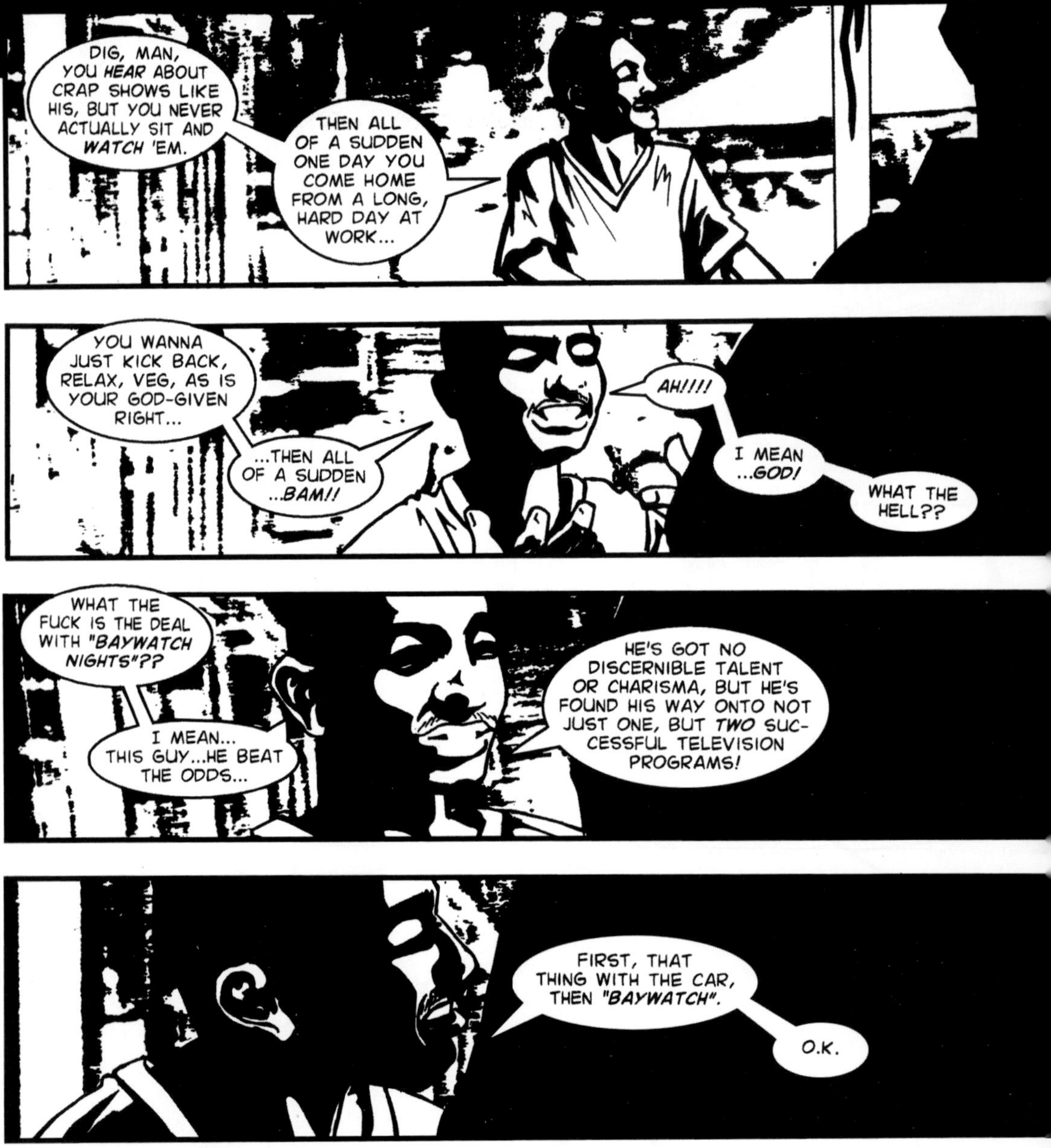
DIG, MAN, YOU HEAR ABOUT CRAP SHOWS LIKE HIS, BUT YOU NEVER ACTUALLY SIT AND WATCH 'EM.
THEN ALL OF A SUDDEN ONE DAY YOU COME HOME FROM A LONG, HARD DAY AT WORK...
YOU WANNA JUST KICK BACK, RELAX, VEG, AS IS YOUR GOD-GIVEN RIGHT...
...THEN ALL OF A SUDDEN ...BAM!!
AH!!!!
I MEAN ...GOD!
WHAT THE HELL??
WHAT THE FUCK IS THE DEAL WITH "BAYWATCH NIGHTS"??
I MEAN... THIS GUY...HE BEAT THE ODDS...
HE'S GOT NO DISCERNIBLE TALENT OR CHARISMA, BUT HE'S FOUND HIS WAY ONTO NOT JUST ONE, BUT TWO SUC-CESSFUL TELEVISION PROGRAMS!
FIRST, THAT THING WITH THE CAR, THEN "BAYWATCH".
O.K.

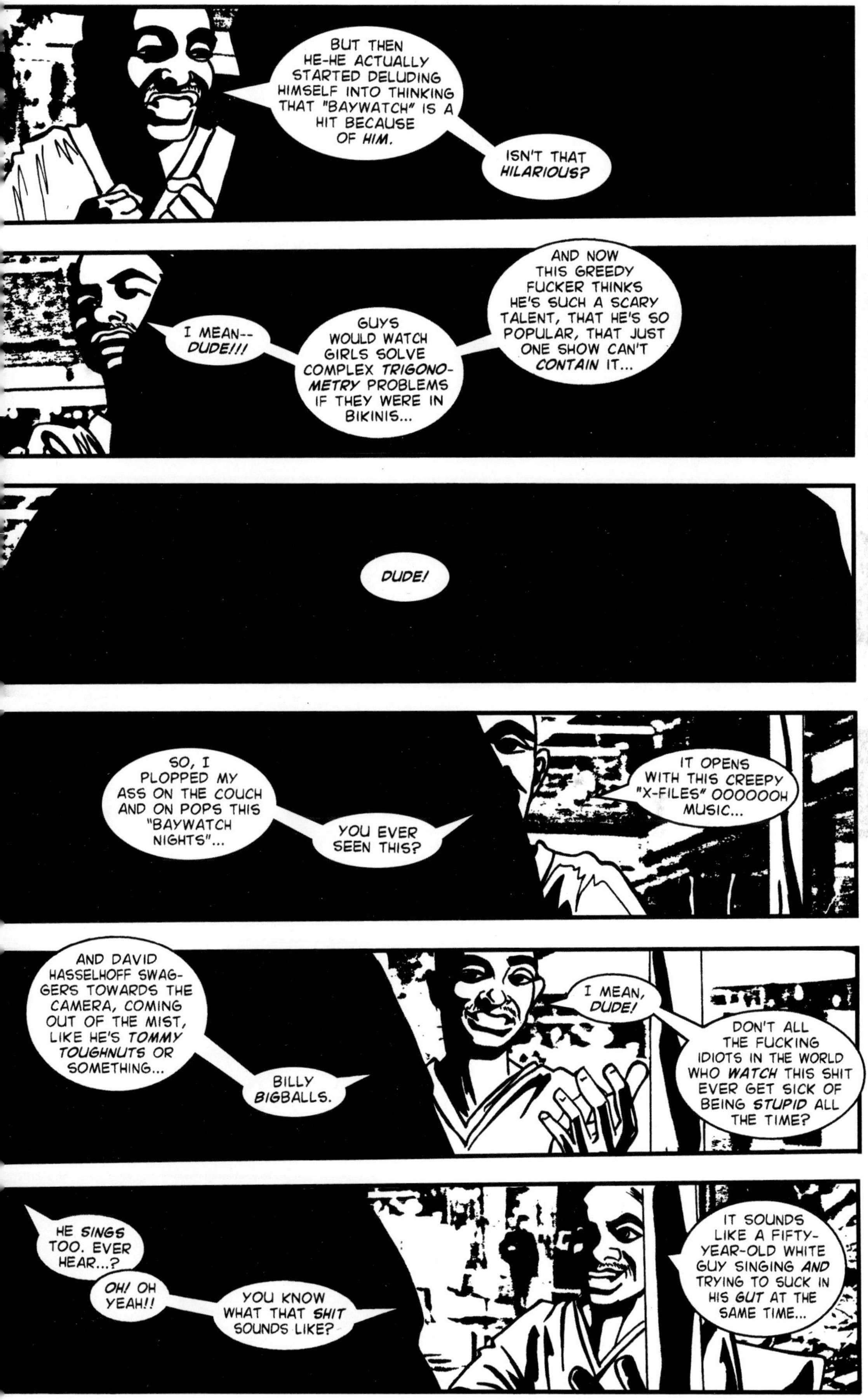
BUT THEN HE-HE ACTUALLY STARTED DELUDING HIMSELF INTO THINKING THAT "BAYWATCH" IS A HIT BECAUSE OF *HIM.*
ISN'T THAT *HILARIOUS?*
I MEAN-- *DUDE!!!*
GUYS WOULD WATCH GIRLS SOLVE COMPLEX *TRIGONOMETRY* PROBLEMS IF THEY WERE IN BIKINIS...
AND NOW THIS GREEDY FUCKER THINKS HE'S SUCH A SCARY TALENT, THAT HE'S SO POPULAR, THAT JUST ONE SHOW CAN'T *CONTAIN* IT...
DUDE!
SO, I PLOPPED MY ASS ON THE COUCH AND ON POPS THIS "BAYWATCH NIGHTS"...
YOU EVER SEEN THIS?
IT OPENS WITH THIS CREEPY "X-FILES" OOOOOOH MUSIC...
AND DAVID HASSELHOFF SWAGGERS TOWARDS THE CAMERA, COMING OUT OF THE MIST, LIKE HE'S *TOMMY TOUGHNUTS* OR SOMETHING...
BILLY BIGBALLS.
I MEAN, *DUDE!*
DON'T ALL THE FUCKING IDIOTS IN THE WORLD WHO *WATCH* THIS SHIT EVER GET SICK OF BEING *STUPID* ALL THE TIME?
HE *SINGS* TOO. EVER HEAR...?
OH! OH YEAH!!
YOU KNOW WHAT THAT *SHIT* SOUNDS LIKE?
IT SOUNDS LIKE A FIFTY-YEAR-OLD WHITE GUY SINGING *AND* TRYING TO SUCK IN HIS *GUT* AT THE SAME TIME...

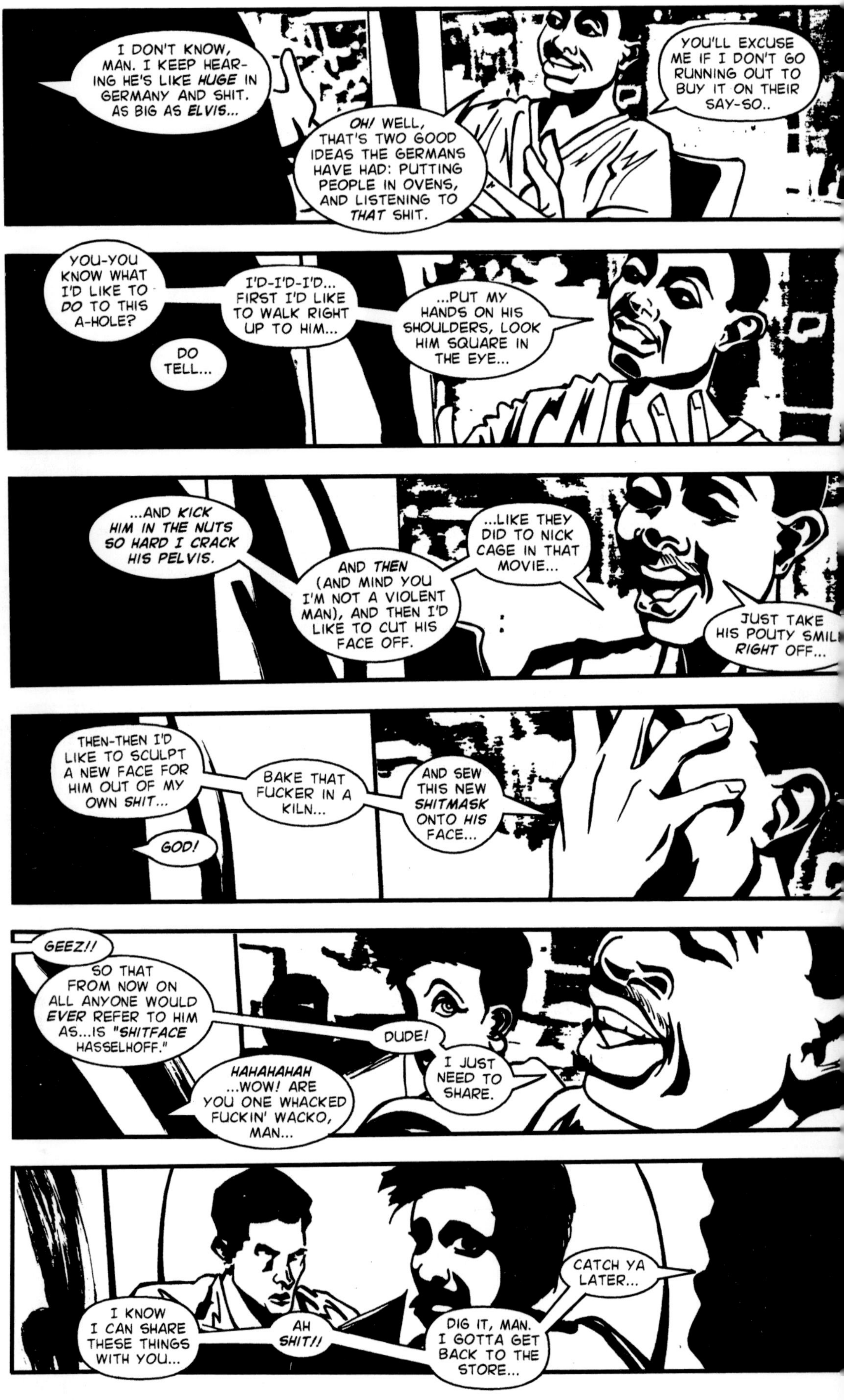
I DON'T KNOW, MAN. I KEEP HEARING HE'S LIKE HUGE IN GERMANY AND SHIT. AS BIG AS ELVIS...
OH! WELL, THAT'S TWO GOOD IDEAS THE GERMANS HAVE HAD: PUTTING PEOPLE IN OVENS, AND LISTENING TO THAT SHIT.
YOU'LL EXCUSE ME IF I DON'T GO RUNNING OUT TO BUY IT ON THEIR SAY-SO..
YOU-YOU KNOW WHAT I'D LIKE TO DO TO THIS A-HOLE?
DO TELL...
I'D-I'D-I'D... FIRST I'D LIKE TO WALK RIGHT UP TO HIM...
...PUT MY HANDS ON HIS SHOULDERS, LOOK HIM SQUARE IN THE EYE...
...AND KICK HIM IN THE NUTS SO HARD I CRACK HIS PELVIS.
AND THEN (AND MIND YOU I'M NOT A VIOLENT MAN), AND THEN I'D LIKE TO CUT HIS FACE OFF.
...LIKE THEY DID TO NICK CAGE IN THAT MOVIE...
JUST TAKE HIS POUTY SMIL RIGHT OFF...
THEN-THEN I'D LIKE TO SCULPT A NEW FACE FOR HIM OUT OF MY OWN SHIT...
GOD!
BAKE THAT FUCKER IN A KILN...
AND SEW THIS NEW SHITMASK ONTO HIS FACE...
GEEZ!!
SO THAT FROM NOW ON ALL ANYONE WOULD EVER REFER TO HIM AS...IS "SHITFACE HASSELHOFF."
DUDE!
I JUST NEED TO SHARE.
HAHAHAHAH ...WOW! ARE YOU ONE WHACKED FUCKIN' WACKO, MAN...
I KNOW I CAN SHARE THESE THINGS WITH YOU...
AH SHIT!!
DIG IT, MAN. I GOTTA GET BACK TO THE STORE...
CATCH YA LATER...

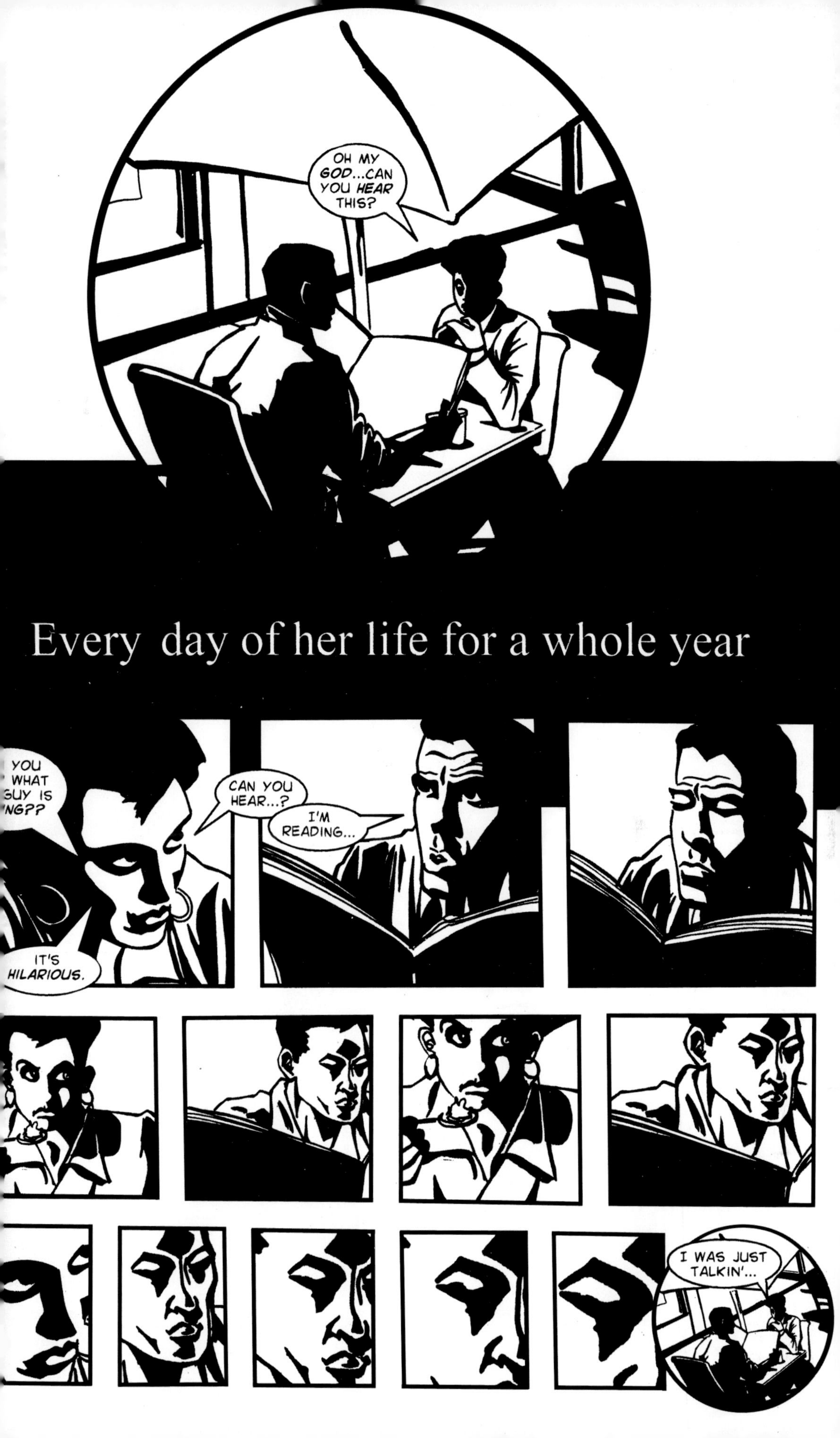
OH MY GOD...CAN YOU HEAR THIS?
Every day of her life for a whole year
IT'S HILARIOUS.
CAN YOU HEAR...?
I'M READING...
I WAS JUST TALKIN'...

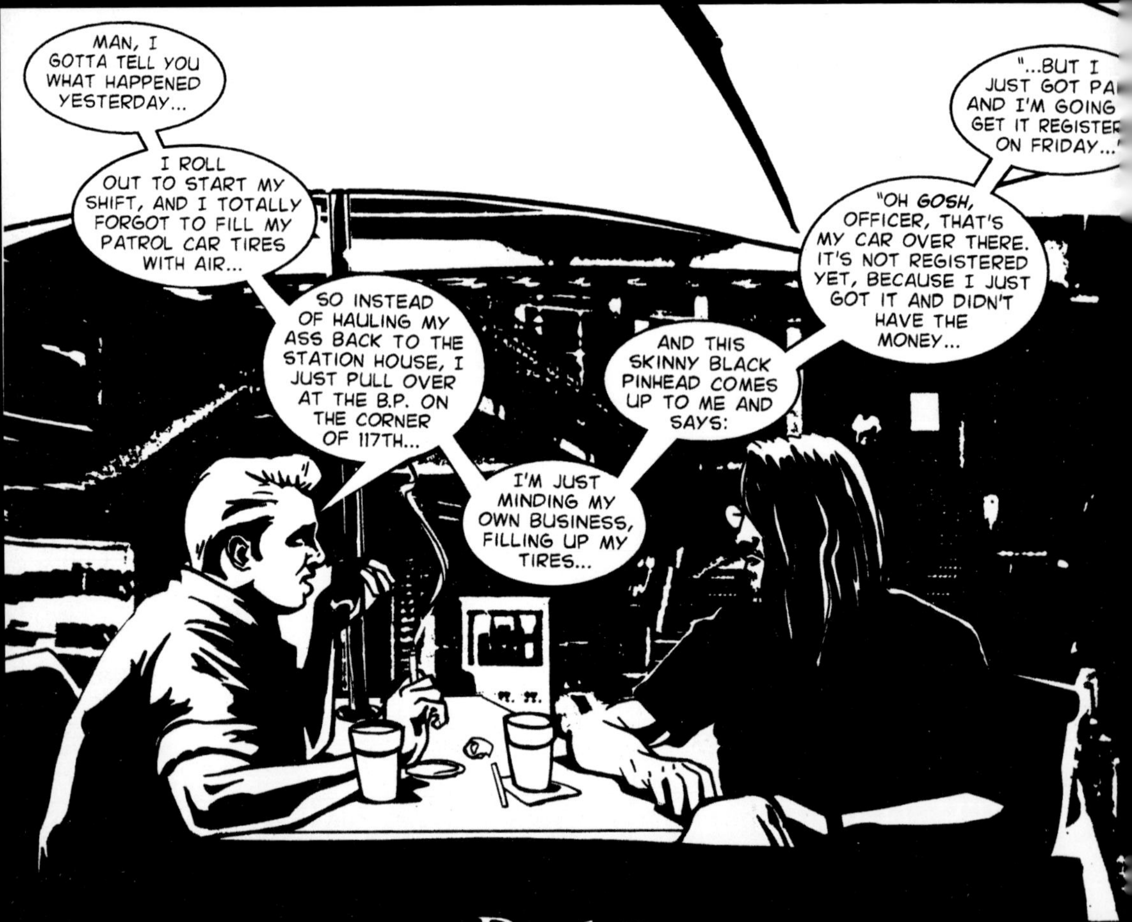
MAN, I GOTTA TELL YOU WHAT HAPPENED YESTERDAY...
I ROLL OUT TO START MY SHIFT, AND I TOTALLY FORGOT TO FILL MY PATROL CAR TIRES WITH AIR...
SO INSTEAD OF HAULING MY ASS BACK TO THE STATION HOUSE, I JUST PULL OVER AT THE B.P. ON THE CORNER OF 117TH...
I'M JUST MINDING MY OWN BUSINESS, FILLING UP MY TIRES...
AND THIS SKINNY BLACK PINHEAD COMES UP TO ME AND SAYS:
"OH *GOSH*, OFFICER, THAT'S MY CAR OVER THERE. IT'S NOT REGISTERED YET, BECAUSE I JUST GOT IT AND DIDN'T HAVE THE MONEY...
"...BUT I JUST GOT PA AND I'M GOING GET IT REGISTER ON FRIDAY..."

Bad Boys

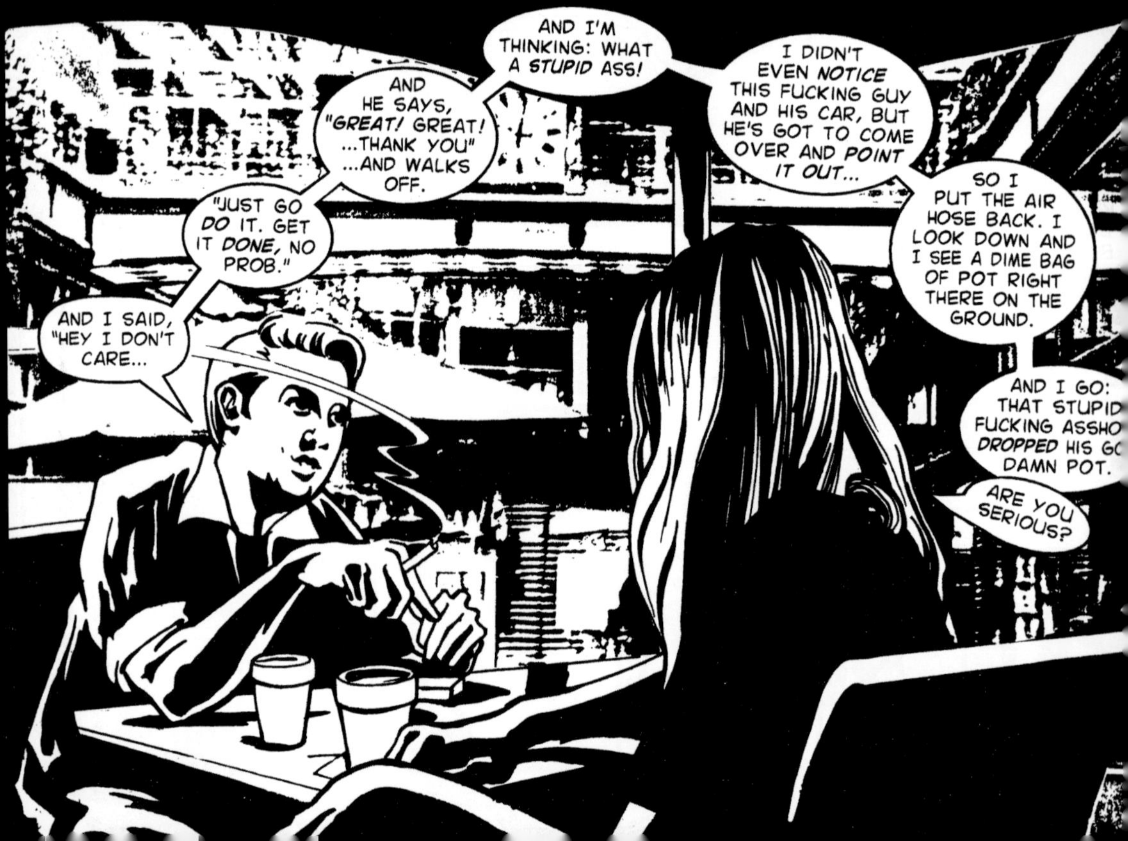
AND I SAID, "HEY I DON'T CARE...
"JUST GO *DO* IT. GET IT *DONE*, NO PROB."
AND HE SAYS, "*GREAT!* GREAT! ...THANK YOU" ...AND WALKS OFF.
AND I'M THINKING: WHAT A *STUPID* ASS!
I DIDN'T EVEN *NOTICE* THIS FUCKING GUY AND HIS CAR, BUT HE'S GOT TO COME OVER AND *POINT IT OUT*...
SO I PUT THE AIR HOSE BACK. I LOOK DOWN AND I SEE A DIME BAG OF POT RIGHT THERE ON THE GROUND.
AND I GO: THAT STUPID FUCKING ASSHO *DROPPED* HIS GO DAMN POT.
ARE YOU SERIOUS?

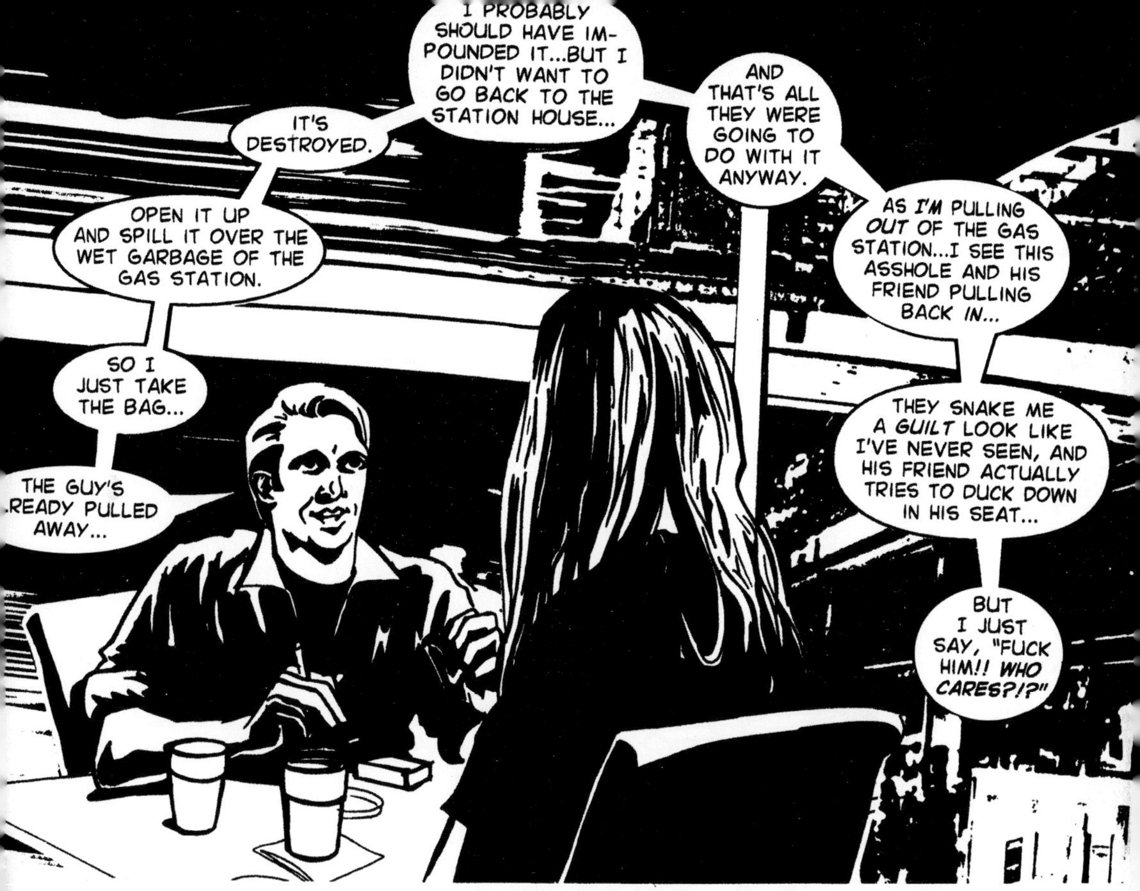
THE GUY'S
READY PULLED AWAY...
SO I JUST TAKE THE BAG...
OPEN IT UP AND SPILL IT OVER THE WET GARBAGE OF THE GAS STATION.
IT'S DESTROYED.
I PROBABLY SHOULD HAVE IM-POUNDED IT...BUT I DIDN'T WANT TO GO BACK TO THE STATION HOUSE...
AND THAT'S ALL THEY WERE GOING TO DO WITH IT ANYWAY.
AS *I'M* PULLING *OUT* OF THE GAS STATION...I SEE THIS ASSHOLE AND HIS FRIEND PULLING BACK *IN*...
THEY SNAKE ME A *GUILT* LOOK LIKE I'VE NEVER SEEN, AND HIS FRIEND ACTUALLY TRIES TO DUCK DOWN IN HIS SEAT...
BUT I JUST SAY, "FUCK HIM!! *WHO CARES?!?"*

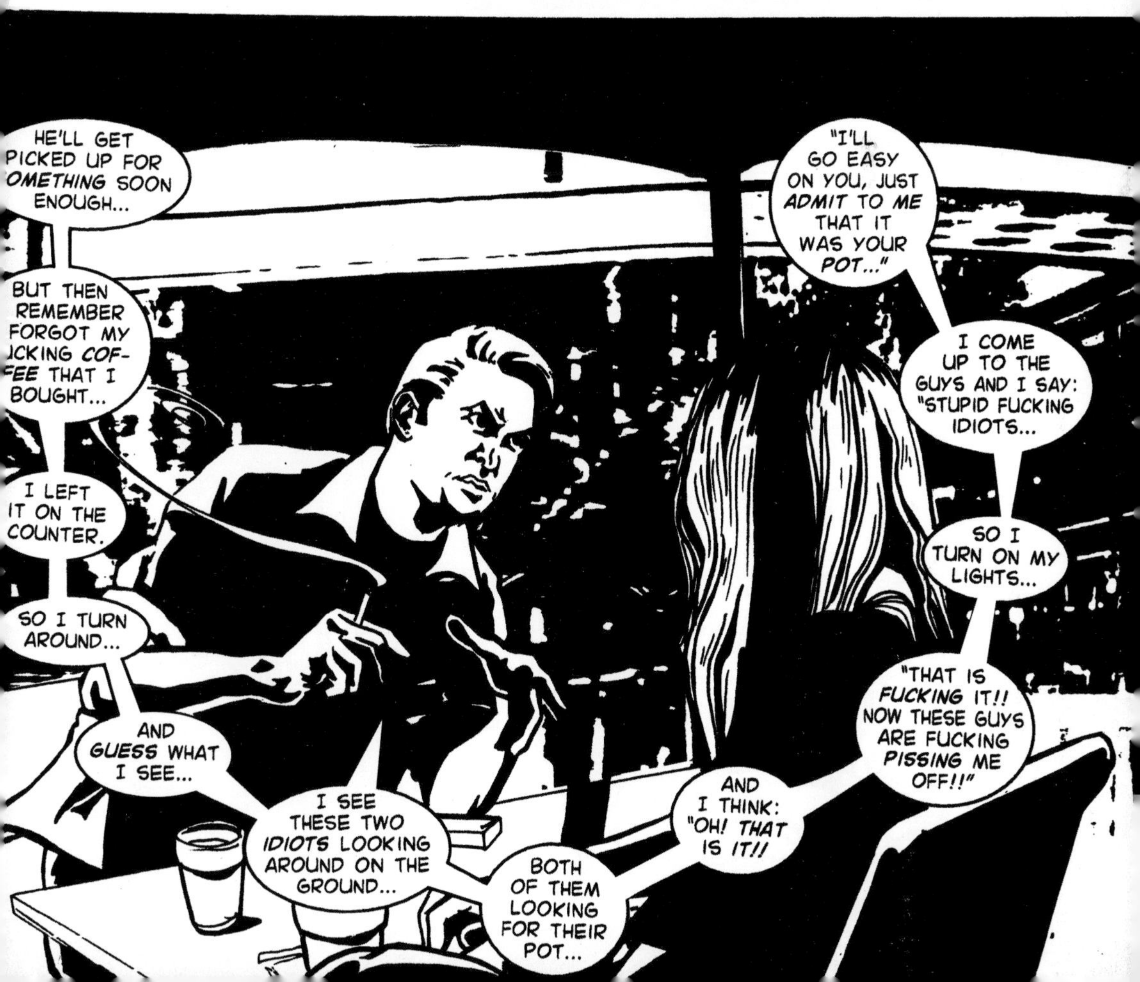
HE'LL GET PICKED UP FOR *OMETHING* SOON ENOUGH...
BUT THEN REMEMBER FORGOT MY ICKING *COF-FEE* THAT I BOUGHT...
I LEFT IT ON THE COUNTER.
SO I TURN AROUND...
AND *GUESS* WHAT I SEE...
I SEE THESE TWO *IDIOTS* LOOKING AROUND ON THE GROUND...
BOTH OF THEM LOOKING FOR THEIR POT...
AND I THINK: "OH! *THAT* IS *IT!!*
"THAT IS *FUCKING* IT!! NOW THESE GUYS ARE FUCKING *PISSING* ME OFF!!"
SO I TURN ON MY LIGHTS...
I COME UP TO THE GUYS AND I SAY: "STUPID FUCKING IDIOTS...
"I'LL GO EASY ON YOU, JUST *ADMIT* TO *ME* THAT IT WAS YOUR *POT*..."

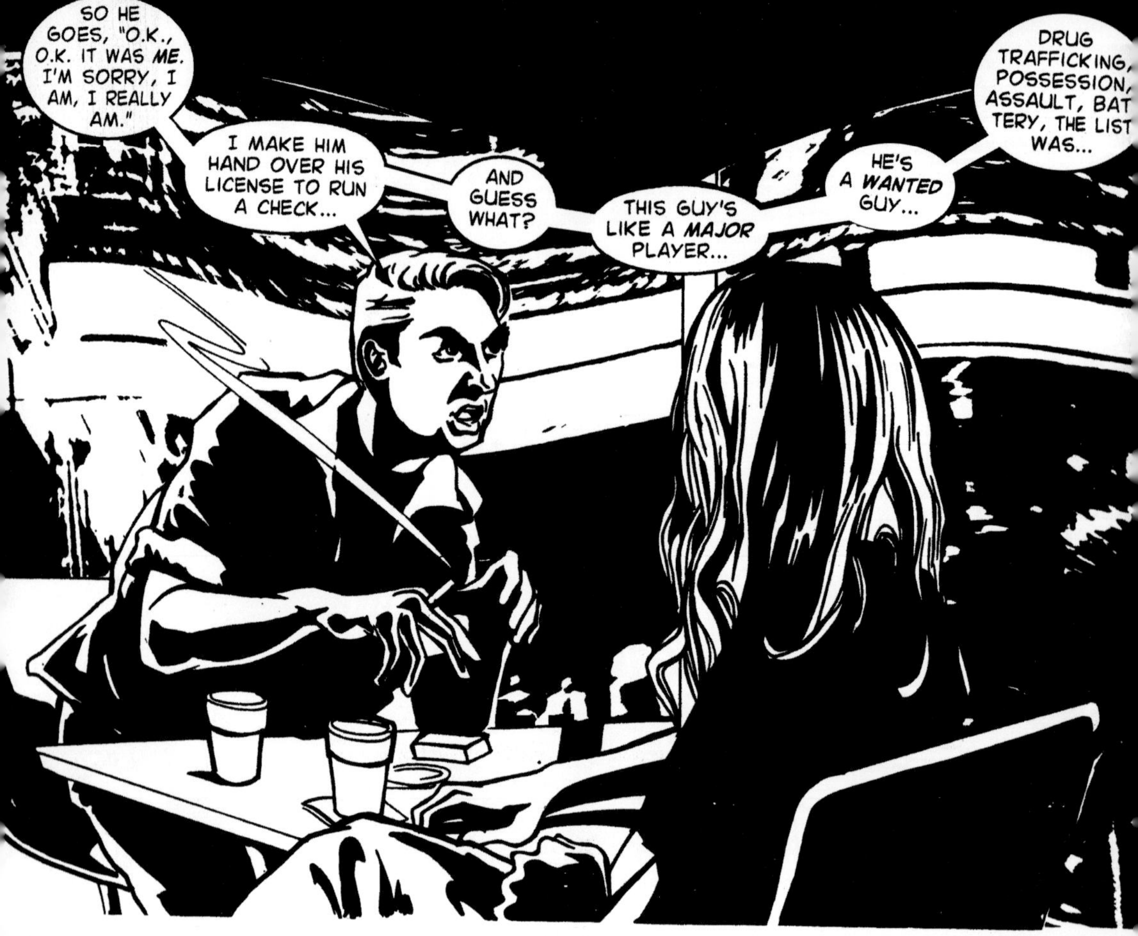
SO HE GOES, "O.K., O.K. IT WAS ME. I'M SORRY, I AM, I REALLY AM."
I MAKE HIM HAND OVER HIS LICENSE TO RUN A CHECK...
AND GUESS WHAT?
THIS GUY'S LIKE A MAJOR PLAYER...
HE'S A WANTED GUY...
DRUG TRAFFICKING, POSSESSION, ASSAULT, BATTERY, THE LIST WAS...

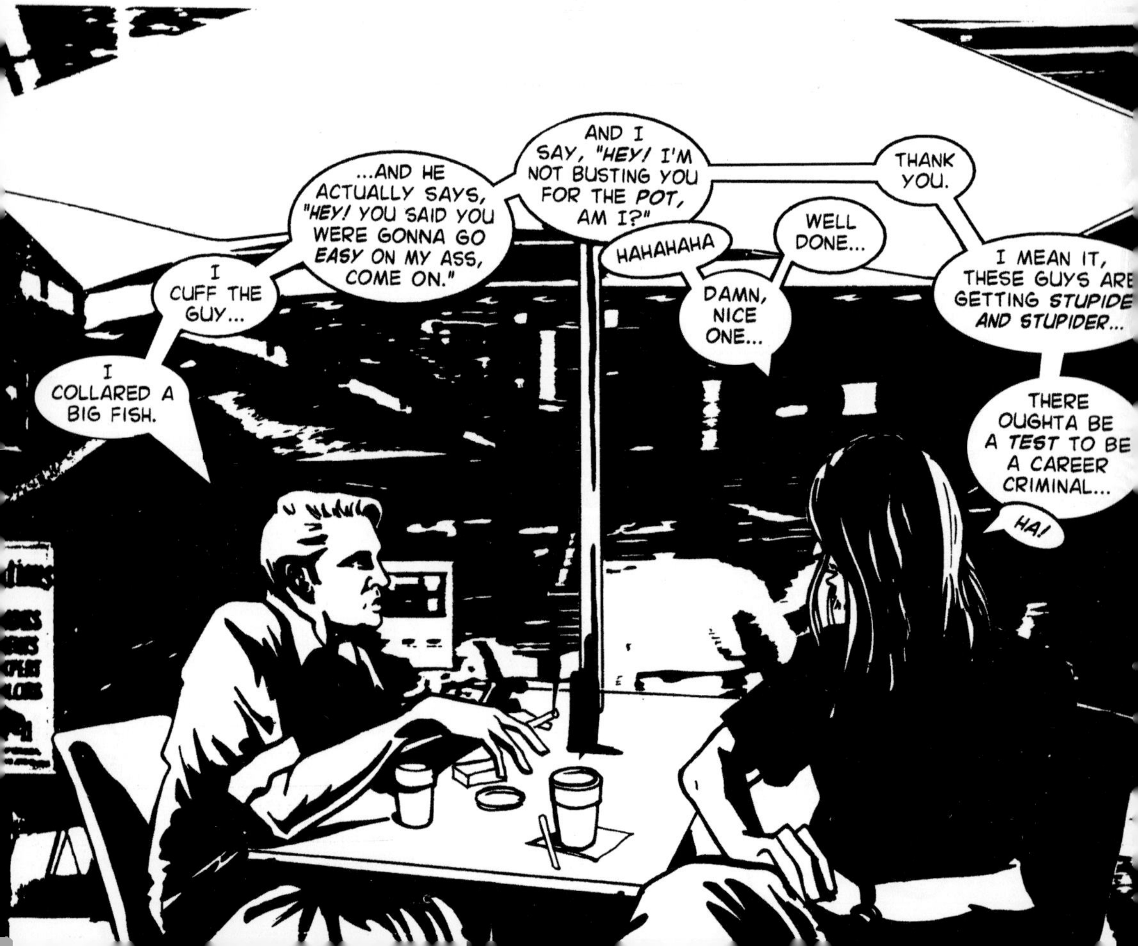
I COLLARED A BIG FISH.
I CUFF THE GUY...
...AND HE ACTUALLY SAYS, "HEY! YOU SAID YOU WERE GONNA GO EASY ON MY ASS, COME ON."
AND I SAY, "HEY! I'M NOT BUSTING YOU FOR THE POT, AM I?"
HAHAHAHA
DAMN, NICE ONE...
WELL DONE...
THANK YOU.
I MEAN IT, THESE GUYS ARE GETTING STUPIDER AND STUPIDER...
THERE OUGHTA BE A TEST TO BE A CAREER CRIMINAL...
HA!

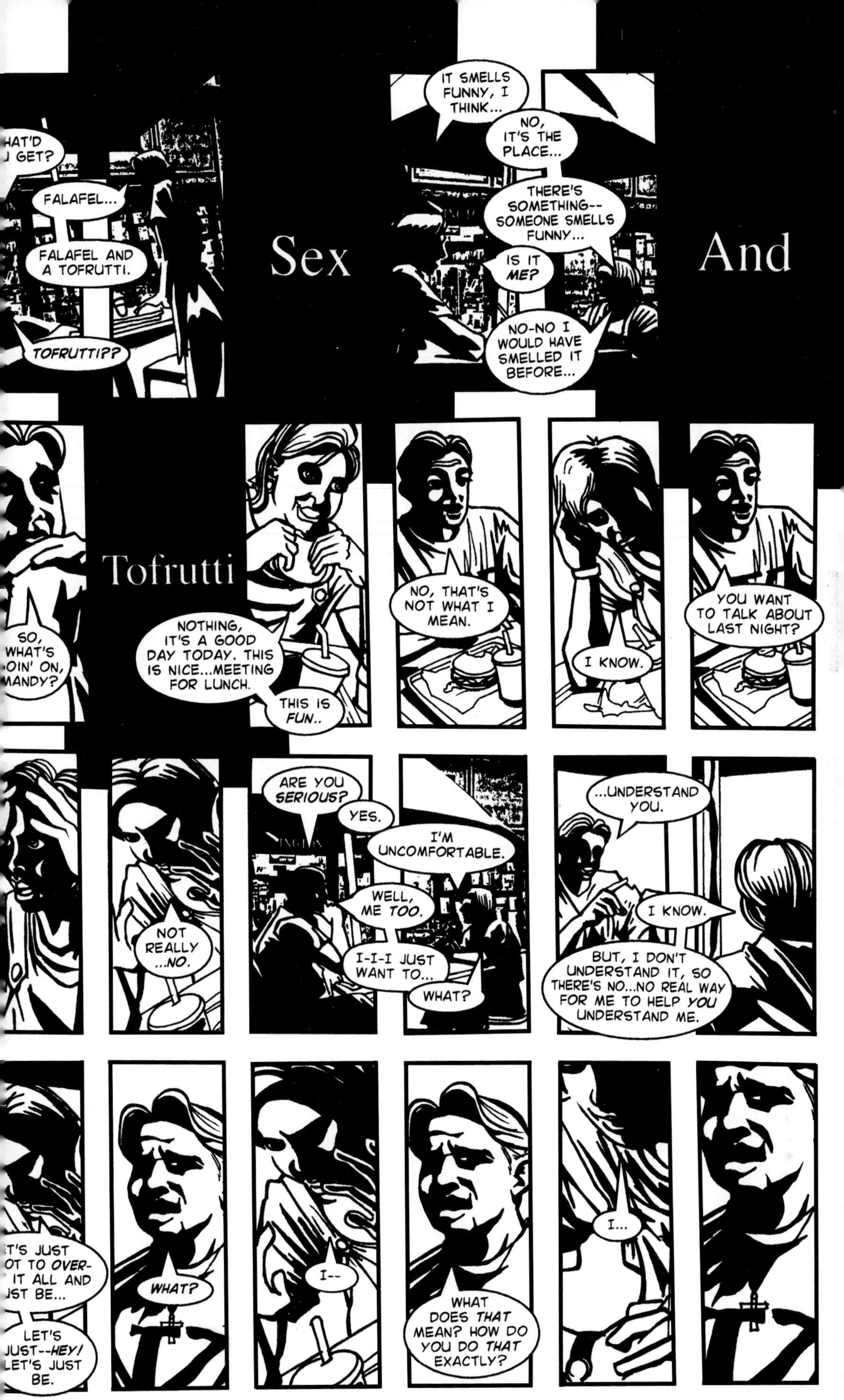

HAT'D
J GET?
FALAFEL...
FALAFEL AND A TOFRUTTI.
TOFRUTTI??
Sex
IT SMELLS FUNNY, I THINK...
NO, IT'S THE PLACE...
THERE'S SOMETHING-- SOMEONE SMELLS FUNNY...
IS IT ME?
NO-NO I WOULD HAVE SMELLED IT BEFORE...
And
Tofrutti
SO, WHAT'S OIN' ON, MANDY?
NOTHING, IT'S A GOOD DAY TODAY. THIS IS NICE...MEETING FOR LUNCH.
THIS IS FUN..
NO, THAT'S NOT WHAT I MEAN.
I KNOW.
YOU WANT TO TALK ABOUT LAST NIGHT?
NOT REALLY ...NO.
ARE YOU SERIOUS?
YES.
I'M UNCOMFORTABLE.
WELL, ME TOO.
I-I-I JUST WANT TO...
WHAT?
...UNDERSTAND YOU.
I KNOW.
BUT, I DON'T UNDERSTAND IT, SO THERE'S NO...NO REAL WAY FOR ME TO HELP YOU UNDERSTAND ME.
T'S JUST OT TO OVER- IT ALL AND JST BE...
LET'S JUST--HEY! LET'S JUST BE.
WHAT?
I--
WHAT DOES THAT MEAN? HOW DO YOU DO THAT EXACTLY?
I...

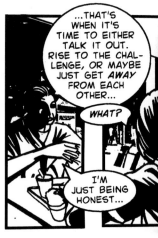

I HAVEN'T PUSHED YOU. I HAVEN'T PRODDED AT YOU.

I--WE'VE BOTH JUST SORT OF ENJOYED THIS. AND THAT'S COOL.

BUT WHEN SHIT HAPPENS LIKE LAST NIGHT...

...THAT'S WHEN IT'S TIME TO EITHER TALK IT OUT. RISE TO THE CHALLENGE, OR MAYBE JUST GET AWAY FROM EACH OTHER...

WHAT?

I'M JUST BEING HONEST...

IS THAT LIKE AN ULTIMATUM?

NO, IT'S JUST.

IT SOUNDS LIKE.

IT'S JUST PRAGMATISM. IT'S FACT.

IT'S TIME TO OPEN UP.

NOW IS THE TIME.

IF YOU DON'T, IT'LL EAT AT US.

IT'LL EAT AT ME.

YOU'LL KNOW IT EATING ME...

AND IT'LL EAT AT US.

AND YOU KNOW WHAT?

I THINK IT'S EATING AT YOU TOO.

I THINK YOU WANT TO TALK ABOUT IT OR YOU WOULDN'T EVEN BE HERE.

YOU KNOW WHAT I'M SAYING...

I KNOW YOU DO.

YOU KNOW...

I THINK. YES, I TH I DO.

I THINK THINGS...A LOT...

I'VE--THERE'S THINGS, THERE'S THOUGHTS THAT I...

IT'S ALL RIGHT...

THAT SCARE ME. THAT CON--SOMETIMES CONSUME ME...

THIS--THIS IS HARD.

I-I'VE NOT SAID THESE THINGS OUT LOUD BEFORE...AND THE WORDS...

THEY DON'T ALWAYS...

I KNOW...

THEY DON'T ALWAYS FIT.

JUST... IT'S O.K.

YOU AR THE LONG I'VE EVER WITH ON GUY...

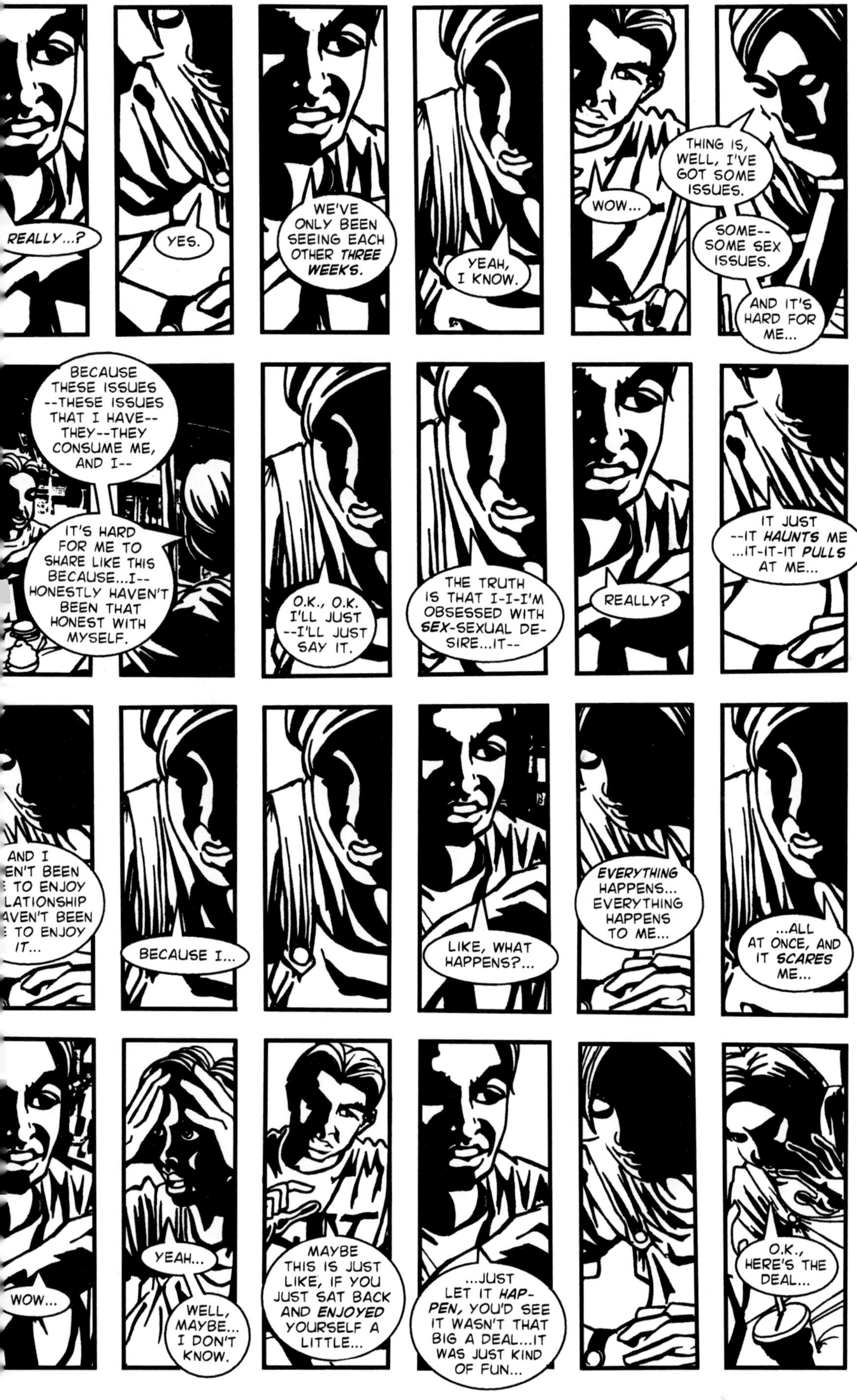

REALLY...?
YES.
WE'VE ONLY BEEN SEEING EACH OTHER THREE WEEKS.
YEAH, I KNOW.
WOW...
THING IS, WELL, I'VE GOT SOME ISSUES.
SOME-- SOME SEX ISSUES.
AND IT'S HARD FOR ME...
BECAUSE THESE ISSUES --THESE ISSUES THAT I HAVE-- THEY--THEY CONSUME ME, AND I--
IT'S HARD FOR ME TO SHARE LIKE THIS BECAUSE...I-- HONESTLY HAVEN'T BEEN THAT HONEST WITH MYSELF.
O.K., O.K. I'LL JUST --I'LL JUST SAY IT.
THE TRUTH IS THAT I-I-I'M OBSESSED WITH SEX-SEXUAL DE-SIRE...IT--
REALLY?
IT JUST --IT HAUNTS ME ...IT-IT-IT PULLS AT ME...
AND I
EN'T BEEN
TO ENJOY
LATIONSHIP
AVEN'T BEEN
TO ENJOY
IT...
BECAUSE I...
LIKE, WHAT HAPPENS?...
EVERYTHING HAPPENS... EVERYTHING HAPPENS TO ME...
...ALL AT ONCE, AND IT SCARES ME...
WOW...
YEAH...
WELL, MAYBE... I DON'T KNOW.
MAYBE THIS IS JUST LIKE, IF YOU JUST SAT BACK AND ENJOYED YOURSELF A LITTLE...
...JUST LET IT HAP-PEN, YOU'D SEE IT WASN'T THAT BIG A DEAL...IT WAS JUST KIND OF FUN...
O.K., HERE'S THE DEAL...

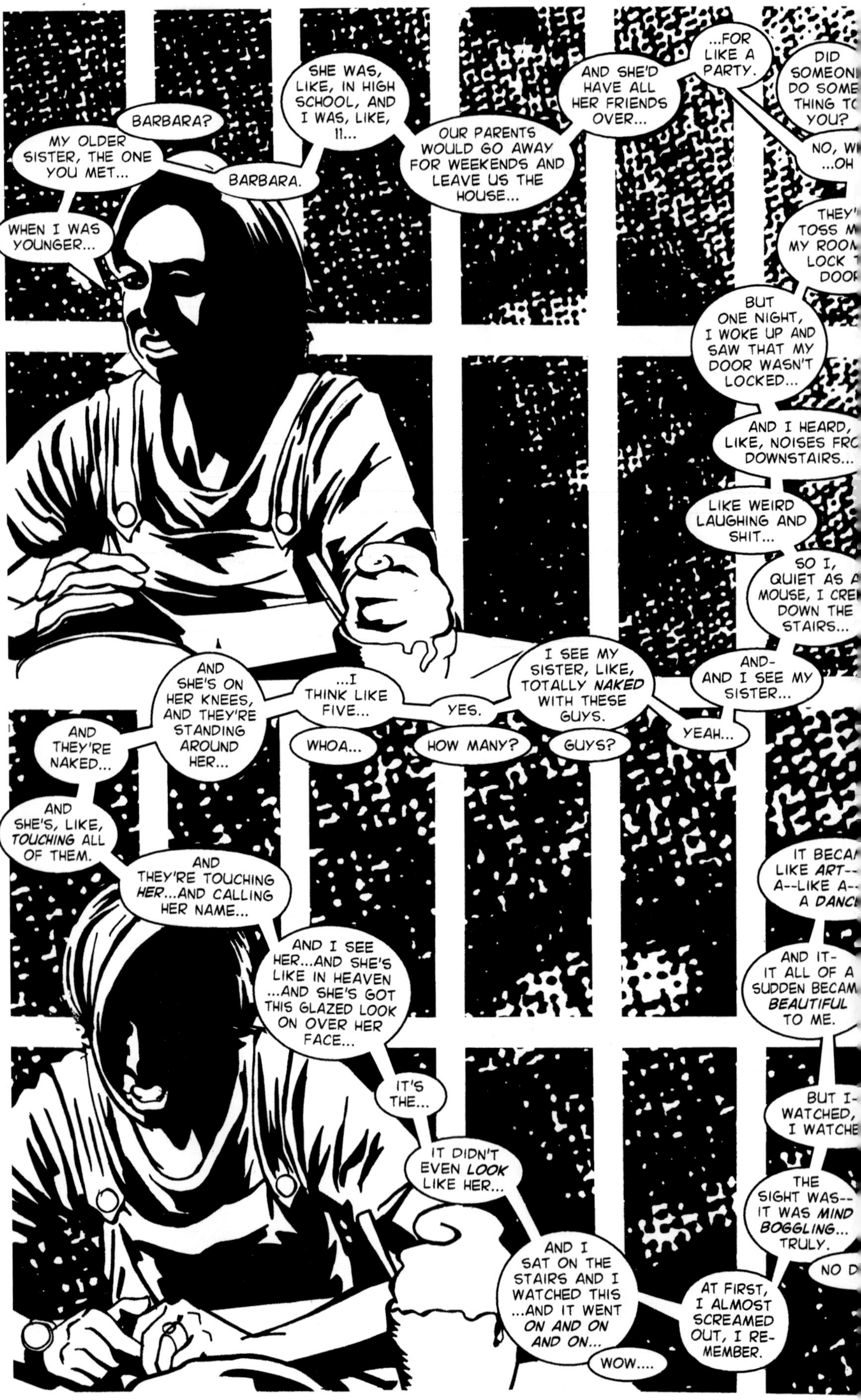
MY OLDER SISTER, THE ONE YOU MET...
BARBARA?
BARBARA.
WHEN I WAS YOUNGER...
SHE WAS, LIKE, IN HIGH SCHOOL, AND I WAS, LIKE, 11...
OUR PARENTS WOULD GO AWAY FOR WEEKENDS AND LEAVE US THE HOUSE...
AND SHE'D HAVE ALL HER FRIENDS OVER...
...FOR LIKE A PARTY.
DID SOMEON DO SOME THING TC YOU?
NO, W ...OH
THEY' TOSS M MY ROOM LOCK T DOOF
BUT ONE NIGHT, I WOKE UP AND SAW THAT MY DOOR WASN'T LOCKED...
AND I HEARD, LIKE, NOISES FRC DOWNSTAIRS...
LIKE WEIRD LAUGHING AND SHIT...
SO I, QUIET AS A MOUSE, I CRE DOWN THE STAIRS...
AND- AND I SEE MY SISTER...
YEAH...
I SEE MY SISTER, LIKE, TOTALLY *NAKED* WITH THESE GUYS.
GUYS?
YES.
HOW MANY?
...I THINK LIKE FIVE...
WHOA...
AND SHE'S ON HER KNEES, AND THEY'RE STANDING AROUND HER...
AND THEY'RE NAKED...
AND SHE'S, LIKE, *TOUCHING* ALL OF THEM.
AND THEY'RE TOUCHING *HER*...AND CALLING HER NAME...
AND I SEE HER...AND SHE'S LIKE IN HEAVEN ...AND SHE'S GOT THIS GLAZED LOOK ON OVER HER FACE...
IT'S THE...
IT DIDN'T EVEN *LOOK* LIKE HER...
AND I SAT ON THE STAIRS AND I WATCHED THIS ...AND IT WENT *ON AND ON AND ON...*
WOW....
AT FIRST, I ALMOST SCREAMED OUT, I RE- MEMBER.
IT BECA LIKE *ART*-- A--LIKE A-- A *DANC*
AND IT- IT ALL OF A SUDDEN BECAM *BEAUTIFUL* TO ME.
BUT I- WATCHED, I WATCHE
THE SIGHT WAS-- IT WAS *MIND BOGGLING*... TRULY.
NO D

I'D NEVER SEEN MY SISTER LOOK SO BEAUTIFUL.

HUH.

SO...

SO MY SISTER IS TRULY AN UNHAPPY PERSON.

YOU'VE MET HER, SHE IS A MISERABLE, UNTRUSTING LOSER.

SO, THE FACT OF THE MATTER THAT I...I HAVEN'T A SEXUAL EXPERIENCE, A SEXUAL THOUGHT...

...WHERE THIS IMAGE, THAT FEELING, THE LOOK ON HER FACE DIDN'T POP INTO MY HEAD...

I-- YOU'RE LOSING ME ON THE BIG PICTURE HERE.

O-- O.K. YOU WANT THE TRUTH...

HERE-HERE IT IS...

I...

I-I-I-DON'T BELIEVE IN GOD.

I DON'T BELIEVE IN HEAVEN. I DON'T BELIEVE IN HELL OR-OR THE DEVIL.

I DON'T BELIEVE IN ANY OF THAT SHIT...

WHAT I DO BELIEVE IN. WHAT I DO DESIRE...WHAT I DO BELIEVE IS REAL...

IS TOUCH.

IS PHYSICAL TOUCH.

I NEED TO-- TO BE HELD AND EX-EXPLORED...

I FIND THAT IT'S ALL I WANT...

IT'S ALL I WANT.

IT'S-IT'S ALL I WANT.

SO, JUST-JUST ALLOW...

NO!! DON'T YOU SEE...?

THAT CAN'T BE ENOUGH.

THAT CAN'T BE IT.

I'VE GOTTA AIM HIGHER, DON'T YOU THINK?

THAN WHAT...?

WHAT?

AIM HIGHER THAN WHAT?

...MAKING YOURSELF HAPPY?

SEE, I DON'T UNDERSTAND YOUR LOGIC.

THE ONE THING YOU *WANT*, THE ONE THING YOU SAY YOU *"BELIEVE"* IN, YOU'RE GOING TO *DENY* YOURSELF...

...BECAUSE YOUR *SISTER* WAS A SLUT IN HIGH SCHOOL AND MARRIED *BADLY*??

NO...

WELL, I-I DON'T THINK-- LISTEN TO THIS... I DON'T THINK *IT IS* THE *ONLY* THING YOU WANT IN LIFE...

I DON'T THINK *IT IS* THE ONLY THING YOU *"BELIEVE"* IN...

WHADAYA THINK OF *THAT?*

I THINK IT'S THE ONLY THING YOU *THINK* ABOUT BECAUSE YOU DENY YOURSELF IT.

HEY!! YOU SAW WHAT HAPPENED LAST NIGHT?

YEAH, I DID...

IT WAS GODDAMN *AMAZING*...

IT WAS *INSANE.*

I KNOW. SO?

SO!!

SO *WHAT??* SO *FUCKIN'* WHAT?

I HATE TO BREAK IT TO YOU, BUT IT'S *SUPPOSED* TO...

I...

IT'S *SUPPOSED* TO BE OUT OF CONTROL.

I...

IT'S SUPPOSED TO BE *WILD* AND UNEXPLAINABLE.

I...

LE YOUR GO

TREAT YOURSELF.

ARE YOU *SCARED* OF IT BECAUSE OF *ME?*

A LITTLE.

WHY?

WHY? 'CAUSE I GET--I GET VERY *COMFORTABLE*...

I GET VERY *RELAXED* AROUND YOU.

I-I LET MY GUARD DOWN...

AND-AND-A I LOSE CONT AND THEN

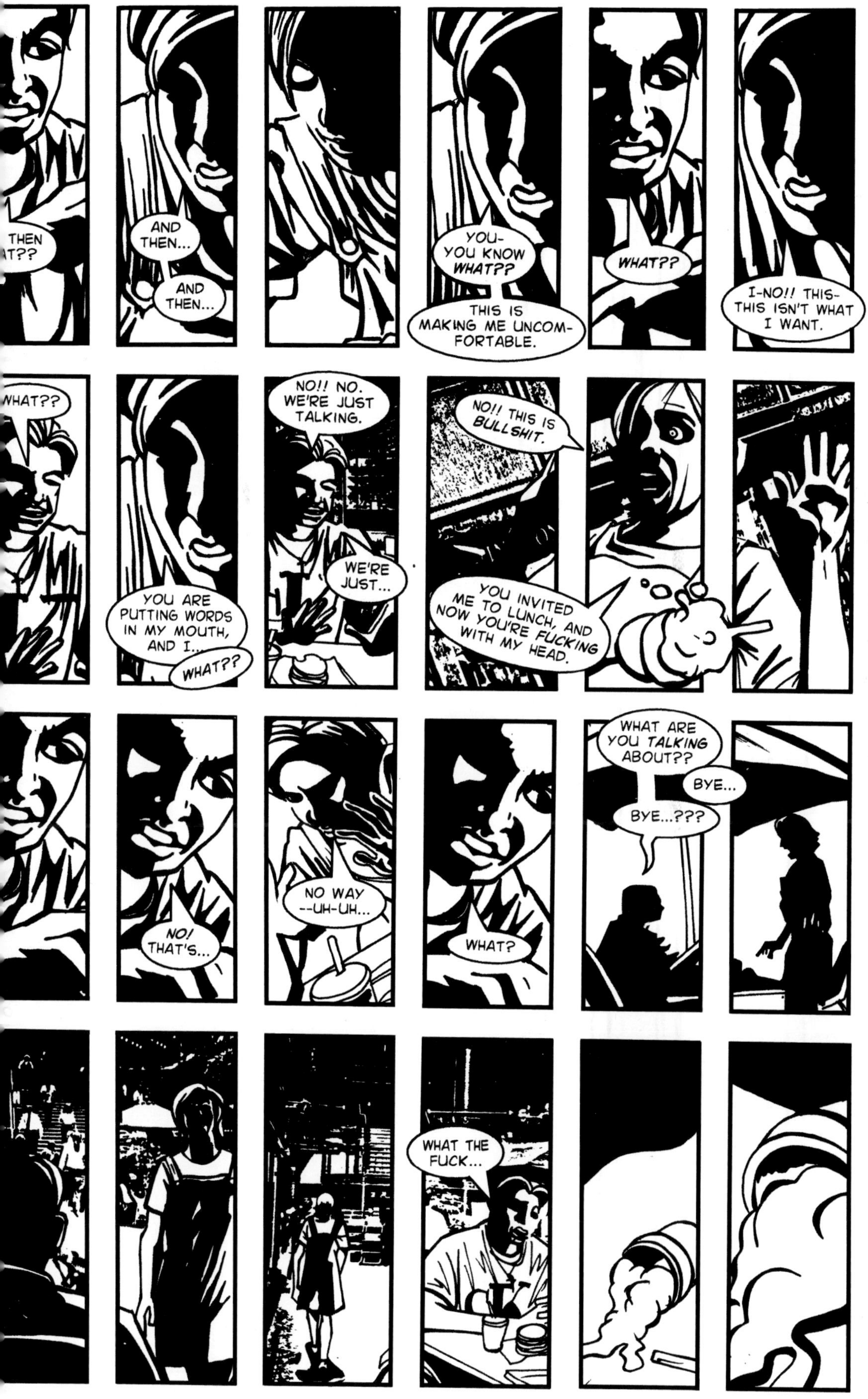
THEN
T??
AND THEN...
AND THEN...
YOU- YOU KNOW WHAT??
THIS IS MAKING ME UNCOMFORTABLE.
WHAT??
I-NO!! THIS- THIS ISN'T WHAT I WANT.
WHAT??
YOU ARE PUTTING WORDS IN MY MOUTH, AND I...
WHAT??
NO!! NO. WE'RE JUST TALKING.
WE'RE JUST...
NO!! THIS IS BULLSHIT.
YOU INVITED ME TO LUNCH, AND NOW YOU'RE FUCKING WITH MY HEAD.
NO! THAT'S...
NO WAY --UH-UH...
WHAT?
WHAT ARE YOU TALKING ABOUT??
BYE...
BYE...???
WHAT THE FUCK...

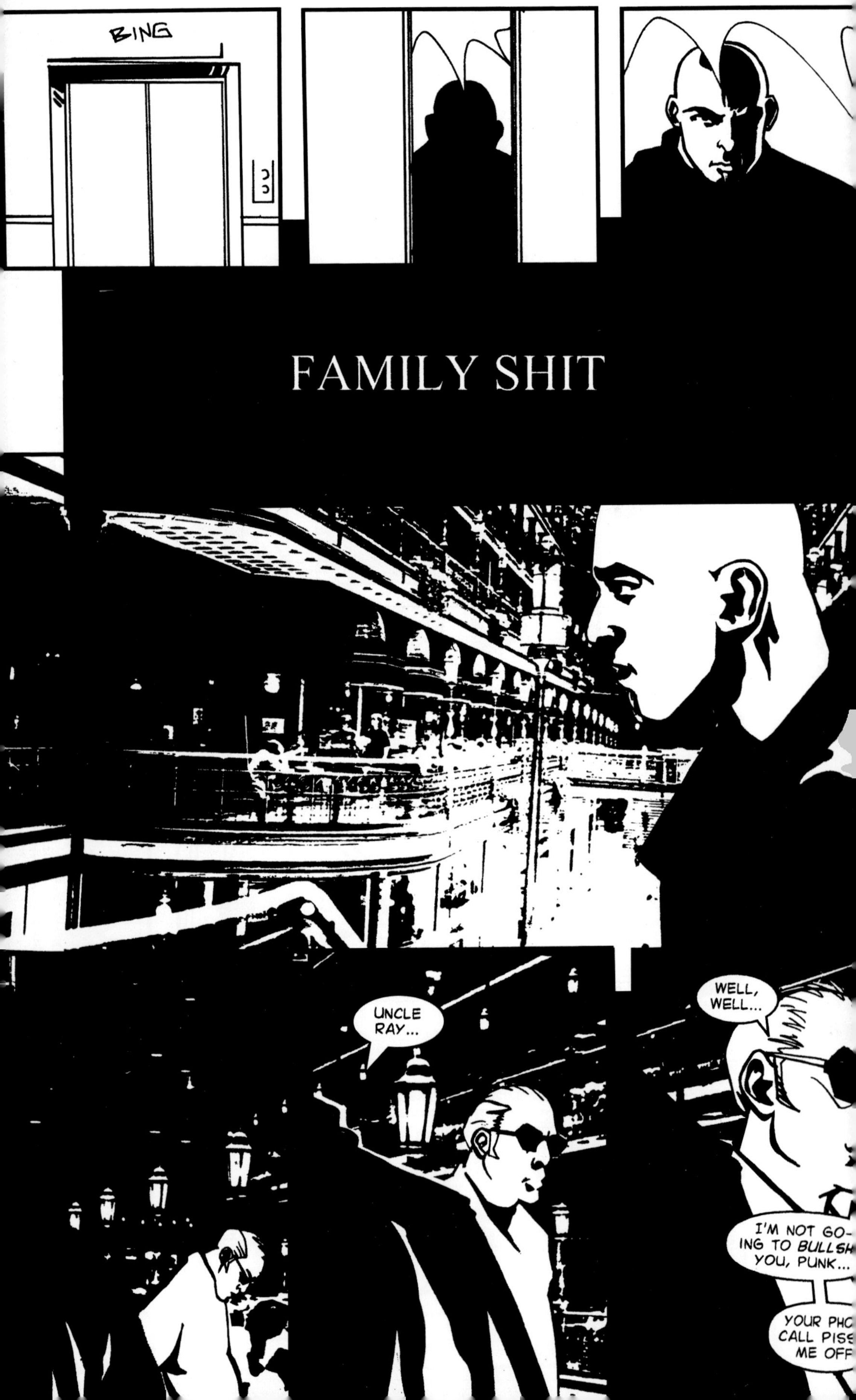
BING
FAMILY SHIT
UNCLE RAY...
WELL, WELL...
I'M NOT GO-ING TO BULLSH YOU, PUNK...
YOUR PHO CALL PISS ME OFF

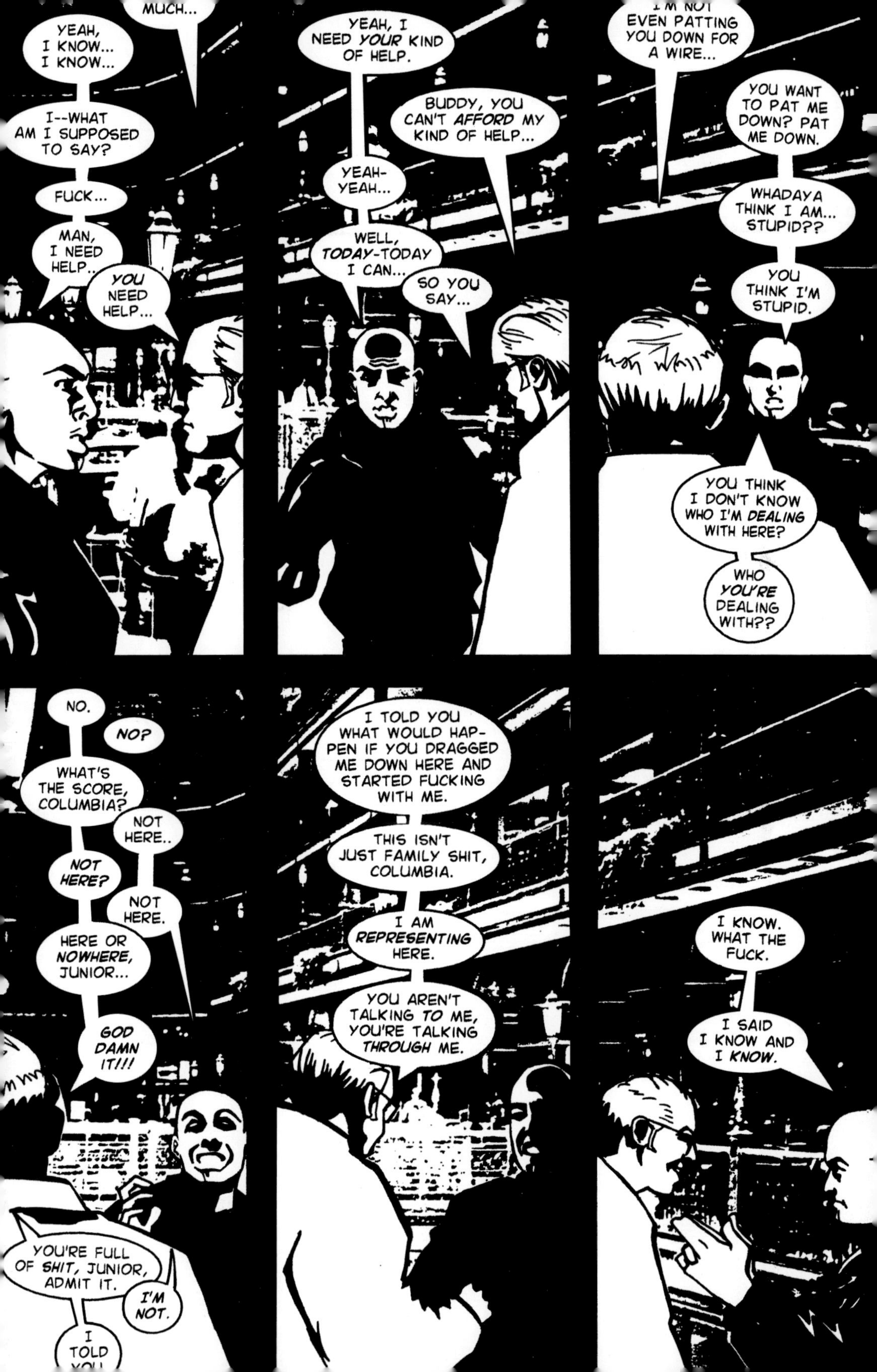
MUCH...
YEAH, I KNOW... I KNOW...
I--WHAT AM I SUPPOSED TO SAY?
FUCK...
MAN, I NEED HELP...
YOU NEED HELP...
YEAH, I NEED YOUR KIND OF HELP.
BUDDY, YOU CAN'T AFFORD MY KIND OF HELP...
YEAH-YEAH...
WELL, TODAY-TODAY I CAN...
SO YOU SAY...
EVEN PATTING YOU DOWN FOR A WIRE...
YOU WANT TO PAT ME DOWN? PAT ME DOWN.
WHADAYA THINK I AM... STUPID??
YOU THINK I'M STUPID.
YOU THINK I DON'T KNOW WHO I'M DEALING WITH HERE?
WHO YOU'RE DEALING WITH??
NO.
NO?
WHAT'S THE SCORE, COLUMBIA?
NOT HERE..
NOT HERE?
NOT HERE.
HERE OR NOWHERE, JUNIOR...
GOD DAMN IT!!!
YOU'RE FULL OF SHIT, JUNIOR, ADMIT IT.
I'M NOT.
I TOLD YOU
I TOLD YOU WHAT WOULD HAP-PEN IF YOU DRAGGED ME DOWN HERE AND STARTED FUCKING WITH ME.
THIS ISN'T JUST FAMILY SHIT, COLUMBIA.
I AM REPRESENTING HERE.
YOU AREN'T TALKING TO ME, YOU'RE TALKING THROUGH ME.
I KNOW. WHAT THE FUCK.
I SAID I KNOW AND I KNOW.

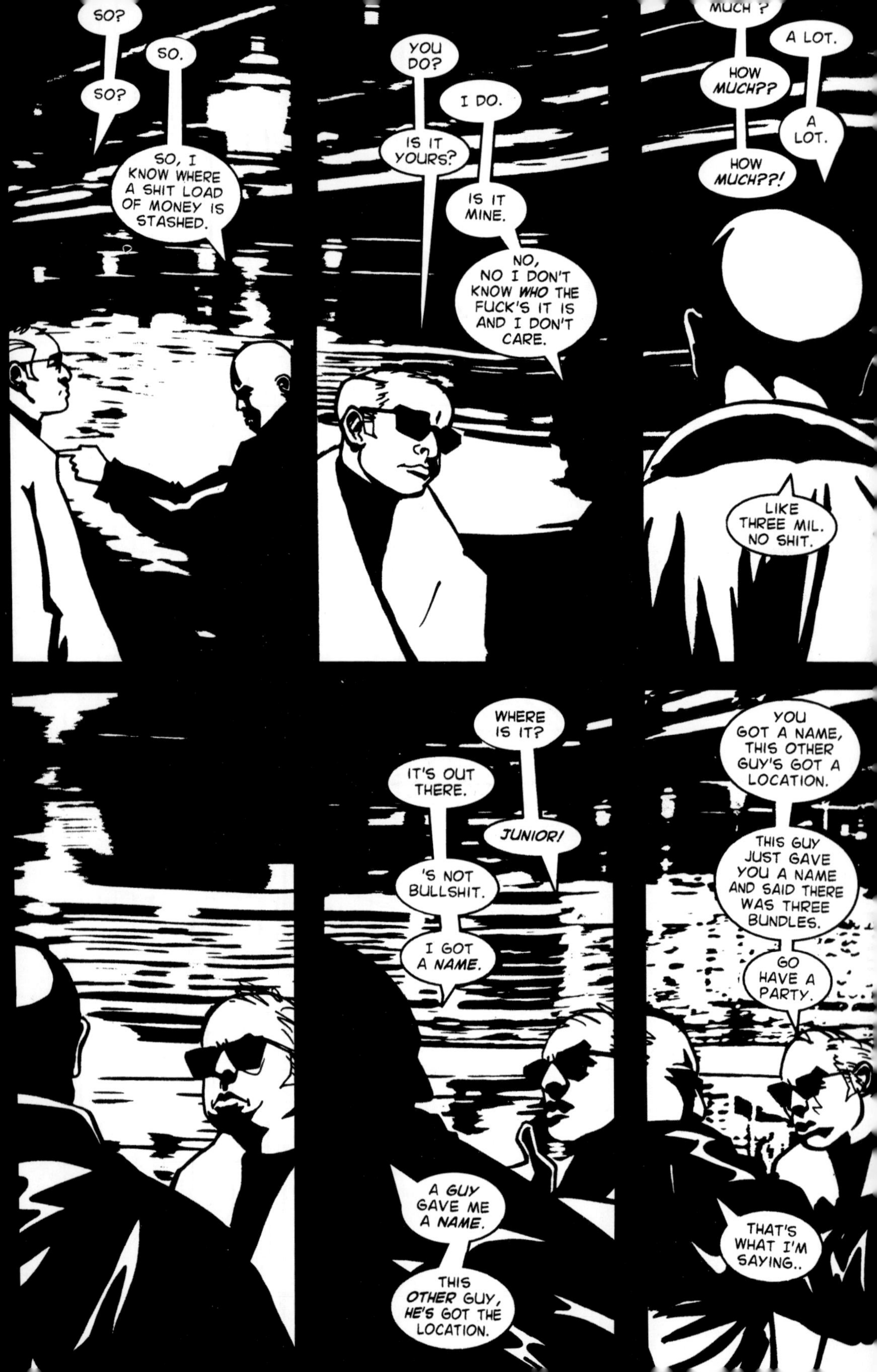
SO?
SO.
SO?
SO, I KNOW WHERE A SHIT LOAD OF MONEY IS STASHED.
YOU DO?
I DO.
IS IT YOURS?
IS IT MINE.
NO, NO I DON'T KNOW WHO THE FUCK'S IT IS AND I DON'T CARE.
MUCH ?
A LOT.
HOW MUCH??
A LOT.
HOW MUCH??!
LIKE THREE MIL. NO SHIT.
WHERE IS IT?
IT'S OUT THERE.
JUNIOR!
'S NOT BULLSHIT.
I GOT A NAME.
A GUY GAVE ME A NAME.
THIS OTHER GUY, HE'S GOT THE LOCATION.
YOU GOT A NAME, THIS OTHER GUY'S GOT A LOCATION.
THIS GUY JUST GAVE YOU A NAME AND SAID THERE WAS THREE BUNDLES.
GO HAVE A PARTY.
THAT'S WHAT I'M SAYING..

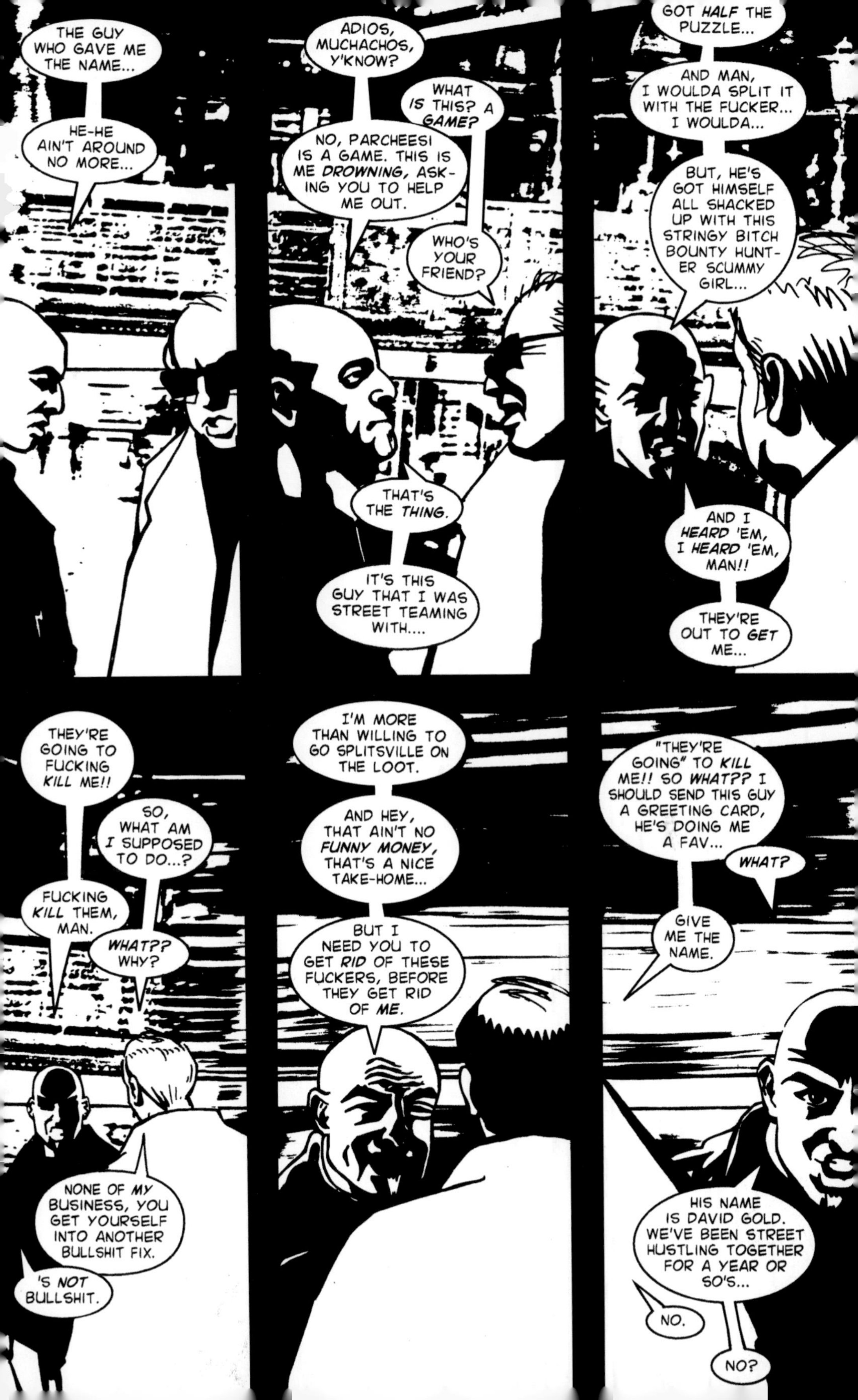
THE GUY WHO GAVE ME THE NAME...
HE-HE AIN'T AROUND NO MORE...
ADIOS, MUCHACHOS, Y'KNOW?
WHAT IS THIS? A GAME?
NO, PARCHEESI IS A GAME. THIS IS ME DROWNING, ASKING YOU TO HELP ME OUT.
WHO'S YOUR FRIEND?
THAT'S THE THING.
IT'S THIS GUY THAT I WAS STREET TEAMING WITH....
GOT HALF THE PUZZLE...
AND MAN, I WOULDA SPLIT IT WITH THE FUCKER... I WOULDA...
BUT, HE'S GOT HIMSELF ALL SHACKED UP WITH THIS STRINGY BITCH BOUNTY HUNTER SCUMMY GIRL...
AND I HEARD 'EM, I HEARD 'EM, MAN!!
THEY'RE OUT TO GET ME...
THEY'RE GOING TO FUCKING KILL ME!!
SO, WHAT AM I SUPPOSED TO DO...?
FUCKING KILL THEM, MAN.
WHAT?? WHY?
NONE OF MY BUSINESS, YOU GET YOURSELF INTO ANOTHER BULLSHIT FIX.
'S NOT BULLSHIT.
I'M MORE THAN WILLING TO GO SPLITSVILLE ON THE LOOT.
AND HEY, THAT AIN'T NO FUNNY MONEY, THAT'S A NICE TAKE-HOME...
BUT I NEED YOU TO GET RID OF THESE FUCKERS, BEFORE THEY GET RID OF ME.
"THEY'RE GOING" TO KILL ME!! SO WHAT?? I SHOULD SEND THIS GUY A GREETING CARD, HE'S DOING ME A FAV...
WHAT?
GIVE ME THE NAME.
HIS NAME IS DAVID GOLD. WE'VE BEEN STREET HUSTLING TOGETHER FOR A YEAR OR SO'S...
NO.
NO?

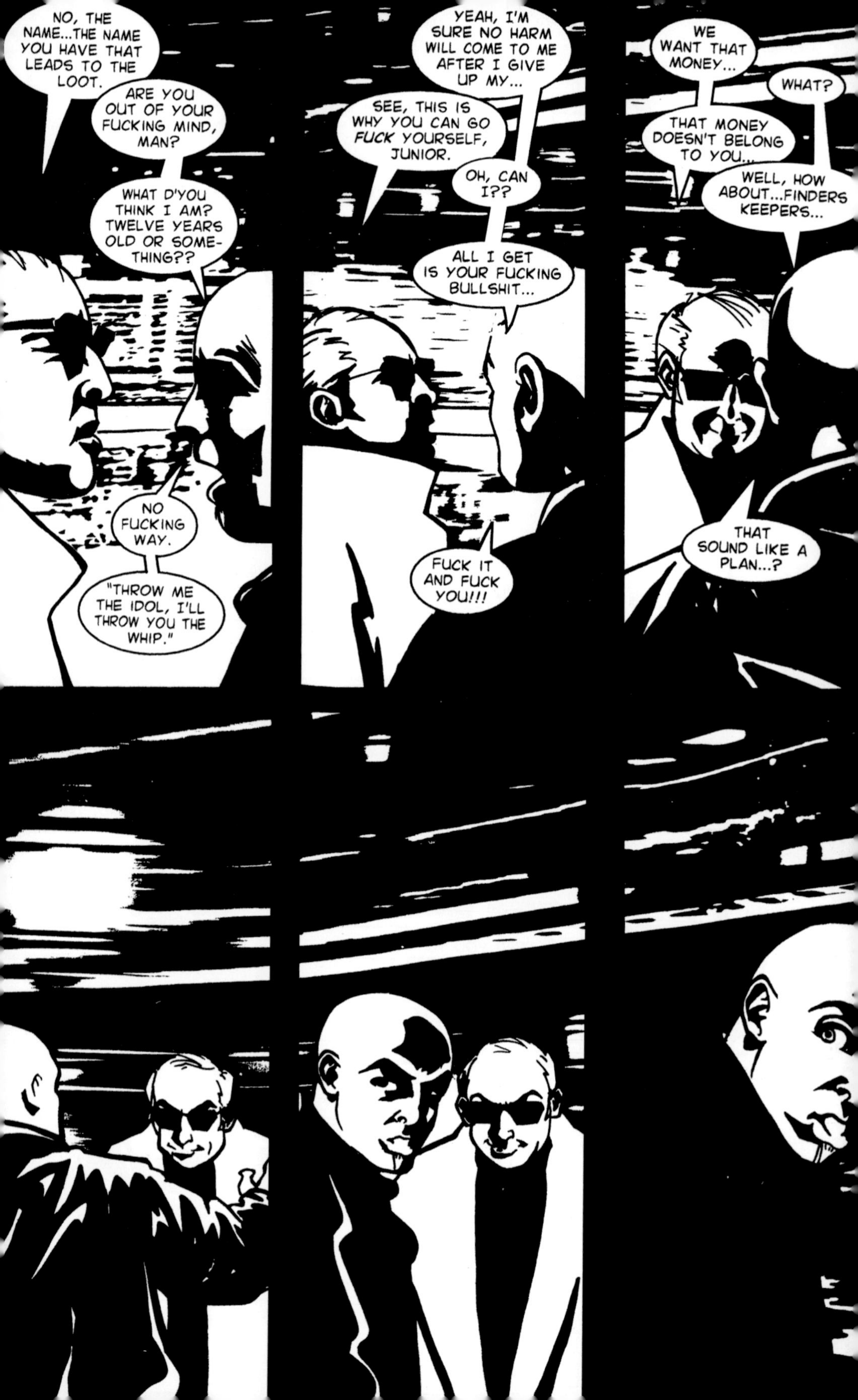
NO, THE NAME...THE NAME YOU HAVE THAT LEADS TO THE LOOT.
ARE YOU OUT OF YOUR FUCKING MIND, MAN?
WHAT D'YOU THINK I AM? TWELVE YEARS OLD OR SOME-THING??
NO FUCKING WAY.
"THROW ME THE IDOL, I'LL THROW YOU THE WHIP."
YEAH, I'M SURE NO HARM WILL COME TO ME AFTER I GIVE UP MY...
SEE, THIS IS WHY YOU CAN GO FUCK YOURSELF, JUNIOR.
OH, CAN I??
ALL I GET IS YOUR FUCKING BULLSHIT...
FUCK IT AND FUCK YOU!!!
WE WANT THAT MONEY...
WHAT?
THAT MONEY DOESN'T BELONG TO YOU...
WELL, HOW ABOUT...FINDERS KEEPERS...
THAT SOUND LIKE A PLAN...?

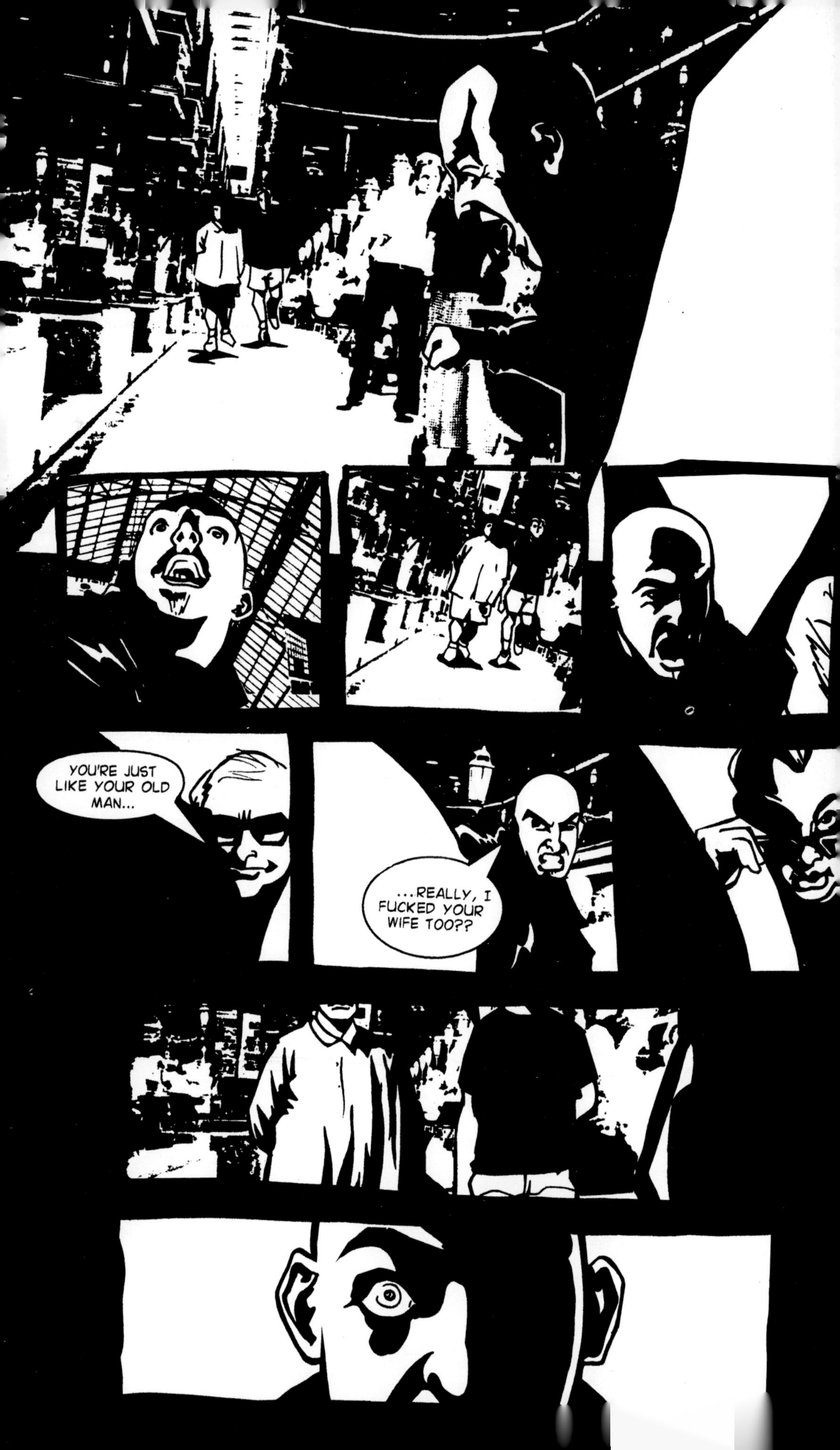
YOU'RE JUST LIKE YOUR OLD MAN...
...REALLY, I FUCKED YOUR WIFE TOO??

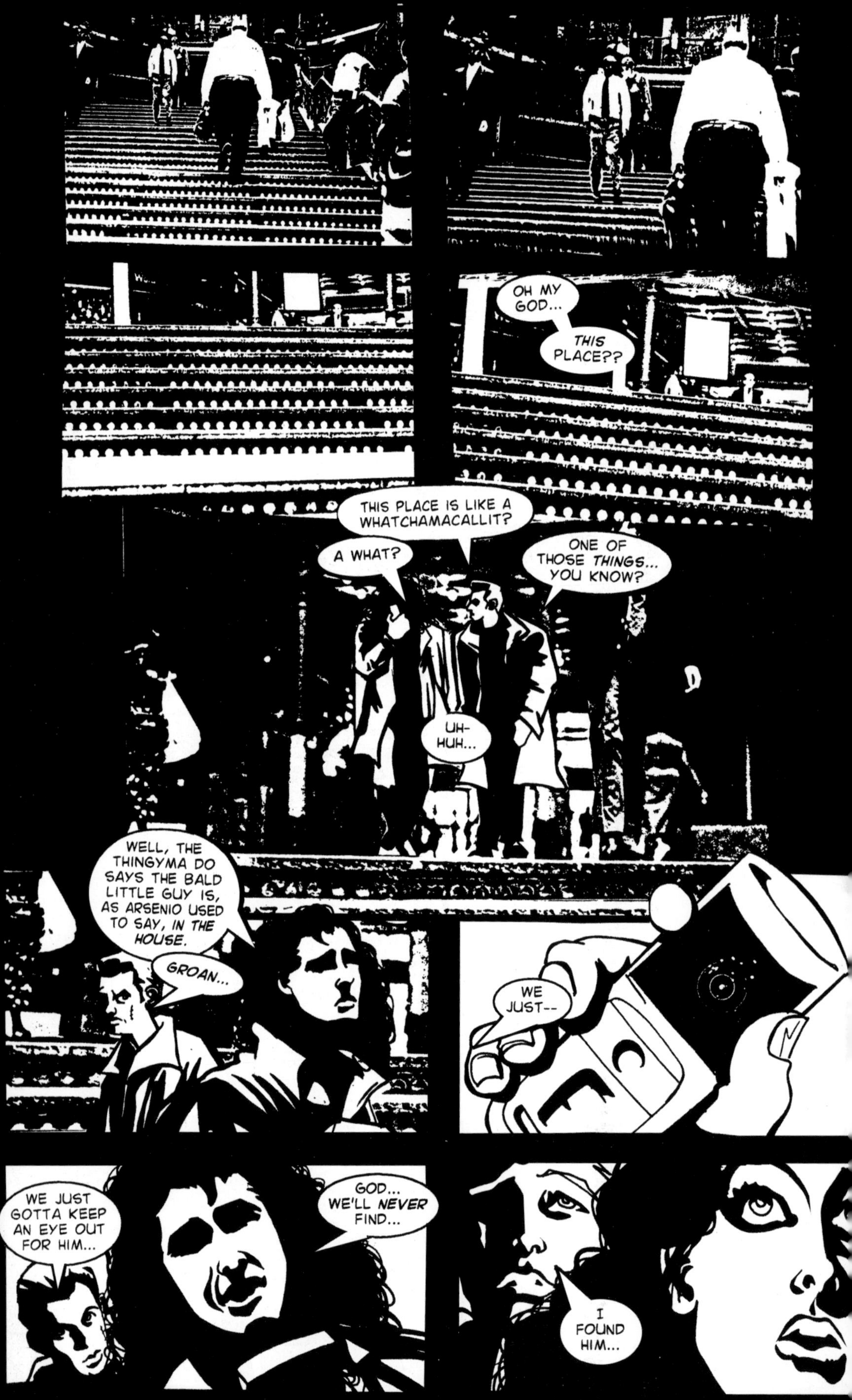
OH MY GOD...
THIS PLACE??
THIS PLACE IS LIKE A WHATCHAMACALLIT?
A WHAT?
ONE OF THOSE THINGS... YOU KNOW?
UH-HUH...
WELL, THE THINGYMA DO SAYS THE BALD LITTLE GUY IS, AS ARSENIO USED TO SAY, IN THE HOUSE.
GROAN...
WE JUST--
WE JUST GOTTA KEEP AN EYE OUT FOR HIM...
GOD... WE'LL NEVER FIND...
I FOUND HIM...

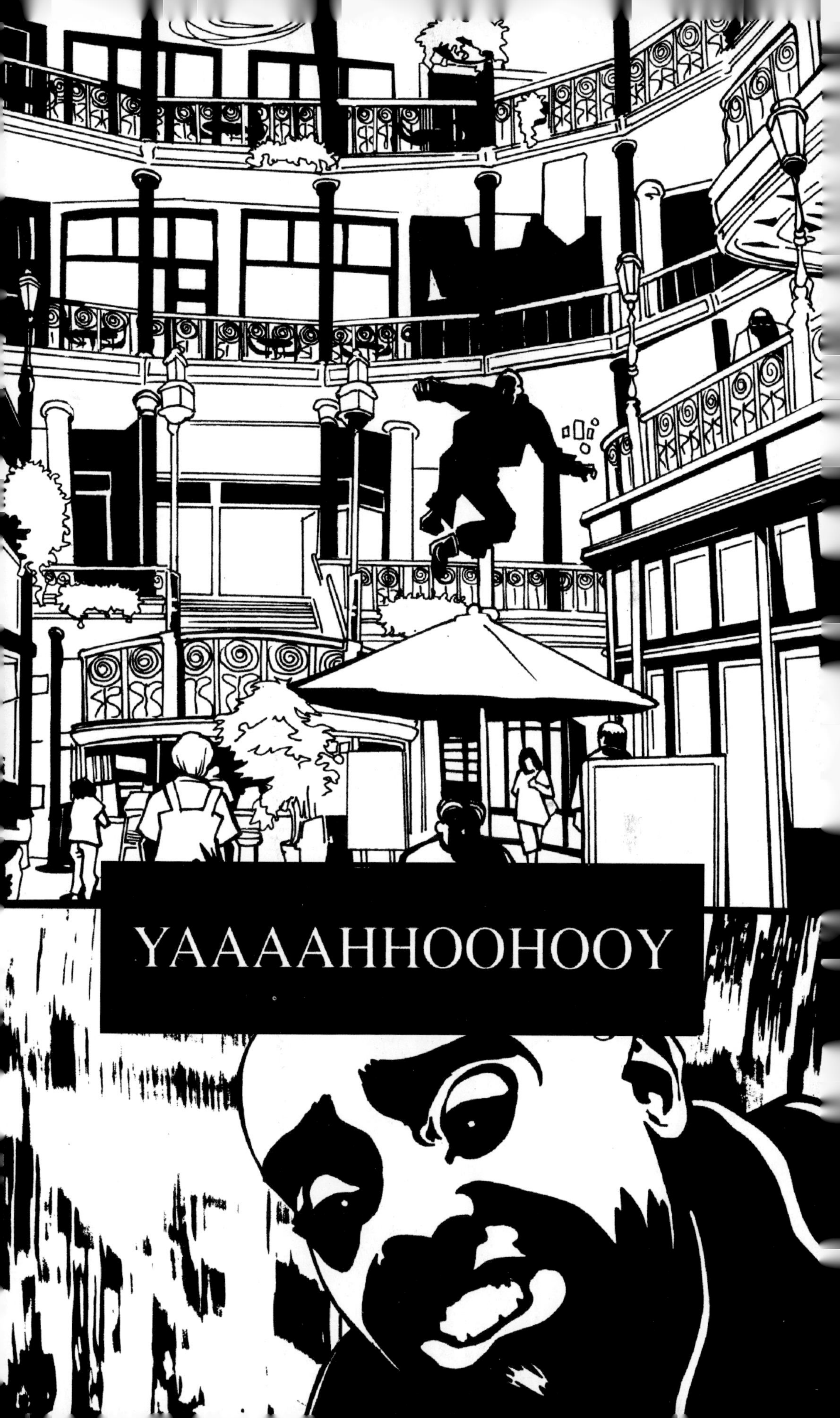
YAAAAHHOOHOOY

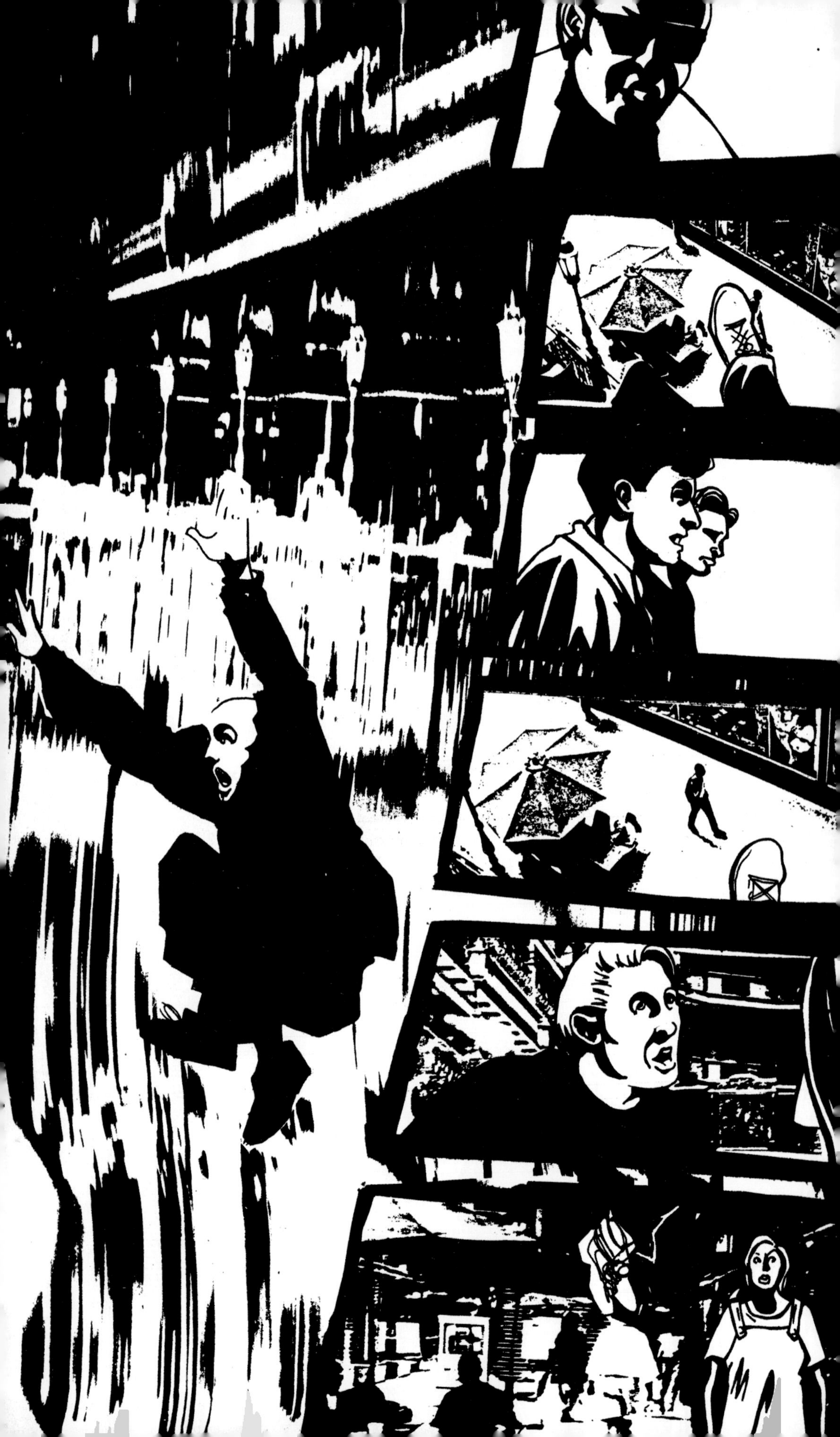

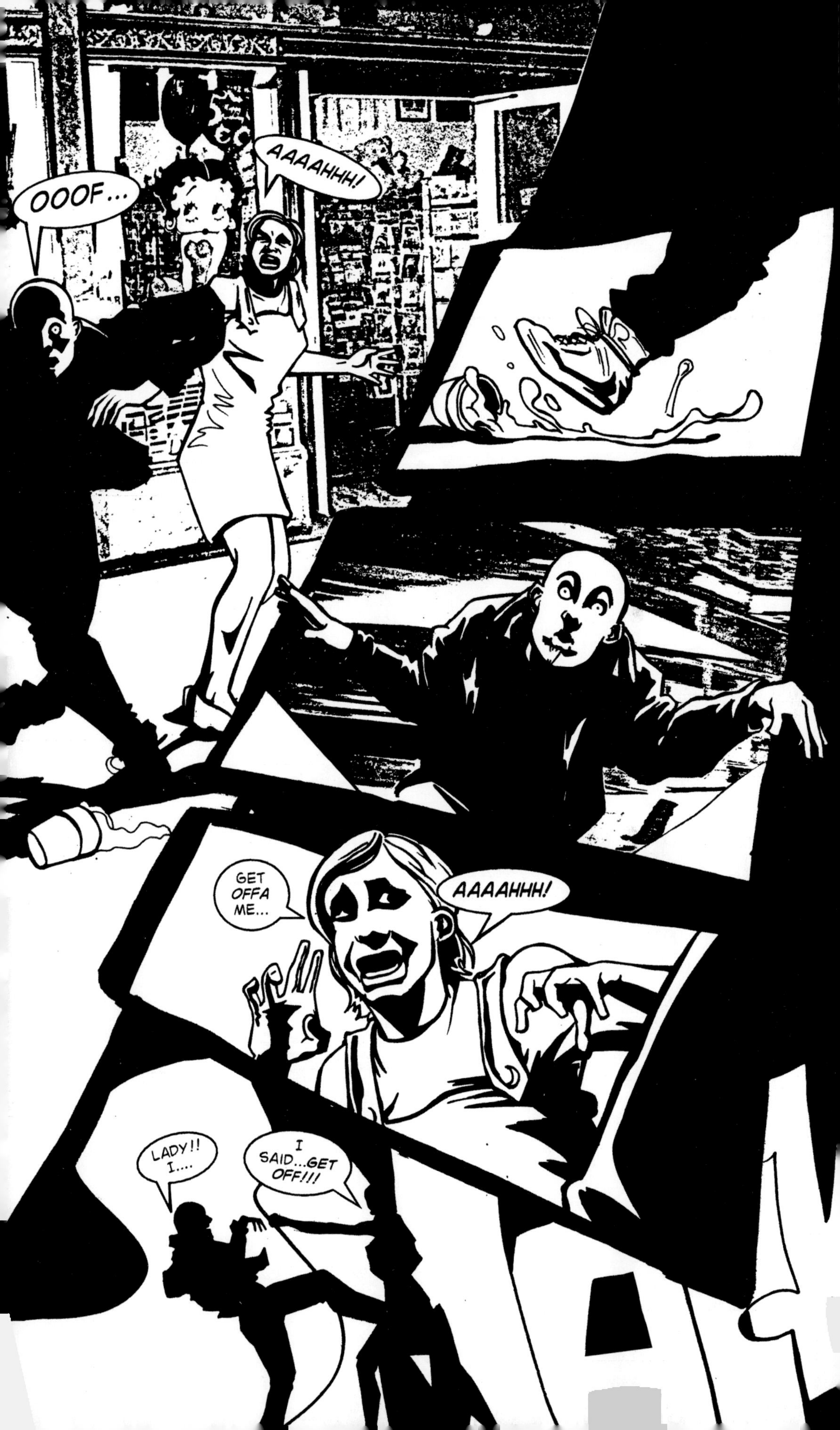
OOOF...
AAAAHHH!
GET OFFA ME...
AAAAHHH!
LADY!! I....
I SAID...GET OFF!!!

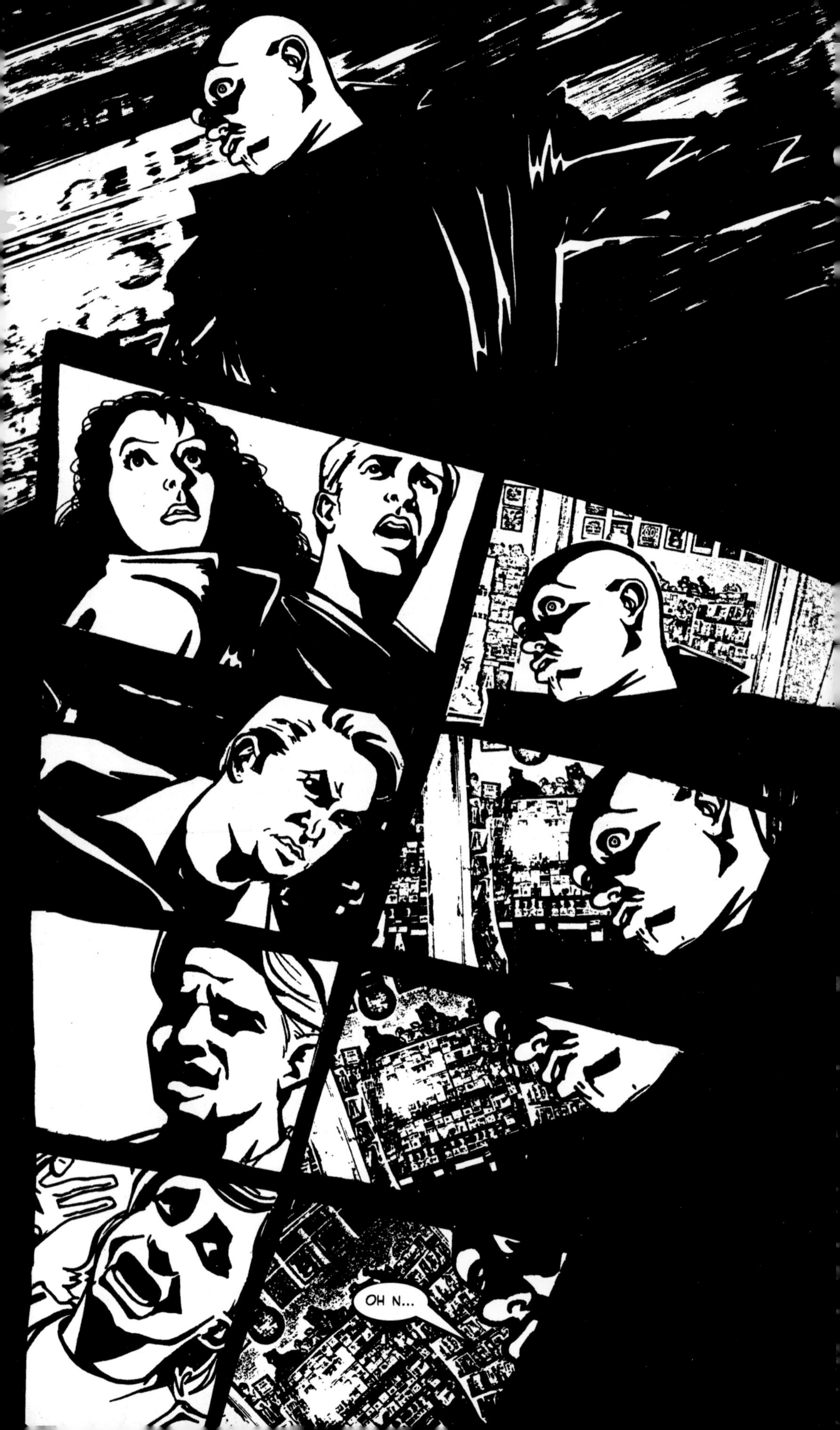
OH N...

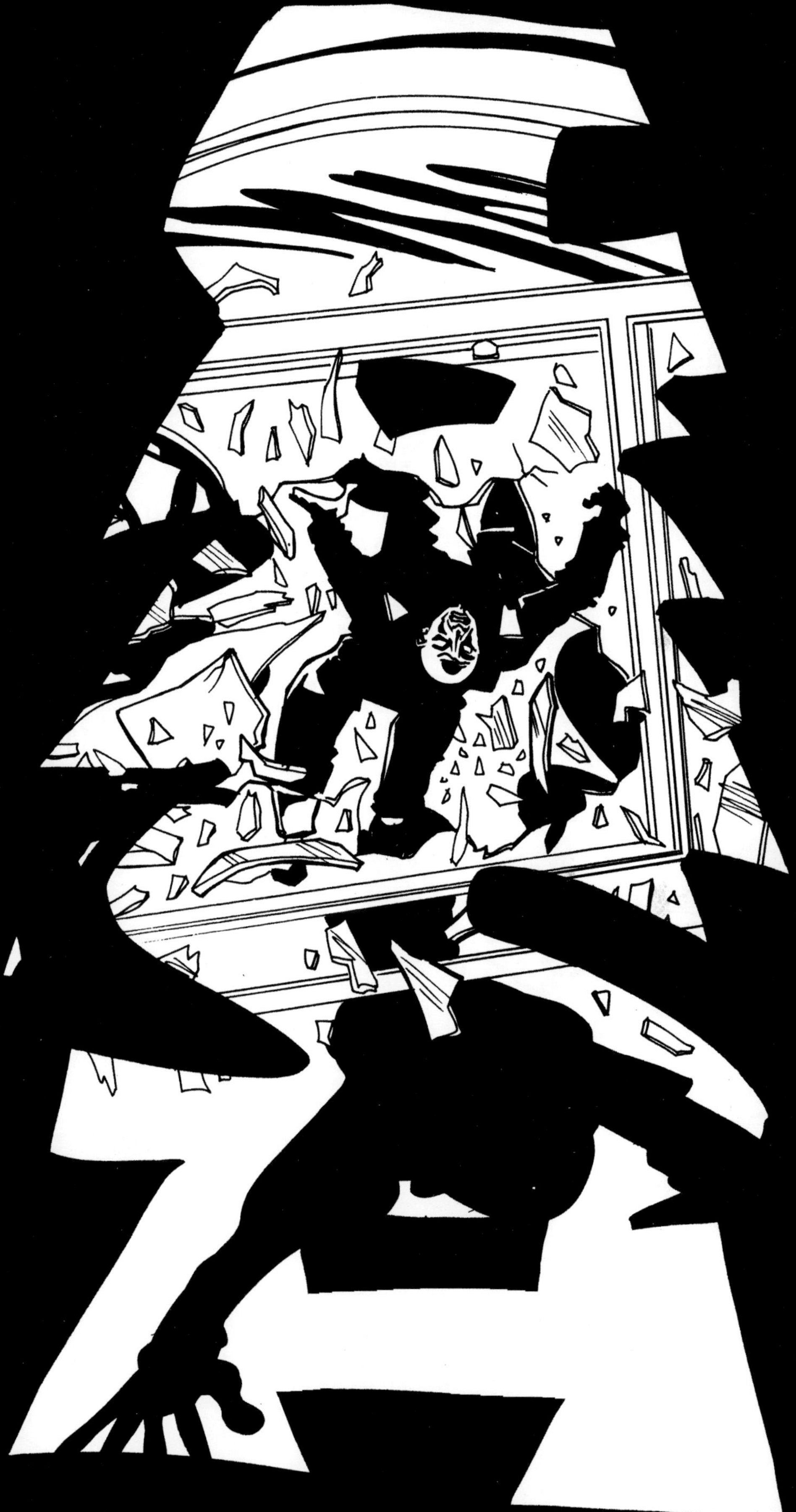

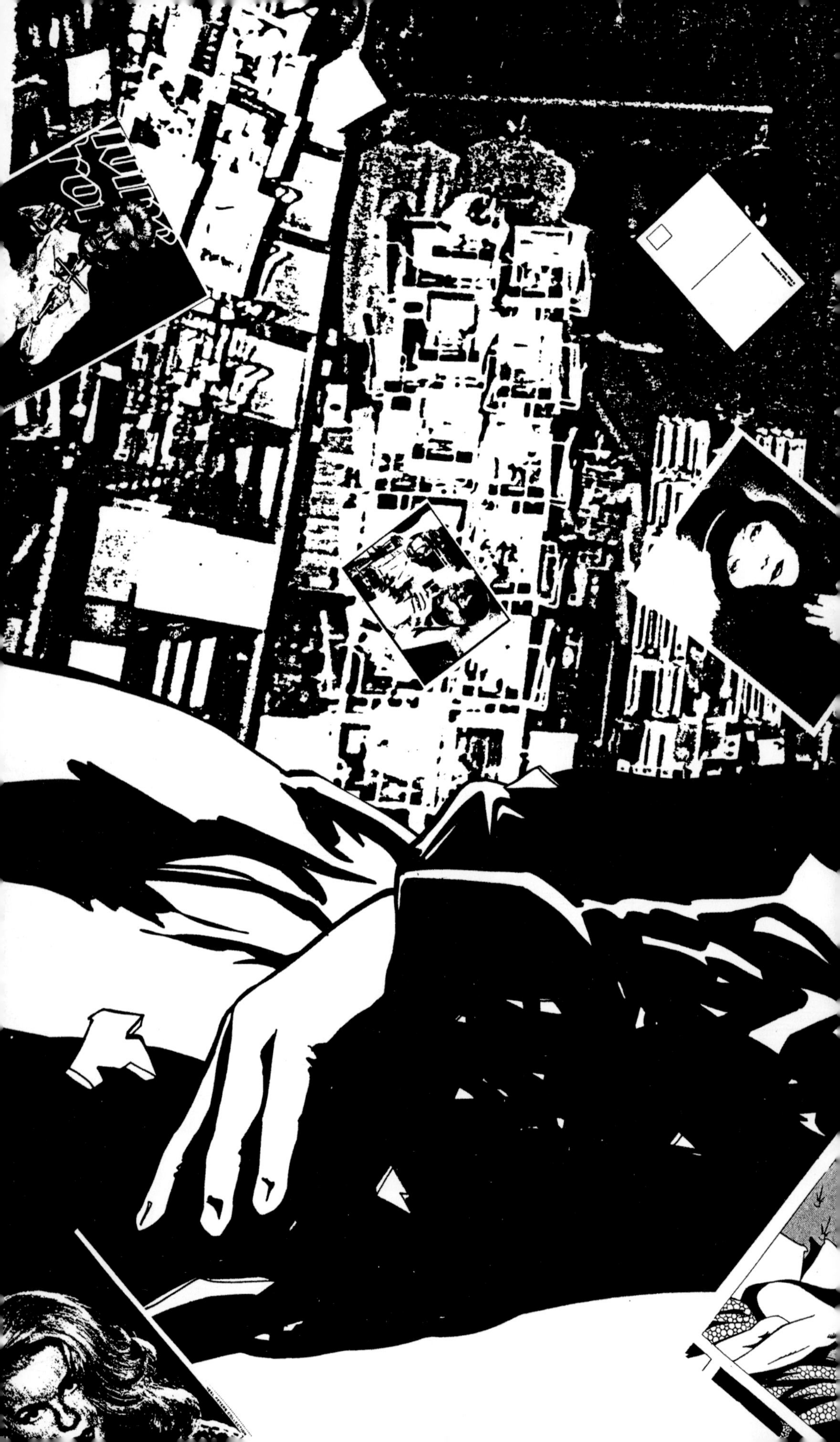

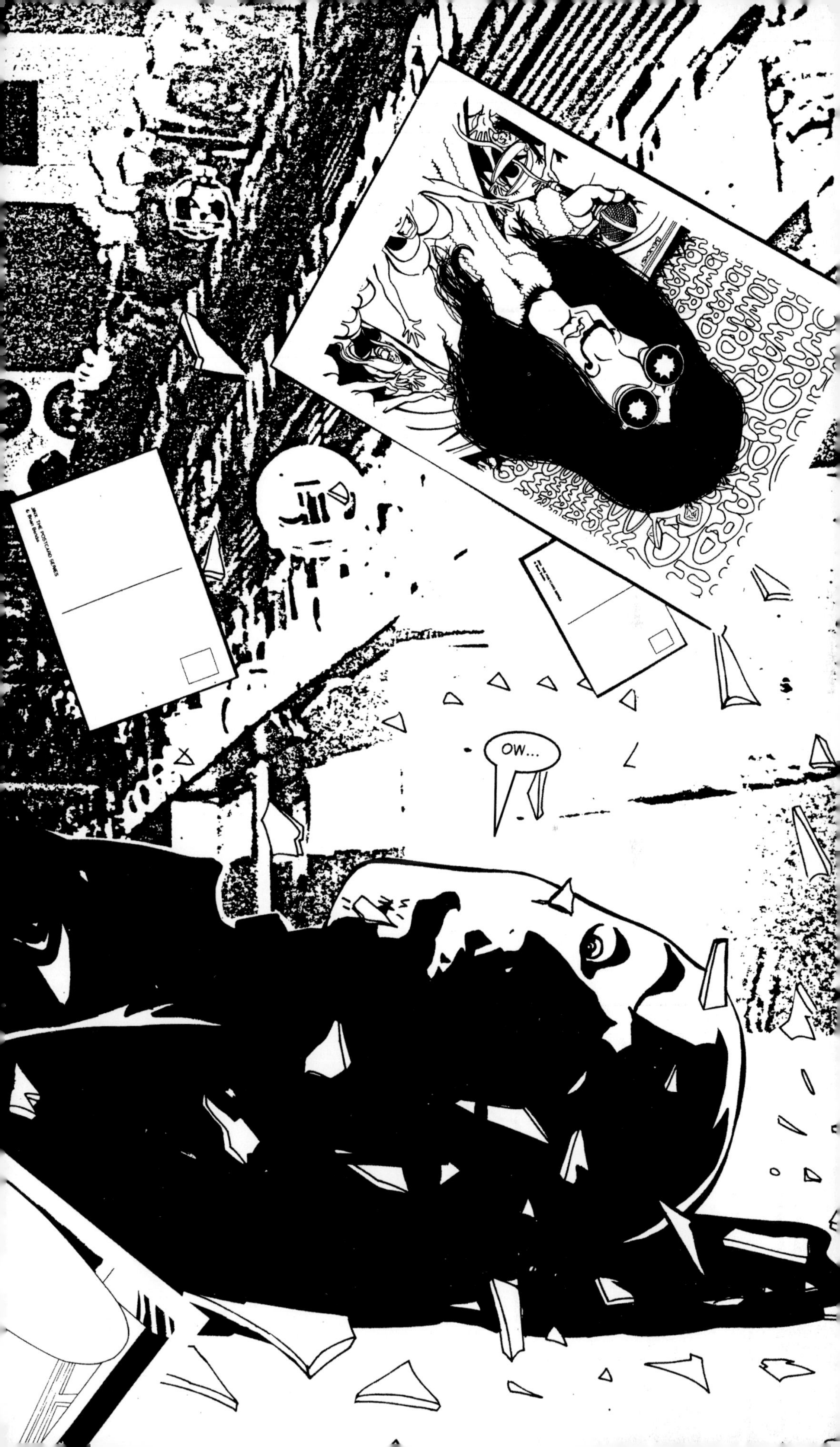
OW...

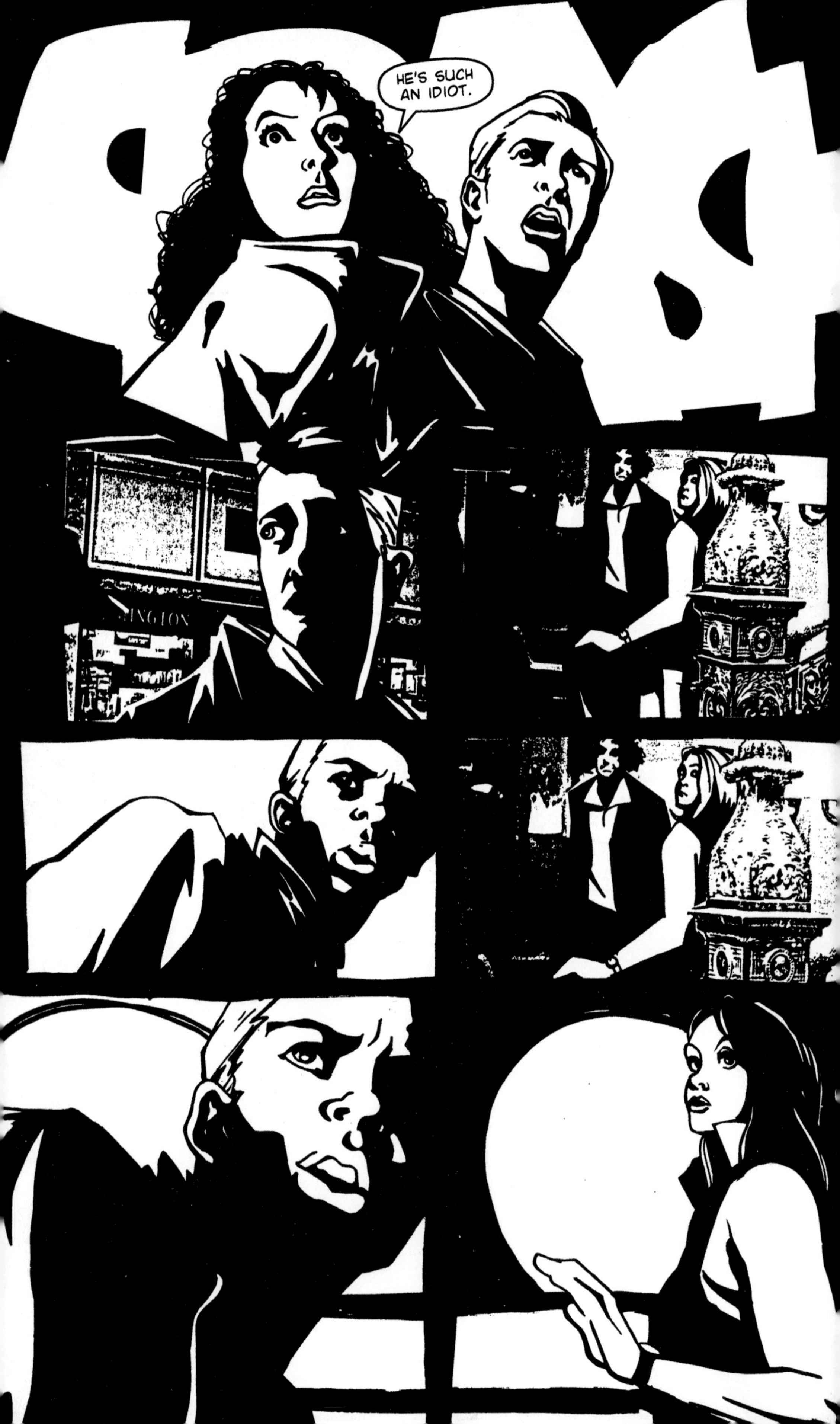
HE'S SUCH AN IDIOT.

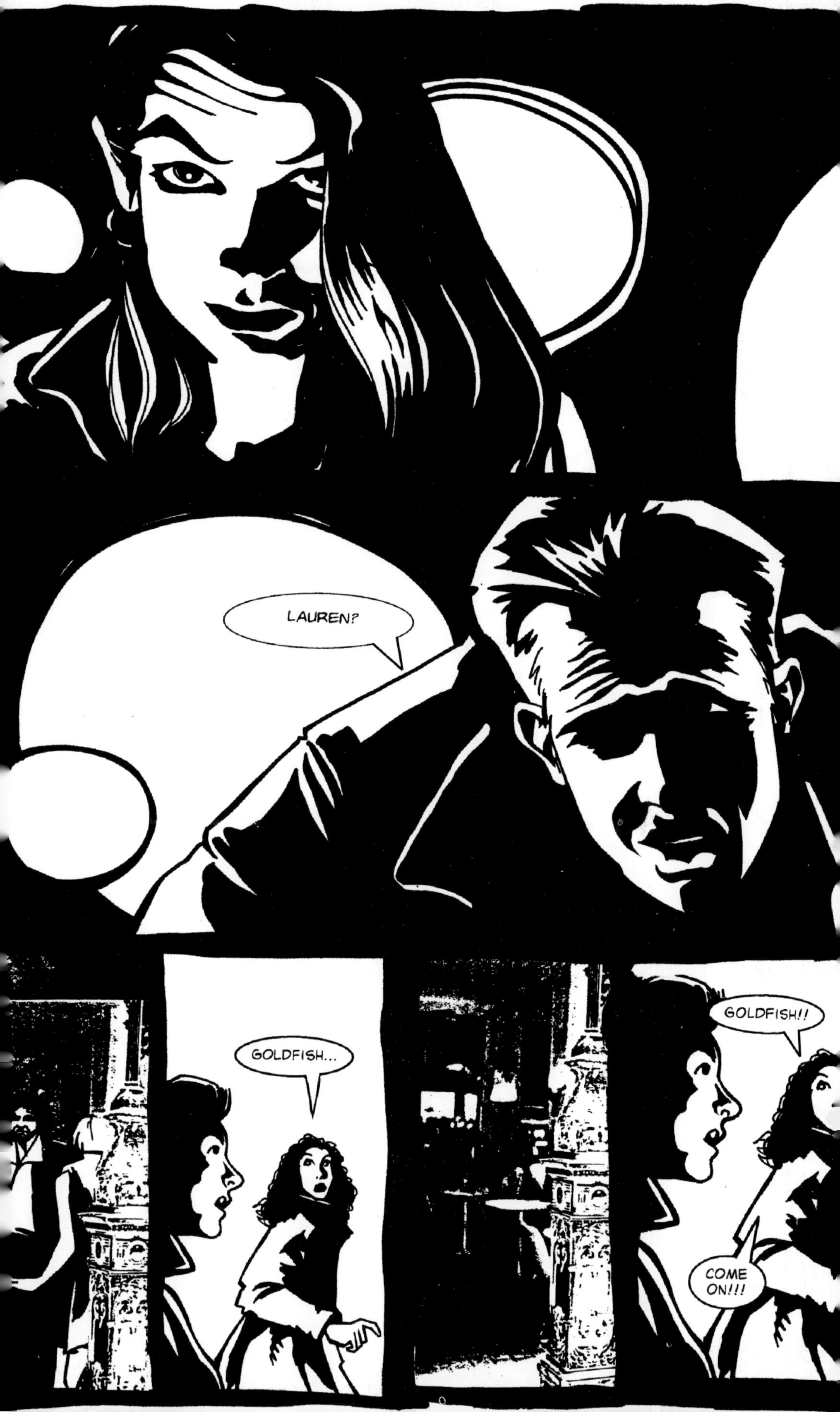
LAUREN?
GOLDFISH...
GOLDFISH!!
COME ON!!!

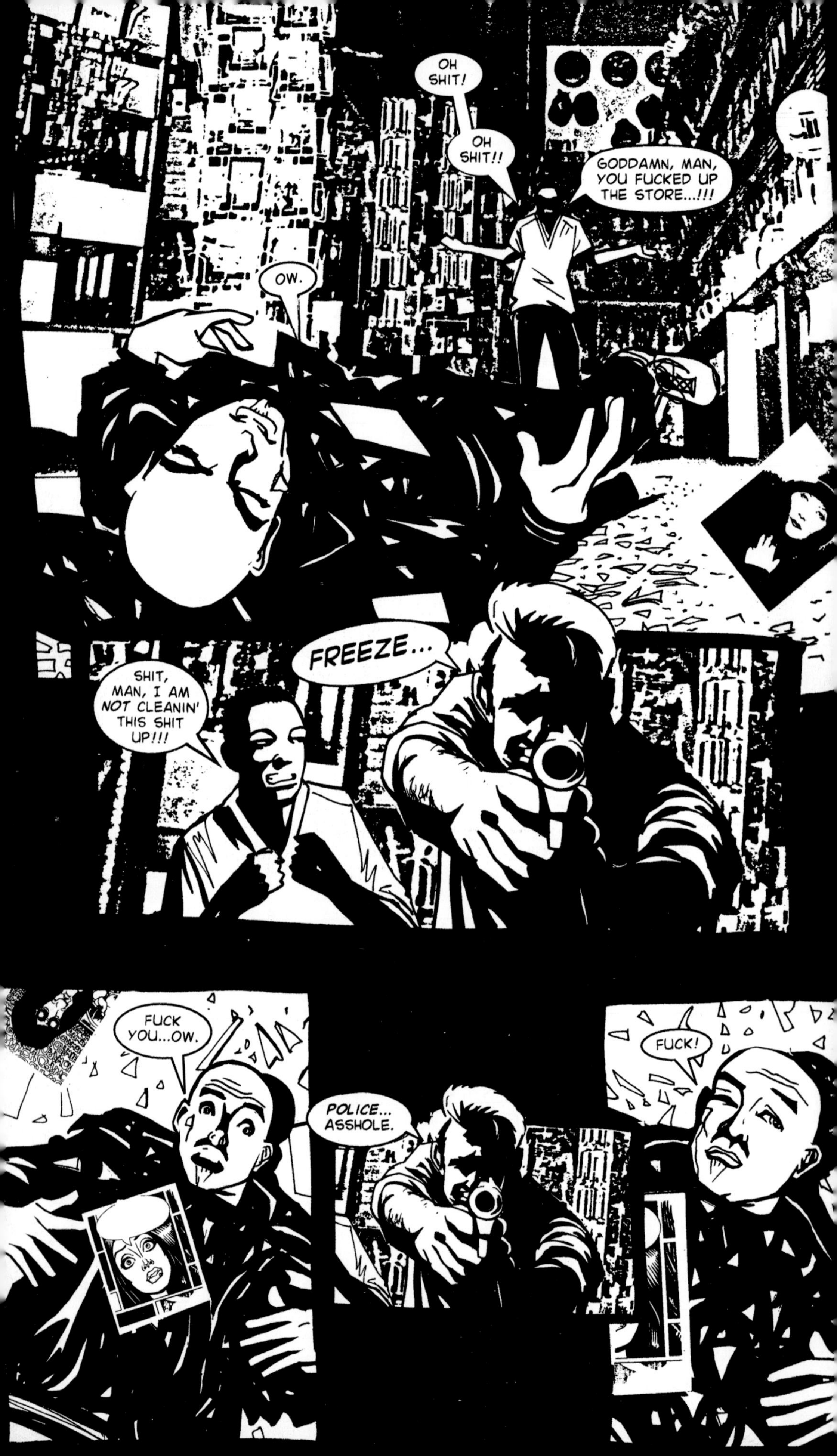
OH SHIT!
OH SHIT!!
GODDAMN, MAN, YOU FUCKED UP THE STORE...!!!
OW.
SHIT, MAN, I AM NOT CLEANIN' THIS SHIT UP!!!
FREEZE...
FUCK YOU...OW.
POLICE... ASSHOLE.
FUCK!

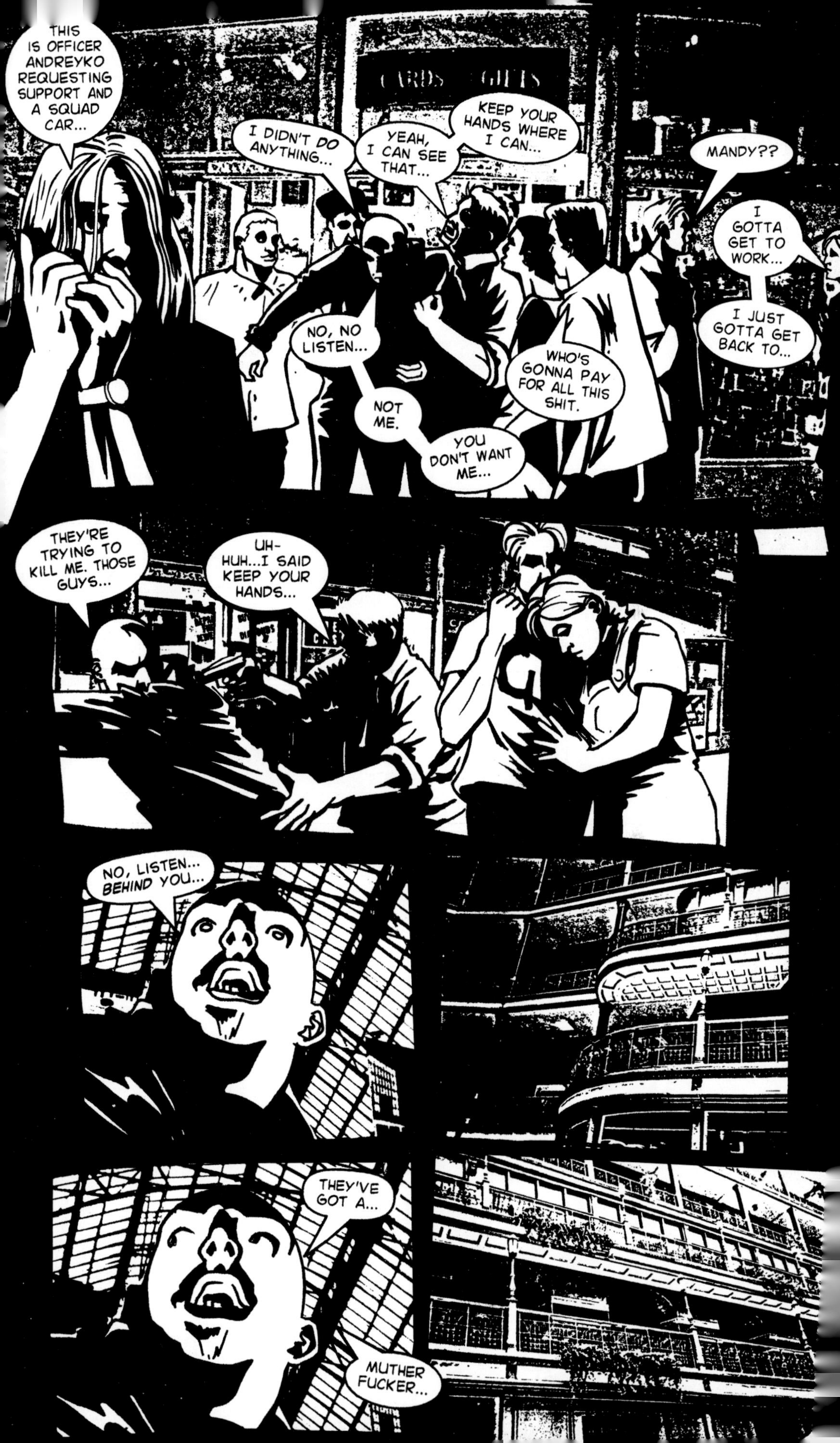
THIS IS OFFICER ANDREYKO REQUESTING SUPPORT AND A SQUAD CAR...
CARDS GIFTS
I DIDN'T DO ANYTHING...
YEAH, I CAN SEE THAT...
KEEP YOUR HANDS WHERE I CAN...
MANDY??
I GOTTA GET TO WORK...
I JUST GOTTA GET BACK TO...
NO, NO LISTEN...
NOT ME.
YOU DON'T WANT ME...
WHO'S GONNA PAY FOR ALL THIS SHIT.
THEY'RE TRYING TO KILL ME. THOSE GUYS...
UH-HUH...I SAID KEEP YOUR HANDS...
NO, LISTEN... BEHIND YOU...
THEY'VE GOT A...
MUTHER FUCKER...

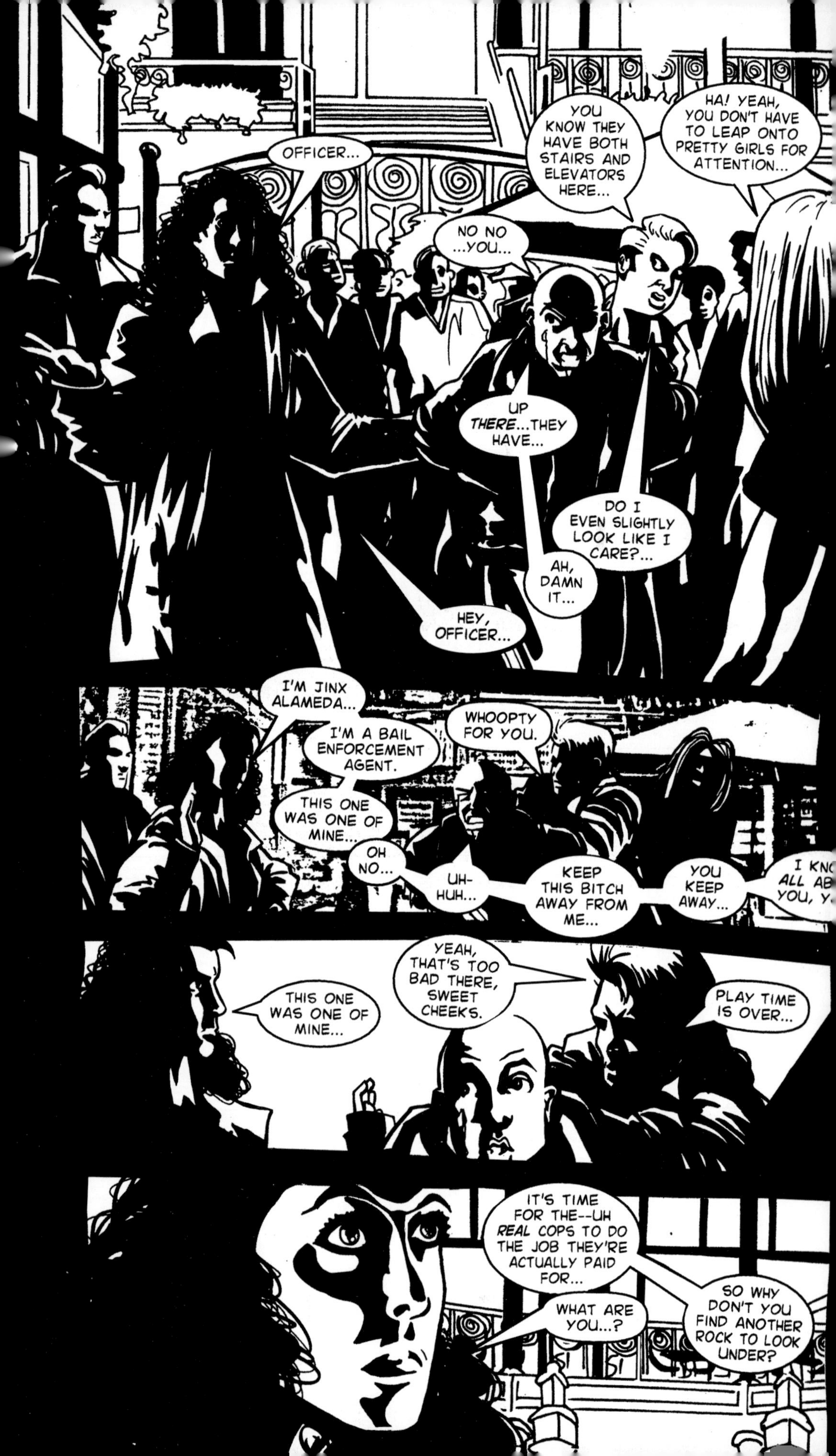
OFFICER...
YOU KNOW THEY HAVE BOTH STAIRS AND ELEVATORS HERE...
HA! YEAH, YOU DON'T HAVE TO LEAP ONTO PRETTY GIRLS FOR ATTENTION...
NO NO ...YOU...
UP THERE...THEY HAVE...
DO I EVEN SLIGHTLY LOOK LIKE I CARE?...
AH, DAMN IT...
HEY, OFFICER...
I'M JINX ALAMEDA...
I'M A BAIL ENFORCEMENT AGENT.
WHOOPTY FOR YOU.
THIS ONE WAS ONE OF MINE...
OH NO...
UH-HUH...
KEEP THIS BITCH AWAY FROM ME...
YOU KEEP AWAY...
THIS ONE WAS ONE OF MINE...
YEAH, THAT'S TOO BAD THERE, SWEET CHEEKS.
PLAY TIME IS OVER...
IT'S TIME FOR THE--UH REAL COPS TO DO THE JOB THEY'RE ACTUALLY PAID FOR...
WHAT ARE YOU...?
SO WHY DON'T YOU FIND ANOTHER ROCK TO LOOK UNDER?

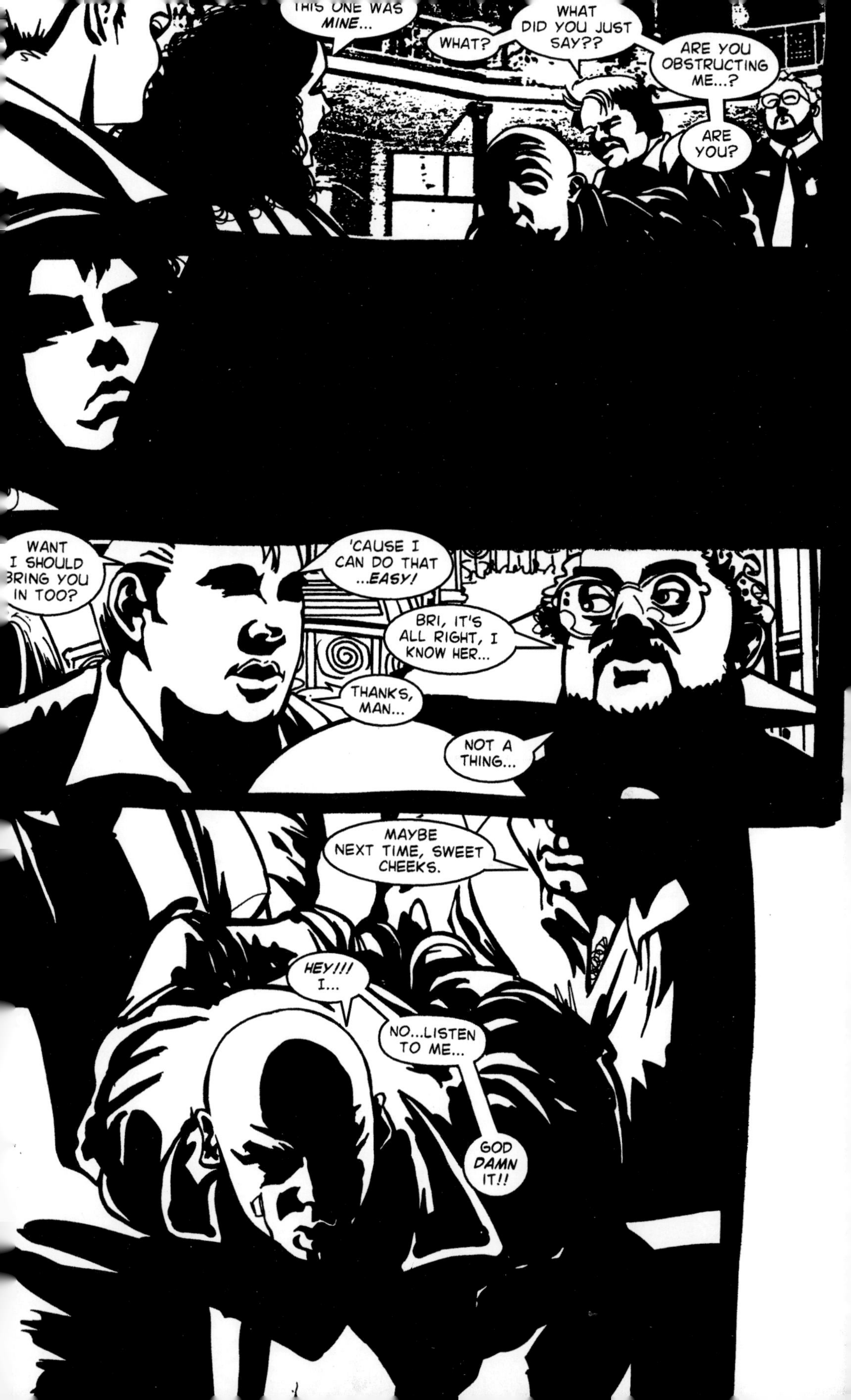
THIS ONE WAS MINE...
WHAT?
WHAT DID YOU JUST SAY??
ARE YOU OBSTRUCTING ME...?
ARE YOU?
WANT I SHOULD BRING YOU IN TOO?
'CAUSE I CAN DO THAT ...EASY!
BRI, IT'S ALL RIGHT, I KNOW HER...
THANKS, MAN...
NOT A THING...
MAYBE NEXT TIME, SWEET CHEEKS.
HEY!!! I...
NO...LISTEN TO ME...
GOD DAMN IT!!

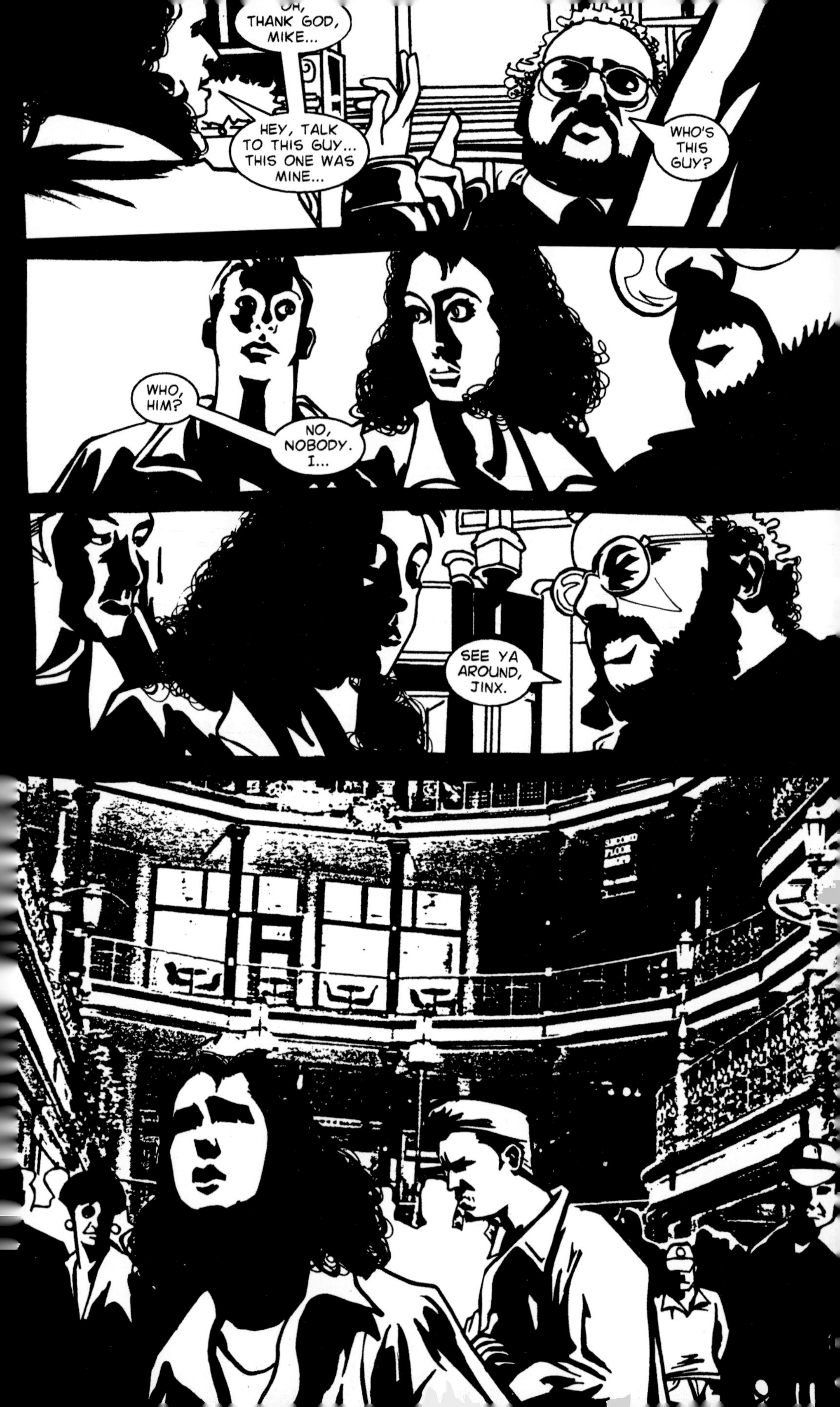

OH, THANK GOD, MIKE...
HEY, TALK TO THIS GUY... THIS ONE WAS MINE...
WHO'S THIS GUY?
WHO, HIM?
NO, NOBODY. I...
SEE YA AROUND, JINX.

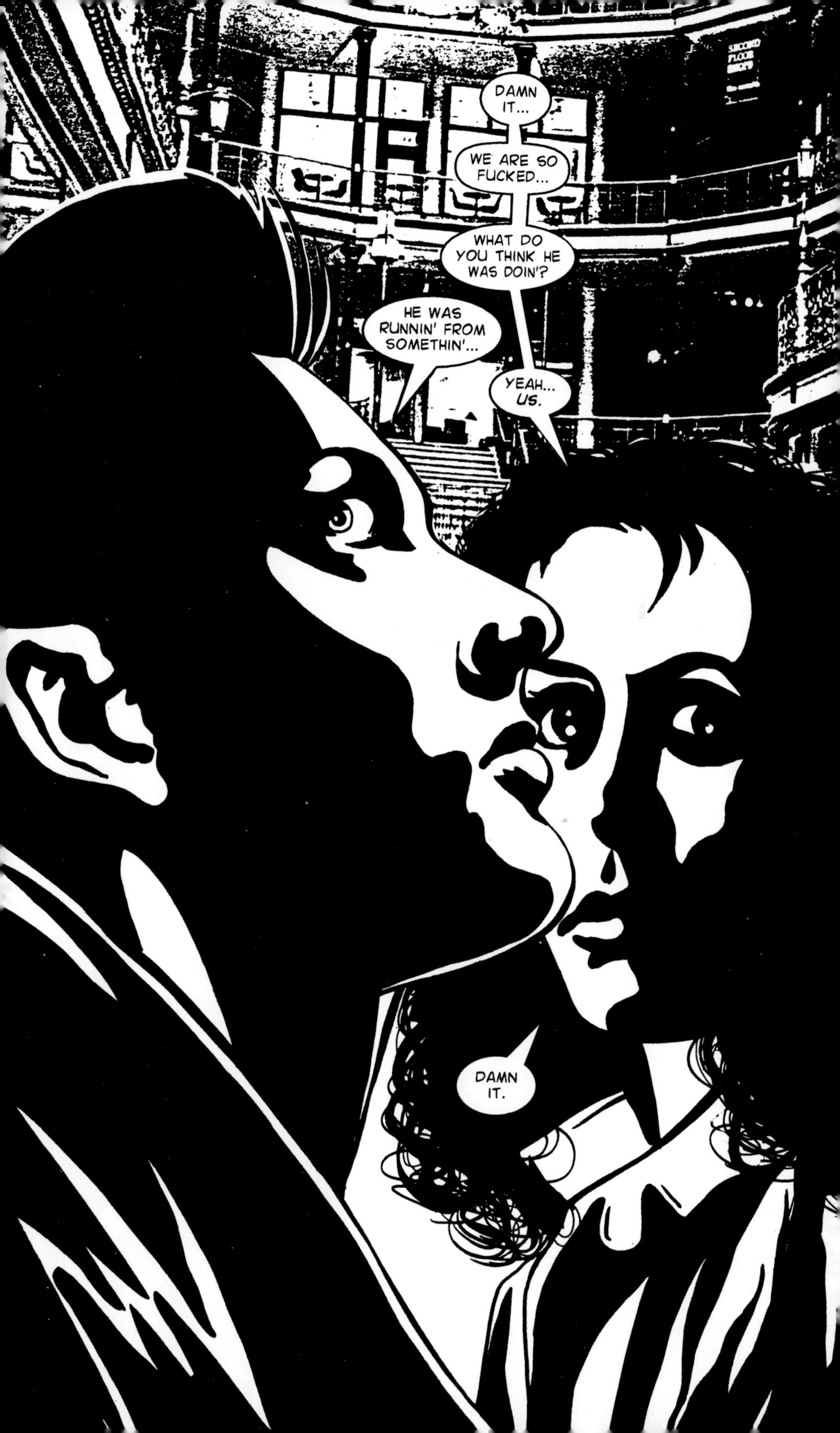
DAMN IT...
WE ARE SO FUCKED...
WHAT DO YOU THINK HE WAS DOIN'?
HE WAS RUNNIN' FROM SOMETHIN'...
YEAH... US.
DAMN IT.

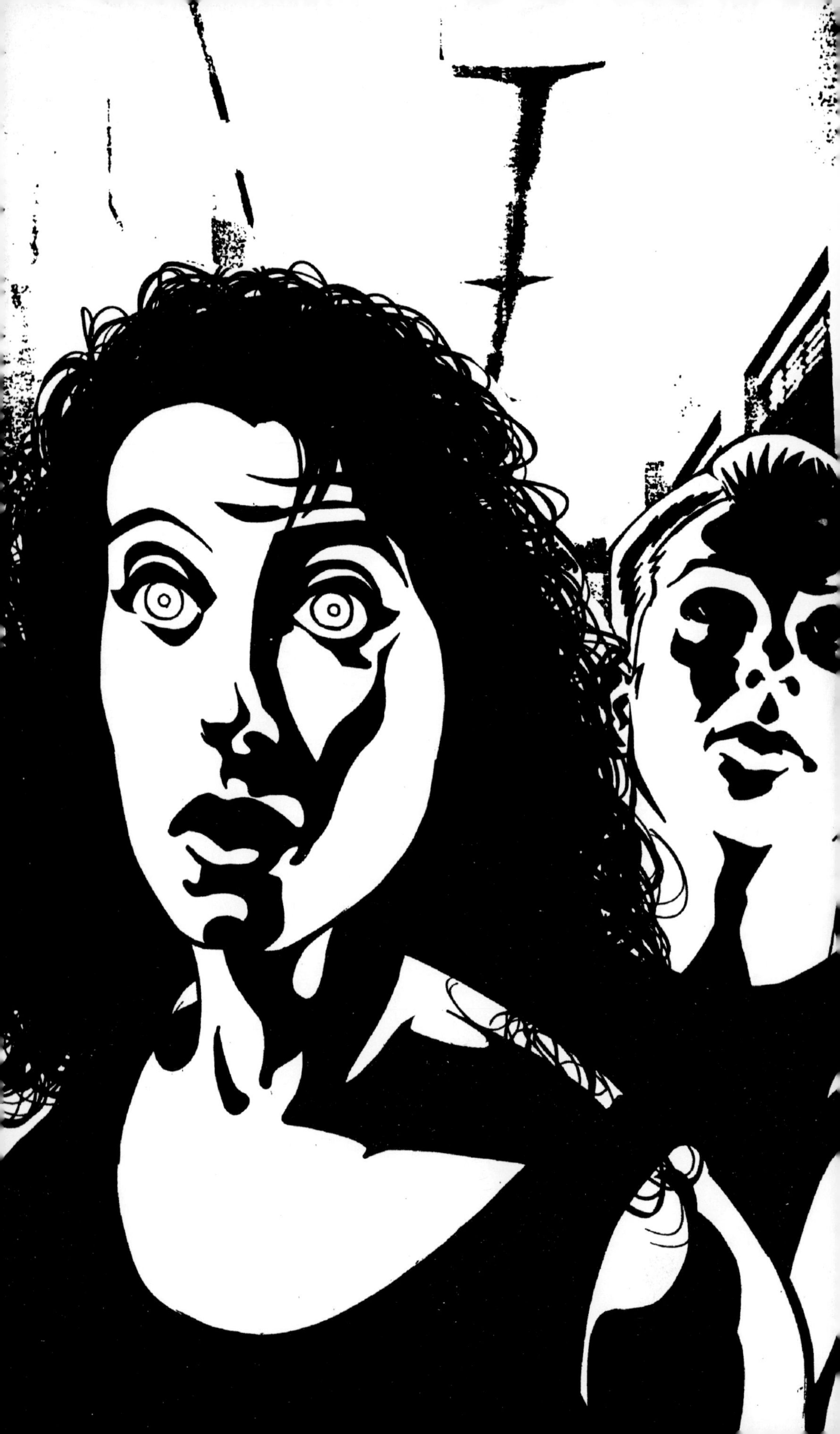

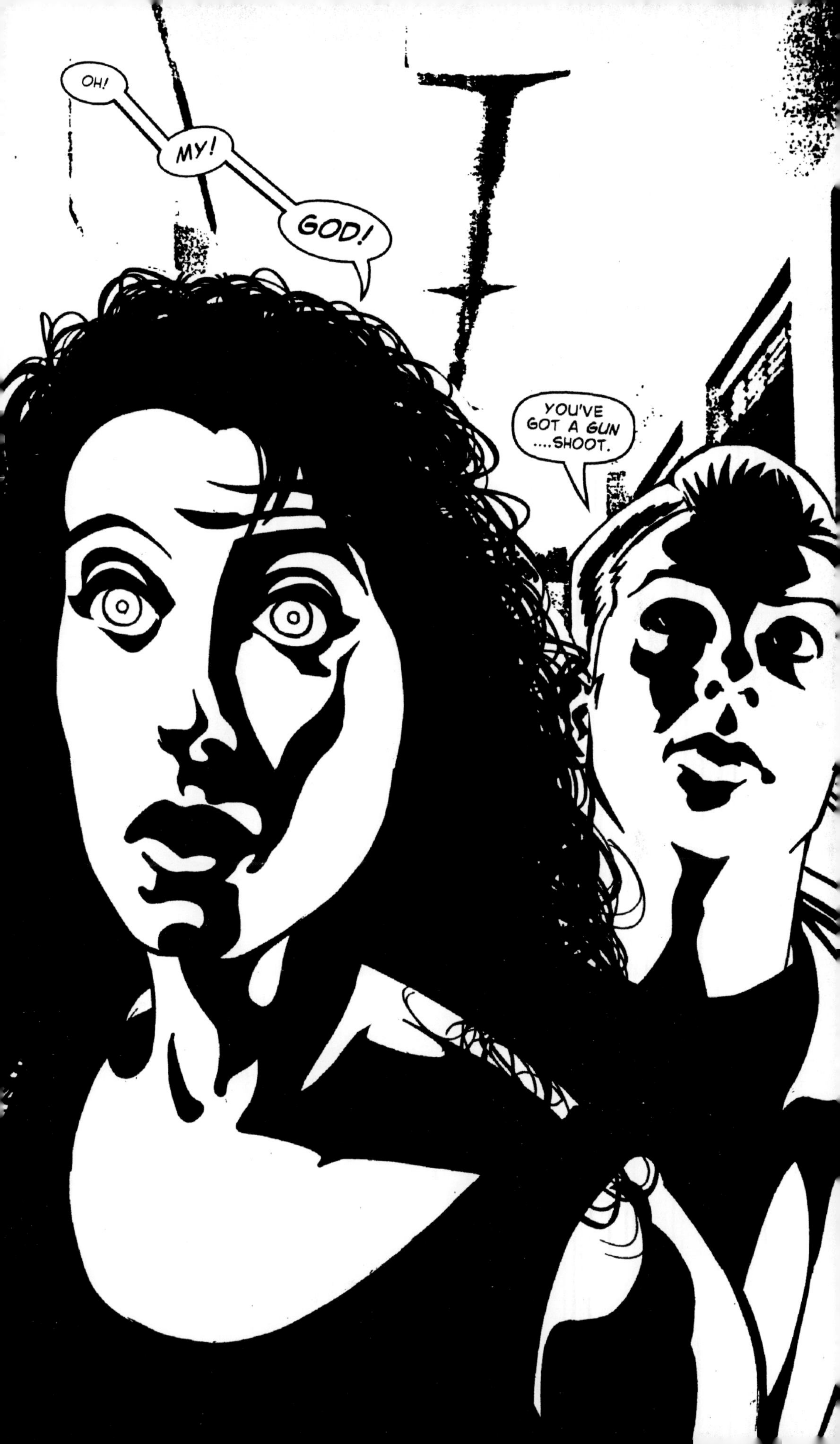
OH!
MY!
GOD!
YOU'VE GOT A GUN ....SHOOT.

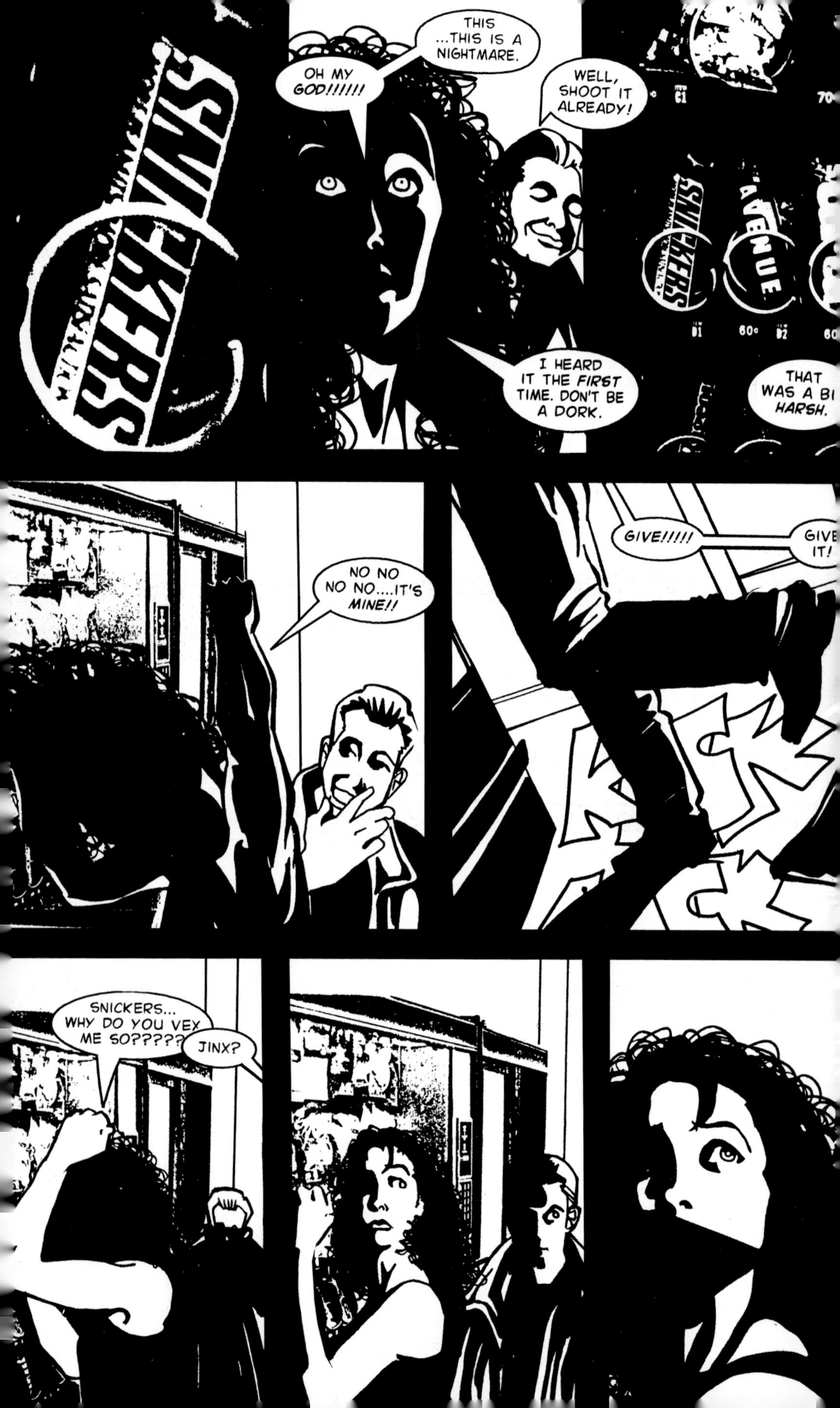
OH MY GOD!!!!!!
THIS ...THIS IS A NIGHTMARE.
WELL, SHOOT IT ALREADY!
I HEARD IT THE FIRST TIME. DON'T BE A DORK.
THAT WAS A BI HARSH.
NO NO NO NO....IT'S MINE!!
GIVE!!!!!
GIVE IT!
SNICKERS... WHY DO YOU VEX ME SO?????
JINX?

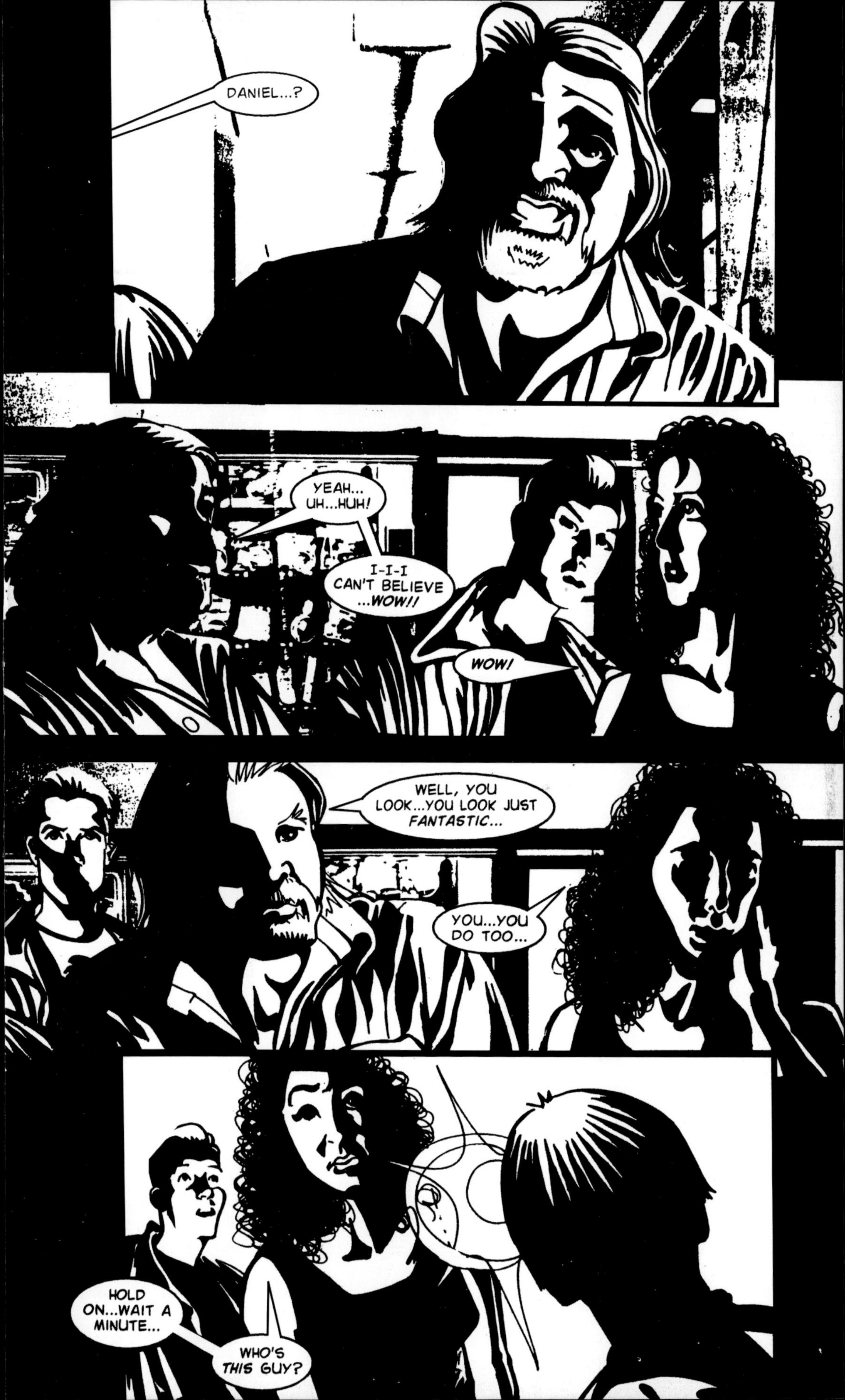
DANIEL...?
YEAH... UH...HUH!
I-I-I CAN'T BELIEVE ...WOW!!
WOW!
WELL, YOU LOOK...YOU LOOK JUST FANTASTIC...
YOU...YOU DO TOO...
HOLD ON...WAIT A MINUTE...
WHO'S THIS GUY?

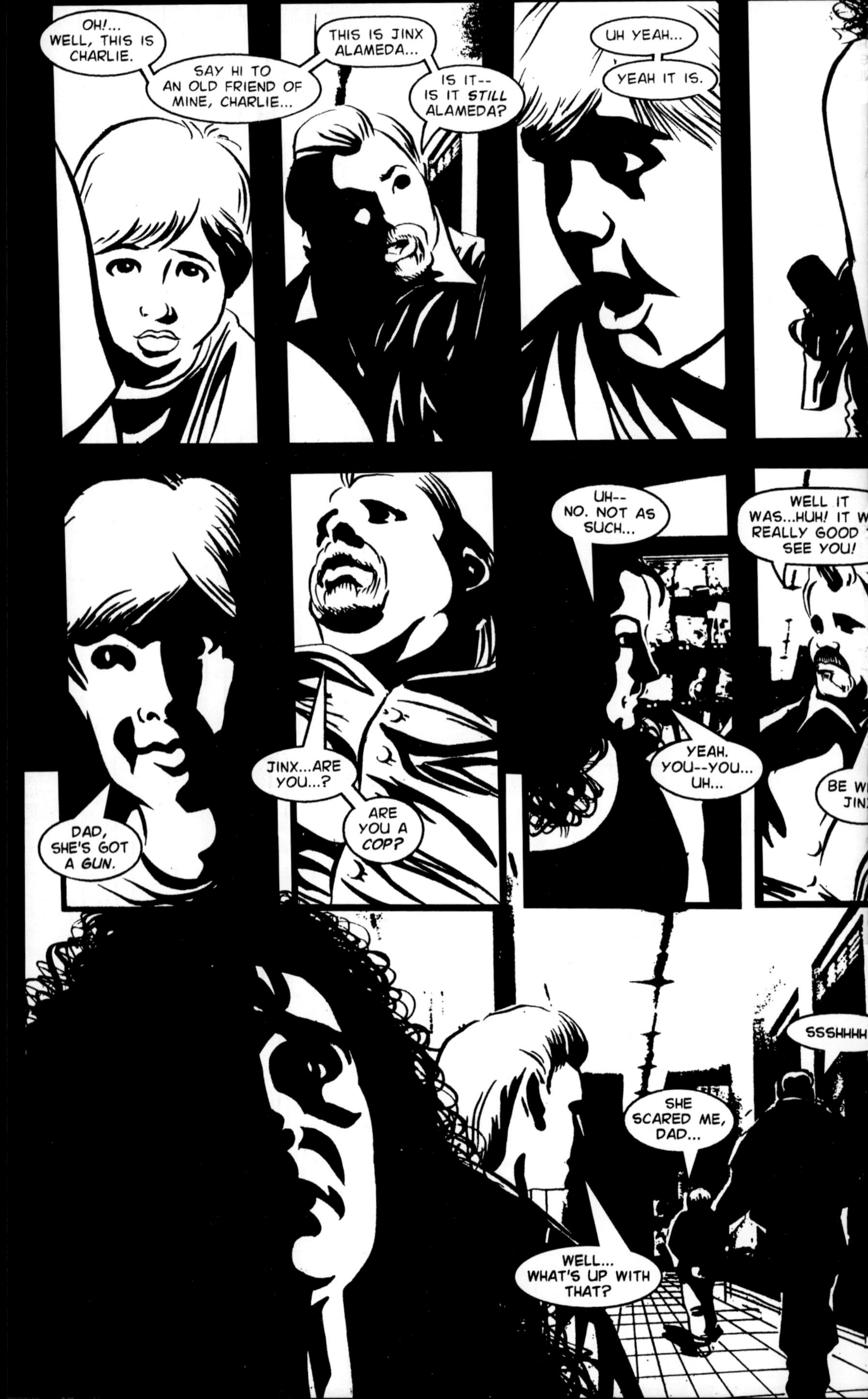
OH!... WELL, THIS IS CHARLIE.
SAY HI TO AN OLD FRIEND OF MINE, CHARLIE...
THIS IS JINX ALAMEDA...
IS IT-- IS IT STILL ALAMEDA?
UH YEAH...
YEAH IT IS.
DAD, SHE'S GOT A GUN.
JINX...ARE YOU...?
ARE YOU A COP?
UH-- NO. NOT AS SUCH...
YEAH. YOU--YOU... UH...
WELL IT WAS...HUH! IT W
REALLY GOOD
SEE YOU!
BE W
SSSHHHH
SHE SCARED ME, DAD...
WELL... WHAT'S UP WITH THAT?

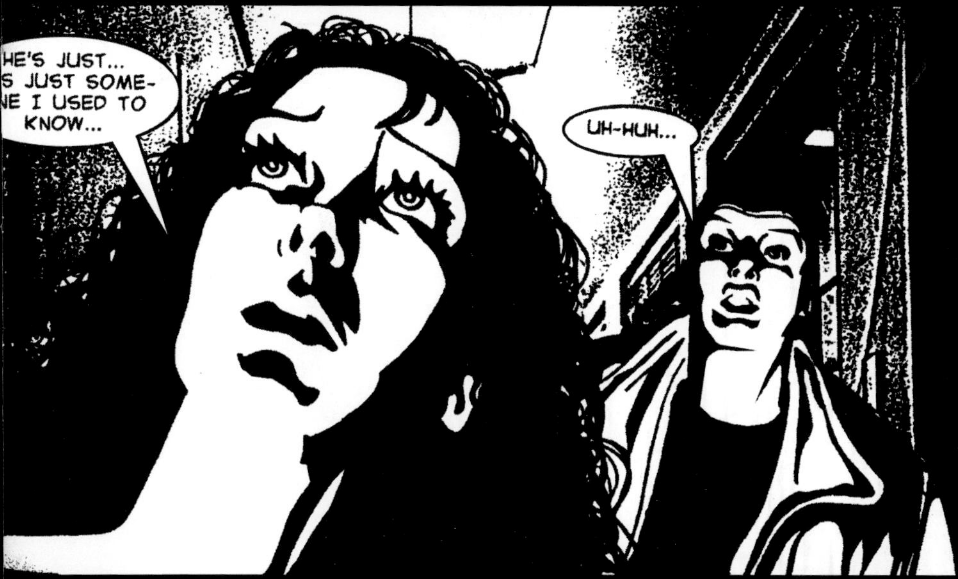
HE'S JUST...
S JUST SOME-
NE I USED TO
KNOW...
UH-HUH...

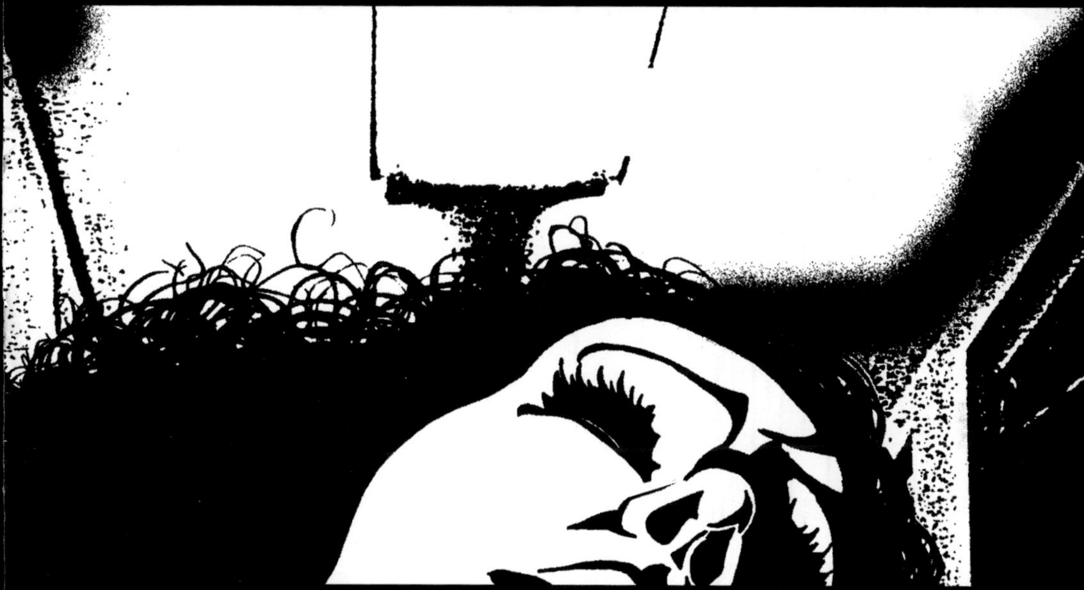

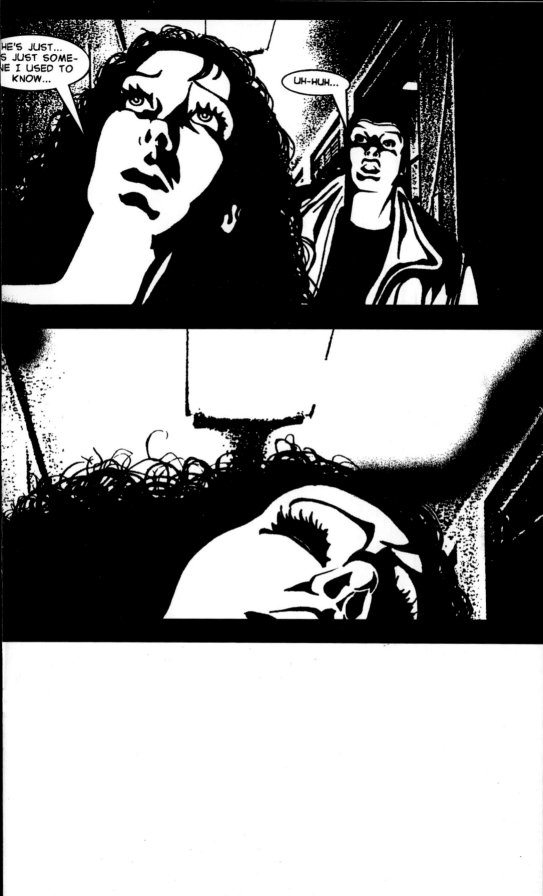

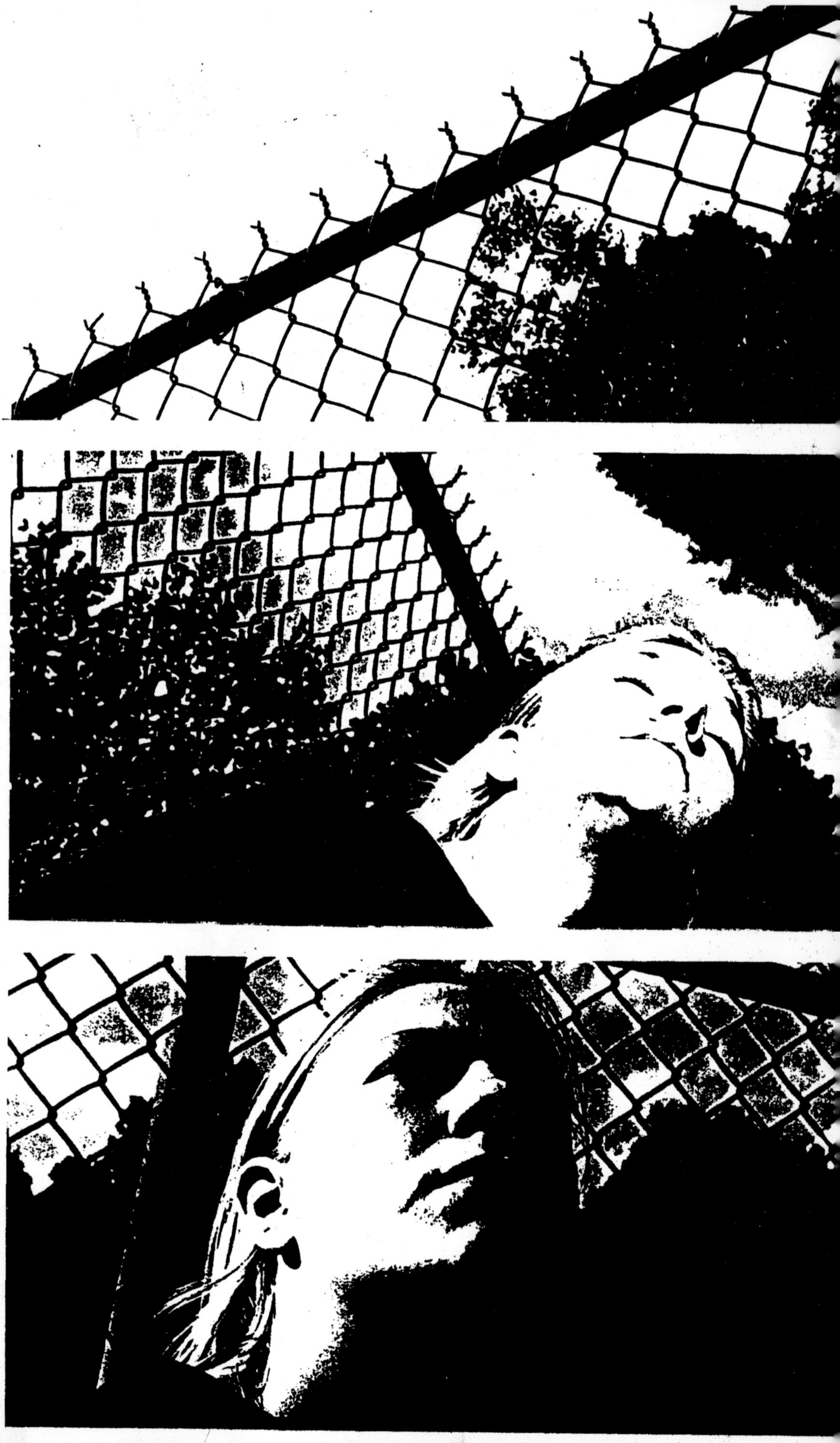

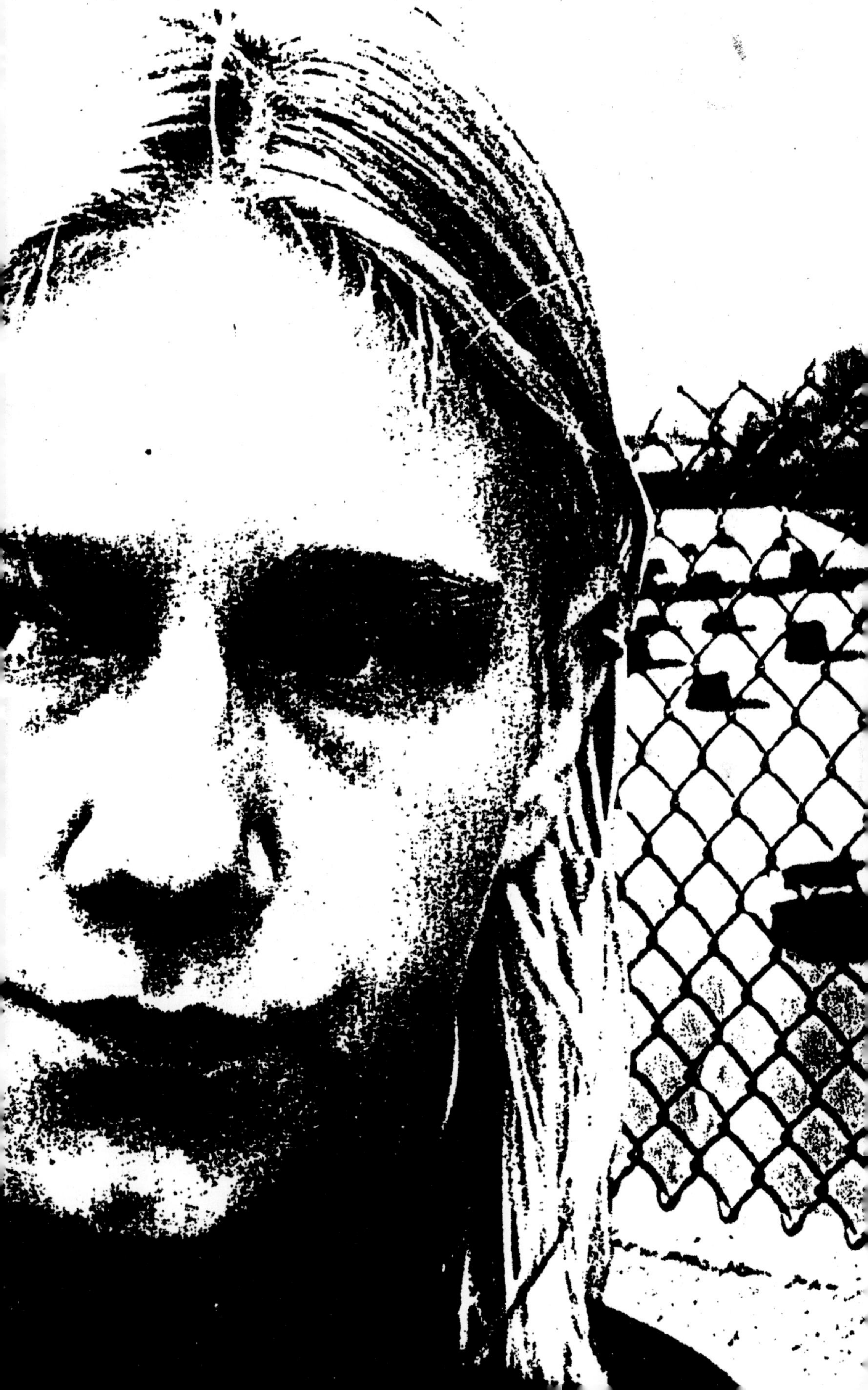

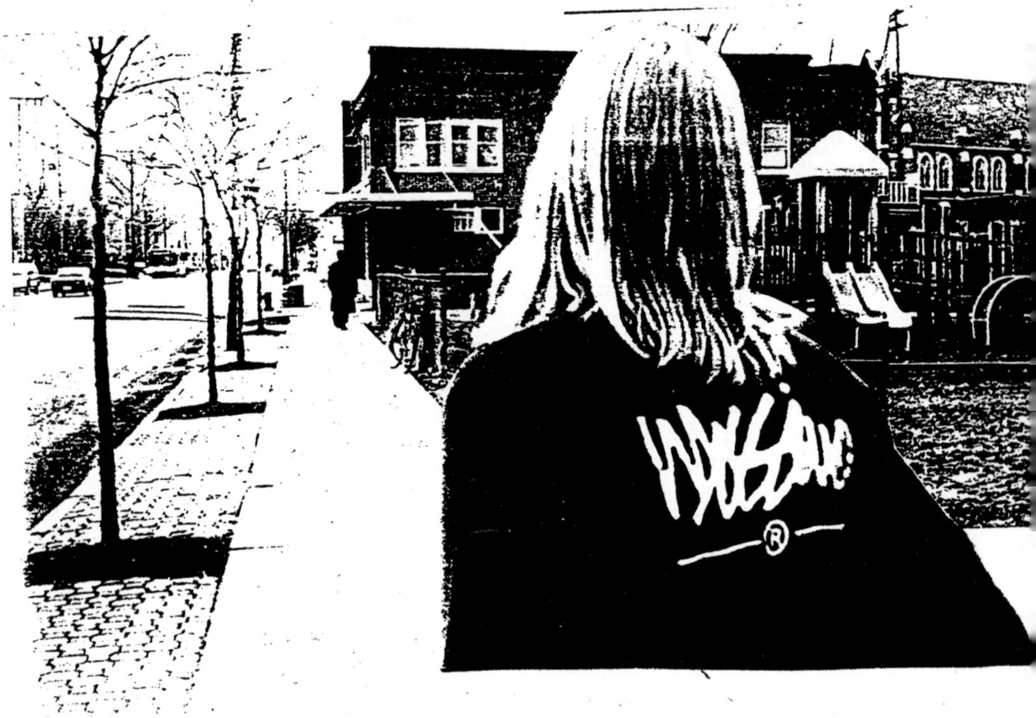

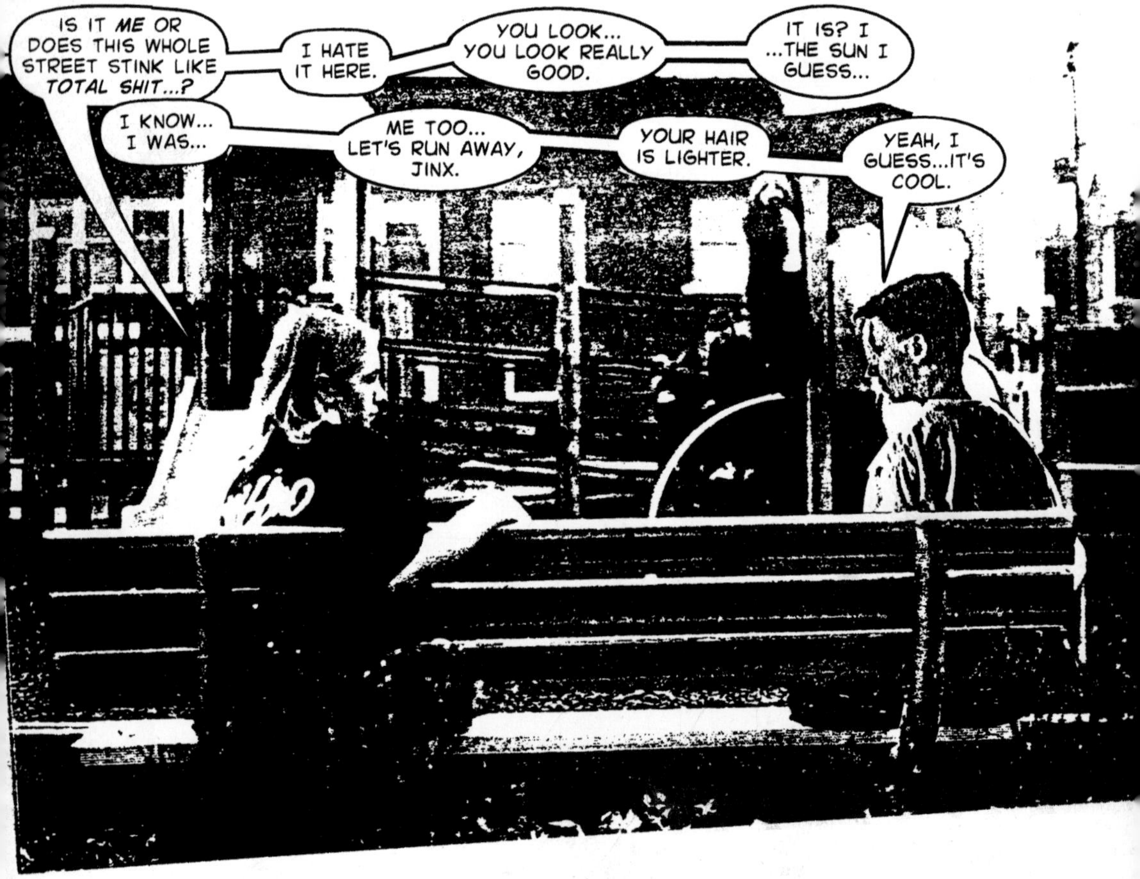

IS IT *ME* OR DOES THIS WHOLE STREET STINK LIKE *TOTAL SHIT*...?
I KNOW... I WAS...
I HATE IT HERE.
ME TOO... LET'S RUN AWAY, JINX.
YOU LOOK... YOU LOOK REALLY GOOD.
YOUR HAIR IS LIGHTER.
IT IS? I ...THE SUN I GUESS...
YEAH, I GUESS...IT'S COOL.

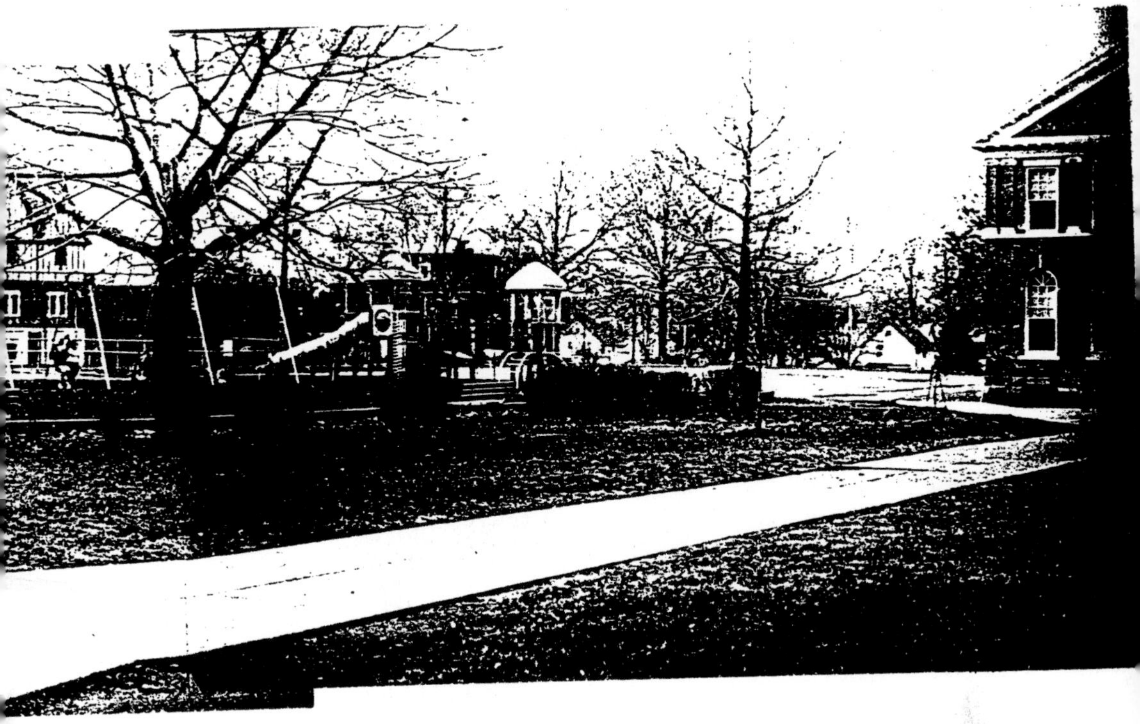

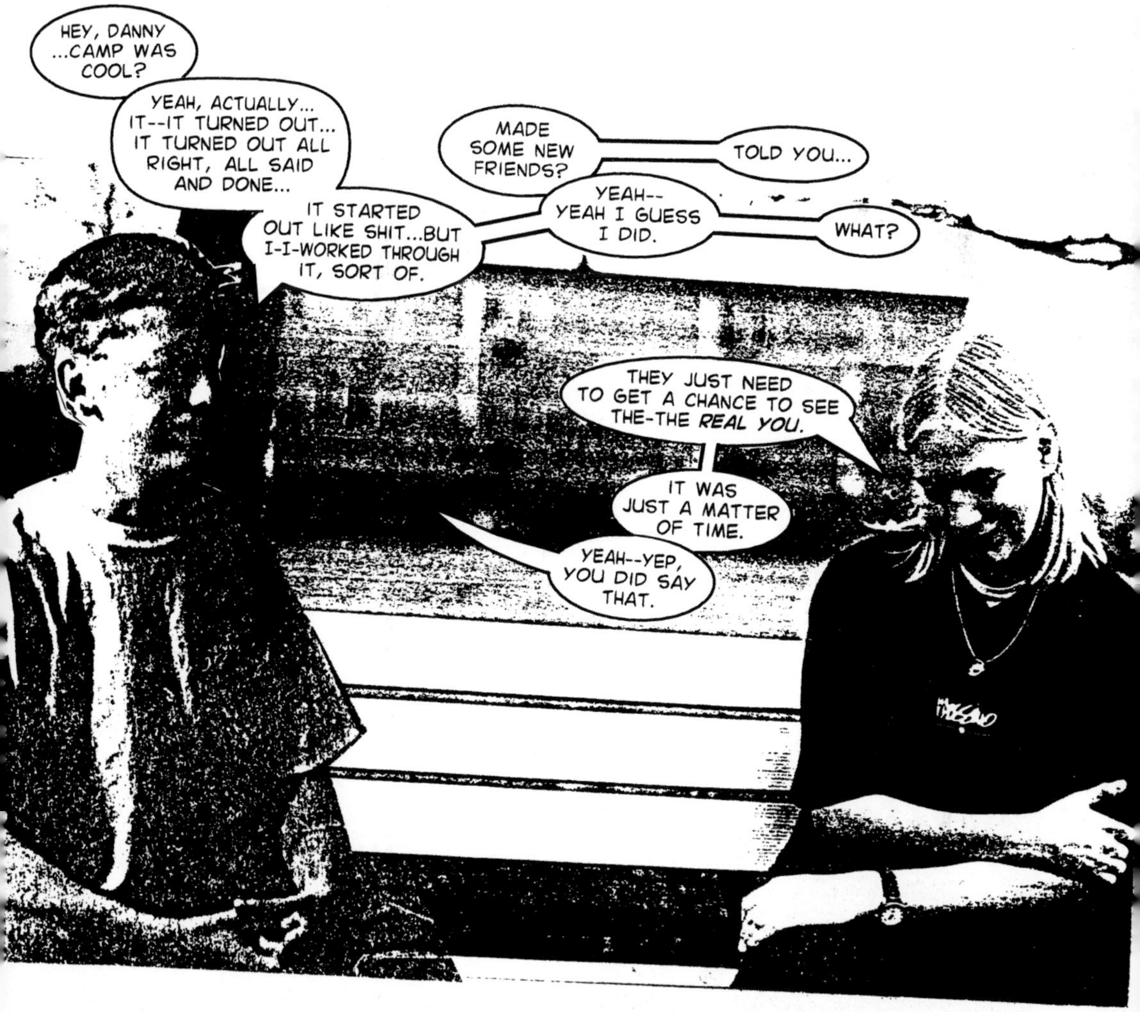
HEY, DANNY ...CAMP WAS COOL?
YEAH, ACTUALLY... IT--IT TURNED OUT... IT TURNED OUT ALL RIGHT, ALL SAID AND DONE...
IT STARTED OUT LIKE SHIT...BUT I-I-WORKED THROUGH IT, SORT OF.
MADE SOME NEW FRIENDS?
TOLD YOU...
YEAH-- YEAH I GUESS I DID.
WHAT?
THEY JUST NEED TO GET A CHANCE TO SEE THE-THE *REAL YOU*.
IT WAS JUST A MATTER OF TIME.
YEAH--YEP, YOU DID SAY THAT.

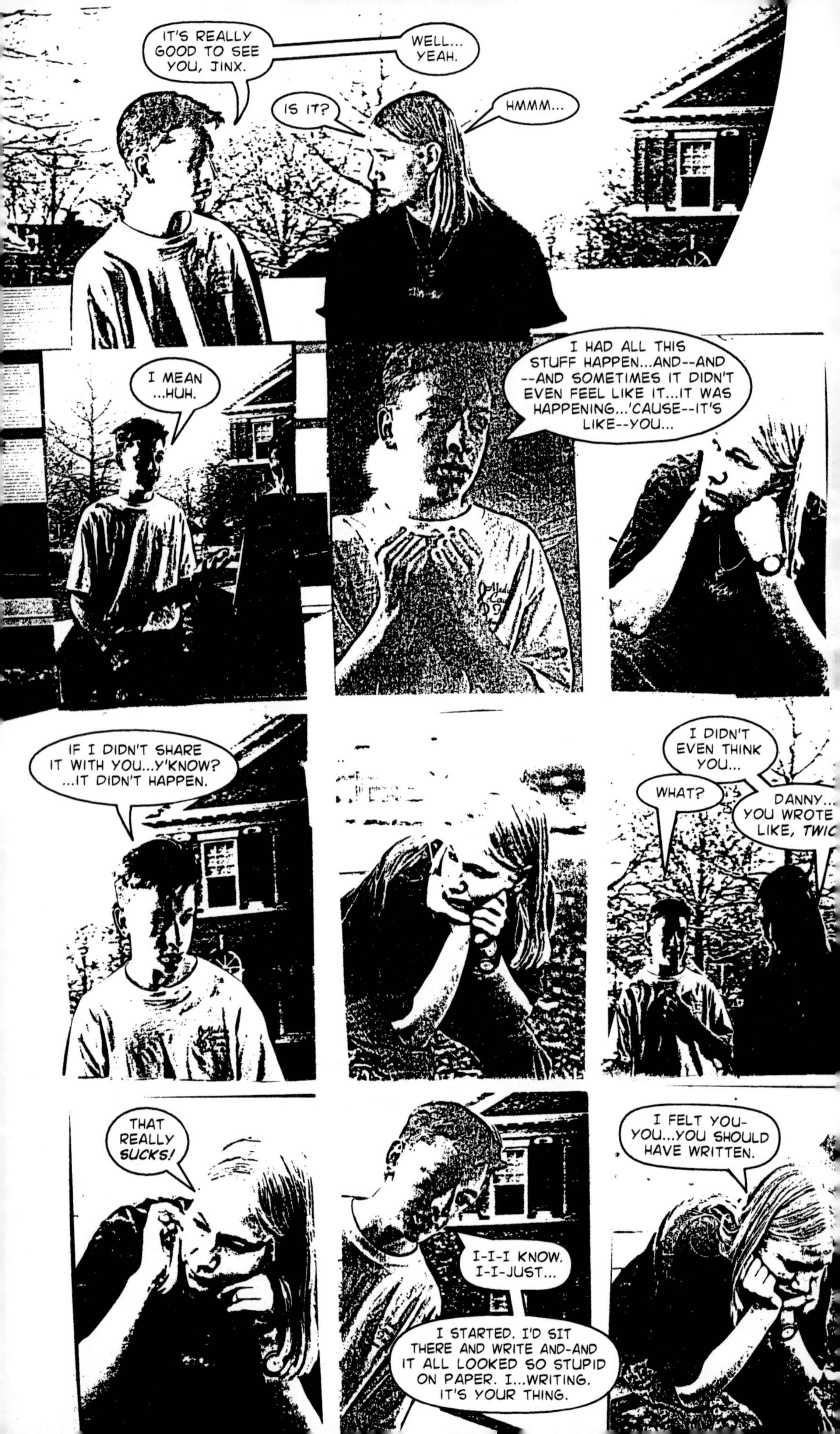
IT'S REALLY GOOD TO SEE YOU, JINX.
WELL... YEAH.
IS IT?
HMMM...
I MEAN ...HUH.
I HAD ALL THIS STUFF HAPPEN...AND--AND --AND SOMETIMES IT DIDN'T EVEN FEEL LIKE IT...IT WAS HAPPENING...'CAUSE--IT'S LIKE--YOU...
IF I DIDN'T SHARE IT WITH YOU...Y'KNOW? ...IT DIDN'T HAPPEN.
I DIDN'T EVEN THINK YOU...
WHAT?
DANNY... YOU WROTE LIKE, *TWIC*
THAT REALLY *SUCKS!*
I-I-I KNOW. I-I-JUST...
I STARTED. I'D SIT THERE AND WRITE AND-AND IT ALL LOOKED SO STUPID ON PAPER. I...WRITING. IT'S YOUR THING.
I FELT YOU- YOU...YOU SHOULD HAVE WRITTEN.

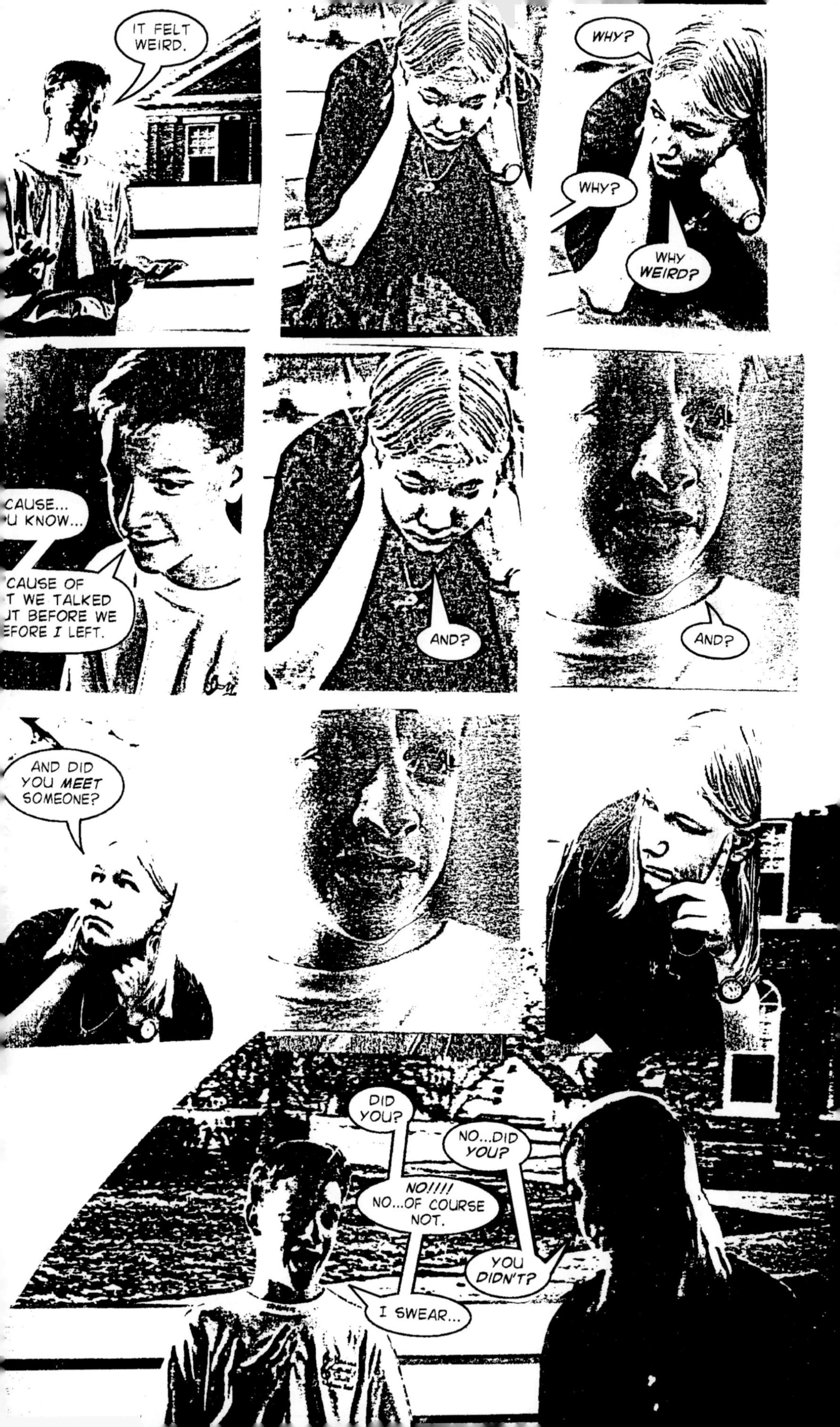
IT FELT WEIRD.
WHY?
WHY?
WHY WEIRD?
CAUSE... U KNOW...
CAUSE OF T WE TALKED JT BEFORE WE EFORE I LEFT.
AND?
AND?
AND DID YOU MEET SOMEONE?
DID YOU?
NO...DID YOU?
NO!!!! NO...OF COURSE NOT.
YOU DIDN'T?
I SWEAR...

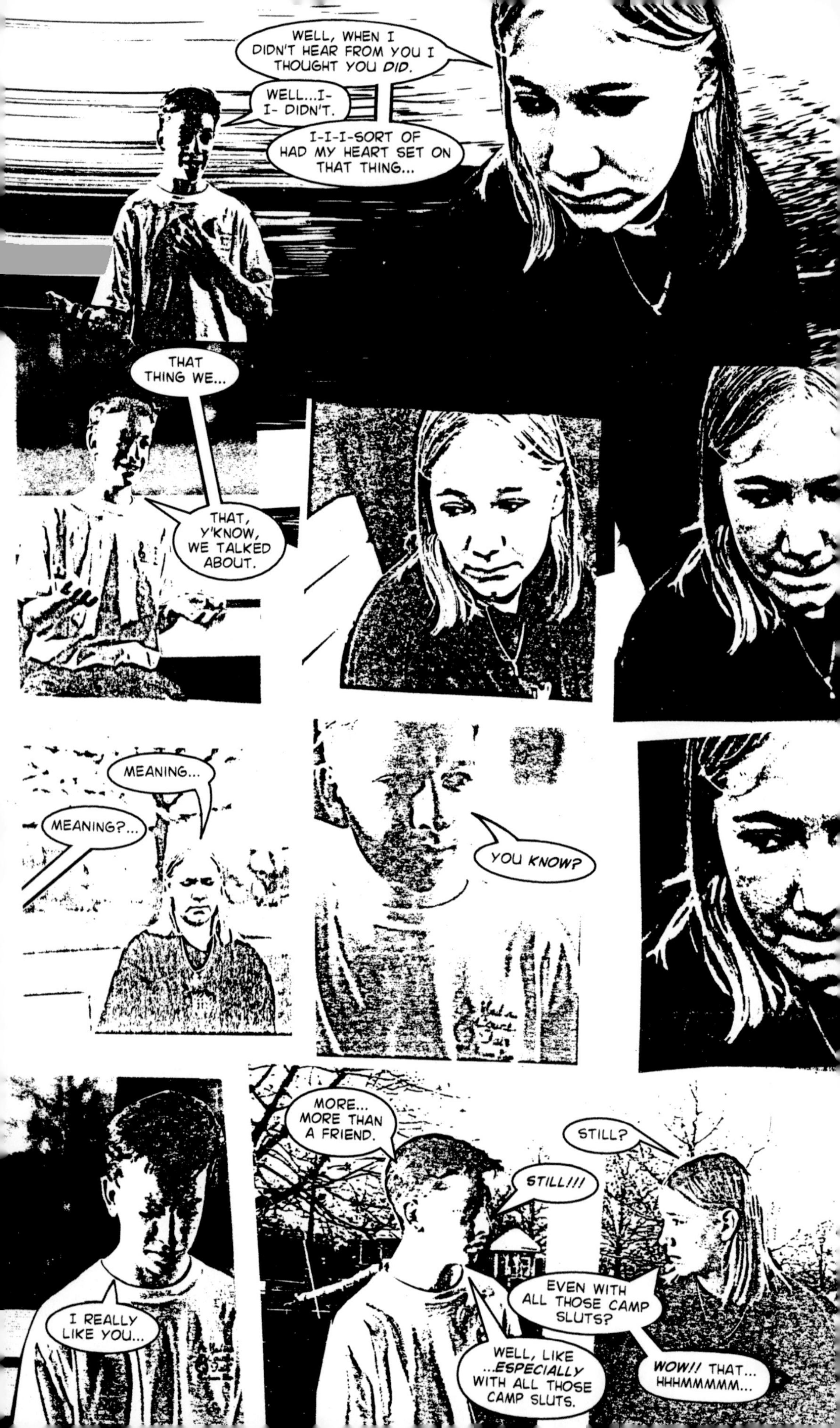
WELL, WHEN I DIDN'T HEAR FROM YOU I THOUGHT YOU DID.
WELL...I- I- DIDN'T.
I-I-I-SORT OF HAD MY HEART SET ON THAT THING...
THAT THING WE...
THAT, Y'KNOW, WE TALKED ABOUT.
MEANING...
MEANING?...
YOU KNOW?
I REALLY LIKE YOU...
MORE... MORE THAN A FRIEND.
STILL?
STILL!!!
EVEN WITH ALL THOSE CAMP SLUTS?
WELL, LIKE ...ESPECIALLY WITH ALL THOSE CAMP SLUTS.
WOW!! THAT... HHHMMMMM...

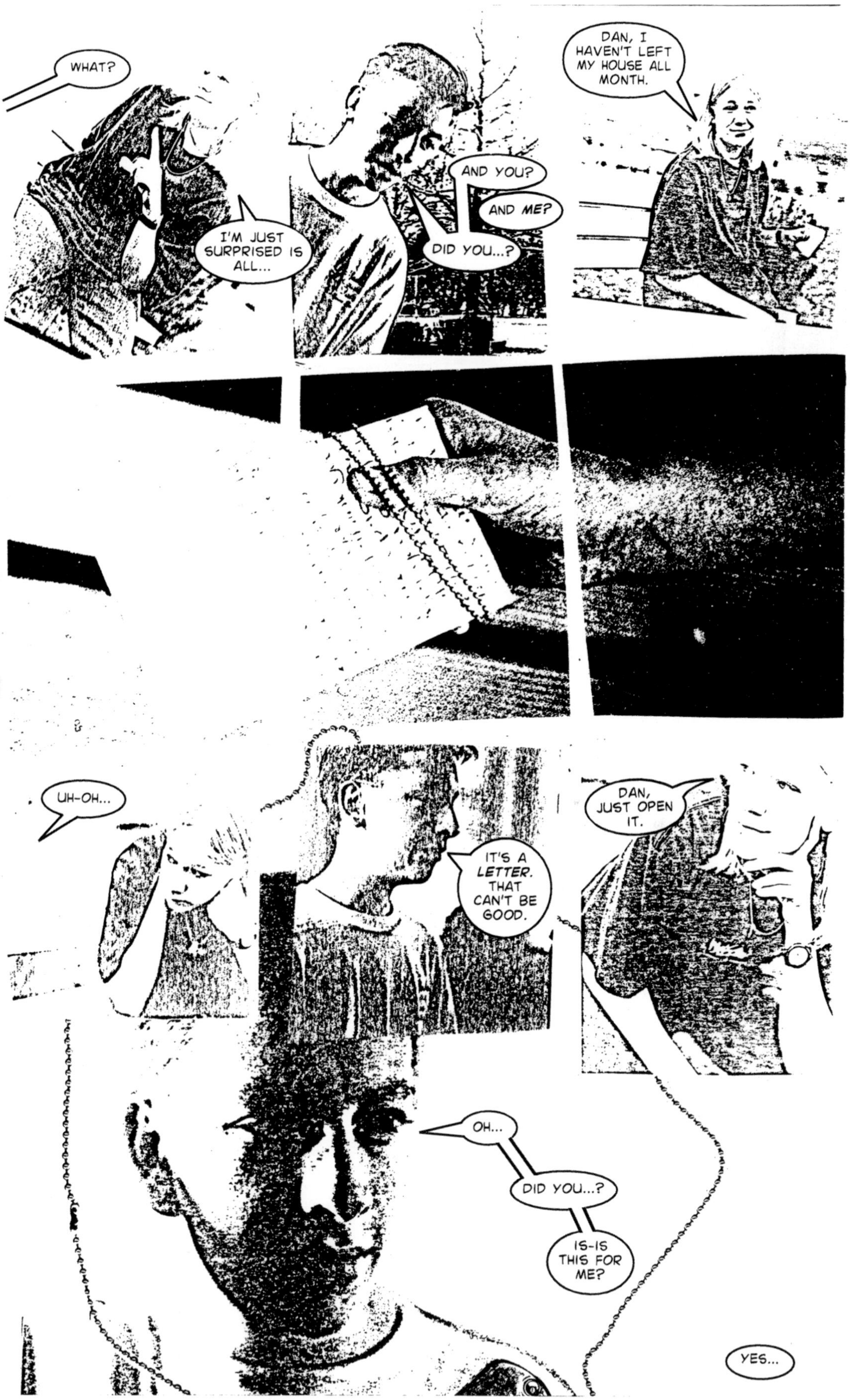
WHAT?
I'M JUST SURPRISED IS ALL...
DID YOU...?
AND YOU?
AND *ME?*
DAN, I HAVEN'T LEFT MY HOUSE ALL MONTH.
UH-OH...
IT'S A *LETTER.* THAT CAN'T BE GOOD.
DAN, JUST OPEN IT.
OH...
DID YOU...?
IS-IS THIS FOR ME?
YES...

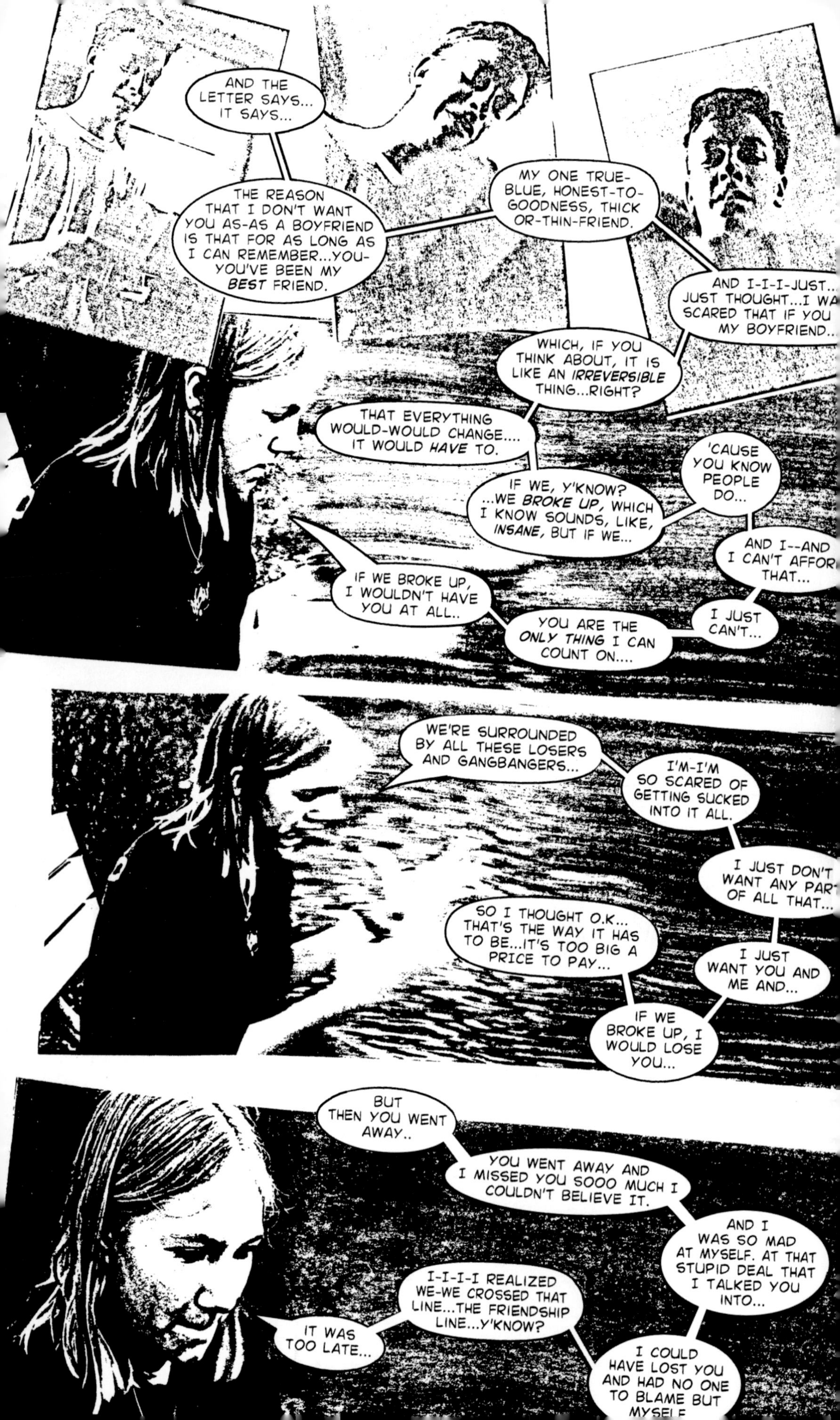
AND THE LETTER SAYS... IT SAYS...
THE REASON THAT I DON'T WANT YOU AS-AS A BOYFRIEND IS THAT FOR AS LONG AS I CAN REMEMBER...YOU-YOU'VE BEEN MY *BEST* FRIEND.
MY ONE TRUE-BLUE, HONEST-TO-GOODNESS, THICK OR-THIN-FRIEND.
AND I-I-I-JUST.. JUST THOUGHT...I WA SCARED THAT IF YOU MY BOYFRIEND..
WHICH, IF YOU THINK ABOUT, IT IS LIKE AN *IRREVERSIBLE* THING...RIGHT?
THAT EVERYTHING WOULD-WOULD CHANGE.... IT WOULD *HAVE* TO.
IF WE, Y'KNOW? ...WE *BROKE UP*, WHICH I KNOW SOUNDS, LIKE, *INSANE*, BUT IF WE...
'CAUSE YOU KNOW PEOPLE DO...
AND I--AND I CAN'T AFFOR THAT...
IF WE BROKE UP, I WOULDN'T HAVE YOU AT ALL..
YOU ARE THE *ONLY THING* I CAN COUNT ON....
I JUST CAN'T...
WE'RE SURROUNDED BY ALL THESE LOSERS AND GANGBANGERS...
I'M-I'M SO SCARED OF GETTING SUCKED INTO IT ALL.
I JUST DON'T WANT ANY PAR OF ALL THAT...
SO I THOUGHT O.K... THAT'S THE WAY IT HAS TO BE...IT'S TOO BIG A PRICE TO PAY...
I JUST WANT YOU AND ME AND...
IF WE BROKE UP, I WOULD LOSE YOU...
BUT THEN YOU WENT AWAY..
YOU WENT AWAY AND I MISSED YOU SOOO MUCH I COULDN'T BELIEVE IT.
AND I WAS SO MAD AT MYSELF. AT THAT STUPID DEAL THAT I TALKED YOU INTO...
I-I-I-I REALIZED WE-WE CROSSED THAT LINE...THE FRIENDSHIP LINE...Y'KNOW?
IT WAS TOO LATE...
I COULD HAVE LOST YOU AND HAD NO ONE TO BLAME BUT

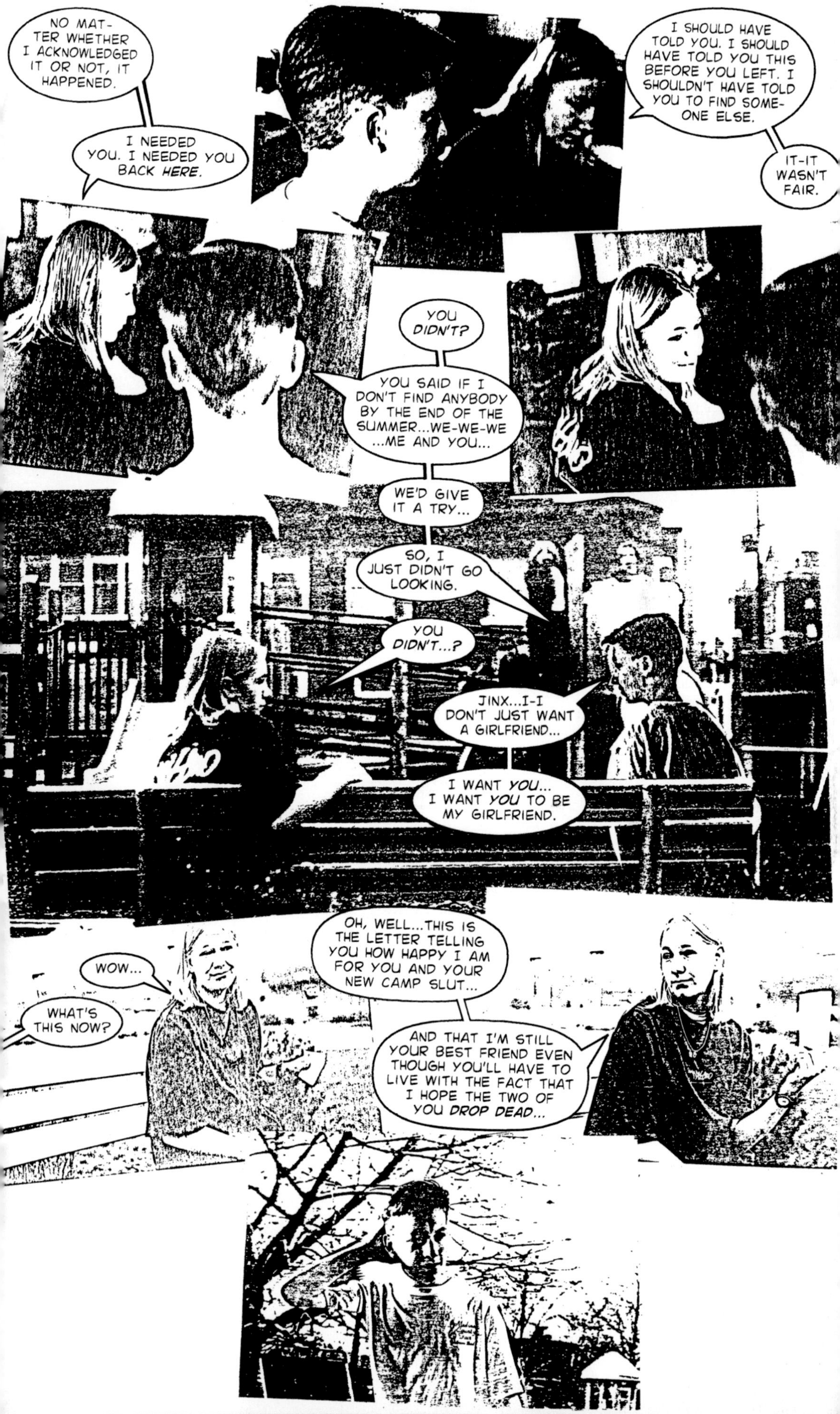

NO MATTER WHETHER I ACKNOWLEDGED IT OR NOT, IT HAPPENED.
I NEEDED YOU. I NEEDED YOU BACK *HERE*.
I SHOULD HAVE TOLD YOU. I SHOULD HAVE TOLD YOU THIS BEFORE YOU LEFT. I SHOULDN'T HAVE TOLD YOU TO FIND SOMEONE ELSE.
IT-IT WASN'T FAIR.
YOU *DIDN'T?*
YOU SAID IF I DON'T FIND ANYBODY BY THE END OF THE SUMMER...WE-WE-WE ...ME AND YOU...
WE'D GIVE IT A TRY...
SO, I JUST DIDN'T GO LOOKING.
YOU *DIDN'T...?*
JINX...I-I DON'T JUST WANT A GIRLFRIEND...
I WANT *YOU*... I WANT *YOU* TO BE MY GIRLFRIEND.
WOW...
WHAT'S THIS NOW?
OH, WELL...THIS IS THE LETTER TELLING YOU HOW HAPPY I AM FOR YOU AND YOUR NEW CAMP SLUT...
AND THAT I'M STILL YOUR BEST FRIEND EVEN THOUGH YOU'LL HAVE TO LIVE WITH THE FACT THAT I HOPE THE TWO OF YOU *DROP DEAD*...

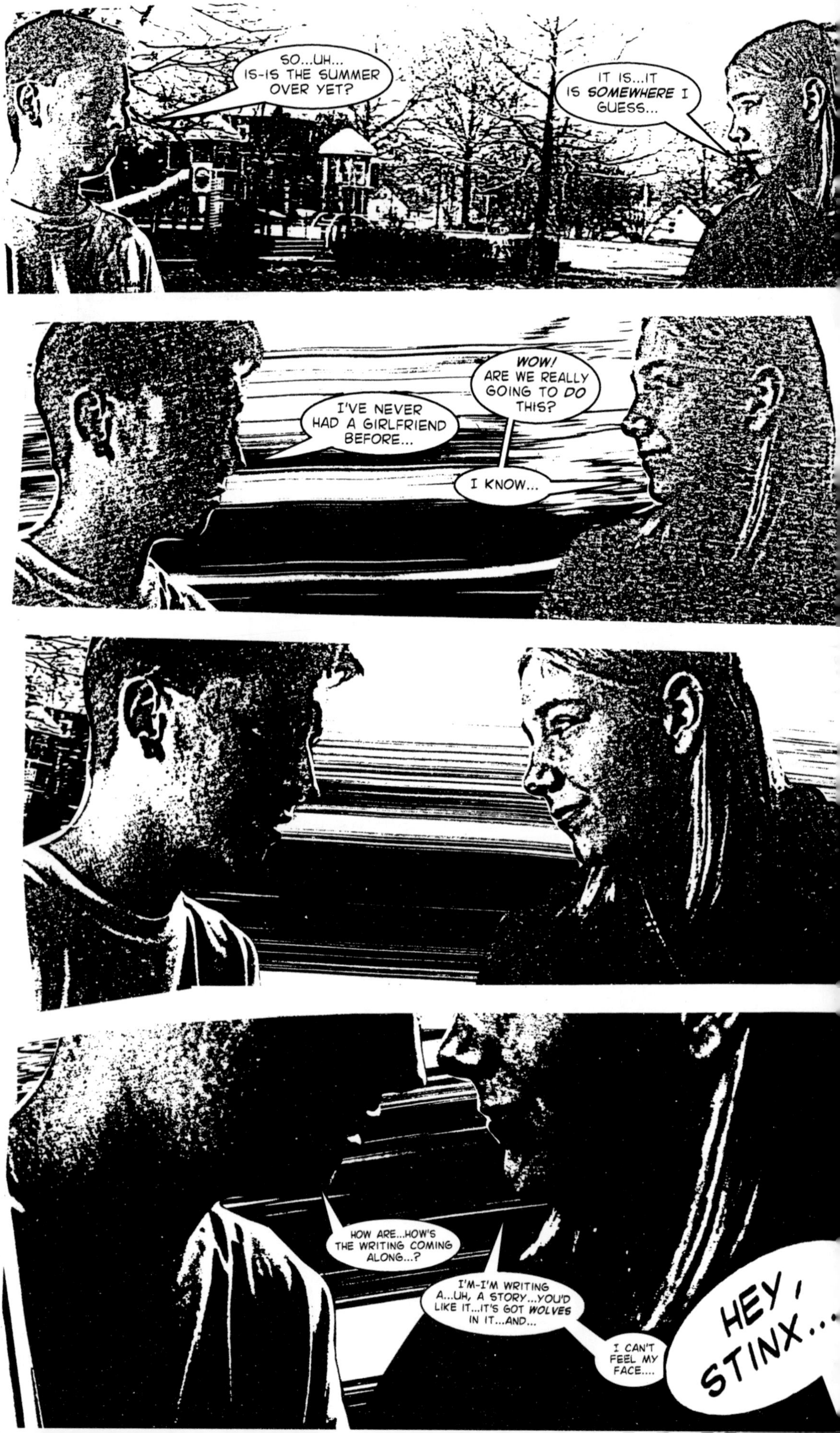
SO...UH... IS-IS THE SUMMER OVER YET?
IT IS...IT IS SOMEWHERE I GUESS...
I'VE NEVER HAD A GIRLFRIEND BEFORE...
WOW! ARE WE REALLY GOING TO DO THIS?
I KNOW...
HOW ARE...HOW'S THE WRITING COMING ALONG...?
I'M-I'M WRITING A...UH, A STORY...YOU'D LIKE IT...IT'S GOT WOLVES IN IT...AND...
I CAN'T FEEL MY FACE....
HEY, STINX...

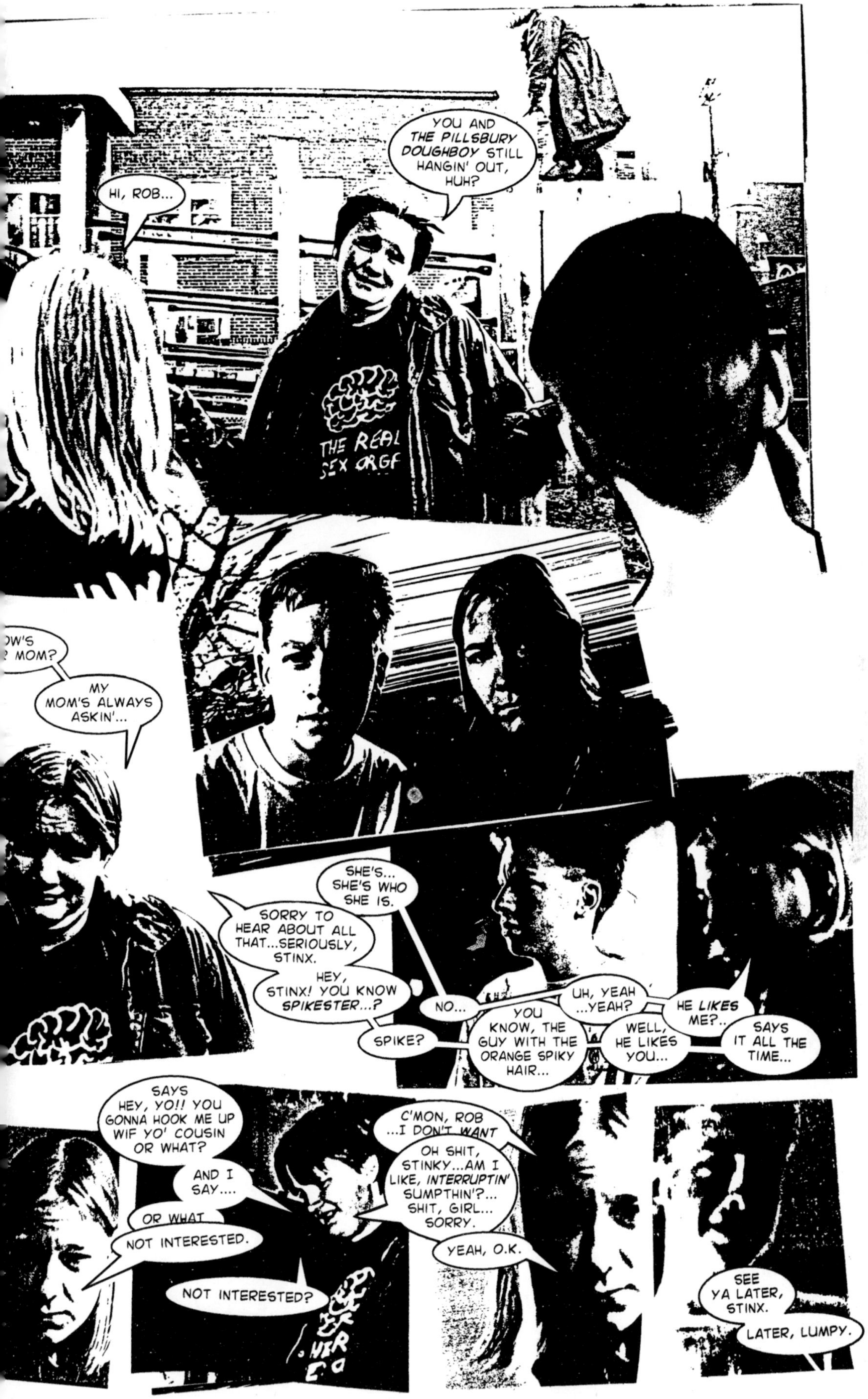

HI, ROB...
YOU AND *THE PILLSBURY DOUGHBOY* STILL HANGIN' OUT, HUH?
OW'S R MOM?
MY MOM'S ALWAYS ASKIN'...
SHE'S... SHE'S WHO SHE IS.
SORRY TO HEAR ABOUT ALL THAT...SERIOUSLY, STINX.
HEY, STINX! YOU KNOW *SPIKESTER*...?
NO...
SPIKE?
UH, YEAH ...YEAH?
YOU KNOW, THE GUY WITH THE ORANGE SPIKY HAIR...
WELL, HE LIKES YOU...
HE *LIKES* ME?..
SAYS IT ALL THE TIME...
SAYS HEY, *YO!!* YOU GONNA HOOK ME UP WIF YO' COUSIN OR WHAT?
AND I SAY....
OR WHAT
NOT INTERESTED.
NOT INTERESTED?
C'MON, ROB ...I DON'T *WANT*
OH SHIT, STINKY...AM I LIKE, *INTERRUPTIN'* SUMPTHIN'?... SHIT, GIRL... SORRY.
YEAH, O.K.
SEE YA LATER, STINX.
LATER, LUMPY.

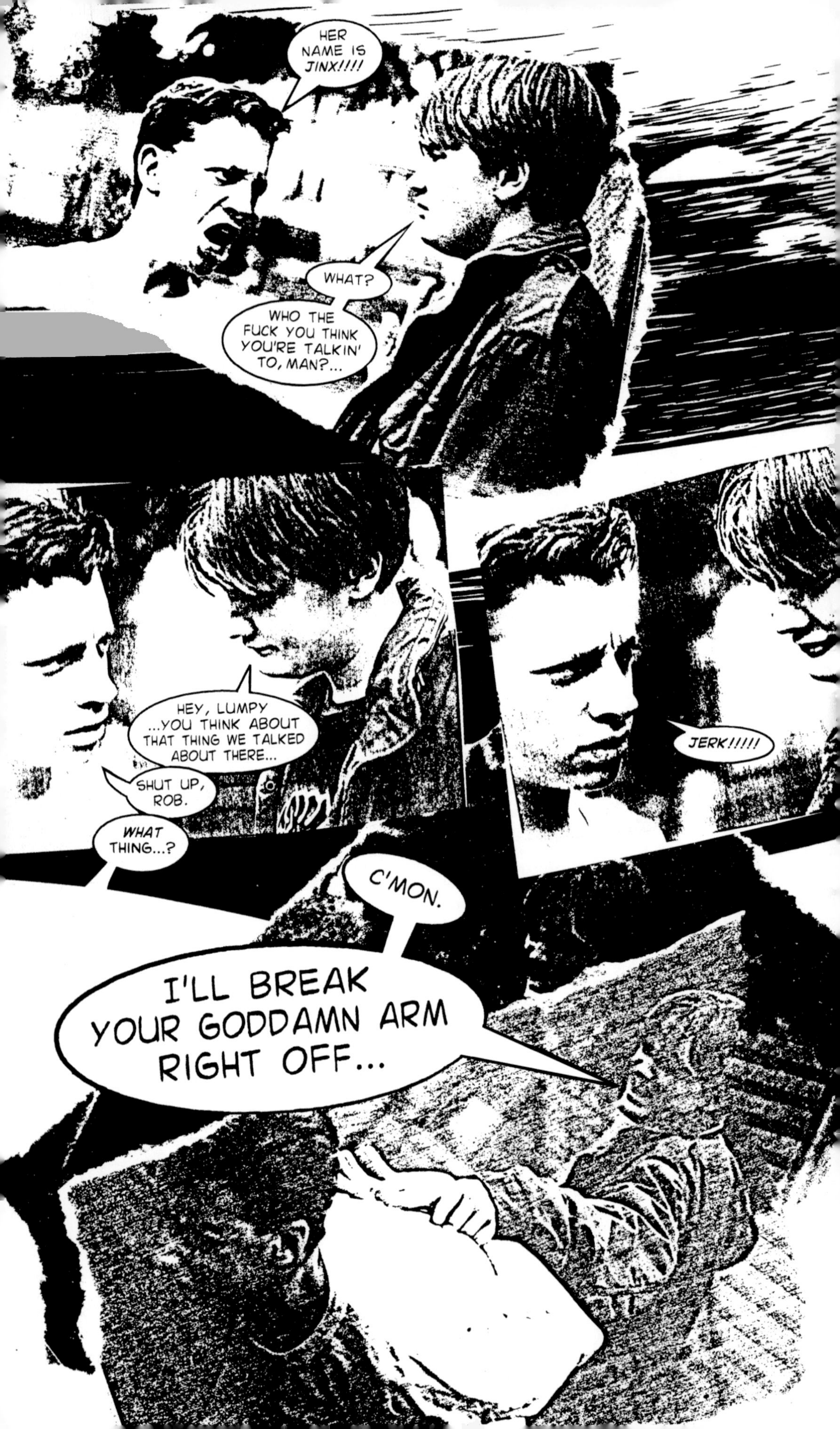
HER NAME IS JINX!!!!
WHAT?
WHO THE FUCK YOU THINK YOU'RE TALKIN' TO, MAN?...
HEY, LUMPY ...YOU THINK ABOUT THAT THING WE TALKED ABOUT THERE...
SHUT UP, ROB.
WHAT THING...?
JERK!!!!!
C'MON.
I'LL BREAK YOUR GODDAMN ARM RIGHT OFF...

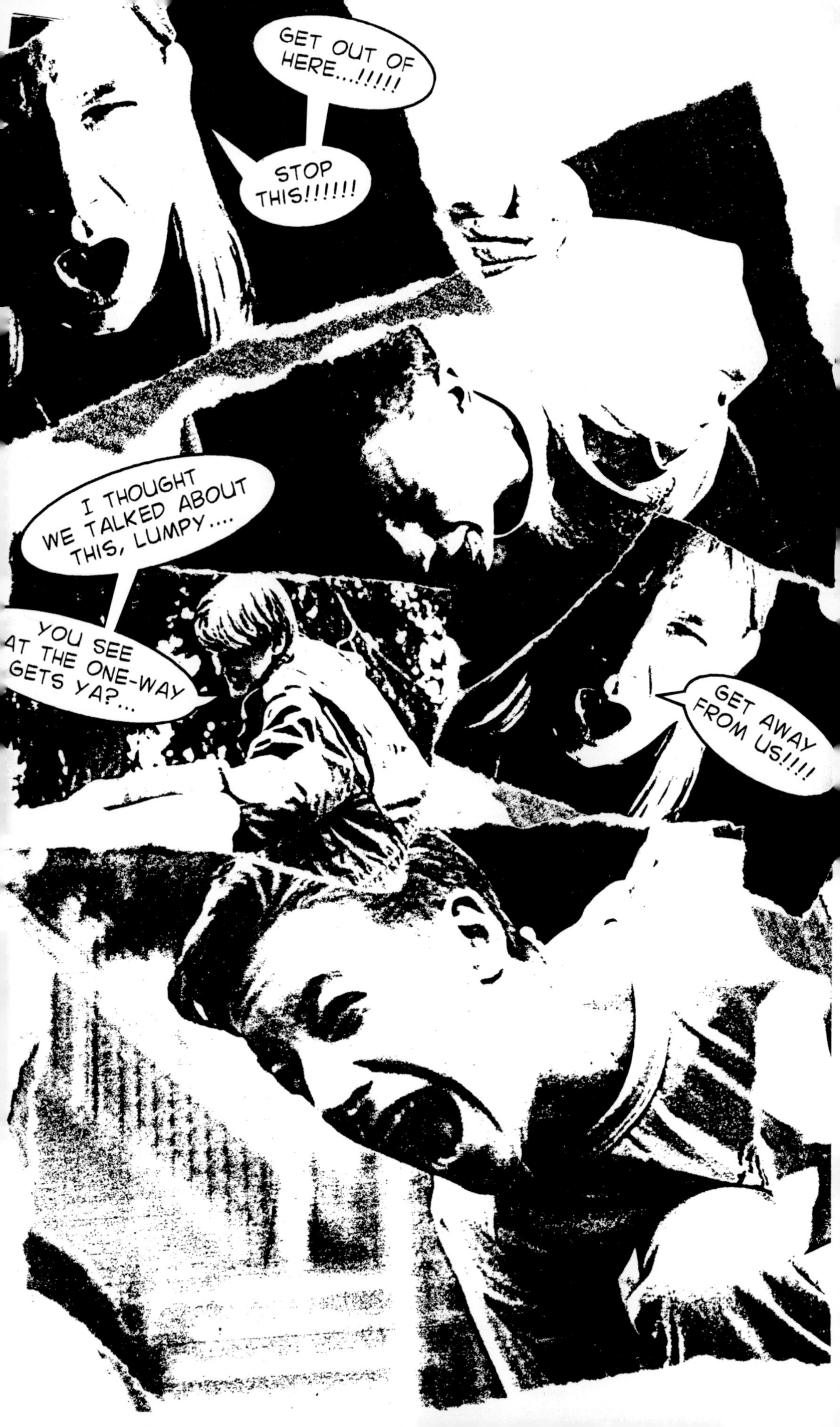
GET OUT OF HERE...!!!!!
STOP THIS!!!!!!
I THOUGHT WE TALKED ABOUT THIS, LUMPY....
YOU SEE AT THE ONE-WAY GETS YA?...
GET AWAY FROM US!!!!

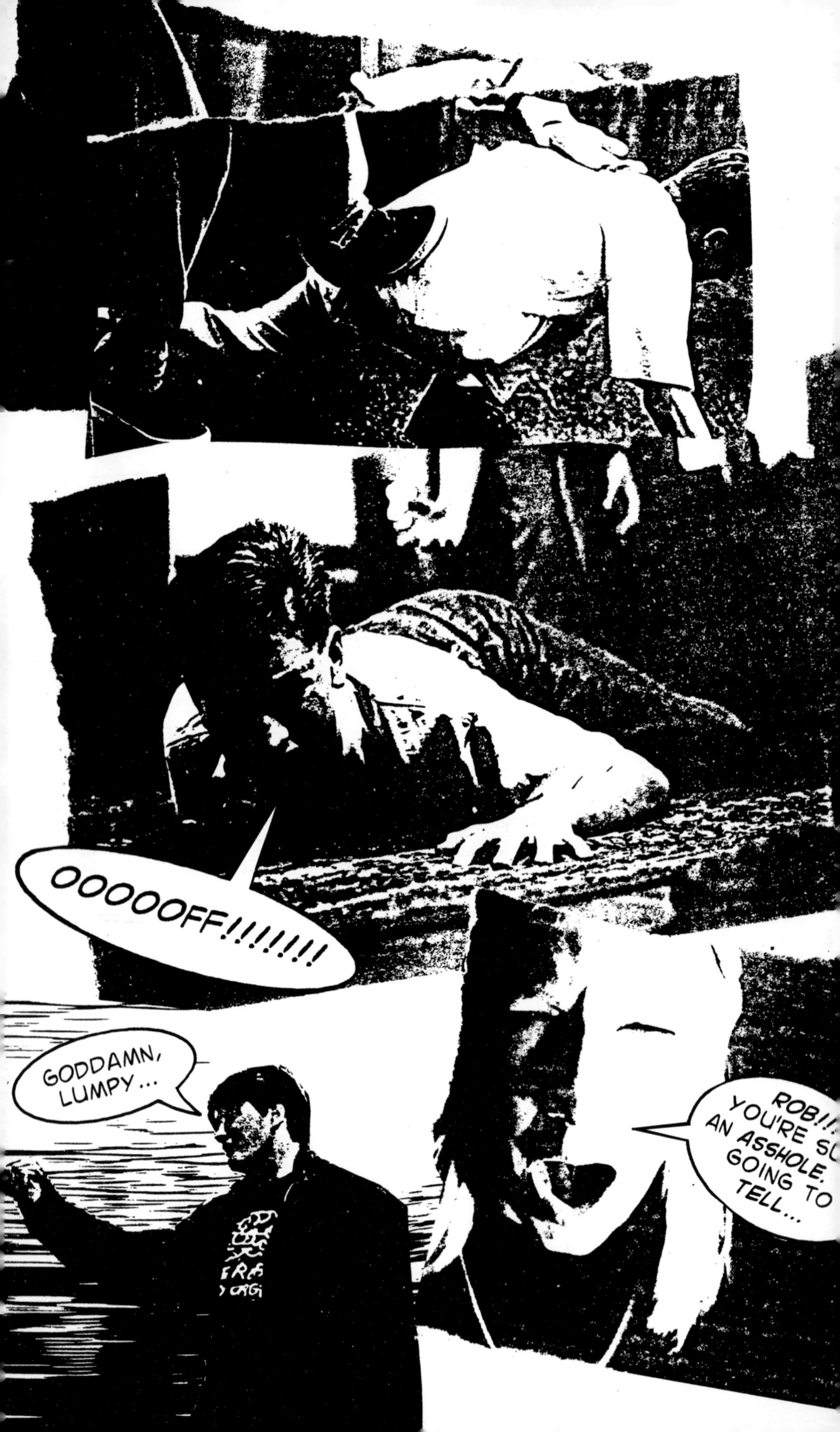
OOOOOOFF!!!!!!!
GODDAMN, LUMPY...
ROB!!! YOU'RE SU AN ASSHOLE. GOING TO TELL...

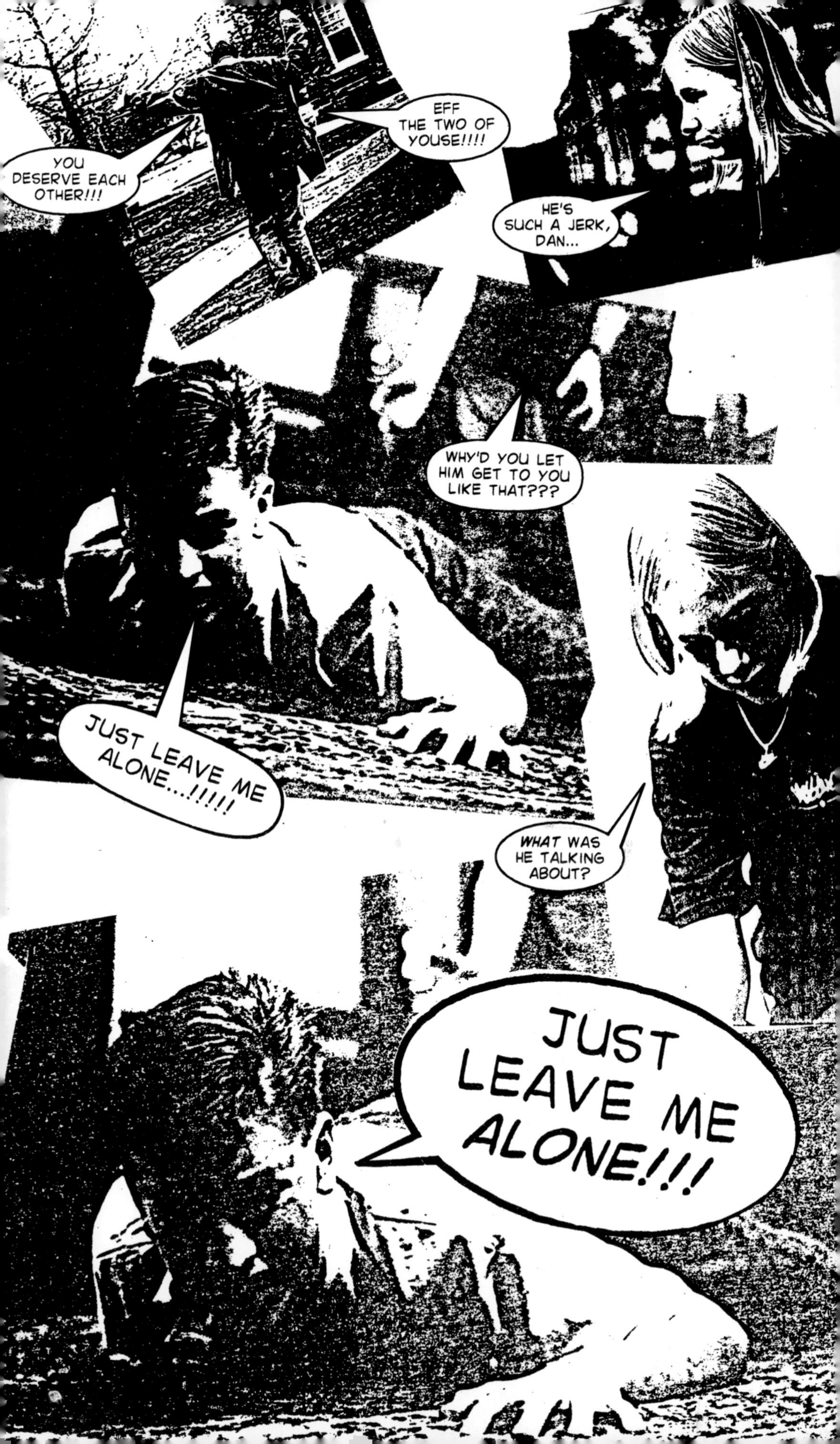

EFF THE TWO OF YOUSE!!!!
YOU DESERVE EACH OTHER!!!
HE'S SUCH A JERK, DAN...
WHY'D YOU LET HIM GET TO YOU LIKE THAT???
JUST LEAVE ME ALONE...!!!!!
WHAT WAS HE TALKING ABOUT?
JUST LEAVE ME ALONE!!!

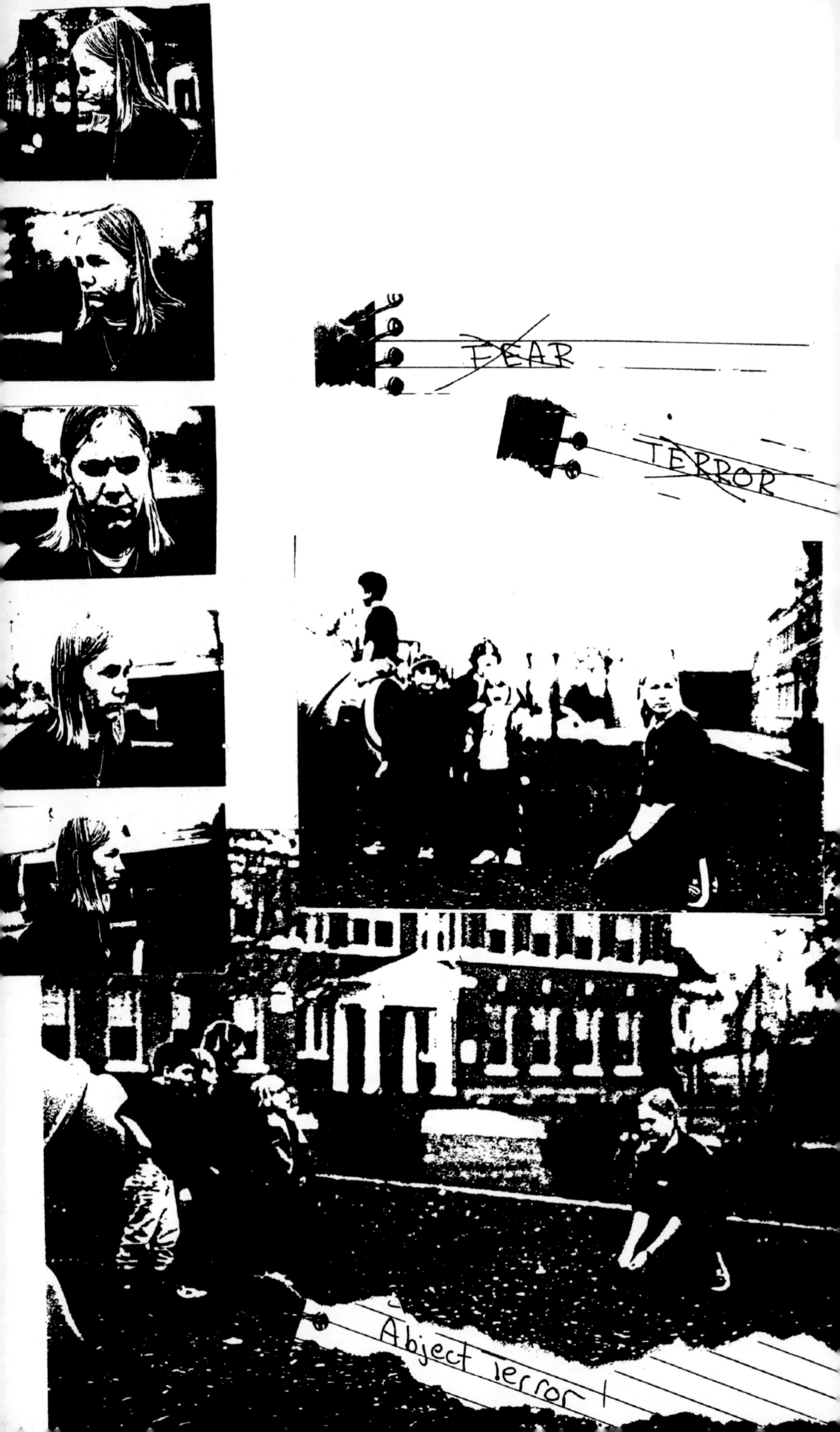
FEAR
TERROR
Abject terror!

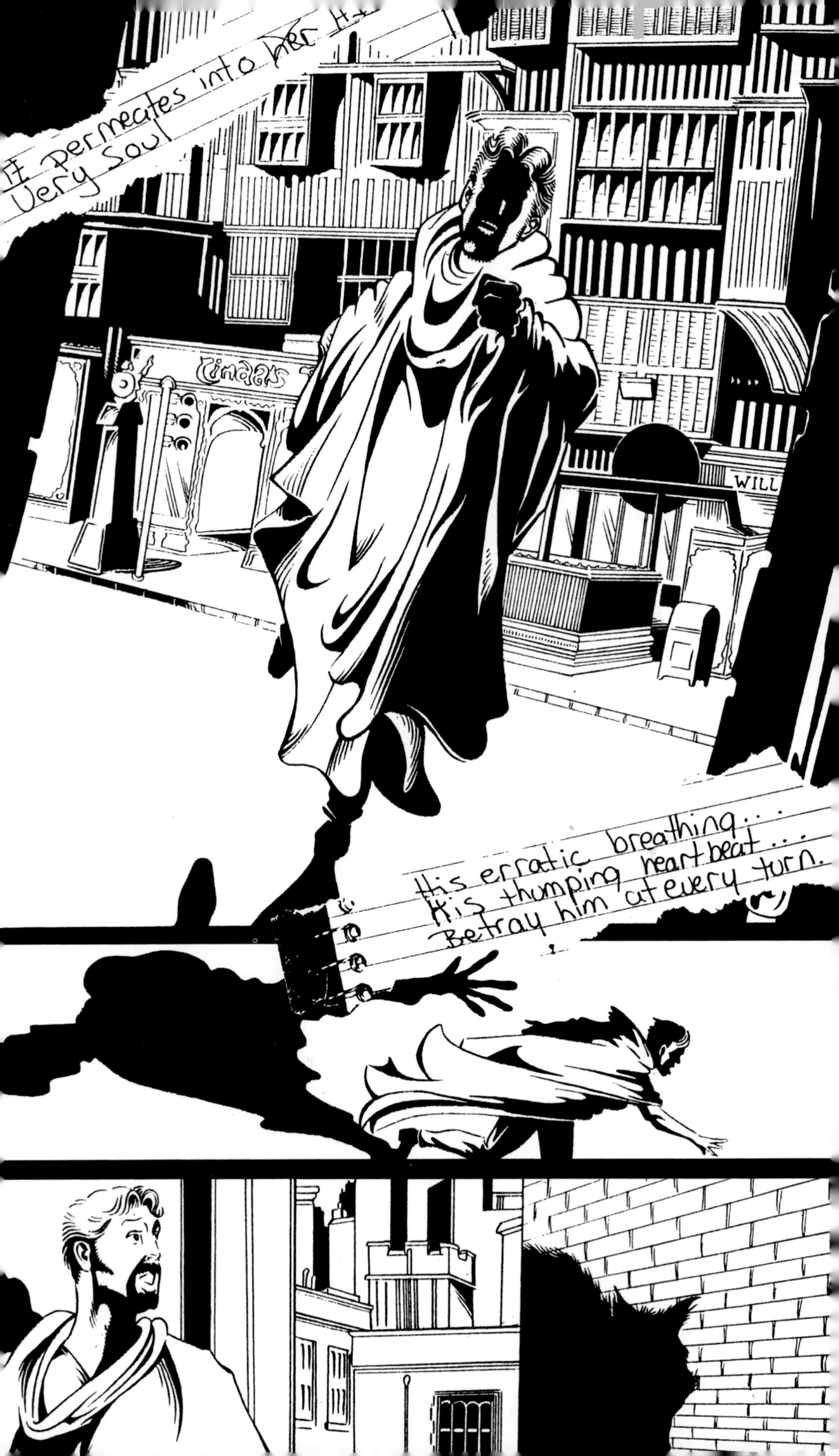
It permeates into her
Very Soul
WILL
His erratic breathing...
His thumping heartbeat...
Betray him at every turn.

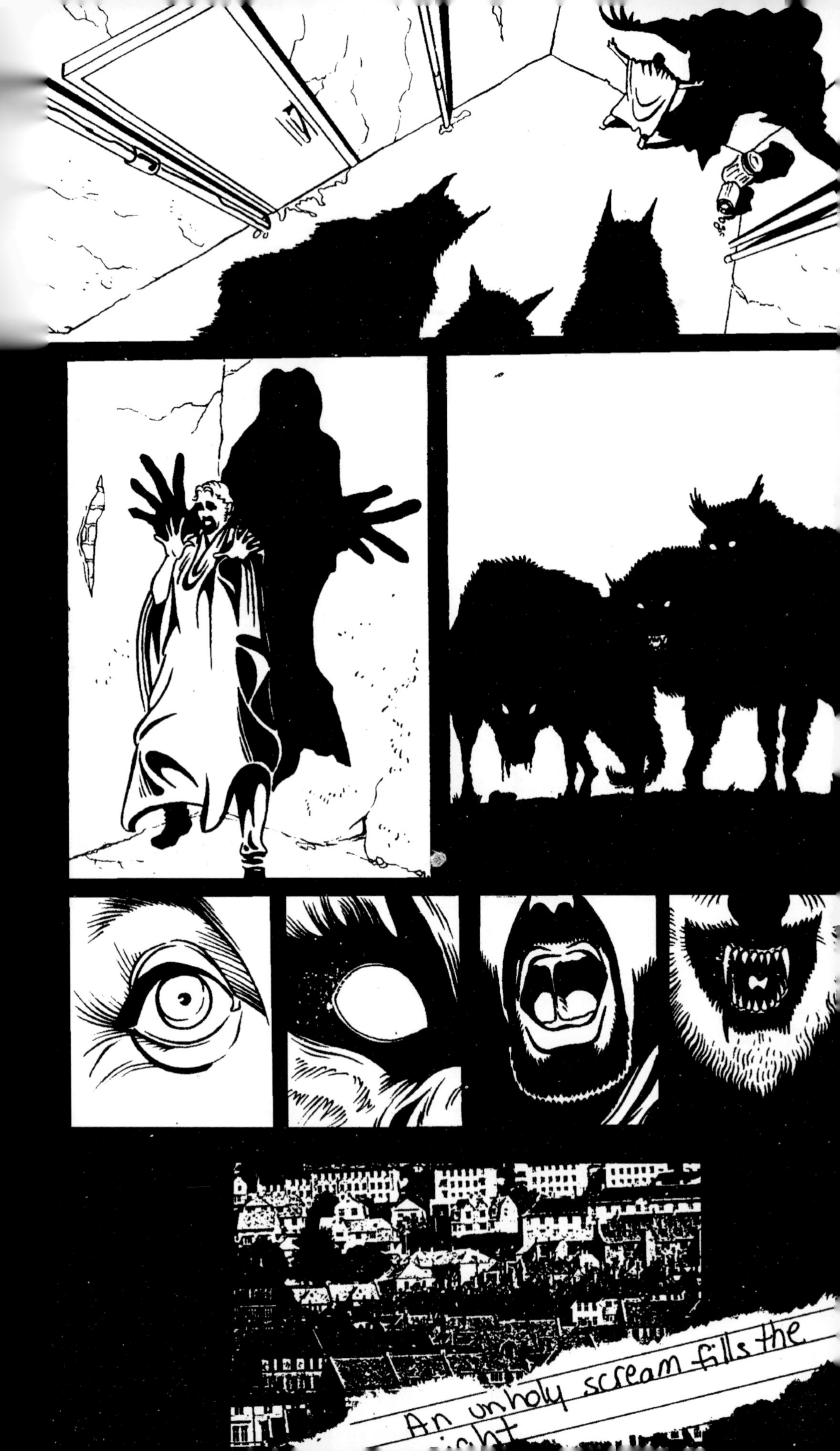
An unholy scream fills the

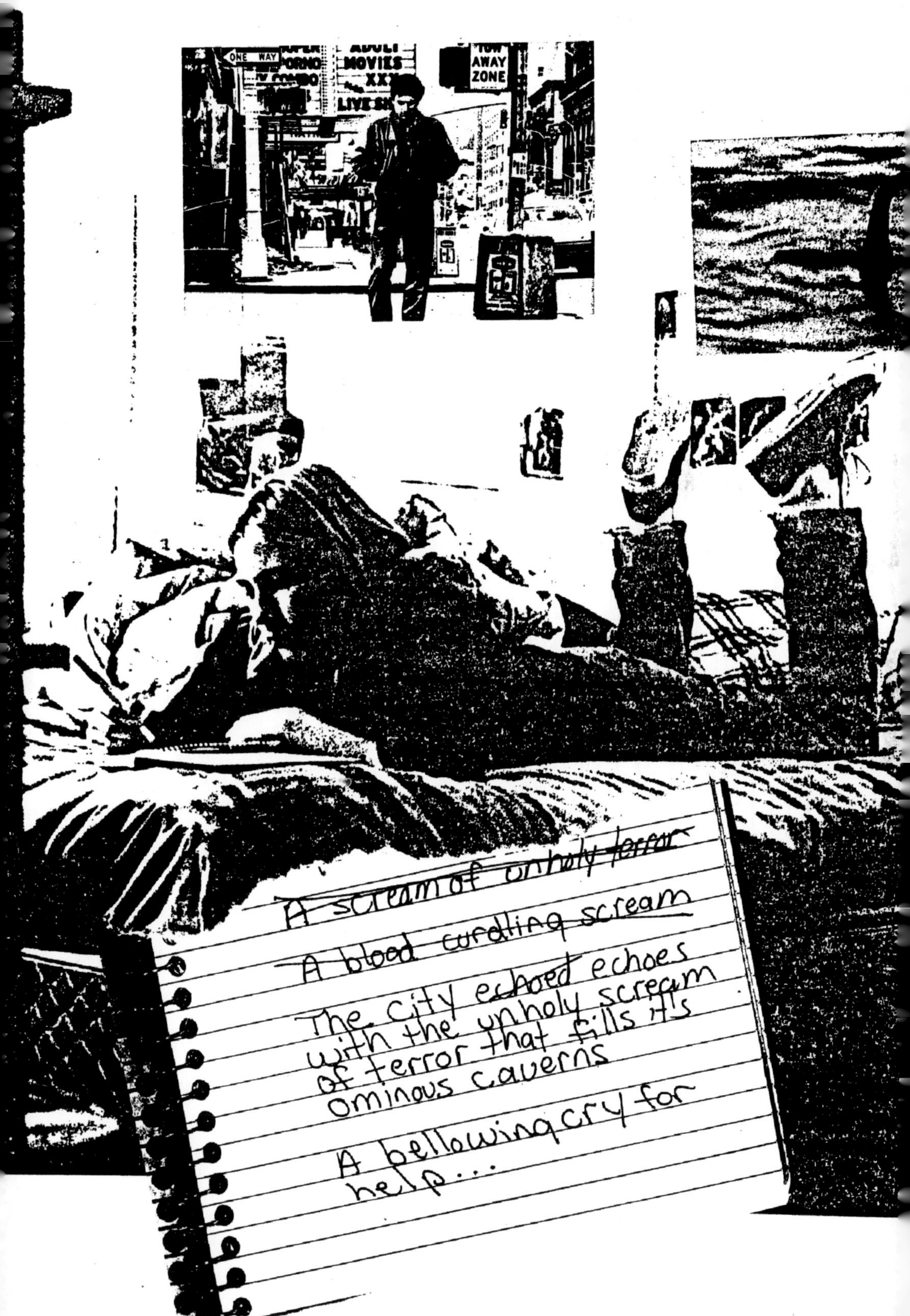
ONE WAY
PORNO
ADULT MOVIES XXX
TOW AWAY ZONE
~~A scream of unholy terror~~
~~A blood curdling scream~~
The city ~~echoed~~ echoes
with the unholy scream
of terror that fills it's
ominous caverns
A bellowing cry for
help...

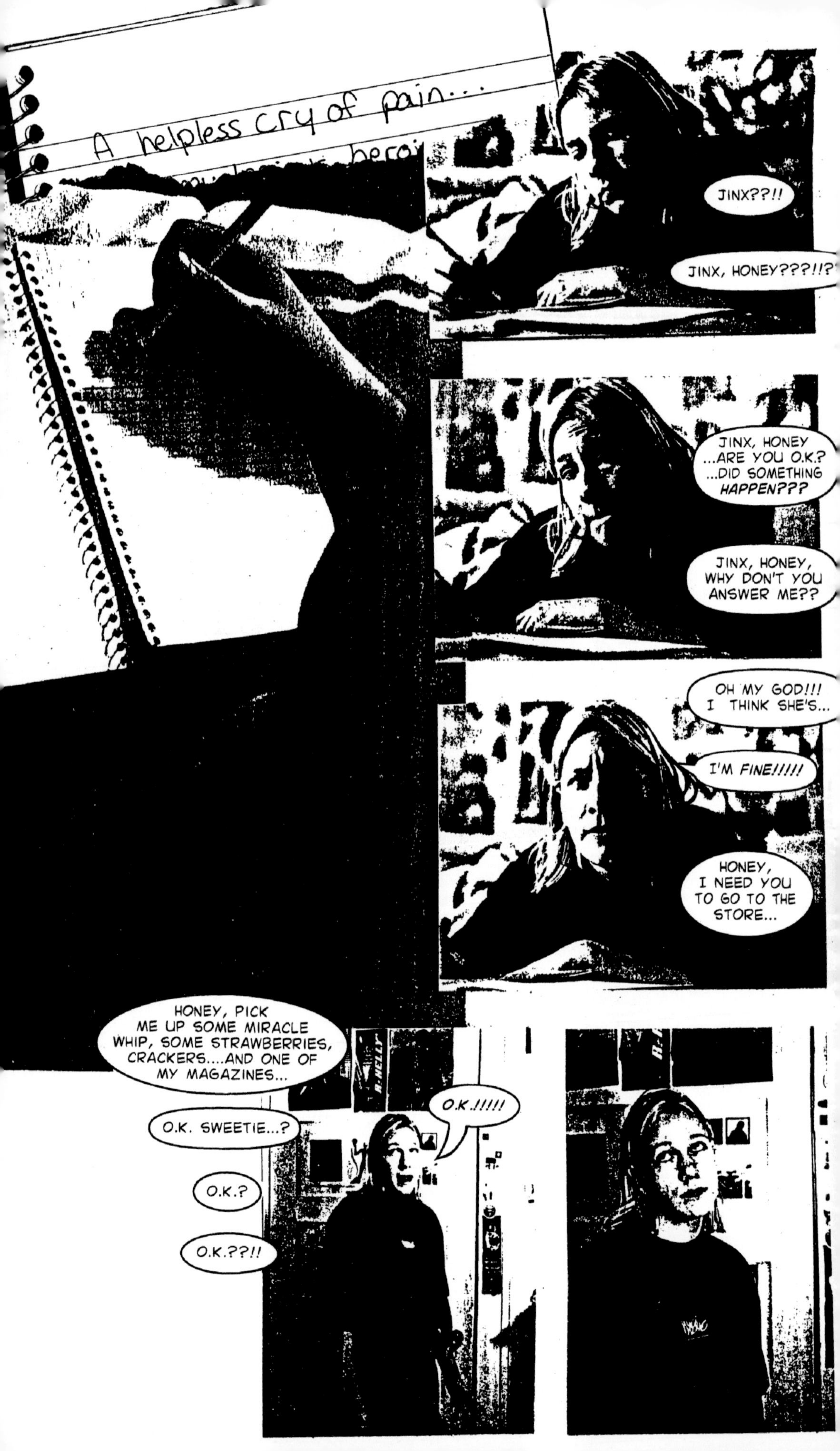
A helpless cry of pain...
JINX??!!
JINX, HONEY???!!?
JINX, HONEY ...ARE YOU O.K.? ...DID SOMETHING HAPPEN???
JINX, HONEY, WHY DON'T YOU ANSWER ME??
OH MY GOD!!! I THINK SHE'S...
I'M FINE!!!!!
HONEY, I NEED YOU TO GO TO THE STORE...
HONEY, PICK ME UP SOME MIRACLE WHIP, SOME STRAWBERRIES, CRACKERS....AND ONE OF MY MAGAZINES...
O.K.!!!!!
O.K. SWEETIE...?
O.K.?
O.K.??!!

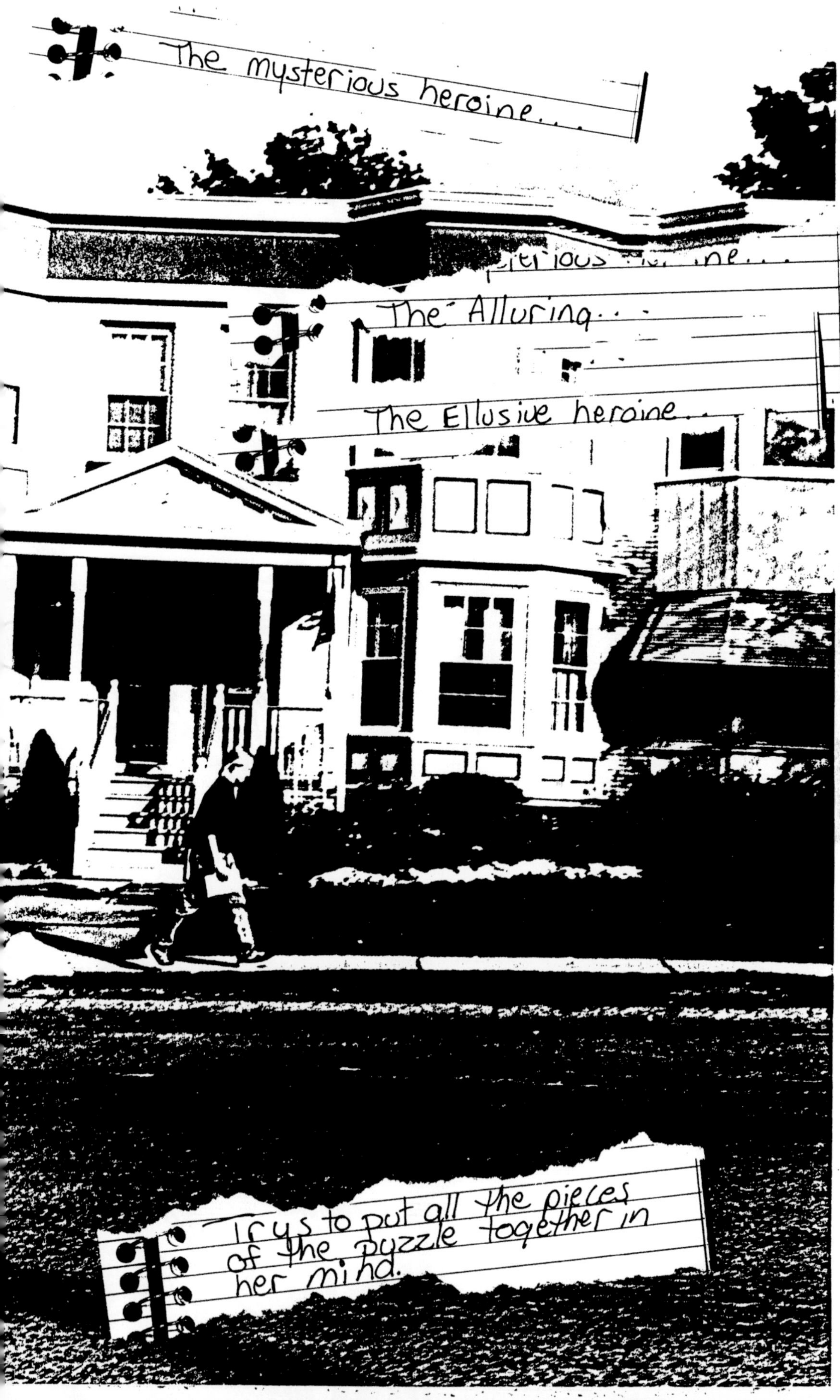
The mysterious heroine...
The Alluring...
The Ellusive heroine...
Trys to put all the pieces of the puzzle together in her mind.

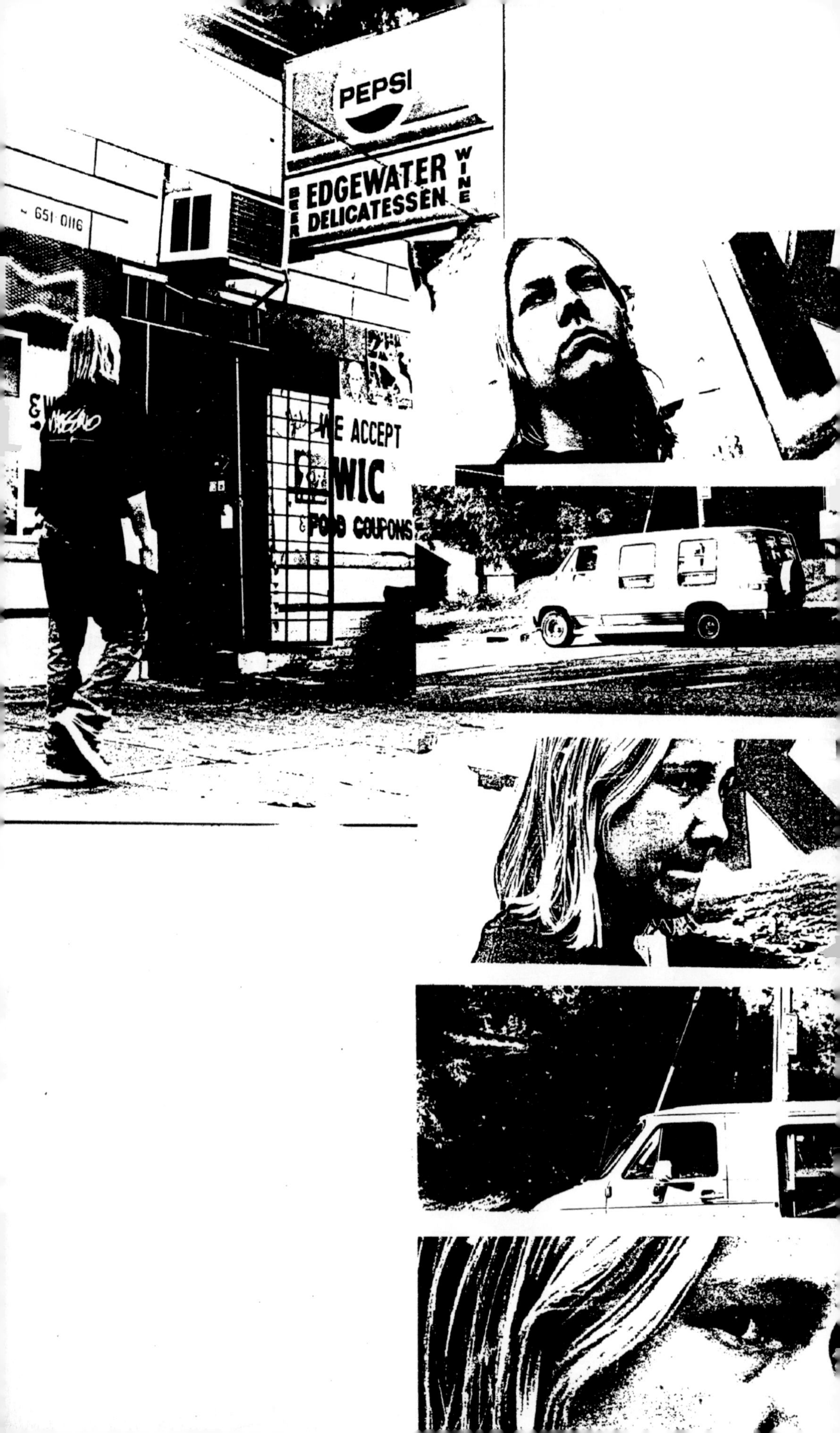
PEPSI
BEER
EDGEWATER DELICATESSEN
WINE
WE ACCEPT
WIC
& FOOD COUPONS

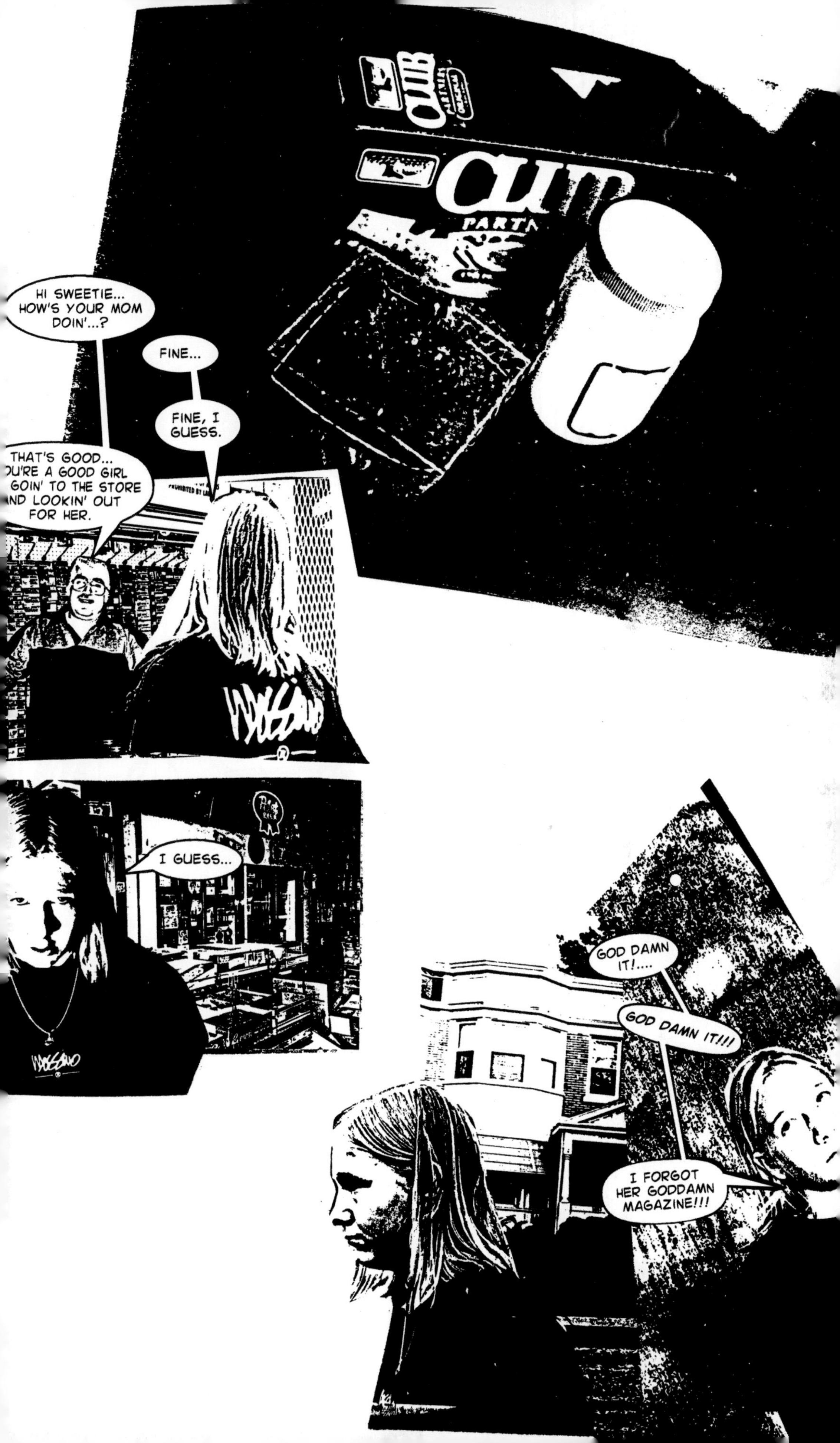
CLUB
PARTN
HI SWEETIE... HOW'S YOUR MOM DOIN'...?
FINE...
FINE, I GUESS.
THAT'S GOOD... OU'RE A GOOD GIRL GOIN' TO THE STORE AND LOOKIN' OUT FOR HER.
I GUESS...
GOD DAMN IT!....
GOD DAMN IT!!!
I FORGOT HER GODDAMN MAGAZINE!!!

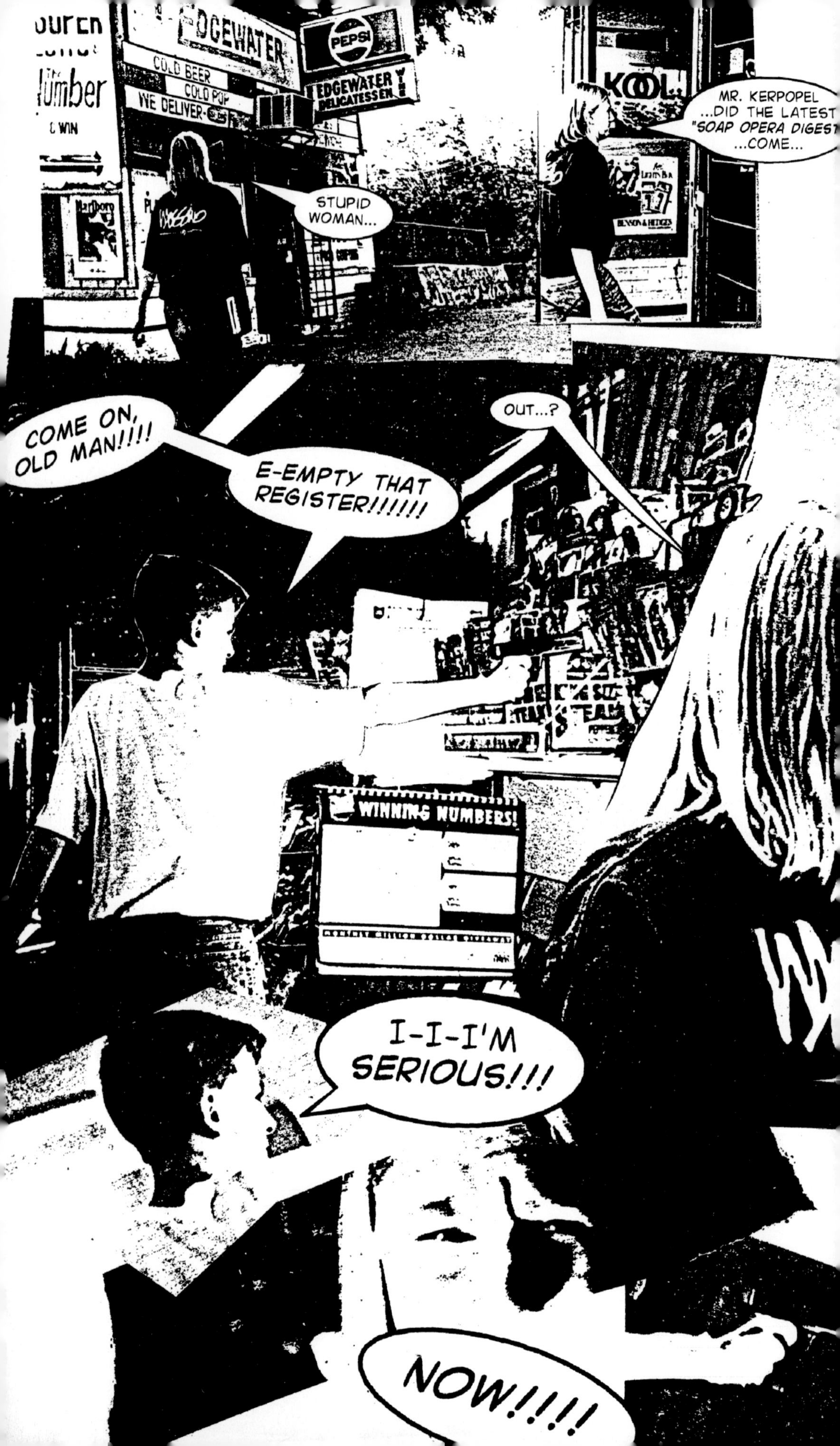
EDGEWATER
COLD BEER
COLD POP
WE DELIVER
PEPSI
EDGEWATER DELICATESSEN
KOOL
STUPID WOMAN...
MR. KERPOPEL ...DID THE LATEST "SOAP OPERA DIGEST" ...COME...
COME ON, OLD MAN!!!!
E-EMPTY THAT REGISTER!!!!!!
OUT...?
WINNING NUMBERS!
I-I-I'M SERIOUS!!!
NOW!!!!!

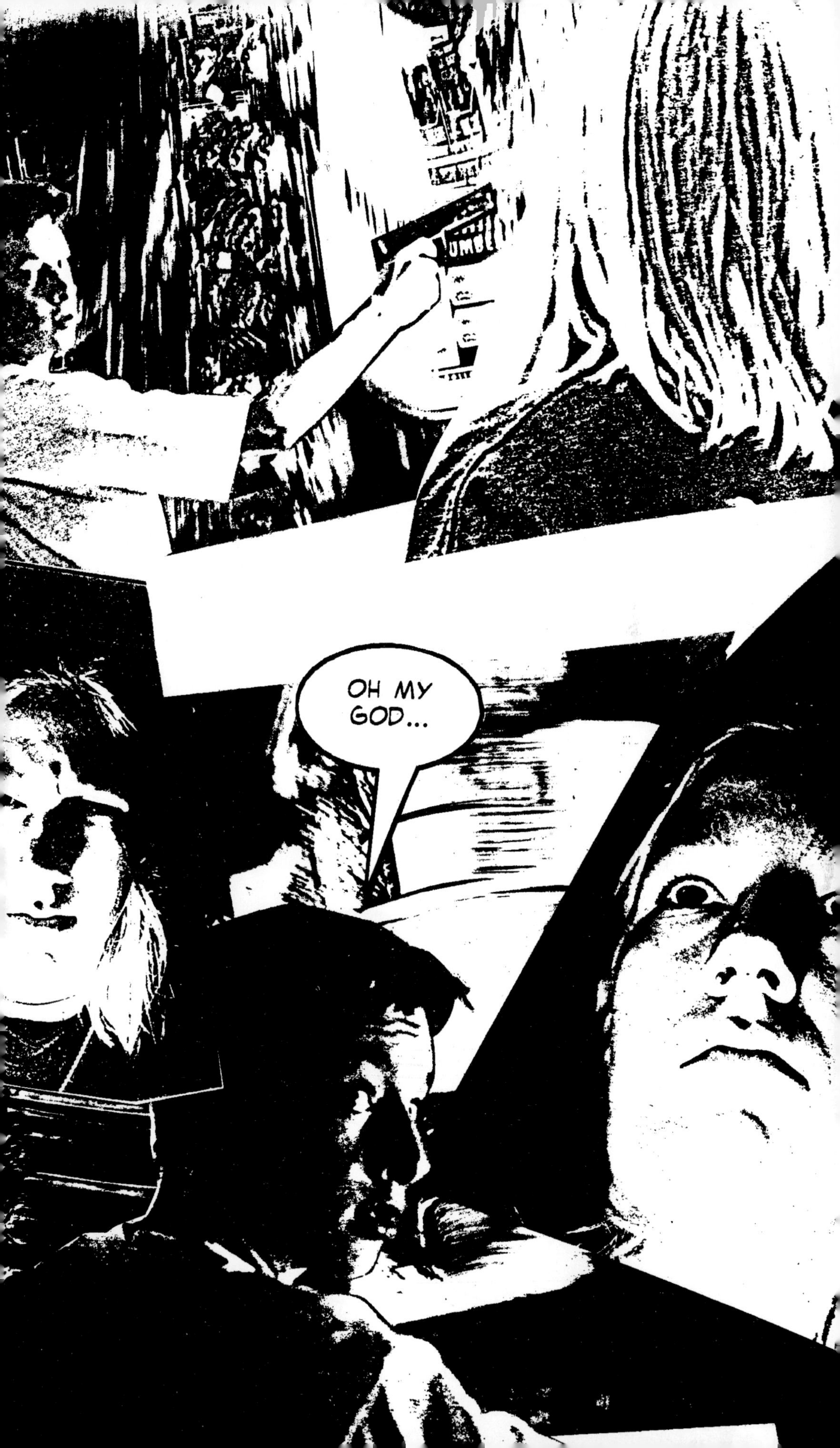
OH MY GOD...

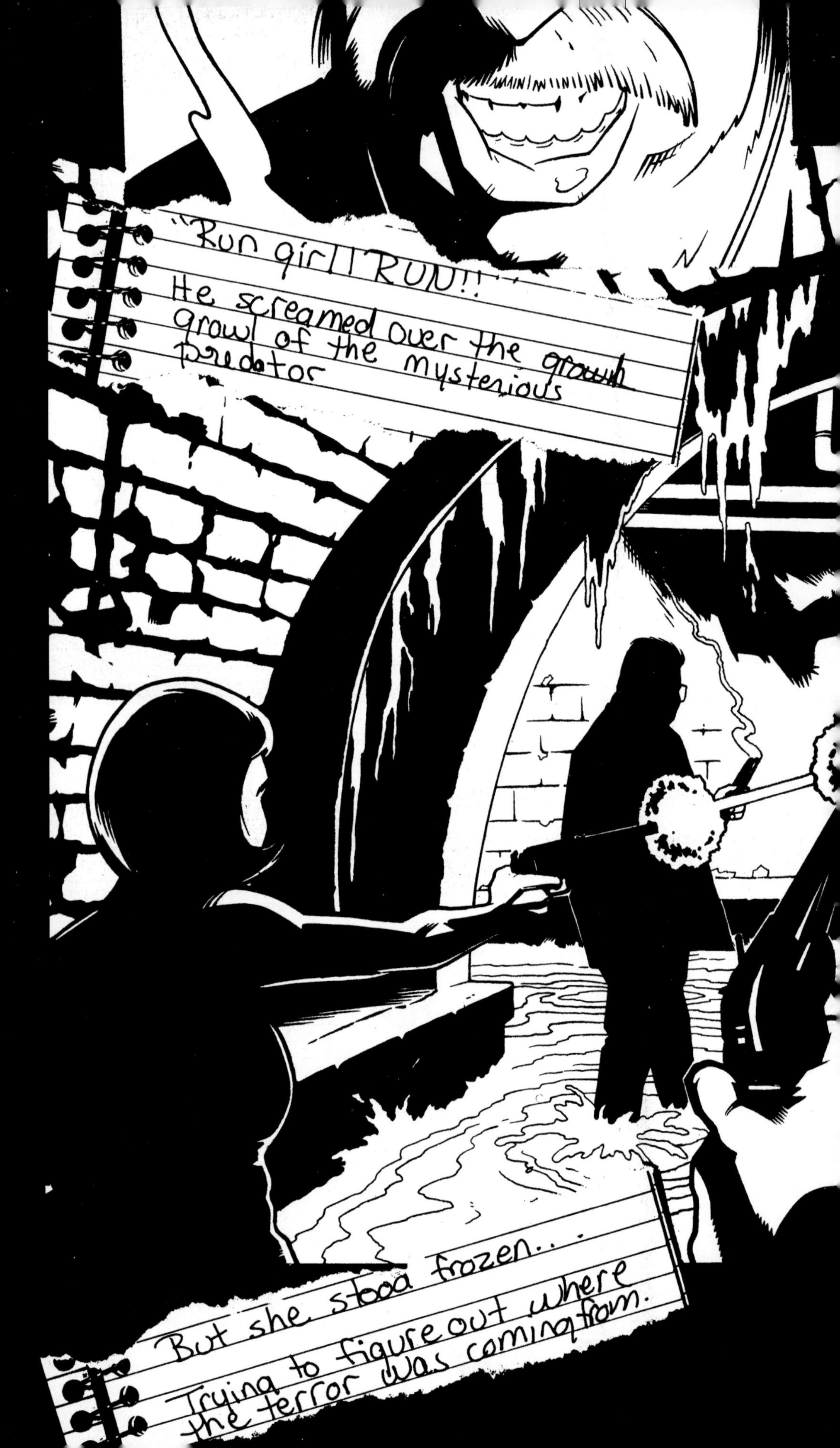
"Run girl! RUN!!"
He screamed over the growl of the mysterious predator
But she stood frozen...
Trying to figure out where the terror was coming from.

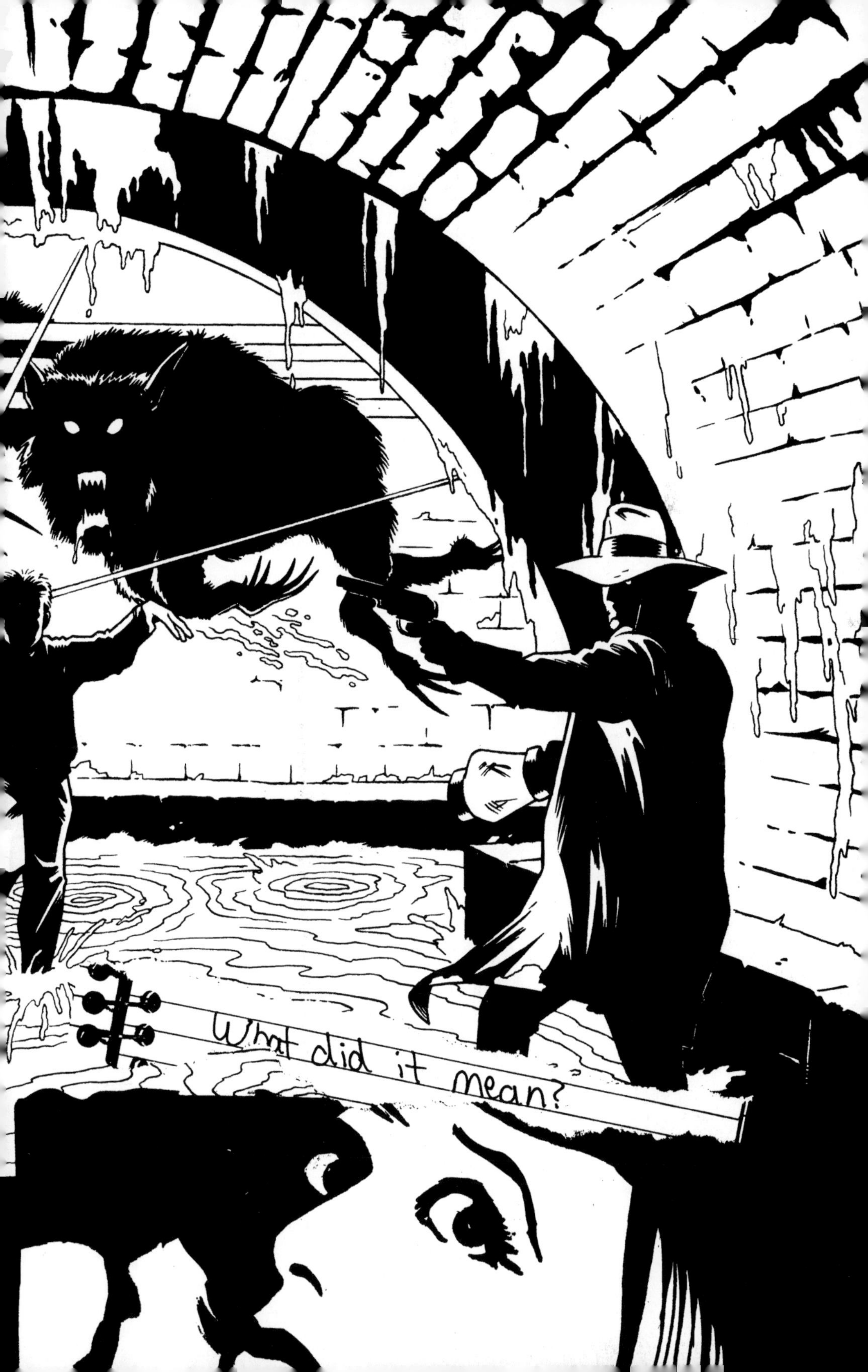
What did it mean?

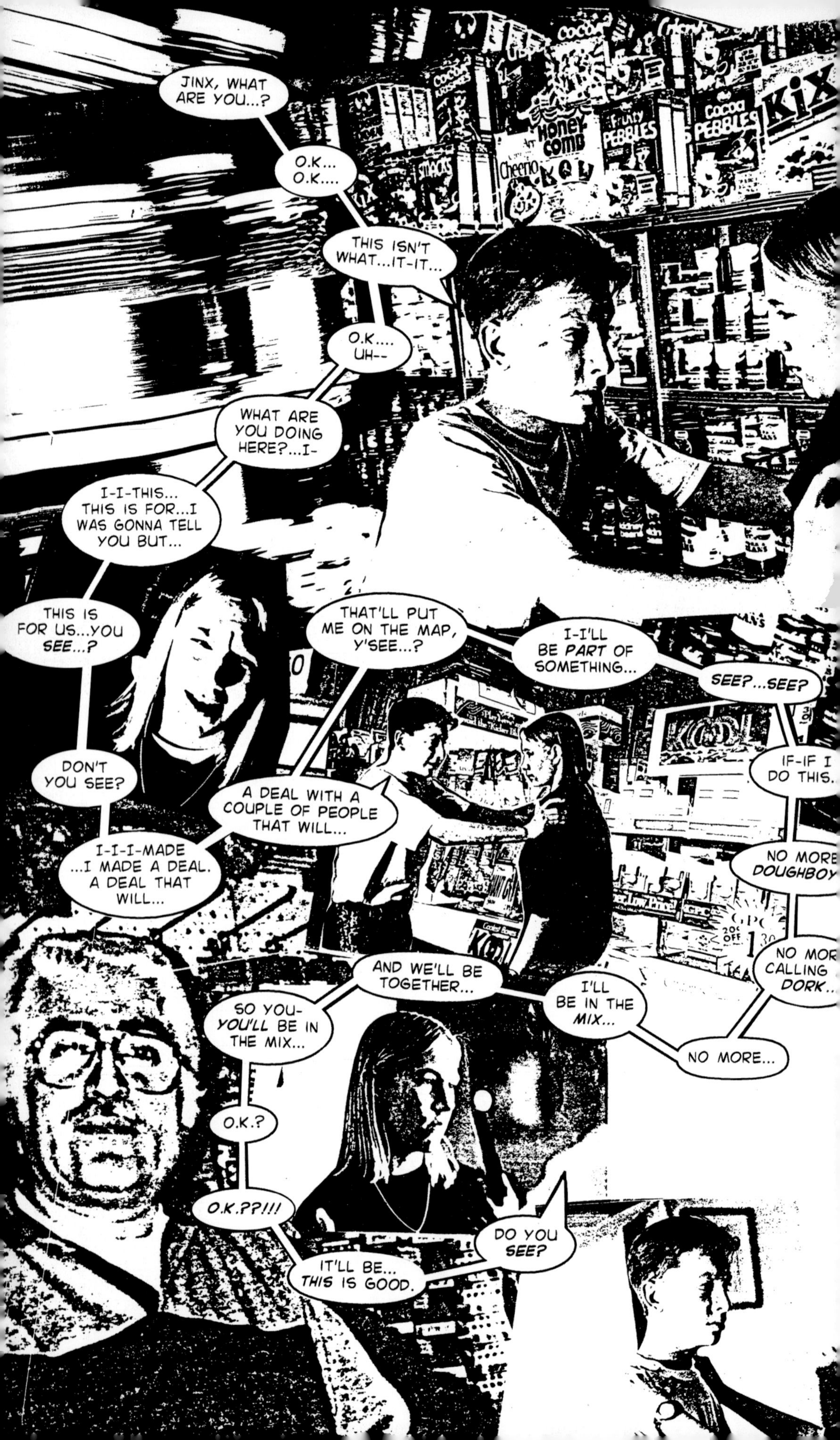
JINX, WHAT ARE YOU...?
O.K... O.K....
THIS ISN'T WHAT...IT-IT...
O.K.... UH--
WHAT ARE YOU DOING HERE?...I-
I-I-THIS... THIS IS FOR...I WAS GONNA TELL YOU BUT...
THIS IS FOR US...YOU SEE...?
DON'T YOU SEE?
I-I-I-MADE ...I MADE A DEAL. A DEAL THAT WILL...
A DEAL WITH A COUPLE OF PEOPLE THAT WILL...
THAT'LL PUT ME ON THE MAP, Y'SEE...?
I-I'LL BE PART OF SOMETHING...
SEE?...SEE?
IF-IF I DO THIS.
NO MORE DOUGHBOY
NO MOR CALLING DORK...
NO MORE...
I'LL BE IN THE MIX...
AND WE'LL BE TOGETHER...
SO YOU- YOU'LL BE IN THE MIX...
O.K.?
O.K.??!!!
IT'LL BE... THIS IS GOOD.
DO YOU SEE?
KiX
Cocoa PEBBLES
Fruity PEBBLES
HONEY COMB
Cheerios

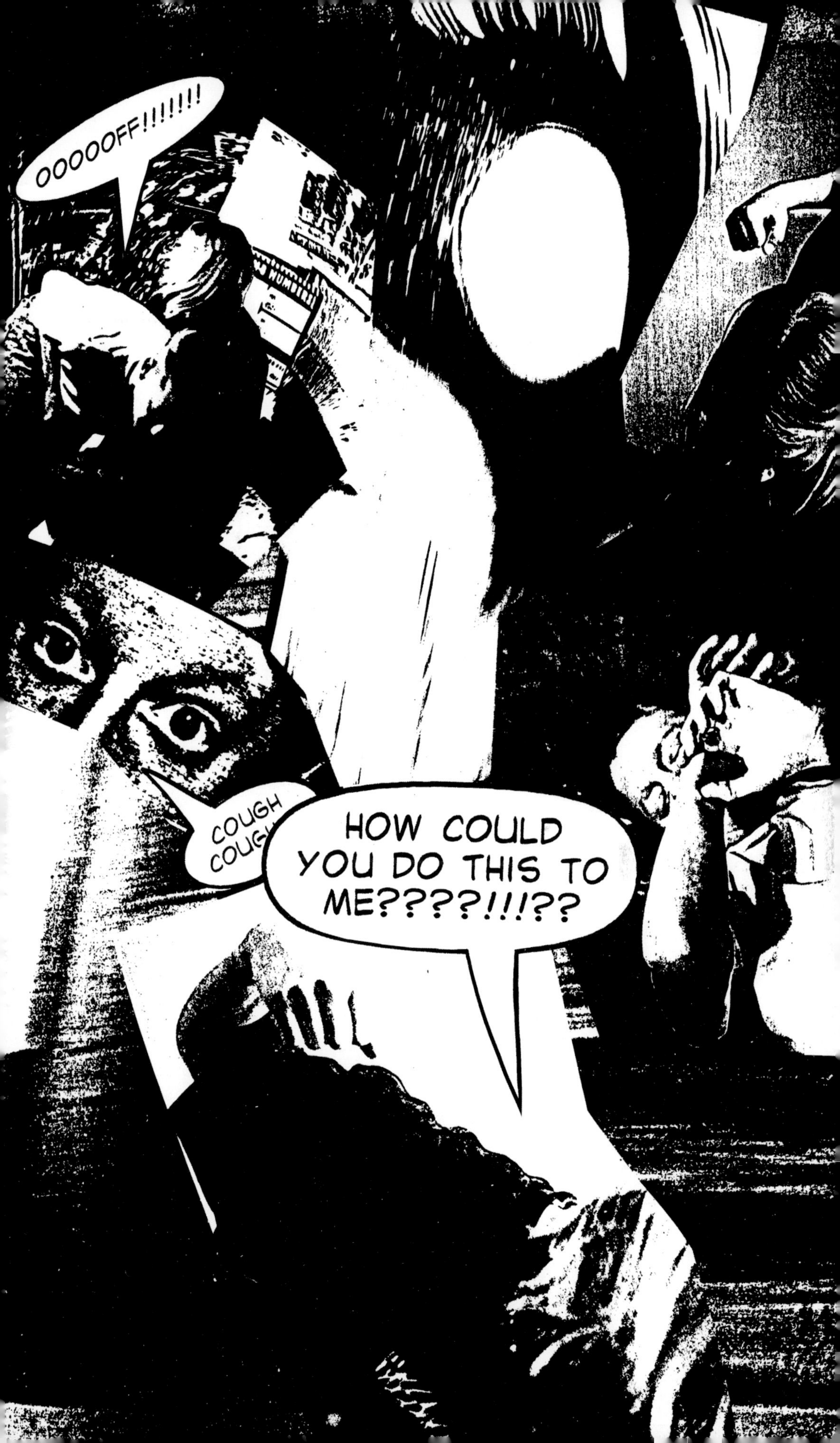
OOOOOOFF!!!!!!!
COUGH
HOW COULD YOU DO THIS TO ME????!!!??

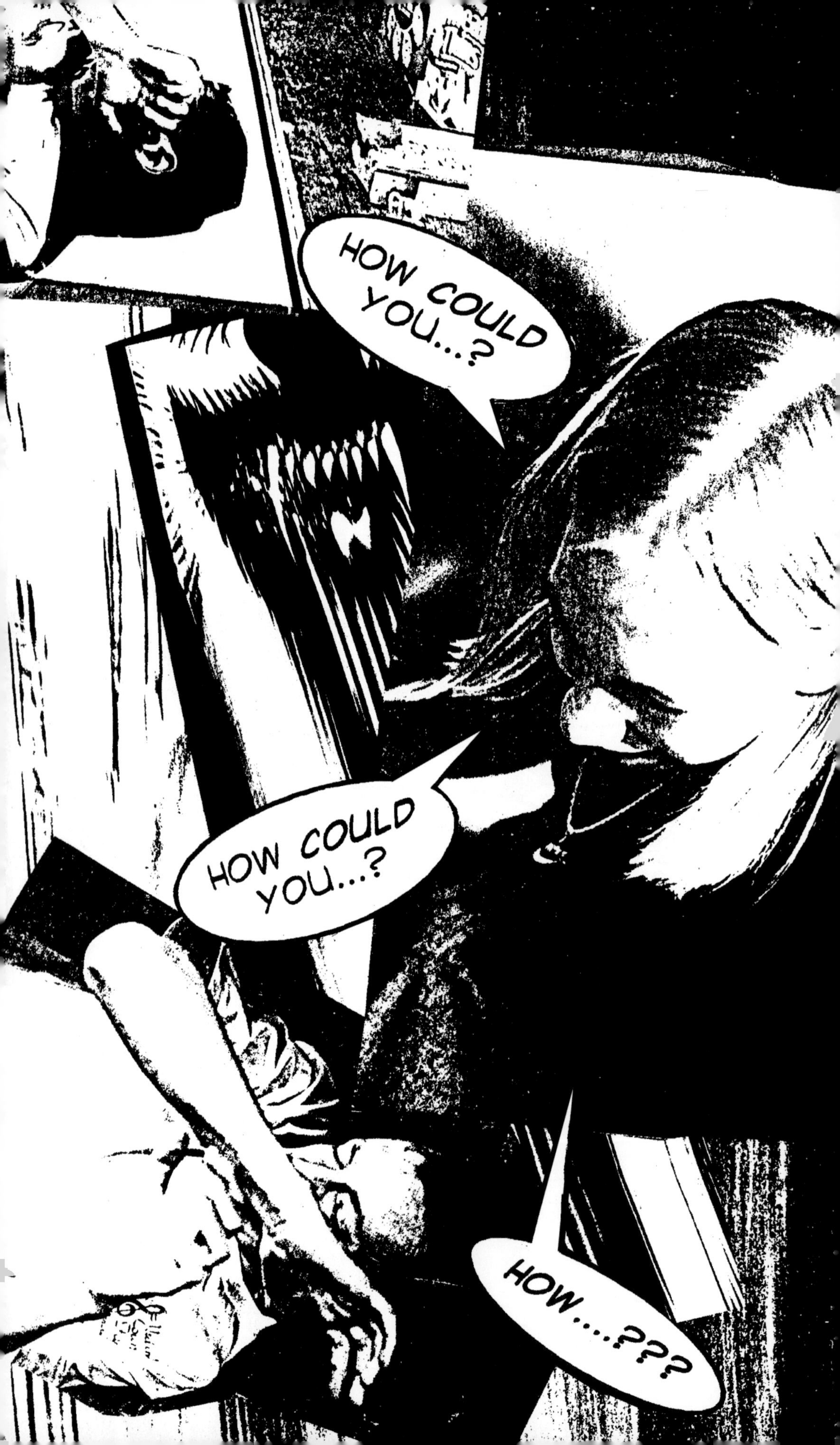
HOW COULD YOU...?
HOW COULD YOU...?
HOW....???

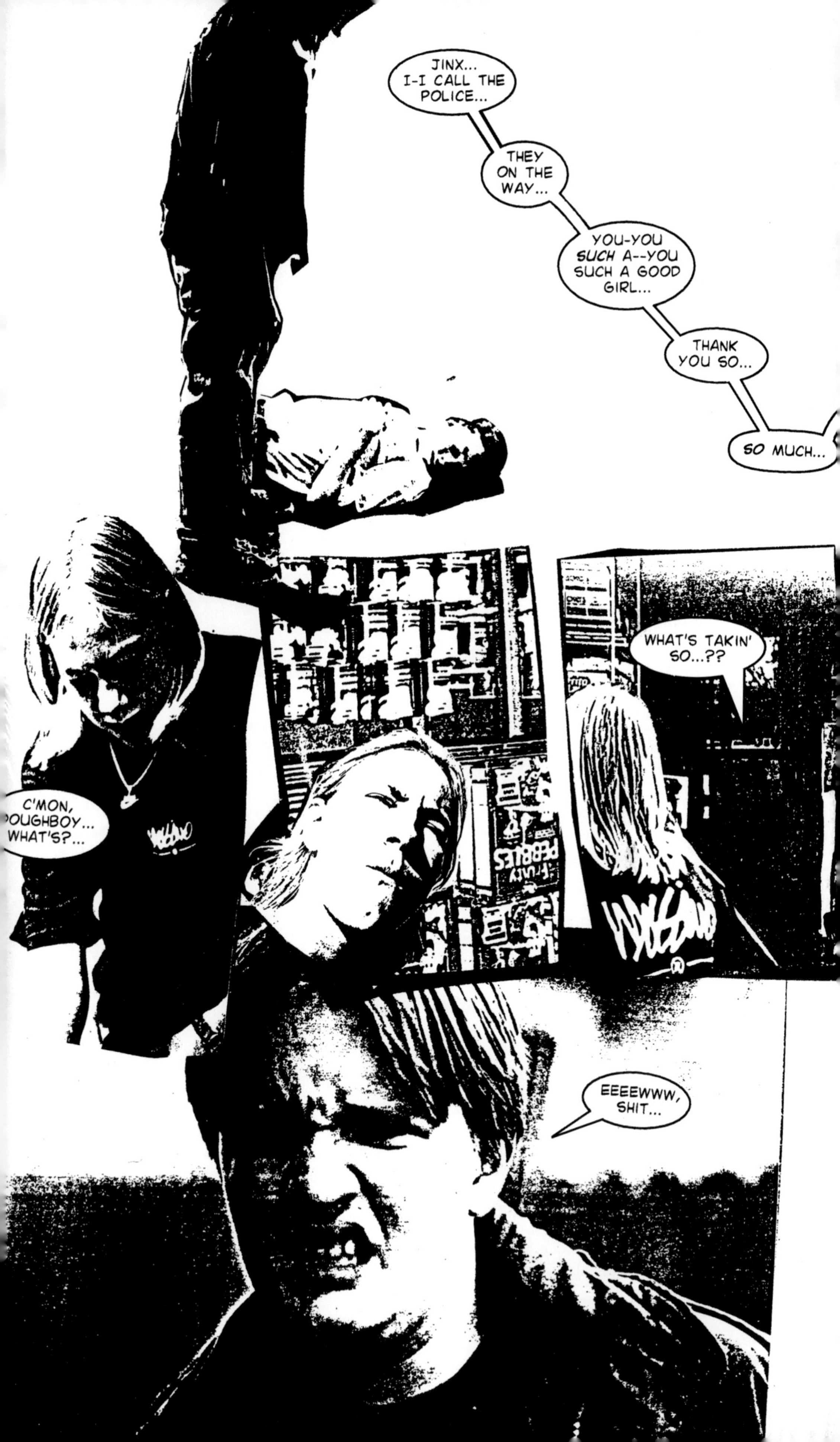
JINX... I-I CALL THE POLICE...
THEY ON THE WAY...
YOU-YOU SUCH A--YOU SUCH A GOOD GIRL...
THANK YOU SO...
SO MUCH...
C'MON, DOUGHBOY... WHAT'S?...
WHAT'S TAKIN' SO...??
EEEEWWW, SHIT...

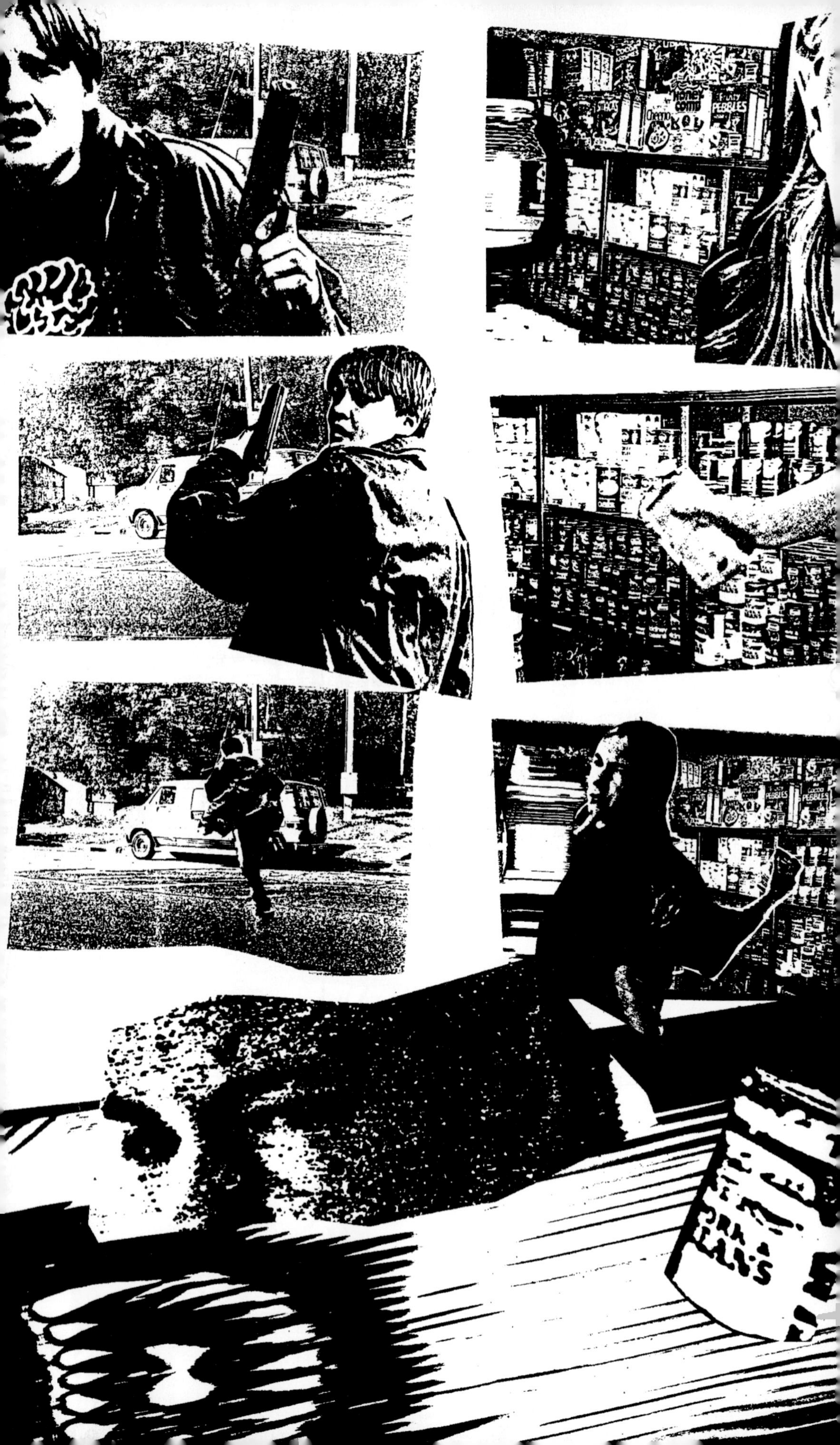
Honey Comb
PEBBLES

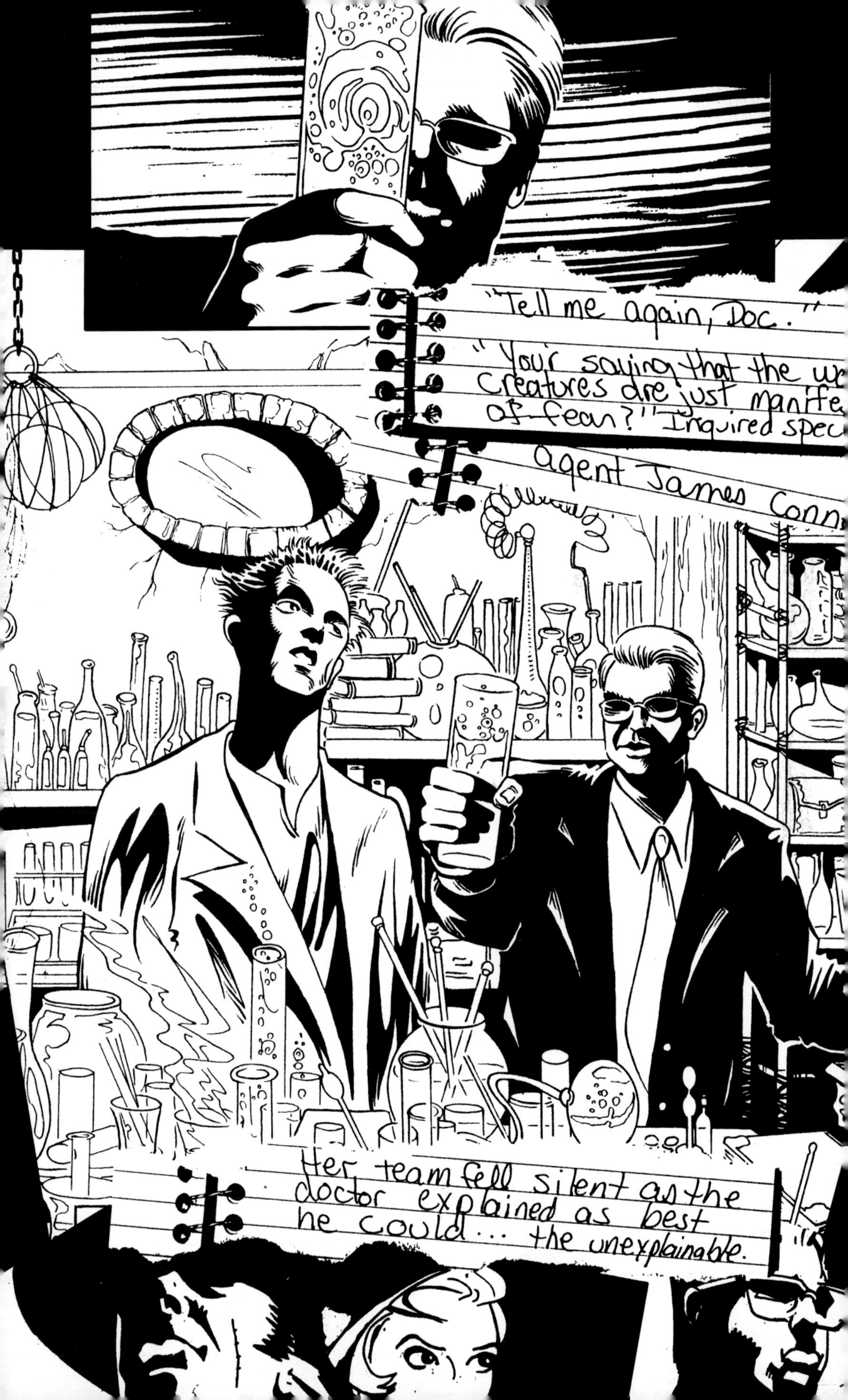
"Tell me again, Doc."
"Your saying that the w
creatures are just manife
of fear?" Inquired spec
agent James Conn
Her team fell silent as the
doctor explained as best
he could... the unexplainable.

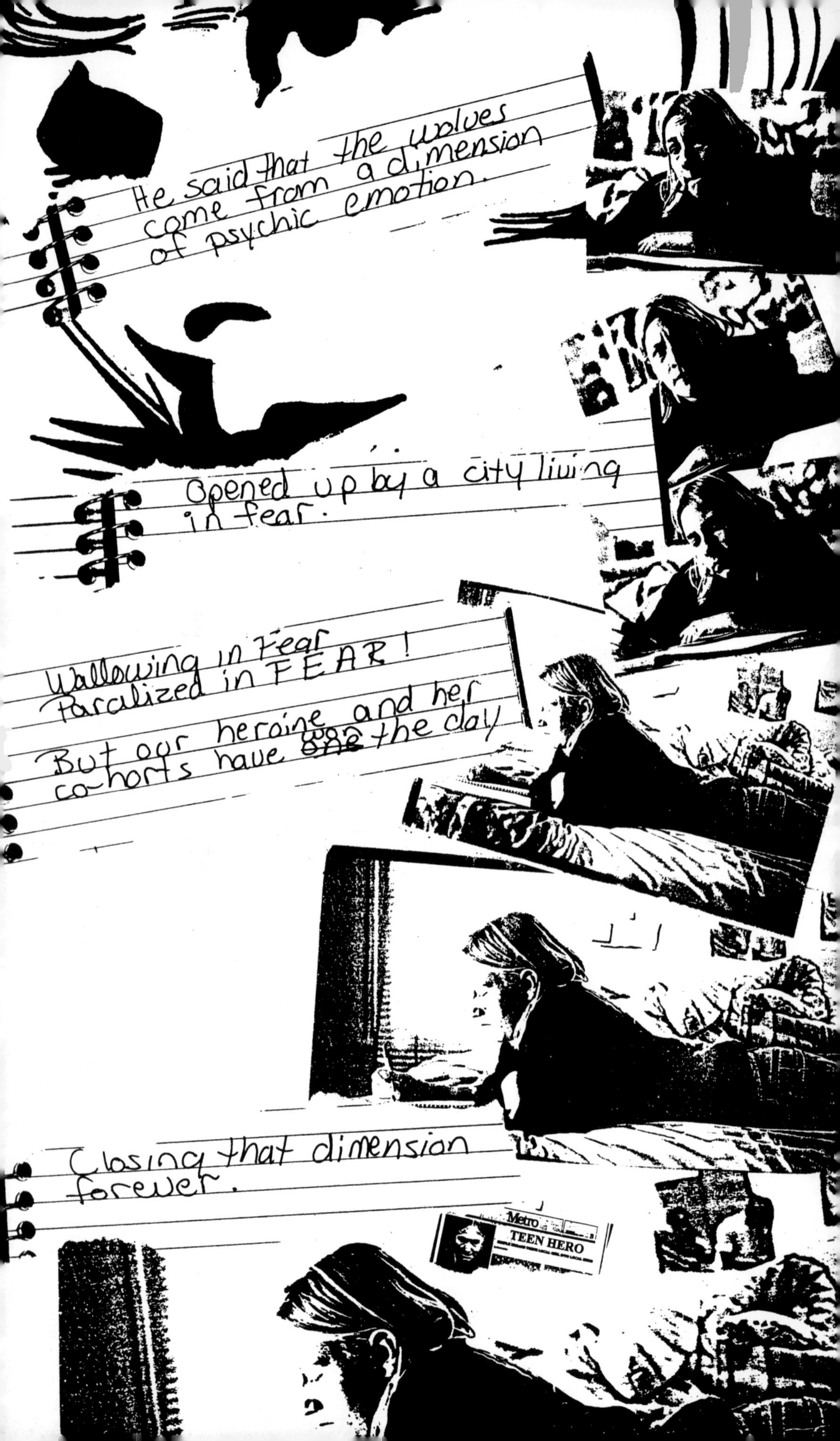
He said that the wolves come from a dimension of psychic emotion.
Opened up by a city living in fear.
Wallowing in Fear
Paralized in FEAR!
But our heroine and her co-horts have won the day
Closing that dimension forever.
Metro
TEEN HERO

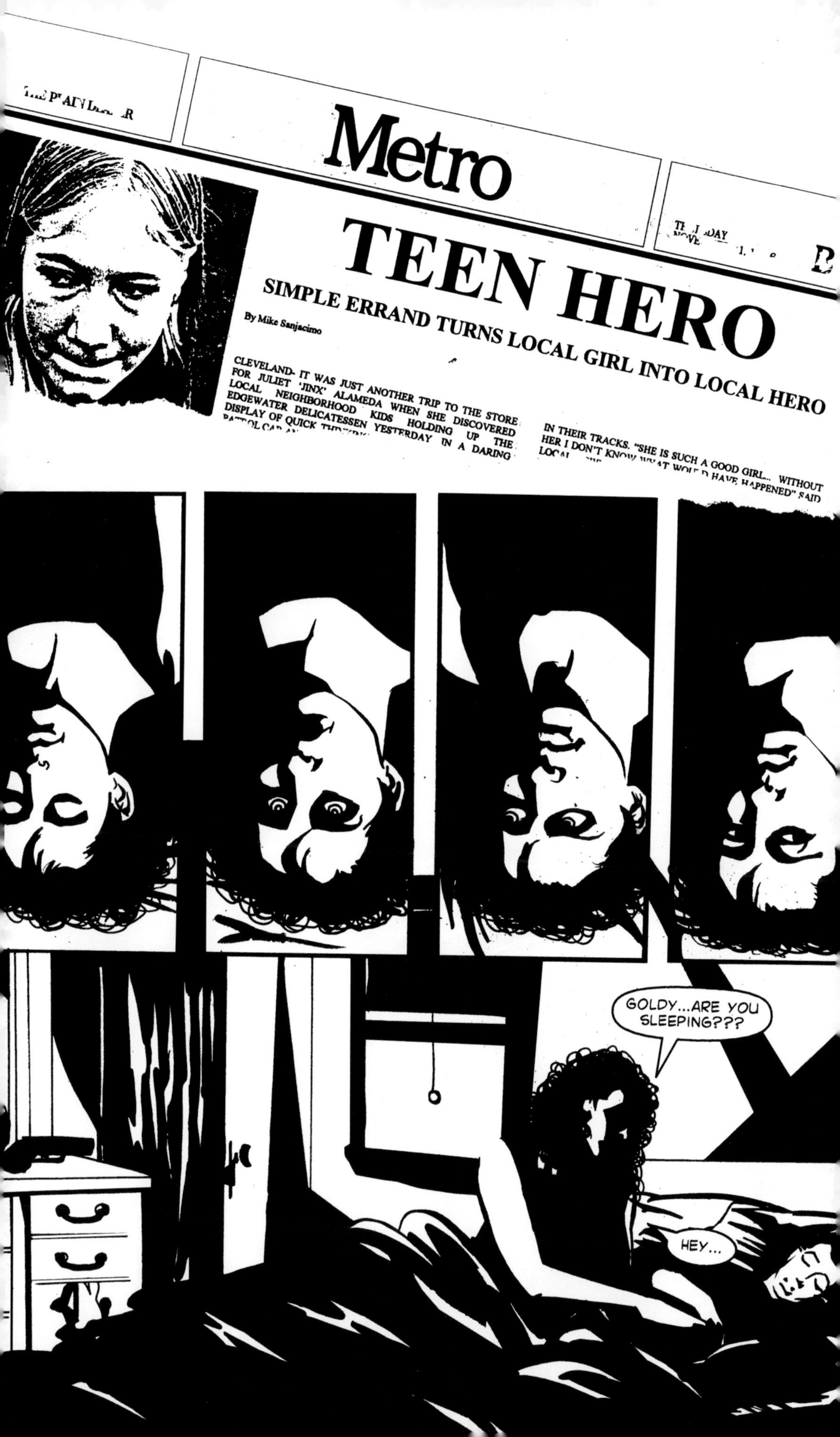
Metro
TEEN HERO
SIMPLE ERRAND TURNS LOCAL GIRL INTO LOCAL HERO
By Mike Sanjacimo
CLEVELAND- IT WAS JUST ANOTHER TRIP TO THE STORE FOR JULIET 'JINX' ALAMEDA WHEN SHE DISCOVERED LOCAL NEIGHBORHOOD KIDS HOLDING UP THE EDGEWATER DELICATESSEN YESTERDAY IN A DARING DISPLAY OF QUICK
IN THEIR TRACKS. "SHE IS SUCH A GOOD GIRL... WITHOUT HER I DON'T KNOW
HAVE HAPPENED" SAID
GOLDY...ARE YOU SLEEPING???
HEY...

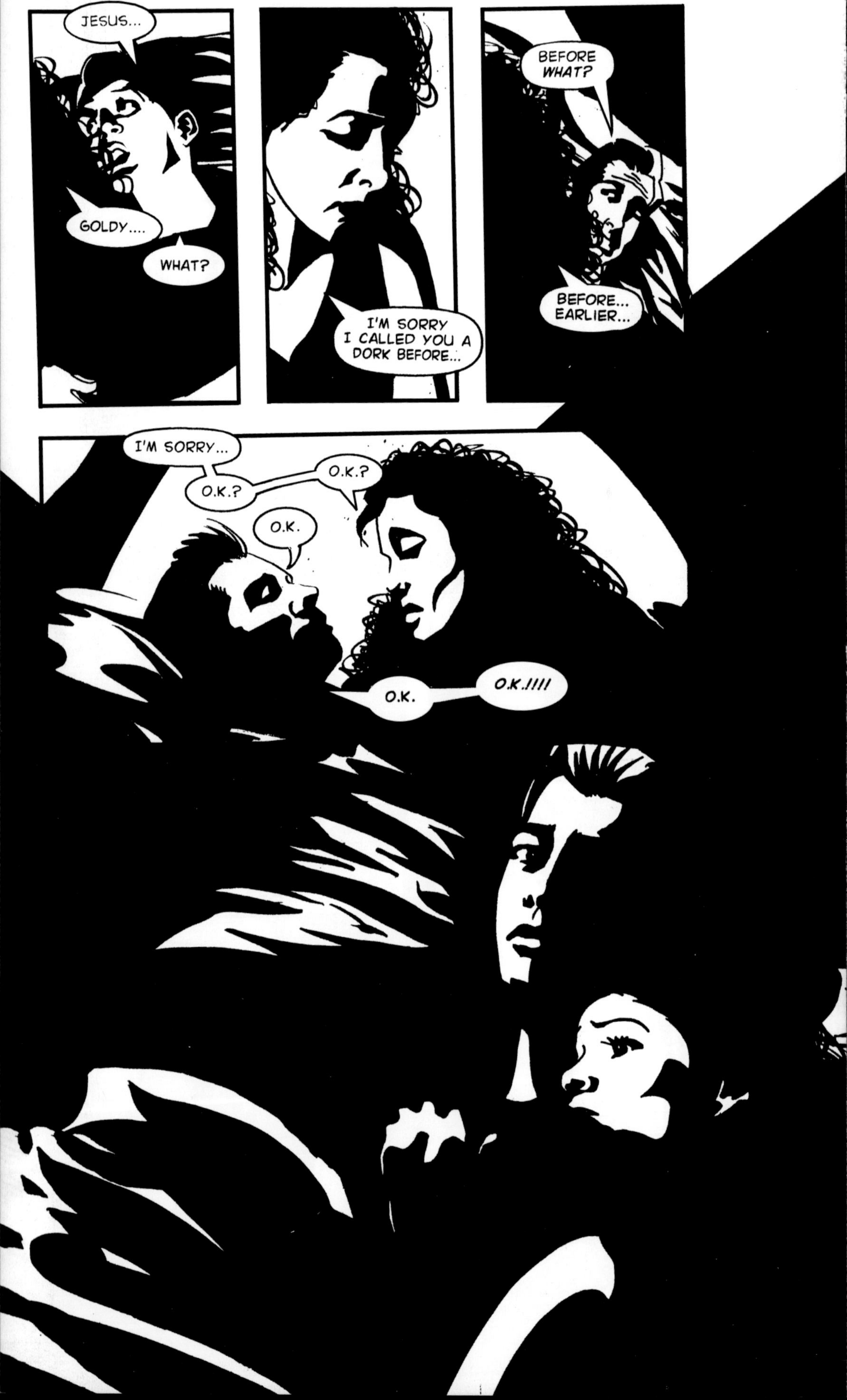
JESUS...
GOLDY....
WHAT?
I'M SORRY
I CALLED YOU A
DORK BEFORE...
BEFORE
WHAT?
BEFORE...
EARLIER...
I'M SORRY...
O.K.?
O.K.?
O.K.
O.K.
O.K.!!!!

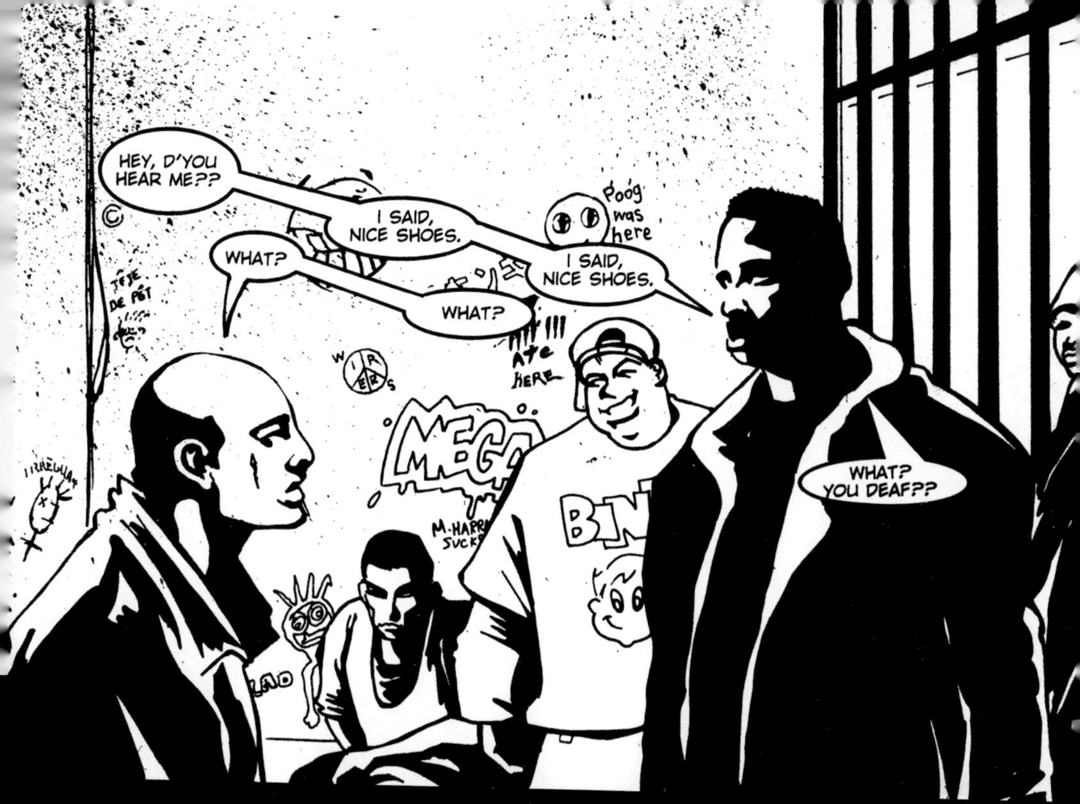
HEY, D'YOU HEAR ME??
I SAID, NICE SHOES.
WHAT?
Poog was here
I SAID, NICE SHOES.
WHAT?
WHAT? YOU DEAF??

Follically challenged

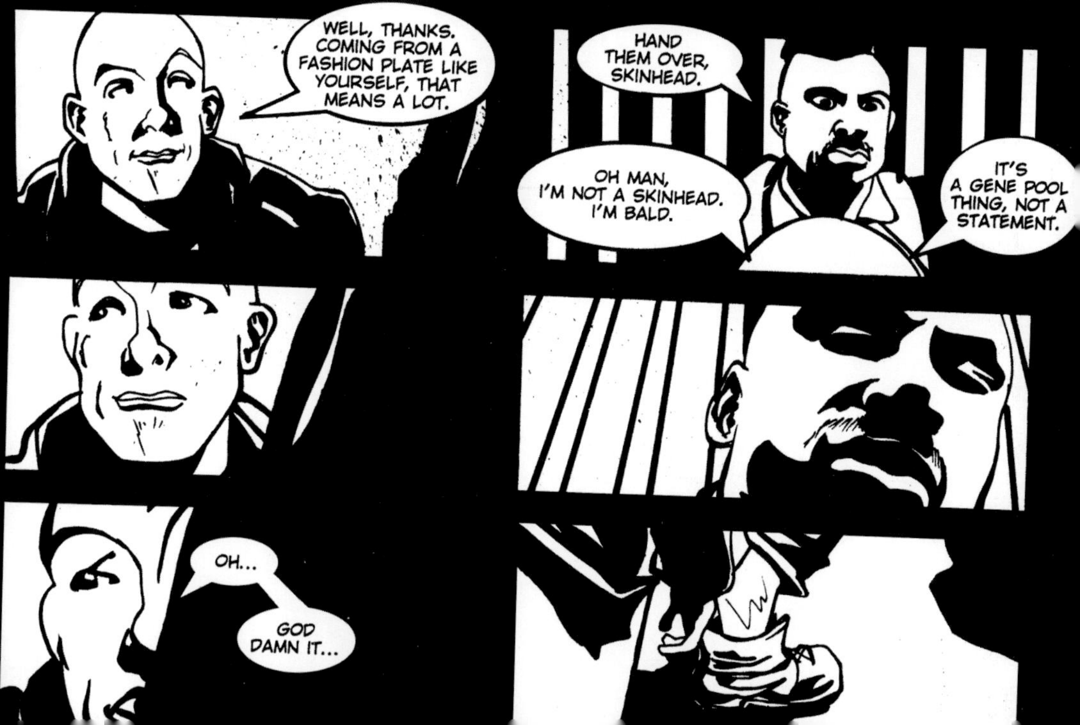
WELL, THANKS. COMING FROM A FASHION PLATE LIKE YOURSELF, THAT MEANS A LOT.
HAND THEM OVER, SKINHEAD.
OH MAN, I'M NOT A SKINHEAD. I'M BALD.
IT'S A GENE POOL THING, NOT A STATEMENT.
OH...
GOD DAMN IT...

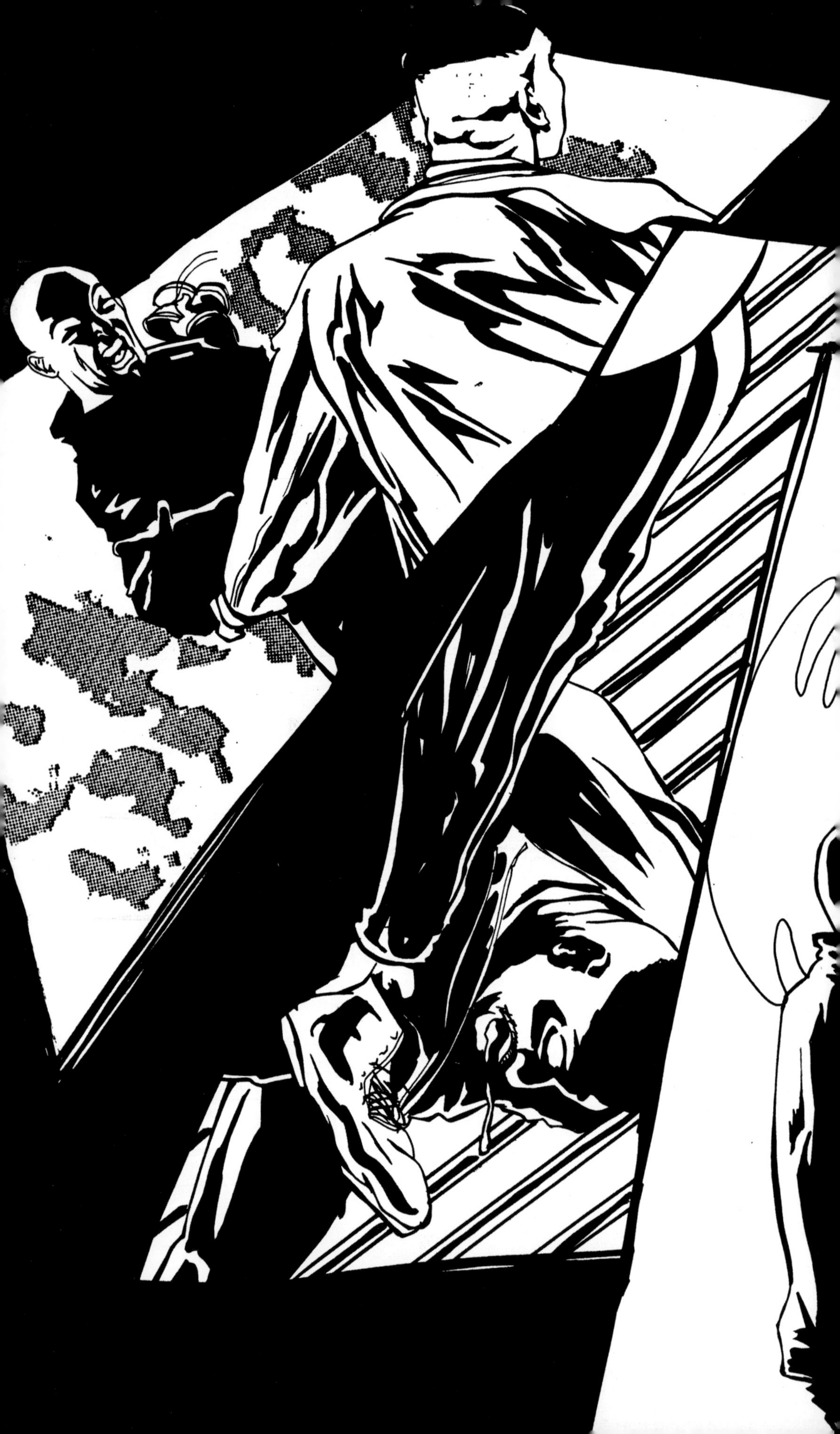

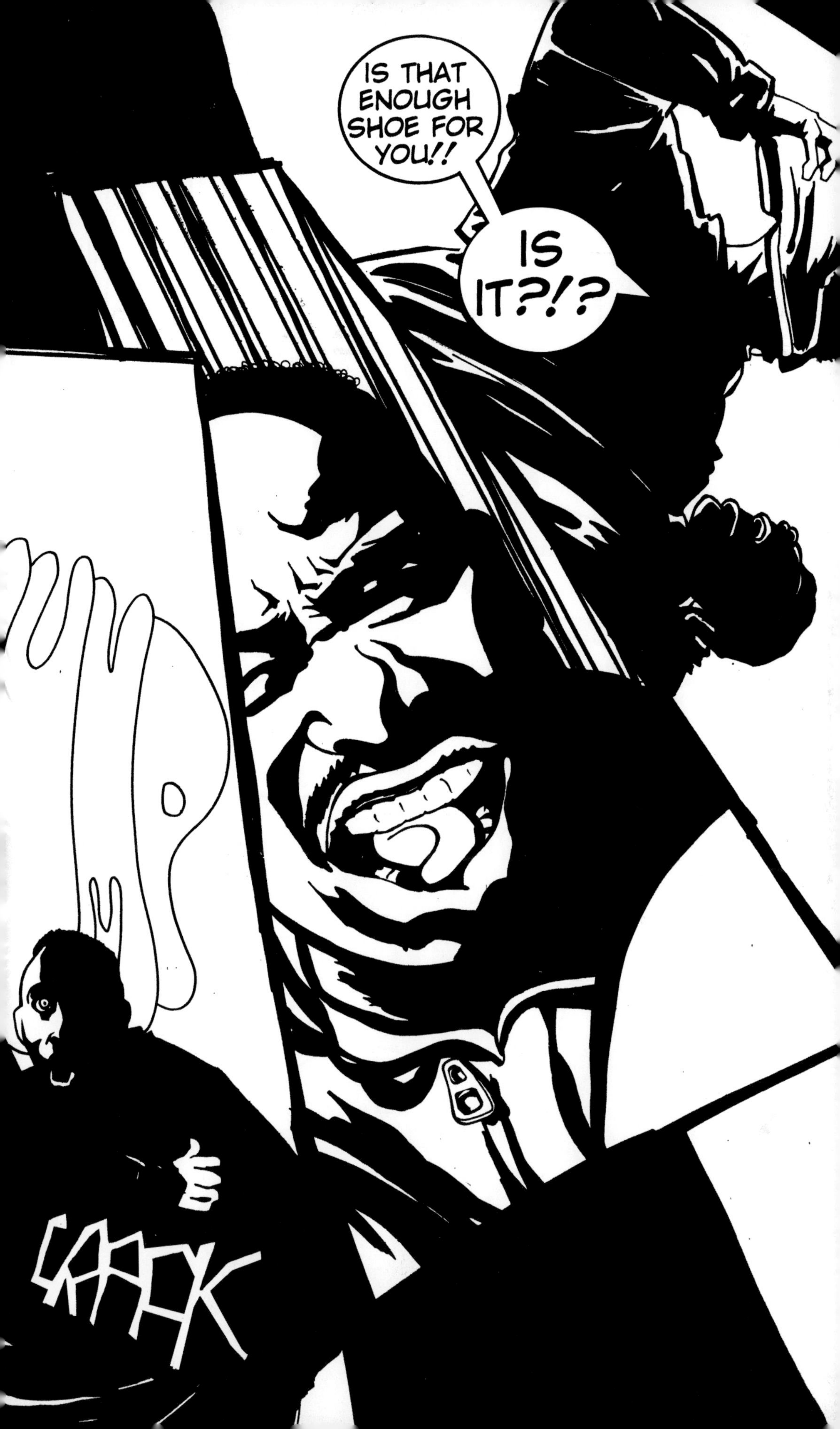
IS THAT ENOUGH SHOE FOR YOU!!
IS IT?!?
CRACK

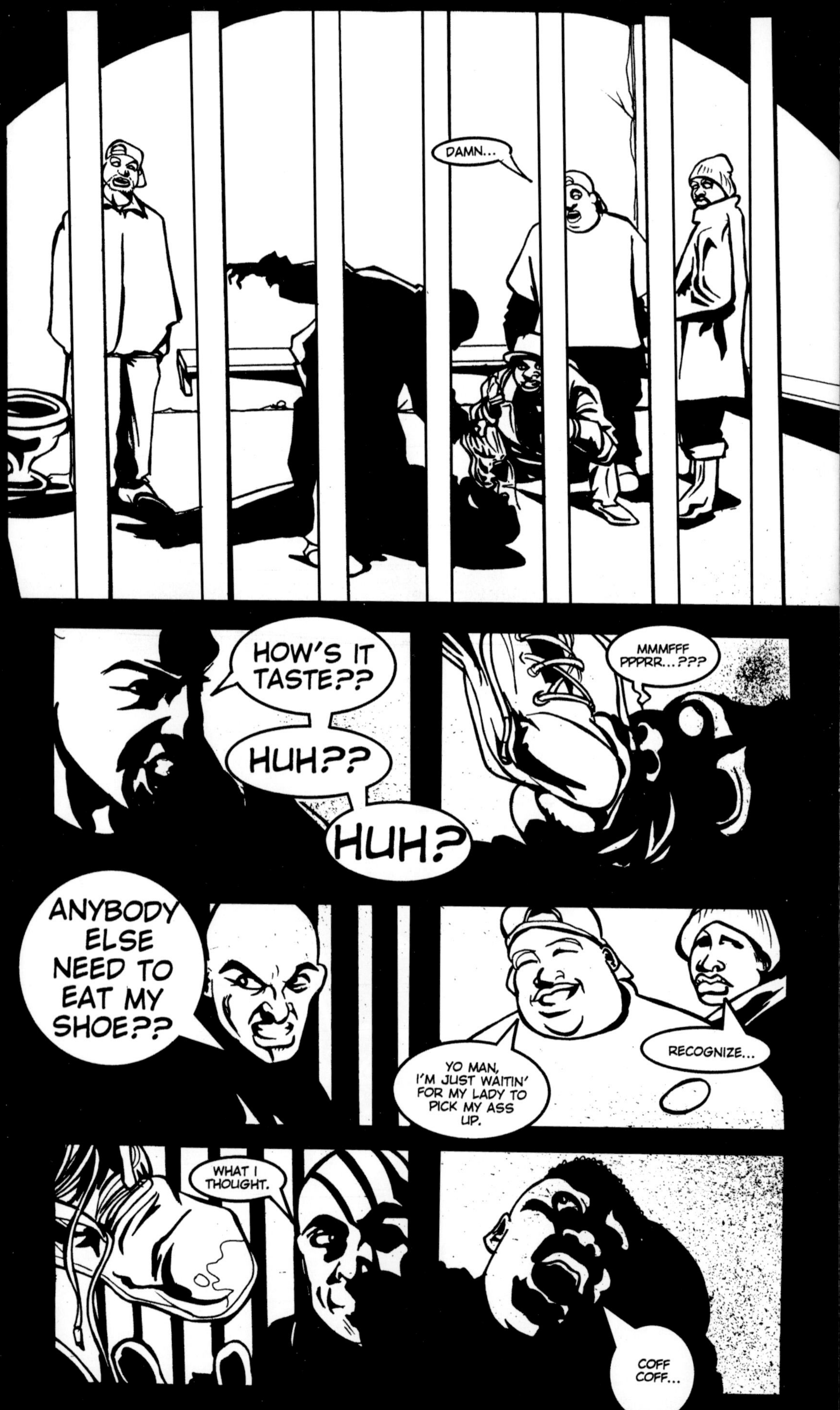
DAMN...
HOW'S IT TASTE??
HUH??
HUH?
MMMFFF PPPRR...???
ANYBODY ELSE NEED TO EAT MY SHOE??
YO MAN, I'M JUST WAITIN' FOR MY LADY TO PICK MY ASS UP.
RECOGNIZE...
WHAT I THOUGHT.
COFF COFF...

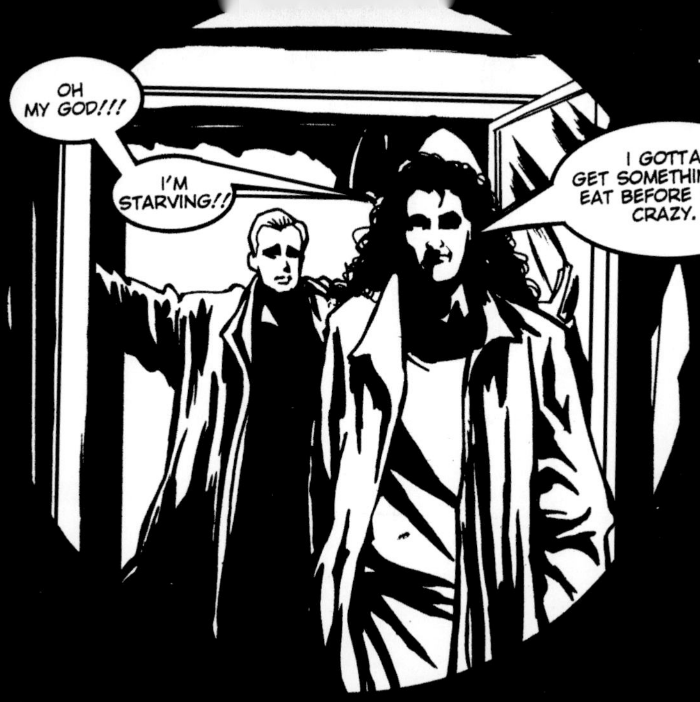
OH MY GOD!!!
I'M STARVING!!
I GOTTA GET SOMETHING TO EAT BEFORE I GET CRAZY.

Low blood sugar

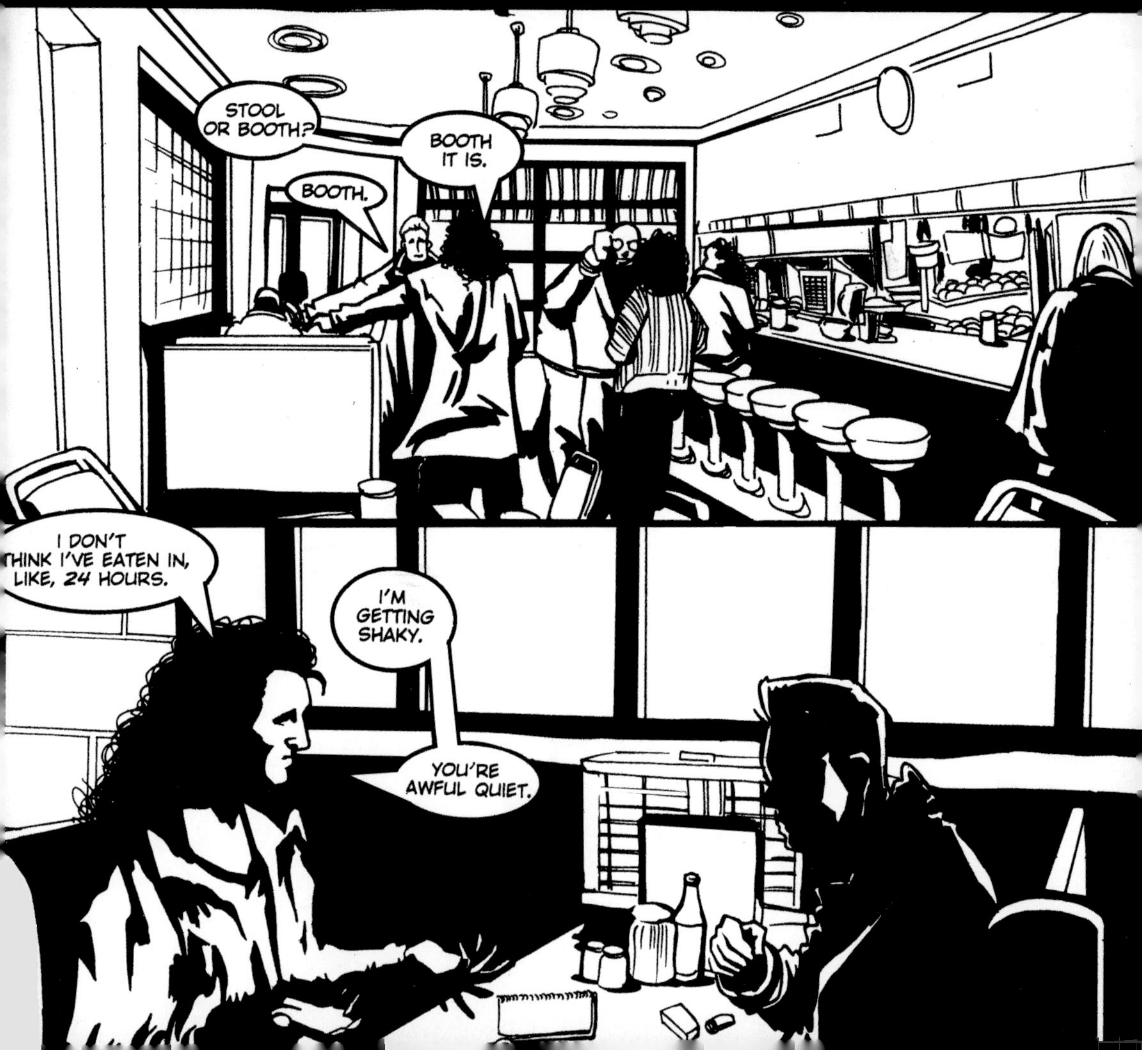
STOOL OR BOOTH?
BOOTH.
BOOTH IT IS.
I DON'T THINK I'VE EATEN IN, LIKE, 24 HOURS.
I'M GETTING SHAKY.
YOU'RE AWFUL QUIET.

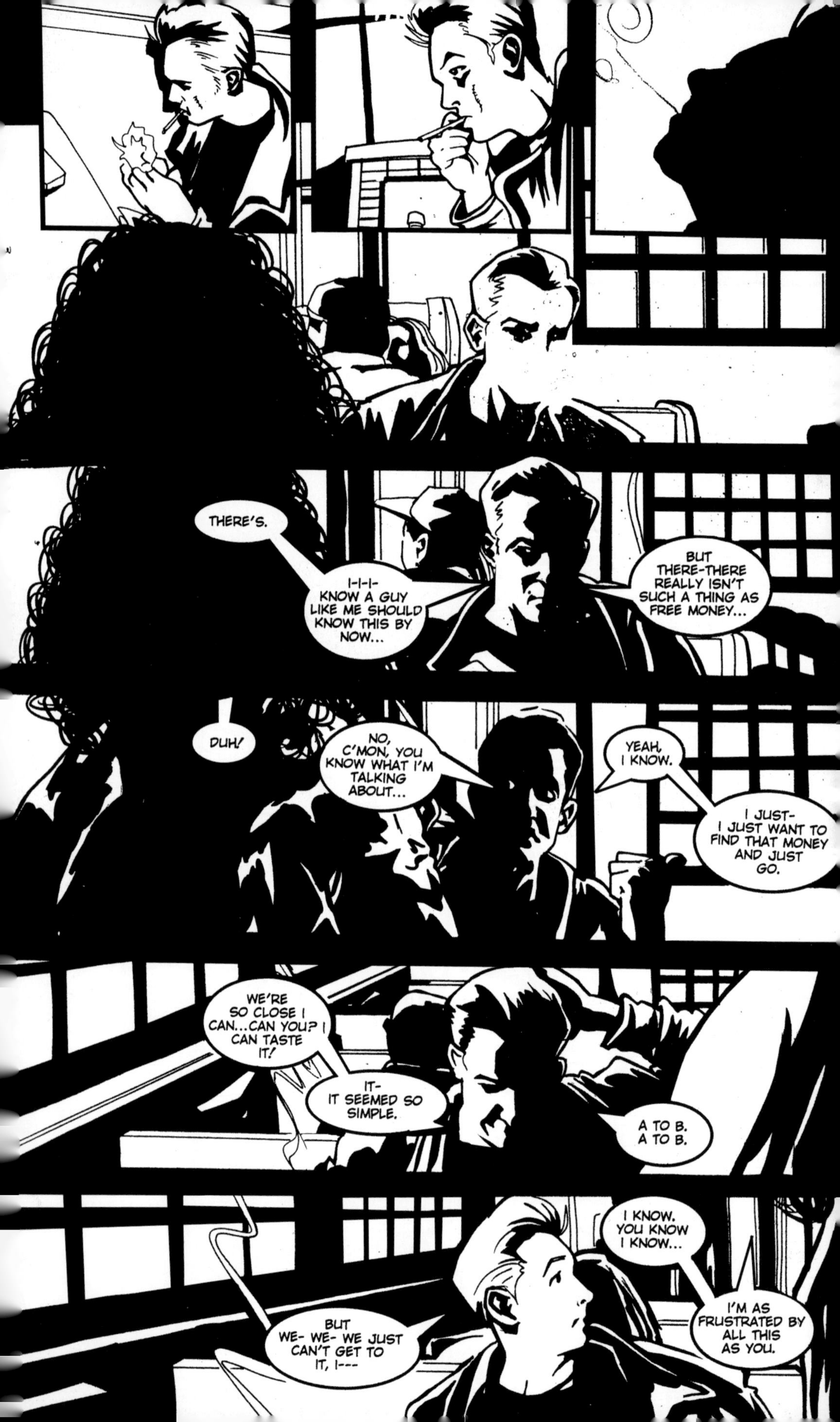
THERE'S.
I-I-I-
KNOW A GUY LIKE ME SHOULD KNOW THIS BY NOW...
BUT THERE-THERE REALLY ISN'T SUCH A THING AS FREE MONEY...
DUH!
NO, C'MON, YOU KNOW WHAT I'M TALKING ABOUT...
YEAH, I KNOW.
I JUST- I JUST WANT TO FIND THAT MONEY AND JUST GO.
WE'RE SO CLOSE I CAN...CAN YOU? I CAN TASTE IT!
IT- IT SEEMED SO SIMPLE.
A TO B. A TO B.
I KNOW. YOU KNOW I KNOW...
BUT WE- WE- WE JUST CAN'T GET TO IT, I---
I'M AS FRUSTRATED BY ALL THIS AS YOU.

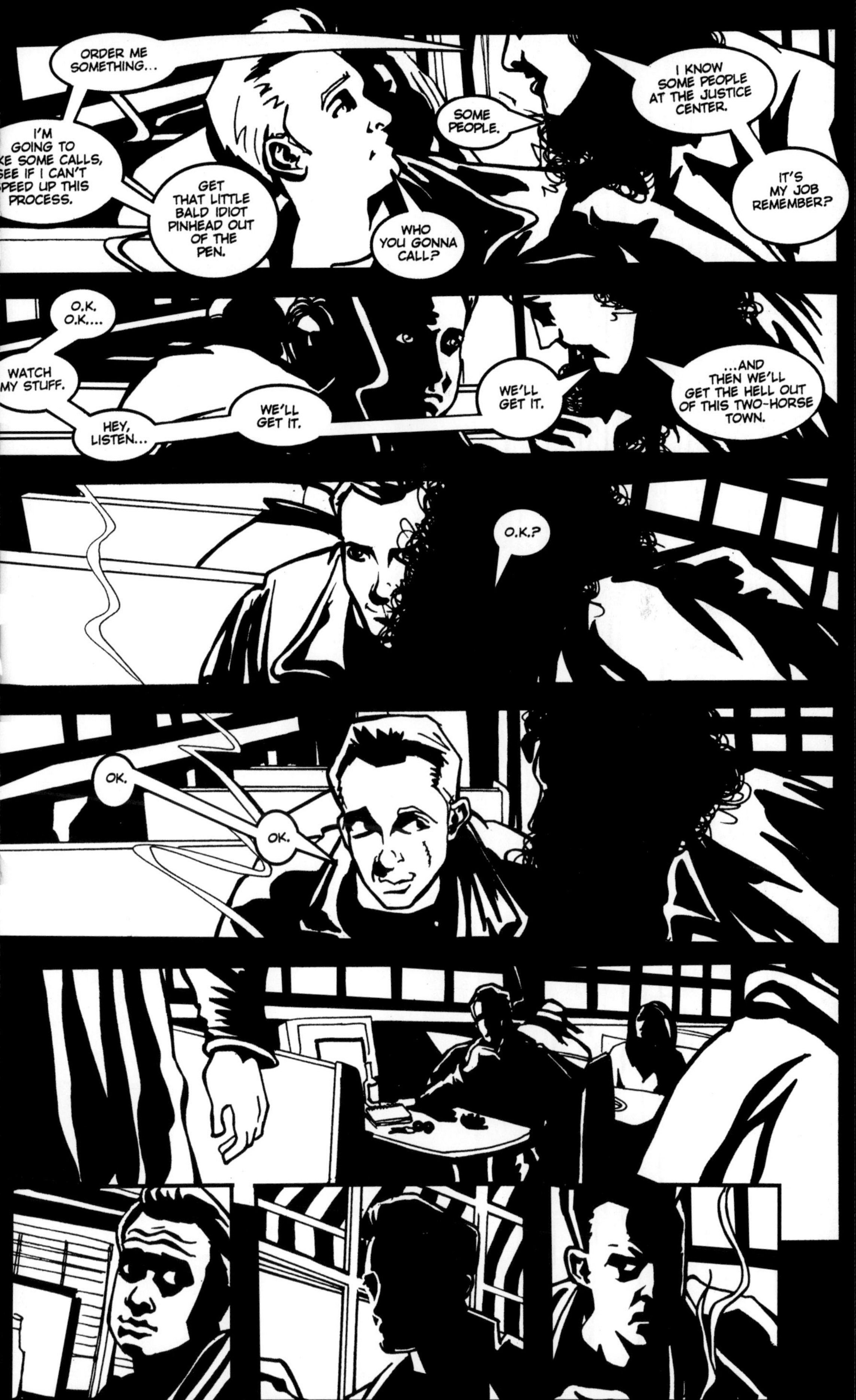
ORDER ME SOMETHING...
I'M GOING TO
KE SOME CALLS,
SEE IF I CAN'T
SPEED UP THIS PROCESS.
GET THAT LITTLE BALD IDIOT PINHEAD OUT OF THE PEN.
WHO YOU GONNA CALL?
SOME PEOPLE.
I KNOW SOME PEOPLE AT THE JUSTICE CENTER.
IT'S MY JOB REMEMBER?
O.K. O.K....
WATCH MY STUFF.
HEY, LISTEN...
WE'LL GET IT.
WE'LL GET IT.
...AND THEN WE'LL GET THE HELL OUT OF THIS TWO-HORSE TOWN.
O.K.?
OK.
OK.

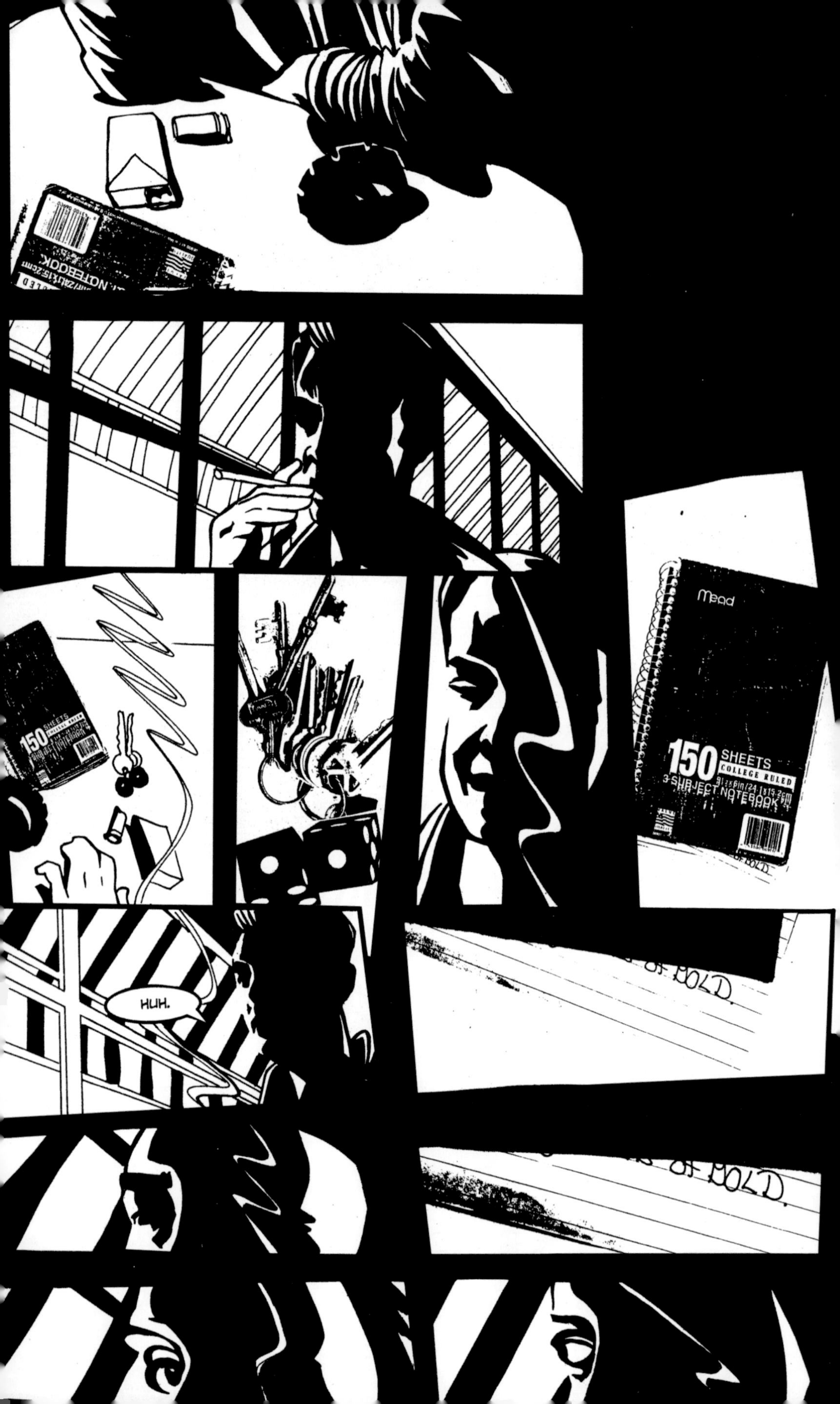
Mead
150 SHEETS
COLLEGE RULED
3 SUBJECT NOTEBOOK
HUH.
OF GOLD.

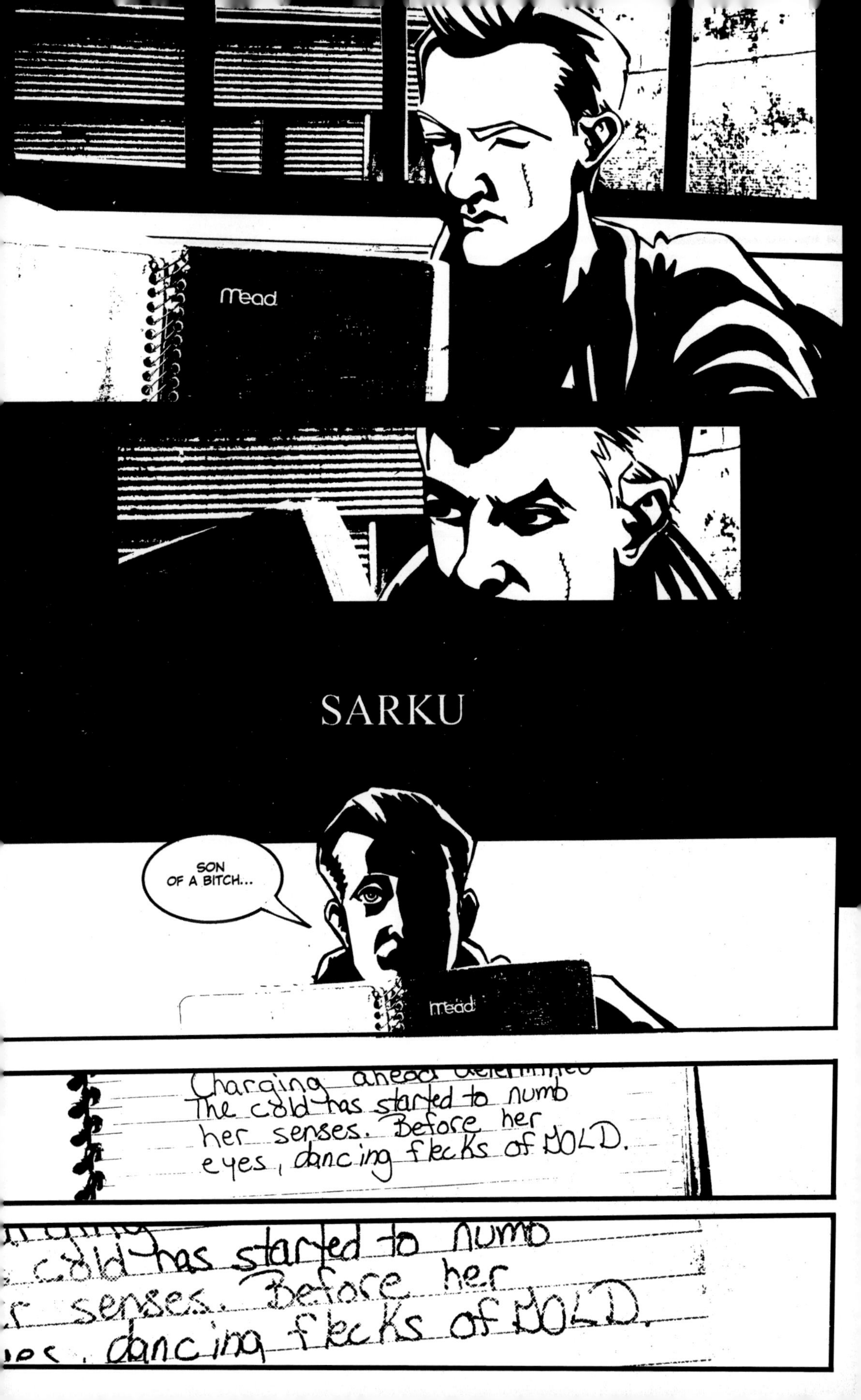
Mead
SARKU
SON OF A BITCH...
Mead
The cold has started to numb
her senses. Before her
eyes, dancing flecks of GOLD.
cold has started to numb
senses. Before her
dancing flecks of GOLD.

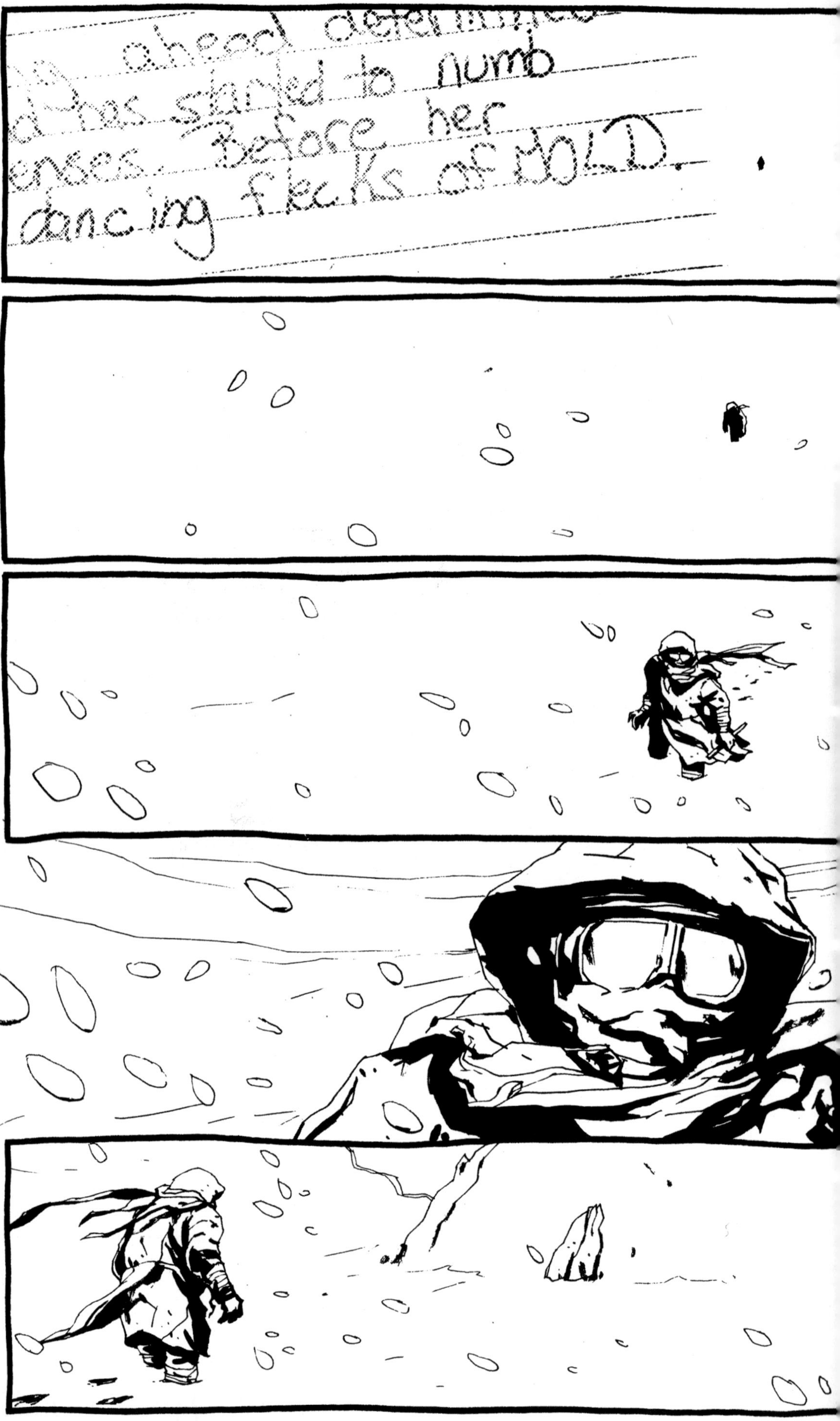
ahead
has started to numb
enses. Before her
dancing flecks of GOLD.

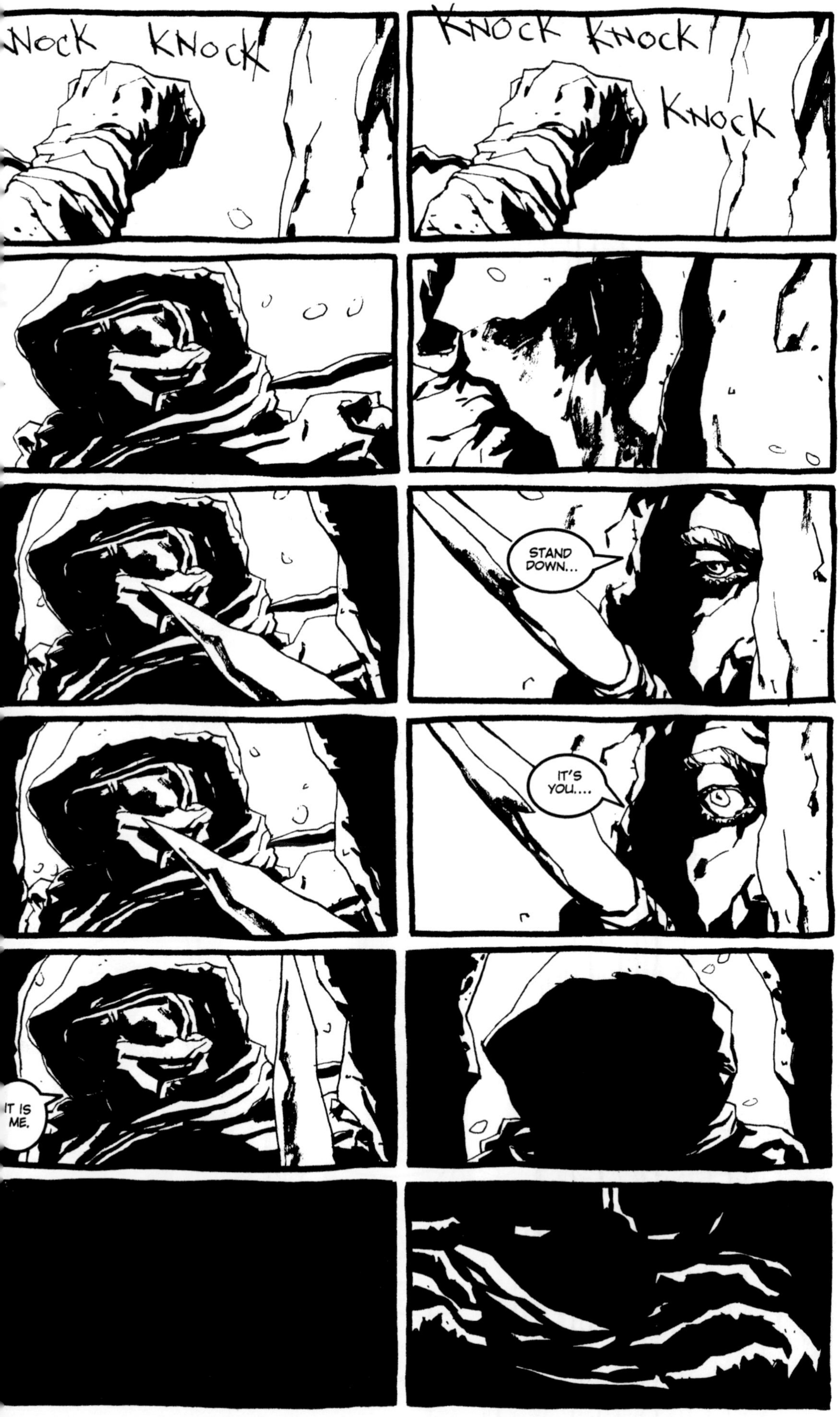
NOCK KNOCK
KNOCK KNOCK
KNOCK
STAND DOWN...
IT'S YOU....
IT IS ME.

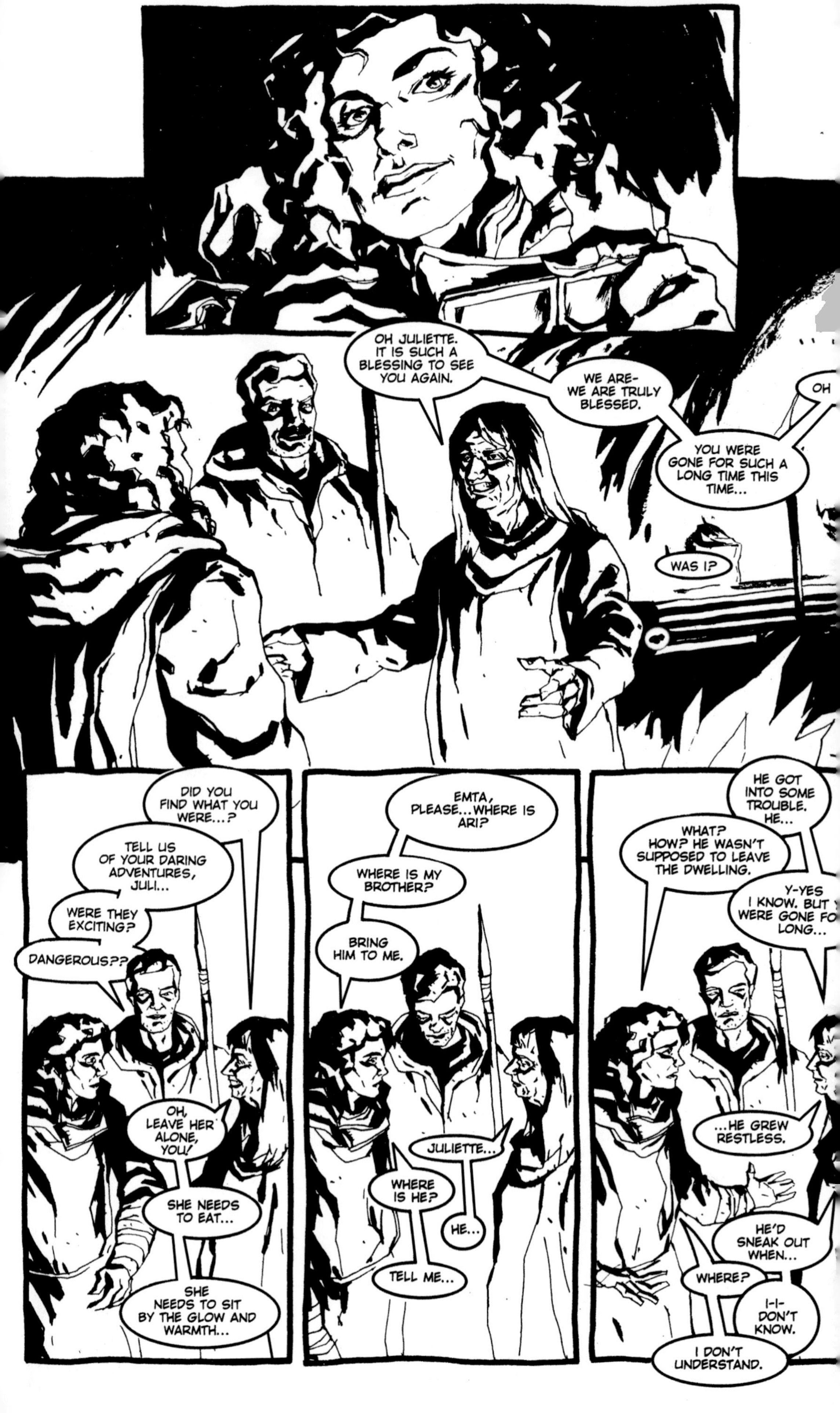
OH JULIETTE. IT IS SUCH A BLESSING TO SEE YOU AGAIN.
WE ARE- WE ARE TRULY BLESSED.
OH
YOU WERE GONE FOR SUCH A LONG TIME THIS TIME...
WAS I?
DID YOU FIND WHAT YOU WERE...?
TELL US OF YOUR DARING ADVENTURES, JULI...
WERE THEY EXCITING?
DANGEROUS??
OH, LEAVE HER ALONE, YOU!
SHE NEEDS TO EAT...
SHE NEEDS TO SIT BY THE GLOW AND WARMTH...
EMTA, PLEASE...WHERE IS ARI?
WHERE IS MY BROTHER?
BRING HIM TO ME.
JULIETTE...
WHERE IS HE?
HE...
TELL ME...
HE GOT INTO SOME TROUBLE. HE...
WHAT? HOW? HE WASN'T SUPPOSED TO LEAVE THE DWELLING.
Y-YES I KNOW. BUT WERE GONE FO LONG...
...HE GREW RESTLESS.
HE'D SNEAK OUT WHEN...
WHERE?
I-I- DON'T KNOW.
I DON'T UNDERSTAND.

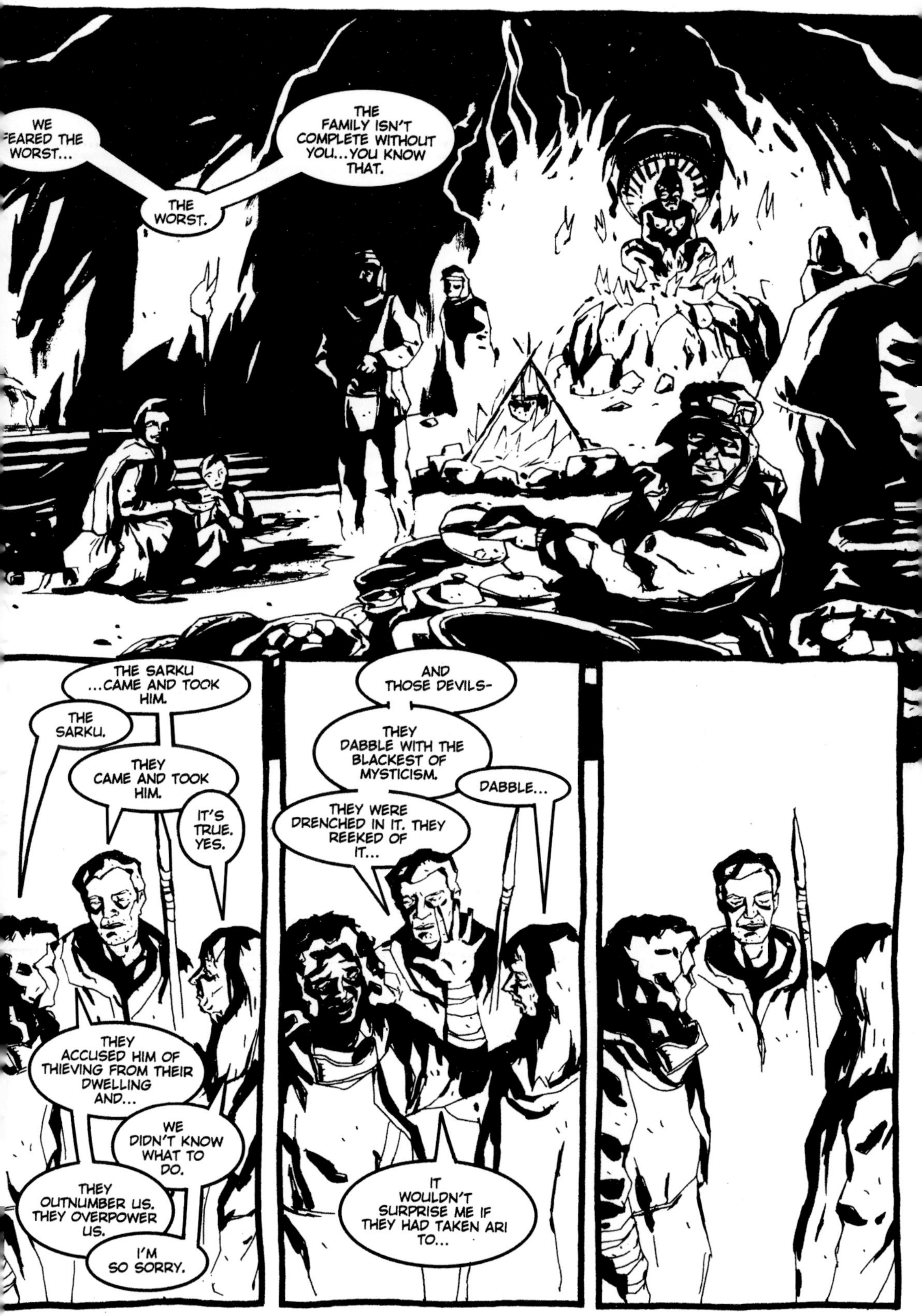
WE FEARED THE WORST...
THE WORST.
THE FAMILY ISN'T COMPLETE WITHOUT YOU...YOU KNOW THAT.
THE SARKU ...CAME AND TOOK HIM.
THE SARKU.
THEY CAME AND TOOK HIM.
IT'S TRUE. YES.
THEY ACCUSED HIM OF THIEVING FROM THEIR DWELLING AND...
WE DIDN'T KNOW WHAT TO DO.
THEY OUTNUMBER US. THEY OVERPOWER US.
I'M SO SORRY.
AND THOSE DEVILS-
THEY DABBLE WITH THE BLACKEST OF MYSTICISM.
DABBLE...
THEY WERE DRENCHED IN IT. THEY REEKED OF IT...
IT WOULDN'T SURPRISE ME IF THEY HAD TAKEN ARI TO...

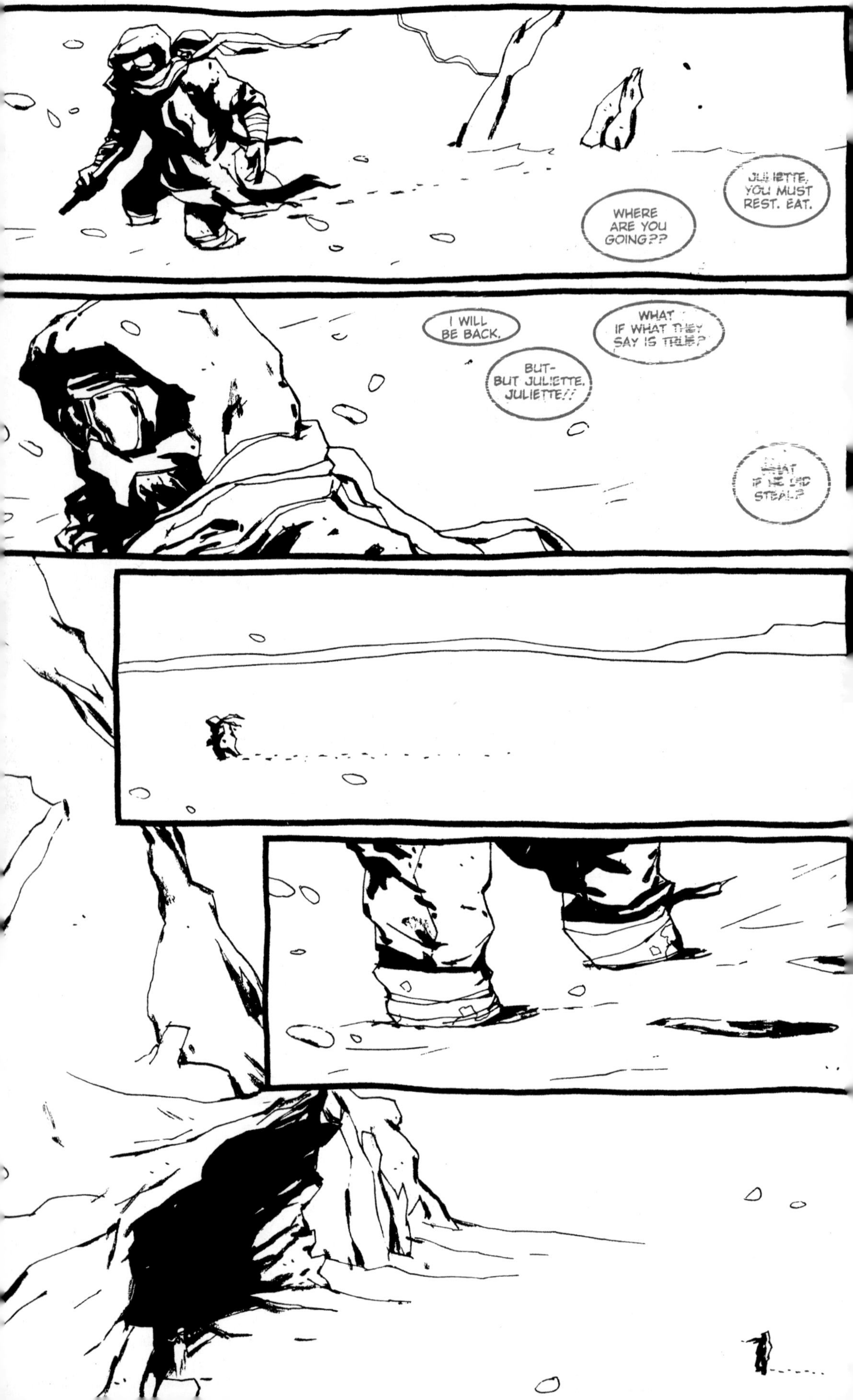
JULIETTE, YOU MUST REST. EAT.
WHERE ARE YOU GOING??
I WILL BE BACK.
BUT- BUT JULIETTE. JULIETTE!!
WHAT IF WHAT THEY SAY IS TRUE?
WHAT IF HE DID STEAL?

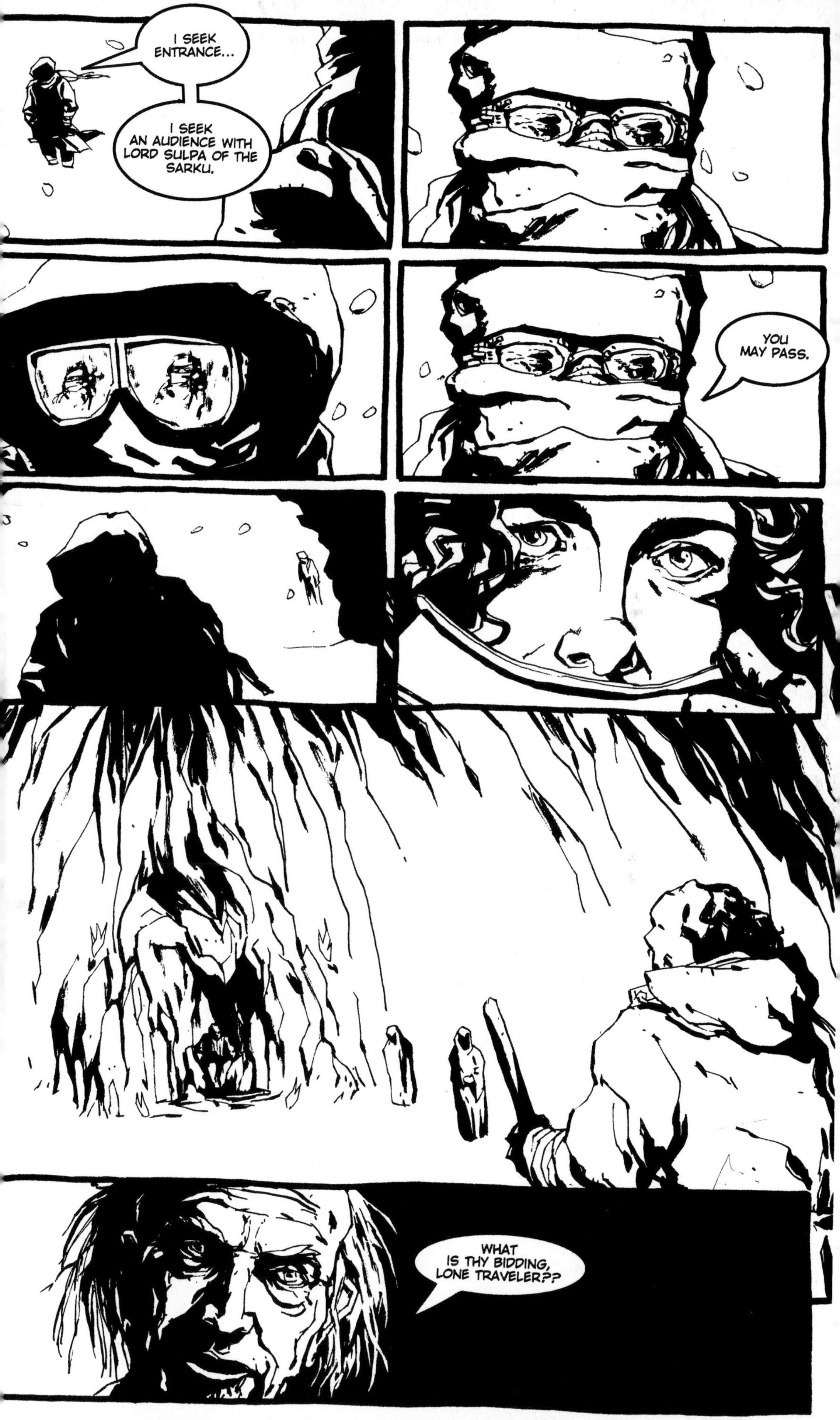
I SEEK ENTRANCE...
I SEEK AN AUDIENCE WITH LORD SULPA OF THE SARKU.
YOU MAY PASS.
WHAT IS THY BIDDING, LONE TRAVELER??

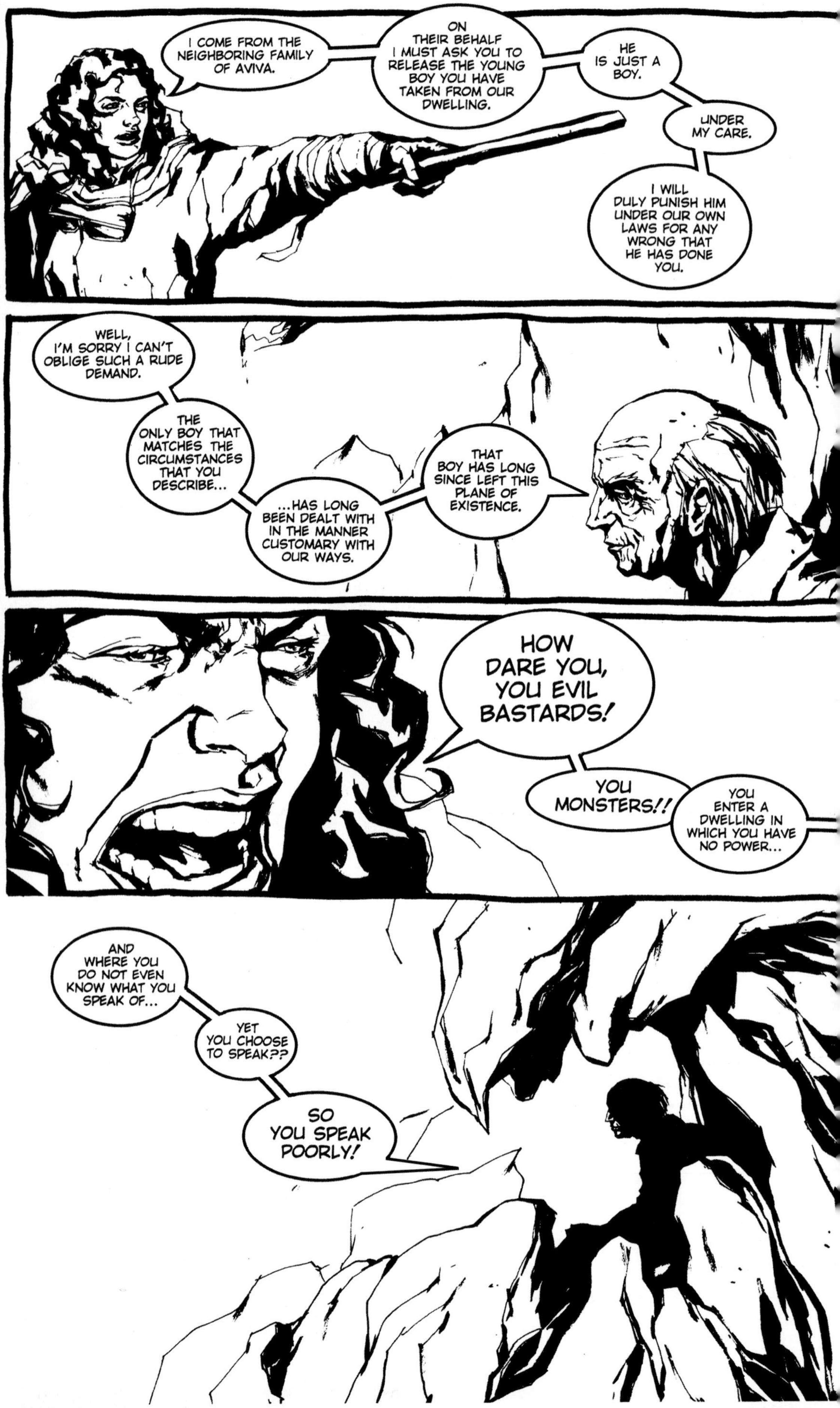

I COME FROM THE NEIGHBORING FAMILY OF AVIVA.
ON THEIR BEHALF I MUST ASK YOU TO RELEASE THE YOUNG BOY YOU HAVE TAKEN FROM OUR DWELLING.
HE IS JUST A BOY.
UNDER MY CARE.
I WILL DULY PUNISH HIM UNDER OUR OWN LAWS FOR ANY WRONG THAT HE HAS DONE YOU.
WELL, I'M SORRY I CAN'T OBLIGE SUCH A RUDE DEMAND.
THE ONLY BOY THAT MATCHES THE CIRCUMSTANCES THAT YOU DESCRIBE...
...HAS LONG BEEN DEALT WITH IN THE MANNER CUSTOMARY WITH OUR WAYS.
THAT BOY HAS LONG SINCE LEFT THIS PLANE OF EXISTENCE.
HOW DARE YOU, YOU EVIL BASTARDS!
YOU MONSTERS!!
YOU ENTER A DWELLING IN WHICH YOU HAVE NO POWER...
AND WHERE YOU DO NOT EVEN KNOW WHAT YOU SPEAK OF...
YET YOU CHOOSE TO SPEAK??
SO YOU SPEAK POORLY!

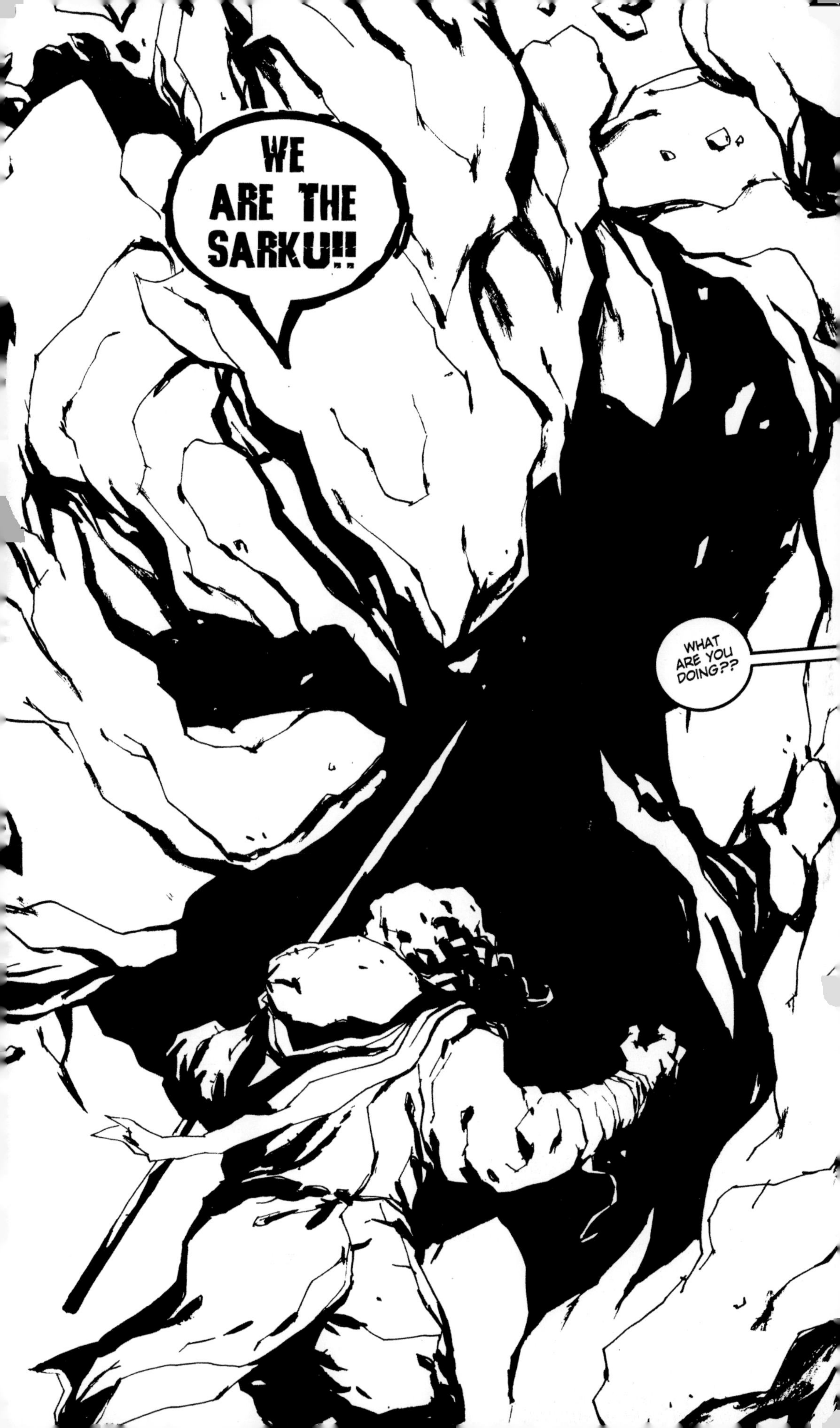
WE ARE THE SARKU!!
WHAT ARE YOU DOING??

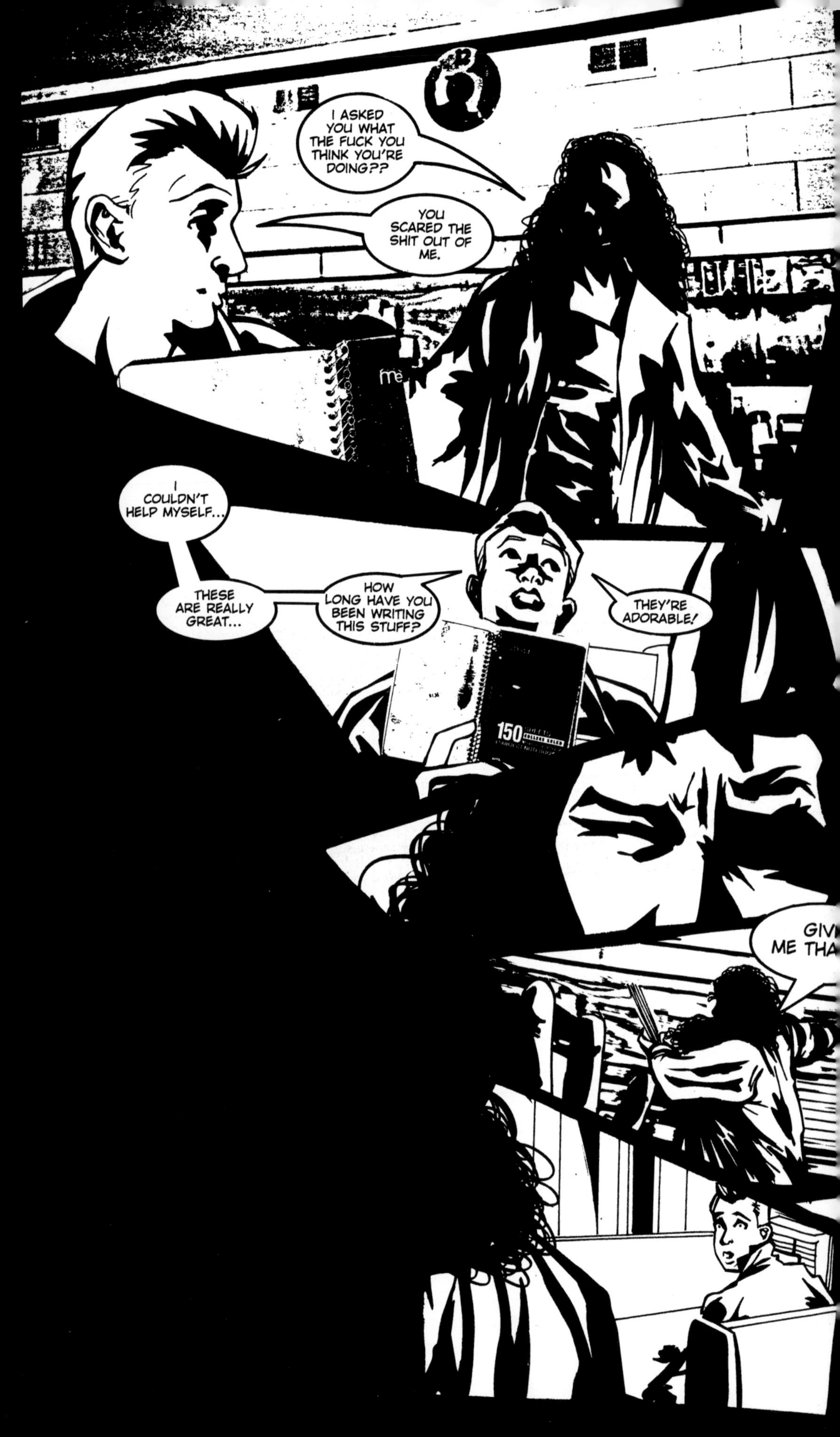
I ASKED YOU WHAT THE FUCK YOU THINK YOU'RE DOING??
YOU SCARED THE SHIT OUT OF ME.
I COULDN'T HELP MYSELF...
THESE ARE REALLY GREAT...
HOW LONG HAVE YOU BEEN WRITING THIS STUFF?
THEY'RE ADORABLE!
GIV
ME THA

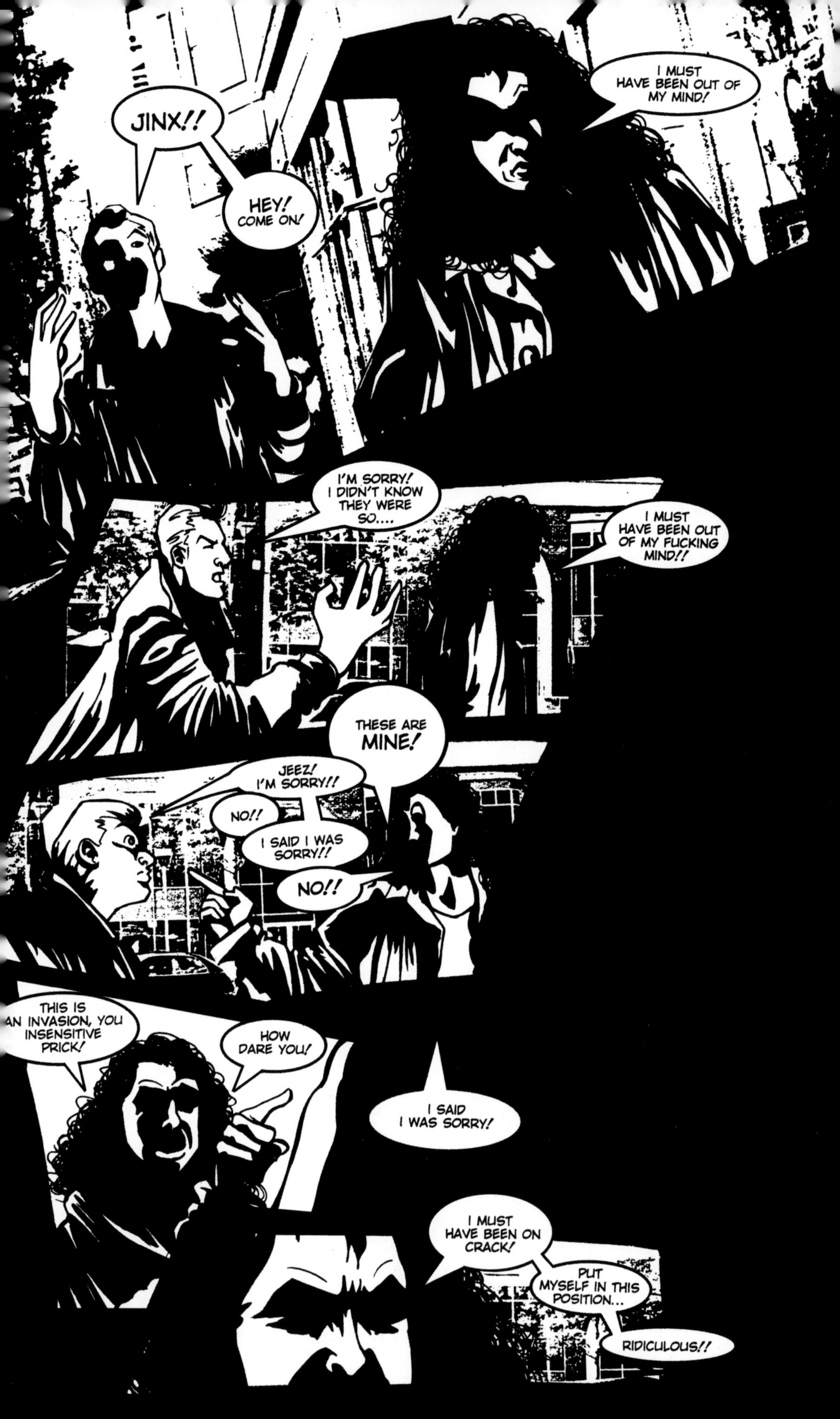
JINX!!
HEY! COME ON!
I MUST HAVE BEEN OUT OF MY MIND!
I'M SORRY! I DIDN'T KNOW THEY WERE SO....
I MUST HAVE BEEN OUT OF MY FUCKING MIND!!
THESE ARE MINE!
JEEZ! I'M SORRY!!
NO!!
I SAID I WAS SORRY!!
NO!!
THIS IS AN INVASION, YOU INSENSITIVE PRICK!
HOW DARE YOU!
I SAID I WAS SORRY!
I MUST HAVE BEEN ON CRACK!
PUT MYSELF IN THIS POSITION...
RIDICULOUS!!

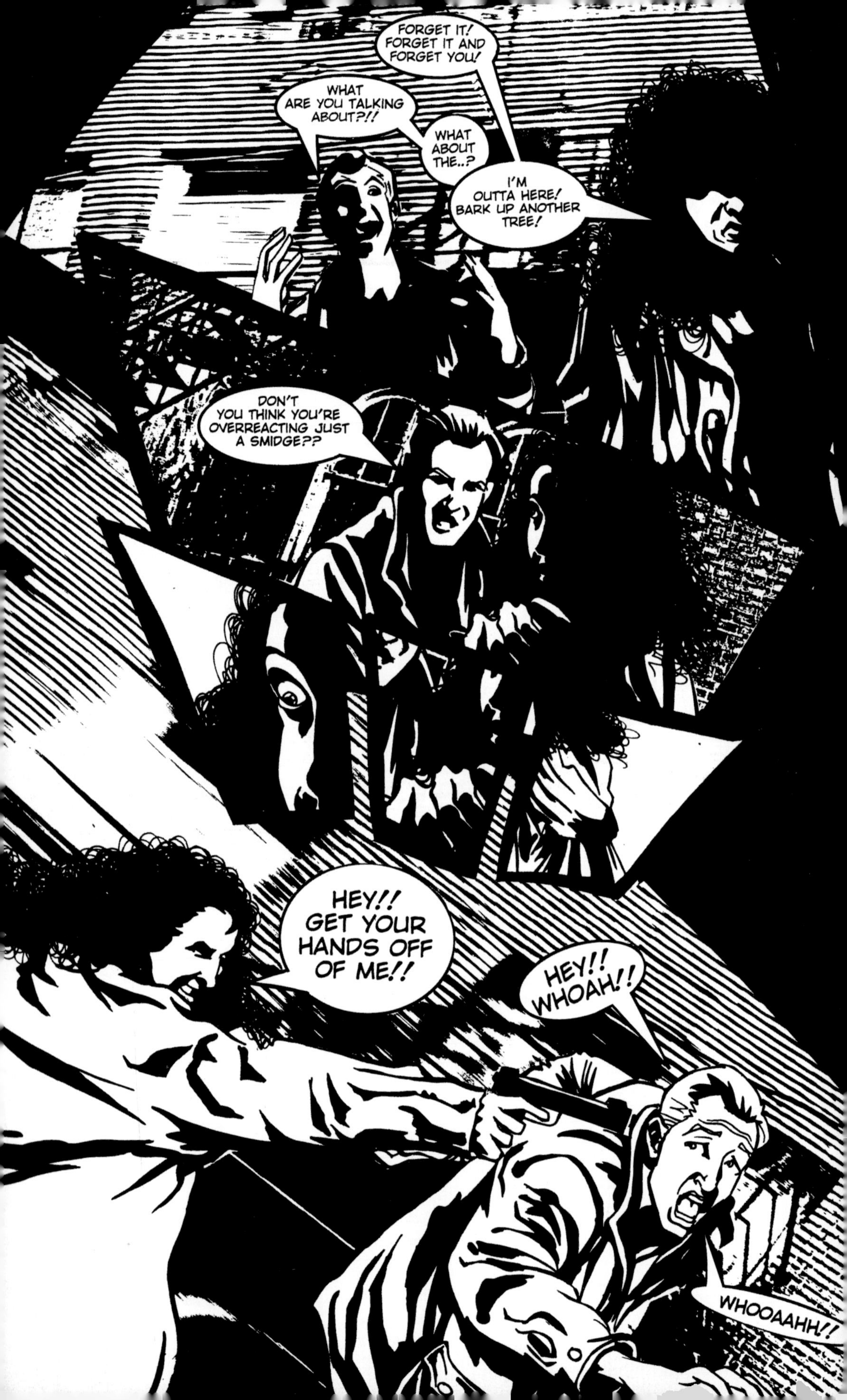
FORGET IT! FORGET IT AND FORGET YOU!
WHAT ARE YOU TALKING ABOUT?!!
WHAT ABOUT THE..?
I'M OUTTA HERE! BARK UP ANOTHER TREE!
DON'T YOU THINK YOU'RE OVERREACTING JUST A SMIDGE??
HEY!! GET YOUR HANDS OFF OF ME!!
HEY!! WHOAH!!
WHOOAAHH!!

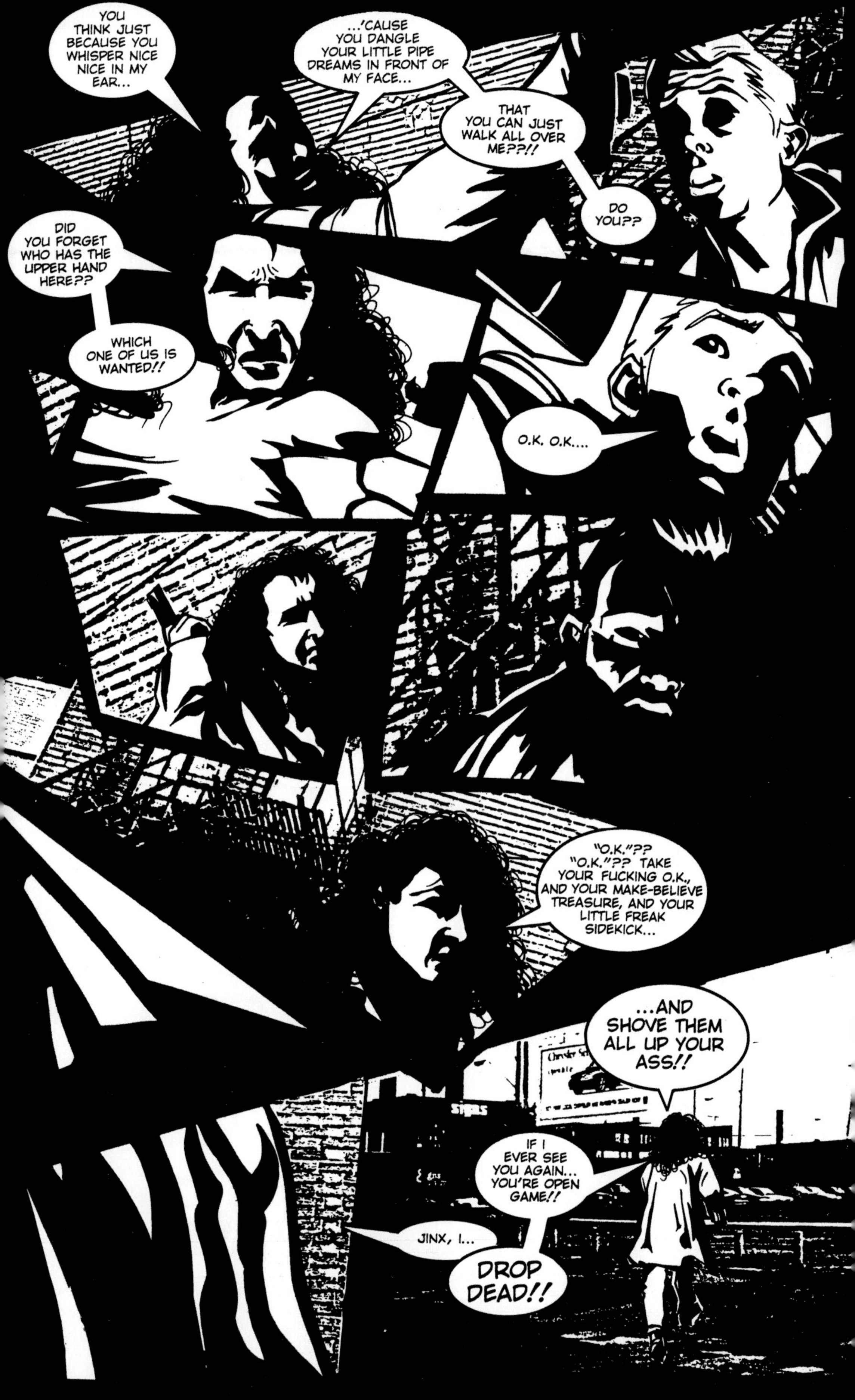
YOU THINK JUST BECAUSE YOU WHISPER NICE NICE IN MY EAR...
...'CAUSE YOU DANGLE YOUR LITTLE PIPE DREAMS IN FRONT OF MY FACE...
THAT YOU CAN JUST WALK ALL OVER ME??!!
DO YOU??
DID YOU FORGET WHO HAS THE UPPER HAND HERE??
WHICH ONE OF US IS WANTED!!
O.K. O.K....
"O.K."?? "O.K."?? TAKE YOUR FUCKING O.K., AND YOUR MAKE-BELIEVE TREASURE, AND YOUR LITTLE FREAK SIDEKICK...
...AND SHOVE THEM ALL UP YOUR ASS!!
IF I EVER SEE YOU AGAIN... YOU'RE OPEN GAME!!
JINX, I...
DROP DEAD!!

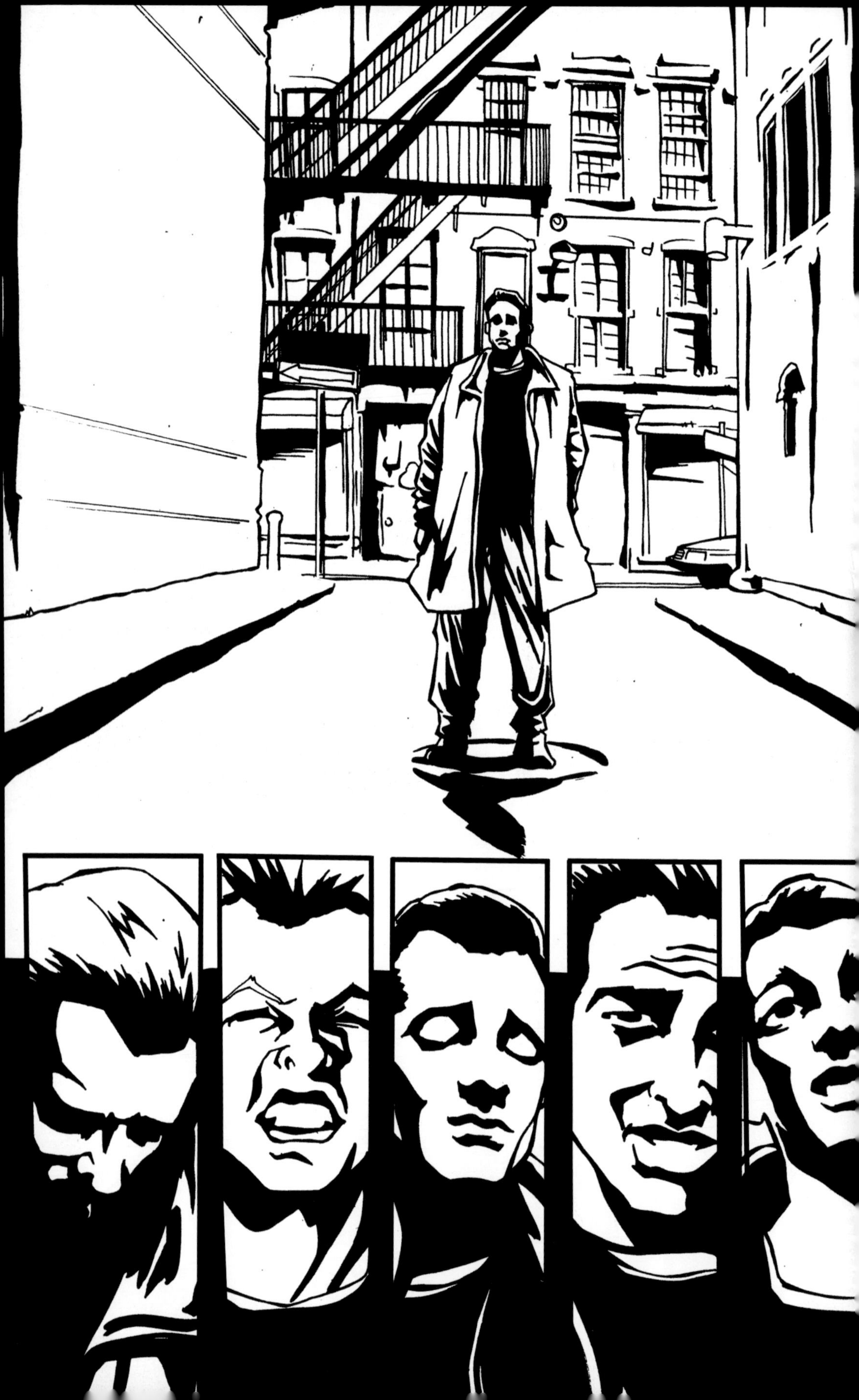

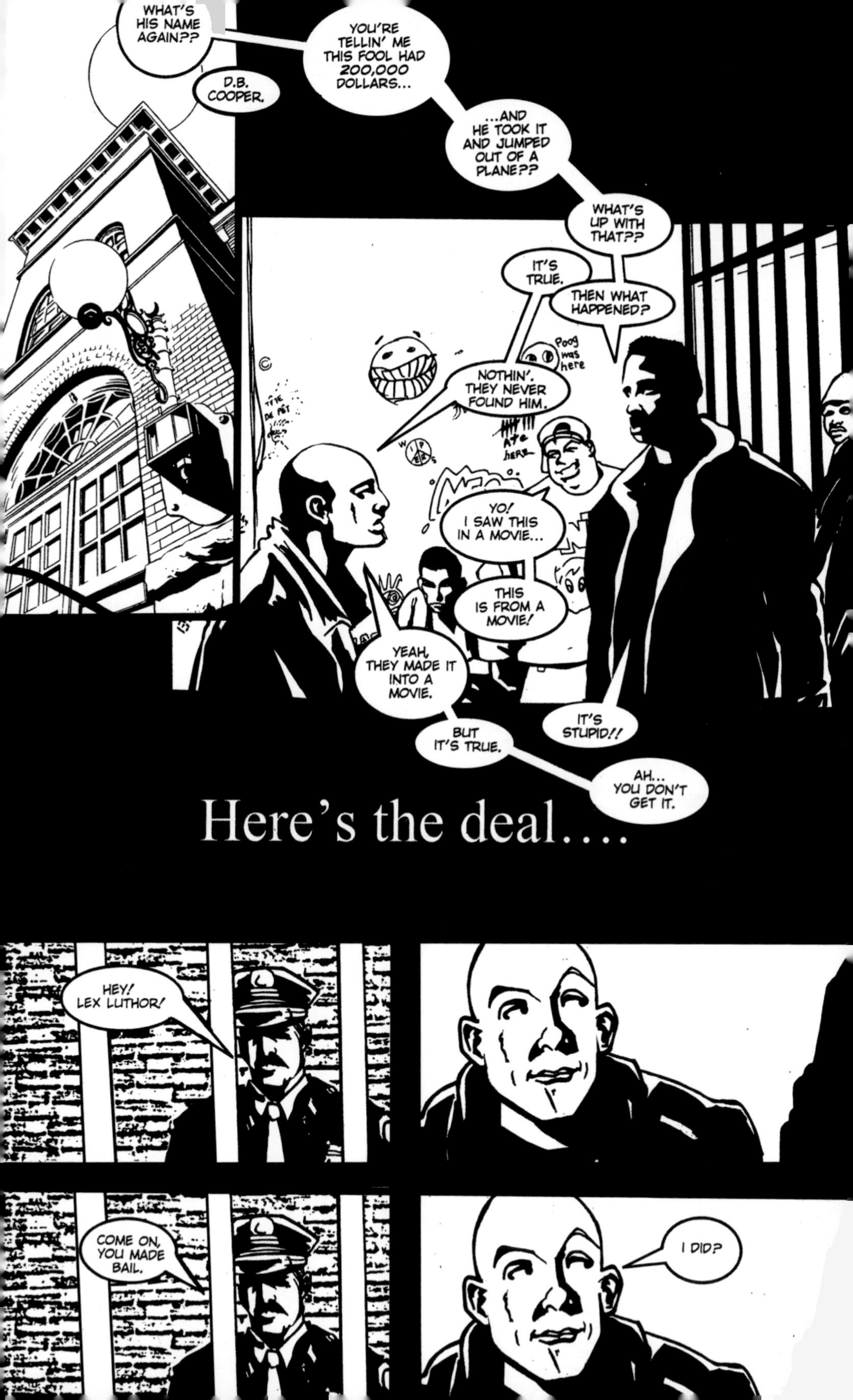

WHAT'S HIS NAME AGAIN??
D.B. COOPER.
YOU'RE TELLIN' ME THIS FOOL HAD 200,000 DOLLARS...
...AND HE TOOK IT AND JUMPED OUT OF A PLANE??
WHAT'S UP WITH THAT??
IT'S TRUE.
THEN WHAT HAPPENED?
NOTHIN'. THEY NEVER FOUND HIM.
Poog was here
YO! I SAW THIS IN A MOVIE...
THIS IS FROM A MOVIE!
YEAH, THEY MADE IT INTO A MOVIE.
IT'S STUPID!!
BUT IT'S TRUE.
AH... YOU DON'T GET IT.
Here's the deal....
HEY! LEX LUTHOR!
COME ON, YOU MADE BAIL.
I DID?

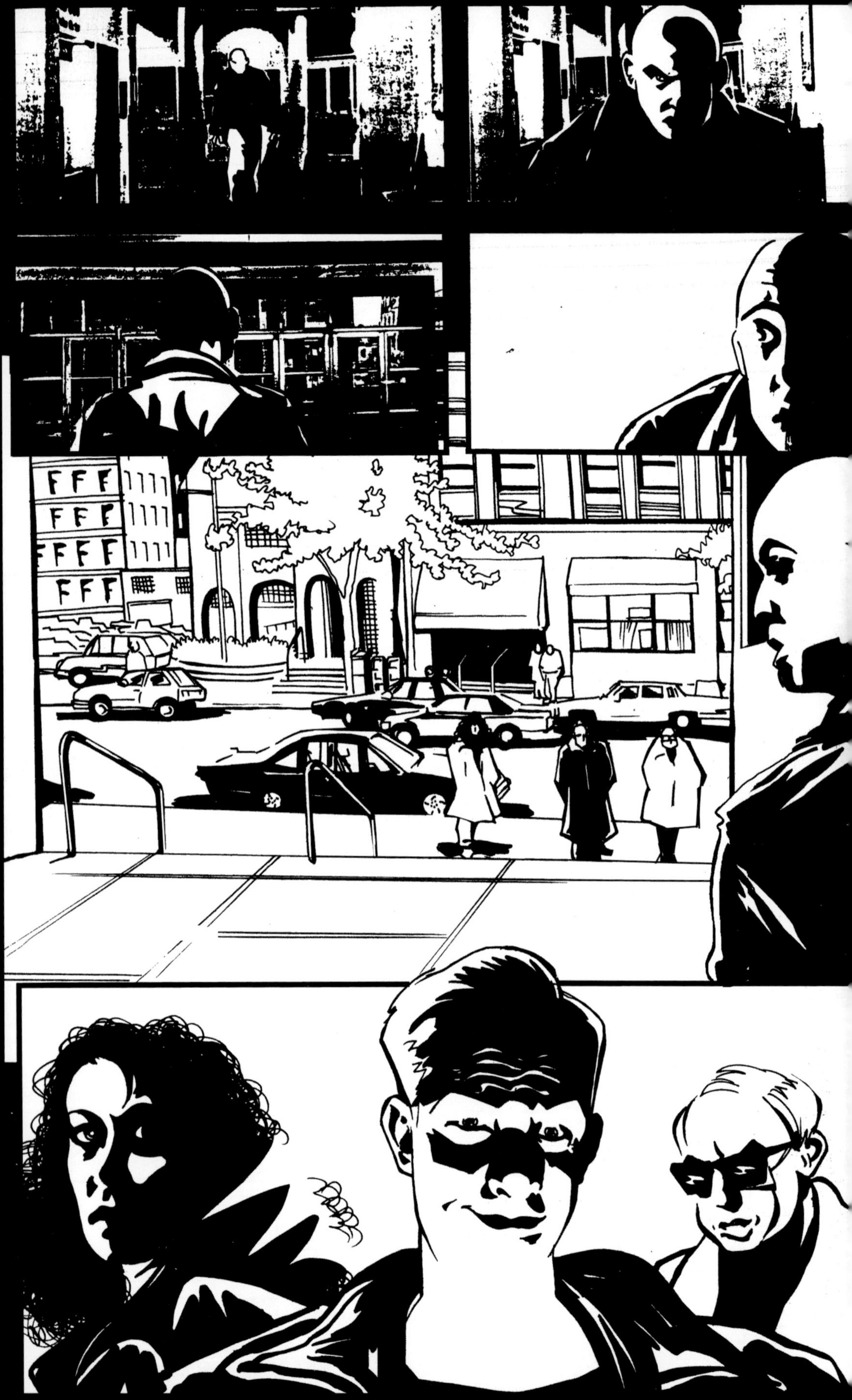

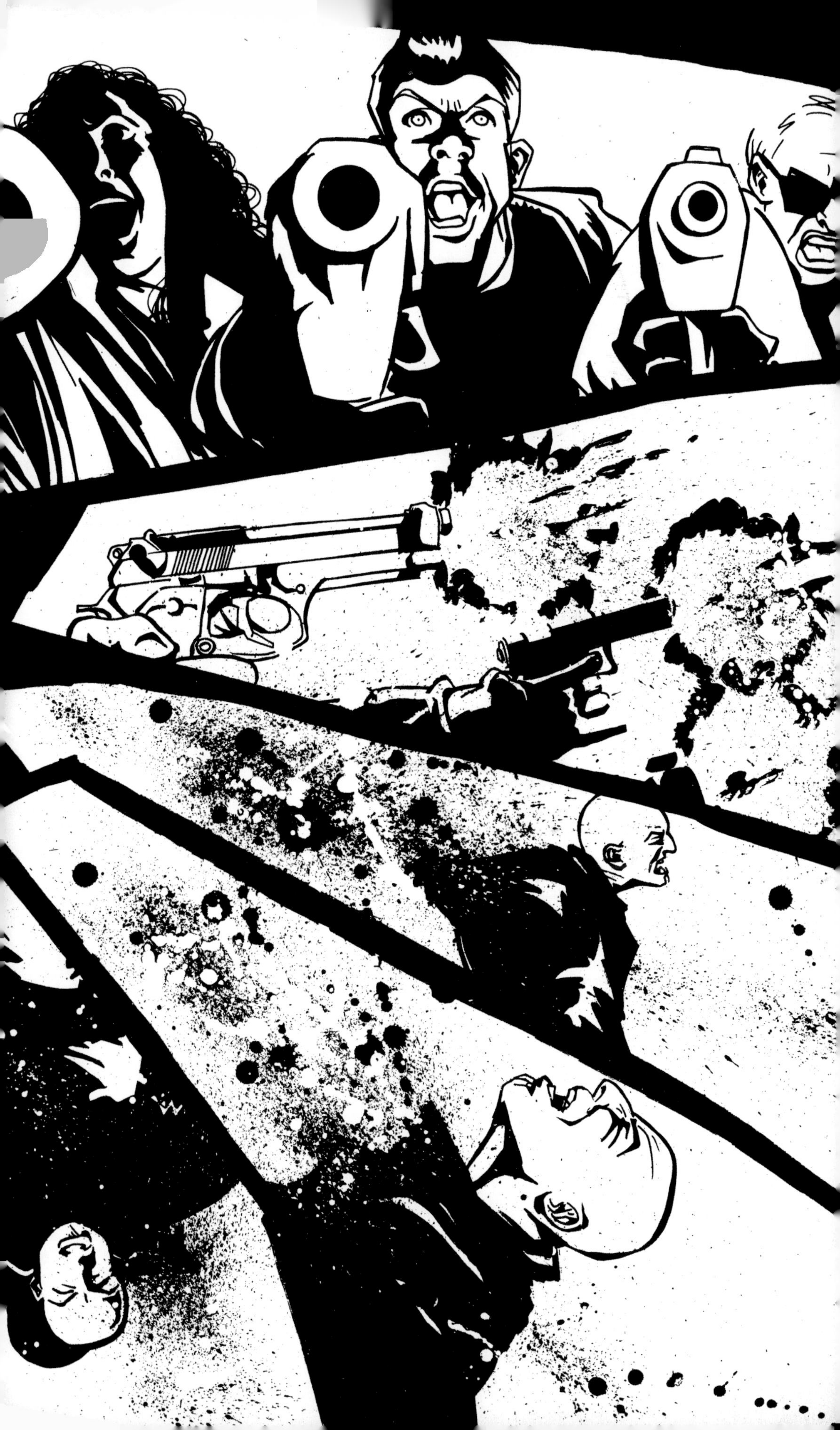

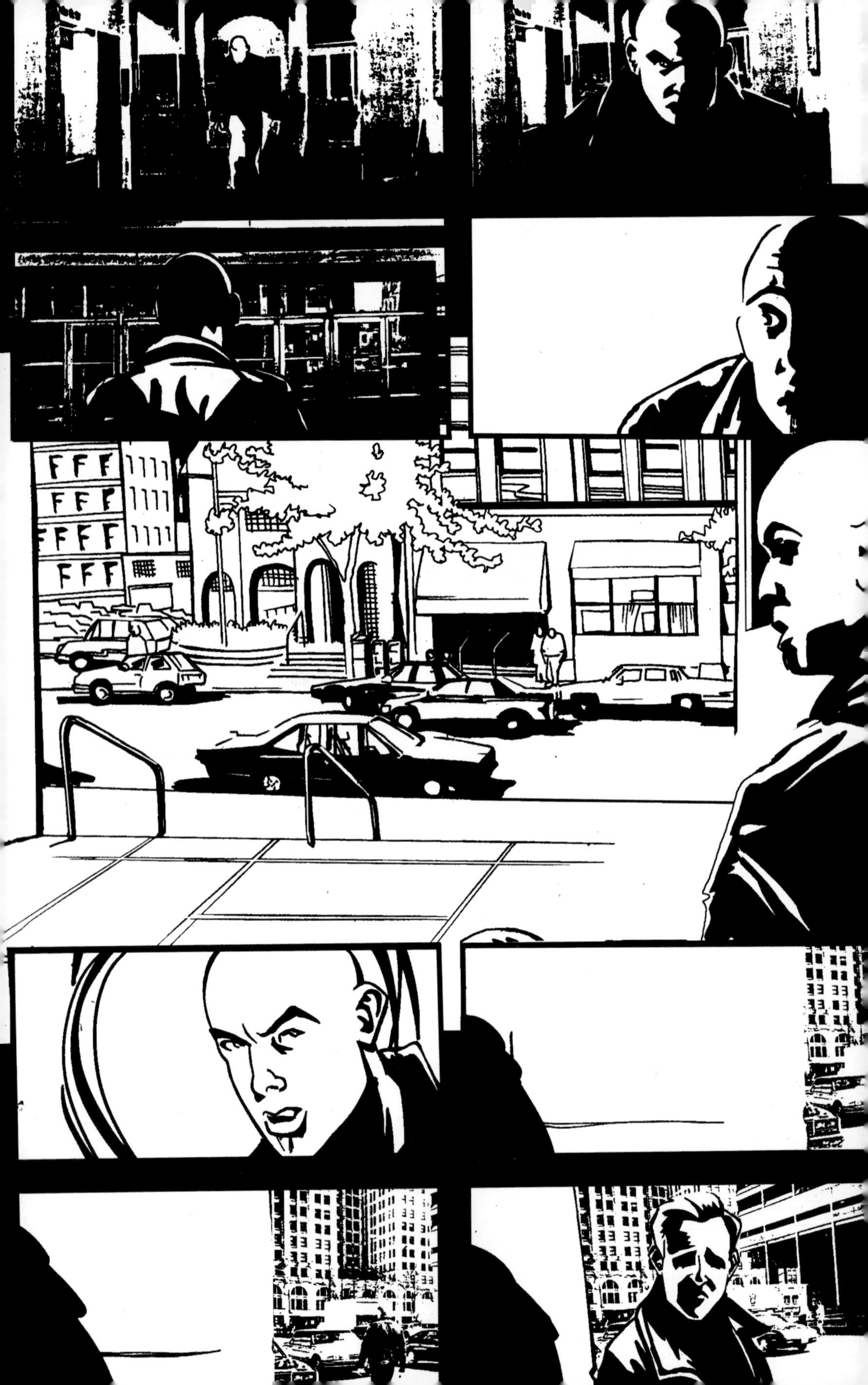

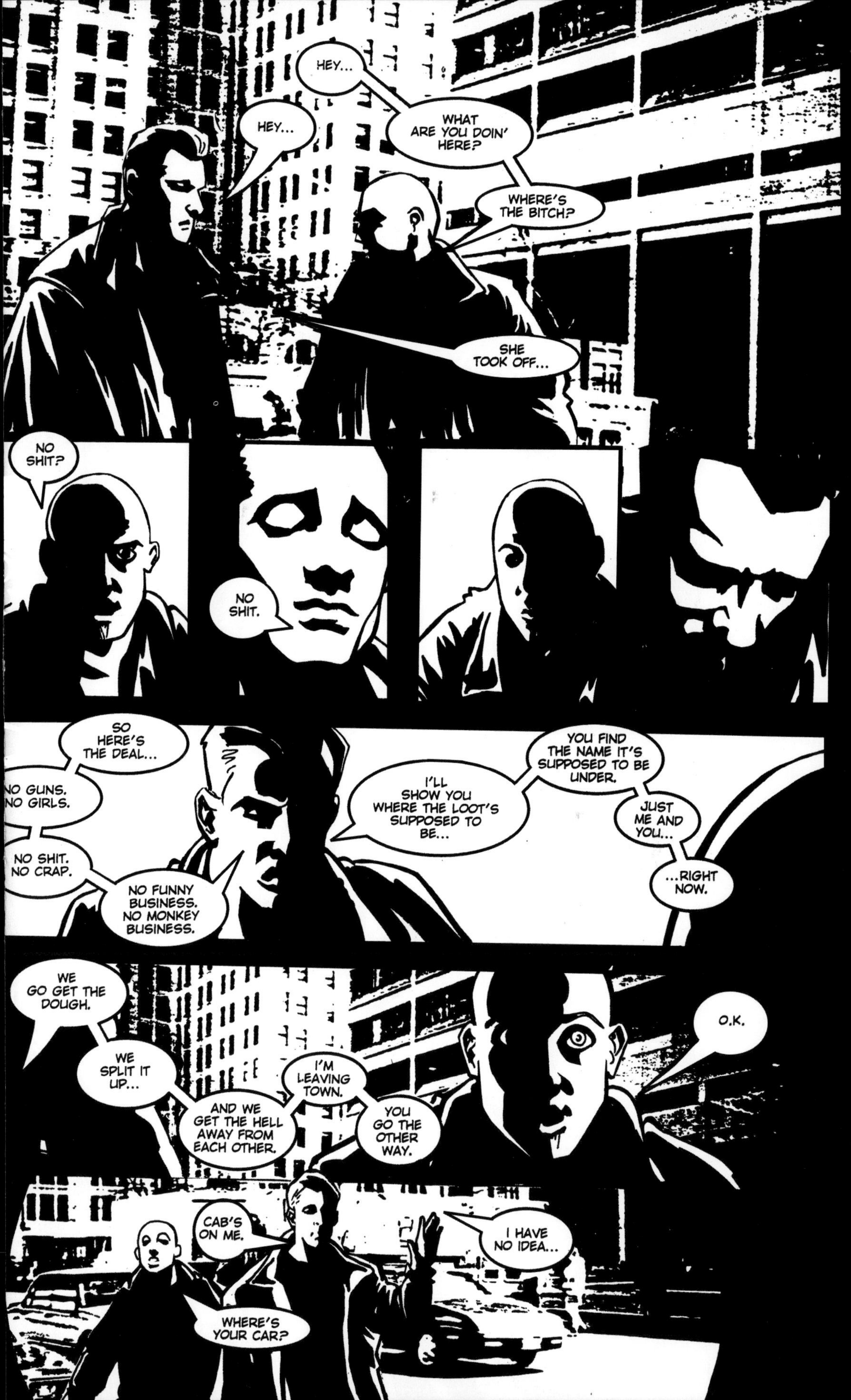
HEY...
HEY...
WHAT ARE YOU DOIN' HERE?
WHERE'S THE BITCH?
SHE TOOK OFF...
NO SHIT?
NO SHIT.
SO HERE'S THE DEAL...
NO GUNS. NO GIRLS.
NO SHIT. NO CRAP.
NO FUNNY BUSINESS. NO MONKEY BUSINESS.
I'LL SHOW YOU WHERE THE LOOT'S SUPPOSED TO BE...
YOU FIND THE NAME IT'S SUPPOSED TO BE UNDER.
JUST ME AND YOU...
...RIGHT NOW.
WE GO GET THE DOUGH.
WE SPLIT IT UP...
AND WE GET THE HELL AWAY FROM EACH OTHER.
I'M LEAVING TOWN.
YOU GO THE OTHER WAY.
O.K.
CAB'S ON ME.
I HAVE NO IDEA...
WHERE'S YOUR CAR?

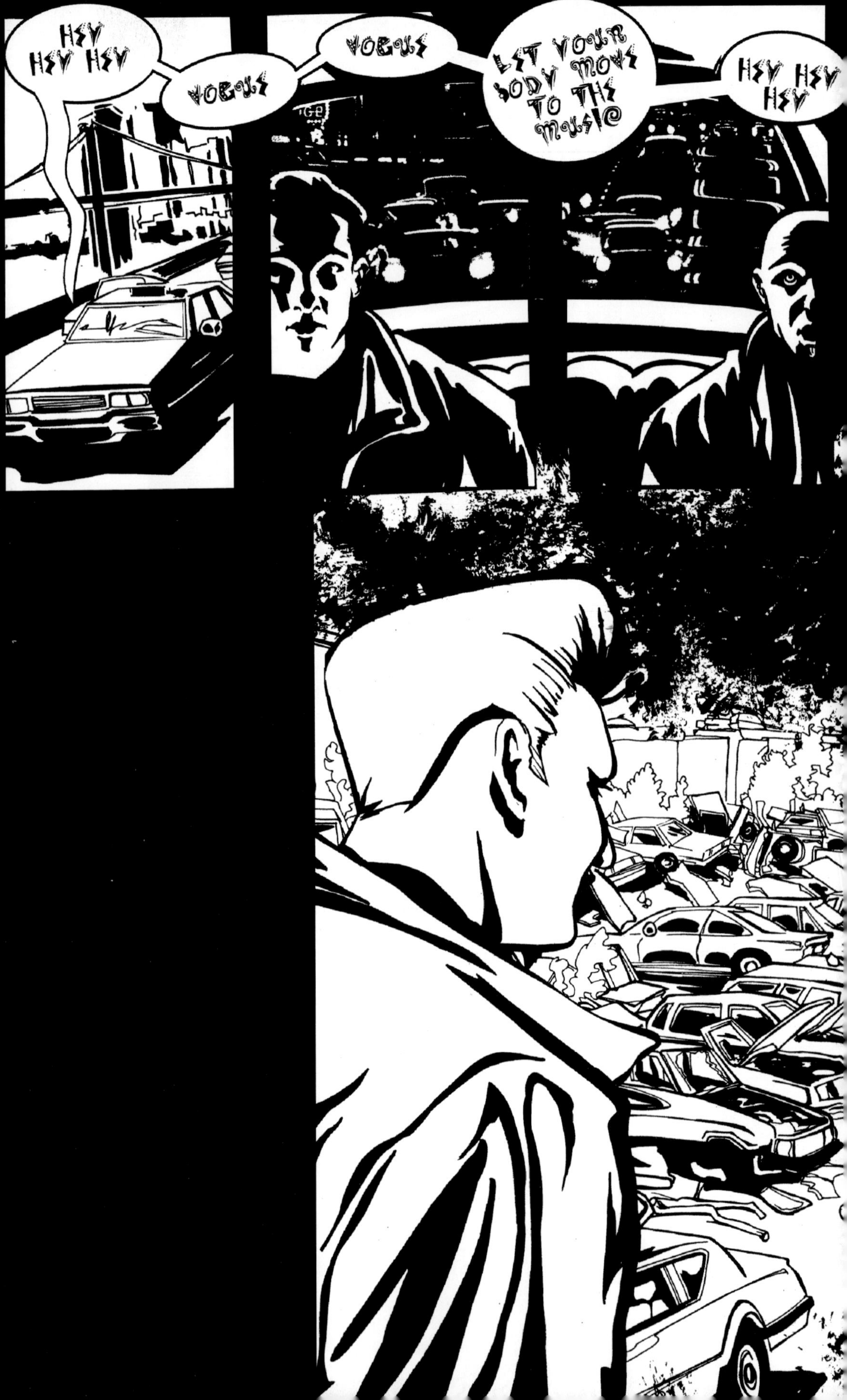
HEY HEY HEY
VOGUE
VOGUE
LET YOUR BODY MOVE TO THE MUSIC
HEY HEY HEY

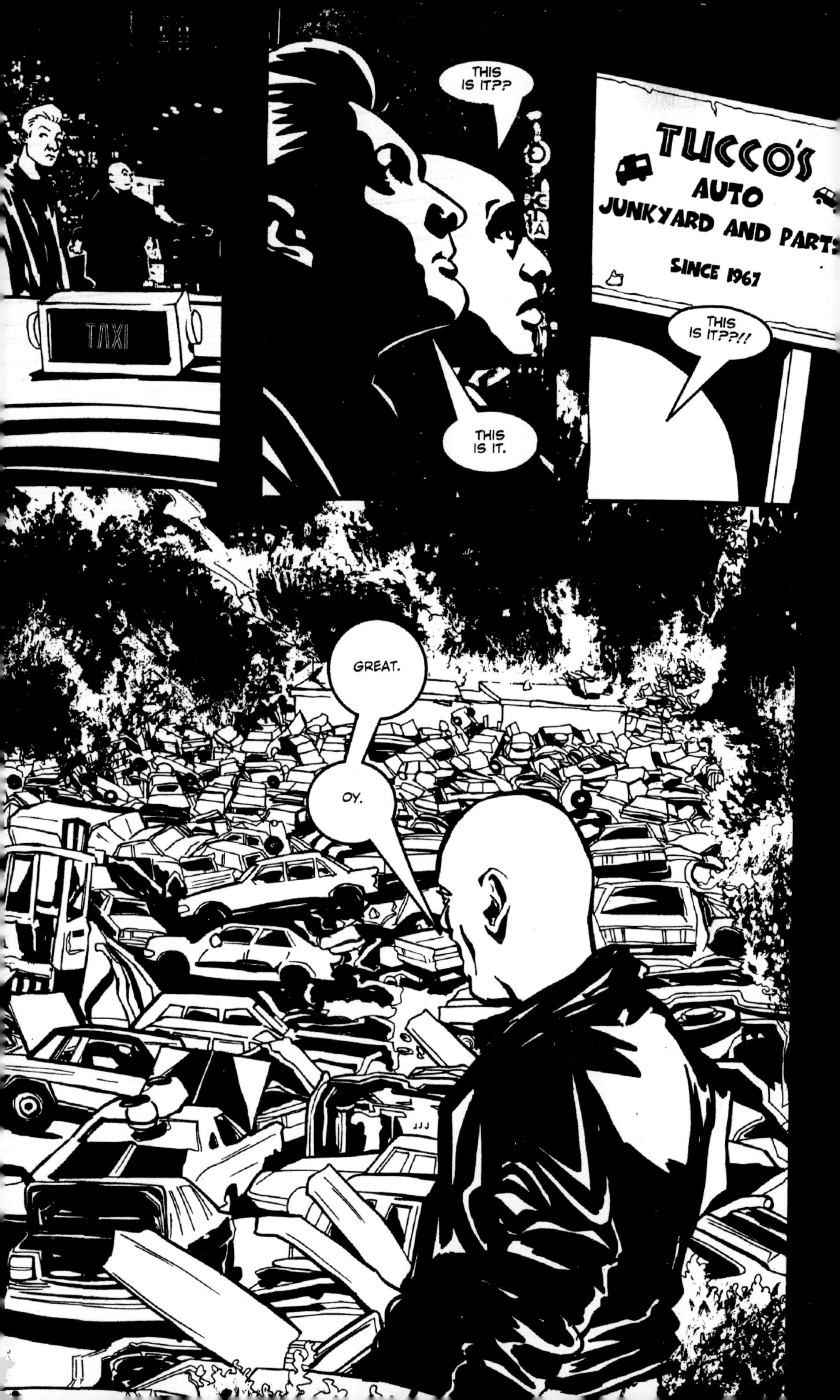
THIS IS IT??
TUCCO'S AUTO JUNKYARD AND PARTS
SINCE 1967
THIS IS IT??!!
THIS IS IT.
GREAT.
OY.

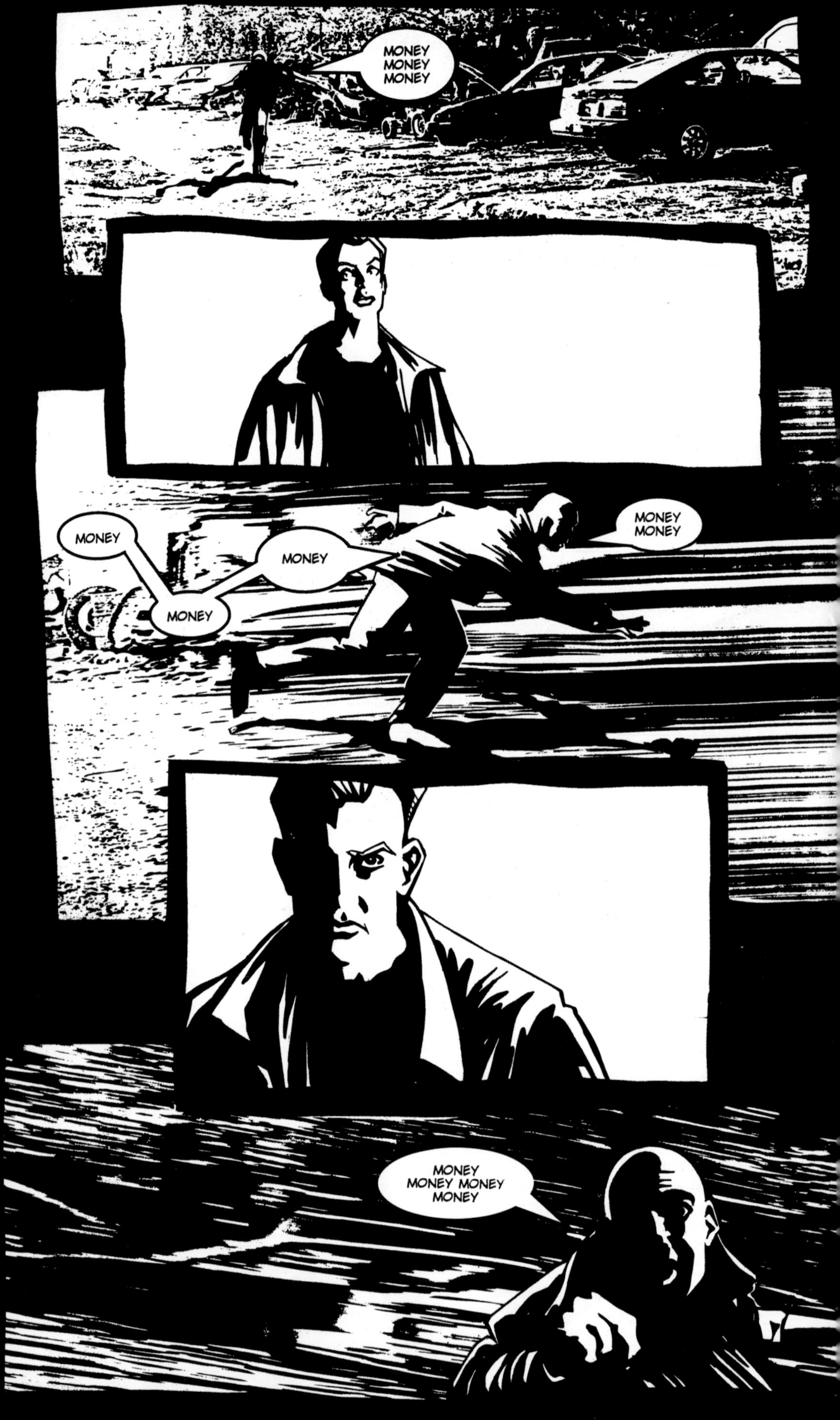
MONEY MONEY MONEY
MONEY
MONEY
MONEY
MONEY MONEY
MONEY MONEY MONEY MONEY

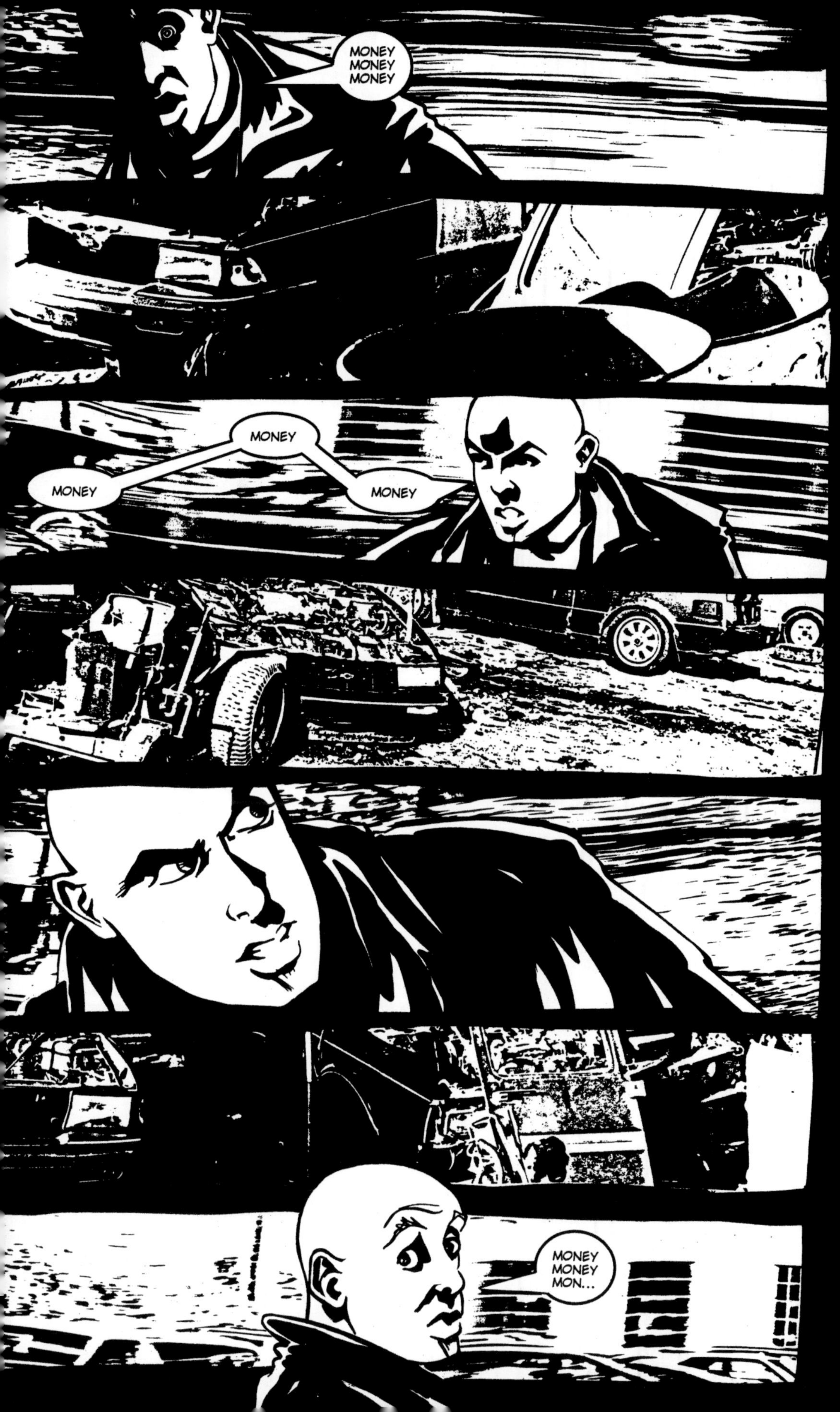
MONEY MONEY MONEY
MONEY
MONEY
MONEY
MONEY MONEY MON...

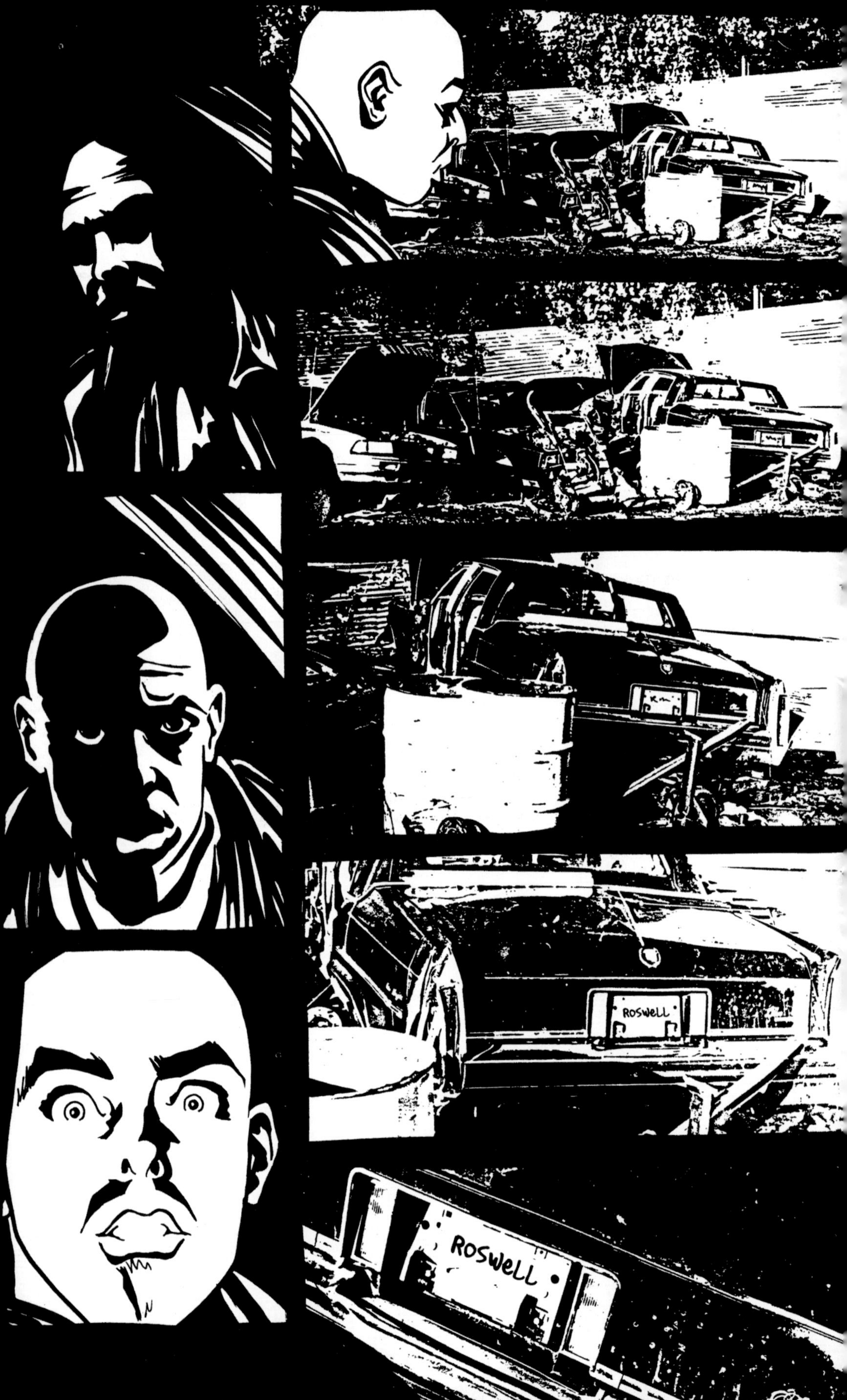
ROSWELL
ROSWELL

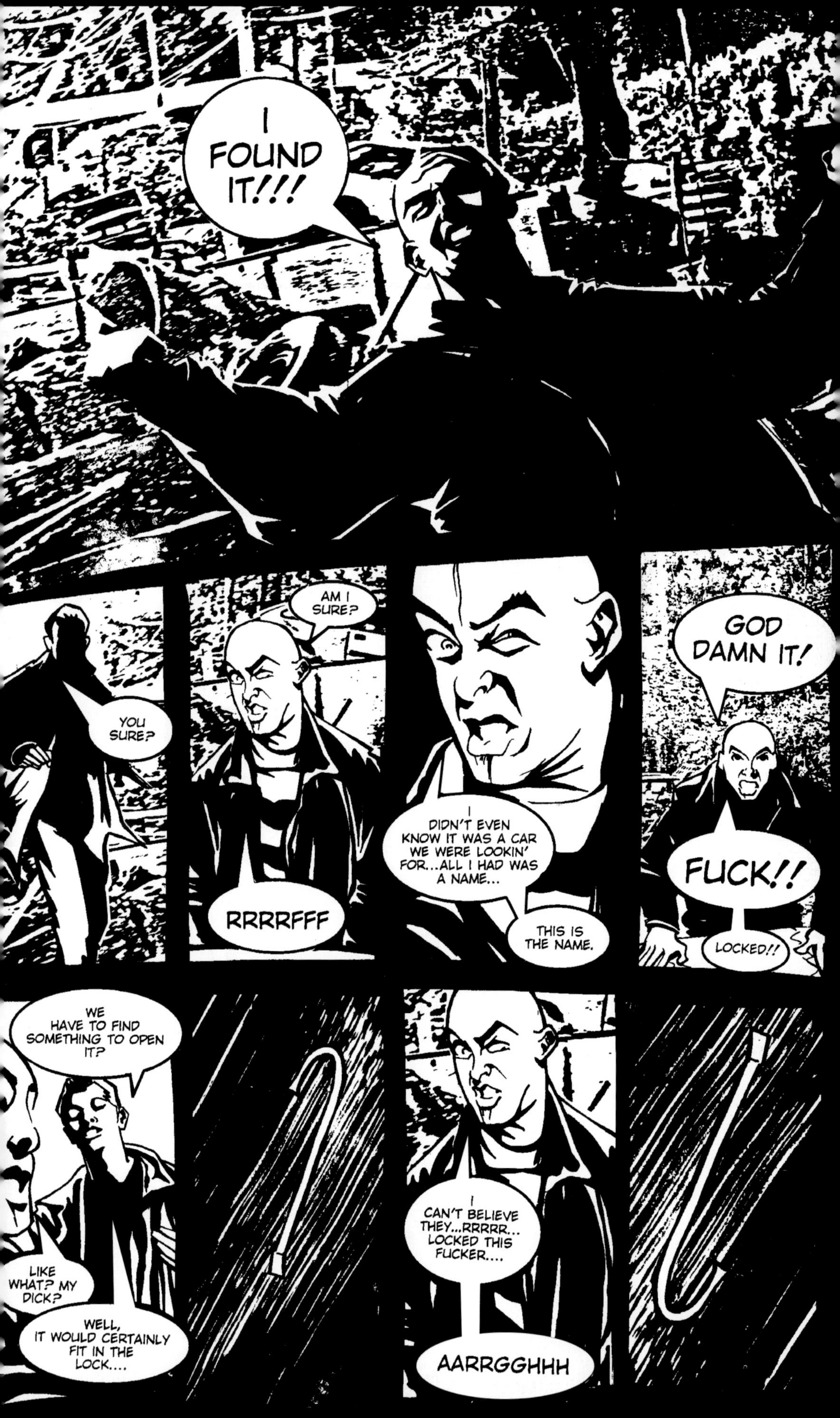
I FOUND IT!!!
YOU SURE?
AM I SURE?
RRRRFFF
I DIDN'T EVEN KNOW IT WAS A CAR WE WERE LOOKIN' FOR...ALL I HAD WAS A NAME...
THIS IS THE NAME.
GOD DAMN IT!
FUCK!!
LOCKED!!
WE HAVE TO FIND SOMETHING TO OPEN IT?
LIKE WHAT? MY DICK?
WELL, IT WOULD CERTAINLY FIT IN THE LOCK....
I CAN'T BELIEVE THEY...RRRRR... LOCKED THIS FUCKER....
AARRGGHHH

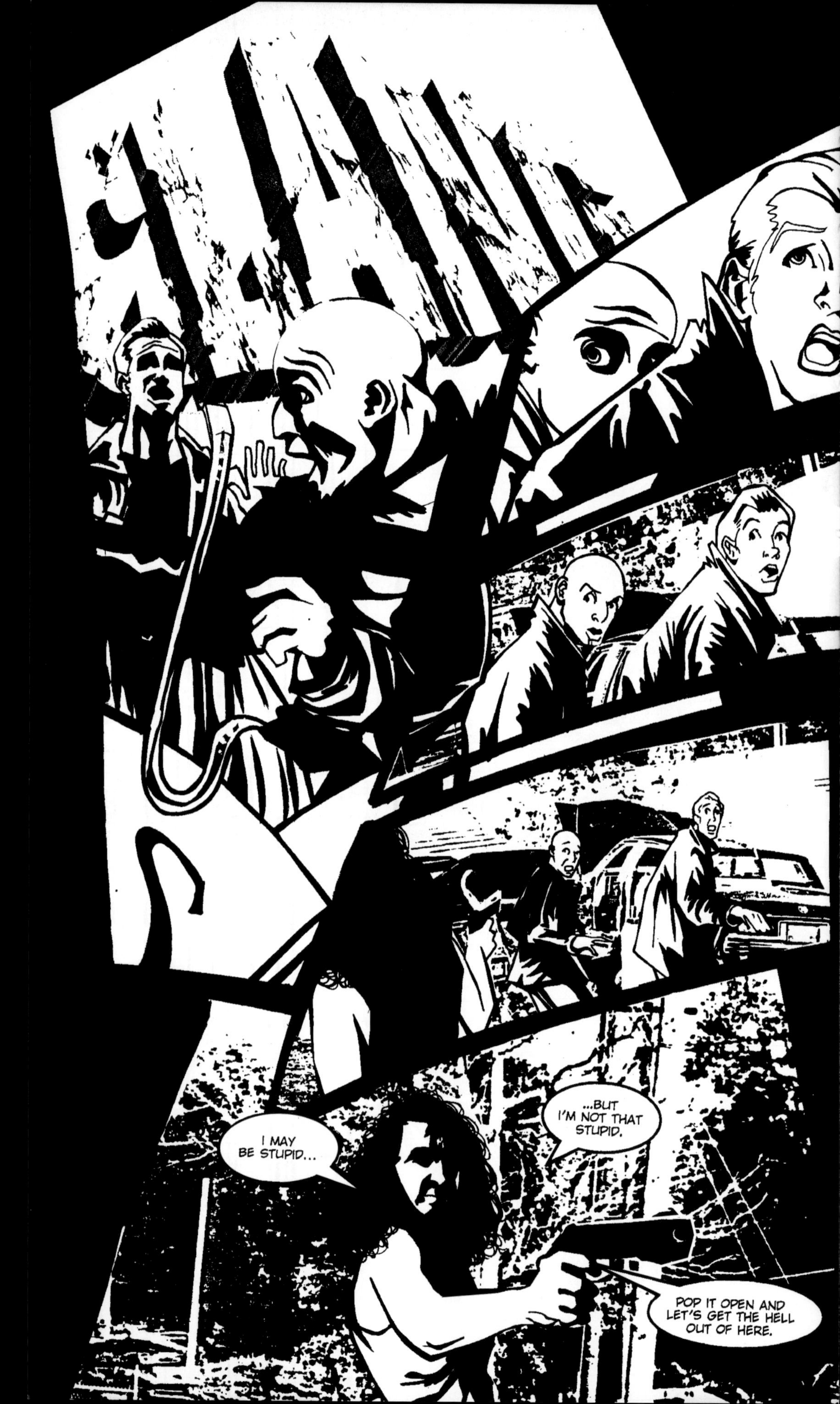
I MAY BE STUPID...
...BUT I'M NOT THAT STUPID.
POP IT OPEN AND LET'S GET THE HELL OUT OF HERE.

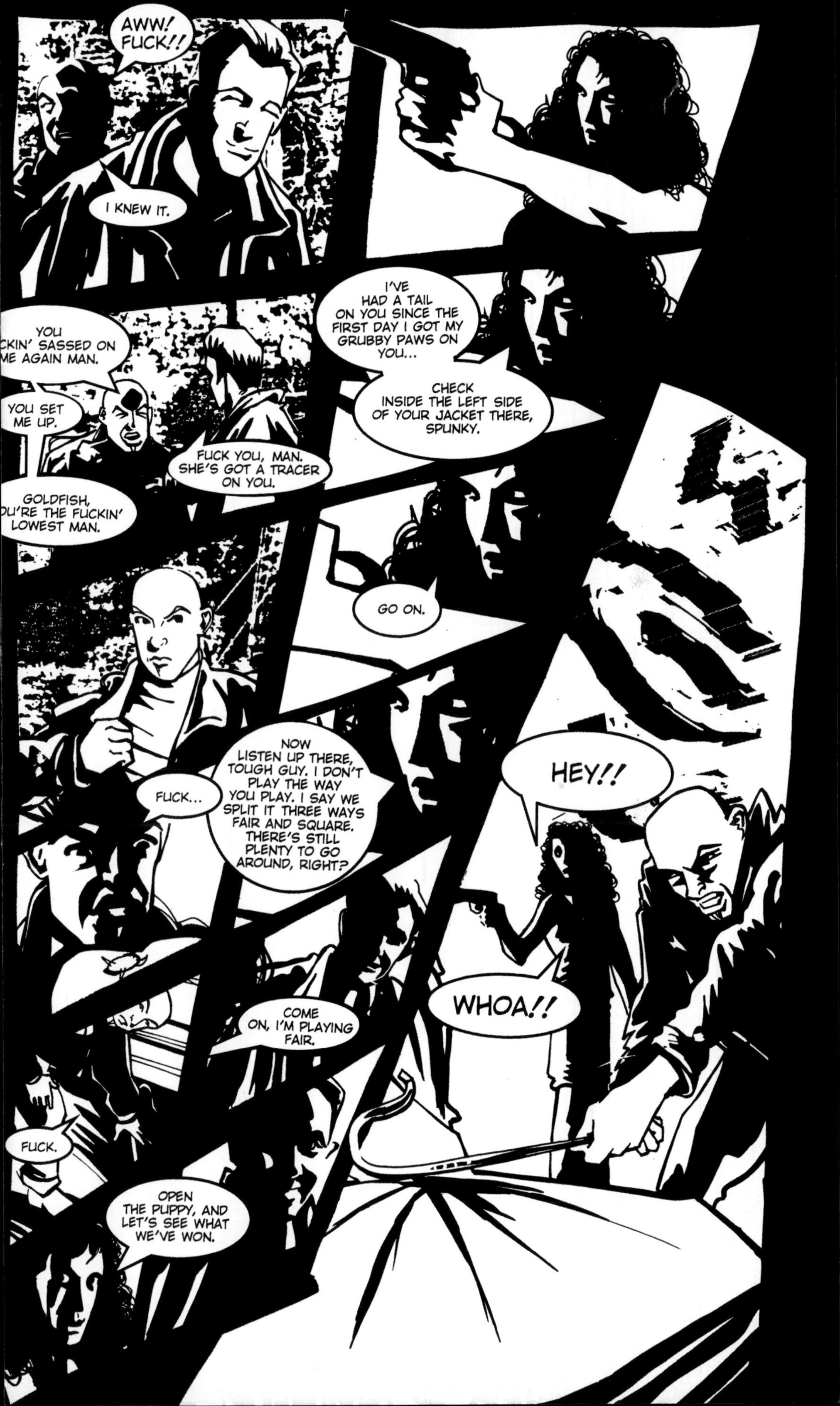
AWW! FUCK!!
I KNEW IT.
I'VE HAD A TAIL ON YOU SINCE THE FIRST DAY I GOT MY GRUBBY PAWS ON YOU...
CHECK INSIDE THE LEFT SIDE OF YOUR JACKET THERE, SPUNKY.
YOU ...CKIN' SASSED ON ...ME AGAIN MAN.
YOU SET ME UP.
FUCK YOU, MAN. SHE'S GOT A TRACER ON YOU.
GOLDFISH, ...U'RE THE FUCKIN' LOWEST MAN.
GO ON.
FUCK...
NOW LISTEN UP THERE, TOUGH GUY. I DON'T PLAY THE WAY YOU PLAY. I SAY WE SPLIT IT THREE WAYS FAIR AND SQUARE. THERE'S STILL PLENTY TO GO AROUND, RIGHT?
COME ON, I'M PLAYING FAIR.
FUCK.
OPEN THE PUPPY, AND LET'S SEE WHAT WE'VE WON.
HEY!!
WHOA!!

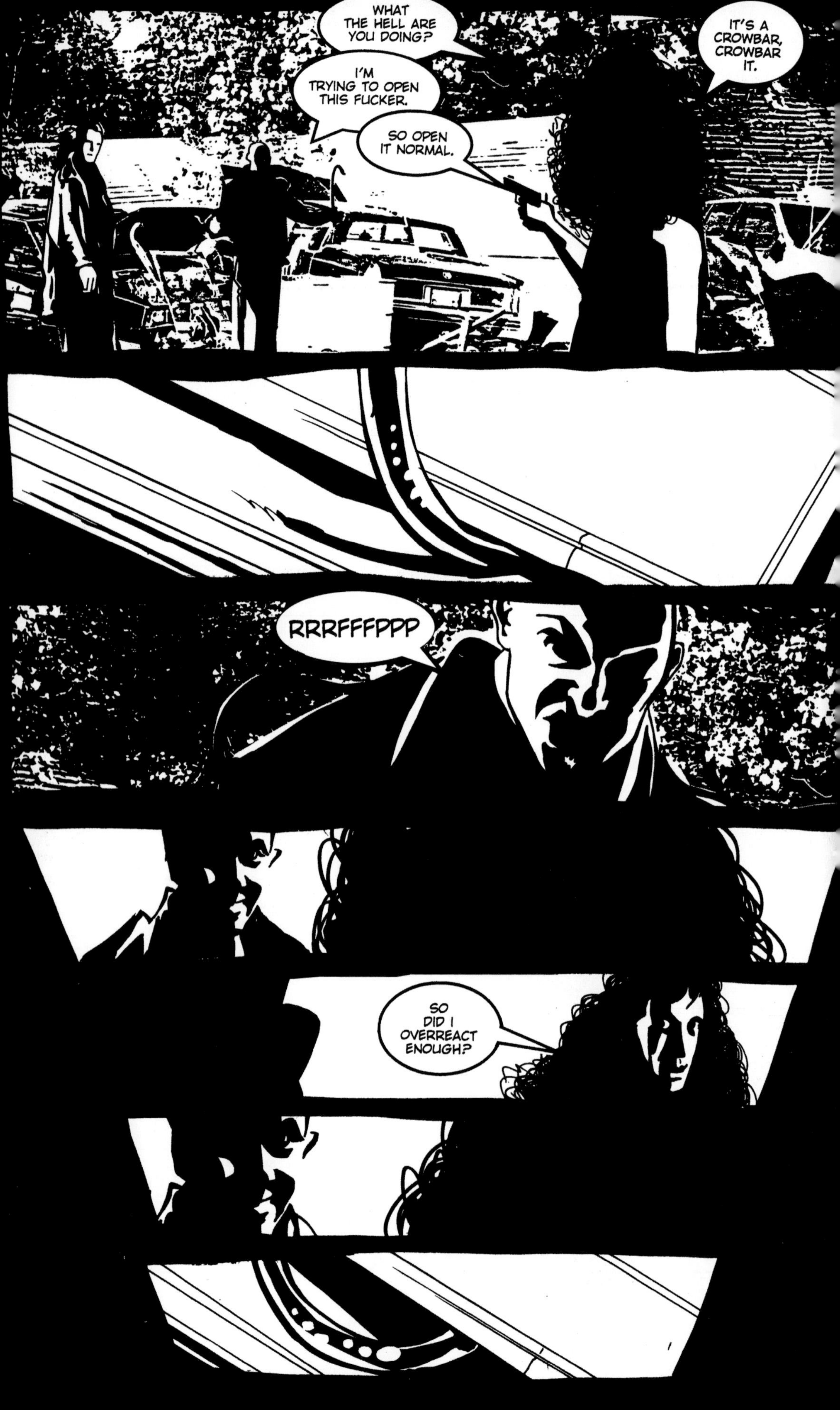
WHAT THE HELL ARE YOU DOING?
I'M TRYING TO OPEN THIS FUCKER.
SO OPEN IT NORMAL.
IT'S A CROWBAR, CROWBAR IT.
RRRFFFPPP
SO DID I OVERREACT ENOUGH?

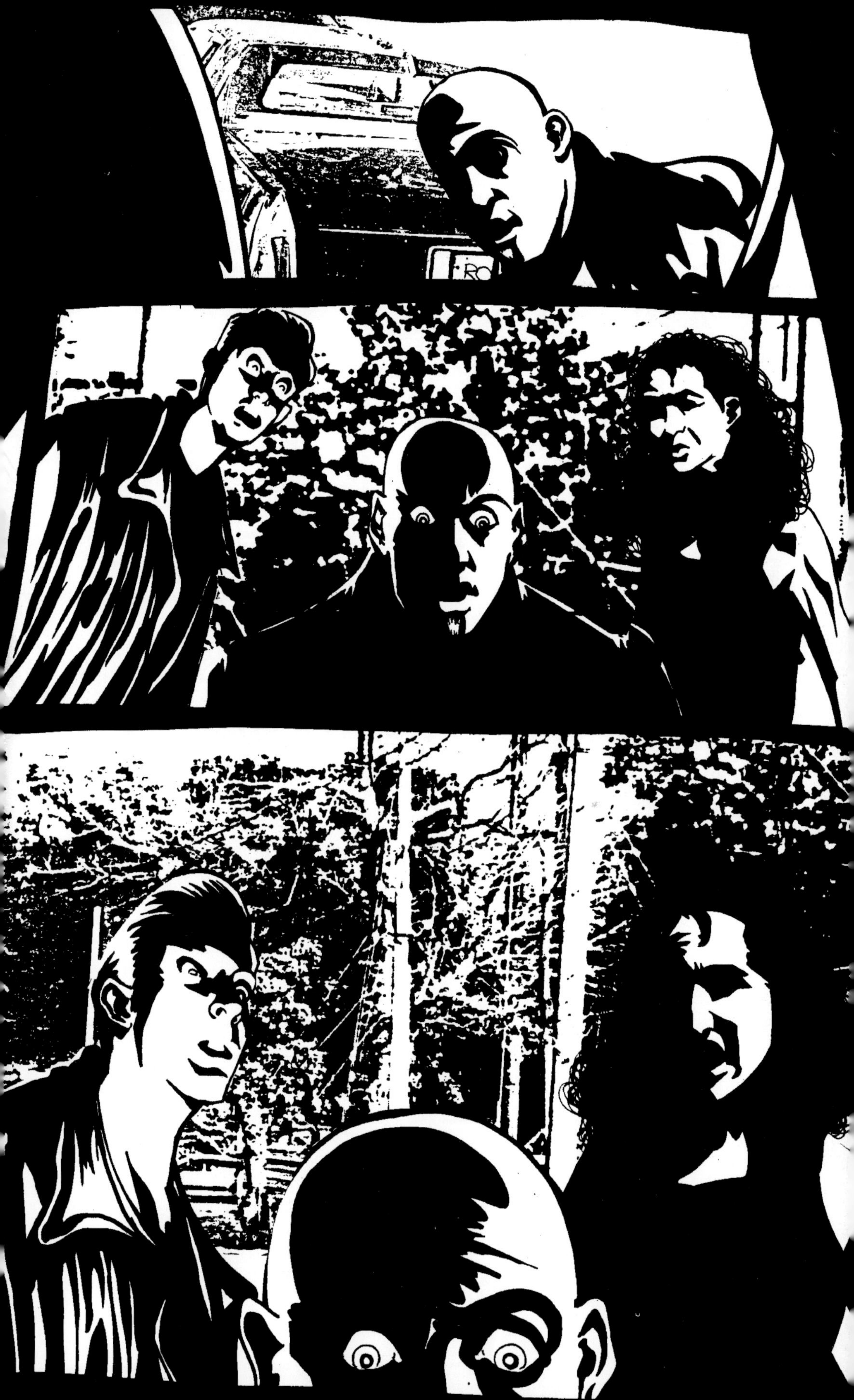

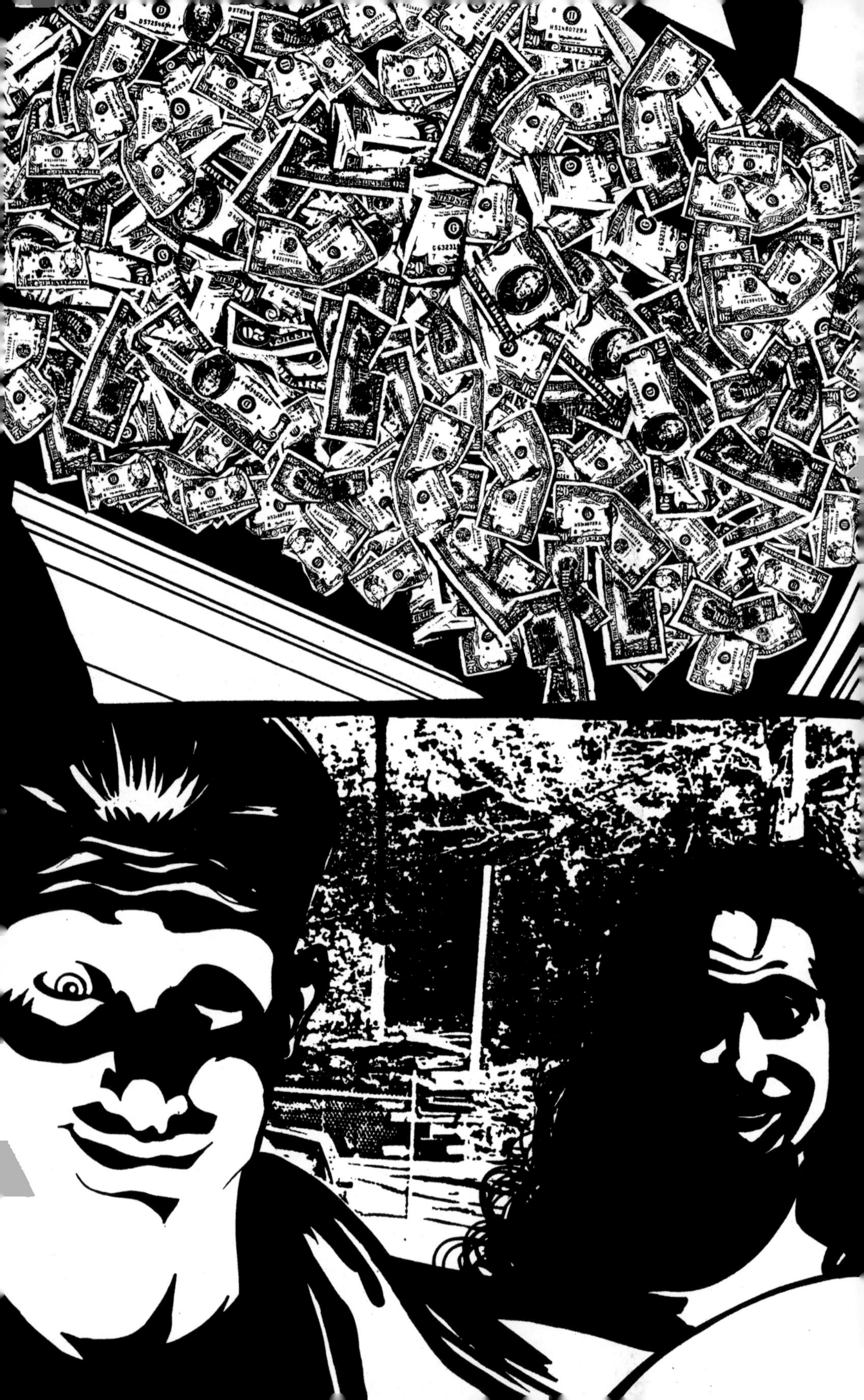

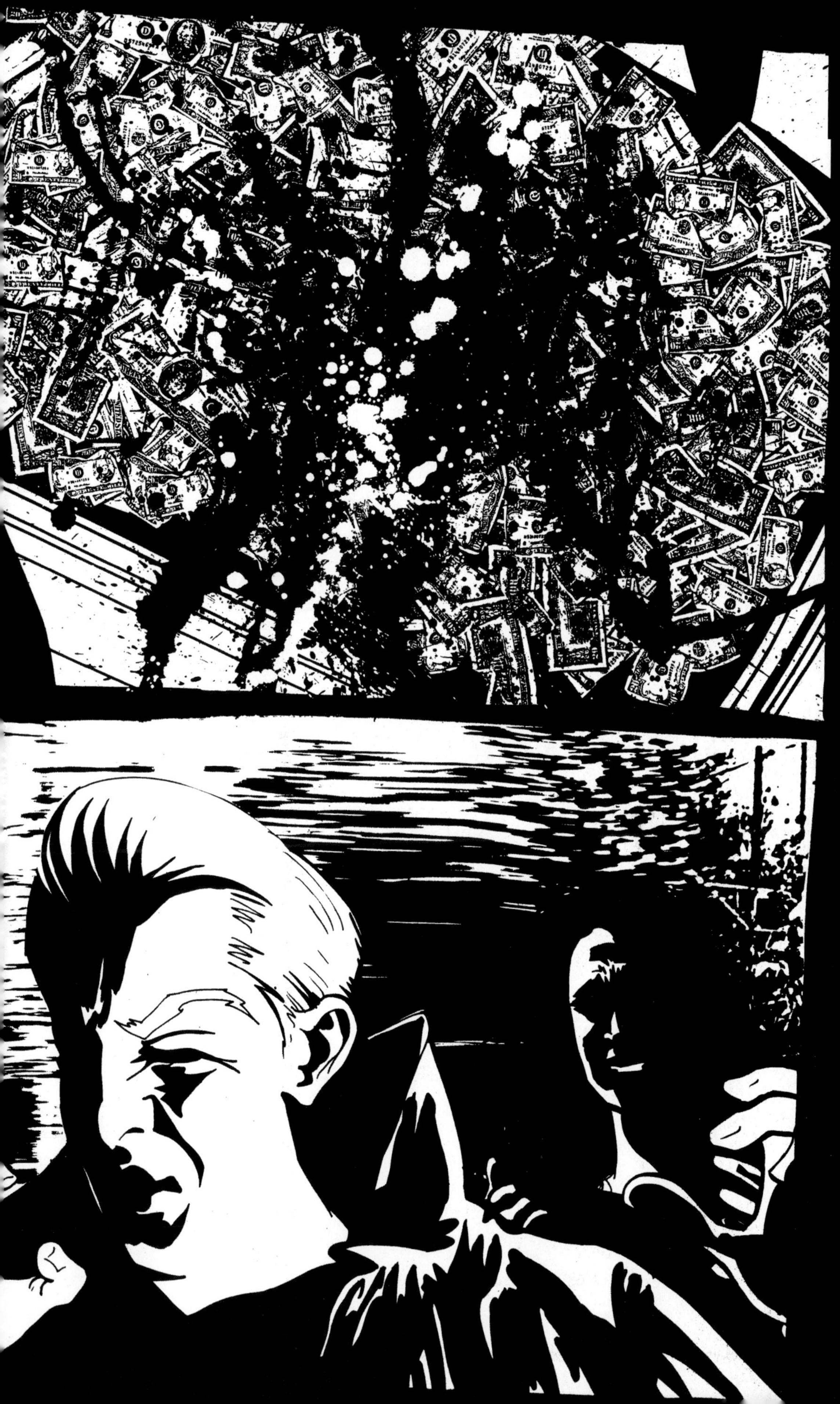

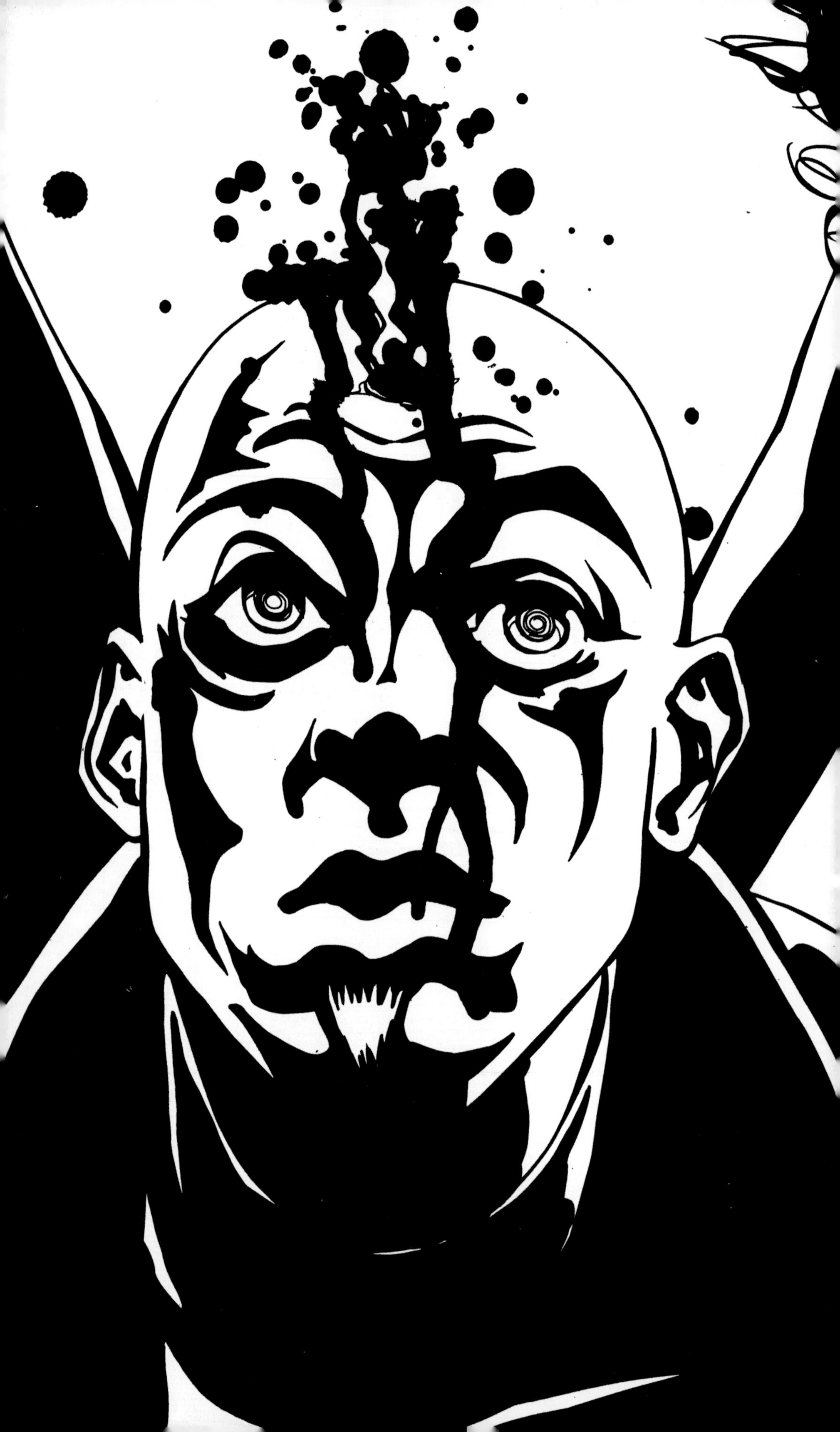

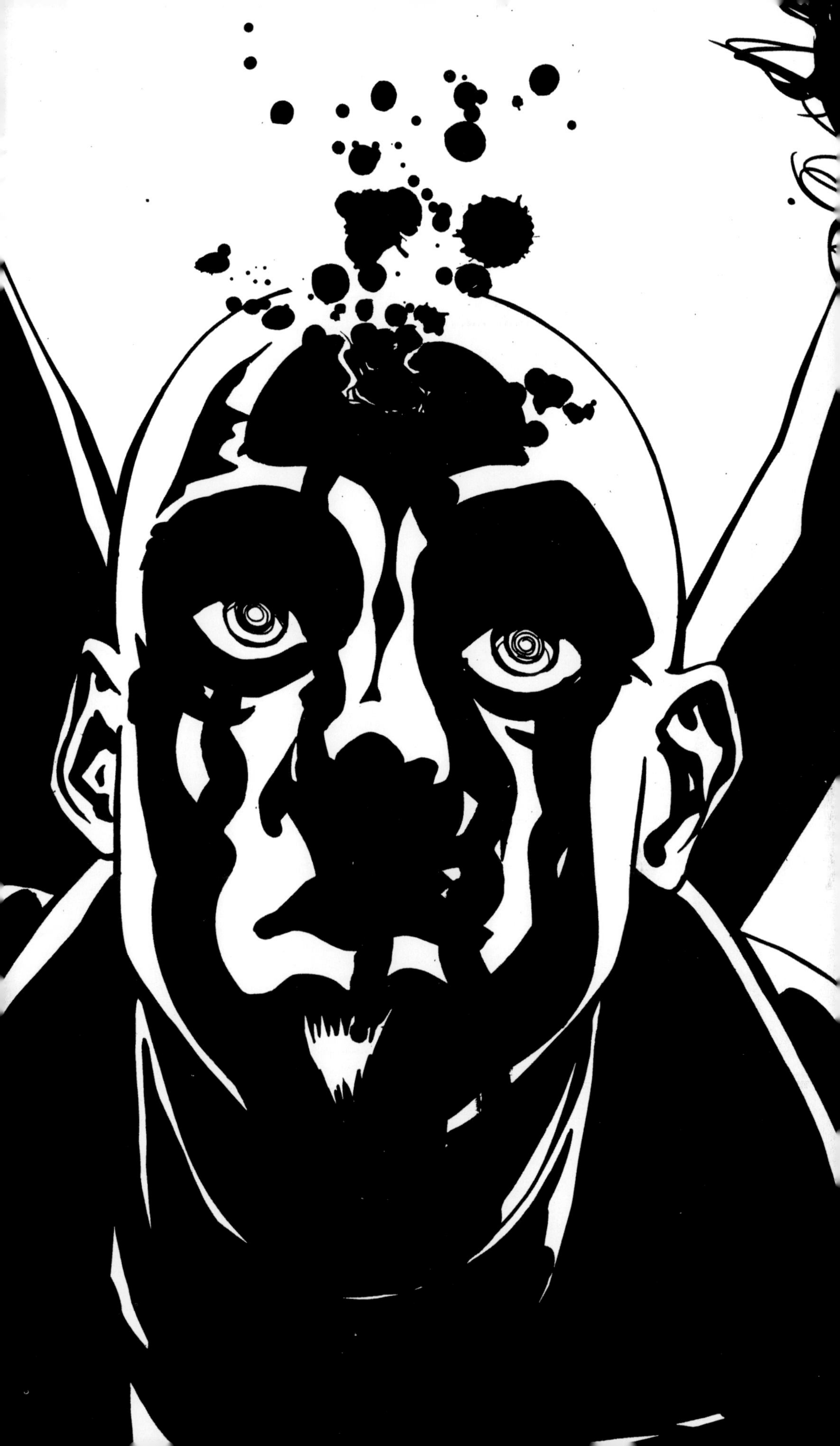

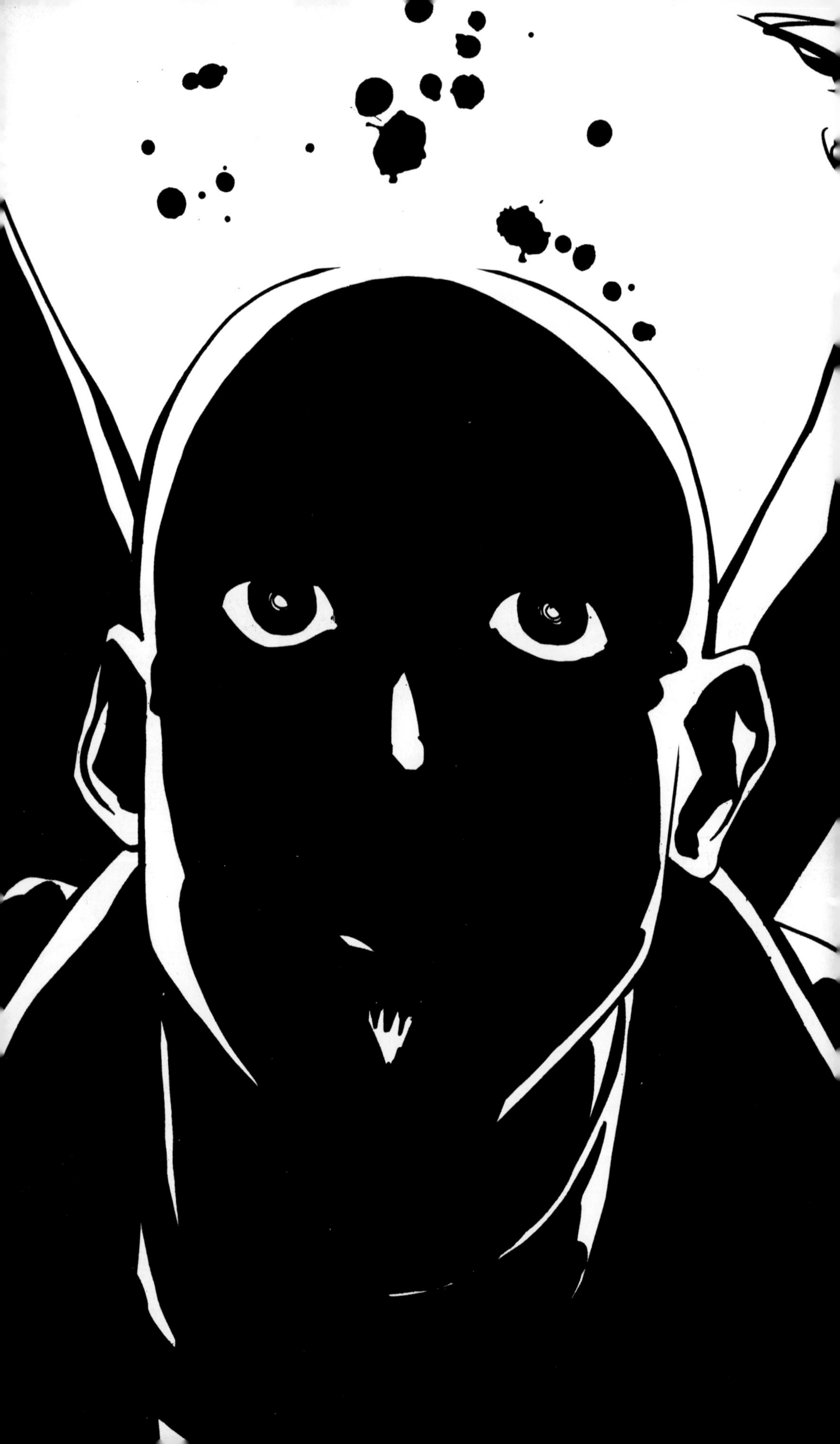

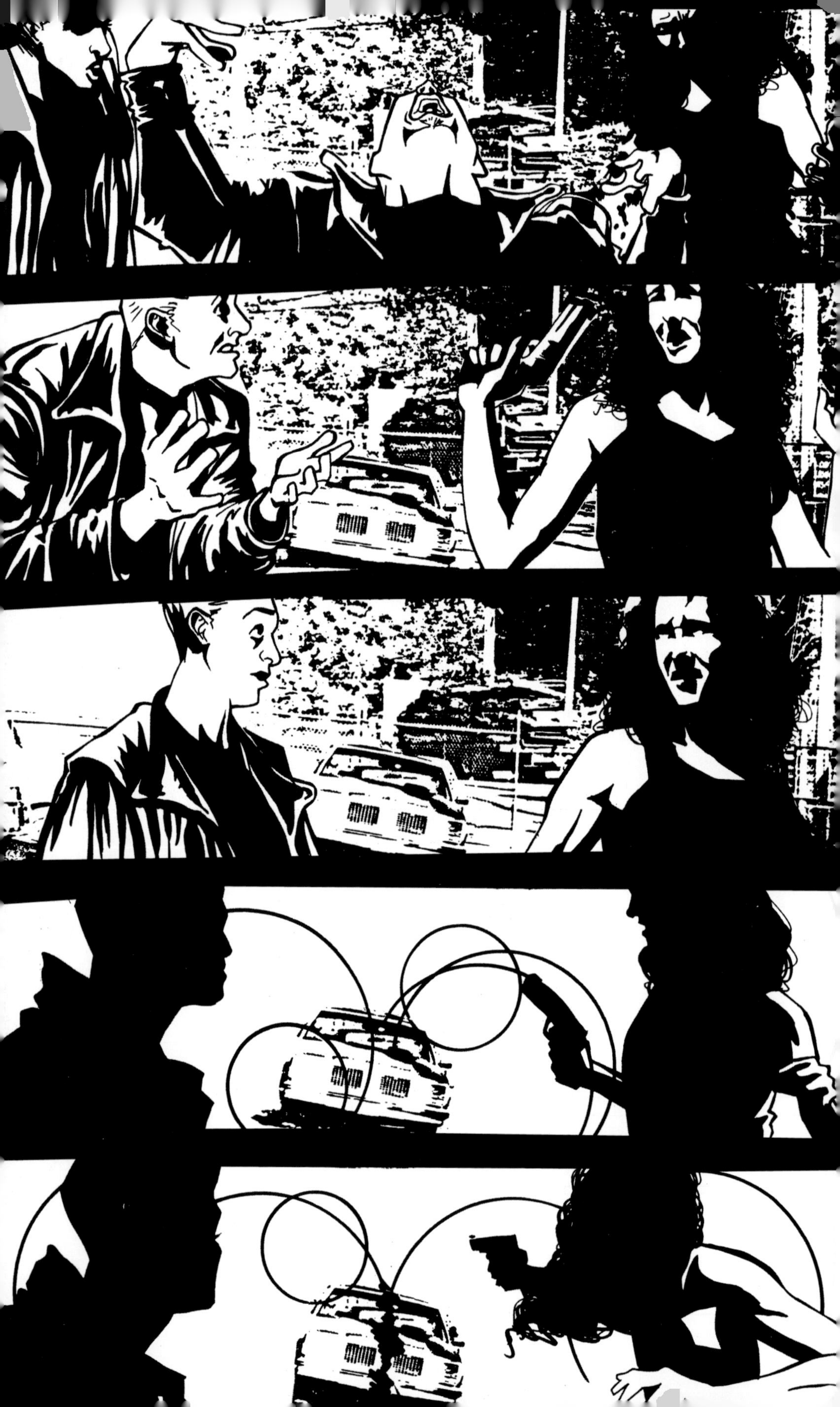

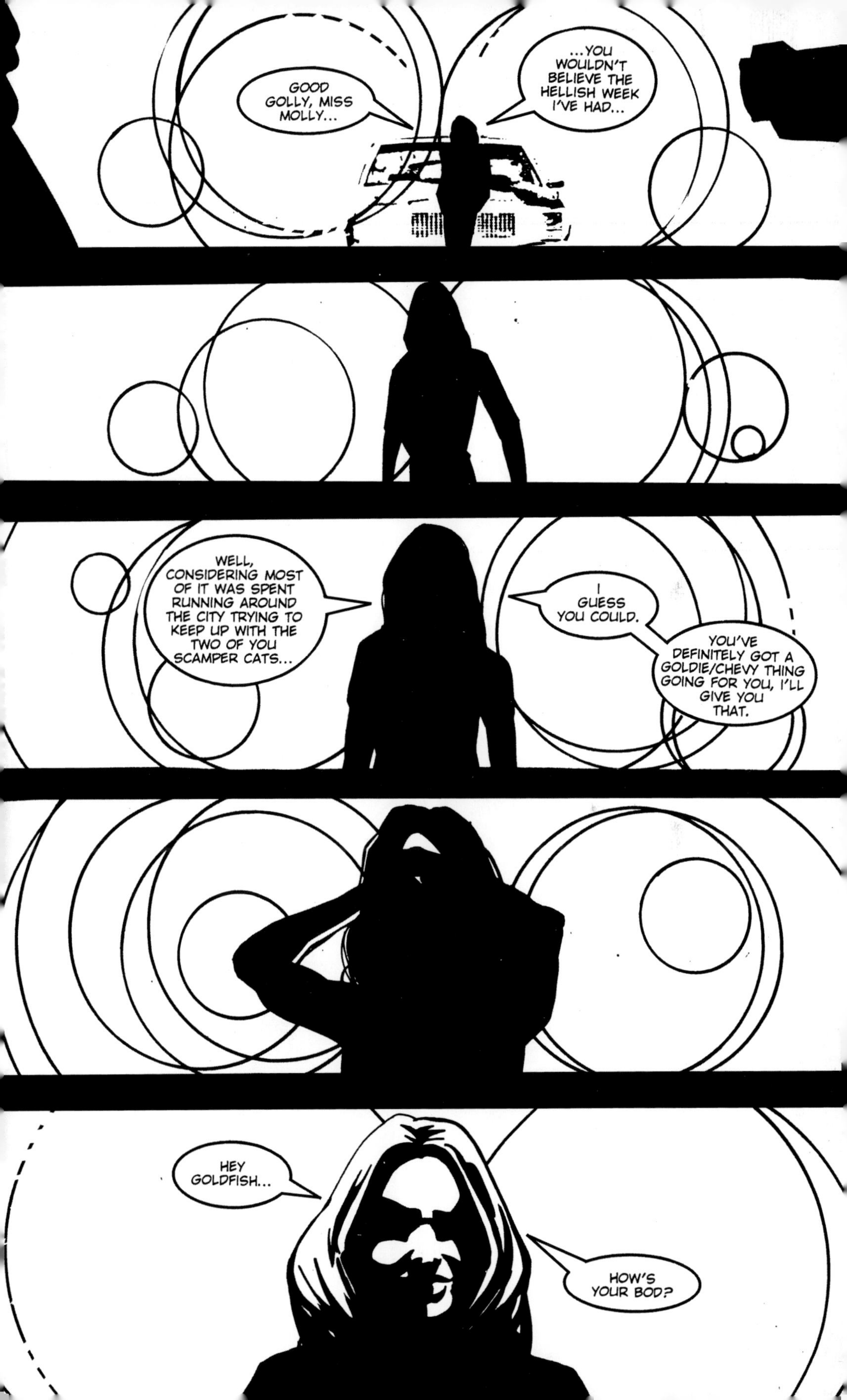
GOOD GOLLY, MISS MOLLY...
...YOU WOULDN'T BELIEVE THE HELLISH WEEK I'VE HAD...
WELL, CONSIDERING MOST OF IT WAS SPENT RUNNING AROUND THE CITY TRYING TO KEEP UP WITH THE TWO OF YOU SCAMPER CATS...
I GUESS YOU COULD.
YOU'VE DEFINITELY GOT A GOLDIE/CHEVY THING GOING FOR YOU, I'LL GIVE YOU THAT.
HEY GOLDFISH...
HOW'S YOUR BOD?

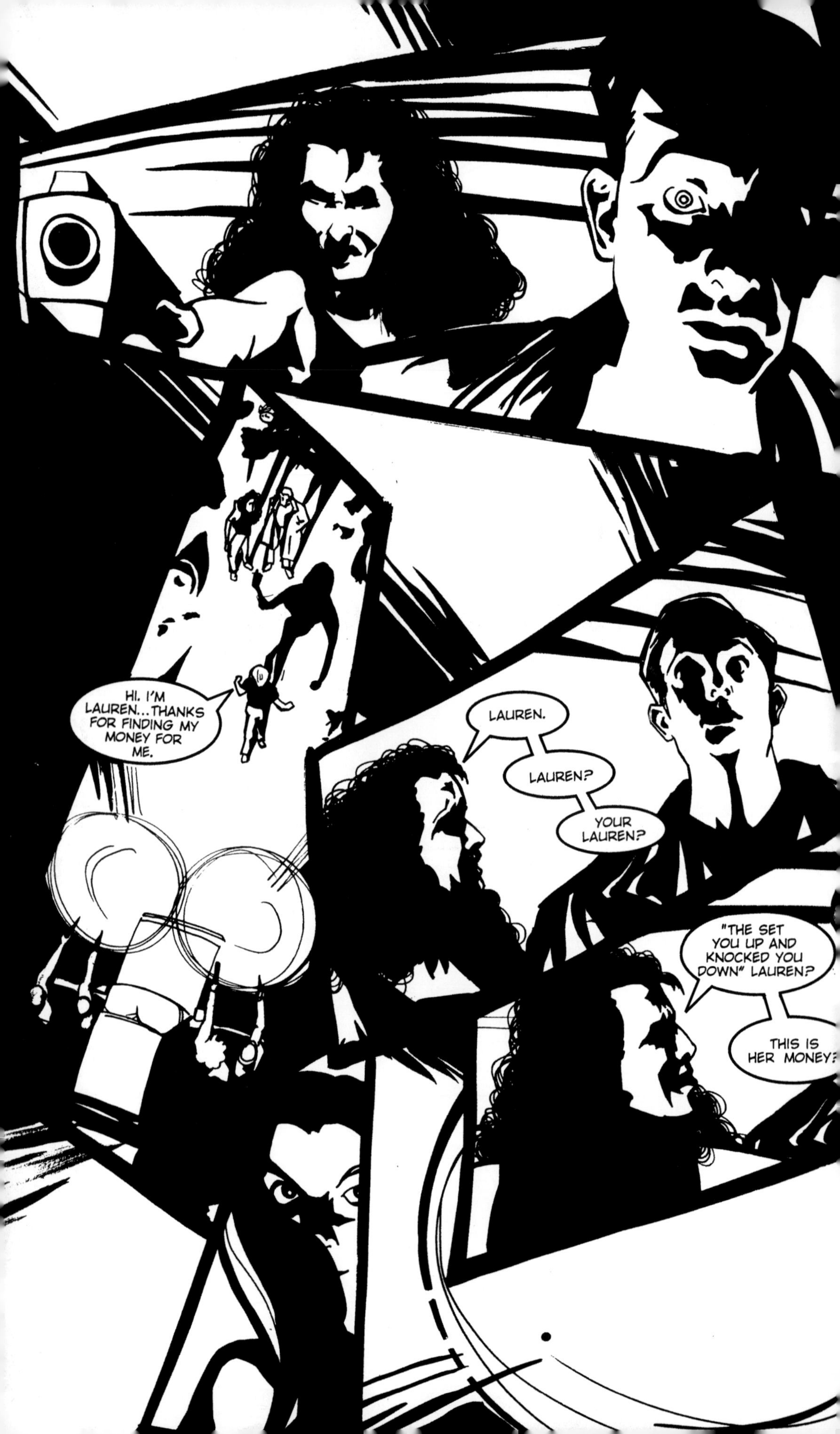
HI. I'M LAUREN...THANKS FOR FINDING MY MONEY FOR ME.
LAUREN.
LAUREN?
YOUR LAUREN?
"THE SET YOU UP AND KNOCKED YOU DOWN" LAUREN?
THIS IS HER MONEY?

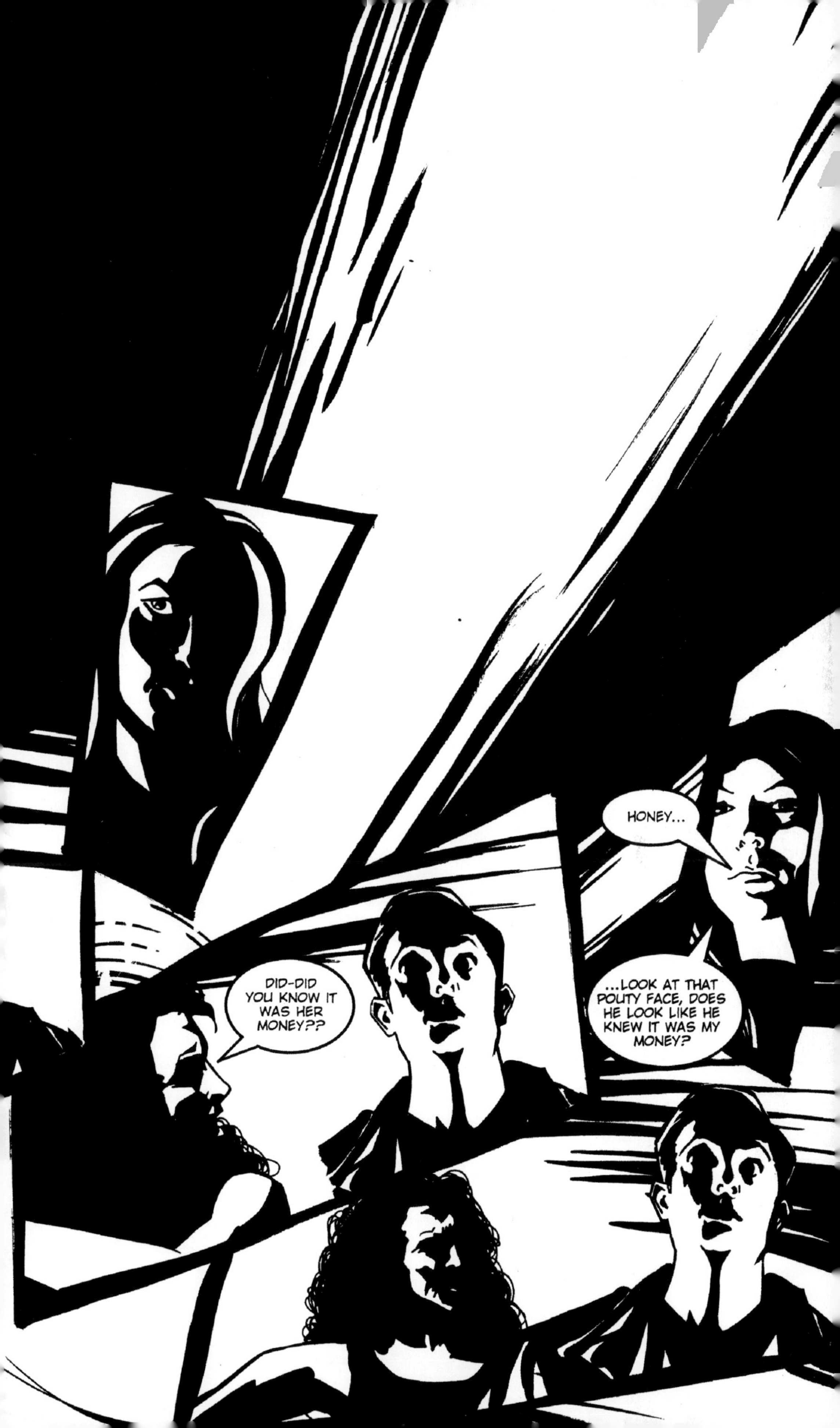
HONEY...
DID-DID YOU KNOW IT WAS HER MONEY??
...LOOK AT THAT POUTY FACE, DOES HE LOOK LIKE HE KNEW IT WAS MY MONEY?

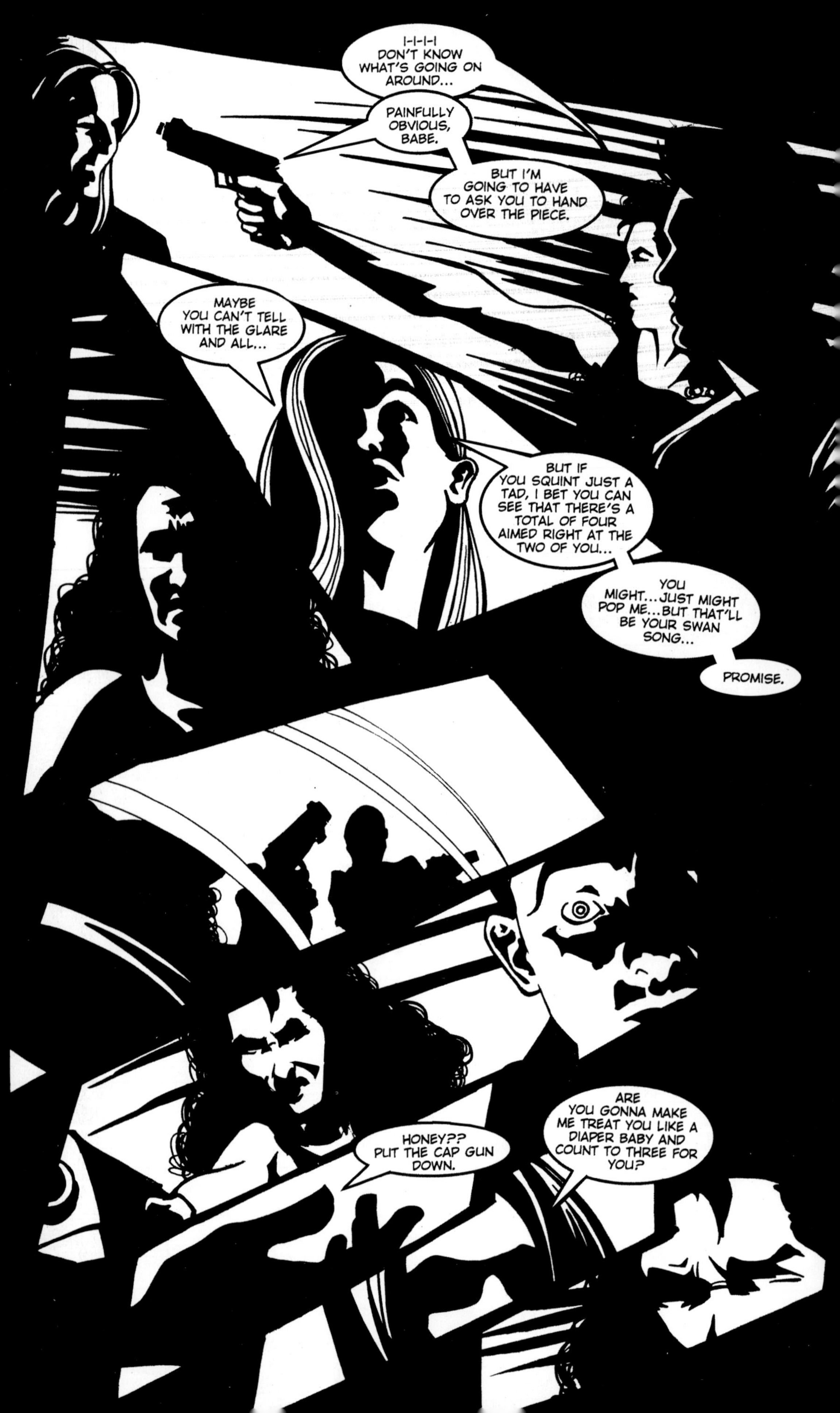
I-I-I-I DON'T KNOW WHAT'S GOING ON AROUND...
PAINFULLY OBVIOUS, BABE.
BUT I'M GOING TO HAVE TO ASK YOU TO HAND OVER THE PIECE.
MAYBE YOU CAN'T TELL WITH THE GLARE AND ALL...
BUT IF YOU SQUINT JUST A TAD, I BET YOU CAN SEE THAT THERE'S A TOTAL OF FOUR AIMED RIGHT AT THE TWO OF YOU...
YOU MIGHT...JUST MIGHT POP ME...BUT THAT'LL BE YOUR SWAN SONG...
PROMISE.
HONEY?? PUT THE CAP GUN DOWN.
ARE YOU GONNA MAKE ME TREAT YOU LIKE A DIAPER BABY AND COUNT TO THREE FOR YOU?

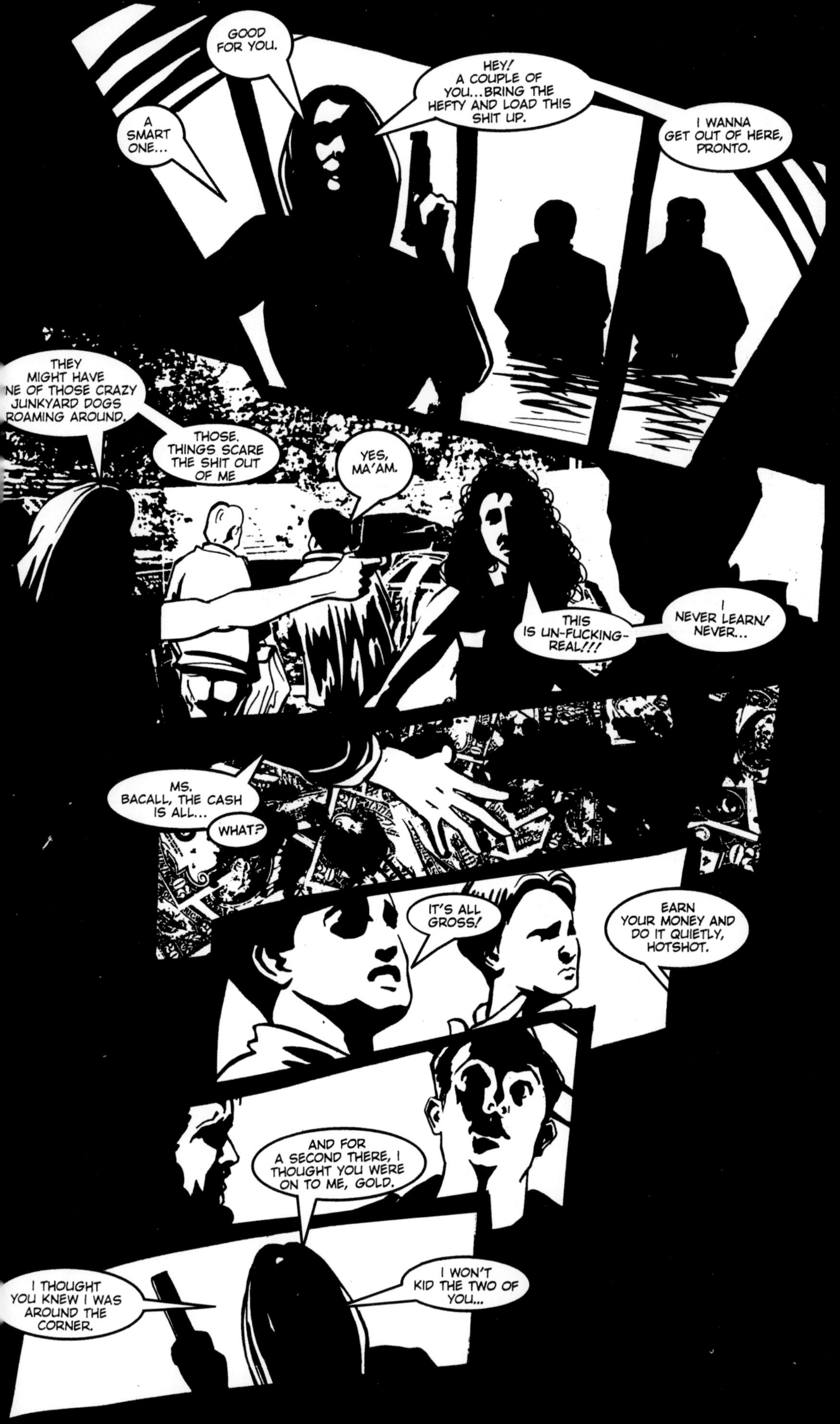
A SMART ONE...
GOOD FOR YOU.
HEY! A COUPLE OF YOU...BRING THE HEFTY AND LOAD THIS SHIT UP.
I WANNA GET OUT OF HERE, PRONTO.
THEY MIGHT HAVE NE OF THOSE CRAZY JUNKYARD DOGS ROAMING AROUND.
THOSE. THINGS SCARE THE SHIT OUT OF ME
YES, MA'AM.
THIS IS UN-FUCKING-REAL!!!
I NEVER LEARN! NEVER...
MS. BACALL, THE CASH IS ALL...
WHAT?
IT'S ALL GROSS!
EARN YOUR MONEY AND DO IT QUIETLY, HOTSHOT.
AND FOR A SECOND THERE, I THOUGHT YOU WERE ON TO ME, GOLD.
I THOUGHT YOU KNEW I WAS AROUND THE CORNER.
I WON'T KID THE TWO OF YOU...

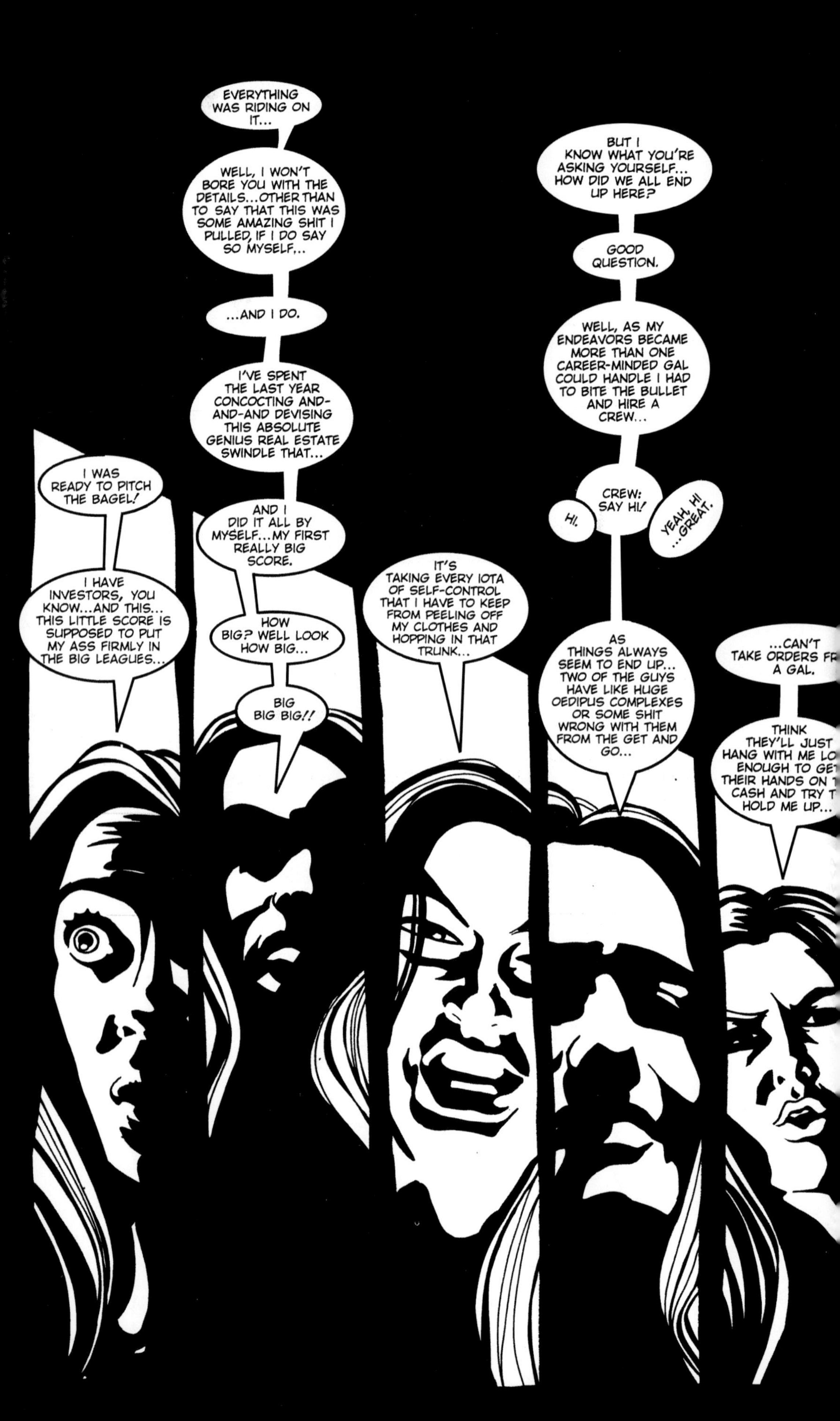

EVERYTHING WAS RIDING ON IT...
WELL, I WON'T BORE YOU WITH THE DETAILS...OTHER THAN TO SAY THAT THIS WAS SOME AMAZING SHIT I PULLED, IF I DO SAY SO MYSELF,...
...AND I DO.
I'VE SPENT THE LAST YEAR CONCOCTING AND-AND-AND DEVISING THIS ABSOLUTE GENIUS REAL ESTATE SWINDLE THAT...
I WAS READY TO PITCH THE BAGEL!
AND I DID IT ALL BY MYSELF...MY FIRST REALLY BIG SCORE.
I HAVE INVESTORS, YOU KNOW...AND THIS... THIS LITTLE SCORE IS SUPPOSED TO PUT MY ASS FIRMLY IN THE BIG LEAGUES...
HOW BIG? WELL LOOK HOW BIG...
BIG BIG BIG!!
IT'S TAKING EVERY IOTA OF SELF-CONTROL THAT I HAVE TO KEEP FROM PEELING OFF MY CLOTHES AND HOPPING IN THAT TRUNK...
BUT I KNOW WHAT YOU'RE ASKING YOURSELF... HOW DID WE ALL END UP HERE?
GOOD QUESTION.
WELL, AS MY ENDEAVORS BECAME MORE THAN ONE CAREER-MINDED GAL COULD HANDLE I HAD TO BITE THE BULLET AND HIRE A CREW...
CREW: SAY HI!
HI.
YEAH, HI ...GREAT.
AS THINGS ALWAYS SEEM TO END UP... TWO OF THE GUYS HAVE LIKE HUGE OEDIPUS COMPLEXES OR SOME SHIT WRONG WITH THEM FROM THE GET AND GO...

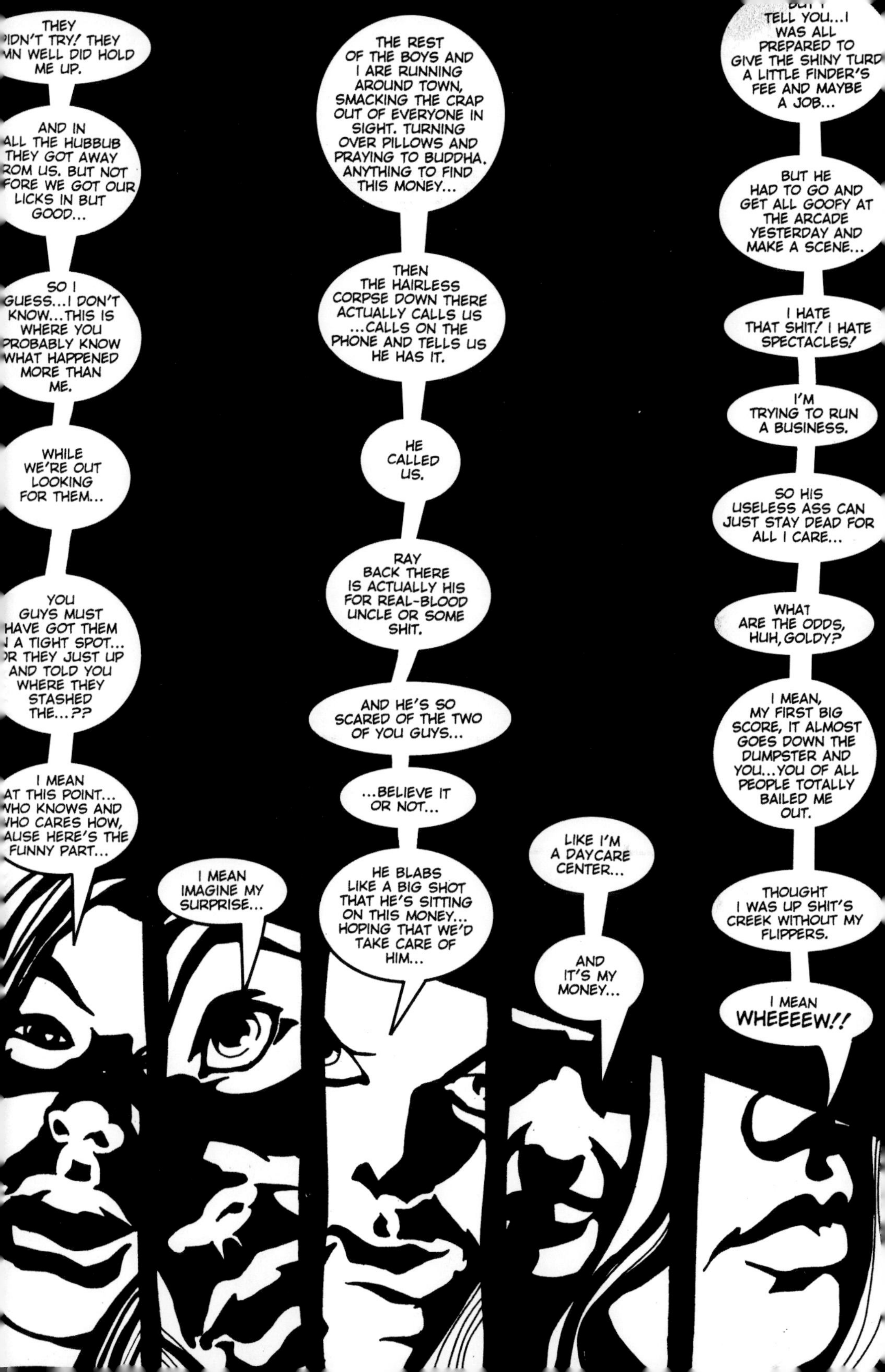

IDN'T TRY! THEY
MN WELL DID HOLD ME UP.
AND IN
ALL THE HUBBUB THEY GOT AWAY
ROM US. BUT NOT
FORE WE GOT OUR LICKS IN BUT GOOD...
SO I GUESS...I DON'T KNOW...THIS IS WHERE YOU
ROBABLY KNOW
WHAT HAPPENED MORE THAN ME.
WHILE WE'RE OUT LOOKING FOR THEM...
YOU GUYS MUST
HAVE GOT THEM
A TIGHT SPOT...
R THEY JUST UP AND TOLD YOU WHERE THEY STASHED THE...??
I MEAN
AT THIS POINT...
HO KNOWS AND
HO CARES HOW,
AUSE HERE'S THE FUNNY PART...
I MEAN IMAGINE MY SURPRISE...
THE REST OF THE BOYS AND I ARE RUNNING AROUND TOWN, SMACKING THE CRAP OUT OF EVERYONE IN SIGHT. TURNING OVER PILLOWS AND PRAYING TO BUDDHA. ANYTHING TO FIND THIS MONEY...
THEN THE HAIRLESS CORPSE DOWN THERE ACTUALLY CALLS US ...CALLS ON THE PHONE AND TELLS US HE HAS IT.
HE CALLED US.
RAY BACK THERE IS ACTUALLY HIS FOR REAL-BLOOD UNCLE OR SOME SHIT.
AND HE'S SO SCARED OF THE TWO OF YOU GUYS...
...BELIEVE IT OR NOT...
HE BLABS LIKE A BIG SHOT THAT HE'S SITTING ON THIS MONEY... HOPING THAT WE'D TAKE CARE OF HIM...
LIKE I'M A DAYCARE CENTER...
AND IT'S MY MONEY...
TELL YOU...I WAS ALL PREPARED TO GIVE THE SHINY TURD A LITTLE FINDER'S FEE AND MAYBE A JOB...
BUT HE HAD TO GO AND GET ALL GOOFY AT THE ARCADE YESTERDAY AND MAKE A SCENE...
I HATE THAT SHIT! I HATE SPECTACLES!
I'M TRYING TO RUN A BUSINESS.
SO HIS USELESS ASS CAN JUST STAY DEAD FOR ALL I CARE...
WHAT ARE THE ODDS, HUH, GOLDY?
I MEAN, MY FIRST BIG SCORE, IT ALMOST GOES DOWN THE DUMPSTER AND YOU...YOU OF ALL PEOPLE TOTALLY BAILED ME OUT.
THOUGHT I WAS UP SHIT'S CREEK WITHOUT MY FLIPPERS.
I MEAN WHEEEEW!!

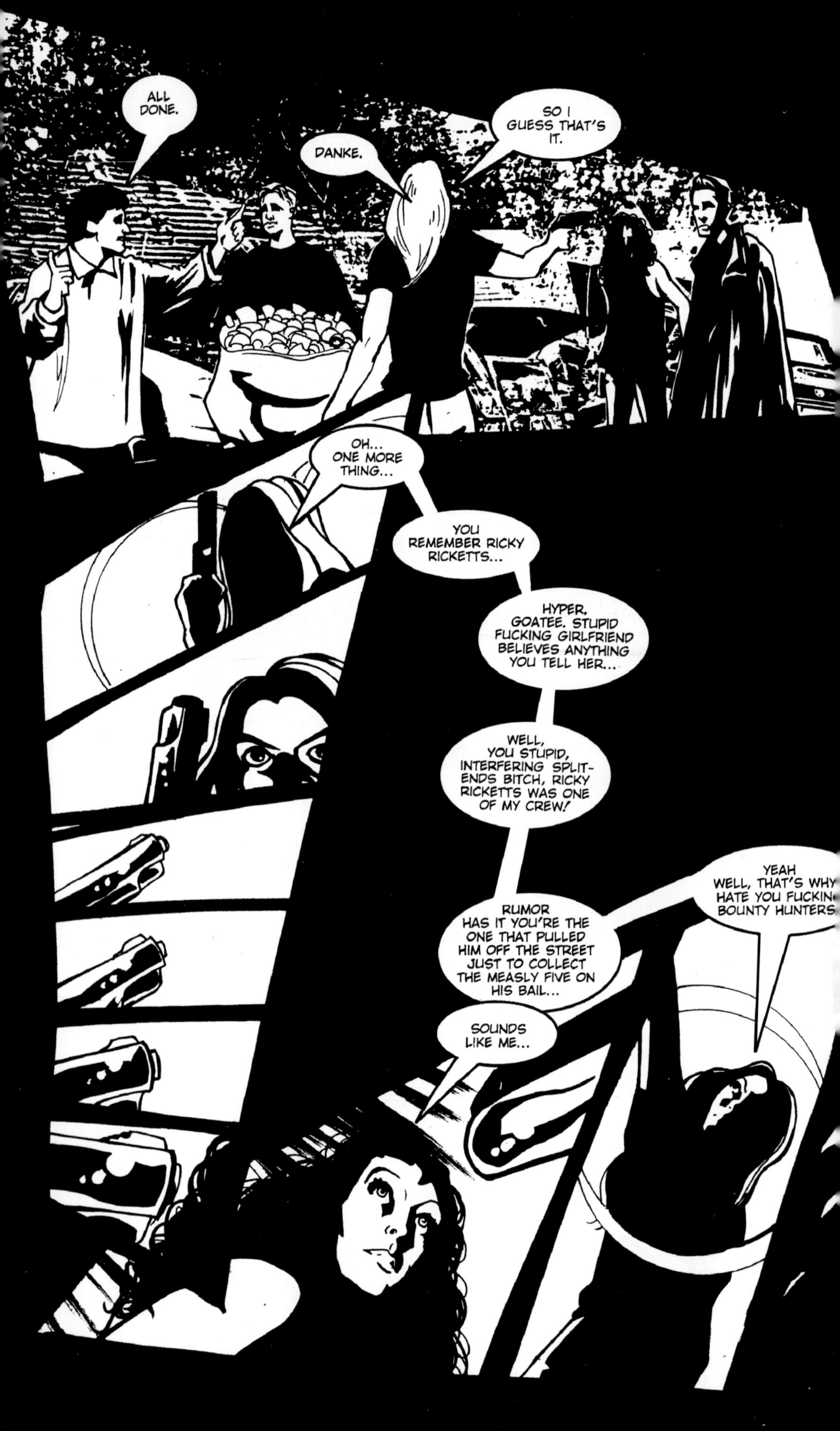
ALL DONE.
DANKE.
SO I GUESS THAT'S IT.
OH... ONE MORE THING...
YOU REMEMBER RICKY RICKETTS...
HYPER. GOATEE. STUPID FUCKING GIRLFRIEND BELIEVES ANYTHING YOU TELL HER...
WELL, YOU STUPID, INTERFERING SPLIT-ENDS BITCH, RICKY RICKETTS WAS ONE OF MY CREW!
RUMOR HAS IT YOU'RE THE ONE THAT PULLED HIM OFF THE STREET JUST TO COLLECT THE MEASLY FIVE ON HIS BAIL...
SOUNDS LIKE ME...
YEAH WELL, THAT'S WHY HATE YOU FUCKIN BOUNTY HUNTERS

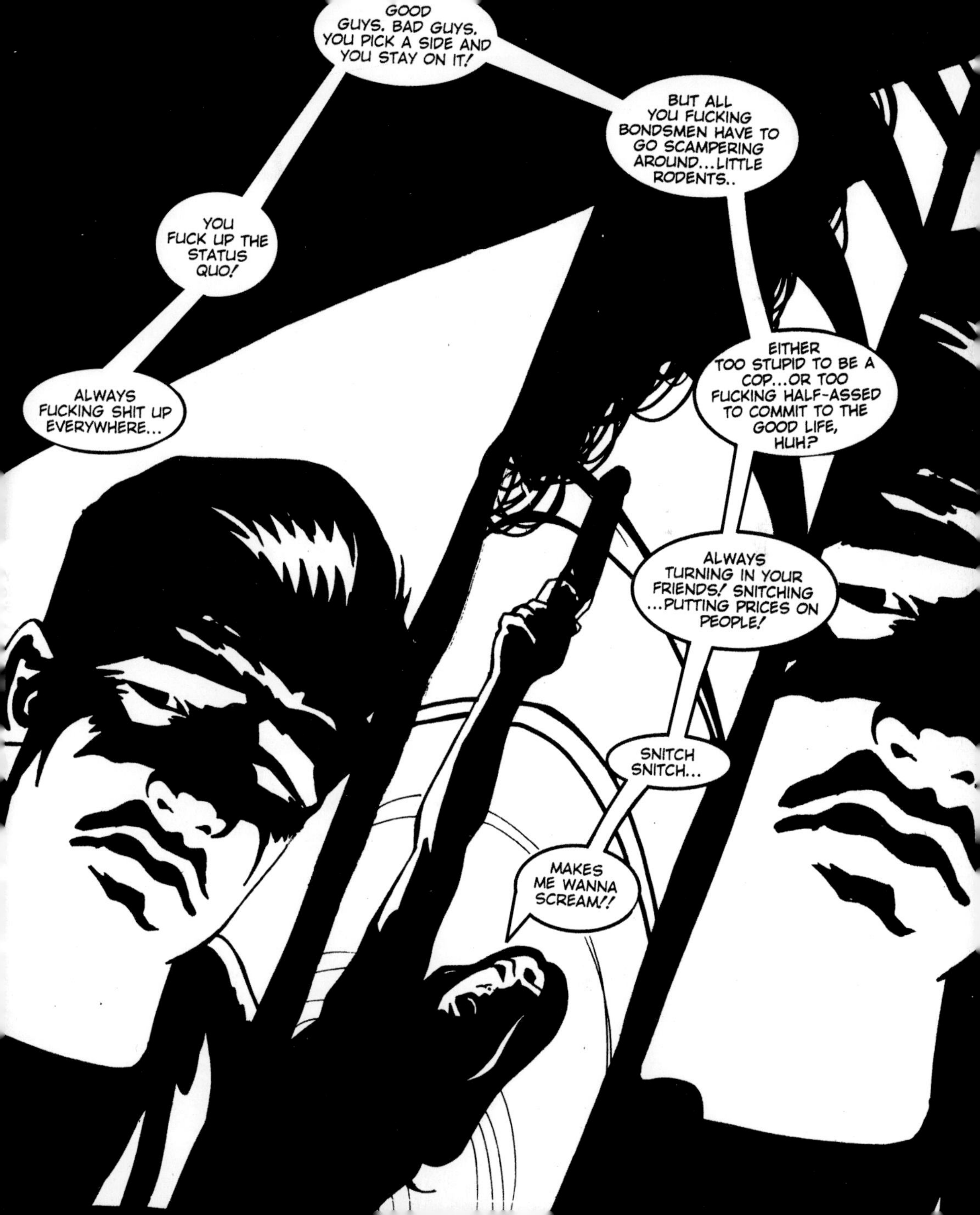

GOOD GUYS. BAD GUYS. YOU PICK A SIDE AND YOU STAY ON IT!
YOU FUCK UP THE STATUS QUO!
ALWAYS FUCKING SHIT UP EVERYWHERE...
BUT ALL YOU FUCKING BONDSMEN HAVE TO GO SCAMPERING AROUND...LITTLE RODENTS..
EITHER TOO STUPID TO BE A COP...OR TOO FUCKING HALF-ASSED TO COMMIT TO THE GOOD LIFE, HUH?
ALWAYS TURNING IN YOUR FRIENDS! SNITCHING ...PUTTING PRICES ON PEOPLE!
SNITCH SNITCH...
MAKES ME WANNA SCREAM!!

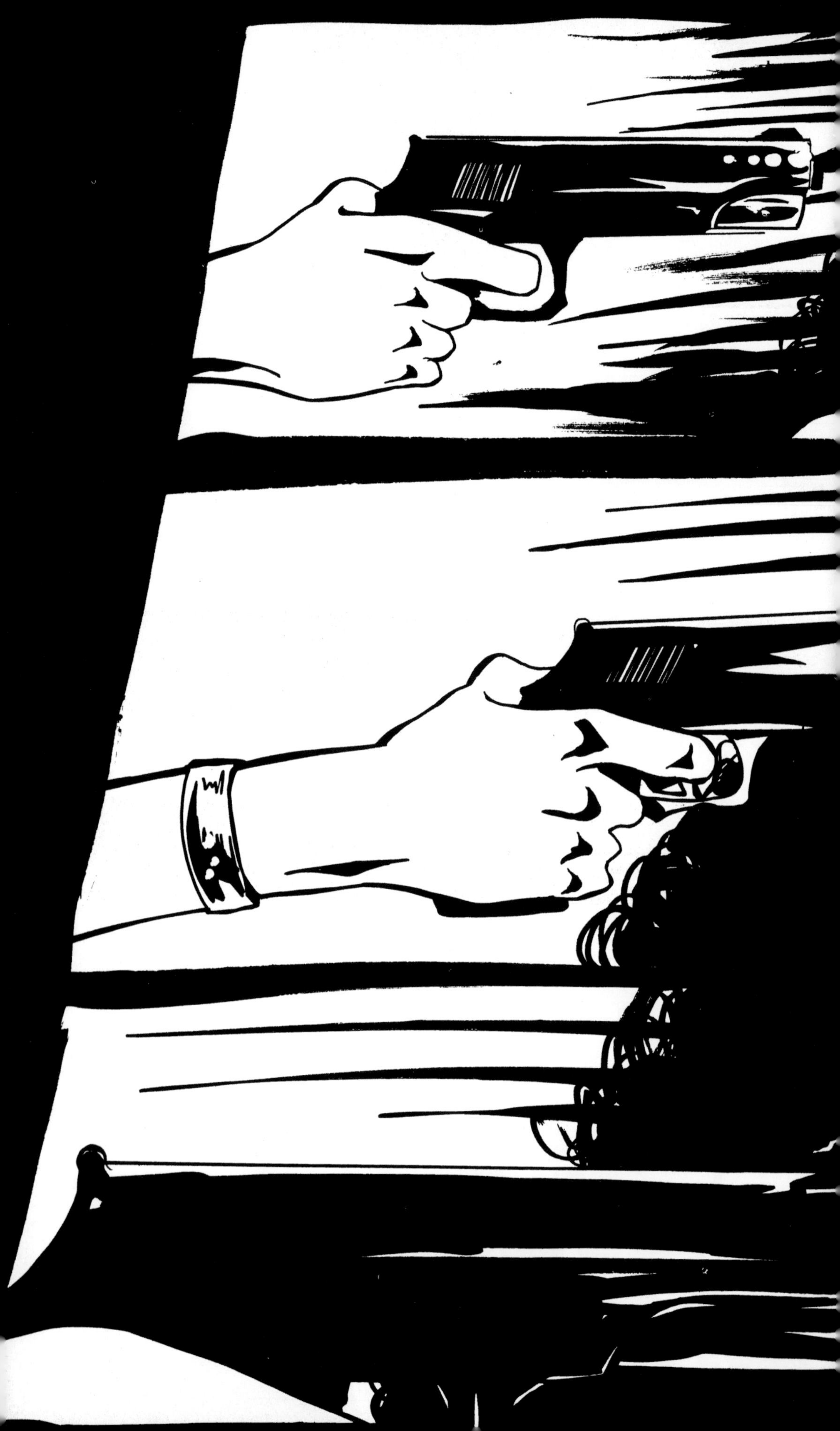

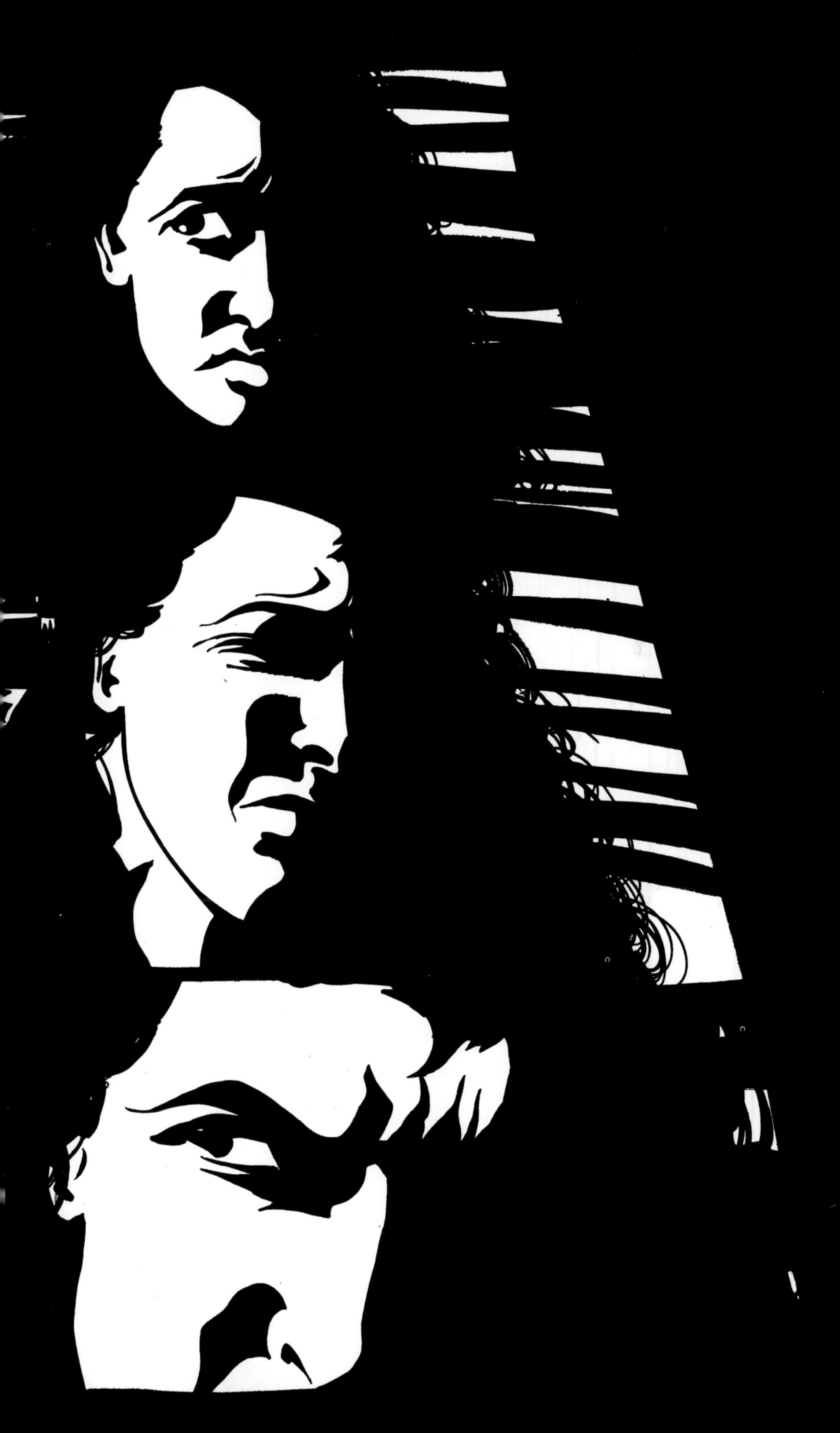

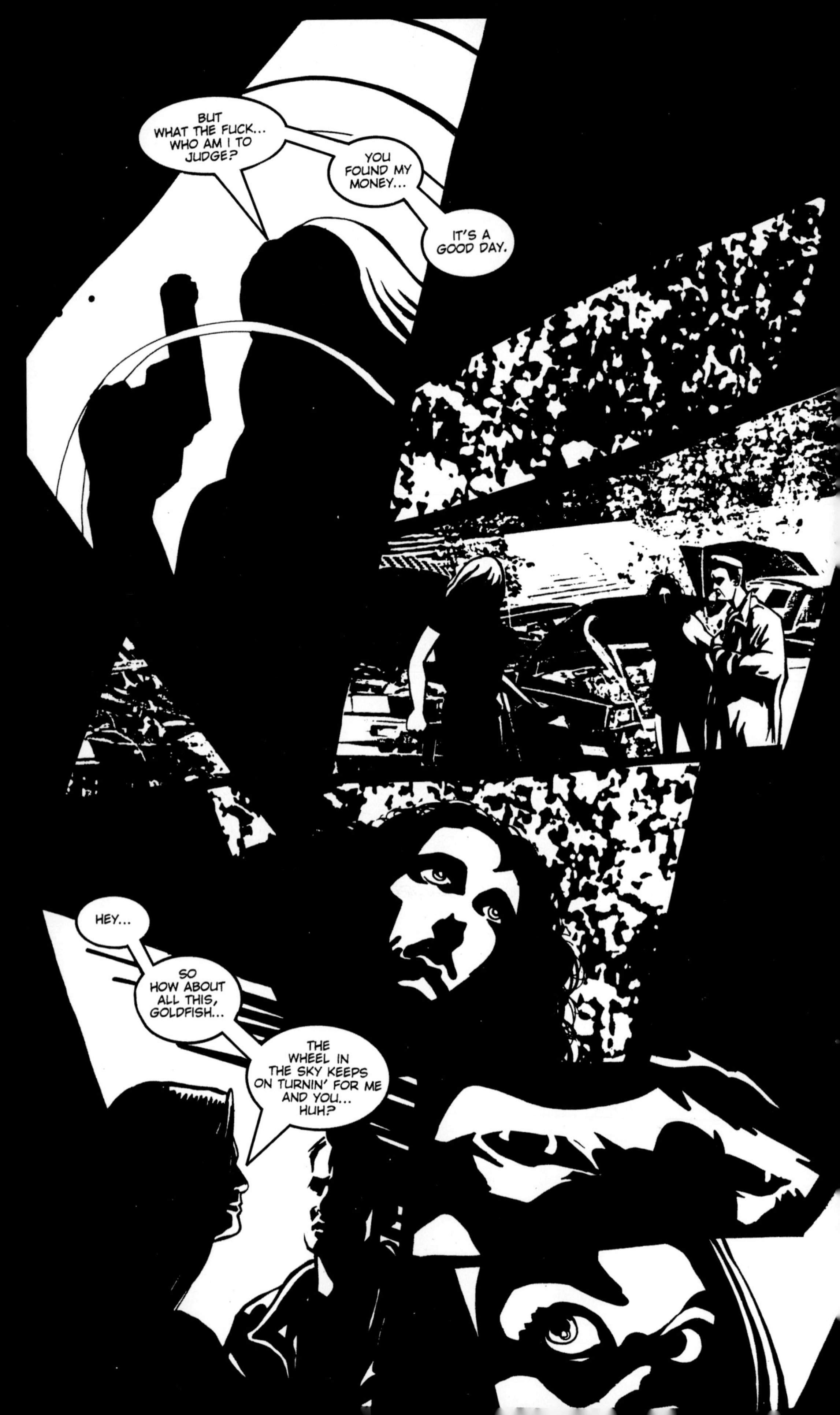
BUT WHAT THE FUCK... WHO AM I TO JUDGE?
YOU FOUND MY MONEY...
IT'S A GOOD DAY.
HEY...
SO HOW ABOUT ALL THIS, GOLDFISH...
THE WHEEL IN THE SKY KEEPS ON TURNIN' FOR ME AND YOU... HUH?

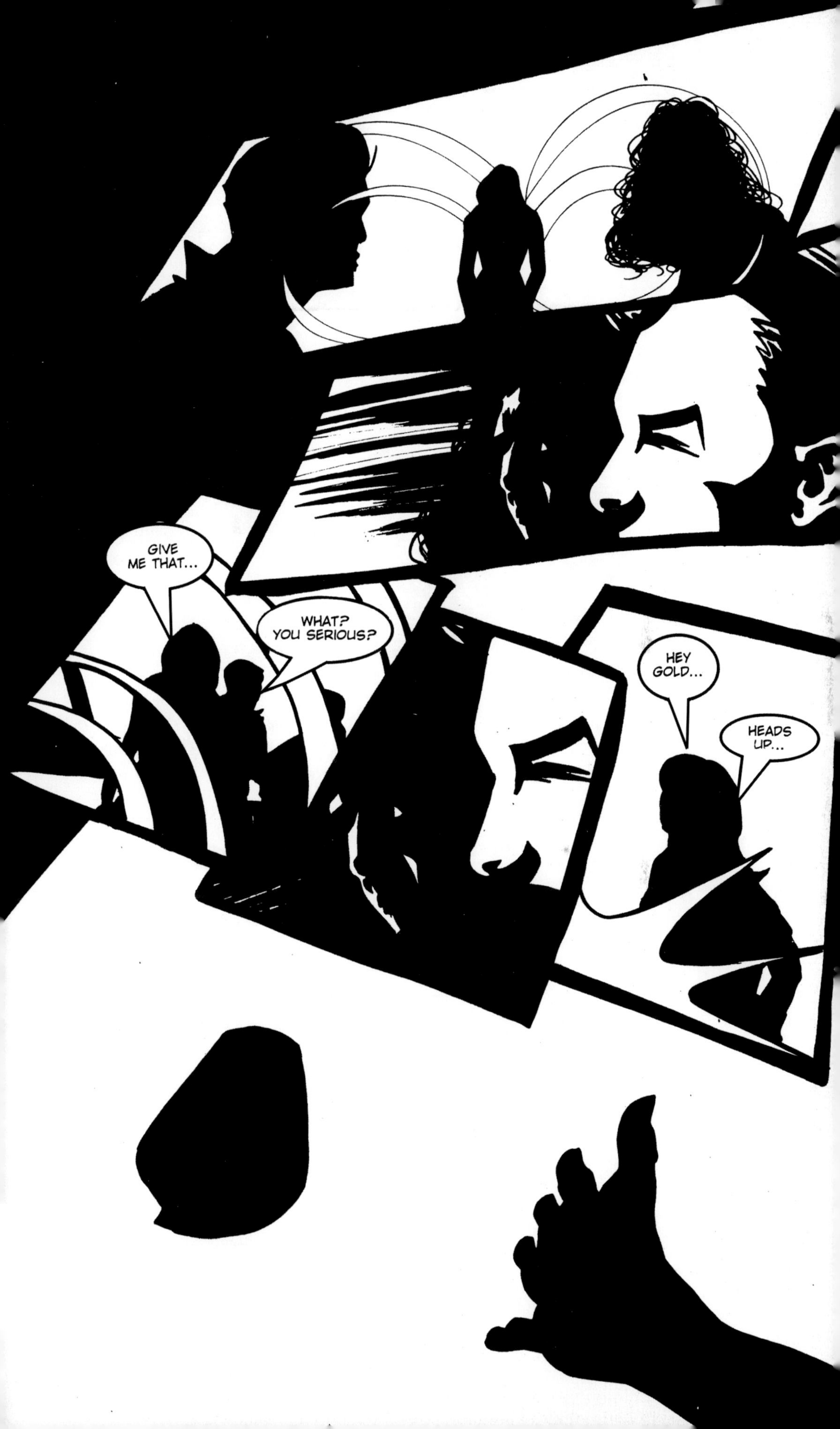
GIVE ME THAT...
WHAT? YOU SERIOUS?
HEY GOLD...
HEADS UP...

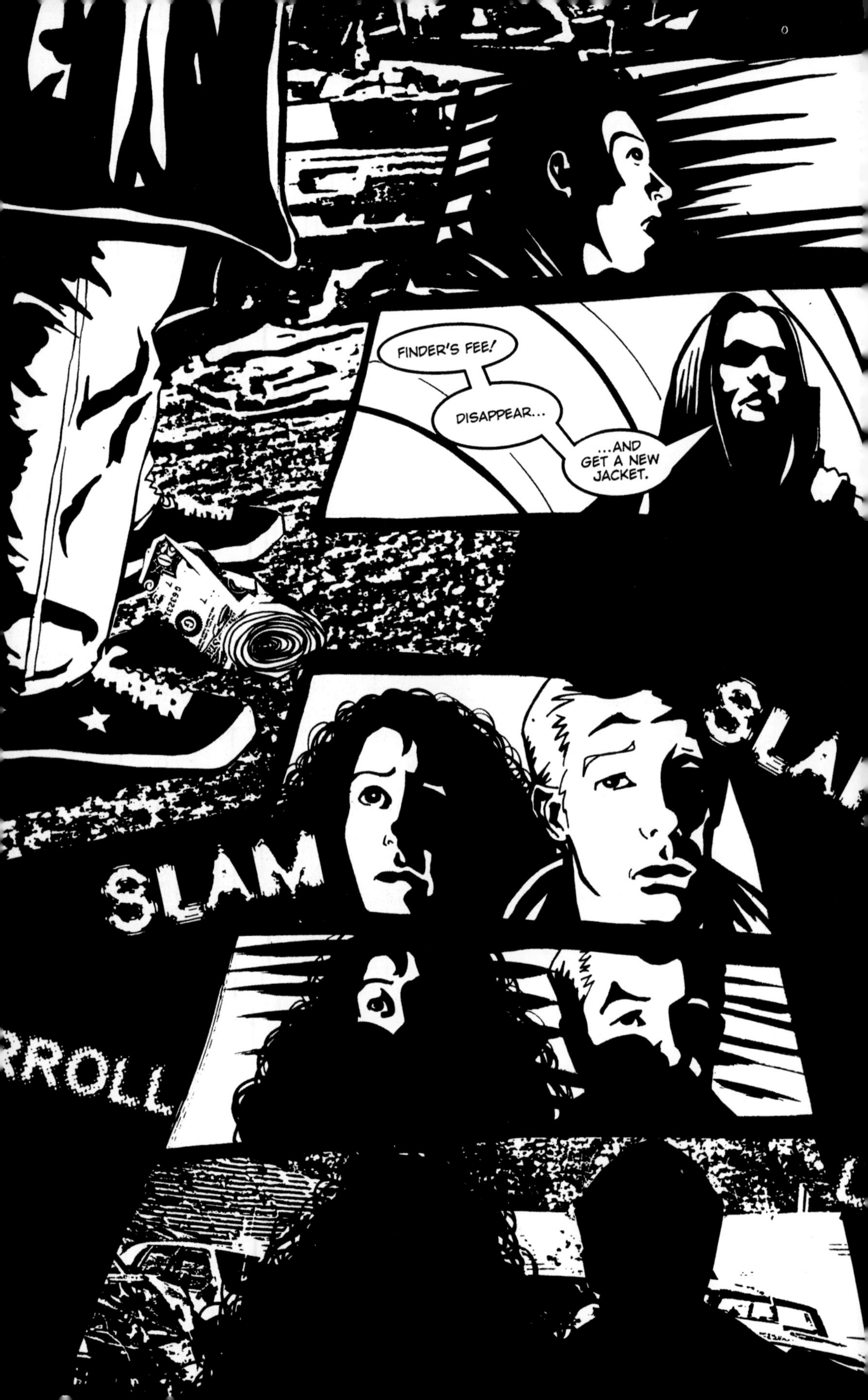
FINDER'S FEE!
DISAPPEAR...
...AND GET A NEW JACKET.
SLAM

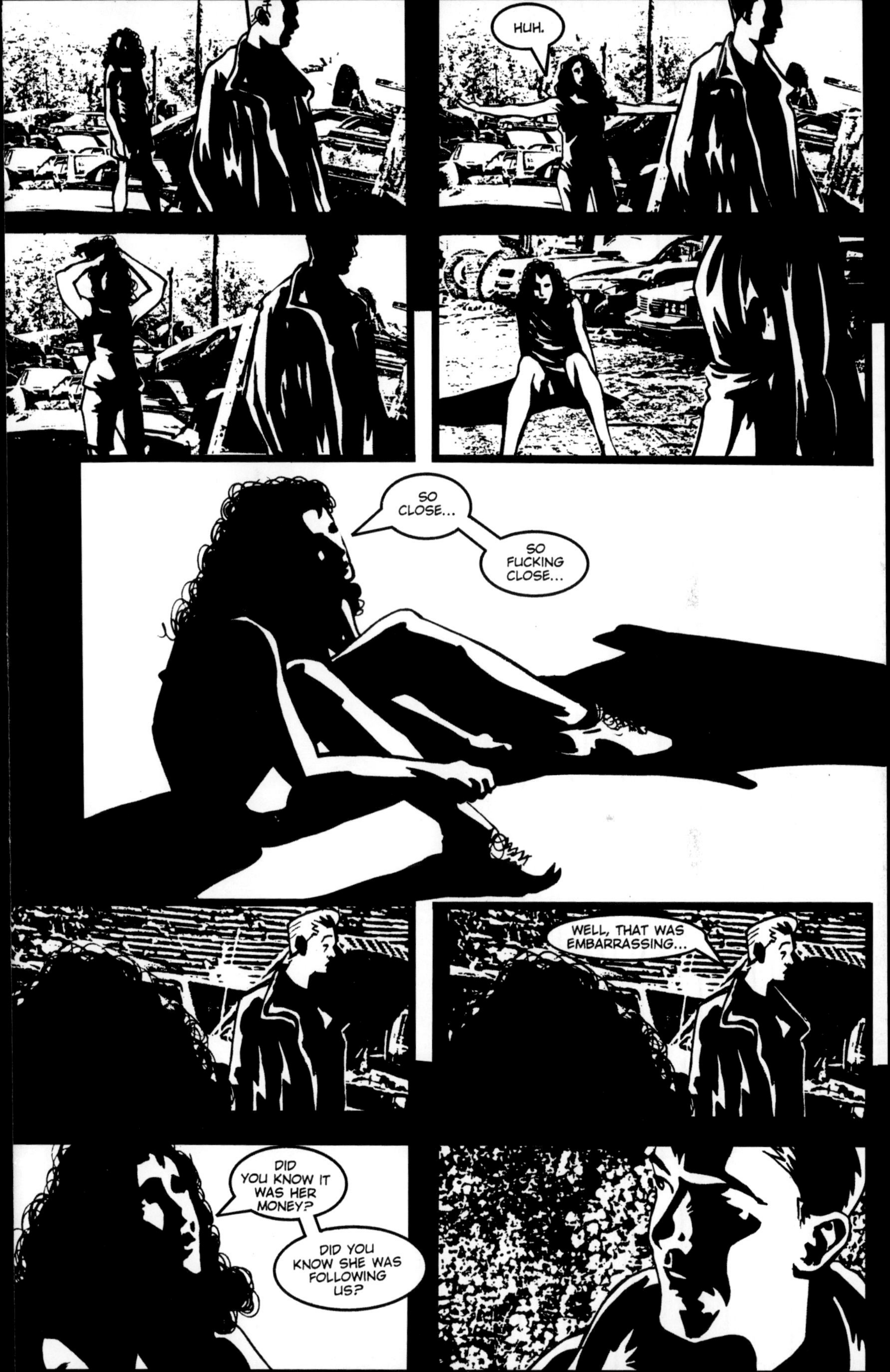
HUH.
SO CLOSE...
SO FUCKING CLOSE...
WELL, THAT WAS EMBARRASSING...
DID YOU KNOW IT WAS HER MONEY?
DID YOU KNOW SHE WAS FOLLOWING US?

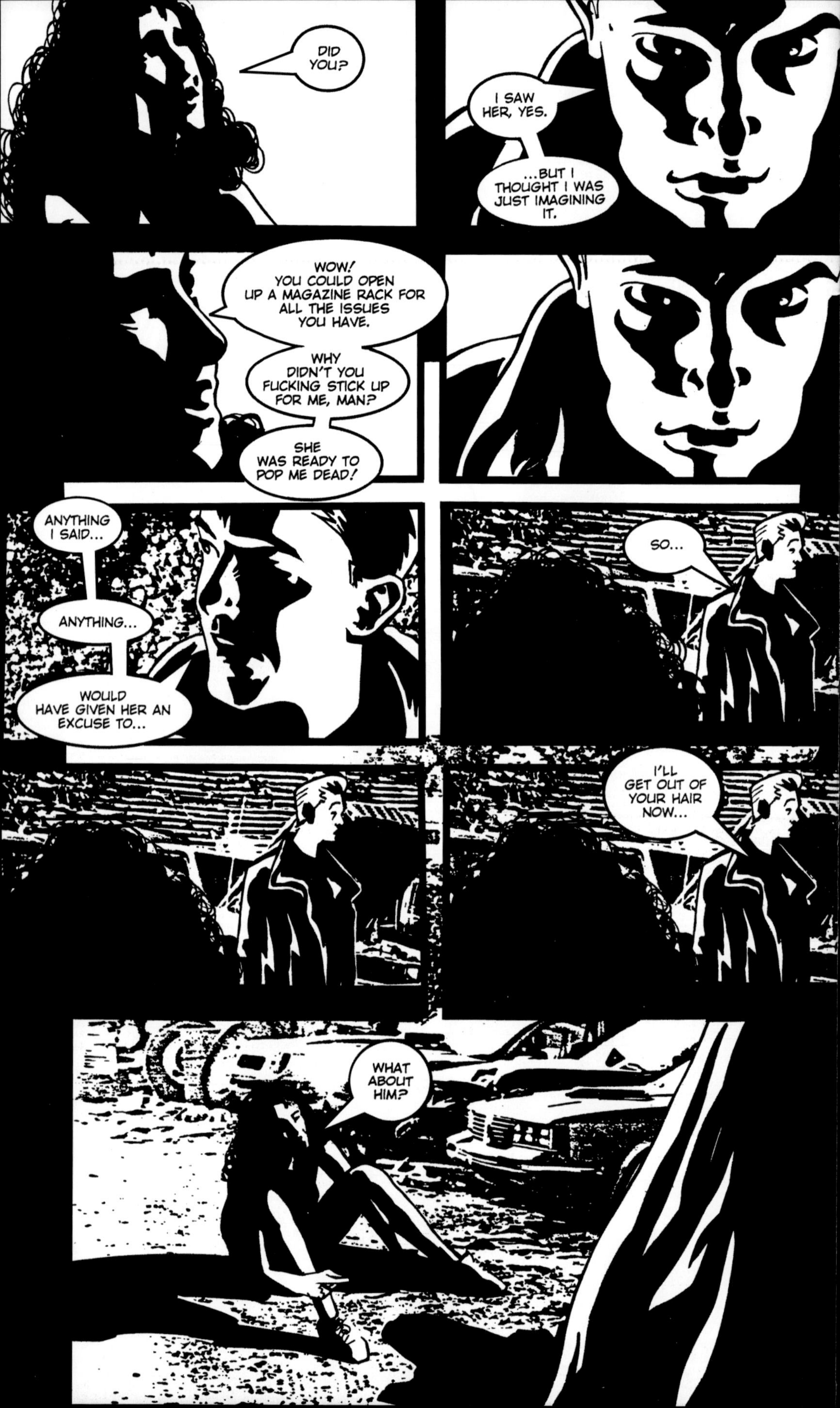
DID YOU?
I SAW HER, YES.
...BUT I THOUGHT I WAS JUST IMAGINING IT.
WOW! YOU COULD OPEN UP A MAGAZINE RACK FOR ALL THE ISSUES YOU HAVE.
WHY DIDN'T YOU FUCKING STICK UP FOR ME, MAN?
SHE WAS READY TO POP ME DEAD!
ANYTHING I SAID...
ANYTHING...
WOULD HAVE GIVEN HER AN EXCUSE TO...
SO...
I'LL GET OUT OF YOUR HAIR NOW...
WHAT ABOUT HIM?

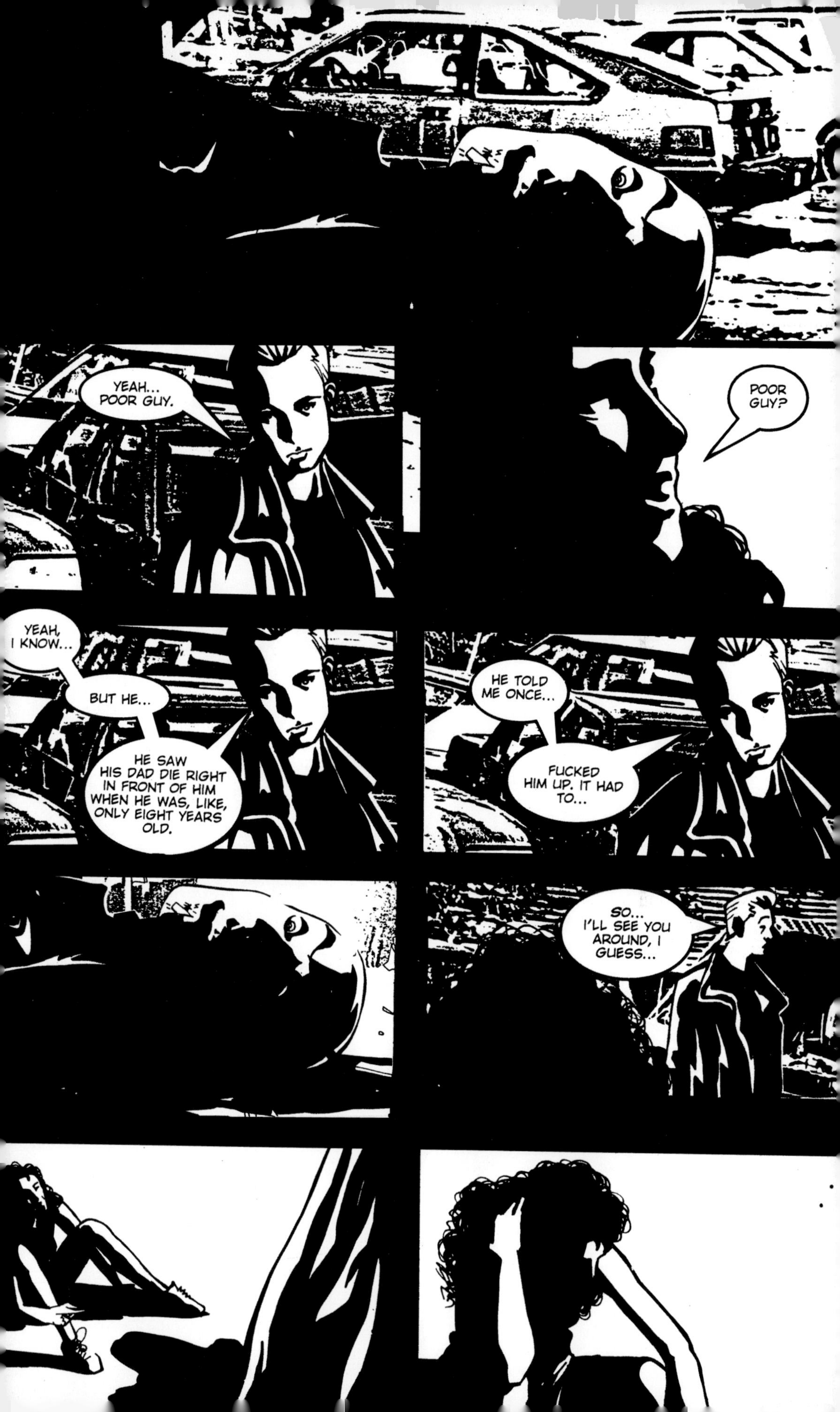
YEAH... POOR GUY.
POOR GUY?
YEAH, I KNOW...
BUT HE...
HE SAW HIS DAD DIE RIGHT IN FRONT OF HIM WHEN HE WAS, LIKE, ONLY EIGHT YEARS OLD.
HE TOLD ME ONCE...
FUCKED HIM UP. IT HAD TO...
SO... I'LL SEE YOU AROUND, I GUESS...

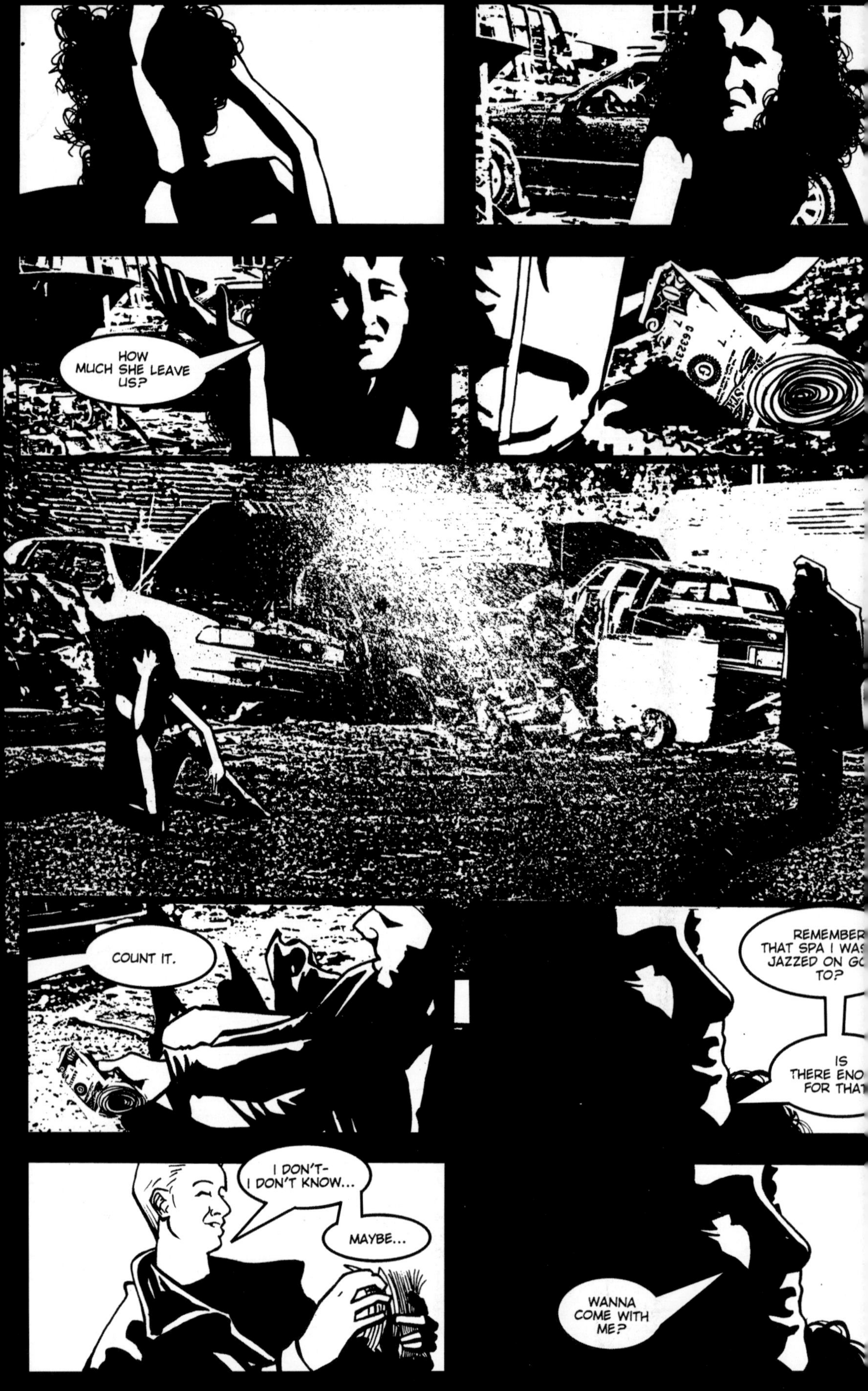
HOW MUCH SHE LEAVE US?
COUNT IT.
REMEMBER THAT SPA I WAS JAZZED ON GO TO?
IS THERE ENO FOR THAT
I DON'T- I DON'T KNOW...
MAYBE...
WANNA COME WITH ME?

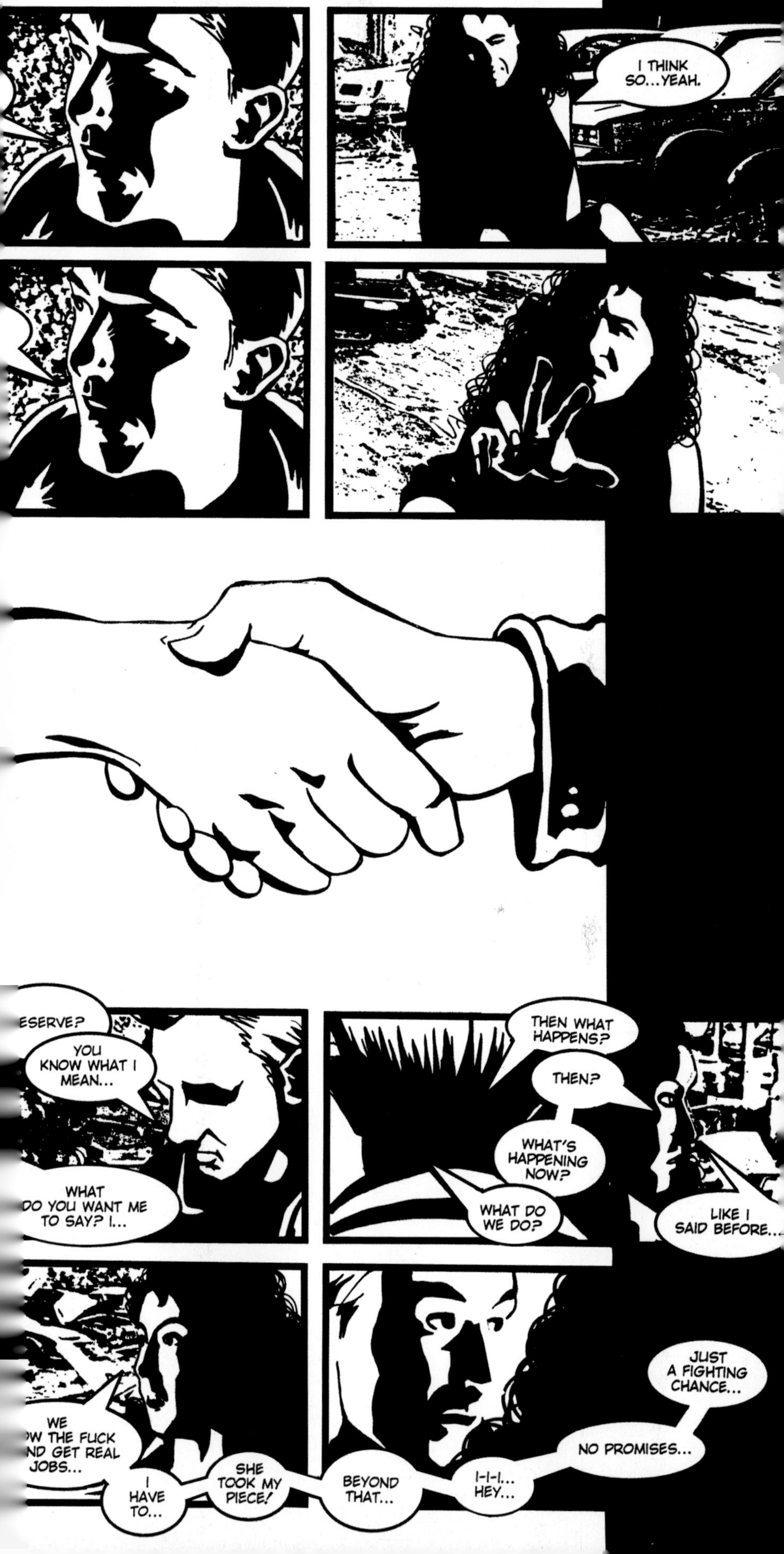
I THINK SO...YEAH.
ESERVE?
YOU KNOW WHAT I MEAN...
WHAT DO YOU WANT ME TO SAY? I...
THEN WHAT HAPPENS?
THEN?
WHAT'S HAPPENING NOW?
WHAT DO WE DO?
LIKE I SAID BEFORE...
WE OW THE FUCK ND GET REAL JOBS...
I HAVE TO...
SHE TOOK MY PIECE!
BEYOND THAT...
I-I-I... HEY...
NO PROMISES...
JUST A FIGHTING CHANCE...

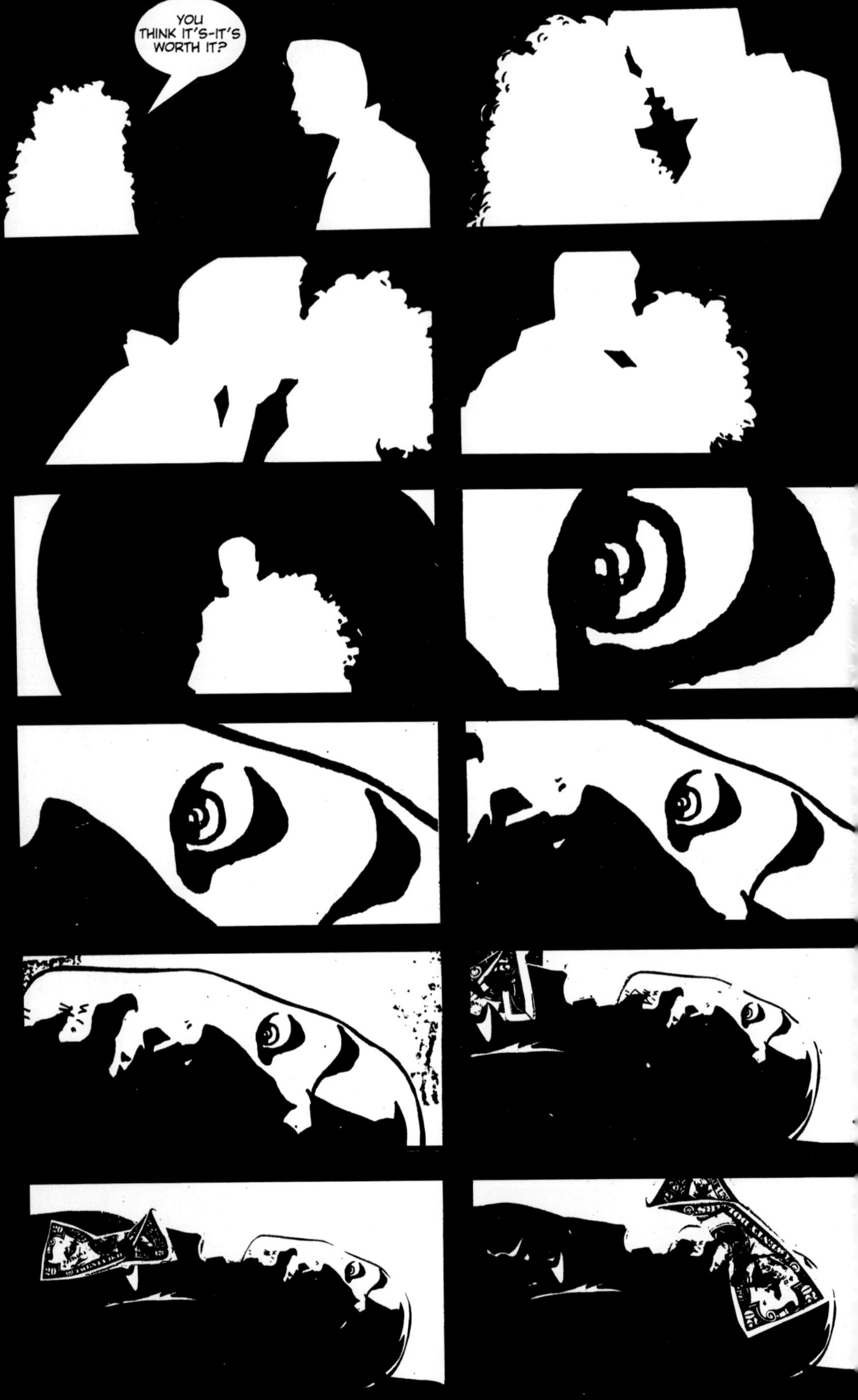
YOU THINK IT'S-IT'S WORTH IT?

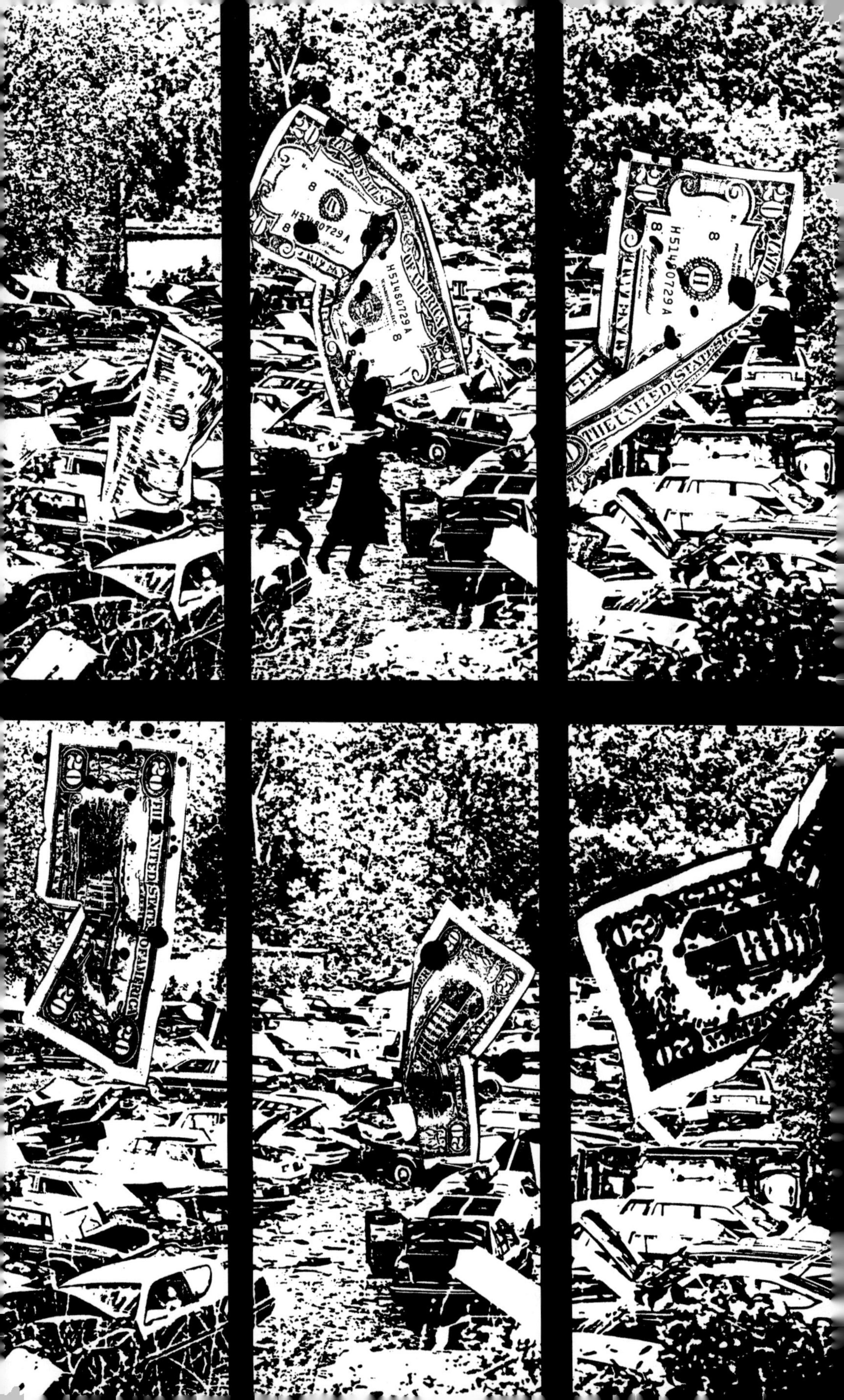
H51460729A
THE UNITED STATES
OF AMERICA

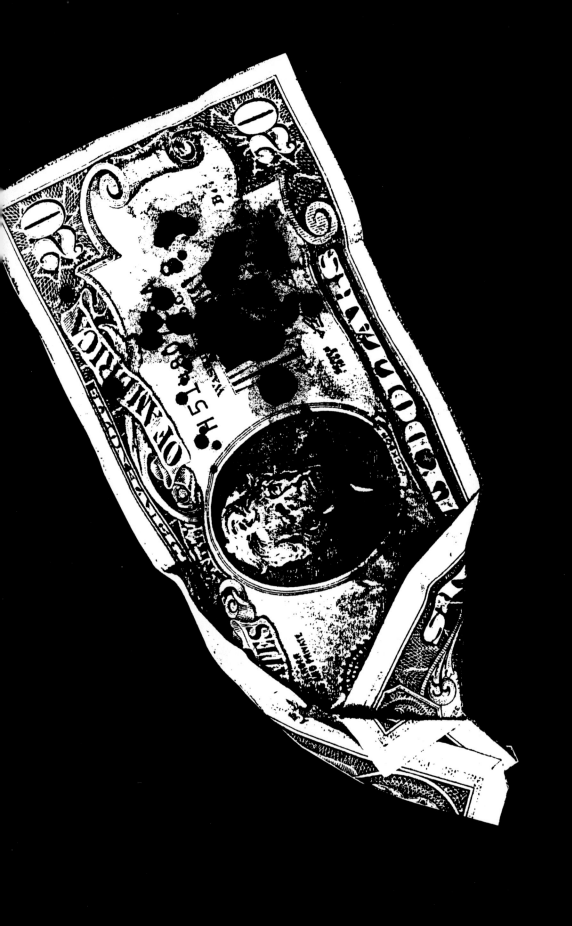

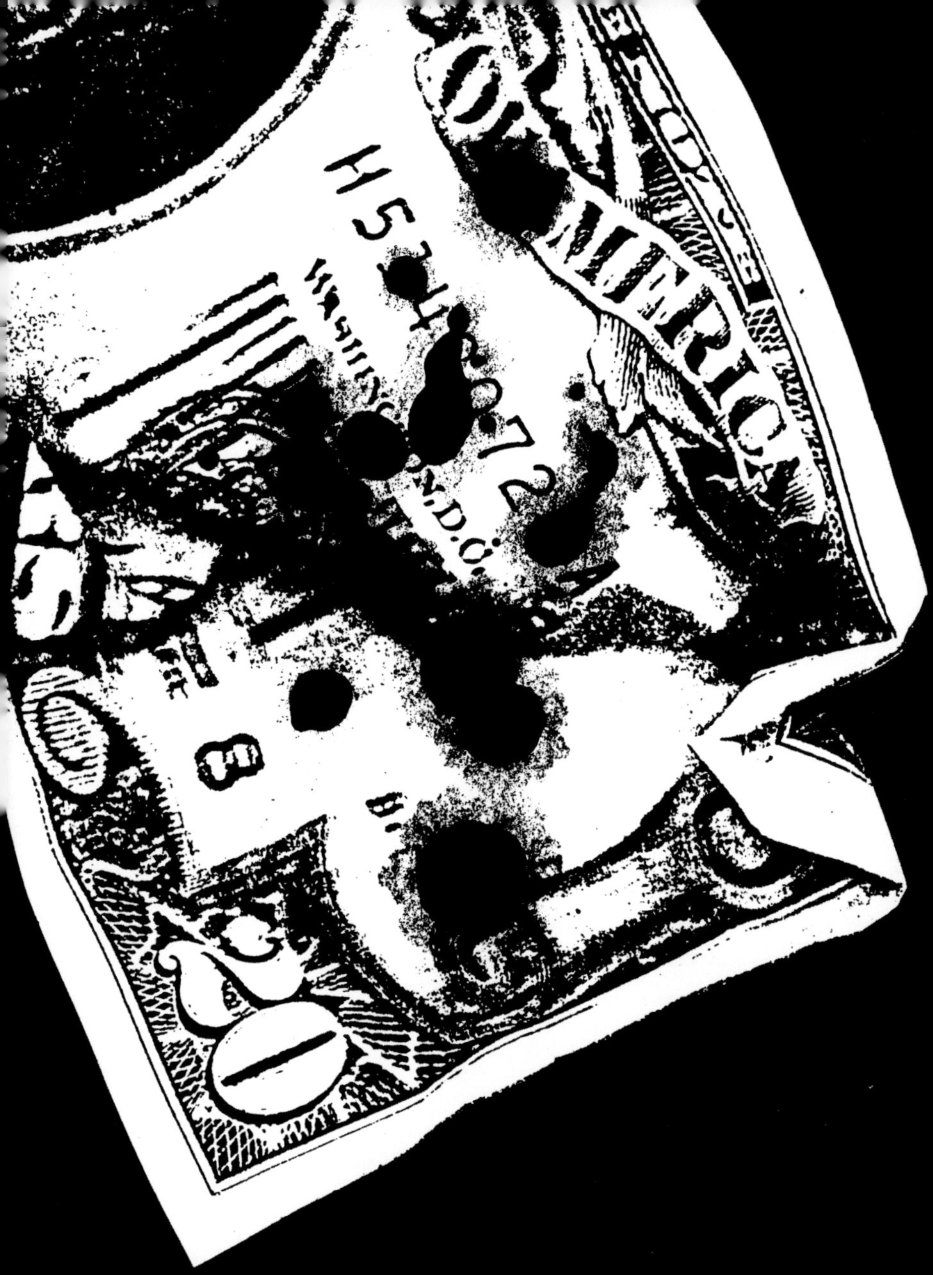

End

JINX SUPPLEMENTAL

THE MAKING OF *JINX*

Welcome to the making-of / behind-the-scenes bonus section. I have had more requests for this material than I've had people ask me if I want fries with that, and trust me, that's a lot of people.

This section isn't a "how to make a comic" section. This is a "how I made a comic" section. The following is a stream of consciousness of philosophies and ideas that I had while making this specific work. At the least it will serve as a sort of creator's journal, to record where my brain was when I created this.

This was originally written soon after this work was completed. I have updated it from its original text for the collected edition.

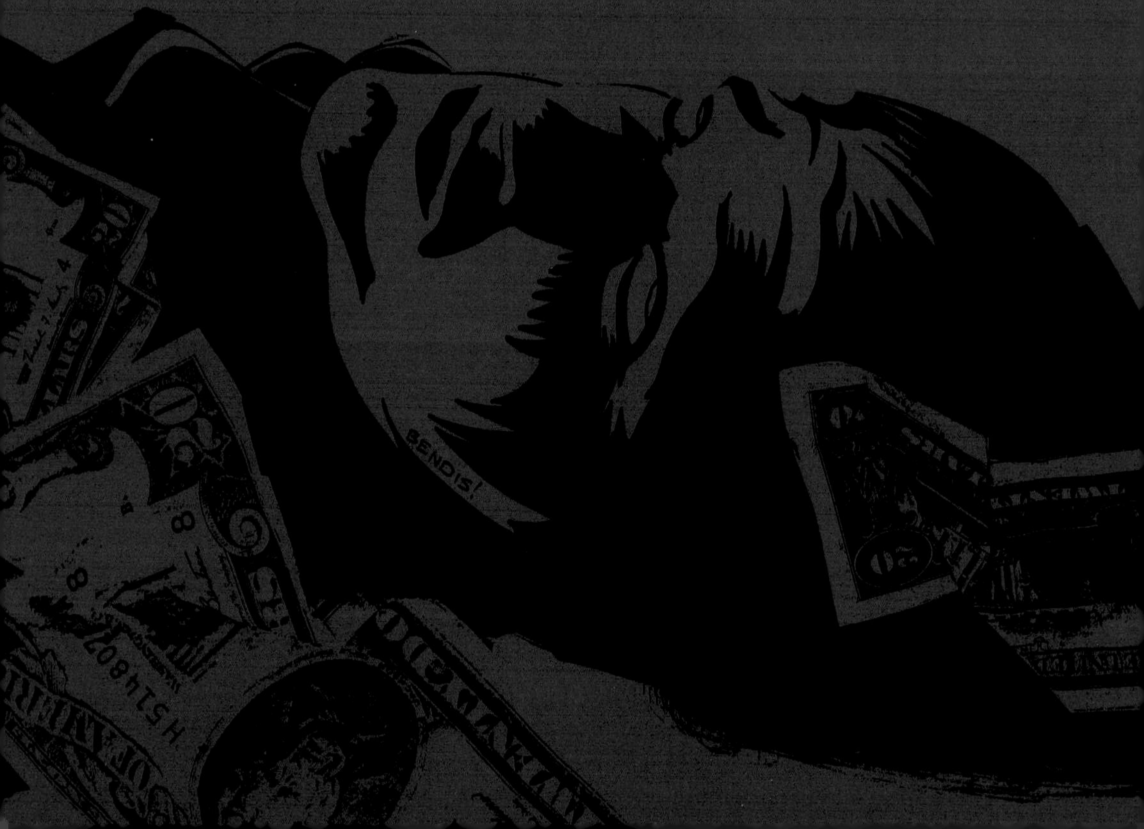
BENDIS!

Early Jinx
drawing.

PREMISE

The premise behind *Jinx* came very easily. After the relative success of my *Goldfish* graphic novel, I had found myself, FINALLY, with the beginnings of something resembling a style. The crime genre had overtaken my entire psyche. I was on fire. What to do next?

Here's what I knew:

I knew that I hadn't finished exploring the relationship of the crime-riddled urban streets and the lawlessness of the Wild West. Which is a huge running theme for me.

I knew I was going to push myself into finally creating a real, albeit dysfunctional, relationship between an adult woman and an adult male, something I had yet to do. My projects always seem to reek of male paranoia. Not on purpose or by design, it just always ended up that way. But I was happily married now, and I should be able to consciously pull that off.

I had fashioned my plot, my motivations, my characters, and their relationships. I knew who Jinx was, where she came from, but I had no damn idea what this woman, who had so captured my imagination, was doing in this world of macho pinheads and greedy fuckups.

I knew I didn't want to make her another grifter. I had done that already with Lauren Bacall in *Goldfish*. And man, I hate the idea of consciously repeating myself à la Woody Allen. I knew I didn't want to make her a cop, because I didn't have anything to say about cops at the time.

So, after whining to my friends about how stuck I was, the great god of stapled comics shined some light my way. I got a call to do a freelance illustration, as often happens. I met this particular client in my local coffee shop that often seconds as the conference room for my studio, and in walked Jinx. In walked this hard, attractive, tank-topped, jeans-clad woman with a shock of hair . . . and packing heat.

I asked her what she did for a living and she said: "I'm a bounty hunter."

I said: "Like De Niro in *Midnight Run*?"

She said: "EXACTLY like De Niro in *Midnight Run*."

And, baby, was I in business. This seedy, odd world of bounty hunting is fascinating and surprisingly underexposed in the world of popular fiction. There have only been two movies that focused on it. And if you think about how many movies have focused on cops and PIs and such, that's an amazingly low number. I had found an untapped well.

And as far as comics went, who was my big competition? *Barb Wire*? HA!

Jinx drawing
used for the
cover of *Comics
Buyer's Guide*.

WRITING

There's a whole lot of so-called "rules" to writing. These rules have been documented time and again by others far more industrious and intelligent than I. Instead I'll give you the mental checklist that runs through my head when I am writing:

WRITE WHAT YOU KNOW. AND IF YOU DON'T KNOW IT, FOR CRYING OUT LOUD, GO RESEARCH IT.

When researching what became Jinx, I talked to a ton of bounty hunters, cops, and others of that ilk. First of all, it is a lot of fun. You get to act like you're a tough guy for a couple of minutes, without having to hurt anybody. Secondly, these people have stories to tell a thousand times more interesting and entertaining than anything you could make up . . . and they are TRUE. There are stories out there for the taking. Your genius is to figure out which ones to tell, and when and where to tell them.

HEY, THAT'S A GOOD IDEA OR FUNNY LINE! IS IT FROM LIFE? YOUR IMAGINATION? OR DID YOU HEAR IT ON T.V.?

The only thing worse than being a hack, is . . . well, there's nothing worse than being a hack, but we do live in a multimedia information superhighway, and it is hard to keep the vision and inspiration pure. But do yourself a favor: at least TRY.

MMMM-MMMM DIALOGUE.

Dialogue is something that I get the most credit for. David Mamet says that having a good ear for dialogue is the professional ability to talk to yourself. I think it is more like: instead of listening to the voices in your head, let them talk to each other while you try to write it all down.

But if anything, my goals for dialogue come from the fact that I so abhor exposition. Information has to be given to the reader, but I always ask myself if this dialogue I have written is something someone would say out loud.

Listen to your friends. I mean, REALLY listen. People do not talk in complete, perfectly structured sentences. People stutter, stammer, start and stop sentences in funny places. This is like music to me. Creating more natural-sounding dialogue for comics is something I take a lot of pride and care in and go to bizarre lengths to achieve. I have had friends act out scenes like they are reading a play.

I know that this style is an acquired taste and every day I learn something new about it, but it is so important to me.

IF IT DOESN'T RING TRUE TO YOU, IT ISN'T GOING TO RING TRUE TO THEM . . . LET THE CHARACTERS DO THEIR THING.

If you build your characters into the fully realized identities they deserve to be, they will dictate their actions to you. Don't force them into situations or conflicts. Real characters run the gamut of human emotion. They have contradicting attitudes, motivations, and ideals. Don't fight it, it's their story. Let them tell it for you.

FREE THERAPY.

There hasn't been one relationship, anxiety, or conundrum in my life that hasn't hugely benefited from the fact that I have a forum in which to address it. Nothing sings to the reader more than when you write from the heart. Seize the opportunity to explore yourself.

FIRST DRAFTS ALWAYS SUCK.

Always.

HA HA HA HA—OH NO!

A lot of writers, especially in comics, throw in every gag they can think of regardless of whether or not they are sacrificing the story momentum or mood of the piece. Anybody can write a gag; the geniuses know where and when it's time to use them or cut them. The *Bowfinger* DVD has some excellent examples of great jokes taken out of a scene for the sake of story. Buy it and study it. It's a real eye opener.

THAT'S WHAT YOUR MOM IS FOR.

Everybody has a mom or grandma to kiss their creative ass. What everybody needs is a core group of close friends and associates that aren't afraid to tell you when it ain't working. Find them and listen. Egos are for losers.

STORY.

The best, and maybe the only truly great, book on writing is *Story* by Robert McKee. There is nothing I am spouting off about here that isn't described perfectly in this amazing book. Buy it, read it, and read it again.

CHARACTER DESIGN

This part is a lot like casting a movie. And yes, I did sleep with myself to get the part.

Luckily, I don't have to worry about designing a silly superhero costume that would never function in real life. But I do have to create identities for realistic people. I have to find a look that you will find appealing and not distracting, that I will want to draw thousands and thousands of times.

It's casting the perfect actor for the part (literally, as I use models). I already had Goldfish's look left over from his book, and I knew Columbia was going to personify my male id. I was perfect for the part of the short, bald loser.

So, all I was left with was Jinx. I wanted Jinx to be one of those women that you don't think too much of initially, but as you get to know her, she gets more and more attractive. I always cast models that run against the grain of my natural style to give my art a more well-rounded world.

Here are a couple of designs that I was pretty close to committing to.

This one is Jinx as a woman of Hispanic or Indian descent. Even though the look appealed to me, I didn't think the ethnicity added anything to the narrative. In fact, I think it would have eventually detracted from it.

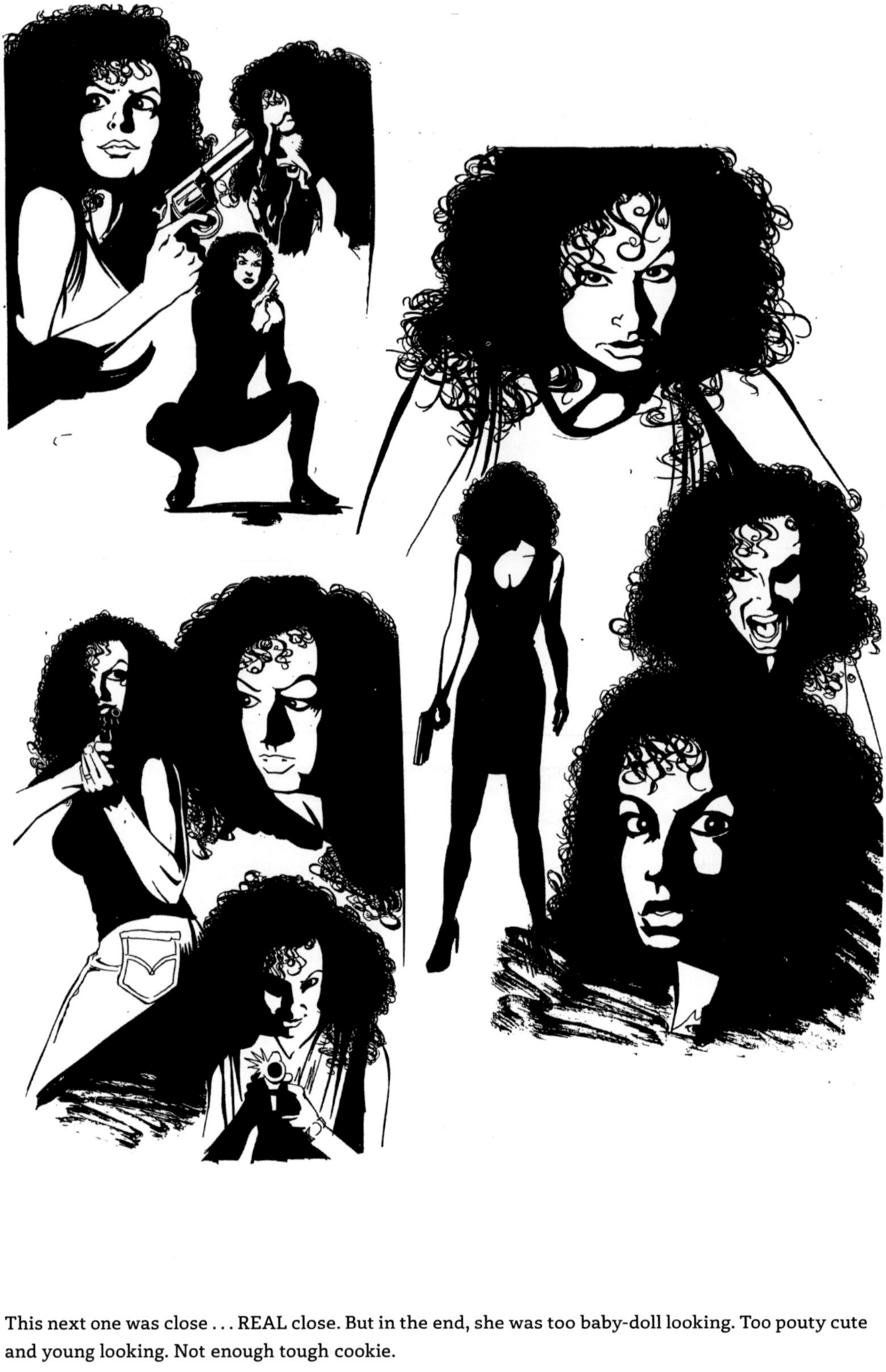

This next one was close . . . REAL close. But in the end, she was too baby-doll looking. Too pouty cute and young looking. Not enough tough cookie.

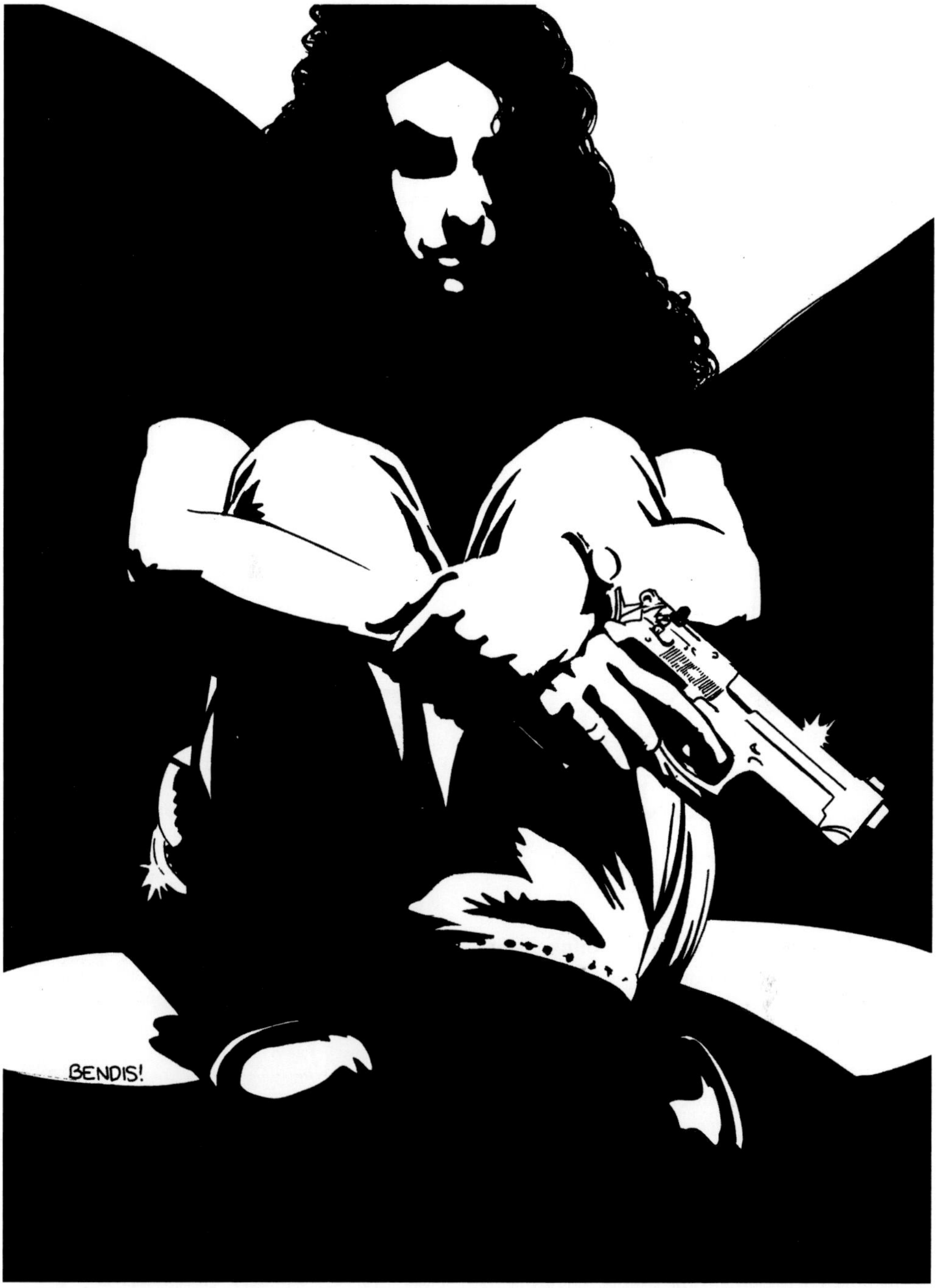
BENDIS!

Then, along came DD Byrne. I had met DD years ago. To be honest, I had an instant crush. She was a member of the Cleveland Ballet, and she was perfect. Her long, angular face made great noir shadows. Her dancer's body gave the impression of a very fit, athletic woman that didn't look like a Stairmaster freak.

And she looked damn good in a tank top!

And once DD got ahold of the character and her motivations, she became the perfect physical actress. BINGO!

MODELS / PHOTO REFERENCE

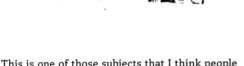

This is one of those subjects that I think people have a misconception about.

First of all, the idea that photo reference is somehow cheating is ridiculous. Remember that nothing is cheating in comics. Comics as a medium is still in its larva stage. The only way to grow is for it to branch out and explore. Worst-case scenario, we fall on our ass. Then we pick ourselves up and try something else.

In my opinion, the only thing that is "cheating" is lifting images, or even ideas, from another artist. I know that this has been said many times and in many different ways, but tracing other people's line art and aping others' style is embarrassing to you and your audience.

Reference is the same as life drawing from a live model. Except that I doubt you have friends that have nothing better to do all day than stand in your studio posing for hours on end. The only thing that I learned in five years of art school is: why HINT at the visual information, when you have the ability to GIVE it? Especially with a book based in the "real world" like mine. Models are an invaluable tool in creating a tone and style that is consistent with the narrative.

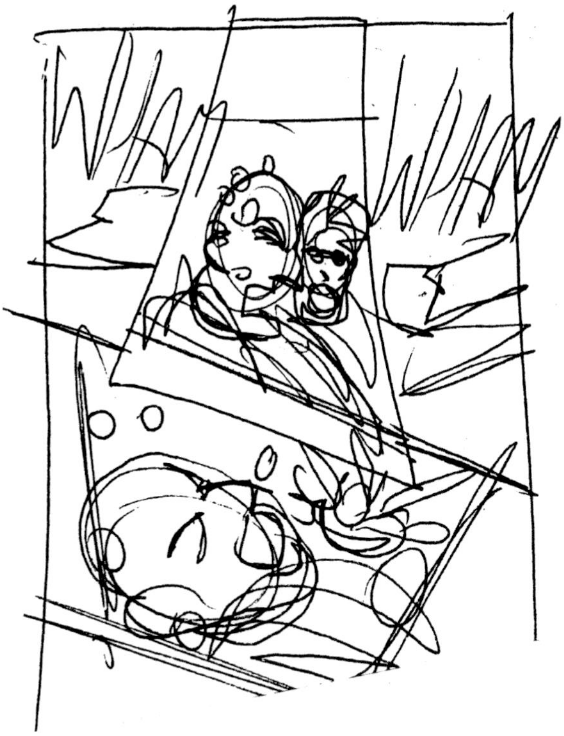

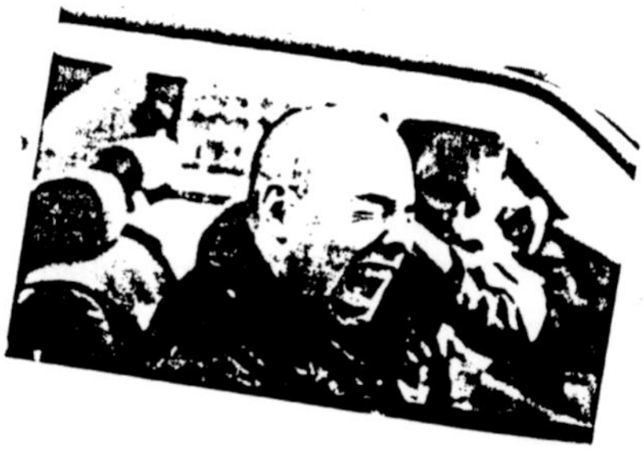

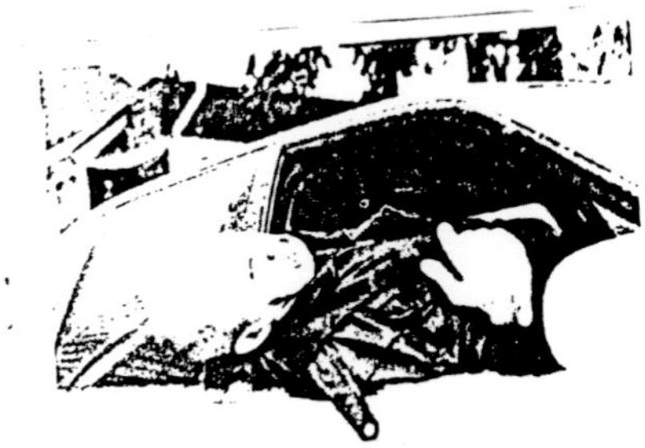

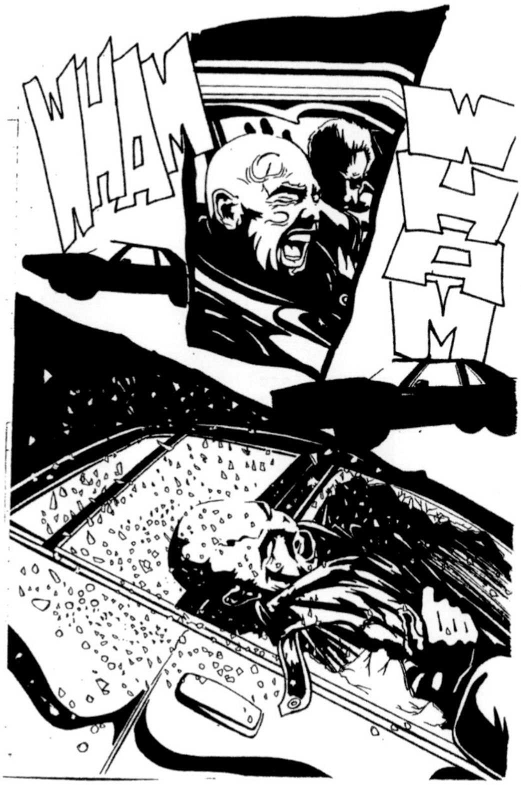

The trick to successful photo reference is to not be a slave to it. The camera has only one eye, a lens, compared to your two eyes. That means that a lot of the camera's basic visual information is untrue. Perspective, foreshortening, and such can all be misperceived by the camera. The key is to know when and where the camera is your friend.

As you see here, you can't just go shoot models. Just like a movie, you have to have a tight game plan. I have a very clear idea of what I'm going to do before I go bothering friends.

I use natural lighting and no flash because it helps me discover new noirish shadows. Also flash photography often creates shapes and shadows where there aren't really any.

The extra step I go to with my models is playing with improvisation situations. I let the models play with the scene, as an actor would. This has uncovered certain body language, a stance and personality, which adds to each character having its own identity.

For example, in my layouts, I might have Jinx and Goldfish holding a coffee cup the same way, basically the way I would. Spending a little extra time with the models will show DD holding a cup one way and John (Goldfish) holding it another. I know that sounds like a little thing, something that nobody would even notice, but trust me, it's not. It's a whole world, a universe, of difference.

Another thing I'm very sensitive to is the static look some artists get from using photo reference. I try very hard to let the shadows and the line work take on a life past the static shot of the model. Plus, I find my constant attempts at following in the footsteps of the great noir cinematographers like John Alton and Gregg Toland immediately abstract the art out of the static "photorealistic" stage.

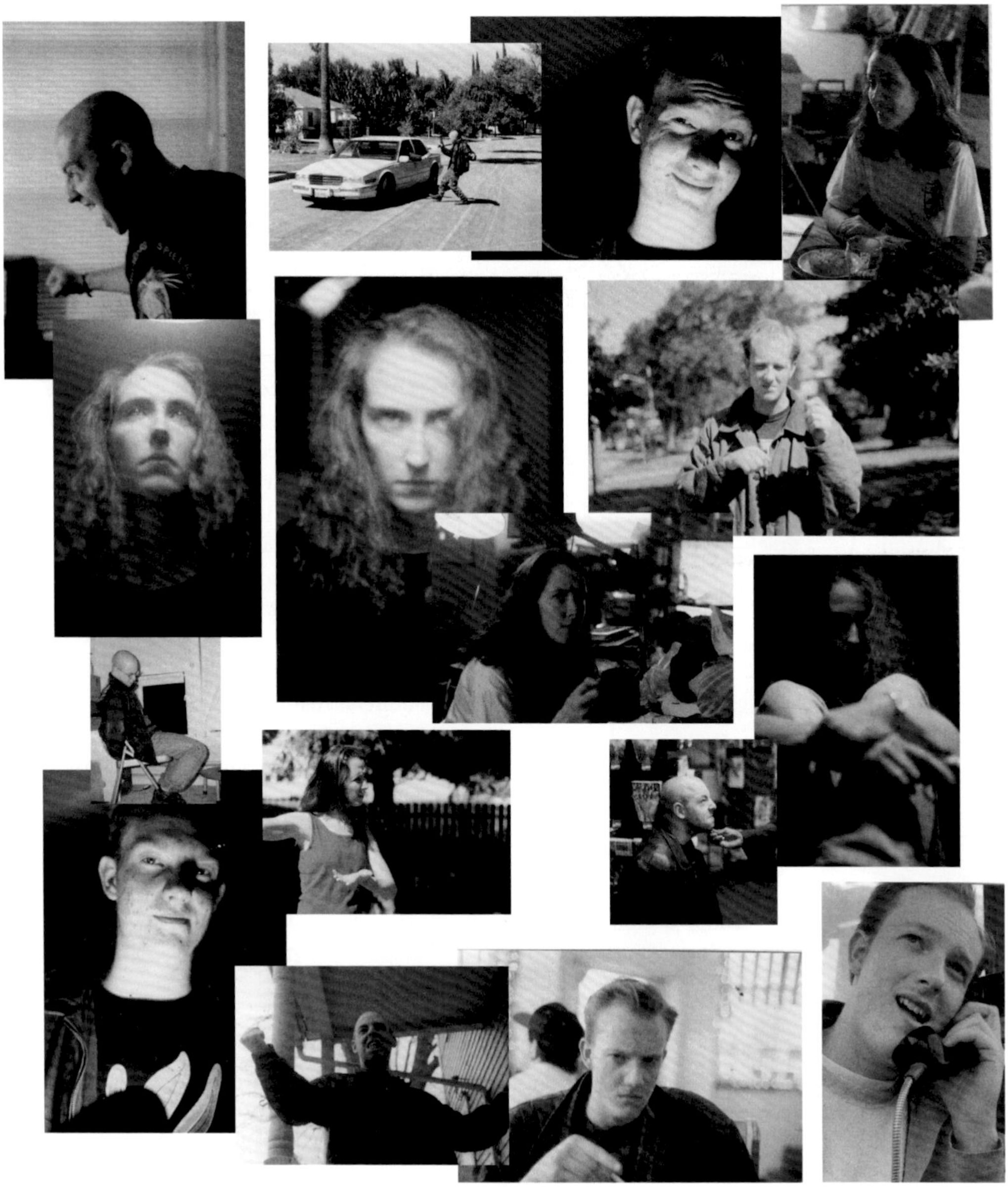

GENERAL SHTUFF

Here's the mantra list of philosophies that I ran through while creating this work . . .

The Bendis Photoshop philosophy (as stolen from *Jurassic Park*): JUST BECAUSE YOU CAN, DOESN'T MEAN YOU SHOULD. Everything in the world is a usable tool for comics, but you should know why you are doing it. Sometimes I look at all the overblown design work in comics and I think: "Put. The. Mouse. DOWN!! You were finished with the piece seven layers ago." Less is more!

The streets are riddled with the dead, bloated carcasses of work from creators that were so sure that theirs was the next BIG THING. Or creators of the mindset of "I'll create a book like so-and-so's. His sells, so will mine." Little do they realize that by the time they finish their book, the winds of pop culture will have already shifted somewhere else. Just create something because you really want to, not because you think it will be popular.

Peter Gabriel said it best: "Commercial success is a fickle mistress. If you go looking for her, she'll avoid you. If you stay true to yourself, she'll come looking for you."

Life imitates art imitating life
Photo shoot for crime comic book ends when real cops arrive

By MICHAEL SANGIACOMO
PLAIN DEALER REPORTER

CLEVELAND — It's getting so a working Joe and a dame can't take a stroll with a rifle and a machete without some screws getting all worked up.

Brian Michael Bendis, a small-time writer with big dreams and a bad haircut, thought he could get a couple of photos of a gorgeous gal on the Lorain-Carnegie Bridge, for the cover of his crime comic book, "Jinx."

But the Cleveland cops had a few ideas of their own, and before he could say "Mickey Spillane," he found himself on the business end of a police special trying to explain that the rifle and the machete were just props and that the dame was a model and that this was all just innocent fun.

Right, and the Flats would be a nice place for a church social.

Well, Bendis got lucky this time. The cop he ran into had an open mind and a slow trigger finger and he let the mug walk scot

free. This time.

Bendis' life came a little too close to imitating the fiction in his crime comics Tuesday evening when he ran afoul of Cleveland police on the bridge.

Two officers got the wrong idea when they saw Bendis and another man standing on the bridge with a young woman, handcuffs, a machete, fake blood, and a realistic-looking air rifle.

Police pulled guns and some tense moments followed.

"I could not explain things fast enough," Bendis said. "I know how it must have looked to the police, and don't blame them at all for the way they acted. They pulled their guns on us and eventually threw me and my photographer in the police cars while they talked to our model. Fortunately, she was able to explain everything."

Bendis was accompanied by Rona Kudroff, 25, of Beachwood, and photographer John Skrtic, 20, of Cleveland. Skrtic was taking a

photo of Kudroff staring wistfully at the skyline. The props were to be used in later photos.

"We figured we'd grab a quick shot or two and get out of there," said Bendis, 27. "Someone saw the rifle and the woman and called the police, thinking there was a problem."

The next thing he knew, a wailing police cruiser roared up, lights flashing. And officers looking very serious were pointing guns at them.

"I lead a boring life," Bendis said. "I spend 90 percent of my time fabricating situations like this. But when it happened, I didn't know what to do."

An officer, with an unkind reference to his shaved head, ordered Bendis to put down his camera.

"So I tried to explain that it was just a camera and the officer got very upset," he said. "Everyone started yelling and then I heard him say I had to the count of three to put it down and put my hands

RICHARD T. CONWAY / PLAIN DEALER

Brian Bendis: "They pulled their guns on us and eventually threw me and my photographer in the police cars while they talked to our model."

up and it struck me that I should shut up and do it."

There is a bright side.

"I got a million dollars worth of ideas and dialogue," Bendis said.

When all is said and done, it's your name on the title. It is your work in the book. It is your ass on the line, and it is probably your life's legacy. So don't succumb to flavor-of-the-month styles and genres and don't underestimate your audience.

And while we're on good rock star quotes, Sting said that rock-and-roll is a bastard art form. What he meant by that is that it is a hybrid art form. When rock-and-roll regurgitates on itself, it fails, but when it looks outside itself and brings in country, jazz, opera, etc., it thrives. It explodes!!

Well, what else is a bastard art form? That's right. It's the same thing with comics. A comic isn't art or writing, it's not painting or line art. It's not poetry or screenwriting. It's all of these things and more. All mixed in together to create the bastard art form of comics. But when comics regurgitates on itself, it fails too. When comics regurgitates on itself, it often feels like that last Michael Keaton clone in the movie *Multiplicity*. There's just something really wrong with it.

Jinx the animated project

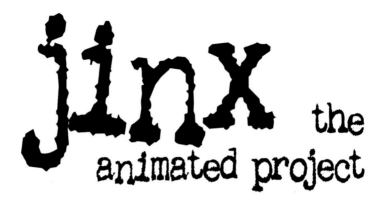

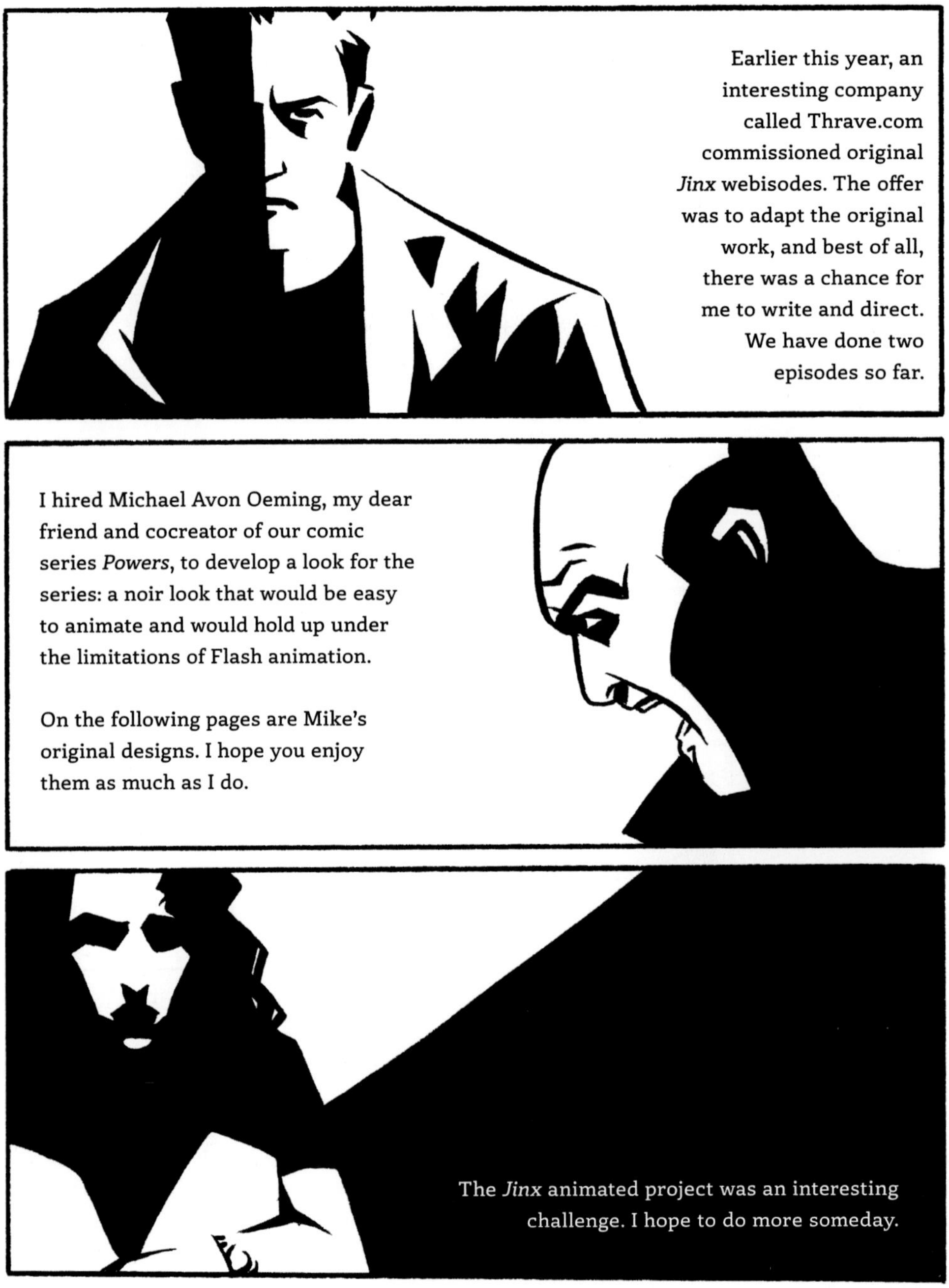
Earlier this year, an interesting company called Thrave.com commissioned original *Jinx* webisodes. The offer was to adapt the original work, and best of all, there was a chance for me to write and direct. We have done two episodes so far.
I hired Michael Avon Oeming, my dear friend and cocreator of our comic series *Powers*, to develop a look for the series: a noir look that would be easy to animate and would hold up under the limitations of Flash animation.
On the following pages are Mike's original designs. I hope you enjoy them as much as I do.
The *Jinx* animated project was an interesting challenge. I hope to do more someday.

AVON 5.00

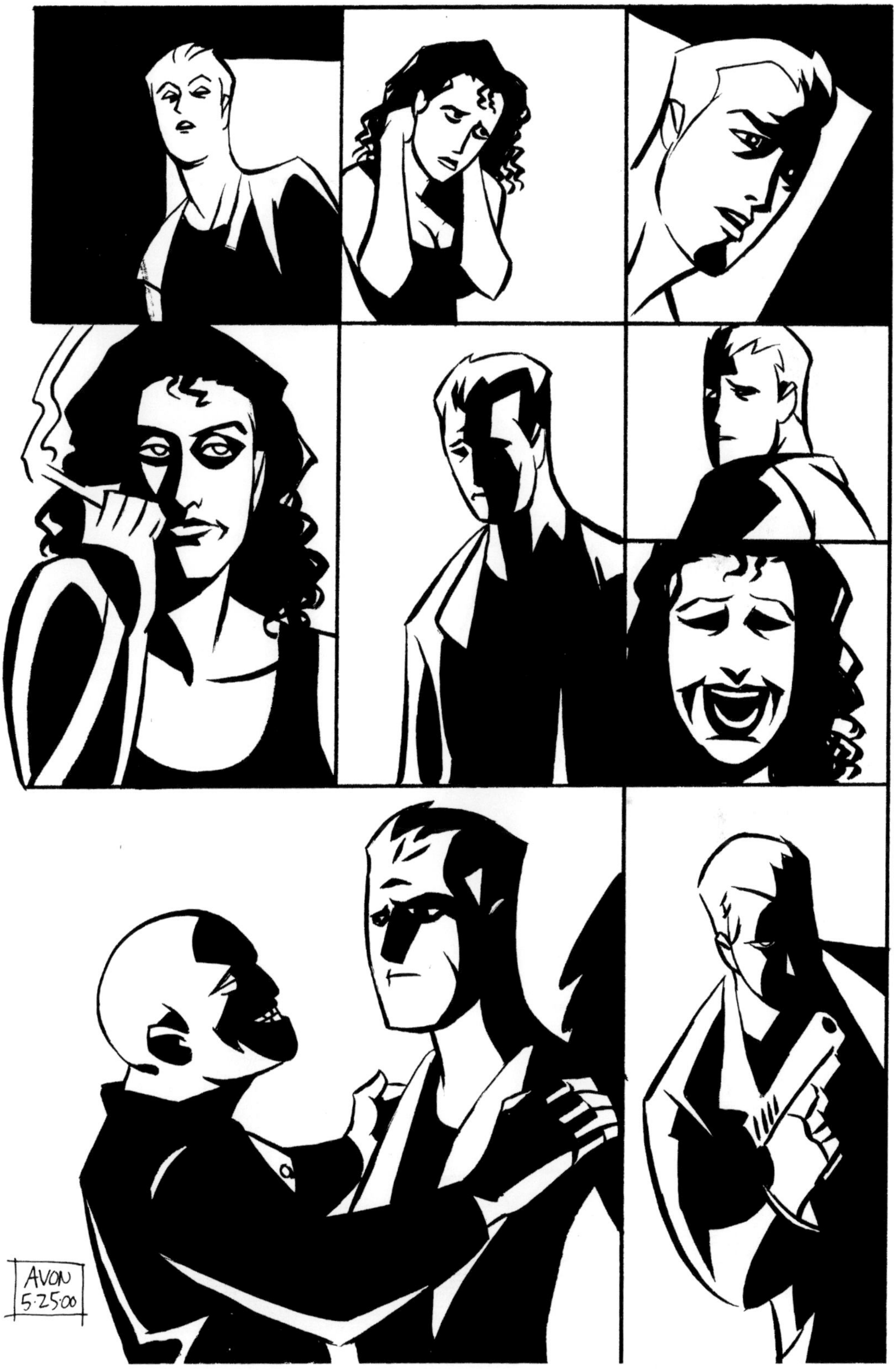
AVON
5·25·00

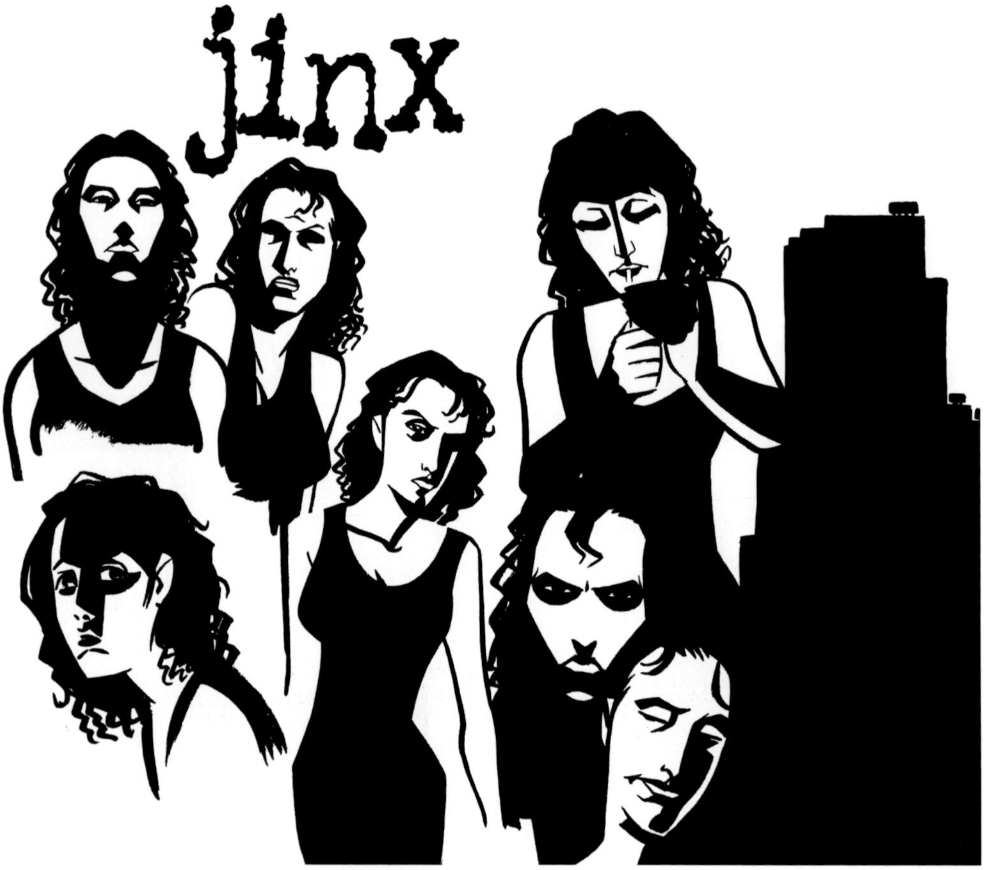
jinx

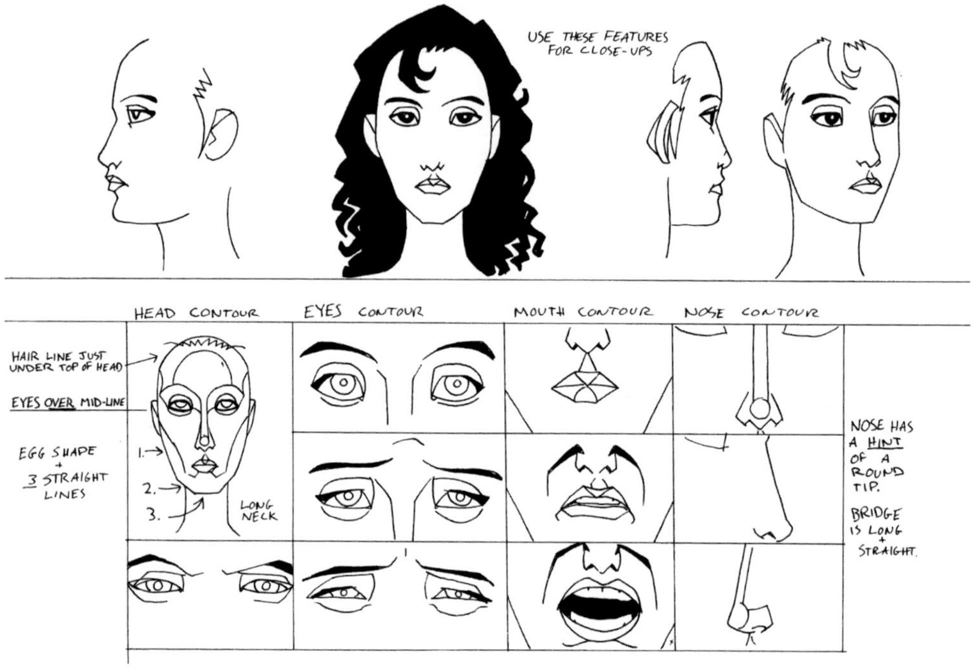
USE THESE FEATURES FOR CLOSE-UPS
HEAD CONTOUR
EYES CONTOUR
MOUTH CONTOUR
NOSE CONTOUR
HAIR LINE JUST UNDER TOP OF HEAD
EYES OVER MID-LINE
EGG SHAPE + 3 STRAIGHT LINES
1.
2.
3.
LONG NECK
NOSE HAS A HINT OF A ROUND TIP.
BRIDGE IS LONG + STRAIGHT.

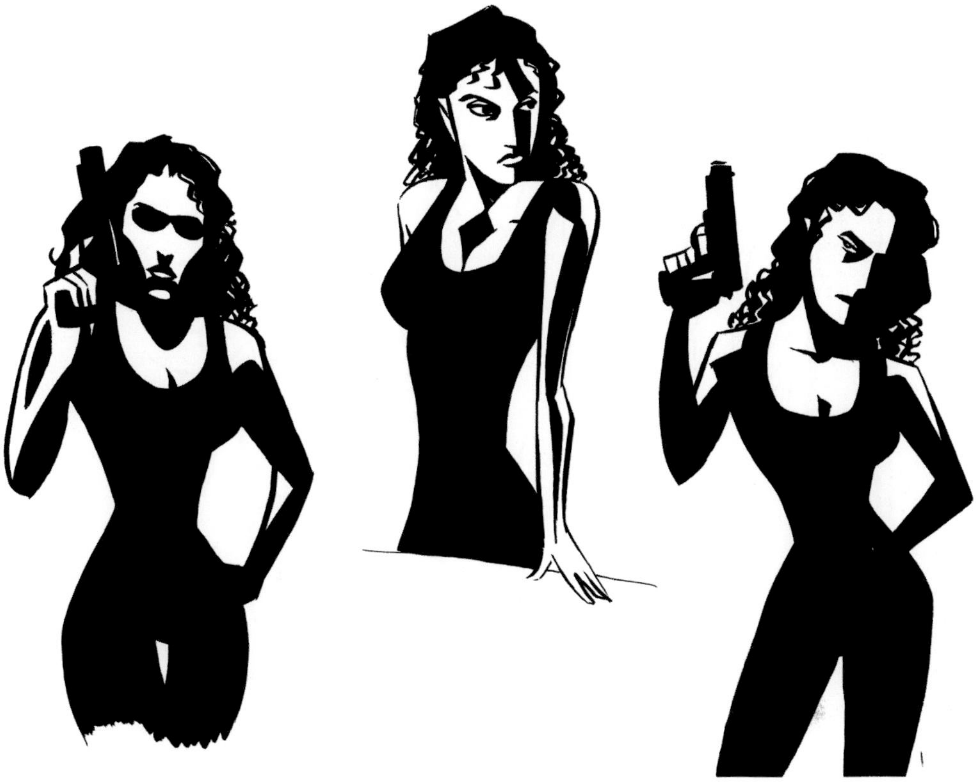

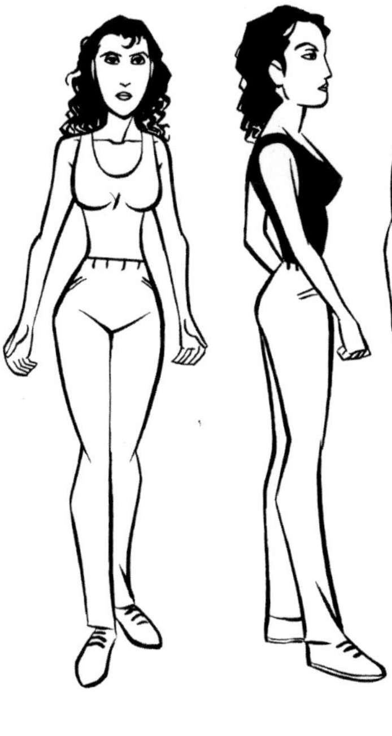

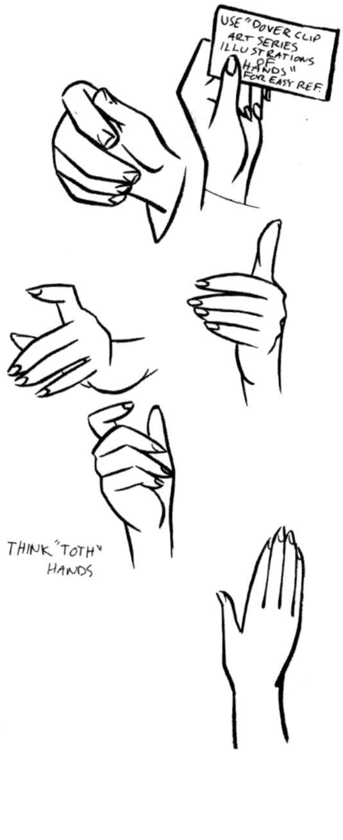
USE "DOVER CLIP ART SERIES ILLUSTRATIONS OF HANDS" FOR EASY REF.
THINK "TOTH" HANDS

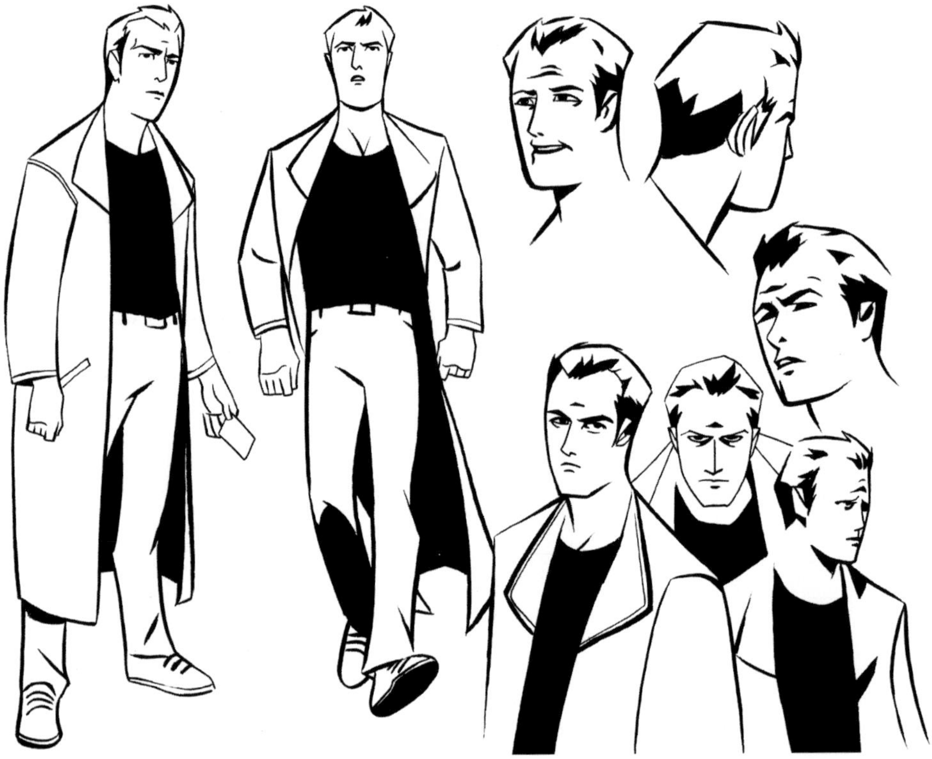

goldfish

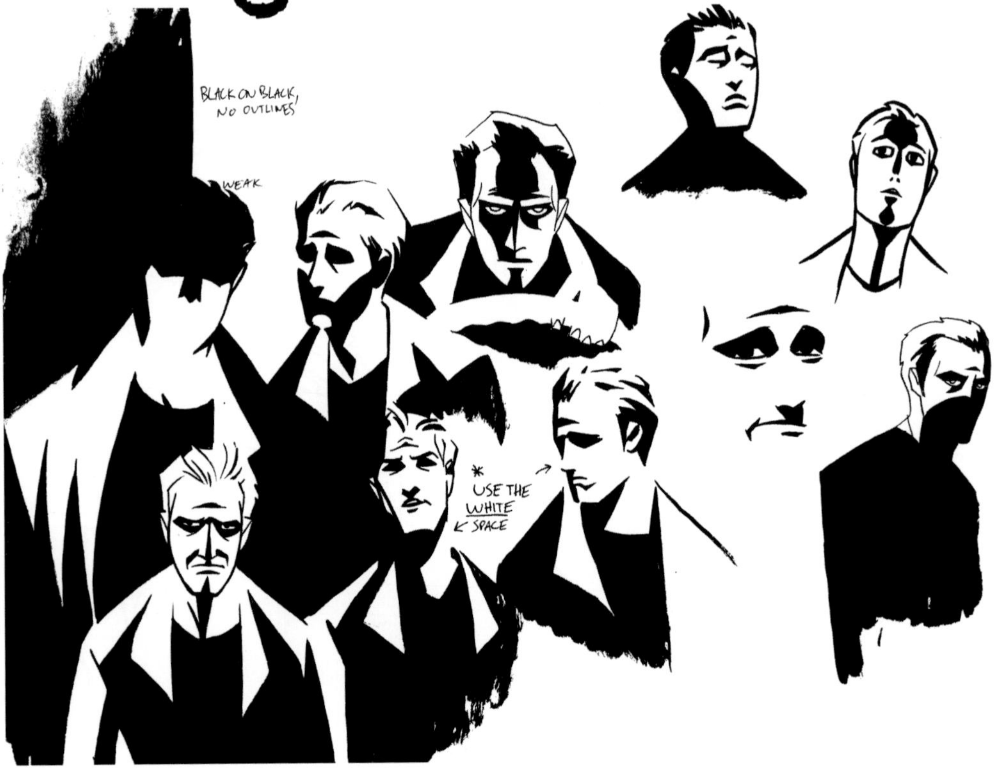
BLACK ON BLACK,
NO OUTLINES
WEAK
* USE THE WHITE SPACE

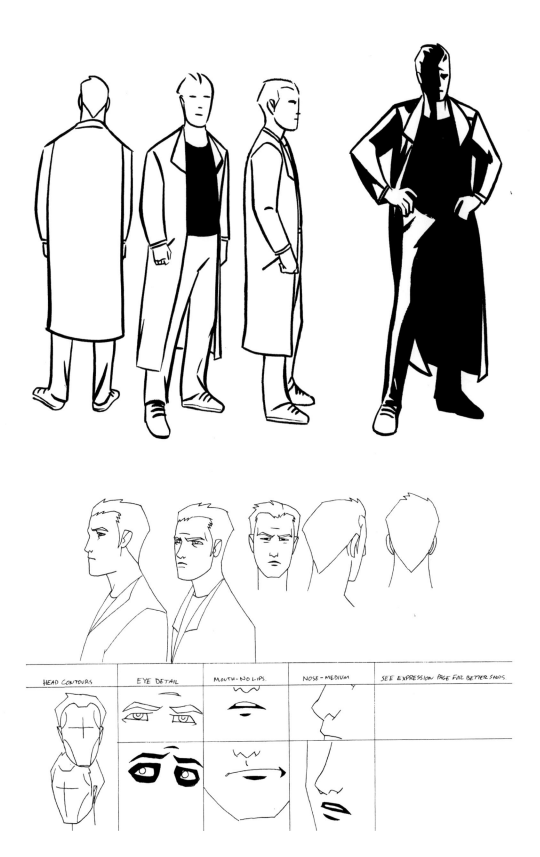

HEAD CONTOURS	EYE DETAIL	MOUTH-NO LIPS.	NOSE - MEDIUM	SEE EXPRESSION PAGE FOR BETTER SHOTS.

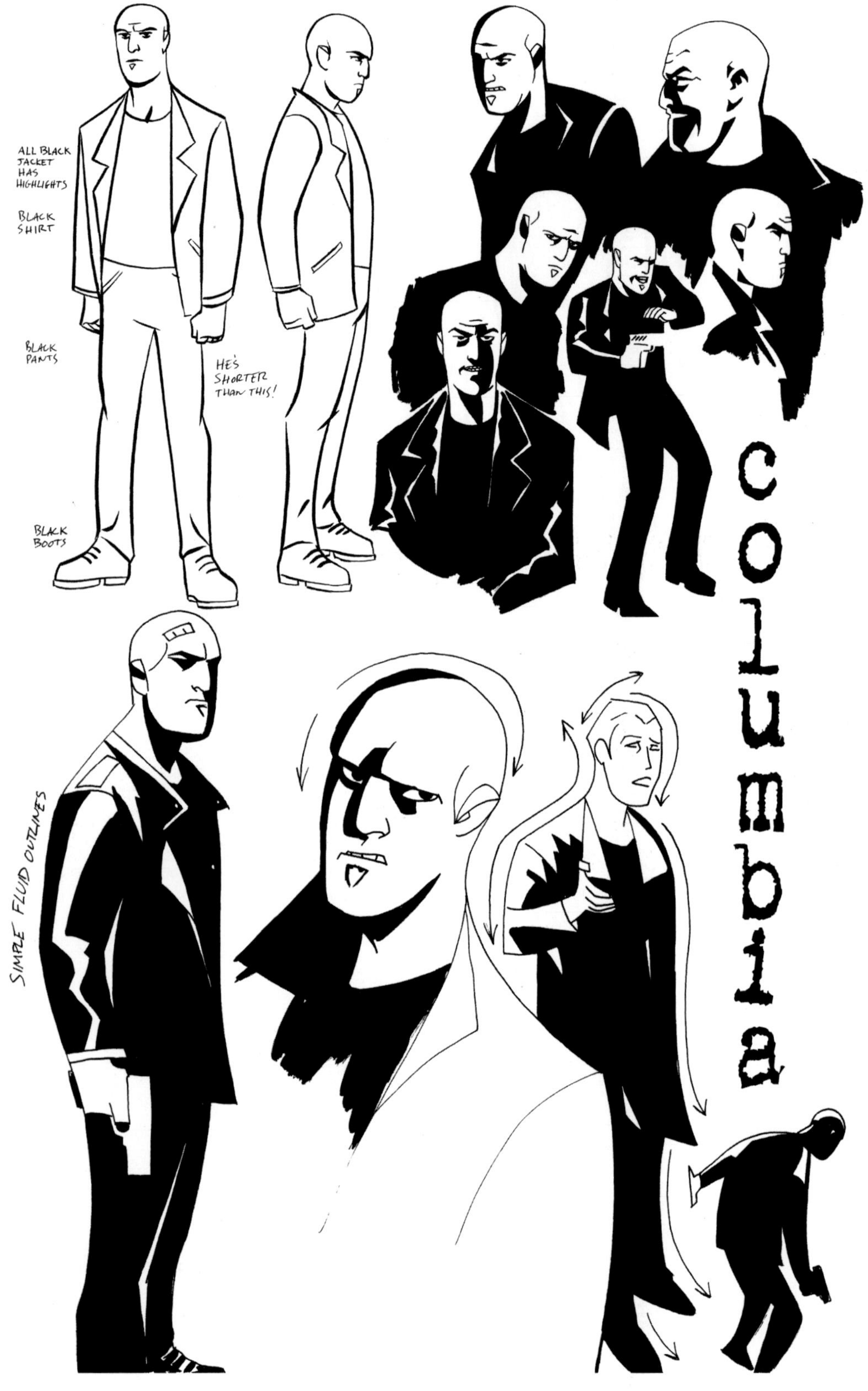
ALL BLACK JACKET HAS HIGHLIGHTS
BLACK SHIRT
BLACK PANTS
BLACK BOOTS
HE'S SHORTER THAN THIS!
SIMPLE FLUID OUTLINES
columbia

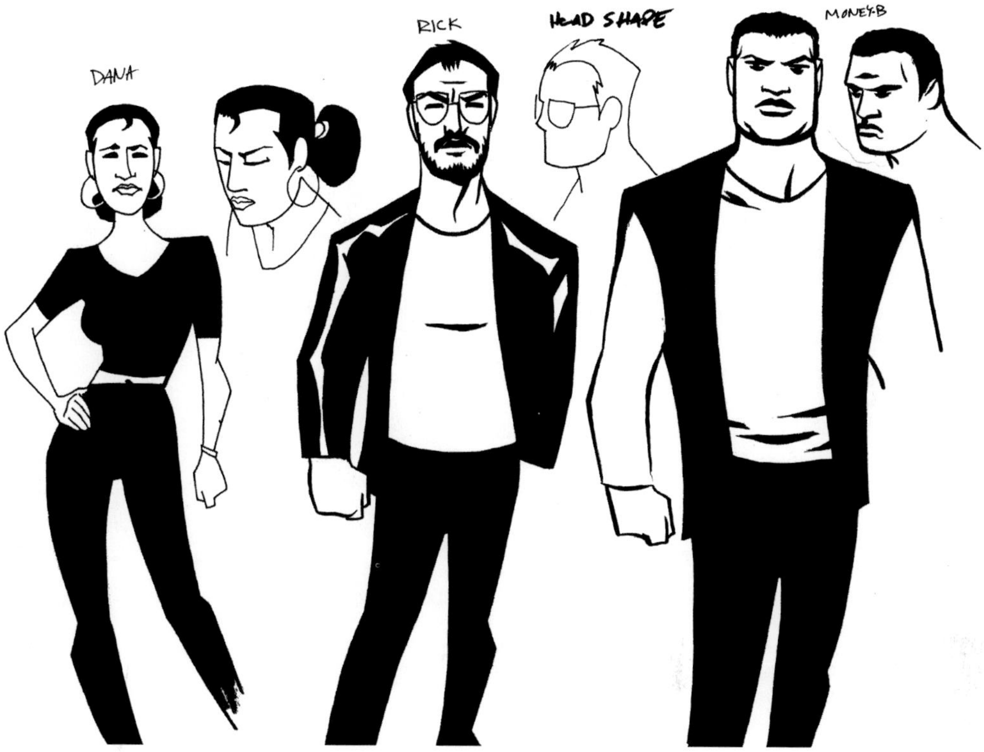
DANA
RICK
HEAD SHAPE
MONEY-B

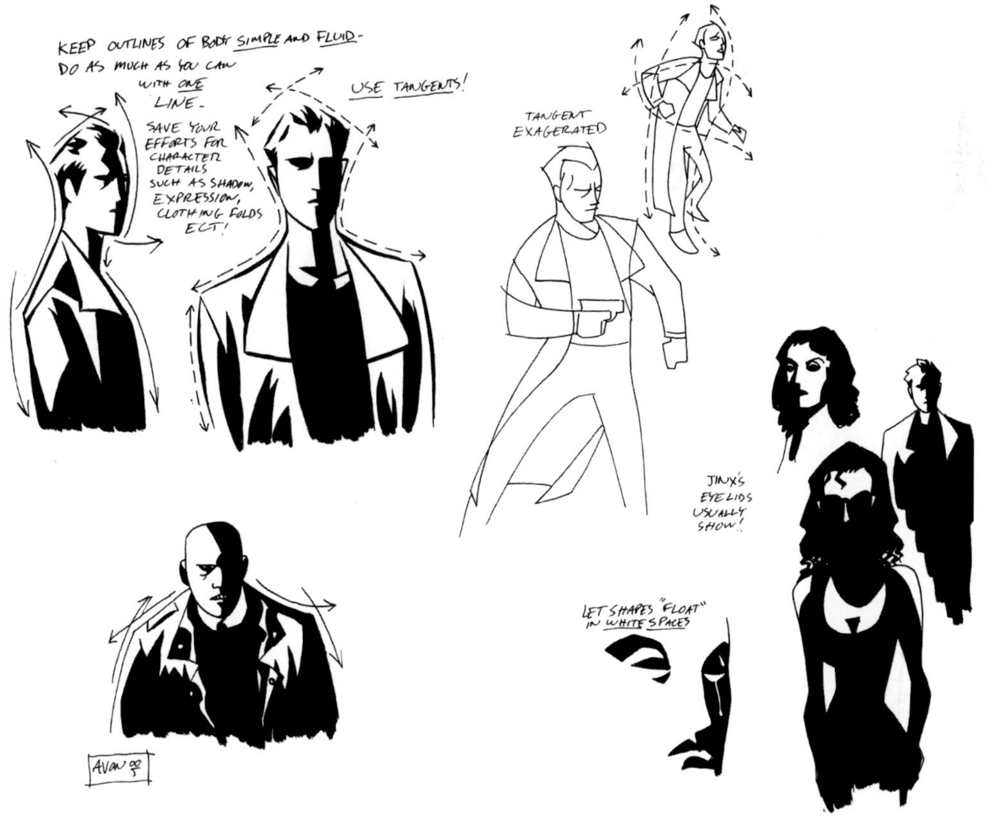
KEEP OUTLINES OF BODY SIMPLE AND FLUID-
DO AS MUCH AS YOU CAN
WITH ONE
LINE.
SAVE YOUR EFFORTS FOR CHARACTER DETAILS SUCH AS SHADOW, EXPRESSION, CLOTHING FOLDS ECT!
USE TANGENTS!
TANGENT EXAGERATED
JINX'S EYELIDS USUALLY SHOW!
LET SHAPES "FLOAT" IN WHITE SPACES

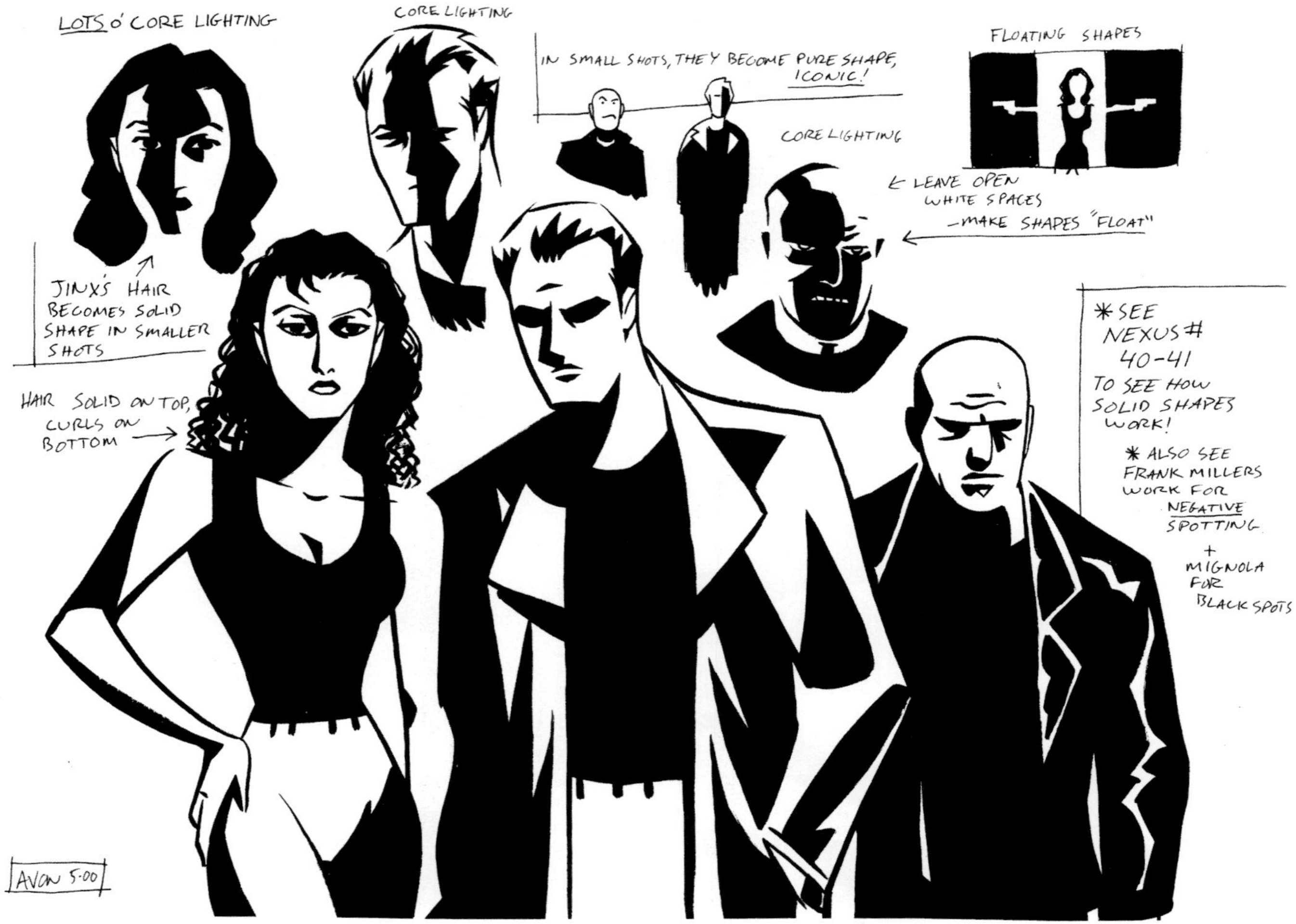
LOTS o' CORE LIGHTING
JINX'S HAIR BECOMES SOLID SHAPE IN SMALLER SHOTS
HAIR SOLID ON TOP, CURLS ON BOTTOM
CORE LIGHTING
IN SMALL SHOTS, THEY BECOME PURE SHAPE, ICONIC!
CORE LIGHTING
FLOATING SHAPES
← LEAVE OPEN WHITE SPACES
—MAKE SHAPES "FLOAT"
* SEE NEXUS # 40-41 TO SEE HOW SOLID SHAPES WORK!
* ALSO SEE FRANK MILLERS WORK FOR NEGATIVE SPOTTING
+ MIGNOLA FOR BLACK SPOTS
AVON 5·00

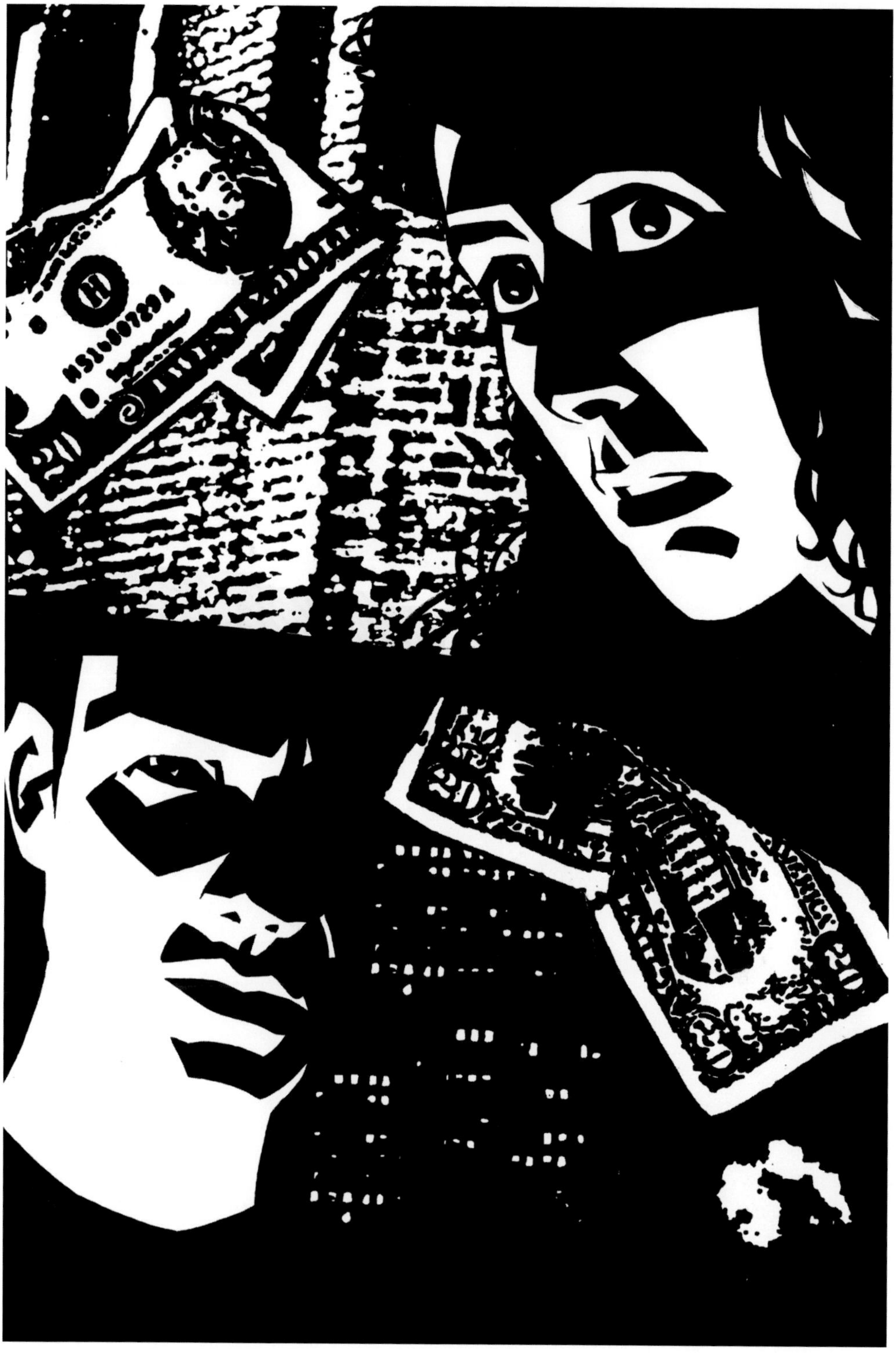

This is a design Mike and I did for promotion. A mixture of the *Jinx* animated look and the xerography collage of the original series. On the following page is the final design, with type. It was used as a full-color postcard.

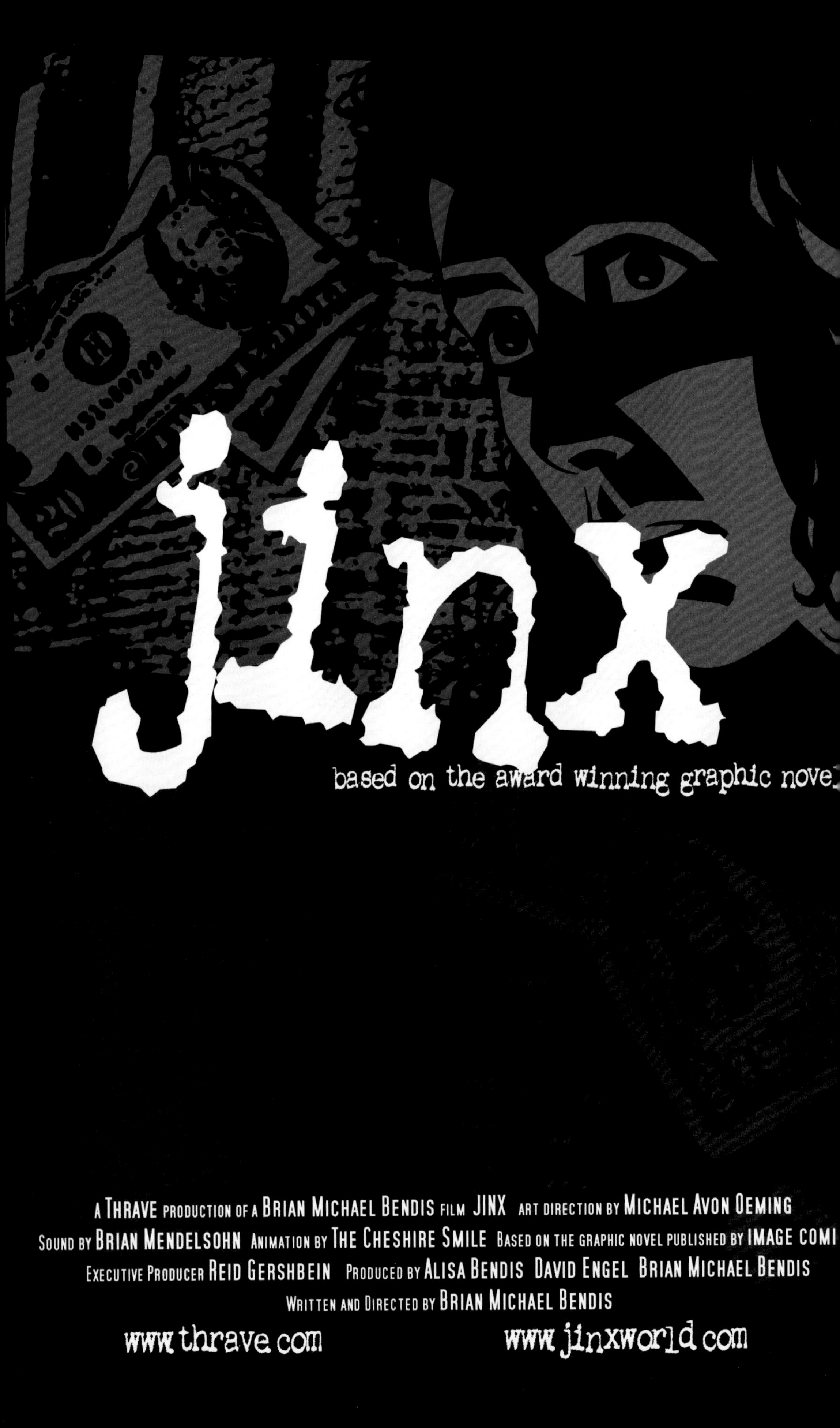
jinx
based on the award winning graphic novel
A THRAVE PRODUCTION OF A BRIAN MICHAEL BENDIS FILM JINX ART DIRECTION BY MICHAEL AVON OEMING
SOUND BY BRIAN MENDELSOHN ANIMATION BY THE CHESHIRE SMILE BASED ON THE GRAPHIC NOVEL PUBLISHED BY IMAGE COMI
EXECUTIVE PRODUCER REID GERSHBEIN PRODUCED BY ALISA BENDIS DAVID ENGEL BRIAN MICHAEL BENDIS
WRITTEN AND DIRECTED BY BRIAN MICHAEL BENDIS
www.thrave.com
www.jinxworld.com

jinx
the animated project

the script

On the following pages is the original screenplay for the two webisodes. It comprises the first couple of chapters of the graphic novel, though there are significant differences between the two.

AVON 5·00

JINX

Teaser script

by Brian Michael Bendis

FADE IN.

EXT. - DOWNTOWN CLEVELAND/ CITY STREET- DAY

Crazy crowded city street scene. Zoom in on...

COLUMBIA, (early 20's) a bald headed, leather jacketed pug,
is running a dice game in front of a trendy coffee shop.

He is entertaining a crowd of five. A couple of skateboard
punks, a guy in an apron, a jogger passing by, and a
Rastafarian.

DIALOGUE IS RAPID FIRE. MUSIC IS INDUSTRIAL RAP MUSIC PLAYING
FROM SOMEONES STEREO IN AN APARTMENT A BLOCK AWAY.

                    COLUMBIA
          What do I look like here- huh? United
          way? Salvation army? Common pappy, what's
          it going to be?

                    JOGGER
          What's the bet again?

                    COLUMBIA
          Even money. I say you won't slice a six
          before a seven or an eight before a
          seven. Your choice, see?

                    JOGGER
          WAIT- I have to roll a six or an eight
          before I roll a seven? I don't know.

                    COLUMBIA
          Alright, alright, alright. Fancy pants,
          Tell ya what: I'll reverse the bet. We'll
          switch sides.

                    JOGGER
          What?

                    COLUMBIA
          I'll- listen. Are you listening? I'll
          roll the six or seven. I'll take it twice
          over, OK I say- I say I'll slam a six and
          an eight before I hit two sevens.

                                        (CONTINUED

CONTINUED:

                        RASTAFARIAN
          No way.

                      SKATE BOARD KID
          You're high.

                     SKATE BOARD KID 2
          Take the bet.

The apron wearer tosses some bills down. A couple of others
go for their wallets and pockets. The other start tossing
bills down

Columbia eyes the cash pile as he shakes the dice.

                         COLUMBIA
          Stand back and watch the magic that is
          me.

Columbia tosses the dice. THE DICE FLY. The dice lands. It's
a seven. The circle looks down on the dice. Everyone but
Columbia smiles.

                        RASTAFARIAN
          Ha ha! What are the odds of that?

Columbia shakes the dice in his hand, serious and worried

                         COLUMBIA
          Six to five.

The dice fly. The dice land. Another seven.

The circle looks down. Columbia turns white as a ghost. The
rest of the crowd erupts in cheers.

                          JOGGER
          Ah ha-ha!! god damn!! I won. I never win
          anything!! I thought you street LOSERS
          were supposed to be good at this.

Columbia scoops up the money BEFORE THE JOGGER CAN REACH IT.

                      JOGGER (CONT'D)
          Hand it over fester!

Columbia stands up to face the group. POINTING IN THE
JOGGER'S FACE.

                         COLUMBIA
                    (to jogger)
          Hold on, what? What did you call me?

                                              (CONTINUED

CONTINUED: (2)

                    JOGGER
          What?

                    COLUMBIA
          Say it again? What did you call me?

                    JOGGER
          That's our money! That's my money.

                    COLUMBIA
          What did you call me?

                    JOGGER
          You mean, loser?

                    COLUMBIA
          LOSER?

                    JOGGER
          YEAH! TOTAL LOSER!! A point you're
          proving for me.

                    COLUMBIA
          Well, let me tell you something here and
          now- I am not a loser-
               (BEAT)
          I am an incredibly sore loser.

Columbia turns tail and runs down the street at top speed.
The circle of marks watches incredulously.

                    JOGGER
          I can't believe he just did that.

INT. APARTMENT- SAME

A young and feisty black woman, Dana, paints her toes and
talks on a cordless at the same time. The apartment is a
tacky explosion of polka dots and patterns.

                    DANA
          Great pair of pumps. Great pair OF- nu-
          uh. Nope. Thirty five bucks. They go with
          the polka dot top that-

The door bell rings. Dana jumps knocking over the nail
polish.

                    DANA (CONT'D)
          SHIT no- hold on. I gotta. Shit!

                                        (CONTINUED

CONTINUED:

Dana keeps the tissues between her toes and hobbles over to the door. She peeps through the peephole. What she sees is curious.

                    DANA (CONT'D)
                 (into phone)
          Hold on. Someone there.

Dana opens the door. Standing in her hallway is JINX Alameda, but she is crying, tissue in hand, and six months pregnant.

                    JINX
          Is Rick here?

                    DANA
          Who might you be?

                    JINX
          Are you Becky?

                    DANA
          Yes.

                    JINX
          I- I need to talk to rick.

                    DANA
          Who are you?

JINX loses control- starts blubbering.

                    JINX
          I thought- I thought I was rick's
          girlfriend- but it seems that I'm just
          some tramp he FUCKED!!

Dana's mouth falls open. The voice on the phone is audible.

                    PHONE
          What? OOOOH shit!

                    JINX
                 (holding her belly)
          ...and now look at me!!

                    PHONE
          OH MY GOODN-

Dana hangs up the phone- her mouth agape.

                    Dana
          What you sayin'?

                                             (CONTINUED

CONTINUED: (2)

> JINX
> I - I don't know what to do? I'm all
> alone. I've got no one. Susie told me he
> might be here-

JINX blows her nose and cries again.

> JINX (CONT'D)
> I'm so ashamed.

Dana is telling into the phone.

> DANA
> Rick?!?!

> RICK
> (on phone)
> What now woman!

> DANA
> I'm going to fucking stab you in the
> neck!

> RICK
> (on phone)
> Better change that tone you-

Dana hangs the phone up.

EXT. DAY.

COLUMBIA IS RUNNING FOR HIS LIFE. BUT HE LOOKS LIKE HE IS
ENJOYING IT.

The circle run after him in at top speed. a stampede of anger
tearing after Columbia. Columbia turns a corner knocking a
woman on her ass.

> COLUMBIA
> OUTTA my way, able!!

The marks are gaining.

> RASTAFARIAN
> ASSHOLE!! You better run!!

Columbia turns another corner. And another corner. But-
Columbia's sneakers actually screech to a stop BECAUSE

...It's a dead end!

(CONTINUED

CONTINUED: (3)

Columbia turns around to face the music. All five marks are at the entrance of the alleyway. Columbia is trapped.

Columbia is gasping for air. So are the marks, except the jogger.

                    COLUMBIA
          Come on guys- it's only money.

The apron wearer picks up a piece of aluminum siding laying against the wall. He hoists it up like a bat.

                    APRON
          Yeah, but see- it's our money!

He lifts up the siding and whacks Columbia in the head with it. The sound of the connect is worse than the hurt.

                    JOGGER
          Hit em again! Hate this fucker!!!

Apron WHOPS Columbia in the back. Columbia loses his footing and fails to the ground. Apron raises the siding to take another whack

                    APRON
          Now, are you going to hand it over or-?

Apron turns isolette. Them back to normal lighting that silhouette again. Strobing light fills the alleyway, everyone turns to face the opening of the alleyway.

The strobing is abstracting everything. a lone figure, a man in as long coat, holding a pistol is standing right outside his car door. He is back lit to the strobing light on top of his squad car.

                    MAN
          Police!! Freeze.

Everyone drops whatever is in their hands. The siding and two skateboards fall to the ground. All hands reach for the sky.

                    JOGGER
          Officer, please! This isn't what you
          think. This guy-

                    MAN
          I know exactly what this is! But today is
          your lucky day. That bald headed prick's
          been workin' this beat for weeks.

          Today- we only want him.
                    (MORE)

                                             (CONTINUED

CONTINUED: (4)

                         MAN (CONT'D)

    So walk away now.

                    SKATE BOARD KID
         No, man, you don't understand this-

                         MAN
         ALRIGHT, UP AGAINST THE WALL!!

                    SKATE BOARD KID
         NO. No - we- we're going.

The apron and the Rastafarian are already on their way out
the door. The skateboarders and the jogger still hesitate.

                         JOGGER
         Bu -

The entire group disperses into the street quickly. Out of
sight. The backlit "officer" holds his position until
everyone has gone far enough away.

Columbia is dizzy and a little punch drunk. It takes him a
couple seconds to get his footing as he tries to stand.

The man pulls the power cord out of the strobing police siren
light on top of his car. He takes the light and tosses it
into the back seat of what we can now clearly see is a beat
up piece of SHIT mobile and not the unmarked police car we
imagined.

The man is not a cop at all, but a young (early 20's), thin,
fair haired, James Deenish guy named GOLDFISH.

FREEZE ON GOLDFISH'S ANNOYED FACE. THE WHITE PARTS OF THE
IMAGE TURN YELLOW. YELLOW AND BLACK.

SCROLL: GOLDFISH

GOLDFISH approaches Columbia and offers him a hand. Columbia
goes to take it, but GOLDFISH slaps his hand away. GOLDFISH
puts his hand back out. Columbia hesitates and drops the
crumbled wad of bills into his hands.

                         GOLDFISH
         Good boy.

Columbia has given up trying to stand for the meanwhile.

                         COLUMBIA
         Jesus! Jesus- GOLDFISH! Take a little
         longer next time.

GOLDFISH straightens and counts the bills.

                                                (CONTINUED

CONTINUED: (5)

>   GOLDFISH
> Trust me friend, if there was ever a guy
> who could use a little slapping around-
> it's you.

>   COLUMBIA
> I'm serious Goldfish. That- that was a
> FUCKING pipe. I could have-

>   GOLDFISH
> It's not a pipe. It's a piece of siding.
> It's like getting hit with a whiffle ball
> bat.

>   COLUMBIA
> What takes you so long?

>   GOLDFISH
> Hey, listen. You're the guy who wants to
> run these kind of cons. You don't want to
> actually learn how to do the dice or spin
> a card.

Columbia finally gets to his feet. GOLDFISH COUNTS THE BILLS.

>   GOLDFISH (CONT'D)
> You don't see me getting my ass spanked
> every other day. Learn a trade. Or hey-
> here a notion. Buy loaded dice like every
> other red blooded American short con
> street hustler..

>   COLUMBIA
> Loaded dice? Where's the skill in that?

FREEZE ON COLUMBIA'S ANNOYED FACE. The white parts of the
image turn blue. Blue and black.

SCROLL: COLUMBIA

INT. DANA'S APARTMENT.

Rick, a straggly haired white guy bursts through the door.
All testosterone and vinegar.

>   RICK
> What the fuck woman?!?!

>   DANA
> Shut your mouth you cheatin' muther
> Fucker!!

                              (CONTINUED

CONTINUED: (6)

Dana points to JINX.

> DANA (CONT'D)
> Who the fuck is that???

JINX is crying into her tissue. She is hunched over crying.
Rick doesn't know what is going on.

He is looking at the hunched over pregnant woman, he is
confused.

> RICK
> I don't know. Who is this?

> DANA
> You tell me ASSHOLE

> RICK
> I've never seen this bitch before in my
> life!!

Rick looks at her. JINX looks up at him.

She hasn't been crying. She has a steely glare. She locks
right onto rick. Dana is confused. Rick knows that his gig is
up

> RICK (CONT'D)
> UH oh.

JINX stands up. She pulls a big sweatshirt out from under her
shirt. She isn't pregnant at all. IN place of the baby, Her
magmum44 is VISIBLE sticking out FROM BETWEEN HER PANTS AND
HER RIPPED STOMACH.

> JINX
> RICKY RICKETTS- you're out on bail for
> attempted armed robbery. You skipped that
> bail. You broke your bond.

She points to the gun sticking out of her pants. IT GLEAMS.

> JINX (CONT'D)
> I'm here to collect you. Shall we?

Rick starts yelling at Dana.

> RICK
> You stupid bitch!! I - I can't fucking
> believe you!!

> DANA
> What's going on?

(CONTINUED

                   RICK
       Stupid!

Rick makes a run for the door.

Money b. BIG BLACK FELLOW. HIS Huge frame fills the entire
door frame. He has his piece out. He is ready for trouble.

                 MONEY B
      This the guy?

                 JINX
      That's the guy.

Dana screams like a scream queen.

                 DANA
     AAAAAAAIIIII!

                 RICK
     Shut up! Shut up you!! BITCH!! WHORE!!
     FUCKING CUN-

Rick turns again, but into JINX sticking her gun right into
HIS nose mid word.

                 JINX
     Ah ah ah. Now that kind of talk I can do
     without all together.

MONEY B grabbed rick ROUGH and cuffs him.

              JINX (CONT'D)
     You got em?

                 MONEY B
     I got em.

MONEY B drags rick out the door. Dana is much drunk from all
of this. JINX turns to console her. She is sincere.

                 JINX
     Listen, honey. Sorry about this. Truly.
     But trust me. I just did you the biggest
     favor of your life. It's like what my mom
     told me the day she bailed on my dad. She
     said to me- she said: "honey, men are
     like cars, no matter how big a piece of
     shit the one you got turns out to be--
     you can always trade up."

JINX is out the door- turns to wave.

                                   (CONTINUED

CONTINUED: (8)

FREEZE ON JINX'S FACE. The white parts of the image turn red.
Red and black.

SCROLL: JINX

                         JINX (CONT'D)
          T.T.F.N

PUNCH FADE TO BLACK.

CREDITS. MUSIC CUE

INT. RED STAR CAFE- SAME

GOLDFISH AND COLUMBIA walk into the fifties style diner. Half
full of party people and late shifters.

Something in the fare corner of the small diner catches
GOLDFISH eye.

He stares awestruck. Columbia's doesn't understand what he is
looking at.

180 pan. We see what GOLDFISH sees. The raven haired JINX.
She sits in the back table. She is writing into a notebook. a
steaming cup of tea on her table. Her arms bare in a black
tank top.

GOLDFISH stares JINX writes in her book. She feels the eyes
on her. She looks up. Warm and inviting. Her big black eyes.

                         GOLDFISH
          Wow.

SCROLL: COMING SOON.

THE GALLERY

During the course of the original series, many of my friends contributed gallery pieces. These were done either for fun or to contribute to the *Jinx* charity special.

I truly believe that the following pages display some of the finest talent of this generation of comic book artists. I hope that you will memorize their names and support whatever title you see them on in the future.

You will also find some odds and ends by me. A little glimpse into some of my favorite xerography work on the series.

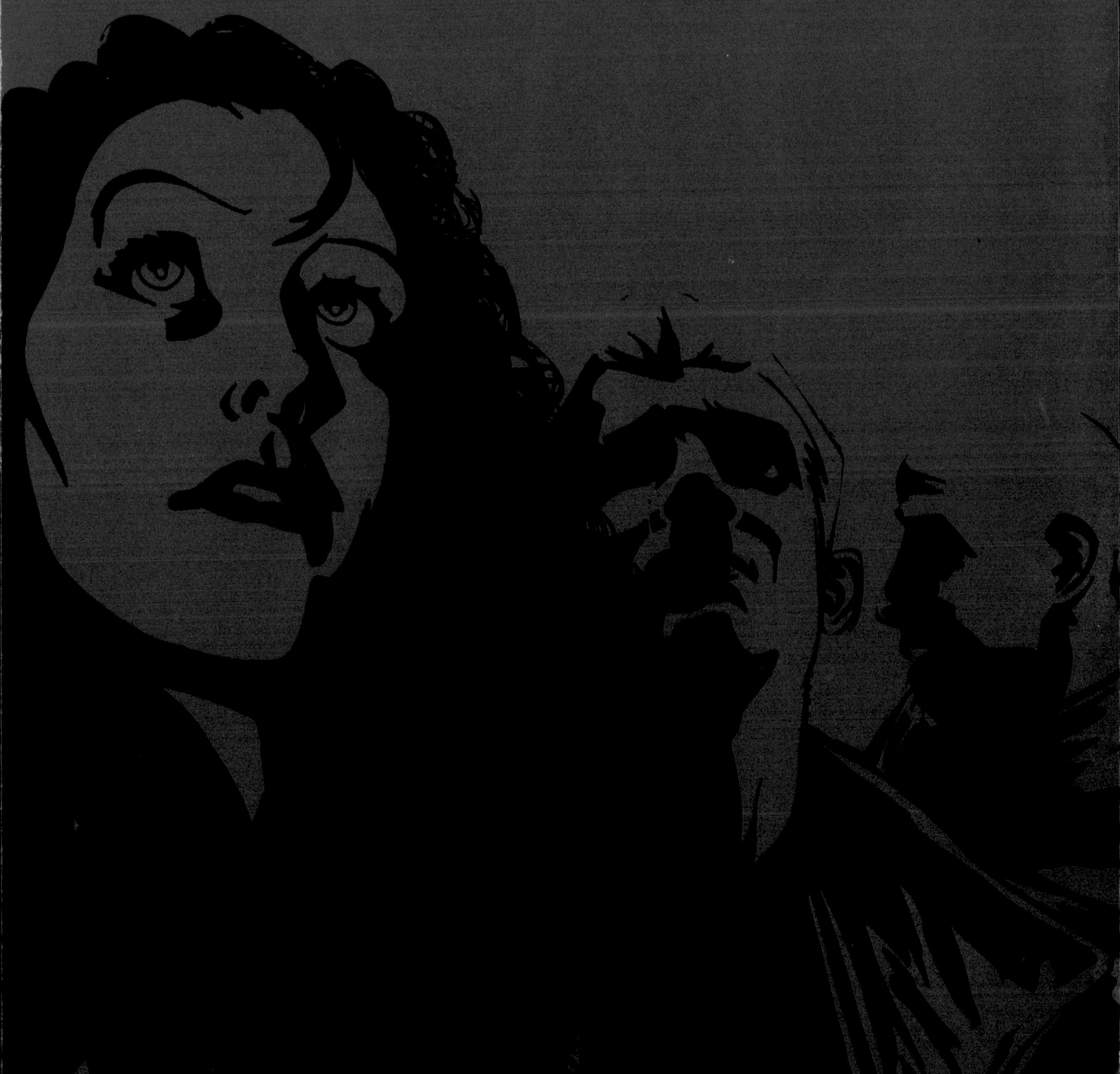

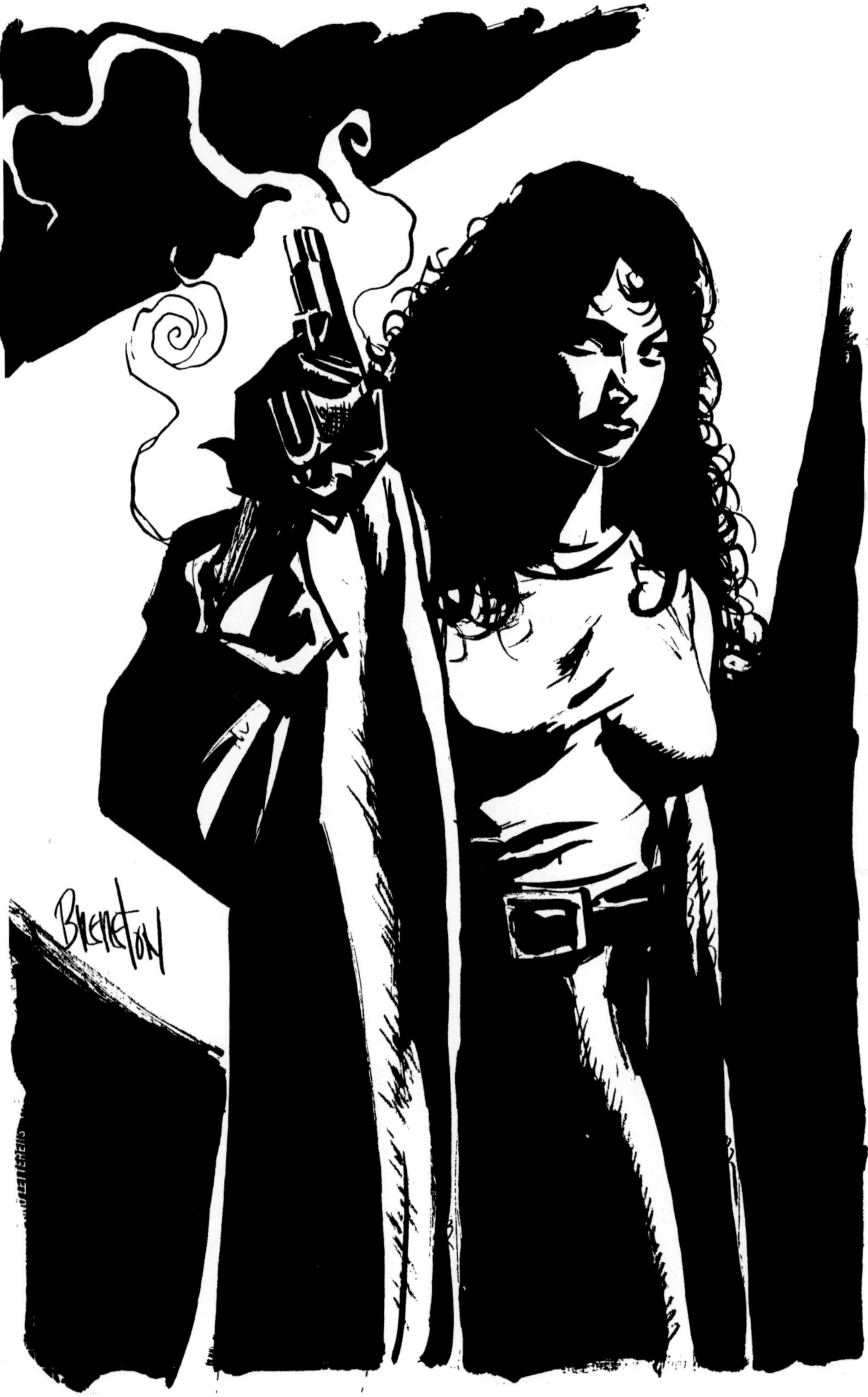
BRERETON

PINUP BY **DAN BRERETON**

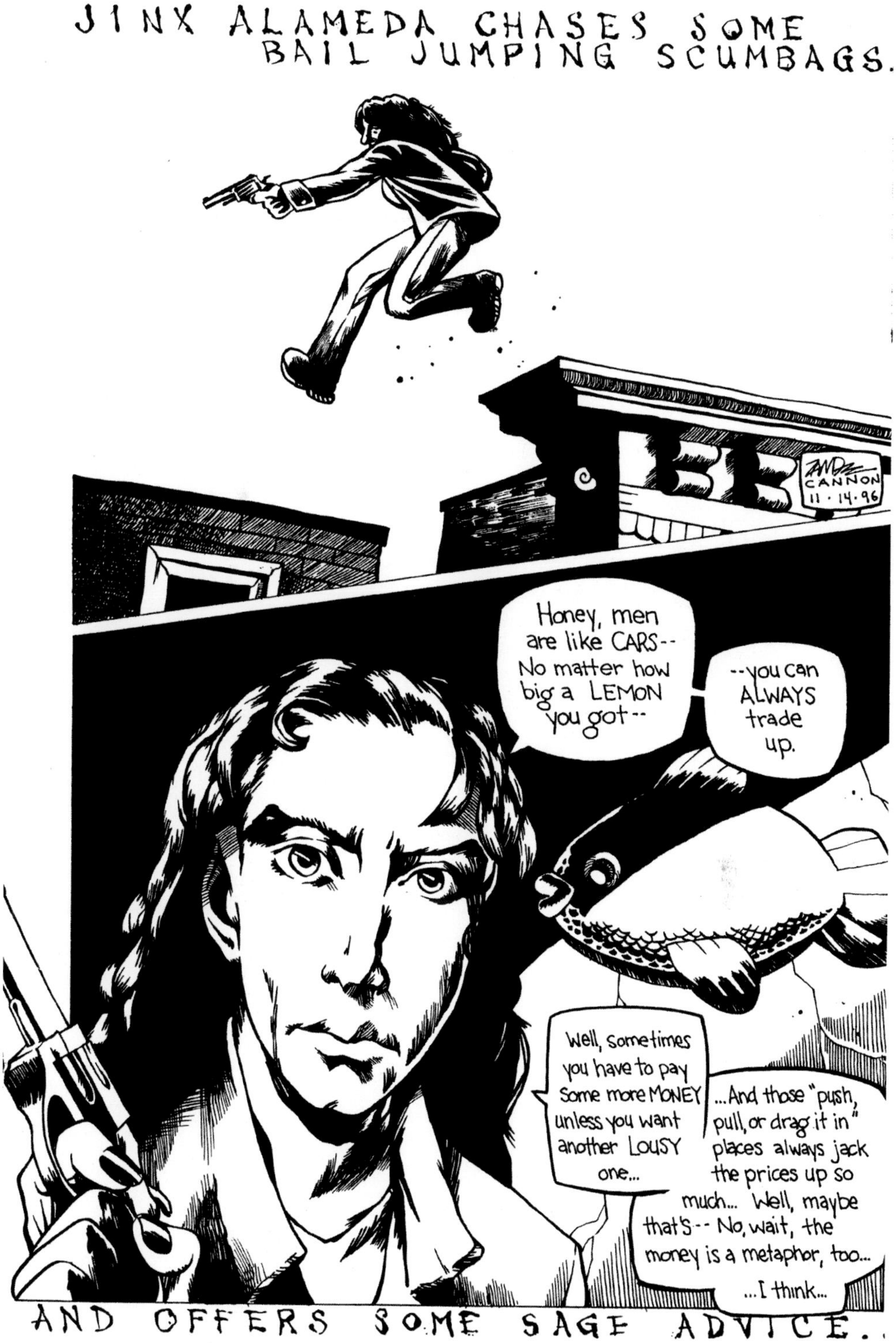
JINX ALAMEDA CHASES SOME BAIL JUMPING SCUMBAGS.
ZANDER CANNON 11·14·96
Honey, men are like CARS-- No matter how big a LEMON you got--
--you can ALWAYS trade up.
Well, sometimes you have to pay some more MONEY unless you want another LOUSY one...
...And those "push, pull, or drag it in" places always jack the prices up so much... Well, maybe that's-- No, wait, the money is a metaphor, too... ...I think...
AND OFFERS SOME SAGE ADVICE...

PINUP BY **ZANDER CANNON**

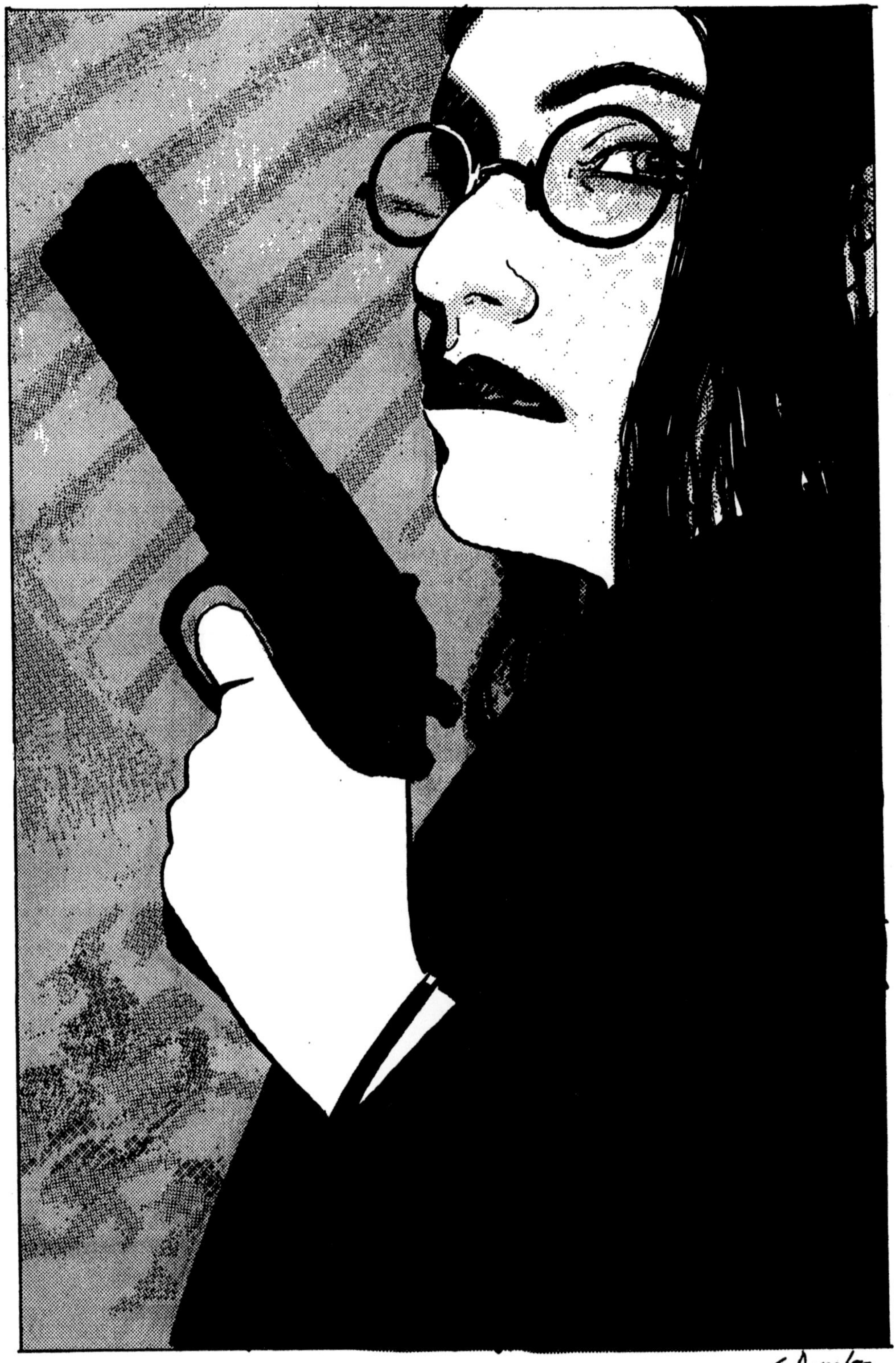

PINUP BY **GUY DAVIS**

WHAT'S REALLY ON THE MIND OF THE INSCRUTABLE JINX?

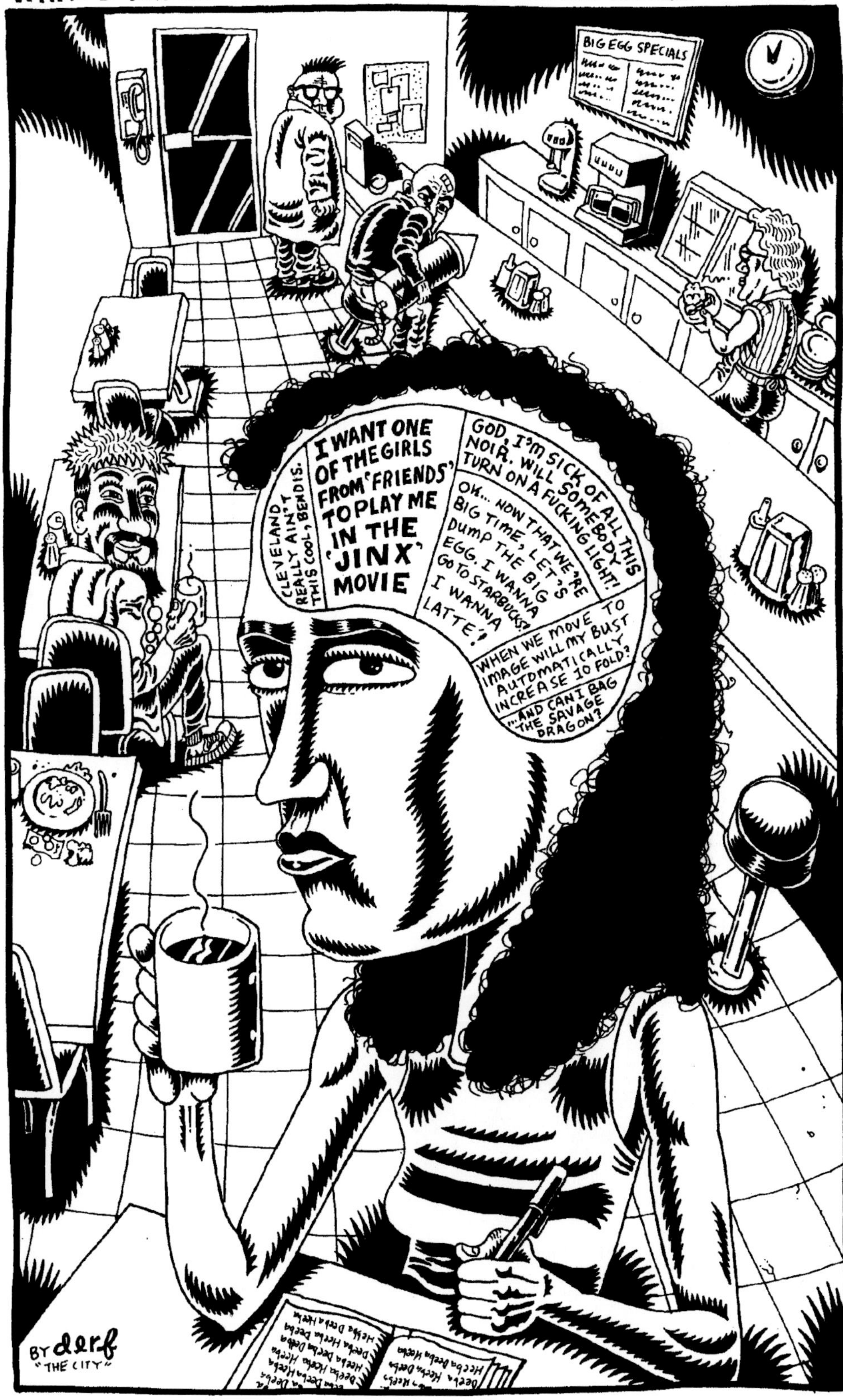

BIG EGG SPECIALS
CLEVELAND REALLY AIN'T THIS COOL, BENDIS.
I WANT ONE OF THE GIRLS FROM 'FRIENDS' TO PLAY ME IN THE 'JINX' MOVIE
GOD, I'M SICK OF ALL THIS NOIR. WILL SOMEBODY TURN ON A FUCKING LIGHT!
OK... NOW THAT WE'RE BIG TIME, LET'S DUMP THE BIG EGG. I WANNA GO TO STARBUCKS! I WANNA LATTE'!
WHEN WE MOVE TO IMAGE WILL MY BUST AUTOMATICALLY INCREASE 10 FOLD?
...AND CAN I BAG THE SAVAGE DRAGON?
BY derf "THE CITY"

PINUP BY **DERF BACKDERF**

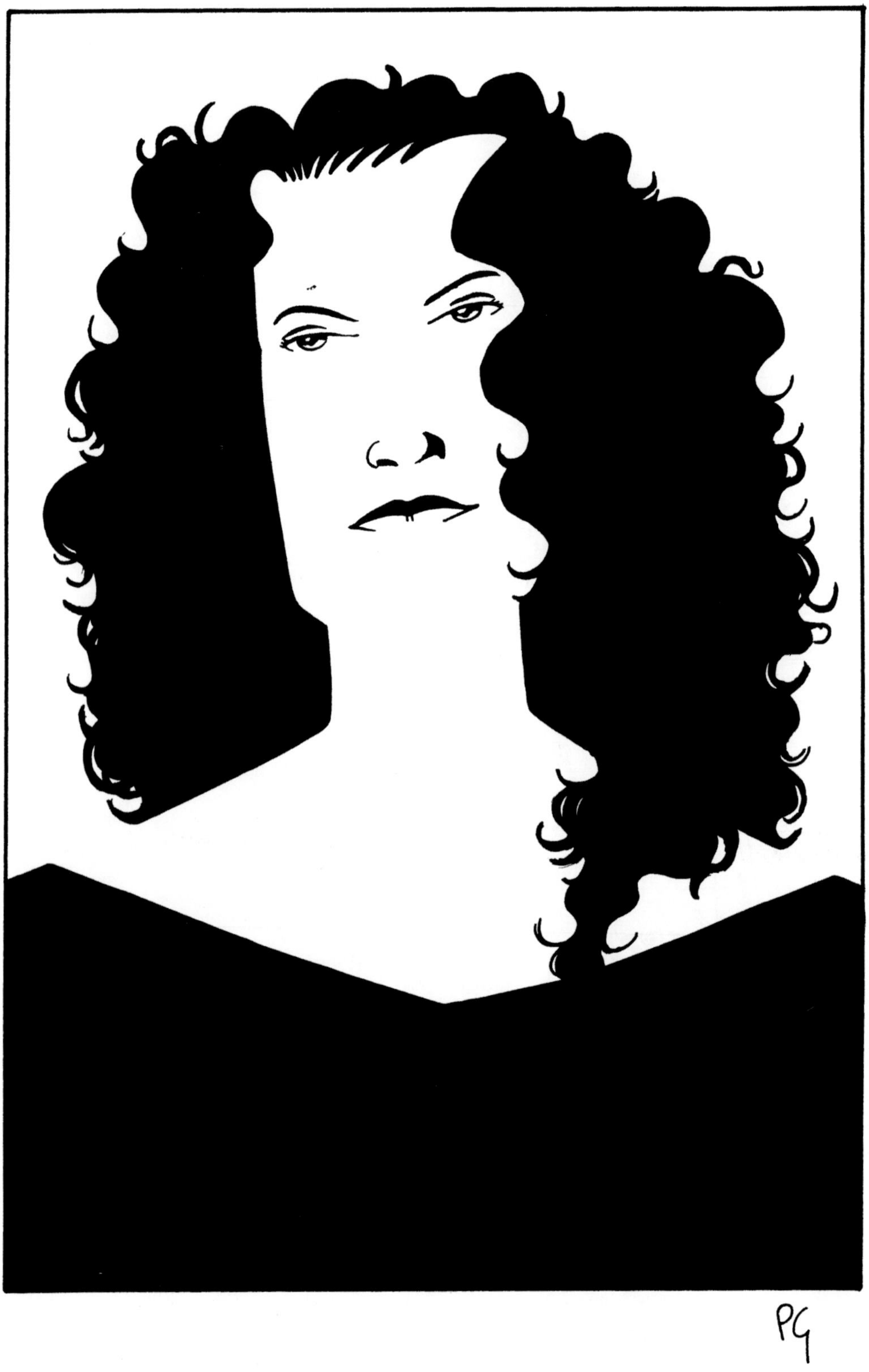
PG

PINUP BY **PAUL GRIST**

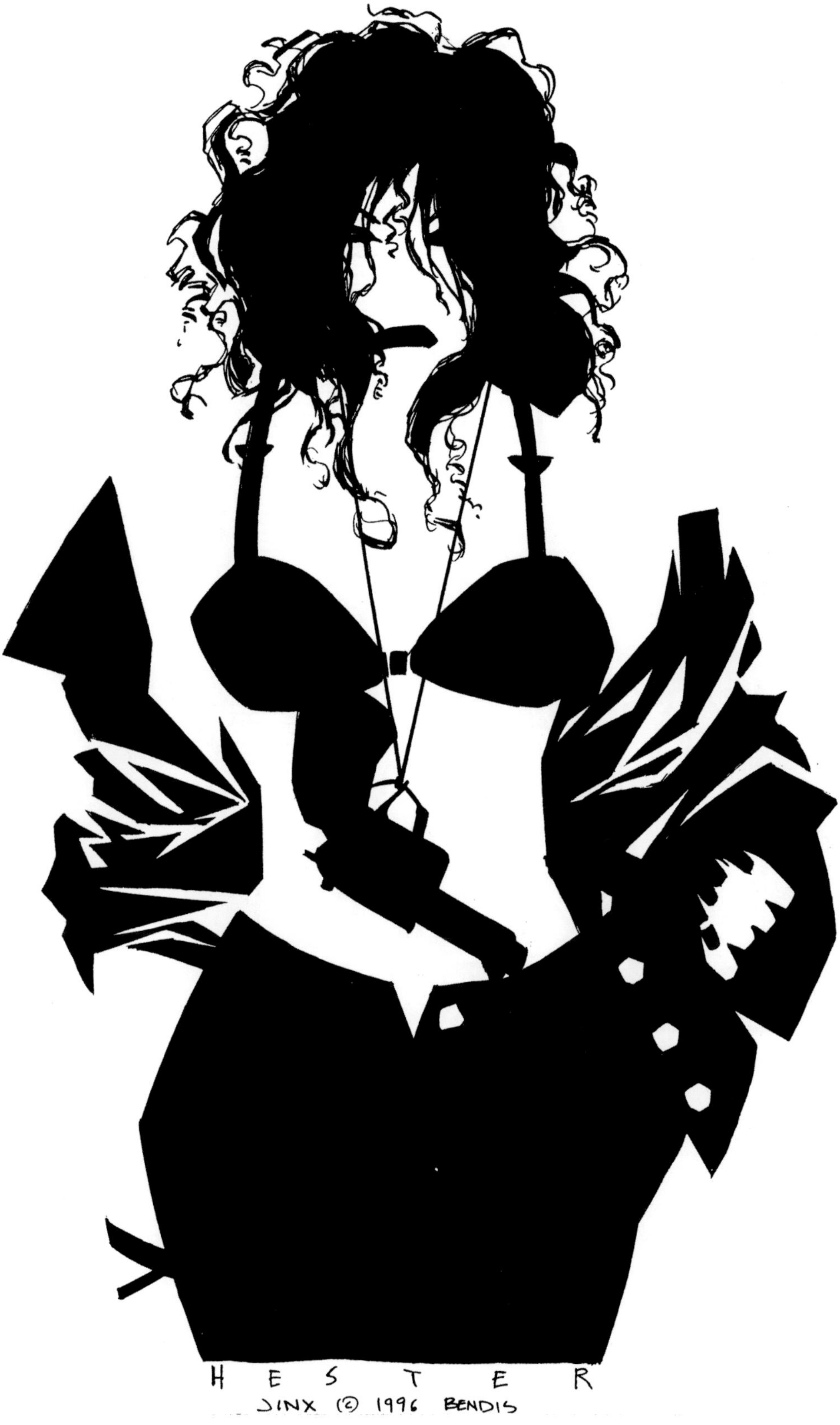
HESTER
JINX © 1996 BENDIS

PINUP BY **PHIL HESTER**

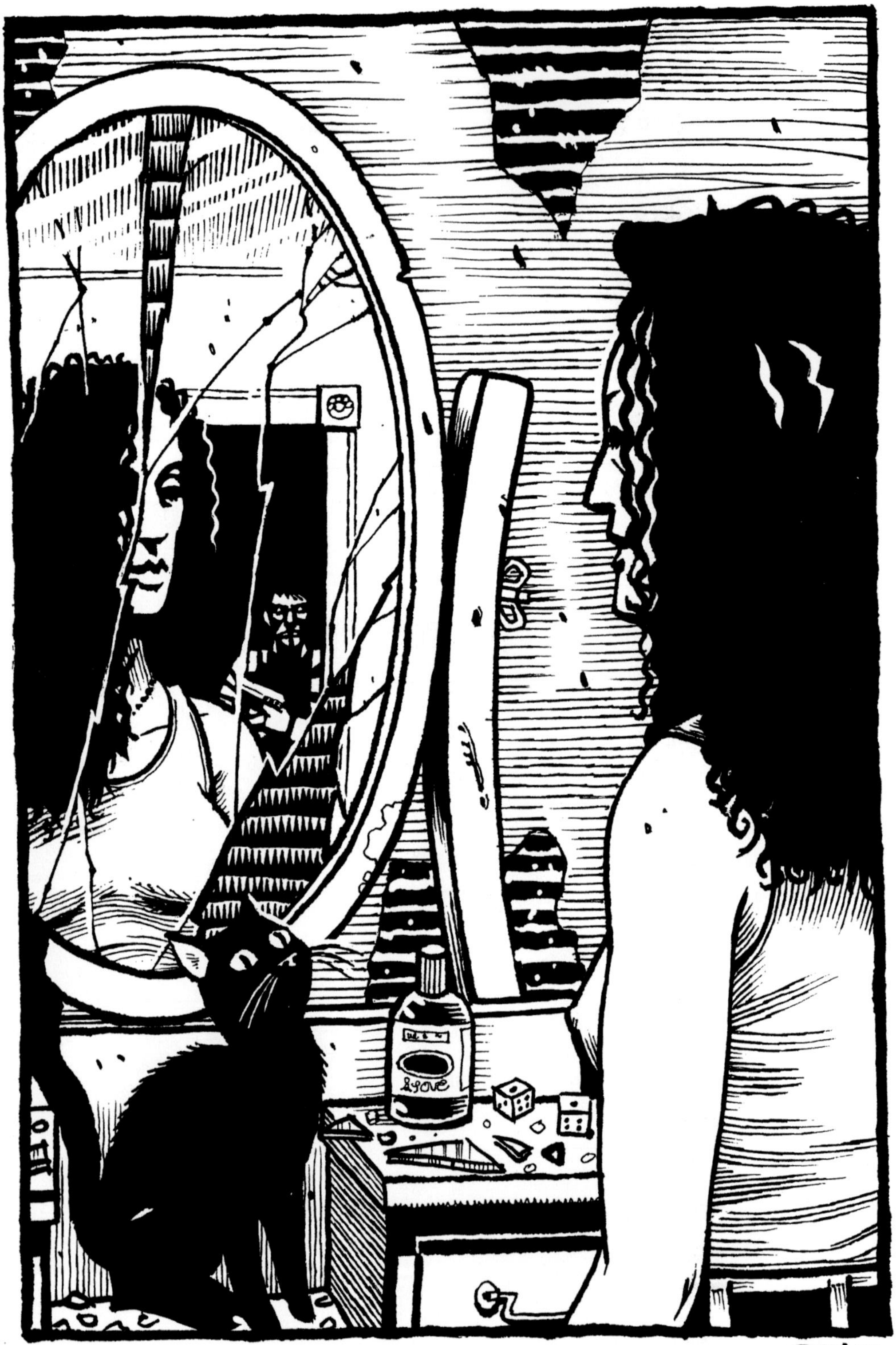
JINX
BEM96©

PINUP BY **BERNIE MIREAULT**

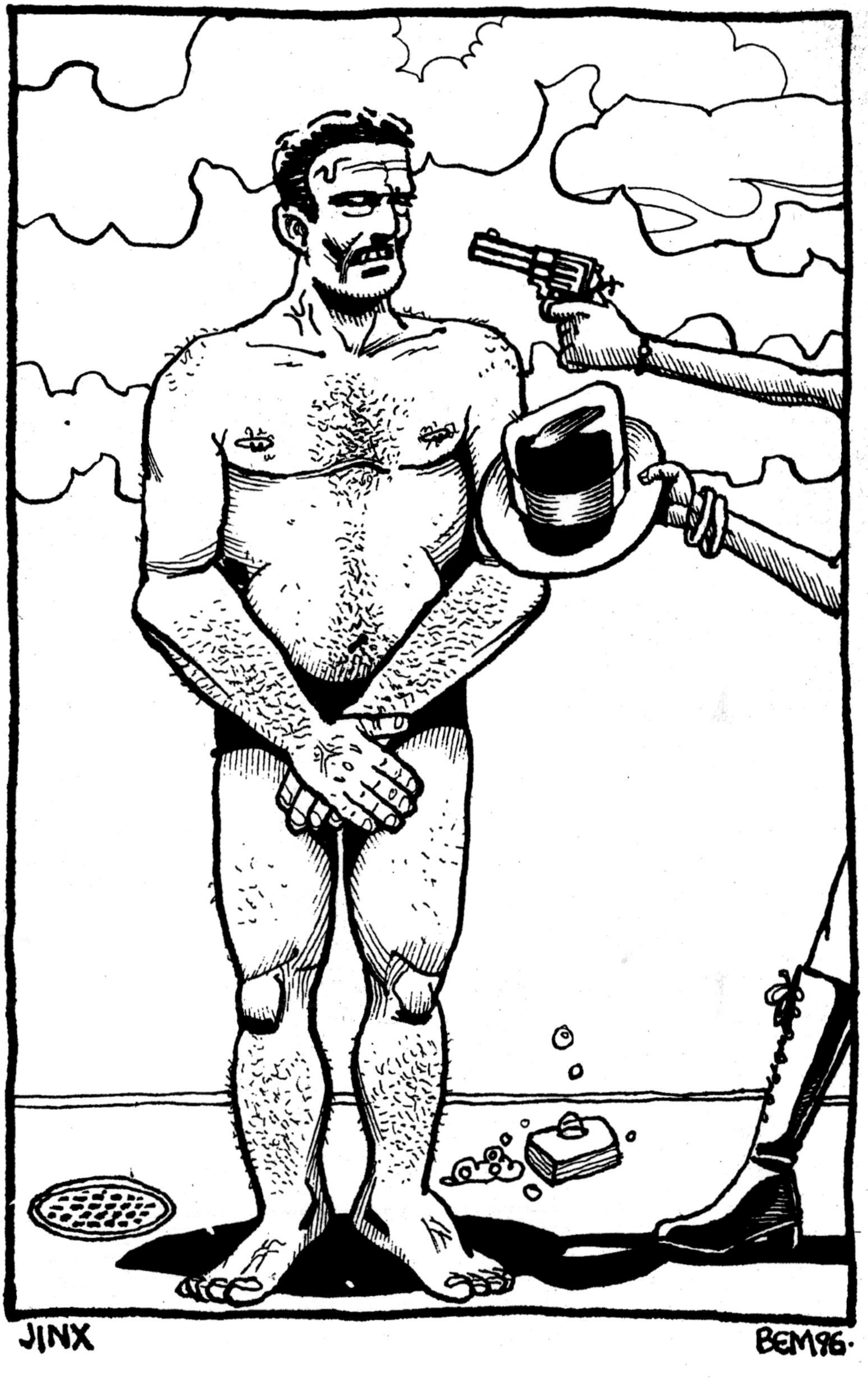
JINX
BEM96.

PINUP BY **BERNIE MIREAULT**

Longshot Comics

Douglas Gethers' Worst Job Yet

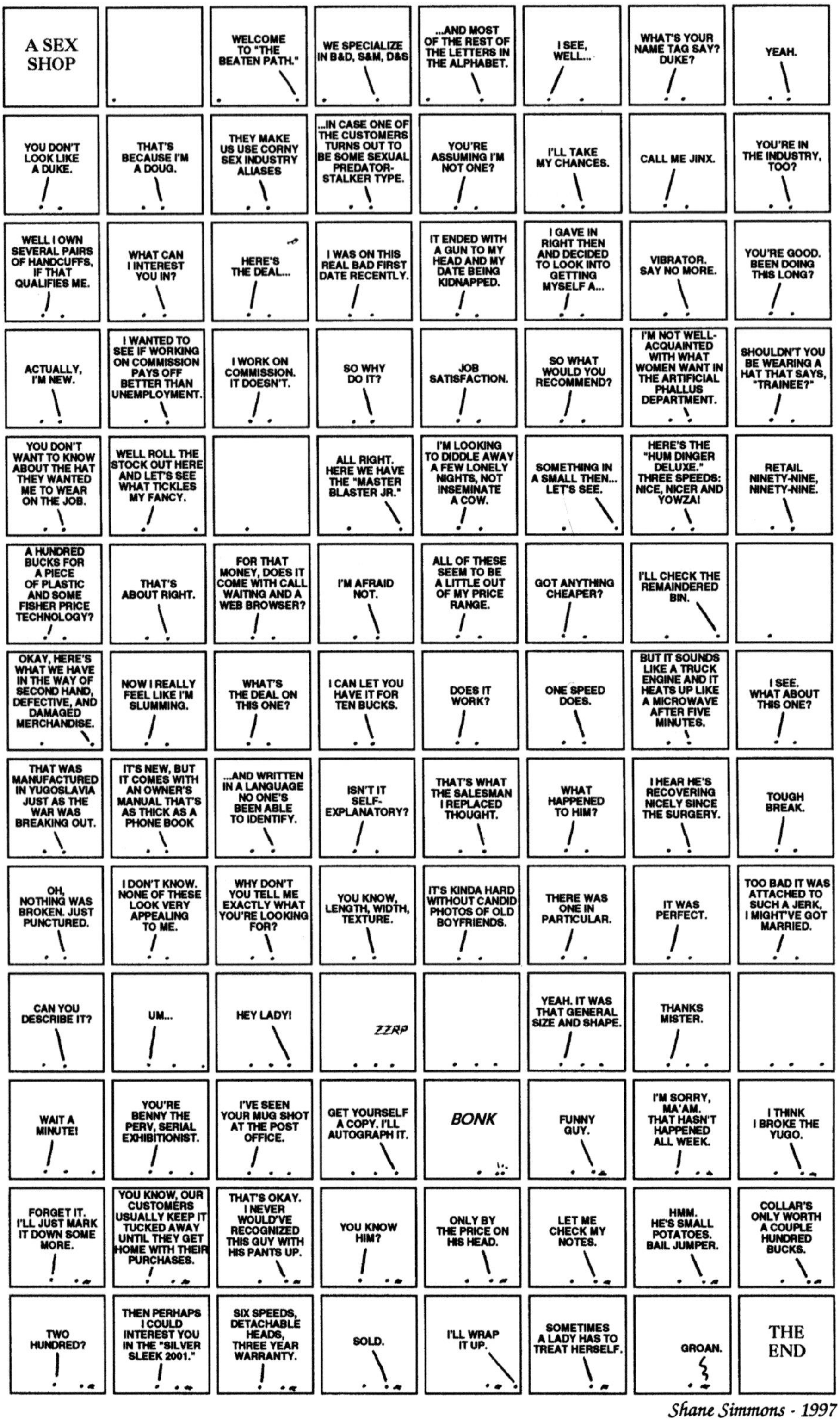
A SEX SHOP
WELCOME TO "THE BEATEN PATH."
WE SPECIALIZE IN B&D, S&M, D&S
...AND MOST OF THE REST OF THE LETTERS IN THE ALPHABET.
I SEE, WELL...
WHAT'S YOUR NAME TAG SAY? DUKE?
YEAH.
YOU DON'T LOOK LIKE A DUKE.
THAT'S BECAUSE I'M A DOUG.
THEY MAKE US USE CORNY SEX INDUSTRY ALIASES
...IN CASE ONE OF THE CUSTOMERS TURNS OUT TO BE SOME SEXUAL PREDATOR-STALKER TYPE.
YOU'RE ASSUMING I'M NOT ONE?
I'LL TAKE MY CHANCES.
CALL ME JINX.
YOU'RE IN THE INDUSTRY, TOO?
WELL I OWN SEVERAL PAIRS OF HANDCUFFS, IF THAT QUALIFIES ME.
WHAT CAN I INTEREST YOU IN?
HERE'S THE DEAL...
I WAS ON THIS REAL BAD FIRST DATE RECENTLY.
IT ENDED WITH A GUN TO MY HEAD AND MY DATE BEING KIDNAPPED.
I GAVE IN RIGHT THEN AND DECIDED TO LOOK INTO GETTING MYSELF A...
VIBRATOR. SAY NO MORE.
YOU'RE GOOD. BEEN DOING THIS LONG?
ACTUALLY, I'M NEW.
I WANTED TO SEE IF WORKING ON COMMISSION PAYS OFF BETTER THAN UNEMPLOYMENT.
I WORK ON COMMISSION. IT DOESN'T.
SO WHY DO IT?
JOB SATISFACTION.
SO WHAT WOULD YOU RECOMMEND?
I'M NOT WELL-ACQUAINTED WITH WHAT WOMEN WANT IN THE ARTIFICIAL PHALLUS DEPARTMENT.
SHOULDN'T YOU BE WEARING A HAT THAT SAYS, "TRAINEE?"
YOU DON'T WANT TO KNOW ABOUT THE HAT THEY WANTED ME TO WEAR ON THE JOB.
WELL ROLL THE STOCK OUT HERE AND LET'S SEE WHAT TICKLES MY FANCY.
ALL RIGHT. HERE WE HAVE THE "MASTER BLASTER JR."
I'M LOOKING TO DIDDLE AWAY A FEW LONELY NIGHTS, NOT INSEMINATE A COW.
SOMETHING IN A SMALL THEN... LET'S SEE.
HERE'S THE "HUM DINGER DELUXE." THREE SPEEDS: NICE, NICER AND YOWZA!
RETAIL NINETY-NINE, NINETY-NINE.
A HUNDRED BUCKS FOR A PIECE OF PLASTIC AND SOME FISHER PRICE TECHNOLOGY?
THAT'S ABOUT RIGHT.
FOR THAT MONEY, DOES IT COME WITH CALL WAITING AND A WEB BROWSER?
I'M AFRAID NOT.
ALL OF THESE SEEM TO BE A LITTLE OUT OF MY PRICE RANGE.
GOT ANYTHING CHEAPER?
I'LL CHECK THE REMAINDERED BIN.
OKAY, HERE'S WHAT WE HAVE IN THE WAY OF SECOND HAND, DEFECTIVE, AND DAMAGED MERCHANDISE.
NOW I REALLY FEEL LIKE I'M SLUMMING.
WHAT'S THE DEAL ON THIS ONE?
I CAN LET YOU HAVE IT FOR TEN BUCKS.
DOES IT WORK?
ONE SPEED DOES.
BUT IT SOUNDS LIKE A TRUCK ENGINE AND IT HEATS UP LIKE A MICROWAVE AFTER FIVE MINUTES.
I SEE. WHAT ABOUT THIS ONE?
THAT WAS MANUFACTURED IN YUGOSLAVIA JUST AS THE WAR WAS BREAKING OUT.
IT'S NEW, BUT IT COMES WITH AN OWNER'S MANUAL THAT'S AS THICK AS A PHONE BOOK
...AND WRITTEN IN A LANGUAGE NO ONE'S BEEN ABLE TO IDENTIFY.
ISN'T IT SELF-EXPLANATORY?
THAT'S WHAT THE SALESMAN I REPLACED THOUGHT.
WHAT HAPPENED TO HIM?
I HEAR HE'S RECOVERING NICELY SINCE THE SURGERY.
TOUGH BREAK.
OH, NOTHING WAS BROKEN. JUST PUNCTURED.
I DON'T KNOW. NONE OF THESE LOOK VERY APPEALING TO ME.
WHY DON'T YOU TELL ME EXACTLY WHAT YOU'RE LOOKING FOR?
YOU KNOW, LENGTH, WIDTH, TEXTURE.
IT'S KINDA HARD WITHOUT CANDID PHOTOS OF OLD BOYFRIENDS.
THERE WAS ONE IN PARTICULAR.
IT WAS PERFECT.
TOO BAD IT WAS ATTACHED TO SUCH A JERK, I MIGHT'VE GOT MARRIED.
CAN YOU DESCRIBE IT?
UM...
HEY LADY!
ZZRP
YEAH. IT WAS THAT GENERAL SIZE AND SHAPE.
THANKS MISTER.
WAIT A MINUTE!
YOU'RE BENNY THE PERV, SERIAL EXHIBITIONIST.
I'VE SEEN YOUR MUG SHOT AT THE POST OFFICE.
GET YOURSELF A COPY. I'LL AUTOGRAPH IT.
BONK
FUNNY GUY.
I'M SORRY, MA'AM. THAT HASN'T HAPPENED ALL WEEK.
I THINK I BROKE THE YUGO.
FORGET IT. I'LL JUST MARK IT DOWN SOME MORE.
YOU KNOW, OUR CUSTOMERS USUALLY KEEP IT TUCKED AWAY UNTIL THEY GET HOME WITH THEIR PURCHASES.
THAT'S OKAY. I NEVER WOULD'VE RECOGNIZED THIS GUY WITH HIS PANTS UP.
YOU KNOW HIM?
ONLY BY THE PRICE ON HIS HEAD.
LET ME CHECK MY NOTES.
HMM. HE'S SMALL POTATOES. BAIL JUMPER.
COLLAR'S ONLY WORTH A COUPLE HUNDRED BUCKS.
TWO HUNDRED?
THEN PERHAPS I COULD INTEREST YOU IN THE "SILVER SLEEK 2001."
SIX SPEEDS, DETACHABLE HEADS, THREE YEAR WARRANTY.
SOLD.
I'LL WRAP IT UP.
SOMETIMES A LADY HAS TO TREAT HERSELF.
GROAN.
THE END
Shane Simmons - 1997

PINUP BY SHANE SIMMONS

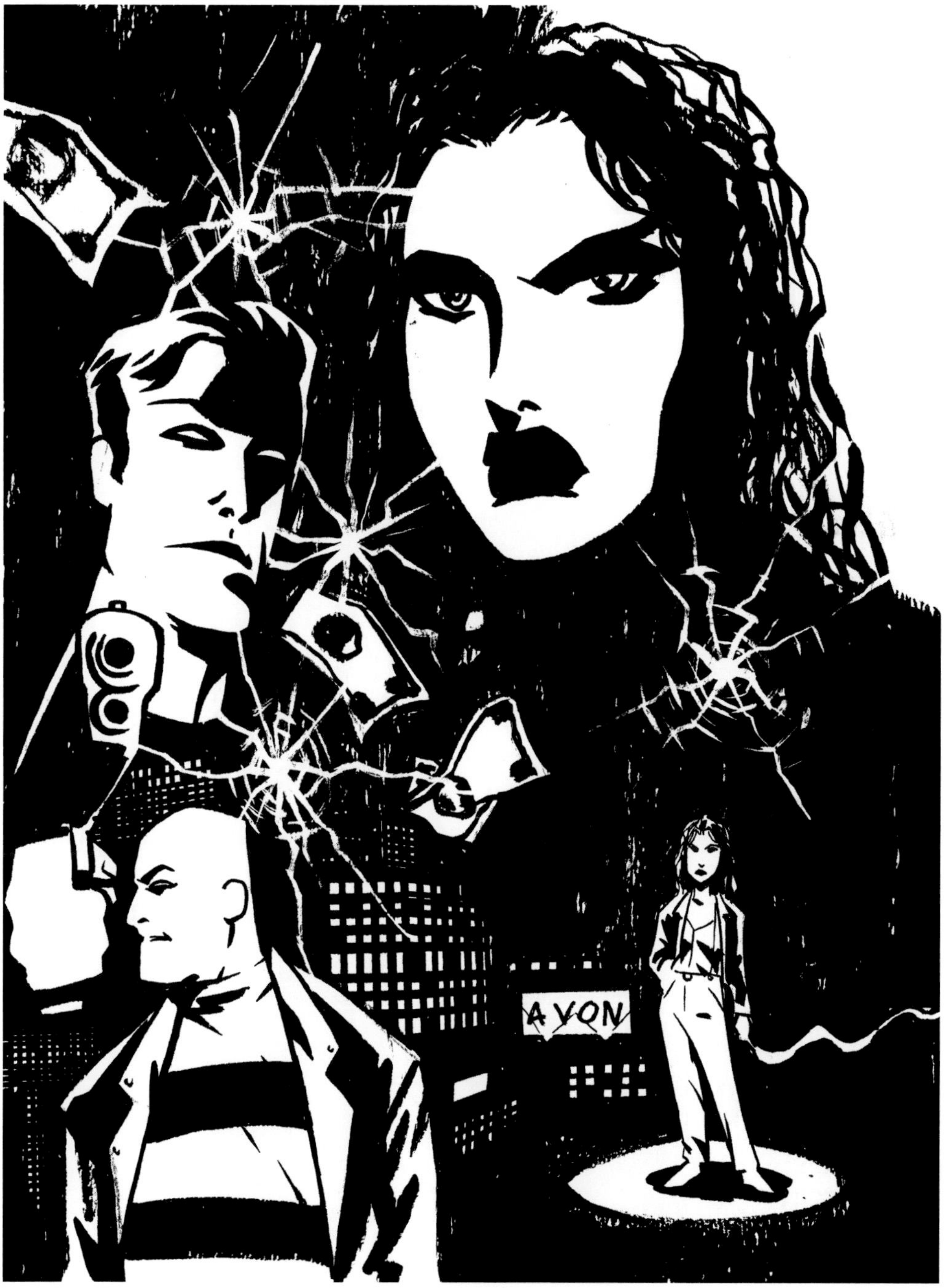
AVON

PINUP BY **MICHAEL AVON OEMING**

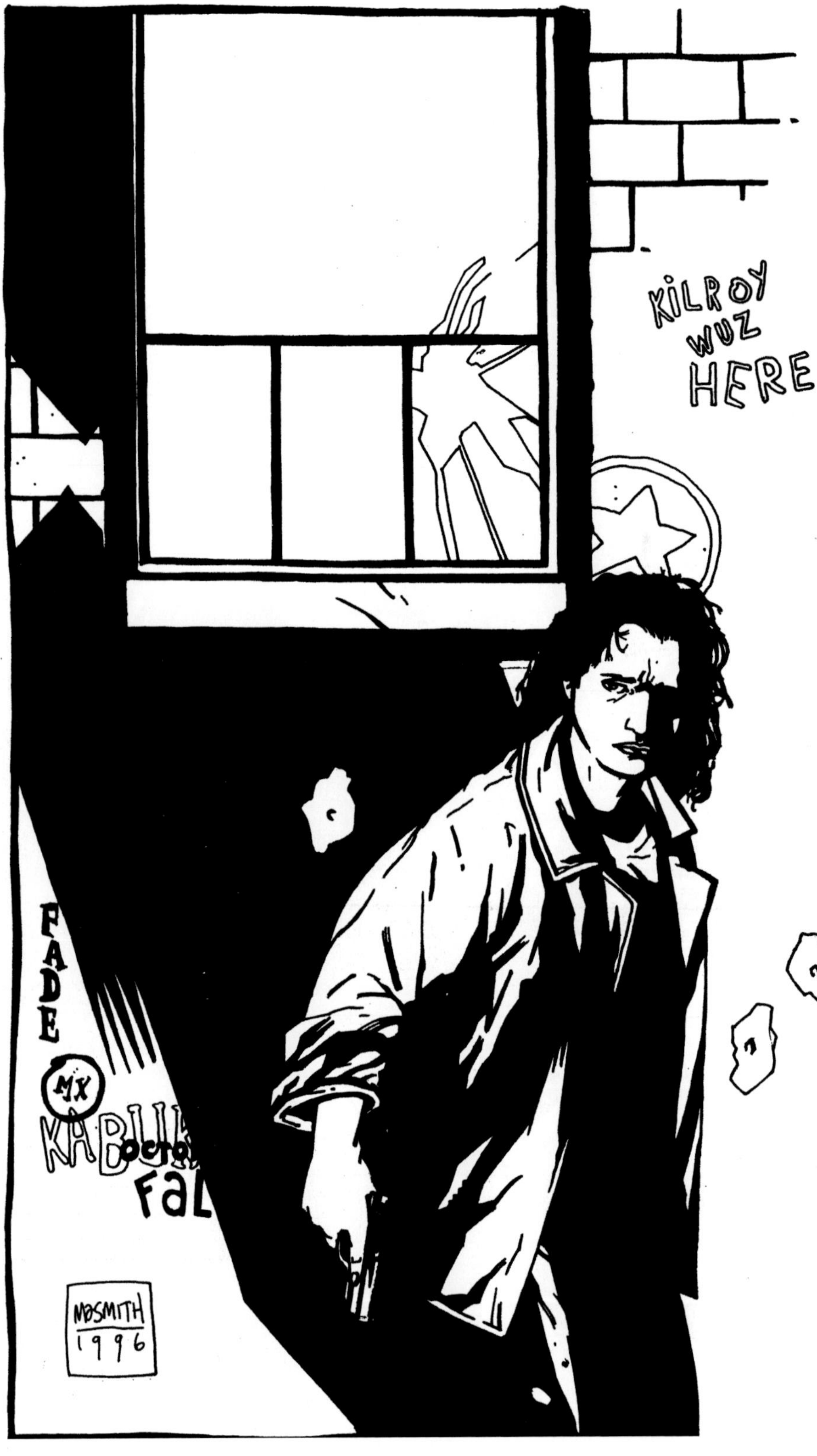
KILROY
WUZ
HERE
FADE
MX
MBSMITH
1996

PINUP BY **MATTHEW SMITH**

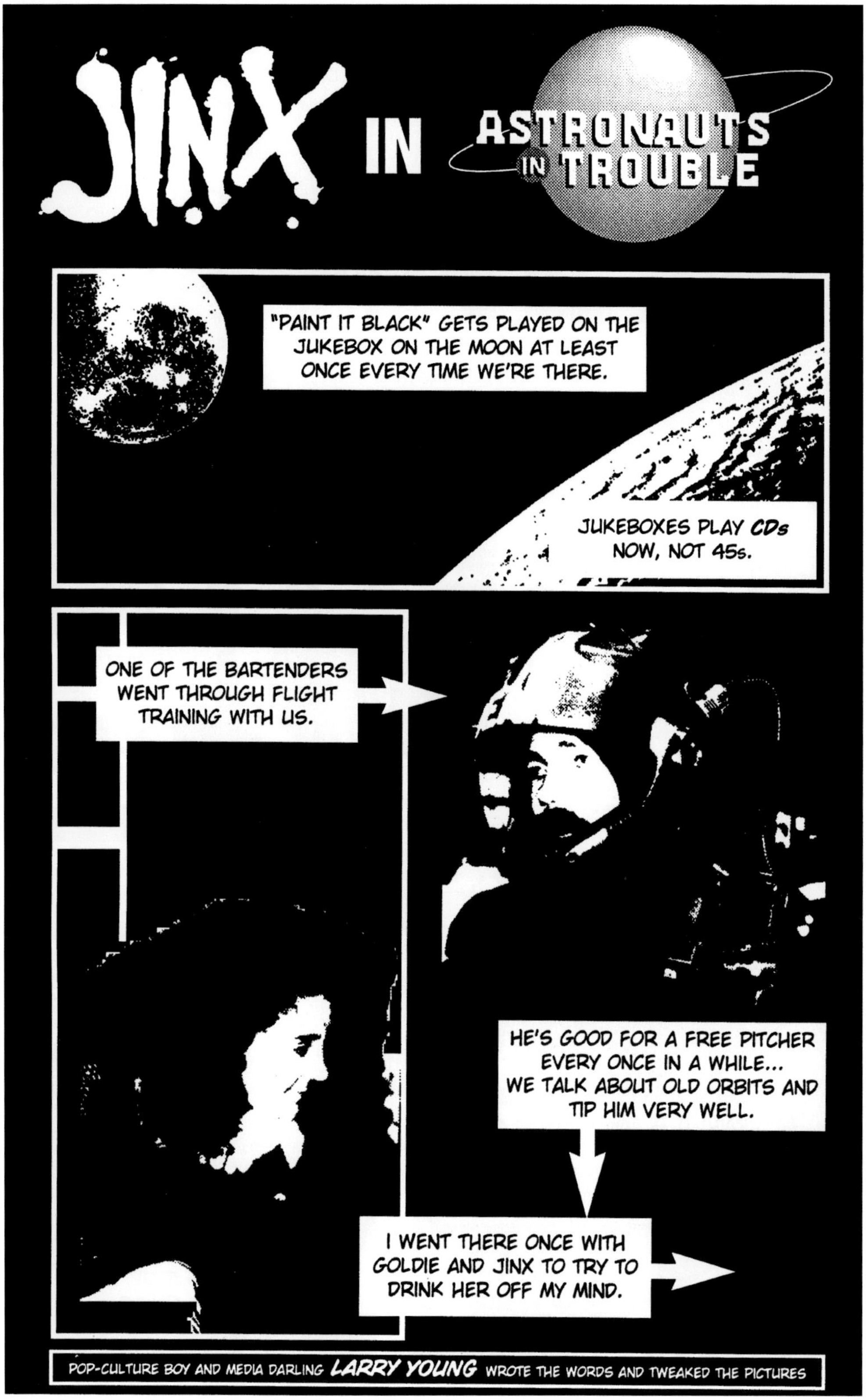
JINX IN
ASTRONAUTS IN TROUBLE
"PAINT IT BLACK" GETS PLAYED ON THE JUKEBOX ON THE MOON AT LEAST ONCE EVERY TIME WE'RE THERE.
JUKEBOXES PLAY *CDs* NOW, NOT 45s.
ONE OF THE BARTENDERS WENT THROUGH FLIGHT TRAINING WITH US.
HE'S GOOD FOR A FREE PITCHER EVERY ONCE IN A WHILE... WE TALK ABOUT OLD ORBITS AND TIP HIM VERY WELL.
I WENT THERE ONCE WITH GOLDIE AND JINX TO TRY TO DRINK HER OFF MY MIND.
POP-CULTURE BOY AND MEDIA DARLING *LARRY YOUNG* WROTE THE WORDS AND TWEAKED THE PICTURES

STRIP BY **LARRY YOUNG**

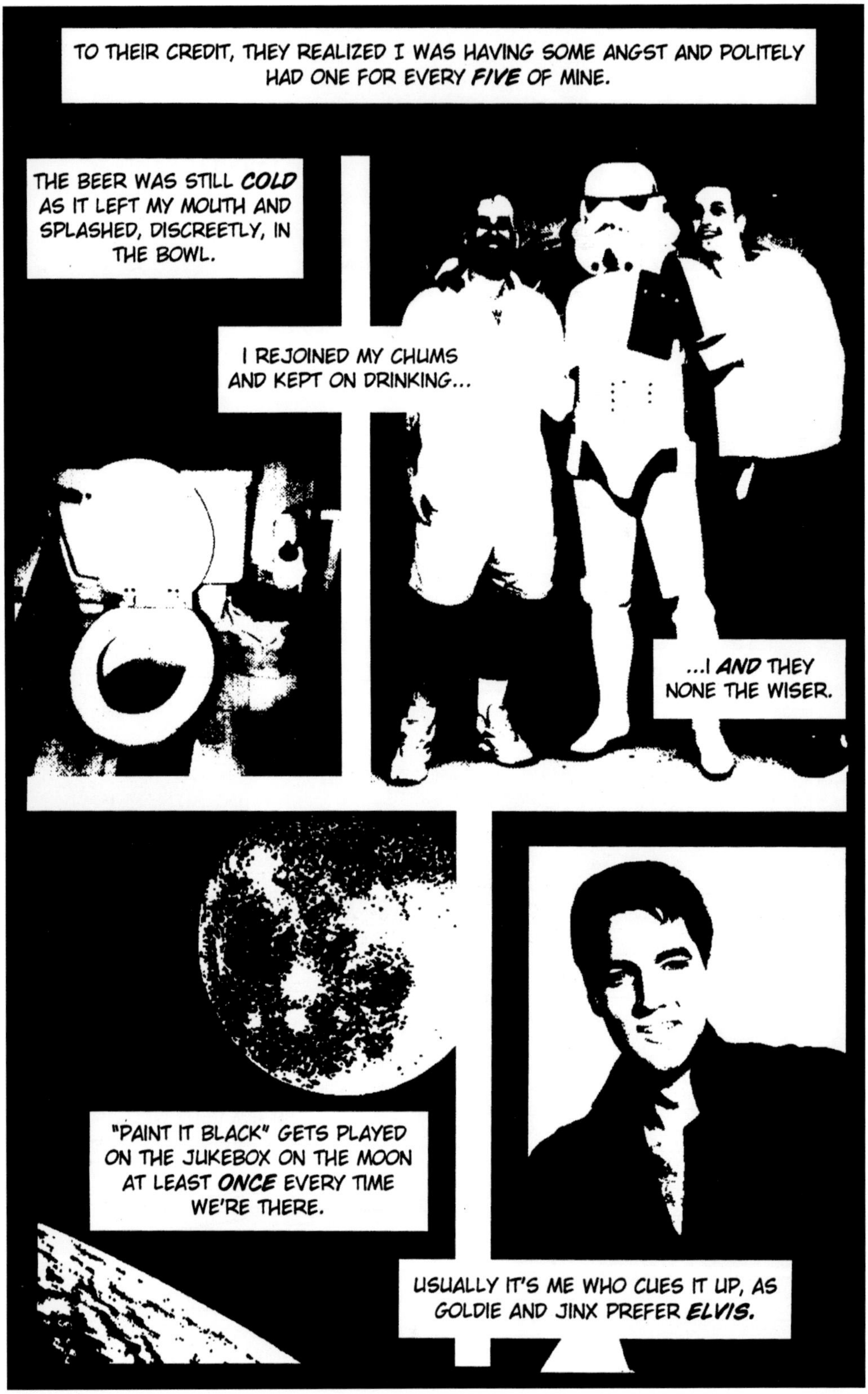
TO THEIR CREDIT, THEY REALIZED I WAS HAVING SOME ANGST AND POLITELY HAD ONE FOR EVERY *FIVE* OF MINE.
THE BEER WAS STILL *COLD* AS IT LEFT MY MOUTH AND SPLASHED, DISCREETLY, IN THE BOWL.
I REJOINED MY CHUMS AND KEPT ON DRINKING...
...I *AND* THEY NONE THE WISER.
"PAINT IT BLACK" GETS PLAYED ON THE JUKEBOX ON THE MOON AT LEAST *ONCE* EVERY TIME WE'RE THERE.
USUALLY IT'S ME WHO CUES IT UP, AS GOLDIE AND JINX PREFER *ELVIS.*

STRIP BY **LARRY YOUNG**

JINX PINUP, MAN!!

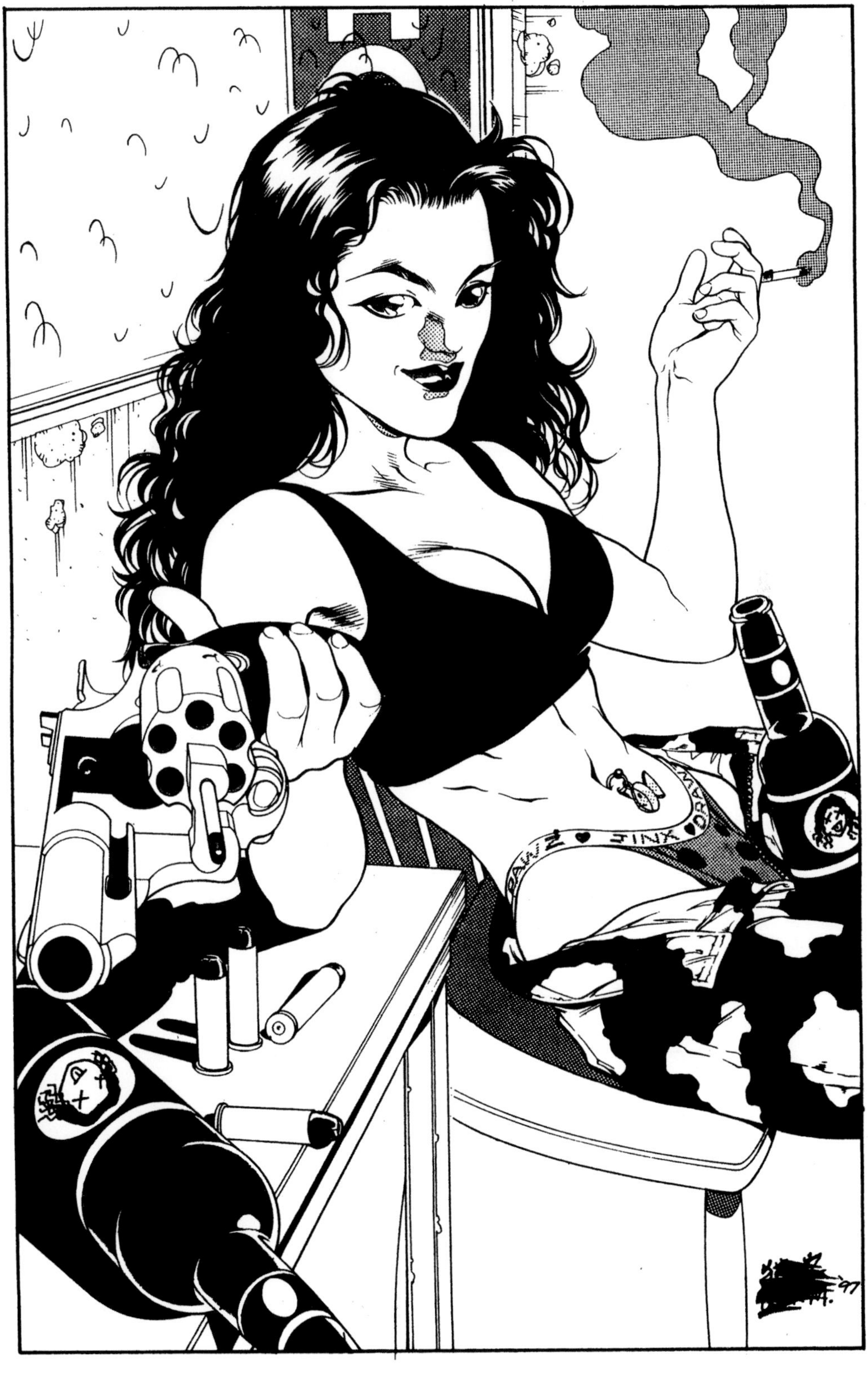
JINX
DRAWNZ
'97

PINUP BY **RICK MAYS**

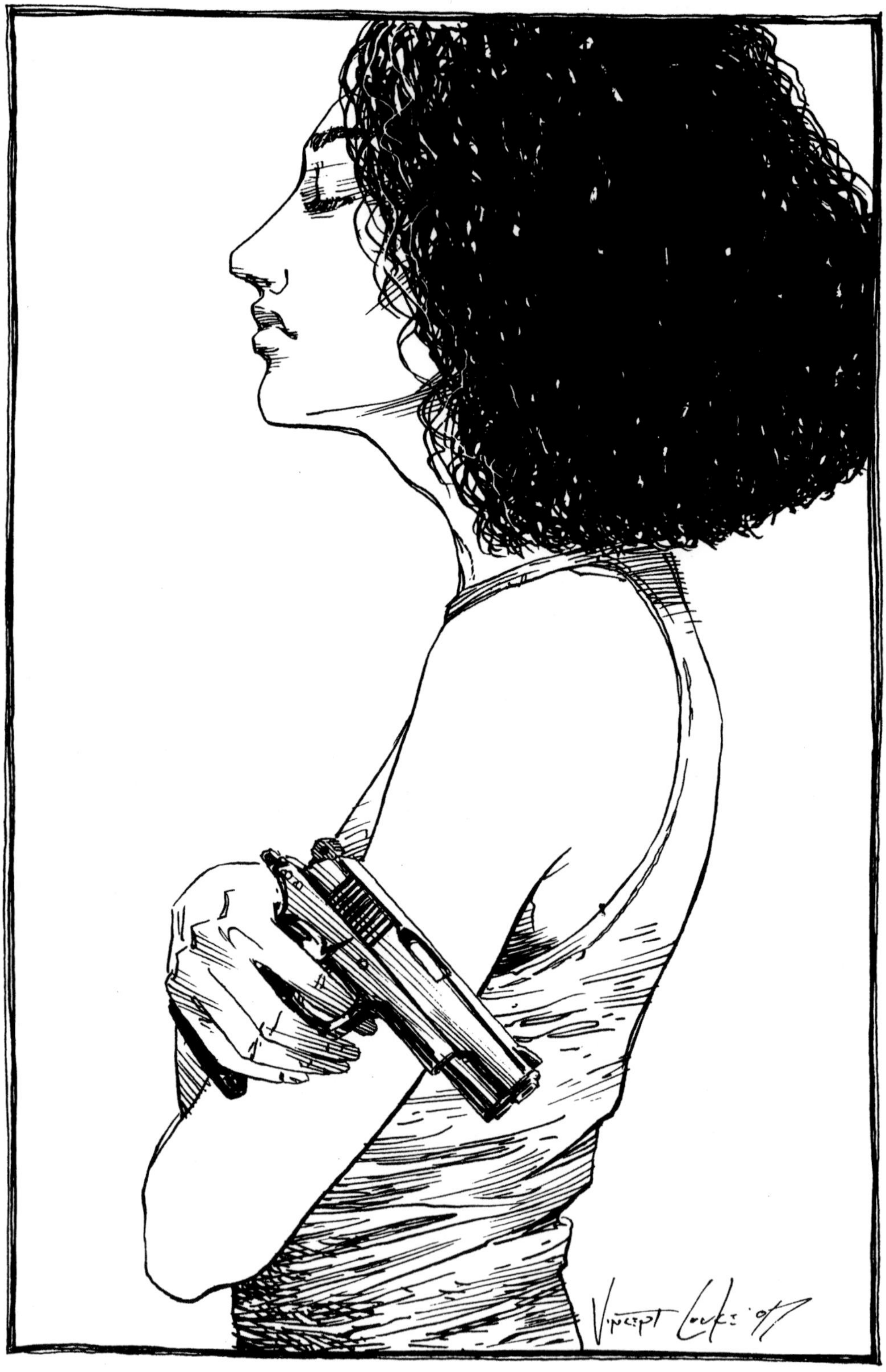
Vincent Locke '07

PINUP BY **VINCENT LOCKE**

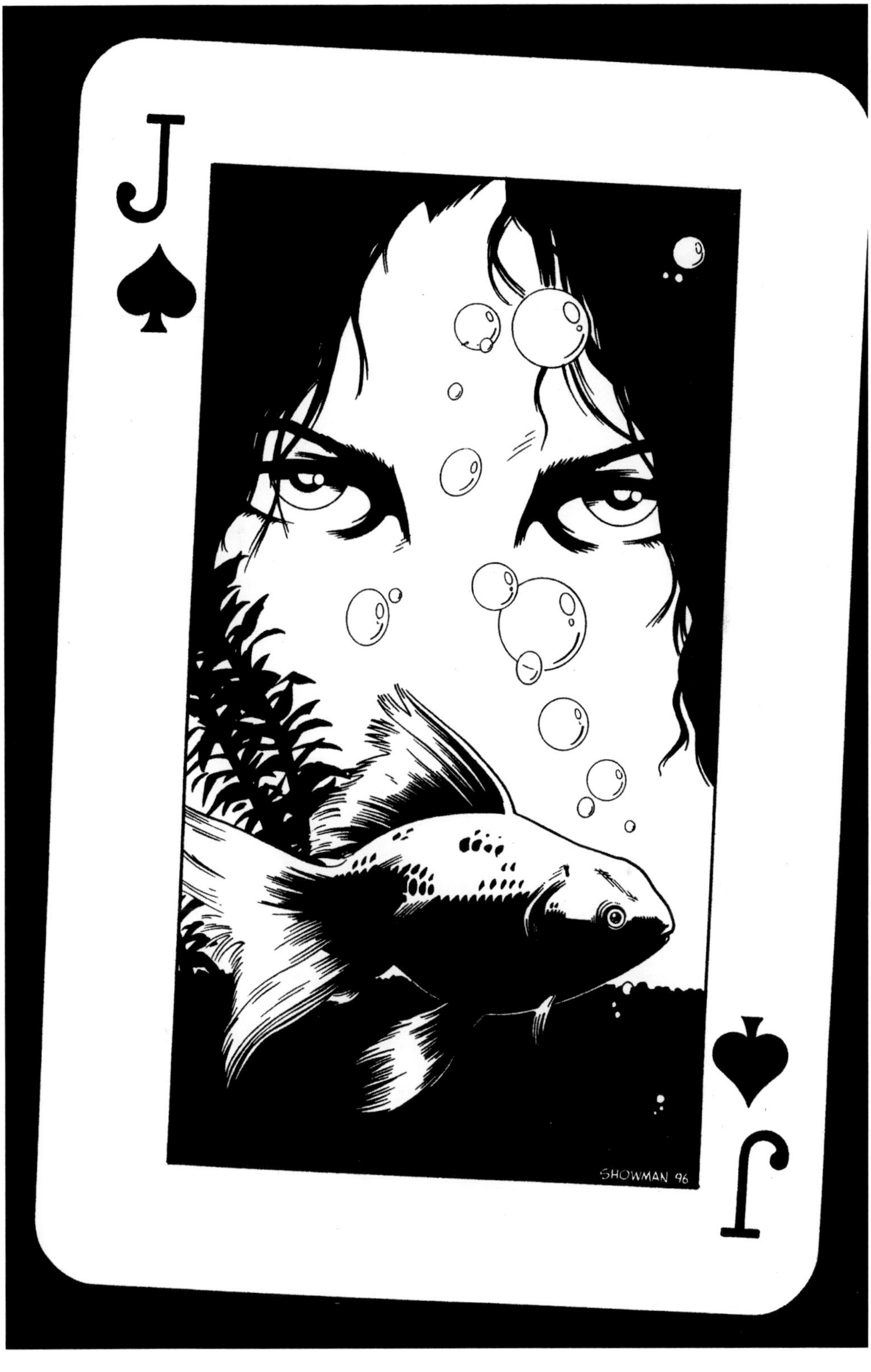
J
J
SHOWMAN 96

PINUP BY **GALEN SHOWMAN**

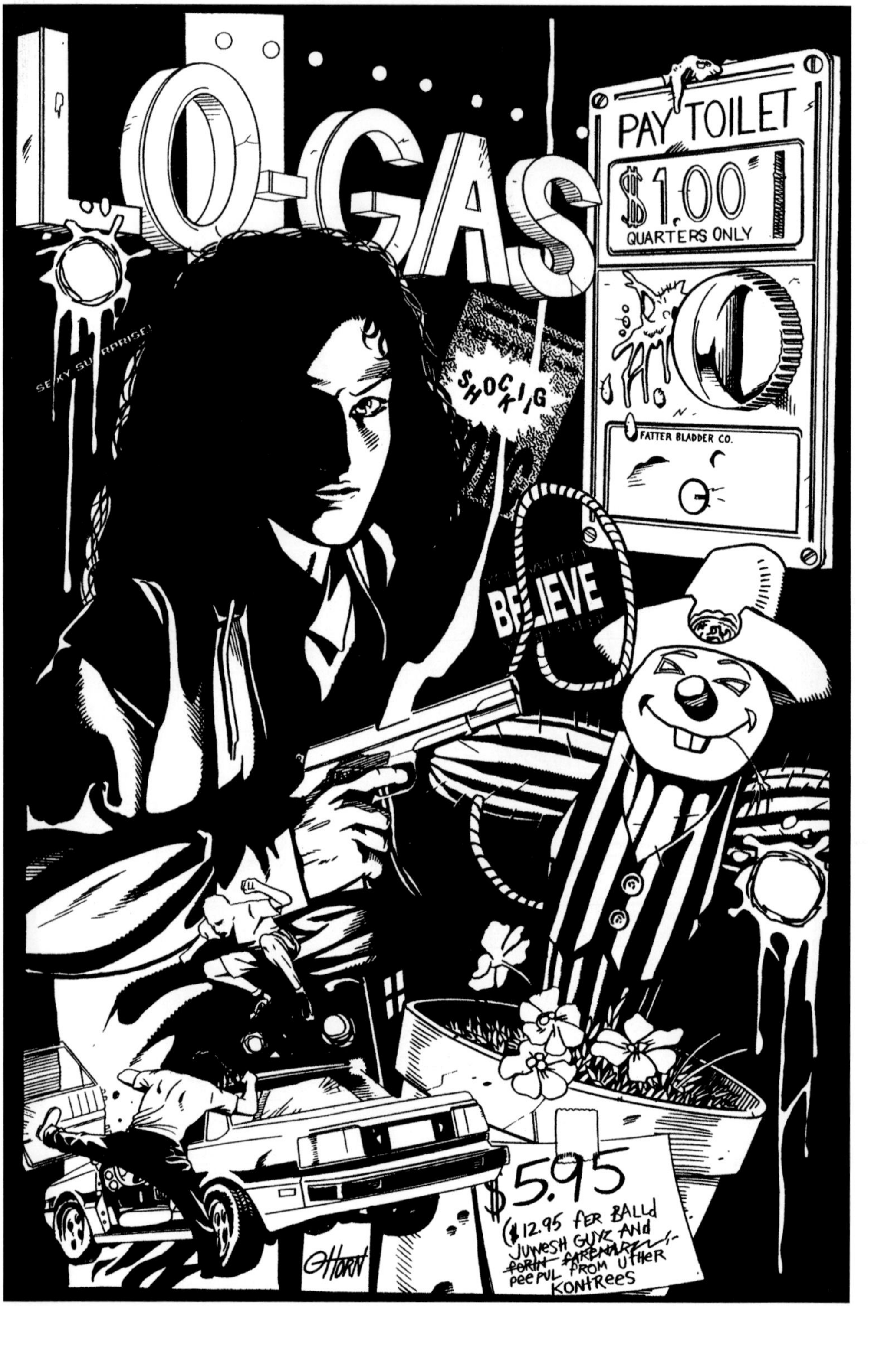
LO-GAS
PAY TOILET
$1.00
QUARTERS ONLY
FATTER BLADDER CO.
BELIEVE
$5.95
($12.95 fer BALLd
JUWESH GUYZ AND
peePUL FROM UtHer
KONtRees

PINUP BY **GREG HORN**

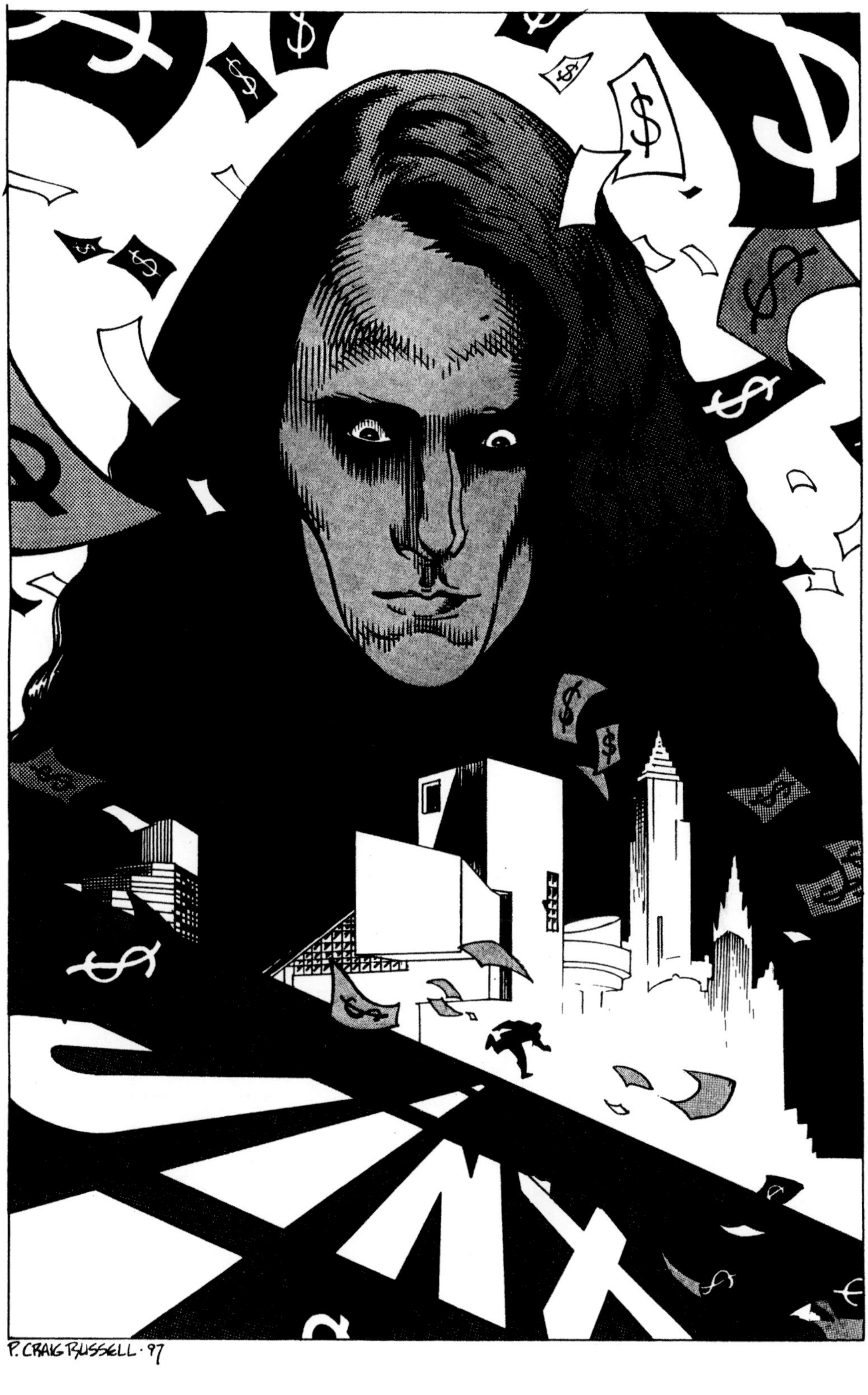
P. CRAIG RUSSELL · 97

PINUP BY **P. CRAIG RUSSELL**

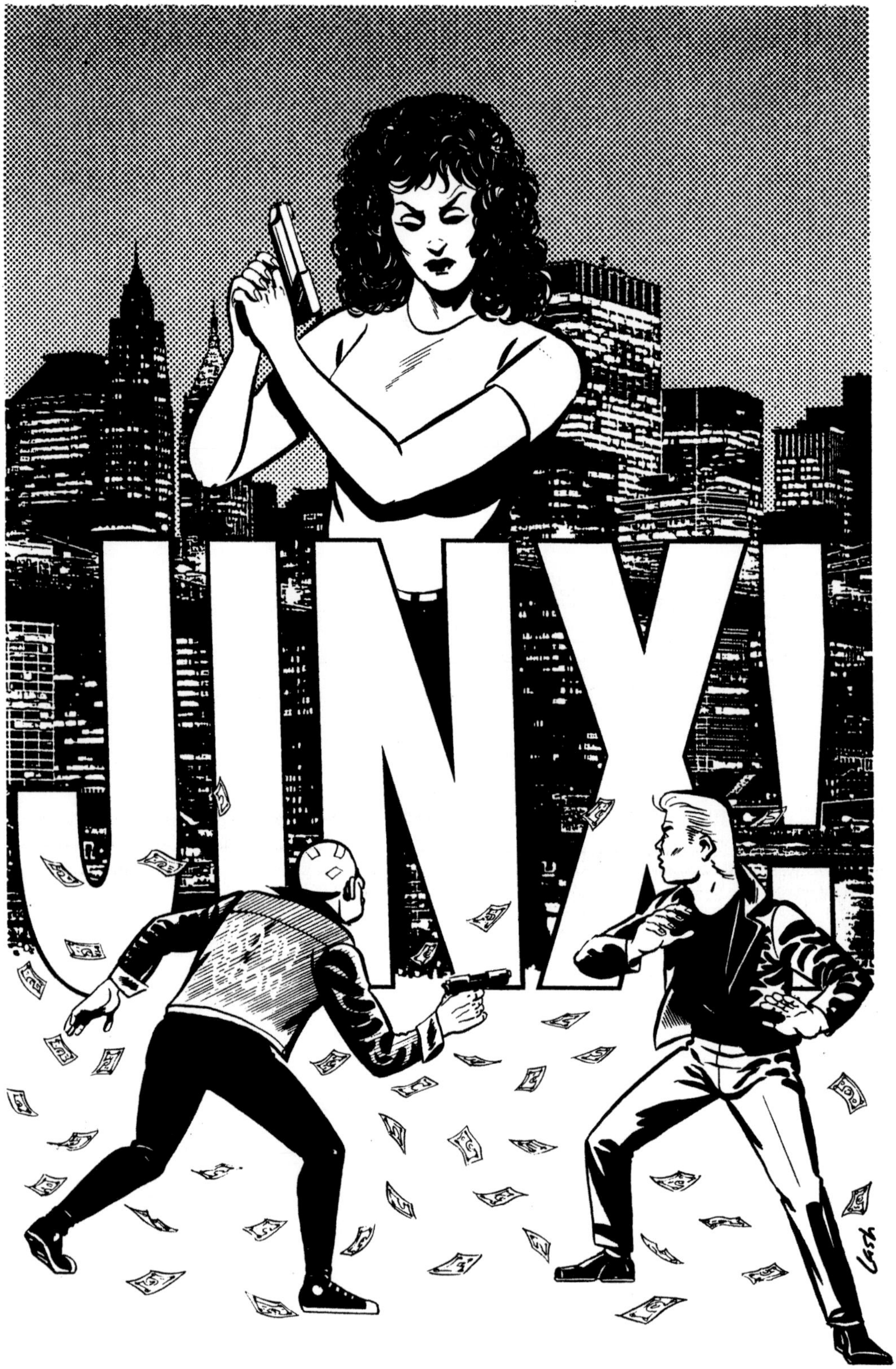
JINX!
LASH

PINUP BY **BATTON LASH**

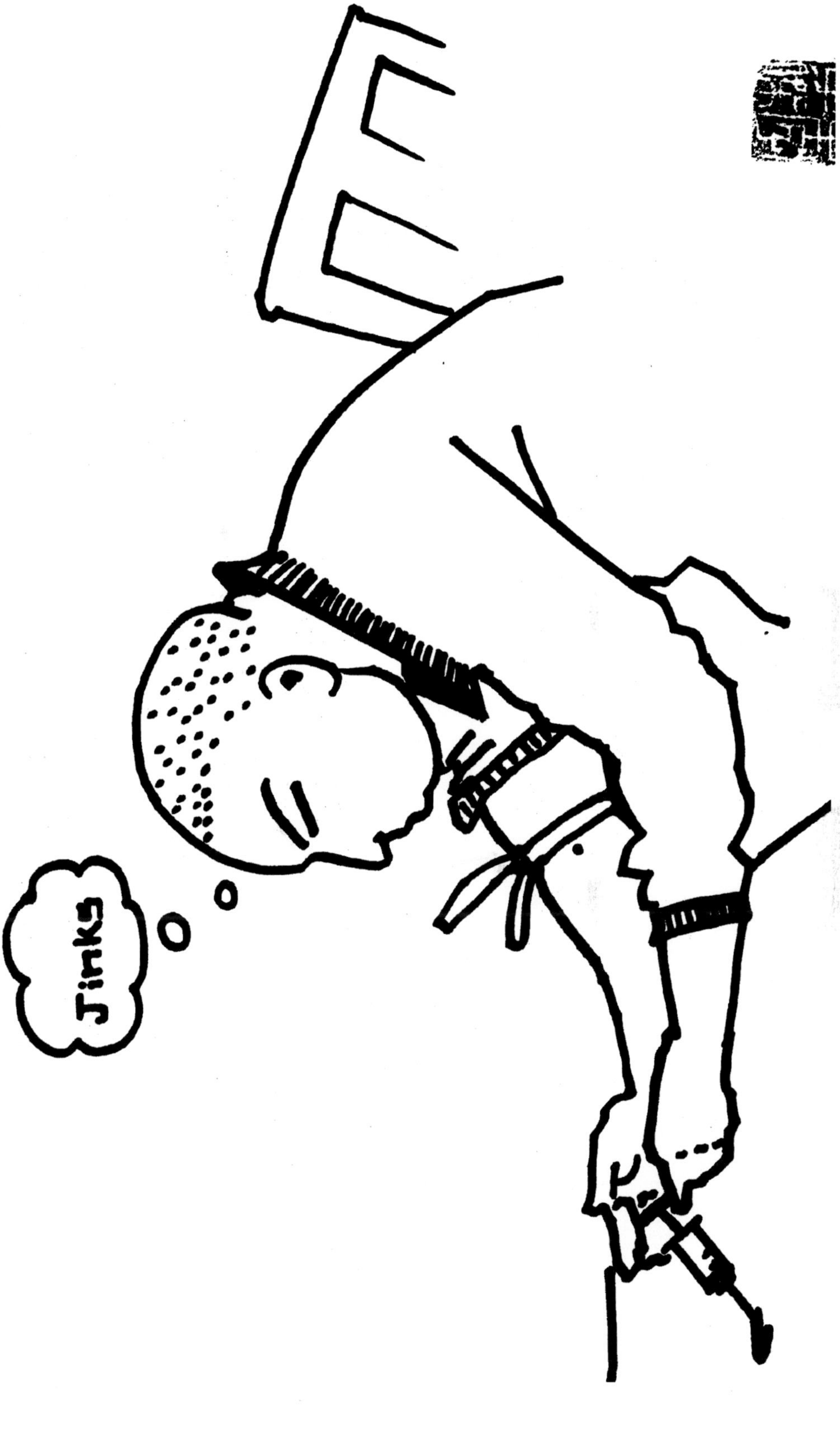
Jinks

PINUP BY **ANDY LEE**

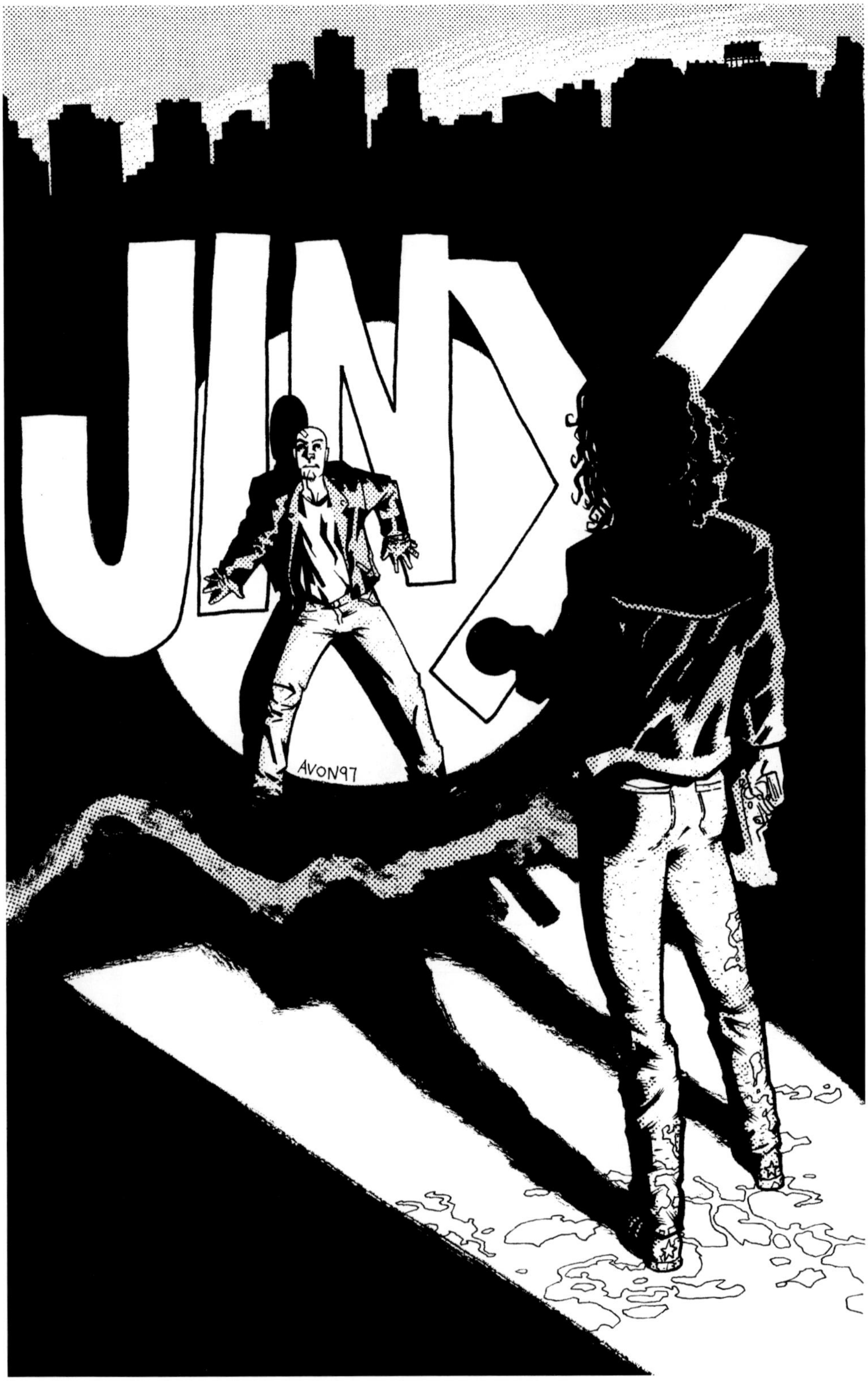
JINX
AVON97

PINUP BY **MICHAEL AVON OEMING**

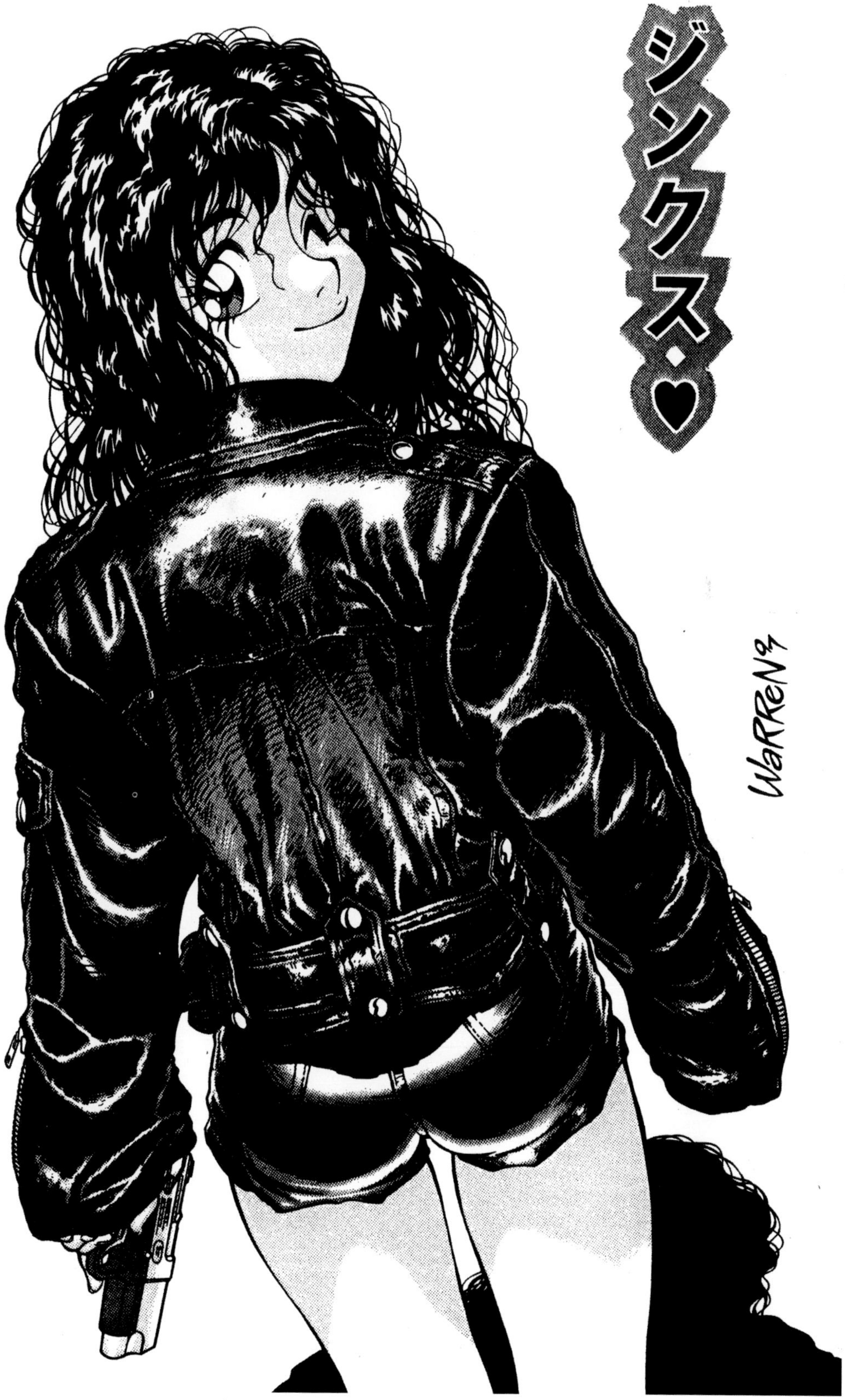
ジンクス・♥
WARREN 97

PINUP BY **ADAM WARREN**

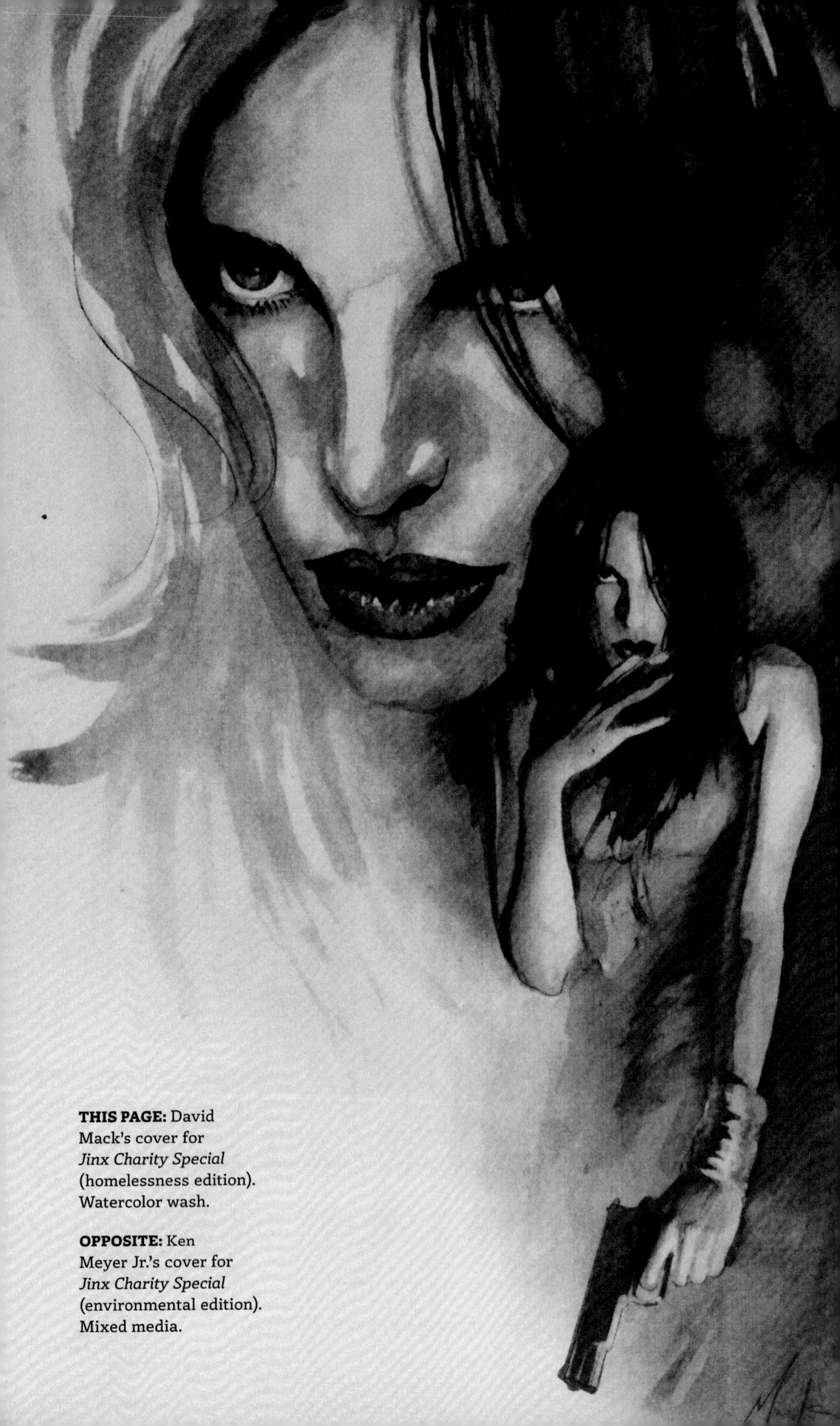

THIS PAGE: David Mack's cover for *Jinx Charity Special* (homelessness edition). Watercolor wash.

OPPOSITE: Ken Meyer Jr.'s cover for *Jinx Charity Special* (environmental edition). Mixed media.

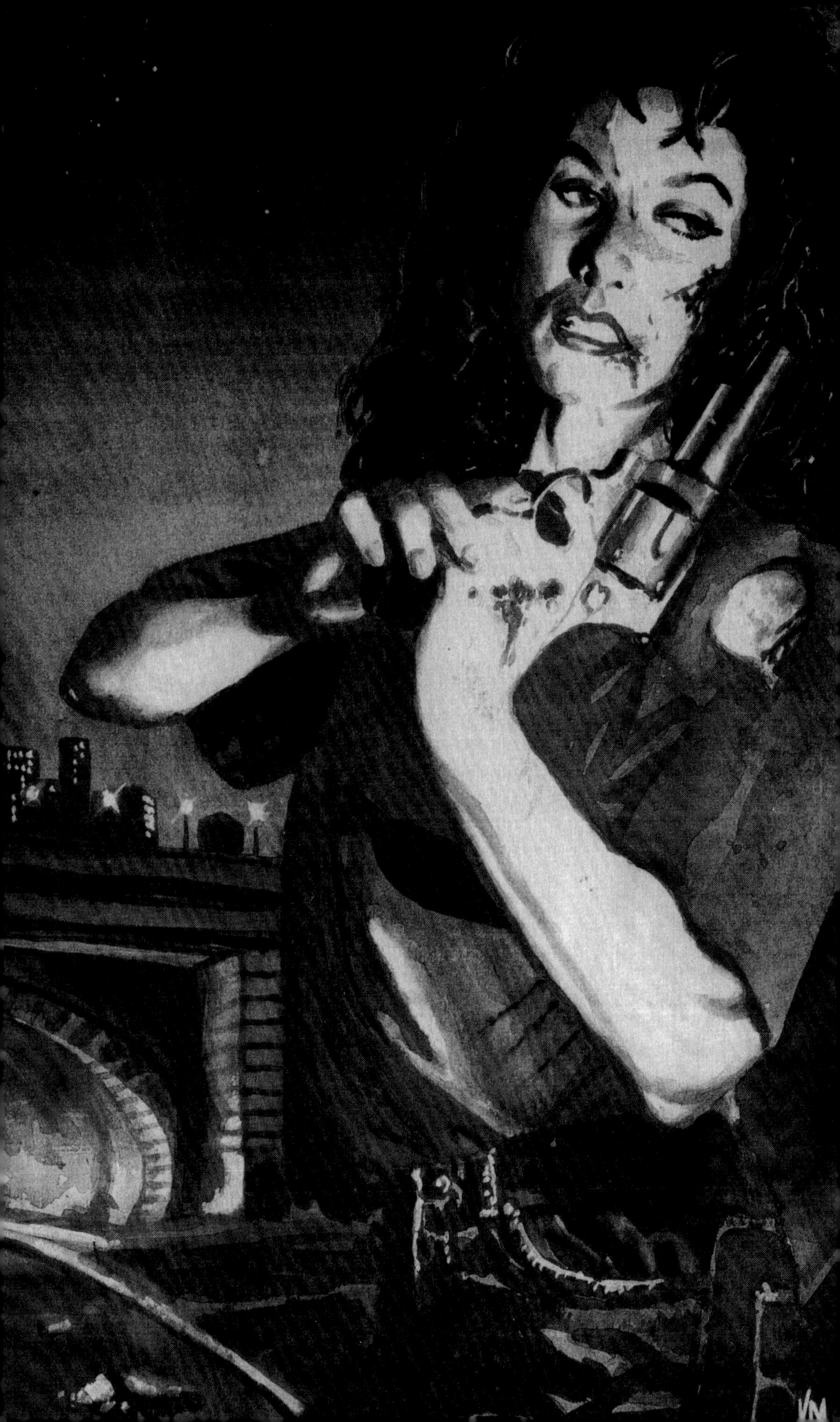

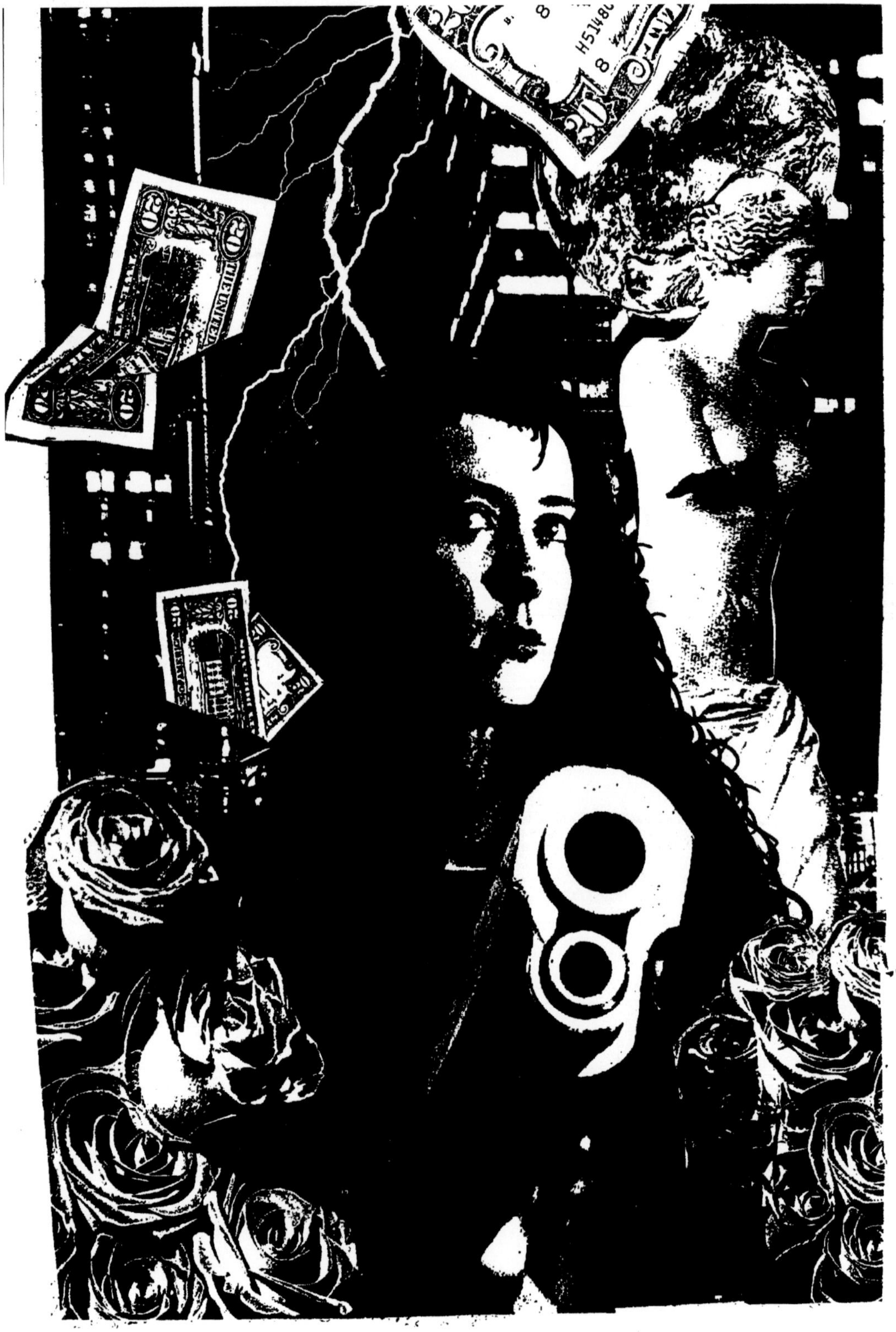

Original unpublished cover for *Jinx* volume 2, issue 1.
Black-and-white xerography photo collage.

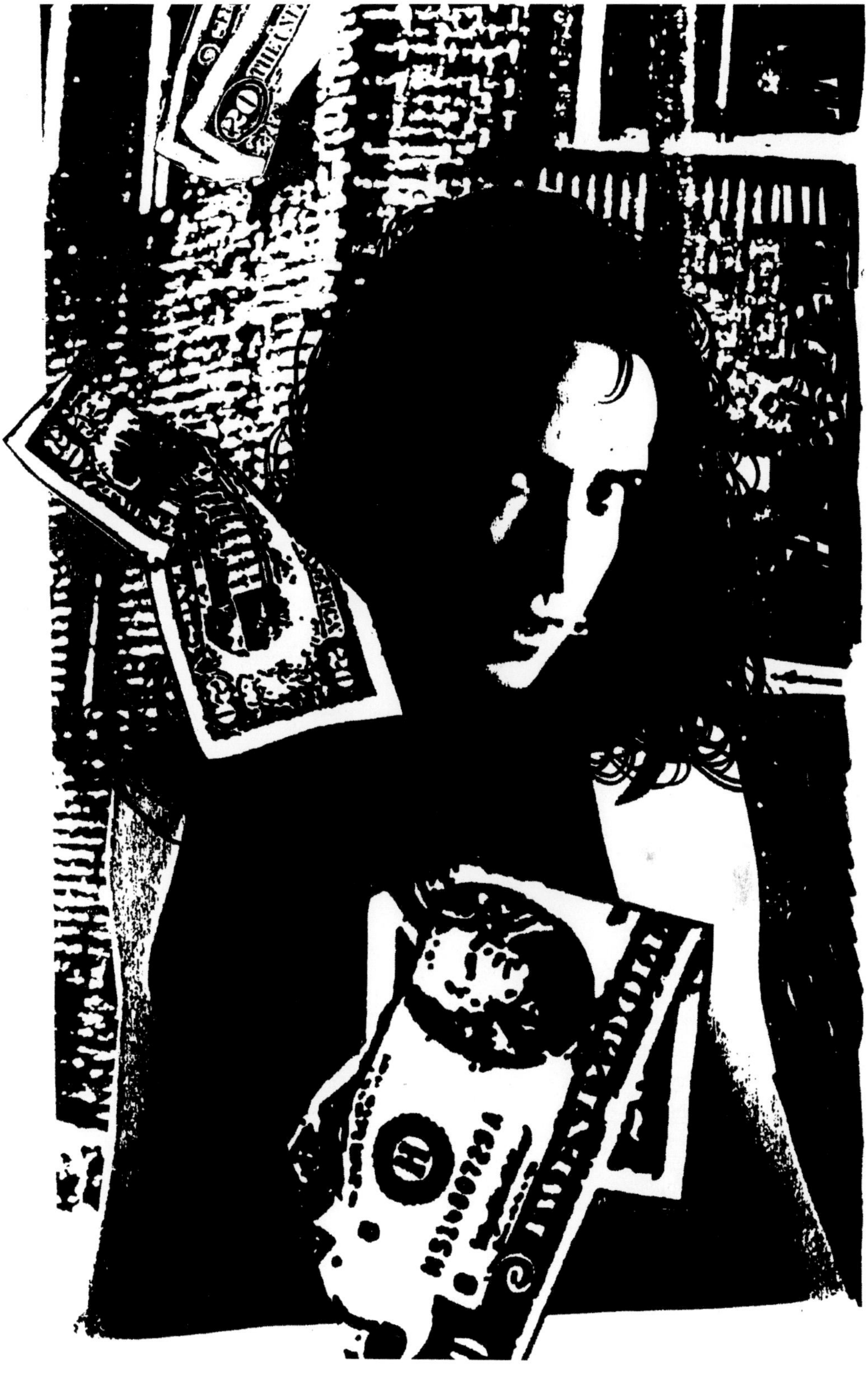

Final cover for *Jinx* volume 2, issue 1.
Black-and-white xerography photo collage.

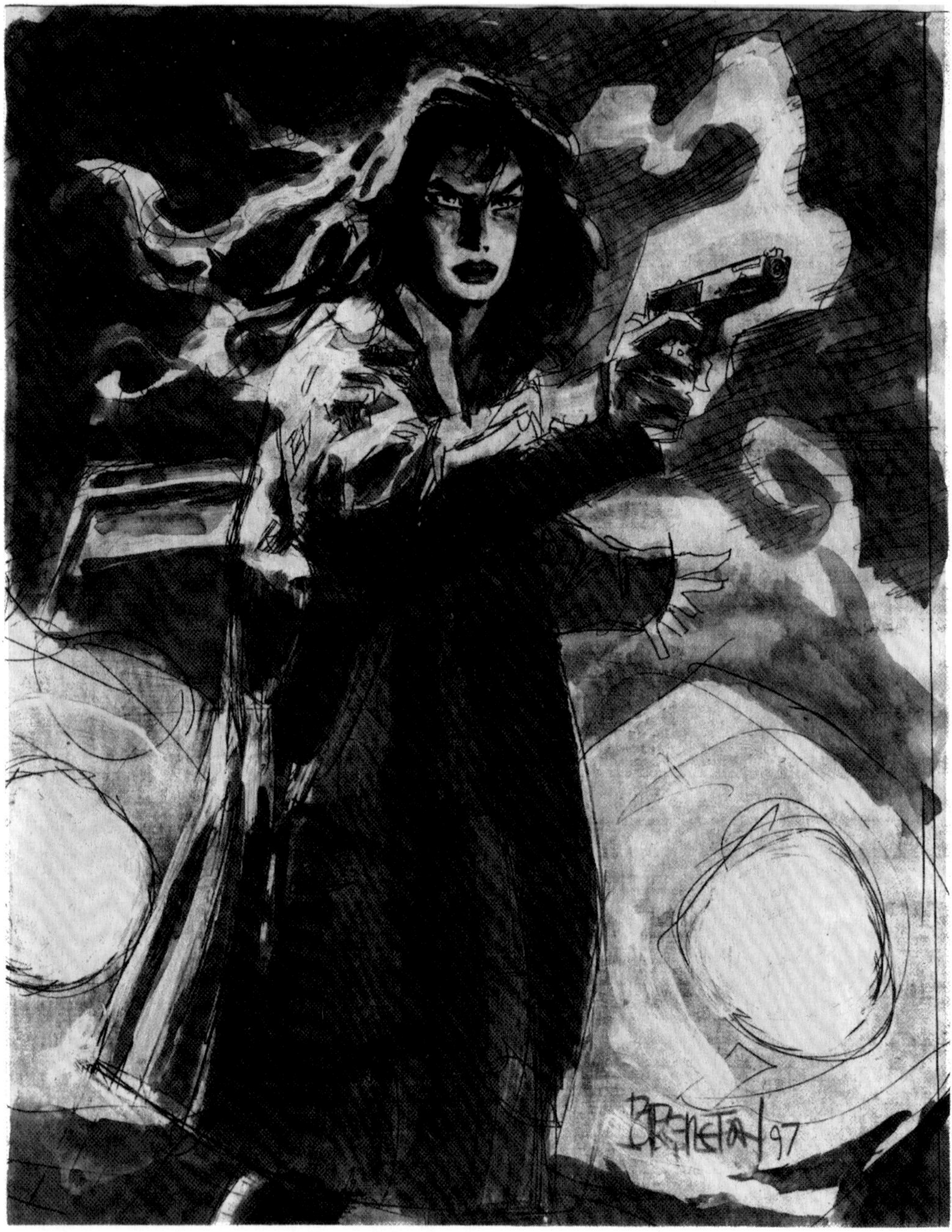
BRERETON 97

THIS PAGE: Original sketch for Dan Brereton's cover for *Jinx* volume 1, issue 5. Wash.

OPPOSITE: Finished cover with type.

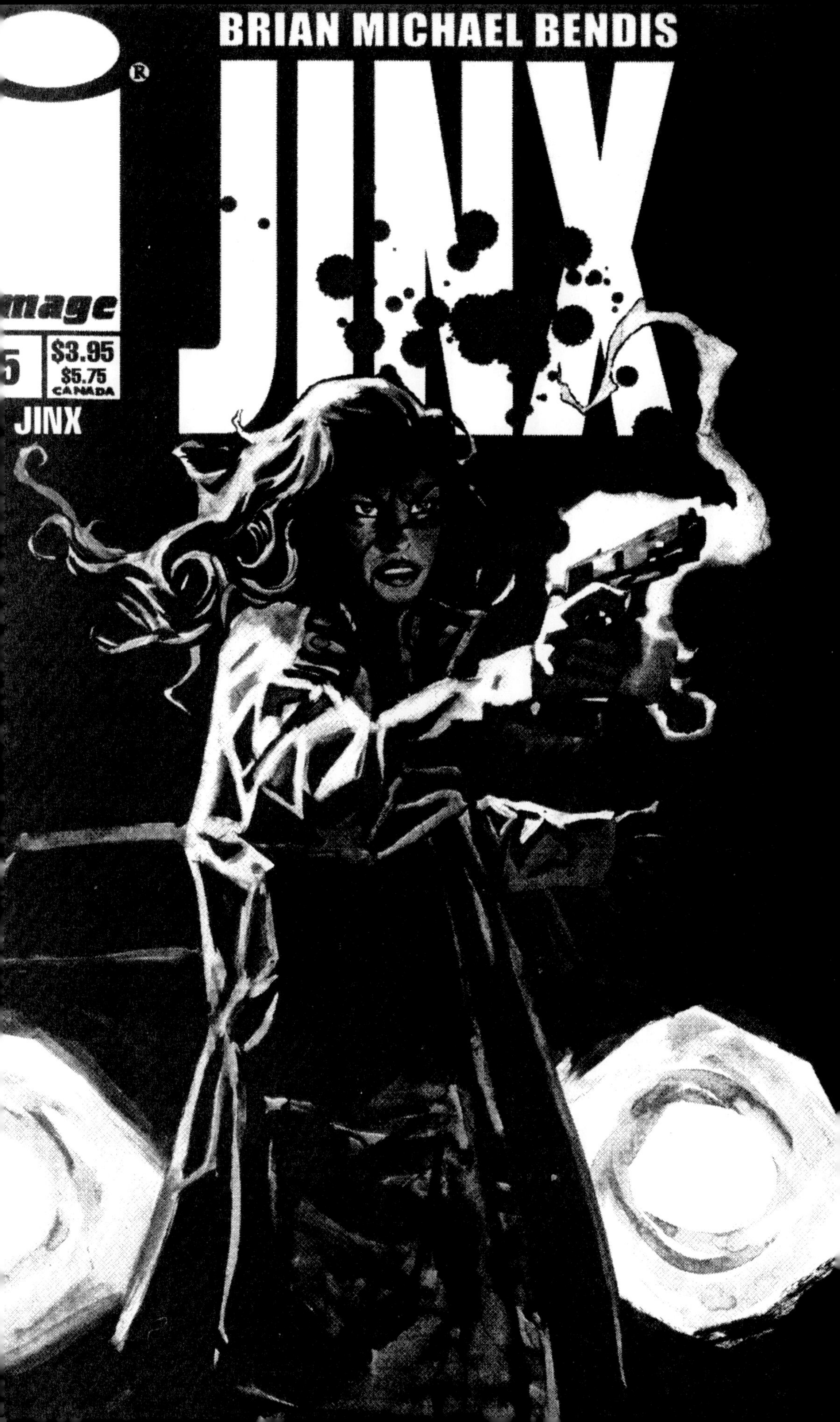
BRIAN MICHAEL BENDIS
JINX
mage
5
$3.95
$5.75
CANADA
JINX

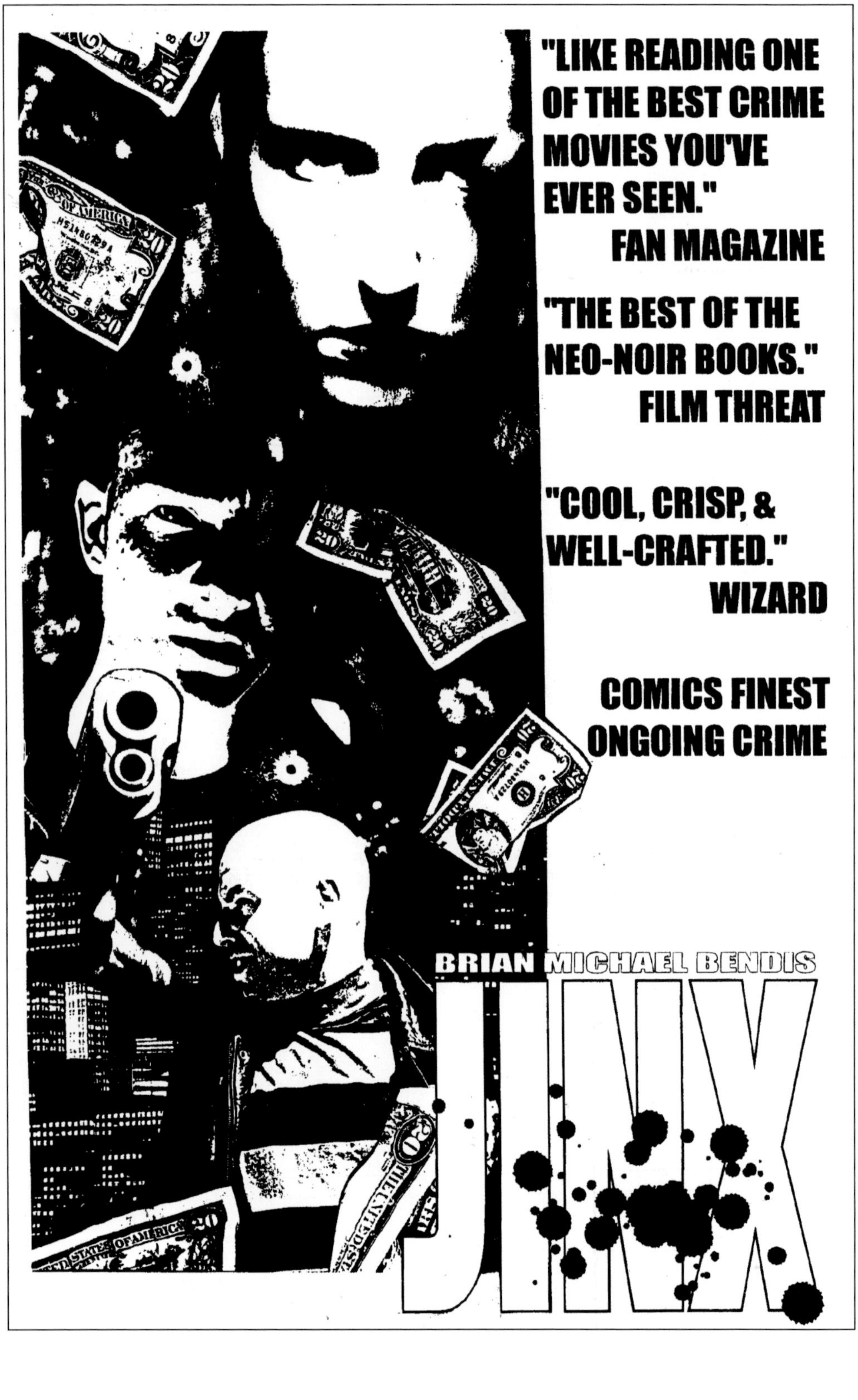
"LIKE READING ONE OF THE BEST CRIME MOVIES YOU'VE EVER SEEN."
FAN MAGAZINE
"THE BEST OF THE NEO-NOIR BOOKS."
FILM THREAT
"COOL, CRISP, & WELL-CRAFTED."
WIZARD
COMICS FINEST ONGOING CRIME
BRIAN MICHAEL BENDIS
JINX

Jinx postcard art.

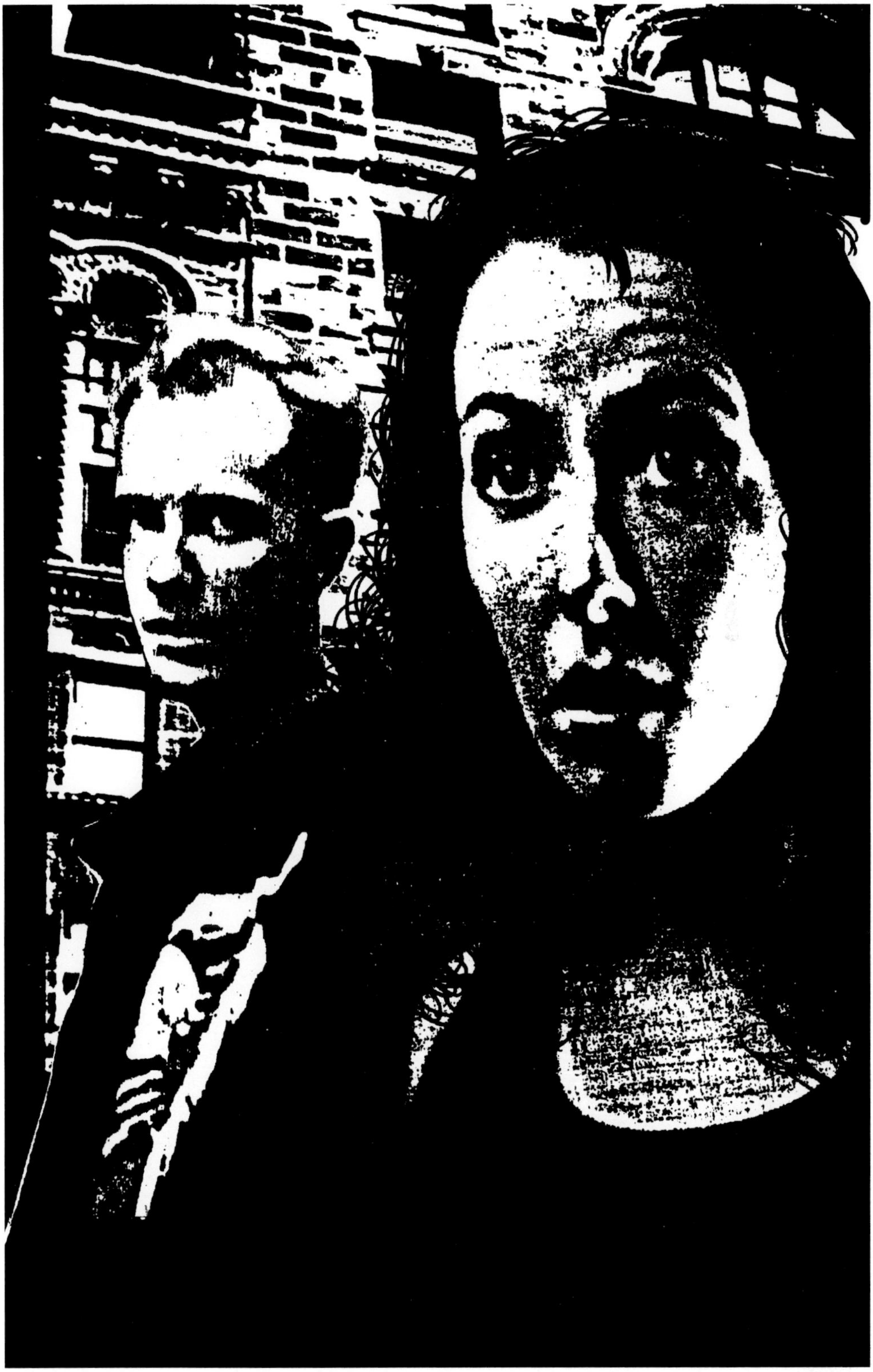

Cover art for *Jinx* volume 2, issue 3.
Black-and-white xerography photo collage.

MODELS

D.D. BYRNE as Jinx

JOHN SKRTIC as Goldfish

SHECKY FINKLESTIENS as Columbia

MIKE SANGIACOMO as Officer Mike

DAVID MACK as Dead Mug #1

JAMES D. HUDNALL as Dead Mug #2

CERAY DOSS as Becky

JARED BENDIS as Ricky Ricketts

MICHAEL JOHNSON as Money B

DAN BERMAN as Street Loser #1

FRISCO as Street Loser #2

MARC ANDREYKO as Reverend Peter

CURTIS as Apollo

KEITH KONAJCIK as Motormouth Mug

TOM ZJABA as Silent Mug

JIMMY WILLIAMS as Danny

MICHAEL HAHN as Young Danny

TIA RACHTEN as Young Jinx

KEVIN SNORELELAND as Rob

and

KYRA KESTER as Lauren Bacall